DON QUIXOTE

THE ORMSBY TRANSLATION, REVISED

BACKGROUNDS AND SOURCES

CRITICISM

A NORTON CRITICAL EDITION

MIGUEL DE CERVANTES

DON QUIXOTE

THE ORMSBY TRANSLATION, REVISED
BACKGROUNDS AND SOURCES
CRITICISM

Edited by
JOSEPH R. JONES
UNIVERSITY OF KENTUCKY
AND
KENNETH DOUGLAS
LATE OF YALE UNIVERSITY

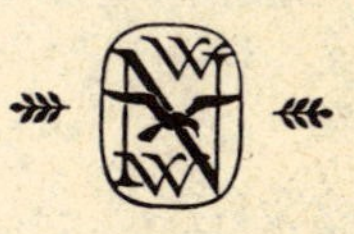

W · W · NORTON & COMPANY
New York *London*

ACKNOWLEDGMENTS

John J. Allen: from *Don Quixote: Hero or Fool?* University of Florida Monographs: Humanities No. 29. Gainesville: University of Florida Press, 1971. Reprinted by permission of the University of Florida Press.
Robert B. Alter: from *Partial Magic: The Novel as a Self-Conscious Genre*, pp. 1–29. Copyright © 1975 by The Regents of the University of California. Reprinted by permission of the University of California Press.
Manuel Durán: from *Cervantes* (Boston: Twayne Publishers, Inc., 1974). Reprinted with the permission of Twayne Publishers, a Division of C. K. Hall & Co., Boston.
Stephen Gilman: "The Apochryphal Quixote," from *Cervantes Across the Centuries*, edited by Angel Flores and J. J. Bernardete (New York: Dryden Press, 1947), pp. 247–253. Reprinted by permission of Gordian Press.
René Girard: from *Deceit, Desire and the Novel* (Baltimore: The Johns Hopkins University Press, 1965), pp. 1–18, 44–52. Reprinted by permission of The Johns Hopkins University Press.
Harry Levin: "The Quixotic Principle: Cervantes and Other Novelists," from *The Interpretation of Narrative*, edited by M. W. Bloomfield (Cambridge: Harvard University Press, 1970). Reprinted by permission of Harry Levin.
Herman Meyer: "Miguel de Cervantes' Don Quixote," in Herman Meyer, *The Poetics of Quotation in the European Novel*, translated by Theodore and Yetta Ziolkowski, pp. 59–71. Copyright © 1968 by Princeton University Press. Reprinted by permission of Princeton University Press.
Vladimir Nabokov: quotation from *King, Queen, Knave*, translated by Dmitri Nabokov (New York: McGraw-Hill Book Company, 1968). Reprinted by permission of McGraw-Hill Book Company.
E. C. Riley: "Teoría literaria," from *Suma cervantina*, edited by J. B. Avalle-Arce and E. C. Riley (London: Tamesis Books, 1973). Reprinted by permission of Germán Bléiberg.
Martín de Riquer: "Cervantes y la caballeresca," from *Suma cervantina*, edited by J. B. Avalle-Arce and E. C. Riley (London: Tamesis Books, 1973). Reprinted by permission of Germán Bléiberg.
Miguel de Unamuno: from *Selected Works of Miguel de Unamuno*, translated by Anthony Kerrigan. Bollingen Series LXXXV, Vol. 3; *Our Lord Don Quixote*, pp. 449–462. Copyright © 1967 by Princeton University Press. Selections from "On the Reading and Interpretation of *Don Quixote*" reprinted by permission.

Library of Congress Cataloging in Publication Data
Cervantes Saavedra, Miguel de, 1547–1616.
Don Quixote: backgrounds and sources, criticisms.
(Norton critical edition)
Bibliography: p.
1. Cervantes Saavedra, Miguel de, 1547–1616. Don Quixote—Addresses, essays, lectures. I. Ormsby, John, 1829–1895. II. Jones, Joseph Ramon, 1935– III. Douglas, Kenneth. IV. Title.
PQ6329.A2 1980 863'.3 79-20762
ISBN 0-393-04514-5
ISBN 0-393-09018-3 pbk.

Printed in the United States of America.

W. W. Norton & Company, Inc., 500 Fifth Avenue, New York, N.Y. 10110
W. W. Norton & Company Ltd., 37 Great Russell Street, London WC1B 3NU

8 9 0

For John Esten Keller, in friendship.

Contents

Preface

This edition was begun by Kenneth Douglas, who, after finishing about two-thirds of his textual revisions of the Ormsby translation, was killed in an accident. W. W. Norton & Company asked me to complete the work begun, make the alterations consistent throughout, and choose the background material and critical essays. It has been a task both pleasant and intellectually profitable—a description which fits few—and I would like to acknowledge my debt to three scholarly gentlemen who, unknown to themselves, have been collaborators in the book which you hold in your hand. It was my daily contact with their first-rate minds over a long period which made my job such a pleasure.

The first and most important is John Ormsby (1829–1895), a brilliant Irishman born in County Mayo, educated at Trinity College, Dublin, and the University of London, in chemistry and law. His real interests were mountain-climbing, exploring, writing, and Spanish literature. Ormsby's knowledge of Spanish was quite remarkable, and he produced the first truly accurate English translation of Cervantes' great novel in 1885. Since I am acutely aware of the difficulties of his task and of the skill with which he carried it through, I hesitate to point out its flaws, if they can be considered such; and I am bound to say that they are mainly the results of outdated scholarship, unpredictable changes in the reading habits and speech of English-speakers, and Ormsby's decision to make his translation as close as possible to Spanish. Advances in scholarship have now shown a few of his renditions to be incorrect; he followed editors whose work on Cervantes' text has been superseded. And he is so careful to copy the language of the original that where possible he follows the actual word order, translates very obscure words into their Elizabethan equivalents, carefully distinguishes among the forms of address (though the distinctions were lost on the readers of 1885, I suspect), and generally chooses to "sacrifice" (as Putnam says) clarity and ease for accuracy. Nevertheless, as Putnam also admits, Ormsby so often found the "inevitable word or expression" in English that it is hard to find a better one. Ormsby's translation has been reprinted at least twenty times, not including abridgments, since 1885.*

* Douglas selected Ormsby's version for its exceptional accuracy and for its well-deserved popularity. Nor is Douglas the only contemporary scholar to try to modernize Ormsby's language. Walter Starkie made a version, incorrectly advertised as a "vigorous new translation," though vigorous it certainly is. An

The second gentleman whose work I have come to know thoroughly is Samuel Putnam (1892–1950), one of the most important American translators of the twentieth century. Putnam knew French, Spanish, Portuguese, and Italian especially well; and his translations of Rabelais, Cervantes, Pirandello, and modern Brazilian literature are justly admired. He was deeply involved in the literature and art of pre-war Paris, where he lived from 1927 to 1934, and his writer's sensitivity to living English as well as to the "classical" languages of Renaissance Europe prepared him in a unique way to render two such subtle authors as Rabelais and Cervantes into modern American idiom.

Putnam had not only Ormsby's work but the benefit of sixty years' accumulation of scholarship at his disposal. His version is often a verbatim copy of Ormsby because Ormsby's is correct and idiomatic and, in most cases, if not the only possible translation, certainly the most obviously natural one. Putnam improves on Ormsby in accuracy once in a while (and I have taken full advantage of these improvements); he is much better in the matter of grammatical antecedents; his notes are models of pertinence and utility; his prose is clear, American-colloquial, and easier to read than Ormsby's. In short, I have nothing but admiration for his splendid translation, and my only objections to it are matters of taste, not adverse criticisms. Putnam makes no attempt to recreate the rhetorical tone of much of the novel, which is by no means always unaffected and natural (in the sense that it is an imitation of everyday speech). Putnam in fact makes Cervantes' prose less self-consciously artful, more colloquial, and easier to follow than it is—or was for Cervantes' early-seventeenth-century readers. Ormsby is, I believe, more faithful to the now quaint-sounding rhetoric. It is a question of degree, and no one has stated the translator's dilemma better than Putnam himself in the preface to his version: to strike a balance between fidelity to the text and idiomatic English, not to "modernize," in the bad sense. In my view, Putnam is slightly heavier on the idiomatic side of the scale in passages where fidelity means a more rhetorical style.

The last of the three collaborators is Kenneth Douglas, a scholar whose speciality was sixteenth-century French. Professor Douglas conceived the idea of this edition and began extensive revisions of Ormsby's language, intending apparently to compare it with the Spanish original later, when he reviewed the Riquer edition of *Don Quixote* for scholarly improvements since Ormsby's day. Unfortunately, his death intervened.

American reader, however, may find Starkie's racy, rural British almost as much a hindrance as Ormsby's neo-Tudor. (I have also compared passages of Ormsby against J. M. Cohen's 1950 Penguin Classic version, and I find that it is a less attractive revision than Starkie's clever version.)

Ormsby aimed his translation at the cultivated Victorian readers who could appreciate the echoes of classical English literary language and whose belletristic education allowed them to read archaic and dialectal prose with ease. Putnam wrote for a similarly cultivated American audience of the late forties, as the scholarly notes (and expensive format) show. The present edition was prepared with the American university student in mind. A glance at the notes of any recent university text of Shakespeare will show the enormous difference in the type of recognition-vocabulary a modern American reader has, and it is futile to ignore this difference between him and any pre-war reader. My experience has taught me that American students by and large look for speed of comprehension and pace, and either they will have both or they will simply stop reading. My goal has been to preserve the flavor of the original as much as possible, including the old-fashioned rhetoric where appropriate, while following current conventions of spelling, punctuation, and paragraphing. Breaking up Ormsby's periodic sentences, supplying antecedents (where Ormsby is accurate but often obscure), and rearranging the clauses in his pseudo-Spanish sentences may rob some passages of nuances or delicate ironies, but the compensation in pace of reading is equal, in my opinion. Reasonable or easily visualized substitutes for rare words avoid additional notes (e.g., on the types of cloth or articles of clothing for which no modern equivalents exist), searching in the dictionary (e.g., for "petronel" or "courbash"), and the annoying pauses in reading which is already slowed by the absolutely necessary explanations. Proverbs are a special case. The text abounds in proverbs, and only a few have familiar equivalents in English. Where possible, I have used rhyming proverbial-sounding translations, if the meaning was obvious. If the sense was not clear, rather than add another footnote (such as Putnam's numerous if useful ones on proverbs), I have put a well-known proverb in its place. In many cases, Sancho's proverbs are supposed to be far-fetched anyway, so I think these substitutions are perfectly justifiable. Oaths are another problem. They are either untranslatable or in Ormsby's rendition are utterly un-American sounding (e.g., "Body o'me!"), so I have changed them freely.

Even more ticklish is the rendering of Don Quixote's version of the language found in his books of chivalry. It is not always easy to say just where Don Quixote's speech begins to be bookish and quaint and where it is merely elevated but normal. Cervantes makes good use of this ambiguity. I have eliminated the familiar address ("thou," "ye," etc.) in ordinary conversation but used it as the equivalent of Don Quixote's chivalrous language when I thought it enhanced the effect.

Finally, while making no apologies, I acknowledge that the result of all these revisions is still not the ideal translation. Just as Ormsby and his illustrious followers compromised when they tried to make a very old book full of irony, jokes, and a dazzling collection of tricks of style, sound smooth, natural, and profound for readers of their day, Professor Douglas and I have compromised to the demands of the audience which we set out to attract to our favorite book.

JOSEPH R. JONES

Spanish Names and Pronunciation

With a few traditional exceptions (Quixote, Seville, Roland, etc.), names and words appear in their modern Spanish forms in this edition. The following rules of pronunciation are simplified for readers unfamiliar with Cervantes' tongue.

Spanish Vowels and Diphthongs	*English Approximation*	*Examples*
a	f*a*ther	S*a*ncho
e	cr*e*pe	P*e*dro
i	mach*i*ne	C*i*d
o	s*o*	Quix*o*te
u	tr*u*e	M*u*rcia
au	h*ow*	L*au*ra
ie	*yea*	S*ie*rra, Bab*ie*ca
ua	*wa*ter	Yang*ua*s
ue, üe	s*ue*de	Pis*ue*rga, Yang*üe*sans
ui	*we*	R*ui*dera
exceptions:		
gue	*gay*	*Gue*vara
gui	*ghee*	*Gui*llermo
que	*kay*	Palome*que*
qui	*key*	*Qui*xote

Spanish Consonants	*English Approximation*	*Examples*
c *before* e, i.	*th*ree	el Cid
z	*th*ree	Panza, Zoraida
g *before* e, i	*h*ot	Genil, Gil
j	*h*ot	Jerez
h	(silent)	Hernández, Haldudo
ll	mi*ll*ion	Ola*ll*a
ñ	ca*ny*on	señor, doña
s	ki*ss* (not rose)	Ambrosio

Spanish Accent: Words ending in a vowel, *n*, or *s* receive a stress on the next-to-last syllable: *San*cho, Mari*tor*nes. Words ending in any consonant except *n* or *s* receive a stress on the last syllable: se*ñor*, Vi*var*, re*al*. Any exceptions have a written accent-mark: Ara*gón*, Nico*lás*, *Pé*rez, marave*dí*, Gri*sós*tomo.

The Text of
The Ingenious Gentleman Don Quixote of La Mancha

Note

The title in Spanish is *El ingenioso hidalgo Don Quixote de la Mancha.* No one knows quite what Cervantes meant by *ingenioso.* It seems an odd epithet to apply to a madman—if he *was* mad—and it has been rendered in English translations as "witty," "imaginative," "visionary," and, of course, "ingenious." "Whimsical" might be a possibility; and one German translator has used *scharfsinnig,* "clever."

The word *hidalgo,* "gentleman," in the title indicates hereditary gentility of birth. It is the lowest grade of nobility in the Spanish caste system, and it meant that one was descended from "old Christians" (i.e., had no Jewish or Moorish ancestors) and persons who had not engaged in the trades. An *hidalgo* had certain privileges, the most important of which was that he was exempt from taxation; on the other hand, he was not allowed to work for pay and was required to live off investments, property, or the patronage of another aristocrat.

Part of the humor of *Don Quixote* for a contemporary reader was that when Alonso Quijano, an *hidalgo,* lost his wits, he assumed the title Don Quixote—*don* ("sir," roughly) being reserved for titled noblemen, their heirs, and high ecclesiastics. The custom of using *don* indiscriminately with anyone who looked like a gentleman was the source of much satire. In the title of Part II, published in 1615, the word *hidalgo* is replaced by *caballero,* "knight" literally, but also equivalent to "gentleman."

The title page says that Cervantes "composed" the work, though the Spanish word *compuesto* may mean, loosely, "written," as well as composed, compiled, arranged, etc. The reader will learn in the first chapters that Cervantes poses as a researcher who has gathered the rather confusing accounts of Don Quixote's exploits. In Cervantes' own sequel, published in 1615, the title page says simply, "by Miguel de Cervantes Saavedra, author of the first part."

The Ingenious Gentleman Don Quixote of La Mancha

by

Miguel de Cervantes Saavedra

Dedicated to the Duke of Béjar,
Marquis of Gibraleón,
Count of Benalcázar and Bañares,
Viscount of La Puebla de Alcocer,
Lord of the Towns of Capilla, Curiel, and Burgillos.

1605
With Copyright

Printed in Madrid by Juan de la Cuesta.
For sale at the shop of Francisco de Robles,
bookseller to the king our lord.

to anyone else for correcting and pricing until the aforesaid book has been corrected and priced by our Council. This done, and not until then, he may print the aforesaid beginning and first sheet, and he shall then print this our permit and approval, price, and errata, on pain of incurring those penalties contained in the laws and decrees of these our realms. And we command those of our Council and all other judges whomsoever to obey and fulfill this our permit and its contents. Dated Valladolid, September 26, 1604.

I, THE KING.

By order of the King our lord: Juan de Amezqueta.

Dedication

To the Duke of Béjar

Marquis of Gibraleón, Count of Benalcázar and Bañares, Viscount of La Puebla de Alcocer, Lord of the Towns of Capilla, Curiel, and Burguillos[1]

Confident of the courteous reception and honors that Your Excellency bestows on all sorts of books, as a prince so inclined to favor the fine arts, chiefly those which by their nobility do not submit to the service and bribery of the vulgar, I have decided to publish *The Ingenious Gentleman Don Quixote of La Mancha* in the shelter of Your Excellency's most illustrious name. And with the obeisance I owe to such grandeur, I beg you to receive it graciously under your protection, so that in this shadow, though deprived of those precious ornaments of elegance and erudition that clothe works composed in the houses of those who know, it may dare appear with assurance before the judgment of some who, trespassing the bounds of their own ignorance, condemn with more rigor and less justice the writings of others. It is my earnest hope that Your Excellency's wisdom will consider my honorable purpose and will not disdain the littleness of so humble a service.[2]

1. The duke whose patronage is sought in this dedication, Don Alonso de Zúñiga y Sotomayor, was twenty-eight years old at the date of *Don Quixote*'s first edition. By extending a moderate protection to some obscure authors, he had attained a certain reputation as a lover of letters and friend of writers.
2. Cervantes borrowed portions of this dedication from one to the Marquis of Ayamonte with which Fernando de Herrera headed his annotated edition of Garcilaso's works and from the introduction by Francisco de Medina for the same book. The address thus concocted was of little avail, for the duke died in 1619, and no record is preserved of his doing anything in favor of the man who bestowed immortality on his name by attaching it to such a book.

Prologue

Idle reader: you may believe me, without my having to swear, that I would have liked this book, as it is the child of my brain, to be the fairest, gayest, and cleverest that could be imagined. But I could not counteract Nature's law that everything shall beget its like; and what, then, could this sterile, uncultivated wit of mine beget but the story of a dry, shriveled, eccentric offspring, full of thoughts of all sorts and such as never came into any other imagination—just what might be begotten in a prison, where every misery is lodged and every doleful sound makes its dwelling?[3] Tranquillity, a cheerful retreat, pleasant fields, bright skies, murmuring brooks, peace of mind, these are the things that go far to make even the most barren muses fertile and cause them to bring into the world offspring that fill it with wonder and delight.

Sometimes when a father has an ugly, unattractive child, the love he bears him so blindfolds his eyes that he does not see its defects; on the contrary, he considers them marks of intelligence and charm and talks of them to his friends as wit and grace. I, however—for though I pass for the father, I am the stepfather of Don Quixote—have no desire to go with the current of custom or to implore you, dearest reader, almost with tears in my eyes, as others do, to pardon or excuse the defects you may perceive in this child of mine. You are neither its relative nor its friend, your soul is your own and your will as free as any man's, you are in your own house and master of it as much as the king of his taxes, and you know the common saying, "A man's home is his castle"[4]—all of which exempts and frees you from every consideration and obligation. And you can say what you will about the story without fear of being abused for any ill or rewarded for any good you may say of it.

My wish would be simply to present it to you plain and unadorned, without the embellishment of a prologue or the lengthy catalogue of the usual sonnets, epigrams, and eulogies, such as are commonly put at the beginning of books. For I can tell you, though composing it cost me considerable effort, I found nothing harder than the making of this prologue you are now reading. Many times I took up my pen to write it, and many I laid it down again, not knowing what to write. One of these times, as I was pondering with the paper before me, a pen behind my ear, my elbow on the desk, and my cheek in my hand, thinking of what I should say, there came in unexpectedly a certain lively, clever friend of mine, who, seeing

3. Cervantes was in prison in Seville in 1597 and again in 1602. But the language of this sentence is sufficiently ambiguous to allow for both a literal and a purely metaphorical interpretation.

4. Putnam suggests this as an equivalent for the original: "Under my cloak, I kill [*or* I rule] the king."

me so deep in thought, asked the reason; to which I, making no mystery of it, answered that I was thinking of the prologue I had to write for the story of Don Quixote, which so troubled me that I had a mind not to write any at all—nor even publish the achievements of so noble a knight.

"For, how could you expect me not to feel uneasy about what that ancient lawgiver they call the Public will say when it sees me, after slumbering so many years in the silence of oblivion, coming out now with all my years upon my back, and with a book as dry as a bone, devoid of invention, meager in style, poor in conceits, wholly wanting in learning and doctrine, without quotations in the margin or annotations at the end, after the fashion of other books I see, which, though on fictitious and profane subjects, are so full of maxims from Aristotle and Plato and the whole herd of philosophers that they fill the readers with amazement and convince them that the authors are men of learning, erudition, and eloquence. And then, when they quote the Holy Scriptures, anyone would say they are St. Thomases or other doctors of the Church, observing as they do a decorum so ingenious that in one sentence they describe a distracted lover and in the next deliver a devout little sermon that it is a pleasure and a treat to hear and read. Of all this there will be nothing in my book, for I have nothing to quote in the margin or to note at the end, and still less do I know what authors I follow in it, to place them at the beginning, as all do, under the letters A, B, C, beginning with Aristotle and ending with Xenophon or Zoilus or Zeuxis, though one was a slanderer and the other a painter. Also my book must do without sonnets at the beginning, at least sonnets whose authors are dukes, marquises, counts, bishops, ladies, or famous poets. Though if I were to ask two or three friendly tradesmen, I know they would give me some, and such that the productions of those that have the highest reputation in our Spain could not equal.[5]

"In short, my friend," I continued, "I am determined that Señor Don Quixote shall remain buried in the archives of his own La Mancha until Heaven provides someone to garnish him with all those things he stands in need of; because I find myself, through my incapacity and want of learning, unequal to supplying them, and because I am by nature indolent and lazy about hunting for authors to say what I myself can say without them. Hence, my friend, the cogitation and abstraction you found me in, and what you have heard from me is sufficient cause for it."

Hearing this, my friend, giving himself a slap on the forehead

5. Cervantes, in this portion of the introduction, appears to be criticizing Lope de Vega (1562–1635), Spain's greatest dramatist, whose works often display these pedantic characteristics.

and breaking into a hearty laugh, exclaimed, "Before God, brother, now am I disabused of an error in which I have been living all this long time I have known you, all through which I have taken you to be shrewd and sensible in all you do; but now I see you are as far from that as the heaven is from the earth. Is it possible that things of so little moment and so easy to set right can occupy and perplex a ripe wit like yours, accustomed to break through and crush far greater obstacles? By my faith, this comes, not of any want of ability, but of too much indolence and too little thinking. Do you want to know if I am telling the truth? Well, then, pay attention to me, and you will see how, in the opening and shutting of an eye, I sweep away all your difficulties and supply all those deficiencies which you say check and discourage you from bringing before the world the story of your famous Don Quixote, the light and mirror of all knight-errantry."

"Say on," said I, listening to his talk. "How do you propose to make up for my diffidence and reduce to order this chaos of perplexity I am in?"

To which he answered, "Your first difficulty, about the sonnets, epigrams, or complimentary verses which you lack for the beginning and which ought to be by persons of importance and rank, can be removed if you yourself take a little trouble to write them. You can afterwards baptize them and give them any name you like, fathering them on Prester John of the Indies or the Emperor of Trebizond, who I know were said to have been famous poets. And even if they were not, and any pedants or bachelors should attack you and question the fact, don't let it bother you two *maravedís'* worth, for even if they prove a lie against you, they cannot cut off the hand you wrote it with.

"As to references in the margin to the books and authors from whom you take the maxims and sayings you put into your story, all you have to do is work in any sentence or scraps of Latin you may happen to know by heart, or at any rate that will not give you much trouble to look up. Thus when you speak of freedom and captivity, you can insert *Non bene pro toto libertas venditur auro*;[6] and then refer in the margin to Horace, or whoever said it. Or, if you allude to the power of death, you can bring in *Pallida mors æquo pulsat pede pauperum tabernas,/Regumque turres.*[7]

"If it is the friendship and the love God commands us to feel towards our enemy, go at once to the Holy Scriptures, which you can do with a very small amount of research, and quote no less than the words of God himself: *Ego autem dico vobis: diligite inimicos*

6. Roughly, "One should not sell his liberty for any price." The saying comes from medieval fable collections, not from Horace.

7. "Pale death strikes without distinction the hovels of the poor and the towers of kings." Horace.

vestros.[8] If you speak of evil thoughts, turn to the Gospel: *De corde exeunt cogitationes malæ.*[9] If of the fickleness of friends, there is Cato, who will give you his couplet: *Donec eris felix multos numerabis amicos,/Tempora si fuerint nubila, solus eris.*[1] With these and such like bits of Latin they will take you for a grammarian at all events, and that nowadays is no small honor and profit.

"With regard to adding annotations at the end of the book, you may safely do it in this way. If you mention any giant in your book, arrange for it to be the giant Goliath, and with this alone, which will cost you almost nothing, you have a grand note, for you can put *The giant Golias or Goliath was a Philistine whom the shepherd David slew by a mighty stone-cast in the Terebinth valley, as is related in the Book of Kings,* in the chapter where you find it written.

"Next, to prove yourself a man of erudition in polite literature and a cosmographer, manage to mention the river Tagus in your story, and there you are at once with another fine annotation, setting forth *The river Tagus was so called after a King of Spain: it has its source in such and such a place and falls into the ocean, kissing the walls of the famous city of Lisbon, and it is a common belief that it has golden sands,* etc.

"If you should have anything to do with robbers, I will give you the story of Cacus, for I know it by heart; if with loose women, there is the Bishop of Mondoñedo, who will lend you Lamia, Laida, and Flora, any reference to whom will bring you great credit; if with hard-hearted ones, Ovid will furnish you with Medea; if with witches or enchantresses, Homer has Calypso, and Virgil Circe; if with valiant captains, Julius Cæsar himself will lend you himself in his own *Commentaries,* and Plutarch will give you a thousand Alexanders. If you should deal with love, and if you have a smattering of Italian, you can go to Leon the Hebrew, who will supply you to your heart's content; or if you should not care to go to foreign countries, you have at home Fonseca's *Of the Love of God,* in which is condensed all that you or the most imaginative mind can want on the subject.

"In short, all you have to do is to manage to quote these names or refer to these stories I have mentioned, and leave it to me to insert the annotations and quotations, and I swear by all that's good to fill your margins and use up four sheets at the end of the book.

"Now let us come to those references to authors which other

8. "But I say unto you, love your enemies . . ." (Matthew 5:44).
9. "From out of the heart proceed evil thoughts . . ." (Matthew 15:19).
1. "While you are prosperous, you will have many friends; but when times are troubled, you will be alone." Ovid, not Dionysius Cato. The substitution of the word *felix* for *sospes* in the original may be another ironical allusion to Lope de Vega, whose full name was Félix Lope de Vega y Carpio.

books have and you need for yours. The remedy for this is very simple: you have only to look up some book that quotes them all, from A to Z as you say yourself, and then insert the very same list in your book, and though the deception may be obvious, because you had so little need to make use of them, that is no matter; there will probably be some stupid enough to believe that you have made use of them all in this simple, straightforward story of yours. At any rate, if it answers no other purpose, this long catalogue of authors will serve to give instant authority to your book.

"Besides, no one will trouble himself to verify whether you have followed them or whether you have not, since it cannot possibly matter to him; especially as, if I understand it correctly, this book of yours has no need of any of those things you say it lacks, for it is, from beginning to end, an attack upon the books of chivalry, of which Aristotle never dreamed or St. Basil said a word or Cicero had any knowledge. Nor do the niceties of truth nor the observations of astrology come within the range of its fanciful nonsense; nor have geometrical measurements or refutations of the arguments used in rhetoric anything to do with it; nor does it have any reason to preach to anybody, mixing up things human and divine, a sort of motley in which no Christian understanding should dress itself. It has only to avail itself of imitation in its writing, and the more perfect the imitation the better the work will be. And as this piece of yours aims at nothing more than to destroy the authority and influence which books of chivalry have in the world and with the public, there is no need for you to go begging for aphorisms from philosophers, precepts from Holy Scripture, fables from poets, speeches from orators, or miracles from saints, but merely to take care that your sentences flow musically, pleasantly, and plainly, with clear, proper, and well-placed words, setting forth your purpose to the best of your power, and putting your ideas intelligibly, without confusion or obscurity.

"Strive, too, that in reading your story the melancholy may be moved to laughter, and the merry made merrier still; that the simple shall not be wearied, that the judicious shall admire the invention, that the grave shall not despise it, or the wise fail to praise it. Finally, keep your aim fixed on the destruction of that ill-founded edifice of the books of chivalry, hated by so many yet praised by many more; for if you succeed in this you will have achieved no small success."

In profound silence I listened to what my friend said, and his observations made such an impression on me that, without attempting to question them, I admitted their soundness, and out of them I determined to make this prologue, in which gentle reader, you will perceive my friend's good sense, my good fortune in finding such an adviser in such a time of need, and why you find—to your relief—the story of Don Quixote of La Mancha so straightforward and free of extraneous matter. This famous knight is held by all the inhabitants of the district of the Campo de Montiel to have been the chastest lover and the bravest knight that has for many years been seen in that region. I have no desire to magnify the service I am rendering to you in making you acquainted with so renowned and honored a knight, but I do desire your thanks for the acquaintance you will make with the famous Sancho Panza, his squire, in whom, to my thinking, I have given you condensed all the squirely virtues that are scattered throughout the swarm of the vain books of chivalry. And so may God give you health and not forget me. *Vale.*

[Preliminary Verses]

Urganda the Unknown[2]

To the book of Don Quixote of La Mancha

If to be welcomed by the good,
O Book, thou make thy steady aim,
No empty chatterer will dare
To question or dispute thy claim.
But if perchance thou hast a mind
To win of idiots approbation,
Lost labor will be thy reward,
Though they'll pretend appreciation.

They say a goodly shade he finds
Who shelters 'neath a goodly tree;
And such a one thy kindly star
In Béjar hath provided thee:
A royal tree whose spreading boughs
A show of princely fruit display;
A tree that bears a noble Duke,
The Alexander of his day.

Of a Manchegan gentleman
Thy purpose is to tell the story,
Relating how he lost his wits
O'er idle tales of love and glory,
Of ladies, arms, and cavaliers:
A new Orlando Furioso—
Innamorato, rather—who
Won Dulcinea del Toboso.

Put no vain emblems on thy shield
Or pompous coats-of-arms display.[3]
A modest dedication make,
And give no scoffer room to say,
"What! Alvaro de Luna[4] here?
Or is it Hannibal again?
Or does King Francis at Madrid
Once more of destiny complain?"[5]
Since Heaven it hath not pleased on thee
Deep erudition to bestow,

2. Urganda is a personage in the romance *Amadis of Gaul* who is rather like a female Merlin. She derived her title (which might also be translated "the Unrecognized") from her ability to change her appearance at will.

3. This is probably another jibe at Lope de Vega, who claimed descent from a legendary Spanish hero, and who printed his coat-of-arms with a motto which may also be alluded to at the end of this strophe.

4. A fifteenth-century statesman whose spectacular rise, fall, and execution made his name proverbial for the instability of worldly success.

5. Francis I spent a year in captivity in Madrid after the battle of Pavia.

Or black Latino's gift of tongues,[6]
No Latin let thy pages show.
Ape not philosophy or wit,
Lest those who really comprehend,
Wry fraces make and, whispering, ask,
"Why offer flowers to me, my friend?"[7]

Be not a meddler; no affair
Of thine the life thy neighbors lead.
Be prudent; oft the random jest
Recoils upon the jester's head.
Thy constant labor let it be
To earn thyself an honest name,
For fooleries preserved in print
Are perpetuity of shame.

A further counsel bear in mind:
If that thy roof be made of glass,
It shows small wit to pick up stones
To pelt the people as they pass.
Win the attention of the wise,
And give the thinker food for thought;
For he who writes frivolities,
Will but by simpletons be sought.

Amadís of Gaul[8]

To Don Quixote of La Mancha

SONNET

Thou that didst imitate that life of mine,
When I in lonely sadness on the great
Rock Peña Pobre sat disconsolate,
In self-imposèd penance there to pine;
Thou, whose only drink the bitter brine
Of thine own tears, and who without a plate
Of silver, copper, tin, in lowly state
Off the bare earth and on earth's fruits didst dine;
Live thou, of thine eternal glory sure.
So long as on the round of that fourth sphere
The bright Apollo shall his coursers steer,
In thy renown thou shalt remain secure,
Thy country's name in story shall endure,
And thy sage author stand without a peer.

6. Juan Latino, a self-educated Negro slave in the Duke of Sessa's household, became a freedman and professor of rhetoric and Latin at Granada, where he died in 1573.

7. "Flower" is underworld jargon for a swindle or trick.

8. Don Quixote's principal model, the hero of the most famous Spanish romance of chivalry. In a celebrated episode, Amadís, in disgrace with his beloved, retires to a desolate island, Peña Pobre ("Wretched Rock"), to die. Don Quixote imitates this "penance" in Part I, Ch. XXV.

Don Belianís of Greece[9]

To Don Quixote of La Mancha

SONNET

In slashing, hewing, cleaving, word and deed,
I was the foremost knight of chivalry,
Stout, bold, expert, as e'er the world did see;
Thousands from the oppressor's wrong I freed;
Great were my feats, eternal fame their meed;
In love I proved my truth and loyalty;
The hugest giant seemed a dwarf to me;
Ever to knighthood's laws gave I good heed.
My mastery the Goddess Fortune owned,
And even Chance, submitting to control,
Grasped by the forelock, yielded to my will.
Yet, though above yon hornèd moon enthroned
My fortune seems to sit, Quixote, still
Envy of thy achievements fills my soul.

The Lady Oriana[1]

To Dulcinea del Toboso

SONNET

Oh, fairest Dulcinea, could it be!—
It is a pleasant fancy to suppose so—
That Miraflores changed to El Toboso,
And London's town to that which shelters thee!
Oh, could mine but acquire that livery
Of countless charms thy mind and body show so!
Or him, now famous grown—thou mad'st him grow so—
Thy knight, in some dread combat could I see!
Oh, would I had resisted Amadís
By exercise of such coy chastity
As led thee Don Quixote to dismiss!
Then would my heavy sorrow turn to joy;
None would I envy, all would envy me,
And happiness be mine without alloy.

Gandalín, Squire of Amadís of Gaul

To Sancho Panza, squire of Don Quixote

SONNET

All hail, illustrious man! Fortune, when she
Bound thee apprentice to the squirely trade,

9. Belianís of Greece was the hero of another romance by Jerónimo Fernández, published in 1547 and continued in 1579.

1. Oriana, the beloved and eventually the wife of Amadís. Her castle, Miraflores, was within two leagues of London.

Her care and tenderness of thee displayed,
Shaping thy course from misadventure free.
No longer now doth proud knight-errantry
Regard with scorn the sickle and the spade;
Of towering arrogance less count is made
Than of plain esquire-like simplicity.
I envy thee thy Dapple, and thy name,
And those packsaddles thou wast wont to stuff
With comforts that thy providence proclaim.
Excellent Sancho! hail to thee again!
To thee alone the Ovid of our Spain
Does homage with the rustic kiss and cuff.[2]

From Donoso, the Motley Poet[3]

To Sancho Panza and Rocinante

[ON SANCHO]

I am the esquire Sancho Pan—
Who served Quixote of La Man—;
But from his service I retreat—,
Resolved to pass my life discreet—;
For Villadiego, called the Si—,
Maintained that only in reti—
Was found the secret of well-be—,
According to the *Celesti*—:[4]
A book divine, except for sin—
By speech too plain, in my opin—.

TO ROCINANTE

I am that Rocinante fa—,
Great-grandson of great Babie—,[5]
Who, all for being lean and bon—,
Had Don Quixote for an own—;
But if I matched him well in weak—,
I never took scant feedings meek—,
But kept myself in corn by steal—,
A trick I learned from Lazaril—,
When with a piece of straw so neat—
The blind man of his wine he cheat—.[6]

2. "Rustic kiss and cuff" refers to a practical joke which lies in inducing an unsuspecting person to kiss the joker's hand and then giving him a cuff on the cheek as he stoops. It is not clear who is meant by the Spanish Ovid.

3. Donoso, a surname but also an adjective meaning "witty," is a fictitious poet. Ormsby imitates the Spanish verse-form which rhymes only the accented syllable of each word and omits the rest. The reference to "Villadiego the Si[lent] is an allusion to an expression which means to flee from danger.

4. *Celesti[na]* is the title of a late-fifteenth-century Humanistic comedy, the main character of which is an old bawd.

5. Babieca, the famous charger of the Cid.

6. An allusion to the novel *Lazarillo de Tormes* (1544) and the trick by which the hero secured a portion of his master's wine.

Orlando Furioso[7]

To Don Quixote of La Mancha

SONNET

If thou art not a Peer, peer thou hast none;
  Among a thousand Peers thou art a peer;
  Nor is there room for one when thou art near,
Unvanquished victor, great unconquered one!
Orlando, by Angelica undone,
  Am I; o'er distant seas condemned to steer,
  And to Fame's altars as an offering bear
Valor respected by Oblivion.
I cannot be thy rival, for thy fame
  And prowess rise above all rivalry,
    Albeit both bereft of wits we go.
But, though the Scythian or the Moor to tame
  Was not thy lot, still thou dost rival me:
    Love binds us in a fellowship of woe.

The Knight of Phoebus[8]

To Don Quixote of La Mancha

SONNET

My sword was not to be compared with thine
  Phœbus of Spain, marvel of courtesy,
Nor with thy famous arm this hand of mine
  That smote from east to west as lightnings fly.
  I scorned all empire, and that monarchy
The rosy east held out did I resign
  For one glance of Claridiana's eye,
The bright Aurora for whose love I pine.
A miracle of constancy my love;
  And banished by her ruthless cruelty,
    This arm had might the rage of Hell to tame.
But, Gothic Quixote, happier thou dost prove,
    For thou dost live in Dulcinea's name,
  And famous, honored, wise, she lives in thee.

From Solisdán[9]

To Don Quixote of La Mancha

SONNET

Your fantasies, Quixote, it is true,
  That crazy brain of yours have quite upset,

7. Orlando, the hero of an Italian romance in verse, *The Madness of Roland*, by Ariosto. Roland, or Orlando, was one of the Twelve Peers of Charlemagne's court, and the infidelity of his beloved Angelica unhinged his mind. He is in some ways a model for Don Quixote.

8. The Knight of Phoebus is the hero of

But aught of base or mean hath never yet
Been charged by any in reproach to you.
Your deeds are open proof in all men's view;
For you went forth injustice to abate,
And for your pains sore drubbings did you get
From many a rascally and ruffian crew.
If fairest Dulcinea, your heart's queen,
Be unrelenting in her cruelty,
If still your woe be powerless to move her,
In such hard case your comfort let it be
That Sancho was a sorry go-between:
A booby he, hard-hearted she, and you no lover.

Dialogue

Between Babieca and Rocinante

SONNET

B. "How comes it, Rocinante, you're so lean?"
R. "I'm underfed, with overwork I'm worn."
B. "But what becomes of all the hay and corn?"
R. "My master gives me none; he's much too mean."
B. "Come, come, you show ill-breeding, sir, I ween;
'T is like an ass your master thus to scorn."
R. "*He* is an ass, will die an ass, an ass was born;
Why, he's in love; what's plainer to be seen?"
B. "To be in love is folly?"—*R.* "No great sense."
B. "You're metaphysical."—*R.* "From want of food."
B. "Rail at the squire, then."—*R.* "Why, what's the good?
I might indeed complain of him, I grant ye,
But, squire or master, where's the difference?
They're both as sorry hacks as Rocinante."

---

a romance by Diego Ortúñez de Calahorra, printed at Zaragoza in 1562 and later continued by other authors. The reference below to "Gothic" means "descended from the Gothic conquerors" of the fifth and sixth centuries, an exaggerated compliment.

9. Solisdán is either an invention of Cervantes or a printer's error for Solimán, the name of the Turkish sultan and also of the fictitious emperor of Trapisonda, father of the Claridiana mentioned in the previous poem and in the author's Prologue.

Table of the Chapters Contained in This Famous History of the Valorous Knight Don Quixote of La Mancha*

First Part of the Ingenious Gentleman Don Quixote of La Mancha

Second Part of the Ingenious Gentleman Don Quixote of La Mancha

* In the first edition of *Don Quixote*, this Table of Contents was at the end of the book, as is still the custom in Spanish-speaking countries.

Third Part of the Ingenious Gentleman Don Quixote of La Mancha

Fourth Part of the Ingenious Gentleman Don Quixote of La Mancha

End of the Table

The First Part of
The Ingenious Gentleman
Don Quixote of La Mancha

Chapter I

WHICH TREATS OF THE CHARACTER AND PURSUITS OF THE FAMOUS GENTLEMAN DON QUIXOTE OF LA MANCHA

In a village of La Mancha,[1] which I prefer to leave un-named, there lived not long ago one of those gentlemen that keep a lance in the lance-rack, an old shield, a lean hack, and a greyhound for hunting. A stew of rather more beef than mutton, hash on most nights, bacon and eggs on Saturdays, lentils on Fridays, and a pigeon or so extra on Sundays consumed three quarters of his income. The rest went for a coat of fine cloth and velvet breeches and shoes to match for holidays, while on weekdays he cut a fine figure in his best homespun. He had in his house a housekeeper past forty, a niece under twenty, and a lad for the field and marketplace, who saddled the hack as well as handled the pruning knife. The age of this gentleman of ours was bordering on fifty. He was of a hardy constitution, spare, gaunt-featured, a very early riser, and fond of hunting. Some say that his surname was Quixada or Quesada (for there is no unanimity among those who write on the subject), although reasonable conjectures tend to show that he was called Quexana. But this scarcely affects our story; it will be enough not to stray a hair's breadth from the truth in telling it.

You must know that the above-named gentleman devoted his leisure (which was mostly all the year round) to reading books of chivalry—and with such ardor and avidity that he almost entirely abandoned the chase and even the management of his property. To such a pitch did his eagerness and infatuation go that he sold many an acre of tillage land to buy books of chivalry to read, bringing home all he could find.

But there were none he liked so well as those written by the famous Feliciano de Silva, for their lucidity of style and complicated conceits were as pearls in his sight, particularly when in his reading he came upon outpourings of adulation and courtly chal-

1. "In a village of La Mancha" is a line from an old ballad. Cervantes probably had no specific village in mind, but the burlesque verses at the end of Part I, by the members of the Academy of Argamasilla, and the naming of Argamasilla de Alba as Don Quixote's town in the sequel of Part I written by Fernández de Avellaneda, have caused it to be identified since the seventeenth century as the place which the author preferred to leave unnamed.

lenges. There he often found passages like "*the reason of the unreason with which my reason is afflicted so weakens my reason that with reason I complain of your beauty;*" or again, "*the high heavens, that of your divinity divinely fortify you with the stars, render you deserving of the desert your greatness deserves.*"[2]

Over this sort of folderol the poor gentleman lost his wits, and he used to lie awake striving to understand it and worm out its meaning; though Aristotle himself could have made out or extracted nothing, had he come back to life for that special purpose. He was rather uneasy about the wounds which Don Belianís[3] gave and received, because it seemed to him that, however skilled the surgeons who had cured him, he must have had his face and body covered all over with seams and scars. He commended, however, the author's way of ending his book, with a promise to go on with that interminable adventure, and many a time he felt the urge to take up his pen and finish it just as its author had promised. He would no doubt have done so, and succeeded with it too, had he not been occupied with greater and more absorbing thoughts.

Many an argument did he have with the priest of his village (a learned man, and a graduate of Sigüenza[4]) as to which had been the better knight, Palmerín of England or Amadís of Gaul. Master Nicolás, the village barber, however, used to say that neither of them came up to the Knight of Phœbus, and that if there was any that could compare with *him* it was Don Galaor, the brother of Amadís of Gaul, because he had a spirit equal to every occasion, and was no wishy-washy knight or a crybaby like his brother, while in valor he was not a whit behind him.

In short, he became so absorbed in his books that he spent his nights from sunset to sunrise, and his days from dawn to dark, poring over them; and what with little sleep and much reading his brain shriveled up and he lost his wits.[5] His imagination was stuffed with all he read in his books about enchantments, quarrels, battles, challenges, wounds, wooings, loves, agonies, and all sorts of impossible nonsense. It became so firmly planted in his mind that the whole fabric of invention and fancy he read about was true, that to

2. The first passage quoted is from *Don Florisel de Niquea*, by Feliciano de Silva, the volumes of which appeared in 1532, 1536, and 1551. The second is from *Olivante de Laura*, printed in 1564 at Barcelona without author's name (Antonio de Torquemada).

3. *Don Belianís de Grecia*, by the Licentiate Jerónimo Fernández; first and second part, 1547, third and fourth, 1579. One Spanish commentator on *Don Quixote* (Clemecín) counted 101 serious wounds received by Belianís in vols. I and II alone.

4. The priest (*cura* in Spanish) is addressed afterwards as "Licentiate" which may mean that he was also a graduate in civil law. Sigüenza was one of the "minor universities." These granted degrees which were often laughed at by the Spanish humorists.

5. A contemporary reader would understand that the madness of Don Quixote is a result of excessive mental activity and not enough of his usual exercise, which caused the moisture of the brain to dry up. Don Quixote as described by Cervantes is a man of hot, dry temperament. Such persons were thought to be prone to manias.

him no history in the world was better substantiated. He used to say the Cid Ruy Díaz was a very good knight but that he was not to be compared with the Knight of the Burning Sword who with one backstroke cut in half two fierce and monstrous giants. He thought more of Bernardo del Carpio because at Roncesvalles he slew Roland in spite of enchantments, availing himself of Hercules' trick when he strangled Antæus the son of Terra in his arms. He approved highly of the giant Morgante, because, although of the giant breed which is always arrogant and ill-mannered, he alone was affable and well-bred. But above all he admired Reinaldos of Montalbán, especially when he saw him sallying forth from his castle and robbing everyone he met, and when beyond the seas he stole that image of Mohammed which, as his history says, was entirely of gold. To have a bout of kicking at that traitor of a Ganelon he would have given his housekeeper, and his niece into the bargain.[6]

In a word, his wits being quite gone, he hit upon the strangest notion that ever madman in this world hit upon. He fancied it was right and requisite, no less for his own greater renown than in the service of his country, that he should make a knight-errant of himself, roaming the world over in full armor and on horseback in quest of adventures. He would put into practice all that he had read of as being the usual practices of knights-errant: righting every kind of wrong, and exposing himself to peril and danger from which he would emerge to reap eternal fame and glory. Already the poor man saw himself crowned by the might of his arm Emperor of Trebizond at least. And so, carried away by the intense enjoyment he found in these pleasant fancies, he began at once to put his scheme into execution.

The first thing he did was to clean up some armor that had belonged to his ancestors and had for ages been lying forgotten in a corner, covered with rust and mildew. He scoured and polished it as best he could, but the one great defect he saw in it was that it had no closed helmet, nothing but a simple morion.[7] This deficiency, however, his ingenuity made good, for he contrived a kind of half-helmet of pasteboard which, fitted on to the morion, looked like a whole one. It is true that, in order to see if it was strong and fit to withstand a cut, he drew his sword and gave it a couple of slashes, the first of which undid in an instant what had taken him a week to do. The ease with which he had knocked it to pieces disconcerted him somewhat, and to guard against the danger he set to work again, fixing bars of iron on the inside until he was satisfied with its

6. Ganelon, the archtraitor of the Charlemagne legend.

7. A morion was an old-fashioned soldier's helmet with a brim, covering the top of the head, of the sort usually seen in pictures of the Spanish *conquistadores* of America. Don Quixote wants a helmet with a visor which covers the entire head; this would be more medieval, aristocratic, and knightly.

strength. Then, not caring to try any more experiments with it, he accepted and commissioned it as a helmet of the most perfect construction.

He next proceeded to inspect his nag, which, with its cracked hoofs and more blemishes than the steed of Gonela, that "*tantum pellis et ossa fruit*,"[8] surpassed in his eyes the Bucephalus of Alexander or the Babieca of the Cid. Four days were spent in thinking what name to give him, because (as he said to himself) it was not right that a horse belonging to a knight so famous, and one with such merits of its own, should be without some distinctive name. He strove to find something that would indicate what it had been before belonging to a knight-errant, and what it had now become. It was only reasonable that it should be given a new name to match the new career adopted by its master, and that the name should be a distinguished and full-sounding one, befitting the new order and calling it was about to follow. And so, after having composed, struck out, rejected, added to, unmade, and remade a multitude of names out of his memory and fancy, he decided upon calling it Rocinante. To his thinking this was a lofty, sonorous name that nevertheless indicated what the hack's status had been before it became what now it was, the first and foremost of all the hacks in the world.[9]

Having got a name for his horse so much to his taste, he was anxious to get one for himself, and he spent eight days more pondering over this point. At last he made up his mind to call himself Don Quixote,[1]—which, as stated above, led the authors of this veracious history to infer that his name quite assuredly must have been Quixada, and not Quesada as others would have it. It occurred to him, however, that the valiant Amadís was not content to call himself Amadís and nothing more but added the name of his kingdom and country to make it famous and called himself Amadís of Gaul. So he, like a good knight, resolved to add on the name of his own region and style himself Don Quixote of La Mancha. He believed that this accurately described his origin and country, and that he did it honor by taking its name for his own.

So then, his armor being furbished, his morion turned into a helmet, his hack christened, and he himself confirmed, he came to the conclusion that nothing more was needed now but to look for a lady to be in love with, for a knight-errant without love was like a tree without leaves or fruit, or a body without a soul.

"If, for my sins, or by my good fortune," he said to himself, "I come across some giant hereabouts, a common occurrence with knights-errant, and knock him to the ground in one onslaught, or

8. "It was nothing but skin and bones." Gonela was a famous Italian jester and author of a joke book.

9. *Rocín:* "work-horse." *Ante:* "formerly" or "foremost."

1. *Quixote*—or, as it is written in modern Spanish, *quijote*—means the piece of armor that protects the thigh.

cleave him asunder at the waist, or, in short, vanquish and subdue him, will it not be well to have some one I may send him to as a present, that he may come in and fall on his knees before my sweet lady, and in a humble, submissive voice say, 'I am the giant Caraculiambro, lord of the island of Malindrania, vanquished in single combat by the never sufficiently extolled knight Don Quixote of La Mancha, who has commanded me to present myself before your grace, that your highness may dispose of me at your pleasure'?"

Oh, how our good gentleman enjoyed the delivery of this speech, especially when he had thought of some one to call his lady! There was, so the story goes, in a village near his own a very good-looking farm-girl with whom he had been at one time in love, though, so far as is known, she never knew it nor gave a thought to the matter. Her name was Aldonza Lorenzo, and upon her he thought fit to confer the title of Lady of his Thoughts. Searching for a name not too remote from her own, yet which would aim at and bring to mind that of a princess and great lady, he decided upon calling her Dulcinea del Toboso, since she was a native of El Toboso. To his way of thinking, the name was musical, uncommon, and significant, like all those he had bestowed upon himself and his belongings.[2]

Chapter II

WHICH TREATS OF THE FIRST SALLY THE INGENIOUS DON QUIXOTE MADE FROM HOME

Once these preliminaries had been settled, he decided to wait no longer before putting his project into effect, for he was afflicted by the thought of how much the world would suffer because of his tardiness. Many were the wrongs that had to be righted, grievances redressed, injustices made good, abuses removed, and duties discharged. So, without informing anyone of his intentions, and without anybody seeing him, one morning before dawn (which was one of the hottest of the month of July) he put on his suit of armor, mounted Rocinante with his patched-up helmet on, grasped his shield, took his lance, and by the back door of the yard sallied forth upon the plain. It gave him immense pleasure and satisfaction to see with what ease he had inaugurated his great purpose.

Scarcely did he find himself upon the open plain, however, when a terrible thought struck him, one all but enough to make him

2. The humor of all these names is lost on English readers. "Don Quixote" suggests "Lanzarote" (Lancelot), but the *-ote* ending in Spanish is also suggestive of boorishness or rusticity. La Mancha is arid, flat, farm country, utterly different from the mysterious forests or exotic lands of the romances of chivalry. Many of the towns have names which are likewise unromantic and rustic: Argamasilla means "mortar," El Toboso means "limestone region," etc. Aldonza Lorenzo is an archetypically rustic name. Perhaps one might compare the situation by imagining an Arthurian romance in a setting of the American West, with its dust, heat, commonplace names, and so on.

abandon the enterprise at the very outset. It occurred to him that he had not been dubbed a knight and that according to the law of chivalry he neither could nor ought to bear arms against any knight; and that even if he had been, still he ought, as a novice knight, to wear white armor, without a device upon the shield until his prowess had earned him one. These reflections made him waver in his purpose, but his craziness being stronger than any reasoning, he made up his mind to have himself dubbed a knight by the first one he came across. In this he would be following the example of others in the same situation, as he had read in the books that brought him to this pass. As for white armor, he resolved, on the first opportunity, to scour his until it was whiter than an ermine. Having thus comforted himself, he pursued his way, taking that which his horse chose, for in this he believed lay the essence of adventures.

As our new-fledged adventurer paced along, he kept talking to himself. "Who knows," he said, "whether in time to come, when the veracious history of my famous deeds is made known, the sage who writes it, when he has to set forth my first sally in the early morning, may not do it after this fashion? 'Scarce had the rubicund Apollo spread o'er the face of the broad spacious earth the golden threads of his bright hair, scarce had the little birds of painted plumage attuned their notes to hail with dulcet and mellifluous harmony the coming of the rosy Dawn, that, deserting the soft couch of her jealous spouse, was appearing to mortals at the gates and balconies of the Manchegan horizon, when the renowned knight Don Quixote of La Mancha, quitting the lazy down, mounted his celebrated steed Rocinante and began to traverse the ancient and famous Fields of Montiel,' " which in fact he was actually traversing.

"Happy the age, happy the time," he continued, "in which shall be made known my deeds of fame, worthy to be molded in brass, carved in marble, limned in pictures, for a memorial for ever. And thou, O sage magician, whoever thou art, to whom it shall fall to be the chronicler of this wondrous history, forget not, I entreat thee, my good Rocinante, the constant companion of my ways and wanderings."

Then he broke out again, as if he were really lovesick, "O Princess Dulcinea, lady of this captive heart, a grievous wrong hast thou done me to drive me forth with scorn, and with inexorable obduracy banish me from the presence of thy beauty. O lady, deign to hold in remembrance this heart, thy vassal, that thus in anguish pines for love of thee."

So he went on stringing together these and other absurdities, all of the sort his books had taught him, imitating their language as well as he could. All the while he rode so slowly and the sun mounted so rapidly and with such heat that it was enough to melt his brains if he had any. Nearly all day he traveled without anything remarkable happening to him. This plunged him in despair, for he was eager to encounter at the earliest moment someone on whom to test the valor of his mighty arm.

Some writers declare that the first adventure he met with was that of Puerto Lápice, while others say it was that of the windmills. But what I have ascertained on this point, and what I have found written in the annals of La Mancha, is that he was on the road all day, and towards nightfall his hack and he found themselves dead tired and hungry. Looking all around to see if he could discover any castle or shepherd's hut where he might refresh himself and satisfy his needs, he perceived not far out of his way an inn. It was as welcome as a star guiding him to the portals, if not the palaces, of his redemption; and quickening his pace he reached it just as night was falling.

At the door were standing two young women, party girls as they call them, on their way to Seville with some mule drivers who had chanced to halt that night at the inn. As everything our adventurer thought, saw, or imagined seemed to him to be fashioned and to happen on the same lines as what he had been reading, the moment he saw the inn he pictured it to himself as a castle with its four turrets and pinnacles of shining silver, not forgetting the drawbridge and moat and every feature usually ascribed to such castles. To this inn, which to him seemed a castle, he advanced, and at a short distance from it he checked Rocinante, expecting that some dwarf would mount the battlements to proclaim by sound of trumpet the arrival of a knight at the castle. But seeing they were slow about it and that Rocinante was in a hurry to reach the stable, he made for the inn door. There he perceived the two misguided damsels, who seemed to him to be two fair maidens or lovely ladies taking their ease at the castle gate.

At this moment it so happened that a swineherd who was going through the harvested fields collecting a drove of pigs (for, without any apology, that is what they are called) gave a blast on his horn to bring them together. Forthwith it seemed to Don Quixote to be what he was expecting, the signal of some dwarf announcing his arrival, and so with prodigious satisfaction he rode up to the inn and to the ladies. Seeing a man of this sort approaching in full armor and with lance and shield, they fearfully turned back toward the inn. But Don Quixote, guessing their fear by their flight, raised his pasteboard visor and disclosed his dry, dusty face. He addressed them with a courteous air and in a gentle voice.

"Flee not, your ladyships, nor fear ye any harm," he said, "for it belongs not nor pertains to the order of knighthood which I profess to harm anyone, much less highborn maidens as your appearance proclaims you to be." The girls were looking at him and straining their eyes to make out the features which the clumsy visor obscured, but when they heard themselves called maidens, a thing so much out of their line, they could not restrain their laughter. At this Don Quixote took offense. "Modesty becomes the fair, and moreover laughter that has little cause is great folly," he declared. "This, however, I say not to pain or anger you, for my desire is none other than to serve you."

The incomprehensible language and the unpromising looks of our cavalier only increased the ladies' laughter, and that increased his irritation. Matters might have gone farther if at that moment the innkeeper had not come out. Being a very fat man, he was a very peaceful one. When he saw this grotesque figure clad in armor that did not match any more exactly than did his saddle, bridle, lance, shield, or breastplate, he felt inclined to join the damsels in their outburst of merriment. He was awed by all this complicated weaponry, however, and decided to keep a civil tongue in his head.

"Señor knight," he said, "if your worship wants lodging, excepting the bed (for there is not one in the inn), there is plenty of everything else here."

Don Quixote noted the respectful bearing of the warden of the fortress (for so innkeeper and inn seemed in his eyes). "Sir Castellan," he replied, "for me anything will suffice, for 'My armor is my only wear, My only rest the fray.'" The innkeeper fancied Don Quixote had called him Castellan because he took him for a "worthy of Castile."[1] In actual fact he was an Andalusian, one of those from the strand of San Lúcar, as crafty a thief as Cacus[2] and as full of tricks as a student or a page.

"In that case," said he, "'Your bed is on the flinty rock, Your sleep to watch alway.'[3] So you may dismount and count on enough opportunities for sleeplessness under this roof for a twelvemonth, not to say for a single night."

With this, he advanced to hold the stirrup for Don Quixote, who got down with great difficulty and exertion, for he had not broken his fast all day. He then instructed the innkeeper to take great care of his horse, as he was the best bit of flesh that ever ate bread in this world. The landlord eyed him over but did not find him as good as Don Quixote said, or even half as good. However, he put him up in the stable and returned to see what might be wanted by his guest. The damsels, who had by this time made their peace with the gentleman, were now relieving him of his armor. They had taken off his breastplate and backpiece, but they neither knew nor saw how to open the throat-piece or remove his make-shift helmet. It had

1. These jokes depend on the various meanings of *castellano*: "Castilian," "castle warden," and, in underworld slang, "thief."

2. In Roman legend, Cacus was a giant son of Vulcan, who robbed the Italians of their cattle. His name is proverbial in Spanish for "thief."

3. In the lines above, Don Quixote quotes a popular ballad; in these, the landlord takes up the same ballad, with amusing aptness.

been fastened with green ribbons which, since the knots could never be undone, would have to be cut. This however he would not by any means consent to, and so he remained all the evening with his helmet on, the funniest and oddest figure that can be imagined. Since he took the shop-worn trollops who were removing his armor to be ladies of high degree belonging to the castle, he addressed them with great sprightliness:

> " 'Oh, never, surely, was there knight
> So served by hand of dame,
> As served was he, Quixote called,
> When from his town he came,
> With maidens waiting on himself,
> Princesses on his hack'

—or Rocinante, for that, my ladies, is my horse's name, and Don Quixote of La Mancha is my own. For though I had no intention of declaring myself until my achievements in your service and honor had made me known, the necessity of adapting that old ballad about Lancelot to the present occasion has given you the knowledge of my name altogether prematurely. A time, however, will come for your ladyships to command and me to obey, and then the might of my arm will show my desire to serve you."

The girls, who were not used to hearing rhetoric of this sort, had nothing to say in reply and only asked him if he wanted anything to eat. "I would gladly eat a bit of something," said Don Quixote, "for I feel it would be very beneficial."

The day happened to be a Friday, and in the whole inn there was nothing but some pieces of the salt fish they call in Castile *abadejo*, in Andalusia *bacallao*, in some places *curadillo*, and in others "troutlet." So they asked him if he thought he could eat troutlet, for there was no other fish to give him. "If there are troutlets enough," said Don Quixote, "they will be the same thing as a whole trout. It is all one to me whether I am given eight *reales* in small change or a piece-of-eight. Moreover, it may be that these troutlets are like veal, which is better than beef, or kid, which is better than goat. But whatever it may be, let it come quickly, for the burden and pressure of arms cannot be borne without support to the inside."

They set a table for him at the door of the inn for the sake of the air, and the host brought him a portion of ill-soaked and worse cooked cod, and a piece of bread as black and moldy as his own armor. A laughable sight it was to see him eating, for having his helmet on and the visor up, he could not with his own hands put anything into his mouth unless some one else placed it there, and this service one of the ladies rendered him. But to give him anything to drink was impossible, or would have been, had not the landlord bored a reed, and putting one end in his mouth poured the wine into him through the other. All this he bore with patience rather than sever the ribbons of his helmet.

While this was going on there came up to the inn a swinegelder who, as he approached, sounded his reed pipe four or five times. Don Quixote, consequently, became completely convinced that he was in some famous castle, and that they were regaling him with music, and that the codfish was trout, the bread the whitest, the wenches ladies, and the landlord the castellan of the castle. In view of all this, he concluded that his resolve and sortie had been to some avail. Yet it still distressed him to think he had not been dubbed a knight, for it was plain to him he could not lawfully engage in any adventure without receiving the order of knighthood.

Chapter III

WHEREIN IS RELATED THE DROLL WAY IN WHICH DON QUIXOTE HAD HIMSELF DUBBED A KNIGHT

Harassed by this reflection, he wasted no time on the scanty supper always found in such inns, and when it was finished he called the landlord. Having shut himself up in the stable with him, Don Quixote fell on his knees before him. "From this spot I rise not, valiant knight," he declared," "until thy courtesy grant me the boon I seek, one that will redound to thy praise and the benefit of the human race." Seeing his guest at his feet and hearing a speech of this kind, the landlord stood staring at him in bewilderment without knowing what to do or say. He entreated Don Quixote to rise, but all to no purpose until he had agreed to grant the boon demanded.

"I looked for no less, my lord, from thy High Magnificence," replied Don Quixote, "and I have to tell thee that the boon I have asked and which thy liberality has granted is that thou shalt dub me knight tomorrow morning. Tonight I shall watch my arms in the chapel of this thy castle and tomorrow, as I have said, what I so much desire will be accomplished. It will enable me lawfully to roam through all the four quarters of the world seeking adventures on behalf of those in distress, as is the duty of chivalry and of knights-errant like myself, whose ambition is directed to such deeds."

The landlord, as has been mentioned, was something of a wag. He had already some suspicion of his guest's lack of wits, and to hear talk of this kind quite convinced him. To provide sport for the night he determined to humor Don Quixote. So he told him he was quite right in pursuing the object he had in view, and that such a motive was natural and becoming in cavaliers as distinguished as he seemed and his gallant bearing showed him to be. As for the landlord himself, in his younger days he had followed the same honorable calling, roaming in quest of adventures in various parts of the world, among others the curing-grounds and Riarán suburbs of Málaga, the red light district of Seville, the Little Market of Segovia, Olivera Square in Valencia, Rondilla Lane in Granada, the Strand of San Lúcar, the Horse Fountain of Córdoba, the taverns of Toledo,[1] and sundry other localities. There he had proved the nimbleness of his feet and the lightness of his fingers, doing many wrongs, courting many widows, ruining a few maidens and swindling a few minors, and, in short, bringing himself under the notice of almost every tribunal and court of justice in Spain. But at last he had retired to this castle of his, where he was living upon his property and upon that of others. Here he received all knights-errant of whatever rank or condition they might be, all for the great love he bore them and that they might share their substance with him in return for his benevolence.

He told Don Quixote, moreover, that in this castle of his there was no chapel in which he could watch over his armor, as it had been pulled down in order to be rebuilt. Yet in a case of necessity it might, he knew, be watched anywhere, and vigil might be held that night in a courtyard of the castle. In the morning, God willing, the requisite ceremonies might be performed so as to have him dubbed a knight, and so thoroughly dubbed that nobody could be more so.

Then he asked if he had any money with him, to which Don Quixote replied that he had not a cent, as in the histories of knights-errant he had never read of any of them carrying any. On this point the landlord told him he was mistaken, for, though not recorded in the histories, because in the author's opinion there was no need to mention anything so obvious and necessary as money and clean shirts, it was not to be supposed therefore that they did not carry them. He might regard it as certain and established that all knights-errant (about whom there were so many full and unimpeachable books) carried well-furnished purses in case of emergency, and likewise carried shirts and a little box of ointment to cure the wounds they received. For in those plains and deserts where they engaged in combat and came out wounded, there was not always someone to cure them, unless indeed they had for a friend some sage magician to aid them at once by fetching through the air on a cloud some damsel or dwarf with a vial of water of such power that by tasting one drop of it they were cured of their hurts and wounds in an instant and left as sound as if they had not received any harm whatever. In case this should not occur, the knights of old took care to see that their squires were provided with money and other requisites, such as bandages and ointments for

1. The localities mentioned were famous meeting places for delinquents, prostitutes, itinerant workers, gamblers, etc.

healing purposes. And when it happened that knights had no squires (which was rarely and seldom the case) they themselves carried everything in very slim saddlebags that were hardly seen on the horse's croup, as if it were something else of more importance. Unless for some such reason, carrying saddlebags was not very favorably regarded among knights-errant. He therefore advised him (and, as his godson so soon to be, he might even command him) never from that time forth to travel without money and the usual requirements, and he would find how useful they were when he least expected it.

Don Quixote promised to follow his advice scrupulously, and it was arranged forthwith that he should watch over his armor in a large yard at one side of the inn. So, collecting it all together, Don Quixote placed it on a trough that stood by the side of a well, and putting his shield on his arm, he grasped his lance and began with a stately air to march up and down in front of the trough. As he began his march night began to fall.

The landlord told all the people in the inn about his guest's craziness, the watching of the armor, and the dubbing ceremony to come. Full of wonder at so strange a form of madness, they flocked to see it from a distance and observed with what composure he sometimes paced up and down, or sometimes, leaning on his lance, gazed on his armor without taking his eyes off it for ever so long. As the night closed in with a light from the moon so brilliant that it might vie with the source from which it was borrowed, everything the novice knight did was plainly seen by all.

Meanwhile one of the mule drivers who were in the inn saw fit to water his team, making it necessary to remove Don Quixote's armor, as it lay on the trough. But the knight, seeing the other approach, hailed him in a loud voice.

"O thou," he said, "whoever thou art, rash knight that comest to lay hands on the armor of the most valorous errant that ever girt on sword, have a care what thou dost. Touch it not unless thou wouldst lay down thy life as the penalty of thy rashness." The mule driver gave no heed to these words, though for the sake of his health it would have been advisable to do so. He seized the armor by the straps and flung it some distance from him. At this, Don Quixote raised his eyes to heaven, and appeared to fix his thoughts upon his lady Dulicinea. "Aid me, lady mine," he entreated, "in this the first encounter that presents itself to this breast which thou holdest in subjection. Let not thy favor and protection fail me in this first jeopardy."

Having made these and similar declarations, he dropped his shield and lifted his lance with both hands. With it he dealt such a blow on the driver's head that he stretched him on the ground, so stunned that had he followed it up with a second there would have been no need of a surgeon to cure the mule driver. This done, Don Quixote picked up his armor and began walking up and down with the same serenity as before.

Shortly after this another mule driver, unaware of what had happened (for the first one still lay senseless), came out with the same intention of watering his mules. He too was proceeding to remove the armor in order to clear the trough, when Don Quixote, without uttering a word or imploring aid from anyone, once more dropped his shield and once more lifted his lance. Without actually smashing the second driver's head to bits, he made more than three pieces of it, for he laid it open in four quarters. At the noise, all the people in the inn ran to the spot, and among them the landlord. Seeing this, Don Quixote braced his shield on his arm and laid his hand on his sword. "O Lady of Beauty," he exclaimed, "strength and support of my faint heart, it is time for thee to turn the eyes of thy greatness on this thy captive knight on the brink of so mighty an adventure."

By this he felt himself so inspired that he would not have flinched if all the carriers in the world had assailed him. The comrades of the wounded, perceiving the plight they were in, began from a distance to shower stones on Don Quixote. He screened himself as best he could with his shield, for he did not dare to move away from the trough and leave his armor unprotected. The landlord shouted to them to leave him alone, for he had already told them that the knight was mad and as a madman would not be accountable even if he killed them all. Still louder shouted Don Quixote, calling them knaves and traitors, and the lord of the castle, who allowed knights-errant to be treated in this fashion, a villain and a low-born knight whom, had he received the order of knighthood, he would call to account for his treachery. "But of you," he cried, "base and vile rabble, I make no account; fling, strike, come on, do all ye can against me, ye shall see what the reward of your folly and insolence will be." This he uttered with so much spirit and boldness that he filled his assailants with a terrible fear, and it was as much for this reason as at the persuasion of the landlord that they quit stoning him. He allowed them to carry off the wounded and then, with the same calmness and composure as before, resumed the watch over his armor.

The pranks his guest was indulging in were not at all to the landlord's liking. So he determined to cut matters short and confer upon him at once the accursed order of knighthood before any further misadventure could happen. Going up to him, he apologized for the rudeness which, without his knowledge, had been shown by these low people, who, however, had been well punished for their audacity. As he had already explained, he said, there was no chapel in the castle, nor was it needed for what remained to be done. As he understood the ceremonial of the order, the whole point of being dubbed a knight lay in the accolade and in the slap on the shoulder, and that could be administered in the middle of a field. Don Quixote had now done all that was needful as to watching the armor, for all requirements were satisfied by a watch of two hours only, while he had been at it more than four. Don Quixote believed it all, telling the landlord that he stood there ready to obey and that the matter should be concluded as rapidly as possible. For, if he were again attacked, and felt himself to be dubbed knight, he would not, he thought, leave a soul alive in the castle, except such as out of respect he might spare at the landlord's bidding.

Thus warned and menaced, the castellan forthwith brought out a book in which he entered the amounts of straw and barley sold to the mule drivers. With a lad carrying a candle-stump, and the two damsels already mentioned, he returned to where Don Quixote stood and ordered him to kneel down. Then he read from his account book as if he were repeating some devout prayer. In the middle of his delivery he raised his hand and gave Don Quixote a sturdy blow on the neck, and then, with the knight's own sword, a smart slap on the shoulder, all the while muttering between his teeth as if he were saying his prayers. Having done this, he directed one of the ladies to gird on the sword, which she did with great self-possession and gravity. Of both of these a plentiful supply was needed, lest a burst of laughter should signal each stage of the ceremony; but what they had already seen of the novice knight's prowess kept their laughter within bounds.

"May God make your worship a very fortunate knight and grant you success in battle," said the worthy lady, as she girded him with the sword. Don Quixote asked her name so that he might from that time forward know to whom he was indebted for the favor he had received, as he meant to confer upon her some share of the honor the might of his arm would bring. She answered with great humility that she was called La Tolosa, and that she was the daughter of a cobbler of Toledo who lived in the stalls of Sancho Bienaya Square and that wherever she might be, she would serve and esteem him as her lord. Don Quixote replied that she would do him a favor by henceforward assuming the "Don" and calling herself Doña Tolosa. She promised she would, the other damsel buckled on his spur, and there followed almost the same conversation as with the lady of the sword. He asked her name, and she said it was La Molinera and that she was the daughter of a respectable miller of Antequera. Don Quixote asked her also to adopt the "Don" and call herself Doña Molinera, offering her further services and favors.[2]

Having thus, with hot haste and speed, brought to a conclusion these unprecedented ceremonies, Don Quixote was on tenterhooks

2. Prostitutes did in fact use the title *doña* ("lady" or "madam").

until he could see himself on horseback sallying forth in quest of adventures. Saddling and mounting Rocinante, he embraced his host and thanked him for his kindness in knighting him. The language he employed was so extraordinary that it is impossible to convey an idea of it. The landlord, to get him out of the inn, replied with no less rhetoric though with shorter words, and without asking him to pay the bill let him go with a "Godspeed."

Chapter IV

OF WHAT HAPPENED TO OUR KNIGHT WHEN HE LEFT THE INN

Day was dawning when Don Quixote left the inn, so happy, so gallant, so exhilarated at finding himself now dubbed a knight, that his joy almost burst the girth of his horse. However, recalling the advice of his host as to what he should carry with him, especially money and shirts, he determined to go home and provide himself with all, and also with a squire. He planned to hire a farmer who was a neighbor of his, a poor man with a family, but very well qualified for the job of squire to a knight. With this in mind, he turned his horse's head toward his village, and Rocinante, thus reminded of his old quarters, stepped out so briskly that he hardly seemed to tread the earth.

He had not gone far when out of a thicket on his right there seemed to come feeble cries as of some one in distress. "Thanks be to heaven," he exclaimed, as soon as he had heard them, "for the favor it accords me. Already I am offered the opportunity of fulfilling the obligation I have undertaken and gathering the fruit of my ambition. These cries come no doubt from some man or woman in want of help and needing my aid and protection."

Turning his reins, he headed Rocinante in the direction from which the cries seemed to come. He had gone but a few paces into the wood when he saw a mare tied to an oak. Tied to another and stripped from the waist upwards was a youth of about fifteen years of age, from whom the cries came. Nor were they without cause, for a lusty farmer was flogging him with a belt and following up every blow with scoldings and commands. "Your mouth shut and your eyes open!" he kept repeating, while the youth answered, "I won't do it again, master! By God's passion I won't do it again, and I'll take better care of the flock in the future."

When he saw what was going on, Don Quixote angrily intervened. "Discourteous knight," he called out, "it ill becomes thee to assail one who cannot defend himself. Mount thy steed and take thy lance" (for there was a lance[1] leaning against the oak to which the mare was tied), "and I will make thee know that thou art behaving as a coward."

1. Lances were and are used as cattle prods by mounted herdsmen.

The farmer, seeing before him this figure in full armor brandishing a lance over his head, gave himself up for dead. "Sir Knight," he answered meekly, "this boy I am punishing is my servant. I employ him to watch a flock of sheep I keep in these parts, but he is so careless I lose one every day. When I punish him for his carelessness—or cheating—he says I do it out of stinginess, to avoid paying him the wages I owe him. Before God and on my soul, he lies."

"In my presence thou utterest 'he lies,' base clown?" said Don Quixote. "By the sun that shines on us I have a mind to run thee through with this lance. Pay him at once without another word. If not, by the God that rules us I will make an end of thee, and annihilate thee on the spot. Release him instantly."

The farmer hung his head and without a word untied his servant. Don Quixote asked the boy how much his master owed him.

He replied that it was nine months at seven *reales* a month. Don Quixote added it up, found that it came to seventy-three *reales*,[2] and told the farmer to pay it immediately, if he did not want to die for it.

The trembling rustic replied that as he lived and by the oath he had sworn (though he had not sworn any) it was not that much. There were to be taken into account and deducted three pairs of shoes he had given the boy, and a *real* for two blood-lettings when he was sick.

"That is all very well," said Don Quixote, "but let the shoes and the blood-lettings stand as compensation for the blows you have given him without any cause. For if he ruined the hide of the shoes you paid for, you have damaged that of his body, and if the barber took blood from him when he was sick, you have drawn it when he was sound. So on that score he owes you nothing."

"The difficulty is, Sir Knight, that I have no money here. Let Andrés came home with me and I will pay him all, *real* by *real*."

"I go with him!" said the youth. "God forbid! No, señor, not for the world; for once alone with me, he would flay me like a Saint Bartholomew."

"He will do nothing of the kind," said Don Quixote. "I have only to command, and he will obey me. And as he has sworn to me by the order of knighthood which he has received, I leave him free and guarantee the payment."

"Consider what you are saying, señor," said the youth. "This master of mine is not a knight nor has he received any order of knighthood. He is Juan Haldudo[3] the Rich of Quintanar."

2. Don Quixote's calculation is, of course, wrong. A *real* ("royal") was a silver coin about the size of an American quarter, weighing 3.20 to 3.38 grams. It was equivalent to thirty-four copper *maravedís* in Cervantes' day. It was usually minted in pieces-of-eight, eight-*real* coins, which had become the standard unit.

3. *Haldudo* means "skirted" or "wearing long or full skirts." Don Quixote takes it to be an unflattering nickname.

"That matters little," replied Don Quixote. "There may be Haldudos who are knights. Moreover, everyone is the son of his works."

"That is true," said Andrés. "But this master of mine—of what works is he the son, when he refuses me the wages of my sweat and labor?"

"I do not refuse, brother Andrés," said the farmer. "Be good enough to come along with me, and I swear by all the orders of knighthood there are in the world to pay you as I have agreed, *real* by *real*, and perfumed at that."

"You may omit the perfume," said Don Quixote. "Give it to him in *reales*, and I shall be satisfied. See that you do as you have sworn; if not, by the same oath, I swear to come back and hunt you down and punish you. And I shall find you, even if you hide as cleverly as a lizard. If you desire to know who it is that lays this command upon you, that you may be more firmly bound to obey it, know that I am the valorous Don Quixote of La Mancha, the undoer of wrongs and injustices. So, God be with you, and keep in mind what you have promised and sworn under those penalties that have been already declared to you."

So saying, he gave Rocinante the spur and was soon out of reach. The farmer followed him with his eyes, and when he saw that he had cleared the wood and was no longer in sight, he turned to his boy Andrés. "Come here, my son," he said, "I want to pay you what I owe you, as that undoer of wrongs has commanded me."

"My oath on it," said Andrés, "your worship will be well advised to obey the command of that good knight, may he live a thousand years! As he is a valiant and just judge, by St. Roque, if you do not pay me, he will come back and do as he said."

"My oath on it, too," said the farmer. "But as I have a strong affection for you, I want to add to the debt in order to add to the payment." And he seized him by the arm, tied him up again, and gave him such a flogging that he left him for dead.

"Now, Master Andrés," said the farmer, "call on the undoer of wrongs. You will find he won't undo that, though I am not sure that I have quite done with you, for I have a good mind to flay you alive." But at last he untied him and gave him leave to go look for his judge so that the sentence pronounced might be carried out.

Andrés went off rather down in the mouth, swearing he would go to look for the valiant Don Quixote of La Mancha. He would tell him exactly what had happened, and all would have to be repaid him sevenfold. But for all that he went off weeping, while his master stood there laughing.

Thus did the valiant Don Quixote right that wrong. Thoroughly satisfied with what had taken place, as he considered he had made a very happy and noble beginning with his knighthood, he took the road towards his village in perfect self-content.

"Well mayest thou this day call thyself fortunate above all on earth, O Dulcinea del Toboso, fairest of the fair!" he said in a low voice. "For it has fallen to thy lot to hold subject and submissive to thy full will and pleasure a knight so renowned as is and will be Don Quixote of La Mancha, who, as all the world knows, yesterday received the order of knighthood, and hath today righted the greatest wrong and grievance that ever injustice conceived and cruelty perpetrated, who hath today plucked the rod from the hand of yonder ruthless oppressor so wantonly lashing that tender child."

He now came to a road branching in four directions, and immediately he was reminded of those crossroads where knights-errant used to stop to consider which road they should take. In imitation of them he halted for a while, and after having deeply considered it, he gave Rocinante his head, submitting his own will to that of his hack, who followed out his first intention, which was to make straight for his own stable.

After he had gone about two miles Don Quixote perceived a large party of people, who, as afterwards appeared, were some Toledo traders, on their way to buy silk at Murcia. There were six of them coming along under their umbrellas, with four mounted servants and three muleteers on foot. Scarcely had Don Quixote caught sight of them when the fancy possessed him that this must be some new adventure. To help him imitate as far as he could those armed encounters he had read of in his books, here seemed to come one made on purpose, and he decided to act. So with lofty bearing and determination he fixed himself firmly in his stirrups, got his lance ready, and brought his shield before his breast. Planting himself in the middle of the road, he stood waiting the approach of these knights-errant, as he now held them to be. When they had come near enough to see and hear, he made a haughty gesture. "All the world stop," he cried out, "unless all the world confess that in all the world there is no maiden fairer than the Empress of La Mancha, the peerless Dulcinea del Toboso."

The traders halted at the sound of this language and the sight of the strange figure that uttered it, and from both figure and language they at once guessed the craziness of their owner. They wished to find out, however, just what sort of avowal was being demanded, and one of them, who was rather fond of a joke and very sharp-witted, made reply. "Sir Knight," he said, "we do not know who this good lady is that you speak of. Show her to us, for if she is of such beauty as you suggest, with all our hearts and without any pressure we will confess the truth that you have required of us."

"If I were to show her to you," replied Don Quixote, "what merit would ye have in confessing a truth so manifest? The essential point is that without seeing her ye must believe, confess, affirm, swear, and defend it. Else ye have to do with me in battle, monstrous, arrogant rabble that ye are. Come ye on, one by one as the order of knighthood requires, or all together as is the custom and vile usage of your breed. Here do I bide and await you, relying on the justice of the cause I maintain."

"Sir Knight," replied the trader, "I entreat your worship in the name of this present company of princes, to save us from burdening our consciences with the confession of a thing we have never seen or heard of. Moreover, it is one much to the prejudice of the Empresses and Queens of the Alcarria and Estremadura.[4] Let your worship be pleased to show us some portrait of this lady, though it be no bigger than a grain of wheat. For one can judge the cloth by the sample, and in this way we shall be satisfied and easy, and you will be content and pleased. Indeed I believe we are already so far agreed with you that even though her portrait should show her blind in one eye, and distilling vermilion and sulphur from the other, we would nevertheless, to gratify your worship, say all in her favor that you desire."

"She distills nothing of the kind, vile rabble," said Don Quixote, burning with rage, "nothing of the kind, I say, but ambergris and civet in cotton.[5] Nor is she one-eyed or humpbacked, but straighter than a Guadarrama spindle. Now ye must pay for the blasphemy ye have uttered against beauty like that of my lady."

So saying, he charged with leveled lance against the one who had spoken, with such fury and fierceness that, if luck had not contrived that Rocinante should stumble midway and come down, it would have gone hard with the rash trader. Down went Rocinante, and over went his master, rolling along the ground for some distance. When he tried to rise he could not do so, being encumbered with lance, shield, spurs, helmet, and the weight of his old armor.

"Fly not, cowards and caitiffs!" he kept saying, all the while struggling to get up. "Stay, for not by my fault, but my horse's, am I stretched here."

One of the party's muleteers, who could not have had much good nature in him, hearing the poor prostrate man blustering in this style, was unable to refrain from giving him an answer on his ribs. Coming up to him he seized his lance, broke it in pieces, and with one piece began so to belabor our Don Quixote that, notwithstanding and in spite of his armor, he milled him like a measure of wheat. His masters called out not to lay on so hard and to leave him alone, but the muleteer's blood was up. He would not abandon the game until he had vented the rest of his wrath, and, gathering up the remaining fragments of the lance, he finished by hurling

4. Two thinly populated, backward regions. The sharp-witted merchant has immediately seen the absurdity of Don Quixote's "Empress of La Mancha."

5. Ambergris and civet are fragrant secretions of the sperm whale and civet cat, once popular in perfume. Civet was imported packed in cotton.

them at the unhappy victim. For his part, through the storm of sticks that rained on him he never ceased threatening heaven and earth and the brigands, for such they seemed to him.

At last the muleteer was tired, and the traders continued their journey, taking with them matter for talk about the poor fellow who had been cudgeled. He, when he found himself alone, made another effort to rise. But if he was unable when whole and sound, how was he to rise after having been thrashed and well nigh knocked to pieces? Yet he considered himself fortunate, as it seemed to him that this was a real knight-errant's mishap and entirely, he believed, the fault of his horse. However, battered in body as he was, to rise was beyond his power.

Chapter V

IN WHICH THE NARRATIVE OF OUR KNIGHT'S MISHAP IS CONTINUED

Finding, then, that, in fact he could not move, he thought of having recourse to his usual remedy, which was to think of some passages in his books. His madness brought to his mind Baldwin and the Marquis of Mantua, when Carloto left Baldwin wounded on the mountain side. The story is known by heart by the children, not forgotten by the young men, and lauded and even believed by the old folk. Yet for all that it is not a whit truer than the miracles of Mohammed. This seemed to him to fix exactly the situation in which he found himself; so, making a show of severe suffering, he began to roll on the ground and with feeble breath repeat the very words which the wounded knight of the wood is said to have uttered:

> Where art thou, lady mine, that thou
> My sorrow dost not rue?
> Thou canst not know it, lady mine,
> Or else thou art untrue.

And so he went on with the ballad as far as the lines:

> O noble Marquis of Mantua,
> My Uncle and liege lord!

As chance would have it, when he had got to this line there happened to come by a peasant from his own village, a neighbor of his, who had been to the mill with a load of wheat. He, seeing the knight stretched there, came up to him and asked him who he was and what was the matter with him that he complained so mournfully.

Don Quixote was firmly persuaded that this was the Marquis of

Mantua, his uncle. So the only answer he made was to go on with his ballad, in which he told the tale of his misfortune and of the loves of the Emperor's son and his wife, all exactly as the ballad sings it.

The peasant stood amazed at hearing such nonsense, and relieving him of the visor, already battered to pieces by blows, he wiped Don Quixote's face, which was covered with dust. As soon as he had done so he recognized him. "Señor Quixada," he said (so he appears to have been called when he was in his senses and had not yet changed from a quiet country gentleman into a knight-errant), "who has brought your worship to this pass?" But to all questions the other only went on with his ballad.[1]

Seeing this, the good man removed as well as he could the breastplate and backpiece to see if Don Quixote had any wound, but he could perceive no blood or any mark whatever. He then attempted to raise him from the ground and with no little difficulty hoisted him on his donkey, which seemed to him to be a steadier mount. Collecting the arms, and even the splinters of the lance, he tied them on Rocinante. Leading the horse by the bridle and the ass by the halter he took the road for the village, very sad to hear what absurd stuff Don Quixote was talking.

Don Quixote was no less grieved, for what with blows and bruises he could not sit upright on the ass. From time to time he sent up sighs to heaven, so that once more the peasant felt impelled to ask what ailed him. It could have been only the devil that put into his head tales that matched his own adventures, for now, forgetting Baldwin, he recalled the Moor, Abindarráez, when the governor of Antequera, Rodrigo de Narváez, took him prisoner and carried him away to his castle. As a consequence, when the peasant again asked him how he was and what ailed him, he gave him for reply the same words and phrases that the captive Abindarráez gave to Rodrigo de Narváez, just as he had read the story in the *Diana* of Jorge de Montemayor where it is written. He applied it to his own case so aptly that the peasant went along cursing his fate that he had to listen to such a lot of nonsense. However, it enabled him to reach the conclusion that his neighbor was mad, and so he made haste to reach the village to escape the tiresome harangue.

"Señor Don Rodrigo de Narváez," said Don Quixote, when at last he had reached the end, "your worship must know that this fair Jarifa I have mentioned is now the lovely Dulcinea del Toboso, for

1. "The action in this chapter seems to have been suggested by an anonymous farce, *Entremés de los romances*, in which a peasant, overwrought from reading ballads, loses his mind and goes about imitating his heroes. This chapter of *Don Quixote* coincides with the farce on many points (including the verses quoted), and the unfortunate peasant gets a beating, like Don Quixote. It seems plausible to assume that Cervantes conceived some of the fundamental traits of *Don Quixote* from his knowledge of the farce." (Martín de Riquer.)

whom I have done, am doing, and will do the most famous deeds of chivalry that in this world have been seen, are to be seen, or ever shall be seen."

"Señor—sinner that I am!" rejoined the peasant, "cannot your worship see that I am not Don Rodrigo de Narváez nor the Marquis of Manta, but Pedro Alonso your neighbor, and that your worship is neither Baldwin nor Abindarráez, but the worthy gentleman Señor Quixada?"

"I know who I am," replied Don Quixote, "and I know that I may be not only those I have named, but all the twelve Peers of France and even all the Nine Worthies,[2] since my achievements surpass all that they have done all together and each of them on his own account."

With this talk and more of the same kind they reached the village just as night was beginning to fall. But the peasant waited until it was a little later, so that the battered gentleman might not be seen riding in such a shameful way. At what seemed to him the proper time he entered the village and went to Don Quixote's house, which he found all in confusion. There were the priest and the village barber, who were great friends of Don Quixote, and his housekeeper was speaking to them in a loud voice.

"What," she asked, "does your worship think can have befallen my master, Señor Licentiate Pero Pérez?"—for so the priest was called. "It is three days now since anything has been seen of him, or the hack, or the shield, lance, or armor. Miserable me! I am certain of it, and it is as true as that I was born to die, that these accursed books of chivalry he has and reads so constantly have upset his reason. For now I remember having often heard him saying to himself that he would become a knight-errant and go all over the world in quest of adventures. To the devil and Barabbas with such books, that have brought to ruin in this way the finest mind in all La Mancha!"

The niece said the same and, indeed, more. "You must know, Master Nicolás"—for that was the name of the barber—"it was often my uncle's way to stay up two days and nights together poring over these unholy books of misadventures. After that he would fling the book away and snatch up his sword and fall to slashing the walls. When he was tired out he would say he had killed four giants like four towers; and the sweat that flowed from him when he was weary he said was the blood of the wounds he had received in battle; and then he would drink a great jug of cold water and become calm and quiet, saying that this water was a most

2. The twelve peers were legendary knights of Charlemagne's court. The nine "worthies" are Joshua, David, Judas Maccabaeus, Hector, Alexander, Caesar, Arthur, Charlemagne, and Geoffrey of Bouillon (leader of the First Crusade).

precious potion which the sage Esquife,[3] a great magician and friend of his, had brought him. But I take all the blame myself for never having told your worships of my uncle's crazy notions, that you might put a stop to them before things had come to this pass, and burn all these accursed books—for he has a great number—that richly deserve to be burned like heretics."

"I say so too," said the priest, "and by my faith tomorrow shall not pass without public judgment upon them. May they be condemned to the flames lest they lead those that read to behave as my good friend seems to have behaved."

All this the peasant heard, and from it he understood at last what was the matter with his neighbor, so he began calling aloud, "Open, your worships, to Señor Baldwin and the Marquis of Mantua, who comes badly wounded, and to Señor Abindarráez, the Moor, whom the valiant Rodrigo de Narváez, the governor of Antequera, brings captive."

At these words they all hurried out, and when they recognized their friend, master, and uncle, who had not yet dismounted from the ass because he could not, they ran to embrace him.

"Stop!" said he, "for I am sore wounded through my horse's fault. Carry me to my couch, and if possible send for the wise Urganda to cure and see to my wounds."

"See there! plague on it!" cried the housekeeper at this. "Didn't my heart tell me what my master's problem was? To bed with your worship at once, and we will try to cure you here without fetching that Hurgada.[4] A curse I say once more, and a hundred times more, on those books of chivalry that have brought your worship to such a state."

They carried him to bed at once. After searching for his wounds they could find none, but he said they were all bruises from having had a severe fall with his horse Rocinante when in combat with ten giants, the biggest and the boldest to be found on earth.

"So!" said the priest, "are there giants in the act? By the sign of the Cross I will burn them tomorrow before the day is over."

They put a host of questions to Don Quixote, but his only answer to all was—give him something to eat, and leave him to sleep, for that was what he needed most. They did so, and the priest questioned the peasant at great length as to how he had found Don Quixote. He told him, and related the nonsense he had talked when found and on the way home. All this made the priest the more eager to do what he did the next day, which was to summon his friend the barber, Master Nicolás, and go with him to Don Quixote's house.

3. The magician Alquife, whose unfamiliar name is misquoted by the niece. *Esquife* in Spanish means "skiff."

4. *Hurgada* (the *h* is silent) means "poked" and has vulgar connotations.

Chapter VI

OF THE DIVERTING AND IMPORTANT SCRUTINY WHICH THE PRIEST AND THE BARBER MADE IN THE LIBRARY OF OUR INGENIOUS GENTLEMAN

He was still sleeping, so the priest asked the niece for the keys of the room containing the books that were the authors of all this mischief, and very gladly she gave them. They all went in, the housekeeper with them, and found more than a hundred volumes of big books very well bound, and some other small ones. The moment the housekeeper saw them, she turned and ran out of the room, and came back immediately with a bowl of holy water and a sprinkler.

"Here, your worship," she said, "sprinkle this room, and don't let any of the whole swarm of magicians in these books bewitch us, in revenge for our planning to banish them from the world."

The simplicity of the housekeeper made the priest laugh, and he directed the barber to give him the books one by one to see what they were about, as there might be some among them that did not deserve the penalty of fire.

"No," said the niece, "there is no reason for showing mercy to any of them; they have every one of them done mischief. Better fling them out of the window into the courtyard and make a pile of them and set fire to them, or else carry them into the yard, where a bonfire can be made without the smoke giving any annoyance." The housekeeper said the same, so eager were they both for the slaughter of those innocents, but the priest would not agree to it without first reading at least the titles.

The first that Master Nicolás put into his hand was *The four books of Amadís of Gaul.* "This seems a mysterious thing," said the priest, "for, as I have heard say, this was the first book of chivalry printed in Spain, and from this all the others derive their birth and origin.[1] So it seems to me that we ought inexorably to condemn it to the flames as the founder of so vile a sect."

"No, sir," said the barber, "for I too have heard say that this is the best of all the books of this kind ever written, and so, as something matchless in its own line, it ought to be pardoned."

"True," said the priest, "and for that reason let its life be spared for the present. Let us see that other next to it."

"It is," said the barber, "*The Exploits of Esplandián,* the lawful son of Amadís of Gaul."[2]

"Then indeed," said the priest, "the merit of the father must not be attributed to the son. Take it, mistress housekeeper, open the

1. A revision of a late medieval romance by Garci Rodríguez de Montalvo, published in Zaragoza in 1508. It was the most important but not actually the first romance of chivalry printed in Spain.

2. *Las sergas de Esplandián* (1510) forms the fifth book of the Amadís series, and is the composition of Rodríguez de Montalvo.

window, fling it into the yard, and lay the foundation for the bonfire we are to make."

The housekeeper obeyed with great satisfaction, and the worthy Esplandián went flying into the yard to await in all patience the fire that was in store for him.

"Proceed," said the priest.

"The next one," said the barber, "is *Amadís of Greece*. In fact, it seems to me that all on this side are of the same Amadís lineage."

"Then to the yard with the whole lot of them," said the priest. "To be able to burn Queen Pintiquiniestra, and the shepherd Darinel and his eclogues, and the bedeviled and involved discourses of his author, I would burn with them the father who begot me, if he were going about in the guise of a knight-errant."[3]

"I am of the same mind," said the barber.

"And so am I," added the niece.

"In that case," said the housekeeper, "here, into the yard with them!"

They were handed to her, and as there were so many she spared herself the staircase, and flung them down out of the window.

"What is that thick tome there?" said the priest.

"This," said the barber, "is *Don Olivante de Laura*."

"The author of that book," said the priest, "also wrote *The Garden of Flowers*, and truly there is no deciding which of the two books is the more truthful, or, to put it better, the less lying. All I can say is, send this one into the yard as a swaggering fool."[4]

"This next one is *Florismarte of Hircania*," said the barber.

"Señor Florismarte[5] here?" said the priest. "Then by my faith it's to the yard with him, in spite of his marvelous birth and fantastic adventures, for the stiffness and dryness of his style deserve nothing else. Into the yard with him and the other, mistress housekeeper."

"With all my heart, señor," said she, and executed the order with great delight.

"This," said the barber, "is *The Knight Platir*."[6]

"An old book," said the priest, "but I find no reason for clemency in it. Send it after the others without appeal."

3. *Amadís de Grecia*, by Feliciano de Silva (1530), the ninth book of the Amadís series. Pintiquiniestra was Queen of Sobradisa, and Darinel was a shepherd and wrestler of Alexandria.

4. *Olivante de Laura*, by Antonio de Torquemada, appeared first at Barcelona in 1564. The *Jardín de flores* (Salamanca, 1570), a treatise of wonders natural and supernatural, was translated into English as *The Spanish Mandeville of Miracles or the Garden of Curious Flowers* (London, 1600), a title which may seem to justify the priest's criticism. Cervantes made use of the book in the First Part of *Persiles and Sigismunda*, and in the Second Part of *Don Quixote*.

5. *Historia del muy animoso y esforçado príncipe Felixmarte de Yrcania;* the hero is also called Florismarte. It was by Melchor Ortega, of Ubeda, and appeared at Valladolid in 1556.

6. *Platir* is the fourth book of the Palmerín series. The hero is the son of Primaleón, and grandson of Palmerín de Oliva. Its author is unknown. It appeared first at Valladolid in 1533.

This was done, and another book was opened. They saw it was entitled *The Knight of the Cross.*[7]

"For the sake of the book's holy name," said the priest, "its ignorance might be excused. But they say, 'behind the cross there's the devil.' To the fire with it."

"And this," said the barber, taking down yet another book, "is *The Mirror of Chivalry.*"

"I know you, your worship," said the priest. "That is where Señor Reinaldos of Montalbán figures with his friends and comrades, greater thieves than Cacus, and the Twelve Peers of France with the veracious historian Turpin. However, I am not for condemning them to more than perpetual banishment, because, at any rate, they have some share in the work of the famous Matteo Boiardo. From them too the Christian poet Ludovico Ariosto wove his web, to whom, if I find him here, and speaking any language but his own, I shall show no pity whatever. But if he speaks his own tongue I will have nothing but respect for him."[8]

"Well, I have him in Italian," said the barber, "but I do not understand him."

"Little good would it do you if you did understand him," said the priest. "And on that score we might have excused the Captain[9] if he had not brought him into Spain and turned him into a Castilian. He robbed him of a great deal of his natural force, and so do all those who try to turn books written in verse into another language. With all the pains they take and all the cleverness they show, they never can reach the level attained in the original language. In short, I say that this book, and any others to be found that deal with these French matters, should be thrown into or deposited in some dry well, until after more reflection it is settled what is to be done with them. Yet I except one, *Bernardo del Carpio,* that is going about, and another called *Roncesvalles.* For these, if they come into my hands, shall pass at once into those of the housekeeper, and from hers into the fire without any reprieve."[1]

To all this the barber gave his assent, and looked upon it as right and proper, being persuaded that the priest was so staunch to the Faith and loyal to the Truth that he would not for the world say anything in conflict with them. He opened another book and saw it was *Palmerín de Oliva,* and beside it was another called *Palmerín of England.*

7. *The Knight of the Cross* appeared in two parts: the first in Valencia in 1521, under the title of *Lepolemo,* and by Alonso de Salazar; the second, with the achievements of *Leandro el Bel,* the son of Lepolemo, by Pedro de Luxán, in 1526.

8. *The Mirror of Chivalry—Espejo de caballerías*—was published at Seville in three parts, 1533–50. It is a prose translation of Boiardo's widely admired verse-romance on the exploits of Roland (Orlando in Italian).

9. The captain Gerónimo Jiménez de Urrea, who translated Ariosto's *Orlando furioso* into Spanish verse and took great liberties with the text.

1. The condemned books are by Agustín Alonso, of Salamanca (Toledo, 1585), and Francisco Garrido de Villena (Valencia, 1555).

"Let the Olive be made firewood of at once and burned until no ashes even are left," said the priest. "But let that Palm of England be kept and preserved as a thing unique, and let a casket be made for it like that which Alexander found among the spoils of Darius and set aside for the safekeeping of the works of the poet Homer. This book, my friend, is to be esteemed for two reasons, first because it is very good, and secondly because it is said to have been written by a wise and witty king of Portugal.[2] All the adventures at the Castle of Miraguarda are excellent and skilfully contrived. The language is polished and clear and displays great propriety and judgment by closely observing and mirroring the style of every speaker. So then, provided it seems good to you, Master Nicolás, I say let this and *Amadís of Gaul* be spared the fire. As for all the rest, let them perish without further question or query."

"No, my friend," said the barber, "for the book I am holding is the famous *Don Belianís*."[3]

"Well," said the priest, "that and the second, third, and fourth parts all stand in need of a little rhubarb to purge their excess bile, and they must be cleared of all the stuff about the Castle of Fame and other greater affectations. To that end let them be allowed the overseas clause[4] and, to the degree they mend their ways, so shall mercy or justice be accorded them. In the meantime, friend, keep them in your house and let no one read them."

"With all my heart," said the barber. And not caring to tire himself with reading more books of chivalry, he told the housekeeper to take all the big ones and throw them into the yard. It was not said to one dull or deaf, but to one who enjoyed burning them more than cleaning out the biggest and finest cobwebs.[5] So, seizing about eight at a time, she flung them out of the window.

In carrying so many together she let one fall at the feet of the barber. Curious to know whose it was, he picked it up and found it to read, *History of the Famous Knight, Tirante the White*.[6] "God bless me!" said the priest with a shout, "*Tirante the White* here! Hand it over, friend, for in it I have found a treasury of enjoyment and a mine of recreation. Here is Don Quirieleison of Montalbán, a valiant knight, and his brother Tomás of Montalbán, and the

2. *Palmerín de Oliva*, the founder of the Palmerín series of romances, was first printed at Salamanca in 1511. Nothing certain is known of the author. *Palmerín de Inglaterra* ("of England") was by Francisco de Moraes.

3. *Belianís de Grecia*, already mentioned in the first chapter as one of Don Quixote's special studies.

4. The "overseas clause" was the allowance of time granted in the case of persons beyond the seas, when sued or indicted, to enable them to appear and show cause why judgment should not be given against them.

5. The text says that the housekeeper was more anxious to burn the offensive books than to *echar una tela, por grande y delgada que fuera*. Ormsby and others translate this as "weave cloth" or "weave a tapestry," which seems illogical. Perhaps the text is faulty.

6. *Los cinco libros del esforçado e inuencible cauallero Tirante el Blanco de Roca Salada. Cauallero de la Garrotera*, the translation into Castilian of the romance *Tirant lo Blanch*, first published in Catalan at Valencia in 1490, by Joanot Martorell and Martí Joán de Galba.

knight Fonseca, with the battle the bold Tirante fought with the mastiff, and the witticisms of the damsel Placerdemivida, and the loves and wiles of the widow Reposada, and the empress in love with the squire Hipólito. In truth, my friend, by right of its style it is the best book in the world. Here knights eat and sleep, and die in their beds, and make their wills before dying, and a great deal more of which there is nothing in all the other books. Nevertheless, I say he who wrote it, for deliberately composing such fooleries, deserves to be sent to the galleys for life.[7] Take it home with you and read it, and you will see that what I have said is true."

"As you wish," said the barber. "But what are we to do with these little books that are left?"

"These must be not chivalry but poetry," said the priest, and opening one he saw it was the *Diana* of Jorge de Montemayor.[8]

"These," he said, supposing all the others to be of the same sort, "do not deserve to be burned like the others, for they neither do nor can do the mischief the books of chivalry have done, being intellectual books that can hurt no one."

"Ah, señor!" said the niece. "Your worship had better order these to be burned as well as the others. For it would be no wonder if, after being cured of his chivalry disorder, my uncle, by reading these, took a fancy to turn shepherd and range the woods and fields singing and piping; or, what would be still worse, to turn poet, which they say is an incurable and infectious malady."

"The damsel is right," said the priest, "and it will be well to put this stumbling block and temptation out of our friend's way. To begin, then, with the *Diana* of Montemayor. It is my opinion it should not be burned, but that everything about the sage Felicia and the magic water should be removed, together with almost all the longer pieces of verse. Let it keep, and welcome, its prose and the honor of being the first book of the kind."

"Next in order," said the barber, "is the *Diana*, entitled the *Second Part*, by the Salamancan, and this other has the same title, and its author is Gil Polo."

"As for the Salamancan's," replied the priest, "let it swell the number of the condemned in the yard, and let Gil Polo's be preserved as if it came from Apollo himself. But come, my friend, make haste, for it is growing late."[9]

"This book," said the barber, opening another, "is the ten books

7. The text here is obscure, and its meaning may depend on a pun: "sent to the galleys" should perhaps be understood as "printed." It would therefore mean: "Nevertheless, I say he who wrote it, since he did it for amusement only, deserves to be reprinted." (Martín de Riquer.)

8. *Los siete libros de la Diana de Jorge de Montemayor* (Valencia, 1558?).

9. The "Salamancan" was Alonso Pérez, who published a continuation of the *Diana* at Alcalá de Henares in 1564, but Gil Polo's, printed the same year at Valencia, has been generally preferred. The pun on Polo and Apollo is not so obvious in English.

of the *Fortune of Love*, written by Antonio de Lofraso, a Sardinian poet."[1]

"By the holy orders I have received," said the priest, "since Apollo has been Apollo, and the Muses have been Muses, and poets have been poets, so funny and absurd a book as this has never been written. In its way it is the best and the most singular of all of this species that have as yet appeared, and he who has not read it may be sure he has never read what is delightful. Hand it over, friend, for I am happier at having found it than if they had given me a cassock of Florentine cloth." And he put it aside with extreme satisfaction.

"These that come next," the barber went on, "are *The Shepherd of Iberia*, *The Nymphs of Henares*, and *The Enlightenment of Jealousy*."[2]

"Then all we have to do," said the priest, "is to hand them over to the secular arm[3] of the housekeeper. Ask me not why, or we shall never have done."

"This next is the *Pastor de Fílida*."[4]

"No shepherd that," said the priest, "but a highly polished courtier. Let it be preserved as a precious jewel."

"This large one here," said the barber, "is called *The Treasury of various Poems*."[5]

"If there were not so many of them," said the priest, "they would be more admired. This book must be weeded and cleansed of certain vulgarities mixed in with its excellences. Let it be preserved because the author is a friend of mine, and out of respect for other more heroic and loftier works that he has written."

"This," continued the barber, "is the *Lyrics of López de Maldonado*."[6]

"The author of that book, too," said the priest, "is a great friend of mine, and his verses from his own mouth are the admiration of all who hear them, for such is the sweetness of his voice that he enchants when he chants them. He runs on rather too long in his eclogues, but what is good was never yet plentiful. Let it be kept with those that have been set apart. But what book is that next to it?"

"The *Galatea* of Miguel de Cervantes," said the barber.

"That Cervantes has been for many years a great friend of mine,

1. The *Fortuna d'Amor*, appeared at Barcelona in 1573.

2. The books here referred to are *El pastor de Iberia*, by Bernardo de la Vega (Seville, 1591); the *Nimphas y pastores de Henares*, by Bernardo González de Bovadilla (Alcalá de Henares, 1587); and the *Desengaño de celos*, by Bartolomé López de Enciso (Madrid, 1586).

3. An allusion to the Inquisition. This ecclesiastical tribunal investigated crimes against religion and then handed the culprits over to the *brazo secular* or ordinary tribunal that was to execute the sentence.

4. The *Pastor de Fílida* (Madrid, 1582), by Luis Gálvez de Montalvo.

5. *Tesoro de varias poesías por Pedro de Padilla* (Madrid, 1580).

6. Madrid, 1586.

and to my knowledge he has had more experience in reverses than in verses. His book is not without imagination; it presents us with something but brings nothing to a conclusion. We must wait for the Second Part he has promised; perhaps it will show enough improvement to win the unrestricted praise that is now denied it. In the meantime, my good friend, keep it shut up in your own quarters."

"Very good," said the barber. "Now there come three together, the *Araucana* of Don Alonso de Ercilla, the *Austríada* of Juan Rufo, Justice of Córdoba, and the *Montserrate* of Christóbal de Virués, the Valencian poet."[7]

"These three books," said the priest, "are the best that have been written in Castilian in heroic verse, and they may compare with the most famous of Italy. Let them be preserved as the richest treasures of poetry that Spain possesses."

The priest was tired and would not look into any more books, and so he decided that, "contents uncertified," all the rest should be burned. But just then the barber held open one, called *The Tears of Angélica.*

"I should have shed tears myself," said the priest when he heard the title, "had I ordered that book to be burned, for its author[8] was one of the famous poets of the world, not to say Spain, and was very happy in the translation of some of Ovid's fables."

Chapter VII

OF THE SECOND SALLY OF OUR WORTHY KNIGHT DON QUIXOTE OF LA MANCHA

At this instant Don Quixote began shouting out. "Here, here, valiant knights! Here is need for you to put forth the might of your strong arms, for they of the court are gaining the mastery in the tourney!"

Called away by this noise and outcry, they proceeded no farther with the scrutiny of the remaining books, and so it is thought that *The Carolea, The Lion of Spain,* and *The Deeds of the Emperor,* written by Don Luis de Avila,[1] went to the fire unseen and unheard. For no doubt they were among those remaining, and perhaps if the priest had seen them they would not have undergone so severe a sentence.

7. These three are examples of Spanish epic poetry. The *Araucana* of Ercilla (Madrid, 1569, 1578, 1590); the *Austríada,* which appeared first at Madrid in 1584, on the life and achievements of Don John of Austria; and the *Montserrate* (Madrid, 1588) of the dramatist Virués.

8. Luis Barahona de Soto.

1. The books referred to are the *Carolea* of Gerónimo Sempere (1560), in verse, which deals with the victories of Charles V; the *León de España,* by Pedro de la Vezilla (1586), is a poem on the history of the city of León; the work of Avila is a prose commentary on the wars against the Protestants of Germany.

When they reached Don Quixote, he was already out of bed and was still shouting and raving and slashing and cutting all around, as wide awake as if he had never slept. They closed in on him and by force got him back to bed, and after a while he became somewhat calmer.

"Of a truth, Señor Archbishop Turpin,"[2] he said, addressing the priest, "it is a great disgrace for us who call ourselves the Twelve Peers so carelessly to allow the knights of the court to gain the victory in this tourney. We the adventurers had carried off the honor on the three former days."

"Hush, friend," said the priest. "God willing, the luck may turn, and what is lost today may be won tomorrow. For the present let your worship have a care of your health, for it seems to me that you are over-fatigued, if not badly wounded."

"Wounded no," said Don Quixote, "but bruised and battered no doubt, for that bastard Don Roland has cudgeled me with the trunk of an oak tree, and all for envy, because he sees that I alone rival him in his achievements. But I would not call myself Reinaldos of Montalbán did he not pay me for it, in spite of all his enchantments, as soon as I rise from this bed. For the present let them bring me something to eat, for that, I feel, will better serve my purpose. Leave it to me to avenge myself."

They did as he wished, giving him something to eat, and once more he fell asleep, leaving them marveling at his madness.

That night the housekeeper burned to ashes all the books that were in the yard and in the whole house. Some must have been consumed that deserved preservation in everlasting archives, but their fate and the indifference of the examiner did not permit it, and so in them was verified the proverb that the innocent sometimes suffer for the guilty.

One of the remedies which the priest and the barber immediately applied to their friend's disorder was to close off and wall up the room where the books were, so that when he got up he should not find them. Possibly the cause being removed the effect might cease, and they could say that a magician had carried them off, room and all. So it was done speedily. Two days later Don Quixote got up, and the first thing he did was to go and look at his books. Being unable to find the room where he had left it, he wandered to and fro looking for it. He came to the place where the door used to be, and tried it with his hands, and turned and twisted his eyes in every direction without saying a word. But after a good while he asked his housekeeper whereabouts was the room that held his books.

The housekeeper had been already well instructed in what she was to answer. "What room or what in the world is your worship

2. Turpin, Charlemagne's chaplain and Archbishop of Rheims, claimed as author of the *Chronicle of Charlemagne.*

looking for?" she asked. "There are neither room nor books in this house now, for the devil himself has carried all away."

"It was not the devil," said the niece, "but a magician who came on a cloud one night after the day your worship left here. He dismounted from a serpent that he rode and entered the room. What he did there I don't know, but after a little while he made off, flying through the roof, and left the house full of smoke. And when we went to see what he had done we saw neither book nor room. But we remember very well, the housekeeper and I, that in a loud voice the old villain said as he was leaving that, because of a private grudge against the owner of the books and the room, he had done mischief in that house that would be discovered later. He said too that his name was the Sage Muñatón."

"He must have said Frestón,"[3] said Don Quixote.

"I don't know whether he called himself Frestón or Fritón," said the housekeeper. "I only know that his name ended with 'ton.' "

"So it does," said Don Quixote, "and he is a sage magician, a great enemy of mine, who has a grudge against me because he knows by his arts and lore that in time I am to engage in single combat with a knight whom he befriends and that I am to conquer, and he will be unable to prevent it. For this reason he endeavors to do me all the ill turns that he can, but I promise him it will be hard for him to oppose or avoid what is decreed by Heaven."

"Who doubts that?" said the niece. "But, uncle, who mixes you up in these quarrels? Would it not be better to remain at peace in your own house instead of roaming the world looking for impossible adventures, never considering that many go for wool and come back shorn?"

"Oh, my dear niece," replied Don Quixote, "how little you understand the matter. Ere they shear me I shall have plucked away and stripped off the beards of all who dare to touch only the tip of a hair of mine."

The two were unwilling to make any further answer, as they saw that his anger was kindling.

In short, then, he remained at home fifteen days very quietly without showing any signs of a desire to take up with his former delusions. During this time he held lively discussions with his two friends, the priest and the barber, concerning his insistence that knights-errant were what the world stood most in need of, and that through him was to be accomplished the revival of knight-errantry. The priest sometimes contradicated and sometimes agreed with him, for if he had not observed this precaution he would have been unable to bring him to reason.

Meanwhile, Don Quixote was making overtures to a peasant,

3. A magician, the reputed author of *Belianís de Grecia.*

a neighbor of his, a good man (if that title can be given to one who is poor), but with very little grey matter in his skull. Finally, Don Quixote convinced him with such persuasions and promises that the poor rustic made up his mind to sally forth with him and serve him as squire. Don Quixote, among other things, told him he ought to be ready to go with him gladly, because any moment an adventure might occur that might win an island in the twinkling of an eye and leave him governor of it. On these and the like promises Sancho Panza (for so the peasant was called) left wife and children and engaged himself as squire to his neighbor.

Don Quixote next set about getting some money. By selling one thing and pawning another, and making a bad bargain in every case, he got together a fair sum. He provided himself with a shield, which he begged as a loan from a friend, and, restoring his battered helmet as best he could, he warned his squire Sancho of the day and hour he intended to set out, so that the squire might provide himself with what he thought most needful. Above all, the knight charged him to take saddlebags with him. Sancho said he would, and that he meant to take also a very good ass he had, as he was not much given to going on foot.

About the ass, Don Quixote hesitated a little, trying to call to mind any knight-errant taking with him a squire mounted on assback, but no instance occurred to his memory. Nevertheless, he decided to take him, intending to furnish him with a more honorable mount when the chance was offered of appropriating the horse of the first discourteous knight he encountered. Himself he provided with shirts and such other things as he could, according to the advice the innkeeper had given him.

All this being done and without taking leave, Sancho Panza of his wife and children, or Don Quixote of his housekeeper and niece, they sallied forth, unseen by anybody, from the village one night. In the course of it they made so much headway that by daylight they believed themselves safe from discovery, even should search be made for them.

Sancho rode his ass like a patriarch, with his saddlebags and wineskin, longing to see himself soon governor of the island his master had promised him. Don Quixote decided upon taking the same route and road he had taken on his first journey, over the plain of Montiel. He traveled it with less discomfort than on the last occasion, for, as it was early morning and the rays of the sun fell on them obliquely, the heat did not distress them.

"Your worship will take care, Señor Knight-errant," Sancho Panza admonished his master, "not to forget about the island you have promised me, for be it ever so big I'll be equal to governing it."

To which Don Quixote replied, "You must know, friend Sancho Panza, that is was a practice very much in vogue with the knights-errant of old to make their squires governors of the islands or kingdoms they won. I am determined that there shall be no failure on my part in so liberal a custom; on the contrary, I mean to improve upon it, for they sometimes, and perhaps most frequently, waited until their squires were old. Then, when they had had enough of service and hard days and worse nights, they gave them some title or other, of count, or at the most marquis, of some valley or province more or less. But if you live and I live, it may well be that before six days are over, I may have won some kingdom that has others dependent upon it. That will be just the thing to enable you to be crowned king of one of them. Nor need you count this wonderful, for things and chances fall to the lot of such knights in ways so unexampled and unexpected that I might easily give you even more than I promise."

"In that case," said Sancho Panza, "if I should become a king by one of those miracles your worship speaks of, even Juana Gutiérrez, my old lady, would come to be queen and my children princes."

"Well, who doubts it?" said Don Quixote.

"I doubt it," replied Sancho Panza, "because for my part I am persuaded that if God should shower down kingdoms on earth, not one of them would fit the head of Mari Gutiérrez. Let me tell you, señor, she is not worth two *maravedís* as a queen. Countess will fit her better, and that only with God's help."

"Leave it to God, Sancho," Don Quixote rejoined, "for he will give her what suits her best. But do not undervalue yourself so much as to be content with anything less than the governorship of a province."

"I will not, señor," answered Sancho, "specially as I have a man of such quality for a master in your worship, who will know how to give me all that will be suitable for me and that I can bear."

Chapter VIII

OF THE GOOD FORTUNE WHICH THE VALIANT DON QUIXOTE HAD IN THE TERRIBLE AND UNDREAMED-OF ADVENTURE OF THE WINDMILLS, WITH OTHER OCCURRENCES WORTHY TO BE FITLY RECORDED

At this point they came in sight of thirty or forty windmills that are on that plain.

"Fortune," said Don Quixote to his squire, as soon as he had seen them, "is arranging matters for us better than we could have hoped. Look there, friend Sancho Panza, where thirty or more monstrous giants rise up, all of whom I mean to engage in battle and slay, and with whose spoils we shall begin to make our fortunes. For this is righteous warfare, and it is God's good service to sweep so evil a breed from off the face of the earth."

"What giants?" said Sancho Panza.

"Those you see there," answered his master, "with the long arms, and some have them nearly two leagues long."

"Look, your worship," said Sancho. "What we see there are not giants but windmills, and what seem to be their arms are the vanes that turned by the wind make the millstone go."

"It is easy to see," replied Don Quixote, "that you are not used to this business of adventures. Those are giants, and if you are afraid, away with you out of here and betake yourself to prayer, while I engage them in fierce and unequal combat."

So saying, he gave the spur to his steed Rocinante, heedless of the cries his squire Sancho sent after him, warning him that most certainly they were windmills and not giants he was going to attack. He, however, was so positive they were giants that he neither heard the cries of Sancho, nor perceived, near as he was, what they were.

"Fly not, cowards and vile beings," he shouted, "for a single knight attacks you."

A slight breeze at this moment sprang up, and the great vanes began to move.

"Though ye flourish more arms than the giant Briareus,[1] ye have to reckon with me!" exclaimed Don Quixote, when he saw this.

So saying, he commended himself with all his heart to his lady Dulcinea, imploring her to support him in such a peril. With lance braced and covered by his shield, he charged at Rocinante's fullest gallop and attacked the first mill that stood in front of him. But as he drove his lance-point into the sail, the wind whirled it around with such force that it shivered the lance to pieces. It swept away with it horse and rider, and they were sent rolling over the plain, in sad condition indeed.

Sancho hastened to his assistance as fast as the ass could go. When he came up he found Don Quixote unable to move, with such an impact had Rocinante fallen with him.

"God bless me!" said Sancho, "did I not tell your worship to watch what you were doing, because they were only windmills? No one could have made any mistake about it unless he had something of the same kind in his head."

"Silence, friend Sancho," replied Don Quixote. "The fortunes of war more than any other are liable to frequent fluctuations. Moreover I think, and it is the truth, that that same sage Frestón who carried off my study and books, has turned these giants into mills in

1. Mythological giant who had a hundred arms.

order to rob me of the glory of vanquishing them, such is the enmity he bears me. But in the end his wicked arts will avail but little against my good sword."

"God's will be done," said Sancho Panza, and helping him to rise got him up again on Rocinante, whose shoulder was half dislocated. Then, discussing the adventure, they followed the road to Puerto Lápice, for there, said Don Quixote, they could not fail to find adventures in abundance and variety, as it was a well-traveled thoroughfare. For all that, he was much grieved at the loss of his lance, and said so to his squire.

"I remember having read," he added, "how a Spanish knight, Diego Pérez de Vargas by name, having broken his sword in battle, tore from an oak a ponderous bough or branch. With it he did such things that day, and pounded so many Moors, that he got the surname of Machuca,[2] and he and his descendants from that day forth were called Vargas y Machuca. I mention this because from the first oak I see I mean to tear such a branch, large and stout. I am determined and resolved to do such deeds with it that you may deem yourself very fortunate in being found worthy to see them and be an eyewitness of things that will scarcely be believed."

"Be that as God wills," said Sancho, "I believe it all as your worship says it. But straighten yourself a little, for you seem to be leaning to one side, maybe from the shaking you got when you fell."

"That is the truth," said Don Quixote, "and if I make no complaint of the pain it is because knights-errant are not permitted to complain of any wound, even though their bowels be coming out through it."

"If so," said Sancho, "I have nothing to say. But God knows I would rather your worship complained when anything ailed you. For my part, I confess I must complain however small the ache may be, unless this rule about not complaining applies to the squires of knights-errant also."

Don Quixote could not help laughing at his squire's simplicity, and assured him he might complain whenever and however he chose, just as he liked. So far he had never read of anything to the contrary in the order of knighthood.

Sancho reminded him it was dinner time, to which his master answered that he wanted nothing himself just then, but that Sancho might eat when he had a mind. With this permission Sancho settled himself as comfortably as he could on his beast, and taking out of the saddlebags what he had stowed away in them, he jogged along behind his master munching slowly. From time to time he took a pull at the wineskin with all the enjoyment that the

2. From *machucar*, "to pound or crush." There was a popular ballad about this feat.

thirstiest tavernkeeper in Málaga might have envied. And while he went on in this way, between gulps, he never gave a thought to any of the promises his master had made him, nor did he rate it as hardship but rather as recreation going in quest of adventures, however dangerous they might be.

Finally they settled down for the night among some trees. From one of them Don Quixote plucked a dry branch to serve as a lance, fixing on it the head he had removed from the broken one. All that night Don Quixote lay awake thinking of his lady Dulcinea, in conformity with what he had read in his books, how many a night in the forests and deserts knights used to lie sleepless, borne up by the memory of their mistresses.

Sancho Panza spent it thus: having his stomach full of something stronger than chicory water he slept straight through. If his master had not called him, neither the rays of the sun beating on his face nor all the cheery notes of the birds welcoming the approach of day would have had power to waken him. On getting up he tried the wineskin and found it somewhat less full than the night before. This grieved his heart because it did not seem likely they would remedy the deficiency readily. Don Quixote did not care to break his fast, for, as has been already said, he confined himself to savory recollections for nourishment.

They returned to the road they had set out on leading to Puerto Lápice, and at three in the afternoon they came in sight of it. "Here, brother Sancho Panza," said Don Quixote when he saw it, "we may plunge our hands up to the elbows in what they call adventures. But bear in mind, even should you see me in the greatest danger in the world, you must not put a hand to your sword in my defense. Not, that is, unless you perceive that the assailants are rabble or low-born persons, for in that case you may very properly aid me. But if they are knights, you are on no account permitted or allowed by the laws of knighthood to help me until you have been dubbed a knight."

"Most certainly, señor," replied Sancho, "your worship will be fully obeyed in this matter. Especially since I am of a peaceful disposition and no friend to mixing in squabbles and quarrels. It is true that as regards the defense of my own person I don't intend to give much attention to those laws, for laws human and divine allow each one to defend himself against any assailant whatever."

"That I grant," said Don Quixote, "but as for aiding me against knights, you must restrain your natural impetuosity."

"I will do so, I promise you," answered Sancho, "and will keep this law as carefully as Sunday."

While they were thus talking there appeared on the road two friars of the order of St. Benedict, mounted on two dromedaries, for the two mules they rode on were every bit as tall. The friars wore traveling masks[3] and carried umbrellas, and behind them came a coach accompanied by four or five persons on horseback and two muleteers on foot. In the coach there was, as was afterwards learned, a Biscayan lady on her way to Seville, where her husband was about to embark for the Indies where a lofty position awaited him. The friars, though going the same way, were not in her company.

"Either I am mistaken," said Don Quixote to his squire, the moment he set eyes on them, "or this is going to be the most famous adventure that has ever been seen. Those black shapes we see there must be, and doubtless are, magicians who are carrying off some stolen princess in that coach, and with all my might I must undo this wrong."

"This will be worse than the windmills," said Sancho. "Look, señor, those are friars of St. Benedict, and the coach plainly belongs to some travelers. I tell you to reconsider, and don't let the devil mislead you."

"I have told you already, Sancho," replied Don Quixote, "that on the subject of adventures you know little. What I say is the truth, as you shall see presently."

So saying, he advanced and posted himself in the middle of the road along which the friars were coming.

"Devilish and unnatural beings," he cried aloud, as soon as he thought they had come close enough to hear him, "release instantly the highborn princesses whom ye are carrying off by force in this coach, else prepare to meet a speedy death as the just punishment of your evil deeds."

The friars pulled up and stood wondering at the appearance of Don Quixote as well as at his words.

"Señor Knight," they answered him, "we are not devilish or unnatural, but two brothers of St. Benedict following our road, nor do we know whether or not there are any captive princesses in this coach."

"No soft words with me, for I know you, lying rabble," said Don Quixote. Without waiting for a reply he spurred Rocinante and with leveled lance charged the first friar with great fury and determination. If the friar had not flung himself off the mule, he would have been brought to the ground against his will and seriously wounded, if not killed outright. The second brother, seeing how his comrade was treated, drove his heels into his enormous mule and made off across the country faster than the wind.

When he saw the friar on the ground, Sancho Panza dismounted briskly from his ass, rushed towards him, and began to strip off his habit. At that instant the friars' muleteers came up and asked what

3. The two Benedictine monks, in their black habits, were wearing these masks to protect themselves from dust and sunburn, since a tanned face was unfashionable. The masks, used by well-to-do travelers, are mentioned several times in the course of the novel.

he was stripping him for. Sancho answered them that this fell to him lawfully as spoil of the battle which his lord Don Quixote had won. The muleteers had little sense of humor and did not understand all this about battles and spoils. So, seeing that Don Quixote was some distance off talking to the travelers in the coach, they fell upon Sancho, knocked him down, and leaving hardly a hair in his beard belabored him with kicks and left him stretched breathless and senseless on the ground. Without any more delay they helped the friar to mount and he, trembling, terrified, and pale, as soon as he found himself in the saddle, spurred after his companion, who was standing at a distance watching the result of the onslaught. Then, not caring to wait for the end of the affair just begun, they pursued their journey making the sign of the cross oftener than if they had the devil after them.

Don Quixote was, as has been said, speaking to the lady in the coach. "My beauteous lady," said he, "thou mayest now dispose of thy person as may be most in accordance with thy pleasure, for the pride of thy ravishers lies prostrate on the ground through this strong arm of mine. And lest thou shouldest be pining to know the name of thy deliverer, know that I am called Don Quixote of La Mancha, knight-errant and adventurer, and captive to the peerless and beautiful lady Dulcinea del Toboso. In return for the service thou hast received of me, I ask no more than that thou shouldst return to El Toboso, and on my behalf present thyself before that lady and tell her what I have done to set thee free."

One of the squires in attendance upon the coach, a Biscayan, was listening to all Don Quixote was saying. Perceiving that he would not allow the coach to go on, but was saying it must return at once to El Toboso, the Biscayan went up to Don Quixote and seized his lance, addressing him in bad Castilian and worse Biscayan.[4] "Go away; good riddance, gentleman. By God that made me, if you no leave coach I kill you or I not Basque."

Don Quixote understood him quite well, and answered him very quietly. "If thou wert a gentleman, as thou art none, I should have already chastised thy folly and rashness, miserable creature."

"I no gentleman!" exclaimed the Biscayan. "I swear to God like Christian you lying. If you throw lance and draw sword, soon see who better man. Basque on land on sea gentleman, by devil, and you lying if you say different."

" 'We'll see about that, said Agrajes,' " replied Don Quixote. Throwing his lance on the ground he drew his sword, slipped his shield on his arm, and attacked the Biscayan, bent upon taking his life.

The Biscayan would have liked to dismount from his mule, when he saw Don Quixote advancing. But it was one of those sorry crea-

4. The language of the "Biscayan" provinces of northeastern Spain is Basque. The broken Spanish of Basques was frequently satirized in Cervantes' day.

tures let out for hire, and he had no choice but to draw his sword. Luckily for him, however, he was near the coach, from which he was able to snatch a cushion that served him as a shield. And they went at one another as if they had been mortal enemies. The others tried to make peace between them, but could not, for the Biscayan declared in his disjointed phrases that if they did not let him finish his battle he would kill his mistress and everyone that tried to prevent him. The lady in the coach, amazed and terrified at what she saw, ordered the coachman to pull away a little, and set herself to watch this severe struggle. In the course of it the Biscayan smote Don Quixote a mighty stroke on the shoulder over the top of his shield, which, had he not been wearing armor, would have cleft him to the waist.

Feeling the weight of this prodigious blow, Don Quixote cried aloud. "O lady of my soul, Dulcinea, flower of beauty," he said, "come to the aid of this thy knight, who, in fulfilling his obligations to thy beauty, finds himself in this extreme peril."

To say this, to lift his sword, to shelter himself well behind his shield, and to assail the Biscayan was the work of an instant, for he was determined to venture all upon a single blow. The Biscayan, seeing how he attacked, was convinced of his courage by his spirited bearing, and resolved to follow his example. So he waited for Don Quixote, keeping well under cover of his cushion. But he could not execute any sort of maneuver with his mule which, dead tired and never meant for this kind of game, could not stir a step.

On, then, as we have said, came Don Quixote against the wary Biscayan, with uplifted sword, firmly resolved to split him in half. On his side the Biscayan waited for him sword in hand and protected by his cushion. All present stood trembling, anxiously waiting the result of the blows that threatened to fall, while the lady in the coach and the rest of her following were making a thousand vows and offerings to all the images and shrines of Spain, that God might deliver her squire and all of them from the great peril in which they found themselves.

But at this point of crisis, the author of the history leaves the battle in suspense, spoiling the whole episode.[5] The excuse he offers is that he could find nothing more written about these achievements of Don Quixote than what has already been told. It is true the second author of this work[6] was unwilling to believe that so interesting a history could have been allowed to lapse into oblivion, or that learned persons in La Mancha could have been so undiscerning as not to preserve in their archives or registries some documents referring to this famous knight. Since such was his conviction, he did not despair of discovering the conclusion of this pleasant history. He did this, heaven favoring him, in a way to be related in the Second Part.

5. Cervantes is parodying the suspense-raising effects of the romances of chivalry.
6. Cervantes himself.

The Second[1] Part of The Ingenious Gentleman Don Quixote of La Mancha

Chapter IX

IN WHICH IS CONCLUDED AND FINISHED THE TERRIFIC BATTLE BETWEEN THE GALLANT BISCAYAN AND THE VALIANT MANCHEGAN

In the First Part of this history we left the valiant Biscayan and the renowned Don Quixote with drawn swords uplifted, ready to deliver two such furious slashing blows that if they had landed squarely, they would at the least have split and cleft the combatants asunder from top to toe and laid them open like a pomegranate. At this suspenseful point the delightful history came to a stop and remained curtailed with no indication from the author where the missing part could be found.

This distressed me greatly, because the pleasure derived from reading this small portion turned to vexation at the thought of how slight a chance I had of ever finding the larger portion required, or so it seemed to me, to complete such an interesting tale. It struck me as impossible and against all precedent that no scholarly person should have undertaken to record these marvelous achievements. Such a lack never afflicted those knights-errant who, 'as folks do say, set out adventures seeking.' Each one of them had one or two scribes seemingly created for the purpose. They not only recorded knightly deeds but wrote down the knights' most trifling thoughts and whimsies, however secret they might be. No, such a good knight could not have incurred the misfortune never to have met with what Platir and others like him had in abundance. And so I could not bring myself to believe that such a gallant tale had been left maimed and mutilated. I laid the blame on Time, devourer and destroyer of all things, which had either concealed or consumed it.

On the other hand, it struck me that, since among his books there had been found such modern ones as *The Enlightenment of Jealousy* and the *Nymphs and Shepherds of Henares*, his story must likewise be modern. Thus, though it might not be written, it might

1. Cervantes divided the volume now called *Don Quixote*, Part I, into four parts; but when he published his continuation, he did not make any internal divisions except chapters.

exist in the memory of the people of his village and of those in the neighborhood. This reflection kept me perplexed and longing to know really and truly the whole life and wondrous deeds of our famous Spaniard, Don Quixote of La Mancha, light and mirror of Manchegan chivalry, the first in our age and in these evil days to devote himself to the labor and exercise of the arms of knight-errantry; who righted wrongs, succored widows, and protected damsels, of the kind that used to ride about, whip in hand, on their palfreys, with all their virginity, from mountain to mountain and valley to valley. If it were not for some ruffian, or boor with a hood and hatchet, or monstrous giant, that raped them, there were in days of yore damsels that at the end of eighty years, in all which time they had never slept a day under a roof, went to their graves as pure as the mothers that bore them.

I say, then, that in these and other respects our gallant Don Quixote is worthy of everlasting and notable praise. Nor should praise be withheld even from me, for the labor and pains spent in searching for the conclusion of this delightful history. I know well, nevertheless, that if Heaven, chance, and good fortune had not helped me, the world would have remained deprived of an entertainment and pleasure that may well occupy the attentive reader for a couple of hours or so.

This is how the discovery was made. One day, as I was in the Alcaná[2] of Toledo, a boy came up to sell some notebooks and old papers to a silk dealer. As I am fond of reading even scraps of paper in the streets, my natural bent led me to take up one of the notebooks the boy had for sale. I saw it was in characters which I recognized as Arabic but, despite that, was unable to read. I looked about to see if there was any Spanish-speaking Morisco[3] at hand to read them for me, and I had no great difficulty in finding such an interpreter. Indeed, even had I sought one for an older and better language,[4] I could have found him. In short, chance provided me with one.

When I told him what I wanted and put the book into his hands, he opened it in the middle and read a little. Then he began to laugh. I asked him what he was laughing at, and he replied that it was at something in a note written in the margin of the book. I asked him to tell me what it was.

"In the margin, as I told you," he replied, still laughing, is written: " '*This Dulcinea del Toboso so often mentioned in this history, had, they say, the best hand of any woman in all La Mancha for salting pigs.*' "

2. A marketplace in Toledo in the neighborhood of the cathedral.
3. The Moriscos were the descendants of North African invaders, who kept their language and religion until they were expelled in 1609 and again in 1613.
4. I.e., Hebrew. Unconverted Jews had been expelled in 1492. Cervantes is alluding to the false converts who formed an important part of the Toledan merchant class.

When I heard Dulcinea del Toboso named, I was struck with surprise and amazement, for it occurred to me at once that these notebooks contained the history of Don Quixote. With this idea I urged him to read the beginning, and he did so, turning the Arabic into Castilian at sight. He told me it meant, "*History of Don Quixote of La Mancha, written by Cide Hamete Benengeli,*[5] *an Arab historian.*"

It required great caution to hide the joy I felt when the title of the book reached my ears. Snatching it from the silk dealer, I bought all the papers and notebooks from the boy for half a *real*. If he had had his wits about him and had known how eager I was, he might have safely calculated on making more than six *reales* by the bargain. I withdrew at once with the Morisco into the cathedral cloister and begged him to translate all these notebooks relating to Don Quixote into the Castilian tongue, without omitting or adding anything. In payment, I offered him whatever he pleased. He was satisfied with fifty pounds of raisins and two bushels of wheat, and promised to translate them faithfully and with all despatch. But to make the matter easier, and not to let such a precious find out of my hands, I took him to my house, where in little more than a month and a half he translated the whole just as it is set down here.

In the first notebook an artist had depicted the battle between Don Quixote and the Biscayan to the very life. They were planted in the same attitude as the history describes, their swords raised, and the one protected by his shield, the other by his cushion. The Biscayan's mule was so true to nature that it could be seen to be a hired one a bowshot off. The Biscayan had an inscription under his feet which said, "*Don Sancho de Azpeitia,*" which no doubt must have been his name; and at the feet of Rocinante was another that said, "*Don Quixote.*" Rocinante was marvelously portrayed, so long and thin, so lank and lean, with so much backbone and so far gone in consumption, that he showed plainly with what judgment and propriety the name of Rocinante had been bestowed upon him. Near him was Sancho Panza holding the halter of his ass, at whose feet was another label that said, "*Sancho Zancas,*" and according to the picture, he must have had a big belly, a short body, and long shanks, for which reason, no doubt, the names of Panza and Zancas were given him, for by these two surnames the history several times calls him.[6] Some other trifling particulars might be mentioned, but they are all of slight importance and have nothing to do with the faithful telling of the story, and no story can be bad so long as it is true.

If any objection can be raised as to its truth, it can only be because its author was an Arab, since lying is very common among those of that nation. Yet, as they are such enemies of ours, he is

5. *Benengeli*: "eggplant."

6. *Panza*: "paunch"; *zancas*: "shanks."

more likely to have erred by diminishing rather than by overstating the case. And this is my own opinion. For, where he could and should have licensed his pen to praise so worthy a knight, he seems to me deliberately to have written nothing. This is ill done and worse contrived, for it is the business and duty of historians to be exact, truthful, and wholly free from passion. Neither interest nor fear, hatred nor love, should make them swerve from the path of truth, whose mother is history, rival of time, storehouse of deeds, witness for the past, example and counsel for the present, and warning for the future. In this I know will be found all the entertainment that can be desired, and if any good quality is lacking, I maintain it is the fault of its hound of an author and not of the subject. To be brief, its Second Part, according to the translation, began in this way:

With trenchant swords upraised and poised on high, it seemed as though the two valiant and wrathful combatants stood threatening heaven and earth and hell, so bold was their mien. The fiery Biscayan was the first to strike a blow, delivering it with such force and fury that, had not the sword turned in its course, that single stroke would have sufficed to end the bitter struggle and all the adventures of our knight. But that good fortune which reserved him for greater things turned aside the sword of his adversary so that, though it smote him upon the left shoulder, it did him no more harm than to strip all that side of its armor, carrying away a great part of his helmet with half of his ear. It all fell to the ground with a fearful din, leaving him in sorry plight.

Good God! Who could properly describe the rage that filled the heart of our Manchegan, when he saw himself dealt with in this fashion? All that can be said is that he again raised himself in his stirrups and, grasping his sword more firmly with both hands, came down on the Biscayan with such fury, smiting him full over the cushion and over the head, that even so good a shield proved useless. It was as if a mountain had fallen on him, and he began to bleed from nose, mouth, and ears, reeling as if about to fall backwards from his mule. No doubt he would have done so had he not flung his arms about its neck. At the same time, however, he slipped his feet out of the stirrups and then unclasped his arms. The mule, frightened by the terrible blow, made off across the plain, and with a few plunges flung its master to the ground. Don Quixote stood looking on very calmly. When he saw the other fall, he leaped from his horse and with great briskness ran toward him. He held the point of his sword to his eyes and bade him surrender, or he would cut his head off. The Biscayan was so stunned that he was unable to answer a word, and he would have fared ill, so blinded by rage was Don Quixote, had it not been for the ladies in the coach. They had been watching the combat in great terror, and now they hastened to where he stood and implored him with earnest entreaties to grant them the great grace and favor of sparing their squire's life. To this Don Quixote responded with much gravity and dignity.

"In truth, fair ladies," he said, "I am well content to do what you ask of me, but it must be on one condition and understanding. This knight must promise me to go to the village of El Toboso, and on my behalf present himself before the peerless lady Dulcinea, so that she may deal with him as shall be most pleasing to her."

The terrified and disconsolate ladies, without discussing Don Quixote's demand or asking who Dulcinea might be, promised that their squire should do all that had been commanded.

"Then, on the faith of that promise," said Don Quixote, "I shall do him no further harm, though he greatly deserves it."

Chapter X

OF THE PLEASANT DISCOURSE THAT PASSED BETWEEN DON QUIXOTE AND HIS SQUIRE SANCHO PANZA[1]

By this time Sancho had got up, rather the worse for the handling he had received from the friars' muleteers, and was watching the battle of his master, Don Quixote. In his heart he was praying that it might be God's will to grant him the victory and so enable him to win some island. Then Sancho could become its governor, as had been promised. Seeing, therefore, that the struggle was over and that his master was remounting Rocinante, he approached to hold the stirrup. Before Don Quixote could mount, Sancho went down on his knees before him, took his hand, and kissed it.

"May it please your worship, Señor Don Quixote," he said, "to give me the government of the island which has been won in this hard fight. Be it ever so big, I feel myself well able to govern it as much and as properly as anyone in the world who has ever governed islands."

"You must take notice, brother Sancho," Don Quixote replied, "that this adventure and those like it are not adventures for winning but are merely crossroad encounters. Nothing is to be won except a broken head or an ear the less. Just have patience, for adventures will arise from which I may make you not only a governor, but something more."

Sancho gave him many thanks and again kissed his hand and the skirt of his mailed tunic. He helped him to mount Rocinante, and mounting his ass himself, proceeded to follow his master, who was

1. Cervantes apparently devised the chapter headings after completing the work, and the heading for this chapter is inaccurate: "Of what else happened to Don Quixote with the Bisacayan and of the danger in which he stood with a crowd of Yangüesans." The headings themselves, whether an afterthought or not, parody the style of those in romances of chivalry.

setting a lively pace. He had neither taken leave nor said anything further to the ladies in the coach, and now he turned into a nearby wood. Sancho followed at his ass's fastest trot, but Rocinante stepped out so briskly that, seeing himself left behind, he had to call to his master to wait. Don Quixote did so, reining in Rocinante until his weary squire could catch up. "It seems to me, señor," said Sancho, "that it would be prudent for us to go and take sanctuary in some church.[2] Seeing how badly mauled you left the man you were fighting, it will be no wonder if they tell the Holy Brotherhood[3] of the affair and have us arrested. Faith, if they do, before we come out of jail we'll have to sweat for it."

"Silence," said Don Quixote. "Where have you ever seen or heard that a knight-errant has been arraigned before a court of justice, however many homicides he may have committed?"

"I know nothing about those," answered Sancho, "nor in my life have I had anything to do with one. I only know that the Holy Brotherhood deals with those who fight in the fields, and in that other matter I don't meddle."

"Then you need have no uneasiness, my friend," said Don Quixote, "for I will deliver you out of the hands of the Chaldeans, not to say those of the Brotherhood. But tell me on your life, have you ever seen a more valiant knight than I in all the known world? Have you read in history of any who has or had higher mettle in attack, more spirit in maintaining it, more dexterity in wounding or skill in overthrowing?"

"The truth is," answered Sancho, "that I have never read any history, for I can neither read nor write. But what I will bet is that a more daring master than your worship I have never served in all the days of my life, and God grant that your worship doesn't have to pay for this daring in the way I have said. What I beg of your worship is to take care of your wound, because a great deal of blood is flowing from that ear, and I have here some bandages and a little white ointment in the saddlebags."

"All that might be well dispensed with," said Don Quixote, "if I had remembered to make a vial of the balm of Fierabrás,[4] for time and medicine are saved by one single drop."

"What vial and what balm is that?" said Sancho Panza.

"It is a balm," answered Don Quixote, "the recipe for which I

2. Fugitives could not be arrested inside a church.

3. Established by Ferdinand and Isabel in 1496 as a police force destined to maintain public order, especially outside towns, and to fight highwaymen. The Brotherhood had power to judge and punish criminal offenders. The members of the force were called *cuadrilleros* (see Chapter XVI).

4. Fierabrás, in the legends of the Twelve Peers, was a Saracen giant who stole from Rome the miraculous liquid with which Jesus was embalmed, which instantly healed wounds.

have in my memory, with which one need have no fear of death or dread dying of any wound. And so when I make it and give it to you, all you have to do—when in some battle you see they have cut me in half through the middle of the body, as is wont to happen frequently—is, neatly and with great deftness, before the blood congeals, to place that portion of the body that has fallen to the ground upon the other half which remains in the saddle, taking care to fit it on evenly and exactly. Then you must give me to drink just two drops of the balm I have mentioned, and you shall see me become sounder than an apple."

"If that is so," said Panza, "I renounce forthwith the government of the promised island. All I desire in payment for my many and faithful services is that your worship give me the recipe for this priceless liquid. I am convinced it will be worth more than two *reales* an ounce anywhere and I need no more in order to pass the rest of my life in ease and honor. But I need to know if it costs much to make it."

"For less than three *reales*, six quarts of it may be made," said Don Quixote.

"Sinner that I am!" said Sancho. "Then why does your worship put off making it and teaching it to me?"

"Be calm, friend," answered Don Quixote. "Greater secrets I mean to teach you, and greater favors will I bestow upon you. For the present let us see to the dressing, for my ear pains me more than I could wish."

Sancho took out some bandages and ointment from the saddlebags. But when Don Quixote saw how his helmet was shattered, he almost took leave of his senses.

"I swear," he said, clapping his hand on his sword and raising his eyes to heaven, "by the Creator of all things and the four Gospels in their fullest extent, I will do as the great Marquis of Mantua did when he swore to avenge the death of his nephew Baldwin, and that was not to eat bread from a tablecloth nor embrace his wife, and other points which, though I cannot now call them to mind, I here accept as stated, until I take complete vengeance upon the man who has committed such an offense against me."

"Señor Don Quixote," said Sancho, when he heard this, "your worship should bear in mind that if the knight has done what was commanded, presenting himself before my lady Dulcinea del Toboso, he will have done all that he was bound to do. He deserves no further punishment unless he commits some new offense."

"You have spoken well and hit the point," answered Don Quixote. "And so I revoke the oath with respect to taking fresh vengeance on him. But I make and confirm it anew, and will lead the life I have said, until such time as I take by force from some knight another helmet such as this and as good. Do not think, Sancho, that I am making idle threats when I say so. I have someone to imitate in the matter, since the very same thing happened in the case of Mambrino's helmet, which cost Sacripante so dear."[5]

"Señor," replied Sancho, "your worship should send all such oaths to the devil, for they are an obstacle to salvation and harmful to the conscience. Just tell me now: if for several days to come we meet no man armed with a helmet, what are we to do? Is the oath to be kept in spite of all the inconvenience and discomfort it will be to sleep in your clothes and not to sleep in a house, and a thousand other penances contained in the oath of that old fool the Marquis of Mantua, which your worship is now wanting to revive? Let your worship observe that there are no men in armor traveling on any of these roads, nothing but mule drivers and wagon drivers, who not only do not wear helmets, but probably never heard tell of them all their lives."

"You are wrong there," said Don Quixote, "for we shall not have been more than two hours at these crossroads before we see more men in armor than came to Albraca to win the fair Angelica."[7]

"Enough," said Sancho. "So be it then. God grant us success, and that the time for winning that island which is costing me so dear may soon come, and then let me die."

"I have already told you, Sancho," said Don Quixote, "not to feel any uneasiness on that score. For if an island should be lacking, there is the kingdom of Denmark, or of Soliadisa, which will fit you as a ring fits the finger, and even better. You will enjoy yourself all the more on terra firma. But let that happen in its own good time. See if you have anything for us to eat in those saddlebags, because we must soon go in quest of some castle where we may lodge tonight. There we will make the balm I told you about, for I swear to God, this ear is giving me great pain."

"I have an onion and a little cheese and a few scraps of bread," said Sancho, "but they are not fit for a valiant knight like your worship."

"How little you know about that," answered Don Quixote. "I would have you know, Sancho, that it is the glory of knights-errant to go without eating for a month, and even when they do eat, that it should be of what comes first to hand. This would have been clear to you, had you read as many histories as I have. Though they are very many, among them all I have found no mention made of knights-errant eating, unless by accident or at some sumptuous banquets prepared for them, and the rest of the time they passed in dalliance. And though it is plain they could not do without eating and

5. Mambrino, a Moorish king in the *Orlando* of Boiardo, whose enchanted helmet was won by Rinaldo. (It was Dardinel, however, not Sacripante, whom it cost so dear.)

7. The siege of Albraca is one of the incidents in the *Orlando* of Boiardo.

performing all the other natural functions, because, in fact, they were men like ourselves, it is plain too that, wandering as they did the most part of their lives through woods and wilds and without a cook, their most usual fare would be rustic viands such as those you now offer me. So that, friend Sancho, let not that distress you which pleases me, and do not seek to reform the world or change the customs of knight-errantry."

"Pardon me, your worship," said Sancho, "for, as I cannot read or write, as I said just now, I neither know nor comprehend the rules of the profession of chivalry. From now on I will stock the saddlebags with every kind of dry fruit for your worship, since you are a knight. As for myself, since I am not one, I will furnish them with poultry and other more substantial things."

"I do not say, Sancho," replied Don Quixote, "that it is imperative for knights-errant not to eat anything else but the fruits you speak of, only that this is their more usual diet, with certain herbs they found in the fields which they knew and I know too."

"A good thing it is," answered Sancho, "to know those herbs, for to my thinking it will be needful some day to put that knowledge into practice."

Here he took out what he said he had brought, and the pair made their repast peaceably and sociably. But they were anxious to find quarters for the night and did not linger over their poor dry fare. They soon mounted and made haste to reach some habitation before night set in. But daylight failed, and also the hope of succeeding in their object, just as they reached the huts of some goatherds, and so they determined to pass the night there. It was as distressing to Sancho not to have reached a house as it was to his master's satisfaction to sleep under the open heaven, for he fancied that each time this happened to him he was performing an act that strengthened his claim to knighthood.

Chapter XI

OF WHAT BEFELL DON QUIXOTE WITH CERTAIN GOATHERDS

He was cordially welcomed by the goatherds, and Sancho, having seen to Rocinante and the ass as best he could, drew near the fragrance that came from some pieces of salted goat simmering in a pot on the fire. Though he would have liked at once to see if they were ready to be transferred from pot to stomach, he refrained from doing so as the goatherds removed them from the fire. Laying sheepskins on the ground, they quickly spread their rude table, and with signs of hearty good will invited them both to share what they had. Around the skins six of the men belonging to the fold seated themselves, having first with rough politeness urged Don Quixote to take a seat on a trough which they placed upside down for him. Don Quixote seated himself, and Sancho remained standing to serve the cup, which was made of horn.

"So that you may see, Sancho," said his master, when he saw him standing, "how much good there is in knight-errantry, and how those who practice it are on the high road to speedy honors and the world's esteem, I want you to seat yourself here at my side in these good people's company. I want you to be as though one with me, your master and natural lord, and to eat from my plate and drink from the same vessel as I. For the same may be said of knight-errantry as of love, that it levels all."

"Many thanks," said Sancho, "but let me tell your worship that provided I have enough to eat, I can eat it as well, or better, standing, and by myself, than seated alongside an emperor. Indeed, if truth were told, what I eat in my corner without refinements or fuss tastes better to me, even though it's bread and onions, than turkey at those other tables where I am forced to chew slowly, drink little, wipe my mouth every minute, and cannot sneeze or cough if I want or do other things that liberty and privacy allow. So, señor, exchange these honors which your worship would offer me as a servant and follower of knight-errantry, and let me have other things which I may find of more use and advantage. While acknowledging that they have been duly received, I renounce all such honors from this moment to the end of the world."

"Nevertheless," said Don Quixote, "you must seat yourself, because whosoever humbleth himself God doth exalt."

Seizing him by the arm, he forced him to sit down beside him.

The goatherds did not understand this jargon about squires and knights-errant, and all they did was to eat in silence and stare at their guests, who with great elegance and appetite were stowing away pieces as big as one's fist. When the meat course was finished, they spread upon the sheepskins a great heap of dried acorns, and with them they put down a half cheese harder than any mortar. All this while the horn was not idle, for it went around constantly, now full, now empty, like the bucket of a water-wheel. With no trouble at all they soon drained one of the two wineskins that could be seen. When Don Quixote had quite appeased his appetite he took up a handful of the acorns. Contemplating them attentively, he embarked on a discourse very much like what follows.

"Happy the age, happy the time, to which the ancients gave the name of golden, not because in the fortunate age the gold so coveted in this our iron one was gained without toil, but because they that lived in it knew not the two words "*mine*" and "*thine*"! In that blessed age all things were in common; to win the daily food no labor was required of anyone save to stretch forth his hand and gather it from the sturdy oaks that stood generously inviting him with their sweet ripe fruit. The clear streams and running brooks yielded their savory limpid waters in noble abundance. The busy and sagacious bees fixed their republic in the clefts of the rocks and hollows of the trees, offering without interest the plenteous produce of their fragrant toil to every hand. The mighty cork trees, with no obligation save to their own courtesy, shed the broad light bark that served at first to roof the houses supported by rude stakes, a protection against the inclemency of heaven alone. Then all was peace, all friendship, all concord; as yet the curved plow's heavy share had not dared to rend and pierce the tender bowels of our first mother who, without compulsion, yielded from every portion of her broad fertile bosom all that could satisfy, sustain, and delight the children that then possessed her. Then it was that the innocent and fair young shepherdess roamed from vale to vale and hill to hill, with flowing locks and no more garmets than were needful modestly to cover what modesty seeks and ever sought to hide. Nor were their ornaments like those in use today, set off by Tyrian purple and silk tortured in endless fashions, but the wreathed leaves of the green dock and ivy, wherewith they went as bravely and becomingly decked as our court ladies with all the rare and far-fetched artifices that idle curiosity has taught them. Then the love-thoughts of the heart clothed themselves simply and naturally as the heart conceived them, without endeavoring to commend themselves by forced and rambling verbiage. Fraud, deceit, or malice had then not yet mingled with truth and sincerity. Justice held her ground, undisturbed and unassailed by the efforts of favor and of interest that now so much impair, pervert, and beset her. Arbitrary law had not yet established itself in the mind of the judge, for then there was no cause to judge and no one to be judged. Maidens and modesty, as I have said, wandered at will alone and unattended, without fear of insult from lawlessness or libertine assault, and if they were undone it was of their own will and pleasure. But now in this hateful age of ours not one is safe, not though some new labyrinth like that of Crete conceal and surround her. Even there the pestilence of gallantry will make its way to them through chinks or on the air by the zeal of its accursed importunity, and, in spite of all seclusion, lead them to ruin. In defense of these, as time advanced and wickedness increased, the order of knights-errant was instituted, to defend maidens, to protect widows, and to succor the orphans and the needy. To this order I belong, brother goatherds, to whom I return thanks for the hospitality and kindly welcome you offer me and my squire. For though by natural law all living are bound to show favor to knights-errant, yet, seeing that without knowing this obligation you have welcomed and feasted me, it is right that with all the goodwill in my power I should thank you for yours."

All this long harangue (which might very well have been omitted) our knight delivered because the acorns they gave him reminded him of the golden age. Thus the whim seized him to address all this unnecessary speech to the goatherds, who listened to him gaping in amazement without saying a word in reply. Sancho likewise held his peace and ate acorns and paid repeated visits to the second wineskin, which they had hung up on a cork tree to keep the wine cool.

Don Quixote spent more time talking than in eating the supper, and when he had finished, one of the goatherds spoke. "In order that your worship, señor knight-errant, may say more truthfully that we show you hospitality with ready goodwill," he said, "we will give you amusement and pleasure by having one of our comrades sing. He will be here before long, and he is a very intelligent young man and deeply in love, and what is more he can read and write and play on the fiddle to perfection."

The goatherd had hardly done speaking when the notes of the fiddle reached their ears, and shortly after, the player arrived. He was a very good-looking young man of about twenty-two. His comrades asked him if he had eaten, and he replied that he had.

"In that case, Antonio," said the man who had already spoken of him, "you may as well do us the pleasure of singing a little, so that the gentleman, our guest, may see that even in the mountains and woods there are musicians. We have told him of your accomplishments, and we want you to show them and prove that what we say is true. So sit down and sing that ballad about your love that your uncle the priest wrote for you, and that was so much liked in the town."

"With all my heart," said the young man, and without waiting for more urging he seated himself on the trunk of a felled oak, and tuning his fiddle, presently began to sing these words.

ANTONIO'S BALLAD

Thou dost love me well, Olalla;
  Well I know it, even though
Love's mute tongues, thine eyes, have never
  By their glances told me so.

For I know my love thou knowest;
  Therefore thine to claim I dare:
Once it ceases to be secret,
  Love need never feel despair.

True it is, Olalla, sometimes
  Thou hast all too plainly shown
That thy heart is brass in hardness,
  And thy snowy bosom stone.

Yet for all that, in thy coyness,
  And thy fickle fits between,
Hope is there—at least the border
  Of her garment may be seen.

Lures to faith are they, those glimpses,
  And to faith in thee I hold;
Kindness cannot make it stronger,
  Coldness cannot make it cold.

If it be that love is gentle,
  In thy gentleness I see
Something holding out assurance
  To the hope of winning thee.

If it be that in devotion
  Lies a power hearts to move,
That which every day I show thee,
  Helpful to my suit should prove.

Many a time thou must have noticed—
  If to notice thou dost care—
How I go about on Monday
  Dressed in all my Sunday wear.

Love's eyes love to look on brightness;
  Love loves what is gaily drest;
Sunday, Monday, all I care is
  Thou shouldst see me in my best.

No account I make of dances,
  Or of strains that pleased thee so,
Keeping thee awake from midnight
  Till the cocks began to crow;

Or of how I roundly swore it
  That there's none so fair as thou;
True it is, but as I said it,
  By the girls I'm hated now.

For Teresa of the hillside
  At my praise of thee was sore;
Said, "You think you love an angel;
  It's a monkey you adore;

"Caught by all her glittering trinkets,
  And her borrowed braids of hair,
And a host of made-up beauties
  That would Love himself ensnare."

'T was a lie, and so I told her,
  And her cousin at the word
Gave me his defiance for it;
  And what followed thou hast heard.

Mine is no high-flown affection,
Mine no passion *par amours*—
As they call it—what I offer
Is an honest love, and pure.

Binding cords the holy Church has,
Cords of softest silk they be;
Put thy neck beneath the yoke, dear;
Mine will follow, thou wilt see.

Else—and once for all I swear it
By the saint of most renown—
If I ever quit the mountains,
'T will be in a friar's gown.

Here the goatherd brought his song to an end. Though Don Quixote entreated him to sing more, Sancho had no mind that way, being more inclined for sleep than for listening to songs.

"Your worship," he said to his master, "will do well to decide at once where you intend pass the night, for the labor these good men do all day does not allow them to spend the night in singing."

"I understand you, Sancho," replied Don Quixote. "I perceive clearly that those visits to the wineskin demand compensation in sleep rather than in music."

"It's sweet to us all, blessed be God," said Sancho.

"I do not deny it," replied Don Quixote, "but settle down where you will. Those of my calling are more becomingly employed in keeping watch than in sleeping. Yet it would be well if you would dress this ear of mine again, for it is giving me more pain than it should."

Sancho did as he was asked, but one of the goatherds, seeing the wound, told him not to be uneasy, as he would apply a remedy with which it would be soon healed. Gathering some leaves of rosemary, of which there was a great quantity there, he chewed them and mixed them with a little salt. Then he applied them to the ear and secured them firmly with a bandage, giving the assurance that no other treatment would be required. And so it proved.

Chapter XII

OF WHAT A GOATHERD RELATED TO THOSE WITH DON QUIXOTE

Just then another young man came up. He was one of those who brought the provisions from the village. "Do you know what is going on in the village, comrades?" he asked.

"How could we know?" replied one of them.

"Well, then, I must tell you," continued the young man, "that this morning the famous student-shepherd called Grisóstomo died.

It is rumored that he died of love for that stubborn girl Marcela, the daughter of Guillermo the Rich. She's the girl who wanders about in these lonely places in the dress of a shepherdess."

"Are you talking about Marcela?" said one.

"That's the one I mean," answered the goatherd. "And the best of it is, he has directed in his will that he is to be buried in the fields, like a Moor, and at the foot of the rock where the Corktree Spring is. The story goes (and they say he himself said so) that it was there he first saw her. And he left other directions which the clergy of the village say should not and must not be obeyed, because they smack of paganism. To all that his great friend Ambrosio the student, who like him went about dressed as a shepherd, replies that everything must be carried out to the last detail according to Grisóstomo's order. It has the whole village in commotion, but it's being said that everything will be done that Ambrosio and his friends the shepherds want to have done. Tomorrow they are coming to bury him where I said with great ceremony. I am sure it will be something worth seeing. At least I will certainly go, even if I knew I should not return to the village tomorrow."

"We will do the same," answered the goatherds, "and draw lots to see who must stay to mind everybody's goats."

"That was well said, Pedro," said one, "though there will be no need to take the trouble; I will stay behind. But don't imagine it's generosity or that I'm not curious. The splinter that stuck in my foot the other day won't let me walk."

"We thank you just the same," said Pedro.

Don Quixote asked Pedro to tell him about the dead man and about the shepherdess. Pedro replied that all he knew was that the dead man was a wealthy gentleman from a village in the region. He had been a student at Salamanca for many years, after which he returned to his village with the reputation of being very learned and deeply read. "Above all," Pedro continued, "they said he was learned in the science of the stars and of what went on yonder in the heavens and the sun and the moon. He would tell us about the crips of the sun and moon to the exact time."

"*Eclipse* it is called, friend, not *crips*, the darkening of those two luminaries," said Don Quixote. But Pedro would not trouble himself with trifles and went on with his story.

"Also he foretold when the year was going to be one of abundance or estility."

"*Sterility*, you mean," said Don Quixote.

"Sterility or estility," answered Pedro, "it is all the same in the end. And I can tell you that in this way his father and friends who believed him grew very rich. They did as he advised them. He would say, 'Sow barley this year, not wheat. This year you may sow chick-peas and not barley. The next there will be a full olive crop, and the three following not enough for a drop will be harvested.' "

"That science is called astrology," said Don Quixote.

"I don't know what it is called," replied Pedro, "but I know that he knew all this and more besides. But, to finish, not many months after he returned from Salamanca, he appeared one day dressed as a shepherd with his crook and sheepskin coat, having discarded the long gown he wore as a scholar. And at the same time Ambrosio, a great friend of his and a fellow student, also adopted shepherd's attire. I forgot to say that the dead Grisóstomo was a great man for writing verses. He made up carols for Christmas Eve and plays for Corpus Christi, which the young men of our village acted, and all said they were excellent. When the villagers saw the two scholars so unexpectedly appearing in shepherds' dress they were lost in wonder, and couldn't guess what had led them to make so extraordinary a change. About this time Grisóstomo's father died, leaving him heir to a large amount of property in chattels as well as in land, no small number of cattle and sheep, and a large sum of money. Of all this the young man was left absolute owner, and indeed he deserved it all, for he was a very good comrade, and kind-hearted, and a friend of worthy people, and had a face like a benediction. Soon it became known that he had changed his clothing for no other reason than to wander about these lonely places after the Marcela our lad here mentioned a while ago, the shepherdess poor dead Grisóstomo had fallen in love with. And let me tell you now, for it is well you should know, what sort of girl she is. Perhaps, and even without any perhaps, you will not have heard anything like it all the days of your life, though you should live more years than Sarna."[1]

"Say Sarah," said Don Quixote, unable to endure the goatherd's confusion of words.

"Sarna lives long enough," answered Pedro. "And if, señor, you must find fault with words at every step, we won't reach the end in a year."

"Pardon me, friend," said Don Quixote, "but, as there is such a difference between *sarna* and Sarah, I mentioned it. However, you have answered well, for *sarna* lives longer than Sarah. Go on with your story, and I will make no more objections."

"I was saying, my dear sir," said the goatherd, "that in our village there was a farmer even richer than Grisóstomo's father. He was named Guillermo, and God bestowed upon him, over and above great wealth, a daughter at whose birth her mother died. She was the most respected woman in this neighborhood. I can see her now with that heavenly face. She was active, besides, and kind to the poor, for which I trust her soul is in bliss with God this very

1. *Más años que sarna*: "older than itch." Don Quixote supposes Pedro to mean Sarah, the wife of Abraham.

moment in the other world. Her husband Guillermo died of grief at the loss of so good a wife, leaving his daughter Marcela, young and rich, to the care of an uncle of hers, a priest who officiated in our village.

"The girl grew up to be so beautiful that it reminded us of her mother, who had been very beautiful, yet it was thought that the daughter would be even more so. When she reached the age of fourteen or fifteen, whoever beheld her blessed God for having made her so beautiful, and most of them were hopelessly in love with her. Her uncle kept her in great seclusion and retirement, but for all that the fame of her great beauty spread so that both for that reason and for her great wealth, her uncle was asked, solicited, and importuned, to give her in marriage. It was not only those of our town who did so, but people from many leagues around, and some among them of the highest quality. He, being a good Christian man, desired to give her in marriage at once, seeing her to be old enough. But he was unwilling to do so without her consent—not that he had an eye to the gain and profit the custody of the girl's property brought him while he put off her marriage. And, faith, this was said in praise of the good priest in more than one set in the town. For you should know, Sir Errant, that in these little villages everything is talked about and everything is criticized. You may rest assured, as I do, that a priest must be unusually good if his parishoners feel obliged to speak well of him, especially in villages."

"That is the truth," said Don Quixote. "But go on, for the story is very good, and you, good Pedro, tell it with very good grace."

"May the grace of the Lord be with me," said Pedro, "for that is the important thing. To proceed, I will tell you that though the uncle recounted and described for his niece the qualities of each individual among all those who had asked for her in marriage, and though he begged her to marry and make a choice according to her own taste, she always gave the same answer. No, she had no desire to marry just yet, and being so young she did not think she was fit to bear the burden of matrimony. Since, to all appearances, these were reasonable excuses, her uncle ceased to urge her and waited till she was rather older and could mate herself to her own liking. For, said he—and he said quite right—parents are not to settle children in life against their will.

"But when one least looked for it, lo and behold one day the demure Marcela makes her appearance as a shepherdess. And despite her uncle and all those in the town who tried to dissuade her, she took to the fields with the other shepherd lasses of the village and tended her own flock. And so, since she appeared in public and her beauty could be seen openly, I could not tell you how many rich youths, gentlemen and peasants, have adopted Grisóstomo's clothes and go about in the fields paying court to her. One of these, as has been already mentioned, was our dead friend who, they say, not only loved but adored her. But you must not suppose, because Marcela chose a life of such liberty and independence, and with so little or rather no privacy, that she has provided any occasion, or the semblance of one, to besmirch her purity and modesty. On the contrary, so great is the vigilance with which she watches over her honor, that not one of all those who court and woo her has boasted, or could truthfully boast, that she has given him the smallest hope of obtaining his desire. She does not avoid or shun the shepherds' society and conversation, and treats them courteously and kindly. But should one of them declare his intention to her, though it be no less proper and holy than matrimony, she flings him from her like a catapult. And with this kind of disposition she does more harm in this country than if the plague had broken out in it. Her affability and her beauty draw on the hearts of those that associate with her to love and court her, but her scorn and forthright rebuffs bring them to the brink of despair. So they don't know what to say, except loudly to declare her cruel and hard-hearted, along with other expressions that well describe her character.

"If you should remain here for any time, señor, you would hear the hills and valleys resound with the laments of her rejected suitors. Not far from here is a spot where there are a coupld of dozen tall beeches, and each one of them has the name of Marcela carved and written on its smooth bark. A crown's carved above the name on some of the trees as though her lover would say more plainly that Marcela wore and deserved the crown of all human beauty. Here one shepherd is sighing, there another is lamenting; there love songs are heard, here despairing elegies. One passes all the hours of the night seated at the foot of some oak or rock, and there, without having closed his weeping eyes, the sun finds him in the morning bemused and bereft of sense. Another without relief or respite to his sighs, stretched on the burning sand in the full heat of the sultry summer noontime, makes his appeal to the compassionate heavens. Over one and the other, over these and all, the beautiful Marcela triumphs in careless freedom. And all of us who know her are waiting to see what will come of her pride, and what fortunate man will succeed in taming a nature so formidable and winning so supreme a beauty.

"All I have told you being so well-established, I am certain that what they say of the cause of Grisóstomo's death, as our lad told us, is no less true. And so I advise you, señor, to attend his burial tomorrow. It will be well worth seeing, for Grisóstomo had many friends, and it is not half a league from here to where he directed he should be buried."

"I will make a point of it," said Don Quixote, "and I thank you for the pleasure you have given me by relating so interesting a tale."

"Oh," said the goatherd, "I do not know even the half of what has happened to the lovers of Marcela, but perhaps tomorrow we may fall in with some shepherd on the road who can tell us. And now it will be well for you to go and sleep under shelter, for the night air may hurt your wound, though with the remedy I have applied there is nothing to be feared."

Sancho Panza, who was sending the goatherd's loquacity to the devil, also begged his master to go into Pedro's hut to sleep. Don Quixote did so, and passed all the rest of the night thinking of his lady Dulcinea, in imitation of the lovers of Marcela. Sancho Panza settled himself between Rocinante and his ass, and slept, not like a lover who had been discarded, but like a man who had been soundly kicked.

Chapter XIII

IN WHICH IS ENDED THE STORY OF THE SHEPHERDESS MARCELA, WITH OTHER INCIDENTS

But hardly had day begun to show itself through the windows of the east, when five of the six goatherds came to rouse Don Quixote. They told him that if he was still of a mind to go and see the famous burial of Grisóstomo they would keep him company. Don Quixote, who desired nothing better, got up and ordered Sancho to saddle horse and ass at once. This he did briskly, and with equal dispatch they all set out on their way.

They had gone less than a mile when, at a place where two paths met, they saw coming toward them some six shepherds. They were dressed in black sheepskins and their heads were crowned with garlands of cypress and bitter oleander. Each man carried a stout holly staff in his hand, and along with them came two gentlemen on horseback in handsome traveling dress, and accompanied by three servants on foot. Courteous salutations were exchanged, and by inquiring which way each party was going, they learned that all were bound for the burial site. So they went on their way together.

One of those on horseback addressed his companion.

"It seems to me, Señor Vivaldo," he said, "that we may consider well spent the time required to attend this remarkable funeral. Remarkable it cannot fail to be, judging by the strange things these shepherds have told us of the dead shepherd and the murderous shepherdess."

"I think so too," replied Vivaldo, "and I would delay not just one day but four in order to see it."

Don Quixote asked them what it was they had heard about Marcela and Grisóstomo. The traveler answered that they had met the shepherds that morning, and seeing them dressed in this mournful fashion they had asked why they appeared in such a guise. One of them answered, describing the strange behavior and the beauty of a shepherdess called Marcela, the loves of her many suitors, and the death of that Grisóstomo whose burial they were about to witness. In short, he repeated everything Pedro had related to Don Quixote.

This topic was dropped, and the man called Vivaldo began another by asking Don Quixote what induced him to go thus armed in so peaceful a region.

"The exercise of my calling," replied Don Quixote, "does not allow or permit me to travel in any other manner. Easy life, enjoyment, and repose were invented for soft courtiers, but toil, unrest, and arms were invented and made for those alone whom the world calls knights-errant, of whom I, though unworthy, am the least of all."

The instant they heard this, they all concluded he was mad. The better to settle the point and discover what kind of madness his was, Vivaldo proceeded to ask him what knights-errant meant.

"Have not your worships," replied Don Quixote, "read the annals and histories of England, in which are recorded the famous deeds of King Arthur, whom we in our popular Castilian invariably call King Artús? With regard to him it is an ancient tradition, universally accepted as true all over the kingdom of Great Britain, that this king did not die, but was changed by magic into a raven. In due time he is to return to reign and recover his kingdom and scepter. That is why it cannot be proved from that time to this that any Englishman ever killed a raven. Well, then, in the time of this good king the famous order of chivalry of the Knights of the Round Table was instituted, and the amours of Lancelot of the Lake with Queen Guinevere occurred, precisely as they are related. The go-between and confidante was the highly honorable lady Quintañona, whence came that ballad so well known and widely spread in our Spain—

> O never surely was there knight
> So served by hand of dame,
> As served was he Sir Lancelot hight
> When he from Britain came—

with all the sweet and delectable unfolding of his achievements in love and war. Handed down from that time, this order of chivalry went on extending and spreading itself over many and various parts of the world. In it, famous and renowed for their deeds, were the mighty Amadís of Gaul with all his sons and descendants to the fifth generation, and the valiant Felixmarte of Hircania, and the never sufficiently praised Tirante el Blanco. In our own days almost we have seen and heard and talked with the invincible knight Don Belianís of Greece. That, sirs, is what it means to ge a knight-errant, and that is the order of chivalry I have spoken of. As I have already said, I, though a sinner, have made profession of it. What the aforesaid knights professed that same do I profess, and so I go through these solitudes and wilds seeking adventures, with mind resolved to set my arm and person against the worst perils that fortune may offer, in aid of the weak and needy."

These words were enough to convince the travelers that Don Quixote was out of his senses and to reveal the sort of madness that ruled him. They felt the same astonishment at this that everyone felt on first becoming acquainted with it. Vivaldo, being a person of great shrewdness and with a merry disposition, decided to while away the short journey they said was required to reach the mountain burial site by providing the occasion for him to utter further absurdities.

"It seems to me, Señor Knight-errant," he said to him, "that your worship has chosen one of the most austere professions in the world. I imagine even that of the Carthusian monks is not so austere."

"Equally austere it may perhaps be," replied our Don Quixote, "but I am very much inclined to doubt whether the world is equally in need of it. For, if truth be told, the soldier who carries out his captain's orders does no less than the captain who gives the order. What I mean is that churchmen in peace and quiet pray heaven for the world's welfare, but we soldiers and knights put into effect what they pray for. We defend it with the might of our arms and the edge of our swords, not under shelter but in the open air and exposed to the intolerable rays of the summer sun and the piercing frosts of winter. Thus we are God's ministers on earth and the arms that implement his justice. And as the business of war and all that it involves cannot be conducted without sweat, toil, and exertion, it follows that those professionally engaged in it undoubtedly must exert themselves more than those who in absolute peace and quiet continually pray to God to help the weak.

"I am not saying, nor do I entertain the thought, that the knight-errant's calling is as good as that of the monk in his cell. I merely infer from what I myself endure that it is beyond a doubt more laborious and more belabored, both hungrier and thirstier, and more wretched, ragged, and lice-ridden. There is no reason to doubt that the knights-errant of yore endured much hardship in the course of their lives. And if some of them by the might of their arms did rise to be emperors, in faith it cost them dear in blood and sweat. And if those who reached that rank had not had magicians and sages to help them, they would have been completely baulked in their ambition and disappointed in their hopes."

"That is my opinion too," replied the traveler. "But one thing among many others seems to me very wrong in knights-errant, and that is that when they find themselves about to undertake some mighty, perilous adventure and in manifest danger of losing their lives, they never think at that very moment of commending themselves to God, as every good Christian in such peril should do. Instead, they commend themselves to their ladies with as much devotion as if these ladies were their gods. This strikes me as savoring somewhat of paganism."

"Sir," answered Don Quixote, "that cannot on any account be omitted, and any knight-errant who acted otherwise would be disgraced. For it is usual and customary, in knight-errantry, that the knight-errant who engages in any great feat of arms with his lady before him should turn his eyes towards her softly and lovingly. It is as though he were entreating her to favor and protect him in the hazardous venture he is about to undertake. Even though no one should hear him, he is bound to say certain words under his breath, commending himself to her with all his heart. We have innumerable instances of this in the histories. But it should not lead one to suppose that they fail to commend themselves to God, for they will have time and opportunity to do so while engaged in their task."

"Nevertheless," answered the traveler, "I still feel some doubt. I have often read how words will arise between two knights-errant and eventually, their anger being kindled, they wheel their horses around and take a good stretch of field. Then without any more ado they charge at one another at full speed, and in mid-career they commend themselves to their ladies. The encounter usually ends with one knight falling over his horse's haunches pierced through and through by his antagonist's lance. As for the other, only by holding on to his horse's mane can he avoid falling to the ground. I don't see how the dead man could have had time to commend himself to God in the course of so swift an exchange. He would have been better advised not to waste words during the charge commending himself to his lady but to use them to discharge his duties and obligations as a Christian. Moreover, I do not believe that all knights-errant have ladies to commend themselves to, for they are not all in love."

"That is impossible," said Don Quixote. "I say it is impossible there could be a knight-errant without a lady. For such a man it is as natural and proper to be in love as for the heavens to have stars. Quite assuredly no history has ever been written concerning a knight-errant without a lady, for the simple reason that he would be treated not as a legitimate knight but as a bastard. He would have entered this fortress of knighthood not through the door, but over the wall like a thief and a robber."

"Nevertheless," said the traveler, "if I remember rightly, I seem to have read that Don Galaor, brother of the valiant Amadís of Gaul, never had any special lady to whom he might commend himself. Yet he was esteemed nonetheless, and was a very stout and famous knight."

"Sir," declared Don Quixote in reply, "one solitary swallow does not make a summer. Moreover, that knight, as I am aware, was in secret very deeply in love. Besides which, his habit of falling in love with any woman who caught his fancy was a natural bent which he could not control. In short, it is well established that he had one alone whom he made mistress of his will. To her he commended himself very frequently and secretly, for he prided himself on being a discreet knight."

"Then if it is essential that every knight-errant should be in love," said the traveler, "it may be fairly supposed that your worship is in love, since you belong to the order. If you do not pride yourself on being as reticent as Don Galaor, I entreat you as earnestly as I can, on behalf of all this company and of myself, to tell us your lady's name, country, rank, and beauty. She will deem herself fortunate if all the world knows that she is loved and served by such a knight as your worship seems to be."

At this Don Quixote heaved a deep sigh.

"I cannot say positively," he said, "whether my sweet enemy is pleased or not that the world should know I serve her. I can only say in answer to your courteous inquiry that her name is Dulcinea and her country El Toboso, a village of La Mancha. Her rank must be at least that of a princess, since she is my queen and lady, and her beauty superhuman, since all the impossible and fanciful attributes of beauty which the poets apply to their ladies are verified in her. Her hairs are gold, her forehead Elysian fields, her eyebrows rainbows, her eyes suns, her cheeks roses, her lips coral, her teeth pearls, her neck alabaster, her bosom marble, her hands ivory, her fairness snow, and what modesty conceals from sight is such, I think and imagine, as rational reflection can only extol but not compare."

"We should like to know her lineage, race, and ancestry," said Vivaldo.

"She is not," answered Don Quixote, "of the ancient Roman Curtii, Caii, or Scipios, nor of the modern Colonnas or Orsini, nor of the Moncadas or Requesenes of Catalonia, nor yet of the Rebellas or Villanovas of Valencia; Palafoxes, Nuzas, Rocabertis, Corellas, Lunas, Alagones, Urreas, Foces, or Gurreas of Aragon; Cerdas, Manriques, Mendozas, or Guzmás of Castile; Alencastros, Pallas, or Meneses of Portugal. But she is of those of El Toboso of La Mancha, a lineage that though modern, may furnish a source of gentle blood for the most illustrious families of the ages that are to come. None may dispute this with me save on the condition that Zerbino placed at the foot of the trophy of Orlando's arms, saying,

> 'These let none move
> Who dareth not his might with Roland prove.' "[1]

"Although mine is of the Cachopíns of Laredo," said the traveler, "I will not venture to compare it with that of El Toboso of La Mancha—though, to tell the truth, no such surname has until now ever reached my ears."

"What!" said Don Quixote, "It has never reached them?"

As the rest of the party went along, they listened with great attention to the conversation of the pair. Even the goatherds and shepherds realized how exceedingly out of his wits our Don Quixote was. Sancho Panza alone thought what his master said was the truth, since he knew who he was and had known him from his birth. His only flicker of doubt concerned the fair Dulcinea del Toboso. Never had he heard mention of any such name or princess, though he lived so close to El Toboso.

Thus they talked as they traveled on, when they saw some twenty shepherds coming down through a gap between two high mountains. All of them were clad in skins of black wool and crowned with garlands. Some of these, as was learned later, were of yew, and the others of cypress. Six of the number were carrying a bier covered with a great variety of flowers and branches.

"They're coming with Grisóstomo's body," said a goatherd, when he saw this. "He gave orders that he should be buried at the foot of the mountain."

At this they hurried on. By the time they reached the spot, those carrying the bier had placed it on the ground. Four of them were wielding sharp pickaxes to hollow out a grave beside a hard rock. Courteous greetings were exchanged, and then Don Quixote and those with him turned to examine the bier. On it they saw, covered with flowers and in shepherd's attire, the body of a man who appeared to be about thirty years of age. Even in death it was clear that in life he had been handsome and of gallant bearing. Around him on the bier itself were laid a number of books and several papers, open and folded. Both the onlookers and those who were preparing the grave, like all the others at the scene, observed a strange silence. Finally one of those who had been carrying the body turned to another.

"Make very sure, Ambrosio," he said, "that this is the place Grisóstomo spoke of, since you are anxious that the provisions of his will should be strictly followed."

"This is the place," answered Ambrosio. "For here my poor

1. *Orlando furioso,* xxiv. 57.

friend often told me the story of his misfortune. It was here, he told me, that for the first time he saw that mortal enemy of the human race. Here, too, for the first time he made known to her his passion, as honorable as it was devoted, and here it was that on the last occasion Marcela utterly scorned and rejected him, so bringing the tragedy of his wretched life to a close. Here, in memory of misfortunes so great, he desired to be laid in the bowels of eternal oblivion."

Then he turned to Don Quixote and the travelers.

"That body, sirs," he continued, "on which you are looking with compassionate eyes, was the abode of a soul on which Heaven bestowed a vast share of its riches. That is the body of Grisóstomo, who was unrivaled in wit, unequaled in courtesy, unapproached in gentle bearing, a paragon of friendship, generous without limit, grave without arrogance, merry without vulgarity, and, in short, first in all that constitutes goodness and second to none in all that makes up misfortune. He loved deeply, he was hated; he adored, he was scorned; he wooed a wild beast, he pleaded with marble, he pursued the wind, he cried to the wilderness, he served ingratitude and for reward was made the prey of death in the midcourse of life, cut short by a shepherdess whom he sought to immortalize in the memory of man. All that, the papers you see could fully prove, had he not commanded me to consign them to the fire after having consigned his body to the earth."

"You would deal with them more harshly and cruelly than their owner himself," said Vivaldo. "It is neither right nor proper to do the will of one who commands what is wholly unreasonable. It would not have been reasonable in Augustus Cæsar, had he permitted the directions left by the divine Mantuan[2] in his will to be carried out. So that, Señor Ambrosio, while you consign your friend's body to the earth, you should not consign his writings to oblivion, for if he gave the order in bitterness of heart, it is not right that you should irrationally obey it. On the contrary, by granting life to those papers, let the cruelty of Marcela live for ever, to serve as a warning in ages to come to all men to shun and avoid falling into such a peril.

"I and all of us here know already the story of your love-stricken and heart-broken friend, and we know too of your friendship, the cause of his death, and the directions he gave at the close of his life. The sad story clearly reveals how great were Marcela's cruelty, Grisóstomo's love, and the loyalty of your friendship. And it reveals the end awaiting those who rashly pursue the path which that insane passion displays before them. Last night we learned of Grisóstomo's death and that he was to be buried here. Out of curiosity and pity

2. I.e., Virgil.

we left our direct road and resolved to come and see for ourselves what had so aroused our compassion when we heard of it. As recompense for that compassion and for our desire to find some remedy, if only that could be found, I beg you, excellent Ambrosio, or at least on my account I entreat you, not to burn those papers but to let me carry away some of them."

Without waiting for the shepherd's answer, he stretched out his hand and took some of those nearest him.

"Out of politeness, señor," said Ambrosio, when he heard this, "I will allow you to keep what you have taken, but it is useless to imagine that I will not burn the remainder."

Vivaldo was eager to see what the papers contained, and he opened one of them at once. It bore the title "Song of Despair."

"That is the last piece the unhappy man wrote," declared Ambrosio on hearing it. "So that you may see, señor, to what a pass his misfortunes brought him, read it aloud. You will have time enough, while we are waiting for the grave to be dug."

"I will do so willingly," said Vivaldo. Since the bystanders were no less curious, they all gathered around him while he read in a loud voice the poem that follows.

Chapter XIV

WHEREIN ARE INSERTED THE DESPAIRING VERSES OF THE DEAD SHEPHERD, TOGETHER WITH OTHER INCIDENTS NOT LOOKED FOR

GRISÓSTOMO'S SONG

Since thou dost in thy cruelty desire
The ruthless rigor of thy tyranny
From tongue to tongue, from land to land proclaimed,
The very Hell will I constrain to lend
This stricken breast of mine deep notes of woe
To serve my need of fitting utterance.
And as I strive to body forth the tale
Of all I suffer, all that thou hast done,
Forth shall the dread voice roll, and bear along
Shreds from my vitals torn for greater pain.
Then listen, not to dulcet harmony,
But to a discord wrung by mad despair
Out of his bosom's depths of bitterness,
To ease my heart and plant a sting in thine.

The lion's roar, the fierce wolf's savage howl,
The horrid hissing of the scaly snake,
The awesome cries of monsters yet unnamed,
The crow's ill-boding croak, the hollow moan
Of wild winds wrestling with the restless sea,

The wrathful bellow of the vanquished bull,
The plaintive sobbing of the widowed dove,
The envied owl's[1] sad note, the wail of woe
That rises from the dreary choir of Hell,
Commingled in one sound, confusing sense,
Let all these come to aid my soul's complaint,
For pain like mine demands new modes of song.

No echoes of that discord shall be heard
Where Father Tagus rolls, or on the banks
Of olive-bordered Betis;[2] to the rocks
Or in deep caverns shall my plaint be told,
And by a lifeless tongue in living words;
Or in dark valleys or on lonely shores,
Where neither foot of man nor sunbeam falls;
Or in among the poison-breathing swarms
Of monsters nourished by the sluggish Nile.
For, though it be to solitude remote
The hoarse vague echoes of my sorrows sound
Thy matchless cruelty, my dismal fate
Shall carry them to all the spacious world.

Disdain hath power to kill, and patience dies
Slain by suspicion, be it false or true;
And deadly is the force of jealousy;
Long absence makes of life a dreary void;
No hope of happiness can give repose
To him that ever fears to be forgot;
And death, inevitable, waits in hall.
But I, by some strange miracle, live on
A prey to absence, jealousy, disdain;
Racked by suspicion as by certainty;
Forgotten, left to feed my flame alone.
And while I suffer thus, there comes no ray
Of hope to gladden me athwart the gloom;
Nor do I look for it in my despair;
But rather clinging to a cureless woe,
All hope do I abjure for evermore.

Can there be hope where fear is? Were it well,
When far more certain are the grounds of fear?
Ought I to shut mine eyes to jealousy,
If through a thousand heart-wounds it appears?
Who would not give free access to distrust,
Seeing disdain unveiled, and—bitter change!—
All his suspicions turned to certainties,
And the fair truth transformed into a lie?
Oh, thou fierce tyrant of the realms of love,

1. The owl was the only bird that witnessed the Crucifixion, and it became for that reason an object of envy to the other birds, so much so that it cannot appear in the daytime without being persecuted.

2. Tagus is the Tajo river; Betis, the Guadalquivir.

Oh, Jealousy! Put chains upon these hands,
And bind me with thy strongest cord, Disdain.
But, woe is me! Triumphant over all,
My sufferings drown the memory of you.

And now I die, and since there is no hope
Of happiness for me in life or death,
Still to my fantasy I'll fondly cling.
I'll say that he is wise who loveth well,
And that the soul most free is that most bound
In thraldom to the ancient tyrant Love.
I'll say that she who is mine enemy
In that fair body hath as fair a mind,
And that her coldness is but my desert,
And that by virtue of the pain he sends
Love rules his kingdom with a gentle sway.
Thus, self-deluding, and in bondage sore,
And wearing out the wretched shred of life
To which I am reduced by her disdain,
I'll give this soul and body to the winds,
All hopeless of a crown of bliss in store.

Thou whose injustice hath supplied the cause
That makes me quit the weary life I loathe,
As by this wounded bosom thou canst see
How willingly thy victim I become,
Let not my death, if haply worth a tear,
Cloud the clear heaven that dwells in thy bright eyes;
I would not have thee expiate in ought
The crime of having made my heart thy prey;
But rather let thy laughter gaily ring
And prove my death to be thy festival.
Fool that I am to bid thee! Well I know
Thy glory gains by my untimely end.

And now it is the time; from Hell's abyss
Come thirsting Tantalus, come Sisyphus
Heaving the cruel stone, come Tityus
With vulture, and with wheel Ixion[3] come,
And come the sisters of the ceaseless toil;
And all into this breast transfer their pains,
And (if such tribute to despair be due)
Chant in their deepest tones a doleful dirge
Over a corse unworthy of a shroud.
Let the three-headed guardian of the gate[4]
And all the monstrous progeny of hell
The doleful concert join: a lover dead
Methinks can have no fitter obsequies.

3. Mythological figures tortured by the gods: Tantalus, with food and water always out of reach; Sisyphus, with the endless labor of pushing a stone uphill; Tityus, with having his liver devoured by vultures; Ixion, with the eternal turning of the wheel to which he was bound.

4. The three sisters are the Fates; the three-headed dog is Cerberus, guardian of Hades.

Song of despair, grieve not when thou art gone
Forth from this sorrowing heart: my misery
Brings fortune to the cause that gave thee birth;
Then banish sadness even in the tomb.

Grisóstomo's poem found favor with the listeners, though the reader said it did not seem to him to agree with what he had heard of Marcela's reserve and propriety. In it Grisóstomo complained of jealousy, suspicion, and absence, all to the prejudice of the good name and fame of Marcela. To this Ambrosio replied as one who knew well his friend's most secret thoughts.

"Señor," he said, "to lift that doubt I should tell you that when the unhappy man wrote this poem he was away from Marcela. He had voluntarily separated himself, to see if absence would affect him as it usually does. As everything distresses and every fear besets the banished lover, so imaginary jealousies and suspicions, dreaded no less than if they were true, tormented Grisóstomo. Thus the truth of Marcela's virtuous reputation remains unshaken, and with her envy itself should not and cannot find any fault save that of being cruel, somewhat haughty, and very scornful."

"That is true," said Vivaldo. And he was about to read another of the papers he had preserved from the fire when he was stopped by, as it seemed, a marvelous vision that unexpectedly rose before their eyes. On the summit of the rock where they were digging the grave there appeared the shepherdess Marcela, so beautiful that her beauty exceeded its reputation. Those who had never till then beheld her gazed upon her in wonder and silence, and those who were accustomed to see her were not less amazed than those who had never seen her before. But the instant Ambrosio saw her he addressed her with manifest indignation.

"Have you come, by chance, cruel basilisk of these mountains," he cried, "to see if in your presence blood will flow from the wounds of this wretched being your cruelty has robbed of life? Or have you come to exult over your cruel exploits, or like another pitiless Nero, to look down from that height upon the ruin of his Rome in embers, or in your arrogance to trample on this ill-fated corpse, as the ungrateful daughter trampled on the corpse of her father Tarquin?[5] Tell us quickly why you have come, or what you seek. Since I know that in his thoughts Grisóstomo never failed to obey you in life, I will make all those who call themselves his friends obey you, though he is dead."

"I have not come, Ambrosio, for any of the purposes you name," replied Marcela. "I wish to defend myself and to prove how unrea-

5. Ambrosio's classical references: the basilisk killed with its look; Nero is supposed to have enjoyed the burning of Rome, about which there was a popular ballad; and Tullia's desecration of her father's corpse was the subject of another well-known ballad. It was widely believed that a victim's corpse would bleed in the presence of the murderer.

sonable are those who blame me for their sorrow and for Grisóstomo's death. Therefore I ask all of you here to give me your attention, for it will not take much time or many words to bring the truth home to persons of sense.

"Heaven, you say, has made me beautiful, and so much so that in spite of yourselves my beauty leads you to love me. Because of the love you show me, you say, and even urge, that I am duty bound to love you. By the natural understanding which God has given me, I know that everything beautiful attracts love, but I cannot see how, because of being loved, that which is loved for its beauty is bound to love that which loves it. Besides, it may happen that the lover of that which is beautiful may be ugly, and ugliness being detestable, it is very absurd to say, 'I love you because you are beautiful; you must love me though I am ugly.'

"But supposing beauty to be equal on both sides, it does not follow that inclination must be therefore alike, for it is not every beauty that excites love, some only pleasing the eye without arousing affection. If every sort of beauty were to excite love and win the heart, the will would wander vaguely to and fro unable to make choice of any. Since there is an infinity of beautiful objects, there must be an infinity of inclinations, and true love, I have heard it said, is indivisible and must be voluntary and not compelled. If this is true, as I believe, why would you have me bend my will by force, for no other reason than that you say you love me?

"But tell me: had Heaven made me ugly, as it has made me beautiful, could I rightly complain if you did not love me? Remember, too, that my beauty was no choice of mine. Heaven of its bounty gave it to me, such as it is, without my asking or choosing. And just as the viper, though it can kill, does not deserve to be blamed for the poison it carries, since this is a gift of nature, neither do I deserve reproach for being beautiful. For beauty in a modest woman is like fire at a distance or a sharp sword. The one does not burn, the other does not cut those who do not come too near. Honor and virtue are the adornments of the mind, without which the body has no right to pass for beautiful, however beautiful it may be. But if modesty is one of the virtues that lend a special grace and charm to mind and body, why should she who is loved for her beauty part with her modesty to gratify a man who for his pleasure alone strives with all his might and energy to rob her of it?

"I was born free, and that I might live in freedom I chose the solitude of the fields. In the trees of the mountains I find society, the clear waters of the brooks are my mirrors, and to the trees and waters I make known my thoughts and charms. I am a fire afar off, a sword laid aside. Those whom I have inspired with love by letting them see me, I have by words undeceived. If their longings live on hope—and I have given none to Grisóstomo or to any other—it cannot justly be said that the death of anyone is my doing. It was his own obstinacy rather than my cruelty that killed him. And if the reproach is raised against me that his wishes were honorable, and that therefore I was bound to yield, I make this reply.

"When, on this very spot where now his grave has been made, he declared to me his purity of purpose, I told him that my resolve was to live in perpetual solitude and that the earth alone should enjoy the fruits of my withdrawal and the spoils of my beauty. If, after my frank avowal, he chose to persist against all hope and steer against the wind, what wonder is it that he should sink in the depths of his infatuation? If I had encouraged him, I would be false; if I had gratified him, I would have acted against my own better resolution and purpose. He was persistent in spite of warning, he despaired without being hated.

"Consider now whether it is reasonable to blame me for his suffering. Let the man who has been deceived complain, let him yield to despair whose hopes were raised only to be proved vain, let him flatter himself whom I shall entice, let him boast whom I shall accept. But let no man call me cruel or murderous to whom I make no promise, upon whom I practice no deception, whom I neither entice nor welcome. It has not been so far the will of Heaven that I should love by fate, and to expect me to love by choice is idle.

"Let this general declaration serve for each of my suitors on his own account. Let it be understood from this time forth that if anyone dies for me it is not out of jealousy or misery. She who loves no one can give no cause for jealousy to anyone, and outspokenness should not be confused with scorn. Let him who calls me wild beast and basilisk leave me alone as something noxious and evil. Let him who calls me ungrateful withhold his attentions; let him who calls me wayward, seek not my acquaintance; let him who calls me cruel, pursue me not. This wild beast, this basilisk, this ungrateful, cruel, wayward being has no longing of any kind to seek, serve, know, or follow them.

"If Grisóstomo's impatience and violent passion killed him, why should my modest behavior and circumspection be blamed? If I preserve my purity in the company of the trees, why should he who would have me preserve it among men seek to rob me of it? I have, as you know, wealth of my own and do not covet the wealth of others. My taste is for freedom, and I have no liking for constraint; I neither love nor hate anyone; I do not deceive one or court the other, or trifle with one or play with another. The modest conversation of the village shepherd girls and the care of my goats are my recreation. My desires are bounded by these mountains, and if they ever wander hence it is to contemplate the beauty of the heavens, steps by which the soul travels to its primeval abode."

With these words, she turned, without waiting for a reply, and entered the thickest part of a nearby wood. All present were lost in admiration, as much at her good sense as at her beauty. Some, who had been wounded by the irresistible shafts launched by her bright eyes, made as though they would follow her, not heeding the frank declaration they had heard. Seeing this, and deeming it a fitting occasion to exercise his chivalry in aid of distressed damsels, Don Quixote laid his hand on the hilt of his sword.

"Let no one, whatever his rank or condition," he exclaimed in a clear, loud voice, "dare to follow the beautiful Marcela, under pain of incurring my fierce indignation. She has shown by clear and satisfactory arguments that little or no blame lies with her for the death of Grisóstomo, and she has shown how far she is from yielding to the wishes of any of her lovers. For this reason, instead of being followed and persecuted, she should in justice be honored and esteemed by all the good people of the world, for she shows that she is the only woman in it that holds to such a virtuous resolution."

Whether it was because of the threats of Don Quixote, or because Ambrosio told them to fulfil their duty to their good friend, none of the shepherds moved or stirred from the spot. Having finished the grave and burned Grisóstomo's papers, they laid his body in it, not without many tears from those who stood by. They closed the grave with a heavy stone, until a slab which Ambrosio said he was planning to have made, with an epitaph reading as follows, was ready:

Beneath the stone before your eyes
The body of a lover lies;
In life he was a shepherd swain,
In death a victim to disdain.
Ungrateful, cruel, coy, and fair,
Was she that drove him to despair,
And Love hath made her his ally
For spreading wide his tyranny.

All then strewed upon the grave a profusion of flowers and branches, expressed their condolence with his friend Ambrosio, and took their leave. Vivaldo and his companion did the same; and Don Quixote said farewell to his hosts and to the travelers. They invited him to come with them to Seville, this being a convenient place for finding adventures, which rose up in every street and around every corner oftener than anywhere else. Don Quixote thanked them for their advice and for wishing to do him a favor. But he refused for the present, saying he could not go to Seville until he had cleared all these mountains of the highwaymen and robbers who were said to infest them. In view of his good intentions the travelers were unwilling to urge him further. So, once more bidding him farewell, they left him and went on their way. As they traveled they did not fail to discuss the story of Marcela and Grisóstomo, as well as the madness of Don Quixote. He, for his part, resolved to go in quest of the shepherdess Marcela and offer her all the services he could render. But things did not turn out as he expected, according to the account given in this veracious history, of which the Second Part ends here.

The Third Part of The Ingenious Gentleman Don Quixote of La Mancha

Chapter XV

IN WHICH IS RELATED THE UNFORTUNATE ADVENTURE THAT DON QUIXOTE FELL IN WITH WHEN HE FELL OUT WITH CERTAIN HEARTLESS YANGUESANS

The sage Cide Hamete Benengeli relates that as soon as Don Quixote took leave of his hosts and all those who had attended the burial of Grisóstomo, he and his squire rode into the wood they had seen Marcela enter. After having wandered for more than two hours in all directions without finding the shepherdess, they drew rein in a meadow covered with tender grass. Alongside ran a pleasant cool stream that irresistibly invited them to linger during the sultry hours of midday, which by this time was growing oppressive. Don Quixote and Sancho dismounted and turned Rocinante and the ass loose to feed on the abundant grass. Then they ransacked the saddlebags, and without any ceremony very peacefully and sociably master and servant made a meal of their contents.

Sancho had not thought it worth while to hobble Rocinante, feeling sure, from what he knew of his staid, continent temperament, that all the mares in the Córdoba pastures would not lead him into error. Chance, however, and the devil, who is not always asleep, so ordained it that a drove of Galician ponies was feeding in the valley. They belonged to some Yangüesan[1] carriers, who habitually take their midday rest with their teams in places where grass and water are plentiful, and the spot chosen by Don Quixote suited the Yangüesans' purpose very well.

It was at this moment that Rocinante took a fancy to disport himself with the ladies. Abandoning his usual gait and demeanor as he scented them, and without asking leave of his master, he broke into a brisk little trot and hastened to make known his wishes. They, however, seemed to prefer their pasture to him, and greeted him so effectively with their heels and teeth that they soon broke his girths and left him naked without a saddle to cover him. But

1. I.e., of Yanguas, a district in the north of Old Castile, near Logroño.

what must have affected him more was that the carriers, seeing the violence he was offering their mares, came running up armed with stakes.[2] They so belabored him that they brought him badly battered to the ground.

By this time Don Quixote and Sancho, who had witnessed the drubbing of Rocinante, arrived panting.

"So far as I can see, friend Sancho," said Don Quixote, "these are not knights but base persons of low birth. I mention this because you can lawfully aid me in taking due vengeance for the insult offered Rocinante before our eyes."

"What the devil vengeance can we take," answered Sancho, "if they are more than twenty, and we no more than two, or, indeed, perhaps not more than one and a half?"

"I count for a hundred," replied Don Quixote.

Without another word he drew his sword and attacked the Yangüesans, and incited and impelled by his master's example, Sancho did the same. To begin with, Don Quixote delivered a slash at one of them that laid open his leather jacket, together with a great portion of his shoulder.

The Yangüesans, seeing themselves assaulted by only two men while they were so many, seized their stakes and hemmed in the two on either side. Then they began to lay on with great zeal and energy. The second blow, in fact, brought Sancho to the ground, and Don Quixote fared the same way. All his skill and high mettle availed him nothing, for fate decreed he should fall at the feet of Rocinante, who had not yet risen—serving to show how furiously stakes can pound in angry boorish hands. Then, seeing the mischief they had done, the Yangüesans loaded their team with all possible haste and pursued their journey, leaving the two adventurers a sorry sight and in a sorrier mood.

Sancho was the first to come to, and finding himself close to his master he called to him in a weak and doleful voice, "Señor Don Quixote, ah, Señor Don Quixote!"

"What is it, brother Sancho?" answered Don Quixote in the same feeble, suffering tone.

"If it were possible," answered Sancho Panza, "I would like your worship to give me a couple of sips of that potion of Fear-o'-brass if you have any on hand. Perhaps it will serve for broken bones as well as for wounds."

"If I only had it here, wretch that I am, what more would we want?" said Don Quixote. "But I swear to you, Sancho Panza, on the faith of a knight-errant, before two days are over, unless fortune orders otherwise, I mean to have it in my possession, or my hand will have lost its cunning."

2. Used by the horse drivers in loading their beasts to prop up the pack on one side while they are adjusting the balance on the other.

"But how long does your worship think it will be before we will have the use of our feet?" answered Sancho Panza.

"For myself I cannot guess how long," said the battered knight. "But I assume all the blame, for I had no business raising my sword against men not dubbed knights like myself. So I believe that because I transgressed the laws of chivalry, the God of battles has allowed this chastisement to befall me. Consequently it is well, brother Sancho, for you to listen carefully to the matter I am about to mention, for it closely concerns the welfare of us both. And that is, when you see us slighted by rabble of this sort, do not wait till I draw sword against them, for I shall not do so. But you may draw your sword and chastise them to your heart's content. If any knights should come to their aid and defense, I will defend you and assail them with all my might; and you have already had a thousand signs and proofs of the might of my strong arm."

Such was the poor gentleman's arrogance, because of his victory over the stout Biscayan. But Sancho did not so fully approve his master's admonition as to let it pass unanswered. "Señor," he said, "I am a man of peace, meek and quiet. I can put up with any affront because I have a wife and children to support and bring up. So let your worship also receive a hint, since it cannot be made a command, that on no account will I draw sword against either peasant or knight. And here before God I forgive the insults offered me, whether they have been, are, or shall be offered by high or low, rich or poor, noble or commoner, not excepting any rank or condition whatsoever."

"I wish," said his master in response to all this, "that I had breath enough to speak rather more easily, and that the pain I feel in my side would abate. Then I would explain to you, Panza, the mistake you are making. Come now, you sinner, suppose the wind of fortune, hitherto so adverse, should turn in our favor, filling the sails of our desires so that safely and without impediment we reach harbor in one of those islands I have promised you. What would your situation be if, upon winning it, I made you lord over it? Why, you will make it well-nigh impossible, since you are not a knight, have no desire to be one, and possess neither the courage nor the will to avenge insults or defend your authority. You must realize that in newly conquered kingdoms and provinces the minds of the inhabitants are never so quiet nor so well disposed to their new lord that they may not make some move to reverse matters once more. They may, as the expression goes, try their luck once again. So the new ruler must have good sense to enable him to govern, and valor to attack and defend himself, whatever may befall."

"In what has now befallen us," answered Sancho, "I'd have been well pleased to have that good sense and that valor your worship speaks of. But I swear on the faith of a poor man, I am more fit for poultices than for arguments. See if your worship can get up, and let us help Rocinante, though he does not deserve it, for he was the main cause of all this thrashing. I never thought it of Rocinante, for I took him to be a virtuous person and as quiet as myself. Indeed, what they say is right, that it takes a long time to come to know people, and that nothing is sure in this life. Who would have said that, after the mighty slashes your worship gave that unlucky knight-errant, there would come posthaste and on their very heels such a storm of sticks as has descended on our shoulders?"

"Yet yours, Sancho," replied Don Quixote, "ought to be used to such squalls. But mine, it is plain, since they were reared in soft cloth and fine linen, must feel more keenly the pain of this mishap. Did I not imagine—why do I say imagine?—did I not know of a certainty that all these annoyances are very necessary accompaniments of the calling of arms, I would lie down here and die of pure vexation."

"Señor," his squire replied, "as these mishaps are the rewards harvested through chivalry, tell me if they happen very often, or if they have their own fixed times for coming to pass. Because it seems to me that after two harvests we shall be no good for the third, unless God in his infinite mercy helps us."

"Be informed, friend Sancho," answered Don Quixote, "that the life of knights-errant is subject to a thousand dangers and reverses, and neither more nor less remote is the immediate possibility that knights-errant may become kings and emperors. Experience has shown this to be true for many different knights with whose histories I am thoroughly acquainted. I could tell you now, if pain would allow it, of some who by simple might of arm have risen to the high stations I have mentioned. And these same knights, both before and after, experienced various misfortunes and miseries. For the valiant Amadís of Gaul fell into the power of his mortal enemy Arcaláus the magician, who, it is positively asserted, held him captive and gave him more than two hundred lashes with the reins of his horse while he was tied to one of the pillars of a court. Moreover, there is an anonymous author of no small authority who says that the Knight of Phœbus was caught when a trapdoor opened under his feet in a certain castle. After this fall he found himself bound hand and foot in a deep pit underground, where they gave him one of those things they call enemas, of sand and ice water, that well-nigh finished him. If he had not been helped in that dire extremity by a sage, a great friend of his, it would have gone ill with the poor knight. So I may well suffer in company with such worthy people, for greater were the indignities they had to suffer than those we now suffer.

"I would have you know, Sancho, that wounds caused by any instruments that chance to be in hand cause no indignity. This is expressly laid down in the law of the duel. For instance, if the cobbler strikes someone with his last, though it is in fact a piece of wood, it cannot for that reason be maintained that the man he struck has been cudgeled. I say this lest you should imagine that because we have been drubbed in this affray we have therefore suffered an indignity. For the arms those men used to belabor us were nothing more than their stakes. Not one of them, so far as I remember, carried rapier, sword, or dagger."

"They gave me no time to see that much," answered Sancho. "Hardly had I laid hand on my sword when they signed the cross on my shoulders with their sticks so vigorously that they took away sight from my eyes and strength from my feet, stretching me where I now am lying. Here I am not distressed by the thought of whether all those stake-blows were an indignity or not, whereas the pain of the blows does distress me, for they will remain as deeply imprinted on my memory as on my shoulders.

"For all that, let me tell you, brother Panza," said Don Quixote, "that there is no recollection to which time does not put an end, and no pain which death does not remove."

"And what greater misfortune can there be," replied Panza, "than one that must wait for time to end it and death to remove it? If our mishap were one of those that are cured with a couple of poultices, it would not be so bad. But I am beginning to think that all the plasters in a hospital would scarcely be enough to put us right."

"No more of that! Pluck strength out of weakness, Sancho, as I mean to do," rejoined Don Quixote. "Let us see how Rocinante is, for it seems to me that not the least share of this mishap has befallen the poor beast."

"There is nothing surprising about that," replied Sancho, "since he is a knight-errant too. What I wonder at is that my beast should have come off scot-free while we end up with broken ribs."

"Fortune always leaves a door open in adversity in order to provide relief," said Don Quixote. "I say that because this little beast may now take the place of Rocinante and bear me to some castle where I may be cured of my wounds. Moreover I shall not consider it dishonorable to be so mounted, for I remember having read how good old Silenus, tutor and instructor of the merry god of laughter, when he entered the city of the hundred gates,[3] was very satisfied to be mounted on a handsome ass."

"It may be true that he went mounted as your worship says," answered Sancho, "but there is a great difference between riding in like a gentleman and going slung like a sack of garbage."

"Wounds received in battle confer honor instead of taking it away. So say no more, friend Panza," replied Don Quixote. "But as

3. Boeotian Thebes; the god of laughter is Bacchus.

I told you before, get up as best you can and put me on your beast in whatever way suits you. Let us leave before night overtakes us in these wilds."

"And yet I have heard your worship say," observed Panza, "that it is most fitting for knights-errant to sleep in wastes and deserts, and that they esteem it very good fortune."

"That is," said Don Quixote, "when they cannot help it, or when they are in love. So true is this that some knights have remained two years on rocks, in sunshine and shade and all the inclemencies of heaven, without their ladies knowing anything of it. One of these was Amadís, when, under the name of Beltenebros, he dwelt on the Wretched Rock for—I know not if it was eight years or eight months, for I am not very sure of the reckoning. At any rate he stayed there doing penance because of some pique the Princess Oriana had against him. But no more of this now, Sancho. Make haste before a mishap like Rocinante's befalls the ass."

"The very devil would be in it in that case," said Sancho. And letting off thirty "ohs," and sixty sighs, and a hundred and twenty maledictions and execrations on whosoever it was that had brought him there, he raised himself, stopping halfway bent like a Turkish bow, unable to stand upright. But despite all his pains he saddled his ass, who too had gone astray somewhat, yielding to the excessive license of the day. He next raised up Rocinante who, had he possessed a tongue to complain with, most assuredly would have outdone Sancho and his master.

At long last, Sancho fixed Don Quixote on the ass and secured Rocinante with a leading rein. Taking the ass by the halter, he proceeded more or less in the direction in which it seemed to him the high road might be. As chance was conducting their affairs for them from good to better, he had not gone a short league when the road came in sight, and on it he perceived an inn, which to his annoyance Don Quixote insisted with delight was a castle. Sancho contended that it was an inn, and his master that it was no inn but a castle. The dispute lasted so long that before the point was settled they had time to reach it, and into it Sancho entered with all his team and without any further controversy.

Chapter XVI

OF WHAT HAPPENED TO THE INGENIOUS GENTLEMAN IN THE INN WHICH HE TOOK TO BE A CASTLE

The innkeeper, seeing Don Quixote slung across the ass, asked Sancho what was wrong with him. Sancho answered that it was nothing, only that he had fallen down from a cliff and had his ribs a little bruised. The innkeeper had a wife whose disposition was unusual in a woman of her calling, for she was kind-hearted and felt for the sufferings of her neighbors. So she at once set about looking after Don Quixote and made her young daughter, who was a very pretty girl, help take care of her guest. There was also a servant in the inn, an Asturian lass with a broad face, flat head, and snub nose, blind in one eye and not very sound in the other. The elegance of her shape, to be sure, made up for all her defects. She measured no more than five feet from head to foot, and her shoulders, which weighed her down somewhat, made her contemplate the ground more than she would have liked.

This graceful lass, then, helped the young girl, and the two made up a very bad bed for Don Quixote in a garret that showed clear signs of having formerly served for many years as a hayloft. In it was also quartered a mule driver,[1] whose bed was placed a little beyond our Don Quixote's. Though it was made only of the pack-saddles and cloths of his mules, he had much the advantage of it, as Don Quixote's bed consisted simply of four rough boards on two not very even trestles. For thinness, the mattress might have passed for a quilt, and it was full of pellets which, had they not been identifiable as wool through the holes, would to the touch have seemed pebbles in hardness. The two sheets were as stiff as leather, and anyone who chose might have counted the threads in the coverlet without missing a single one.

On this accursed bed Don Quixote stretched himself, and the innkeeper's wife and daughter soon covered him with poultices from top to toe, while Maritornes—for that was the name of the Asturian—held the light for them. While she was applying poultices to him the innkeeper's wife, observing how full of bruises Don Quixote was in some places, remarked that this had more the look of blows than of a fall.

It was not blows, Sancho said, but the rock had many points and projections, and each of them had left its mark. "Please, señora," he added, "manage to save some of those soft bandages, as there will be someone to use them, for my back is rather sore too."

"Then you must have fallen also," said the innkeeper's wife.

"I did not fall," said Sancho Panza, "but from the shock I got at seeing my master fall, my body aches so that I feel as if I had had a thousand whacks."

"That may well be," said the young girl, "for I have dreamed many a time that I was falling down from a tower and never coming to the ground. When I awoke from the dream I was as weak and shaken as if I had really fallen."

"That is the point, señora," replied Sancho Panza. "Without

1. In Cervantes' day, freight-hauling and cheap public transportation between cities were provided by pack-animals, usually mules, under the guidance of muleteers (drivers, carriers, etc.). The drivers were a tough lot, rather like modern-day "truckers," and were often of Morisco extraction, like this one.

dreaming, and being more awake than I am now, I find myself with almost as many bruises as my master, Don Quixote."

"What is the gentleman's name?" asked Maritornes the Asturian.

"Don Quixote of La Mancha," answered Sancho Panza, "and he is a knight-adventurer, and one of the best and stoutest that have been seen in the world for a long time."

"What is a knight-adventurer?" said the lass.

"Are you so new in the world that you don't know?" answered Sancho Panza. "Well then, let me tell you, sister, that a knight-adventurer is a thing that gets beaten up one minute and becomes an emperor the next minute, who today is the most miserable and needy being in the world, and tomorrow will have the crowns of two or three kingdoms to give his squire."

"Then how is it," said the innkeeper's wife, "that belonging to so good a master as this, you have not, to judge by appearances, even so much as a county?"

"It is too soon yet," answered Sancho, "for we have only been gone a month in quest of adventures. So far we have met with nothing that can be called one; sometimes when one thing is looked for, another is found. However, if my master Don Quixote gets well of this wound, or fall, and I am left none the worse for it, I would not change my expectations for the best title in Spain."

To all this conversation Don Quixote was listening very attentively. He sat up in bed as well as he could and took the innkeeper's wife by the hand. "Believe me, fair lady," he said to her. "Thou mayest call thyself fortunate in having in this castle of thine sheltered my person, which is such that, if I do not myself praise it, it is because of what is commonly said, that self-praise is demeaning. But my squire will inform thee who I am. I only tell thee that I shall preserve for ever inscribed on my memory the service thou hast rendered me in order to tender thee my gratitude while life shall last. Would to Heaven love held me not so enthralled and subject to its laws and to the eyes of that fair ingrate whom I name under my breath, but that those of this lovely damsel might be the masters of my liberty."

The innkeeper's wife, her daughter, and the worthy Maritornes listened in bewilderment to the words of the knight-errant. They understood about as much as if he had been talking Greek, though they could perceive that his remarks were all meant as expressions of goodwill and compliments. Not being accustomed to this kind of language, they stared at him and wondered to themselves, for he seemed a man of a different sort from those they were used to. Thanking him in their tavernkeeper's language for his civility they left him, while the Asturian gave her attention to Sancho, who needed it no less than his master.

The mule driver had made an arrangement with her for recreation that night, and she had given him her word that when the guests were quiet and the family asleep she would come to him and do whatever he wanted. And it is said of this good lass that she never made promises of this kind without fulfilling them, even though she made them in the woods and without any witness present. For she prided herself greatly on being a lady and held it no disgrace to be employed as servant in an inn, because, she said, misfortunes and bad luck had brought her to that position.[2]

Don Quixote's hard, narrow, wretched, rickety bed stood first in this star-lit stable, and close beside it Sancho made his, consisting merely of a rush mat and a blanket that looked as if it was of threadbare canvas rather than wool. Next to these two beds was that of the driver, made up, as has been said, of the packsaddles and all the trappings of the two best mules he had, though there were twelve of them, sleek, plump, and in prime condition. He was one of the rich carriers of Arévalo, according to the author of this history, who particularly mentions this carrier because he knew him very well, and they even say was in some degree a relation of his. Besides, Cide Hamete Benengeli was a historian of great scrupulousness and accuracy in all things, as is very evident, since he did not neglect those already mentioned, however trifling and insignificant they might be.

His example might be followed by those grave historians who relate transactions so curtly and briefly that we hardly get a taste of them, all the substance of the work being left in the inkpot out of carelessness, perverseness, or ignorance. A thousand blessings on the author of *Tablante de Ricamonte* and that of the other book in which the deeds of Count Tomillas are related; with what minuteness they describe everything![3]

To proceed, then. After having paid a visit to his team and given them their second feed, the mule driver stretched himself on his packsaddles and lay waiting for his conscientious Maritornes. Sancho was by this time covered with plasters and had lain down. Though he tried to sleep, the pain of his ribs would not let him, while Don Quixote with *his* pains had his eyes as wide open as a hare's. The inn was sunk in silence, and there was no light anywhere except from a lantern that hung burning in the middle of the gateway.

This strange stillness and the thoughts, ever present to our knight's mind, of the incidents described at every turn in the books that were the cause of his misfortune, delivered up his imagination

2. Natives of the old northern Spanish kingdoms like Asturias all claimed to descend from aristocratic ancestors. Cervantes and other authors satirized such pretensions to "honor" as Maritornes'.

3. *La corónica de los nobles caualleros Tablante de Ricamonte & de Don Jofré hijo del Conde Donasón* (Toledo, 1513), translated from a French romance. The deeds of the Count Tomillas are recounted in the *Historia de Enrique de Oliva, rey de Iherusalem, emperador de Constantinopla* (Sevilla, 1498).

to the most extraordinary delusion that one could possibly conceive. He fancied himself installed in a famous castle (for, as has been said, all the inns he lodged in were castles to his eyes), and that the daughter of the innkeeper was daughter of the lord of the castle. She, captivated by his gentle bearing, had fallen in love with him and had promised to come to his bed for a while that night without the knowledge of her parents. Regarding all this fantasy of his own fabrication as solid fact, he began to feel uneasy and to consider the perilous risk which his virtue was about to encounter. He therefore resolved in his heart to commit no treason to his lady Dulcinea del Toboso, even though queen Guinevere herself and dame Quintañona should appear before him.

While he was taken up with these peculiar notions, the time and the hour came—an unlucky hour for him—for the Asturian's arrival. Clad in her nightgown, with bare feet and hair gathered in a cheap hairnet, with noiseless and cautious steps, she entered the chamber where the three were quartered, in search of the carrier. But scarcely had she reached the door when Don Quixote perceived her, sat up in his bed in spite of his plasters and his aching ribs, and stretched out his arms to receive his beauteous damsel. The Asturian, who advanced, crouching and in silence, with hands outstretched to touch her lover, ran into the arms of Don Quixote.

Grasping her tightly by the wrist and drawing her towards him, while she dared not utter a word, he made her sit down on the bed. Then he felt her nightgown, and though it was of burlap it appeared to him to be of the finest and softest silk. On her wrists she wore some glass beads, but to him they had the sheen of precious Orient pearls. Her hair, which rather resembled a horse's mane, to him seemed threads of the brightest gold of Araby whose refulgence dimmed the sun itself. Her breath, which no doubt smelled of yesterday's stale salad, to his thinking diffused a sweet aromatic fragrance.

In short, he drew her imaginary portrait with the same features and in the same style as he had seen in his books, where some princess, smitten by love, came with all the adornments that are here recorded, to see the sorely wounded knight. And so great was poor Don Quixote's blindness that neither touch, nor smell, nor anything else about the good lass that would have made any but a mule driver vomit, were enough to undeceive him. On the contrary, he was persuaded he had the goddess of beauty in his arms, and he grasped her firmly.

"Would that I found myself, lovely and exalted lady," he went on to say, in a low, tender voice, "in a position to repay the favor that thou, by the sight of thy great beauty, hast granted me. But fortune, which is never weary of persecuting the good, has chosen to place me upon this bed, where I lie so bruised and broken that, though my inclination would gladly comply with thine, it is impossible. Besides, to this impossibility another yet greater is to be added, which is the faith that I have pledged to the peerless Dulcinea del Toboso, sole lady of my most secret thoughts. Were it not that this stood in the way, I should not be so insensible a knight as to miss the happy opportunity which thy generosity has offered me."

Maritornes was fretting and sweating at finding herself held so fast by Don Quixote, and not understanding or heeding the words he addressed to her, she tried without speaking to free herself. The worthy carrier, whose wicked thoughts kept him awake, was aware of his girlfriend the moment she entered the door, and was listening attentively to all Don Quixote said. Jealous that the Asturian should have broken her word with him for another, he crept nearer to Don Quixote's bed and stood quietly to see what would come of this talk which he could not understand. When he perceived the wench struggling to get free and Don Quixote striving to hold her, not liking the joke, he raised his arm and delivered such a terrible blow to the lank jaws of the amorous knight that he bathed his mouth in blood. Not satisfied with this, he climbed on Don Quixote's ribs and tramped all over them at a pace faster than a trot.

The bed, being rather shaky and not very firm on its feet, was unable to support the additional weight of the carrier and collapsed with a mighty crash. At this the innkeeper awoke and at once concluded that it must be some brawl of Maritornes', because after calling loudly to her, he got no answer. With this suspicion he got up and lighting a lamp hastened to the quarter where he had heard the disturbance. The wench, in her fright and panic upon seeing that her master was coming—for his temper was terrible—made for the bed of Sancho Panza, who still slept. Crouching on it, she huddled herself up into a ball.

"Where are you, you strumpet?" exclaimed the innkeeper as he entered. "Of course this is some of your work."

At this moment Sancho awoke, and feeling this mass almost on top of him fancied it was a nightmare and began punching in all directions. A number of punches fell on Maritornes who, irritated by the pain and flinging modesty aside, repaid Sancho so amply that she woke him up in spite of himself. He, finding himself so handled by whom he knew not, raised himself up as well as he could and grappled with Maritornes. Between the two of them began the most stubborn and amusing skirmish in the world.

The carrier, however, perceiving by the light of the innkeeper's lamp what was happening to his ladylove, abandoned Don Quixote and ran to bring her the help she needed. The innkeeper headed the same way but with a different intention, for he wanted to chastise the lass, believing beyond a doubt that she was alone responsible for all the music. And so, as the saying is, the cat beat the rat, the rat the rope, the rope the stick, and the carrier pounded Sancho, Sancho the lass, she him, and the innkeeper her, and all worked away so briskly that they did not give themselves a moment's rest. And the best of it was that the innkeeper's lamp went out, and as they were left in the dark, they all pounded on one another so unmercifully that there was not a sound spot left where a hand could light.

It so happened that there was lodging that night in the inn an officer of what they call the old Holy Brotherhood of Toledo.[2] He also heard the extraordinary noise of the conflict, seized his staff of office and the tin case with his warrants, and made his way in the dark into the room.

"Stop in the name of the law!" he cried. "Stop in the name of the Holy Brotherhood!"

The first person he came upon was the battered Don Quixote, who lay stretched senseless on his back on his broken-down bed. As the officer was feeling about in the dark, his hand fell on the knight's beard. He kept on shouting, "Help in the name of the law!"

But when he realized that the man he had laid hold of did not move or stir, he concluded that he was dead and that those in the room were his murderers. With this suspicion he raised his voice still higher. "Shut the inn gate," he cried. "See that no one goes out; they have killed a man here!" This cry startled them all and each abandoned the struggle at whatever point it had reached when the voice made itself heard. The innkeeper retreated to his room, the carrier to his packsaddles, the lass to her quarters. Only the unlucky Don Quixote and Sancho were unable to move from where they were. The officer let go Don Quixote's beard at this juncture and went out to look for a light, so that he might search for and apprehend the culprits. Not finding any, for the innkeeper had purposely extinguished the lantern as he returned to his room, the officer was compelled to make his way to the hearth, where after much time and trouble he lit another lamp.

Chapter XVII

IN WHICH ARE CONTAINED THE INNUMERABLE TROUBLES WHICH THE BRAVE DON QUIXOTE AND HIS GOOD SQUIRE SANCHO PANZA ENDURED IN THE INN, WHICH TO HIS MISFORTUNE HE TOOK TO BE A CASTLE

By this time Don Quixote had regained consciousness, and in the same tone of voice in which he had called to his squire the day

2. See note 3, Chapter X.

before when he lay stretched "in the vale of the stakes,"[1] he began calling to him now. "Sancho, my friend, are you asleep? Are you asleep, friend Sancho?"

"How can I sleep, for God's sake," replied Sancho, discontented and bitter, "when all the devils in hell have been after me tonight?"

"Assuredly you are right in that," answered Don Quixote, "for either I know little about it, or this castle is enchanted. I will tell you—but you must swear not to reveal what I am about to say until after my death."

"I swear," answered Sancho.

"I ask this," continued Don Quixote, "because I hate taking away anyone's good name."

"I swear," replied Sancho, "to hold my tongue about it till the end of your worship's days, and God grant I may be able to let it out tomorrow."

"Do I treat you so badly, Sancho," said Don Quixote, "that you would see me dead so soon?"

"It's not that," replied Sancho, "but because I hate keeping things long, and I don't want them to turn rotten in storage."

"At any rate," said Don Quixote, "I have more confidence in your affection and good nature. So I would have you know that tonight there befell me one of the strangest adventures that I could describe. You should be aware, if I am to tell it briefly, that a little while ago the daughter of the lord of this castle came to me, the most elegant and beautiful damsel that could be found in many a wide stretch of earth. What could I not relate concerning the charms of her person, her lively wit, and other secret matters which, to maintain the fealty I owe my lady Dulcinea del Toboso, I shall leave untouched and unspoken! I will say only that fate may have envied the great boon good fortune had accorded me or, more probably and as I have already said, this castle is enchanted. Just as she and I were engaged in the sweetest and most amorous discourse there came, without my seeing or knowing whence, a hand attached to the arm of some huge giant, which planted such a blow on my jaws that they were bathed in blood. Then I was pummeled so severely as to be left in worse shape than yesterday when the carriers, because of Rocinante's unseemly behavior, did us the harm you know of. So I conjecture that some enchanted Moor must be guarding the treasure of this damsel's beauty, and that it is not for me."

"Nor for me either," said Sancho, "for more than four hundred Moors have so thrashed me that the beating with the stakes was fun and games compared to it. But tell me, señor, what do you call this

1. An allusion to the mule drivers' stakes and to a popular ballad which began with this line.

excellent and rare adventure that has left us in such a state? Though your worship was not so bad off, holding in your arms the incomparable beauty you spoke of. But what did I get except the heaviest whacks I think I ever had in my life? Unlucky me and the mother that bore me! For I am no knight-errant and never expect to be one, yet out of each piece of ill-luck the heavier part falls on me."

"Were you thrashed too?" asked Don Quixote.

"Didn't I just tell you so? Curses on my ancestral tribe!" said Sancho.

"Don't be upset, friend," said Don Quixote, "for I will now make the precious balm that will cure us in the twinkling of an eye."

By this time the officer of the Holy Brotherhood had succeeded in lighting the lamp, and he came in to see the man he thought had been killed. Sancho caught sight of him at the door, wearing only his nightshirt, with a scarf around his head and a lamp in his hand, and a very forbidding expression.

"Señor," Sancho said to his master, "can this by any chance be the enchanted Moor coming back to thrash us some more, if there's still something left unthrashed?"

"It cannot be the Moor," answered Don Quixote, "for those under enchantment do not let anyone see them."

"If they can't be seen, they let themselves be felt," said Sancho. "My shoulders can testify to that."

"Mine could speak too," said Don Quixote, "but that is not a sufficient reason for believing that what we see is the enchanted Moor."

The officer came up and was amazed to find them conversing so quietly. Don Quixote, to be sure, still lay on his back unable to move, on account of his bruises and bandages.

"Well, how goes it, my good man?" said the officer, approaching.

"I would speak more politely, if I were you," replied Don Quixote. "Is it the custom in these parts to address knights-errant thus, you blockhead?"

The officer, finding himself so disrespectfully treated by such a sorry-looking individual, lost his temper. Raising the lamp full of oil, he dealt Don Quixote a blow on the head that inflicted a horrid bruise. Then, with everything plunged in darkness, he went out.

"That is certainly the enchanted Moor, señor," said Sancho Panza. "He keeps the treasure for others, and reserves his fists and his lamp-swinging for us."

"That is the truth," answered Don Quixote. "And there is no use bothering oneself about these enchantments or being angry or vexed at them. Since these beings are invisible and phantasmal, there is no one from whom we can exact vengeance, do what we may. Get up, Sancho, if you can, call the warden of this fortress, and have him give me a little oil, wine, salt, and rosemary to make the salutary balm, for indeed I believe I have great need of it. I am losing much blood from the wound that the phantom gave me."

Sancho got up with aching bones and went off in the dark to find the innkeeper. He met the officer, who wanted to see what had become of his enemy. "Señor," he said to him, "whoever you are, do us the favor and kindness to give us a little rosemary, oil, salt, and wine. It is needed to cure one of the best knights-errant on earth. He is lying on the bed over there, having been wounded by the enchanted Moor who is in this inn."

The officer, hearing such talk, judged him to be out of his senses. As day was beginning to break, he opened the inn gate and called the landlord, telling him what the good man wanted. The landlord provided what was requested, and Sancho brought it to Don Quixote who, his hands on his head, was bewailing the pain of the blow from the lamp. This had done him no more harm than to raise a couple of rather large lumps, and what he took for blood was only the sweat pouring out because of all he had gone through during the turbulence that had just ended.

In short, he took the ingredients, of which he made a compound, mixing them all and boiling them a good while until it seemed to him they had reached perfection. Then he asked for a vial to pour it into, and as there was none in the inn, he decided to put it in a tin oil can or container of which the host made him a free gift. Over the oil can he repeated more than eighty Our Fathers and as many more Hail Marys, Salve Reginas, and Creeds, accompanying each word with a cross by way of benediction. Present at all this were Sancho, the innkeeper, and the officer. As for the carrier, he was now peacefully engaged in attending to his mules.

This being accomplished, Don Quixote felt anxious to test on himself, on the spot, the powers of this precious balm, as he held it to be. So he drank nearly a quart of what could not be poured into the oil can and remained in the vessel in which it had been boiled. But scarcely had he finished drinking when he began to vomit so violently that nothing was left in his stomach. What with the pangs and spasms of vomiting, he broke into a profuse sweat. So he told them to cover him up and leave him alone, which they did.

He fell asleep, and wakened more than three hours later. So great was his bodily relief, and so much less pain did he feel from his bruises, that he thought himself quite cured. He truly believed he had hit upon the balm of Fierabrás, and that with this remedy he could henceforward confront, without the least fear, any kind of destruction, battle, or combat, no matter how perilous.

Sancho Panza, who also regarded his master's recovery as miraculous, begged him for the considerable quantity of liquid that was left in the pot. Don Quixote consented, and he, taking it with both hands, in good faith and with a better will, gulped down and drained off very little less than his master. But the fact is that poor Sancho's stomach was inevitably less delicate than that of his master. So, before he could vomit, he was seized with such nausea and retchings, and such sweats and faintness, that really and truly he believed his last hour had come. Finding himself so racked and tormented, he cursed the balm and the thief that had given it to him.

"It is my belief, Sancho," said Don Quixote, seeing him in this state, "that this mischief has occurred because you have not been dubbed a knight. I am convinced this liquor cannot be good for any others."

"If your worship knew that," retorted Sancho "—woe is me and all my kindred!—why did you let me taste it?"

At this moment the beverage took effect, and the poor squire began to discharge at both ends at such a rate that the rush mat on which he had thrown himself and the canvas blanket he had covering him were fit for nothing afterwards. He sweated and perspired with such spasms and convulsions that not only he himself but all present thought his end had come. This tempest and tribulation lasted about two hours, and at the end of this time he was left, not like his master, but so weak and exhausted that he could not stand.

Don Quixote, however, who, as has been said, felt himself relieved and well, was eager to depart at once in quest of adventures. It seemed to him that all the time he lingered was a deprivation for the world and those in it who stood in need of his help and protection, and all the more since he had the security and confidence his balm afforded him. So, urged by this impulse, he saddled Rocinante himself and put the packsaddle on his squire's beast. He also helped Sancho to dress and to mount the ass. Once that was done, he mounted his horse and passing by a corner of the inn where there was a pike, he picked it up so that it might serve him for a lance. All those in the inn, who numbered more than twenty, stood watching him. The innkeeper's daughter was also observing him, and he too never took his eyes off her. From time to time he heaved a sigh that seemed to come up from the depths of his breast. But everyone thought it must be due to the pain in his ribs, or those at least thought so who had seen him being bandaged the night before.

As soon as they were both mounted and near the gate of the inn, he called to the innkeeper and said in a very grave and measured voice, "Many and great are the favors, Señor Warden, that I have received in this thy castle. I remain under the deepest obligation to be grateful to thee all the days of my life. If I can repay them by avenging thee of any arrogant foe who may have wronged thee, know that my calling is no other than to aid the weak, to avenge those who suffer wrong, and to chastise perfidy. Search thy memory. If thou findest anything of this kind, thou needest only tell me of it, and I promise thee by the order of knighthood which I have received to procure thee satisfaction and reparation to the utmost of thy desire."

The innkeeper spoke with equal calmness. "Sir Knight," he said, "I do not want your worship to avenge me of any wrong, because when any is done me I can take what vengeance seems good to me. All I want is for you to pay the bill you ran up in the inn last night, as well for the straw and barley for your two beasts, and for supper and beds."

"Then this is an inn?" said Don Quixote.

"And a very respectable one," said the innkeeper.

"I have been under a misapprehension all this time," answered Don Quixote. "In truth I thought it was a castle, and not a bad one. But since it appears that it is not a castle but an inn, all that can be done now is for you to excuse the payment. I cannot contravene the rule of knights-errant, of whom I know as a fact (and up to the present have read nothing to the contrary) that they never paid for lodging or anything else in any inn where they might be. For any hospitality offered them is their due by law and right, in return for the insufferable toil they endure in seeking adventures by night and by day, in summer and in winter, on foot and on horseback, in hunger and thirst, cold and heat, exposed to all the inclemencies of heaven and all the hardships of earth."

"That is no concern of mine," replied the innkeeper. "Pay me what you owe me, and let us have no more talk of chivalry, for all I care about is to get my money."

"You are a stupid, malicious innkeeper," said Don Quixote.

Putting spurs to Rocinante and resting his pike on his shoulder he rode out of the inn before anyone could stop him and pushed on some distance without looking to see if his squire was following him.

When the innkeeper saw him go without paying, he ran to get payment from Sancho, who declared that as his master would not pay neither would he. Since he was squire to a knight-errant, the same rule and reason held good for him as for his master with regard to not paying anything in inns and hostelries. At this the innkeeper grew angry, threatening to compel him if he did not pay, and in a way he would not like. To this Sancho made answer that by the law of chivalry his master had received he would not pay a cent if it cost him his life. The excellent and ancient usage of knights-errant was not going to be violated by him, nor should the squires of such as were yet to come into the world ever complain of him or reproach him with breaking so just a privilege.

The unfortunate Sancho's ill-luck so ordered it that among the company in the inn were four woolcarders from Segovia, three needlemakers from the Horse Fountain district of Córdoba, and two lodgers from the Fair district of Seville. They were lively fellows all, well-disposed, fond of a joke, and playful. Almost as if instigated and moved by a common impulse, they closed in on Sancho and dismounted him from his ass, while one of them went in for the blanket off the host's bed. But after flinging him into it they looked up and saw that the ceiling was somewhat lower than was required for their work. So they decided to go out into the yard, which was bounded only by the sky. There, putting Sancho in the middle of the blanket, they began to toss him high, having fun with him as they would with a dog during Mardi Gras time.

The cries of the poor blanket-tossed wretch were so loud that they reached the ears of his master who halted to listen attentively. He was certain that some new adventure was coming, until it became obvious that the noise was made by his squire. Wheeling about he came up to the inn at a laborious gallop. Finding it shut, he rode around it to see if he could find some way of getting in. But as soon as he came to the wall of the yard, which was not very high, he discovered the unpleasant game that was being played with his squire. He saw him rising and falling in the air with such grace and nimbleness that, had his rage allowed him, it is my belief he would have laughed.

He tried to climb from his horse on to the top of the wall, but he was so bruised and battered that he could not even dismount. And so, still on horseback, he began to utter such challenges and insults at those who were blanketing Sancho that no one could write them down accurately. But they brought about no stay in the laughter or the labor. Nor did the flying Sancho cease his lamentations, which he mingled now with threats and now with entreaties but all to little or no purpose. Finally, from pure weariness, they left off.

Then they brought him his ass, and mounting him on top of it they put his jacket around him. The compassionate Maritornes, seeing him so exhausted, sought to refresh him with a jug of water. So that it might be cool, she fetched it from the well. Sancho took it, but as he was raising it to his mouth he was stopped by the cries of his master.

"Sancho, my son," Don Quixote called out, "do not drink water. Do not drink it, my son, for it will kill you. See, here I have the blessed balm"—he held up the flask of liquor—"two drops of which will certainly restore you."

At these words Sancho rolled his eyes upward.

"Can it be," he said in an even louder voice, "that your worship has forgotten I am not a knight? Or do you want me to end by vomiting up whatever bowels are left me after last night? Keep your liquid in the name of all the devils, and leave me to myself!"

At one and the same instant he left off talking and began drinking. But as at the first sip he perceived it was water he did not care to go on with it, and he begged Maritornes to fetch him some wine. This she did with a right good will, and paid for it with her own money. For indeed they say of her that, though she was in that line of work, there was some faint and distant resemblance to a Christian about her. When Sancho had finished drinking, he dug his heels into the ass. The gate of the inn was thrown open, and he rode out very well pleased at having paid nothing and established his point, though it had been at the expense of his usual sureties, his shoulders. It is true that the innkeeper detained his saddlebags in payment of what was owing, but Sancho took off in such a flurry that he never missed them. The innkeeper, as soon as he saw Sancho go, wanted to bar the gate, but the blanketers would not agree to it. They were fellows who would not have cared two pennies for Don Quixote, even had he been really one of the knights-errant of the Round Table.

Chapter XVIII

IN WHICH IS RELATED THE DISCOURSE SANCHO PANZA HELD WITH HIS MASTER, DON QUIXOTE, AND OTHER ADVENTURES WORTH RELATING

When Sancho reached his master he was so limp and faint that he could not urge his beast on.

"I have now come to the conclusion, good Sancho," said Don Quixote, seeing the state he was in, "that this castle or inn is beyond a doubt enchanted. What else can those be, who have so atrociously diverted themselves with you, but phantoms or beings from another world? I hold this to be confirmed by the fact that, when I was near the wall of the yard witnessing the acts of your sad tragedy, it was beyond my power to climb it, nor could I even dismount from Rocinante, because they no doubt had me enchanted. For I swear to you by my knightly faith that if I had been able to climb up or dismount, I would have avenged you in such a fashion that those braggart thieves would have remembered their jest forever, even though, in so doing, I would be contravening the laws of chivalry. As I have often told you, these laws do not permit a knight to lay hands on anyone not a knight save in case of urgent and great necessity in defense of his own life and person."

"I would have avenged myself too if I could," said Sancho, "whether I had been dubbed knight or not, but I couldn't. For my part I am persuaded those who played this prank on me were neither phantoms nor enchanted, as your worship says, but men of flesh and bone like ourselves. They all had names, for I heard them called out when they were tossing me. One was called Pedro Martínez, and another Tenorio Hernández, and the innkeeper, I heard, was called Juan Palomeque the Left-handed. So that, señor, you could not leap over the yard wall or dismount from your horse for some reason other than enchantments. And what I can clearly see from all this is that these adventures we seek will in the end lead us into such misadventures that we won't know which is our right foot. The best and wisest thing, as best I can understand it, would be for us to return home, now that it is harvest time, and attend to our business, and give up wandering from pillar to post, as the saying is."

"How little you know about chivalry, Sancho," replied Don Quixote. "Hold your peace and have patience, for the day will come when you will see with your own eyes what an honorable thing it is to wander in the pursuit of this calling. Now tell me, what greater pleasure can there be in the world, or what delight can equal that of winning a battle and triumphing over one's enemy? None, beyond all doubt."

"Very likely," answered Sancho, "though I don't know it. All I know is that since we have been knights-errant, or since your worship has been one (for I have no right to count myself one of so honorable a number) we have never won any battle except the one with the Biscayan, and even out of that your worship came minus half an ear and half a helmet. From that time till now it has been all beatings and more beatings, punches and more punches. I got the blanketing into the bargain, carried out by enchanted persons on whom I can have no revenge. So I do not know what the 'delight,' as your worship calls it, of conquering an enemy is like."

"That is what vexes me and no doubt vexes you, too, Sancho," replied Don Quixote. "But henceforward I will endeavor to have at hand some sword so cunningly made that no kind of enchantments can affect him who carries it. It is even possible that fortune may procure for me the sword that belonged to Amadís when he was called 'The Knight of the Burning Sword.' It was one of the best swords that ever knight in the world possessed. For, besides having the power I have mentioned, it cut like a razor, and there was no armor, however strong and enchanted it might be, that could resist it."

"It would be my luck," said Sancho, "that even if that happened and your worship found some such sword, it would turn out like the balm to be serviceable and good for dubbed knights only. And squires can lump it."

"Fear not, Sancho," said Don Quixote. "Heaven will deal better by you."

Thus Don Quixote and his squire were talking as they rode along, when Don Quixote perceived approaching them on the road they were following, a large and thick cloud of dust.

"This is the day, O Sancho," he said, when he had noticed this, "which will reveal the boon my fortune reserves for me. This, I say, is the day when as much as on any other shall be displayed the might of my arm and when I shall do deeds that will remain written in the book of fame for all ages to come. Do you see the cloud of dust that rises yonder? Well, all that is churned up by a vast army composed of various and countless nations that comes marching there."

"In that case there must be two," said Sancho, "because on this opposite side there is another cloud of dust."

Don Quixote turned to look and found it true. He rejoiced exceedingly, for he concluded that two armies were about to meet and clash in the midst of that broad plain. At all times and seasons his fancy was full of the battles, enchantments, adventures, reckless feats, loves, and challenges that are recorded in the books of chivalry, and everything he said, thought, or did had reference to such things. Now the cloud of dust he had seen was raised by two great flocks of sheep coming along the same road in opposite directions, which, because of the dust, did not become visible until they drew near. But Don Quixote asserted so positively that they were armies that Sancho was led to believe it. "Well, what are we to do, señor?" he asked.

"Do?" said Don Quixote. "Give aid and assistance to the weak and needy. And you should know, Sancho, that the army coming toward us is conducted and led by the mighty emperor Alifanfarón, lord of the great isle of Trapobana. The other advancing behind me is the army of his enemy the king of the Garamantas, Pentapolín of the Bare Arm, for he always goes into battle with his right arm bare."

"But why are these two lords such enemies?"

"They are at enmity," replied Don Quixote, "because this Alifanfarón is a furious pagan and is in love with the daughter of Pentapolín, who is a very beautiful and moreover gracious lady, and a Christian. Her father is unwilling to bestow her upon the pagan king unless he first abandons the religion of his false prophet Mohammed, and adopts his own."

"By my beard," said Sancho, "Pentapolín does quite right, and I will help him as much as I can."

"In that you will be doing your duty, Sancho," said Don Quixote. "For to engage in battles of this sort it is not necessary to be a dubbed knight."

"That I can well understand," answered Sancho. "But where will we put this ass so as to be sure to find him after the fray is over? I believe it has not been the custom to go into battle on a mount of this kind."

"That is true," said Don Quixote. "What you had best do with him is let him go free, even if he gets lost, for the horses we shall have when we emerge victorious will be so many that even Rocinante will run a risk of being exchanged for another. But pay attention and watch, for I wish to give you some account of the chief knights accompanying the two armies. So that you may better see and observe, let us withdraw to the hill that rises yonder, from where both armies may be seen."

They did so and placed themselves on a rising ground from which the two flocks that to Don Quixote seemed armies might have been plainly seen, if the clouds of dust they raised had not obscured them and blinded the sight. Nevertheless, seeing in his imagination what he did not see and what did not exist, he began to speak in a loud voice.

"The knight you see over there in yellow armor, who bears upon his shield a lion crowned crouching at the feet of a damsel, is the valiant Laurcalco, lord of the Silver Bridge. The knight in armor with flowers of gold, who bears on his shield three silver crowns on an azure field, is the dreaded Micocolembo, grand duke of Quirocia. That other of gigantic frame, on his right hand, is the ever dauntless Brandabarbarán of Boliche, lord of the three Arabias, who for armor wears that serpent skin, and has for a shield a gate which, according to tradition, is one of those of the temple that Samson brought to the ground when by his death he revenged himself upon his enemies. But turn your eyes to the other side, and you shall see in front and in the van of this other army the ever victorious and never vanquished Timonel of Carcajona, prince of New Biscay, who comes in armor with arms quartered azure, green, white, and yellow, and bears on his shield a cat on a field tawny with a motto which says *Miau,* which is the beginning of the name of his lady, who according to report is the peerless Miaulina, daughter of the duke Alfeñiquén of the Algarve. The other, who weighs down and presses the loins of that powerful charger and bears arms white as snow and a shield blank and without any device, is a novice knight, a Frenchman by birth, Pierre Papin by name, lord of the baronies of Utrique. That other, who with iron-shod heels strikes the flanks of that nimble parti-colored zebra, and for arms bears azure vair,[1] is the mighty duke of Nerbia, Espartafilardo of the Forest, who bears for device on his shield an asparagus plant with a motto in Castilian that says, *My fortune creeps.*"

And so he went on naming a number of knights of one squadron or the other out of his imagination, and for all he improvised arms,

1. "Azure vair": an alternating blue and white pattern resembling the markings of *vair,* a heraldic term for "squirrel's pelt."

colors, devices, and mottoes, carried away by the illusions of his unheard-of madness.[2]

"People of divers nations compose this squadron in front," he went on without a pause. "There are those who drink of the sweet waters of the famous Xanthus, who scour the woody Massilian plains, who sift the pure fine gold of Arabia Felix, who enjoy the famed cool banks of the crystal Thermodon, who in many and various ways turn aside the streams of the golden Pactolus, the Numidians, faithless in their promises, the Persians renowned in archery, the Parthians and Medes who fight as they retreat, the Arabs who ever shift their dwellings, the Scythians as cruel as they are fair, the Ethiopians with pierced lips, and an infinity of other nations whose features I recognize and descry, though I cannot recall their names. In the other squadron come those who drink of the crystal streams of the olive-bearing Betis, who make smooth their countenances with the water of the ever rich and golden Tagus, who rejoice in the fertilizing flow of the divine Genil, who roam the Tartesian plains abounding in pasture, who take their pleasure in the Elysian meadows of Jerez, the rich Manchegans crowned with ruddy ears of corn, the wearers of iron, old relics of the Gothic race, those who bathe in the Pisuerga renowned for its gentle current, who feed their herds along the spreading pastures of the winding Guadiana famed for its hidden course, who tremble with the cold of the pine-clad Pyrenees or the dazzling snows of the lofty Apennine. In a word, as many as all Europe includes and contains."

Good God, what a number of countries and nations he named! To each he gave its proper attributes with marvelous readiness, brimful and saturated with what he had read in his lying books! Sancho Panza hung upon his words without speaking, and from time to time turned in an effort to see the knights and giants his master was describing; and as he could not make out one of them, he said to him:

"Devil take it, señor, if there's a sign of any man or knight or giant in the whole thing. Maybe it's all enchantment, like the phantoms last night."

"How can you say that!" answered Don Quixote. "Do you not hear the neighing of the steeds, the braying of the trumpets, the roll of the drums?"

"I hear nothing but the bleating of ewes and sheep," said Sancho.

It was true, for by this time the two flocks had come close.

2. The names and places described in this paragraph are, obviously, parodies of similar catalogues in the romances of chivalry. The next two imaginary groups ("this squadron in front" and "the other squadron") of knights come from classical geography (Xanthus, the river of Troy, the Massilian plains of Africa, etc.), and from Spain: Betis is the Guadalquivir River which flows past Seville; Tagus is the Tajo, a river which surrounds Toledo; Genil is a river near Granada, etc.

"The fear you feel, Sancho," said Don Quixote, "prevents you from seeing or hearing correctly, for one of the effects of fear is to derange the senses and make things appear different from what they are. If your fear is so great, withdraw to one side and leave me to myself, for alone I suffice to bring victory to the side I choose to aid."

So saying he gave Rocinante the spur, and bracing his lance, shot down the slope like a thunderbolt.

"Come back, Señor Don Quixote," shouted Sancho after him. "I swear to God they are sheep and ewes you are charging! Come back! Unlucky the father that begot me! What madness is this! Look, there is no giant, nor knight, nor cats, nor arms, nor shields quartered or whole, nor vair azure or bedeviled. What are you doing? Sinner that I am before God!"

But Don Quixote would not turn back, despite all these entreaties. On the contrary, he went forward.

"Ho, knights," he shouted out, "ye who follow and fight under the banners of the valiant emperor Pentapolín of the Bare Arm, follow me all. Ye shall see how easily I shall give him his revenge over his enemy Alifanfarón of the Trapobana."

So saying, he dashed into the midst of the squadron of ewes and began spearing them with as much spirit and intrepidity as if he were transfixing mortal enemies in earnest. The shepherds and drovers accompanying the flock shouted to him to desist. Seeing it was no use, they unloosed their slings and began to greet him with stones as big as one's fist. Don Quixote gave no heed to the stones but kept on galloping in all directions.

"Where art thou, proud Alifanfarón?" he called. "Come and face me. I am a single knight who would test thy valor in single combat and make thee breathe thy last as a penalty for the wrong thou hast done the valiant Pentapolín Garamanta."

At this point a water-smoothed rock struck him on the side and caved in a couple of his ribs. Feeling himself so assaulted, and surely imagining himself slain or badly wounded, he remembered his potion. He pulled out his flask, put it to his mouth, and began to pour the contents into his stomach. But before he could swallow what seemed to him enough, another pebble came flying. It struck him directly on the hand with such force that the flask was smashed to pieces. On its course it knocked three or four teeth and molars out of his mouth and badly crushed two fingers. The impact of these blows was such that, despite himself, the poor knight fell off his horse. The shepherds came up and felt sure they had killed him. So in great haste they gathered their flock together, took up the dead beasts, of which there were more than seven, and left without making any further inquiry.

All this time Sancho stood on the hill watching the crazy feats his master was performing, and tearing his beard and cursing the hour and occasion when fortune had brought them together. When he saw Don Quixote lying on the ground and realized the shepherds had gone, he came down the slope to where he was and found him in a pitiable condition, though not unconscious.

"Didn't I tell you to come back, Señor Don Quixote," he asked, "and that you were attacking not armies but herds of sheep?"

"That's how my enemy, that thieving magician, can alter and falsify things," answered Don Quixote. "Be informed, Sancho, that it is a very easy matter for his sort to make us believe what they choose. And this malignant being who persecutes me, envious of the glory he knew I would win in this battle, turned the squadrons of the enemy into flocks of sheep. At any rate, do this much, I beg you, Sancho, to undeceive yourself, and grasp that what I say is true. Mount your ass and follow them quietly, and you will see that when they have gone some little distance they will return to their original shape. Ceasing to be sheep, they will become men exactly as I described them to you. But do not go just yet, for I want your help and assistance. Come here, and see how many of my teeth and molars are missing, for I feel as if not one was left in my mouth."

Sancho came so close that he almost put his eyes into his master's mouth. It was at this very moment that the balm acted on Don Quixote's stomach, which discharged its contents, with more force than a musket, right into the beard of the compassionate squire.

"Holy Mary!" cried Sancho, "what has happened to me? Clearly this sinner is mortally wounded, since he is vomiting blood from the mouth."

Closer investigation revealed, however, by color, taste, and smell, that it was not blood but the balm from the flask he had seen him drink. He was overcome with such loathing that, his stomach turning, he vomited up his insides over his master, leaving both of them in a fine mess indeed. Sancho ran to his ass for something with which he could clean himself and take care of his master. But when he failed to find his saddlebags, he well-nigh took leave of his senses. Cursing himself yet once again, in his heart he resolved to leave his master and return home, even though he forfeited the wages for his service and all hopes of the promised island.

Don Quixote now rose, putting his left hand to his mouth to keep his teeth from falling out altogether. With the other hand he laid hold of Rocinante's bridle—so loyal and well-behaved was the creature that he had never stirred from his master's side—and made his way to where the squire stood leaning over his ass with hand on cheek, as though in deep dejection.

"Bear in mind, Sancho," said Don Quixote, when he saw him standing there so obviously depressed, "that one man is no more than another unless he does more than another. All these tempests that befall us are signs that fair weather is coming shortly and that things will go well with us, for it is impossible for good or evil to last for ever. Hence it follows that, since evil has lasted so long, good must be now at hand. So you must not distress yourself at the misfortunes which happen to me, since you have no share in them."

"Had no share?" replied Sancho. "Was it any other than my father's son who was tossed in a blanket yesterday? And did they belong to any other but myself—the saddlebags that are missing today with all my treasures?"

"What! Are the saddlebags missing, Sancho?" asked Don Quixote.

"Yes, they are missing," answered Sancho.

"In that case there will be nothing for us to eat today," replied Don Quixote.

"That would be so," answered Sancho, "If there were none of the herbs your worship says you know in these meadows, those which supply the needs of knights-errant as unlucky as your worship."

"For all that," answered Don Quixote, "I would rather have just now a quarter of a loaf of bread, or a loaf and a couple of herrings' heads than all the herbs described by Dioscorides, even with Doctor Laguna's notes. Nevertheless, Sancho the Good, mount your beast and come along with me, for God, who provides for all things, will not fail us (especially since we are so active in his service). For he fails not the gnats of the air, nor the worms of the earth, nor the tadpoles of the water, and is so merciful that he maketh his sun to rise on the good and on the evil, and sendeth rain on the unjust and on the just."

"Your worship would make a better preacher than knight-errant," said Sancho.

"Knights-errant knew and ought to know everything, Sancho," said Don Quixote. "There were knights-errant in former times as well qualified to deliver a sermon or discourse in the middle of an encampment as if they had graduated from the University of Paris. Thereby we may see that the lance has never blunted the pen, nor the pen the lance."

"Well, be it as your worship says," replied Sancho. "Let us be off now and find some shelter for the night, and God grant it may be somewhere where there are no blankets, or blanket-tossers, or phantoms, or enchanted Moors. For if there are, may the devil take the whole concern."

"Ask that of God, my son," said Don Quixote, "and lead on where you will, for this time I leave our lodging to your choice. But stretch out your hand and feel with your finger how many of my teeth and molars are missing from this right side of the upper jaw, for it is there I feel the pain."

Sancho put in his fingers and felt around.

"How many molars did your worship have on this side?" he asked.

"Four," replied Don Quixote, "besides the wisdom tooth, all whole and quite sound."

"Mind what you are saying, señor."

"I say four, if not five," answered Don Quixote, "for never in my life have I had tooth or molar pulled, nor has any fallen out or been destroyed by any decay or abcess."

"Well, then," said Sancho, "in this lower side your worship has no more than two molars and a half, and in the upper neither a half nor any at all, for it is all as smooth as the palm of my hand."

"Luckless man that I am!" said Don Quixote, hearing the sad news his squire conveyed. "I would rather have had an arm hacked off, provided it was not the sword-arm. I tell you, Sancho, a mouth without teeth is like a mill without a millstone, and a tooth is more to be prized than a diamond. But we who profess the austere order of chivalry must risk all this. Mount, friend, and lead the way, and I will follow you at whatever pace you wish."

Sancho did as he was bid, proceeding in the direction in which he thought he might find shelter without turning off the high road, which was very much traveled there. As they went along, then, at a slow pace—for the pain in Don Quixote's jaws kept him uncomfortable and ill-suited for speed—Sancho thought it well to amuse and divert him by talk of some kind. Among the things he said to him was the matter to be recounted in the following chapter.

Chapter XIX

OF THE SHREWD DISCOURSE WHICH SANCHO HELD WITH HIS MASTER, AND OF THE ADVENTURE THAT BEFELL HIM WITH A DEAD BODY, TOGETHER WITH OTHER NOTABLE OCCURRENCES

"It seems to me, señor, that all these misadventures that have happened to us lately have been a punishment for the offense your worship committed against the order of chivalry by not keeping the oath you made not to eat bread off a tablecloth or embrace the queen, and all else your worship swore to observe until you had taken Malandrino's helmet, or whatever the Moor is called, for I don't remember very well."

"You are quite right, Sancho," said Don Quixote, "but to tell the truth, it had escaped my memory. And you may be sure that the affair of the blanket occurred because you failed to remind me of it in time. But I will make amends, for there are ways of arranging everything in the order of chivalry."

"Did I swear something, then?" asked Sancho.

"It makes no difference that you swore no oath," said Don Quixote. "It is enough that I can see you may not be clear of involvement. And whether it be so or not, it will do no harm to provide ourselves with a remedy."

"In that case," said Sancho, "let your worship take care not to forget the remedy as you did the oath. Perhaps the phantoms may have a mind to amuse themselves with me again or even with your worship, if they see you so obstinate."

As they were talking of this and other matters, night overtook them on the road before they could reach or discover any place of shelter. What made it still worse was that they were dying of hunger, for along with the saddlebags they had lost their entire larder and commissariat. To make their misfortune complete, they met with an adventure which, without any stretching of the imagination, really seemed to be one. The night had grown quite dark, but for all that they pushed on, for Sancho felt sure that as the road was the king's highway they might reasonably expect to find some inn within a league or two.

Thus they were going along, the night being dark, the squire hungry, and the master not averse to eating, when they saw coming towards them on the road a great number of lights which looked exactly like stars in motion. Sancho was taken aback at the sight of them, nor was Don Quixote altogether unafraid. The one pulled up his donkey by the halter, the other his hack by the bridle, and they stood still, watching anxiously to see what all this would turn out to be. They found that the lights were approaching them, and the nearer they came the greater they seemed, a spectacle which made Sancho shake like a man dosed with mercury, and Don Quixote's hair stand on end. However, he regained his spirits to some extent.

"This, Sancho," he said, "will no doubt be a most mighty and perilous adventure, in which I will need to put forth all my valor and resolution."

"Unlucky me!" answered Sancho "If this adventure has to do with phantoms, as I am beginning to think, where can I find the ribs to withstand it?"

"Phantoms or not," said Don Quixote, "I will not let them touch a thread of your garments. If they played tricks with you last time, it was because I was unable to leap the walls of the yard. But now we are on a wide plain, where I can wield my sword as I please."

"And if they enchant and cripple you as they did the last time," said Sancho, "what difference will the open plain make, one way or the other?"

"For all that," replied Don Quixote, "I entreat you, Sancho, keep a good heart, for experience will show you what mine is worth."

"I will, please God," answered Sancho.

The two of them withdrew to one side of the road and set about observing closely what all these moving lights might be. Very soon afterwards they made out some twenty men in white surplices, all on horseback and with lighted torches in their hands. This awe-inspiring spectacle completely extinguished Sancho's courage, and his teeth began to chatter like those of a man with a fit of malarial chills. His heart sank and his teeth chattered even more when behind them a litter covered over with black could be seen advancing, followed by six more mounted figures in mourning down to the very feet of their mules. It was plain they were not horses because of their slow pace. As the men in surplices came along they muttered to themselves in a low plaintive tone. This strange spectacle at such an hour and in such a solitary place was quite enough to strike terror into Sancho's heart, and even into his master's. And (except in Don Quixote's case) it actually did so, for all Sancho's resolution had now broken down. With his master it was just the opposite, for his imagination immediately represented all this to him vividly as an adventure from one of his books.

He took it into his head that the litter was a bier on which some slain or badly wounded knight was being carried. To avenge him was a task reserved for Don Quixote alone. So, without further reasoning, he laid his lance in rest, fixed himself firmly in his saddle, and with gallant spirit and bearing took up his position in the middle of the road where the white-surpliced men would necessarily pass.

Waiting until he saw them near at hand, he raised his voice. "Halt, knights, or whosoever ye may be," he said, "and render me account of who ye are, whence ye come, where ye go, and what it is ye carry upon that bier. To judge by appearances, either ye have done some wrong or some wrong has been done you, and it is fitting and necessary that I should know, either that I may chastise you for the evil ye have done, or that I may avenge you for the injury inflicted upon you."

"We are in a hurry," answered one of the men in white, "and the inn is far off. We cannot stop to give you the account as you demand." He spurred his mule and went on his way.

Don Quixote was mightily provoked by this answer and seized the mule by the bridle. "Halt and be more mannerly," he said, "and provide the account I have demanded. Otherwise ye must all do battle with me."

The mule was shy and was so frightened at having her bridle seized that she reared up and flung her rider to the ground over her haunches. An attendant on foot, seeing the white-robed man fall, began to insult Don Quixote, who was moved to anger. Without any more ado, he braced his lance and charged one of the men in mourning and brought him badly wounded to the ground. As he wheeled around upon the others, the agility with which he attacked and routed them was a sight to see. It seemed as if wings had that instant grown upon Rocinante, so lightly and proudly did he bear himself. The men in white were all timid and unarmed, so they speedily made their escape from the fray. As they set off at a run across the plain with their lighted torches, they looked like maskers on some gala or festival night. The mourners, too, in disarray and tangled in the mule's trappings and their long cassocks, were unable to move themselves, and so with entire safety to himself Don Quixote pounded them all and drove them off against their will. They all thought it was not a man but a devil from hell, come to carry away the dead body they had in the litter.

Sancho, beholding all this, was astounded by his lord's intrepidity. "Clearly," he said to himself, "this master of mine is no less bold and valiant than he says he is."

Lying on the ground near the first man whom the mule had thrown was a burning torch, whose light enabled Don Quixote to see him. Going up to him he presented the point of the lance to his face and called on him to yield himself prisoner, if he did not wish to be killed.

"I am prisoner enough as it is," replied the prostrate man. "I cannot stir, for one of my legs is broken. I entreat you, if you are a Christian gentleman, not to kill me. That would be a grave sacrilege, for I am a licentiate and have taken my first orders."

"Then what the devil brought you here, if you are a churchman?" said Don Quixote.

"What, señor?" said the other. "My bad luck."

"Then still worse awaits you," said Don Quixote, "if you do not give satisfactory replies to the questions I already asked you."

"You shall be soon satisfied," said the licentiate. "I must tell you that though just now I said I was a licentiate, I am only a bachelor,[1] and my name is Alonzo López. I am a native of Alcobendas, I come from the city of Baeza with eleven others, those priests who fled with the torches. We are going to the city of Segovia with the dead body in that litter. It belonged to a gentleman who died in Baeza, where he was interred, and now, as I said, we are taking his bones to their final burial-place in Segovia, where he was born."

"And who killed him?" asked Don Quixote.

"God, by means of a malignant fever that took him," answered the bachelor.

"In that case," said Don Quixote, "the Lord has relieved me of the task of avenging his death, had any other slain him. But since he was slain by him who slew him, one can only remain silent and shrug one's shoulders, and I should do the same were he to slay me. I would have your reverence know that I am a knight of La Mancha, Don Quixote by name, and it is my business and call-

1. "Bachelor" and "licenciate" indicate persons who have university degrees roughly equivalent to our bachelor's and master's degrees.

ing to roam the world straightening out wrongs and redressing injuries."

"I do not understand the part about straightening out wrongs," said the bachelor, "for from straight you have made me crooked, leaving me with a broken leg that will never be set straight all the days of its life. The injury you have redressed in my case has left me so injured that I will remain unredressed forever. It was the height of misadventure for me to fall in with you, on your search for adventures."

"Things do not all happen in the same way," answered Don Quixote. "It all came about, Sir Bachelor Alonzo López, because of your traveling by night, dressed in those surplices, with lighted torches, praying and covered with mourning so that naturally you looked like something evil and from the other world. I could not avoid doing my duty, which was to attack you, and I should have done it even had I known for certain that you were the very devils of hell, as I certainly believed and took you to be."

"As my fate has so willed it," said the bachelor, "I entreat you, sir knight-errant, whose errand has been such an evil one for me, to help me to get from under this mule. One of my legs is held fast between the stirrup and the saddle."

"I might have talked on till tomorrow," said Don Quixote. "How long were you going to wait before telling me of your distress?"

He at once called to Sancho, who, however, had no mind to come, as he was busy unloading a pack mule, well laden with provisions which these worthy gentlemen had brought with them. Sancho made a bag of his coat, and getting together as much as he could and as the bag would hold, he loaded his beast. Then he hastened to obey his master's call and helped him to remove the bachelor from under the mule. Putting him on her back he handed him the torch, and Don Quixote told him to follow his companions and beg their pardon for the wrong he could not avoid doing them.

"If by chance these gentlemen want to know who was the hero that did them so much harm, your worship may tell them," said Sancho, "that he is the famous Don Quixote of La Mancha, otherwise called the Knight of the Mournful Countenance."

The bachelor took his leave, and Don Quixote asked Sancho what had induced him to call him the "Knight of the Mournful Countenance," especially at that time.

"I will tell you," answered Sancho. "It was because I was looking at you for some time by the light of the torch held by that unfortunate man, and just now your worship really has the ugliest face I ever saw: it must be due either to exhaustion from this combat or else to the lack of teeth and molars."

"It is not that," replied Don Quixote, "but because the sage whose duty it doubtless is to write the history of my achievements must have thought it proper that I should take some distinctive name, as did all knights of yore. One was called 'He of the Burning Sword,' another 'He of the Unicorn,' this one 'He of the Damsels,' that one 'He of the Phoenix,' another 'The Knight of the Griffin,' and another 'He of the Death's-head,' and by these names and designations they were known all over the world. So I say that the sage aforesaid must have put it into your mouth and mind just now to call me 'The Knight of the Mournful Countenance,' as I intend to call myself from this day forward. And that the name may fit me better, I mean, when the opportunity offers, to have a very mournful countenance painted on my shield."

"There is no reason, señor, to waste time or money on having a face painted," said Sancho. "All that's necessary is for your worship to uncover your own and turn toward those who look at you. Without anything further, either image or shield, they will call you 'Him of the Mournful Countenance.' Believe me, I am telling you the truth, for I assure you, señor, and all in good humor, that hunger and the loss of your teeth have given you such an ugly face that just as I said, the mournful picture will not be missed."

Don Quixote laughed at Sancho's joke. Nevertheless he resolved to adopt that name and have his shield or buckler painted as he had imagined it.

At this moment the bachelor returned and addressed himself to Don Quixote.[2]

"I forgot to mention," he said, "that your worship is excommunicated for having laid violent hands on a holy thing, *juxta illud, Si quis, suadente diabolo,* etc."[3]

"I do not understand your Latin," answered Don Quixote, "but I know that I did not lay hands, only this pike. Besides, I did not think I was committing an assault upon priests or things of the Church, which, like a Catholic and faithful Christian, as I am, I respect and revere, but upon phantoms and specters from the other world. Even so, I remember how the Cid Ruy Díaz fared when he broke the chair of that king's ambassador before his Holiness the Pope, who excommunicated him for it; and yet the good Cid Rodrigo de Vivar bore himself that day like a very noble and valiant knight."

After listening to this the bachelor took his departure, as has been said, without any rejoinder.

Don Quixote wanted to see whether the body in the litter consisted of bones or not, but Sancho would not agree to that.

"Señor," he said, "you have come out of this perilous adventure more safe and sound than from any other I have seen. Yet these

2. This line is an editorial addition to explain the unexpected reappearance of the bachelor.
3. "According to that [decree which begins] 'If anyone, at the prompting of the devil . . .'" This refers to a canon of the Council of Trent which excommunicates persons who harm clergymen.

people, though beaten and routed, may feel ashamed and humiliated when they reflect how they have let themselves be vanquished by one single man. If they should pull themselves together and come back to look for us, they could cause us trouble. The ass is properly loaded; the mountains are near at hand; we are hungry. All we have to do is retreat at a reasonable walk and, as the saying is, 'Let the dead man sleep; a live one has to eat.' "

And leading his ass, he begged his master to follow. Feeling that Sancho was right, Don Quixote did so without saying a word in reply. They proceeded some little distance between two hills and found themselves in a wide and secluded valley. There they dismounted and Sancho unloaded his beast. Stretched upon the green grass, with hunger for sauce, they breakfasted, dined, lunched, and supped all at once, satisfying their appetites with more than one slice of cold meat which the dead man's clerical companions (who seldom put themselves on short allowance) had brought with them on their pack mule.

But another piece of ill-luck befell them, which Sancho considered the worst of all, and that was that they had no wine to drink or even water to moisten their lips. As thirst tormented them, Sancho, observing that the meadow where they sat was full of green and tender grass, said what will be told in the following chapter.

Chapter XX

OF THE UNEXAMPLED AND UNHEARD-OF ADVENTURE WHICH WAS ACHIEVED BY THE VALIANT DON QUIXOTE OF LA MANCHA WITH LESS PERIL THAN ANY EVER ACHIEVED BY ANY FAMOUS KNIGHT IN THE WORLD

"This grass, señor, proves that there must be some spring or brook near here to give it moisture. It would be well to move a little farther on. We'll soon find some place to quench the terrible thirst that tortures us. It is even harder to bear than hunger."

The advice seemed good to Don Quixote, so he took Rocinante by the bridle while Sancho took the ass by the halter, after packing away the remains of the supper. They advanced up the meadow feeling their way, for in the darkness of the night they could see nothing. But they had not gone two hundred paces when a loud noise struck their ears, as though of water falling from great high rocks. The sound cheered them greatly, and they came to a halt, trying to make out the direction from which it came. But now another commotion assailed their ears, diluting the pleasure they had in listening to the water, and especially Sancho's, since he was by nature timid and faint-hearted. They heard, I say, strokes that fell with a measured beat, and a certain rattling of iron and chains.

Together with the furious din of the water, it would have struck terror into any heart but Don Quixote's.

The night was dark, as has been said, and they had reached a spot among some tall trees whose leaves, stirred by a gentle breeze, made a low ominous sound. What with the solitude, the place, the darkness, the noise of the water, and the rustling of the leaves, everything inspired awe and dread, more especially since they noticed that the strokes did not cease, nor the wind lull, nor morning approach. To all this might be added their ignorance as to where they were. But Don Quixote, supported by his intrepid heart, leaped on Rocinante, and slipping his shield on his arm, brought his pike to the ready.

"Friend Sancho, know that I by Heaven's will have been born in this our iron age to revive in it the age of gold, or the golden as it is called. I am he for whom perils, mighty achievements, and valiant deeds are reserved. I am, I say again, he who is to revive the Knights of the Round Table, the Twelve of France, and the Nine Worthies, and he who is to consign to oblivion the Platirs, the Tablantes, the Olivantes and Tirantes, the Phoebuses and Belianíses, with the whole herd of famous knights-errant of days gone by, performing in these in which I live such exploits, marvels, and feats of arms as shall obscure their brightest deeds. Thou dost mark well, faithful and trusty squire, the gloom of this night, its strange silence, the dull confused murmur of those trees, the awful sound of that water in quest of which we came, that seems as though it were precipitating and dashing itself down from the lofty Mountains of the Moon, and that incessant hammering that strikes and hurts our ears. These things all together and each of itself are enough to instil fear, dread, and dismay into the breast of Mars himself, much more into one not used to hazards and adventures of the kind.

"Well, then, all this that I depict for thee is but an incentive and stimulant to my spirit, making my heart burst in my bosom through eagerness to engage in this adventure, arduous as it promises to be. Therefore tighten Rocinante's girths a little, and God be with thee. Wait for me here three days and no more, and if in that time I do not come back, thou canst return to our village, whence to do me a favor and service, thou wilt go to El Toboso, where thou shalt say to my incomparable lady Dulcinea that her captive knight has died in attempting things that might make him worthy of being called hers."

When Sancho heard his master's words he began to weep in the most pathetic way.

"Señor," he said, "I do not know why your worship wants to attempt this dreadful adventure. It is night now, no one sees us here, we can easily turn around and take ourselves out of danger, even if we don't drink for three days to come. As there is no one to see us, all the less will there be anyone to call us cowards. Besides, I have heard the priest of our village, whom your worship knows well, preach that 'he who seeks danger perishes in it.' So it is not right to tempt God by trying so tremendous a feat from which there can be no escape except by a miracle, and Heaven has performed enough of them for your worship in delivering you from being blanketed as I was, and bringing you out victorious and safe and sound from among all those enemies that were with the dead man. If all this does not move or soften that hard heart, let it be moved by this thought and reflection, that you will have hardly left this spot when from pure fear I shall give my soul up to anyone that will take it. I left home and wife and children to come and serve your worship, trusting to do better and not worse. But as 'greed bursts the bag' it has torn my hopes open, for just as I had them highest about getting that wretched, unlucky island your worship has so often promised me, I see that instead and in exchange for it you mean to desert me now in a place so far from human contact. For God's sake, master, let not so great an injustice be done to me.[1] And if your worship will not entirely give up attempting this feat, at least put it off till morning. According to what I learned when I was a shepherd, dawn cannot be more than three hours off, because the Little Dipper is overhead and its handle shows that it's midnight."

"How can you see, Sancho," said Don Quixote, "where the handle is, or where this dipper is that you talk of, when the night is so dark that not a star can be seen in the whole heaven?"

"That's true," said Sancho, "but fear has many eyes and sees things underground, not to mention what's above in the heavens. Besides, there is good reason to believe that day is approaching."

"Let it do as it chooses," replied Don Quixote. "It shall not be said of me now or at any time that tears or entreaties turned me aside from fulfilling knightly usage. So I beg you, Sancho, to hold your peace, for God, who has put it into my heart to undertake now this so unexampled and terrible adventure, will take care to watch over my safety and console your sorrow. What you have to do is to tighten Rocinante's girths well and wait here, for I shall come back shortly, alive or dead."

When Sancho realized that this was his master's final resolve, and saw how little his tears, counsels, and entreaties prevailed, he decided to employ his own ingenuity and compel him, if he could, to wait till daylight. So, while tightening the girths of the horse, quietly and without being noticed he tied Rocinante's hind legs with the ass's halter. Thus when Don Quixote tried to depart he could not, as the horse could only move by jumps.

1. In the Spanish, Sancho begins to imitate Don Quixote's antiquated language when speaking of knight-errantry.

"See there, señor!" said Sancho Panza, when he saw the success of his trick. "Heaven, moved by my tears and prayers, has so ordered it that Rocinante cannot stir. If you are obstinate, and spur and hit him, you will only provoke fortune, and kick, as they say, against the pricks."

Don Quixote grew desperate at this, but the more he drove his heels into the horse, the less he stirred him. Not having any suspicion of the hobbling, he felt inclined to resign himself and wait till daybreak or until Rocinante could move, for he was firmly convinced that all this was caused by something other than Sancho's ingenuity. "As that is so, Sancho," he said to him, "and as Rocinante cannot move, I am content to wait till dawn smiles upon us, even though I weep while it delays its coming."

"There is no need to weep," answered Sancho, because "I will amuse your worship by telling stories from now till daylight, unless you would rather dismount and lie down to sleep a little on the green grass after the fashion of knights-errant. You would be fresher when day comes and the moment arrives for attempting the extraordinary adventure that awaits you."

"Why talk about dismounting or sleeping?" said Don Quixote. "Do you take me for one of those knights who rest in the presence of danger? Sleep, you who are born to sleep, or do as you will, for I will act as I think most consistent with my character."

"Don't be angry, master," replied Sancho. "That is not what I meant."

Coming close to him he laid one hand on the pommel and the other on the rear of the saddle so that he held his master's left thigh in his embrace. So greatly afraid was he of the strokes which still resounded with a regular beat that he did not dare move a finger's width away from him. Don Quixote then suggested he tell some amusing story as he had proposed, and Sancho replied that he would if only his terror at the noises would allow it.

"Still," said he, "I will try to tell a story which, if I can manage to relate it, and nobody interferes, is the best of stories. Your worship, pay attention, because I am going to begin: 'Once upon a time' and 'may good fortune come to all who hear, and harm to him who seeks it.' Your worship should know that the ancients didn't begin their tales just as each one pleased. It was a maxim of Cato Zonzorino[2] the Roman, that says 'harm to him who seeks it.' And it fits this situation like a ring on a finger, to show that your worship should stand still and not go looking for trouble anywhere and that we should go back by some other road, since nobody forces us to follow this in which so many terrors beset us."

2. I.e. Cato Censorino—Cato the Censor; but Sancho's impression was that the name was derived from *zonzo*, "stupid."

"Go on with your story, Sancho," said Don Quixote, "and leave the choice of our road to my care."

"I say then," continued Sancho, "that in a village of Extremadura there was a goat-shepherd—that is to say, one who tended goats —which shepherd or goatherd, as my story goes, was called Lope Ruiz, and this Lope Ruiz was in love with a shepherdess called Torralba, which shepherdess called Torralba was the daughter of a rich cattle man, and this rich cattle man—"

"If that is the way you tell your tale, Sancho," said Don Quixote, "repeating everything you are going to say twice, you will not finish in two days. Go straight on with it, and tell it like a reasonable man, or else say nothing."

"Tales are always told in my part of the country in the very way I am telling this," answered Sancho, "and I cannot tell it in any other, nor is it right of your worship to ask me to adopt new customs."

"Tell it as you will," replied Don Quixote. "And since fate ordains that I cannot help listening, go on with your tale."

"And so my dear master" continued Sancho, "as I have said, this shepherd was in love with Torralba the shepherdess, who was a wild, buxom lass with something of the look of a man about her, for she had a little moustache. I can see her now."

"Then you knew her?" said Don Quixote.

"I didn't know her," said Sanchgo, "but the man who told me the story said it was so true and certain that when I told it to someone else I could safely declare and swear I had seen it all myself. Anyway, as time went on, the devil, who never sleeps and puts everything in confusion, contrived that the love the shepherd felt for the shepherdess turned into hatred and ill-will. And the reason, according to gossip, was that she gave him cause to be a wee bit jealous—in fact she had crossed the line and trespassed on forbidden ground. So much did the shepherd hate her from that time forward that in order to escape from her, he determined to leave the country and go where he would never set eyes on her again. Torralba, when she found herself spurned by Lope, was immediately smitten with love for him, though she had never loved him before."

"That is the natural way of women," said Don Quixote, "to scorn the one that loves them, and love the one that hates them. Go on Sancho."

"It came to pass," said Sancho, "that the shepherd carried out his intention, and driving his goats before him made his way across the plains of Extremadura to pass over into the Kingdom of Portugal. Torralba, who knew of it, went after him, and walking barefoot followed him at a distance, with a pilgrim's staff in her hand and a pack over her shoulder, in which she carried, it is said, a bit of mirror and a piece of a comb and some little container or other of paint for her face. But whatever it was she carried, I am not going to trouble myself to prove it. All I say is, that the shepherd, they say, came with his flock to cross over the river Guadiana, which was at that time swollen and almost overflowing its banks, and at the spot he came to there was neither ferry nor boat nor anyone to carry him or his flock to the other side. At this he was much troubled, because he saw Torralba was approaching and would give him great annoyance with her tears and entreaties. However, he went looking around until he discovered a fisherman who had alongside of him a boat so small that it could only hold one person and one goat. But anyway Lope spoke to the fisherman and agreed with him to carry himself and his three hundred goats across. The fisherman got into the boat and carried one goat over; he came back and carried another over; he came back again, and again brought over another —let your worship keep count of the goats the fisherman is taking across, for if one escapes my memory there will be an end of the story, and it will be impossible to tell another word of it. To proceed, I should tell you that the landing place on the other side was muddy and slippery, and the fisherman lost a great deal of time in going and coming. Still he returned for another goat, and another, and another."

"Take it for granted he brought them all across," said Don Quixote, "and don't keep going and coming in this way, or you will not finish bringing them over in a year."

"How many have gone across so far?" said Sancho.

"How the devil do I know?" replied Don Quixote.

"There you are," said Sancho. "I told you you must keep a good count. Well then, by God, there is an end of the story, for there is no going any farther."

"How can that be?" said Don Quixote. "Is it so essential to the story to know exactly how many goats have crossed over, so that if there is a mistake of one in the reckoning, you can't go on with it?"

"No señor, not a bit," replied Sancho, "for when I asked your worship to tell me how many goats had crossed, and you answered you did not know, at that very instant all I had to say went right out of my memory, and, faith, it was very good and entertaining."

"So, then," said Don Quixote, "the story has come to an end?"

"As much as my mother has," said Sancho.

"In truth," said Don Quixote, "you have told one of the rarest stories, tales, or histories, that anyone in the world could have imagined. And such a way of telling it and ending it was never seen nor will be in a lifetime, though I expected nothing else from your excellent understanding. But I do not wonder at it, for perhaps the ceaseless pounding has confused your wits."

"All that may be," replied Sancho, "but I know that as to my story, all that can be said is that it ends there where the mistake in the count of the passage of the goats begins."

"Let it end where it will, well and good," said Don Quixote, "and let us see if Rocinante can move." Again he spurred him, and again Rocinante made jumps and stayed where he was, so well tied was he.

Just then, whether it was the cold of the morning that was now approaching, or that he had eaten something laxative at supper, or that it was only natural (as is most likely), Sancho felt a desire to do what no one could do for him. But so great was the fear that had penetrated his heart, he dared not separate himself from his master by as much as the black of his nail. Not to do what he needed to do was, however, also impossible; so what he did to settle the question was to remove his right hand, which held the back of the saddle, and with it to untie gently and silently the string which held up his breeches, so that they at once fell down around his feet like fetters. He then raised his shirt as well as he could and stuck out his hind quarters, no slim ones.

But once he had accomplished this, which he fancied was all he need do to get out of this terrible dilemma and discomfort, another still greater difficulty presented itself. It seemed to him impossible to relieve himself without making some noise or sound, and he ground his teeth and squeezed his shoulders together, holding his breath as much as he could. But in spite of his precautions he was unlucky enough after all to make a little noise, not at all like the noise that was causing him so much fear.

"What was that noise, Sancho?" asked Don Quixote when he heard it.

"I don't know, señor," answered the squire. "It must be something new, for adventures and misadventures don't stop, once they start."

Again he tried his luck, succeeding so well that without any further noise or disturbance he was lightened of the burden that had given him so much discomfort. But as Don Quixote's sense of smell was as acute as his hearing, and as Sancho was so closely linked with him that the fumes rose almost in a straight line, it could not be but that some should reach his nostrils. No sooner had they arrived than he protected his nose by compressing it between his fingers.

"Sancho," he said in a rather snuffly tone, "it strikes me you are in terrible fear."

"I am," answered Sancho, "but how does your worship notice that now more than ever?"

"Because just now you smell stronger than ever, and not of ambergris," answered Don Quixote.

"Very likely," said Sancho, "but that's not my fault but your worship's, for leading me around at inconvenient times and through such strange places."

"Then go back three or four paces, my friend," said Don Quixote, all the time with his fingers to his nose, "and for the future pay more attention to your person and to what you owe mine. For it is my great familiarity with you that has bred this contempt."

"I'll bet," replied Sancho, "that your worship thinks I have done something I ought not with my person."

"The less said, the better, friend Sancho," returned Don Quixote.

With this and other talk of the same sort master and servant passed the night. At last Sancho, perceiving that daybreak was near, very cautiously untied Rocinante and tied up his breeches. As soon as Rocinante found himself free, though by nature he was not at all spirited, he seemed to feel some discomfort and began pawing. For as to bucking, begging his pardon, he did not know what it meant. Don Quixote, then, observing that Rocinante could move freely, took it as a good sign and a signal he should attempt the dread adventure.

By this time day had fully dawned and everything showed distinctly. Don Quixote saw that he was among some tall trees, chestnuts, which cast a very deep shade. He could hear, too, that the sound of the strokes had not ceased, but was unable to make out what caused it. So without any further delay he let Rocinante feel the spur. Once more taking leave of Sancho, he told him to wait for him there three days at most, as he had said before. If he had not returned by that time, Sancho might feel sure it had been God's will that Don Quixote should end his days in that perilous adventure. He again repeated the message and commission which Sancho was to convey to his lady Dulcinea. Nor, he said, should Sancho be uneasy as to the payment for his services, for before leaving home Don Quixote had made his will, in which full recompense was provided for in the matter of wages, in due proportion to the time served. But if God delivered him safe, sound, and unhurt out of that danger, then Sancho might look upon the promised island as much more than certain. Sancho began to weep afresh on again hearing the affecting words of his good master, and resolved to stay with him until the final outcome and conclusion of the business.

From these tears and this honorable resolve of Sancho Panza's the author of this history infers that he must have been of good birth and at least an old Christian.[3] The feeling he displayed touched his master a little, but not so much as to make him show any weakness. On the contrary, he hid what he felt as well as he

3. An "old Christian" was one who had no trace of Moorish or Jewish blood in his veins.

could and began to approach the place from where the sound of the water and of the pounding seemed to come.

Sancho followed him on foot, leading by the halter, as he usually did, the ass which was his constant comrade in prosperity or adversity. Advancing some distance through the shady chestnut trees, they came upon a little meadow at the foot of some high rocks, down which a mighty rush of water flung itself. At the foot of the rocks were some rudely constructed houses looking more like ruins than houses. From them, obviously, proceeded the din and clatter that went on unceasingly. Rocinante took fright at the noise of the water and of the blows. After quieting him, Don Quixote advanced step by step towards the houses, commending himself with all his heart to his lady, imploring her support in this formidable enterprise, and on the way begging God, too, not to forget him. Sancho never left his side, stretching his neck as far as he could and peering between Rocinante's legs to see if he could make out what was causing him such fear and apprehension.

On they went another hundred paces or so when, turning a corner, the true cause, beyond the possibility of any mistake, of the horrendous and terrifying noise which had kept them in a state of suspense and fear all night appeared plain and obvious. And it was —I hope, dear reader, that you will not be disappointed and annoyed—six fulling hammers which were making all the din with the alternate strokes.[4]

When Don Quixote saw what it was, he was struck dumb and paralyzed from head to foot. Sancho glanced at him and saw him with his head bent down upon his breast, plainly mortified. Don Quixote glanced at Sancho and saw him with cheeks puffed out and his mouth full of laughter, obbviously on the point of exploding. In spite of his vexation, the knight could not help laughing at the sight of his squire, and when Sancho saw his master begin, he let go so heartily that he had to hold his sides with both hands to keep himself from bursting with laughter. Four times he stopped, and four times his laughter broke out afresh with undiminished violence. At this Don Quixote grew furious, above all when he heard Sancho repeat his own words.

"Friend Sancho," declaimed Sancho mockingly," "know that I by Heaven's will have been born in this our iron age to revive in it

4. A fulling mill was a machine used in finishing woolen cloth, which was folded (wetted with soap, urine, or a special clay and water mixture) and laid in a trough. A series of heavy wooden piles pounded it for hours—as much as twenty hours for coarse materials—flattening and polishing it. The piles were raised straight up and dropped on end, one after another, by means of a water-driven cogwheel, so that a steady rhythm was maintained (about one blow per second, according to Diderot's *Encyclopédie,* in which the machines are described and illustrated), and no doubt a number of fulling hammers made a thunderous noise, increased by that of the rushing water in the mill race and rattling machinery.

the age of gold, or the golden as it is called. I am he for whom perils, mighty achievements, and valiant deeds are reserved."

And he went on repeating the words Don Quixote had uttered the first time they heard the awful strokes.

Don Quixote, seeing that Sancho was making fun of him, was so mortified and vexed that he lifted up his pike and gave him two such blows that if he had caught them on his head instead of his shoulders, there would have been no wages to pay, unless perhaps to his heirs. Sancho, seeing that his jest had such unfortunate results, and fearing his master might carry it still further, spoke to him very humbly. "Calm yourself, sir," he said, "for by God I was only joking."

"Well, if you are joking I am not," replied Don Quixote. "Look here, sir joker: suppose this has been some perilous adventure and not fulling hammers. Do you not think I have shown the courage necessary to venture and to succeed? Am I bound, by any chance, gentleman that I am, to know and distinguish sounds and tell whether or not they come from fulling mills? Perhaps, furthermore, as happens to be the case, I have never in my life seen one, unlike you, common peasant that you are, who were born and bred among them? But turn me these six hammers into six giants, and hurl them forth to beard me, one by one or all together. Then only, if I do not knock them head over heels, make all the fun of me you like."

"No more of that, señor," returned Sancho. "I admit I went a little too far with the joke. But tell me, your worship, now that we've made peace (and may God bring you out of all adventures as safe and sound as he has brought you out of this one), wasn't the great fear we were in something to laugh at, and isn't it a good story? At least *my* fear, for as to your worship, I see now that you neither know nor understand what fear or dismay is."

"I do not deny," said Don Quixote, "that what happened to us may be worth laughing at, but it is not worth making a story about, for not everyone is shrewd enough to put things in the right place."

"At any rate," said Sancho, "your worship knew how to put the point of your pike in the right place when you aimed at my head and hit me on the shoulders, thanks be to God and to me for dodging so promptly. But let that pass, for it will come out in the wash. I have heard say 'he loves you well that makes you weep,' and, too, that it is usual with great lords after any hard words to give a servant a pair of breeches. But I do not know what they give after blows, unless maybe that knights-errant after blows give islands, or kingdoms on the mainland."

"It may be in the dice," said Don Quixote, "that all you say will come true. Overlook the past, for you are shrewd enough to know that our first impulses are beyond our control. For the future bear one thing in mind, and see to it you curb and restrain your loquacity in my company. In all the books of chivalry I have read, and they are innumerable, I never met with a squire who talked so much to his lord as you do to yours. In fact I feel it to be a great fault of yours and of mine; yours, that you have so little respect for me and mine, that I do not make myself more respected. There was Gandalín, the squire of Amadís of Gaul, who was Count of the Ínsula Firme. We read of him that he always addressed his lord with his cap in his hand, his head bowed down, and his body bent double, *more turquesco*.[5] And what shall we say of Gasabal, the squire of Galaor? He was so silent that in order to convey the greatness of his marvelous taciturnity his name is only once mentioned in the whole of that history, which is as long as it is truthful. From all I have said you will gather, Sancho, that there must be a difference between master and servant, between lord and lackey, between knight and squire. So from this day forward we must observe more respect and take less liberties, for in whatever way I may be provoked with you, 'it will be bad for the pitcher.'[6] The favors and benefits I have promised you will come in due time, and if they do not, your wages at least will not be lost, as I have already told you."

"All that your worship says is very well," said Sancho, "but I'd like to know (in case the time of favors should not come, and it might be necessary to fall back upon wages) how much did the squire of a knight-errant get in those days, and did they agree by the month or by the day, like bricklayers?"

"I do not believe," replied Don Quixote, "that such squires were ever on wages, but were dependent on favor. If I have mentioned yours in the sealed will I left at home, it was with a view to what may happen. For as yet I do not know how chivalry will turn out in these wretched times of ours, and I do not wish my soul to suffer for trifles in the other world. I would have you know, Sancho, that in this world no condition is more hazardous than that of adventurers."

"That is true," said Sancho, "since the mere noise of the hammers of a fulling mill can disturb and disquiet the heart of such a valiant errant adventurer as your worship. But you may be sure I will not open my lips henceforward to make light of anything of your worship's, but only to honor you as my master and natural lord."

"By so doing," replied Don Quixote, "you shall live long on the face of the earth, for next to parents, masters are to be respected as though they were parents."

5. "In Turkish fashion."
6. The proverb in full is, "whether the pitcher hits the stone or the stone hits the pitcher, it's bad for the pitcher."

Chapter XXI

WHICH TREATS OF THE EXALTED ADVENTURE AND RICH PRIZE OF MAMBRINO'S HELMET, TOGETHER WITH OTHER THINGS THAT HAPPENED TO OUR INVINCIBLE KNIGHT

About this time a light rain began to fall, and Sancho wanted to go into the fulling mills, but the clumsy joke had inspired so great a loathing of them in Don Quixote that he would not enter on any account. So turning aside to the right they came upon another road like the one they had taken the night before. A little while later Don Quixote caught sight of a man on horseback on whose head was something that shone like gold. The moment he saw him he turned to speak to Sancho.

"I think, Sancho," he said, "that no proverb whatsoever is untrue, since all are maxims drawn from experience itself, mother of all the sciences, especially that one that says, 'Where one door shuts, another opens.' I say this because if last night fortune barred the door to what we were looking for, deceiving us with the fulling mills, it now opens wide before us another better more certain adventure. If I fail to enter it, it will be my own fault, and I cannot blame it on my ignorance of fulling mills or the darkness of the night. I say this because, if I do not err, coming toward us is one who wears on his head the helmet of Mambrino, concerning which I swore the oath you know of."

"Watch what you say, your worship, and still more what you do," said Sancho, "for I don't want any more fulling mills to finish off pounding and knocking out our senses."

"The devil take you," said Don Quixote. "What has a helmet to do with fulling mills?"

"I don't know," replied Sancho, "but, faith, if I could speak the way I used to, perhaps I could give some reasons that would make your worship see you are mistaken."

"How can I be mistaken in what I say, unbelieving traitor?" returned Don Quixote. "Tell me, do you not see yonder knight coming towards us on a dappled grey steed, with a helmet of gold upon his head?"

"What I see and make out," answered Sancho, "is only a man on a grey ass like my own, with something shining on his head."

"Well, that is the helmet of Mambrino," said Don Quixote. "Stand to one side and leave me alone with him. You shall see how, without saying a word, to save time, I shall end this adventure and acquire the helmet I have so longed for."

"I will take care to get out of the way," said Sancho, "but God grant, I say once more, that it may be what you say and not fulling mills."

"I have told you, brother, on no account to mention those fulling mills to me again," said Don Quixote, "or I swear—and I say no more—to full the soul out of you."

Sancho held his peace, fearing his master might carry out the oath he had hurled at him so forthrightly.

These are the facts concerning the helmet, steed, and knight that Don Quixote saw. In the neighborhood were two villages, one so small that it had neither apothecary's shop nor barber, while the other nearby village had both. So the barber of the larger served the smaller, and in this smaller village was a sick man who required to be bled and another man who wanted to be shaved. On this errand the barber was going, carrying with him a brass basin. But as luck would have it, on the way it began to rain, and not to spoil his hat, which probably was a new one, he put the basin on his head. Since it was clean, it glittered at half a league's distance.

He rode on a grey ass, as Sancho said, and this was why Don Quixote could imagine them to be a dapple-grey steed and a knight with a golden helmet. For he made everything he saw fall in with his crazy chivalry and aberrant notions. When he saw the poor "knight" draw near, without parleying with him he bore down upon him at Rocinante's top speed and with the pike pointed low. He was fully determined to run him through and through, and he galloped up to him at full tilt.

"Defend thyself, miserable being," he cried out, "or yield of thine own accord what is so reasonably my due."

The barber, who without any expectation or apprehension saw this apparition coming down upon him, had no way of avoiding the stroke of the lance except to let himself fall off his donkey. No sooner had he touched the ground than he sprang up more nimbly than a deer and sped across the plain faster than the wind.

The basin was left lying on the ground, to Don Quixote's satisfaction. He remarked that the pagan had shown his discretion by imitating the beaver, which, when overtaken by hunters, bites and tears off what it instinctively knows they want.[1] He ordered Sancho to pick up the helmet.

"By God," said Sancho, as he took it in his hands, "the basin is a good one, and worth a *real* if it is worth a cent." He handed it to his master, who immediately put it on his head, turning it around, now this way, now that, in search of a proper fit.

"Clearly," he said, when he failed to find it, "the pagan to whose

1. Its testicles, according to popular lore. Beavers were hunted for the excretion of glands in the groin (not the testicles), from which an expensive perfume was made.

measure this famous headpiece was first forged must have had a very large head. But the worst of it is that half of it is missing."

When Sancho heard him call the basin a headpiece he was unable to restrain his laughter, but remembering his master's wrath he checked himself in the midst of it.

"What are you laughing at, Sancho?" said Don Quixote.

"I am laughing," said he, "to think of the great head the pagan must have had who owned this helmet, for it looks exactly like a regular barber's basin."

"Do you know what I suspect, Sancho?" said Don Quixote. "This wonderful piece of this enchanted helmet must by some strange accident have come into the hands of someone unable to recognize or realize its value. Not knowing what he did, and seeing it to be of the purest gold, he must have melted down one half for the sake of what it might be worth and used the other to make this, which, as you say, is like a barber's basin. Be that as it may, to me who recognize it, the transformation makes no difference. I will set it to rights at the first village where there is a blacksmith, and in such a way that the helmet the god of smithies forged for the god of battles shall not surpass it or even come up to it. In the meantime I will wear it as best I can, for something is better than nothing. All the more so, since it will be quite enough to protect me from a stoning."

"That is," said Sancho, "if it is not shot with a sling as they were in the battle of the two armies, when they signed the cross on your worship's teeth and smashed the flask with that blessed potion that made me vomit my bowels up."

"It does not grieve me much to have lost it," said Don Quixote, "for you know, Sancho, that I have the recipe in my memory."

"So have I," answered Sancho, "but if ever I make it or try it again as long as I live, may this be my last hour. Moreover, I do not intend to put myself in a situation where I may need it, for I mean, with all my five senses, to keep myself from being wounded or from wounding anyone. As to being blanketed again I say nothing, for it is hard to prevent mishaps of that sort, and if they come there is nothing for it but to squeeze our shoulders together, hold our breath, shut our eyes, and let ourselves go where luck and the blanket may send us."

"You are a bad Christian, Sancho," said Don Quixote on hearing this, "for once an injury has been done you, you never forget it. But you should know that noble and generous hearts attach no importance to trifles. What lame leg have you got by it, what broken rib, what cracked head, that you cannot forget that jest? For jest and sport it was, properly regarded, and had I not seen it in that light I would have returned and done more mischief in revenging you than the Greeks did for the kidnap of Helen—who, if she were alive now, or if my Dulcinea had lived then, would assuredly not be so famous for her beauty as she is."

At this he heaved a sigh and sent it aloft.

"Let it pass for a jest," said Sancho, "as it can't be revenged in earnest, but I know what sort of jest and earnest it was, and I know it will never be rubbed out of my memory any more than off my shoulders. But putting that aside, will your worship tell me what we are to do with this dapple-grey steed that looks like a grey ass, left by that Martino that your worship knocked off it? From the way he took to his heels and bolted, he is not likely ever to come back for it; and by my beard the grey is a good one."

"I have never been in the habit," said Don Quixote, "of despoiling those I vanquish, nor is it the practice of chivalry to take away their horses and leave them to go on foot, unless indeed the victor has lost his own in the combat, in which case it is lawful to take the horse of the vanquished as having been won in lawful war. Therefore, Sancho, leave this horse, or ass, or whatever you will have it to be, for when its owner sees we have gone he will come back for it."

"God knows I'd like to take it," returned Sancho, "or at least to change it for my own, which does not seem to me so good. The laws of chivalry are strict indeed, since they can't be stretched to let one ass be changed for another. I should like to know if I might at least change trappings."

"I am not quite certain about that," answered Don Quixote, "and the matter being doubtful, pending better information, I say you may change them, if you have urgent need of them."

"So urgent is it," answered Sancho, "that if they were for my own person I could not want them more."

Forthwith, authorized by this license, he effected the *mutatio capparum*,[2] dressing his beast up and making quite an improvement in its appearance. This done, they broke their fast on the remains of the spoils of war plundered from the baggage mule and drank from the brook that flowed from the fulling mills. Yet they did not cast a glance in that direction, so much did they loathe them for the alarm they had caused. Then, all anger and gloom removed, Don Quixote and Sancho mounted and, without taking any particular road (not to choose one being proper for true knights-errant), they set out, guided by Rocinante's will. This bore along with it that of his master, not to say that of the ass, which always followed Rocinante wherever he led, loving and sociably. Nevertheless they returned to the high road, and pursued it at random without any other aim.

"Señor," said Sancho to his master, as they traveled along in this

2. The "change of hoods," when cardinals put on purple hoods in place of the usual red ones. (Cervantes explains this in his novelette, "The Dialogue of the Dogs.") Here it means simply he exchanged the trappings of the asses. As Ormsby says, there is a certain audacious humor in applying the term to asses.

fashion, "would your worship give me permission to speak to you a little? For since you laid that hard command of silence on me, I've had several things on my chest, and I have one on the tip of my tongue that I've got to get off."

"Say on, Sancho," said Don Quixote, "and be brief in your discourse, for there is no pleasure in one that is long."

"Well, señor," returned Sancho, "I say that for several days I have been considering how little one earns or profits by going in search of these adventures that your worship seeks in these wilds and crossroads. Even if you win and carry out the most perilous ones, there is no one to see or hear of them, and so they must be left untold forever, to the loss of your worship's goal and the credit they deserve. Therefore it seems to me it would be better (saving your worship's better judgment) if we were to serve some emperor or other great prince who may have some war on hand, in whose service your worship can prove the worth of your person, your great might, and greater understanding. When he sees this, the lord in whose service we may be will be obliged to reward us, each according to his merits, and there you will surely find some one to put your achievements in writing and so preserve their memory for ever. Of my own deeds I say nothing, as they will not go beyond squirely limits. Yet I make bold to say that, if it is the practice in chivalry to record the achievements of squires, I think mine won't be left out."

"There is merit in what you say, Sancho," answered Don Quixote, "but before that point is reached one must roam the world, as though on probation, and seek adventures. By achieving some, so great a name and fame may be acquired that, when he arrives at the court of some great monarch, the knight may be already known by his deeds. Then the boys, the instant they see him enter the city gate, may all follow him and surround him, crying, 'This is the Knight of the Sun'—or 'the Serpent,' or any other title under which he may have achieved great deeds. 'This,' they will say, 'is he who vanquished in single combat the gigantic Brocabruno of mighty strength, he who delivered the great Mameluke of Persia out of the long enchantment under which he had been for almost nine hundred years.' So from one to another they will go proclaiming his achievements.

"And presently, at the tumult of the boys and the others, the king of that kingdom will appear at the windows of his royal palace and behold the knight, recognizing him by his arms and the device on his shield. 'What ho!' he will at once say, as a matter of course. 'Forth all ye, the knights of my court, to receive the flower of chivalry who cometh hither!' At this command all will issue forth, and he himself, advancing halfway down the stairs, will embrace the knight closely, and salute him, kissing him on the cheek. Then he will lead him to the queen's chamber, where the knight will find her with the princess her daughter, who will be one of the most beautiful and accomplished damsels that could with the utmost pains be discovered anywhere in the known world. Straightway it will come to pass that she will fix her eyes upon the knight and his upon her, and each will seem to the other something more divine than human, and without knowing how or why they will be taken and entangled in the inextricable toils of love and sorely distressed in their hearts not to see any way of making their pains and sufferings known by speech. Thence they will lead him, no doubt, to some richly adorned chamber of the palace where, having removed his armor, they will bring him a rich mantle of scarlet wherewith to robe himself. If he looked noble in his armor he will look still more so in a quilted vest. When night comes he will sup with the king, queen, and princess. And all the time he will never take his eyes off her, stealing stealthy glances, unnoticed by those present, and she will do the same, and with equal cautiousness, being, as I have said, a damsel of great discretion. The tables being removed, suddenly through the door of the hall there will enter a hideous and diminutive dwarf followed by a fair dame, between two giants, who comes with a certain adventure, the work of an ancient sage; and he who shall achieve it shall be deemed the best knight in the world.

"The king will then command all those present to attempt it, but none will bring it to a successful conclusion save the visiting knight, to the great enhancement of his fame. At this the princess will be overjoyed and will esteem herself happy and fortunate in having fixed and placed her thoughts so high. And the best of it is that this king, or prince, or whatever he is, is engaged in a very bitter war with another as powerful as himself, and the visiting knight, after having spent some days at his court, requests leave to go and serve him in the said war. The king will grant it very readily, and the knight will courteously kiss his hands for the favor done him.

"That night he will take leave of his lady the princess at the grating of the chamber where she sleeps, which looks upon a garden, and at which he has already many times conversed with her, the go-between and confidante in the matter being a damsel much trusted by the princess. He will sigh, she will swoon, the damsel will fetch water, much distressed because morning approaches, and for the honor of her lady she would not that they were discovered. At last the princess will come to herself and will present her white hands through the grating to the knight, who will kiss them a thousand and a thousand times, bathing them with his tears. It will be arranged between them how they are to inform each other of their good or evil fortunes, and the princess will entreat him to make his absence as short as possible, which he will promise to do with many oaths. Once more he kisses her hands, and takes his leave in such grief that he is well-nigh ready to die.

"He betakes him to his chamber, flings himself on his bed, cannot sleep for sorrow at parting, rises early in the morning, goes to take leave of the king, queen, and princess, and as he takes his leave of the pair, he is told that the princess is indisposed and cannot receive a visit. The knight thinks it is from grief at his departure, his heart is pierced, and he is hardly able to keep from showing his pain. The confidante is present, observes all, goes to tell her mistress, who listens with tears and says that one of her greatest distresses is not knowing who this knight is and whether he is of kingly lineage or not. The damsel assures her that so much courtesy, gentleness, and gallantry of bearing as her knight possesses could not exist in any save one who was royal and illustrious. Her anxiety is thus relieved, and she strives to be of good cheer lest she should excite suspicion in her parents, and at the end of two days she appears in public.

"Meanwhile the knight has taken his departure. He fights in the war, conquers the king's enemy, wins many cities, triumphs in many battles, returns to the court, sees his lady where he was wont to see her, and it is agreed that he shall demand her in marriage of her parents as the reward of his services. The king is unwilling to give her, since he does not know who the knight is, but nevertheless, whether carried off or in whatever other way it may be, the princess comes to be his bride, and her father comes to regard it as very good fortune. For it so happens that this knight is proved to be the son of a valiant king of some kingdom, I know not what, for I fancy it is not likely to be on the map. The father dies, the princess inherits, and in two words the knight becomes king.

"And here comes in at once the bestowal of rewards upon his squire and all who have aided him in rising to so exalted a rank. He marries his squire to a damsel of the princess's, who will be, no doubt, the one who was confidante in their amour, and is daughter of a very great duke."[3]

"That's what I want, plain and simple!" said Sancho. "That's what I'm waiting for. For all this, word for word, is in store for your worship under the title of the Knight of the Mournful Countenance."

"You need not doubt it, Sancho," replied Don Quixote, "for in the same manner, and by the same steps as I have described here, knights-errant rise and have risen to be kings and emperors. All we require now is to find out what king, Christian or pagan, is at war and has a beautiful daughter. But there will be time enough to think of that, for, as I have told you, fame must be won in other quarters before setting out for the court.

3. Cervantes gives here an epitome, and without extravagant caricature, of a typical romance of chivalry, e.g., *Tirant lo Blanc*, a famous fifteenth-century Catalan romance.

"There is another thing, too, that is lacking. Supposing we find a king who is at war and has a beautiful daughter, and that I have won incredible fame throughout the universe. Still I do not know how it can be made out that I am of royal lineage, or even second cousin to an emperor, for the king will not be willing to give me his daughter in marriage unless he is first thoroughly satisfied on this point, however much my famous deeds may deserve it. By this deficiency I fear I shall lose what my arm has fairly earned. True it is I am a gentleman from a respectable family, of estate and property, and entitled to the privilege of five hundred *sueldos*.[4] It may be that the sage who shall write my history will so clear up my ancestry and pedigree that I may find myself fifth or sixth in descent from a king. For I would have you know, Sancho, that there are two kinds of lineages in the world. Some there are who trace and derive their descent from kings and princes, but time has reduced them little by little until they end in a point like a pyramid upside down. Others who spring from the common herd go on rising step by step until they come to be great lords. Thus the difference is that the former were what they no longer are, and the others are what previously they were not. Of these I may be one, so that after investigation my origin may prove great and famous, with which the king, my father-in-law to be, ought to be satisfied. Should he not be, the princess will so love me that even though she well knew me to be the son of a water-carrier, she will take me for her lord and husband in spite of her father. If not, then it comes to seizing her and carrying her off where I please, for time or death will put an end to the wrath of her parents."

"On that score," said Sancho, "certain cruel people say, 'Never ask as a favor what you can take by force.' Though it would fit better to say, 'A fast escape is better than the intercessions of honest men.' I say so because if my lord the king. your worship's father-in-law, will not condescend to give you my lady the princess, there is nothing for it but, as your worship says, to kidnap her and carry her off. But the trouble is that until peace is made and you come into the peaceful enjoyment of your kingdom, the poor squire is famishing as far as rewards go, unless the confidante damsel that is to be his wife comes with the princess, and with her he tides over his bad luck until Heaven orders things otherwise. For his master, I suppose, may as well give her to him at once for a lawful wife."

"Nobody can object to that," said Don Quixote.

"Then since that may be," said Sancho, "there is nothing to do but to commend ourselves to God, and let fortune take what course it will."

4. According to some authorities, this passage refers to a special privilege which certain gentlemen enjoyed, a gift of 500 *sueldos* (an ancient coin) for the military service of an ancestor. Others believe it refers to special retributions for injuries.

"God guide it according to my wishes and your wants," said Don Quixote, "and let the man who thinks he is unworthy be unworthy."

"In God's name let it be so," said Sancho. "I am an old Christian, and that's enough to make me eligible to be a count."

"And more than enough," said Don Quixote. "Even if you were not, it would make no difference, because I being the king can easily give you nobility without purchase or service rendered by you. For when I make you a count, then you are at once a gentleman. People may say what they will, but by my faith they will have to call you 'your lordship,' whether they like it or not."

"Not a doubt of it, and I'll know how to carry the tittle," said Sancho.

"You should say *title*, not *tittle*," said his master.

"So be it," answered Sancho. "I say I will know how to behave, because in fact I was once a summoner in a confraternity, and the summoner's gown looked so well on me that everybody said I looked impressive enough to be the president of the confraternity. What will happen, when I put a duke's robe on my back, or dress myself in gold and pearls like a count? I believe they'll come a hundred leagues to see me."

"You will look well," said Don Quixote, "but you must shave your beard often, for you let it grow so thick and rough and unkempt, that if you do not shave it every second day at least, they will see what you are at the distance of a musket shot."

"What more is needed," said Sancho, "than to have a barber, and keep him in the house on wages? And if it should be necessary, I will make him follow me around like a nobleman's groom.

"Why, how do you know that noblemen have grooms behind them?" asked Don Quixote.

"I will tell you," answered Sancho. "Years ago I was in the capital for a month and there I saw a very small gentleman taking a walk who they said was a very great man, and a man following him on horseback at every turn he took, just as if he was his tail. I asked why he didn't join the little man, instead of always going behind him. They answered me that he was his groom, and that it was the custom with nobles to have such persons behind them, and ever since then I have known it so well that I have never forgotten it."

"You are right," said Don Quixote, "and in the same way you may take your barber with you. Customs did not come into use all together, nor were they all invented at once, and you may be the first count to have a barber to follow him. Indeed, it requires more trust to let a barber shave one's beard than to let a groom saddle one's horse."

"Let the barber business be my lookout," said Sancho, "and let your worship's be to try to become a king and make me a count."

"So it shall be," answered Don Quixote, and raising his eyes he saw what will be told in the following chapter.

Chapter XXII

OF THE FREEDOM DON QUIXOTE CONFERRED ON MANY UNFORTUNATE PERSONS WHO AGAINST THEIR WILL WERE BEING TAKEN WHERE THEY HAD NO WISH TO GO

Cide Hamete Benengeli, the Arab and Manchegan author, relates in this most grave, high-sounding, minute, delightful, and original history that after the discussion between the famous Don Quixote of La Mancha and his squire Sancho Panza which is set down at the end of chapter twenty-one, Don Quixote raised his eyes and saw coming along the road he was following some dozen men on foot strung together by the neck, like beads, on a great iron chain, and all with manacles on their hands. With them there came also two men on horseback and two on foot. Those on horseback had wheel-lock muskets; those on foot had javelins and swords.

"That is a chain of galley slaves," said Sancho, as soon as he saw them, "on the way to the galleys by force of the king's orders."

"How so, by force?" asked Don Quixote. "Is it possible that the king uses force against anyone?"

"I didn't say that," answered Sancho, "but that these are people condemned for their crimes to serve by force in the king's galleys."

"In fact," replied Don Quixote, "however it may be, these people are being taken by force, and not of their own will."

"True," said Sancho.

"Then if so," said Don Quixote, "here is a case for the exercise of my office, to put down force and to succor and help the wretched."

"Your worship should consider," said Sancho, "that justice, which is the king himself, is not using force or doing wrong to such persons, but punishing them for their crimes."

The chain of galley slaves had by this time come up, and Don Quixote in very courteous language asked those in charge to be good enough to tell him the reason or reasons for their conducting these people in this manner. One of the guards on horseback answered that they were galley slaves belonging to his majesty, that they were going to the galleys, and that that was all there was to be said and all he had any business to know.

"Nevertheless," replied Don Quixote, "I should like to know from each of them separately the reason of his misfortune." He added more to the same effect to induce them to tell him what he wanted, and he was so polite that the other mounted guard answered him.

"Though we have here the register and certificate of the sentence of every one of these wretches, this is no time to take them out or read them. Come and ask the men themselves. They can tell if they choose, and they will, for these fellows enjoy dirty tricks and talking about them."

With this permission, which Don Quixote would have taken even had they not granted it, he approached the chain and asked the first for what offenses he was now in such a sorry state.

The prisoner made answer that it was for being a lover.

"For that only?" replied Don Quixote. "Why, if they send people to the galleys for being lovers, I might have been rowing in them long ago."

"The love is not the sort your worship is thinking of," said the galley slave. "Mine was for a washerwoman's basket of clean linen which I loved so well and held so close in my embrace, that if the arm of the law had not forced it from me, I would never have let it go of my own will to this moment. I was caught in the act, there was no occasion for torture, the case was settled, they treated me to a hundred lashes on the back, and three years in the *gurapas* besides, and that was the end of it."

"What are *gurapas*?" asked Don Quixote.

"*Gurapas* are galleys," answered the galley slave, who was a young man of about twenty-four, and said he was a native of Piedrahita.

Don Quixote asked the same question of the second, who made no reply, so downcast and melancholy was he; but the first answered for him.

"He, sir," he said, "goes because he is a 'canary,' I mean as a musician and a singer."

"What!" said Don Quixote, "for being musicians and singers are people sent to the galleys too?"

"Yes, sir," answered the galley slave, "for there is nothing worse than singing when you're in trouble."

"On the contrary, I have heard say," said Don Quixote, "that 'singing cheers and drives away tears.' "

"Here it is the reverse," said the galley slave, "for he who sings once, weeps all his life."

"I do not understand it," said Don Quixote. But one of the guards explained.

"Sir," he said, "to these wicked men, 'to sing when you're in trouble' means to confess under torture. They put this sinner to the torture, and he confessed his crime, which was being a *cuatrero*, that is a cattle-stealer, and on his confession they sentenced him to six years in the galleys, besides two hundred lashes that he has already had on the back. And he is always dejected and downcast because the other thieves that were left behind and those who march here insult him, and snub, and jeer, and despise him for confessing and not having courage enough to say no. For say they, '*Nay* has no more letters in it than *yea*,' and a culprit is well off when life or death depends on his own tongue and not on that of witnesses or evidence. To my thinking they are not very wrong."

"And I think so too," answered Don Quixote.

Passing on to the third he asked him what he had asked the others, and the man answered very readily and unconcernedly. "I am going for five years to their ladyships the *gurapas* for the want of ten ducats."

"I will give twenty with pleasure to get you out of that trouble," said Don Quixote.

"That," said the galley slave, "is like a man having money at sea when he is dying of hunger and has no way of buying what he wants. I say so because if at the right time I had had those twenty ducats that your worship now offers me, I would have greased the notary's pen and quickened the attorney's wit with them, so that today I should be in the middle of the plaza of the Zocodover at Toledo, and not on this road coupled like a greyhound. But God is great. Patience—there, that's enough."

Don Quixote passed on to the fourth, a man of venerable aspect with a white beard which reached below his breast, who on hearing himself asked the reason of his being there began to weep without answering a word. But the fifth galley slave acted as his interpreter. "This worthy man," he said, "is going to the galleys for four years, after having made the usual rounds in ceremony and on horseback."[1]

"You mean," said Sancho Panza, "I take it, that he has been exposed to shame in public."

"Just so," replied the galley slave, "and the offense for which they gave him that punishment was having been a marriage-broker, or rather, a body-broker I mean, in short, that this gentleman has been convicted as a go-between and for having besides a certain touch of the sorcerer about him."

"If that touch had not been thrown in," said Don Quixote, "he would not deserve, as a simple go-between, to row in the galleys, but rather to command and be admiral of them. The office of go-between is no ordinary one, being the office of persons of discretion,

1. Malefactors were paraded through the streets on horseback, sometimes tarred-and-feathered, preceded by a crier and followed by the hangman, who whipped them as they went. The ceremony is frequently alluded to in the picaresque novels.

one very necessary in a well-ordered state, and only to be exercised by persons of good birth.[2] Indeed, there ought to be an inspector and overseer of them, as in other trades, and a recognized number, as with the brokers in the stock exchange. In this way many of the evils would be avoided which are caused by this office and calling being in the hands of stupid and ignorant people, such as silly women and young and inexperienced pages and hangers-on, who on the most urgent occasions, and when ingenuity is needed, let the opportunity grow cold, and know not which is their right hand. I should like to go farther and give reasons to show that it is advisable to select those who are to hold so necessary an office in the state, but this is not the fit place for it. Some day I will expound the matter to someone able to see to and rectify it. All I say now is, that the additional fact of his being a sorcerer has removed the sorrow it gave me to see these white hairs and this venerable countenance in so painful a position on account of his being a go-between. Though I know well there are no sorceries in the world that can move or compel the will as some simple persons believe, for our will is free, nor is there herb or charm that can force it. All that certain silly women and quacks do is to turn men mad with potions and poisons, pretending that they have power to cause love, for, as I say, it is an impossibility to compel the will."

"It is true," said the good old man, "and indeed, sir, as far as the charge of sorcery goes I was not guilty. As to that of being a pimp I cannot deny it, but I never thought I was doing any harm by it, for my only object was that all the world should enjoy itself and live in peace and quiet, without quarrels or troubles. But my good intentions were unavailing to save me from going where I never expect to come back from, with this weight of years upon me and a urinary ailment that never gives me a moment's ease." He fell to weeping as before, and such compassion did Sancho feel for him that he took out a *real* from his bosom and gave it to him in alms.

Don Quixote went on and asked another what his crime was, and the man answered with no less but rather much more sprightliness than the last one.

"I am here because I carried the joke too far with a couple of girl cousins of mine, and with a couple of sisters who were not mine. In short, I carried the joke so far with them all that it ended in such a complicated increase of kindred that nobody could make it clear. It was all proved against me; I got no favor; I had no money; I was near having my neck stretched. They sentenced me to the galleys

2. Don Quixote is not defending pimps, as *alcahuete* is sometimes rendered, but the go-between of romances of chivalry and sentimental novels, in which the lovers invariably depend upon young maids, pages, or timorous dueñas to deliver their love letters, messages, and so on. But *alcahuete* means procurer also, and the humor of this passage depends on Don Quixote's innocent interpretation of the old pimp's crimes.

for six years. I accepted my fate; it is the punishment of my fault. I am a young man; let life only last, and with that all will come right. If you, sir, have any way of helping these poor wretches, God will repay you in heaven, and we on earth will take care to pray for the life and health of your worship, that they may be as long and as good as your amiable appearance deserves."

This one was in the dress of a student, and one of the guards said he was a great talker and a very elegant Latin scholar.

Behind all these there came a man of thirty, a very personable fellow, except that one of his eyes turned in a little towards the other. He was bound differently from the rest, for attached to his leg was a chain so long that it was wound all around his body. There were two rings on his neck, one attached to the chain, the other to what they call a "keep-friend" or "prop."[3] From this hung two irons reaching to his waist with two manacles fixed to them in which his hands were secured by a big padlock, so that he could neither raise his hands to his mouth nor lower his head to his hands. Don Quixote asked why this man carried so many more chains than the others. The guard replied that it was because he alone had committed more crimes than all the rest put together, and was so daring and such a villain, that though they marched him in that fashion they did not feel sure of him, but were in dread of his making his escape.

"What serious crimes can he have committed," said Don Quixote, "if they have not deserved a heavier punishment than being sent to the galleys?"

"He goes for ten years," replied the guard, "which is the same thing as civil death, and all that needs be said is that this good fellow is the famous Ginés de Pasamonte, otherwise called Ginesillo de Parapilla."

"Gently, señor commissary," said the galley slave at this, "let us have no fixing of names or surnames. My name is Ginés, not Ginesillo, and my family name is Pasamonte, not Parapilla as you say. Let each one mind his own business, and he will be doing enough."

"Speak with less impertinence, señor high-and-mighty thief," replied the commissary, "if you don't want me to make you hold your tongue in spite of yourself."

"It is easy to see," returned the galley slave, "that a man has to do what God ordains, but some one will find out some day whether I am called Ginesillo de Parapilla or not."

"Don't they call you that, you liar?" said the guard.

"They do," returned Ginés, "but I will make them stop calling me that or I will pull out my beard. If you, sir, have anything to give us, give it to us at once, and God speed, for you are becoming

3. A kind of yoke which forced the prisoner to hold his head up.

tiresome with all this inquisitiveness about the lives of others. If you want to know about mine, let me tell you I am Ginés de Pasamonte, whose life has been written by these fingers."

"He is telling the truth," said the commissary, "for he has himself written his story as grand as you please, and has left the book in the prison pawned for two hundred *reales*."

"And I mean to take it out of pawn," said Ginés, "even if it were in for two hundred ducats."

"Is it that good?" said Don Quixote.

"It's so good," replied Ginés, "that it will show up *Lazarillo de Tormes*, and all of that kind that have been written or ever will be written.[4] All I will say about it is that it deals with facts, and facts so neat and amusing that no lies could match them."

"And what is the title of the book?" asked Don Quixote.

"The *Life of Ginés de Pasamonte*," replied the subject of it.

"And is it finished?" asked Don Quixote.

"How can it be finished," said the other, "when my life is not yet finished? All that is written is from my birth down to the point when they sent me to the galleys this last time."

"Then you have been there before?" said Don Quixite.

"In the service of God and the king I have been there for four years before now, and I know by this time what the biscuit and the lash are like," replied Ginés. "And it is no great grievance to me to go back to them, for there I shall have time to finish my book. I have still many things left to say, and in the galleys of Spain there is more than enough leisure—not that I need much for what I have to write, for I have it by heart."

"You seem a clever fellow," said Don Quixote.

"And an unfortunate one," replied Ginés. "For misfortune always persecutes good wit."

"It persecutes rogues," said the commissary.

"I told you already to go easy, señor commissary," said Pasamonte. "Their lordships never gave you that staff to mistreat us wretches here, but to conduct and take us where his majesty orders you. If not, by the life of—but never mind. It may be that some day the stains made in the inn will come out in the wash. Let everyone hold his tongue and behave well and speak better. And now let us march on, for we have had quite enough of this entertainment."

The commissary lifted his staff to strike Pasamonte in return for

4. At the time Cervantes was writing, the only book of picaresque fiction that had appeared besides *Lazarillo de Tormes* was Alemán's *Guzmán de Alfarache* (Madrid, 1599), at which it has been suggested this passage is aimed. Its hero is sent to the galleys like Ginés de Pasamonte, and at an inn on the road, he ingratiates himself with the commissary by presenting him with a stolen pig. This incident seems to fit exactly the allusion by Pasamonte below. There was also a Gerónimo de Pasamonte, author of an autobiography, who may be Cervantes' model.

his threats, but Don Quixote came between them and begged him not to mistreat him, as it was not too much to allow one who had his hands tied to have his tongue a trifle free. Then he turned to the whole chain of galley slaves.

"From all you have told me, dear brethren," he said, "I see clearly that though they have punished you for your faults, the punishments you are about to endure do not give you much pleasure, and that you go to them very much against the grain and against your will. Perhaps this man's weakening courage under torture, that man's want of money, the other's lack of friends, and lastly the perverted judgment of the judge may have been the cause of your ruin and of your failure to obtain the justice you had on your side. All this presents itself now to my mind, urging, persuading, and even compelling me to demonstrate in your case the purpose for which Heaven sent me into the world. It caused me to profess the order of chivalry to which I belong and to take the vow to give aid to those in need and who are oppressed by the strong. But as I know that it is a mark of prudence not to do by foul means what may be done by fair, I will ask these gentlemen, the guards and commissary, to be so good as to release you and let you go in peace. There will be no lack of others to serve the king under more favorable circumstances, and it seems to me unjust to make slaves of those whom God and nature have made free.

"Moreover, sirs of the guard," added Don Quixote, "these poor fellows have done nothing to you. Let each answer for his own sins, for there is a God in Heaven who will not forget to punish the wicked or reward the good. And it is not fitting that honest men should be the instruments of punishment inflicted on others, when they themselves are in no way involved. This request I make thus gently and quietly, so that, if you comply with it, I may have reason for thanking you. But if you will not voluntarily comply, this lance and sword together with the might of my arm shall compel you to comply with it by force."

"What nonsense!" said the commissary. "A fine piece of pleasantry he has come out with at last! He wants us to let the king's prisoners go, as if we had any authority to release them, or he to order us to do so! Go your way, sir, and good luck to you. Put that basin straight that you've got on your head, and don't go looking for three feet on a cat."

"'Tis you that are the cat, rat, and rascal," replied Don Quixote.

Matching word with action, he fell upon the commissary so suddenly that without giving him time to defend himself he brought him to the ground badly wounded with a lance thrust. It was lucky for Don Quixote that this was the man with the musket. The other guards stood thunderstruck and amazed at this unexpected event, but recovering their presence of mind, those on horseback seized their swords, and those on foot their javelins, and attacked Don Quixote, who was waiting for them with great calmness. No doubt it would have gone badly with him if the galley slaves, seeing the chance of liberating themselves, had not succeeded in breaking the chain on which they were strung.

Such was the confusion that the guards, at one moment rushing at the galley slaves who were breaking loose and at the next attacking Don Quixote who was waiting for them, did nothing effective. Sancho, for his part, gave a helping hand to release Ginés de Pasamonte, who was the first to leap forth upon the plain free and unfettered. Attacking the prostrate commissary, he took from him his sword and the musket. By aiming at one and leveling at another he, without ever discharging it, drove every one of the guards off the field. They took to flight in order to escape both Pasamonte's musket and the showers of stones the freed galley slaves were raining upon them. Sancho was greatly upset at the affair, because he anticipated that those who had fled would report the matter to the Holy Brotherhood, who at the summons of the alarm bell would at once sally forth in quest of the offenders. He said so to his master and entreated him to leave the place at once and go into hiding in the mountains close by.

"That is all very well," said Don Quixote, "but I know what must be done now." Calling together all the galley slaves, who were now running riot and had stripped the commissary to the skin, he collected them around him to hear what he had to say and addressed them as follows.

"To be grateful for benefits received is the mark of persons of good birth, and one of the sins most offensive to God is ingratitude. I say so because, sirs, ye have already clearly witnessed the benefit ye have received from me. In return I desire, and it is my good pleasure that, laden with the chain I have taken off your necks, ye at once proceed to the city of El Toboso, and there present yourselves before the lady Dulcinea del Toboso, and say to her that her knight, he of the Mournful Countenance, commends himself to her. And recount to her in full detail all the particulars of this notable adventure, up to the recovery of your longed-for liberty. This having been done, ye may go where ye will, and good fortune attend you."

Ginés de Pasamonte replied on behalf of all. "That which you, sir, our deliverer, demand of us," he said, " is of all impossibilities the most impossible to comply with. We cannot go together along the roads, but only singly and separate, and each one his own way, endeavoring to hide ourselves in the bowels of the earth to escape the Holy Brotherhood, which, no doubt, will come out in search of us. What your worship may do, and fairly do, is to change this service and tribute as regards the lady Dulcinea del Toboso for a certain quantity of Hail Marys and Creeds which we will say for your worship's intention. This is a condition that can be complied with by night and by day, running or resting, in peace or in war. But to imagine that we are going now to return to the flesh-pots of Egypt, I mean to take up our chain and set out for El Toboso, is to imagine that it is now night, though it is not yet ten in the morning. To ask this of us is like asking pears of the elm tree."

"Then by all that's good," said Don Quixote, now stirred to wrath, "Don son of a bitch, Don Ginesillo de Paropillo, or whatever your name is, you will have to go yourself alone, with your tail between your legs and the whole chain on your back."

Pasamonte, who was anything but meek, by this time was thoroughly convinced that Don Quixote was not quite right in his head, since he had carried out his crazy notion of setting them free. Hearing himself insulted in this fashion, he gave the wink to his companions. They, as they retreated, began to shower stones on Don Quixote at such a rate that he was quite unable to protect himself with his shield, and poor Rocinante no more heeded the spur than if he had been made of brass. Sancho planted himself behind his donkey and thus sheltered himself from the hailstorm that poured on both of them. Don Quixote was unable to shield himself so thoroughly, and more pebbles than I could count struck him full on the body with such force that they brought him to the ground.

The instant he fell, the student pounced upon him, snatched the basin from his head, and with it struck three or four blows on his shoulders, and as many more on the ground, knocking it almost to pieces. They then stripped him of a jacket that he wore over his armor, and they would have stripped off his stockings if his leg-armor had not prevented them. They took Sancho's coat, leaving him in his shirtsleeves. Then, dividing among themselves the remaining spoils of battle, they went each one his own way, more anxious about keeping clear of the Holy Brotherhood they dreaded than about burdening themselves with the chain or presenting themselves before the lady Dulcinea del Toboso. The ass and Rocinante, Sancho and Don Quixote, were all that were left upon the spot. The ass stood with drooping head, serious and shaking his ears from time to time as if he thought the storm of stones that assailed them was not yet over. Rocinante lay stretched beside his master, for he too had been brought to the ground by a stone. Sancho was stripped and trembling with fear of the Holy Brotherhood. And Don Quixote fumed at finding himself treated thus by the very persons for whom he had done so much.

Chapter XXIII

OF WHAT BEFELL DON QUIXOTE IN THE SIERRA MORENA, WHICH WAS ONE OF THE RAREST ADVENTURES RELATED IN THIS VERACIOUS HISTORY

"I have always heard it said, Sancho," said Don Quixote, when he saw how he had been treated, "that to do good to boors is to throw water into the sea. If I had believed your words, I would have avoided this trouble. But it is done now; we must simply be patient and take warning for the future."

"You worship will take warning as much as I am a Turk," returned Sancho. "But since you say this mischief might have been avoided if you had believed me, believe me now, and a still greater one will be avoided. For I tell you chivalry is of no account with the Holy Brotherhood, and they wouldn't give two cents for all the knights-errant in the world. I can tell you I seem to hear their arrows whistling past my ears this minute."

"You are a coward by nature, Sancho," said Don Quixote, "but lest you should say I am obstinate and never do as you advise, this once I will take your advice and withdraw before the fury you dread so much. But it must be on one condition, that never, in life or death, will you say to anyone that I retired or withdrew from this danger out of fear, but only because of your entreaties. If you say otherwise you will lie, and from this time to that, and from that to this, I give you the lie, and say you lie and will lie every time you think so or say so. And answer me not again, for at the mere thought of withdrawing or retiring from any danger, above all from this, which does seem to carry some little shadow of fear about it, I am ready to take my stand here and await alone, not only the Holy Brotherhood you talk of and dread, but the brothers of the twelve tribes of Israel, and the Seven Maccabees, and Castor and Pollux, and all the brothers and brotherhoods in the world."

"Señor," replied Sancho, "to retire is not to flee, and there is no wisdom in waiting when danger outweighs hope. Wise men justifiably preserve themselves today for tomorrow and do not risk all in one day. And let me tell you, though I am coarse and a peasant, I have got some notion of what they call sensible conduct; so don't repent of having taken my advice. Mount Rocinante if you can, and if not I will help you, and follow me, for my mother-wit tells me we have more need of legs than hands just now."

Don Quixote mounted without replying, and with Sancho leading the way on his donkey, they entered the Sierra Morena, which was close by. It was Sancho's intention to cross it entirely and come out again at El Viso or Almodóvar del Campo, after hiding for some days among its crags so as to escape the Brotherhood, should it come to look for them. He was encouraged in this by perceiving that the stock of provisions carried by the ass had come safe out of the fray with the galley slaves, a circumstance that he regarded as a miracle, seeing how they pillaged and ransacked.[1]

As for Don Quixote, his heart rejoiced as he advanced amid the mountains, for they seemed to him just the place for the adventures he was in quest of. They brought to mind the marvelous adventures that had befallen knights-errant in similar solitudes and wilds, and he went along reflecting on these things, so absorbed and transported by them that he had no thought for anything else. Nor had Sancho any other concern, now that he fancied he was traveling in a safe region, than to satisfy his appetite with what remained from the clerical spoils. So he marched behind his master sitting sideways on his mount, emptying the sack and packing his paunch. For as long as he could go that way, he would not have given a penny to meet with another adventure.

While so engaged he raised his eyes and saw that his master had halted and was trying with the point of his pike to lift some bulky object lying on the ground. Sancho hastened to join him to give aid if that were needed. He reached Don Quixote just as with the point

1. The following passage does not appear in the first edition, in which there is no allusion to the loss of Sancho's mount until the middle of Ch. XXV, where, without any explanation of how it happened, Cervantes speaks of Dapple as having been lost. When the second edition was in the press, an attempt was made to remedy the oversight, and the printer, apparently, supplied this passage. The references to the ass as if still in Sancho's possession (nine or ten in number) were left unaltered, though the first of them occurs only four or five lines after the inserted passage. In the third edition of 1608 some of these inconsistencies were removed, and in the Second Part Cervantes refers to the matter and charges the printer with the blunder.

"That night they reached the very heart of the Sierra Morena, where it seemed prudent to Sancho to pass the night and even some days, at least as many as the stores he carried might last, and so they encamped between two rocks and among some cork trees; but fatal destiny, which, according to the opinion of those who have not the light of the true faith, directs, arranges, and settles everything in its own way, so ordered it that Ginés de Pasamonte, the famous knave and thief who by the virtue and madness of Don Quixote had been released from the chain, driven by fear of the Holy Brotherhood, which he had good reason to dread, resolved to take hiding in the mountains; and his fate and fear led him to the same spot to which Don Quixote and Sancho Panza had been led by theirs, just in time to recognize them and leave them to fall asleep; and as the wicked are always ungrateful, and necessity leads to evildoing, and immediate advantage overcomes all considerations of the future, Ginés, who was neither grateful nor well-principled, made up his mind to steal Sancho Panza's donkey, not troubling himself about Rocinante, as being a prize that was no good either to pawn or sell. While Sancho slept he stole his donkey, and before day dawned he was far out of reach.

Aurora made her appearance bringing gladness to the earth but sadness to Sancho Panza, for he found that his Dapple was missing, and seeing himself bereft he began the saddest and most doleful lament in the world, so loud that Don Quixote awoke at his exclamations and heard him saying, "O son of my bowels, born in my very house, my children's plaything, my wife's joy, the envy of my neighbors, relief of my burdens, and lastly, half supporter of myself, for with the twenty-six *maravedis* you earned me daily I met half my charges."

Don Quixote, when he heard the lament and learned the cause, consoled Sancho with the best arguments he could, entreating him to be patient and promising to give him a letter of exchange ordering three out of five ass-colts that he had at home to be given to him. Sancho took comfort at this, dried his tears, suppressed his sobs, and returned thanks for the kindness shown him by Don Quixote."

of the pike he was raising a saddle-pad with a valise attached to it. Both were half or indeed wholly rotten and torn, but so heavy were they that Sancho had to help lift them. His master ordered him to see what the valise contained, and Sancho did so with great alacrity. Though the valise was secured by a chain and padlock, its torn and rotten condition allowed him to see its contents, which were four shirts of fine cloth, and other linen articles as exquisite as they were clean. In a handkerchief he found a small heap of gold crowns.

"Blessed be all Heaven," he exclaimed, as soon as he saw them, "for sending us an adventure that is good for something!"

Searching further he found a little memorandum book richly bound. Don Quixote asked him for this, telling him to take the money and keep it for himself. Sancho kissed his hands for the favor and emptied the valise of its linen, which he stowed away in the provision sack.

"It seems to me, Sancho," Don Quixote observed, after he had reflected on the whole matter, "for it cannot be otherwise, that some traveler must have lost his way in these mountains and been attacked and slain by wicked men. Then they brought him to this remote spot to bury him."

"That cannot be," answered Sancho, "because if they had been robbers they would not have left this money."

"You are right," said Don Quixote, "and I cannot guess or explain what this may mean. But wait, let us see if there is anything written in this memorandum book which may enable us to discover what we want to know."

He opened it, and the first thing he found in it was a sonnet, written roughly but in a very good hand. He read it aloud so that Sancho might hear it, and found that it ran as follows:

SONNET

Or Love is lacking in intelligence,
  Or to the height of cruelty attains,
  Or else it is my doom to suffer pains
Beyond the measure due to my offense.
But if Love be a God, it follows thence
  That he knows all, and certain it remains
  No God loves cruelty. Then who ordains
This penance that enthrals while it torments?
It were a falsehood, Chloe, thee to name;
  Such evil with such goodness cannot live;
And against Heaven I dare not charge the blame.
  I only know it is my fate to die.
  To him who knows not whence his malady,
  A miracle alone a cure can give.

"There is nothing to be learned from that poem," said Sancho, "unless from the clue that's in it, one can solve the whole matter."

"What clue is that?" said Don Quixote.

"I thought your worship spoke of a clue in it," said Sancho.

"I said Chloe,"[2] replied Don Quixote, "and that, no doubt, is the name of the lady of whom the author of the sonnet complains. Faith, he must be a reasonably good poet, or I know little of the craft."

"Then your worship understands poetry too?"

"Better than you realize," replied Don Quixote, "as you shall see when you carry a letter written in verse from beginning to end to my lady Dulcinea del Toboso. I would have you know, Sancho, that all or most of the knights-errant in days of yore were great troubadours and great musicians, for both of these accomplishments, or more properly speaking gifts, are the especial preserve of lovers-errant. Yet it is true the verses of the knights of old have more spirit than neatness in them."

"Read more, your worship," said Sancho, "and you will find something that will enlighten us."

Don Quixote turned the page. "This is prose and seems to be a letter," he said.

"An ordinary letter, señor?"

"To judge from the beginning it seems to be a love letter," replied Don Quixote.

"Then read it aloud, your worship," said Sancho, "for I am very fond of love stories."

"With all my heart," said Don Quixote, and reading it aloud as Sancho had requested him, he found it ran thus:

Your false promise and my sure misfortune carry me to a place whence the news of my death will reach your ears before the words of my complaint. Ungrateful one, you have rejected me for one more wealthy but not more worthy, but if virtue were esteemed wealth I should neither envy the fortunes of others nor weep for misfortunes of my own. What your beauty raised up your deeds have laid low; the former induced me to believe you were an angel, the latter reveal to me that you are a woman. Peace be with you who have sent war to me, and Heaven grant that your husband's deceptions remain ever hidden from you, so that you may not repent what you have done, nor I reap a revenge I would not have.

"There is less to be gathered from this than from the verses," said Don Quixote, when he had finished the letter, "except that he who wrote it is some rejected lover." Turning over nearly all the pages of the book he found more verses and letters, some of which he could read, while others he could not. But they were all made up

2. The original sonnet says *Fili*, "Phyllis," and Sancho confuses it with *hilo*, "thread," or "clue."

of complaints, laments, misgivings, desires and aversions, favors and rejections, while some were rapturous and some doleful.

As Don Quixote was examining the book, Sancho examined the valise. There was not a corner in the whole of it or in the pad that he did not search, peer into, and explore, not a seam he did not rip or tuft of wool he did not pick to pieces, lest anything should escape for want of care and pains. Such was the greed excited in him by the discovery of the crowns, which amounted to nearly a hundred; and though he found no more booty, he held the blanketings, the vomiting of balm, the benedictions of the stakes, carriers' fisticuffs, missing saddlebags, stolen coat, and all the hunger, thirst, and weariness he had endured in the service of his good master, cheap at the price. He considered himself more than fully repaid by the gift of the treasure-trove.

The Knight of the Mournful Countenance was still very anxious to find out who the owner of the valise could be. Judging by the sonnet and the letter, from the money in gold and the fineness of the shirts, he conjectured that he must be some lover of distinction whom the scorn and cruelty of his lady had driven to a desperate course. But as in that uninhabited and rugged spot there was no one to be seen whom he could question, he saw nothing else for it but to push on, taking whatever road Rocinante chose—which was wherever he could find a path—firmly persuaded that among these wilds he could not fail to meet some rare adventure.

As he went along, then, occupied with these thoughts, he perceived on the top of a knoll that rose before their eyes a man who sprang from rock to rock and from one clump of underbrush to another with marvelous agility. As well as Don Quixote could make out, he was unclad, with a thick black beard, long tangled hair, and bare legs and feet. His thighs were covered by breeches apparently of tawny velvet but so ragged that they showed his skin in several places. He was bareheaded, and despite the speed, as has been said, with which he went by, the Knight of the Mournful Countenance observed and noted all these trifles. Though Don Quixote made the attempt, he was unable to follow him, for Rocinante in his feebleness could not advance over such rough ground; and he was, moreover, slow-paced and sluggish by nature. Don Quixote at once came to the conclusion that this was the owner of saddle-pad and valise, and he made up his mind to go in search of him, even though he should have to wander a year in the mountains before finding him. So he directed Sancho to take a short cut over one side of the mountain, while he himself went by the other, and perhaps by this means they might encounter the man who had passed so quickly out of their sight.

"I could not do that," said Sancho, "for when I leave your worship fear at once lays hold of me and assails me with all sorts of panics and fancies. And let what I now say be a notice that from this time forth I am not going to stir a finger's width from your presence."

"It shall be so," said he of the Mournful Countenance, "and I am very glad that you are willing to rely on my courage, which will never fail you, even though the soul in your body fails you. So come on now behind me slowly as best you can, and keep your eyes peeled. Let us make the circuit of this ridge, and perhaps we shall come upon the man we saw. No doubt he is none other than the owner of what we found."

"It would be far better," said Sancho in answer to this, "not to look for him. If we find him, and he happens to be the owner of the money, it is clear that I have to give it back. It would be better, therefore, not to go to this needless trouble. I'll keep possession of it until in some other less meddlesome and officious way the real owner can be discovered. And perhaps that will be after I have spent it, and then the king will exempt me from repayment."

"You are wrong in that, Sancho," said Don Quixote, "for now that we suspect who the owner is and have him almost before us, we are bound to seek him and make restitution. If we do not seek him, the strong suspicion we have as to his being the owner makes us as guilty as if he were so. So, friend Sancho, let not our search for him cause you any uneasiness, for my uneasiness will be relieved if we find him."

So saying he gave Rocinante the spur, and Sancho followed him on his usual mount. After they had partly made the circuit of the mountain, they found lying in a ravine, dead and half devoured by dogs and pecked by jackdaws, a mule saddled and bridled. All this still further strengthened their suspicion that he who had fled was the owner of the mule and the saddle-pad.

As they stood looking at it they heard a whistle like that of a shepherd watching his flock, and suddenly on their left there appeared a great number of goats. Behind them on the summit of the mountain was the goatherd in charge of them, a man advanced in years. Don Quixote called aloud to him and begged him to come down to where they were standing. He shouted in return, asking what had brought them to that spot, seldom or never trodden except by the feet of goats, or of the wolves and other wild beasts that roamed around. Sancho in return bade him come down, and they would explain all to him. The goatherd descended and reached the place where Don Quixote stood.

"I will wager," he said, "that you are looking at the hack mule that lies dead in the hollow there, and, faith, it has been lying there now these six months. Tell me, have you come upon its master about here?"

"We have come upon nobody," answered Don Quixote, "nor on

anything except a saddle-pad and a little valise that we found not far from here."

"I found it too," said the goatherd, "but I would not lift it nor go near it for fear of some ill-luck or being accused of theft. The devil is crafty, and things rise up under one's feet to make one fall without knowing why or wherefore."

"That's exactly what I say," said Sancho. "I found it too, and I would not go within a stone's throw of it; I left it there, and there it lies just as it was, for I don't want any problems."[3]

"Tell me, my good man," said Don Quixote, "do you know who is the owner of this property?"

"All I can tell you," said the goatherd, "is that about six months ago, more or less, there arrived at a shepherd's hut three leagues, perhaps, away from this place, a young man of well-bred appearance and manners. He was mounted on that same mule which lies dead here, and with the same saddle-pad and valise which you say you found and did not touch. He asked us what part of these mountains was the most rugged and remote. We told him that it was where we now are, and so in truth it is, for if you push on half a league farther, perhaps you will not be able to find your way out. I am wondering how you managed to come here, for there is no road or path that leads to this spot.

"I say, then, that on hearing our answer the youth turned about and made for the place we pointed out to him, leaving us all impressed with his good looks and wondering at his question and the haste with which we saw him retreat into the mountains. After that we saw him no more, until some days afterwards he crossed the path of one of our shepherds and, without saying a word, came up to him and gave him several cuffs and kicks. Then he turned to the donkey that was carrying our provisions and took all the bread and cheese, and having done this he made off back again into the mountains with extraordinary swiftness. When some of us goatherds heard of this we went in search of him for about two days through the remote regions in these mountains and finally found him hiding in the hollow of a large thick cork tree.

"He came out to meet us very gently with his clothing now torn and his face so changed and tanned by the sun that we hardly recognized him. Only his clothes, though torn, convinced us, from our recollection of them, that he was the person we were looking for. He saluted us courteously and in a few well-spoken words told us not to wonder at seeing him going about in this state, since he was obliged to do so in order to work out a penance which for his many sins had been imposed upon him. We asked him to tell us who he was, but we were never able to find out from him. We begged him,

3. Literally, "I don't want a dog with a bell," a rhyming proverb.

too, when he needed food, which he could not do without, to tell us where we could find him, as we would bring it to him with all goodwill and readiness. Or if this were not to his taste, at least he should come and ask us for it and not take it by force from the shepherds.

"He thanked us for the offer, begged our pardon for the recent assault, and promised for the future to ask for food in God's name without doing violence to anybody. As for the place where he lived, he said he had no other than whatever chance offered when night overtook him. His words ended in an outburst of weeping so bitter that we who listened to him would have been stones had we not wept along with him, when we compared what we saw of him the first time with what we saw now. For, as I said, he was a graceful and gracious young man, and his courteous and polished language showed him to be of good birth and courtly breeding. Though we who were listening to him were all country people, his gentle manners were enough to make that plain, even to us.

"But in the midst of his conversation he stopped and became silent, keeping his eyes fixed upon the ground for some time. We stood still, waiting anxiously to see what would come of this abstraction. And we felt sorry for him, for from his behavior, now staring at the ground with fixed gaze and eyes wide open without moving an eyelid, and then closing them, compressing his lips and raising his eyebrows, we could plainly see that a fit of madness of some kind had come over him. Before long he showed that what we imagined was the truth, for he arose in a fury from the ground where he had thrown himself and attacked the man nearest him with such rage and fierceness that, if we had not dragged him off, he would have beaten or bitten him to death. 'Oh faithless Fernando,' he kept exclaiming, 'now you'll pay the penalty of the wrong you have done me. These hands will tear out that heart of yours, abode and dwelling of all iniquity, but above all of deceit and fraud.' To these he added other words that all in effect upbraided this Fernando and accused him of treachery and faithlessness.

"With great difficulty we forced him to release his hold, and without another word he rushed off, plunging in among the bushes and brambles so as to make it impossible for us to follow. This leads us to suppose that madness overcomes him from time to time and that some one called Fernando must have done him a grievous wrong, as the condition to which it has brought him seems to show. All this has since been confirmed on the many occasions when he has crossed our path. At one time he begs the shepherds to give him some of the food they carry, at another he takes it from them by force. For when there is a fit of madness upon him, even though the shepherds offer it freely, he will not accept it but snatches it from them by dint of blows. But when he is in his senses, he begs it for the love of God, courteously and civilly, and receives it with many thanks and not a few tears.

"And to tell you the truth, sirs," continued the goatherd, "it was yesterday that we decided, I and four of the lads, two of them hired men and the other two friends of mine, to go in search of him until we find him. When we do we will take him, either by force or with his consent, to the town of Almodóvar, eight leagues from here. There we will try to cure him, if indeed his malady admits of a cure, or to find out when he is in his senses who he is and if he has relatives whom we may tell of his misfortune. This, sirs, is all I can say in answer to your question. You can be sure that the owner of the articles you found is the young man you saw pass by with such nimbleness and so naked."

Don Quixote had already described how he had seen the man go bounding along the mountain side, and he was now filled with amazement at what the goatherd told him and more eager than ever to discover who the unhappy madman was. In his heart he resolved, as he had done before, to search for him all over the mountain, not leaving a corner or cave unexamined until he had found him. But chance arranged matters better than he expected or hoped, for at that very moment, the youth he wished to find made his appearance, emerging from a gorge near where they stood. He came along talking to himself in a way that would have been unintelligible near at hand, and much more so at a distance. He was dressed in the way that has been described, except that as he drew near, Don Quixote perceived that the tattered vest he wore still smelled of amber. From which he concluded that anyone wearing such garments could not be of very low rank.

As he came near, the youth greeted them in a harsh, hoarse voice but with great courtesy. Don Quixote returned his greeting with equal politeness. Dismounting from Rocinante, he advanced with well-bred bearing and grace to embrace him, and he held him for some time close in his arms as if he had known him for a long time. The other, whom we may call the Ragged Knight of the Disreputable Countenance,[4] as Don Quixote was that of the Mournful Countenance, submitted to the embrace and then pushed him back a little. Placing his hands on Don Quixote's shoulders, he stood gazing at him as if seeking to see whether he knew him, no less amazed, perhaps, at the sight of the face, figure, and armor of Don Quixote than Don Quixote was at the sight of him. To be brief, the first to speak after the embrace was the Ragged One, and he said what will be told farther on.

4. Cervantes again plays with the convention of the romances of chivalry in giving the unknown gentleman an epithet. The ambiguity of *caballero*, which means both "knight" and "gentleman," is lost in English.

Chapter XXIV

IN WHICH IS CONTINUED THE ADVENTURE OF THE SIERRA MORENA

The history relates that Don Quixote listened to the ill-starred knight of the Sierra with the utmost attention:

"Whoever you are, señor," he began, "for I do not know you, I certainly thank you for the proofs of kindness and courtesy you have shown me. Would I were in a condition to respond to the cordial reception you have given me with something more than good will. But my fate grants me no other means of returning kindnesses done me save the hearty desire to repay them."

"My desire," replied Don Quixote, "is to be of service to you. Indeed, I had resolved not to leave these mountains until I had found you, and learned from you whether any kind of relief can be found for the sorrow under which, to judge by your strange existence, you seen to labor. I would have searched for you with all possible diligence, if that had been necessary. And if your misfortune should be one of those that refuse all consolation, it was my purpose to lament and mourn alongside you, so far as I could, for it is still some comfort in misfortune to find a fellow sufferer. If, then, my good intentions deserve any reciprocal courtesy, I entreat you, señor, by the courtesy you clearly possess in such a high degree, and by whatever you love or have loved best in life, to tell me who you are and the cause that has brought you to live or die in these solitudes like a brute beast, where you dwell in a manner so unsuited to your station, as is shown by your dress and appearance. And I swear," added Don Quixote, "by the order of knighthood which I have received, and by my vocation of knight-errant, if you gratify me in this, to serve you with all the zeal my calling demands, either in relieving your misfortune if it admits of relief, or in joining you in lamenting it as I promised."

The Knight of the Thicket, hearing the Knight of the Mournful Countenance talk in this strain, did nothing but stare at him, and stare at him again, and again survey him from head to foot.

"If you have anything to give me to eat," he said, after he had thoroughly examined him, "for God's sake give it to me. After I have eaten I will do all you ask in return for the good will you have shown me."

Sancho delved in his sack, and the goatherd in his pouch, to provide the Ragged One with sustenance. He ate what they gave him like a half-witted creature, so hastily that he took no time between mouthfuls, and gorged rather than swallowed. While he ate neither he nor those watching him uttered a word. As soon as he had finished he made signs to them to follow, and he led them to a green meadow which lay a little farther off round the corner of a rock. On reaching it he stretched himself upon the grass and the others did the same, all keeping silence.

"If you wish me, sirs," said the Ragged One after he had settled himself comfortably, "to relate briefly the dreadful extent of my misfortunes, you must promise not to break the thread of my sad story with any question or other interruption, for the instant you do so, the tale I tell will come to an end."

These words reminded Don Quixote of the tale his squire had told him, when he failed to keep count of the goats that had crossed the river and the story remained unfinished. But to return to the Ragged One:

"I give you this warning," he went on, "because I wish to pass briefly over the story of my misfortunes. Recalling them to memory only serves to add fresh ones, and the less you question me the sooner I shall finish the account, though I shall not fail to relate anything of importance in order to satisfy your curiosity completely."

Don Quixote gave the promise for himself and the others, and with this assurance the Ragged One began as follows:

"My name is Cardenio, my birthplace one of the best cities of this Andalusia, my family noble, my parents rich, my misfortune so great that my parents must have wept and my family grieved over it. Their wealth provided no alleviation, for fortune's gifts can do little to relieve reverses inflicted by Heaven. In that same region there dwelled a heavenly creature on whom love had bestowed all the glory I could desire. Such was the beauty of Luscinda, a girl as noble and as rich as I. Yet she was more fortunate, and she exhibited less constancy than my honest passion deserved. This Luscinda I loved, worshiped, and adored from my earliest and tenderest years, and she loved me with all the innocence and sincerity of childhood. Our parents were aware of our feelings and were not sorry to perceive them, for they saw clearly that as they ripened they must lead at last to a marriage between us. This seemed almost pre-ordained by the equality of our birth and wealth.

"We grew up, and our mutual love grew also, so that Luscinda's father felt bound for propriety's sake to refuse me admission to his house. In this perhaps he imitated the parents of that Thisbe so often sung by the poets, and the refusal simply added love to love and flame to flame. For though they forced silence on our tongues they could not impose it on our pens, which can reveal the heart's secrets to a loved one more freely than speech. Often the presence of the beloved disturbs the firmest will and strikes dumb the boldest tongue. Heavens, how many letters did I write her, and how many dainty modest replies did I receive! How many songs and love poems did I compose in which my heart declared and made known its feelings, described its ardent longings, reveled in its recollections, and dallied with its desires! At length growing impatient and sensing how my heart languished with longing to see her, I resolved to carry out what seemed to me the best plan for winning my desired and merited reward, and I asked her father for her hand in lawful marriage. His answer was that he thanked me for the desire I showed to honor him and to consider myself honored by the bestowal of his treasure. Yet, since my father was alive, it was his right to make this request, for if it were not altogether his wish and desire, Luscinda would not be taken or given by stealth. I thanked him for his kindness, reflecting that what he said was reasonable and that my father would assent as soon as I told him. With this in mind, I went the very same instant to tell him what I desired.

"When I entered the room I found him standing with an open letter in his hand. Before I could utter a word, he handed it to me. 'By this letter you will see, Cardenio,' he said, 'how strong is Duke Ricardo's inclination to favor you.'

"This Duke Ricardo, as you, sirs, probably know already, is a grandee of Spain[1] whose lands are situated in the richest part of Andalusia. I read the letter, which was couched in terms so flattering that even I felt it would be wrong of my father not to comply with the duke's request. This was that I should be sent immediately to him, as he wished me to become the companion, not the servant, of his eldest son. He would take it upon himself to place me in a position worthy of the esteem in which he held me. On reading the letter my voice failed me. 'Two days hence you will depart, Cardenio, in accordance with the duke's wish,' said my father, whereupon I grew even more speechless. 'Give thanks to God, who is opening a road on which you may attain what I know you deserve,' he said, adding further words of fatherly counsel.

"The time for my departure arrived. One night I spoke to Luscinda, telling her all that had occurred. I also told her father, entreating him to permit some delay and to defer disposing of her hand until I saw what Duke Ricardo wanted of me. He gave me his word, and she confirmed it with countless vows and swoonings.

"Finally I presented myself to the duke. He received me and treated me so kindly that very soon envy began to do its work, the old servants coming to regard the duke's inclination to favor me as an injury to themselves. But the one to whom my arrival gave the greatest pleasure was the duke's second son, Fernando by name, a gallant youth, of noble, generous, and armorous disposition, who very soon made so intimate a friend of me that it was remarked by everybody. Though the elder was attached to me and showed me kindness, he did not carry his affectionate treatment to the same length as Don Fernando.

1. A nobleman of the highest rank, enjoying the privilege of remaining covered in the presence of the sovereign. The first time the *grandes* were introduced to the king, they donned a special cap before the whole court.

"It so happened, then, that as between friends no secret remains unshared, and as the favor I enjoyed with Don Fernando had grown into friendship, he made all his thoughts known to me, and in particular a love affair which troubled his mind a little. He was deeply in love with a peasant girl, a vassal of his father's, the daughter of wealthy parents, and she was so beautiful, modest, discreet, and virtuous, that no one who knew her was able to decide in which respect she was most highly gifted or most excelled. The attractions of the beautiful peasant girl raised the passion of Don Fernando to such a point that, in order to gain his object and overcome her virtuous resolutions, he determined to pledge his word to her to become her husband, for to attempt it in any other way was to attempt an impossibility. Bound to him as I was by friendship, I strove by the best arguments and the most forcible examples I could think of to dissuade him from such a course. But perceiving I produced no effect, I resolved to make Duke Ricardo, his father, acquainted with the matter. Don Fernando, being sharp-witted and shrewd, foresaw and apprehended this, however, for he realized that my duty as a good servant obliged me not to keep concealed anything so injurious to the honor of my lord the duke. So, to mislead and deceive me, he told me he could find no better way of effacing from his mind the beauty that so enslaved him than by absenting himself for some months. He wanted this to be done by both of us going to my father's house under the pretext, as he would tell the duke, of examining and buying some fine horses in my city, which produces the best horses in the world.[2]

"When I heard him say this, even if his resolution had not been praiseworthy, I would have hailed it as one of the happiest that could be imagined. My affection prompted me, for I saw what a favorable opportunity it offered me to return and see my Luscinda. With this thought and wish, I commended his idea and encouraged his plan. I advised him to put it into execution as quickly as possible, since absence undeniably produces its effect despite the most deeply rooted feelings. Later I was to learn that, when he said this, he had already slept with the peasant girl under the title of husband, and sought an opportunity to make it known with safety to himself, for he dreaded what his father the duke would do when he heard of this folly.

"With young men love is for the most part nothing more than lust, which, as its final goal is enjoyment, comes to an end once the goal is reached. Thus it happens that what seems to be love takes flight, as it cannot pass the limit set by nature, which sets no limit to true love. What I mean is that after Don Fernando had enjoyed this peasant girl, his passion subsided and his eagerness cooled. Thus, while at first he had feigned a wish to absent himself

2. Córdoba, famous for its horses.

in order to cure his love, he was now in reality anxious to go to avoid keeping his promise.

"The duke gave him permission and ordered me to accompany him. We arrived at my city, and my father gave him the reception due to his rank. I saw Luscinda without delay, and though it had not been dead or deadened, my love gathered fresh life. To my sorrow, I told the story to Don Fernando, for I thought that because of the great friendship he bore me I should conceal nothing from him. So warmly did I extoll her beauty, her gaiety, and her wit, that my praises excited in him the desire to see a girl adorned by such attractions. To my misfortune, I satisfied his wish, showing her to him one night by the light of a taper at a window where we used to talk to one another. As she appeared to him in her dressing-gown, she drove all the beauties he had previously seen out of his recollection. Speech failed him, he lost his senses, he was spellbound and in the end love-smitten, as you will see in the course of the story of my misfortune. To inflame still further his passion, which he hid from me and revealed to Heaven alone, it so happened that one day he found a note of hers entreating me to demand her of her father in marriage. So delicate, so modest, and so tender was it, that on reading it he told me that in Luscinda alone were combined all the charms of beauty and understanding that were distributed among all the other women in the world.

"It is true, and I admit it now, that though I knew what good cause Don Fernando had to praise Luscinda, it gave me uneasiness to hear these praises from his mouth. I began to fear and, with reason, to distrust him, for there was no moment when he was not ready to talk of Luscinda. He would start the subject himself even though he dragged it in by the hair, thus causing in me a certain amount of jealousy. Not that I feared for the constancy or faith of Luscinda, but still my fate aroused forebodings in me, despite her reassurances. Don Fernando contrived always to read the letters I sent Luscinda and her answers to me, claiming that he enjoyed the wit and sense of both. One day Luscinda happened to ask me for a book of chivalry to read, *Amadís of Gaul*, of which she was very fond—"

"Had your worship told me at the beginning of your story that the Lady Luscinda was fond of books of chivalry," said Don Quixote, as soon as he heard a book of chivalry mentioned, "no other praise would have been needed to impress on me the superiority of her understanding. It could not have been of the excellence you describe had a taste for such delightful reading been wanting. So, as far as I am concerned, you need waste no more words in describing her beauty, worth, and intelligence. On merely hearing what her taste was, I declare her to be the most beautiful and the most intelligent woman in the world. And I wish your worship had, along with *Amadís of Gaul,* sent her the worthy *Don Rugel of Greece*, for I know the Lady Luscinda would greatly relish Daraida and Geraya, and the shrewd sayings of the shepherd Darinel, and the admirable verses of his bucolics, sung and delivered by him with such sprightliness, wit, and ease. But a time may come when this omission can be rectified, and to do so your worship need do no more than to come with me to my village. There I can give you more than three hundred books which are the delight of my soul and the entertainment of my life—though it occurs to me that I have got none of them now, thanks to the spite of wicked and envious enchanters. But pardon me for having broken our promise not to interrupt your discourse. When I hear chivalry or knights-errant mentioned, I can no more help talking about them than the rays of the sun can help giving heat, or those of the moon moisture. Pardon me, therefore, and proceed, for that is more to the purpose now."

While Don Quixote was saying this, Cardenio let his head fall on his breast and seemed plunged in deep thought. And though Don Quixote twice begged him go on with his story, he neither looked up nor uttered a word in reply. Yet after a while he raised his head. "I cannot get rid of the idea," he said, "nor will anyone in the world remove it or make me think otherwise. Only a blockhead would fail to assert or believe that that arrant knave Doctor Elisabat was not sleeping with Queen Madásima."

"That is not true, my oath upon it," said Don Quixote in high wrath, turning upon him angrily, as his way was. "And it is a very great slander, or rather villainy, for Queen Madásima was a very illustrious lady. It is not to be supposed that so exalted a princess would sleep with a quack, and whoever maintains the contrary lies like a great scoundrel. I will force him to acknowledge it, on foot or on horseback, armed or unarmed, by night or by day, or as he likes best."

Cardenio was looking at him steadily, and his mad fit having now come upon him, he had no inclination to go on with his story. Nor would Don Quixote have listened to it, so much did what had been said about Madásima disgust him. Strange to say, he stood up for her as if she were in earnest his true, natural lady. This was the pass to which his unholy books had brought him. Now when Cardenio, being mad, as I said, heard himself given the lie and called a scoundrel and other insulting names, he did not relish the jest. Snatching up a stone that he found near him, he struck such a blow on Don Quixote's breast that he laid him on his back. Sancho Panza, seeing his master treated thus, attacked the madman with his closed fist. But the Ragged One met him with a blow of his fist that stretched him at his feet. Then he stepped on him, to have the satisfaction of crushing his ribs, and the goatherd, who came to the rescue, shared the same fate. Having beaten and pummeled them all, he left them and quietly withdrew to his hiding place on the mountain.

Sancho rose, and in his rage at having been so belabored without deserving it, ran to take vengeance on the goatherd. He accused him of not having warned them that this man was at times taken with a mad fit, for if they had known it they would have been on their guard to protect themselves. The goatherd replied that he had said so, and that if Sancho had not heard him, that was no fault of his. Sancho retorted, and the goatherd rejoined, and the altercation ended by their seizing each other by the beard and exchanging such fisticuffs that if Don Quixote had not made peace between them, they would have knocked one another to pieces.

"Leave me alone, Sir Knight of the Mournful Countenance," said Sancho, grappling with the goatherd, "for this fellow is a peasant like myself and no dubbed knight. I can safely take satisfaction for the affront he has offered me, fighting with him hand to hand like an honest man."

"That is true," said Don Quixote, "but I know that he is not to blame for what has happened."

With this he pacified them, and again asked the goatherd if it would be possible to find Cardenio, as he felt the greatest eagerness to know the end of his story. The goatherd told him, as he had told him before, that there was no knowing for sure where his lair was, but if Don Quixote wandered about much in that neighborhood, he could not fail to fall in with him either in or out of his senses.

Chapter XXV

WHICH TREATS OF THE STRANGE THINGS THAT HAPPENED TO THE VALLIANT KNIGHT OF LA MANCHA IN THE SIERRA MORENA, AND OF HIS IMITATION OF THE PENANCE OF BELTENEBROS

Don Quixote took leave of the goatherd and once more mounting Rocinante bade Sancho follow him. This he did very discontentedly, with his donkey. They proceeded slowly, making their way into the most rugged part of the mountains. Sancho was all the while dying to have a talk with his master and longing for him to begin, so that there should be no breach of the injunction laid upon him.

"Señor Don Quixote," he said to him at last, being unable to remain silent any longer, "give me your worship's blessing and dismissal. I'd like to go home at once to my wife and children, for with them I can at least talk and converse as much as I like. To compel me to go through these lonely places day and night and not speak to you when I have the urge is burying me alive. If luck would have it that animals spoke as they did in the days of Aesop, it would not be so bad, because I could talk to my donkey about whatever came into my head and so put up with my bad luck. But it is a hard thing and unbearable for a man to go seeking adventures all his life and get nothing but kicks and blanketings, brickbats and punches, and with all this to have to sew up his mouth without daring to say what is in his heart, just as if he were dumb."

"I understand you, Sancho," replied Don Quixote. "You are dying to have the interdict I placed upon your tongue removed. Consider it removed, and say what you will while we are wandering in these mountains."

"So be it," said Sancho. "Let me speak now, for God knows what will happen next. And to take advantage of the permission at once, I ask what made your worship stand up so for that Queen Magimasa, or whatever her name is, or what did it matter whether that abbot was a friend of hers or not? If your worship had let that pass—and you were not a judge in the matter—it is my belief the madman would have gone on with his story, and the blow from the stone and the kicks and more than half a dozen punches would have been escaped."

"I swear, Sancho," answered Don Quixote, "if you knew as I do what an honorable and illustrious lady Queen Madásima was, you would say I had great patience not to break in pieces the mouth that uttered such blasphemies, for a very great blasphemy it is to say or imagine that a queen has become the lover of a bone-setter. The truth of the story is that that Doctor Elisabat whom the madman mentioned was a person of great prudence and sound judgment, and served as governor and physician to the queen. But to suppose she was his mistress is nonsense deserving very severe punishment, and as a proof that Cardenio did not know what he was saying, remember when he said it, he was out of his wits."

"That is what I say," said Sancho. "There was no occasion for minding the words of a madman. If good luck had not helped your worship and he had sent that stone at your head instead of at your breast, we would have been in fine shape for standing up for my lady, God confound her! And then, wouldn't Cardenio have gone free as a madman?"

"Against men in their senses or against madmen," said Don Quixote, "every knight-errant is bound to stand up for the honor of women, whoever they may be, much more for queens of such high degree and dignity as Queen Madásima. I have a particular regard for her on account of her amiable qualities. Besides being extremely beautiful, she was very wise and very patient under her misfortunes, of which she had many, and the counsel and society of Doctor Elisabat were a great help to her in enduring her afflictions with wisdom and resignation. Hence the ignorant and ill-disposed common people took occasion to say and think that she was his mistress. They lie, I say it once more, and all who think and say so will lie two hundred times more."

"I neither say nor think so," said Sancho. "It's their affair. They'll have their reward. No doubt they have already rendered account to God whether they were lovers or not. I come from my vineyard, I know nothing. I am not fond of prying into other people's lives. A fool and his money are soon parted. Naked I came, naked I remain: I neither lose nor gain. And if they were lovers, what is that to me? People are always looking for something that's not there. And who can stop them? Besides they slandered God himself."

"God bless me," said Don Quixote, "what a set of absurdities you are stringing together! What has what we are talking about got to do with the proverbs you are threading one after the other? For God's sake hold your tongue, Sancho, and henceforward prod the ass and don't meddle in what does not concern you. You must understand with all your five senses that everything I have done, am doing, or shall do, is well founded on reason and in conformity with the rules of chivalry, for I understand them better than all the knights in the world that profess them."

"Señor," replied Sancho, "is it a good rule of chivalry that we should go astray through these mountains without path or road, looking for a madman who when he is found will perhaps take a fancy to finish what he began, not his story, but your worship's head and my ribs, and end by breaking them for us?"

"Peace, I say again, Sancho," said Don Quixote, "for let me tell you it is not so much the desire of finding that madman that leads me into these regions. My aim is to achieve here something that will win me eternal name and fame throughout the known world. It shall be such that thereby I shall set the seal on all that can make a knight-errant perfect and famous."

"And is this achievement very perilous?"

"No," replied the Knight of the Mournful Countenance, "because the dice may roll seven instead of snake-eyes. All will depend on your dilgence."

"On my diligence!" said Sancho.

"Yes," said Don Quixote, "for if you return soon from the place where I am about to send you, my penance will be soon over, and my glory will soon begin. But as it is not right to keep you any longer in suspense and hanging on my words, I would have you know, Sancho, that the famous Amadís of Gaul was one of the most perfect knights-errant. I am wrong to say he was *one*. He stood alone, the first, the only one, the lord of all that were in the world in his time. A fig for Don Belianís and for all who say he equaled him in any respect, for, my oath upon it, they are deceiving themselves! I say, too, that when a painter desires to become famous in his art, he endeavors to copy the originals of the finest painters that he knows. The same rule holds good for all the most important crafts and callings that serve to adorn a state. Thus must he who would be esteemed prudent and patient imitate Ulysses, in whose person and labors Homer presents to us a lively picture of prudence and patience. Virgil, too, shows us in the person of Æneas the virtue of a dutiful son and the sagacity of a brave and skilful captain. These are not represented or described as they were, but as they ought to be, so as to leave the example of their virtues to posterity. In the same way Amadís was the pole star, day star, sun of valiant and devoted knights, whom all we who fight under the banner of love and chivalry are bound to imitate. This, then, being so, I consider, friend Sancho, that the knight-errant who imitates him most closely come nearest to reaching the perfection of chivalry.

"Now one of the instances in which this knight most conspicuously showed his prudence, worth, valor, endurance, fortitude, and love, was when he withdrew, rejected by the Lady Oriana, to do penance upon Wretched Rock, changing his name into that of Beltenebros,[1] a name assuredly significant and appropriate to the life which he had voluntarily adopted. So, as it is easier for me to imitate him in this than in cleaving giants asunder, cutting off serpents' heads, slaying dragons, routing armies, destroying fleets, and breaking enchantments, and as this place is so well suited for a similar purpose, I must not allow the opportunity to escape which now so conveniently offers me its forelock."

"What is it," said Sancho, "that your worship means to do in such an out-of-the-way place as this?"

"Have I not told you," answered Don Quixote, "that I mean to imitate Amadís here, playing the victim of despair, the madman, the maniac? Thus at the same time I imitate the valiant Don Roland, when at the fountain he had evidence of the fair Angelica's having disgraced herself with Medoro and through grief went mad. He pulled up trees, muddied the waters of the clear springs, slew shepherds, destroyed flocks, burned down huts, leveled houses, dragged mares about, and perpetrated a hundred thousand other outrages worthy of everlasting renown and record.[2] And though I have no intention of imitating Roland, or Orlando, or Rotolando (for he went by all these names), step by step in all the mad things he did, said, and thought, I will make a rough copy to the best of my power of all that seems to me most essential. But perhaps I shall content myself with the simple imitation of Amadís, who without giving way to any mischievous madness but merely to tears and sorrow, gained as much fame as the most famous."

1. *Bel*: "handsome"; *tenebros*: "dark" or "obscure."

2. References to Ariosto's *Orlando furioso*.

"It seems to me," said Sancho, "that the knights who behaved in this way had provocation and cause for their crazy actions and penances. But what cause has your worship for going mad? What lady has rejected you, or what evidence have you found to prove that the lady Dulcinea del Toboso has been trifling with Moor or Christian?"

"There is the point," replied Don Quixote, "and that is the beauty of my plan. No thanks to a knight-errant for going mad when he has cause; the thing is to go crazy without any provocation, and to let my lady know, if I do this without any excuse, what I would do if I had one. Moreover I have abundant cause in the long separation I have endured from my lady till death, Dulcinea del Toboso, for as you heard the shepherd Ambrosio say the other day, in absence all ills are felt and feared. So, friend Sancho, waste no time in advising me against so rare, so happy, and so unheard-of an imitation. Mad I am and mad I must be, until you return with the answer to a letter I mean to send by you to my lady Dulcinea. If it be such as my constancy deserves, my insanity and penance will come to an end, and if it be to the opposite effect, I shall become mad in earnest. Being so, I shall suffer no more. Thus in whatever way she may answer, I shall escape from the struggle and affliction in which you will leave me, either to enjoy in my senses the boon you bear me, or as a madman not to feel the evil you bring me. But tell me, Sancho, have you got Mambrino's helmet safe? I saw you take it up from the ground when that ungrateful wretch tried to break it in pieces but could not, by which the fineness of its temper is shown."

"By the living God, Sir Knight of the Mournful Countenance," said Sancho in answer, "I cannot stand or tolerate patiently some of the things your worship says. From them I am beginning to suspect that all you tell me about chivalry, and winning kingdoms and empires, and giving islands, and bestowing other rewards and dignities after the custom of knights-errant, must all be made up of wind and lies, and all pigments or figments, or whatever we may call them. What would anyone think who heard your worship calling a barber's basin Mambrino's helmet without ever seeing the mistake all this time, but that whoever says and maintains such things must have his brains addled? I have the basin in my sack all dented, and I am taking it home to have it mended; to trim my beard in it, if, by God's grace, I am allowed to see my wife and children some day or other."

"Look here, Sancho," said Don Quixote, "by him you swore by just now I swear you have the least understanding that any squire in the world has or ever had. Is it possible that all this time you have been going about with me you have never found out that all things concerning knights-errant seem to be illusions and nonsense and ravings, and to be done topsy-turvy? And not because it really is so, but because there is always a swarm of enchanters around us who change and alter everything with us and turn things as they please, and according as they are disposed to aid or destroy us. Thus what seems to you a barber's basin seems to me Mambrino's helmet, and to another it will seem something else. And rare foresight it was in the sage who is on my side to make what is really and truly Mambrino's helmet seem a basin to everybody, for since it is held in such estimation, all the world would pursue me to rob me of it. But when they see it is only a barber's basin, they do not take the trouble to obtain it, as was plainly shown by the man who tried to break it and left it on the ground without taking it. But my faith, had he known what it is, he would never have left it behind. Keep it safe, my friend, for just now I have no need of it. Indeed, I shall have to take off all this armor and remain as naked as I was born, if I decide to follow Roland rather than Amadís in my penance."[3]

Thus talking they reached the foot of a high mountain which stood like an isolated peak among the others that surrounded it. Past its base there flowed a gentle brook, all around it spread a meadow so green and luxuriant that it was a delight to the eyes to look upon it, and forest trees in abundance, and shrubs and flowers, added to the charms of the spot. Upon this place the Knight of the Mournful Countenance fixed his choice for the performance of his penance and, as he beheld it, exclaimed in a loud voice as though he were out of his senses, "This is the place, oh ye heavens, that I select and choose for bewailing the misfortune in which ye yourselves have plunged me. This is the spot where the overflowing of mine eyes shall swell the waters of yon little brook, and my deep and endless sighs shall stir unceasingly the leaves of these mountain trees, in testimony and token of the pain my persecuted heart is suffering. Oh, ye rural deities, whoever ye be that haunt this lone spot, give ear to the complaint of a wretched lover whom long absence and brooding jealousy have driven to bewail his fate among these wilds, and to complain of the hard heart of that fair and ungrateful one, the end and limit of all human beauty! Oh, ye wood nymphs and dryads that dwell in the thickets of the forest, so may the nimble wanton satyrs by whom ye are vainly wooed never disturb your sweet repose, help me to lament my hard fate or at least weary not at listening to it! Oh, Dulcinea del Toboso, day of my night, glory of my pain, guide of my path, star of my fortune, so may heaven grant thee in full all thou seekest of it, bethink thee of the place and condition to which absence from thee has brought me, and make that return in kindness that is due to my fidelity! Oh, lonely trees, that from this day forward shall bear me company in my soli-

3. *Orlando furioso*, canto xxiii st. 130 ff.

tude, give me some sign by the gentle movement of your boughs that my presence is not distasteful to you! Oh, thou, my squire, pleasant companion in my prosperous and adverse fortunes, fix well in thy memory what thou shalt see me do here, so that thou mayest relate and report it to the sole cause of all."

So saying he dismounted from Rocinante, and in an instant relieved him of saddle and bridle and gave him a slap on the rump. "He gives thee freedom," he said, "who is bereft of it himself, oh steed as excellent in deed as thou art unfortunate in thy lot. Begone where thou wilt, for thou bearest written on thy forehead that neither Astolfo's hippogriff nor the famed Frontino that cost Bradamante so dear could equal thee in speed."[4]

"Good luck to him who has saved us the trouble of stripping the packsaddle off Dapple," said Sancho, when he saw this.[5] "By my faith he would not have gone without some little pats and something said in his praise. Though if he were here I wouldn't let anyone strip him, because there would be no reason, since he wasn't in love or desperate, nor was his master, which I was while it was God's pleasure. And indeed, Sir Knight of the Mournful Countenance, if my departure and your worship's madness are to come off in earnest, it will be as well to saddle Rocinante again so that he can take the place of Dapple, because it will save me time in going and returning. If I go on foot I don't know when I'll get there or when I'll get back, as I am, in truth, a bad walker."

"I declare, Sancho," returned Don Quixote, "it shall be as you wish, for your plan does not seem to me a bad one. Three days from now you will depart, for I wish you to observe in the meantime what I do and say for her sake, so that you may be able to tell it."

"But what more have I to see besides what I have seen?" said Sancho.

"Much do you know about it!" said Don Quixote. "I now have got to tear my garments, to scatter about my armor, knock my head against these rocks, and more of the same sort of thing, which you must witness."

"For the love of God," said Sancho, "be careful, your worship, how you give yourself those knocks on the head, for you may come across such a rock, and in such a way, that the very first may put an end to this whole business of penance. And in my opinion, if knocks on the head seem necessary to you and this affair can't be done without them, you might be content—as the whole thing is pretended and counterfeit and a joke—you might be content, I say,

4. The hippogriff was the winged horse with eagle head on which Astolfo went in quest of information about Orlando. Frontino was the name of the mount of Ruggiero, Bradamante's lover. All appear in Ariosto's *Orlando furioso*.

5. This is the earliest reference, in the first edition of Part I, to the stolen ass. Apparently Cervantes intended to insert the theft in this chapter.

with giving them to yourself in the water, or against something soft, like cotton. Leave it all to me, for I'll tell my lady that your worship knocked your head against a point of rock harder than a diamond."

"I thank you for your good intentions, friend Sancho," answered Don Quixote, "but I would have you know that all these things I am doing are not in jest, but very much in earnest. Anything else would be a transgression of the ordinances of chivalry, which forbid us to tell any lie whatever under the penalties due to apostasy. To do one thing instead of another is just the same as lying, so my knocks on the head must be real, solid, and valid, without trickery or exaggeration. And it will be needful to leave me some bandages to dress my wounds, since fortune has compelled us to do without the balm we lost."

"It was worse losing the ass," replied Sancho, "for with him bandages and all were lost. But I beg your worship not to remind me again of that accursed potion, for my soul, not to say my stomach, turns at hearing the very name of it. And I beg you, too, to consider the three days you allowed me for seeing the mad things you do as having already passed, because I have as good as seen them and judged them, and I will tell wonderful stories to my lady. So write the letter and send me off at once. I am anxious to return and take your worship out of this purgatory where I am leaving you."

"Purgatory do you call it, Sancho?" said Don Quixote. "Rather call it hell, or even worse if there be anything worse."

"For one who is in hell," said Sancho, "*nulla est retentio*,[5] as I have heard say."

"I do not understand what *retentio* means," said Don Quixote.

"*Retentio*," answered Sancho, "means that whoever is in hell never comes or can come out of it, which will be the opposite case with your worship, unless my legs don't work—that is if I have spurs to wake up Rocinante. Let me once get to El Toboso and into the presence of my lady Dulcinea, and I will tell her such things of the crazy doings and mad actions (for it's all the same) that your worship has done and is still doing that I will manage to make her softer than a glove though I find her harder than a cork tree. And with her sweet and honeyed answer I will come back through the air like a sorcerer and take your worship out of this purgatory that seems to be hell but is not, as there is hope of getting out of it—which, as I have said, those in hell don't have, and I believe your worship will not say anything to the contrary."

"That is true," said he of the Mournful Countenance, "but how shall we manage to write the letter?"

"And the ass-colt order too," added Sancho.

5. Sancho misquotes a phrase from the funeral rites, "For in hell there is no redemption [*nulla est redemptio*]."

"All shall be included," said Don Quixote, "and as there is no paper, it would be well to write it on the leaves of trees, as the ancients did, or on the tablets of wax, though that would be as hard to find just now as paper. But it has just occurred to me how it may be conveniently and even more than conveniently written, and that is in the notebook that belonged to Cardenio. You will take care to have it copied on paper, in a good hand, at the first village you come to where there is a schoolmaster, or if not, any sacristan will copy it. But be sure you do not give it to any notary to copy, for they write a legal hand that Satan could not make out."

"But what is to be done about the signature?" said Sancho.

"The letters of Amadís were never signed," said Don Quixote.

"That is all very well," said Sancho, "but the order must be signed, and if it is copied, they will say the signature is false, and I'll be left without ass-colts."

"The order shall go signed in the same book," said Don Quixote, "and on seeing it my niece will raise no difficulty about obeying it. As to the love letter, you can put by way of signature, '*Yours till death, the Knight of the Mournful Countenance.*' And it will be no great matter if it is in some other person's hand, for as well as I recollect, Dulcinea can neither read nor write, nor in the whole course of her life has she seen handwriting or letter of mine. My love and hers have been always platonic, not going beyond a modest look, and even that so seldom that I can safely swear I have not seen her four times in all these twelve years I have been loving her more than the light of these eyes that the earth will one day devour. And perhaps even of those four times she has not once perceived that I was looking at her, such is the retirement and seclusion in which her father Lorenzo Corchuelo and her mother Aldonza Nogales have brought her up."

"Well, well!" said Sancho. "So Lorenzo Corchuelo's daughter is the lady Dulcinea del Toboso, otherwise called Aldonza Lorenzo?"

"She it is," said Don Quixote, "and she it is that is worthy to be lady of the whole universe."

"I know her well," said Sancho, "and let me tell you she can fling a crowbar as well as the strongest lad in all the town. Praise God, but she is a sensible girl, sturdy and tall, strong as an ox, and fit to be helpmate to any knight-errant that is or is to be, who may make her his lady. By God, she's tough! And what a voice! I can tell you one day she posted herself on the top of village belfry to call some laborers that were in a ploughed field of her father's, and though they were better than half a league off they heard her as well as if they were at the foot of the tower. And the best part is that she is not a bit prudish; she's like a city-bred girl; she jokes with everybody and has a grin and a wisecrack for everything. So, Sir Knight of the Mournful Countenance, I say you not only may and ought to do crazy things for her sake, but you have a perfect right to give way to despair and hang yourself. No one who hears of it but will say you did well, though the devil should take you. And I wish I were on my road already, simply to see her, for it's been a long time since I saw her, and she must be changed by now, because staying out in the fields always and the sun and the air spoil women's looks greatly. But I must confess the truth to your worship, Señor Don Quixote. Until now I have been mistaken, for I believed truly and honestly that the lady Dulcinea must be some princess your worship was in love with, or some person great enough to deserve the rich presents you have sent her, such as the Biscayan and the galley slaves, and many more no doubt, for your worship must have won many victories in the time when I was not yet your squire. But all things considered, what good can it do the lady Aldonza Lorenzo, I mean the lady Dulcinea del Toboso, to have the vanquished men your worship sends or will send coming to her and going down on their knees before her? Because may be when they came she'd be combing flax or threshing on the threshing floor, and they'd be ashamed to see her, and she'd laugh, or resent the present."

"I have before now told you many times, Sancho," said Don Quixote, "that you talk too much and that with a dull wit you are always striving at sharpness. But to show you what a fool you are and how rational I am, I would have you listen to a short story. Be informed that a certain widow, fair, young, independent, and rich, and above all free and easy, fell in love with a sturdy strapping young lay-brother. His superior came to know of it and one day spoke to the worthy widow by way of brotherly remonstrance. 'I am surprised, señora,' he said, 'and not without good reason, that a woman of such high standing, so fair, and so rich as you are, should have fallen in love with such a common, low, stupid fellow as So-and-so, when in this house there are so many masters, graduates, and divinity students from among whom you might cloose as if they were a lot of pears, saying this one I'll take, that I won't take.' She replied to him with great sprightliness and candor, 'My dear sir,' said she, 'you are very much mistaken, and your ideas are very old-fashioned, if you think that I have made a bad choice in So-and-so, fool as he seems. Because for all I want with him, he knows as much and more philosophy than Aristotle.'

"In the same way, Sancho, for all I want with Dulcinea del Toboso, she is just as good as the most exalted princess on earth. It is not to be supposed that all those poets who sang the praises of ladies under the fancy names they give them had any such mistresses. Do you believe that the Amarillises, the Phyllises, the Sylvias, the Dianas, the Galateas, the Fílidas, and all the rest of them, that the books, the ballads, the barber's shops, the theaters are full of, were really and truly ladies of flesh and blood, and mistresses of those that glorify and have glorified them? Nothing of the kind; they only invent them for the most part to furnish a subject for their verses, and that they may pass for lovers or for men valiant enough to be so. So it suffices me to think and believe that the good Aldonza Lorenzo is fair and virtuous. And as to her pedigree, it is very little matter, for no one will examine into it for the purpose of conferring any order upon her,[6] and I, for my part, reckon her the most exalted princess in the world.

"You should know, Sancho, if you do not know, that two things alone beyond all others are incentives to love, and these are great beauty and a good name. These two things are to be found in Dulcinea in the highest degree, for in beauty no one equals her and in good name few approach her. To put the whole thing in a nutshell, I persuade myself that all I say is as I say, neither more nor less, and I picture her in my imagination as I would have her to be, as well in beauty as in condition. Helen approaches her not nor does Lucretia come up to her, nor any other of the famous women of times past, Greek, Barbarian, or Latin. And let each say what he will, for if in this I am taken to task by the ignorant, I shall not be censured by the critical."

"I say that your worship is entirely right," said Sancho, "and that I am an ass. I do not know how the name of ass came into my mouth, for a rope is not to be mentioned in the house of a man who has been hanged. But now for the letter, and then, good-bye, I'm leaving."

Don Quixote took out the notebook, and, retiring to one side, very deliberately began to write the letter. When he had finished it he called to Sancho, saying he wished to read it to him so that he might commit it to memory, in case of losing it on the road; for with evil fortune like his anything might be expected. "Write it two or three times there in the book," replied Sancho, "and give it to me, and I will carry it very carefully. To expect me to keep it in my memory is all nonsense, for I have such a bad one that I often forget my own name. But repeat it to me, anyway. I'd like to hear it. I'll bet it's perfect."

"Listen," said Don Quixote. "This is what it says."

DON QUIXOTE'S LETTER
TO DULCINEA DEL TOBOSO

" 'Sovereign and exalted Lady: He who is pierced by the point of absence and wounded to the heart's core sends thee, sweetest Dulcinea del Toboso, the health that he himself enjoys not. If

6. Proof of *hidalguía*—the first degree of nobility—was necessary before the military orders of Santiago, Alcántara, Calatrava, or Montesa could be conferred.

thy beauty despises me, if thy worth is not for me, if thy scorn is my affliction, though I be sufficiently long-suffering, hardly shall I endure this anxiety, which, besides being oppressive, is protracted. My good squire Sancho will relate to thee in full, fair ingrate, dear enemy, the condition to which I am reduced on thy account. If it be thy pleasure to give me relief, I am thine. If not, do as may be pleasing to thee, for by ending my life I shall satisfy thy cruelty and my desire.

"Thine till death,

The Knight of the Mournful Countenance. ' "

"By the life of my father," said Sancho, when he heard the letter, "it's the deepest thing I ever heard. I'll be damned if your worship doesn't say everything as you like in it! And how well you fit 'The Knight of the Mournful Countenance' into the signature. I declare your worship is as smart as the devil, and there is nothing you don't know."

"Everything is needed for the calling I follow," said Don Quixote.

"Now then," said Sancho, "let your worship put the order for the three ass-colts on the other side, and sign it very plainly, so they'll recognize it at first sight."

"By all means," said Don Quixote, and when he had written it, he read it to this effect:

"Dear Niece: In accordance with this order, please pay to Sancho Panza, my squire, three of the five ass-colts which I left at home in your charge. Said three ass-colts to be paid and delivered for the same number received here on account and duly recorded and upon presentation of this receipt turned over to him. Done in the heart of the Sierra Morena, the twenty-seventh of August of this present year."

"That will do," said Sancho. "Now let your worship sign it."

"There is no need to sign it," said Don Quixote, "but merely to put my flourish,[7] which is the same as a signature, and enough for three asses, or even three hundred."

"I can trust your worship," returned Sancho "Let me go and saddle Rocinante. Be ready to give me your blessing, for I intend to go at once without seeing the fooleries your worship is going to do. I'll say I saw you do so many that she will not want any more."

"At any rate, Sancho," said Don Quixote, "I should like—and there is reason for it—I should like you, I say, to see me stripped to the skin and performing a dozen or two insanities, which I can get done in less than half an hour. Having seen them with your own eyes, you can then safely swear to the rest you intend to add. And I promise you you will not tell of as many as I intend to perform."

7. The *rúbrica,* or flourish, which is always a part of a Spanish signature. Note how cleverly Don Quixote avoids using his real name.

"For the love of God, master," said Sancho, "don't let me see your worship stripped. It will upset me, and I won't be able to keep from tears, and my head aches so with all I shed last night for Dapple that I am not fit to begin any new crying. But if it is your worship's pleasure that I should see some insanities, do them in your clothes, short ones, and some that are appropriate for this situation, for I myself need nothing of the sort, and, as I have said, it will be a saving of time for my return, which will be with the news your worship desires and deserves. If not, let the lady Dulcinea look out! If she doesn't answer reasonably, I swear as solemnly as I can that I'll kick and punch the answer out of her stomach. Why should a knight-errant as famous as your worship go mad without rhyme or reason for a—? Her ladyship had better not make me say it, for by God I will speak, regardless of the consequences. I am pretty good at that! Little does she know me. Faith, if she knew me she'd be in awe of me."

"In faith, Sancho," said Don Quixote, "to all appearance you are no sounder in your wits than I."

"I am not so crazy," answered Sancho, "but I have a worse temper. But apart from all this, what has your worship to eat until I come back? Will you go out on the road like Cardenio to take it from the shepherds?"

"Let not that anxiety trouble you," replied Don Quixote, "for even if I had it, I should not eat anything but the herbs and the fruits which this meadow and these trees may yield me. The real heart this business of mine lies in not eating and in performing other mortifications."

"Do you know what I am afraid of? That I may not be able to find my way back to this spot where I am leaving you, it is such an out-of-the-way place."

"Observe the landmarks well," said Don Quixote, "for I will try not to go far from this neighborhood, and I will even take care to climb the highest of these rocks to see if I can behold you returning. However, lest you miss me and lose your way, the best plan will be to cut some branches of the broom that grows so abundantly about here, and as you go, to lay them at intervals until you have come out on the plain. These will serve you, like the thread in the labyrinth of Theseus, as marks and signs for finding me when you return."

"So I will," said Sancho Panza, and having cut some, he asked his master's blessing. Not without many tears on both sides he took his leave and mounted Rocinante, Don Quixote earnestly bidding him to have as much care of the animal as of his own person.

Sancho set out for the plain, strewing at intervals the branches of broom as his master had advised. And so he departed, though Don Quixote kept begging him to watch while he carried out a couple of mad pranks. He had not gone a hundred paces, however, when he turned and said, "I must say, señor, your worship was right in saying that in order to be able to swear without a weight on my conscience that I had seen you do mad things, it would be well for me to see one, at any rate—though your worship's remaining here has let me see a very big one."

"Did I not tell you so?" said Don Quixote. "Wait, Sancho, and I will do them in a jiffy."

Hastily pulling off his breeches, he stripped himself to his skin and his shirt, and without more ado did a couple of capers in the air and a couple of somersaults, heels over head. In order not to see such a display a second time, Sancho wheeled Rocinante around and felt easy and satisfied in his mind that he could swear to his master's madness. And so we will let him follow his road until his return, which was a quick one.

Chapter XXVI

IN WHICH ARE CONTINUED THE REFINEMENTS WITH WHICH DON QUIXOTE PLAYED THE PART OF A LOVER IN THE SIERRA MORENA

Returning to the behavior of the Knight of the Mournful Countenance now that he was alone, the history says that when Don Quixote had finished doing the somersaults or capers, naked from the waist down and clothed from the waist up, and saw that Sancho had gone off without pausing to witness any more crazy feats, he climbed up to the top of a high rock. There he reflected once again on a matter he had several times before considered without ever coming to any conclusion, namely whether it would be better and more to his purpose to imitate the outrageous madness of Roland or the melancholy madness of Amadís.

"What wonder is it," he said, as he communed with himself, "if Roland was so good a knight and so valiant as everyone says when, after all, he was enchanted? Nobody could kill him save by thrusting a long pin into the sole of his foot, and he always wore shoes with seven iron soles. Yet cunning devices did not avail him against Bernardo del Carpio, who knew all about them and strangled him in his arms at Roncesvalles.[1] But putting the question of his valor aside, let us come to his losing his wits. It is certain that he did lose them because of the proofs that chance provided and the information the shepherd gave that Angelica had slept more than two siestas with Medoro, a little curly-headed Moor who was page to Agramante. If he was persuaded that this was true and that his lady had wronged him, it is no wonder that he should go mad. But how am I

1. Bernardo del Carpio is the hero of a Spanish epic tradition which is the counterpart of the French and Italian tales about Roland. Roncesvalles (Roncevaux in French) is the site of Bernardo's triumph over Charlemagne's army and Roland.

to imitate him in his madness, unless I also have a similar occasion? For my Dulcinea, I will venture to swear, never saw a Moor in her life, as he really is, in his proper costume, and today she is just as her mother bore her. I should plainly be doing her a wrong if I imagined anything else and went mad with the same kind of madness as Roland the Furious.

"On the other hand, I know that Amadís of Gaul, without losing his senses and without doing anything mad, acquired no less fame as a lover than did the most famous. For, according to his history, after being rejected by his lady Oriana, who had ordered him not to appear in her presence until it should be her pleasure, all he did was to retire to Wretched Rock. There, in the company with a hermit, he took his fill of weeping until Heaven sent him relief in the midst of his great grief and need. And if this be true, as it is, why should I now take the trouble to strip stark naked or do mischief to these trees which have done me no harm, or why am I to disturb the clear waters of these brooks which will give me drink whenever I have a mind? Long live the memory of Amadís, and let him be imitated so far as is possible by Don Quixote of La Mancha, of whom it will be said, as was said of another, that if he did not achieve great things he died in attempting them. If I am not repulsed or rejected by my Dulcinea, it is enough for me, as I said, to be absent from her. And so, now to business! Come to my memory, ye deeds of Amadís, and show me how I am to begin to imitate you. I know already that what he chiefly did was to pray and commend himself to God. But what am I to do for a rosary, for I have not got one?"

Then it occurred to him that he might make one by tearing a great strip off the tail of his shirt, which was hanging down, and making eleven knots on it, one bigger than the rest. This he used as a rosary all the time he was there, during which he repeated countless Hail Marys. But what distressed him greatly was the absence of another hermit who might confess him and offer him consolation. So he solaced himself by pacing up and down the little meadow and writing and carving on the bark of the trees and on the fine sand a multitude of verses all reflecting his sadness, and some in praise of Dulcinea. But when he was found there afterwards, the only complete and legible verses that could be discovered were those that follow:

Ye on the mountain side that grow,
  Ye green things all, trees, shrubs, and bushes,
Are ye aweary of the woe
  That this poor aching bosom crushes?
If it disturb you, and I owe
  Some reparation, it may be a
Defence for me to let you know

Quixote's tears are on the flow,
And all for distant Dulcinea
Del Toboso.

The loyalest lover time can show,
Doomed for a lady-love to languish,
Among these solitudes doth go,
A prey to every kind of anguish.
Why Love should like a spiteful foe
Thus use him, he hath no idea,
But barrels full—this doth he know—
Quixote's tears are on the flow,
And all for distant Dulcinea
Del Toboso.

Adventure-seeking doth he go
Up rugged heights, down rocky valleys,
But hill or dale, or high or low,
Mishap attendeth all his sallies:
Love still pursues him to and fro,
And plies his cruel scourge—ah me! a
Relentless fate, an endless woe.
Quixote's tears are on the flow,
And all for distant Dulcinea
Del Toboso.

The addition of "Del Toboso" to Dulcinea's name gave rise to no little laughter among those who found the above lines, for they suspected Don Quixote must have fancied that unless he added "del Toboso" when he introduced the name of Dulcinea the verse would be unintelligible, and this was indeed the fact, as later admitted. He wrote many more, but, as has been said, these three stanzas were all that could be plainly and perfectly deciphered. In this way, and by sighing and calling on the fauns and satyrs of the woods and the nymphs of the streams, and Echo, moist and mournful, to answer, console, and hear him, as well as looking for herbs to sustain him, he passed his time until Sancho's return. Had that been delayed three weeks, rather than three days, the Knight of the Mournful Countenance would have been so altered that his own mother would not have known him. And here it will be well to leave him, wrapped up in sighs and verses, to relate how Sancho Panza fared on his mission.

As for him, he came out on the high road and made for El Toboso, the next day reaching the inn where the mishap of the blanket had fallen him. As soon as he recognized it he felt as if he were once more flying through the air, and he could not bring himself to enter it. Yet it was an hour when he might well have done so, for it was dinner time and he longed to taste something hot, as it had been all cold fare with him for many days past. The craving drove him to approach the inn, still undecided whether to go in or not. As he hesitated thus two persons came out who at once recognized him.

"Señor licentiate," said one to the other, "is not the man on the horse Sancho Panza who, as our adventurer's housekeeper told us, went off with her master as his squire?"

"It is indeed," said the licentiate, "and that is our friend Don Quixote's horse."

If they knew him so well, it was because they were the priest and the barber of his own village who had scrutinized and passed sentence upon the books. As soon as they recognized Sancho Panza and Rocinante they approached, for they were anxious to hear of Don Quixote.

"Friend Sancho Panza," said the priest, calling him by name, "where is your master?"

Sancho recognized them at once and decided he would say nothing about the place and the state in which he had left his master. So he replied that his master was in a certain place intent upon a certain matter of great importance to him which he could not disclose for the eyes in his head.

"No, no," said the barber, "if you don't tell us where he is, Sancho Panza, we will suspect (as we suspect already) that you have murdered and robbed him, for here you are mounted on his horse. In fact, you must produce the master of the nag, or else take the consequences."

"There is no need of threats with me," said Sancho, "for I am not a man to rob or murder anybody. Let his own fate or the God who made him kill each one. My master is having a fine time doing penance in the middle of these mountains."

Then he told them, right out and without stopping, how he had left him, what adventures had befallen him, and how he was carrying a letter to the lady Dulcinea del Toboso, the daughter of Lorenzo Corchuelo, with whom Don Quixote was over head and heels in love. They were both amazed at what Sancho Panza told them, for though they were aware of Don Quixote's madness and of its nature, each time they heard of it they were filled with fresh wonder. They then asked Sancho Panza to show them the letter he was carrying to the lady Dulcinea del Toboso. He said it was written in a notebook and that his master's directions were that he should have it copied on paper at the first village he came to. On this, the priest said if Sancho showed it to him, he himself would make a fair copy of it. Sancho put his hand into his bosom in search of the notebook but could not find it. If he had been searching until now, he could not have found it, for Don Quixote had kept it and had never given it to him, nor had he himself thought of asking for it. When Sancho discovered he could not find the book, his face grew deadly pale, and in great haste he again felt his body all over. Seeing plainly it was not to be found, without more ado he seized his beard with both hands and pulled out half of it, and then, as quick as he could and without stopping, gave himself a dozen cuffs on the face and nose till they were bathed in blood.

Seeing this, the priest and the barber asked him what had happened to him that he should give himself such rough treatment.

"What could have happened to me?" replied Sancho, "but that I have lost, from one hand to the other, in a moment, three ass-colts, each of them as big as a castle?"

"How is that?" said the barber.

"I have lost the notebook," said Sancho, "that contained the letter to Dulcinea and an order signed by my master in which he directed his niece to give me three ass-colts out of four or five he had at home," and he went on to tell them about the loss of Dapple.

The priest consoled him, telling him that when his master was found, he would get him to renew the order and make another draft on paper, as was usual and customary. Those made in notebooks were never accepted or honored.

Sancho comforted himself with this and said if that were so, the loss of Dulcinea's letter did not trouble him much, for he had it almost by heart, and it could be taken down from him wherever and whenever they liked.

"Repeat it then, Sancho," said the barber, "and we will write it down afterwards."

Sancho Panza stopped to scratch his head to bring back the letter to his memory. He balanced himself now on one foot, now the other, one moment staring at the ground, the next at the sky. He almost gnawed off half the end of a finger while they waited in suspense for him to begin. "By God, señor licentiate," he said, after a long pause, "devil if I can recollect anything from the letter. But it said at the beginning, 'Exalted and stubborn Lady.' "

"It cannot have said 'stubborn,' " said the barber, "but 'superhuman' or 'sovereign.' "

"That's it," Sancho. "Then, as well as I remember, it went on, 'He who is wounded and wanting of sleep and pierced, kisses your worship's hands, thankless and very ungrateful beauty.' And it said something or other about sending her health and sickness, and from that it went on until it ended with 'Yours till death, the Knight of the Mournful Countenance.' "

It gave the two of them no little amusement to see what a good memory Sancho had, and they complimented him greatly on it and begged him to repeat the letter a couple of times more, so that they too might learn it by heart to write it later. Sancho repeated it three times, and as he did, uttered three thousand more absurdities. Then he told them more about his master, but he never said a word about the blanketing he himself had suffered in that inn, into which he refused to enter. He told them, moreover, how his lord, if he received a favorable answer from the lady Dulcinea del Toboso, would set about trying to make himself an emperor, or at least a monarch. They had planned it between them, and with Don Quixote's personal worth and the might of his arm, it was an easy thing to achieve. And when he became one, Don Quixote was to make a marriage for him (for he would be a widower by that time, as a matter of course) and was to give him as a wife one of the damsels of the empress, the heiress of some rich and grand state on the mainland, having nothing to do with islands of any sort, for he did not care for them now.

All this Sancho delivered with so much composure—wiping his nose from time to time—and with so little common sense that his two hearers were again filled with wonder at the force of Don Quixote's madness, that could run away with his poor man's reason. They did not care to waste their effort trying to disabuse him of his error, as they considered that since it did not in any way hurt his conscience, it would be better to leave him in it, and they would have all the more amusement in listening to his foolishness. So they told him to pray to God for his lord's health, as it was a very likely and a very feasible thing for him in course of time to come to be an emperor, as he said, or at least an archbishop or some other dignitary of equal rank.

"If fortune, sirs," said Sancho in reply, "should so order things that my master should feel inclined, instead of being an emperor, to become an archbishop, I would like to know what archbishops-errant give their squires?"

"They give them," said the priest, "some simple benefice or parish, or some place as sacristan which brings them a good fixed income, not counting the altar fees, which may be reckoned at as much more."

"But for that," said Sancho, "the squire must be unmarried and must at least know how to help at mass. If that is so, woe is me, for I am married already, and I don't know the first letter of the ABC. What will become of me if my master takes a notion to become an archbishop and not an emperor, as is usual and customary with knights-errant?"

"Don't worry, friend Sancho," said the barber, "for we will entreat your master, and advise him, even urging it upon him as a case of conscience, to become an emperor and not an archbishop, because it will be easier for him as he is more valiant than learned."

"That is what I thought," said Sancho, "though I can tell you he is fit for anything. What I mean to do is to pray our Lord to place him where it may be best for him, and where he may be able to bestow most favors upon me."

"You speak like a man of sense," said the priest, "and you will be acting like a good Christian. But what must be done now is to take steps to coax your master out of that useless penance you say he is performing. We had better go into this inn to consider what plan to adopt, and also to dine, for it is now time."

Sancho said that they could go in but that he would wait there outside, and that he would tell them afterwards the reason why he was unwilling and why it did not suit him to enter it. But he begged them to bring him out something to eat, and to let it be hot, and also to bring barley for Rocinante. They left him and went in, and shortly afterwards the barber brought him out something to eat. Later after they had between them carefully thought over what they should do to carry out their project, the priest hit upon an idea very well adapted to humor Don Quixote and effect their purpose. The notion, as the priest explained to the barber, was that he himself would put on the disguise of a wandering damsel, while the barber should try as best he could to pass for a squire. They would proceed to where Don Quixote was, and the priest, pretending to be an aggrieved and distressed damsel, would ask a boon of him, which as a valiant knight-errant he could not refuse to grant. The boon he meant to ask was that Don Quixote should accompany "her" to the place she would conduct him, in order to redress a wrong which a wicked knight had done her. At the same time she would entreat him not to require her to remove her mask, nor ask her any question touching her circumstances until he had righted her with the wicked knight.

He had no doubt that Don Quixote would comply with any request made in these terms and that in this way they might lead him away and restore him to his own village, where they would try to find out if his extraordinary madness could in any way be cured.

Chapter XXVII

OF HOW THE PRIEST AND THE BARBER PROCEEDED WITH THEIR SCHEME; TOGETHER WITH OTHER MATTERS WORTHY OF RECORD IN THIS GREAT HISTORY

The priest's plan did not seem a bad one to the barber—indeed, far from it—so they immediately started to carry it out. They borrowed a skirt and veil from the innkeeper's wife, leaving her in pledge a new cassock of the priest's, and the barber made a beard out of a grey-brown or red oxtail in which the innkeeper used to stick his comb. His wife asked them what they wanted these things for, and the priest told her in a few words about the madness of Don Quixote and how this disguise was intended to get him away from the mountain where he was at present. The innkeeper and his wife immediately came to the conclusion that the madman—the balm-man and master of the blanket-tossed squire—had been their guest, and they told the priest all that had occurred between them, not omitting what Sancho had kept silent about.

Finally the innkeeper's wife dressed up the priest in a style that left nothing to be desired. She put on him a woolen skirt with black-velvet stripes four inches wide, all slashed, and a bodice of green velvet set off by a binding of white satin, which as well as the skirt must have been made in the time of King Wamba.[1] The priest would not let them adorn his head, but put on his head a little quilted linen cap which he used for a nightcap. He bound his forehead with a strip of black silk, while with another he made a mask that concealed his beard and face very well. He then put on his hat, which was broad enough to serve him for an umbrella, and enveloping himself in his cloak seated himself woman-fashion on his mule. The barber mounted his beast wearing a beard reaching down to the waist, that was a mingled red and white, for it was, as has been said, the tail of a clay-red ox.

They took leave of all, and of the good Maritornes, who, sinner that she was, promised to pray a rosary of prayers that God might grant them success in such an arduous and Christian undertaking. But hardly had he left the inn when it struck the priest that he was doing wrong in rigging himself out in that fashion, as it was an indecorous thing for a priest to dress himself that way even though much might depend upon it. He said so to the barber and begged him to change dresses, as it was fitter the barber should be the distressed damsel, while he himself would play the squire's part, which would be less derogatory to his dignity. Otherwise he was resolved to have nothing more to do with the matter, and let the devil take Don Quixote.

Just at this moment Sancho came up, and seeing the pair in such a costume he was unable to restrain his laughter. The barber, however, agreed to do as the priest wished, and, altering their plan, the priest went on to instruct him how to play his part and what to say to Don Quixote to induce and compel him to follow them and leave the hideout he had chosen for his idle penance. The barber told him he could manage it properly without any instruction, and as he did not care to dress himself up until they were near where Don Quixote was, he folded up the garments, and the priest adjusted his beard, and they set out under the guidance of Sancho Panza.

1. Wamba, a king of the Gothic line, who reigned from 672 to 680.

He, as he went along, told them of the encounter with the madman they met in the Sierra, yet he said nothing about finding the valise or of what it contained. Despite his simplicity, the lad was a trifle covetous.

The next day they reached the place where Sancho had put down the broom branches as marks to direct him to where he had left his master. Recognizing it, he told them that this was the entrance and that they would do well to dress themselves, if that was required to deliver his master. They had already told him that the way they were rigged out and dressed was of the highest importance, if they were to rescue his master from the pernicious life he had adopted. And they strictly forbade him to tell his master who they were or that he knew them. Should Don Quixote ask, as ask he would, if he had given the letter to Dulcinea, Sancho should say that he had, and that, as she did not know know how to read, she had given an answer by word of mouth, saying that she commanded him, on pain of her displeasure, to come and see her at once and that it was a very important matter. In this way, and also because of what they were planning to tell him, they felt sure he could be restored to a better way of life and induced to take immediate steps to become an emperor or monarch, for there was no fear of his becoming an archbishop.

All this Sancho listened to and fixed well in his memory. He thanked them heartily for their decision to advise his master to become an emperor instead of an archbishop, for he felt sure that, when it came to bestowing rewards on their squires, emperors could do more than archbishops-errant. He said, too, that it would be as well for him to go on ahead of them to find the knight and give him his lady's answer, for that might be enough to bring him from the place without putting them to all this trouble. They approved of what Sancho proposed, and resolved to wait for him until he brought back word that his master had been found. Sancho pushed on into the ravines, leaving them in a spot through which flowed a little gentle rivulet, and where the rocks and trees afforded a cool and grateful shade.

It was an August day when the heat in those parts is intense, and the hour was three in the afternoon, all of which made the spot more inviting and tempted them to wait there for Sancho's return. Thus they were reposing in the shade when a voice, unaccompanied by the notes of any instrument but sweet and pleasing in its tone, reached their ears. They were not a little astonished at this, as the place did not seem to be a likely one for so fine a singer. Though it is often said that shepherds of rare voice are to be found in the woods and fields, this is rather a flight of the poet's fancy than the truth. They were even more surprised to realize that what they heard were not verses of shepherd rustics but of polished courtiers.

This was demonstrated by the following verses, which were those they heard sung.

What makes my quest of happiness seem vain?
Disdain.
What bids me to abandon hope of ease?
Jealousies.
What holds my heart in anguish of suspense?
Absence.
If that be so, then for my grief
Where shall I turn to seek relief,
When hope on every side lies slain
By Absence, Jealousies, Disdain?

What the prime cause of all my woe doth prove?
Love.
What at my glory ever looks askance?
Chance.
Whence is permission to afflict me given?
Heaven.
If that be so, I but await
The stroke of a resistless fate,
Since, working for my woe, these three,
Love, Chance, and Heaven, in league I see.

What must I do to find a remedy?
Die.
What is the lure for love when coy and strange?
Change.
What, if all fail, will cure the heart of sadness?
Madness.
If that be so, it is but folly
To seek a cure for melancholy:
Ask where it lies; the answer saith
In Change, in Madness, or in Death.

The hour, the summer season, the solitary place, the voice and skill of the singer, all contributed to the wonder and delight of the two listeners, who remained still waiting to hear something more. Finding, however, that the silence continued some little time, they resolved to go in search of the musician who sang with so fine a voice. But just as they were about to do so, they were checked by the same voice, which once more fell upon their ears, singing this sonnet:

SONNET

When heavenward, holy Friendship, thou didst go
Soaring to seek thy home beyond the sky,
And take thy seat among the saints on high,
It was thy will to leave on earth below

Thy semblance, and upon it to bestow
Thy veil, wherewith at times hypocrisy,
Parading in thy shape, deceives the eye,
And makes its vileness bright as virtue show.
Friendship, return to us, or force the cheat
That wears it now, thy livery to restore,
By aid whereof sincerity is slain.
If thou wilt not unmask thy counterfeit,
This earth will be the prey of strife once more,
As when primeval discord held its reign.

The song ended with a deep sigh, and again the listeners remained waiting attentively for the singer to resume. But perceiving that the music had now turned to sobs and heart-rending moans, they determined to find out who the unhappy being could be whose voice was as rare as his sighs were piteous. They had not proceeded far when on turning the corner of a rock they discovered a man of the same aspect and appearance as Sancho had described to them when he told them the story of Cardenio. He showed no astonishment when he saw them but stood still with his head on his breast like one in deep thought, without raising his eyes after the first glance when they suddenly came upon him.

The priest, being aware of his misfortune and having recognized him by the description, then went up to him. In a few sensible words, for he was a well-spoken man, he entreated and urged him to quit a life of such misery lest he should end it there—and that would be the greatest of all misfortunes. Cardenio was then in his right mind, free from any attack of that madness which so frequently carried him away. Seeing them dressed in a fashion so unusual among the frequenters of those wilds, he could not help showing some surprise, especially when he heard them speak of his case as if it were a well-known matter, as the priest's words gave him to understand.

"I see plainly, sirs, whoever you may be," he said in reply, "that Heaven, whose care it is to help the good, and even the wicked very often, here, in this remote spot, cut off from human contact, sends me those, little though I deserve it, who would show me by many and forcible arguments how unreasonable is the life I am leading, and would induce me to seek out some better place to dwell. But since they know that if I escape this evil, I shall fall into another still greater, perhaps they will set me down as weak-minded or devoid of reason, which is worse. Nor would that be any wonder, for I myself realize that the recollection of my misfortunes has so powerful an effect and contributes and works so mightily to my ruin that despite myself I become at times like a stone, without feeling or consciousness. I sense the truth of it when they tell me and show me proofs of the things I have done when the terrible fit comes over me. All I can do is bewail my lot in vain, idly curse my destiny, and excuse my madness by telling to any that care to hear, how it came about. No reasonable beings will wonder at the effects after they have learned the cause. If they cannot help me at least they will not blame me, and the repugnance they feel at my wild ways will turn into pity for my woes. If, sirs, you should have come here with the same design as others, I entreat you, before you proceed with your cogent arguments, to hear the story of my countless misfortunes. Perhaps, when you have heard it, you will spare yourselves the trouble you would take in providing consolation for grief that is beyond the reach of it."

As they both desired nothing more than to hear from his own lips the cause of his suffering, they entreated him to tell it, promising not to do anything for his relief or comfort that he did not wish. At that the unhappy gentleman began his sad story in nearly the same words and manner he had used in telling it to Don Quixote and the goatherd a few days before, when, because of Doctor Elisabat and Don Quixote's scrupulous observance of what was due to chivalry, the tale was left unfinished, as this history has already recorded. Now, fortunately, the mad fit held off and allowed him to reach the end. Thus, when he came to the incident of the note which Don Fernando had found in the volume of *Amadís of Gaul*, Cardenio said that he remembered it perfectly and that it was expressed in these words:

LUSCINDA TO CARDENIO

" 'Every day I discover merits in you that oblige and compel me to hold you in higher estimation. So if you desire to relieve me of this obligation without cost to my honor, you may easily do so. I have a father who knows you and loves me dearly and who will put no constraint on my inclination. He will grant what will be reasonable for you to desire, if you value me as you say and as I believe you do.'

"This letter induced me, as I told you, to demand Luscinda in marriage, and it also led Don Fernando to look on Luscinda as one of the most discreet and prudent women of the day. It was this letter that aroused in him the desire to ruin me before my desire could be realized. I told Don Fernando that all Luscinda's father was waiting for was that my father should ask him for her, and that I did not dare to propose it, out of fear that he would not consent—not because he did not know perfectly well of Luscinda's rank, goodness, virtue, and beauty, or failed to see that her qualities would do honor to any family in Spain. But I was aware that he did not wish me to marry so soon, before seeing what the Duke Ricardo would do for me. In short, I told him I did not venture to mention it to my father because of this hindrance and also in view of many others that held me back, though I did not know precisely what they were. It seemed to me simply that what I desired was never to come to pass.

"To all this Don Fernando answered that he would take it upon himself to speak to my father and persuade him to speak to Luscinda's father. O, ambitious Marius! O, cruel Catiline! O, wicked Sylla! O, perfidious Ganelon! O, treacherous Vellido! O, vindictive Julian![2] O, covetous Judas! Traitor, cruel, vindictive, and perfidious, how had this poor wretch failed in his fidelity, who so frankly showed you the secrets and the joys of his heart? What offense did I commit? What words did I utter or what counsels did I give which did not aim at advancing your honor and welfare? But, woe is me, why do I complain? For sure it is that when misfortunes spring from the stars, they fall upon us from on high with such fury and violence that no power on earth can check their course nor human ingenuity stay their coming. Who could have thought that Don Fernando, a highborn gentleman, intelligent, bound to me by gratitude for my services, and who could win the object of his love wherever he might set his affections, could have become so obdurate, as they say, as to rob me of my one ewe lamb that was not even yet in my possession? But laying aside these useless and unavailing reflections, let us take up the broken thread of my unhappy story.

"To proceed, then. Since Don Fernando saw that my presence thwarted the execution of his treacherous and wicked design, he resolved to send me to his elder brother under the pretext of asking for money to pay for six horses. With the sole intent of sending me away that he might the better carry out his infernal scheme, he had purchased the horses the very day he offered to speak to my father, and he now desired me to fetch the purchase price. Could I have anticipated this treachery? Could I by any chance have suspected it? So far was I from doing so that I offered with the greatest pleasure to go at once, out of satisfaction at the good bargain I had made.

"That night I spoke with Luscinda and told her what had been agreed upon with Don Fernando, and how I had strong hopes of our fair and reasonable wishes being realized. She, as unsuspicious as I was of the treachery of Don Fernando, urged me to try to return speedily, as she believed the fulfilment of our desires would be delayed only so long as my father put off speaking to hers. I know not why it was that on saying this to me her eyes filled with tears, and a lump came in her throat that prevented her from uttering one word of all those which, it seemed to me, she was striving to

2. Marius, Catiline, and Sylla are Roman "traitors." Ganelon or Galalon betrayed Roland and the Peers at Roncesvalles; Vellido or Bellido Dolfos treacherously murdered King Sancho II of Castile; and Count Julian, governor of Ceuta, in 710 called the Arabs into Spain to revenge himself on King Roderick for having seduced his daughter Florinda.

utter. I was astonished at this unusual turn, which I never before observed in her. We had always talked, whenever good fortune and my ingenuity gave us the chance, with the greatest gaiety and cheerfulness, without mingling in our words any tears, sighs, jealousies, doubts, or fears. On my side, I praised my good fortune that Heaven should have given her to me to love, I glorified her beauty, I extolled her worth and her understanding. She paid me back by praising in me what in her love for me she thought worthy of praise. Besides, we had a hundred thousand trifles and doings of our neighbors and acquaintances to talk about, and the utmost extent of my boldness was to take, almost by force, one of her fair white hands and carry it to my lips, as well as the closeness of the low grating that separated us allowed me. But the night before the unhappy day of my departure she wept, she moaned, she sighed, and she withdrew leaving me filled with perplexity and amazement, overwhelmed at the sight of such strange and affecting signs of grief and sorrow in Luscinda. But not to dash my hopes, I ascribed it all to the depth of her love for me and the pain that separation gives those who love tenderly. At last I took my departure, sad and dejected, my heart filled with fancies and suspicions, but not knowing well what it was I suspected or fancied—omens clearly pointing to the sad event and misfortune that was awaiting me.

"I reached the place where I had been sent, gave the letter to Don Fernando's brother, and was kindly received but not promptly dismissed. He desired me to wait, very much against my will, eight days in some place where the duke his father was not likely to see me, as his brother wrote that the money was to be sent without his knowledge. All this was a scheme devised by the treacherous Don Fernando, for his brother had no lack of money and could have sent me back at once.

"This command exposed me to the temptation of disobying it, as it seemed to me impossible to endure life for so many days separated from Luscinda, especially after leaving her in the sorrowful mood I have described to you. Nevertheless as a dutiful servant I obeyed, though I felt it would be at the cost of my well-being. But four days later a man sought me out and gave me a letter. The address indicated that it was from Luscinda, and the writing was hers. I opened it with fear and trepidation, persuaded that it must be something serious that had impelled her to write to me when at a distance, as she seldom did so when I was near. Before reading it I asked the man who it was that had given it to him, and how long he had been upon the road. He told me that as he happened to be passing through one of the streets of the city at the hour of noon, a very beautiful lady called to him from a window, and with tears in her eyes said to him hurriedly, 'Brother, if you are, as you seem to be, a Christian, for the love of God I entreat you to have this letter dispatched without a moment's delay to the place and person named in the address, for they are well known. By doing so you will render a great service to our Lord, and that you may experience no inconvenience in doing so, take what is in this handkerchief.' 'With this,' said he, 'she threw out of the window a hankerchief in which were tied up a hundred *reales* and this gold ring which I bring here together with the letter I have given you. Then, without waiting for any answer, she left the window, though not before she saw me take the letter and the handkerchief. I had let her know by signs that I would do as she asked. Seeing myself so well paid for the trouble I would have in bringing it, and knowing by the address that it was intended for you (for señor, I know you very well), and also unable to resist that beautiful lady's tears, I resolved to trust no one else, but to come myself and give it to you. In sixteen hours from the time when it was given to me I made the journey which, as you know, is eighteen leagues.'

"All the while the good-natured improvised courier was telling me this, I hung upon his words, my legs trembling under me so that I could scarcely stand. However, I opened the latter and read these words:

> 'Don Fernando has fulfilled the promise he gave you to urge your father to speak to mine, but much more to his own satisfaction than to your advantage. I have to tell you, señor, that he has demanded me in marriage, and my father, led away by what he considers Don Fernando's superiority over you, has so cordially favored his suit that the betrothal is to take place two days from now, with such secrecy and so privately that the only witnesses are to be the Heavens above and a few members of the household. Picture to yourself the state I am in, and reflect whether it is urgent for you to come. The outcome of this matter will show you whether I love you or not. God grant this may come to your hand before mine is forced to link itself with that of the man who keeps so ill the faith that he has pledged.'

"Such, in brief, were the words of the letter, which made me set out at once without waiting any longer for reply or money. For I now saw clearly that it was not the purchase of horses but the pursuit of his own pleasure that had made Don Fernando send me to his brother. The exasperation I felt against Don Fernando, joined with the fear of losing the prize I had won by so many years of love and devotion, lent me wings. Almost flying, I reached home the next day, at the very time I could speak with Luscinda. I arrived unobserved and left the mule on which I had come at the house of the worthy man who had brought me the letter. Fortune for once was pleased to be so kind that I found Luscinda at the grating that was the witness of our loves. She recognized me at once, and I her, but not as we ought to have recognized one another. But who in all the world can boast of having fathomed or understood the wavering mind and unstable nature of a woman? Indeed no one. As soon as Luscinda saw me she said, 'Cardenio, I am in my bridal dress, and the treacherous Don Fernando and my covetous father are waiting for me in the hall with the other witnesses, who shall witness my death before they witness me bethrothal. Do not be distressed, my friend, but find a way to be present at this sacrifice, and if my words will not prevent it, I have a concealed dagger which will prevent more deliberate violence by putting an end to my life and giving you a first proof of the love I have borne and bear you.' I replied to her distractedly and hastily, in fear lest I should not have time to reply. 'May your words be verified by your deeds, lady,' I said, 'and if you have a dagger to save your honor, I have a sword to defend you or kill myself, if fortune should be against us.'

"I think she could not have heard all of this, for I perceived that they called her away in haste, as the bridegroom was waiting. Now the night of my sorrow set in, the sun of my happiness went down, I felt my eyes bereft of sight, my mind of reason. I could not enter the house, nor was I capable of any movement. Yet reflecting how important it was that I should be present at whatever took place on the occasion, I nerved myself as best I could and went in. I well knew all the entrances and exits, and besides, with all the suppressed excitement that pervaded the house no one took notice of me. So, without being seen, I succeeded in placing myself in the recess formed by a window of the hall itself. I was hidden by the ends and borders of two tapestries, from between which I could see, without being seen, all that took place in the room. Who could describe the agitation I suffered as I stood there, the thoughts that came to me, the reflections that passed through my mind? They were such as cannot be told, nor would it be well to do so. Suffice it to say that the bridegroom entered the hall in his usual dress, without ornament of any kind. As groomsman he had with him a cousin of Luscinda's, and except for the servants of the house there was no one else in the chamber. Soon afterwards Luscinda came out from an antechamber, attended by her mother and two of her damsels, arrayed and adorned as became her rank and beauty, and in full festival and ceremonial attire. My anxiety and distraction did not allow me to observe or notice particularly what she wore. I could only perceive the colors, which were crimson and white, and the glitter of the gems and jewels on her veil and apparel. Yet these were surpassed by the rare beauty of her lovely auburn hair that vied with the precious stones and the light of the four torches that stood in the hall to shed a brighter gleam than all. Oh memory, mortal foe of my peace, why bring before me now the incomparable beauty of that adored enemy of mine? Would it not be better, cruel memory, to remind me of what she then did so that, stirred by a wrong so glaring, I may seek, if not vengeance, at least to rid myself of life? Do not grow weary, sirs, of listening to these digressions. My sorrow is not one of those that can or should be told tersely and briefly, for to me each incident seems to call for many words."

To this the priest replied that not only were they not weary of listening to him, but that the details he mentioned interested them greatly, since they were of a kind by no means to be omitted and deserved the same attention as the main story.

"To proceed, then," continued Cardenio. "When all were assembled in the hall, the priest of the parish came in and took the pair by the hand to perform the requisite ceremony. At the words, 'Will you, Señora Luscinda, take Señor Don Fernando, here present, for your lawful husband, as the holy Mother Church ordains?' I thrust my head and neck out from between the tapestries, and with strained attention and throbbing heart set myself to listen to Luscinda's answer, awaiting from her reply the sentence of death or the grant of life. Oh, that I had but dared at that moment to rush forward crying aloud, 'Luscinda, Luscinda, beware what you are doing! Remember what you owe me, reflect that you are mine and cannot be another's, that your 'I do' will end my life in that same instant. O, treacherous Don Fernando, robber of my glory, death of my life! What are you seeking? Remember that you can not as a Christian attain the object of your wishes, for Luscinda is my bride and I am her husband!' Fool that I am! Now that I am far away and out of danger, I say I should have done what I did not do. Now that I have let myself be robbed of my precious treasure, I curse the robber on whom I might have taken vengeance, had I as much heart for it as for bewailing my fate. In short, since I was then a coward and a fool, it is little wonder if I am now dying of shame, stricken with remorse, and mad.

"The priest stood waiting for Luscinda's answer, but she withheld it for a long time. Just as I thought she would take out the dagger to save her honor or was struggling for words to declare the truth on my behalf, I heard her say in a faint and feeble voice, 'I will.' Don Fernando said the same, and gave her the ring, and thus they stood linked by a knot that could never be untied. The bridegroom then approached to embrace his bride, and she, pressing her hand upon her heart, fell fainting in her mother's arms. It only remains for me to tell you the state I was in when with that consent I saw all my hopes mocked, Luscinda's words and promises proved falsehoods, and the recovery of the prize I had just lost rendered impossible forever. I stood stupefied, wholly abandoned, it seemed, by Heaven, and proclaimed the enemy of the earth that bore me, for the air refused me breath for my sighs, and the water moisture for my tears. Fire alone increased its strength, so that my whole frame glowed with rage and jealousy. Everyone was thrown into confusion when Luscinda fainted, and as her mother was unlacing her to give her air, a sealed paper was discovered in her bosom. Don Fernando seized it at once and began to read it by the light of a torch. As soon as he had read it he sat in a chair, resting his cheek on his hand in the attitude of one deep in thought, taking no part in the efforts being made to revive his bride.

"Seeing the whole household in confusion, I ventured to come out regardless whether I were seen or not. If I had been seen, I was determined to perform some frenzied deed that would prove to all the world the righteous indignation filling my breast by punishing the treacherous Don Fernando and even the fickle breast of the unconscious traitress. But my fate was doubtless reserving me for greater sorrows, if such there be, for it so ordered that just then I had enough and to spare of the reason which since has failed me. And so, without seeking to take vengeance on my greatest enemies, which could have been done easily, as all thought of me was far from their minds, I resolved to take vengeance on myself. I would inflict on myself the pain they deserved, and perhaps with even greater severity than if I had slain them. For sudden pain is soon over, but that which is prolonged by tortures slays eternally without ending life.

"In a word, I went out of the house and reached that of the man with whom I had left my mule. I made him saddle it for me, mounted without bidding him farewell, and rode out of the city like another Lot, not daring to turn my head to look back upon it. When I found myself alone in the open country, screened by the darkness of the night and tempted by the stillness to give vent to my grief without fear of being heard or seen, I broke silence and raised my voice to invoke curses upon Luscinda and Don Fernando, as if I could thus avenge the wrong they had done me. I called her cruel, ungrateful, false, thankless, but above all covetous, since my enemy's wealth had blinded the eyes of her affection, so that turning from me she had transferred it to a man to whom fortune had been more generous and liberal. And yet, in the midst of this outburst of execration and upbraiding, I found excuses for her, saying it was no wonder that a young girl in the seclusion of her parents' house, trained and schooled to obey them always, should have been ready to yield to their wishes when they offered her for a husband a gentleman of such distinction, wealth, and noble birth. Had she refused to accept him she would have been thought out of her senses or suspected of having placed her affections elsewhere, which would have done injury to her fair name and fame. But then again, I said, had she declared I was her husband, they would have seen that in choosing me she had not chosen so ill that they could not pardon her. Before Don Fernando had made his offer, they themselves—if their desires had been ruled by reason—could not have desired a more eligible husband for their daughter than I was. And she, before taking the last fatal step and giving her hand, might easily have said that I had already given her mine, for then I should have come forward to support any such declaration of hers. In short, I came to the conclusion that feeble love, little reflection, great ambition, and a craving for rank had made her forget the words she had used to deceive me, whom firm hopes and honorable passion had buoyed up and encouraged.

"Thus agitated and thus soliloquizing, I journeyed onward for the remainder of the night. By daybreak I had reached one of the passes in these mountains, where I wandered for three days more without taking any path or road. At last I came to some meadows lying on one side or other of the mountains, and there I asked some herdsmen in what direction the most rugged part of the range lay. They told me that it was in this part, and I set out for it at once, intending to end my life here. But as I was making my way among the crags, my mule dropped dead through fatigue and hunger, or, as I think more likely, in order to have done with the worthless burden it was carrying. I was left on foot, worn out, famished, with no one to help me and no thought of seeking help. So I lay stretched on the ground, how long I cannot say, after which I rose up free of all hunger.

"Beside me I found some goatherds, who no doubt had relieved me in my need, for they told me how they had found me and how I had been raving in a way that plainly showed I had lost my reason. Since then I am conscious that I am not always in full possession of it, at times being so deranged and crazed that I do a thousand mad things, tearing my clothes, crying aloud in these lonely places, cursing my fate, and idly calling on the dear name of her who is my enemy. All I seek is to end my life in lamentation, and when I recover my senses I am so exhausted and weary that I can scarcely move. Usually my dwelling is the hollow of a cork tree large enough to shelter this miserable body, and the herdsmen and goatherds who frequent these mountains are moved by compassion and furnish me with food, which they leave by the wayside or on the rocks, where they think I may perhaps pass and find it. So, even though I may be out of my senses at the time, the wants of nature teach me what I need to sustain me and make me crave it and take it eagerly. At other times, so they tell me when they find me in a rational mood, I come out upon the road, and though they would gladly give it to me, I snatch food by force from the shepherds bringing it from the village to their huts.

"Thus do I pass the wretched life that remains to me, until it shall be Heaven's will to bring it to a close, or to affect my memory so that I no longer recollect Luscinda's beauty and treachery, or the wrong done me by Don Fernando. If Heaven should do this without depriving me of life, I will turn my thoughts into some better channel. If not, I can only implore it to have full mercy on my soul, for in myself I feel no power or strength to release my body from this woeful pass in which of my own accord I have placed it.

"Such, sirs, is the dismal story of my misfortune. Say if you think it can be told with less emotion than you have seen in me and do not trouble yourselves to counsel or urge on me what reason suggests might offer me relief, for it will avail me no more than the medicine prescribed by a wise physician avails the sick man who will not take it. I have no wish for health without Luscinda, and since it is her pleasure to be another's when she is or should be mine, let it be my pleasure to be a prey to misery when I might have enjoyed happiness. By her fickleness she sought to make my ruin irretrievable. I will strive to gratify her wishes by seeking destruction. It will make plain to generations to come that I alone was left without that of which all others in misfortune have a superabundance. To them the impossibility of being consoled is itself a consolation, while to me it brings greater sorrows and sufferings, for I think that even in death there will be no end of them."

Here Cardenio brought to a close his long discourse and story, no less full of misfortune than of love. But just as the priest was going to pronounce some words of comfort, he was stopped by a voice that reached his ear, saying in melancholy tones what will be told in the Fourth Part of this narrative. For at this point the sage and sagacious historian, Cide Hamete Benengeli, brought the Third to a conclusion.

The Fourth Part of The Ingenious Gentleman Don Quixote of La Mancha

Chapter XXVIII

WHICH TREATS OF THE STRANGE AND DELIGHTFUL ADVENTURE THAT BEFELL THE PRIEST AND THE BARBER IN THE SAME SIERRA

Happy and fortunate were the times when that most daring knight Don Quixote of La Mancha sallied forth into the world. Because of his so noble resolve to seek to revive and restore to the world the long-lost and almost defunct order of knight-errantry, we now enjoy in this age of ours, so poor in merry entertainment, not only the charm of his true history, but also of the tales and episodes contained in it. These, in their way, are no less pleasing, ingenious, and truthful than the history itself which, resuming its thread, carded, spun, and wound, relates that just as the priest was about to console Cardenio, he was interrupted by a voice he heard speaking in a plaintive tone.

"O God!" it was saying, "could this place perchance serve as a secret grave for the weary load of this body I bear so unwillingly? It could indeed, unless the solitude these mountains promise deceives me. Woe is me! What company can be so pleasing to my mind as these rocks and thickets that permit me to complain to Heaven of my misfortune, rather than human companionship, since there is no one on earth from whom I might seek counsel in doubt, comfort in sorrow, or relief in distress!"

All this was heard distinctly by the priest and those with him. It seemed to them to be uttered close by, as indeed it was; so they got up to look for the speaker. Before they had gone twenty paces they discovered behind a rock, and seated at the foot of an ash tree, a youth in the dress of a peasant. They were unable at the moment to see his face, as he was leaning forward and bathing his feet in the brook that flowed past. They approached so silently that he did not notice them, for he was utterly intent on bathing his feet, which shone like two pieces of shining crystal among the stones of the brook. This whiteness and beauty struck them with surprise, for such feet did not seem intended to crush clods or follow the plow and the oxen, as their owner's dress would suggest. So, finding they had not been noticed, the priest, who was in front, made a sign to the other two to conceal themselves behind some fragments of rock. This they did, watching closely what the youth was doing.

He had on a drab-colored double cape, tightly belted to his body with a white towel, and woolen breeches and leggings, with a cap on his head, all of the same color. The leggings were rolled up as far as the middle of the leg, which seemed truly to be of pure alabaster.

As soon as he had finished washing his beautiful feet, he wiped them with a kerchief he took from under the cap. As he removed it, he raised his face, and those watching had the occasion to see a beauty so exquisite that Cardenio addressed the priest in a whisper.

"As this is not Luscinda," he said, "it is no human creature but a divine being."

The youth then took off the cap and, as he shook his head from side to side, there broke loose and spread out a mass of hair that the beams of the sun might have envied. In this way they learned that what had seemed a peasant was a lovely woman, the most beautiful the eyes of two of them had ever beheld. It would have been true even of Cardenio, if he had not seen and known Luscinda, for he afterwards declared that only Luscinda's beauty could compare with this. The long auburn tresses not only covered her shoulders, but concealed her all around beneath their masses, such was their length and abundance. Except for the feet, nothing of her form was visible. She now used her hands as a comb, and if her feet had seemed like bits of crystal in the water, her hands looked like pieces of driven snow among her locks.

All this increased not only the admiration of the three beholders, but their anxiety to learn who she was. With this in mind they resolved to show themselves, and at the stir they made in getting upon their feet, the beautiful girl raised her head. Parting her hair from before her eyes with both hands, she looked to see who had made the noise, and the instant she perceived them she started to her feet. Without waiting to put on her shoes or gather up her hair, she hastily snatched up a bundle she had beside her, perhaps containing clothes. Startled and alarmed, she tried to flee, but before she had gone six paces she fell to the ground, for her delicate feet were unable to bear the roughness of the stones. Seeing this, the three hastened towards her, and the priest was the first to speak.

"Stop, señora, whoever you may be," he said, "for those you see here only desire to be of service to you. There is no need for you to flee so ill-advisedly, for your feet cannot bear it, nor will we allow it."

Taken by surprise and bewildered, she made no reply. They, however, came nearer, and the priest took her hand.

"What your dress would hide, señora," the priest went on, "is revealed to us by your hair. It is clear proof that no trifling cause can have disguised your beauty in a garb so unworthy and sent it into solitudes like these. We have had the good fortune to find you, if not to relieve your distress, at least to offer you comfort. For no distress, so long as life lasts, can be so oppressive or reach such a height that the sufferer refuses to listen to comfort offered with good intention. And so, señora, or señor, or whatever you prefer to be, dismiss the fears aroused by the sight of us and acquaint us with your good or evil fortunes. From all of us together, or from each one of us, you will receive sympathy in your trouble."

While the priest was speaking, the disguised young woman stood as if spellbound, looking at them without opening her lips or uttering a word, like a village rustic who has suddenly been shown something he has never seen before. But after the priest had added some further words to the same effect, she sighed deeply and broke her silence.

"Since the solitude of these mountains has been unable to conceal me," she said, "and the loosening of my disheveled hair will not allow my tongue to lie, it would be idle for me now to make any further pretense. If you were to believe me, you would believe more out of courtesy than for any other reason. This being so, I thank you, sirs, for the offer you have made, which forces me to comply with your request. Yet I fear the narration of my misfortunes will arouse in you as much concern as compassion, for you will be unable to suggest any remedy or any consolation. However, so that no doubt as to my honor may remain in your minds, now that you have discovered me to be a woman and have seen me to be young, alone, and thus attired, I feel bound to tell you things that taken together or separately would be enough to destroy any good name, and which I would willingly keep secret if I could."

All this she who now stood revealed as a lovely woman delivered without any hesitation, with so much ease, and in so sweet a voice that they were no less charmed by her intelligence than by her beauty. As they again repeated their offers and begged her to fulfil her promise, she first modestly covered her feet and gathered up her hair. Then, without further pressing, she seated herself on a stone with the three gathered around her, and after an effort to restrain some tears that came to her eyes, she began to tell her story in a clear, steady voice.

"In Andalusia there is a town from which a duke takes a title, making him one of those who are called Grandees of Spain. This nobleman has two sons, the elder heir to his estates and apparently to his good qualities. The younger is heir to I know not what, unless it be the treachery of Vellido and the falsehood of Ganelon. My parents, who are this lord's vassals, are lowly in origin but so wealthy that if birth had conferred as much on them as fortune, they would have had nothing left to desire, and I would have had no reason to fear trouble like that in which I now find myself, for it may be that my ill fortune can be attributed to their lack of noble birth. It is true that they are not so lowly that they have any reason to be ashamed of their condition, but neither are they so high as to efface the impression I have that their humble birth led to my misfortune. In short, they are peasants, plain homely people, without any taint of disreputable blood, and, as the saying is, old rusty Christians, but so rich that by their wealth and sumptuous way of life they are coming by degrees to be considered gentlefolk by birth, and even noble. The wealth and nobility they thought most of, however, was having me for their daughter. As they have no other child to make their heir and are affectionate parents, I was pampered as few daughters are pampered by their parents.

"I was the mirror in which they beheld themselves, the staff of their old age, and on me, with submission to Heaven, all their wishes centered. My own desires were in accordance with theirs, for I knew their worth, and as I was mistress of their hearts, I was mistress also of their possessions. At my bidding they engaged or dismissed their servants, through my hands passed the accounts and returns of what was sown and reaped, and I had under my care the oil-mills, the wine-presses, the count of the flocks and herds, the beehives, all in short that a rich farmer like my father has or can have. I acted as steward and mistress with a diligence on my part and satisfaction on theirs that I cannot well describe. As for the leisure hours left me after I had given the needed orders to the head-shepherds, overseers, and other laborers, I spent in those occupations that are not only allowable but necessary for young girls, such as the needle, embroidery cushion, and spindle. If I desisted for a while in order to refresh my mind, I found recreation in reading some devotional book or playing the harp, for experience taught me that music soothed the troubled mind and relieves weariness of spirit. Such was the life I led in my parents' house, and if I have depicted it thus minutely, it is not out of ostentation, or to let you know that I am rich, but that you may see how, without any fault of mine, I have fallen from the happy condition I have described to the misery I am in at present. The truth is that I led this busy life in a retirement that might have seemed monastic, and unseen, as I thought, by any except the servants of the house. When I went to mass it was so early in the morning, and I was so closely attended by my mother and the women of the household, and so thickly veiled and so shy, that my eyes scarcely saw more than the ground I trod on. Despite all this the eyes of love, or idleness, more properly speaking, that not even the lynx's can rival, discovered me, with the persistence of Don Fernando. For that is the name of the younger son of the duke I told you of."

The moment the speaker mentioned the name of Don Fernando, Cardenio changed color and broke into a sweat, with such signs of emotion that the priest and the barber, who observed it, feared he would break out in one of the mad fits which they heard attacked him sometimes. But Cardenio showed no further agitation and remained quiet, fixing an attentive gaze on the peasant girl, for he began to suspect who she was. She, however, failed to notice the excitement of Cardenio and went on with her story.

"He had hardly set eyes on me, when, as he admitted afterwards, he was smitten with a violent love for me, as his behavior plainly showed. But to shorten the long recital of my woes, I will say nothing of all the devices used by Don Fernando to make known his passion. He bribed all the household, he gave and offered gifts and presents to my parents. Every day was like a holiday or a celebration in our street, and at night no one could sleep for the music. Countless love letters reached me, no one knew how, and they were filled with tender pleadings and pledges, and contained more promises and oaths than they had letters of the alphabet. All this not only did not soften me, it hardened my heart against him as if he had been my mortal enemy and as if everything he did to make me yield were done with the opposite intention.

"Not that Don Fernando's gallantries were disagreeable to me, or that I found his persistence tiresome. It gave me a certain satisfaction to find myself so sought and prized by a gentleman of such distinction, and I was not displeased at seeing my praises in his letters. For however ugly we women may be, it seems to me it always pleases us to hear ourselves called beautiful. But my own sense of right was opposed to all this, as well as the repeated advice of my parents, who now very plainly perceived Don Fernando's purpose, for he cared very little if all the world knew it. They told me they trusted and confided their honor and good name to my virtue and rectitude alone and urged me to consider the disparity between Don Fernando and myself. I might conclude from this that his intentions, whatever he might say to the contrary, had his own pleasure as their goal rather than my advantage. If I were at all eager to set up a barrier against his unreasonable wooing, they were ready, they said, to marry me at once to anyone I preferred, either from the leading people of our own town or among those in the neighborhood. In view of their wealth and my good name, a match might be looked for in any quarter. This suggestion and their sound advice strengthened my resolution, and I never gave Don Fernando a word in reply that could hold out to him any hope of success, however remote.

"All this caution of mine, which he must have taken for coyness, had apparently the effect of increasing his wanton appetite. That is the name I gave to his passion for me, for had it been what he declared it to be, you would not now hear of it because there would be no occasion for me to tell you. At length he learned that my parents were contemplating marriage for me in order to end his hopes of possessing me, or at least to secure additional protectors to watch over me. This news or this suspicion led him to act in the way you shall hear. One night I was in my chamber with no other companion than a maid who waited on me, and with the doors carefully locked lest my honor should be imperiled through my carelessness. I neither know nor can imagine how it happened, but despite all this seclusion and these precautions, and in the solitude and silence of my retreat, I found him standing before me. The apparition so astounded me that it deprived my eyes of sight and my tongue of speech. I was unable to utter a cry nor, I think, did he give me time to utter one, as he immediately approached me and took me in his arms. Overwhelmed as I was, I was powerless to defend myself. He then began to make such protestations to me that I do not know how falsehood could have adorned them to seem so like the truth. The traitor contrived that his words should be vouched for by his tears, and his sincerity by his sighs.

"I, a young girl, alone in the midst of my family, and without experience of such situations, began, I do not know quite how, to think that all these lying protestations were true. Yet his sighs and tears moved me to nothing more than pure compassion. Thus, as the first feeling of bewilderment passed away, I began in some degree to recover myself and spoke to him with more courage than I thought was in me.

"I declared, 'If, as I am now in your arms, señor,' I were in the claws of a fierce lion, and my deliverance could be procured by doing or saying anything to the prejudice of my honor, that would no more be in my power than it would be possible to undo the past. So then, though you hold my body clasped in your arms, I hold my soul secured by virtuous intentions, very different from yours, as you will see if you attempt to carry them into effect by force. I am your vassal, but I am not your slave; your nobility neither has nor should have any right to dishonor or degrade my humble birth. Low-born peasant that I am, I have my self-respect as much as you, a lord and gentleman. Your violence will be to no purpose with me, your wealth will have no weight, your words will have no power to deceive me, nor your sighs or tears to soften me. If I were to find any of the things I mention in the man my parents give me as a husband, his will would be mine, and mine in conformity with his. Since my honor would be preserved even though my inclinations were not gratified, I would willingly grant him what you, señor, now seek to obtain by force. And I say this lest you should suppose that any but my lawful husband shall ever win anything of me.'

" 'If that,' said this disloyal gentleman, 'is the only scruple you feel, fairest Dorotea' (for that is the name of this unhappy being), 'see how I now give you my hand to be yours. Let Heaven, from which nothing is hidden, and the image of Our Lady you have here, be witnesses of this pledge.' "

When Cardenio heard her say she was called Dorotea, he showed fresh agitation and felt convinced of the truth of his former suspicion. But he was unwilling to interrupt the story and wished to hear the end of what he already all but knew.

"What!" he said. "Is Dorotea your name, señora? I have heard of another of the same name who can perhaps match your misfortunes. But proceed, and later I may tell you something that will astonish you as much as it will excite your compassion."

Dorotea was struck by Cardenio's words as well as by his strange and miserable attire. She begged him, if he knew anything concerning her, to tell her at once, for if fortune had bestowed any blessing on her it was the courage to hear whatever calamity might befall. She felt sure that nothing affecting her could add in any degree to what she endured already.

"I would not let the occasion pass, señora," replied Cardenio, "of telling you what I think, if what I suspect were the truth. But so far there has been no occasion, nor it is of any importance to you to know it."

"Be that as it may," replied Dorotea, "what happened in my story was that Don Fernando, taking an image that stood in the chamber, placed it as a witness of our betrothal. Employing the most binding words and extravagant oaths, he gave me his promise to become my husband. Before he had finished pledging himself I advised him to consider well what he was doing and to think of the anger his father would feel when he saw him married to a peasant girl who was one of his vassals. I told him not to be blinded by my beauty, such as it was, for that was insufficient to excuse his transgression, and if in the love he bore me he wished me any kindness, it would be to let my destiny follow its course at the level my station in life required. For marriages so unequal never bring happiness, nor do they long continue to offer the enjoyment they begin with.

"All that I now repeat I said to him, and much more which I cannot recollect. But it by no means induced him to forego his purpose, since he who has no intention of paying does not worry over difficulties when he is striking the bargain. At the same time I debated the matter briefly in my own mind. 'I shall not be the first,' I said to myself, 'who has risen through marriage from a lowly to a lofty station, nor will Don Fernando be the first led by beauty or, as is more likely, a blind attachment, to marry below his rank. Consequently, since I am introducing no new usage or practice, I may as well avail myself of the honor that chance offers me. Even though his inclination for me should not outlast the attainment of his wishes, I shall, after all, be his wife before God. If I strive to repel him by scorn, I can see that, fair means failing, he is in a mood to use force, and I shall be left dishonored and with no way of proving my innocence to those who cannot know how innocently I find myself in this position. For what arguments would persuade my parents that this gentleman entered my chamber without my consent?'

"All these questions and answers passed through my mind in a moment. But it was the oaths of Don Fernando, the witnesses he appealed to, the tears he shed, and lastly the charms of his person and his high-bred grace—accompanied by such signs of genuine love, they might well have conquered a heart even more unattached and modest than mine—which more than all else began to influence me and lead me unawares to my ruin. I summoned my maid, so that there might be a witness on earth besides those in Heaven. Once again Don Fernando repeated his oaths, invoked as witnesses new saints as well as the former ones, called down upon himself a thousand curses hereafter should he fail to keep his promise, shed more tears, redoubled his sighs, and pressed me closer in his arms, from which he had never allowed me to escape. So I was left by my maid, and I ceased to be one, and he became a traitor and a perjured man.

"The day which followed the night of my misfortune did not come so quickly, I imagine, as Don Fernando wished, for when desire has attained its object, the greatest pleasure is to fly from the scene of pleasure. I say so because Don Fernando left me hastily and, through the scheming of my maid, by whom indeed he had been admitted, made his way to the street before daybreak. On taking leave of me he told me, though with less earnestness and fervor than when he came, that I might rest assured of his faith and of the sanctity and sincerity of his oaths. To confirm his words, he drew a valuable ring off his finger and placed it upon mine. He then took his departure and I was left, whether sorrowful or happy, I cannot say. All I can say is, I was left agitated and troubled in mind and almost bewildered by what had taken place. I had not the spirit, or else it did not occur to me, to chide my maid for her treachery in concealing Don Fernando in my chamber, for as yet I was unable to make up my mind whether what had befallen me was for good or evil. I told Don Fernando at parting that, as I was now his, he might see me on other nights in the same way, until it should be his pleasure to let the matter become known. Except the following night, however, he came no more, nor for more than a month could I catch a glimpse of him in the street or in church, while I wearied myself searching for the opportunity. Yet I knew he was in the town and almost every day was out hunting, a pastime he was very fond of. I remember well how sad and dreary those days and hours were to me, and I remember well how I began to doubt as they went by, and even to lose confidence in the faith of Don Fernando. And I remember, too, how my maid heard those words reproving her audacity that she had not heard before, and how I was forced to constrain my tears and the expression of my face, for I could not give my parents cause to ask me why I was so melancholy, and so feel driven to invent falsehoods in reply. But this was suddenly brought to an end, for the time came when all such considerations were disregarded, when there was no further question of honor, when my patience gave way and the secret of my heart became widely known. The reason was that a few days later it was reported in the town that Don Fernando had been married in a neighboring city to an extremely beautiful girl, the daughter of parents of distinguished position, though not so rich that her portion would entitle her to look for so brilliant a match. It was said, too, that her name was Luscinda, and that at the betrothal some strange things had happened."

Cardenio heard the name of Luscinda, but he only shrugged his shoulders, bit his lips, bent his brows, and before long let two streams of tears escape from his eyes. Dorotea, however, did not interrupt her story.

"When this sad news reached my ears," she said "instead of being struck with a chilll, my heart burned with such wrath and fury that I could scarcely restrain myself from rushing out into the streets, crying aloud and openly proclaiming the perfidy and treachery of which I was the victim. But this transport of rage was for the time checked by the decision I reached and carried out the same night. That was to put on these clothes which I got from a servant of my father's, a shepherd, to whom I confided the whole of my misfortune and whom I begged to accompany me to the city where I heard my enemy was. Though he remonstrated with me for my boldness and condemned my resolve, when he saw how intent I was, he offered to accompany me, as he said, to the end of the world.

"I at once packed up a woman's dress in a linen pillow case, together with some jewels and money to provide for emergencies. In the silence of the night, without informing my treacherous maid, I left the house. Accompanied by my servant and abundant anxieties, I set out on foot for the city. Yet I was borne as though on wings by my eagerness to reach it, not to prevent what I presumed to be already done, but at least to call upon Don Fernando to tell me with what conscience he had done it. I reached my destination in two days and a half, and on entering the city inquired for the house of Luscinda's parents.

"The first person I asked gave me more in reply than I sought to know, for he showed me the house and told me all that had occurred at the betrothal of the daughter of the family. The affair had attained such notoriety in the city that it was the talk of every knot of idlers in the street. He said that on the night of Don Fernando's betrothal with Luscinda, as soon as she had consented to be his bride by saying 'I do,' she had fainted dead away. When the bridegroom approached to unlace the bosom of her dress to give her air, he found a paper in her own handwriting, in which she said and declared that she could not be Don Fernando's bride because she was already Cardenio's. He, according to the man's account, was a gentleman of distinction of the same city. If she had accepted Don Fernando, she wrote, it was only in obedience to her parents. In short, he said, the words of the paper made it clear she meant to kill herself on the completion of the betrothal and gave her reasons for putting an end to herself. All this was confirmed, it was said, by a dagger they found somewhere in her clothes.

"On seeing this, Don Fernando, persuaded that Luscinda had trifled with him, made a fool of him, and slighted him, attacked her before she had recovered from her swoon. He tried to stab her with the dagger they had found, and he would have succeeded had not her parents and those who were present prevented him. It was said, moreover, that Don Fernando went away at once and that Luscinda did not recover from her collapse until the next day, when she told her parents how she was really the bride of that Cardenio I have mentioned. I learned besides that Cardenio, according to report, had been present at the betrothal and that, when he saw her betrothed, contrary to his expectation, he had fled the city in despair. He left behind him a letter declaring the wrong Luscinda had done him and his intention of going where no one should ever see him again. All this was a matter of notoriety in the city, and everyone spoke of it, especially when it became known that Luscinda was missing from her father's house and from the city. Nor could she be found anywhere, to the alarm of her parents, who did not know what they should do to find her. What I learned revived my hopes, and I was better pleased not to have found Don Fernando than to find him married, for it seemed to me that the door was not yet entirely shut on relief in my case. I thought that perhaps Heaven had put this impediment in the way of the second marriage to lead him to recognize his obligations under the former one, and to reflect that as a Christian he was bound to consider his soul above all human desires. All this passed through my mind, and I comfortlessly strove to comfort myself, indulging in faint and distant hopes of cherishing that life I now abhor.

"But while I was in the city, uncertain what to do, as I could not find Don Fernando, I heard notice given by the public crier offering a great reward to anyone who could find me, and giving particulars of my age and of the very dress I wore. And I heard it said that the lad who came with me had taken me away from my father's house, a thing that cut me to the heart, for it showed how low my good name had fallen. It was not enough that I should lose it by my flight, but they must add with whom I had fled, and he being so much beneath me and so unworthy of my consideration. The instant I heard the notice I left the city with my servant, who now began to show signs of wavering in his fidelity to me, and the same night, for fear of discovery, we entered the most thickly wooded part of these mountains. But, as is commonly said, one evil calls up another, and the end of one misfortune is apt to be the beginning of one still greater, and so it proved in my case. For my worthy servant, until then so faithful and trusty, when he found me in this lonely spot, was moved more by his own villainy than by my beauty and sought to take advantage of the opportunity which these wilds seemed to offer. With little shame and less fear of God and respect for me he began to make overtures to me, and finding that I replied to the effrontery of his proposals with justly severe language, he laid aside the entreaties which he had employed at first and began to use violence. But just Heaven, that seldom fails to watch over and aid good intentions, so aided mine that with my slight strength and with little exertion I pushed him over a precipice, where I left him, whether dead or alive I do not know. Then, with greater speed than seemed possible in my terror and fatigue, I made my way into the mountains, without any other thought or purpose but that of hiding there and escaping my father and those he had dispatched in search of me. I cannot say how many months have elapsed since this intention brought me here. I met a herdsman who engaged me as his servant at a place in the heart of the mountains. All this time I have been serving him as a hired hand, always trying to stay out in the fields to hide the locks which have now unexpectedly betrayed me. But all my care and pains were unavailing, for my master made the discovery that I was not a man and harbored the same base designs as my servant. Since fortune does not always supply a remedy in cases of difficulty, and no precipice or ravine was at hand down which to fling the master and cure his passion, as I had in the servant's case, I thought it a lesser evil to leave him and again conceal myself among these crags, than to test my strength and persuasiveness. So, as I say, once more I went into hiding and sought some place where with sighs and tears I might implore Heaven to have pity on my misery and grant me help and strength to escape from it or let me die in the wilds, leaving no trace of an unhappy being who, by no fault of hers, has furnished matter for talk and scandal at home and abroad."

Chapter XXIX

WHICH TREATS OF THE AMUSING DEVICE AND METHOD ADOPTED TO EXTRICATE OUR ENAMORED KNIGHT FROM THE EXTREMELY SEVERE PENANCE HE HAD IMPOSED UPON HIMSELF.[1]

"Such, sirs, is the true story of my sad adventures. Judge for yourselves whether the sighs and lamentations you heard and the tears that flowed from my eyes had not sufficient cause even if I had indulged in them more freely. And if you consider the nature of my misfortune you will see that consolation is idle, as there is no possible remedy for it. All I ask of you is something you may easily and reasonably do, and that is to show me where I may pass my life unharassed by the dread of being discovered by those in search of me. For though the great love my parents have for me makes me feel sure of being welcomed by them, so great is my feeling of shame at the mere thought that I cannot present myself before them as the maiden I was, that I had rather banish myself from their sight for ever than look them in the face, knowing that they see my face stripped of the purity they had a right to expect in me."

With these words she became silent, and the color that overspread her face showed plainly the pain and shame that filled her heart. In their hearts the listeners felt as much pity as wonder at her misfortunes, and the priest was just about to offer her some consolation and advice when Cardenio forestalled him. "So then, señora," he said, "you are the fair Dorotea, the only daughter of the rich Clenardo?" Dorotea was astonished at hearing her father's name, and at the miserable appearance of the man who mentioned it, for it has already been related how wretchedly clad Cardenio was.

"And who may you be, my friend," she rejoined, "who seem to know my father's name so well? For so far, if I remember rightly, I have not mentioned it in the whole story of my misfortunes."

"I am that unhappy being, señora," replied Cardenio, "whom Luscinda, as you have said, declared to be her husband. I am the unfortunate Cardenio, whom the wrong-doing of the person who brought you to your present condition has reduced to the state you see me in, bare, ragged, deprived of all human comfort, and what is worse, of reason. That I possess only when it pleases Heaven for some short space to retore it to me. I, Dorotea, am he who witnessed the wrong done by Don Fernando and waited to hear the 'I do' by which Luscinda proclaimed herself to be his betrothed. I am he who had not courage enough to see how her fainting fit ended or what came of the paper that was found in her bosom, because my heart had not the fortitude to endure so many strokes of ill-for-

1. The headings of Chapters xxix and xxx are reversed in the first edition.

tune at once. So, unable to bear it, I went from the house, leaving a letter with my host, which I entreated him to place in Luscinda's hands. I came to these wilds with the resolve to end the life I hated as if it were my mortal enemy. But fate would not rid me of it, contenting itself with robbing me of my reason, perhaps to preserve me for the good fortune I have had in meeting you. For if what you have just told us is true, as I believe it to be, Heaven may yet have in store for both of us a happier outcome to our misfortunes than we anticipate. Seeing that Luscinda cannot marry Don Fernando, since she is mine, as she herself has so openly declared, and since Don Fernando cannot marry her as he is yours, we may reasonably hope that Heaven will restore to us what is ours, as it is still in existence and as yet neither alienated nor destroyed. And as this consolation springs from hope which is neither remote nor based on wild fancy, I entreat you, señora, to form new and worthier resolutions in your mind, as I mean to do in mine, and prepare yourself to look forward to happier fortunes. For I swear to you by the faith of a gentleman and a Christian not to desert you until I see you in possession of Don Fernando. If my words cannot induce him to recognize his obligation to you, I will avail myself of the right which my rank as a gentleman gives me and with just cause challenge him on account of the injury he has done you—not with respect to my own wrongs, which I shall leave to Heaven to avenge, while I on earth devote myself to yours."

Dorotea, utterly amazed by Cardenio's words, and not knowing how to return thanks for such an offer, attempted to kiss his feet. But Cardenio would not permit it, and the priest spoke for both of them. He commended Cardenio's sound reasoning and lastly begged, advised, and urged them to come with him to his village, where they might furnish themselves with what they needed and undertake to discover Don Fernando or restore Dorotea to her parents or do what seemed to them most advisable. Cardenio and Dorotea thanked him and accepted his kind offer. The barber, who had been listening to all attentively and in silence, said some kindly words also, and with no less goodwill than the priest offered his services in any way that might be of use. He also explained to them in a few words what had brought them there and the strange nature of Don Quixote's madness and how they were waiting for his squire, who had gone in search of him. Like the recollection of a dream, the quarrel he had had with Don Quixote came back to Cardenio's memory, and he described it to the others. But he was unable to say what the dispute was about.

At this moment they heard a shout and recognized it as coming from Sancho Panza. Not finding them where he had left them, he was calling aloud to them. They went to meet him, and in answer to their inquiries about Don Quixote, he told them how he had found him stripped to his shirt, lank, yellow, half dead with hunger, and sighing for his lady Dulcinea. Although told that she commanded him to leave that place and come to El Toboso, where she was expecting him, Don Quixote had answered that he was determined not to appear in the presence of her beauty until he had done deeds to make him worthy of her favor. If this went on, Sancho said, his master ran the risk of not becoming an emperor as in duty bound, or even an archbishop, which was the least he could be, and for this reason they ought to consider how to get him away from there. In reply the priest said that there was no reason for alarm, for they would fetch him away in spite of himself. He then told Cardenio and Dorotea of how they proposed to cure Don Quixote, or at any rate to take him home. Hearing this, Dorotea said that she could play the distressed damsel better than the barber, especially as she had with her the dress in which to do it to perfection. They might trust her so to act the part that it would fit in perfectly with their plan. She had read a great many books of chivalry and knew exactly the style in which afflicted damsels begged boons of knights-errant.

"In that case," said the priest, "all we need do is to set about it at once, for beyond a doubt fortune is declaring itself in my favor. It has unexpectedly opened up the prospect of relief for you, while easing our own path to what we need."

Dorotea then took out of her pillow case a dress of thin woolen material and a green mantilla of some other fine material and a necklace and other ornaments out of a little box. With these she arrayed herself in an instant so that she looked like a great lady. All this and more, she said, she had taken from home in case of need, but had had no occasion to make use of it until that moment. They were all highly delighted with her grace, air, and beauty, and declared that Don Fernando must be a man of poor taste to reject such charms. But the one who admired her most was Sancho Panza, for it seemed to him, and indeed it was true, that in all his life he had never seen such a lovely creature. He asked the priest with great eagerness who this beautiful lady was and what she was doing in so isolated a spot.

"This fair lady, brother Sancho," replied the priest, "is no less a personage than the heiress in the direct male line of the great kingdom of Micomicón. She has come to beg a boon of your master, for she would have him redress a wrong or injury that a wicked giant has done her. Because of the fame your master has acquired far and wide as a good knight, this princess has come from Guinea to seek him."

"A lucky search and a lucky find!" said Sancho Panza. "Especially if my master has the good fortune to redress that injury and right that wrong and kill that son of a bitch of a giant your worship speaks of. And kill him he will if he meets him, unless he happens to be a ghost, for my master has no power at all against ghosts. But one thing among others I would beg of you, señor licentiate, is to prevent my master from taking a notion to be an archbishop, for that is what I'm afraid of. Your worship could recommend him to marry this princess at once, for in this way he will be disqualified from taking archbishop's orders. He will easily come into his empire, and I'll get what I want. I have been thinking over the matter carefully, and by what I can find out it will not do for my master to become an archbishop, because I am no good for the Church, since I am married. And for me, having wife and children, to set about obtaining dispensations so that I could obtain income from the Church would be endless work. So, señor, it all turns on my master's marrying this lady—I do not know what she's called, so I can't call her by her name."

"She is called the Princess Micomicona," said the priest, "for as her kingdom is Micomicón, it is clear that must be her name."[2]

"There's no doubt of that," replied Sancho, "for I have known many to take their name and title from the place where they were born and call themselves Pedro of Alcalá, Juan of Úbeda, and Diego of Valladolid. It may be that over there in Guinea queens have the same way of taking the names of their kingdoms."

"So it may," said the priest. "And as for your master's marrying, I will do all in my power to bring it about."

Sancho was as much pleased at this as the priest was amazed at his simplicity and at seeing what a hold on his imagination the absurdities of his master had taken, for he had evidently persuaded himself that Don Quixote was going to be an emperor.

By this time Dorotea had seated herself on the priest's mule and the barber had fitted the oxtail beard to his face. They now told Sancho to lead them to where Don Quixote was, warning him not to say that he knew either the priest or the barber, since whether or not his master became an emperor entirely depended on his not recognizing them. Neither the priest nor Cardenio, however, saw fit to go with them. Cardenio did not want to remind Don Quixote of the quarrel he had with him, and there was no necessity for the priest's presence just yet. So they allowed the others to go on before them, while they themselves followed slowly on foot. The priest did not forget to tell Dorotea how to behave, but she said they might make their minds easy, as everything would be done exactly as the books of chivalry required and described.

They had gone about three-quarters of a league when they discovered Don Quixote in a rocky waste, clothed by this time, but without his armor. As soon as Dorotea saw him and was assured by

2. Micomicón, a silly name invented by Cervantes, suggests the words *mico*, "monkey," and *cómico*, "comical."

Sancho that that was Don Quixote, she whipped her "palfrey," and the well-bearded barber followed her. On reaching him, her squire sprang from his mule and came forward to receive her in his arms. She, dismounting with great ease of manner, advanced to kneel before the feet of Don Quixote, and though he strove to raise her up, she addressed him while still kneeling.

"From this spot I will not rise, O valiant and courageous knight," she said, "until your goodness and courtesy grant me a boon which will redound to the honor and renown of your person and render a service to the most disconsolate and afflicted damsel the sun has ever seen. If the might of your strong arm corresponds to the repute of your immortal fame, ye are bound to aid the helpless being who, led by the fragrance of your renowned name, has come from far distant lands to seek your aid in her misfortunes."

"I will not answer a word, beauteous lady," replied Don Quixote, "nor will I listen to anything further concerning you until ye rise from the earth."

"I will not rise, señor," answered the afflicted damsel, "unless of your courtesy the boon I ask is first granted me."

"I grant and accord it," said Don Quixote, "provided without detriment or harm to my king, my country, or her who holds the key of my heart and freedom, it may be complied with."

"It will not be to the detriment or harm of any of them, my worthy lord," said the afflicted damsel.

Here Sancho Panza drew close to his master's ear and spoke to him very softly. "Your worship may very safely grant the boon she asks," he said, "it's nothing at all: only to kill a big giant. And she who asks it is the exalted Princess Micomicona, queen of the great kingdom of Micomicón of Ethiopia."

"Let her be who she may," replied Don Quixote, "I will do what is my bounden duty, and what my conscience bids me, in conformity with what I have professed," and he turned to the damsel, "Let your great beauty rise," he said, "for I grant the boon which ye would ask of me."

"Then what I ask," said the damsel, "is that your magnanimous person accompany me at once whither I will conduct you, and that ye promise not to engage in any other adventure or quest until ye have avenged me of a traitor who, against all human and divine law, has usurped my kingdom."

"I repeat that I grant it," replied Don Quixote. "And so, lady, ye may from this day forth lay aside the melancholy that distresses you and let your failing hopes gather new life and strength, for with the help of God and of my arm ye will soon see yourself restored to your kingdom, and seated upon the throne of your ancient and mighty realm, notwithstanding and despite of the felons who would gainsay it. And now to work, for in delay there is apt to be danger."

The distressed damsel strove with much insistence to kiss his hands, but Don Quixote, who was in all things a polished and courteous knight, would by no means allow it. He made her rise and embraced her with great courtesy and politeness, and he ordered Sancho to arm him without a moment's delay and to look to Rocinante's girths. Sancho took down the armor, which was hanging on a tree like a trophy, and having seen to the girths he armed his master in a trice.

"Let us be gone in the name of God," exclaimed Don Quixote, as soon as he found himself armed, "to bring aid to this great lady."

The barber was all this time on his knees and at great pains to hide his laughter and not let his beard fall, for had it fallen maybe their fine scheme would have come to nothing. But now that the boon was granted and Don Quixote had so promptly prepared to set out in compliance with it, he rose and took his lady's hand, and between them they placed her upon the mule. Don Quixote then mounted Rocinante, and the barber settled himself on his beast, Sancho being left to go on foot, which made him feel anew the loss of his Dapple, since now he needed him. But he bore all with cheerfulness, being persuaded that his master had now fairly started and was just on the point of becoming an emperor. He felt no doubt at all that he would marry this princess and be king of Micomicón at least. The only thing that troubled him was the reflection that this kingdom was in the land of the blacks, and that the people they would give him for vassals would be all black. But for this he soon found a remedy in his fancy.

"What is it to me," he said to himself, "if my vassals are blacks? All I have to do is make a cargo of them and take them to Spain, where I can sell them and get ready money for them and with it buy some title or some office in which to live in comfort the rest of my life. Unless you go to sleep and haven't the brains or skill to arrange matters, you could sell three, six, or ten thousand vassals while you're talking about it! By God I'll catch 'em, big and little, or as best I can, and no matter how black, I'll turn them into silver and gold. Let 'em think I'm dumb!" And so he jogged on, so occupied with his thoughts and easy in his mind that he forgot all about the hardship of traveling on foot.

Cardenio and the priest were watching all this from behind some bushes, not knowing how to join the others. But the priest, who was very clever, soon hit upon a solution, and with a pair of scissors, which he carried in a case, he quickly cut off Cardenio's beard. Putting on him a sleeveless grey jacket of his own, he gave him a black cape, leaving himself in his breeches and vest, while Cardenio's appearance was so changed that he would not have recognized himself in a mirror. Having done this, though the others had gone on ahead while they were disguising themselves, they easily came out on the high road before them, for the brambles and awkward places they encountered did not allow those on horseback to go as fast as those on foot. They then posted themselves on the level ground at the outlet of the Sierra, and as soon as Don Quixote and his companions emerged from it, the priest began to examine him very deliberately, as though he were trying to recognize him. After having stared at him for some time, he hastened towards him with open arms. "A happy meeting," he exclaimed, "with the mirror of chivalry, my worthy compatriot Don Quixote of La Mancha, the flower and cream of nobility, the protection and relief of the distressed, the quintessence of knights-errant!" So saying he clasped in his arms the knee of Don Quixote's left leg. The latter, astonished at the stranger's words and behavior, looked at him attentively and finally recognized him. He was very much surprised to see him there and made great efforts to dismount. This, however, the priest would not allow.

"Permit me, señor licentiate," Don Quixote said to the priest, "for it is not fitting that I should be on horseback and so reverend a person as your worship on foot."

"On no account will I allow it," said the priest. "Your mightiness must remain on horseback for it is on horseback you achieve the greatest deeds and adventures that have been beheld in our age. As for me, an unworthy priest, it will serve me well enough to mount on the haunches of a mule with these gentlefolk who accompany your worship, if they have no objection. I will fancy I am mounted on the steed Pegasus, or on the zebra or charger that bore the famous Moor, Muzaraque, who to this day lies enchanted in the great hill of Zulema, a little distance from great Complutum."[3]

"Not even that will I consent to, señor licentiate," answered Don Quixote, "and I know it will be the good pleasure of my lady the princess, out of love for me, to order her squire to give up the saddle of his mule to your worship, and he can sit behind if the beast will bear it.'"

"It will, I am sure," said the princess, "and I am sure, too, that I need not order my squire, for he is too courteous and considerate to allow a Churchman to go on foot when he might be mounted."

"That he is," said the barber. He dismounted at once and offered his saddle to the priest, who accepted it without much entreaty. But unfortunately, as the barber was mounting behind, the mule, being as it happened a hired one, which is the same thing as saying

3. Complutum is the Latin name of Alcalá de Henares, not far from Madrid and Cervantes' birthplace.

mean, lifted its hind hoofs and let fly a couple of kicks in the air. They would have made Master Nicolás curse his expedition in quest of Don Quixote had they caught him on the chest or head. As it was, they so took him by surprise that he fell to the ground, paying so little heed to his beard that it fell off. All he could do when he found himself without it was to cover his face hastily with both his hands and moan that his teeth were knocked out.

"By the living God," exclaimed Don Quixote, when he saw all that bundle of beard detached, without jaws or blood, far from the face of the fallen squire. "This is a great miracle! It has knocked off the beard and pulled it off his face as if it had been shaved off deliberately."

The priest, seeing the danger of discovery that threatened his scheme, at once pounced upon the beard and hastened with it to where Master Nicolás lay, still uttering moans. Drawing the barber's head to his breast he attached the beard in an instant, muttering over him some words which he said were a certain special charm for sticking on beards, as they would see. As soon as he had it fixed, he left him, and the squire appeared well bearded and whole as before. At this Don Quixote was utterly astonished and begged the priest to teach him the charm when he had an opportunity. He was convinced that its power must extend beyond the sticking on of beards, for it was clear that where the beard had been stripped off, the flesh must have been torn and lacerated, and if it could heal all that, it must be good for more than beards.

"And so it is," said the priest, and he promised to teach it to him at the first opportunity.

They then agreed that for the present the priest should mount and that the three should ride by turns until they reached the inn, which might be about two leagues from where they were. Thus three of them were mounted, that is to say, Don Quixote, the princess, and the priest, and three were on foot, Cardenio, the barber, and Sancho Panza.

"Let your highness, lady," Don Quixote said to the damsel, "lead on whithersoever is most pleasing to you." But before she could answer the priest spoke.

"Toward what kingdom," he asked, "would your ladyship direct our course? Is it perchance towards that of Micomicón? It must be or else I know little about kingdoms."

She, being quick-witted, understood that she was to answer "Yes."

"Yes, señor," she said, "my way lies towards that kingdom."

"In that case," said the priest, "we must pass right through my village, and there your worship will take the road to Cartagena, where you will be able to embark, fortune favoring. If the wind is fair and the sea smooth and tranquil, in somewhat less than nine years you may come in sight of the great lake Meona, I mean Meotides,[4] which is little more than a hundred days' journey this side of your highness's kingdom."

"Your worship is mistaken, señor," said she, "for it is not two years since I set out from it, and though I never in fact had good weather, nevertheless I am here to behold what I so longed for. That is my lord Don Quixote of La Mancha, whose fame came to my ears as soon as I set foot in Spain. I was impelled to go in search of him, to commend myself to his courtesy and entrust the justice of my cause to the might of his invincible arm."

"Enough; no more praise," said Don Quixote at this, "for I hate all flattery. And though this may not be flattery, still such language is offensive to my chaste ears. I will only say, señora, that whether my arm has might or not, whatever it may or may not have shall be devoted to your service even to death. And now, leaving this to its proper season, I would ask the priest to tell me what it is that has brought him into these parts, alone, unattended, and so lightly clad that I am filled with amazement."

"I will answer that briefly," replied the priest, "by telling you, Señor Don Quixote, that Master Nicolás, our friend and barber, and I were going to Seville to receive some money that a relative of mine who went to the Indies many years ago had sent me. It was not such a small sum, but over sixty thousand pieces-of-eight, full weight, which is something. Passing by this place yesterday, we were attacked by four highway men, who stripped us even to our beards, and them they stripped off so that the barber found it necessary to put on a false one. Even this young man here"—he pointed to Cardenio—"was completely transformed. But the best of it is, the story goes in the neighborhood that those who attacked us belong to a number of galley slaves who, they say, were set free almost on the very same spot by a man of such valor that, in spite of the commissary and of the guards, he released the whole lot of them. Beyond all doubt he must have been out of his senses or be as great a scoundrel as they, or some man without heart or conscience, since he lets the wolf loose among the sheep, the fox among the hens, the fly among the honey. He has defrauded justice and opposed his king and lawful master, for he opposed his just commands. He has, I say, robbed the galleys of their oars, stirred up the Holy Brotherhood, which for many years past has been quiet, and, lastly, has done a deed by which his soul may be lost without any gain to his body."

Sancho had told the priest and the barber of the adventure of the galley slaves which, so much to his glory, his master had achieved. Hence the priest in his allusions made the most of it, to see what would be said or done by Don Quixote, who changed color at every

4. *Meona* means roughly "bed-wetter." *Meotides* refers, presumably, to the Palus Maeotis, now called the Sea of Azov.

word, not daring to say that it was he who had liberated those worthy people.

"These, then," said the priest, "were they who robbed us, and God in his mercy pardon him who would not let them go to the punishment they deserved."

Chapter XXX

WHICH TREATS OF THE SAGACITY OF THE FAIR DOROTEA, WITH OTHER MATTERS PLEASANT AND AMUSING

"By my faith, señor licentiate," said Sancho, the moment the priest had ceased speaking, "it was my master who did the deed. And it wasn't as if I didn't tell him beforehand and warn him to watch out, and that it was a sin to set them free, as they were all on the march there because they were special scoundrels."

"Blockhead!" said Don Quixote at this, "it is no business or concern of knights-errant to inquire whether any person in affliction, in chains, or oppressed that they may meet on the high roads go that way and suffer as they do because of their faults or because of their misfortunes. It only concerns knights-errant to aid persons in need of help, having regard to their sufferings and not to their misdeeds. I encountered a chaplet or string of miserable and unfortunate people and did for them what my knightly order demands of me. As for the rest, be that as it may. Whoever takes objection to it, saving the sacred dignity of our friend the priest and his honored person, I say he knows little about chivalry and lies like the low-born son of a bitch he is, and this I will give him to know to the fullest extent with my sword."

So saying he settled himself in his stirrups and pressed down his helmet, for the barber's basin, which according to him was Mambrino's helmet, he carried hanging at the saddle-bow until he could repair the damage the galley slaves had done it.

Dorotea, who was shrewd and witty, by this time thoroughly understood Don Quixote's crazy disposition, and she realized that all except Sancho Panza were making fun of him. Having observed his irritation and not wanting to be outdone, she spoke. "Sir Knight," she said, "remember the boon you have promised me, and that you must not engage in any other adventure, be it ever so pressing. Calm yourself, for if the priest had known that the galley slaves had been set free by that unconquered arm, he would have taken three stitches in his mouth or even bitten his tongue three times before saying a word indicative of the least disrespect."

"That I swear heartily," said the priest, "and I would have even shaved off half my moustache."

"I will hold my peace, señora," said Don Quixote, "and I will curb the natural anger that had arisen in my breast. Until I have fulfilled my promise, I will proceed in peace and quietness. But in return for this resolve I entreat you to tell me, if you have no objection, what is the nature of your trouble. How many, who, and what are the persons of whom I am to require due satisfaction, and on whom I am to take vengeance on your behalf?"

"That I will do with all my heart," replied Dorotea, "if it will not be wearisome to you to hear of miseries and misfortunes."

"It will not be wearisome, señora," said Don Quixote.

"Well, if that is so," Dorotea answered, "give me your attention." As soon as she said this, Cardenio and the barber drew close, eager to hear what sort of story the quick-witted Dorotea would invent. And Sancho did the same, for he was as much taken in by her as his master. She settled herself comfortably in the saddle, and with the help of coughing and other preliminaries, allowed herself time to think. Then she began her tale with great sprightliness of manner.

"First of all, I would have you know, sirs, that my name is—"

Here she stopped for a moment, for she forgot the name the priest had given her. But he saw what her difficulty was and came to her relief. "It is no wonder, señora," he said, "that your highness should be confused and embarrassed in telling the tale of your misfortunes. Such afflictions often have the effect of depriving the sufferers of memory, so that they do not even remember their own names. This is the case now with your ladyship, who has forgotten that she is called the Princess Micomicona, lawful heiress of the great kingdom of Micomicón. With this cue your highness may now sorrowfully bring to mind whatever you may wish to tell us."

"That is the truth," said the damsel, "but I think from now on I shall have no need of any prompting. I shall bring my true story safe into port, and here it is. The king my father, who was called Tinacrio the Sage, was very learned in what they call magic arts. He became aware by his craft that my mother, who was called Queen Jaramilla, was to die before he did and that soon after he too was to depart this life, and I was to be left an orphan without father or mother. But all this, he declared, did not so much grieve or distress him as his certain knowledge concerning a prodigious giant, the lord of a great island close to our kingdom, Pandafilando of the Lowering Look by name; for it is averred that, though his eyes are properly placed and straight, he always squints out of the corner of his eye as if he were cross-eyed, and this he does out of wickedness to strike fear and terror into those he looks at. My father knew, I say, that this giant on becoming aware of my orphan condition would overrun my kingdom with a mighty force and strip me of all, not leaving me even a small village to shelter me. I could avoid all this ruin and misfortune if I were willing to marry the giant. However, as far as he could see, he never expected that I would agree to a marriage so unequal. He said no more than the truth, for it has never entered my mind to marry him, or any other giant, however great or enormous. My father said, too, that when he was dead, and I saw Pandafilando about to invade my kingdom, I was not to wait and attempt to defend myself, for that would be destructive to me. I should leave the kingdom entirely open to him if I wished to avoid the death and total destruction of my good and loyal vassals, for there would be no possibility of defending myself against the giant's devilish power. And I should, with some of my followers, set out at once for Spain, where I should obtain relief in my distress when I found a certain knight-errant whose fame by that time would extend over the whole kingdom, and who would be called, if I remember rightly, Don Azote or Don Gigote."[1]

" 'Don Quixote,' he must have said, señora," observed Sancho at this, "otherwise called the Knight of the Mournful Countenance."

"That is it," said Dorotea. "He said, moreover, that he would be tall of stature and lank featured, and that on his right side under the left shoulder, or thereabouts, he would have a grey mole with hairs like bristles."

"Here, Sancho my son," said Don Quixote, on hearing this, "lend a hand and help me strip, for I want to see if I am the knight whom that sage king foretold."

"What does your worship want to strip for?" said Dorotea.

"To see if I have the mole your father spoke of," answered Don Quixote.

"There is no occasion to strip," said Sancho, "for I know your worship has just such a mole in the middle of your backbone, which is the mark of a strong man."

"That is enough," said Dorotea, "for with friends we must not look too closely into trifles. Whether it be on the shoulder or on the backbone matters little; it is enough if there is a mole, be it where it may, for it is all the same flesh. No doubt my good father hit the truth in every particular, and I have made a wise decision in commending myself to Don Quixote. He it is my father spoke of, as the features of his countenance match those assigned to this knight by the wide fame he has acquired not only in Spain but in all La Mancha. I had scarcely landed at Osuna when I heard such accounts of his achievements that at once my heart told me he was the very one I had come in search of."

"But how did you land at Osuna, señora," asked Don Quixote, "when it is not a seaport?"

Before Dorotea could reply the priest anticipated her. "The

1. ***Azote:*** **whip;** ***gigote:*** **a stew of chopped meat.**

princess meant to say," he declared, "that after she had landed at Málaga the first place where she heard of your worship was Osuna."

"That is what I meant to say," said Dorotea.

"And that would be only natural," said the priest. "Will your majesty please proceed?"

"There is no more to add," said Dorotea, "except that in finding Don Quixote I have had such good fortune that I already regard myself as queen and mistress of my entire dominion. For out of courtesy and magnanimity he has granted me the boon of accompanying me wherever I may lead him. This will be only to bring him face to face with Pandafilando of the Lowering Look, so that he may slay him and restore to me what has been unjustly usurped. All this must come to pass satisfactorily since my good father Tinacrio the Sage foretold it. He likewise left it declared in writing in Chaldean or Greek characters (for I cannot read them) that if this predicted knight, after having cut the giant's throat, should be disposed to marry me, I was to offer myself at once without demur as his lawful wife and yield him possession of my kingdom together with my person."

"What do you think now, friend Sancho?" said Don Quixote at this. "Do you hear that? Did I not tell you so? See how we have already got a kingdom to govern and a queen to marry!"

"I'll swear to that!" said Sancho. "And to hell with the bastard who won't marry after slitting Señor Pandahilado's[2] windpipe! The queen's not bad, either! I wish the fleas in my bed were like that!"

So saying he cut a couple of capers in the air with every sign of extreme satisfaction and then ran to seize the bridle of Dorotea's mule. Bringing it to a halt, he fell on his knees and begged her to give him her hand to kiss, in token of his acknowledging her as his queen and mistress. Which of the bystanders could have helped laughing to see the madness of the master and the simple-mindedness of the servant? Dorotea gave her hand and promised to make him a great lord in her kingdom, when Heaven should be so good as to permit her to recover and enjoy it. For this Sancho returned thanks, and his words set them all laughing again.

"This, sirs," continued Dorotea, "is my story. It only remains to tell you that of all the attendants I took with me from my kingdom I have none left except this well-bearded squire, for all were drowned in a great tempest we encountered when in sight of port. He and I came to land on a couple of planks as if by a miracle; and indeed the whole course of my life is a miracle and a mystery, as you may have observed. If I have been overly minute in any respect or not as precise as I ought, let it be attributed to what the

2. *Pandafilando*, the absurd name invented by Dorotea, suggests "spinning thread," *filando*. Sancho changes it to "spun," *hilado*, to show his contempt for the evil giant.

licentiate said at the beginning of my tale, that constant and excessive troubles deprive the sufferer of their memory."

"They shall not deprive me of mine, exalted and worthy princess," said Don Quixote, "however great and unexampled those which I shall endure in thy service may be. Here I confirm anew the boon I have promised thee and swear to go with thee to the end of the world, until I find myself in the presence of thy fierce enemy whose haughty head I trust, by the aid of my arm, to cut off with the edge of this—I will not say good sword, thanks to Ginés de Pasamonte, who carried away mine" (this he said under his breath, and then continued). "And when it has been cut off and thou hast been put in peaceful possession of thy realm, it shall be left to thine own decision to dispose of thy person as may be most pleasing to thee. For so long as my memory is occupied, my will enslaved, and my understanding enthralled by her—I say no more —it is impossible for me for a moment to contemplate marriage, even with a Phœnix."

The last words of his master about not wanting to marry were so disagreeable to Sancho that he raised his voice and spoke with great irritation.

"By my oath, Señor Don Quixote," he exclaimed, "you are not in your right senses. How can your worship possibly hesitate in marrying such an exalted princess? Do you think Fortune will offer you such a piece of luck as is offered you now around every corner? Is my lady Dulcinea prettier, perhaps? Certainly not, not half as pretty. I will even go so far as to say she does not come up to the shoe of this one here. A poor chance I've got of becoming a count if your worship is always going to have your head in the clouds. In the devil's name marry, marry, take this kingdom that has been dropped in your lap, and when you are king, make me a marquis or governor of a province, and devil take the rest."

Don Quixote could not bear to hear such blasphemies uttered against his lady Dulcinea. Lifting his pike and without saying anything to Sancho or uttering a word, he gave him two such whacks that he brought him to the ground. Had not Dorotea cried out to him to be merciful, he would have no doubt taken Sancho's life on the spot.

"Do you think," he said to him after a pause, "you vicious peasant, that you can always interfere with me, and that you can always offend and I always pardon? Don't imagine that, impious scoundrel, as beyond a doubt you are, since you have set your tongue wagging against the peerless Dulcinea. Are you not aware, you crude, coarse, vile creature, that, but for the might she infuses into my arm, I should not have strength enough to kill a flea? Say, O scoffer with a viper's tongue, what do you think has won this kingdom and cut off this giant's head and made you a marquis, all of which I consider as already accomplished and decided, but the might of Dulcinea, who uses my arm as the instrument of her achievements? She fights in me and conquers in me, and I live and breathe in her and owe my life and being to her. O scoundrel and son of a whore, how ungrateful you are! You see yourself raised from the dust of the earth to be a titled lord, and the return you make for so great a benefit is to speak evil of her who has conferred it upon you!"

Sancho was not so stunned that he could not hear all his master said. He got up with some degree of nimbleness and ran to place himself behind Dorotea's palfrey. From that position he addressed his master.

"Tell me, señor," he said. "If your worship is resolved not to marry this great princess, it is plain the kingdom will not be yours. And if it is not, can you bestow favors on me? That is what I'm complaining about. Let your worship at any rate marry this queen, now that we've got her here as if rained from heaven. Afterwards you can go back to my lady Dulcinea—there must have been kings in the world who kept mistresses. As to beauty, that's not my concern. And if the truth is to be told, I like them both, though I have never seen the lady Dulcinea."

"What, never seen her, blasphemous traitor!" exclaimed Don Quixote. "Have you not just now brought me a message from her?"

"I mean," said Sancho, "that I did not see her with enough time so that I could take particular notice of her beauty or of her charms point by point. But on the whole, I like her."

"Now I forgive you," said Don Quixote. "And you forgive me the injury I have done you, for our first impulses are not in our control."

"That I see," replied Sancho, "and with me the wish to speak is always the first impulse, and I can't help saying, once at least, what I have on the tip of my tongue."

"For all that, Sancho," said Don Quixote, "watch what you say, for the 'pitcher that goes so often to the well'[3]—I need say no more."

"Well," said Sancho, "God is in heaven and sees all tricks, and He will judge who does most harm, I in not speaking right, or your worship in not doing it."

"That is enough," said Dorotea. "Run, Sancho, kiss your lord's hand and beg his pardon, and henceforward be more circumspect with your praise and abuse. Say nothing in disparagement of that lady Tobosa, of whom I know nothing except that I am her servant. And put your trust in God, for you will assuredly obtain some dignity enabling you to live like a prince."

Sancho advanced hanging his head and begged his master's hand.

3. ". . . leaves its handle or its spout behind"; i.e., sooner or later you get into serious trouble.

Don Quixote presented it to him with dignity, giving him his blessing as soon as he had kissed it. Then he ordered him to go on ahead a little, as he had questions to ask him and matters of great importance to discuss. Sancho obeyed, and when the two had gone some distance in advance, Don Quixote spoke.

"Since your return," he said, "I have had no opportunity or time to ask you for many details concerning your mission and the answer you brought back. Now that chance has granted us the time and opportunity, do not deny me the happiness you can give me with such good news."

"Let your worship ask what you will," answered Sancho, "for I shall find a way out of all as easily as I found a way in. But I implore you, señor, not to be so vengeful in future."

"Why do you say that, Sancho?" said Don Quixote.

"I say it," he returned, "because those blows just now were more because of the quarrel the devil stirred up between us both the other night than for what I said against my lady Dulcinea, whom I love and reverence as I would a relic—though there is nothing of that about her—because she is something belonging to your worship."

'Say no more on that subject if you value your life, Sancho," said Don Quixote, "for it is displeasing to me. I have already pardoned you for that, and you know the common saying, 'for a fresh sin a fresh penance.' "[4]

While the two had been going along conversing in this fashion, the priest told Dorotea that she had shown great cleverness in the story itself, in her concision, and in the resemblance it bore to those of the books of chivalry. She said that she had many times amused herself reading them but that she did not know the situation of the provinces or seaports, and so she had said at random that she had landed at Osuna.

4. In the second edition of Juan de la Cuesta, the recovery of Sancho's mount is inserted at this point:

While this was going on they saw coming along the road a man mounted on an ass. At close quarters, he seemed to be a gipsy, but Sancho Panza, whose eyes and heart were there wherever he saw asses, no sooner beheld the man than he recognized him as Ginés de Pasamonte; and with this clue, he deduced that the mount was his ass. For it was, in fact, Dapple that carried Pasamonte, who to escape recognition and to sell the ass had disguised himself as a gipsy, being able to speak the gipsy language, and many more as well as if they were his own. Sancho saw him and recognized him, and the instant he did so he shouted to him, "Ginesillo, you thief, give up my treasure, release my sweetheart, don't try to hide with my consolation, give up my donkey, leave my delight! Get out of here, you bastard, you thief, and give up what is not yours."

There was no necessity for so many words or insults, for at the first one Ginés jumped down, and at a trot like racing speed made off and got clear of them all. Sancho hastened to his Dapple, and embracing him he said, "How have you been, my happiness, Dapple of my eyes, my friend?" all the while kissing him and caressing him as if he were a human being. The ass held his peace and let himself be kissed and caressed by Sancho without answering a single word. They all came up and congratulated him on having found Dapple, Don Quixote especially, who told him that notwithstanding this, he would not cancel the order for the three ass-colts, for which Sancho thanked him.

"So I noticed," said the priest, "and for that reason I hastened to say what I did, which put all to rights. But is it not strange to see how readily this unhappy gentleman believes all these figments and lies, simply because they are in the style and manner of the absurdities of his books?"

"So it is," said Cardenio, "and so uncommon and without example, that were one to attempt to invent and concoct it in fiction, I doubt if any mind could be keen enough to imagine it."

"But another strange thing about it," said the priest, "is that, apart from the silly things this worthy gentleman says in connection with his madness, when other subjects are dealt with, he can discuss them in a perfectly rational manner, showing that his mind is quite clear and composed. So that, provided his chivalry is not touched on, no one would take him to be anything but a man of thoroughly sound understanding."

While they were holding this conversation, Don Quixote continued his with Sancho.

"Friend Panza," he said, "where our quarrels are concerned let us forgive and forget. Tell me now, setting aside anger and irritation, where, how, and when you found Dulcinea? What was she doing? What did you say to her? What did she answer? How did she look when she was reading my letter? Who copied it out for you? Tell me everything that seems worth knowing, asking, and learning, neither adding nor falsifying to give me pleasure, nor cutting short, lest you should deprive me of it."

"Señor," replied Sancho, "if the truth be told, nobody copied out the letter for me, for I carried no letter at all."

"It is as you say," said Don Quixote, "for I found the notebook in which I wrote it in my own possession two days after your departure. This caused me very great vexation, as I did not know what you would do on finding yourself without any letter. I was convinced you would return from the place where you first missed it."

"So I should have done," said Sancho, "if I had not memorized it when your worship read it to me. I repeated it to a sacristan, who copied it out for me from hearing it, so exactly that he said in all the days of his life, though he had read many a letter of excommunication, he had never seen or read so pretty a letter as that."

"And have you got it still in your memory, Sancho?" said Don Quixote.

"No, señor," replied Sancho, "for as soon as I had repeated it, seeing there was no further use for it, I set about forgetting it. If I recollect any of it, it is that about 'Stubborn,' I mean to say 'Sovereign Lady,' and the end 'Yours till death, the Knight of the Mournful Countenance'; and between these two, I put into it more than three hundred 'my souls' and 'my life's' and 'my eyes.' "

Chapter XXXI

OF THE DELECTABLE DISCUSSION BETWEEN DON QUIXOTE AND SANCHO PANZA, HIS SQUIRE, TOGETHER WITH OTHER INCIDENTS

"None of that is displeasing to me," said Don Quixote. "So continue. You arrived. And what was that queen of beauty doing? Surely you found her stringing pearls or embroidering some heraldic device in gold thread for me, her enslaved knight."

"I did not," said Sancho, "but I found her winnowing two bushels of wheat in the yard of her house."

"Then depend upon it," said Don Quixote, "the grains of that wheat were pearls when touched by her hands. And did you notice, my friend, whether it was white wheat or brown?"

"It was neither, but red," said Sancho.

"Then I promise you," said Don Quixote, "that, winnowed by her hands, beyond a doubt it made the whitest of bread. But go on. When you gave her my letter, did she kiss it? Did she place it on her head?[1] Did she perform any ceremony befitting it, or what did she do?"

"When I went to give it to her," replied Sancho, "she was hard at it swaying from side to side with a lot of wheat she had in the sieve, and she said to me, 'Lay the letter on the top of that sack, friend; I can't read it until I've finished sifting all this."

"Discreet lady!" said Don Quixote. "That was in order to read it at her leisure and enjoy it. Proceed, Sancho. While she was busily engaged, what discourse did she hold with you? What did she ask about me, and what answer did you give? Make haste and tell me all, and don't leave out a single syllable."

"She didn't ask me anything," said Sancho. "But I told her how your worship was doing penance in her service, naked from the waist up, out in these mountains like a savage, sleeping on the ground, not eating bread off a tablecloth or combing your beard, weeping and cursing your fortune."

"In saying I cursed my fortune, you said wrong," said Don Quixote. "I bless it and shall bless it all the days of my life, for it has made me worthy of aspiring to love so lofty a lady as Dulcinea del Toboso."

"And so lofty she is," said Sancho, "that she is six inches taller than I am."

"What! Sancho," said Don Quixote, "did you measure with her?"

"I measured in this way," said Sancho. "When I helped her to

1. An ancient gesture of respect.

put a sack of wheat on the back of an ass, we came so close that I could see she was taller by more than a hand."

"Well," said Don Quixote, "and does she not accompany and adorn this greatness with a thousand million charms of mind! But one thing you will not deny, Sancho. When you came close to her, did you not perceive a Sabean[2] odor, an aromatic fragrance, a delicious something I cannot find a name for, I mean a redolence, an exhalation, as if you were in the shop of some skilled glovemaker?"[3]

"All I can say is," said Sancho, "that I did notice a little odor, somewhat mannish. She must have been all in a sweat from the hard work, which has toughened her up."

"It could not be that," said Don Quixote. "You must have been suffering from cold in the head or must have smelled yourself. For I know well how she smells—that rose among thorns, that lily of the field, that liquid amber."

"Maybe so," replied Sancho. "I often get from myself the same odor which seemed to come from her grace the lady Dulcinea. But that's no wonder; one devil is just like another."

"Well then," continued Don Quixote, "now she has done sifting the wheat and has sent it to the mill. What did she do when she read the letter?"

"As for the letter," said Sancho, "she didn't read it, because she said she could neither read nor write. Instead, she tore it up into small pieces, saying she did not want to let anyone read it so that her secrets wouldn't become known in the village, and that what I had told her by word of mouth about the love your worship had for her and the extraordinary penance you were doing for her sake was enough. And finally she told me to tell your worship that she kissed your hands and had a greater desire to see you than to write to you. Therefore she entreated and commanded you, on receipt of this message, to come out of those bushes and stop this foolishness and to set out at once for El Toboso, unless something of greater importance should happen, for she had a great desire to see your worship. She laughed a lot when I told her how your worship was called The Knight of the Mournful Countenance. I asked her if that Biscayan you conquered the other day had been there, and she told me he had, and that he was an honest fellow. I asked her too about the galley slaves, but she said she had not seen any as yet."

"So far all goes well," said Don Quixote. "But tell me what jewel did she give you when you took your leave, in return for the tidings you brought of me? For it is a usual and ancient custom with knights and ladies errant to give the squires, damsels, or dwarfs who

2. Sabean: from Saba or Sheba, an area famous for perfume.

3. Fine gloves were made of heavily scented leather.

bring tidings of their ladies to the knights, or of their knights to the ladies, some rich jewel as recompense for good news and acknowledgment of the message."

"That is very likely," said Sancho, "and a good custom it was, to my mind. But that must have been in days gone by, for now it would seem to be the custom only to give a piece of bread and cheese. That was what my lady Dulcinea gave me over the top of the yard-wall when I said good-bye to her; and it was sheep's-milk cheese into the bargain."

"She is generous in the extreme," said Don Quixote, "and if she did not give you a jewel of gold, it must have been because she did not have one on hand. But a gift is welcome whenever it comes. I shall see her, and all shall be made right.

"But do you know what amazes me, Sancho? It seems to me you must have gone and come through the air, for you have taken little more than three days to go to El Toboso and return, though it is more than thirty leagues distant. This inclines me to think that the sage magician who is my friend and watches over my interests (of necessity there has to be one, or else I should not be a bona fide knight-errant), this magician, I say, must have helped you to travel without your knowledge. For some of these sages will pick up a knight-errant sleeping in his bed, and without his knowing now or in what way he wakes up the next day more than a thousand leagues away from the place where he went to sleep. If it were not for this, knights-errant would not be able to give aid to one another in peril, as they do at every turn. For a knight happens to be fighting in the mountains of Armenia with some dragon or fierce serpent or another knight, and he is getting the worst of the battle and is at the point of death. But when he least expects it, there suddenly appears on a cloud or chariot of fire, another knight, a friend of his, who just before had been in England, and who takes his part and delivers him from death. At night he finds himself back in his own quarters eating supper very much to his satisfaction, and yet from one place to the other will have been two or three thousand leagues. And all this is done by the craft and skill of the sage enchanters who take care of those valiant knights. So, friend Sancho, I find no difficulty in believing that you may have gone from here to El Toboso and returned in such a short time. As I have said, some friendly sage must have carried you through the air without your perceiving it."

"That must have been it," said Sancho, "because Rocinante certainly went like a gipsy's donkey with quicksilver in his ears."[4]

"Quicksilver indeed!" said Don Quixote. "And in addition, a legion of devils, who can travel and make others travel without

4. Alluding to a common device of the gipsy dealers to improve the pace of a beast for sale.

being weary, exactly as the whim seizes them. But putting this aside, what do you think I ought to do about my lady's command to go and see her? For though I feel bound to obey her mandate, I feel too that I am debarred by the boon I have accorded the princess who accompanies us, and the law of chivalry compels me to have regard for my word in preference to my inclination. On the one hand the desire to see my lady pursues and harasses me; on the other my solemn promise and the glory I shall win in this enterprise urge and call me. But what I think I shall do is to travel with all speed and quickly reach the place where this giant is, cut off his head on my arrival, and establish the princess peacefully in her realm. Then I shall return forthwith to behold the light that lightens my senses and offer such excuses that she will come to approve of my delay, for she will see that it entirely tends to increase her glory and fame. All that I have won, am winning, or shall win by arms in this life comes to me of the favor she extends to me, and because I am hers."

"Ah! what a sad state your worship's brains are in!" said Sancho. "Tell me, señor, do you mean to travel all that way for nothing and pass up and lose a match as profitable and aristocratic as this, where for a dowry they give a kingdom that in sober truth I have heard say is more than twenty thousand leagues around and abounds with all things necessary to support human life, and is bigger than Portugal and Castile put together? Keep your mouth shut, for the love of God! Blush for what you have said, and take my advice, and forgive me, and marry at once in the first village where there is a priest. If not, here is our own priest who will do the business beautifully. Remember, I am old enough to give advice, and what I say now fits the case perfectly. 'A bird in hand is worth two in the bush,' and 'he who has the good and chooses the bad must not feel upset at the troubles he'll have.' "[5]

"Look here, Sancho," said Don Quixote. "If you are advising me to marry, in order that I may become king as soon as I have killed the giant and be able to confer favors and give you what I have promised, let me tell you this. I shall be able very easily to satisfy your desires without marrying, for before going into battle, I will stipulate that, if I emerge victorious, even if I do not marry, they shall give me a portion of the kingdom. Thus I may bestow it on anyone I choose, and when they give it to me, whom would you have me bestow it upon but you?"

"Of course," said Sancho. "But let your worship take care to choose it on the seacoast, so that if I don't like the life I may be able to ship off my black vassals and deal with them as I have said. Don't bother going to see my lady Dulcinea now, but go and kill this

5. Sancho garbles the proverb so that it sounds silly in Spanish; we have translated the sense of the real proverb but lost the humor.

giant and let us finish off this business. By God, it strikes me it will be one of great honor and profit."

"You have hit the mark, Sancho," said Don Quixote. "I will take your advice and accompany the princess before going to see Dulcinea. But I counsel you not to say anything to anyone, or to those who are with us, about what we have considered and discussed. Since Dulcinea is so decorous that she does not wish her thoughts to be known, it is not right that I, or anyone acting on my behalf, should disclose them."

"Well then, if that is so," said Sancho, "why does your worship make all those you vanquish present themselves before my lady Dulcinea? This amounts to signing your name to it that you love her and are her lover. And as those who go must kneel before her and say they come from your worship to submit themselves, how can the thoughts of both of you be hid?"

"O, how silly and simple you are!" said Don Quixote. "Do you not see, Sancho, that this tends to embellish her renown? You must realize that by our chivalrous standards, it is a high honor for a lady to have many knights-errant in her service. Yet their thoughts never go beyond serving her for her own sake, and they look for no other reward for their great and true devotion than her readiness to accept them as her knights."

"It is with that kind of love," said Sancho, "I have heard preachers say we ought to love our Lord, for himself alone, without being moved by the hope of glory or the fear of punishment. Though for my part, I would rather love and serve him for what he could do."

"The devil take you for a peasant!" said Don Quixote. "What shrewd things you say at times! One would think you had been to school."

"By my faith, I cannot even read."

Master Nicolás here called out to them to wait a while, as the other travelers wanted to halt and drink at a little spring. Don Quixote drew up, much to Sancho's satisfaction, for he, by this time, was weary of telling so many lies and fearful his master might catch him tripping.

Though he knew that Dulcinea was a peasant girl from El Toboso, he had never seen her in all his life. Cardenio had now put on the clothes which Dorotea was wearing when they found her, and though they were not very good, they were far better than those he discarded. They dismounted together by the side of the spring, and with the provisions the priest had bought at the inn they appeased to some extent their keen appetites.

While they were so occupied, a youth chanced to pass by. He stopped to examine the party at the spring and the next moment ran to Don Quixote and clasped him around the legs. "O, señor, do you not know me?" he said and began to weep copiously. "Look at me well. I am that lad Andrés your worship released from the oak tree where I was tied."

Don Quixote recognized him, and taking his hand he turned to those present. "This will show your worships," he said, "how important it is to have knights-errant to redress the wrongs and injuries done by tyrannical and wicked men in this world. Some days ago, as I was passing through a wood, I heard cries and piteous complaints as though from a person in pain and distress. I immediately hastened, impelled by my bounden duty, in the direction from where the plaintive accents seemed to proceed. I found tied to an oak this lad who now stands before you, at which I heartily rejoice, for his testimony will not let me depart from the truth in any particular. He was, I say, tied to an oak, naked from the waist up, and a boor, who I afterwards learned was his master, was flaying him with the reins of his mare. As soon as I saw him, I asked the reason for so cruel a flagellation. The boor replied that he was flogging this child because he was his servant and guilty of carelessness due to dishonesty rather than stupidity. At that the boy said, 'Señor, he flogs me only because I ask for my wages.' In reply his master made some sort of speech in explanation but, though I listened to it, I did not accept it. In short, I compelled the fellow to unbind him and to swear he would take him home and pay him *real* by *real*, and perfumed into the bargain. Is not all this true, Andrés my son? Did you not observe with what authority I commanded him, and with what humility he promised to do all I enjoined, specified, and required of him? Answer without hesitation, and tell these gentlemen what took place, so they may see that it is as great an advantage as I say to have knights-errant abroad."

"All your worship has said is quite true," answered the lad. "But the end of the business turned out just the opposite of what your worship supposes."

"How, the opposite?" said Don Quixote. "Did not the boor pay you then?"

"Not only did he not pay me," replied the lad, "but as soon as your worship had left the wood and we were alone, he tied me up again to the same oak and gave me a fresh flogging, until I looked like Saint Bartholomew. With every stroke he gave me, he followed up with some jest or gibe about having made a fool of your worship, and if it hadn't been for the pain I was suffering, I would have laughed at the things he said. In short, he left me in such a condision that I have been until now in a hospital getting cured of the injuries which that wicked peasant inflicted on me. For all this your worship is to blame, for if you had gone your own way and not come where there was no call for you or meddled in other people's affairs, my master would have been content with giving me one or two dozen lashes and would have then untied me and paid me what he owed. But when your worship insulted him so unreasonably and gave him so many hard words, his anger was aroused. And as he could not revenge himself on you, as soon as he saw you had gone, the storm burst upon me in such a way that I feel as if I will never be a man again."

"The mischief," said Don Quixote, "lay in my going away, for I should not have gone until I had seen you paid. I ought to have known by long experience that there is no peasant who will keep his word if he finds it inconvenient to do so. But you remember, Andrés, that I swore if he did not pay you I would search for him and find him, though he were to hide himself in the whale's belly."

"That is true," said Andrés. "But it was of no use."

"You shall see now whether it is of use or not," said Don Quixote. So saying, he got up hastily and bade Sancho bridle Rocinante, who was browsing while they were eating. Dorotea asked him what he intended to do. He replied that he meant to go in search of this peasant and chastise him for such iniquitous conduct, and see Andrés paid to the last farthing, despite and in the teeth of all the peasants in the world. She replied that he must remember how he had promised not to engage in any enterprise until he had concluded hers. Since he knew this better than anyone, he should restrain his ardor until his return from her kingdom.

"That is true," said Don Quixote, "and Andrés must have patience until my return, as you say, señora. But I once more swear and promise not to stop until I have seen him avenged and paid."

"I have no faith in those oaths," said Andrés. "I would rather have something to help me to get to Seville than all the revenges in the world. If you have anything to eat that I can take with me, give it to me, and God be with your worship and all knights-errant, and may their errands turn out as well for themselves as they have for me."

Sancho took a piece of bread and another of cheese from his store and gave them to the lad. "Here, take this, brother Andrés," he said, "for we have all of us a share in your misfortune."

"Why, what share have you got?"

"This share of bread and cheese I am giving you," answered Sancho. "God knows whether I'll ever need it myself or not, for I would have you know, friend, that we squires to knights-errant have to bear a great deal of hunger and hard luck, and even other things more easily felt than told."

Andrés seized his bread and cheese, and seeing that nobody gave him anything more, bowed his head, and took hold of the road, as the saying is. However, he had a word to say before he left. "For the love of God, sir knight-errant, if you ever meet me again, though you may see them cutting me to pieces, give me no aid, but leave me to my misfortune. It will not be so great that a greater will not come to me by being helped by your worship, on whom and all the knights-errant that have ever been born God send his curse."

Don Quixote was getting up to chastise him, but Andrés took to his heels at such a pace that no one attempted to follow him. Don Quixote was very crestfallen at Andrés' story, and the others had to take great care to restrain their laughter so as not to put him entirely out of humor.

Chapter XXXII

WHICH TREATS OF WHAT BEFELL DON QUIXOTE'S PARTY AT THE INN

When they had finished their good meal, they saddled at once, and the next day, without any adventure worth mentioning, reached the inn that was the object of Sancho Panza's fear and dread. Though he would rather not have entered it, there was no help for it. The innkeeper's wife, the innkeeper, their daughter, and Maritornes, when they saw Don Quixote and Sancho coming, went out to welcome them with signs of hearty satisfaction. Don Quixote responded to this with dignity and gravity and bade them make up a better bed for him than the last time, to which the landlady answered that if he paid better than he did the last time she would give him one fit for a prince. Don Quixote said he would, so they made up a tolerable one for him in the same garret as before. He lay down at once, since he was badly in need of rest and good sense.

No sooner was the door shut on him than the landlady rushed at the barber and seized him by the beard.

"By my faith," she said, "you are not going to make a beard of my tail any longer. You must give it back, for it is a disgrace the way my husband's thing is tossed on the floor—I mean the comb that I used to stick in my good tail."

But for all her tugging the barber would not give it up until the priest told him to let her have it, as there was no further occasion for their stratagem. He might now declare himself and appear in his own character and tell Don Quixote that he had fled to this inn when those thieves the galley slaves robbed him. Should Don Quixote ask for the princess' squire, they could tell him that she had sent the squire on before her to inform the people of her kingdom that she was coming and bringing the deliverer of them all. With that the barber cheerfully restored the tail to the landlady, and at the same time they returned all the accessories they had borrowed to effect Don Quixote's deliverance. All the people in the inn were struck with astonishment at Dorotea's beauty and even at the fine figure of the shepherd Cardenio. The priest made them get ready such fare as the inn could offer, and the landlord, in hope of better payment, served up a tolerably good dinner. All this time Don Quixote was asleep, and they thought it best not to waken him, as sleeping would now do him more good than eating.

While at dinner, the company consisting of the landlord, his wife, their daughter, Maritornes, and all the travelers, they discussed the strange madness of Don Quixote and how he had been found, and the landlady told them what had taken place between him and the muleteer. Then, looking round to see if Sancho was there and seeing he was not, she gave the whole story of his blanketing, which provided them with no little amusement. But when the priest observed that the books of chivalry which Don Quixote had read had turned his brain, the landlord dissented.

"I cannot understand how that can be," he said, "for really to my mind there is no better reading in the world. I have two or three of them, with some other writings, that are the very life, not only of myself, but of other people. When it is harvest time, the reapers flock here on holidays, and there is always one who can read and who takes up one of these books. We gather around him, thirty or more of us, and stay listening to him with such pleasure that it makes our grey hairs grow young again. At least I can say for myself that when I hear of what furious and terrible blows the knights deliver, I have an urge to do the same, and I would enjoy hearing about them night and day."

"And I no less," said the landlady, "because I never have a quiet moment in my house except when you are listening to someone reading. Then you are so taken up that for the time being you forget to scold."

"That is true," said Maritornes. "Faith, I love hearing these things too, for they are very nice, especially when they describe some lady in the arms of her knight under the orange trees, and the dueña who is keeping watch for them dying with envy and fright; all this I say is as sweet as honey."

"And what do you think, young lady?" said the priest, turning to the landlord's daughter.

"I don't know indeed, señor," she said. "I listen too, and to tell the truth, though I do not understand it, I like hearing it. But it is not the blows that my father likes that I like, but the laments the knights utter when they are separated from their ladies. Sometimes they actually make me cry with the pity I feel for them."

"Then you would console them, if it was for you they wept, young lady?" said Dorotea.

"I don't know what I would do," said the girl. "I only know that there are some of those ladies so cruel that their knights call them tigers and lions and a thousand other ugly names. Jesus, I don't know what sort of people can be so unfeeling and heartless that rather than look at a worthy man they leave him to die or go mad. I don't know what is the use of such prudery. If it is for honor's sake, why not marry them? That's all they want."

"Hush, child," said the landlady. "It seems to me you know a great deal about these things, and it is not fit for girls to know or talk so much."

"As the gentleman asked me, I could not help answering him," said the girl.

"Well then," said the priest, "bring me these books, señor landlord, for I would like to see them."

"Certainly," said he, and going into his own room he brought out an old valise secured with a little chain, on opening which the priest found in it three large books and some manuscripts written in a very good hand. The first he opened he found to be *Don Cirongilio of Thrace,* and the second *Don Felixmarte of Hircania,* and the other the *History of the Great Captain Gonzalo Hernández de Córdoba, with the Life of Diego García de Paredes.*[1]

When the priest read the two first titles he looked over at the barber. "We need my friend's housekeeper and niece here now," he said.

"No," said the barber, "I can just as well carry them to the yard or to the hearth, and there is a very good fire there."

"What? Your worship would burn my books!" said the landlord.

"Only these two," said the priest, "*Don Cirongilio* and *Felixmarte.*"

"Are my books heretics or phlegmatics that you want to burn them?" said the landlord.

"Schismatics you mean, friend," said the barber, "not phlegmatics."

"That's it," said the landlord. "But if you want to burn any let it be the one about the Great Captain and Diego García, for I would rather have a child of mine burnt than either of the others."

"Brother," said the priest, "those two books are made up of lies and are full of folly and nonsense. But the account of the Great Captain is a true history and contains the deeds of Gonzalo Hernández of Córdoba, who by his many and great achievements earned the title all over the world of the Great Captain, a famous and illustrious name and deserved by him alone. And this Diego García de Paredes was a distinguished knight of the city of Trujillo in Estremadura, a most gallant soldier, and of such bodily strength that with one finger he stopped a mill-wheel in full motion. Posted with a two-handed sword at the foot of a bridge, he kept the whole of an

1. *Don Cirongilio de Tracia,* by Bernardo de Vargas (Seville, 1545). For *Felixmarte de Hircania* see Chapter VI, Note 5. The *Chronicle of the Great Captain Gonzalo Hernández de Córdoba y Aguilar, to which is added the life of Diego García de Paredes, written by himself* appeared at Seville in 1580. Hernández de Córdoba was a brilliant general whose services against the Moors at Granada and the French in Naples were ungratefully repaid by Ferdinand. García de Paredes was his companion in both campaigns.

immense army from passing over it. He achieved such other exploits that if, instead of his relating them himself with the modesty of a knight who was writing his own history, some free and unbiased writer had recorded them, they would have outshone all the deeds of the Hectors, Achilleses, and Rolands."

"Tell that to my father," said the landlord. "*There's* something to be astonished at! Stopping a mill-wheel! By God, your worship should read what I have read of Felixmarte of Hircania, how with one single backstroke he split five giants in two through the middle as if they had been made of bean-pods like the little friars the children make.[2] Another time he attacked a very great and powerful army, in which there were more than a million six hundred thousand soldiers, all armed from head to foot, and he routed them all as if they had been flocks of sheep. And what do you say to the good Cirongilio of Thrace, who was so bold and courageous? That may be seen in the book, which tells how he was sailing along a river when out of the water a fiery serpent rose up. As soon as he saw it, he flung himself on it and got astride of its scaly shoulders and squeezed its throat with both hands with such force that the serpent, finding itself throttled, could do nothing but sink to the bottom of the river. It carried the knight down with it, for he would not let go. When they got down there, he found himself among palaces and gardens so pretty that it was a wonder to see. And then the serpent changed itself into an ancient old man, who told him such things as were never heard. Say no more, señor, for if you were to hear this, you would go mad with delight. I don't give a hoot for your Great Captain and your Diego García!"

"Our landlord is almost fit to play a second part to Don Quixote," said Dorotea in a whisper to Cardenio, when she heard this.

"I think so," said Cardenio, "for he plainly accepts it as certain that everything those books relate took place exactly as written down. The barefooted friars themselves would not persuade him to the contrary."

"But consider, brother," said the priest once more. "There never was any Felixmarte of Hircania in the world or any Cirongilio of Thrace or any of the other knights of the same sort that the books of chivalry talk of. The whole thing is the fabrication and invention of idle wits, devised by them for the purpose you describe of whiling away the time, as your reapers do when they read. For I swear to you in all seriousness there never were any such knights in the world, and no such exploits or nonsense ever happened anywhere."

"Try that bone on another dog," said the landlord. "As if I did not know how many make five and where my shoe pinches me! Don't think you can feed me with pap, for by God I am no fool. It

2. Made by cutting away part of the pod so as to expose the upper bean, which looks something like a friar's head in the recess of his cowl.

is a good joke for your worship to try and persuade me that everything these good books say is nonsense and lies when they are printed by the license of the Lords of the Royal Council, as if they were people who would allow a lot of lies to be printed, and so many battles and enchantments that they take away one's senses."

"I have told you, friend," said the priest, "that this is done to entertain our idle thoughts. As in well-ordered states games of chess, ball, and billiards are allowed for the diversion of those who do not care, or are not obliged or unable, to work, so books of this kind are allowed to be printed. It is supposed, and indeed is the truth, that there can be nobody so ignorant as to take any of them for true stories. And if it were appropriate and the present company desired it, I could say something about the qualities books of chivalry should possess to be good ones that would be to the advantage and even to the taste of some. I hope the time will come when I can communicate my ideas to someone who may be able to mend matters. In the meantime, señor landlord, believe what I have said. Take your books and do what you will about their truth or falsehood, and much good may they do you. God grant you may not become lame on the same foot your guest Don Quixote limps on."

"No fear of that," returned the landlord. "I won't be so crazy as to make a knight-errant of myself, for I see well enough that things are not what they used to be in those days, when they say those famous knights roamed about the world."

Sancho had made his appearance in the middle of this conversation, and he was very much troubled and cast down by what he heard said about knights-errant being now no longer in vogue and all books of chivalry being foolishness and lies. He resolved in his heart to wait and see what came of this journey of his master's. If it did not turn out as happily as his master expected, he determined to leave him and go back to his wife and children and his ordinary labor.

The landlord was carrying away the valise and the books, but the priest stopped him. "Wait," he said. "I want to see what those papers are that are written in such a good hand."

The landlord took them out and handed them to the priest, who saw that they were a work of about eight sheets of manuscript. At the beginning, in large letters, stood as title "A Story of Ill-advised Curiosity."[3] The priest read three or four lines to himself.

"I must say," he said, "that the title of this story does not seem to me a bad one, and I feel an inclination to read it all."

"Then your reverence should by all means read it," replied the landlord, "for I can tell you that some guests who read it here were

3. There is no concise English translation for the title; the nearest approach to one would be, perhaps, "The inquisitive man who had no business to be so." Putnam's version is the "Story of the One Who Was Too Curious for His Own Good."

very pleased with it and urged me to give it to them. But I would not give it, meaning to return it to the person who forgot the valise, books, and papers here, for maybe he will return some time or other. Though I know I shall miss the books, faith, I mean to return them. Though I am an innkeeper, still I am a Christian."

"You are very right, friend," said the priest. "But for all that, if the story pleases me you must let me copy it."

"With all my heart," replied the host.

While they were talking, Cardenio had taken up the story and begun to read it. He formed the same opinion of it as the priest and begged him to read it so that they might all hear it.

"I would read it," said the priest, "if the time would not be better spent in sleeping."

"It will be rest enough for me," said Dorotea, "to while away the time by listening to some tale. My spirits are not yet tranquil enough to let me sleep even if it were sensible to do so."

"Well, then, in that case," said the priest, "I will read it, if only out of curiosity. Perhaps it may contain something pleasant."

Master Nicolás added his entreaties, and Sancho too. Seeing which, the priest reflected that he would give pleasure to all, including himself.

"Well then," he said, "everyone pay attention, for this is how the story begins."

Chapter XXXIII

IN WHICH IS RELATED THE STORY OF ILL-ADVISED CURIOSITY

"In Florence, a rich and famous city of Italy in the province called Tuscany, lived two gentlemen of wealth and quality, Anselmo and Lotario. So great was their friendship that by way of distinction they were called by all who knew them 'The Two Friends.' They were unmarried, young, of the same age, and of the same tastes, which was enough to account for their reciprocal friendship. Anselmo, it is true, was somewhat more inclined to seek pleasure in love than Lotario, for whom the pleasures of the hunt had more attraction. But on occasion Anselmo would forego his own tastes to yield to Lotario's and Lotario would surrender his to fall in with those of Anselmo, and their inclinations kept pace with such perfect accord that the best regulated clock could not surpass it.

"Anselmo was deeply in love with Camila, a high-born beautiful maiden of the same city. She was the daughter of parents so estimable, and so worthy herself, that he resolved, with the approval of his friend Lotario, without whom he did nothing, to ask for her hand in marriage. Lotario, who transmitted the demand, conducted the negotiation so much to his friend's satisfaction that in a short time Anselmo came to possess the object of his desires. Camila was so happy in having Anselmo as her husband that she unceasingly thanked heaven and Lotario for the good fortune that had befallen her.

"The first few days, since a wedding is usually a time for merry-making, Lotario frequented his friend Anselmo's house as of old, striving to honor him and the occasion and to gratify him in every way he could. But when the wedding days were over and the succession of visits and congratulations had slackened, he purposely ceased visiting Anselmo's house, for it seemed to him, as it would to any sensible man, that friends' houses ought not to be frequented after marriage as they were during their masters' bachelor days. Though true and genuine friendship cannot and should not be in any way suspicious, still a married man's honor is so delicate a matter that it may suffer injury from brothers, to say nothing of friends.

"Anselmo noticed Lotario's absence and complained of it. He declared that if he had known marriage would prevent his enjoying his friend's society as he used to, he would have never married. Furthermore, if the harmony that subsisted between them while he was a bachelor had earned them the pleasing name of 'The Two Friends,' then Lotario should not allow so rare and delightful a title to be lost through needless anxiety to act circumspectly. So Anselmo entreated him, if such a phrase could be used between them, to be once more master of his house and to come in and go out as formerly. He assured Lotario that his wife Camila's only desire or inclination was what he would wish her to have and that Lotario's coldness grieved her, since she knew how sincerely they loved one another.

"To all this and more that Anselmo said to Lotario to persuade him to visit his house in his accustomed way, Lotario replied with so much prudence, sense, and judgment, that Anselmo was satisfied of his friend's good intentions. It was agreed that on two days every week, and on holidays, Lotario should dine with him. But though this arrangement was made, Lotario resolved to follow it only to the extent that he considered in accord with the honor of his friend, whose good name meant more to him than his own. He said, and justly, that a married man upon whom heaven had bestowed a beautiful wife should consider as carefully what friends he brought to his house as what female friends his wife associated with. What cannot be done or arranged in the market-place, in church, at public festivals, or at private devotions (opportunities that husbands cannot always deny their wives), may be easily managed in the house of the female friend or relative in whom most confidence is reposed.

"Lotario said, too, that every married man should have some friend who would point out to him any negligence in his conduct. For it sometimes happens that owing to the husband's deep affection for his wife he does not caution her or, so as not to vex her, refrains from telling her to do or avoid doing certain things, when the contrary behavior might become a matter of honor or reproach for him. Errors of this kind he could easily correct if warned by a friend. But where can one find the friend whose judgment, faithfulness, and loyalty would equal Lotario's demands?

"Truly I cannot say. Lotario alone was such a friend, for with the utmost care and vigilance he watched over his friend's honor and strove to diminish, cut down, and reduce the number of occasions he went to the house according to their agreement. He feared that the visits of a wealthy, high-born young man, with the attractiveness he knew was his, at the house of a woman with Camila's beauty might be regarded with suspicion by the malicious inquisitive eyes of the idle public. For though his integrity and reputation might bridle slanderous tongues, still he was unwilling to hazard either his own good name or that of his friend. For this reason he devoted most of the days agreed upon to some other business which he claimed was unavoidable. As a result a great portion of the day was taken up with complaints on one side and excuses on the other. It happened, however, that on one occasion when the two were strolling together outside the city, Anselmo addressed the following words to Lotario.

" 'You may suppose, Lotario my friend, that I am unable to give sufficient thanks for God's favors in making me the son of such parents as mine, in granting so lavishly what are called the gifts of nature as well as those of fortune, and above all for what he has done in giving me you for a friend and Camila for a wife. These two treasures I value, if not as highly as I ought, at least as highly as I am able.

" 'Yet, with all these good things, which generally are all that men need in order to live happily, I am the most discontented and dissatisfied man in the world. I cannot recall when it began, but I have long been harassed and oppressed by a desire so strange and so unusual that I wonder at myself and blame and chide myself when I am alone, and try to stifle it and hide it from my own thoughts. But my success is no greater than if I were endeavoring deliberately to proclaim it before all the world. As, in short, it must come out, I would confide it to your safe keeping, for I feel sure that in this way, and because of your willingness as a true friend to ease my burden, I shall soon find myself freed from the distress it causes me. I know that your concern will give me happiness in the same measure my own folly has caused me misery.'

"Anselmo's words struck Lotario with astonishment, for he could not guess the purpose of such a lengthy preamble. Though he tried to imagine what desire could so trouble his friend, his conjectures were all far from the truth. To relieve the anxiety which this perplexity was causing him, he reproached Anselmo for doing a flagrant injustice to their great friendship by seeking a roundabout way to confide his most hidden thoughts. He well knew that he could count on his friend's advice to allay them, or on his help in carrying them out.

" 'That is the truth,' replied Anselmo, 'and relying on that, I will tell you, Lotario, my friend, that what harasses me is the desire to know whether my wife Camila is as good and as perfect as I think her to be. I cannot assure myself of the truth unless I test her in such a way that the trial may prove the purity of her virtue as the fire proves that of gold. I am convinced, my friend, that a woman is virtuous only to the degree that she is or is not tempted, and that only that woman is strong who resists the promises, gifts, tears, and importunities of earnest lovers. What thanks does a woman deserve for being good if no one urges her to be bad, and what wonder is it that she is reserved and circumspect when no opportunity is given her of going wrong and when she knows she has a husband who will take her life the first time he catches her in an impropriety? I do not therefore hold the woman who is virtuous through fear or want of opportunity in the same esteem as her who comes out of temptation and trial with a crown of victory.

" 'So, for these reasons and many others that I could give to justify and support my opinion, I want my wife Camila to undergo this trial and be refined and tested in the fire of finding herself wooed by one entitled to aim so high. If she comes out, as I know she will, victorious from this struggle, I shall look upon my good fortune as unequaled, I shall be able to say that the cup of my desire is full, and that the virtuous woman of whom the sage says "Who shall find her?"[1] has fallen to my lot. If the result is contrary to my expectations, the satisfaction of knowing that I have been right in my opinion will enable me to bear without complaint the pain which my so dearly bought experience will naturally cause me. And, as no argument you can advance in opposition to my wish will dissuade me from carrying it into effect, it is my desire, friend Lotario, that you should consent to become the instrument carrying out my intent. I will make available to you the necessary occasions, and nothing shall be lacking that I may think necessary for the pursuit of a virtuous, honorable, modest, and high-minded woman. Among other reasons, I am induced to entrust this arduous task to you on reflecting that, if Camila should be conquered by you, the conquest will not be pushed to extremes, but only far enough for me to consider as good as done what will not be done, out of respect. Thus I shall not be wronged in any way except through intention, and my wrong will remain buried in the integrity

1. "Who can find a virtuous woman? for her price is far above rubies." Proverbs 31:10.

of your silence which, I know well, will match the silence of death in what concerns me. If, therefore, you would have me enjoy what can be called life, you will at once undertake this amorous struggle, not lukewarmly or slothfully, but with the energy and zeal that my desire demands, and with the loyalty our friendship assures me of.'

"Thus did Anselmo declare himself to Lotario, who listened so attentively that, apart from what has already been recorded, he did not open his lips until the other had finished. Then perceiving that Anselmo had no more to say, he regarded him for a while, as one would regard something never before seen that excited wonder and amazement.

" 'I cannot persuade myself, Anselmo my friend,' he said, 'that you have not been speaking in jest. Had I thought you were speaking seriously, I would not have allowed you to go so far but would have cut short your long harangue by refusing to listen. I truly suspect that either you do not know me, or I do not know you. Yet I know well you are Anselmo, and you know that I am Lotario. The misfortune appears to be that you are not the Anselmo you used to be and must have thought that I am not the Lotario I ought to be. The things you have said to me do not come from the Anselmo who was my friend, nor is what you ask of me a request that should be made of the Lotario you know. True friends ought to test and use their friends, as a poet has said, *usque ad aras*,[2] whereby he meant that they will not employ their friendship in things contrary to God's will.

" 'If this, then, was a heathen's feeling about friendship, how much more should it be a Christian's, since he is aware that the divine must not be forfeited for the sake of any human friendship? And if a friend should go so far as to put aside his duty to Heaven to fulfil his duty to his friend, it should not be in matters that are trifling or of little moment, but in such as affect the friend's life and honor. Now tell me, Anselmo, in which of these two are you imperiled, that I should risk so much to accommodate you and do the detestable thing you ask me to do? Neither one nor the other! Quite the contrary, you ask me, as I understand it, to labor mightily to rob you of honor and life and to rob myself of them at the same time. For if I take away your honor it is plain I take away your life, as a man without honor is worse than dead. And being the instrument, at your own insistence, of so much wrong done you, shall not I, too, be left without honor, and consequently without life? Listen to me, Anselmo my friend, and have the patience not to answer until I have said what occurs to me about the promptings of your desire, for there will be time enough for you to reply and for me to listen.'

" 'Agreed,' said Anselmo. 'Say what you will.'

2. ***Usque ad aras*****: "as far as the altar."**

" 'It seems to me, Anselmo,' Lotario went on, 'that your present state of mind is like that of the Moors, who can never be brought to see the error of their creed by quotations from the Holy Scriptures or by reasons based upon speculation or founded upon the articles of faith. They must have examples that are palpable, easy, intelligible, capable of proof, not admitting of doubt, with mathematical demonstrations that cannot be denied, like, "*If equals are subtracted from equals, the remainders are equal.*" If they do not understand this in words, as indeed they do not, it has to be shown them with the hands, and put before their eyes, and even with all this, no one succeeds in convincing them of the truth of my holy religion.

" 'This same procedure I shall have to adopt with you, for the desire which has sprung up in you is absurd and remote from everything that has a semblance of reason. So I feel it would be a waste of time to try to reason with you in your folly, for at present I will give it no other name. I am even tempted to abandon you to this folly as punishment for your wicked desire, but the friendship I bear you, which will not allow me to desert you in such manifest deadly danger, keeps me from dealing so harshly with you. So that you may see this clearly, Anselmo, tell me: have you not said I must force my suit upon a modest woman, decoy one that is virtuous, make overtures to one that is pure-minded, and court one that is prudent? Yes, you have told me this. If you know, then, that you have a wife who is modest, virtuous, pure-minded, and prudent, what are you seeking? And if you believe she will triumph over all my attacks—as doubtless she would—what higher titles do you think you can bestow upon her than those she now possesses, or in what way will she be better then than she is now? Either you do not really hold her to be what you say she is, or you do not know what you are asking. If you do not hold her to be what you say, why seek to test her instead of treating her as guilty in whatever way you find best? But if she is as virtuous as you believe, it is an outrageous proceeding to make trial of truth itself, for, once tested, it cannot be esteemed more highly than before. Thus it is conclusively proved that to attempt things from which we may derive harm rather than advantage is the doing of unreasoning and reckless minds, especially when we are not forced or compelled to attempt such things, which even viewed from afar it is clearly madness to attempt.

" 'Difficulties are attempted either for the sake of God or for the sake of the world, or for both. Those undertaken for God's sake are those which the saints undertake when they attempt to live the lives of angels in human bodies. Those undertaken for the sake of the world are those of the men who traverse such a vast expanse of water, such a variety of climates, so many strange countries, to acquire what are called the blessings of fortune. Those undertaken for the sake of God and the world together are those of brave soldiers, who no sooner see in the enemy's wall a breach as wide as a cannon ball could make than, casting aside all fear, without hesitating or heeding the manifest peril, borne onward by the desire of defending their faith, their country, and their king, they fling themselves dauntlessly into the midst of the thousand opposing deaths that await them.

" 'Such are the things that men habitually attempt, and there is honor, glory, and gain in attempting them, however difficult and perilous they may be. But what you declare you wish to undertake will win you neither the glory of God nor the blessings of fortune nor fame among men. Even if it should turn out as you desire, you will be no happier, richer, or more honored than you are now. But if it should be otherwise you will be reduced to misery greater than can be imagined, for then it will avail you nothing to reflect that no one is aware of the misfortune that has befallen you. The fact that you know it yourself will suffice to torture and crush you. In confirmation of the truth of what I say, let me repeat a stanza written by the famous poet Luigi Tansillo at the end of the first part of his *Tears of Saint Peter.*[3] This is how it goes.

> The anguish and the shame but greater grew
> In Peter's heart as morning slowly came;
> No eye was there to see him, well he knew,
> Yet he himself was to himself a shame;
> Exposed to all men's gaze or screened from view,
> A noble heart will feel the pang the same;
> A prey to shame the sinning soul will be,
> Though none but heaven and earth its shame can see.

Thus by keeping it secret you will not escape sorrow, but rather will shed tears unceasingly. If not tears from the eyes, they will be tears of blood from the heart, like those shed by the simple doctor our poet tells us of, who tried the test of the cup which the wise Rinaldo, who was better advised, refused to touch.[4] Though this may be a poetic fiction it contains a moral lesson worthy of attention, study, and imitation. Moreover, what I am about to say will enable you to see the great error you are seeking to commit.

" 'Tell me, Anselmo, if Heaven or good fortune had made you master and lawful owner of a diamond of the finest quality, of an excellence and purity that had satisfied all the jewelers who had seen it, and who had proclaimed as with one voice that for purity, quality, and fineness it was all a stone of the kind could possibly be; suppose, too, that you yourself shared this belief, since you knew nothing to the contrary; would it be a reasonable desire to take the

3. Translated into Castilian by Luis Gálvez de Montalvo, Cervantes' friend (Toledo, 1587).

4. A reference to Ariosto's *Orlando furioso*, canto 43.

diamond and place it between an anvil and a hammer, in order by mere force of blows and strength of arm to find out if it were as hard and as fine as they said? If you did, and if the stone should resist so foolish a test, that would add nothing to its value or reputation. If it were broken, as might occur, would not all be lost? Undoubtedly it would, leaving its owner to be judged a fool in the opinion of all.

" 'Anselmo my friend, look on Camila as a most precious diamond, valued as such no whit less by you than by others, and see how senseless it is to run the risk of her being broken. If she remains intact she can rise to no more than her present value, and if she gives way and is unable to resist, consider now how you will be deprived of her, and with what justification you will reproach yourself for having caused her ruin and your own. Remember no jewel in the world is so precious as a chaste and virtuous woman, and that the whole honor of women consists in their good repute. Since your wife's, as you know, is unexcelled, why should you seek to call its truth into question?

" 'Remember, my friend, that woman is an imperfect animal. Impediments should not be placed in her way to make her trip and fall; they should be removed and her path left clear of all obstacles. Thus she may run her course unhindered and be free to attain the desired perfection, which consists in being virtuous. Naturalists tell us that the ermine is a little animal with a fur of purest white and that when the hunters wish to capture it, they use this artifice. Having noted the places which it frequents and passes, they stop the way to them with mud. Then they frighten the ermine and drive it towards this spot. When the ermine comes to the mud it halts and lets itself be taken captive, rather than pass through the mire and spoil and sully its whiteness, which it values more than life and liberty. The virtuous and chaste woman is an ermine, and the virtue of modesty is whiter and purer than snow. He who wishes her not to lose it but to keep and preserve it must follow a course unlike that employed with the ermine. He must not put before her the mire of the gifts and attentions of persevering lovers, because perhaps—and even without a perhaps—she may not, unaided, have the virtue and natural strength to pass through these impediments and tread them under foot. They must be removed, and the brightness of virtue and the inherent beauty of an unblemished reputation must be set before her.

" 'A virtuous woman, too, is like a mirror of clear shining crystal, liable to be tarnished and dimmed by every breath that touches it. She must be treated as relics are: adored, not touched. She must be protected and prized as one protects and prizes a fair garden full of flowers and roses, whose owner allows no one to trespass or pluck a blossom. It must suffice others that from afar and through the iron grating they may enjoy its fragrance and its beauty. Finally, let me repeat some verses that come to mind. I heard them in a modern comedy, and it seems to me they concern the point we are discussing. A prudent old man was advising another, the father of a young girl, to lock her up, watch over her, and keep her in seclusion. He used the following arguments, among others.

> Woman is a thing of glass;
> But her brittleness 'tis best
> Not too curiously to test:
> Who knows what may come to pass?
>
> Breaking is an easy matter,
> And it's folly to expose
> What you cannot mend to blows,
> What you can't make whole to shatter.
>
> This, then, all may hold as true,
> And the reason's plain to see;
> For if Danaës there be,
> There are golden showers too.[5]

" 'All that I have said so far, Anselmo, has been with reference to yourself. Now it is right for me to say something of my own situation. If I speak at length, you must pardon me, for in view of the labyrinth you have entered, and from which you would have me extricate you, this is unavoidable.

" 'You look on me as your friend, yet you would rob me of my honor, a desire wholly inconsistent with friendship. Not only do you aim at this, but you would have me rob you of yours. That you would rob me of it is undeniable, for when Camila sees me paying court to her as you insist I should, she will certainly regard me as a man without honor or principle, since what I am trying to do so conflicts with the sense of my own worth and with your friendship. That you would have me rob you of it is also undeniable, for Camila, hearing herself thus entreated, will suppose I have detected in her a frivolity that encourages me to reveal my base desire. But if she considers herself dishonored, her dishonor affects you through your association with her, and following on this we witness a common occurrence.

" 'The husband of the adulterous woman, though he may not be aware of or be in the least responsible for his wife's dereliction, or though through carelessness or negligence he may never have had it in his power to guard against his misfortune, nevertheless is stigmatized. He goes by a vile and reproachful name and is regarded with contempt instead of pity by all who know of his wife's guilt, though

5. From an unknown play, perhaps Cervantes' *La Confusa*, now lost. Jupiter, in the form of a rain of gold, begot Perseus on Danaë, who was shut in a tower by her father.

they see that his misfortune is not his own fault, but is due to the lust of a vicious spouse. But I will tell you why with good reason dishonor attaches to the husband of the unchaste wife, though he knows nothing of this, is not to blame, and has done nothing or provided any cause that would provoke her infidelity. And do not tire of listening to me, for it will be advantageous for you.

" 'When God created our first parent in the earthly paradise, the Holy Scripture says that he plunged Adam into a deep sleep and while he slept took a rib from his left side forming out of this our mother Eve. When Adam awoke and beheld her he said, "This is flesh of my flesh, and bone of my bone." And God said "For this shall a man leave his father and his mother, and they shall be two in one flesh." Then was instituted the divine sacrament of marriage, with such binding ties that death alone can loose them. Such is the force and power of this miraculous sacrament that it makes two different persons one and the same flesh. It brings about even more when the virtuous are married, for though they have two souls they have but one will. Hence it follows that as the flesh of the wife is one with her husband's flesh, the stains that befall her or the injuries she incurs affect the husband's flesh, though he, as I have said, may have given no cause for them.

" 'For as the pain of the foot or any bodily member is felt by the whole body, because all is one flesh, as the head feels the hurt to the ankle without having caused it, so the husband, being one with her, shares his wife's dishonor. As all worldly honor or dishonor comes of flesh and blood, and the erring wife's is of that kind, the husband must unavoidably shoulder his share and be looked on as dishonored without knowing it.

" 'Consider, then, Anselmo, the risk you run in seeking to disturb the peace enjoyed by your virtuous wife. Consider how empty and ill-advised is the curiosity that would rouse up passions now reposing peacefully in the breast of your chaste wife. Reflect that you are staking all to win but little and that what you will lose is so much I leave it undescribed, not having the words to express it. But if all I have said is not enough to turn you from your vile purpose, you must seek some other instrument for your dishonor and misfortune. I will not consent to act thus, even though I lose your friendship, the greatest loss I can conceive.'

"Having said this, the wise and virtuous Lotario was silent, and Anselmo, troubled in mind and deep in thought, was unable for a while to utter a word in reply. At length he spoke.

" 'Lotario my friend,' he said, 'I have listened attentively, as you have seen, to all you have had to say. Your arguments, examples, and comparisons reveal your great intelligence and the pinnacle of true friendship you have reached. I see, too, and admit that if I am not guided by your view and follow my own, I am flying from the good and pursuing evil. This being so, you must realize that I now labor under the infirmity women sometimes suffer from, when the craving seizes them to eat clay, plaster, charcoal, and even worse things disgusting to look at and much more so to eat. So some device must be found to cure me, and this can easily be achieved if only you will begin, even though in a lukewarm and make-believe fashion, to pay court to Camila. She will not be so amenable that her virtue will give way at the first attack, and with this mere attempt I shall rest satisfied, while you will have done what our friendship obliges you to do, not only by giving me life, but by persuading me not to discard my honor.

" 'This you are bound to do for one reason alone, namely, that since I am indeed resolved to apply this test, you may not properly allow me to reveal my weakness to another and so imperil the honor you are striving to keep me from losing. If your own honor does not stand as high as it ought in the estimation of Camila while you pay court to her, that is of little or no importance. In a little while, when you have found in her the fidelity we expect, you can tell her the plain truth about our stratagem and so regain your place in her esteem. Since you venture so little, and in the doing afford me so much satisfaction, do not refuse to undertake it, even if further objections occur to you. For, as I have said, if you will only make a beginning I will look on the matter as settled.'

"Lotario saw that Anselmo's resolve could not be shaken. He did not know what further examples to offer or arguments to put forward in order to dissuade him, and he saw how he was threatening to confide his pernicious scheme to someone else. So to avoid a greater evil he resolved to gratify him and to do what he asked, with the intention of arranging things so as to satisfy Anselmo without disturbing Camila's peace of mind. So in reply he told Anselmo to mention his plan to no one else, for he would undertake the task and set about it as soon as he pleased. Anselmo embraced Lotario warmly and affectionately, thanking him for his offer as if he had done him some great favor. They agreed that a start should be made the next day. Anselmo would give Lotario the time and opportunity to converse alone with Camila and would provide him with money and jewels to offer her. He suggested, too, that he should entertain her with music and write verses in her praise, and if he was unwilling to take the trouble of composing them, Anselmo offered to do it himself. Lotario agreed to all with an intention very different from what Anselmo supposed, and with this understanding they returned to Anselmo's house. There they found Camila awaiting her husband anxiously and uneasily, for he was later than usual in returning.

"Lotario went back to his own house, and Anselmo remained in his, as well satisfied as his friend was troubled, for Lotario could see no satisfactory way out of this ill-advised business. That night, however, he thought of a plan that might deceive Anselmo without doing Camila any harm. The next day he went to dine with his friend and was welcomed by Camila, who showed him great cordiality, for she knew the affection her husband felt for him. When dinner was over and the cloth removed, Anselmo told Lotario to stay with Camila while he attended to some urgent business, since he would return in an hour and a half. Camila begged him not to go, and Lotario offered to accompany him, but nothing could persuade Anselmo. On the contrary, he wished that Lotario should wait for him, as he had a matter of great importance to discuss with him. At the same time he ordered Camila not to leave Lotario alone until he came back. In short he contrived to put so good a face on the reason, or the folly, of his absence that no one could have suspected it was a pretense.

"Anselmo went away and Camila and Lotario were left alone at the table, for the rest of the household had gone to dinner. Lotario saw himself in the arena as his friend had desired, and facing an enemy who by her beauty alone could vanquish a squadron of armed knights. Judge whether he had good reason to fear. But what he did was to lean his elbow on the arm of the chair and his cheek upon his hand and, asking Camila's pardon for his ill manners, he said he wished to take a nap until Anselmo returned. Camila in reply said he could repose more at his ease in the drawing room than in his chair and suggested he should go in and sleep there. Lotario refused and remained asleep where he was. Anselmo, on his return, found Camila in her own room and Lotario asleep. Thus he imagined that his absence had lasted long enough to give them time for conversation and even for sleep, and he was all impatience that Lotario should wake up, so that he might go out with him and ask him what success he had had.

"Everything happened just as he wished. Lotario awoke, the two left the house, and Anselmo asked what he was anxious to know. Lotario, in reply, told him he had not thought it advisable to declare himself entirely the first time. So he had merely praised Camila's charms, telling her that all the city spoke of nothing else but her beauty and wit, for this seemed to him an excellent way of first gaining her goodwill and disposing her to listen with pleasure the next time. He thus availed himself of the device the devil uses when he would deceive someone who is on the alert. For he, the angel of darkness, transforms himself into an angel of light and, under a fair appearance, at last reveals himself and effects his purpose, if his wiles have not been discovered at the outset. All this gave great satisfaction to Anselmo, who said he would provide the same opportunity every day, but without leaving the house, for he would find things to do at home so that Camila should not detect the plot.

"In this way several days went by, and Lotario, without uttering a word to Camila, reported to Anselmo that he had talked with her without ever being able to draw from her the slightest indication of consent to anything dishonorable, or even a sign or shadow of hope. He said that, on the contrary, she threatened to inform her husband of it, if he did not abandon his wicked plan.

" 'So far so good,' said Anselmo. 'Camila has thus far resisted words; now we must see how she will resist deeds. Tomorrow I will give you two thousand gold crowns for you to offer or even present, and the same amount to buy jewels to lure her. Women are fond of dressing well and wearing fashionable clothes, and all the more so if they are beautiful, however chaste they may be. If she resists this temptation, I will be satisfied and will give you no more trouble.'

"Lotario replied that now he had begun, he would carry it out to the end, though he could see he was to come out of it wearied and vanquished. The next day he received the four thousand crowns, and with them four thousand perplexities, for he did not know what new falsehood to utter. In the end he made up his mind to tell Anselmo that Camila stood as firm against gifts and promises as against words and that there was no use in taking any further trouble, for the time was all spent to no purpose.

"But chance would have it otherwise and so ordered it that Anselmo, having left Lotario and Camila alone as on other occasions, shut himself in a room, listening and watching through the keyhole to see what occurred between them. He observed that for more than half an hour Lotario did not utter a word to Camila, nor was he going to utter a word though he were to stay there for an age. So he concluded that what his friend had told him about Camila's answers was all invention and falsehood, and to make sure of this, he came out, called Lotario to one side, and asked him what news he had and in what frame of mind Camila was. Lotario replied that he was not willing to go on with the business, for she had answered him so angrily and harshly that he had no heart to say anything more to her.

" 'Ah, Lotario, Lotario,' said Anselmo, 'how badly you carry out your obligations to me and misuse the great confidence I placed in you! I have been watching through the keyhole, and I have seen that you did not say a word to Camila. Thus I conclude that on previous occasions you did not speak to her either. If this is so, as no doubt it is, why do you deceive me, or craftily seek to deprive me of the means I might find of attaining my desire?'

"Anselmo said no more, but he had said enough to cover Lotario with shame and confusion. The latter, feeling as though his honor were threatened by his having been detected in a lie, swore to Anselmo that from that moment he would strive to satisfy him, without any deceit, as Anselmo would see if he had the curiosity to watch. Yet he need not take the trouble, for the pains that would be taken to satisfy him would remove all suspicions from his mind. Anselmo believed him, and to provide an opportunity that would be exempt from any interruption, he decided to spend eight days away from home. So he went to the house of a friend who lived in a village not far from the city, and he so arranged it, to account for his departure to Camila, that the friend should send him a very pressing invitation.

"Unhappy, shortsighted Anselmo, what are you doing, what are you plotting, what are you devising? Consider how you are working against yourself, plotting your own dishonor, and devising your own ruin. Your wife Camila is virtuous, you possess her in peace and quietness, no one threatens your happiness, her thoughts wander not beyond the walls of your house, you are her heaven on earth, the object of her wishes, the fulfilment of her desires, the measure wherewith she measures her will, making it conform in all things to yours and Heaven's. If, then, the mine of her honor, beauty, virtue, and modesty offers you without labor all the wealth it contains and that you can wish for, why must you dig the earth in search of fresh veins, of new unknown treasure, risking the collapse of all, since it rests on the feeble props of her weak nature? Consider that from him who seeks impossibilities even that which is possible may with justice be withheld, as was better expressed by a poet who said:

> 'Tis mine to seek for life in death,
> Health in disease seek I,
> I seek in prison freedom's breath,
> In traitors loyalty.
>
> So Fate, that ever scorns to grant
> A grace or boon to me,
> Since what can never be I want,
> Denies me what might be.

"The next day Anselmo departed for the village, after telling Camila that during his absence Lotario would look after his house and dine with her, and that she was to treat him as she would himself. Camila was distressed, as a discreet and right-minded woman would be, at her husband's orders and urged him to remember how improper it was that anyone should occupy his seat at the table during his absence. If he acted thus from lack of confidence that she would be able to manage his house, let him try her this time, and experience would show him that she was equal to greater responsibilities. Anselmo replied that it was his pleasure to have it so and that she had only to submit and obey. Camila said she would do so, though against her will.

"Anselmo left, and the next day Lotario came to his house, where Camila offered him a friendly and modest welcome. But she never let Lotario see her alone, for she was always attended by her men and women servants, especially by a handmaid of hers, Leonela by name. She was much attached to her, for they had been brought up together from childhood in her father's house, and she had kept her after her marriage with Anselmo. The first three days Lotario did not speak to Camila, though he might have done so when they removed the cloth and the servants retired to dine hastily. Such were Camila's orders, and Leonela had even been instructed to dine earlier than Camila and never to leave her side. She, however, her mind being fixed upon things more to her taste, and needing this time and occasion for her own pleasures, did not always obey her mistress's commands. On the contrary she left them alone, as if they had ordered her to do so. But Camila's modest bearing, the calmness of her countenance, and her total composure were enough to bridle Lotario's tongue.

"But the influence exerted by the many virtues of Camila in imposing silence on Lotario's tongue proved mischievous for both of them, for if his tongue was silent his thoughts were busy and could dwell at leisure upon the perfections of Camila's goodness and beauty one by one. These were charms enough to awaken love in a marble statue, not to say a heart of flesh. Lotario gazed upon her when he might have been speaking to her and thought how worthy of being loved she was. Thus reflection began little by little to assail his allegiance to Anselmo, and a thousand times he thought of withdrawing from the city and going where Anselmo should never see him nor he see Camila. But already the delight he found in contemplating Camila, prevented and detained him. He made an effort to constrain himself, struggling to repel and repress the pleasure he found in contemplating Camila, and when alone he blamed himself for his weakness, calling himself a bad friend and even a bad Christian. Then he argued the matter and compared himself with Anselmo, always reaching the conclusion that Anselmo's folly and rashness had been worse than his own faithlessness, and that if he could excuse his intentions as easily before God as with man, he had no reason to fear any punishment for his offense.

"In short, the beauty and goodness of Camila, joined with the opportunity which the blind husband had placed in his hands, overcame Lotario's loyalty. Heeding nothing save the object of his desires, after Anselmo had been absent for three days, during which he had waged a ceaseless struggle with his passion, he began to voice his love for Camila with so much vehemence and warmth of language that she was overwhelmed with amazement. All she could do was rise to her feet and retire to her room without answering him a word.

"But this rebuff did nothing to weaken, in Lotario, the hope which always springs up with love. On the contrary, his passion for Camila increased while she, on discovering in him what she had never expected, did not know what to do. Considering it neither safe nor right to give him the opportunity of speaking to her again, she resolved to send, that very night, one of her servants with a letter to Anselmo, in which she wrote the following words.

Chapter XXXIV

IN WHICH IS CONTINUED THE STORY OF ILL-ADVISED CURIOSITY

" 'It is commonly said that an army makes a poor showing without its general and a castle without its warden, and I say that a young married woman looks still worse without her husband unless there are very good reasons for it. I find myself so ill at ease without you and so incapable of enduring this separation, that unless you return quickly I shall have to go for relief to my parents' house, even if I leave yours without a protector. For the protector you have left me, if indeed he deserved that title, has, I think an eye for his own pleasure rather than for what concerns you. As you are a man of discernment I need say no more to you, nor indeed is it fitting I should say more.'

"Anselmo received this letter and gathered that Lotario had already begun his task and that Camila must have replied to him as he himself would have wished. Delighted beyond measure on learning this, he sent word to her not to leave his house on any account, as he would very shortly return. Camila was astonished at Anselmo's reply, which placed her in greater preplexity than before. She neither dared to remain in her own house, nor yet to go to her parents, for if she stayed her virtue was imperiled, and if the left she was opposing her husband's commands.

"Finally she decided upon what was the worse course for her, resolving not to fly from Lotario's presence, so as not to give her servants food for gossip. She now began to regret having written thus to her husband, fearing he might imagine that Lotario had discovered in her some frivolousness which had impelled him to lay aside the respect he owed her. However, being confident of her rectitude, she put her trust in God and in her own virtuous intentions, which would enable her to resist in silence all Lotario's solicitations without informing her husband so as not to involve him in any quarrel or trouble. She even began to consider how to excuse

Lotario to Anselmo, if he should inquire what had induced her to write that letter.

"With these resolutions, which were more honorable than judicious or effectual, she spent the next day listening to Lotario. He wooed her so ardently that her firmness began to waver, and her virtue had enough to do to rescue her eyes, lest they should reveal the tender compassion which Lotario's tears and appeals had awakened in her bosom. Lotario observed all this, and it inflamed him all the more. In short he felt that while Anselmo's absence afforded time and opportunity he must lay siege to the fortress, and so he assailed her self-esteem with praises of her beauty, for there is nothing that more quickly overcomes and levels the castle towers of fair women's vanity than vanity itself, borne upon the tongue of flattery. In fact with the utmost assiduity he undermined the rock of her purity with such skillful devices that even if Camila had been of brass she would have fallen. He wept, he entreated, he promised, he flattered, he importuned, he pretended with so much feeling and apparent sincerity, that he overthrew Camila's virtuous resolves and won the triumph he least expected and most longed for.

"Camila yielded, Camila fell. But what wonder if Lotario's friendship could not stand firm? This clear example shows us that the passion of love is to be conquered only by flying from it and that no one should engage in a struggle with an enemy so mighty, for divine strength is needed to overcome his human power. Leonela alone knew of her mistress's weakness, for the two false friends and new lovers were unable to conceal it. Lotario preferred not to tell Camila what Anselmo had had in mind, or that it was Anselmo who had made the outcome possible. Lotario did not want Camila to undervalue his love and think that it was by chance and unintentionally, and not of his own accord, that he had wooed her.

"A few days later Anselmo returned to his house and failed to notice that it was lacking in the very thing he had treated so lightly and esteemed so highly. He went at once to see Lotario and found him at home. They embraced each other, and Anselmo asked for the tidings of his life or his death.

" 'The tidings I have to give you Anselmo my friend,' said Lotario, 'are that you possess a wife worthy to be the pattern and crown of all good wives. The words I addressed to her were carried away by the wind, my promises despised, and my presents refused, while the feigned tears I shed were turned into open ridicule. In short, Camila is both the essence of all beauty and the treasure-house where purity dwells and gentleness and modesty abide with all the virtues that can confer praise, honor, and happiness upon a woman. Take back your money, my friend. Here it is, and I had

had no need to touch it, for Camila's chastity does not yield to things so base as gifts or promises. Be content, Anselmo, and refrain from seeking further proof. As you have passed dryshod through the sea of doubts and suspicions that are and may be held concerning women, do not plunge again into the deep ocean of new embarrassments or with another pilot make trial of the goodness and strength of the ship that Heaven has granted you for your passage across the sea of this world. Consider yourself now safe in port, moor yourself with the anchor of sound reflection, and rest in peace until you are called upon to pay that debt which no nobility on earth can escape paying.'

"Anselmo was completely satisfied by Lotario's words and believed them as fully as if they had been spoken by an oracle. Nevertheless he begged him not to abandon the undertaking, if only for the sake of curiosity and amusement. Yet, from this point on, Lotario need not strive as earnestly as before. All Anselmo wished him to do was to write some verses to her, praising her under the name of Chloris. Anselmo would tell Camila that Lotario was in love with a lady to whom he had given that name so that he might sing her praises with the decorum due to her modesty. If Lotario were unwilling to take the trouble of writing the verses, Anselmo would compose them himself.

" 'That will not be necessary,' said Lotario, 'for the muses are not such enemies of mine that they disdain to visit me now and then in the course of the year. Tell Camila what you have proposed about a pretended love affair of mine, and as for the verses, I will write them. If they are not as good as the subject deserves, at least they will be the best I can produce.'

"An agreement to this effect was made between the friends, the one ill-advised and the other treacherous. Anselmo, returning to his house, asked Camila the question she already wondered he had not asked before—why she had felt obliged to write the letter she had sent him. Camila replied that it had seemed to her that Lotario looked at her somewhat more freely than when Anselmo had been at home. But now she was undeceived and believed it was only her own imagination, for Lotario now avoided seeing her or being alone with her. Anselmo told her she might be quite easy about that, for he knew that Lotario was in love with a damsel of rank in the city whom he celebrated under the name of Chloris, and that even if he were not, his fidelity and their great friendship left no room for fear. Had not Camila, however, been informed beforehand by Lotario that this love for Chloris was a pretense and that he himself had told Anselmo of it so that he might sometimes voice the praises of Camila herself, no doubt she would have fallen into the despairing toils of jealousy. Being forewarned, she received the startling news without uneasiness.

"The next day, as the three were at table, Anselmo asked Lotario to recite something of what he had composed for his mistress Chloris, for as Camila did not know her, he might safely say what he liked.

" 'Even if she did know her,' returned Lotario, 'I would hide nothing, for when a lover praises his lady's beauty and accuses her of cruelty, he casts no imputation upon her fair name. At any rate, all I can say is that yesterday I wrote a sonnet on the ingratitude of this Chloris, which goes thus:

SONNET

At midnight, in the silence, when the eyes
  Of happier mortals balmy slumbers close,
  The weary tale of my unnumbered woes
To Chloris and to Heaven is wont to rise.
And when the light of day returning dyes
  The portals of the east with tints of rose,
  With undiminished force my sorrow flows
In broken accents and in burning sighs.
And when the sun ascends his star-girt throne,
  And on the earth pours down his midday beams,
    Noon but renews my wailing and my tears;
And with the night again goes up my moan.
  Yet ever in my agony it seems
    To me that neither Heaven nor Chloris hears.'

"The sonnet pleased Camila, and still more Anselmo, for he praised it and said the lady was excessively cruel, since she made no return for sincerity so manifest. On which Camila said, 'Then all that lovesick poets say is true?'

" 'As poets they do not tell the truth,' replied Lotario, 'but as lovers they are as truthful as they are incapable of expressing what they feel.'

" 'There is no doubt of that,' observed Anselmo, anxious to support and uphold Lotario's ideas with Camila, who was as unaware of his design as she was deeply in love with Lotario. So, taking delight in anything that was his, and knowing that his thoughts and writings had her for their object and that she herself was the real Chloris, she asked him to repeat some other sonnet or verses if he recollected any.

" 'I do,' replied Lotario, 'but I do not think it as good as the first one, or, more correctly speaking, it is even worse. But you can easily judge, for it is this.

SONNET

I know that I am doomed; death is to me
  As certain as that thou, ungrateful fair,
  Dead at thy feet shouldst see me lying, ere

My heart repented of its love for thee.
If buried in oblivion I should be,
  Bereft of life, fame, favor, even there
  It would be found that I thy image bear
Deep graven in my breast for all to see.
This like some holy relic do I prize
  To save me from the fate my truth entails,
    Truth that to thy hard heart its vigor owes.
Alas for him that under lowering skies,
  In peril o'er a trackless ocean sails,
    Where neither friendly port nor pole star shows.'

"Anselmo praised this second sonnet too, as he had praised the first. Thus he went on adding link after link to the chain with which he was binding himself and making his dishonor secure. When Lotario was doing most to dishonor Anselmo, Anselmo told him he was most honored, so that with each step that Camila descended towards the depths of her abasement, she mounted, in Anselmo's opinion, towards the summit of virtue and fair fame.

" 'I am ashamed to think, my dear Leonela,' said Camila on one occasion, when she happened to be alone with her maid, 'how lightly I have valued myself that I did not compel Lotario to purchase at least by some expenditure of time, that full possession of myself I so quickly yielded him of my own free will. I fear he will note only my pliancy or frivolity and not consider the irresistible influence he brought to bear on me.'

" 'Do not let that trouble you, my lady,' said Leonela, 'for it does not take away the value of the thing given or make it the less precious to give it quickly, if it is really valuable and worthy of being prized. People even have the saying that "he who gives quickly gives twice." '

" 'They say also,' said Camila, 'that "what costs little is valued less." '

" 'That saying does not hold good in your case,' replied Leonela, 'for love, as I have heard say, sometimes flies and sometimes walks. With one it runs, with another it moves slowly; some it cools, others it burns, some it wounds, others it slays. It begins the course of its desires and at the same moment completes and ends it. In the morning it will lay siege to a fortress and by night will have taken it, for there is no power that can resist it. So what are you in dread of, what do you fear, when the same must have befallen Lotario, love having chosen the absence of my master as the instrument for subduing us? It was absolutely necessary to complete then what love had decided before Anselmo had time to return and by his presence cause the work to be left unfinished. Love has no better agent for carrying out his designs than opportunity, and of opportunity he avails himself in all his feats, especially at the outset. All this I know well myself, more by experience than by hearsay, and some day, señora, I will enlighten you on the subject, for I am of your flesh and blood too. Moreover, lady Camila, you did not surrender yourself or yield so quickly. First you saw Lotario's whole soul in his eyes, in his sighs, in his words, his promises, and his gifts, and by it and his good qualities perceived how worthy he was of your love. This, then, being the the case, do not let these scrupulous and prudish ideas trouble your imagination, but be assured that Lotario prizes you as you do him, and be content and satisfied that as you are caught in the noose of love, it is one of worth and merit that has taken you, and one that has not only the four S's that they say true lovers ought to have,[1] but a complete alphabet. Listen to me and you will see how I can repeat it by rote. He is, to my eyes and thinking, Amiable, Brave, Courteous, Distinguished, Elegant, Fond, Gay, Honorable, Illustrous, Loyal, Manly, Noble, Open, Polite, Quickwitted, Rich, and the S's according to the saying, and then Tender, Veracious—X does not suit him, for it is a rough letter—Y has been given already, and Z, Zealous for your honor.'[2]

"Camila laughed at her maid's alphabet and perceived her to be more experienced in love affairs than she had said. This she admitted, confessing to Camila that she was having a love affair with a young man of good birth of the same city. Camila was uneasy at this, fearing it might in some way endanger her honor, and she asked whether her intrigue had gone beyond words. Her maid, with little shame and much effrontery, said it had, for it is certain that ladies' imprudences make servants shameless. When they see their mistresses make a false step, they think nothing of going astray themselves, or of letting it be known.

"Camila could do no more than entreat Leonela to say nothing about her mistress's doings to the young man she called her lover and to conduct her own affairs secretly lest Anselmo or Lotario should hear of them. Leonela said she would, but kept her word in such a way that she confirmed Camila's fear of losing her reputation because of her maid's behavior. For this abandoned, bold Leonela, as soon as she perceived that her mistress was no longer acting as she had previously done, had the audacity to bring her lover into the house, confident that even if her mistress saw him she would not dare to expose him. The sins of mistresses give rise to this mischief among others; thus they make themselves the slaves of their own servants, whose laxities and depravities they are forced to hide.

"This was the case with Camila, who perceived not once but

1. The four *S*'s that should qualify a lover were *sabio, solo, solícito, secreto*: "wise, unattached, persistent, discreet."
2. This is a free translation of Leonela's list. *I* was also used in print as a sign for the sound of *J* and was interchangeable with *Y*. There were no *K* or *W*. *U* and *V* were interchangeable in print. The "rough" *X* at this period was beginning to stand for the Modern Spanish strongly aspirated h-sound.

many times that Leonela was with her lover in some room of the house. Yet not only did she not dare to chide her, she afforded her opportunities for concealing him and removed all hindrances, lest he should be seen by her husband. She was unable, however, to prevent Lotario from seeing him on one occasion, as he sallied forth at daybreak. Lotario, not knowing who he was, at first took him for a ghost. But as soon as he saw him hasten away, muffling his face with his cloak and carefully concealing himself, he rejected this foolish idea and adopted another, which would have ruined everything if Camila had not hit upon a remedy. It did not occur to Lotario that the man he had seen issuing at such an untimely hour from Anselmo's house could have entered it on Leonela's account, nor did he even remember there was such a person as Leonela. All he thought was that as Camila had been light and yielding with him, she had been equally so with another. For the erring woman's sin brings this further penalty with, it, that her honor is distrusted even by the man to whose overtures and persuasions she has yielded. He believes her to have surrendered more easily to others and gives immediate credence to every suspicion that comes into his mind.

"All Lotario's good sense seems to have failed him at this juncture, and all his prudent maxims escaped his memory. For without once reflecting rationally, and without more ado, he hastened to speak to Anselmo, who had not yet got out of bed. In his impatience and in the blind, jealous rage that gnawed his heart, he was dying to revenge himself upon Camila, who had done him no wrong.

" 'Anselmo,' he said to him, 'I must tell you that for several days past I have been in a quandry, trying to keep silent about a matter it is no longer possible or right I should conceal from you. You should know that Camila's fortress has surrendered and is ready to submit to my will. If I have been slow to reveal this to you, it was in order to see if it was some light caprice of hers or if she sought to test me in order to discover whether my wooing of her, done with your permission, was intended seriously. I thought, too, that if she were what she ought to be and what we both believed her to be, she would have told you of my advances before now. But in view of her delay, I believe the promise she made me that the next time you are away from the house she will meet me in the storage room where you keep your valuables.' Camila used, indeed, to meet him there.

" 'But I do not wish you to rush precipitously to vengeance, for the sin is as yet only committed in intention, and Camila may change her mind before the time agreed upon and, instead, be filled with contrition. Since until now you have always followed my advice wholly or in part, be sure to take the advice I am about to give you so that, without mistake and with mature deliberation, you may satisfy yourself as to the best course. Pretend to go away for two or three days as you have done on other occasions, and contrive to hide yourself in the storeroom. The tapestries and other things there make it easy for you to remain hidden, and then you will see with your own eyes, and I with mine, what Camila's intention is. If it should be a guilty one, which may be feared rather than expected, then with silence, prudence, and discretion you yourself can avenge the wrong done you.'

"Anselmo was amazed, overwhelmed, and astounded at Lotario's words, which came at a time when he least expected to hear them, for he had regarded Camila as having triumphed over the pretended attacks of Lotario and was beginning to enjoy the glory of her victory. He remained silent for a considerable time, looking on the ground with fixed gaze.

" 'You have behaved, Lotario,' he said at last, 'as I expected of your friendship. I will follow your advice in everything, and you, do as you see fit, and keep this secret as you see it must be kept in such unexpected circumstances.'

"Lotario gave his word, but after leaving Anselmo he was filled with remorse over what he had said to him. He realized how foolishly he had acted, as he could have revenged himself upon Camila in some less cruel and degrading way. He cursed his want of sense, condemned his hasty resolution, and did not know how he could undo the mischief or find some acceptable solution. At last he decided to tell Camila everything, and as there was no lack of opportunity for doing so, he found her alone the same day. But she, as soon as the chance presented itself, spoke to him first.

" 'Lotario my love,' she said, 'I must tell you of the sorrow in my heart which fills it so that it seems ready to burst. It will be a wonder if it does not, for Leonela's audacity has now reached such a pitch that every night she conceals a gallant of hers in this house and remains with him till morning, at the cost of my reputation. For this is at the mercy of anyone who happens to see him leave my house at such untimely hours. But what distresses me is that I cannot punish or chide her, for her awareness of our intrigue prevents my saying anything about hers, though I am dreading that some catastrophe will come of it.'

"As Camila said this Lotario at first imagined it was a trick, to persuade him that the man he had seen going out was Leonela's lover and not hers. But when he saw how she wept and suffered and begged him to help her, he realized she was telling the truth, and this heightened his confusion and remorse. However, he told Camila not to be alarmed, as he would find a way to check Leonela's insolence. At the same time he told her what, in his jealous rage, he had said to Anselmo and how Anselmo had hidden himself in the storeroom so that he might see how poorly Camila preserved her fidelity to him. Lotario entreated her pardon for this madness and asked her advice as to how to remedy the situation so that he could emerge from the intricate labyrinth in which his imprudence had placed him.

"Camila was angered and appalled by what Lotario told her, and with great good sense she reproved him and condemned his base design and the foolish and mischievous resolution he had made. But as woman has by nature a nimbler wit than man for good and for evil, though it is apt to fail when she sets out deliberately to reason, Camila on the spur of the moment thought of a way to remedy what was to all appearances irremediable. She told Lotario to arrange that the next day Anselmo should conceal himself in the place he mentioned, for thereby she hoped to make sure that in the future they could enjoy themselves without any apprehension. Without revealing her plan to him entirely she told him to be careful, as soon as Anselmo was concealed, to come to her when Leonela called him. To everything Camila would say, Lotario should answer as he would have answered had he not known that Anselmo was listening. Lotario begged her to explain her intention fully, so that he could do what he saw was needful with greater assuredness and prudence.

" 'I tell you,' said Camila, 'there is nothing to be concerned about except to reply to whatever I ask,' for she did not wish to explain to him beforehand what she meant to do, fearing he might be unwilling to follow out an idea which seemed to her such a good one and might try to devise some other less practicable plan.

"Lotario went away, and the next day Anselmo, pretending to go to his friend's country house, took his departure, and then returned. He had no trouble hiding himself, for Camila and Leonela took care to give him the opportunity.

"So he placed himself in hiding in the state of agitation it may be imagined a man would feel who expected to see the entrails of his honor laid bare before his eyes and who was about to lose the supreme blessing he thought he possessed in his beloved Camila. Having made sure Anselmo was in his hiding place, Camila and Leonela entered the store-room and the instant she set foot within it Camilla heaved a deep sigh. 'Ah! dear Leonela,' she said, 'would it not be better, before I do what I am unwilling you should know, for fear you may try to prevent it, that you should take Anselmo's dagger, which I asked you for, and pierce this vile heart of mine? But no, there is no reason why I should suffer the punishment of another's fault. First I must find out what it is that the bold licentious eyes of Lotario have seen in me that could have encouraged him to disclose a design so base, without regard for his friend and for my honor. Go to the window, Leonela, and call him, for no doubt he is in the street waiting to carry out his vile project. But mine, cruel though it is, but honorable, shall be carried out first.'

" 'Ah, señora,' said the crafty Leonela, who knew her part, 'what is it you want to do with this dagger? Can it be that you mean to take your own life, or Lotario's? Whichever you mean to do, it will lead to the loss of your reputation and good name. It is better to dissemble the wrong done you and not give this wicked man the chance of entering the house now and finding us alone. Consider, señora: we are weak women, and he is a man, and a determined one. As he comes with such a base purpose and urged on by blind passion, perhaps before you can carry out your resolve he may do what will be worse for you than taking your life. Confound my master, Anselmo, for giving such authority in his house to this shameless fellow! And supposing you kill him, señora, as I suspect you mean to do, what shall we do with him when he is dead?'

" 'What, my friend?' replied Camila. 'We shall leave him for Anselmo to bury. He will look on it as a light task to hide his own infamy underground. Fetch Lotario, and hurry, for all the time I delay in avenging my wrong seems to me an offense against the loyalty I owe my husband.'

Anselmo was listening to all this, and every word that Camila uttered made him change his mind. But when he heard the decision to kill Lotario his first impulse was to emerge from hiding to avert such a disaster. Yet in his anxiety to see the outcome of a resolution so bold and virtuous, he restrained himself, intending to come out in time to prevent the deed. At this moment Camila, throwing herself upon a bed that was close by, swooned away, and Leonela began to weep bitterly.

" 'Woe is me!' cried Leonela, 'that I should be fated to have dying here in my arms the flower of virtue upon earth, the crown of true wives, the pattern of chastity!' She uttered more to the same effect, so that anyone who heard her would have taken her for the most tender-hearted and faithful handmaid in the world, and her mistress for another persecuted Penelope.

" 'Why do you not go, Leonela,' said Camila, who was not long in recovering from her fainting fit, 'and summon this friend, the falsest to his friend the sun ever shone upon or night concealed? Away, run, haste, speed, lest the fire of my wrath burn itself out with delay and the righteous vengeance that I hope for melt away in menaces and curses.'

" 'I am just going to call him, señora,' said Leonela. 'But you must first give me the dagger, lest during my absence you should give cause to all who love you to weep all their lives.'

" 'Go in peace dear Leonela, I will not do so,' said Camila, 'for rash and foolish as I may be to your mind, in defending my honor I shall not be so rash as that Lucretia who, they say, killed herself without having done anything wrong and without having first killed the man responsible for her misfortune. I shall die, if I am to die, but it must be after full vengeance upon him who has brought me here to weep over audacity that no fault of mine gave birth to.'

"Leonela required much urging before she would go to summon Lotario, but at last she went, and while awaiting her return Camila continued, as if speaking to herself. 'Good God!' she exclaimed, 'would it not have been more prudent to have repulsed Lotario, as I have done many a time before, than to allow him, as I am now doing, to think me unchaste and vile, even for the short time I must wait until I undeceive him? No doubt it would have been better, but I should not be avenged, nor my husband's honor vindicated, should he find so clear and easy an escape from the consequences of his depravity. Let the traitor pay with his life for the temerity of his wanton wishes, and let the world know (if ever it should come to know) that Camila not only preserved her allegiance to her husband, but avenged him of the man who dared to wrong him. Still, I think it might be better to reveal this to Anselmo. But then I called his attention to it in the letter I wrote to him in the country. If he did nothing to prevent the mischief I there pointed out to him, I suppose that out of pure goodness of heart and trustfulness he would not and could not believe that any thought against his honor could dwell in the breast of so staunch a friend. Nor indeed did I myself believe it for many days, nor could I have ever believed it if his insolence had not gone so far as to make it manifest by open presents, lavish promises, and ceaseless tears. But why do I argue thus? Does a bold determination stand in need of arguments? Surely not. Then down with traitors! Vengeance, to my aid! Let the false one approach, advance, die, yield up his life, and then befall what may. Pure I came to him whom Heaven bestowed upon me, pure I shall have him. At the worst I shall be bathed in my own chaste blood and in the foul blood of the falsest friend that friendship ever saw in the world.' As she uttered these words she paced the room holding the unsheathed dagger, with such irregular and disordered steps and such gestures that one would have supposed her to have lost her senses and taken her for some violent desperado instead of a delicate woman.

"Anselmo, hidden behind some tapestries where he had concealed himself, saw and was amazed by everything. He already felt that what he had seen and heard was a sufficient answer to even greater suspicions, and he would have been now well pleased if the proof Lotario's coming would provide were dispensed with, as he feared some sudden mishap. But as he was on the point of coming out to embrace and undeceive his wife, he paused, for he saw Leonela returning with Lotario. Camila, when she saw Lotario, drew a long line on front of her on the floor with the dagger.

" 'Lotario,' she said, 'pay attention to my words. If you should dare to cross this line, or even approach it, the instant I see you attempt it I will pierce my bosom with this dagger. Before you utter a word I desire you to listen to a few from me, and afterwards you can reply as you choose. First I want you to tell me, Lotario, if you know my husband Anselmo, and in what light you regard him. Secondly, I want to know if you know me too. Answer me this, without embarrassment or reflecting deeply on your answer, for I ask you no riddles.'

"Lotario was not so dull that he had failed to grasp Camila's intention from the first moment when she directed him to have Anselmo hide himself. Therefore he fell in with her idea so readily and promptly that between them they made the imposture look more true than truth.

" 'I did not think, fair Camila,' such was his reply, 'that you sent for me to ask questions so remote from the aim I have in coming here. But if you are doing so in order to defer the promised reward, you might have put it off still longer, for the longing for happiness gives the more distress the nearer comes the hope of gaining it. But lest you should say I do not answer your questions, I say that I know your husband Anselmo, and that we have known each other from our earliest years. I will not speak of what you too know, of our friendship, so that I may not compel myself to testify against the wrong that love, the mighty excuse for greater errors, makes me inflict upon him. You I know and hold in the same estimation as he does, for otherwise I would not, for any lesser reward, have acted against what I owe my station and the holy laws of true friendship, now broken and violated by me through that powerful enemy, love.'

" 'If you confess that,' returned Camila, 'mortal enemy of all that rightly deserves to be loved, with what face do you dare to come before one you know to be the mirror in which her husband sees himself, and into which you should look in order to see how unworthily you wrong him? But, woe is me, I now comprehend what has made you give so little heed to what you owe yourself. It must have been some frivolity of mine, for I will not call it immodesty, as I did not proceed from any deliberate intention, but from some heedlessness such as women are guilty of through inadvertence when they think they have no occasion for reserve. But tell me, traitor, when did I by word or sign give a reply to your entreaties that could awaken in you a shadow of hope of attaining your base wishes? When were not your declarations of love sternly and scornfully rejected and rebuked? When were your frequent pledges and still more frequent gifts believed or accepted? Yet, since I am convinced that no one can long persevere in the attempt to win love unsustained by some hope, I am willing to attribute to myself the blame for your assurance, for no doubt some thoughtlessness of mine has all this time fostered your hopes. Therefore will I punish myself and inflict upon myself the penalty your guilt deserves. And so that you may see that being so relentless to myself I cannot possibly behave otherwise to you, I have sent for you to witness the sacrifice I mean to offer the injured honor of my honored husband, wronged by you with all the diligence you were capable of, and by me too through lack of caution in avoiding every occasion, if I have given any, of encouraging and sanctioning your base designs. Once more I say the suspicion I have, that some imprudence of mine aroused these lawless thoughts in you, is what causes me most distress. This too is what I desire to punish with my own hands, for if any other means were used, my error might become more widely known. But before I do so, in dying I mean to inflict death and take with me one who will fully satisfy my longing for the revenge I cherish. For I shall see, wherever I go, how the penalty is inflicted by inflexible, unswerving justice on the man who has placed me in so desperate a position.'

"As she uttered these words, with incredible energy and swiftness she dashed at Lotario with the naked dagger, so clearly intent on burying it in his breast that he was almost uncertain whether these demonstrations were real or feigned. He needed all his skill and strength to prevent her from striking him; and with such reality did she act this strange farce and mystification that, to give it the semblance of truth, she determined to stain it with her own blood. Realizing—or pretending to realize—that she could not wound Lotario, she said, 'It seems that Fate will not grant my just desire complete satisfaction, but it will not be able to keep me from satisfying it partially at least.' With that she made an effort to free the hand with the dagger which Lotario held in his grasp, and she succeeded in releasing it. Then, directing the point to a place where it could not inflict a deep wound, she plunged it into her left side high up close to the shoulder, and allowed herself to fall to the ground as if in a faint.

"Leonela and Lotario stood amazed and astounded at the catastrophe, and seeing Camila stretched on the ground and bathed in her blood they were still uncertain as to the true nature of the act. Lotario, terrified and breathless, ran in haste to pluck out the dagger, but when he saw how slight the wound was he was relieved of his fears and once more admired the subtlety, coolness, and ready wit of the fair Camila. In order to play his part more convincingly, he began to utter profuse and doleful lamentations over her body as if she were dead, invoking curses not only on himself but also on the man responsible for placing him in such a position. Knowing that his friend Anselmo heard him, he spoke in such a way as to make a listener feel much more pity for Lotario himself than for Camila, even though she were supposed to be dead.

"Leonela took her up in her arms and laid her on the bed, entreating Lotario to find someone to attend to her wound in secret, and at the same time asking him what they should say to Anselmo about his lady's wound, if he should chance to return before it was healed. He replied they might say what they liked, for he was not in a state to give advice that would be of any use. All he could tell her was to try to stop the bleeding, as he was going where he should never more be seen, and with every appearance of deep grief and sorrow he left the house. But when he found himself alone and where there was nobody to see him, he crossed himself unceasingly, lost in wonder at the adroitness of Camila and the consistent acting of Leonela. He reflected how convinced Anselmo would be that he had a second Portia[3] for a wife, and he looked forward anxiously to meeting Anselmo in order to rejoice together over falsehood and truth the most craftily veiled that could be imagined.

"Leonela, as he told her, staunched her lady's blood, which was no more than enough to support her deception. Washing the wound with a little wine, she bound it up to the best of her ability, talking all the time she was tending her in a strain that, even if nothing else had been said before, would have assured Anselmo that he had in Camila a model of purity. To Leonela's words Camila added her own, calling herself cowardly and lacking courage since, at the time she had most need of it, she had not enough to rid herself of the life she so much loathed. She asked her attendant's advice as whether or not she ought to inform her beloved husband of all that had happened, but Leonela told her to say nothing about it, since this would oblige him to take vengeance on Lotario. He could do so only at great risk to himself, and it was the duty of a true wife not to provoke her husband to quarrel but, on the contrary, to spare him all dissension as far as possible.

"Camila replied that she believed Leonela was right and that she would follow her advice, but at any rate it would be well to consider how she was to explain the wound to Anselmo, for he could not help seeing it. Leonela answered that she did not know how to tell a lie even in jest.

" 'Then how can I, my dear?' said Camila, 'for I would not dare to forge or keep up a falsehood if my life depended on it. If we can

3. Portia, Brutus' wife, killed herself at her husband's death.

think of no escape from this difficulty, it will be better to tell him the plain truth than that he should find us out in an untrue story.'

" 'Have no qualms, señora,' said Leonela. 'Between this time and tomorrow I will think of what we must say to him, and perhaps the wound being where it is it can be hidden from his sight, and Heaven will be pleased to aid us in a purpose so good and honorable. Calm yourself, señora, and endeavor to moderate your excitement lest my master find you agitated. Leave the rest to my care and God's, who always supports good intentions.'

"Anselmo had with the deepest attention listened to and seen played out the tragedy of the death of his honor, which the performers acted with such wonderfully convincing truth that it seemed they had become the realities of the parts they played. He longed for night and an opportunity of escaping from the house to go and see his good friend Lotario, and with him give vent to his joy over the precious pearl he had gained in having established his wife's purity. Both mistress and maid took care to give him time and opportunity to get away, and he took advantage of it to make his escape. At once he went in quest of Lotario, and it would be impossible to describe how he embraced him when he found him and the things he said to him in the joy of his heart and the praises he bestowed upon Camila. Lotario listened to all this without being able to show any pleasure, for he could not forget how deceived his friend was and how dishonorably he had wronged him. Though Anselmo could see that Lotario was not glad, still he imagined it was only because he had left Camila wounded and had been himself the cause of it. So among other things he told him not to be distressed about Camila's accident, for, as they had agreed to hide it, the wound was evidently trifling. That being so, Lotario had no cause for fear, but should henceforward be of good cheer and rejoice like Anselmo himself who, thanks to Lotario's adroitness, found himself raised to the greatest height of happiness he could ever have hoped for. He could desire no better pastime than making verses in praise of Camila that would preserve her name for all time to come. Lotario applauded his intention and proposed to help him in raising a monument so glorious.

"And so Anselmo was left the most willingly hoodwinked man there could be in the world. He himself, persuaded he was conducting the instrument of his glory, led home by the hand the man who had utterly destroyed his good name. Camila received him with averted countenance, though with smiles in her heart. The deception was carried on for some time, until at the end of a few months Fortune turned her wheel and the guilt which had been until then so skilfully concealed was published abroad, and Anselmo paid with his life the penalty of his ill-advised curiosity."

Chapter XXXV

WHICH BRINGS THE STORY OF ILL-ADVISED CURIOSITY TO A CLOSE AND TREATS OF THE HEROIC AND PRODIGIOUS BATTLE DON QUIXOTE HAD WITH CERTAIN SKINS OF RED WINE[1]

There remained but little more of the story to be read, when Sancho Panza burst forth in wild excitement from the garret where Don Quixote was lying. "Run, sirs! quick," he shouted, "and help my master, who is in the thick of the toughest and stiffest battle I ever laid eyes on. By the living God he has given the giant, the enemy of my lady the Princess Micomicona, such a slash that he has sliced his head clean off as if it were a turnip."

"What are you talking about, brother?" said the priest, pausing as he was about to read the remainder of the story. "Are you in your senses, Sancho? How the devil can that be, when the giant is two thousand leagues away?"

Here they heard a loud noise in the chamber and Don Quixote shouting out, "Stop, theif, brigand, villain. Now I have thee, and thy scimitar shall not avail thee!" And then it seemed as though he were slashing vigorously at the wall.

"Don't stop to listen," said Sancho, "but go in and separate them or help my master. Though there's probably no need of that now; no doubt the giant is dead by this time and giving account to God of this past wicked life. I saw the blood flowing on the ground and the head cut off and fallen on one side, and it is as big as a large wineskin."

"May I die," said the landlord at this, "if Don Quixote or Don Devil has not slashed some of the skins full of red wine that were standing by his bed. The spilled wine must be what this good fellow takes for blood."

So saying he went into the room and the rest after him, and there they found Don Quixote in the strangest costume in the world. He was in his shirt, which was not long enough in front to cover his thighs completely and was about four inches shorter behind. His legs were very long and lean, covered with hair, and anything but clean; on his head he had a little greasy red cap that belonged to the innkeeper; around his left arm he had rolled the blanket of the bed, to which Sancho, for reasons best known to himself, owed a grudge; and in his right hand he held his unsheathed sword, with which he was slashing about on all sides, uttering exclamations as if he were actually fighing some giant. The

1. In the first edition, the reference to Don Quixote's battle with the wineskins (which occurs in this chapter) appears by mistake in the heading of Chapter XXXVI.

best of it was his eyes were not open, for he was fast asleep and dreaming that he was doing battle with the giant. For his imagination was so worked up by the adventure he was going to accomplish that it made him dream he had already reached the kingdom of Micomicón and was engaged in combat with his enemy. Believing he was raining blows on the giant, he had given so many sword cuts to the skins that the whole room was full of wine.

Seeing this, the landlord was so enraged that he rushed at Don Quixote and with his clenched fist began to pummel him in such a way that if Cardenio and the priest had not dragged him off, he would have brought the war with the giant to an end. But in spite of everything, the poor gentleman never woke until the barber brought a great pot of cold water from the well and dashed it all over his body, on which Don Quixote woke up, but not so completely as to understand what was the matter. Dorotea, seeing how short and slight his attire was, would not go in to witness the battle between her champion and her opponent. As for Sancho, he went searching all over the floor for the head of the giant.

"I see now," he said, when he failed to find it, "that it's all enchantment in this house. For the last time, on this very spot where I am now, I got ever so many punches and blows without knowing who gave them to me or being able to see anybody. Now this head is not to be seen anywhere about, though I saw it cut off with my own eyes and the blood running from the body as if from a fountain."

"What blood and fountains are you talking about, enemy of God and his saints?" said the landlord. "Don't you see, you thief, that the blood and the fountain are only these skins here that have been stabbed and the red wine swimming all over the room? And I wish I saw the soul of him that stabbed them swimming in hell."

"I know nothing about that," said Sancho. "All I know is it will be my bad luck that through not finding this head my county will melt away like salt in water." For Sancho awake was worse than his master asleep, so much had his master's promises affected him.

The innkeeper was beside himself at the indifference of the squire and the mischievous doings of the master. He swore it would not be like the last time, when they went without paying, and that their privileges of chivalry would not hold good this time, to let one or other of them off without paying, even to the cost of the patches that would have to be put on the damaged wineskins. The priest was holding Don Quixote's hands, for he, fancying he had now ended the adventure and was in the presence of the Princess Micomicona, had knelt down in front of the priest. "Exalted and famous lady," he said, "your highness may live from this day forth fearless of any harm this base being could do you. And I too from this day forth am released from the promise I gave you, since by the help of God on high and by the favor of her by whom I live and breathe, I have fulfilled it so successfully."

"Didn't I say so?" said Sancho on hearing this. "You see I wasn't drunk. There you see my master has already made bacon out of the giant. 'There *will* be a bullfight.'[2] My county is a sure thing!"

Who could have helped laughing at the absurdities of the pair, master and servant? And laugh they did, all except the landlord, who cursed himself. But at length the barber, Cardenio, and the priest managed with no small trouble to get Don Quixote on the bed, and he fell asleep with every appearance of excessive weariness. They left him to sleep and came out to the gate of the inn to console Sancho Panza on not having found the head of the giant. But they had far more trouble pacifying the landlord who was furious at the sudden death of his wineskins, while his wife screamed and shouted, "At an evil moment and in an unlucky hour he came into my house, this knight-errant. I wish that I had never set eyes on him, for what he has cost me. The last time he went off without paying the overnight charges against him for supper, bed, straw, and barley, for himself and his squire and a horse and an ass, saying he was a knight adventurer—God send unlucky adventures to him and all the adventurers in the world—and therefore not required to pay anything, because that's the way it was stated in the knight-errantry tariff. And then, all because of him, the other gentleman came and carried off my tail and gives it back with more than two *cuartillos*'[3] worth of damage, all stripped of its hair, so that it is no use to my husband. And then, to top it all off, to burst my wineskins and spill my wine! I wish I saw his own blood spilled! But let him not deceive himself, for, by the bones of my father and the ghost of my mother, they shall pay me down every cent or my name is not what it is and I am not my father's daughter."

All this and more to the same effect the innkeeper's wife delivered with great irritation, and her good maid Maritornes backed her up, while the daughter held her peace and smiled from time to time. The priest smoothed matters by promising to make good all losses to the best of his power, not only as regarded the wineskins but also the wine, and above all the depreciation of the tail which they set such store by. Dorotea comforted Sancho, telling him that she pledged herself, as soon as it appeared certain that his master had decapitated the giant and she found herself peacefully established in her kingdom, to bestow upon him the best county there was in it. With this Sancho consoled himself and assured the princess she might rely upon it that he had seen the head of the giant and that in fact it had a beard that reached its waist, and that if it was not to be seen now, it was because everything that happened in that

2. "*¡Ciertos son los toros!*" Said when something doubtful appears as a certainty.
3. A *cuartillo* is the fourth part of a *real.*

house occurred by means of enchantment, as he himself had proved the last time he had stayed there. Dorotea said she fully believed it, and that he need not be uneasy, for all would go well and turn out as he wished.

Now that everyone had been calmed down, the priest was anxious to go on with the story, as he saw there was but little more left to read. Dorotea and the others begged him to finish it, and he, as he was willing to please them, and enjoyed reading it himself, continued the tale.

"The result was that with the confidence Anselmo felt in Camila's virtue, he lived happy and free from anxiety, while Camila purposely looked coldly on Lotario, so that Anselmo might suppose her feelings towards him to be the opposite of what they were. The better to back up this position, Lotario begged to be excused from coming to the house, as Camila's displeasure at his presence could plainly be seen. But the hoodwinked Anselmo said he would on no account allow such a thing, and so in a thousand ways he became the author of his own dishonor, while he believed he was insuring his happiness. Meanwhile the satisfaction with which Leonela saw herself authorized to carry on her love-affair reached such a height that, regardless of everything else, she followed her inclinations blindly, feeling confident that her mistress would shield her, and even show her how to manage it safely. At last one night Anselmo heard footsteps in Leonela's room, and on trying to enter to see who it was, he found that the door was held shut. This made him all the more determined to open it, so exerting his strength, he forced it open and entered the room in time to see a man leaping through the window into the street. He ran quickly to seize him or discover who he was, but could do neither one nor the other, for Leonela flung her arms around him. 'Calm down, sir,' she said. 'Don't get upset or run after the man who jumped out the window. He belongs to me, and in fact he is my husband.'

"Anselmo would not believe it, but in blind rage drew a dagger and threatened to stab Leonela, ordering her to tell the truth or he would kill her. She was so terrified that she did not realize what she was saying. 'Do not kill me, señor,' she pleaded, 'for I can tell you things more important than any you can imagine.'

" 'Then tell me at once or you will die,' said Anselmo.

" 'It would be impossible for me now,' said Leonela, 'I am so upset. Leave me till tomorrow, and then what you hear from me will fill you with astonishment. But rest assured that the person who leaped through the window is a young man of this city, who has given me his promise to become my husband.'

"Anselmo calmed down and did not mind waiting as she had asked, for he never expected to hear anything against Camila, since he was so content with and sure of her virtue. So he left the room, locking Leonela inside and telling her not to come out until she had told him all she had to reveal. He went at once to see Camila, informing her of all that had passed between him and her maid, and of the promise she had made to reveal to him of matters of grave importance.

"There is no need to relate whether Camila was agitated or not, for so great was her fear that feeling sure, as she had good reason to do, that Leonela would tell Anselmo all she knew of her faithlessness, she had not the courage to wait and see if her suspicions were confirmed. So that very night, as soon as she thought Anselmo had fallen asleep, she packed up her most valuable jewels and some money, and without being observed by anybody escaped from the house and went to Lotario's. She told him what had occurred and begged him to lead her to some safe place or to fly with her where Anselmo could not find them. All this reduced Lotario to such a state of perplexity that he could not say a word to Camila in reply, and he was even less able to decide what to do. At length he resolved to conduct her to a convent where a sister of his was prioress. Camila agreed, and with all the speed the circumstances demanded Lotario took her to the convent and left her there and then himself left the city without informing anyone of his departure.

"As soon as daylight came Anselmo got up, being eager to learn what Leonela had to tell him, and did not notice that Camila was missing. He hastened to the room where he had locked Leonela in, opened the door and entered, but found no Leonela. All he found was some knotted sheets hanging out the window, a plain proof that she had let herself down from it and escaped. He returned, uneasy in mind, to tell Camila, but not finding her in bed or anywhere in the house he was lost in amazement. He asked the servants of the house about her, but none of them could give him any explanation.

"As he was searching for Camila he happened to notice that her boxes were lying open and that the greater part of her jewels were gone. Now he became fully aware of his disgrace and could see that Leonela was not the cause of his misfortune. So just as he was, without dressing completely, he went off, sad at heart and dejected, to acquaint his friend Lotario with his distress. When he failed to find him and the servants reported that he had been absent from his house all night and had taken all his money with him, Anselmo felt as though he were losing his senses. And to round off everything, when he returned to his own house he found it empty, for each and every one of his servants, male and female, had deserted it. He did not know what to think or say or do, and his reason seemed to be deserting him little by little. He reviewed his position and saw himself in a moment left without wife, friend, or servants, abandoned, he felt, by the heaven above him and, worse than all else, robbed of his honor, for in Camila's disappearance he saw his own ruin. After long reflection, he resolved to go to his friend's village, where he had been staying while providing opportunities for this misfortune to be contrived against him. He locked the doors of his house, mounted his horse, and with a broken spirit set out on his journey. But he had hardly gone halfway when, harassed by his thoughts, he had to dismount and tie his horse to a tree, where he collapsed, moaning with sorrow. There he remained till nearly nightfall, when he observed a man approaching on horseback from the city. After greeting him, he asked what was the news in Florence.

" 'The strangest news for many a day,' replied the townsman, for it is reported that Lotario, the great friend of the wealthy Anselmo, who lived at San Giovanni, last night carried off Camila, the wife of Anselmo, who also has disappeared. All this has been told by a maid-servant of Camila's, whom the governor found last night lowering herself by a sheet from the windows of Anselmo's house. I cannot say precisely how the affair came to pass. All I know is that the whole city is wondering at the occurrence, for no one could have expected such a thing, seeing the intimate friendship that existed between them. It was so great, they say, that they were called "The Two Friends." '

" 'Is it known at all,' said Anselmo, 'what road Lotario and Camila took?' "

" 'Not in the least,' said the townsman, 'though the governor has been very active in searching for them.'

" 'God speed you, señor,' said Anselmo.

" 'God be with you,' said the townsman and went his way.

"This dreadful news almost robbed Anselmo not only of his senses but of his very life. He got up as best he could and reached the house of his friend, who as yet knew nothing of Anselmo's misfortune; but seeing him arrive so pale, worn, and haggard, he realized that something terrible must have happened. Anselmo asked to be allowed to retire and to be given writing materials. This was done, and he was left lying down and alone, for he had requested this, and even that the door should be locked. Finding himself alone, the thought of his misfortune so weighed on his mind that he knew with absolute certainty that his life was drawing to a close. Thus he resolved to leave behind him an explanation of his strange end. He began to write, but before he could put down all he meant to say, his breath failed him, and he yielded up his life, a victim to the suffering his ill-advised curiosity had brought upon him.

"The master of the house, noticing that though the hour was late Anselmo did not call, decided to go in and ascertain if his condition was growing worse. He found him lying on his face, his body partly in the bed, partly on the writing table, on which he lay with the written page open and the pen still in his hand. After calling him and receiving no answer, his host approached him and took him by the hand, only to find that it was cold, and he realized that Anselmo was dead. Greatly surprised and distressed, he summoned the household to witness the sad fate which had befallen Anselmo. Then he read the paper, which he knew to be in the dead man's handwriting and which contained these words:

" 'A foolish and ill-advised desire has robbed me of life. If the news of my death should reach Camila's ears, let her know that I forgive her, for she was not bound to perform miracles, nor ought I to have required them of her. And since I have been the author of my own dishonor, there is no reason why—'

"Anselmo had written no more, and thus it was plain that at this point, before he could finish what he had to say, he had breathed his last. The next day his friend sent word of his death to his relatives, who had already learned of his misfortune and also knew of the convent where Camila had gone. She was almost ready to accompany her husband on his last journey, not because the news of his death had reached her, but because she had been told of her lover's departure. Although a widow, she refused, it is said, either to leave the convent or take the veil, until, not long afterwards, word came that Lotario had been killed in a battle in which M. de Lautrec had been recently engaged with the Great Captain Gonzalo Fernández de Córdoba[4] in the kingdom of Naples, to which her too late repentant lover had gone. On learning this, Camila took the veil and shortly afterwards died, worn out by grief and melancholy. This was how all three of them ended, an end that was the consequence of an ill-advised beginning."

"I like this story," said the priest, "but I cannot persuade myself to believe it. If it's sheer invention then the author's invention is at fault, for it is impossible to imagine any husband so foolish as to desire such a costly experiment. If it had been represented as occurring between a gallant and his mistress, it might have happened; but between husband and wife it is altogether too implausible. As to the way in which the story is told, however, I have no fault to find."

Chapter XXXVI

WHICH TREATS OF MORE CURIOUS INCIDENTS THAT OCCURRED AT THE INN

The landlord had been standing at the gate of the inn, and at this moment he called out. "Here comes a fine troop of guests," he said. "If they stop here we can say *gaudeamus*."[1]

4. Martín de Riquer identifies this as the battle of Cerignola, 1503.

1. "Let us rejoice" (Latin).

"What sort are they?" asked Cardenio.

"Four men," said the landlord, "riding with short stirrups, with lances and shields, and all with black masks.[2] With them is a woman in white on a sidesaddle, whose face is also veiled, and two attendants on foot."

"Are they very near?" said the priest.

"So near," answered the landlord, "that they are about to arrive.

Hearing this Dorotea covered her face, and Cardenio retreated into Don Quixote's room. Hardly had they time to do so before the whole party the innkeeper had described entered the inn, and the four men on horseback, who were of well-bred appearance and bearing, dismounted. They came forward to take down the woman who was riding sidesaddle, and one of them taking her in his arms placed her in a chair near the entrance of the room where Cardenio was hiding. All this time neither she nor they had removed their masks or spoken a word. Only after she sat down did the woman heave a deep sigh and let her arms fall, as though she were ill and weak. The attendants on foot then led the horses away to the stable.

Observing this, the priest, his curiosity aroused by people garbed in such a way and preserving such silence, went to where the servants were standing and asked one of them what he wanted to know.

"Faith, sir," the man replied, "I cannot tell you who they are. I only know they seem to be people of distinction, particularly the gentleman who advanced to take in his arms the lady you saw. I say this because all the rest show him respect, and nothing is done except what he directs and orders."

"And who is the lady?" asked the priest.

"That I cannot tell you either," said the servant, "for I have not seen her face all the way. I have indeed heard her sigh many times and utter such groans that she seems to be giving up the ghost every time. But it is no wonder if we do not know any more than we have told you, as my comrade and I have only been in their company two days. They met us on the road and begged us to accompany them to Andalusia, promising to pay us well."

"And have you heard any of them called by his name?" asked the priest.

"No, indeed," replied the servant. "They all preserve an amazing silence on the road, for not a sound is to be heard among them except the poor lady's sighs and sobs, which make us pity her. We feel sure that wherever it is she is going, it is against her will, and as far as one can judge from her dress, she is a nun or, what is more likely, about to become one. Perhaps it is because taking the vows is not of her own free will that she is so unhappy as she seems to be."

2. Travelers' masks, to protect the face from sunburn and dust.

"That may well be," said the priest, and leaving them he returned to where Dorotea was. She, hearing the veiled lady sigh, was moved by natural compassion and went up to her.

"What are you suffering from, señora?" she said. "If it should be anything women are familiar with and know how to relieve, I offer you my services with all my heart."

To this the unhappy lady made no reply. And though Dorotea repeated her offers more earnestly, she still kept silence, until the gentleman with the mask who, the servant said, was obeyed by the rest, approached and spoke to Dorotea. "Do not give yourself the trouble, señora, of making any offers to that woman, for it is her way to give no thanks for anything that is done for her. And do not try to make her answer unless you want to hear some lie from her lips."

"I have never told a lie," was the immediate reply of the lady who had been silent until then. "On the contrary, it is because I am so truthful and so ignorant of deceit that I am now in this miserable condition. This I call you yourself to witness, for it is my unstained truth that has made you false and a liar."

Cardenio heard these words clearly and distinctly, being quite close to the speaker, for there was only the door of Don Quixote's room between them. The instant he did so, he uttered a loud exclamation. "Good God!" he cried. "What do I hear? What voice is this that has reached my ears?"

Startled at the voice, the lady turned her head. Since she did not see the speaker, she stood up and attempted to enter the room. But observing this, the gentleman held her back so that she could not move a step. In her agitation and sudden movement, the silk veil covering her face fell off and disclosed a countenance of incomparable and marvelous beauty, but pale and terrified. For she kept turning her eyes everywhere she could direct her gaze with an eagerness that made her look as if she had lost her senses. This excited the pity of Dorotea and all who beheld her, though they did not know what motivated it.

The gentleman grasped her firmly by the shoulders and, being so intent on holding her back, was unable to put a hand to his mask which was slipping and, a moment later, fell off.

Dorotea, who was holding the lady in her arms, raised her eyes and saw that the gentleman was her husband Don Fernando. The instant she recognized him, with a long, plaintive cry from the depths of her heart, she fell backwards in a faint. But for the barber, who was standing close by and caught her in his arms, she would have fallen to the ground. The priest at once hastened to uncover her face and throw water on it, and as he did so Don Fernando, for he it was who held the other lady in his arms, recognized her and stood as if frozen by the sight. Not for this, however, did he relax his grasp of Luscinda, for it was she who was struggling to release herself from his hold, having recognized Cardenio by his voice, as he had recognized her. Cardenio also heard Dorotea's cry as she fell, and imagining that it came from his Luscinda, burst forth in terror from the room. The first thing he saw was Don Fernando with Luscinda in his arms. Don Fernando, too, knew Cardenio at once, and all three, Luscinda, Cardenio, and Dorotea,[3] stood in silent amazement, scarcely knowing what had happened to them.

They gazed at one another without speaking, Dorotea at Don Fernando, Don Fernando at Cardenio, Cardenio at Luscinda, and Luscinda at Cardenio. The first to break silence was Luscinda, who turned to Don Fernando. "Leave me, Señor Don Fernando," she said, "for the sake of what you owe yourself. If no other reason will induce you, leave me to cling to the wall of which I am the ivy, to the support from which neither your insistence, nor your threats, nor your promises, nor your gifts have been able to detach me. See how Heaven, by ways strange and hidden from our sight, has brought me face to face with my true husband; and well you know by dearly bought experience that death alone can efface him from my memory. May this plain declaration lead you, since you can do nothing else, to turn your love into rage, your affection into resentment, and so to take my life. If I yield it up in the presence of my beloved husband, I count it well expended. By my death he may be convinced that I kept my faith to him to the last moment of my life."

Meanwhile Dorotea had come to herself and had heard Luscinda's words, which enabled her to divine who Luscinda was. But seeing that Don Fernando did not yet release this lady or make any reply, she summoned up all the resolution she could and went to kneel at his feet. Then, shedding a flood of bright and touching tears, she spoke to him.

"If, my lord," she said, "the beams of that sun you hold eclipsed in your arms did not dazzle and rob your eyes of sight, you would have seen by this time that she who kneels at your feet is, so long as you will have it so, the unhappy and unfortunate Dorotea. I am that lowly peasant girl whom you, in your goodness or for your pleasure, would raise high enough to call herself yours. I am she who in the seclusion of innocence led a contented life until, at the voice of your persistence and your true and tender passion, as it seemed, she opened the gates of her modesty and surrendered to you the keys of her liberty. The gift was accepted by you but thanklessly, as is clearly shown by my forced retreat to the place where you now find me, and by your appearance under the circumstances in which I see you. Nevertheless, I would not have you

3. Only a few lines back Dorotea had fainted, and a little farther on she comes to herself.

suppose that I have come here driven by my shame, for I was urged on only out of grief and sorrow at seeing myself forgotten by you. It was your will to make me yours, and you so followed your will that now, even though you regret it, you cannot help being mine. Consider, my lord, that the incomparable affection I bear you may compensate for the beauty and noble birth for which you would desert me. You cannot be the beautiful Luscinda's because you are mine, nor can she be yours because she is Cardenio's. And it will be easier, remember, to bend your will to love one who adores you, than to lead one to love you who now abhors you. You addressed yourself to my inexperience, you laid siege to my virtue, you were not unaware of my station in life, and well you know how I yielded wholly to your will. There is no ground or reason for you to plead deception. If this is so, as it is, and if you are a Christian as you are a gentleman, why do you with such subterfuges put off making me as happy in the end as you did at first? And if you will not have me for what I am, true and lawful wife, at least take and accept me as your slave, for so long as I am yours I will count myself happy and fortunate. Do not by deserting me let my shame become the talk of the gossips in the streets, do not make the old age of my parents miserable. The loyal services they as faithful vassals have ever rendered your family do not merit such a return, and if you think it will debase your blood to mingle it with mine, reflect that there is little or no nobility in the world that has not traveled the same road, and that in illustrious lineages it is not the woman's blood that counts. Reflect, moreover, that true nobility consists in virtue, and if you are lacking in that, refusing me what in justice you owe me, then even my claims to nobility are higher than yours. To make an end, señor, these are my last words to you. Whether you like it or not, I am your wife. Your words are witness, which must not and ought not to be false, if you pride yourself on that for want of which you scorn me. Witness is the pledge which you gave me, and witness is Heaven, which you yourself called to witness the promise you had made me. And if all this should fail, your own conscience will not fail to lift up its silent voice in the midst of all your gaiety to vindicate the truth of what I say and mar your highest pleasure and enjoyment."

All this and more the injured Dorotea delivered with such earnest feeling and such tears that all present, even those who came with Don Fernando, were constrained to join her in them. Don Fernando listened to her without replying, until, ceasing to speak, she gave way to such sobs and sighs that only a heart of brass would not have been softened by the sight of so great sorrow. Luscinda stood regarding her with no less compassion for her sufferings than admiration for her intelligence and beauty and would have gone to her to say some words of comfort but was prevented by Don Fernando's grasp, which held her fast. He, overwhelmed with confusion and astonishment, after regarding Dorotea for some moments with a fixed gaze, released Luscinda and opened his arms wide.

"You have conquered, fair Dorotea," he said, "you have conquered, for it is impossible to have the heart to deny the united force of so many truths."

Luscinda, in her feebleness, was about to fall to the ground when Don Fernando released her. But Cardenio, who stood near, having retreated behind Don Fernando to escape recognition, cast fear aside and, regardless of what might happen, ran forward to support her. "If Heaven in its compassion," he cried, as he clasped her in his arms, "is willing to let you rest at last, mistress of my heart, true, constant, and fair, nowhere can you rest more safely than in these arms that now receive you, and received you before, when fortune permitted me to call you mine."

At these words Luscinda looked up at Cardenio, at first beginning to recognize him by his voice and then satisfying herself by gazing at him that it was he. Hardly knowing what she did, and heedless of all considerations of decorum, she flung her arms around his neck and pressed her face close to his. "Yes, my dear lord," she said, "you are the true master of this your slave, even though contrary fate may interpose again and fresh dangers threaten this life that hangs on yours."

A strange sight was this for Don Fernando and those that stood around, and they were filled with surprise at an incident so unlooked for. Dorotea fancied that Don Fernando changed color and looked as though he meant to take vengeance on Cardenio, for she observed him put his hand to his sword. The instant the idea struck her, with remarkable quickness she clasped him around the knees, kissing them and holding him so as to prevent his moving.

"What is it you mean to do," she said, while her tears continued to flow, "my only refuge, in this unforeseen event? Your wife is at your feet, and she whom you would have for your wife is in the arms of her husband. Reflect whether it is fitting for you or possible for you to undo what Heaven has done, or whether it is becoming in you to seek to raise to be your mate the woman who in spite of every obstacle, and strong in her truth and constancy, is before your eyes, bathing with the tears of love the face and bosom of her lawful husband. For God's sake I entreat you, for your own sake I implore you, do not let this open manifestation rouse your anger. Rather may it calm it so as to allow these two lovers to live in peace and quiet without any interference from you so long as Heaven permits. In so doing you will prove the generosity of your lofty noble spirit, and the world will see that with you reason has more influence than passion."

All the time Dorotea was speaking, Cardenio, though he held

Luscinda in his arms, never took his eyes off Don Fernando. He was determined, if he saw him make any hostile movement, to try to defend himself and resist as best he could all who might assail him, though it should cost him his life. But now Don Fernando's friends, as well as the priest and the barber, who had been present all the while, not forgetting the worthy Sancho Panza, ran forward. Gathered around Don Fernando, they besought him to have a due regard for Dorotea's tears, and not to dash her reasonable hopes, since, as they firmly believed, what she said was but the truth. And they urged him to observe that it was not, as it might seem, by accident, but by a special disposition of Providence that they had all met in a place where no one could have expected a meeting.

He should bear in mind, the priest told him, that only death could part Luscinda from Cardenio. Even if some sword were to separate them they would think their death most happy, and in a case that could not be remedied his wisest course was, by constraining and overcoming himself, to show a generous mind and of his own accord allow these two to enjoy the happiness Heaven had granted them. He urged him also to turn his gaze on the beauty of Dorotea, and he would see that few if any could equal much less excel her, while to her beauty should be added her modesty and the surpassing love she bore him. But besides all this, he reminded Fernando that if he prided himself on being a gentleman and a Christian, he could not do otherwise than keep his plighted word. In doing so he would obey God and meet the approval of all sensible people, who know and recognize that beauty enjoys the privilege, provided virtue accompany it, of exalting itself to any rank, without any slur upon the man who places it upon an equality with himself. Furthermore, when the potent sway of passion asserts itself, so long as there is no mixture of sin in it, he who gives way to it is not to be blamed.

To be brief, they added to these so many other forcible arguments that Don Fernando's manly heart, being after all nourished by noble blood, was touched and yielded to the truth which, even had he wished it, he could not contradict. To show his submission and his acceptance of the good advice that had been offered, he stooped down and embraced Dorotea.

"Rise, dear lady," he said to her, "it is not right that what I hold in my heart should be kneeling at my feet. And if until now my deeds have not reflected what I own to be the truth, it may have been by Heaven's decree in order that, by seeing the constancy of your love, I might learn to value you as you deserve. What I beg of you is not to reproach me with my transgression and grievous wrong-doing, for the same cause and force that drove me to make you mine impelled me to struggle against being yours. To prove this, turn and look at the eyes of the now happy Luscinda, and you will see in them an excuse for all my errors. As she has found and gained the object of her desires, and I have found in you what satisfies all my wishes, may she live in peace and contentment as many happy years with her Cardenio, as on my knees I pray Heaven to allow me to live with my Dorotea." With these words he once more embraced her and pressed his face to hers with so much tenderness that he could barely prevent his tears from completing the proof of his love and repentance in the sight of all. Not so Luscinda and Cardenio and almost all the others, for they shed so many tears, some in their own happiness, some at that of the others, that one would have supposed a heavy calamity had fallen upon them all. Even Sancho Panza was weeping, though afterwards he said he only wept because he saw that Dorotea was not, as he believed, the queen Micomicona, from whom he expected such great favors. Their wonder as well as their weeping lasted some time, and then Cardenio and Luscinda went and fell on their knees before Don Fernando, giving him thanks for the favor he had done them in language so grateful that he did not know how to respond. So, raising them up, he embraced them with every mark of affection and courtesy.

He then asked Dorotea how she had managed to reach a place so far from her own home. She, in a few well-chosen words, told all that she had previously related to Cardenio. This so delighted Don Fernando and his companions that they wished the story had been longer, so charmingly did Dorotea describe her misadventures. When she had finished, Don Fernando recounted what had happened to him in the city after he had found in Luscinda's bosom the paper in which she declared that she was Cardenio's wife and never could be his. He said he meant to kill her, and would have done so had he not been prevented by her parents, and that he left the house full of rage and shame, and resolved to avenge himself when a more convenient opportunity should offer. The next day he learned that Luscinda had disappeared from her father's house and that no one could tell where she had gone. Finally, at the end of some months, he discovered that she was in a convent and meant to remain there all the rest of her life, if she could not share it with Cardenio. As soon as he had learned this, he took these three gentlemen as his companions and arrived at the place where she was. But he avoided speaking to her, fearing that if it were known he was there, stricter precautions would be taken in the convent. Watching a time when the porter's lodge was open, he left two of his companions to guard the gate while he and the third entered the convent in quest of Luscinda. They found her in the cloisters in conversation with one of the nuns and, carrying her off without giving her time to resist, reached a place with her where they provided themselves with everything needed for taking her away. All which they were able to do in complete safety, as the convent was in the country at a considerable distance from the city. He added that when Luscinda found herself in his power, she lost consciousness, and after coming to, did nothing but weep and sigh without speaking a word. Thus in silence and tears they reached the inn, which for him was reaching heaven where all the mischances of earth are over and at an end.

Chapter XXXVII

IN WHICH IS CONTINUED THE STORY OF THE FAMOUS PRINCESS MICOMICONA, WITH OTHER DROLL ADVENTURES

To all this Sancho listened with no little sorrow at heart seeing how his hopes for a title were fading away and going up in smoke and how the fair Princess Micomicona had turned into Dorotea and the giant into Don Fernando while his master was sleeping tranquilly, totally unconscious of all that had occurred. Dorotea was unable to persuade herself that her present happiness was not all a dream, Cardenio was in a similar state of mind, and Luscinda's thoughts ran in the same direction. Don Fernando gave thanks to Heaven for the favor shown him and for having been rescued from the intricate labyrinth in which he had been brought so near the destruction of his good name and of his soul. In short, everybody in the inn was full of contentment and satisfaction at the happy outcome of such a complicated and hopeless business. The priest as a sensible man made sound reflections upon the whole affair and congratulated each upon his good fortune. But the one in the highest spirits and good humor was the landlady because of the promise Cardenio and the priest had given her to pay for all the losses and damage she had sustained because of Don Quixote. Sancho, as has been already said, was the only one who was distressed, unhappy, and dejected. So with a long face, he went in to his master, who had just awakened.

"Sir Mournful Countenance," he said to him, "your worship may as well sleep on as much as you like, without troubling yourself about killing any giant or restoring her kingdom to the princess. For that is all over and settled now."

"I should think it was," replied Don Quixote, "for I have had the most prodigious and stupendous battle with the giant that I ever remember having had all the days of my life. With one backstroke —swish!—I brought his head tumbling to the ground, and so much blood gushed forth from him that it ran in rivulets over the earth like water."

"Like red wine, your worship should say," replied Sancho, "because I would have you know, if you don't know it, that the dead giant is a punctured wineskin and the blood twenty-four gallons of red wine that it had in its belly and the cut-off head is the bitch that bore me, and the devil take it all!"

"What are you talking about, you fool?" said Don Quixote. "Are you in your senses?"

"Let your worship get up," said Sancho, "and you will see the nice business you have made of it and what we have to pay. And you will see the queen turned into a private lady called Dorotea, and other things that will astonish you, if you understand them."

"I shall not be surprised at anything of the kind," returned Don Quixote. "For if you remember the last time we were here, I told you that everything that happened here was a matter of enchantment. It would be no wonder if it were the same now."

"I could believe all that," replied Sancho, "if my blanketing was the same sort of thing also. Only it wasn't, but real and genuine, because I saw the landlord, who is here today, holding one end of the blanket and tossing me up to the skies very neatly and smartly, and with as much laughter as strength. And when you recognize people, I am of the opinion, stupid and sinful as I am, that there is no enchantment about it at all but a great deal of bruising and bad luck."

"Well, God will give a remedy," said Don Quixote. "Hand me my clothes and let me go out, for I want to see these transformations and things you speak of."

Sancho fetched his clothes, and while Don Quixote was dressing, the priest gave Don Fernando and the others present an account of the knight's madness and of the stratagem they had used to get him away from his 'Wretched Rock,' where he fancied he must remain because of his lady's scorn. He described to them also nearly all the adventures that Sancho had mentioned, at which they marveled and laughed long, for it seemed to them, as it did to everyone, the strangest form of madness a crazy intellect could devise. The priest went on to point out that Dorotea's good fortune now prevented her from collaborating with them further, and that they would have to hit upon some other way of getting him home.

Cardenio proposed carrying out the scheme already begun and suggested that Luscinda might well take over Dorotea's part.

"No," said Don Fernando, "that must not be, for I want Dorotea to follow out this idea of hers. If the worthy gentleman's village is not very far off, I shall be happy if I can do anything for his condition."

"It is not more than two days' journey from here," said the priest.

"Even if it were more," said Don Fernando, "I would gladly travel so far for the sake of doing so good a work."

At this moment Don Quixote came out in full panoply, with Mambrino's helmet, all dented as it was, on his head, his shield on his arm, and leaning on his staff or pike. The strange figure he presented filled Don Fernando and the rest with amazement, as they contemplated his lean yellow face half a league long, his odd collection of armor, and the solemnity of his deportment. They stood silent waiting to see what he would say, and he, fixing his eyes on the fair Dorotea addressed her with great gravity and composure.

"I am informed fair lady by my squire here that thy greatness has been annihilated and thy being abolished, since, from a queen and lady of high degree as thou wast formerly, thou hast turned into a private maiden. If this has been done by the command of the magician king thy father through fear that I should not afford thee the aid thou needest and art entitled to, I may tell thee he did not and does not know what he does and was little versed in the annals of chivalry. If he had read and gone through them as attentively and slowly as I have, he would have found at every turn that knights of less renown than mine have accomplished things more difficult. It is no great matter to kill a whelp of a giant, however arrogant he may be. Not many hours past I myself was engaged with one, and—I will not speak of it, lest they say I am lying. Time, however, that reveals all, will tell the tale when we least expect it."

"You were engaged with a couple of wineskins, and not a giant," said the innkeeper at this. But Don Fernando told him to hold his tongue and not to interrupt.

"I say in conclusion, high and disinherited lady," Don Quixote continued, "that if thy father has brought about this metamorphosis in thy person for the reason I have mentioned, thou shouldst not attach any importance to it. There is no peril on earth through which my sword will not force a way and with it, before many days are over, I will bring thy enemy's head to the ground and place on thine the crown of thy kingdom."

Don Quixote said no more and waited for the reply of the princess. She knew of Don Fernando's determination to carry on the deception until Don Quixote had been conveyed to his home and responded with much gravity and ease of manner. "Whoever told you, valiant Knight of the Mournful Countenance, that I had undergone any change or transformation did not tell you the truth, for I am the same as I was yesterday. It is true that certain strokes of good fortune, that have given me more than I could have hoped for, have made some alteration in me. But I have not therefore ceased to be what I was before, nor have I lost the fixed desire to avail myself of your valiant and unvenerable arm. And so, señor, let your goodness reinstate the father that begot me in your good opinion, and be assured that he was a wise and prudent man, since by his craft he found out such a sure and easy way of remedying my misfortune. For I believe, señor, that had it not been for you, I should never have lit upon the good fortune I now possess. In this I am saying what is perfectly true, as most of the gentlemen present can fully testify. All that remains is to set out on our journey tomorrow, for today we could not travel far. For the rest of the happy outcome I am looking forward to, I trust to God and the valor of your heart."

So spoke the sprightly Dorotea. On hearing her, Don Quixote turned to Sancho with an angry air. "I declare, Sancho, my boy," he said to him, "that you are the biggest little scoundrel in Spain. Did you not tell me just now, you worthless thief, that the princess had been turned into a maiden called Dorotea, and that the head which I am persuaded I cut off from a giant was the bitch that bore you, and other nonsense that put me in the greatest perplexity I have ever been in all my life? I vow"—and here he looked to heaven and gound his teeth—"I have a mind to wreak havoc on you, in a way that will teach sense for the future to all lying squires of knights-errant in the world."

"Let your worship be calm, señor," returned Sancho, "for it may well be that I have been mistaken as to the change of the lady princess Micomicona. But as to the giant's head, or at least as to the stabbing of the wineskins and the blood being red wine, I make no mistake, as sure as there is a God. The wounded skins are there at the head of your worship's bed, and the wine has made a lake of the room. If not, you will see when you have to pay the piper—I mean when his worship the inkeeper calls for all the damages. For the rest, I am heartily glad that her ladyship the queen is as she was, for it concerns me as much as anyone."

"I tell you again, Sancho, you are a fool," said Don Quixote. "Forgive me, and that will do."

"That will do," said Don Fernando. "Let us say no more about it. As her ladyship the princess proposes to set out tomorrow because it is too late today, so be it, and we will spend the evening in pleasant conversation. Tomorrow we will all accompany Señor Don Quixote, for we wish to witness the valiant and unparalleled achievements he is about to perform in the course of the mighty enterprise he has undertaken."

"It is I who shall wait upon and accompany you," said Don Quixote. "I am much gratified by the favor bestowed upon me and the good opinion held of me, which I shall strive to justify at the cost of my life, or even more, if it can possibly cost me more."

Many were the compliments and expressions of politeness that passed between Don Quixote and Don Fernando. But they were brought to an end by a traveler who at this moment entered the inn. From his attire he seemed to be a Christian lately come from the country of the Moors, for he was dressed in a short smock of blue cloth with short sleeves and without a collar. His breeches were also of blue linen, and his cap of the same color, and he wore date-colored short boots and had a Moorish cutlass slung from a strap across his breast. Behind him, mounted on an ass, came a woman dressed in Moorish fashion, with her face covered and a veil on her head. She was wearing a little brocaded cap and a mantle that covered her from her shoulders to her feet. The man was of a robust and well-proportioned frame, in age a little over forty, rather swarthy in complexion, with a long mustache and a handsome beard. In short, his appearance was such that if he had been well dressed, he would have been taken for a person of quality and good birth.

On entering, he asked for a room, and when they told him there was none in the inn, he seemed distressed, and approaching the woman who by her dress seemed to be a Moor, he took her down from the saddle in his arms. Luscinda, Dorotea, the landlady, her daughter, and Maritornes, attracted by the strange and to them entirely new costume, gathered around her. Dorotea, who was always kindly, courteous, and quick-witted, had noticed that both she and the man who had brought her were annoyed at not finding a room. "Do not be put out, señora," she said to her, "by the discomfort and want of luxuries here, for it is the way of roadside inns to be without them. Still, if you will be pleased to share our lodging with us"—and she pointed to Luscinda—" perhaps you might have found worse accomodation in the course of your journey."

To this the veiled lady made no reply. All she did was to rise from her seat, crossing her hands upon her bosom, bowing her head, and bending her body as a sign that she returned thanks. From her silence they concluded that she must be a Moor and unable to speak a Christian tongue.

At this moment the captive[1] came up, having been until now otherwise engaged. He saw they all were standing around his companion and that she made no reply to what had been said to her. "Ladies," he declared, "this damsel hardly understands my language and can speak only that of her own country. So she cannot reply to what was asked."

"Nothing has been asked of her," returned Luscinda. "She has only been offered our company for this evening and a share of the quarters we occupy. She will be made as comfortable as the circumstances allow, with the good will we are bound to show all strangers

1. Cervantes' readers would assume that anyone in "Moorish" garb—"a Christian lately come from the country of the Moors"—was a ransomed or escaped captive.

in need of it, especially if it be a woman to whom the service is rendered."

"On her part and my own, señora," replied the captive, "I kiss your hands, and I esteem highly, as I ought, the favor you have offered. On such an occasion and coming from persons of your appearance, it is, clearly, a very great one."

"Tell me, señor," said Dorotea, "is this lady a Christian or a Moor? Her dress and her silence lead us to imagine that she is what we could wish she was not."

"In dress and outwardly," said he, "she is a Moor, but at heart she is a thoroughly good Christian, for she has the greatest desire to become one."

"Then she has not been baptized?" returned Luscinda.

"There has been no opportunity for that," replied the captive, "since she left Algiers, her native country and home. Up to the present she has not found herself in any such imminent danger of death as to make it necessary to baptize her before she has been instructed in all the ceremonies our holy mother Church ordains. But, please God, before long she shall be baptized with the solemnity befitting her quality, which is higher than her dress or mine indicates."

By these words he aroused the desire, in all who heard him, to know who the Moorish lady and the captive were. But no one liked to ask just then, seeing that it was better to help them rest at that moment than to question them about their lives. Dorotea took the Moorish lady by the hand and led her to a seat beside herself, where she requested her to remove her veil. The lady looked at the captive as if to ask him what they meant and what she was to do. He said to her in Arabic that they asked her to take off her veil, and thereupon she removed it and disclosed a countenance so lovely that to Dorotea she seemed more beautiful than Luscinda and to Luscinda more beautiful than Dorotea, and all the bystanders felt that if any beauty could compare with theirs, it was the Moorish lady's, and there were even those who were inclined to give it somewhat the preference. And as it is the privilege and charm of beauty to win the heart and secure good will, all forthwith became eager to show kindness and attention to the lovely Moor.

Don Fernando asked the captive what her name was, and he replied that it was Lela Zoraida; but the instant she heard him, she guessed what the Christian had asked. "No, no Zoraida," she said hastily, with some displeasure and energy, "María, María!" giving them to understand that she was called "María" and not "Zoraida."

These words, and the touching earnestness with which she uttered them, drew more than one tear from some of the listeners, particularly the women, who are by nature tender-hearted and compassionate. "Yes, yes, María, María," said Luscinda, embracing her affectionately, to which the Moor replied "Yes, yes, María, Zoraida *macange*," which means "not Zoraida."

Night was now approaching, and by the orders of those with Don Fernando, the innkeeper had taken pains to prepare the best supper that was in his power. The hour having arrived, they all took their seats at a long table like a refectory table, for round or square there was none in the inn. The seat of honor at the head of it, though he would have refused, they assigned to Don Quixote, who desired the Princess Micomicona to place herself by his side, as he was her protector. Luscinda and Zoraida took their places next to her, opposite to them were Don Fernando and Cardenio, and next to the captive and the other gentlemen, and by the side of the ladies, the priest and the barber. And so they dined in high enjoyment, which was increased when they observed Don Quixote stop eating, and, moved by an impulse like that which made him deliver himself at such length when he supped with the goatherds, begin to address them.

"Verily, gentlemen, if we reflect upon it," he said, "great and marvelous are the things seen by those who make profession of the order of knight-errantry. Who in the world, if he entered the gate of this castle at this moment and saw us as we are here, would suppose or imagine us to be what we are? Who would say that the lady beside me was the great queen that we all know her to be or that I am the Knight of the Mournful Countenance, trumpeted far and wide by the mouth of Fame? Now there can be no doubt that this art and calling surpasses all those that mankind has invented and is the more deserving of being held in honor in proportion as it is the more exposed to peril.

"Away with those who assert that letters have the pre-eminence over arms. I will tell them, whosoever they may be, that they know not what they say. The reason which such persons commonly advance and upon which they chiefly rest is that the labors of the mind are greater than those of the body, and that arms give employment to the body alone—as if the calling were a porter's trade, for which nothing more is required than sturdy strength, or as if, in what we who profess them call arms, there were not included acts of vigor whose execution requires high intelligence, or as if the soul of the warrior, when he has an army or the defense of a city under his care, did not exert itself as much by mind as by body. Consider whether by bodily strength it is possible to learn or guess the intentions of the enemy, his plans, stratagems, or obstacles, or to ward off impending mischief. All these are the work of the mind, and in them the body has no share whatever.

"Since, therefore, arms have need of the mind, as much as letters, let us see now which of the two minds, that of the man of letters[2] or that of the warrior, has most to do. This will be seen by the end and goal each seeks to attain, for that purpose is the more estimable which has for its aim the nobler object. The end and goal of letters —I am not speaking now of divine letters, the aim of which is to raise and direct the soul to heaven, for with an end so infinite no other can be compared—I speak of humane letters, the end of which is to establish distributive justice, give to every man that which is his, and see and take care that good laws are observed. That end is undoubtedly noble, lofty, and deserving of high praise, but not such as should be given to that sought by arms, which have for their end and object peace, the greatest boon that men can desire in this life.

"The first good news the world and mankind received was that which the angels announced on the night that was our day, when they sang in the air, 'Glory to God in the highest, and peace on earth to men of good will.' And the salutation which the great Master of heaven and earth taught his disciples and chosen followers when they entered any house, was to say, 'Peace be on this house.' And many other times he said to them, 'My peace I give unto you, my peace I leave you, peace be with you,' a jewel and a precious gift given and left by such a hand, a jewel without which there can be no happiness either on earth or in heaven. This peace is the true goal of war, and war is only another name for arms. This, then, being admitted, that the goal of war is peace, and that so far it has the advantage over the goal of letters, let us turn to the bodily labors of the man of letters, and those of him who follows the profession of arms, and see which are the greater."

Don Quixote delivered his discourse in such a manner and in such correct language, that for the time being, he made it impossible for any of his hearers to consider him a madman. On the contrary, as they were mostly gentlemen, to whom arms are an appurtenance by birth, they listened to him with great pleasure.

"Here, then, I say," he continued, "is what the student has to undergo. First of all poverty—not that all are poor, but to put the case as strongly as possible. And when I have said that he endures poverty, I think nothing more need be said about his hard fortune, for he who is poor has no share of the good things of life. This poverty he suffers from in various ways, hunger, or cold, or nakedness, or all together. But for all that, it is not so extreme but that he gets something to eat, though it may be at somewhat unseasonable hours and from the leavings of the rich. For the greatest misery of the student is what they themselves call 'living on soup,'[3] and there

2. "Man of letters," *letrado*, as will be seen, means one devoted to jurisprudence.

3. Monasteries regularly provided free soup for the needy, including poor students, who were called *sopistas*, from *sopa*, "soup."

is always some neighbor's brazier or hearth for them, which, if it does not warm, at least tempers the cold to them, and lastly, they sleep comfortably at night under a roof. I will not go into other particulars, as for example lack of shirts, and no superabundance of shoes, thin and threadbare garments, and gorging themselves to surfeit in their voracity when good luck has treated them to a banquet of some sort.

"By the road I have described, rough and hard, stumbling here, falling there, getting up again to fall again, they reach the rank they desire, and that once attained, we have seen many who have passed these Syrtes[4] and Scyllas and Charybdises, as if borne flying on the wings of favoring fortune. We have seen them, I say, ruling and governing the world from a seat of authority, their hunger turned into satiety, their cold into comfort, their nakedness into fine raiment, their sleep on a mat into repose in fine linen and damask, the justly earned reward of their virtue. But, contrasted and compared with what the warrior undergoes, all they have undergone falls far short of it, as I am now about to show."

Chapter XXXVIII

WHICH TREATS OF THE CURIOUS DISCOURSE DON QUIXOTE DELIVERED ON ARMS AND LETTERS

"As we began in the student's case with poverty and its accompaniments," said Don Quixote, continuing his discourse, "let us see now if the soldier is richer. We shall find that in poverty itself there is no one poorer, for the soldier is dependent on his miserable pay, which comes late or never, or else on what he can plunder, seriously imperiling his life and conscience. Sometimes his nakedness will be so great that a ragged leather jacket serves him for uniform and shirt, and in the depth of winter he has to defend himself against the inclemency of the weather in the open field with nothing better than the breath of his mouth, which I need not say, coming from an empty place, must come out cold, contrary to the laws of nature. To be sure, he looks forward to the approach of night to make up for all these discomforts on the bed that awaits him. This, unless by his own fault, never sins by being over-narrow, for he can measure out on the ground as many feet as he likes, and roll about to his heart's content without any fear of the sheets slipping off.

"Then suppose the day and hour have come for taking his degree in his calling. Suppose the day of battle has arrived, when they put on him a mortar board of bandages, to mend some bullet hole, perhaps, that has gone through his temples or left him with a crippled

4. Syrtes, a dangerous sand bank off the coast of North Africa, and like Scylla and Charybdis, a classical synonym for a hidden danger or a known but unavoidable risk.

arm or leg. Or if this does not happen, and merciful Heaven watches over him and keeps him safe and sound, he may be in the same poverty he was in before, go through more engagements and more battles, and come victorious out of all before he betters himself. But miracles of that sort are seldom seen. For tell me, sirs, if you have ever reflected on it, by how much do those who have gained by war fall short of the number of those who have perished in it? No doubt you will reply that there can be no comparison, that the dead cannot be numbered, while the living who have been rewarded do not go beyond some hundreds.

"All this is reversed in the case of men of letters; for by their legitimate earnings, to say nothing of the others, they all find means of support. Thus, though the soldier has more to endure, his reward is much less. But against all this it may be argued that it is easier to reward two thousand men of letters than thirty thousand soldiers, for the former may be remunerated by giving them posts which inevitably are bestowed on men of their calling, while the latter can only be recompensed out of the property of the master they serve. But this impossibility only strengthens my argument.

"Putting this, however, aside, for it is a puzzling question and difficult to resolve, let us return to the superiority of arms over letters, a matter still in dispute, so many are the arguments put forward on each side. Besides those I have mentioned, letters say that without them, arms cannot maintain themselves, for war, too, has its laws and is governed by them, and laws belong to the domain of letters and men of letters. To this arms make answer that without them, laws cannot be maintained, for by arms states are defended, kingdoms preserved, cities protected, roads made safe, seas cleared of pirates. In short, if it were not for them, states, kingdoms, monarchies, cities, ways by sea and land would be exposed to the violence and confusions which war brings with it, so long as it lasts and is free to make use of its privileges and powers. And then it is plain that whatever costs most is valued and deserves to be valued most. To attain to eminence in letters costs a man time, sleepless nights, hunger, nakedness, headaches, indigestion, and other things of the sort, some of which I have already referred to. But for a man to come in the ordinary course of things to be a good soldier costs him all the student suffers, and in an incomparably higher degree, for at every step he runs the risk of losing his life. What dread of want or poverty that can assail the student can compare with what the soldier feels when, beleaguered in some stronghold, mounting guard in some trench, or on the walls, he knows that the enemy is tunneling towards the post where he is stationed. He cannot under any circumstances retire or flee from the imminent danger that threatens him. All he can do is to inform his captain, who may try to remedy it by a counter-mine. Then the soldier stands his ground in fear and expectation of the moment when he will fly up to the clouds without wings and descend into the deep against his will.

"If this seems a trifling risk, let us see whether it is equaled or surpassed by the encounter of two galleys prow to prow, in the midst of the open sea, locked and entangled one with the other, when the soldier has no more standing room that two feet of plank on the ramming prow. He sees himself threatened by as many ministers of death as there are gunbarrels of the foe pointed at him, not a lance length from his body, and sees too that with the first heedless step he will go down to visit the profundities of Neptune's bosom. Still with dauntless heart, urged on by honor that nerves him, he makes himself a target for all that musketry and struggles to cross that narrow path to the enemy's ship. What is still more marvelous, no sooner has one gone down into the depths he will never rise from till the end of the world, than another takes his place. And if he too falls into the sea that waits for him like an enemy, another and another will succeed him without a moment's pause between their deaths. Such courage and daring are the greatest that all the hazards of war can show.

"Happy the blest ages that knew not the dread fury of those devilish engines of artillery, whose inventor I am persuaded is in hell receiving the reward of his diabolical invention. He made it easy for a base and cowardly arm to take the life of a gallant gentleman. For, he knows not how or whence, in the height of the ardor and enthusiasm that stir brave hearts, there may come some random bullet, discharged perhaps by one who fled in terror at the explosion when he fired off his accursed machine, which in an instant puts an end to the projects and cut off the life of one who deserved to live for ages to come. When I reflect on this, I am almost tempted to say that in my heart I repent of having adopted this profession of knight-errant in so detestable an age. For though no peril can make me fear, it distresses me to think that powder and lead may rob me of the opportunity of making myself famous and renowned throughout the known earth by the might of my arm and the edge of my sword. But Heaven's will be done. If I succeed in my attempt, I shall be all the more honored, as I have faced greater dangers than the knights-errant of yore exposed themselves to."

All this lengthy discourse Don Quixote delivered while the others dined, forgetting to raise a morsel to his lips, though Sancho more than once told him to eat his supper, as he would have time enough afterwards to say all he wanted. It aroused fresh pity in those who had heard him to see a man of apparently sound sense, and with rational views on every subject he discussed, so hopelessly lacking in it when his wretched unlucky chivalry was in question. The priest told him he was quite right in all he had said in favor of arms and that he himself, though a man of letters and a university graduate, was of the same opinion.

They finished their supper, the cloth was removed, and the innkeeper's wife, her daughter, and Maritornes were getting Don Quixote of La Mancha's garret ready, where the women were to be quartered by themselves for the night. Don Fernando begged the captive to tell them the story of his life, for it could not fail to be strange and interesting, to judge by the hints he had let fall on his arrival in company with Zoraida. To this the captive replied that he would very willingly comply, only he feared his tale would not give them as much pleasure as he wished; nevertheless, not to gainsay them, he would tell it. The priest and the others thanked him and added their entreaties. He, having been so urged, said there was no occasion to ask, where a command carried such weight. "If your worships will give me your attention you will hear a true story which, perhaps, fictitious ones constructed with ingenious and studied art cannot come up to," he added.

At these words, they settled in their places and maintained a deep silence. Seeing them waiting on his words in mute expectation, the captive began to speak in a pleasant quiet voice.

Chapter XXXIX

WHEREIN THE CAPTIVE RELATES HIS LIFE AND ADVENTURES

"My family had its origin in a village in the mountains of León. Nature had been kinder and more generous to it than fortune, though in the general poverty of those communities my father passed for being even a rich man. He would have been so in reality had he been as clever in preserving his property as he was in spending it. This tendency towards liberality he had acquired from having been a soldier in his youth, for the soldier's life is a school in which the miser becomes free-handed and the free-handed prodigal. If any soldiers are to be found who are stingy, they are freaks of rare occurrence. My father went beyond liberality and bordered on prodigality, a disposition by no means advantageous to a married man who has children to succeed to his name and position. My father had three, all sons, and all of sufficient age to choose a profession. Finding, then, that he was unable to resist his propensity, he decided to remove the instrument and cause of his prodigality and lavishness—his property—without which Alexander himself would have seemed parsimonious. So, calling us all three aside one day into a room, he addressed us somewhat in this fashion.

" 'My sons, to assure you that I love you, no more need be known or said than that you are my sons. To encouraged a suspicion that I do not love you, no more is needed than the knowledge that I have no self-control as far as preservation of your inheritance is concerned. Therefore, that you may for the future feel sure I love you like a father and have no wish to ruin you like a stepfather, I propose to do what I have for some time back considered and after mature deliberation decided upon. You are now of an age to marry or at least to choose of a calling that will bring you honor and profit when you are older. What I have resolved to do is to divide my property into four parts. Three I will give to you, to each his portion by rights, and the other I will keep to live on and support myself for whatever remainder of life Heaven may be pleased to grant me. But I want each of you on taking possession of his share to follow one of the paths I will indicate. In this Spain of ours there is a proverb, to my mind very true—as they all are, being short aphorisms drawn from long practical experience—and the one I refer to says, "The church, or the sea, or the king's house." As much as to say, in plainer language, whoever wants to flourish and become rich, let him enter the church or go to sea, adopting commerce as his calling, or go into the king's service in his household, for they say, "Better a king's crumb than a lord's favor." I say so because it is my will and pleasure that one of you should become a scholar, another a merchant, and the third serve the king in the wars, for it is a difficult matter to gain admission to his service in his household, and if war does not bring much wealth, it confers great distinction and fame. Eight days hence I will give you your full shares in money, without defrauding you of a penny, as you will see in the end. Now tell me if you are willing to follow out my idea and advice as I have laid it before you.'

"He called upon me as the eldest to answer. After urging him not to strip himself of his property but to spend it as he pleased, for we were young men able to gain our living, I consented to comply with his wishes. Mine, I said, were to follow the profession of arms and thereby serve God and my king. My second brother, after making a similar protestation, decided he would go to the Indies and invest his portion in trade. The youngest, and in my opinion the most talented, said he would rather enter the church or go to complete his studies at Salamanca. As soon as we had come to an understanding and chosen our professions, my father embraced us all, and in the short time he mentioned carried out all he had promised. When he had given to each his share, which as well as I remember was three thousand ducats apiece in cash (for an uncle of ours bought the estate and paid for it in cash, not to let it go out of the family), we all three on the same day took leave of our good father. At the same time, as it seemed to me inhuman to leave my father with such scanty means in his old age, I induced him to take two of my three thousand ducats, as the remainder would be enough to provide me with all a soldier needed. My two brothers, moved by my example, gave him each a thousand ducats, so that there was left for my father four thousand ducats in money, besides three thousand, the value of the portion that fell to him, which he preferred to retain in land instead of selling it. Finally, as I said, we took leave of him and of our uncle whom I have mentioned, not without sorrow and tears on both sides, and they besought us to let them know whenever an opportunity offered how we fared, whether well or ill. We promised to do so, and when he had embraced us and given us his blessing, one set out for Salamanca, the other for Seville, and I for Alicante, where I had heard there was a Genoese vessel taking in a cargo of wool for Genoa.

"It has now been some twenty-two years since I left my father's house, and all that time, though I have written several letters, I have had no news whatever of him or of my brothers. My own adventures during that period I will now relate briefly.

"I embarked at Alicante, reached Genoa after a prosperous voyage, and proceeded to Milan, where I provided myself with arms and a few soldier's accessories. It was my intention to go and take service in Piedmont, but as I was already on the road to Alessandria della Paglia, I learned that the great Duke of Alba was on his way to Flanders. I changed my plans, joined him, served under him in his campaigns, was present at the deaths of the Counts Egmont and Horn, and was promoted to be ensign under a famous captain of Guadalajara, Diego de Urbina by name.[1] Some time after my arrival in Flanders news came of the league that his Holiness Pope Pius V of happy memory had made with Venice and Spain against the common enemy, the Turk, who had just then with his fleet taken the famous island of Cyprus, which belonged to the Venetians, a loss deplorable and disastrous. It was known as a fact that the Most Serene Don Juan of Austria, natural brother of our good King Philip, was coming as commander-in-chief of the allied forces, and rumors were abroad of the vast preparations which were being made. All this stirred my heart and filled me with a longing to take part in the anticipated campaign, and though I had reason to believe, and almost certain promises, that on the first opportunity that presented itself I would be promoted to captain, I preferred to leave everything and go to Italy. It was my good fortune that Don Juan had just arrived at Genoa and was going on to Naples to join the Venetian fleet, as he afterwards did at Messina. I may say, in short, that I took part in that glorious expedition,[2] promoted by this time to be a captain of infantry, to which honorable charge my good luck rather than my merits raised me. And that day—so fortunate for Christendom, because then all the nations of the

1. Cervantes served under this man at the battle of Lepanto.

2. The battle of Lepanto, October 7, 1571.

earth were disabused of their error in imagining the Turks to be invincible on sea—on that day, I say, on which the Ottoman pride and arrogance were broken, among all who there were made happy (for the Christians who died that day were happier than those who remained alive and victorious), I alone was miserable. For, instead of the naval crown that I might have expected had it been in Roman times, on the night that followed that famous day I found myself with fetters on my feet and manacles on my hands.

"It happened in this way. Uchalí,[3] the king of Algiers, a daring and successful corsair, having attacked and taken the leading Maltese galley (only three knights being left alive in it, and they badly wounded), the chief gallery of Giovanni Andrea,[4] on board of which I and my company were placed, came to its relief. Doing as I was bound to do in such a case, I leaped on board the enemy's galley, which, sheering off from that which had attacked it, prevented my men from following me. So I found myself alone in the middle of my enemies, who were in such numbers that I was unable to resist—in short I was taken, covered with wounds. Uchalí, as you know, sirs, made his escape with his entire squadron, and I was left a prisoner in his power, the only sad being among so many filled with joy, and the only captive among so many free. For there were fifteen thousand Christians, all rowers in the Turkish fleet, that regained their longed-for liberty that day.

"They carried me to Constantinople, where the Grand Turk, Selim, made my master supreme commander at sea for having done his duty in the battle and carried off as evidence of his bravery the standard of the Order of Malta. The following year, which was the year seventy-two, I found myself at Navarino rowing in the leading galley with the three lanterns.[5] There I saw how the opportunity of capturing the whole Turkish fleet in port was lost; for all the marines and Janissaries[6] that belonged to it were sure that they were about to be attacked inside the very harbor. They had their kits and *pasamaques*, or shoes, ready to flee at once on shore without waiting to be attacked, in so great fear did they stand of our fleet. But Heaven ordered it otherwise, not for any fault or neglect of the general who commanded on our side, but for the sins of Christendom and because it was God's will and pleasure that we should always have instruments of punishment to chastise us. As it was, Uchalí took refuge at Modón, which is an island near Navarino, and landing his forces, fortified the mouth of the harbor and waited quietly until Don Juan retired. On this expedition was taken the galley called the *Prize*, whose captain was a son of the famous corsair Barbarossa. It was taken by the chief Neapolitan galley called the *She-*

3. A famous Italian renegade who was captured and then converted to Islam.
4. Giovanni Andrea Doria, nephew of the great Andrea Doria.
5. The distinguishing mark of the admiral's galley.
6. The elite troops of the Turkish army.

Wolf, commanded by that thunderbolt of war, that father of his men, that successful and unconquered captain Don Alvaro de Bazán, Marquis of Santa Cruz. I cannot resist telling you what took place at the capture of the *Prize*.

"The son of Barbarossa was so cruel and treated his slaves so badly that when those who were at the oars saw that the *She-Wolf* galley was bearing down upon them and gaining upon them, they all at once dropped their oars. They seized their captain who stood on the stage at the end of the gangway shouting to them to row hard, and they passed him on from bench to bench, from the poop to the prow, biting him, so that before he had got much past the mast, his soul had already gone to hell. So great, as I said, was the cruelty with which he treated them and the hatred with which they hated him.

"We returned to Constantinople, and the following year, seventy-three, it became known that Don Juan had seized Tunis and taken the kingdom from the Turks. He placed Muley Hamet in possession, putting an end to the hopes which Muley Hamida, the cruelest and bravest Moor in the world, entertained of returning to reign there. The Grand Turk took the loss greatly to heart, and with the cunning which all his race possesses, he made peace with the Venetians (who were much more eager for it than he was). The following year, seventy-four, he attacked La Goleta[7] and the fort which Don Juan had left half built near Tunis.

"While all these events were occurring, I was laboring at the oar without any hope of freedom. At least I had no hope of obtaining it by ransom, for I was firmly resolved not to write to my father telling him of my misfortunes.

"At length La Goleta fell, and the fort fell. There were seventy-five thousand regular Turkish soldiers and more than four hundred thousand Moors and Arabs from all parts of Africa gathered there, and in the train of all this great host were such munitions and engines of war, and so many ditch-diggers that with their hands they might have covered La Goleta and the fort with handfuls of earth. The first to fall was La Goleta, until then considered impregnable, and it fell, not by any fault of its defenders, who did all that they could and should have done, but because experiment proved how easily entrenchments could be made in the desert sand. For water used to be found at eighteen inches depth, while the Turks found none at two yards. So by means of a quantity of sandbags, they raised their fortifications so high that they overlooked the walls of the fort, firing on them from above, so that no one was able to make a stand or maintain the defense.

"It was a common opinion that our men should not have shut themselves up in La Goleta but should have waited in the open at

7. The fort commanding the entrance, the "gullet," to the lagoon of Tunis.

the landing-place. But those who say so talk from a distance and with little knowledge of such matters, for if in La Goleta and in the fort there were barely seven thousand soldiers, how could such a small number, however resolute, come out and hold their own against numbers like those of the enemy? And how is it possible to help losing a stronghold that is not relieved, above all when surrounded by a host of determined enemies in their own country? But many thought, and I thought so too, that it was special favor and mercy which Heaven showed to Spain in permitting the destruction of that source and hiding place of mischief, that devourer, sponge, and moth of countless money, uselessly wasted there to no other purpose except preserving the memory of its capture by the invincible Charles V. As if to make that eternal, as it is and will be, these stones were needed to support it!

"The fort also fell, but the Turks had to win it inch by inch, for the soldiers who defended it fought so gallantly and stoutly that the number of the enemy killed in twenty-two general assaults exceeded twenty-five thousand. Of three hundred that remained alive, not one was taken unwounded, a clear and manifest proof of their gallantry and resolution and how sturdily they had defended themselves and held their post. A small fort or tower which was in the middle of the lagoon under the command of Don Juan Zanoguera, a Valencian gentleman and a famous soldier, capitulated upon terms. They took prisoner Don Pedro Puertocarrero, commandant of La Goleta, who had done all in his power to defend his fortress, and took the loss of it so much to heart that he died of grief on the way to Constantinople, where they were carrying him a prisoner. They also took the commandant of the fort, Gabrio Cerbellón by name, a Milanese gentleman, a great engineer and a very brave soldier.

"In these two fortresses perished many persons of note, among whom was Pagano Doria, knight of the Order of St. John, a man of generous disposition, as was shown by his extreme liberality to his brother, the famous Giovanni Andrea Doria. What made his death the more sad was that he was slain by some Arabs to whom, seeing that the fort was now lost, he entrusted himself, and who offered to conduct him in the disguise of a Moor to Tabarca, a small fort or station on the coast held by the Genoese employed in the coral fishery. These Arabs cut off his head and carried it to the commander of the Turkish fleet, who proved on them the truth of our Castilian proverb, that 'though the treason may please, the traitor is hated.' They say he ordered those who brought him the present to be hanged for not having brought him alive.

"Among the Christians who were taken in the fort was one named Don Pedro de Aguilar, a native of some town in Andalusia. He had been ensign in the fort, a soldier of great repute and rare intelligence, who had in particular a special gift for what they call poetry. I say so because his fate brought him to my galley and to my bench and made him a slave to the same master. Before we left the port, this gentleman composed two sonnets by way of epitaphs, one on La Goleta and the other on the fort. Indeed, I may as well repeat them, for I know them by heart and I think they will be liked rather than disliked."

The instant the captive mentioned the name of Don Pedro de Aguilar, Don Fernando looked at his companions and they all three smiled. "Before your worship proceeds any further," said one of them, when the sonnets were mentioned, "I entreat you to tell me what became of that Don Pedro de Aguilar you have spoken of."

"All I know is," replied the captive, "that after having been in Constantinople two years, he escaped in the disguise of an Albanian, in company with a Greek spy. Whether he regained his liberty or not I cannot tell, though I presume he did, because a year afterwards I saw the Greek at Constantinople, though I was unable to ask him what the result of the journey was."

"Well you are right," returned the gentleman, "for that Don Pedro is my brother, and he is now in our village in good health, rich, married, and with three children."

"Thanks be to God for all the mercies he has shown him," said the captive, "for to my mind there is no happiness on earth to compare with recovering lost liberty."

"And what is more," said the gentleman, "I know the sonnets my brother made."

"Then let your worship repeat them," said the captive, "for you will recite them better than I can."

"With all my heart," said the gentleman. "The one about La Goleta goes like this."

Chapter XL

IN WHICH THE STORY OF THE CAPTIVE IS CONTINUED

SONNET

"Blest souls, that, from this mortal husk set free,
  In guerdon of brave deeds beatified,
  Above this lowly orb of ours abide
Made heirs of heaven and immortality,
With noble rage and ardor glowing ye
  Your strength, while strength was yours, in battle plied,
  And with your own blood and the foeman's dyed
The sandy soil and the encircling sea.
It was the ebbing lifeblood first that failed
The weary arms; the stout hearts never quailed.
  Though vanquished, yet ye earned the victor's crown:

Though mourned, yet still triumphant was your fall;
For there ye won, between the sword and wall,
In Heaven glory and on earth renown."

"That is it exactly, according to my recollection," said the captive.

"Well then, the one about the fort," said the gentleman, "if my memory serves me, goes thus:

SONNET

Up from this wasted soil, this shattered shell,
Whose walls and towers here in ruin lie,
Three thousand soldier souls took wing on high,
In the bright mansions of the blest to dwell.
The onslaught of the foeman to repel
By might of arm all vainly did they try,
And when at length 'twas left them but to die,
Wearied and few the last defenders fell.
And this same arid soil hath ever been
A haunt of countless mournful memories,
As well in our day as in days of yore.
But never yet to Heaven it sent, I ween,
From its hard bosom purer souls than these,
Or braver bodies on its surface bore."

The sonnets were not displeasing, and the captive rejoiced at the news they gave him of his comrade. Then he went on with his tale.

"La Goleta and the fort being thus in their hands, the Turks gave orders to dismantle La Goleta—for the fort was reduced to such a state that there was nothing left to level—and to do the work more quickly and easily they mined it in three places. But nowhere were they able to blow up the part which seemed to be the least strong, that is to say, the old walls, while all that remained standing of the new fortifications that the Little Friar[1] had made came to the ground with the greatest ease. Finally the fleet returned victorious and triumphant to Constantinople, and a few months later my master died. He was called Uchalí, alias Uchalí Fartax, which means in Turkish 'the scabby renegade.' That he was, for it is the practice with the Turks to name people from some defect or virtue they may possess. The reason is that there are among them only four surnames belonging to families tracing their descent from the Ottoman house, and the others, as I have said, take their names and surnames either from bodily blemishes or moral qualities. This 'scabby one' rowed at the oar as a slave of the Grand Turk for fourteen years, and when over thirty-four years of age, in resentment at having been struck by a Turk while at the oar, turned renegade and renounced his faith in order to be able to revenge himself. Such

1. Jacome Paleazzo, the royal engineer.

was his valor that, without owing his advancement to the base ways and means by which most favorities of the Grand Turk rise to power, he came to be king of Algiers and afterwards sea commander, which is the third highest place in the realm. He was a Calabrian by birth and a worthy man morally, and he treated his slaves with great humanity. He had three thousand of them, and after his death they were divided, as he directed by his will, between the Grand Turk (who is heir of all who die and shares with the children of the deceased) and his renegades.

"I fell to the lot of a Venetian renegade who, when a cabin boy on board a ship, had been taken by Uchalí and was so much beloved by him that he became one of his most favored youths. He came to be the most cruel renegade I ever saw. His name was Hassan Pasha, and he grew very rich and became king of Algiers. With him I went there from Constantinople, rather glad to be so near Spain, not that I intended to write to anyone about my unhappy lot, but to see if fortune would be kinder to me in Algiers than in Constantinople, where I had attempted in a thousand ways to escape without ever finding a favorable time or chance. In Algiers I resolved to seek other means of effecting the purpose I cherished so dearly, for the hope of obtaining my liberty never deserted me. When in my plots and schemes and attempts the result did not answer my expectations, without giving way to despair I immediately began to look out for or think up some new hope to support me, however faint or feeble it might be.

"In this way I lived on, shut up in a building or prison called by the Turks a *baño,* in which they confine the Christian captives, the king's as well as those belonging to private individuals, and also what they call those of the *almacén,* which is as much as to say the slaves of the municipality, who serve the city in the public works and other employments. Captives of this kind recover their liberty with great difficulty, for, as they are public property and have no particular master, there is no one with whom to bargain for their ransom, even though they may have the means. To these *baños,* as I have said, some private individuals of the town are in the habit of bringing their captives, especially when they are to be ransomed. There they can keep them in safety and comfort until their ransom arrives. The king's captives also, those that are going to be ransomed, do not go out to work with the rest of the crew, except when their ransom is delayed. For then, to make them write for it more urgently, they compel them to work and go for wood, which is no light labor.

"I, however, was one of those held for ransom, for when it was discovered that I was a captain, although I declared my scanty means and lack of fortune, nothing could dissuade them from including me among the gentlemen and those waiting to be ransomed. They put a chain on me, more as a mark of this than to keep me safe, and so I spent my life in that *baño* with several other gentlemen and persons of quality marked out as held for ransom. Though at times, or rather almost always, we suffered from hunger and scanty clothing, nothing distressed us so much as hearing and seeing at every turn the unexampled and unheard-of cruelties my master inflicted upon the Christians. Every day he hanged a man, impaled one, cut off the ears of another, and all with so little provocation, or so entirely without any, that the Turks acknowledged he did it for its own sake and because he was by nature murderously disposed toward the whole human race.

"The only one that fared at all well with him was a Spanish soldier, a certain de Saavedra[2] by name. To him he never gave a blow himself, or ordered a blow to be given, or addressed a hard word, although this Saavedra had done things that will dwell in the memory of the people there for many a year, and all to recover his liberty. For the least of the many things he did we all dreaded that he would be impaled, and he himself was in fear of it more than once. Time does not allow it, but I could tell you now something of what that soldier did that would interest and astonish you much more than the narration of my own tale.

"To go on with my story. The courtyard of our prison was overlooked by the windows of the house belonging to a wealthy Moor of high position. These, as is usual in Moorish houses, were rather loopholes than windows and besides were covered with thick and close latticework. It so happened, then, that as I was one day on the terrace of our prison with three other comrades, seeing, to pass away the time, how far we could leap with our chains. We were alone, all the other Christians having gone out to work. I chanced to raise my eyes, and from one of these little closed windows I saw a reed appear with a cloth attached to the end of it, and it kept waving to and fro and moving as if making signs to us to come and take it. We watched it, and one of those who were with me went and stood under the reed to see whether they would let it drop or what they would do. As he did so the reed was raised and moved from side to side, as if they meant to say 'no' by a shake of the head. The Christian came back, and it was again lowered, making the same movements as before. Another of my comrades went, and with him the same happened as with the first, and then the third went forward, but with the same result as the first and second. Seeing this, I wanted to try my luck, and as soon as I came under the reed it was dropped and fell inside the *baño* at my feet. I hastened to untie the cloth, in which I observed a knot, and in this were ten *cianís*, which are coins of gold alloy, current among the Moors, and each worth ten *reales* of our money.

2. Cervantes himself.

"Needless to say I rejoiced over this godsend, and my joy was not less than my wonder as I tried to imagine how this good fortune could have come to us, but to me specially, for the evident unwillingness to drop the reed for any but me showed that it was for me the favor was intended. I took my welcome money, broke the reed, and returned to the terrace, and looking up at the window, I saw a very white hand, for they opened and shut it very quickly. From this we gathered or presumed that it must be some woman living in that house that had done us this kindness, and to show that we were grateful for it, we made salaams after the fashion of the Moors, bowing the head, bending the body, and crossing the arms on the breast. Shortly afterwards, at the same window a small cross made of reeds was put out and immediately withdrawn. This sign led us to believe that some Christian woman was a captive in the house and that it was she who had been so good to us. But the whiteness of the hand and the bracelets we had seen made us dismiss that idea, though we thought it might be one of the Christian renegades whom their masters very often take as lawful wives, and gladly, for they prefer them to the women of their own nation. In all our conjectures we were wide of the truth, so from that time forward our sole occupation was watching and gazing at the window where the cross had appeared to us, as if it were our pole star. At least fifteen days passed without our seeing either it or the hand or any other sign whatever. Meanwhile, we attempted as best we could to discover who it was that lived in the house and whether there was any Christian renegade in it, but nobody could ever tell us anything more than that he who lived there was a rich Moor of high position, Agi Morato by name, formerly warden of La Pata Fortress, an office of high dignity among them. But when we least thought it was going to rain any more *cianís* from that quarter, we saw the reed suddenly appear with another cloth tied in a large knot attached to it, and this at a time when, as on the former occasion, the *baño* was deserted and unoccupied.

"We made the same test as before, each of the same three going forward before I did, but the reed was delivered to none but me, and on my approach it was let drop. I untied the knot and I found forty Spanish gold crowns with a paper written in Arabic, and at the end of the writing there was a large cross drawn. I kissed the cross, took the crowns, and returned to the terrace, and we all made our salaams. Again the hand appeared. I made signs that I would read the paper, and then the window was closed. We were all puzzled, though filled with joy at what had taken place, and as none of us understood Arabic, great was our curiosity to know what the paper contained, and still greater the difficulty of finding someone to read it. At last I resolved to confide in a renegade, a native of Murcia, who professed a very great friendship for me and had given pledges that bound him to keep any secret I might entrust to him.

"It is the custom with some renegades, when they intend to return to Christian territory, to carry about them certificates from captives of quality testifying, in whatever form they can, that such and such a renegade is a worthy man who has always shown kindness to Christians and is anxious to escape on the first opportunity that may present itself. Some obtain these testimonials with good intentions, others put them to a cunning use. For when they raid Christian territory; if they get lost or taken prisoner, they produce their certificates and say that these papers reveal their aim in coming, which was to remain on Christian ground, and that with this in mind they had joined the Turks in their foray. In this way they escape their captors' rage and make their peace with the Church, without any harm, and then when they have the chance, they return to Barbary to become what they were before. Others, however, procure these papers and make use of them honestly and remain on Christian soil. This friend of mine, then, was one of these renegades that I have described. He had certificates from all our comrades, in which we testified in his favor as strongly as we could. If the Moors had found the papers, they would have burned him alive.

"I knew that he understood Arabic very well and could not only speak but also write it. But before I disclosed the whole matter to him, I asked him to read for me this paper which I had found by accident in a hole in my cell. He opened it and remained some time examining it and muttering to himself as he translated it. I asked him if he understood it, and he told me he did perfectly well and that if I wished him to tell me its meaning word for word, I must give him pen and ink that he might do it more satisfactorily. We at once gave him what he required, and he set about translating it bit by bit.

" 'All that is here in Spanish is what the Moorish paper contains,' he said, when he had finished, 'and you must bear in mind that when it says "Lela Marién" it means "Our Lady the Virgin Mary." '

"We read the paper and it ran thus:

> " 'When I was a child my father had a slave who taught me to pray the Christian prayer in my own language and told me many things about Lela Marién. The Christian died, and I know that she did not go to the fire, but to Allah, because since then I have seen her twice, and she told me to go to the land of the Christians to see Lela Marién, who had great love for me. I do not know how to go. I have seen many Christians, but except yourself none has seemed to me to be a gentleman. I am young and beautiful and have plenty of money to take with me. See if you can arrange for us to go, and if you desire it, you will be my husband there, and if you do not desire it, it will not distress me, for Lela

Marién will find me some one to marry me. I myself have written this. Have a care to whom you give it to read. Trust no Moor, for they are all untrustworthy. I am greatly troubled on this account, for I would not have you confide in anyone, because if my father knew it, he would at once fling me down a well and cover me with stones. I will put a thread on the reed. Tie the answer to it, and if you have no one to write for you in Arabic, tell it to me by signs, for Lela Marién will make me understand you. She and Allah and this cross, which I often kiss as the captive bade me, protect you.'

"Judge, sirs, whether the words or this paper gave us reason for surprise and joy. Both were so great that the renegade perceived that the paper had not been found by chance but had been in reality addressed to some one of us. He begged us, if what he suspected were the truth, to trust him and tell him all, for he would risk his life for our freedom. So saying he took out from his breast a metal crucifix, and with many tears swore by the God the image represented, in whom, sinful and wicked as he was, he truly and faithfully believed, to be loyal to us and keep secret whatever we chose to reveal to him. For he thought and almost foresaw that, by means of her who had written that paper. he and all of us would obtain our liberty and he himself obtain the object he so much desired, his restoration to the bosom of the Holy Mother Church, from which by his own sin and ignorance he was now severed like a corrupt limb. The renegade said this with so many tears and such signs of repentance that with one consent we all agreed to tell him the whole truth of the matter, and so we gave him a full account, without concealing anything. We pointed out to him the window at which the reed appeared, so that he was thus able to note the house, and he resolved to ascertain with particular care who lived in it. We agreed also that it would be advisable to answer the Moorish lady's letter, and the renegade without a moment's delay took down the words I dictated to him. They were exactly what I shall tell you, for nothing of importance that took place in this affair has escaped my memory or ever will while life lasts. This, then, was the answer returned to the Moorish lady.

" 'The true Allah protect you, Lady, and that blessed Marién who is the true mother of God and who has put it into your heart to go to the land of the Christians, because she loves you. Entreat her to show you how you can execute the command she gives you, for she is compassionate and assuredly will do so. On my own part, and on that of all these Christians with me, I promise to do all we can for you, even to death. Do not fail to write and inform me what you intend to do, and I will always answer you. For the great Allah has given us a Christian captive who can speak and write your language well, as this paper shows.

Without fear, therefore, you can tell us whatever you wish. As to what you say, that if you reach the land of the Christians you will be my wife, I give you my promise upon it as a good Christian, and you must know that Christians keep their promises better than do the Moors. Allah and Marién his mother watch over you, my lady.'

"The paper being written and folded, I waited two days until the *baño* was empty as before, when I went at once to the usual walk on the terrace to see if there were any sign of the reed. This was not long in making its appearance, and as soon as I saw it, though I could not see who had let it down, I showed the paper as a sign to attach the thread. But this was already fixed to the reed, and to it I tied the paper, and shortly afterwards our star once more made its appearance with the white flag of peace, the little bundle. It was dropped, and I picked it up and found in the cloth, in gold and silver coins of all sorts, more than fifty crowns, which fifty times more strengthened our joy and doubled our hope of gaining our liberty.

"That very night our renegade returned. He said he had learned that the Moor we had been told of lived in that house, that his name was Agi Morato, that he was enormously rich, and that he had one only daughter, the heiress of all his wealth. It was the general opinion throughout the city that she was the most beautiful woman in Barbary, and several of the viceroys who came there had sought her for a wife, but that she had been always unwilling to marry. He had learned, moreover, that she had a Christian slave who was now dead. All this agreed with the contents of the paper. We at once took counsel with the renegade as to the means to be adopted to carry of the Moorish lady and bring us all to Christian territory. In the end it was agreed that for the present we should wait for a second communication from Zoraida (for that was her name, though now she desires to be called María), because we saw clearly that she alone could find a way out of all these difficulties. When we had decided upon this, the renegade told us not to be uneasy, for either he would lose his life or succeed in setting us free.

"For four days the *baño* was filled with people, so that the reed failed to appear, but at last, when the *baño* was again empty as usual, it appeared with the cloth so swelling that it promised a happy birth. Reed and cloth came down to me, and I found another paper and a hundred crowns in gold, without any other coin. The renegade was present, and in our cell we gave him the paper to read. He declared this to be its meaning.

" 'I cannot think of a plan, señor, for our going to Spain, nor has Lela Marién shown me one, though I have asked

> her. All that can be done is for me to give you plenty of money in gold from this window. With it ransom yourself and your friends, and let one of you go to the land of the Christians and there buy a boat and come back for the others. He will find me in my father's garden, which is at the Babazón gate near the seashore, where I shall spend the whole summer with my father and my servants. You can carry me away from there by night without any danger and bring me to the boat. And remember you are to be my husband, else I will pray to Marién to punish you. If you cannot trust anyone to go for the boat, ransom yourself and go, for I know you will return more surely than any other, for you are a gentleman and a Christian. Try to become acquainted with the garden. When I see you strolling down below, I will know that the *baño* is empty and I will give you abundance of money. Allah protect you, señor.'

"These were the contents of the second paper, and on hearing them, each declared himself willing to be the ransomed one, and promised to go and return with scrupulous good faith. I too made the same offer, but to all this the renegade objected, saying that he would not on any account consent to one being set free before all went together. Experience had taught him how badly those who have been set free keep promises made in captivity. Captives of distinction frequently tried this plan, paying the ransom of a man who was to go to Valencia or Majorca with enough money to equip a boat and return for those who had ransomed him. But no such man had ever returned, for recovered liberty and the dread of losing it again efface from the memory every obligation in the world. To prove the truth of what he said, he told us briefly what had happened to a certain Christian gentleman almost at that very time, the strangest case that had ever occurred even there, where astonishing and marvelous things are happening every instant.

"In short, he declared that what could and ought to be done was to give to him the money intended for the ransom of one of us Christians. Then he could buy a boat in Algiers under the pretext of becoming a merchant and trader at Tetuan and along the coast. Once master of the vessel, it would be easy for him to hit on some way of getting us all out of the *baño* and putting us on board, especially if the Moorish lady gave, as she had promised, money enough to ransom all, because once free, it would be the easiest thing in the world for us to embark even in open day. But the greatest difficulty was that the Moors forbid any renegade to buy or own any craft except a large vessel for going on roving expeditions. They fear that anyone who buys a small vessel, especially if he be a Spaniard, only wants to escape to Christian territory. This however he could get over by arranging with an ex-Aragonese Moor to join with him in the purchase of the vessel and in the profit on the cargo. Under cover of this he could become master of the vessel, and then he considered all the rest as accomplished.

"Though to me and my comrades it seemed better to send to Majorca for the vessel as the Moorish lady suggested, we did not dare oppose him. We were afraid that if we did not do as he said, he would denounce us and place us in danger of losing all our lives by disclosing our dealings with Zoraida, for whose life we would have all given our own. We therefore resolved to put ourselves in the hands of God and in the renagade's, and at the same time an answer was given to Zoraida. She was informed that we would do all she recommended, for she had given as good advice as if Lela Marién had delivered it, and that it depended on her alone whether we were to defer the business or put it in execution at once. I renewed my promise to be her husband, and thus the next day that the *baño* chanced to be empty, she at different times gave us by means of the reed and cloth two thousand gold crowns and a paper. In this she said that the next *jumá,* that is to say Friday, she was going to her father's garden, but that before she went she would give us more money. If it were not enough, we were to let her know, as she would give us as much as we asked, for her father had so much he would not miss it, and besides she kept all the keys.

"We at once gave the renegade five hundred crowns to buy the vessel, and with eight hundred I ransomed myself, giving the money to a Valencian merchant who happened to be in Algiers at the time. He had me released on his word, pledging that on the arrival of the first ship from Valencia he would pay my ransom. If he had given the money at once it would have made the king suspect that my ransom money had been in Algiers for a long time and that the merchant, for his own profit, had kept it secret. In fact my master was so difficult to deal with that I dared not on any account pay down the money at once. The Thursday before the Friday on which the fair Zoraida was to go to the gardens, she gave us a thousand crowns more. Warning us of her departure, she begged me, if I were ransomed, to find out at once where her father's garden was and in any event to seek an opportunity of seeing her there. I answered in a few words that I would do so and that she must remember to commend us to Lela Marién with all the prayers the captive had taught her.

"This having been done, steps were taken to ransom our three comrades, so that they could leave the *baño*. Otherwise, if they saw me ransomed and themselves still imprisoned, even though the money was forthcoming, they might make a disturbance about it and the devil prompt them to do something that might harm Zoraida. Though I need not perhaps have feared this from men of their standing, I was unwilling to run any risk in the matter. So I had them ransomed just as I was, handing over all the money to the merchant so that he might offer security with safety and confidence. Nevertheless, I did not confide our plans and our secret to him, for that might have been dangerous.

Chapter XLI

IN WHICH THE CAPTIVE STILL CONTINUES HIS ADVENTURES

"Before fifteen days were over our renegade had already purchased an excellent vessel with room for more than thirty persons. To make the transaction safe and lend it plausibility, he thought it advisable to make a voyage to a place called Shershel, thirty leagues from Algiers on the Orán side, where there is an extensive trade in dried figs. Two or three times he made this voyage in company with the *tagarino* already mentioned. The Moors of Aragón are called *tagarinos* in Barbary, and those of Granada *mudéjares*, but in the kingdom of Fez, they call *mudéjar* Moors *elches*, and they are the people the king chiefly employs in war.

"To proceed. Every time he passed with his boat he anchored in a cove that was not two crossbow shots from the garden where Zoraida was waiting. There the renegade, together with the two Moorish lads that rowed, used to station himself purposely, either going through his prayers, or else rehearsing as a part what he meant to perform in reality. Thus he would go to Zoraida's garden and ask for fruit, which her father gave him, not knowing who he was. As he afterwards told me, he tried to speak to Zoraida and tell her who he was and that by my orders he was to take her to the land of the Christians, so that she might feel satisfied and easy. Yet he had never been able to do so, for the Moorish women do not allow themselves to be seen by any Moor or Turk unless their husband or father commands it. With Christian captives, however, they permit freedom of conversation and communication, even more than might be considered proper. But for my part I would have been sorry if he had spoken to her, for perhaps it might have alarmed her to hear her affairs discussed by renegades.

"But God, who ordered it otherwise, granted no opportunity for our renegade's well-meant purpose. The latter saw how safely he could go to Shershel and return, and that he could anchor when and how and where he liked, and that the *tagarino* his partner had no will but his own. Now that I was ransomed, all we had to do was to find some Christians to row, so he told me to look out for any I would be willing to take, over and above those who had been ransomed. I was to engage them for the next Friday, the day he fixed for our departure. On this I spoke to twelve Spaniards, all stout rowers and men who could most easily leave the city. It was no easy matter to find so many just then, because there were twenty ships out on a cruise and they had taken all the rowers with them. Indeed they would not have been found, had not their master remained at home that summer without going to sea in order to finish a small galley he had in the shipyards. To these men I said nothing more than that the next Friday in the evening they were to come out stealthily one by one and hang around Agi Morato's garden, waiting for me there until I came. These directions I gave each one separately with orders that if they saw any other Christians there they were not to say anything to them except that I had directed them to wait at that spot.

"This preliminary having been settled, another still more necessary step had to be taken. This was to let Zoraida know how matters stood, so that she might be prepared and forewarned and not taken by surprise, if we were suddenly to seize her before she thought the Christians' vessel could have returned. I decided, therefore, to go to the garden to see whether I could speak to her, and the day before my departure I went there under the pretense of gathering herbs. The first person I met was her father, who addressed me in the language that all over Barbary and even in Constantinople is the medium between captives and Moors. It is neither Morisco nor Castilian, nor of any other nation, but a mixture of all languages, by means of which we can all understand one another. In this sort of language, I say, he asked me what I wanted in his garden, and to whom I belonged. I replied that I was a slave of Arnaúte Mamí[1] (for I knew for certain that he was a very great friend of his), and that I wanted some herbs to make a salad. He asked me then whether I were to be ransomed or not and what my master demanded of me. While these questions and answers were proceeding, the fair Zoraida, who had already noticed me, came out of the house in the garden. As Moorish women are by no means particular about letting themselves be seen by Christians, or, as I have said before, at all coy, she had no hesitation in coming to where her father stood with me. Moreover her father, seeing her approaching slowly, called to her to come. It would be beyond my power now to describe to you the great beauty, the nobility, and the rich brilliant attire of my beloved Zoraida as she presented herself before my eyes. I will content myself with saying that more pearls hung from her beautiful neck, her ears, and her hair than she had hairs on her head. On her ankles, which as is customary were bare, she had *carcajes* (as bracelets or anklets are called in Morisco) of the purest gold, set with so many diamonds that she told me afterwards her father valued them at ten thousand *doblas*, and those she had on her wrists were worth as much more. The pearls were in profusion and very fine, for the highest display and adornment of

1. The captor of the Sol galley on which Cervantes and his brother Rodrigo were returning to Spain.

the Moorish women is decking themselves with rich pearls and seed-pearls, and of these there are therefore more among the Moors than among any other people. Zoraida's father had the reputation of possessing a great number, and the finest in all Algiers, and of possessing also more than two hundred thousand Spanish crowns. She, who is now mistress of me only, was mistress of all this.

"Whether thus adorned she would have been beautiful or not, and what she must have been in her prosperity, may be imagined from the beauty remaining after so many hardships. As everyone knows, the beauty of some women has its times and its seasons and is increased or diminished by chance causes. Naturally, the emotions of the mind will heighten or impair it, though indeed more frequently they totally destroy it. In a word she presented herself before me that day attired with the utmost splendor and supremely beautiful. At any rate, she seemed to me the most beautiful object I had ever seen, and when, besides, I thought of all I owed her, I felt as though I had before me some heavenly being come to earth to bring me relief and happiness.

"As she approached, her father told her in his own language that I was a captive belonging to his friend Arnaúte Mamí and that I had come for salad greens.

"She took up the conversation, and in that mixture of tongues I have spoken of she asked me if I was a gentleman and why I was not ransomed.

"I answered that I was already ransomed, and that by the price it might be seen what value my master set on me, as I had given one thousand five hundred *zoltanís*[2] for my freedom. 'Had you been my father's, she replied, 'I can tell you I would not have let him part with you for twice as much, for you Christians always tell lies about yourselves and make yourselves out poor to cheat the Moors.'

" 'That may be, lady,' said I, 'but indeed I dealt truthfully with my master, as I do and mean to do with everybody in the world.'

" 'And when do you depart?' said Zoraida.

" 'Tomorrow, I think,' said I, 'for there is a vessel here from France which sails tomorrow, and I think I will go in her.'

" 'Would it not be better,' said Zoraida, 'to wait for the arrival of ships from Spain and go with them and not with the French, who are not your friends?'

" 'No,' said I, 'though if there were news that a vessel were coming from Spain it is true I might, perhaps, wait for it. However, it is more likely I will depart tomorrow, for my longing to return to my country and to those I love is so great it will not allow me to wait for another opportunity, however convenient, if it requires delay.'

2. An Algerian coin.

" 'No doubt you are married in your own country,' said Zoraida, 'and for that reason you are anxious to see your wife.'

" 'I am not married,' I replied, 'but I have given my promise to marry on my arrival there.'

" 'And is she beautiful, the lady to whom you have given it?' said Zoraida.

" 'So beautiful,' said I, 'that, to describe her worthily and tell you the truth, she is very like you.'

"At this her father laughed very heartily. 'By Allah, Christian,' he said, 'she must be very beautiful if she is like my daughter, the most beautiful woman in all this kingdom. Look at her well, and you will see I am telling the truth.'

"Zoraida's father, being the better linguist, helped to interpret most of these words and phrases, for though she spoke the bastard language which, as I have said, is used there, she expressed her meaning more by signs than by words.

"While we were still talking of this and other matters, a Moor came running up, exclaiming that four Turks had leaped over the fence or wall of the garden and were gathering the fruit though it was not yet ripe. The old man was alarmed, and Zoraida too, for the Moors usually and, as it were instinctively, have a dread of the Turks. In particular they fear the soldiers, who are so insolent and overbearing toward their Moorish subjects that they treat them worse than if they were their slaves. 'Daughter,' said Zoraida's father, 'return to the house and shut yourself in while I go and speak to these dogs. And you, Christian, pick your herbs and go in peace, and Allah bring you safe to your own country.'

"I bowed, and he went away to look for the Turks, leaving me alone with Zoraida, who made as if she were about to retire as her father had ordered her. But the moment he was concealed by the trees of the garden, she turned to me with her eyes full of tears. '*Ámexi, cristiano, ámexi*?' she asked—that is to say, 'Are you going, Christian, are you going?'

" 'Yes, lady,' I answered, "but not without you, come what may. Be on the watch for me on the next *jumá* and do not be alarmed when you see us, for most surely we will go to the land of the Christians.'

"This I said in such a way that she understood everything perfectly. Then, throwing her arms around my neck, she began with feeble steps to move towards the house. But as fate would have it —and it might have been very unfortunate if Heaven had not ordered it otherwise—just as we were moving on in the way I have described, with her arm round my neck, her father returned after having sent away the Turks. He saw how we were walking and we realized that he had seen us. But Zoraida was alert and quick-witted enough to leave her arm where it was. She even drew closer to me and laid her head on my breast, bending her knees a little and giving every sign of having fainted. I, at the same time, acted as though I were supporting her against my will. Her father came running up, and seeing his daughter in this state asked what was the matter with her. She did not reply. 'No doubt she fainted in alarm at the entrance of those dogs,' he said. As he was taking her from me and drawing her to his own breast, she sighed, her eyes still wet with tears.

" '*Ámexi, cristiano, ámexi*'—'Go, Christian, go,' she repeated. 'There is no need, daughter,' her father rejoined, for the Christian to go, for he has done you no harm and the Turks have gone. Feel no alarm, there is nothing to hurt you, for as I say, the Turks at my request have gone back the way they came.'

" 'It was they who terrified her, as you said, señor,' said I to her father. 'But since she tells me to go, I have no wish to displease her. Peace be with you, and with your leave I will come back to this garden for herbs if need be, for my master says there are nowhere better herbs for salad than here.'

" 'Come back for any you may need," replied Agi Morato. 'My daughter does not speak thus because she is displeased with you or any Christian. She only meant that the Turks should go, not you, or that it was time for you to gather your herbs.'

"With this I at once took my leave, and she, looking as though her heart were breaking, retired with her father. While pretending to look for herbs I made the round of the garden at my ease, and studied carefully all the approaches and outlets and the security of the house and everything that could be taken advantage of to make our task easy. This done, I went and related all that had occurred to the renegade and my comrades.

"Impatiently I looked forward to the hour when, all fear at an end, I would possess the prize which fortune held out to me, the fair and lovely Zoraida. The time passed finally, and the day we so longed for arrived. All of us abided by the plan which, after careful consideration and many a long discussion, we had decided on, and we succeeded as fully as we could have wished. On the Friday following the day when I spoke to Zoraida in the garden, the renegade anchored his vessel at nightfall almost opposite the spot where she was. The Christians who were to row were ready and in hiding in different places nearby. They were waiting for me, anxious and elated, and eager to attack the vessel they had before their eyes, for they did not know the renegade's plan but expected to gain their liberty by force of arms and by killing the Moors on board.

"As soon, then, as I and my comrades made our appearance, all those in hiding came out and joined us. It was now the time when the city gates are shut, and no one was to be seen anywhere outside. When we were together, we debated whether it would be better first to go for Zoraida or to make prisoners of the Moors who rowed in the vessel. While we were still hesitating our renegade came up asking what delayed us. Now was the time, with all the Moors off their guard and most of them asleep. We told him why we hesitated, but he said it was of more importance first to secure the boat, which could be done with the greatest ease and without any danger, and then we could go for Zoraida. We all approved of what he said, and so without further delay, and guided by him, we made for the vessel. He leaped on board first and drew his cutlass. 'Let no one stir,' he said in Morisco, 'if he does not want it to cost him his life.'

"By this time almost all the Christians were on board, and the Moors, who lacked courage when they heard their captain speak in this way, had no heart for a fight. Without anyone taking up arms —of which, indeed, they had hardly any—without a word they let themselves be bound by the Christians, who threatened to slaughter them all if they raised any outcry.

"This accomplished, and half of our party remaining to keep guard over them, the rest of us, again taking the renegade as our guide, hastened towards Agi Morato's garden. As good luck would have it, when we tried the gate it opened as easily as if it had not been locked. Thus, in absolute quiet and silence, we reached the house without being perceived by anybody. The lovely Zoraida was watching for us at a window, and as soon as she perceived that there were people there, she asked in a low voice if we were *nizarini,* as much as to say or ask if we were Christians. I answered that we were and begged her to come down. As soon as she recognized me, she did not delay an instant, but without a word came down immediately, opened the door and appeared before us all. She was so beautiful and so richly attired that I cannot attempt to describe her.

"The moment I saw her I took her hand and kissed it, and the renegade and my two comrades did the same. The rest, who knew nothing of the circumstances, did as they saw us do, thinking it only gratitude and thanks to her for giving us our liberty. The renegade asked her in the Morisco language if her father was in the house. She replied that he was and that he was asleep.

" 'Then we will have to waken him and take him with us,' said the renegade, 'and everything of value in this villa.'

" 'No,' said she, 'my father must not on any account be touched, and there is nothing in the house except what I shall take, and that will be quite enough to enrich and satisfy all of you. Wait a little and you'll see.'

"So saying she went in, telling us she would return immediately and bidding us not to make any noise. In the interval I asked the renegade what had passed between them, and when he told me, I declared that nothing should be done except in accordance with the wishes of Zoraida. She now returned with a little trunk so full of gold crowns that she could scarcely carry it. Unfortunately her father awoke while this was going on. Hearing a noise in the garden, he came to the window and realized at once that all those he saw were Christians. So he raised a prodigious hullabaloo.

" 'Christians, Christians! thieves, thieves!' he shouted in Arabic.

"His cries threw us all into the greatest fear and confusion. The renegade saw the danger we were in and knew the undertaking would have to be completed before anyone heard us. So he climbed the stairs with the utmost quickness to where Agi Morato was, and some of our party along with him. I, however, did not dare leave Zoraida, who had fallen almost fainting in my arms.

"To be brief, those who had gone upstairs acted so promptly that in an instant they came down, carrying Agi Morato with his hands bound and a handkerchief tied over his mouth so that he could not utter a word. They warned him at the same time that any attempt to speak would cost him his life. When his daughter caught sight of him, she covered her eyes so as not to see him, and her father was horror-stricken, not knowing how willingly she had placed herself in our hands.

"It was now most essential for us to be on the move, and carefully and quickly we reached the boat, where those remaining on board had waited in great suspense, fearing that some mishap had befallen us. It was barely two hours after night set in when we all boarded the vessel. There the cords were removed from the hands of Zoraida's father and the handkerchief from his mouth, but the renegade once more told him not to utter a word or they would take his life. Seeing his daughter there he began to sigh mournfully, and even more so when he saw how I held her closely embraced and that she lay quiet without resisting or complaining or showing any reluctance. Nevertheless he remained silent, so that they might not carry into effect the repeated threats uttered by the renegade.

"Now that Zoraida was on board and we about to row away, she looked at her father and the other captive Moors. She bade the renegade ask me to do her a favor. She wanted me to release the Moors and set her father at liberty, saying she would rather drown herself in the sea than behold a father who had loved her dearly carried away captive because of her own actions. The renegade repeated this to me, and I replied that I would gladly do so. He protested that this was not advisable, because if they were set on shore they would at once raise the country and stir up the city. Swift cruisers would be sent in pursuit and we would be taken, either by sea or land, without any possibility of escape. The best we could do was to set them free on the first Christian ground we reached.

"On this point we all agreed, and Zoraida, to whom it was

explained, together with the reasons that prevented us from doing as she had asked, was also satisfied. Then in glad silence and with cheerful vigor each of our stout rowers took his oar. Commending ourselves to God with all our hearts, we began to shape our course for the island of Majorca, the nearest Christian land. Owing, however, to the north wind rising a little and the sea growing somewhat rough, it was impossible to keep a straight course for Majorca. We were compelled to coast in the direction of Orán, not without uneasiness on our part that we might be observed from the town of Shershel on that coast, not more than sixty miles from Algiers. We were afraid, too, of meeting one of the small galleys that usually come with goods to Tetuán. Yet each of us for himself and all of us together felt confident that, if we were to meet a merchant ship, provided it was not a cruiser, not only would we not be lost, but we could seize a vessel that would permit us to accomplish our voyage more safely. As we followed our course, Zoraida kept her head between my hands so as not to see her father, and I sensed that she was praying to Lela Marién to help us.

"We might have made about thirty miles when daybreak found us some three musket shots from land, which seemed to us deserted, and without anyone to see us. Nevertheless, by hard rowing we put out a little to sea, for it was now somewhat calmer. After we had gained about two leagues, the word was given to row by turns while we ate something, for the vessel was well provided. But the rowers said it was not a time to take any rest, that food could be served to those who were not rowing, but they would not leave their oars on any account. This was done, but now a stiff breeze began to blow. We were obliged to leave off rowing and make sail at once and steer for Orán, as it was impossible to take any other course. All this was done very promptly, and under sail we ran more than eight miles an hour without any fear, except that we might come across some vessel out on a roving expedition. We gave the Moorish rowers some food, and the renegade comforted them by telling them that they were not held as captives, as we would set them free at the first opportunity. The same was said to Zoraida's father.

" 'Anything else, O Christian,' he replied, 'I might hope for or think likely from your generosity and good behavior. But do not think me so simple as to imagine you will give me my liberty, for you would have never undergone the danger of depriving me of it only to restore it to me so generously, especially as you know who I am and the sum you may expect to receive by freeing me. Only name the amount, and I here offer you all you demand for myself and for my unhappy daughter—or else her alone, for she is the greatest and most precious part of my soul.'

"As he said this he began to weep so bitterly that he filled us all with compassion and forced Zoraida to look at him. When she saw him weeping, she was so moved that she rose from her feet and ran to throw her arms round him and press her face to his. Then they both gave way to such an outburst of tears that several of us were constrained to weep with them.

"But when her father saw her in full dress and with all her jewels about her, he spoke to her in his own language. 'What is the meaning of this, my daughter?' he asked. 'Last night, before this terrible misfortune befell us, I saw you in your everyday house clothes. Now, though you had no time to dress, and though I brought you no joyful tidings that might explain your adorning and bedecking yourself, I see you arrayed in the finest attire I could have given you when fortune was most kind to us. Answer me this, for it causes me greater anxiety and surprise than even this misfortune itself.'

"The renegade interpreted to us what the Moor said to his daughter, but she gave him no answer. When he observed in one corner of the vessel the little trunk in which she used to keep her jewels, which he well knew he had left in Algiers and had not brought to the garden, he was still more amazed. He asked her how the trunk had come into our hands and what was in it. To this the renegade made answer, without waiting for Zoraida to reply. 'Do not bother asking your daughter Zoraida so many questions, señor, for the one answer I will give you will serve for all. I would have you know that she is a Christian and that she has been the file for our chains and our deliverer from captivity. She is here of her own free will, as glad, I imagine, to find herself in this position as one who escapes from darkness into the light, from death to life, and from suffering to glory.'

"Daughter, is this true, what he says?' cried the Moor.

" 'It is," replied Zoraida.

" 'That you are truly a Christian,' said the old man, 'and that you have given your father into the power of his enemies?'

" 'A Christian I am,' Zoraida replied, 'but it is not I who have placed you in this position. It never was my wish to leave you or do you harm, but only to do good to myself.'

" 'And what good have you done yourself, daughter?' said he.

" 'Ask that,' said she, 'of Lela Marién, for she can tell you better than I.'

"The Moor had hardly heard these words when with extraordinary rapidity he flung himself headfirst into the sea. No doubt he would have drowned, had not the long, full garment he wore held him up for a while on the surface of the water. Zoraida cried aloud to us to save him. We all hastened to do so, and seizing him by his robe we drew him in half drowned and unconscious. Zoraida was in such distress at this that she wept over him as piteously and bitterly as though he were already dead. We turned him upon his face, and he vomited a great quantity of water, and at the end of two hours came to.

"Meanwhile the wind had changed, compelling us to head for the land, and we plied our oars to avoid being driven on shore. But it was our good fortune to reach a creek that lies on one side of a small promontory or cape. The Moors call it that of the Cava Rumía, which in our language means 'the wicked Christian woman,' for it is a tradition among them that La Cava, through whom Spain was lost, lies buried at that spot. *Cava* in their language means 'wicked woman,' and *rumía*, 'Christian.' Moreover, they consider it unlucky to anchor there when necessity compels them, and they never do so otherwise. For us, however, it was not the resting place of the wicked woman but a haven of safety for our relief, so much had the sea now got up. We posted a lookout on shore and never let the oars out of our hands, and we ate of the stores the renegade had laid in, imploring God and Our Lady with all our hearts to help and protect us, that we might give a happy ending to a beginning so prosperous. At the entreaty of Zoraida, orders were given to set on shore her father and the other Moors who were still bound, for she could not endure, nor could her tender heart bear to see her father in bonds and her fellow-countrymen prisoners before her eyes. We promised her to do this at the moment of departure, for as it was uninhabited we ran no risk in releasing them at that place.

"Our prayers were not unheard by Heaven, for after a while the wind changed in our favor and made the sea calm, inviting us once more to continue our voyage with a good heart. Seeing this, we unbound the Moors, and one by one put them on shore, at which they were filled with amazement. Then we came to land Zoraida's father, who had now completely recovered his senses.

" 'Why do you think, Christians,' he said, 'that this wicked woman rejoices at your giving me my liberty? Do you think it is because of her affection for me? Not so. It is only because my presence hinders the execution of her base designs. And do not imagine that she has changed her religion because she believes that yours is better than ours. It is only because she knows that immorality is more freely practiced in your country than in ours.' Then he turned to Zoraida, while I and another Christian held him fast by both arms, to prevent his doing some mad act.

" 'Infamous, misguided girl,' he said to her, 'where in your blindness and madness are you going in the hands of these dogs, our natural enemies? Cursed be the hour when I begot you! Cursed the luxury and indulgence in which I reared you!'

"Seeing that he was likely to go on for some time, we made haste to put him on shore, where he continued his maledictions and loud lamentations. He called on Mohammed to pray to Allah to destroy us, to confound us, to make an end of us. When we had made sail and could no longer hear what he said, we could see what he did, how he pulled out his beard and tore his hair and lay writhing on the ground. But once he raised his voice to such a pitch that we were able to hear what he said. 'Come back, dear daughter, come back to shore, I forgive you everything. Let those men have the money, for it is theirs now, and come back to comfort your sorrowing father, who will yield up his life on this barren strand if you abandon him.'

"All this Zoraida heard, and heard with sorrow and tears. 'Allah grant'—this was all she could say in answer—'that Lela Marién, who has made me become a Christian, give you comfort in your sorrow, O my father. Allah knows that I could not do otherwise than I have done and that these Christians bear no responsibility. Even had I wished not to accompany them but to remain at home, I could not have done so, so eagerly did my soul urge me on. This purpose appears no less noble in my eyes than in yours, dear father, it seems wicked.'

"Her father could not hear her as she was saying this, nor could we any longer see him. So, while I consoled Zoraida, we turned our attention to our voyage, which thanks to a breeze from the right point progressed so well we felt sure we would be off the coast of Spain by the following dawn.

"Yet the good seldom or never comes pure and unmixed without some attendant evil that infringes on or overturns it. It may have been due to ill luck or perhaps to the curses the Moor had hurled at his daughter, for these are always to be dreaded, no matter who the father is. In any event, we were in mid-sea and the night about three hours spent. We were running with all sail set and oars lashed, for the favoring breeze saved us the trouble of using them, when we saw by the light of the moon, which shone brilliantly, a square-rigged vessel. It was in full sail close to us, luffing a little and standing across our course, and so close we had to strike sail to avoid running foul of her, while they too turned hard to let us pass. They came to alongside the ship to ask who we were, where we were bound, and where we came from.

" 'Let no one answer,' our renegade said, for the questions had been asked in French. 'No doubt these are French corsairs who plunder all comers.'

"Acting on this warning no one answered a word, but after we had gone a little ahead and the vessel was now lying to leeward, suddenly they fired two guns. Apparently both had been loaded with chain-shot, for one cut our mast in half and brought down both it and the sail into the sea. The other, discharged at the same moment, sent a ball into our vessel amidships, piercing the hull completely, but without doing any further damage. Finding ourselves sinking we began to shout for help, asking those in the ship to pick us up as we were drowning. They struck their sails, and lowering a skiff or boat, as many as a dozen Frenchmen, well armed with muskets and ready to fire, got into it and came alongside. Seeing how few we were and that our vessel was going down, they took us in, telling us that the blame lay with our incivility in refusing them an answer. Our renegade took the trunk containing Zoraida's wealth and dropped it into the sea without anyone noticing.

"In short we went on board with the Frenchmen who, having found out all they wanted to know about us, stripped us of everything we had, as if they had been our bitterest enemies. From Zoraida they took even the anklet she wore on her feet. But the distress they caused her did not affect me so much as the fear that after stealing her rich and precious jewels they would go on to rob her of the most precious jewel she valued above all else.

"However, the desires of these people are restricted to money, though in their covetousness they are insatiable. On this occasion it went so far that they would have taken even the clothes we wore as captives, if they had been worth anything. Some of them wanted to throw us all into the sea wrapped in a sail. They intended to trade at several Spanish ports, giving themselves out as Bretons, and if they brought us alive they would be punished as soon as the robbery was discovered.

"But the captain—it was he who had plundered my beloved Zoraida—declared himself satisfied with the prize he had got. He said he would not touch at any Spanish port but would pass the Straits of Gibraltar by night, or as best he could, and make for La Rochelle, from which he had sailed. So it was agreed that we should have the skiff belonging to their ship and all we needed for the short voyage ahead of us. This was done the next day after we had sighted the Spanish coast. This sight, together with the joy we felt, enabled us to forget all our sufferings and miseries as completely as if we had never experienced them. Such is the delight of recovering lost liberty.

"It may have been about midday when they placed us in the boat, giving us two kegs of water and some biscuit. The captain, moved by some streak of compassion, gave some forty gold crowns to the lovely Zoraida as she was about to embark, and he would not let his men take from her the garments she has on now. We got into the boat, returning them thanks for their kindness to us and showing ourselves grateful rather than indignant. They stood out to sea, steering for the straits, while we, using no compass other than the land we had before us, set ourselves to row with such energy that by sunset it seemed to us we might easily land before the night was far advanced.

"But the moon did not show that night, the sky was clouded, and we did not know where we were. So we did not think it prudent to make for the shore, as several of us advised. They declared we ought to run ourselves ashore even if it turned out to be rocks and far from any habitation, for this would end the fears we could not help entertaining of vessels of the Tetuán corsairs. These set out from Barbary at nightfall and are on the Spanish coast by daybreak, where they usually take some prize and then go home to sleep in their own houses. Of the conflicting views, the one adopted was that we should approach gradually and land where we could, if the sea was sufficiently calm. This was done, and a little before midnight we drew near to the foot of a huge and lofty mountain at the base of which there was a narrow space on which to land conveniently. We ran our boat up on the sand, whereupon we all sprang out and kissed the ground. Shedding tears of joyful satisfaction, we returned thanks to God our Lord for his incomparable goodness to us on our voyage. We took the provisions our of the boat and drew it up on the shore. Then we climbed a long way up the mountain, for even there we could not feel easy in our hearts or persuade ourselves that Christian soil lay beneath our feet.

"The dawn came more slowly, I think, than we could have wished. Having made our way to the summit, we strained our eyes to see if any habitation or any shepherds' huts could be discovered; yet neither dwelling, nor human being, nor path nor road could we perceive. However, we determined to push on farther, for soon we were bound to meet with someone who could tell us where we were. But what distressed me most was to see Zoraida going on foot over the rough ground. For a while I had carried her on my shoulders, but she was more wearied by my weariness than rested by the rest and would never again allow me to undergo the exertion, and she walked on very patiently and cheerfully while I led her by the hand.

"We had gone rather less than a quarter of a league when the sound of a little bell fell on our ears, a clear proof that there were flocks close by. Looking about carefully to see if anyone was with them, we observed a young shepherd tranquilly and unsuspiciously trimming a stick with his knife at the foot of a cork tree. We called to him and he, raising his head, sprang nimbly to his feet, for, as we afterwards learned, the renegade and Zoraida were the first his gaze lit upon. Seeing them in Moorish dress, he imagined that all the Moors of Barbary were after him. Plunging with marvelous swiftness into the thicket in front of him, he began to raise a prodigious outcry. 'The Moors—the Moors have landed! To arms, to arms!' he shouted.

"We were quite taken aback by his cries and did not know what to do. But having reflected that the shepherd's shouts would alarm the country and that the mounted coast guard would come at once to see what was the matter, we agreed that the renegade must strip off his Turkish garments. He put on a captive's jacket or coat which one of our party provided at once, though the donor was reduced to his shirt. And so, commending ourselves to God, we followed the road we saw the shepherd take, expecting every moment that the coast guard would be upon us. Our expectation did not deceive us, for not two hours had passed when, as we came out of the brushwood into the open ground, we perceived some fifty mounted men swiftly approaching us at a gallop. As soon as we saw them we stood still, waiting for them, but they, as they came close, were nonplussed to behold a group of poor Christians instead of the Moors they were in quest of. One of them asked if it could be we who were the occasion of the shepherd's having raised the call to arms. I said 'Yes,' and was about to explain what had occurred, where we came from, and who we were. But before I could say anything more, one of the Christians in our party recognized the horseman who had put the question to us.

" 'Thanks be to God, sirs,' he exclaimed, 'for bringing us to such good quarters. If I do not deceive myself, the ground we stand on is that of Vélez Málaga unless, indeed, after all my years of captivity I am unable to recollect that you, señor, who ask who we are, are Pedro de Bustamante, my uncle.'

"The Christian captive had hardly uttered these words, when the horseman threw himself off his horse and ran to embrace the young man.

" 'Nephew of my soul and life!' he cried, 'I recognize you now. Long have I mourned you as dead, I and my sister your mother and all your kin still alive, whom God has been pleased to preserve that they may enjoy the happiness of seeing you. We knew long ago you were in Algiers, and to judge by your garments and those of everyone here, I conclude that you have had a miraculous restoration to liberty.'

" 'It is true,' replied the young man, 'and later we will tell you all.'

"As soon as the horsemen learned that we were Christian captives, they dismounted and offered their horses to carry us to the city of Vélez Málaga, which was a league and a half distant. Some of them, having been told where we had left the boat, went to bring it to the city, and others took us up behind them, Zoraida being placed on the horse of the young man's uncle. The whole town came out to meet us, for by this time they had heard of our arrival from a man who had gone on ahead. They were not astonished to see liberated captives or captive Moors, for people on that coast are well used to see both one and the other. But they were astonished at Zoraida's beauty, which just then was heightened both by the exertion of traveling and out of joy at finding herself on Christian soil, with no remaining fear of being lost. All this had brought such a glow upon her face, that unless my affection for her were deceiving me, I would venture to say that there was not a more beautiful creature in the world—at least, that I had ever seen.

"We went straight to the church to return thanks to God for the mercies we had received, and when Zoraida entered it, she said there were faces there like Lela Marién's. We told her they were images of the Virgin Mary, and as well as he could, the renegade explained to her what they meant and told her she might adore them as if each of them were the very same Lela Marién that had spoken to her. She, having great intelligence and a quick and clear instinct, understood at once everything he said about them. Then they took us away and distributed us all in different houses in town. As for the renegade, Zoraida, and myself, the Christian who came with us brought us to the house of his parents, who had a fair share of the gifts of fortune and who treated us with as much kindness as they did their own son.

"We remained six days in Vélez. At the end of this time, the renegade, having informed himself of what he must do, set out for the city of Granada to restore himself to the sacred bosom of the Church through the medium of the Holy Inquisition. The other released captives took their leave, each going the way that seemed best to him, and Zoraida and I were left alone, with nothing more than the crowns which the Frenchman in his courtesy had bestowed upon Zoraida. With them I bought the beast on which she rides, while I for the present attend her as her father and squire and not as her husband. We are now going to ascertain if my father is living, or if any of my brothers has had better fortune than mine has been. Yet, since Heaven has made me the companion of Zoraida, I think no other lot could be assigned to me, however happy, that I would rather have. The patience with which she endures the hardships that poverty brings with it, and the eagerness she shows to become a Christian, fill me with admiration and bind me to serve her all my life. However, the happiness I feel in seeing myself hers, and her mine, is disturbed and marred by not knowing whether I shall find any corner to shelter her in my own country, or whether time and death may not have made such changes in the fortunes and lives of my father and brothers that, if they are not alive, I shall hardly find anyone who knows me.

"That is all there is to my story, gentlemen. Whether it is interesting or curious, may your better judgments decide. I can only say I would gladly have told it to you more briefly, though my fear of wearying you has made me leave out more than one incident."

Chapter XLII

WHICH TREATS OF WHAT FURTHER TOOK PLACE IN THE INN, AND OF SEVERAL OTHER THINGS WORTH KNOWING

With these words the captive held his peace. "In truth, señor captain," Don Fernando said to him, "the manner in which you have related this remarkable adventure has befitted the novelty and strangeness of the matter. The whole story is curious and uncommon and abounds with incidents that fill the hearers with wonder and astonishment. So great has been our pleasure in listening to it that we would be glad if it were to begin again, even though tomorrow were to find us still occupied with the same tale."

While he said this, Cardenio and the others offered to be of service to him in any way that lay in their power, and in words and language so kind and sincere that the captain was much gratified by their good will. In particular Don Fernando offered, if the captain would go back with him, to get his brother the marquis to become godfather at the baptism of Zoraida, and on his own part, to enable him to return to his own region with the ease and outward appearance that were justly his. For all this the captive returned thanks very courteously, though he would not accept any of their generous offers.

By this time night was falling and, as it did, there came up to the inn a coach attended by some men on horseback. They asked for shelter, but the landlady replied that there was not a hand's breadth of the whole inn unoccupied.

"Well, nevertheless," said one of those who had entered on horseback, "room must be found for his lordship the judge here."

At this name the landlady was taken aback. "Señor," she said "the fact is I have no beds, but if his lordship the judge carries one with him, as no doubt he does, let him come in and welcome. My husband and I will give up our room to accommodate his worship."

"Very good; so be it," said the squire.

In the meantime a man whose dress indicated at a glance the office and post he held got out of the coach. The long robe with ruffled sleeves showed that he was, as his servant said, a judge. He led by the hand a young girl in a traveling dress, apparently about sixteen years of age, so elegant, so beautiful, and so graceful, that all were filled with admiration when she made her appearance. But for having seen Dorotea, Luscinda, and Zoraida, who were there in the inn, they would have fancied that a beauty like this maiden's would have been hard to find. Don Quixote was present at the entrance of the judge with the young lady, and he spoke as soon as he saw him.

"Your honor may with confidence enter and take your ease in

this castle," he said. "Though the accommodation is scanty and poor, there are no quarters so cramped or inconvenient that they cannot make room for arms and letters—above all if arms and letters have beauty for a guide and leader, as letters represented by your honor have in this fair maden. Not only ought castles to throw themselves open and yield themselves up, but rocks should rend themselves asunder and mountains divide and bow themselves down to give her a reception. Enter, your honor, I say, into this paradise, for here ye will find stars and suns to accompany the heaven your honor brings with you, here ye will find arms in their supreme excellence, and beauty in its highest perfection."

The judge was struck with amazement at the language of Don Quixote, and he scrutinized him very carefully, being no less astonished by his appearance than by his talk. But before he could find words to reply, he had a fresh surprise, when he saw opposite him Luscinda, Dorotea, and Zoraida who, having heard of the new guests and of the beauty of the young lady, had come to see her and welcome her. Don Fernando, Cardenio, and the priest, however, greeted him in a more intelligible and polished style. In short, the judge made his entrance in a state of bewilderment, as well with what he saw as what he heard, while the beautiful ladies of the inn gave the beautiful girl a cordial welcome.

On the whole he could perceive that all who were there were people of quality, but with the figure, countenance, and bearing of Don Quixote he was at his wits' end. All civilities having been exchanged and the accommodation at the inn inquired into, it was settled, as it had been settled before, that all the women should retire to the garret already mentioned and that the men should remain outside as if to guard them. The judge, therefore, was very well pleased to allow his daughter, for such the young lady was, to go with the ladies, which she did very willingly. And with part of the innkeeper's narrow bed and half of what the judge had brought with him, they made a more comfortable arrangement for the night than they had expected.

The captive's heart had leaped within him the instant he saw the judge, for somehow it assured him that this was his brother. He asked one of the judge's servants what his name was, and whether he knew from what part of the country he came. The servant replied that he was called the Licentiate Juan Pérez de Viedma, and that he had heard it said he came from a village in the mountains of Léon. From this statement, and from what he himself had seen, he felt convinced that this was his brother who, following his father's advice, had studied law. Excited and rejoicing he called Don Fernando and Cardenio and the priest aside and told them how matters stood, assuring them that the judge was his brother. The servant had further informed him that he was now going to the Indies with the appointment of Judge of the Supreme Court of Mexico. He had learned, too, that the young lady was the judge's daughter, whose mother had died in giving birth to her, and that he was very rich because of the dowry left to him with the daughter. The captive asked their advice as to how he should make himself known, or whether, when he had made himself known, his brother would be ashamed of him, seeing him so poor, or would receive him with a warm heart.

"Leave it to me to find out that," said the priest. "Though there is no reason for supposing, señor captain, that you will not be kindly received, because the merit and wisdom revealed by your brother's bearing make it unlikely that he will proven haughty or insensible or that he will not know how to estimate the accidents of fortune at their proper value."

"Still," said the captain, "I would prefer not to make myself known abruptly, but in some indirect way."

"I have told you already," said the priest, "that I will manage it in a way that will satisfy us all."

By this time supper was ready, and they all took their seats at the table, except the captive and the ladies, who ate by themselves in their own room. In the middle of supper the priest spoke up.

"I had a comrade of your honor's name, Señor Judge," he said, "in Constantinople, where I was a captive for several years. That comrade was one of the most valiant soldiers and captains in the whole Spanish infantry, but he had as large a share of misfortune as of gallantry and courage."

"And what was the captain called, señor?" asked the judge.

"He was called Ruy Pérez de Viedma," replied the priest, "and he was born in a village in the mountains of León. He mentioned a circumstance connected with his father and his brothers which, had it not been told me by so truthful a man as he was, I should have set down as one of those fables old women tell over the fire in winter. He said his father had divided his property among his three sons and had given them words of advice sounder than any of Cato's. But I can say this much, that the choice he made of going to the wars met with such success that, by his gallant conduct and courage and without any help save his own merit, he rose in a few years to be captain of infantry. He saw himself on the highroad and in a position to be made a field commander before long. But Fortune was against him, for where he might have expected her favor he lost it, and with it his liberty, on that glorious day when so many regained their liberty, at the battle of Lepanto. I lost mine at La Goleta, and after a variety of adventures we found ourselves comrades at Constantinople. From there he went to Algiers, where he met with one of the most extraordinary adventures that ever befell anyone in the world."

Here the priest went on to relate briefly his brother's adventure with Zoraida, and to all of it the judge gave such a hearing that never before had he been so attentive a hearer. The priest, however, only went so far as to describe how the Frenchmen plundered those on the boat, and the poverty and distress into which his comrade and the fair Moor had fallen. Concerning them, he said he had been unable to learn their fate, whether they had reached Spain or been carried off to France by the Frenchmen.

The captain, standing a little to one side, was listening to all the priest said, and watching every movement of his brother who, as soon as he perceived the priest had made an end of his story, gave a deep sigh. "Oh, señor," he said, his eyes full of tears, "if you only knew what news you have given me and how it comes home to me, forcing me to show how I feel with the tears that spring from my eyes, in spite of all my wisdom and self-restraint! The brave captain you speak of is my eldest brother. Being of bolder and loftier mind than my other brother or myself, he chose the honorable and worthy calling of arms, one of the three careers our father proposed to us, as your comrade mentioned in the fable you thought he was telling you. I followed the career of letters, in which God and my own exertions have raised me to the position in which you see me. My second brother is in Peru, so wealthy that with what he has sent to my father and me he has fully repaid the portion he took with him. He even put it in my father's hands to gratify his natural generosity, while I too have been enabled to pursue my studies in a more becoming and creditable fashion, and so to attain my present standing. My father is still alive, though dying with anxiety to hear of his eldest son, and he prays God unceasingly that death may not close his eyes until he has looked upon those of his son. But what surprises me is that my brother, with all his common sense, should have failed to send us any news about himelf, either in his troubles and sufferings or in his prosperity. If his father or any of us had known of his captivity, he need not have waited for the miracle of the reed to obtain his ransom. But what alarms me now is not to know whether those Frenchmen let him go free or murdered him to hide the robbery. All this will make me continue my journey, not with the satisfaction in which I began it, but in the deepest melancholy and sadness. Oh dear brother! If I only knew where you were now, I would hasten to seek you out and deliver you from your sufferings, though it were to cost me suffering myself! Oh that I could bring news to our old father that you are alive, even if you should be in the deepest dungeon of Barbary. His wealth and my brother's and my own would set you free! Oh beautiful and generous Zoraida, if only I could repay your goodness to a brother! If only I could be present at the new birth of your soul and at your wedding, which would give us all such happiness!"

All this and more the judge uttered with such deep emotion at the news he had received of his brother that all who heard him shared in it, showing their sympathy with his sorrow. The priest, seeing how well he had succeeded in carrying out his purpose and the captain's wishes, had no desire to keep them unhappy any longer. So he rose from the table and went into the room where Zoraida was. He took her by the hand, and Luscinda, Dorotea, and the judge's daughter followed her. The captain was waiting to see what the priest would do. The priest, taking him with the other hand, advanced with both of them to where the judge and the other gentlemen were sitting. "Let your tears cease to flow, Señor Judge," he said, "and let the wish of your heart be gratified as fully as you could desire, for you have before you your worthy brother and your good sister-in-law. The man you see here is Captain Viedma, and this is the beautiful Moor who has been so good to him. The Frenchmen I told you of have reduced them to the state of poverty you see them in, that you may show your generosity of heart."

The captain ran to embrace his brother, who placed both hands on his breast so as to have a good look at him, holding him a little way off. But as soon as he had fully recognized him, he clasped him in his arms so closely, shedding such tears of heartfelt joy, that most of those present could not help weeping too. The words the brothers exchanged and the emotion they showed can scarcely be imagined, I fancy, much less put down in writing. They told each other in a few words the events of their lives, they showed the true affection of brothers in all its strength, and then the judge embraced Zoraida, putting all he possessed at her disposal. Then he told his daughter to embrace her, and the fair Christian and the lovely Moor drew fresh tears from every eye. And there was Don Quixote observing all these strange proceedings attentively without uttering a word, and attributing the whole to the fantasies of knight-errantry.

Then they agreed that the captain and Zoraida should return with his brother to Seville and send news to his father that the captain had been delivered and found. This would enable the father to be present at the marriage and baptism of Zoraida, for it was impossible for the judge to put off his journey, as he was informed that in a month's time the fleet was to sail from Seville for New Spain, and to miss the passage would have greatly inconvenienced him.

In short, everybody was well pleased and glad at the captive's good fortune, and as now almost two-thirds of the night were past, they resolved to retire to rest for the remainder of it. Don Quixote offered to mount guard over the castle lest they should be attacked by some giant or other malevolent scoundrel, covetous of the great treasure of beauty the castle contained. Those who understood him thanked him for this service, and they gave the judge an account of Don Quixote's extraordinary disposition, with which he was not a little amused. Sancho Panza alone was fuming at the lateness of the hour for going to sleep, and he it was who made himself most comfortable of all, as he stretched himself on the trappings of his donkey. This, as will be told farther on, was to cost him dear.

The ladies, then, having retired to their chamber, and the others having disposed themselves with as little discomfort as they could, Don Quixote sallied out of the inn to act as sentinel of the castle as he had promised. It happened, however, that a little before the approach of dawn a voice so musical and sweet reached the ears of the ladies that it forced them all to listen attentively, but especially Dorotea, who had been awake, and by whose side Doña Clara de Viedma, for so the judge's daughter was called, lay sleeping. No one could imagine who it was that sang so sweetly, and the voice was unaccompanied by any instrument. At one moment it seemed to them as if the singer were in the courtyard, at another in the stable; and as they were all attention, wondering, Cardenio came to the door. "Listen, whoever is not asleep," he said, "and you will hear a muleteer's voice that sings exchantingly."

"We are listening to it already, señor," said Dorotea, whereupon Cardenio went away, and Dorotea, giving all her attention to it, made out that these were the words of the song.

Chapter XLIII

WHEREIN IS RELATED THE PLEASENT STORY OF THE MULETEER, WITH OTHER STRANGE THINGS THAT CAME TO PASS IN THE INN[1]

Ah me, Love's mariner am I
  On Love's deep ocean sailing;
I know not where the haven lies,
  I dare not hope to gain it.

One solitary distant star
  Is all I have to guide me,
A brighter orb than those of old
That Palinurus[2] sighted.

And vaguely drifting am I borne;
  I know not where it leads me;
I fix my gaze on it alone,
  Of all beside it heedless.

1. This chapter heading is missing in the first edition, though it appears in the table of contents with the indication that Ch. XLIII begins with the poem. Some scholars believe Cervantes' started the chapter with the next-to-last paragraph of Ch. XLII which begins, "The ladies, then, . . ."

2. Palinurus was the pilot of Aeneas' boat.

But over-cautious prudery,
And coyness cold and cruel,
When most I need it, these, like clouds,
Its longed-for light refuse me.

Bright star, goal of my yearning eyes
As thou above me beamest,
When thou shalt hide thee from my sight
I'll know that death is near me.

The singer had got so far when it struck Dorotea that it was not fair to let Clara miss hearing such a sweet voice; so, shaking her, she woke her.

"Forgive me, young lady, for waking you," she said, "but I want you to have the pleasure of hearing the best voice you have ever heard, perhaps, in all your life."

Clara awoke quite drowsy, and not understanding at the moment what Dorotea said, asked her what it was. When this was repeated, Clara became attentive at once. But she had hardly heard two lines, as the singer continued, when a strange trembling seized her, as if she were suffering from a severe attack of quartan fever.

"Ah, dear lady of my soul and life!" she said, throwing her arms around Dorotea, "why did you wake me? The greatest kindness fortune could do me now would be to close my eyes and ears so as neither to see or hear that unhappy musician."

"What are you talking about, my dear?" said Dorotea. "Why, they say this singer is a muleteer!"

"No, he is a lord," replied Clara, "and the place he holds so firmly in my heart will never be taken from him, unless he should willingly surrender it."

Dorotea was amazed at the ardent language of the girl, for it seemed to be far beyond any experience of life her tender years could lead one to expect.

"You speak in such a way that I cannot understand you, Señora Clara," she said. "Explain yourself more clearly, and tell me what you are saying about hearts and places and this musician whose voice has so moved you. But do not tell me anything now, for I do not want to lose the pleasure I get from listening to the singer by giving my attention to your distress. I perceive he is beginning to sing a new strain and a new air."

"Let him, in heaven's name," Clara rejoined, and to avoid hearing him she stopped both ears with her hands. This too astonished Dorotea but she turned her attention to the song and found that it ran in this fashion:

Sweet Hope, my stay,
That onward to the goal of thy intent
Dost make thy way,

Heedless of hindrance or impediment,
Have thou no fear
If at each step thou findest death is near.

No victory,
No joy of triumph doth the faint heart know;
Unblessed is he
That a bold front to Fortune dares not show,
But soul and sense
In bondage yieldeth up to indolence.

If Love his wares
Do dearly sell, his right must be confessed;
What gold compares
With that whereon his stamp he hath impressed?
And all men know
What costeth little, that we rate but low.

Love resolute
Knows not the word "impossibility,"
And though my suit
Beset by endless obstacles I see,
Yet no despair
Shall hold me bound to earth while heaven is there.

Here the voice ceased, and Clara's sobs began afresh, all of which whetted Dorotea's curiosity to know what lay behind singing so sweet and weeping so bitter. So she again asked Clara what she had been on the point of saying a little while earlier. Clara, afraid that Luscinda might overhear, wound her arms tightly around Dorotea and put her mouth so close to her ear that no one else could have caught a word.

"This singer, dear señora," she said, "is the son of an Aragonese gentleman, lord of two villages, who lives opposite my father's house at Madrid. My father had curtains over the windows of his house in winter and blinds in summer, yet in some way—I know not how—this gentleman, who was pursuing his studies, saw me, whether in church or elsewhere I cannot tell. In any event he fell in love with me and made me aware of it from the windows of his house. His many tears and gestures compelled me to believe him and even to love him, though I had no idea what he wanted of me. One of the signs he used to make was to link one hand in the other, to indicate he wished to marry me. I should have been glad if that could come about, but being alone and motherless I did not know in whom I could confide. So I left things as they were and showed him no favor, except when my father and the rest of his household were away from home. Then I used to raise the curtain or the blinds and let him see me plainly, which so delighted him that he seemed on the verge of madness. Meanwhile the time came for my father's departure, and the young gentleman became aware of this, though not from me, for I had never been able to tell him of it. He fell sick, of grief I believe and so the day we were going away I could not see him to take farewell of him, were it only with my eyes. But after we had been two days on the road, as we entered a village inn a day's journey from here, I saw him at the inn door in the dress of a muleteer. He was so well disguised, that did I not carry his image graven on my heart I could not have recognized him. But I knew who he was, and it surprised me and made me happy. He watched me, unbeknownst to my father, from whom he always hides when he crosses my path on the road or in the inns where we put up. Since I know who he is, and realize that for love of me he is traveling on foot and undergoing all this hardship, I am ready to die of sorrow. Wherever he sets foot there I set my eyes. I do not know for what purpose he has come, or how he could have got away from his father, who loves him beyond measure, since he has no other heir—and also because it is merited, as you will perceive when you see him. Moreover, I can tell you, everything he sings is out of his own head, for I have heard them say he is a great scholar and poet. What is more, every time I see him or hear him sing, I tremble all over and am fearful that my father will recognize him and come to know of our love. I have never spoken a word to him in my life, yet for all that I love him so that I could not live without him. This, dear señora, is all I have to tell you about the musician whose voice has delighted you so much. By his voice alone you can plainly tell that he is no muleteer, but a lord of hearts and town, as I have told you already."

"Say no more, Doña Clara," said Dorotea at this, at the same time kissing her a thousand times over, "say no more, I tell you, but wait till day comes. Then I trust in God that this affair of yours can be arranged so as to have the happy ending such an innocent beginning deserves."

"Ah, señora," said Doña Clara, "what end can be hoped for when his father is of such lofty position, and so wealthy, that he would think I was not fit to be even a servant to his son, much less wife? And as to marrying without my father's knowledge I would not do it for all the world. I would not ask anything more than for this youth to go back and leave me. Perhaps when I no longer see him, and with the long distance we have to travel, my suffering may become less—though I dare say the remedy I propose will do me very little good. I don't know how the devil this has come about or how this love I have for him began, for I am so young, and he is a mere boy. I really believe we are both of the same age, and I am not sixteen yet. I will be sixteen next Michaelmas Day, my father says."

Dorotea could not help laughing to hear how like a child Doña Clara spoke. "Let us go to sleep now, señora," said she, "for the little of the night that I believe is left to us. God will soon send us daylight, and we will solve all these problems, or it will go hard with me."

With this they fell asleep, and deep silence reigned all through the inn. The only persons not asleep were the landlady's daughter and her servant Maritornes, who knew the weak point of Don Quixote's temperament and also that he was outside the inn mounting guard in armor and on horseback. The pair of them resolved to play some trick upon him, or at any rate to amuse themselves for a while by listening to his nonsense.

It so happened there was not a window in the whole inn that looked outwards except a hole in the wall of a straw-loft, through which they used to throw out the straw. At this hole the two demi-damsels posted themselves and observed Don Quixote on his horse. He was leaning on his pike and from time to time sent forth such deep and doleful sighs that he seemed to pull up his soul by the roots with each of them. And they could hear too how he was speaking in a soft, tender, loving tone. "Oh my lady Dulcinea del Toboso," he said, "perfection of all beauty, summit and crown of discretion, treasure house of grace, depository of virtue, and finally, ideal of all that is good, honorable, and delightful in this world! What is thy grace doing now? Art thou perchance, mindful of thy enslaved knight who of his own free will has exposed himself to such great perils, and all to serve thee? Give me tidings of her, oh luminary of the three faces![3] Perhaps at this moment, envious of hers, you are regarding her, either as she paces to and fro some gallery of her sumptuous palace, or leans over some balcony, meditating how, while preserving her purity and greatness, she may mitigate the tortures this wretched heart of mine endures for her sake, what glory should recompense my sufferings, what repose my toil, and lastly what death my life, and what reward my services? And you, oh sun, that now doubtless are harnessing your steeds in haste to rise betimes and come forth to see my lady; when you see her I entreat you to salute her on my behalf. But have a care, when you see her and salute her, not to kiss her face, for I shall be more jealous of you than you were of that light-footed ingrate[4] that made you sweat and run so on the plains of Thessaly or on the banks of the Peneus (for I do not exactly recollect where it was you did run on that occasion) in your jealousy and love."

Don Quixote had got so far in his pathetic speech when the landlady's daughter began to signal to him. "Señor," she said, "come over here, please."

At these signals and hearing her voice, Don Quixote turned his head and saw by the light of the moon, which then was in its full

3. The moon.

4. Daphne.

splendor, that someone was calling to him from the hole in the wall. To him it seemed to be a window, and what is more, with a gilt grating, as rich castles, such as he believed the inn to be, ought to have. And it immediately suggested itself to his imagination that, as on the former occasion, the fair damsel, the daughter of the lady of the castle, overcome by love for him, was once more endeavoring to win his affections. With this idea, and not to show himself discourteous or ungrateful, he turned Rocinante's head and approached the hole.

"I pity you, beauteous lady," he said, when he saw the two wenches, "that thou shouldst have directed thy thoughts of love to a quarter from whence it is impossible that such a return can be made to thee as is due to thy great merit and gentle birth. Thou must not on this account blame an unhappy knight-errant whom love renders incapable of submission to any other than her whom, the first moment his eyes beheld her, he made absolute mistress of his soul. Forgive me, noble lady, and retire to thy apartment, and do not, by any further declaration of thy passion, compel me to show myself more ungrateful. If, of the love thou bearest me, thou shouldst find that there is anything else in my power wherein I can gratify thee, provided it be not love itself, demand it of me. For I swear to thee by that sweet absent enemy of mine to grant it this instant, though it be that thou requirest of me a lock of Medusa's hair, which was all snakes, or even the very beams of the sun shut up in a vial."

"My mistress wants nothing of that sort, sir knight," said Maritornes at this.

"What then, discreet dueña,[5] is it that your mistress wants?" replied Don Quixote.

"Only one of your fair hands," said Maritornes, "to enable her to vent over it the great passion which has brought her to this loophole, so much to the risk of her honor. For if the lord her father had heard her, the least slice he would cut off her would be her head."

"I should like to see him try!" said Don Quixote. "But he will beware of that, if he does not want to meet the most disastrous end that ever father in the world met for having laid hands on the tender limbs of a lovesick daughter."

Maritornes felt sure that Don Quixote would present the hand she had asked for, and having made up her mind what to do, she got down from the hole and went into the stable. There she took the halter of Sancho Panza's donkey and in all haste returned to the

5. *Dueña* (duenna, in older English) means "matron." In Cervantes' day it was applied to the paid companions and chaperones (often widows and elderly gentlewomen) of aristocratic ladies. Cervantes frequently mocks the stupidity, indiscretion, and ill temper of these high-class servants.

hole just as Don Quixote had stood up on Rocinante's saddle in order to reach the grated window where he supposed the lovelorn damsel to be.

"Lady, take this hand," he said, as he stretched it out, "or rather this scourge of the evil-doers of the earth. Take, I say, this hand which no other hand of woman has ever touched, not even hers who has complete possession of my entire body. I present it to thee, not that thou mayest kiss it, but that thou mayest observe the contexture of the sinews, the close network of the muscles, the breadth and capacity of the veins, whence thou mayest infer what must be the strength of the arm that has such a hand."

"That we shall see presently," said Maritornes, and making a slipknot on the halter, she passed it over his wrist and, coming down from the hole, she tied the other end very firmly to the bolt of the straw-loft door.

"Your grace seems to be grating rather than caressing my hand," Don Quixote exclaimed, when he felt the roughness of the rope on his wrist. "Treat it not so harshly, for it is not to blame for the offense my resolution has given thee, nor is it fair to wreak all thy vengeance on so small a part. Remember that one who loves so well should not revenge herself so cruelly."

But there was nobody now to listen to these words of Don Quixote's, for as soon as Maritornes had tied him, she and the other made off, about to die laughing, leaving him fastened in such a way that he could not release himself.

He was, as has been said, standing on Rocinante, with his arm passed through the hole and his wrist tied to the bolt of the door, and in mighty fear and dread of being left hanging by the arm if Rocinante were to stir one side or the other. So he did not dare to make the least movement, although from the patience and imperturbable disposition of Rocinante, he had good reason to expect that he would stand without budging for a whole century. Finding himself fast, then, and that the ladies had retired, he began to fancy that all this was done by enchantment, as on the former occasion when in that same castle that enchanted Moor of a carrier had beaten him. He cursed in his heart his own want of sense and judgment in venturing to enter the castle again after having come off so badly the first time, it being a settled point with knights-errant that when they have tried an adventure and have not succeeded in it, it is a sign that it is not reserved for them but for others and that therefore they need not try it again. Nevertheless he pulled his arm to see if he could release himself, but it had been made so fast that all his efforts were in vain. It is true he pulled it gently lest Rocinante should move, but try as he might to seat himself in the saddle, he had no choice but to stand upright or pull his hand off.

Then it was he wished for the sword of Amadís, against which no enchantment whatever had any power. Then he cursed his ill fortune. Then he magnified the loss the world would sustain by his absence while he remained there enchanted, for this he believed was beyond all doubt. Then he once more took to thinking of his beloved Dulcinea del Toboso. Then he called to his worthy squire Sancho Panza who, buried in sleep and stretched upon the pack-saddle of his ass, was oblivious, at that moment, of the mother that bore him. Then he called upon the sages Lirgandeo and Alquife[6] to come to his aid. Then he invoked his good friend Urganda to succor him. And then, at last, morning found him in such a state of desperation and perplexity that he was bellowing like a bull, for he had no hope that day would bring any relief to his suffering, which he believed would last for ever, inasmuch as he was enchanted. He was convinced of this by seeing that Rocinante never stirred, either much or little, and he felt sure that he and his horse were to remain in this state, without eating or drinking or sleeping, until the malign influence of the stars passed, or until some other more sage enchanter should disenchant him.

But he was very much deceived in this conclusion, for daylight had hardly begun to appear when there came up to the inn four men on horseback, well equipped and accoutered, with pistols hanging from their saddles. They called out and knocked loudly at the gate of the inn, which was still shut. On seeing this, Don Quixote, from where he was, did not forget to act as sentinel.

"Knights, or squires, or whatever ye be," he said, in a loud, imperious tone, "ye have no right to knock at the gates of this castle. It is plain enough that those within are either asleep or else are not in the habit of throwing open the fortress until the sun's rays have spread over the whole surface of the earth. Withdraw to a distance and wait till it is broad daylight, and then we shall see whether it will be proper or not to open to you."

"What the devil fortress or castle is this," said one, "to make us stand on such ceremony? If you are the innkeeper bid them open for us. We are travelers who only want to feed our horses and go on, for we are in haste."

"Do you think, oh knights, that I look like an innkeeper?" said Don Quixote.

"I don't know what you look like," replied the other, "but I know that you are talking nonsense when you call this inn a castle."

"A castle it is," returned Don Quixote, "indeed, one of the best in this whole province, and it has within it people who have had the scepter in the hand and the crown on the head."

"It would be better if it were the other way," said the traveler, "the scepter on the head and the crown in the hand. And so it will be, if the need arises. But maybe there is some company of players

6. Magicians in the romances *Espejo de príncipes* and *Amadís de Grecia.*

here, with whom it is customary to have those crowns and scepters you speak of. For in so small an inn, and where such silence is kept, I do not believe any people entitled to crowns and scepters can have taken up their quarters."

"You know but little of the world," returned Don Quixote, "since you are ignorant of what commonly occurs in knight-errantry."

But the speaker's comrades, growing weary of the dialogue with Don Quixote, renewed their knocks with such vehemence that the innkeeper, and not only he but everybody in the inn, awoke, and he got up to ask who knocked. It happened at this moment that one of the horses of the four men seeking admittance went to smell Rocinante who, melancholy, dejected, and with drooping ears stood motionless, supporting his sorely stretched master. As he was, after all, flesh, though he looked as if he were made of wood, he could not help giving way and in return smelling the one who had come to offer him attentions. But he had hardly moved at all when Don Quixote lost his footing. Slipping off the saddle, he would have come to the ground but for being suspended by the arm, which caused him such agony that he believed either his wrist would be cut through or his arm torn off. He hung so near the ground that he could just touch it with his feet. This made it all the worse for him, for when he realized how little was required to enable him to plant his feet firmly, he struggled and stretched himself as much as he could to gain a footing, like those undergoing the torture of the strappado, hanging just above the ground, who aggravate their own sufferings by their violent efforts to stretch themselves, deceived by the hope which makes them fancy that with a little more effort they will reach the ground.

Chapter XLIV

IN WHICH ARE CONTINUED THE UNHEARD-OF ADVENTURES AT THE INN

So loud, in fact, were Don Quixote's shouts that the landlord opened the gate of the inn in all haste and came out in dismay, running to see who was uttering such cries. He was joined by those who were outside. Maritornes, who by this time had been roused by the same outcry, suspected what it was and ran to the loft. There without anyone seeing her, she untied the halter by which Don Quixote was suspended, and down he came to the ground in the sight of the landlord and the travelers who, approaching him, asked what was the matter with him that he shouted so. He, without replying a word, took the rope off his wrist, rose to his feet and leaped upon Rocinante. Then he slipped his shield on his arm, put his lance in its socket, and made a wide circuit of the plain, returning at a half-gallop.

"Whoever shall say that I have been enchanted with just cause, provided my lady the Princess Micomicona grants me permission to do so, I give him the lie, challenge him, and defy him to single combat."

The newly arrived travelers were amazed at Don Quixote's words, but the landlord allayed their surprise by telling them who Don Quixote was, and not to mind him as he was out of his senses. They then asked the landlord if by any chance a youth of about fifteen years of age had come to the inn, in the clothing of a muleteer and of such and such an appearance—and they described Doña Clara's suitor. The landlord replied that there were so many people in the inn he had not noticed the person they were inquiring about, but at this point one of them noticed the coach in which the judge had arrived. "He is here, no doubt," he said, "for this is the coach he is following. Let one of us stay at the gate, and the rest go in to look for him, or indeed it might be as well if one of us went around the inn, in case he should try to escape over the wall of the yard."

"So be it," said another, and while two of them went in, one remained at the gate and the fourth made the circuit of the inn. The landlord saw all of this but could not imagine why they were taking all these precautions, though he understood they were looking for the youth they had just described.

It was by this time broad daylight, and for that reason, and also because of the noise Don Quixote had made, everybody was awake and up, but particularly Doña Clara and Dorotea. They had been able to sleep but badly that night, the one from agitation at having her suitor so near her, the other from curiosity to see him. Don Quixote, when he saw that not one of the four travelers took any notice of him or replied to his challenge, was furious and ready to die with indignation and wrath. If he could have found in the ordinances of chivalry that it was lawful for a knight-errant to undertake or engage in another enterprise when he had plighted his word and faith not to involve himself in any until he had made an end of the one to which he was pledged, he would have attacked all of them and would have made them answer in spite of themselves. But considering that it would not become him or be right to begin any new undertaking until he had established Micomicona in her kingdom, he was constrained to hold his peace and wait quietly to see the upshot of those same travelers' investigations. One of them found the youth they were seeking lying asleep by the side of a muleteer, without a thought of anyone coming in search of him, much less finding him. The man laid hold of him by the arm.

"It becomes you well indeed, Señor Don Luis, to be in the dress you wear, just as the bed in which I find you well accords with the luxury in which your mother reared you."

The youth rubbed his sleepy eyes and stared for a while at the man who held him, but presently he recognized him as one of his father's servants. This so took him aback that for some time he could not find or utter a word.

"There is nothing for it now, Señor Don Luis," the servant continued, "but to submit quietly and return home, unless you want my lord, your father, to take his departure for the other world. There can be no other outcome to the grief he feels at your absence."

"But how did my father know that I had gone this way and in these clothes?" said Don Luis.

"It was from a student to whom you confided your intentions," answered the servant. "He revealed them, because he pitied the distress he saw your father suffer when you had gone. So your father dispatched four servants in quest of you, and here we all are at your service, better pleased than you can imagine that we'll be returning so soon and can restore you to eyes that so yearn for you."

"That shall be as I please, or as heaven orders," returned Don Luis.

"What can you please or heaven order," said the other, "except to agree to go back? Anything else is impossible."

The muleteer at whose side Don Luis had been sleeping overheard all this conversation, so he got up and went off to report what had taken place to Don Fernando, Cardenio, and the others, who were dressed by this time. He told them how the man had addressed the youth as "Don," and what words had passed, and how he wanted him to return to his father, which the youth was unwilling to do. With this and what they already knew of the rare voice that heaven had bestowed upon him, they all felt very anxious to know more particularly who he was. They even were disposed to help him if force should be employed against him, so they hastened to where he was still talking and arguing with his servant.

Dorotea at this instant came out of her room with Doña Clara, all in a tremor, in her wake. Calling Cardenio aside, she told him in a few words the story of the musician and Doña Clara, and he at the same time told her what had happened, how the servants sent by the youth's father had sought him out. In telling her this, however, he did not speak low enough, and Doña Clara, hearing what he said, became so upset that had not Dorotea hastened to support her she would have fallen to the ground. Cardenio then asked Dorotea to return to her room, since he would endeavor to straighten out the whole matter, and they did as he had suggested. The four men who had been seeking Don Luis had now come into the inn and surrounded him, while they urged him to return and console his father at once and without a moment's delay. He replied that he could not possibly do so before settling some business that involved his life, his heart, and his honor. The servants insisted, saying that most certainly they would not return without him and that they would take him away whether he liked it or not.

"That you will never do," replied Don Luis, "unless you take me dead—though, no matter how you take me, there will be no life in me."

By this time almost everyone in the inn had been attracted by the dispute, but particularly Cardenio, Don Fernando, his companions, the judge, the barber, and Don Quixote, who now considered there was no necessity for mounting guard over the castle any longer. Since Cardenio was already acquainted with the young man's story, he asked the men who wanted to take him away what their aim was in trying to carry him off against his will.

"Our aim," said one of the four, "is to save the life of his father, who is in danger of losing it because of this gentleman's disappearance."

"Their is no need to make my affairs public here," exclaimed Don Luis, when he heard this. "I am free and will return if it pleases me. If not, none of you can compel me."

"Reason will compel your worship," said the man. "But if it has no power over you, it has power over us, to make us do what we came for and what it is our duty to do."

"Let us hear what the whole affair is about," said the judge at this.

"Do you not know this gentleman, Señor Judge?" replied the man, who knew the judge to be a neighbor of theirs. "He is the son of your neighbor, who has run away from his father's house in clothing so unbecoming his rank, as your honor may perceive."

The judge looked at the youth more carefully, recognized him and embraced him. "What folly is this, Señor Don Luis," he said, "or what can have induced you to come here in this way and in this garb which so ill becomes your rank?"

Tears came into the young man's eyes, and he was unable to utter a word in reply to the judge, who told the four servants not to be uneasy, for all would be satisfactorily settled. Then taking Don Luis by the hand, he drew him aside and asked him why he had come.

But while he was questioning him they heard a loud outcry at the gate of the inn, the reason being that two of the guests who had passed the night there, seeing everybody intent on finding out what the four men wanted, had conceived the idea of going off without paying what they owed. But the landlord, who minded his own affairs more closely than other people's, caught them going out of the gate and demanded his reckoning. With such language did he abuse them for their dishonesty that he drove them to reply with their fists, and they began to lay on him in such a style that the poor man was forced to cry out for help. The landlady and her daughter could see no one more free to give aid than Don Quixote. "Sir knight," the daughter said to him, "by the virtue God has given you, help my poor father, for two wicked men are beating him to a pulp."

"Fair damsel," replied Don Quixote with deliberation and great calm, "at the present moment thy request is inopportune, for I am debarred from involving myself in any adventure until I have brought to a happy conclusion one to which my word has pledged me. But that which I can do for thee I will now mention. Run and tell thy father to stand his ground as well as he can in this battle, and on no account to allow himself to be vanquished, while I go and request permission of the Princess Micomicona to enable me to succor him in his distress. If she grants it, rest assure I will come to his aid."

"Sinner that I am," exclaimed Maritornes, who stood by, "before you have got your permission my master will be in the other world."

"Give me leave, señora, to obtain the permission I speak of," returned Don Quixote. "If I get it, it will matter very little if he is in the other world. I will rescue him thence in spite of all the same world can do, or at any rate I will give thee such a revenge over those who shall have sent him there that thou wilt be more than moderately satisfied."

Without saying anything more he went and knelt before Dorotea, requesting her highness in knightly and errant phrase to be pleased to grant him permission to aid and succor the warden of that castle, who now stood in grievous jeopardy. The princess granted it graciously, and he at once, slipping his shield on his arm and drawing his sword, hastened to the inn gate, where the two guests were still handling the landlord roughly. But as soon as he reached the spot, he stopped short and stood still, though Maritornes and the landlady asked him why he hesitated to help their master and husband.

"I hesitate," said Don Quixote, "because it is not lawful for me to draw sword against persons of squirely condition. Call my squire Sancho to me, for this defense and vengeance are his affair and business."

Thus matters stood at the inn gate, where there was a very lively exchange of fisticuffs and punches, to the grievous damage of the landlord and to the wrath of Maritornes, the landlady, and her daughter, who were furious when they saw the pusillanimity of Don Quixote, and the hard treatment their master, husband, and father was undergoing. But let us leave him there, for he will surely find someone to help him, and if not, let him who attempts more than his strength allows him to do suffer and hold his tongue. Let us go back fifty paces to see what Don Luis said in reply to the judge whom we left questioning him privately as to his reasons for coming on foot and so wretchedly dressed.

In answer the youth, pressing his hand in a way that showed his heart was troubled by some great sorrow, burst into a flood of tears. "Señor," he said, "all I have to tell you is that, from the moment when, through heaven's will and our being near neighbors, I first saw Doña Clara, your daughter and my lady, from that instant I made her the mistress of my will. If your will, my true lord and father, offers no impediment, this very day she shall become my wife. For her I left my father's house, and for her I assumed this disguise, to follow her wherever she goes, as the arrow seeks its mark or the sailor the pole star. She knows nothing more of my passion than what she may have learned from having sometimes seen from a distance that my eyes were filled with tears. You know already, señor, the wealth and noble birth of my parents and that I am their sole heir. If this is a sufficient inducement for you to venture to make me completely happy, accept me at once as your son. For if my father, influenced by other objects of his own, should disapprove of this happiness I have sought for myself, time has more power to alter and change things than human will."

With this the lovelorn youth was silent, while the judge, after hearing him, was astonished, perplexed, and surprised, as well at the manner and intelligence with which Don Luis had confessed the secret of his heart as at the position in which he found himself, not knowing what course to take in a matter so sudden and unexpected. All the answer, therefore, he gave him was to bid him to make his mind easy for the present and arrange with his servants not to take him back that day, so that there might be time to consider what was best for all parties. Don Luis kissed his hands by force, indeed, bathed them with his tears, in a way that would have touched a heart of marble, not to say that of the judge, who, as a shrewd man, had already perceived how advantageous the marriage would be for his daughter. Yet, were it possible, he would have preferred that it should be brought about with the consent of the father of Don Luis who, as he knew, was looking for a title for his son.

The guests had by this time made peace with the landlord, for, by persuasion and Don Quixote's fair words more than by threats, they had paid him what he demanded, and the servants of Don Luis were waiting for the end of the conversation with the judge and their master's decision. Thereupon the devil, who never sleeps, contrived that the barber, from whom Don Quixote had taken Mambrino's helmet, and Sancho Panza the trappings of his ass in exchange for those of his own, should at this instant enter the inn. The said barber, as he led his ass to the stable, observed Sancho Panza engaged in repairing something or other belonging to the packsaddle. The moment he saw it, he knew it, and made bold to attack Sancho.

"Aha, thief, I have caught you!" he exclaimed. "Hand over my basin and my packsaddle and all my trappings that you robbed me of."

Sancho, finding himself so unexpectedly assailed and hearing the abuse poured upon him, seized the packsaddle with one hand and with the other gave the barber a punch that bathed his teeth in blood. The barber, however, was not so ready to let go of the packsaddle. On the contrary, he raised such an outcry that everyone in the inn came running to know what the noise and quarrel were about. "Help, in the name of the king and justice!" he cried. "This thief and highwayman wants to kill me for trying to recover my property."

"You lie," said Sancho. "I am no highwayman. It was in fair war my master Don Quixote won these spoils."

Don Quixote was standing by at the time, highly pleased to see his squire so valorous both in self-defense and on the attack. From that time forth he reckoned him a man of mettle and in his heart resolved to dub him a knight on the first opportunity that presented itself, feeling sure that the order of chivalry would be fittingly bestowed upon him.

"Gentlemen," said the barber in the course of the altercation, along with other things, "this packsaddle is mine as surely as I owe God a death, and I know it as well as if I had given birth to it. Here is my donkey in the stable who will not let me lie. Only try it, and if it does not fit him like a glove, call me a rascal. And what is more, the same day I was robbed of this, they robbed me also of a new brass basin, never yet put to use, that would fetch a crown any day."

At this Don Quixote felt bound to reply. Separating the two by stepping between them, he placed the packsaddle on the ground so that it should be clearly seen until the truth was established.

"Your worships may perceive clearly and plainly," he said, "the error under which this worthy squire lies when he calls a basin what was, is, and shall be the helmet of Mambrino which I won from him in fair war and made myself master of by legitimate and lawful possession. With the packsaddle I do not concern myself, but I may tell you on that head that my squire Sancho asked my permission to strip off the trappings of this vanquished coward's steed, and with it adorn his own. I allowed him, and he took it. As to these trappings having been changed into a packsaddle, I can give no explanation except the usual one, that such transformations occur in adventures of chivalry. To confirm all which, run, Sancho my son, and fetch hither the helmet which this good fellow calls a basin."

"By God, master," said Sancho, "if we have no other proof of our case than what your worship puts forward, Malino's helmet is just as much a basin as this good fellow's trappings are a packsaddle."

"Do as I bid you," said Don Quixote. "Surely everything in this castle cannot be subject to enchantment."

Sancho hastened to fetch the basin. When he had returned with it, Don Quixote took it in his hands.

"Your worships may judge the effrontery of this squire," he said, "when he declares this to be a basin and not the helmet I told you of. I swear by the order of chivalry I profess that this helmet is the identical one I took from him, without anything added to it or removed."

"There is no doubt of that," said Sancho, "for from the time my master won it until now he has only fought one battle in it, when he let loose those unlucky men in chains. And if it had not been for this basin-helmet he would not have come off too well that time, for there was plenty of stone-throwing in that affair."

Chapter XLV

IN WHICH THE DOUBTFUL QUESTION OF MAMBRINO'S HELMET AND THE PACKSADDLE IS FINALLY SETTLED, WITH OTHER ADVENTURES THAT REALLY OCCURRED

"What do you think now, gentlemen," asked the barber, "of the assertion of these worthy persons, who still insist that this is not a basin but a helmet?"

"Whoever says the contrary," said Don Quixote, "I will let him know he lies if he is a knight, and if he is a squire that he lies a thousand times over."

Our own barber, who witnessed all this and was so closely familiar with Don Quixote's temperament, decided to back him in his delusion and stretch out the joke for the amusement of all. So he turned to the other barber.

"Señor Barber," he said, "or whatever you are, you must know that I too am of your profession and have had a license to practice for more than twenty years. I know the tools of the barber's craft very well indeed. I was also a soldier for some time in my youth and know what a helmet is, and a morion, and a headpiece with a visor, and other things about soldiering, I mean about soldiers' arms. And I say—subject to correction and deferring always to sounder judgments—that this piece we have now before us, which this worthy gentleman has in his hands, not only is no barber's basin, but is as far from being one as white is from black and truth from falsehood. I say, moreover, that this, although it is a helmet, is not a complete helmet."

"Certainly not," said Don Quixote, "for half of it is missing, that is to say the beaver."[1]

"It is quite true," said the priest, who had grasped the plan of his friend the barber, and Cardenio together with Don Fernando and his companions agreed that this was so. Even the judge, if he had not been so preoccupied with Don Luis's affair, would have helped to carry on the joke. But he was so wrapped up in his serious concerns that he paid little or no attention to all this banter.

"God bless me!" exclaimed the barber whose leg was being pulled, "is it possible that such an honorable gathering can say that this is not a basin but a helmet? Why, this is a thing that would astonish a whole university, however wise! That will do. If this basin is a helmet, why, then the packsaddle must be a horse's trappings, as this gentleman has said."

"To me it looks like a packsaddle," said Don Quixote, "but I have already said that the question is no concern of mine."

"Whether it is packsaddle or trappings," said the priest, "only Señor Don Quixote can say; for in such matters of chivalry all these gentlemen and I acknowledge his authority."

"By God, gentlemen," said Don Quixote, "so many strange things have happened to me on the two occasions I have stayed in this castle that I will not venture any positive assertion concerning anything in it. For it is my belief that all that goes on within is caused by enchantment. The first time, an enchanted Moor dwelling here gave me sore trouble, nor was Sancho let off lightly by certain underlings of his. Last night I was kept hanging by this arm for nearly two hours, without knowing how or why this misfortune befell me. So that now for me to offer an opinion in such a puzzling matter would be rash and ill-advised. I have already replied to the assertion that this is a basin and not a helmet. As for the question whether this is a packsaddle or harness, I will venture no absolute opinion but leave it to your worships' better judgment. Since you are not dubbed knights like myself, the enchantments of this place may have nothing to do with you. In that case, with unhampered vision, you can see things in this castle as they really are and not as they appear to me."

"There can be no doubt," replied Don Fernando, "that Señor Don Quixote speaks very wisely here and that it is for us to decide the matter. To be on surer ground, I will take the votes of the gentlemen in secret and announce the result clearly and fully."

1. The "beaver," from an Old French word for bib, covered the lower part of the face and the throat.

To those who knew about Don Quixote's foibles, all this afforded great amusement. But to those who knew nothing, it seemed the greatest nonsense in the world—in particular to the four servants of Don Luis as well as to Don Luis himself and to three other travelers who had by chance come to the inn and had the appearance of officers of the Holy Brotherhood, which indeed they were. But the one who above all was at his wits' end was the barber whose basin, there before his very eyes, had been turned into Mabrino's helmet, and whose packsaddle he had no doubt whatever was about to become the splendid trappings of a horse. All laughed to see Don Fernando going from one to another collecting the votes and whispering to them to give him their private opinion whether the treasure over which there had been so much fighting was trappings or packsaddle. After he had taken the votes of those who knew Don Quixote, he said aloud, "The fact is, my good fellow, that I am tired collecting such a number of opinions, for I find that there is not one whom I ask what I desire to know who does not tell me that it is absurd to say that this is the packsaddle of an ass and not the harness of a horse, indeed, of a thoroughbred horse. You must submit, for in spite of you and your donkey this is a harness and not a packsaddle, and you have started and proved your case very badly."

"May I never share heaven," said the second barber, "if your worships are not all mistaken; and may my soul as plainly appear before God as that appears to me to be a packsaddle and not a harness. But, 'laws go,'[2]—I say no more; and indeed I am not drunk, for I am fasting, sinner that I am."

The foolish talk of the barber did not afford less amusement than the absurdities of Don Quixote, who now spoke up.

"There is no more to be done now than for each to take what belongs to him," he declared, "and to what God has given each, may St. Peter add his blessing."

But one of the four servants spoke up. "Unless, indeed, this is a deliberate joke," he said, "I cannot bring myself to believe that men so intelligent as those present are, or seem to be, can venture to declare and assert that this is not a basin and that not a packsaddle. But as I perceive that they do assert and declare it, I can only come to the conclusion that there is some mystery in thus persisting in what is so opposed to the evidence of experience and truth itself. For I swear by"—and here he rapped out a round oath—"all the people in the world will not make me believe that this is not a barber's basin and that a jackass's packsaddle."

"It might easily be a she-ass's," observed the priest.

"It is all the same," said the servant. "That is not the point, but whether it is or is not a packsaddle, as your worships say."

2. "Laws go where kings want them to go."

On hearing this one of the newly arrived officers of the Brotherhood, who had been listening to the dispute and controversy, could no longer restrain his anger and impatience.

"It is a packsaddle," he said, "as sure as my father is my father, and whoever has said or will say anything else must be drunk."

"You lie like a low-born scoundrel," returned Don Quixote, and lifting his pike, which he had never let out of his hand, he delivered such a blow at his head that, had the officer not dodged it, it would have stretched him full length. The pike was shivered in pieces against the ground, and the rest of the officers, seeing their comrade assaulted, raised a shout, calling for help for the Holy Brotherhood. The landlord, who was of the fraternity, ran at once to fetch his staff of office and his sword and ranged himself on the side of his comrades. The servants of Don Luis clustered around him, lest he should escape from them in the confusion. The barber, seeing the house turned upside down, once more laid hold of his packsaddle, and Sancho did the same. Don Quixote drew his sword and charged the officers. Don Luis cried out to his servants to leave him alone and go and help Don Quixote and Cardenio and Don Fernando, who were supporting him. The priest was shouting at the top of his voice, the landlady was screaming, her daughter was wailing, Maritornes was weeping, Dorotea was aghast, Luscinda terror-stricken, and Doña Clara in a faint. The barber pounded Sancho, and Sancho pummeled the barber, while Don Luis gave one of his servants, who ventured to catch him by the arm to keep him from escaping, a cuff that bathed his teeth in blood. The judge tried to help him. Don Fernando was standing on one of the officers and was kicking him heartily, and the landlord raised his voice again calling for help for the Holy Brotherhood, so that the whole inn was nothing but cries, shouts, shrieks, confusion, terror, dismay, mishaps, sword-cuts, fisticuffs, cudgelings, kicks, and bloodshed. And in the midst of all this chaos, complication, and general entanglement, Don Quixote took it into his head that he had been plunged into the thick of the discord of Agramante's camp.[3]

"Hold all," he cried out, in a voice that shook the inn like thunder, "let all sheathe their swords, let all be calm and listen to me as they value their lives!"

All paused at his mighty voice. "Did I not tell you, sirs," he went on, "that this castle was enchanted, and that a legion or so of devils dwelt in it? As proof I call on you to behold with your own eyes how the discord of Agramante's camp has come hither and been transported into the midst of us. See how they fight, there for the sword, here for the horse, on that side for the eagle, on this for the

3. *Orlando furioso*, c. xxvii. Agramante was the chief of the Mohammedan kings assembled at the siege of Paris, of whom Sobrino, mentioned below, was one.

helmet.[4] We are all fighting, and all at cross-purposes. Come then, you, Señor Judge, and you, Señor Priest. Let one of you represent King Agramante and the other King Sobrino, and make peace among us. For by God almighty it is a sorry business that so many persons of distinction as we are should slay one another for such a trifling cause."

The officers, who did not understand Don Quixote's manner of speaking, and found themselves roughly handled by Don Fernando, Cardenio, and their companions, were not to be appeased. The barber was, however; for both his beard and his packsaddle were the worse for the struggle. Sancho like a good servant obeyed the slightest word of his master. The four servants of Don Luis kept quiet when they saw how little they gained by not doing so. The landlord alone insisted that they must punish the insolence of this madman, who at every turn raised a disturbance in the inn. At length the uproar was stilled for the present. The packsaddle remained a horse's harness till the day of judgment, and the basin a helmet and the inn a castle in Don Quixote's imagination.

All having been now pacified and made friends by the persuasiveness of the judge and the priest, the servants of Don Luis began again to urge him to return with them at once. While he was discussing the matter with them, the judge took counsel with Don Fernando, Cardenio, and the priest as to what he ought to do in the case, telling them how things stood and what Don Luis had said to him. It was agreed at length that Don Fernando should tell the servants of Don Luis who he was and that he wanted Don Luis to accompany him to Andalusia, where he would receive from the marquis his brother the welcome his breeding entitled him to. For, otherwise, it was easy to see from the determination of Don Luis that he would not return to his father at present, though they tore him to pieces. On learning the rank of Don Fernando and the resolution of Don Luis, the four then agreed among themselves that three of them should return to tell his father how matters stood. The other would remain in the service of Don Luis and not leave him until they came back for him or his father's orders were known. Thus by the authority of Agramante and the wisdom of King Sobrino all this complication of disputes was smoothed over. But the enemy of concord and hater of peace, feeling himself slighted and made a fool of, and seeing how little he had gained after having involved them all in such an elaborate entanglement, resolved to try his hand once more by stirring up fresh quarrels and disturbances.

This is how it happened. The officers calmed down, on learning the rank of those with whom they had fought, and withdrew from the contest, considering that in any event they were likely to get the

4. The sword, horse, and shield with an eagle come from Ariosto; the helmet is Don Quixote's addition.

worst of the battle. But one of them, the one who had been thrashed and kicked by Don Fernando, recollected that among some warrants he carried for the arrest of certain delinquents, he had one against Don Quixote, whom the Holy Brotherhood had ordered to be arrested for setting the galley slaves free. This was the very thing that Sancho, with good reason, had been fearing. The officer, his suspicions now aroused, decided to ascertain whether Don Quixote's features matched the description. So, taking out a parchment, he found what he was looking for and proceeded to read it slowly, for he was not a good reader. As he made out each word he fixed his eyes on Don Quixote, in order to compare his face with the description in the warrant, and he discovered that beyond a doubt this was the person described. Having made sure of this, he folded up the parchment, took the warrant in his left hand and with his right seized Don Quixote by the collar so tightly that he was choking him. "Help for the Holy Brotherhood!" he shouted. "And so you can be certain I am in earnest about it, read this warrant which says this highwayman is to be arrested."

The priest, taking the warrant, saw that what the officer said was true and that it accurately described Don Quixote's appearance. As for Don Quixote, in a towering rage at finding himself roughly handled by this scoundrelly oaf, with every joint cracking, he clutched the other's throat tightly in both hands. But for the help he received from his comrades, this officer would have gone to his death before Don Quixote released his hold. The landlord, who was duty bound to support his brother officers, at once ran to their aid. The landlady, when she saw her husband involved in yet another brawl, screamed once more and was immediately echoed by Maritornes and the daughter, as she called on heaven and all present for help.

"By the Lord," exclaimed Sancho, seeing what was going on, "it is quite true what my master says about the enchantment of this castle, for it is impossible to live an hour in peace within it!"

Don Fernando separated the officer and Don Quixote and to their mutual relief made them relax their grip, which held fast the coat collar of one adversary and the throat of the other. Despite this, however, the officers clamored for their prisoner and demanded help, so that he might be delivered bound into their power. This was required in the service of the King and of the Holy Brotherhood, on whose behalf they again called for aid and assistance in arresting this robber and highwayman. Don Quixote smiled when he heard these words.

"Come now, base, ill-born brood," he said very calmly "do you name it highway robbery to give freedom to those in bondage, to release captives, to succor the miserable, to raise up the fallen, to relieve the needy? Infamous beings, who by your vile groveling intellects deserve that heaven should not make known to you the virtue that lies in knight-errantry, or reveal the ignorance and sin lying in your refusal to respect the shadow, not to say the presence, of any knight-errant! Come now, band, not of officers, but of thieves, highwaymen with the license of the Holy Brotherhood! Tell me what ignoramus signed a warrant of arrest against such a knight as I? Who was unaware that knights-errant are independent of all jurisdictions, that their law is their sword, their charter their prowess, and their edicts their wills? What fool, I say again, did not know that there are no patents of nobility conferring such privileges or exemptions as a knight-errant acquires the day he is dubbed a knight and takes up the arduous calling of chivalry? What knight-errant ever paid poll-tax, duty, queen's pin-money, king's dues, toll, or ferry? What tailor ever took payment of him for making his clothes? What warden that received him in his castle ever made him pay his bill? What king did not seat him at his table? What damsel was not enamored of him and did not yield herself up wholly to his will and pleasure? And, lastly, what knight-errant has there been, is there, or will there ever be in the world, not bold enough to give, single-handed, four hundred blows to four hundred officers of the Holy Brotherhood if they come his way?"

Chapter XLVI

OF THE NOTABLE ADVENTURE OF THE OFFICERS OF THE HOLY BROTHERHOOD; AND OF THE GREAT FEROCITY OF OUR WORTHY KNIGHT, DON QUIXOTE

While Don Quixote was talking in this vein, the priest was persuading the officers that he was out of his senses, as they might perceive by his deeds and his words, and that they need not press the matter any further. Even if they arrested him and carried him off, they would have to release him at once as a madman. To which the holder of the warrant replied that he had nothing to do with inquiring into Don Quixote's madness but only to execute his superior's orders, and that once taken they might let him go three hundred times if they liked.

"Nevertheless," said the priest, "you must not take him away this time, nor will he, in my opinion, let himself be taken away."

In short, the priest used such arguments, and Don Quixote did such mad things, that the officers would have been more mad than he was if they had not perceived his want of wits. So they thought it best to allow themselves to be pacified and even to act as peacemakers between the barber and Sancho Panza, who still continued their altercation with much bitterness. In the end they, as officers of justice, settled the question by arbitration in such a manner that both sides were, if not perfectly contented, at least to some extent satisfied. For they exchanged the packsaddles, but not the girths or halters, and as to Mambrino's helmet, the priest surreptitiously and without Don Quixote's knowing it paid eight *reales* for the basin, and the barber gave him a receipt and guarantee to make no further demand then or thenceforth for evermore, amen.

These two disputes, which were the most important and gravest, being settled, it only remained for the servants of Don Luis to consent that three of them should return while one was left to accompany Don Luis where Don Fernando desired to take him. Good luck and better fortune, having already begun to solve difficulties and remove obstructions in favor of the lovers and warriors of the inn, saw fit to persevere and bring everything to a happy conclusion. For the servants agreed to do as Don Luis wished and this gave Doña Clara such happiness that no one could have looked into her face just then without seeing the joy of her heart. Zoraida, though she did not fully comprehend all she saw, was grave or gay without knowing why, as she watched and studied the various countenances, but particularly her Spaniard's, whom she followed with her eyes and clung to with her soul. The gift and compensation which the priest gave the barber had not escaped the landlord's notice, and he demanded Don Quixote's payment, together with the amount of the damage to his wineskins and the loss of his wine, swearing that neither Rocinante nor Sancho's donkey should leave the inn until he had been paid to the very last farthing. The priest settled all amicably, and Don Fernando paid, though the judge had also very readily offered to pay the score. All became so peaceful and quiet that the inn no longer reminded one of the discord of Agramante's camp, as Don Quixote said, but of the peace and tranquillity of the days of Octavianus.[1] It was the universal opinion that thanks were due to the great zeal and eloquence of the priest and to the unexampled generosity of Don Fernando.

Finding himself now clear and free of all quarrels, his squire's as well as his own, Don Quixote considered that it would be advisable to continue the journey he had begun and bring to a close that great adventure for which he had been called and chosen. With this high resolve, he went and knelt before Dorotea who, however, would not allow him to utter a word until he had risen. So to obey her he rose.

"It is a common proverb, fair lady," he said, "that 'diligence is the mother of good fortune,' and experience has often shown in important affairs that the earnestness of the negotiator brings the doubtful case to a successful termination. But in nothing does this truth show itself more plainly than in war, where quickness and activity forestall the devices of the enemy and win the victory

1. I.e. Caesar Augustus.

before the foe has time to defend himself. All this I say, exalted and esteemed lady, because it seems to me that for us to remain any longer in this castle now is useless and may be injurious to us in a way that we shall find out some day. For who knows whether your enemy the giant may not have learned by means of secret and diligent spies that I am going to destroy him? If the opportunity be given him, he may fortify himself in some impregnable castle or stronghold, against which all my efforts and the might of my indefatigable arm may avail but little. Therefore, lady, let us, as I say, forestall his schemes by our activity, and let us depart at once in quest of fair fortune, for thy greatness is only kept from enjoying it as fully as thou couldst desire by my delay in encountering thy adversary."

Don Quixote held his peace and said no more, calmly awaiting the reply of the beauteous princess, who answered with commanding dignity and in a style modeled on Don Quixote's own.

"I give ye thanks, sir knight," she said, "for the eagerness ye display, like a good knight who has the natural obligation to succor the orphan and the needy, of aiding me in my sore trouble. Heaven grant that your wishes and mine may be realized, so that ye may see that there are women in this world capable of gratitude. As to my departure, let it be forthwith, for I have no will but yours. Dispose of me entirely in accordance with your good pleasure, for she who has once entrusted to you the defense of her person and placed in your hands the recovery of her dominions must not think of offering opposition to that which your wisdom may ordain."

"On, then, in God's name," said Don Quixote. "When a lady humbles herself to me, I will not lose the opportunity of raising her up and placing her on the throne of her ancestors. Let us depart at once, for the common saying that 'in delay there is danger' lends spurs to my eagerness to take the road. And as neither heaven has created nor hell seen any that can daunt or intimidate me, saddle Rocinante, Sancho, and get ready your donkey and the queen's palfrey. Let us take leave of the castle warden and these gentlemen and depart this very instant."

Sancho, who was standing by all the time, shook his head. "Ah! master, master," he said, " 'there is more mischief in the village than one hears of,' begging the ladies' pardon."

"What mischief can there be in any village, or in all the cities of the world, you booby, that can hurt my reputation?" said Don Quixote.

"If your worship is angry," replied Sancho, "I will hold my tongue and leave unsaid what as a good squire I am bound to say, and what a good servant should tell his master."

"Say what you will," returned Don Quixote, "provided your words are not meant to work upon my fears. For you, if you fear, are behaving like yourself, but I behave like myself in not fearing."

"It is nothing of the sort, as I am a sinner before God," said Sancho, "but I take it to be sure and certain that this lady, who calls herself queen of the great kingdom of Micomicón, is no more so than my mother. If she was what she says, she would not go rubbing noses with a certain member of this group at every instant and in every nook."

Dorotea turned red at Sancho's words, for the truth was that her husband Don Fernando had now and then, when the others were not looking, gathered from her lips some of the reward his love had earned. Sancho, seeing this, had considered that such freedom was more to be found in a courtesan than a queen of a great kingdom. She, being unable or not caring to answer him, let him have his say.

"This I say, señor," he continued, "because, if after we have traveled roads and highways and passed bad nights and worse days, the gentleman now enjoying himself in this inn is to reap the fruit of our labors, there is no need for me to be in a hurry to saddle Rocinante, put the pad on the ass, or get the palfrey ready. It will be better for us to stay quiet and 'let every slut spin her own thread,' and let us go to dinner."

Good God, what indignation possessed Don Quixote when he heard the audacious words of his squire! So great was it that he rejoined with choking voice and stammering tongue and eyes that flashed living fire. "Rascally peasant, boorish, insolent, and ignorant, ill-spoken, foul-mouthed, impudent, backbiter, and slanderer!" he cried. "Have you dared to utter such words in my presence and in that of these illustrious ladies? Have you dared to harbor such gross and shameless thoughts in your muddled imagination? Begone from my presence, you monster, storehouse of lies, hoard of untruths, garner of knaveries, inventor of scandals, publisher of absurdities, enemy of the respect due to royal personages! Begone, show yourself no more before me under pain of my wrath." So saying he knitted his brows, puffed out his cheeks, gazed around him, and stamped on the ground violently with his right foot, showing in every way the rage pent up in his heart. Sancho was so scared and terrified by these words and furious gestures that he would have been glad if the earth had opened that instant and swallowed him. His only thought was to turn around and make his escape from the angry presence of his master.

But the ready-witted Dorotea, who by this time so well understood Don Quixote's humor, undertook to mollify his wrath. "Be not irritated at the absurdities your good squire has uttered, Sir Knight of the Mournful Countenance," she said, "for perhaps he did not utter them without cause. He, with his good sense and Christian conscience, is not likely to bear false witness against anyone. We may therefore believe, without any hesitation, that since, as ye say, sir knight, everything in this castle is brought about by enchantment, Sancho, I say, may have seen, through this diabolical medium, what he says he saw, to the detriment of my modesty."

"I swear by God Omnipotent," exclaimed Don Quixote at this, "your highness has hit the point. Some vile illusion must have come before this sinner of a Sancho that made him see what it would have been impossible to see by any other means than enchantments. For I know well enough, from the poor fellow's goodness and harmlessness, that he is incapable of bearing false witness against anybody."

"True, no doubt," said Don Fernando, "for which reason, Señor Don Quixote, you ought to forgive him and restore him to the bosom of your favor, 'as it was in the beginning,' before illusions of this sort had taken away his senses."

Don Quixote said he was ready to pardon him, and the priest went for Sancho. He came in very humbly, and falling on his knees begged for the hand of his master, who let him take it and kiss it and then gave him his blessing.

"Sancho my son," he said, "now you will realize the truth of what I have many a time told you, that everything in this castle is done by means of enchantment."

"So it is, I believe," said Sancho, "except the affair of the blanket, which came about by ordinary means."

"Do not believe it," said Don Quixote, "for had it been so, I would have avenged you that instant, or even now. But neither then nor now could I do so, not having seen anyone I could punish for it."

They were all eager to learn what the affair of the blanket was, and the landlord gave them a minute account of Sancho's flights, at which they laughed not a little. Sancho would have been embarrassed at this, had not his master once more assured him it was all enchantment. Yet his gullibility never reached so high a pitch that he could persuade himself it was not the plain and simple truth, without any deception whatever about it, that he had been blanketed by beings of flesh and blood and not by visionary and imaginary phantoms, as his master believed and proclaimed.

The illustrious company had now been two days in the inn, and as it seemed to them time to depart, they devised a plan that, without giving Dorotea and Don Fernando the trouble of going back with Don Quixote to his village under pretense of restoring Queen Micomicona, would allow the priest and the barber to carry him away with them as they proposed and the priest to take his madness in hand at home. In furtherance of their plan, they arranged with the owner of an oxcart who happened to be passing to carry him off in the following manner. They constructed a kind of cage with wooden bars, large enough to hold Don Quixote comfortably, and then Don Fernando and his companions, the servants of Don Luis, and the officers of the Brotherhood, together with the landlord, at the directions and advice of the priest, covered their faces and disguised themselves in one way or another. Thus they would seem to Don Quixote quite unlike the persons he had seen in the castle.

This done, in profound silence they entered the room where he was asleep, resting after his recent skirmishes. They advanced to where he was sleeping tranquilly, with no notion of the plot that had been hatched, seized him firmly, and bound him hand and foot. When he awoke with a start, he was unable to move and could only stare in amazement at the strange figures he saw before him. Instantly he gave himself over to the idea his crazed fancy invariably conjured up before him, taking it into his head that all these shapes were phantoms of the enchanted castle and that he himself was unquestionably enchanted, since he could neither move nor help himself. This was precisely what the priest, the concocter of the scheme, expected would happen. Of all those present, only Sancho was simultaneously in his senses and in his own veritable shape, and he, though not far from sharing his master's infirmity, did not fail to perceive who all these disguised shapes were. But he did not dare open his lips until he saw what came of this assault and capture of his master, who also remained silent, waiting to see how this misfortune would turn out.

What happened was that they brought in the cage, shut him up in it, and nailed the bars so firmly they could not be easily burst open. Then they took him on their shoulders, and as they passed out of the room an awful voice—as awful as the barber, not he of the packsaddle but the other, was able to make it—was heard to say, "O Knight of the Mournful Countenance, let not this captivity in which you are placed afflict you, for this must needs be, for the more speedy accomplishment of the adventure in which your great heart has engaged you. The which shall be accomplished when the raging Manchegan lion and the white Tobosan dove shall be linked together, having first humbled their haughty necks to the gentle yoke of matrimony. And from this marvelous union shall come forth to the light of the world brave whelps that shall rival the rampant claws of their valiant father, and this shall come to pass ere the pursuer of the flying nymph shall in his swift natural course have twice visited the starry signs. And you, O most noble and obedient squire that ever bore sword at side, beard on face, or nose to smell with, be not dismayed or grieved to see the flower of knight-errantry carried away thus before your very eyes. For soon, if it so please the Framer of the universe, you will see yourself exalted to such a height that you will not know yourself, and the promises which your good master has made you shall not prove false, and I assure you, on the authority of the sage Mentironiana,[2] that your wages shall be paid you, as you shall see in due season. Follow then the footsteps of the valiant enchanted knight, for it is expedient that you should go to the destination assigned to both of you. As it is not permitted to me to say more, God be with you, for I return to that place I alone know of." As he brought the prophecy to a close, he raised his voice to a high pitch, and then lowered it to such a soft tone, that even those who knew it was all a joke were almost inclined to take what they heard seriously.

Don Quixote was comforted by the prophecy he heard, for he at once grasped its meaning perfectly, perceiving the promise that he should see himself united in holy and lawful matrimony with his beloved Dulcinea del Toboso, from whose blessed womb should proceed the whelps, his sons, to the eternal glory of La Mancha. Being thoroughly and firmly persuaded of this, he lifted up his voice and heaved a deep sigh.

"Oh you, whoever you are," he exclaimed, "who have foretold me so much good, I implore of you that on my part you entreat that sage enchanter who takes charge of my interests, that he leave me not to perish in this captivity in which they are now carrying me away, ere I see fulfilled promises so joyful and incomparable as those which have been now made me. Let this but come to pass, and I shall glory in the pains of my prison, find comfort in these chains wherewith they bind me, and regard this bed whereon they stretch me, not as a hard battlefield but as a soft and happy nuptial couch. And touching the consolation of Sancho Panza, my squire, I rely upon his goodness and rectitude that he will not desert me in good or evil fortune. For if, by his ill luck or mine, it may not happen to be in my power to give him the island I have promised, or any equivalent for it, at least his wages shall not be lost. In my will which is already made, I have declared the sum that shall be paid to him, measured, not by his many faithful services, but by the means at my disposal."

Sancho bowed his head very respectfully and kissed both his master's hands, for, since they were tied together, he could not kiss one only. Then the apparitions lifted the cage upon their shoulders and placed it upon the oxcart.

Chapter XLVII

OF THE STRANGE MANNER IN WHICH DON QUIXOTE OF LA MANCHA WAS ENCHANTED, TOGETHER WITH OTHER REMARKABLE INCIDENTS

"Many grave histories of knights-errant have I read," said Don Quixote, when he saw himself thus caged and hoisted on the cart,

2. A name formed from *mentir*, "to tell lies."

"but never yet have I read, seen, or heard of their carrying off enchanted knights-errant in this fashion, or at the slow pace that these lazy, sluggish animals promise. They always take them away through the air with marvelous swiftness, enveloped in a dark thick cloud, or on a chariot of fire, or perhaps on some hippogriff or other beast of the kind. But to carry me off like this on an oxcart! By God, it puzzles me! But perhaps the chivalry and enchantments of our day take a different course from that of those in days gone by. It may be, too, that as I am a new knight in the world and the first to revive the already forgotten calling of knight-adventurers, they may have newly invented other kinds of enchantments and other modes of carrying off the enchanted. What do you think of the matter, Sancho my son?"

"I don't know what to think," answered Sancho, "not being as well read as your worship in errant writings. But for all that, I venture to say and swear that these apparitions round about us are not quite catholic."[1]

"Catholic! By my father!" said Don Quixote. "How can they be Catholic when they are all devils that have taken fantastic shapes in order to do this and bring me to this condition? If you want to verify this, touch them and feel them, and you will find they have only airy bodies and that their only consistency is appearance."

"By God, master," returned Sancho, "I have touched them already. That devil there, who is so busy, has plump firm flesh, and there's something else about him very different from what I have heard devils are like, for by all accounts they smell of brimstone and other bad smells. But this one smells of amber half a league off." Sancho was here speaking of Don Fernando who, as a gentleman of rank, was very likely perfumed as Sancho said.

"Do not marvel at that, Sancho my friend," said Don Quixote. "Devils are crafty, I can tell you, and even if they do carry odors about with them, they themselves have no smell, because they are spirits. Or if they do have any smell, they cannot smell of anything sweet but of something foul and fetid. The reason is that they carry hell with them wherever they go and can get no ease whatever from their torments. As a sweet smell is a thing that gives pleasure and enjoyment, it is impossible that they can smell sweet. If, then, this devil you speak of seems to smell of amber, either you are deceiving yourself or he wants to deceive you by making you fancy he is not a devil."

Such was the conversation that passed between master and servant. Don Fernando and Cardenio, fearing Sancho might discover their whole scheme, towards which he had already made some progress, decided to hasten their departure. Calling the landlord aside,

1. I.e., not legitimate. Sancho applies the word in this figurative sense, and Don Quixote takes it in the literal.

they ordered him to saddle Rocinante and put the packsaddle on Sancho's donkey, which he did with great alacrity.

In the meantime the priest had arranged that the officers should accompany them as far as his village for a day's pay. Cardenio hung the shield on one side of the bow of Rocinante's saddle and the basin on the other. By the use of signs he commanded Sancho to mount his donkey and take Rocinante's bridle, and at each side of the cart he placed two officers with their muskets. But before the cart was put in motion, out came the landlady and her daughter and Maritornes to bid Don Quixote farewell, pretending to weep with grief at his misfortune.

"Weep ye not, good ladies," said Don Quixote, "for all these mishaps are the lot of those who follow the profession I profess, and if these reverses did not befall me, I should not esteem myself a famous knight-errant. Such things never happen to knights of little renown and fame, because nobody in the world thinks about them. To valiant knights they do happen, for these are envied for their virtue and valor by many princes and other knights who by base means plot to destroy the worthy. Nevertheless, virtue is of herself so mighty that, in spite of all the magic that Zoroaster its first inventor knew, she will come victorious out of every trial and shed her light upon the earth as the sun does upon the heavens. Forgive me, fair ladies, if through inadvertence I have in aught offended you, for intentionally and wittingly I have never done so to any. And pray to God that he deliver me from this captivity to which some malevolent enchanter has consigned me. Should I find myself released therefrom, the favors ye have bestowed upon me in this castle I shall hold in memory, that I may acknowledge, recognize, and requite them as they deserve."

During this exchange between the ladies of the castle and Don Quixote, the priest and the barber bade farewell to Don Fernando and his companions, to the captain, his brother, and the ladies, all of whom were now happy, and in particular to Dorotea and Luscinda. They all embraced one another and promised to let each other know how things went with them. Don Fernando directed the priest where to write to him, to tell him what became of Don Quixote. He assured him that nothing could give him more pleasure than to hear of it, and that he too, on his part, would send word of everything he thought the priest would like to know about his marriage, Zoraida's baptism, Don Luis's affair, and Luscinda's return to her home. The priest undertook to comply scrupulously with his request, and they embraced once more and renewed their promises.

The landlord approached the priest and handed him some papers, saying he had discovered them in the lining of the valise in which the story of "Ill-advised Curiosity" had been found. The priest could take them all, since their owner had not returned. As the landlord could not read, he did not want them himself. The priest thanked him and, opening the papers, he saw at the beginning of the manuscript the words, "Story of Rinconete and Cortadillo," by which he perceived that it was a piece of fiction. As "Ill-advised Curiosity" had been good, he concluded this would be so too, as they were both probably by the same author.[2] So he kept it, intending to read it when he had an opportunity.

He mounted, and his friend the barber did the same. Both wore masks, so as not to be recognized by Don Quixote, and they started out behind the cart. The order of march was as follows. First went the cart with the owner leading it, while at each side of it marched the officers of the Brotherhood, as has been said, with their muskets. Then followed Sancho Panza on his donkey, leading Rocinante by the bridle, and behind all the rest came the priest and the barber on their mighty mules, with faces covered as aforesaid. They maintained a grave and serious air, measuring their pace to suit the slow steps of the oxen. Don Quixote was seated in the cage, with his hands tied and his feet stretched out, leaning against the bars as silent and as patient as if he were a stone statue and not a man of flesh.

Thus slowly and silently they journeyed perhaps two leagues, until they reached a valley which the carter thought a convenient place for resting and feeding his oxen, and he said so to the priest. But the barber was of opinion that they ought to push on a little farther, as at the other side of a hill which appeared close by he knew there was a valley that had more grass and much better than the one where they proposed to halt. His advice was taken and they continued on their way.

Just at that moment, the priest, looking back, saw coming on behind them six or seven men, well mounted and equipped. These soon overtook them, for they were traveling, not at the sluggish, deliberate pace of oxen but like men who rode canons' mules, and in haste to take their noontime rest as soon as possible at the inn which could be seen not a league off. The quick travelers came up with the slow, and courteous salutations were exchanged. One of the newcomers, who was, in fact, a canon of Toledo and master of the others who accompanied him, observing the regular order of the procession, the cart, the officers, Sancho, Rocinante, the priest, and the barber, and above all Don Quixote caged and confined, could not help asking why the man was being transported in that fashion. The badges of the officers had, however, already led them to conclude that he must be some desperate highwayman or other malefactor whose punishment fell within the jurisdiction of the Holy Brotherhood.

2. "Rinconete y Cortadillo" is the third of the *Exemplary Novels* published by Cervantes in 1613.

"Let the gentleman himself tell you the meaning of his going this way, señor," replied one of the officers to whom he had put the question, "for we do not know."

"Perchance, gentlemen," said Don Quixote, who had overheard the conversation, "you are versed and learned in matters of errant chivalry? Because if you are, I will tell you my misfortunes. If not, there is no good in my giving myself the trouble of relating them."

At this the priest and the barber, seeing that the travelers were engaged in conversation with Don Quixote, came forward, in order to answer in such a way as to save their stratagem from being discovered.

"In truth, brother," said the canon, replying to Don Quixote, "I know more about books of chivalry than I do about Villalpando's elements of logic.[3] So if that is all, you may safely tell me what you please."

"In God's name, then, señor," replied Don Quixote, "if that be so, I would have thee know that I am held enchanted in this cage by the envy and fraud of wicked enchanters. For virtue is more persecuted by the wicked than loved by the good. I am a knight-errant, and not one of those whose names Fame has never thought of immortalizing in her record, but of those who, in defiance and in spite of envy itself, and all the magicians that Persia, or Brahmans that India, or Gymnosophists that Ethiopia ever produced, will place their names in the temple of immortality, to serve as examples and patterns for ages to come, whereby knights-errant may see the footsteps in which they must tread if they would attain the summit and crowning point of honor in arms."

"What Señor Don Quixote of La Mancha says," observed the priest, "is the truth, for he is being carried off in this cart under a spell not from any fault or sins of his own, but because of the malevolence of those to whom virtue is odious and valor hateful. This, señor, is the Knight of the Mournful Countenance, if you have ever heard him named, whose valiant achievements and mighty deeds shall be written on lasting brass and imperishable marble, notwithstanding all the efforts of envy to obscure them and malice to hide them."

When the canon heard both the prisoner and the man who was at liberty talk in such a strain he was ready to cross himself in his astonishment. He could not make out what was going on around him, and all his attendants were in the same state of amazement. It was at this point that Sancho Panza, who had drawn near to hear the conversation, set out to make everything plain.

"Well, sirs," he said, "you may like or dislike what I am going to say, but the fact of the matter is, my master, Don Quixote, is about

3. The textbook of "Dialectics" of the University of Alcalá, first printed in 1557 and often reprinted.

as much enchanted as my mother. He is in his full senses, he eats and drinks, and he has to do his business like other men and as he did yesterday, before they caged him. And if that's the case, what do they mean by wanting me to believe that he is enchanted? For I have heard many say that enchanted people neither eat, nor sleep, nor talk, and my master, if you don't stop him, will talk more than thirty lawyers." And with that he turned to the priest.

"Ah, señor priest, señor priest!" he exclaimed, "do you think I don't know you? Do you think I don't guess and see the drift of these new enchantments? Well, I can tell you I know you, even though your face is covered, and I can tell you I am on to you, however you hide your tricks. After all, where envy reigns virtue cannot live, and where there is miserliness there can be no generosity. Devil take it! If it had not been for your worship, my master would be married to the Princess Micomicona this minute, and I would be a count at least, because no less was to be expected, as well from the goodness of my master, him of the Mournful Countenance, as from the greatness of my services. But I see now how true it is what they say in these parts, that the wheel of fortune turns faster than a millwheel, and that those who were up yesterday are down today. I am sorry for my wife and children, for when they might fairly and reasonably expect to see their father return to them a governor or viceroy of some island or kingdom, they will see him come back a stable boy. I have said all this, señor priest, only to urge your paternity to consider that the ill-treatment of my master will be on your conscience. Have a care that God does not call you to account in the next life for making a prisoner of him in this way, and charge against you all the good deeds and acts of mercy that my lord Don Quixote leaves undone while he is a prisoner."

"Incredible!" exclaimed the barber at this. "So you are of the same fraternity as your master, too, Sancho? By God, I begin to see that you will have to keep him company in the cage and be enchanted like him for having caught some of his temperament and chivalry. It was an unlucky moment when you let yourself be seduced by his promises, and an evil hour when that island you long so much for found its way into your head."

"I have not been seduced by anyone," returned Sancho, "nor am I a man to let myself be seduced, if it was by the king himself. Though I am poor, I am an old Christian, and I owe nothing to anybody, and if I want an island, other people want worse things. Each of us is the son of his own works, and being a man I might get to be pope, not to say governor of an island, especially as my master may win so many that he will not know whom to give them to. Watch how you talk, master barber, for shaving is not everything, and all men are not alike. I say this because we all know one another, and nobody's going to throw loaded dice with me. As to the enchantment of my master, God knows the truth. Leave it as it is; it only makes it worse to stir it."

The barber did not wish to answer Sancho lest by his plain speaking he should disclose what the priest and he himself were trying so hard to conceal. The priest, sharing his apprehension, had asked the canon to ride on a little in advance so that he might tell him the mystery of this man in the cage and other things that would amuse him. The canon agreed, and going on ahead with his servants, listened with attention to the account of the character, life, madness, and ways of Don Quixote. The priest described to him briefly the beginning and origin of his derangement and told him the whole story of his adventures up to his being confined in the cage, together with the plan they had of taking him home to see if by any means they could discover a cure for his madness. The canon and his servants were surprised anew when they heard Don Quixote's strange story.

"To tell the truth, señor priest," said the canon, when the account was finished, "I for my part consider what they call books of chivalry to be harmful to the State. And though I myself, led by idle and false taste, have read the beginnings of almost all that have been printed, I never could manage to read any one of them from beginning to end. It seems to me they are all more or less the same, and one has nothing more in it than another, this no more than that. In my opinion this sort of writing and composition is of the same species as the fables they call the Milesian, nonsensical tales that aim solely at giving amusement and not instruction, exactly the opposite of the apologue fables which amuse and instruct at the same time. And though it may be the chief object of such books to amuse, I do not know how they can succeed, when they are so full of such monstrous nonsense. For the enjoyment the mind feels must come from the beauty and harmony which it perceives or contemplates in the things that the eye or the imagination brings before it, and nothing that has any ugliness or disproportion about it can give any pleasure. What beauty, then, or what proportion of the parts to the whole, or of the whole to the parts, can there be in a book or fable where a lad of sixteen cuts down a giant as tall as a tower and makes two halves of him as if he were made of icing? And when they want to give us a picture of a battle, after having told us that there are a million combatants on the side of the enemy, let the hero of the book be opposed to them, and we are expected to believe, whether we like it or not, that this knight wins the victory by the single might of his strong arm. And then what shall we say of the ease with which a born queen or empress will fall into the arms of some unknown wandering knight? What mind, that is not wholly barbarous and uncultured, can find pleasure in reading of how a great tower full of knights sails away across the sea like a ship with a fair wind, and will be tonight in Lombardy and tomorrow morning in the land of Prester John of the Indies, or some other land that Ptolemy never described nor Marco Polo saw?

"If, in answer to this, I am told that the authors of books of this sort wrote them as fiction and therefore are not required to observe niceties of truth, I would reply that fiction is all the better the more it looks like truth, and gives the more pleasure the more probability and possibility there is about it. Plots in fiction should be suited to the understanding of the reader and be constructed in such a way that by solving impossible situations, explaining how great deeds are accomplished, smoothing over difficulties, keeping the mind in suspense, they may surprise, interest, divert, and entertain, so that wonder and delight joined may keep pace one with the other. All this he will fail to effect who shuns verisimilitude and truth to nature, which are the basis of perfection in writing. I have never yet seen any book of chivalry that puts together a connected plot complete in all its members, so that the middle agrees with the beginning, and the end with the beginning and middle. On the contrary, they construct them with such a multitude of members that it seems as though they meant to produce a chimera or monster rather than a well-proportioned figure. And besides all this they are harsh in their style, incredible in their achievements, licentious in their amours, uncouth in their courtly speeches, long-winded in their battles, silly in their arguments, absurd in their travels, and, in short, lacking in anything resembling intelligent art. For this reason they deserve to be banished from the Christian commonwealth as a worthless breed."

The priest listened to him attentively and felt that he was a man of sound understanding and that there was good reason in what he said. So he told him that, being of the same opinion himself, and bearing a grudge against books of chivalry, he had burned all Don Quixote's, which were many. And he gave him an account of the examination he had made of them and of those he had condemned to the flames and those he had spared. The canon was not a little amused, adding that though he had said so much in condemnation of these books, still he found one good thing in them, and that was the opportunity they afforded to a gifted intellect for displaying itself. They presented a wide and spacious field over which the pen might range freely, describing shipwrecks, tempests, combats, battles, portraying a valiant captain with all the qualifications requisite to make one, showing him sagacious in foreseeing the wiles of the enemy, eloquent in speech to encourage or restrain his soldiers, ripe in counsel, rapid in resolve, as bold in biding his time as in pressing the attack; now picturing some sad tragic incident, now some joyful and unexpected event; here a beauteous lady, virtuous, wise, and modest; there a Christian knight, brave and gentle; here a lawless, barbarous braggart; there a courteous prince, gallant and gracious; setting forth the devotion and loyalty of vassals, the greatness and generosity of nobles.

"Or again," said he, "the author may show himself to be an astronomer, or a skilled cosmographer, or musician, or one versed in affairs of state, and sometimes he will have a chance of coming forward as a magician if he likes. He can set forth the craftiness of Ulysses, the piety of Æneas, the valor of Achilles, the misfortunes of Hector, the treachery of Sinon, the friendship of Euryalus, the generosity of Alexander, the boldness of Cæsar, the clemency and truth of Trajan, the fidelity of Zopyrus,[4] the wisdom of Cato, and in short all the faculties that serve to make an illustrious man perfect, now uniting them in one individual, again distributing them among many. If this is done with charm of style and ingenious invention, aiming at the truth as much as possible, he will assuredly weave a web of bright and varied threads that, when finished, will display such perfection and beauty that it will attain the worthiest object any writing can seek, which, as I said before, is to give instruction and pleasure combined. For the unrestricted range of these books enables the author to show his powers, epic, lyric, tragic, or comic, and all the moods the sweet and winning arts of poetry and oratory are capable of, for the epic may be written in prose just as well as in verse."

Chapter XLVIII

IN WHICH THE CANON PURSUES THE SUBJECT OF THE BOOKS OF CHIVALRY, WITH OTHER MATTERS WORTHY OF HIS WIT

"It is as you say, señor canon," said the priest. "And for that reason those who have hitherto written books of the sort deserve all the more censure for writing without paying any attention to good taste or the rules of art, by which they might guide themselves and become as famous in prose as the two princes of Greek and Latin poetry are in verse."

"I myself, at any rate," said the canon, "was once tempted to write a book of chivalry in which all the points I have mentioned were to be observed, and if I must confess the truth, I have more than a hundred sheets written. To see if it came up to my own opinion of it, I showed them to persons who were fond of this kind of reading, to learned and intelligent men as well as to ignorant people who cared for nothing but the pleasure of listening to nonsense. From all I obtained flattering approval, yet I proceeded no farther with it, no less because it seemed to me an occupation

4. Sinon persuaded the Trojans to admit the wooden horse. Euryalus and Nisus were proverbially loyal friends. Zopyrus was a proverbially faithful vassal.

inconsistent with my profession than because I perceived that the fools are more numerous than the wise; and though it is better to be praised by the wise few and mocked by the foolish many, I have no mind to submit myself to the stupid judgment of the silly public, to whom the reading of such books falls for the most part.

"But what most of all made me stay my hand and even abandon all idea of finishing it was an argument I put to myself taken from the plays that are acted nowadays. It was in this wise. If the plays that are now in vogue, both those that are pure invention and those founded on history, are, all or most of them, downright nonsense, having neither head nor tail, and yet the public listens to them with delight, and regards and approves them as perfection when they are far from it, and if the authors who write them and the players who act them say that this is the way they must be, because the public wants them that way and will have nothing else, and that those that have a plan and work out a plot according to the rules of art will only find some half dozen intelligent people to understand them, while all the rest remain blind to the merit of their composition, and that for themselves it is better to earn a living from the many than praise from the few; then my book will fare the same way, after I have burned the midnight oil trying to observe the principles I have spoken of, and I would end up like 'the tailor on the corner.'[1] And though I have sometimes endeavored to convince actors that they are mistaken in adopting this notion, and that they would attract more people and get more credit by producing plays in accordance with the rules of art than by absurd ones, they are so thoroughly wedded to their own opinion that no argument or evidence can wean them from it.

"I remember saying one day to one of these obstinate fellows, 'Tell me, do you remember that a few years ago there were three tragedies acted in Spain, written by a famous poet of these kingdoms, which were so fine that they filled all who heard them with admiration, delight, and interest, the ignorant as well as the wise, the masses as well as the higher orders, and brought in more money to the performers, these three alone, than thirty of the best that have been produced since?'

" 'No doubt,' replied the producer in question, 'you mean *Isabella, Phyllis,* and *Alexandra.*'[2]

" 'Those are the ones I mean,' said I, 'and see if they did not observe the principles of art, and if, by observing them, they failed to show their superiority and please all the world. Thus the fault does not lie with the public that insists on nonsense but with those who don't know how to produce something else. *Ingratitude Revenged* was not nonsense, nor was there any in *Numantia,* nor any

1. A proverb for wasted effort: "Like the tailor on the corner, who sewed for nothing and threw in the thread."

2. By Lupercio Leonardo de Argensola.

to be found in *The Merchant Lover,* nor yet in *The Friendly Fair Foe,*[3] nor in some others that have been written by certain gifted poets, to their own fame and renown, and to the profit of those that produced them.' To these I added some further remarks and left him, I think rather dumbfounded, but not so satisfied or convinced that I could disabuse him of his error."

"You have touched on a subject, señor canon," observed the priest here, "that has awakened an old enmity I have against the plays in vogue at the present day, quite as strong as that which I have against the books of chivalry. For while the drama, according to Tully,[4] should be the mirror of human life, the model of manners, and the image of the truth, those which are presented nowadays are mirrors of nonsense, models of folly, and images of lewdness. For what greater nonsense can there be in connection with what we are now discussing than for an infant to appear in diapers in the first scene of the first act, and in the second a grown up, bearded man? Or what greater absurdity can there be than putting before us an old man as a swashbuckler, a young man as a coward, a lackey using fine language, a page giving sage advice, a king working as a porter, a princess who is a kitchen-maid?

"And then what shall I say of their attention to the time in which the action they represent may or can take place, except that I have seen a play where the first act began in Europe, the second in Asia, the third finished in Africa, and no doubt, had it been in four acts, the fourth would have ended in America, and so it would have been laid in all four quarters of the globe? And if truth to life is the main thing the drama should keep in view, how is it possible for any average understanding to be satisfied when the action is supposed to pass in the time of King Pepin or Charlemagne, and the principal personage in it they represent to be the Emperor Heraclius who entered Jerusalem with the cross and won the Holy Sepulcher, like Godfrey of Bouillon, there being innumerable years between the one and the other? Or, if the play is based on fiction, and historical facts are introduced, or bits of what occurred to different people and at different times are mixed in with it—all, not only without any semblance of probability but with obvious errors that from every point of view are inexcusable? And the worst of it is, there are ignorant people who say that this is perfection and that anything beyond this is affected refinement.

"And then if we turn to sacred dramas—what preposterous miracles they invent! What apocryphal, poorly conceived incidents, attributing to one saint the miracles of another! And even in secular plays they venture to introduce miracles without any reason or

3. *La ingratitud vengada,* a comedy by Lope de Vega; *La Numancia,* a tragedy by Cervantes himself; *El mercader amante,* a comedy by Gaspar de Aguilar; and *La enemiga favorable,* by Francisco Tárraga.

4. Cicero.

object except that they think some such miracle, or 'special effect' as they call it, will come in well to astonish stupid people and draw them to the play. All this discredits the truth and the historical sources, and it heaps opprobrium on the Spanish intellect, for foreigners who scrupulously observe the laws of the drama look upon us as barbarous and ignorant, when they see the absurdity and nonsense of the plays we produce.

"Nor will it be a sufficient excuse to say that the chief object well-ordered governments have in view when they permit plays to be performed in public is to entertain the people with some harmless amusement occasionally, and keep it from those evil humors which idleness is apt to engender, and that, as this may be attained by any sort of play, good or bad, there is no need to lay down laws or bind those who write or act them to make them as they ought to be made, since, as I say, any kind of play may attain the object sought for. To this I would reply that the same end would be, beyond all comparison, better attained by means of good plays than by those that are not so. For after listening to an artistic and properly constructed play, the hearer will come away amused by the jests, instructed by the serious parts, full of admiration at the incidents, his wits sharpened by the arguments, warned by the tricks, all the wiser for the examples, inflamed against vice, and in love with virtue. In all these ways a good play will stimulate the mind of the hearer, however boorish or dull, and of all impossibilities the greatest is that a play endowed with all these qualities will not entertain, satisfy, and please much more than one lacking them, like the greater number of those which are commonly acted nowadays. Nor are the poets who write them to be blamed for this, for there are some among them who are perfectly well aware of their faults and know thoroughly what they ought to do. But as plays have become a salable commodity, they say, and with truth, that the actors will not buy them unless this fashion is followed, and so the poet tries to adapt himself to the requirements of the actor who is to pay him for his work. And that this is the truth may be seen by the countless plays that a most fertile wit[5] of these kingdoms has written, with so much brilliance, so much grace and gaiety, such polished versification, such choice language, such profound reflections, and in a word, so rich in eloquence and elevation of style that he has filled the world with his fame. Yet, because of his desire to suit the taste of the actors, they have not all, as some of them have, come as near perfection as they ought. Others write plays with such carelessness that, after they have been acted, the actors have to fly and abscond, afraid of being punished, as they often have been, for having acted something offensive to some king or other, or insulting to some noble family.

5. Lope de Vega.

"All these evils, and many more that I say nothing of, would be removed if there were some intelligent and sensible person in the capital to examine all plays before they were acted, not only those produced in the capital itself, but all that were intended to be acted in Spain, and without whose approval, seal, and signature no local magistracy should allow any play to be acted. In that case, actors would take care to send their plays to the capital, and could act them in safety, and those who write them would be more careful and take more pains with their work, standing in awe of having to submit it to the strict examination of one who understood the matter. Thus good plays would be produced and the objects they aim at happily attained, no less the amusement of the people than prestige for the Spanish genius, and the actors' interest and safety, since there will be no need to punish them. And if the same or some other person were authorized to examine the newly written books of chivalry, no doubt some would appear with all the perfections you have described, enriching our language with the gracious and precious treasure of eloquence, and driving the old books into obscurity before the light of the new ones that would come out for the harmless entertainment, not merely of the idle but of the very busiest. For the bow cannot be always bent, nor can weak human nature exist without some lawful amusement."

The canon and the priest had proceeded thus far with their conversation when the barber came forward to join them.

"This is the spot, señor licentiate," he said to the priest, "that I said was a good one for fresh and plentiful pasture for the oxen, while we take our siesta."

"And so it seems," returned the priest, and he told the canon what he proposed to do. The canon too made up his mind to halt with them, being attracted by the aspect of the fair valley that lay before their eyes. In order to enjoy it as well as the conversation of the priest, to whom he had begun to take a fancy, and also that he might learn more particulars about Don Quixote's doings, he sent some of his servants on to the inn, which was not far distant, and where they should obtain whatever food there might be for the whole party, as he intended to rest for the afternoon where he was. To this one of the servants replied that the supply mule, which by this time had probably reached the inn, carried provisions enough to make it unnecessary to get anything from the inn except barley.

"In that case," said the canon, "take all the beasts there, and bring the supply mule back."

While this was going on, Sancho, perceiving that he could speak to his master without having the priest and the barber, of whom he had grown distrustful, present all the time, approached the cage in which Don Quixote was placed. "Señor," he said, "to ease my conscience I want to tell you the state of the case as to your enchantment, and that is that these two here, with their faces covered, are the priest of our village and the barber. I suspect they have devised this plan for carrying you off out of pure envy because your worship surpasses them in doing famous deeds. If this should be the truth, it follows that you are not enchanted but hoodwinked and made a fool of. To prove this I want to ask you one thing, and if your answer is what I believe it must be, then you will have laid your finger on the deception, and you will see you are not enchanted but befuddled."

"Ask what you will, Sancho my son," returned Don Quixote, "for I will answer so as to satisfy you fully. When you declare that those riding with us are the priest and the barber, our neighbors and acquaintances, it is very possible that they may seem to be those very persons. But do not on any account believe that they are so in reality and in fact. What you must think and believe is that, if they look like them, as you say, the explanation is that those who have enchanted me have put on this shape and likeness. It is easy for enchanters to assume any form they please, and they may have taken those of our friends in order to deceive you and lead you into a labyrinth of fancies from which even the thread of Theseus could not set you free. They may also have done it to make me hesitant and unable to conjecture the source of the evil that afflicts me. For if, on the one hand, you tell me that the barber and priest of our village are here with us and, on the other, I find myself shut up in a cage, though aware in very truth that no human agency, unless it were supernatural, could have shut me in, what would you have me say or think except that my enchantment is of a sort that transcends all I have ever read of in all the histories that deal with knights-errant that have been enchanted? So you may set your mind at rest that they might be what you say they are, for it is no more true than that I am a Turk. But as for asking me something, say what you wish and I will answer, though you keep on questioning me from now until tomorrow morning."

"May Our Lady help me!" said Sancho, lifting up his voice. "Is it possible that your worship is so thick-skulled and so short of brains that you cannot see that what I say is the simple truth and that malice has more to do with your imprisonment and misfortune that enchantment? But since that's the way things are, I will plainly prove to you that you are not enchanted. Now tell me, may God deliver you from this affliction and you find yourself when you least expect it in the arms of my lady Dulcinea—"

"Enough of this beseeching," said Don Quixote. "Ask whatever you want to know, for I have already told you I will answer with all possible precision."

"That is what I want," said Sancho. "What I would like to know and have you tell me, without adding or leaving out anything but tell the whole truth as one expects it to be told, and as it is told, by all who profess arms, as your worship professes them, under the title of knights-errant—"

"I tell you I will not lie in the least detail," said Don Quixote. "Finish your question, for indeed you weary me with all these asseverations, requirements, and precautions, Sancho."

"I rely on my master's goodness and truthfulness," said Sancho. "And so, because it has to do with what we are talking about, I ask speaking with all reverance, whether since your worship has been shut up and, as you think, enchanted in this cage, you have felt any desire or inclination to do either number one or number two, as the saying is?"

"I do not understand this number one or number two," said Don Quixote. "Explain yourself more clearly, Sancho, if you would have me give a direct answer."

"Can it be," said Sancho, "that your worship does not understand number one and number two? Why, in school that's what they wean the children on. What I mean is, have you any desire to do anything that can't be put off?"

"Ah! now I understand you, Sancho," said Don Quixote. "Yes, often, and this very minute. Get me out of this predicament. Things are already somewhat untidy."

Chapter XLIX

WHICH TREATS OF THE SHREWD CONVERSATION WHICH SANCHO PANZA HELD WITH HIS MASTER DON QUIXOTE

"Aha, I have caught you," said Sancho. "This is what in my heart and soul I was longing to know. Come now, señor, can you deny what is commonly said around here when a person is out of humor, 'I don't know what ails so-an-so, he neither eats, nor drinks, nor sleeps, nor gives a sensible answer to a question; you'd think he was enchanted'? From which one gathers that those who do not eat or drink or sleep or do any of the natural acts I am speaking of are enchanted, but not those that have the desire your worship has, and drink when drink is given to them and eat when there is anything to eat and answer every question that is asked them."

"What you say is true, Sancho," replied Don Quixote, "but I have already told you there are many sorts of enchantments. It may be that in the course of time they have been changed one for another, and now it may be the way with enchanted people to do all that I do, though they did not do so before. So it is vain to argue or draw inferences against customs of former time. I know and feel that I am enchanted, and that is enough to ease my conscience, for it would weigh heavily on it if I thought I was not enchanted and that in a faint-hearted and cowardly way I allowed myself to lie in this cage, defrauding multitudes of the aid I might offer those in need and distress, who at this very moment may be in sore want of my aid and protection."

"Still for all that," replied Sancho, "I say that, for your greater and fuller satisfaction, it would be well if your worship were to try to get out of this prison—and I promise to do all in my power to help and even to take you out of it—and see if you could once more mount your good Rocinante, who seems to be enchanted too, he is so melancholy and dejected. Then we might try our chance in looking for adventures again. If we have no luck, there will be time enough to go back to the cage in which, on the faith of a good and loyal squire, I promise to shut myself up along with your worship, if you are so unfortunate or I so stupid as not to be able to carry out what I say."

"I am content to do as you say, brother Sancho," said Don Quixote, "and when you see an opportunity for effecting my release I will obey you absolutely. But you will see, Sancho, how wrongly you interpret my misfortune."

The knight-errant and errant squire kept up their conversation till they reached the place where the priest, the canon, and the barber, who had already dismounted, were waiting for them. The driver at once unyoked the oxen and left them to roam at large about the pleasant green spot, the freshness of which seemed to invite, not enchanted people like Don Quixote, but wide-awake, sensible people like his squire, who begged the priest to allow his master to leave the cage for a little. If they did not let him out, he said, the prison might not be as clean as decency required for such a gentleman as his master. The priest understood him and said he would gladly comply with his request, only he feared that his master, once freed, would be up to his old tricks and off where nobody could ever find him again.

"I will answer for his not running away," said Sancho.

"And I also," said the canon, "especially if he gives me his word as a knight not to leave us without our consent."

"I give it," said Don Quixote, who was listening to all this. "Moreover, a man enchanted as I am cannot do as he likes with himself. For the enchanter could prevent his moving from one place for three ages, and if he attempted to escape, would bring him back flying." That being so, they might as well release him, particularly as it would be to the advantage of all. If they did not let him out, he protested, he would be unable to avoid offending their nostrils unless they kept their distance.

The canon took his hand, tied though it was, and on Don Quixote's word and promise they unbound him. He rejoiced beyond measure to find himself out of the cage, and his first act was to stretch himself all over. Then he went to where Rocinante was standing and gave him a couple of slaps on the haunches. "I still trust in God and in his blessed mother, O flower and mirror of steeds," he said, "that both of us shall soon see ourselves as we wish to be, you with your master on your back, and I mounted upon you, following the calling for which God sent me into the world." So saying, accompanied by Sancho he withdrew to a retired spot, from which he came back much relieved and more eager than ever to carry out his squire's scheme.

The canon gazed at him, wondering at the extraordinary nature of his madness, having noted that in all his remarks and replies he showed such excellent sense and only lost his stirrups, as has been already said, when the subject of chivalry was broached. So, moved by compassion, he turned to him, as they all sat on the green grass awaiting the arrival of the provisions.

"Is it possible, my dear sir," he asked, "that the dreary and profitless reading of books of chivalry can have so effected your worship's judgment that you fancy yourself enchanted, along with other absurdities as remote from reality as falsehood is from truth? How can any human understanding persuade itself there ever was all that infinity of Amadíses in the world or all that multitude of famous knights, all those emperors of Trebizond, all those Felixmartes of Hircania, all those palfreys and damsels-errant, and serpents, and monsters, and giants, and marvelous adventures, and enchantments of every kind, and battles, and prodigious encounters, splendid costumes, lovesick princesses, squires made counts, amusing dwarfs, love letters, billings and cooings, female knights-errant and, in a word, all that nonsense the books of chivalry contain?

"For myself, I can only say that when I read them, so long as I do not stop to think that all is lies and frivolity, they give me a certain amount of pleasure. But when I come to consider what they are, I fling the very best of them at the wall, and would fling it into the fire if there were one at hand. They richly deserve such punishment as cheats and impostors, out of the range of ordinary toleration, and as founders of heresies and introducers of pernicious customs and teachers that lead the ignorant public to believe and accept as truth all the foolishness they contain. And such is their audacity, they even dare to unsettle the wits of gentlemen of birth and intelligence, as is shown plainly by the way they have served your worship. They have brought you to such a pass that you have to be shut up in a cage and carried on an oxcart as one would carry a lion or a tiger from place to place to make money by showing it.

"Come, Señor Don Quixote, have some compassion for yourself. Return to the bosom of common sense and make use of the liberal share of it that heaven has been pleased to bestow upon you, employing your abundant gifts of mind in some other reading that may serve to benefit your conscience and add to your honor. And if, still led away by your natural bent, you desire to read books of achievements and of chivalry, read the Book of Judges in the Holy Scriptures, for there you will find the grandeur of real events and deeds as true as they are heroic. Lusitania had a Viriatus, Rome a Cæsar, Carthage a Hannibal, Greece an Alexander, Castile a Count Fernán González, Valencia a Cid, Andalusia a Gonzalo Fernández, Estremadura a Diego García de Paredes, Jerez a Garci Pérez de Vargas, Toledo a Garcilaso, Seville a Don Manuel de León, the recounting of whose valiant deeds will entertain and instruct the loftiest minds and fill them with delight and wonder.[1] Here, Señor Don Quixote, will be reading worthy of your sound understanding. From it you will rise learned in history, in love with virtue, strengthened in goodness, improved in manners, brave without rashness, prudent without cowardice—and all to the honor of God, your own advantage, and the glory of La Mancha, whence, I am informed, your worship derives your birth."

Don Quixote listened with the greatest attention to the canon's words. When he realized the canon had finished, he continued to regard him for some time before replying.

"It appears to me, gentle sir, that your worship's discourse is intended to persuade me that there never were any knights-errant in the world and that all the books of chivalry are false, lying, mischievous, and useless to the State, and that I have done wrong in reading them and worse in believing them and still worse in imitating them, when I undertook to follow the arduous calling of knight-errantry which they set forth. For you deny that there ever were Amadíses of Gaul or of Greece, or any other of the knights of whom the books are full."

"It is all exactly as you state it," said the canon.

"You also went on to say," Don Quixote continued, "that books of this kind had done me much harm, inasmuch as they had upset my senses and shut me up in a cage, and that it would be better for me to reform and change my studies and read other truer books which would afford more pleasure and instruction."

"That is it exactly," said the canon.

"Well then," returned Don Quixote, "to my mind it is you who are the one that is out of his wits and enchanted, as you have ventured to utter such blasphemies against a thing so universally acknowledged and accepted as true that whoever denies it, as you

1. Viriatus led the resistance against Roman invaders of Lusitania. Fernán González led the Castilians to independence in the tenth century. Gonzalo Fernández (1453–1515) was the most famous military leader of the reign of Ferdinand and Isabel; and his companion, García de Paredes, was proverbial for his great strength. García Pérez was a thirteenth-century knight who once used a huge branch to batter his Moorish enemies. Garcilaso fought at the conquest of Granada. Manuel de León retrieved a lady's glove from a lion's cage.

do, deserves the same punishment which you say you inflict on the books that irritate you when you read them. For to try to persuade anybody that Amadís and all the other knights-adventurers with whom the books are filled never existed would be like trying to persuade him that the sun does not yield light or ice cold or earth nourishment. What intellect in all the world can persuade another that the story of the Princess Floripes and Guy of Burgundy is not true, or that of Fierabrás and the bridge of Mantible, which happened in the time of Charlemagne.[2] For by all that is good, it is as true as that it is daylight now, and if it is a lie, it must be a lie too that there was a Hector, or Achilles, or Trojan war, or Twelve Peers of France, or Arthur of England, who still lives changed into a raven and is unceasingly looked for in his kingdom. One might just as well try to make out that the history of Guarino Mezquino[3] or of the quest of the Holy Grail is false, or that the loves of Tristram and the Queen Yseult are apocryphal, as well as those of Guinevere and Lancelot, when there are persons who can almost remember having seen the Dame Quintañona, who was the best cupbearer in Great Britain. And so true is this, that I recollect a grandmother of mine on my father's side, whenever she saw any lady in a venerable hood, used to say to me, 'Grandson, that one is like Dame Quintañona.' From this I conclude that she must have known her or at least had managed to see some portrait of her. Then who can deny that the story of Pierres and the fair Magalona is true, when even to this day one may see in the king's armory the pin with which the valiant Pierres guided the wooden horse he rode through the air, and it is a trifle bigger than the pole of a cart?[4] And alongside of the pin is Babieca's saddle, and at Roncesvalles there is Roland's horn, as large as a large beam,[5] whence we may infer that there were Twelve Peers and a Pierres and a Cid and other knights like them, of the sort people commonly call adventurers. Or perhaps I shall be told, too, that there was no such knight-errant as the valiant Lusitanian Juan de Merlo,[6] who went to Burgundy and in the city of Arras fought with the famous lord of Charny, Monsieur Pierres by name, and afterwards in the city of Basle with Monsieur Enrique de Remestán, coming out of both encounters covered with fame and honor, or adventures and challenges achieved and delivered, also in Burgundy, by the valiant Spaniards Pedro Barba and Gutierre Quixada (of whose family I come in the direct male line), when they vanquished the sons of the Count of San Polo.[7] I shall

2. From a romance of the Charlemagne series, translated and published in Spanish in 1589.

3. Another romance about the court of Charlemagne, written in Italian but translated into Spanish in 1527.

4. A Provençal romance translated into Spanish apparently as early as 1519. The flying horse episode, however, does not appear in this work.

5. Roland's famous horn was an elephant's tusk.

6. A knight in the reign of John II of Castile, whose deeds are celebrated by Juan de Mena.

7. Two knights mentioned in the *Crónica de Juan II*.

be told, too, that Don Fernando de Guevara did not go in quest of adventures to Germany, where he engaged in combat with Messire George, a knight of the house of the Duke of Austria.[8] I shall be told that the jousts of Suero de Quiñones, of the *Paso*,[9] and the adventures of Mosén Luis de Falces[1] against the Castilian knight, Don Gonzalo de Guzmán, were mere mockeries, as well as many other achievements of Christian knights of these and foreign realms, which are so authentic and true, that, I repeat, he who denies them must be totally wanting in reason and good sense."

The canon was amazed to hear the medley of truth and fiction Don Quixote uttered, and to see how well acquainted he was with everything relating or belonging to the achievements of his knight-errantry.

"I cannot deny, Señor Don Quixote," he said in reply, "that there is some truth in what you say, especially as regards the Spanish knights-errant. I am willing to grant too that the Twelve Peers of France existed, but I am not disposed to believe that they did all the things that Archbishop Turpin relates of them. For the truth of the matter is they were knights chosen by the kings of France and called 'Peers' because they were all equal in worth, rank, and prowess (at least if they were not they ought to have been), and it was a kind of religious order like those of Santiago and Calatrava in the present day, in which it is assumed that those who take it are valiant knights of distinction and good birth. Just as we say now a Knight of St. John or of Alcántara, they used to say then a Knight of the Twelve Peers, because twelve equals were chosen for that military order. That there was a Cid as well as a Bernardo del Carpio there can be no doubt; but that they did the deeds people say they did, I consider very doubtful. In that other matter of the pin of Count Pierres that you speak of, and say is near Babieca's saddle in the Armory, I confess my sin. I am either so stupid or so short-sighted that, though I have seen the saddle, I have never been able to see the pin, in spite of it being as big as your worship says it is."

"Nevertheless it is there, without any manner of doubt," said Don Quixote, "and what is more, they say it is inclosed in a sheath of cowhide to keep it from rusting."

"All that may be," replied the canon, "but, by the orders I have received, I do not remember seeing it. However, granting it is there, that is no reason why I am bound to believe the stories of all those

8. Another knight of the same time of John II.

9. The *Paso honroso* was one of the most famous feats of chivalry of the Middle Ages. Suero de Quiñones, a knight of León, with nine others, undertook in 1434 to hold the bridge of Orbigo, near Astorga, against all comers for thirty days. Each was to break three lances with every gentleman who presented himself. There were 727 encounters and 166 lances broken.

1. A knight of Navarre mentioned in the *Crónica* of John II and in Zurita's *Annals of Aragon*.

Amadíses and of all that multitude of knights they tell us about, nor is it reasonable that a man like your worship, so worthy, and with so many good qualities, and endowed with such a good understanding, should allow himself to be persuaded that such wild, crazy things as are written in those absurd books of chivalry are really true."

Chapter L

OF THE SHREWD CONTROVERSY BETWEEN DON QUIXOTE AND THE CANON, TOGETHER WITH OTHER INCIDENTS

"What a thing to say!" returned Don Quixote. "Books that have been printed with the king's license and with the approbation of those to whom they have been submitted and which are read with universal delight and extolled by great and small, rich and poor, learned and ignorant, gentle and simple, in a word by people of every sort, of whatever rank or condition they may be—how could they be lies? And above all when they have such an appearance of truth, for they tell us the father, mother, country, kindred, age, place, and the achievements, step by step, and day by day, performed by such a knight or knights! Be silent, sir, utter not such blasphemy. Trust me, I am advising you now to act as a sensible man should. Only read them and you will see the pleasure you will derive from them.

"Come, tell me, can there be anything more delightful than to see, as it were, here now displayed before us a vast lake of bubbling pitch with a host of snakes and serpents and lizards and ferocious and terrible creatures of all sorts swimming about in it, while from the middle of the lake there comes a plaintive voice saying, 'Knight, whosoever thou art who beholdest this dread lake, if thou wouldst win the prize that lies hidden beneath these dusky waves, prove the valor of thy stout heart and cast thyself into the midst of its dark burning waters, else thou shalt not be worthy to see the mighty wonders contained in the seven castles of the seven Fays that lie beneath this black expanse.' And then the knight, almost before the awful voice has ceased, without stopping to consider, without pausing to reflect on the danger to which he is exposing himself, without even relieving himself of the weight of his massive armor, commending himself to God and to his lady, plunges into the boiling lake, and when he least expects it or knows what his fate is to be, he finds himself among flowery meadows, with which the Elysian fields are not to be compared.

"The sky seems more transparent there, and the sun shines with a strange brilliance, and a delightful grove of green leafy trees presents itself to the eyes and charms the sight with its verdure, while the ear is soothed by the sweet untutored melody of the countless birds of gay plumage that flit to and fro among the interlacing branches. Here he sees a brook whose limpid waters, like liquid crystal, ripple over fine sands and white pebbles that look like sifted gold and purest pearls. There he perceives a cunningly wrought fountain of many-colored jasper and polished marble, and here another of rustic fashion where the little mussel-shells and the spiral white and yellow mansions of the snail disposed in studious disorder, mingled with fragments of glittering crystal and mock emeralds, make up a work of varied aspect, where art, imitating nature, seems to have outdone it. Suddenly there is presented to his sight a strong castle or gorgeous palace with walls of massy gold, turrets of diamond and gates of jacinth. In short, so marvelous is its structure that though the materials of which it is built are nothing less than diamonds, carbuncles, rubies, pearls, gold, and emeralds, the workmanship is still more rare.

"And after having seen all this, what can be more charming than to see how a bevy of damsels comes forth from the gate of the castle in gay and gorgeous attire, such that, were I to set myself now to depict it as the histories describe it to us, I should never have done. And then how she who seems to be the first among them all takes by the hand the bold knight who plunged into the boiling lake and, without addressing a word to him, leads him into the rich palace or castle, and strips him as naked as when his mother bore him, and bathes him in lukewarm water, and anoints him all over with sweet-smelling unguents, and clothes him in a shirt of the softest silk, all scented and perfumed, while another damsel comes and throws over his shoulders a mantle which is said to be worth at the very least a city, and even more? How charming it is, then, when they tell us how, after all this, they lead him to another chamber where he finds the tables set out in such style that he is filled with amazement and wonder, to see how they pour out water for his hands distilled from amber and sweet-scented flowers, how they seat him on an ivory chair, to see how the damsels wait on him all in profound silence, how they bring him such a variety of dainties so temptingly prepared that the appetite is at a loss which to select, to hear the music that resounds while he is at table, by whom or whence produced he knows not. And then when the repast is over and the tables removed, for the knight to recline in the chair, picking his teeth perhaps as usual, and a damsel, much lovelier than any of the others, to enter unexpectedly by the chamber door and seat herself by his side and begin to tell him what the castle is, and how she is held enchanted there, and other things that amaze the knight and astonish the readers who are perusing his history.

"But I will not expatiate any further upon this, as it may be gathered from it that whatever part of whatever history of a knight-errant one reads, it will fill the reader, whoever he be, with delight and wonder. Take my advice, sir, and, as I said before, read these books and you will see how they will banish any melancholy you may feel and raise our spirits should they be depressed. For myself I can say that since I have been a knight-errant I have become valiant, polite, generous, well-bred, magnanimous, courteous, dauntless, gentle, patient, and have learned to bear hardships, imprisonments, and enchantments. And though it be such a short time since I have seen myself shut up in a cage like a madman, I hope by the might of my arm, if heaven aids me and fortune does not thwart me, to see myself king of some kingdom where I may be able to show the gratitude and generosity that dwell in my heart. For by my faith, señor, the poor man is incapacitated from showing the virtue of generosity to anyone, though he may possess it in the highest degree, and gratitude that consists of disposition only is a dead thing, just as faith without works is dead. For this reason I should be glad were fortune soon to offer me some opportunity of making myself an emperor, so as to show my heart in doing good to my friends, particularly to this poor Sancho Panza, my squire, who is the best fellow in the world. I would gladly give him a county I have promised him so long, only that I am afraid he has not the capacity to govern his realm."

Sancho had scarcely heard these last words of his master when he said, "Señor Don Quixote, try to give me that county so often promised by you and so long looked for by me, because I promise you there will be no lack of ability in me to govern it. And even if there is, I have heard say there are men in the world who take over estates, paying their lords so much a year. They themselves see to the management while the lord, with his legs stretched out, enjoys the revenue they pay him without troubling himself about anything else. That's what I'll do and not stand around haggling over trifles, but wash my hands of the whole business and enjoy my income like a duke and let things go their own way."

"That, brother Sancho," said the canon, "only holds good as far as the enjoyment of the revenue goes, but the lord of the domain must see to the administration of justice, and here capacity and sound judgment come in, and above all a firm determination to find out the truth. If this should be lacking at the outset, the middle and the end will always go wrong. So God customarily aids the honest intentions of the simple, just as he frustrates the evil designs of the crafty."

"I don't understand those philosophies," replied Sancho Panza. "All I know is, as soon as I have the county, I'll know how to govern it, for I have as much soul as another and as much body as anyone, and I'll be as much king of my realm as any other of his. And being so I would do as I liked, and doing as I liked, I would please myself, and pleasing myself, I would be content, and when a man is content he has nothing more to desire, and when a man has nothing more to desire, there is an end of it. So let the county come, and God be with you, and 'we shall see, as one blind man said to the other.' "

"That is not bad philosophy you are talking, Sancho," said the canon, "but for all that, there is a good deal to be said on this matter of counties."

"I do not know what more need be said," Don Quixote rejoined. "I only follow the example set by the great Amadís of Gaul, when he made his squire count of Firm Island. So, without any scruples of conscience, I can make a count of Sancho Panza, for he is one of the best squires that ever knight-errant had."

The canon was astounded by the coherence that lay behind the nonsense Don Quixote uttered, by the way he had described the adventure of the knight of the lake, and by the impression produced in him by the deliberate lies of the books he read. Lastly, he marveled at the simplicity of Sancho, who desired so eagerly to obtain the county his master had promised him.

By this time the canon's servants, who had gone to the inn to fetch the supply mule, had returned. Making a carpet and the green grass of the meadow serve as a table, everyone sat down to eat in the shade of some trees so that the carter might not be deprived of the advantage of the spot, as has been already said. As they were eating they suddenly heard a loud noise and the sound of a bell that seemed to come from among some brambles and thick bushes that were close by, and at the same instant they observed a beautiful goat, spotted all over black, white, and brown, spring out of the thicket. After it came a goatherd, calling and uttering the usual cries to make it stop or return to the fold. The fleeing goat, scared and frightened, ran toward the company as if seeking their protection and then stood still. When the goatherd arrived he seized it by the horns and began to talk to it as if it were possessed of reason and understanding.

"Oh, Spotty, Spotty," he said, "you're a wanderer! How you have limped along all this time! What wolves frightened you, my daughter? Won't you tell me what is the matter, my beauty? But what else can it be except that you are a female and can't keep still? A plague on your whims and the whims of those you take after! Come back, come back, my darling. If you don't feel happy, at any rate you will be safe in the fold or with your companions. For if you, who are supposed to look after them and lead them, go wandering astray, what will become of them?"

The goatherd's talk amused all who heard it, but especially the canon. "As you live, brother," he said to him, "take it easy, and don't be in such a hurry to drive this goat back to the fold. Since she is a female, as you say, she will follow her natural instinct in spite of all you can do to prevent it. Have a bite and a sip, and that will soothe your irritation, and in the meantime the goat will rest herself," and with these words he handed him the loins of a cold rabbit on the point of a knife.

The goatherd took it with thanks and drank and calmed himself. "I'd be sorry," he said, "if your worships were to take me for a simpleton for having spoken so seriously to this animal, but the truth is there is a certain mystery in the words I used. I am a peasant but not so countrified that I don't know how to behave to men and to beasts."

"That I can well believe," said the priest, "for I know already by experience that the woods breed men of learning, and shepherds' huts harbor philosophers."

"At all events, señor," returned the goatherd, "they shelter men of experience. So that you may see the truth of this and grasp it, though I may seem to put myself forward without being asked, I will, if it will not tire you, sirs, and you will give me your attention for a little, tell you a true story which will confirm this gentleman's declaration"—he pointed to the curate—"as well as my own."

"Seeing that this affair has a certain color of chivalry about it," Don Quixote replied, "I for my part, brother, will hear you most gladly, as will all these gentlemen, because of the high intelligence they possess and their love of curious novelties that interest, charm, and entertain the mind, as I feel quite sure your story will do. So begin, friend, for we are all prepared to listen."

"Count me out," said Sancho. "I'm taking this meat pie to the brook there, where I plan to eat enough for three days. I have heard my lord Don Quixote say that a knight-errant's squire should eat until he can hold no more, whenever he has the chance, because it often happens by accident that they make their way into a wood so thick that they can't find a way out of it for six days. If the man is not well filled or his saddle bags well stored, there he may stay, as very often he does, turned into a dried-up mummy."

"You are right in that, Sancho," said Don Quixote. "Go where you choose and eat all you can, for I have had enough, and only need to refresh my mind, as I shall do by listening to this good fellow's story."

"That is what we shall all do," said the canon, and he begged the goatherd to begin the promised tale.

The goatherd gave the goat which he held by the horns a couple of slaps on the back. "Lie down here beside me, Spotty," he said, "for we have time enough to return to our fold."

The goat seemed to understand him, for as her mastrer seated himself, she stretched herself quietly beside him and looked up in his face to show him she was all attention to what he was going to say, and then in these words he began his story.

Chapter LI

WHICH DEALS WITH WHAT THE GOATHERD TOLD THOSE WHO WERE TAKING DON QUIXOTE HOME

"Three leagues from this valley there is a village which, though small, is one of the richest in the whole region. In it lived a farmer, a very worthy man, and so much respected that, though such deference is the natural accompaniment of riches, he was even more respected for his virtue than for the wealth he had acquired. But what made him still more fortunate, as he himself maintained, was that he had a daughter of such exceeding beauty, rare intelligence, gracefulness, and virtue, that everyone who knew and beheld her marveled at the extraordinary gifts with which heaven and nature had endowed her. As a child she was beautiful, she continued to grow in beauty, and at the age of sixteen she was most lovely. The fame of her beauty began to spread abroad through all the villages around. But why do I say the villages around, merely, when it spread to distant cities and even made its way into the halls of royalty and reached the ears of people of every class, who came from all sides to see her as if to see something rare and curious, or some wonder-working image?

"Her father watched over her and she watched over herself, for there are no locks, or guards, or bolts that can protect a young girl better than her own modesty. The wealth of the father and the beauty of the daughter led many neighbors as well as outsiders to seek her for a wife. But the father, who had so rich a jewel to dispose of, was perplexed and unable to make up his mind to whom among her countless suitors he should entrust her. I was one among the many who had this longing, and, as her father knew me to be of the same town, of pure blood, in the flower of youth, materially well endowed and in mind no less so, I had great hopes of success.

"But in the village there was another equally qualified suitor, so that her father's choice hung in the balance, for he felt that with either of us his daughter would be well situated. So to end his perplexity he resolved to refer the matter to Leandra (for that is the name of the rich young lady who has reduced me to misery), reflecting that, as we were equal in merit, his dear daughter had better choose according to her inclination—a course all fathers might well imitate, when they wish to settle their children in life. I do not mean they should let them choose anything contemptible and bad, but they should confront them with worthy alternatives and then allow them free choice.

"I do not know which Leandra chose, and can only say that her father pointed out to both of us how young his daughter was, and spoke in general terms that neither bound him nor discouraged us. My rival is called Anselmo and I myself Eugenio—that you may know the names of the personages that figure in this tragedy, which is still in suspense, though it is plain it must have a catastrophic end.

"About this time, there arrived in our town a certain Vicente de la Rosa. He was the son of a poor peasant of the town and had returned from service as a soldier in Italy and other countries. A captain who had chanced to pass through our village with his company had carried him off when he was a boy of about twelve, and now twelve years later the young man came back in a soldier's uniform, arrayed in a thousand colors and bedecked all over with glass trinkets and fine steel chains. Today he would appear in one uniform and tomorrow in another, but all flimsy and gaudy, of little substance and less worth. The peasant folk, who are naturally malicious and when they have nothing to do can be malice itself, noticed all this and counted off his finery and jewelry, piece by piece. Thus they discovered that he had three suits of different colors, with garters and stockings to match, but he made so many arrangements and combinations out of them that, unless they had been counted, anyone would have sworn he had displayed more than ten suits of clothes and twenty plumes. Do not regard what I am telling you about his clothes as unimportant or spun out, for they have a great deal to do with the story.

"He used to sit on a bench under the big poplar in our town square, where he would keep us all hanging open-mouthed on the stories he told of his exploits. There was no country on the face of the globe he had not seen or battle he had not been engaged in. He had killed more Moors than can be found in Morocco and Tunis, and fought more single combats according to his own account than Gante and Luna,[1] Diego García de Paredes, and a thousand others he named, and out of all he had come victorious without losing a drop of blood. On the other hand he showed scars of wounds, which, though they could not be seen, he said were gunshot wounds received in various melees and encounters. Lastly, with unheard-of impudence he used to say *vos* to his equals[2] and even those who knew what he was, and declare that his arm was his father and his deeds his pedigree, and that being a soldier he was as

1. Unknown persons. Probably a misprint for Garcilaso.

2. *Vos* ("ye") was an antiquated form of address used with intimates, inferiors, or as an insult.

good as the king himself. And to add to these swaggering ways he was something of a musician and strummed the guitar with such a flourish that some said he made it speak. Nor did his accomplishments end here, for he played the poet too, and on every trifle that happened in the town he composed a ballad a mile long.

"This soldier, then, as I have described him, this Vicente de la Rosa, swaggerer, gallant, musician, and poet, was often seen and watched by Leandra from a window of her house which looked out on the square. The glitter of his showy attire took her fancy, his ballads bewitched her (for he gave away twenty copies of every one he made), and the tales of the exploits he told about himself came to her ears. In short, as the devil no doubt had arranged it, she fell in love with him before he had hit upon the notion of courting her. And as no love affair proceeds so smoothly as that which accords with the lady's inclinations, Leandra and Vicente promptly reached an understanding. Before any of her numerous suitors had realized what her intentions were, she had already carried them out. She left the house of her dearly beloved father—mother she had none—and disappeared from the village with the soldier, who emerged more triumphantly out of this enterprise than out of the many others he laid claim to.

"All the village and all who heard of it were amazed at the affair. I was aghast, Anselmo thunderstruck, her father full of grief, her relations indignant, the authorities all in a ferment, the officers of the Brotherhood in arms. They scoured the roads and searched the woods and in every quarter, and three days later they found the flighty Leandra in a mountain cave, in nothing but underclothes and robbed of all the money and precious jewels she had carried away from home with her. They brought her back to her unhappy father and questioned her about her misfortune. She confessed without pressure that Vicente de la Rosa had deceived her and under promise of marrying her had persuaded her to leave her father's house, as he planned to take her to the richest and most delightful city in the whole world, which was Naples. She, ill-advised and deluded, had believed him and robbed her father and handed over everything to him the night she disappeared. He had carried her away to a rugged mountain and shut her up in the cave where they had found her. She said, moreover, that the soldier, without robbing her of her honor, had taken everything she had and made off, leaving her in the cave.

"This surprised everybody even more. We had no great faith in the young man's continence, but she asserted it with such earnestness that it helped to console her distressed father, who thought nothing of what had been taken since the jewel that once lost can never be recovered had been left to his daughter. The very day Leandra was found, her father removed her from our sight and shut her up in a convent in a neighboring town, in the hope that time may wear away some of the disgrace she has incurred. Leandra's youth furnished an excuse for her fault, at least with those to whom it was of no consequence whether she was good or bad, but those who knew her shrewdness and intelligence did not attribute her sin to ignorance but to impudence and the natural disposition of women, which is for the most part flighty and irresponsible.

"With Leandra out of sight, Anselmo's eyes grew blind or, at any rate, found nothing pleasurable to look at, and mine were plunged in darkness without a gleam that pointed to anything enjoyable while Leandra was away. Our melancholy grew greater and our patience less, as we cursed the soldier's finery and railed at the carelessness of Leandra's father. At last Anselmo and I agreed to leave the village and come to this valley. Here he feeds a great flock of sheep of his own and I a large herd of goats of mine, while we pass our life among the trees, giving vent to our sorrows, together singing the fair Leandra's praises, or upbraiding her, or else sighing alone and pouring forth to heaven our complaints in solitude. Following our example, many more of Leandra's suitors have come to these rude mountains and adopted our mode of life. They are so numerous one would fancy the place had been turned into the pastoral Arcadia, so full is it of shepherds and sheepfolds.

"There is not a spot in it where the name of the fair Leandra is not heard. Here one curses her and calls her capricious, fickle, and immodest, there another condemns her as frail and frivolous; while this pardons and absolves her, that spurns and reviles her; one extols her beauty and another assails her character. In short, all abuse her and all adore her, and to such a pitch has this general infatuation gone that some complain of her scorn without ever having exchanged a word with her, and some even bewail and mourn the raging fever of jealousy, for which she never gave anyone cause. As I have already said, her misconduct was known before her passion. There is no nook among the rocks, no brookside, no shade beneath the trees that is not haunted by some shepherd telling his woes to the breezes. Wherever there is an echo it repeats the name of Leandra, the mountains ring with 'Leandra,' 'Leandra' murmur the brooks, and Leandra keeps us all bewildered and bewitched, hoping without hope and fearing without knowing what we fear.

"Of all this silly set the one that shows the least and also the most sense is my rival Anselmo, for having so many other things to complain of, he only complains of separation. To the accompaniment of a fiddle, which he plays admirably, he sings his complaints in verse that show his ingenuity. I follow another, easier, and to my mind wiser course, and that is to rail at the frivolity of women, at their inconstancy, their double dealing, their broken promises, their unkept pledges, and in short the want of reflection they show in fixing their affections and inclinations. This, sirs, was the reason of words and expressions I made use of to this goat when I came up just now, for as she is a female I have a contempt for her, though she is the best in all my fold. This is the story I promised to tell you, and if I have been tedious in telling it, I will not be slow to serve you. My hut is close by, and I have fresh milk and delicious cheese there, as well as a variety of tasty fruit, no less pleasing to the eye than to the palate."

Chapter LII

OF THE QUARREL THAT DON QUIXOTE HAD WITH THE GOATHERD, TOGETHER WITH THE RARE ADVENTURE OF THE PENITENTS, WHICH WITH AN EXPENDITURE OF SWEAT HE BROUGHT TO A HAPPY CONCLUSION

The goatherd's tale gave great satisfaction to all the hearers, and the canon especially enjoyed it. He had remarked with particular attention the manner of the telling, which was as unlike the manner of a goatherding rustic as it was like that of a polished city wit, and he observed that the priest had been quite right in saying that the woods bred men of learning. They all offered their services to Eugenio, but none showed himself more liberal than did Don Quixote.

"Most assuredly, brother goatherd," he said to him, "if I found myself in a position to attempt any adventure, I would, this very instant, set out on your behalf. I would rescue Leandra from that convent, where no doubt she is kept against her will, in spite of the abbess and all who might try to prevent me, and I would place her in your hands to deal with her according to your will and pleasure, observing, however, the laws of chivalry which lay down that no violence of any kind is to be offered to any damsel. But I trust in God our Lord that the might of one malignant enchanter may not prove so great but that the power of another better disposed may prove superior to it, and then I promise you my support and assistance, as I am bound to do by my profession, which is none other than to give aid to the weak and needy."

The goatherd eyed him, and noticing Don Quixote's sorry appearance and looks he was filled with wonder. So he turned to the barber, who was next to him. "Señor," he asked, "who is this man who cuts such a figure and talks in such a strain?"

"Who could it be," said the barber, "but the famous Don Quixote of La Mancha, the undoer of injustice, the righter of wrongs, the protector of damsels, the terror of giants, and the winner of battles?"

"That," said the goatherd, "sounds like what one reads in the books of the knights-errant, who did all that you say this man does; though it is my belief that either you are joking, or else this gentleman has empty lodgings in his head."

"You are a great scoundrel," said Don Quixote, "and it is you who are empty and a fool. I am fuller than ever was the whorish bitch that bore you." Passing from words to deeds, he picked up a loaf that was near him and threw in the goatherd's face with such force that it flattened his nose. The goatherd did not understand jokes, and finding himself roughly handled in earnest, without the least respect for carpet, tablecloth, or diners, sprang on Don Quixote, seizing him by the throat with both hands. He would no doubt have throttled him, had not Sancho Panza that instant come to the rescue. Grasping the goatherd by the shoulders he threw him down on the table, smashing plates, breaking glasses, and upsetting and scattering everything on it.

Don Quixote, finding himself free, rushed to get on top of the goatherd who, with his face covered with blood, and soundly kicked by Sancho, was on all fours feeling about for one of the table knives to take a bloody revenge with. The canon and the priest, however, prevented him, but the barber so contrived it that he got Don Quixote under the goatherd, who rained down upon him such a shower of punches that the poor knights face streamed with blood as freely as his own. The canon and the priest were bursting with laughter, the officers were capering with delight, and both the one and the other egged them on as they do dogs in a fight. Sancho alone was frantic, for he could not free himself from the grasp of one of the canon's servants, who kept him from going to his master's assistance.

At last, while they were all, with the exception of the two combatants who were mauling each other, in high glee and enjoyment, they heard a trumpet sound a note so doleful that it made them all look in the direction from where the sound seemed to come. But most excited by hearing it was Don Quixote, who very much against his will was under the goatherd and a good deal more than pretty well pummeled.

"Brother devil," he said to him, "for that you must be since you had the might and strength to overcome me, I ask you to agree to a truce for but for an hour. The solemn note of yonder trumpet that falls on our ears seems to me to summon me to some new adventure."

The goatherd, who was by this time tired of pummeling and being pummeled, released him at once. Don Quixote rose to his feet and, turning his eyes to the quarter where the sound had been heard, suddenly saw coming down the slope of a hill several men clad in white, like penitents.

The fact was that the clouds had that year withheld their moisture from the earth, and in all the villages of the district they were organizing processions, rogations, and penances, imploring God to open the hands of his mercy and send the rain. To this end, the people of a nearby village were going in procession to a holy hermitage situated on one side of that valley. When Don Quixote saw the strange garb of the penitents, he did not reflect how often he had seen it before but took it into his head that this was a matter of adventure and that it behooved him alone as a knight-errant to engage in it. He was all the more confirmed in this notion by the idea that an image draped in black which they were carrying was some illustrious lady that these villains and uncouth thieves were carrying off by force. As soon as this occurred to him, he ran with all speed to Rocinante, who was grazing. Taking the bridle and the shield from the saddle-bow, he had him bridled in an instant, and calling to Sancho for his sword he mounted Rocinante and slipped his shield on his arm. "Now, noble company," he exclaimed in a loud voice to those who stood by, "ye shall see how important it is that there should be knights in the world professing the order of knight-errantry. Now, I say, ye shall see, by the deliverance of that worthy lady who is borne captive there, whether knights-errant deserve to be held in estimation."

So saying, he brought his legs to bear on Rocinante—for he had no spurs—and at a full canter (for in all this veracious history we never read of Rocinante actually running) set off to encounter the penitents, while priest, canon, and barber ran to prevent him. But it was out of their power, nor did he even stop for the shouts of Sancho.

"Where are you going, Señor Don Quixote?" he called out after him. "What devils have possessed you to set you against our Catholic faith? Plague take me! Look out! That is a procession of penitents, and the lady they are carrying on the stand there is the blessed image of the immaculate Virgin. Watch what you are doing, señor, for this time it may be said you don't know what you are doing."

Sancho labored in vain, for his master was so bent on reaching these sheeted figures and releasing the lady in black that he did not hear a word. Even had he heard, he would not have turned back if the king had ordered him. He came up to the procession and reined in Rocinante, who was already anxious enough to slacken speed a little.

"Ye who hide your faces," he exclaimed in a hoarse, excited voice, "perhaps because ye are not honest men, pay attention and listen to what I am about to say to you."

The first to halt were those who were carrying the image, and one of the four ecclesiastics who were chanting the litany, struck by the strange figure of Don Quixote, the leanness of Rocinante, and the other ludicrous peculiarities he observed, hastened to reply. "Brother," he said, "if you have anything to say to us, say it quickly, for these brethern are whipping themselves, and we cannot stop, nor is it reasonable that we should stop to hear anything, unless indeed it is short enough to be said in two words."

"I will say it in one," replied Don Quixote, "and it is this, that at once, this very instant, ye release that fair lady whose tears and sad aspect show plainly that ye are carrying her off against her will, and that ye have committed some scandalous outrage against her. I was born into the world to redress all such like wrongs, and I will not permit you to advance another step until ye have restored her to the liberty she pines for and deserves."

From these words all the hearers concluded that he must be a madman and began to laugh heartily. Their laughter acted like gunpowder on Don Quixote's fury, for without another word he drew his sword and made a rush at the stand. One of those supporting it left the burden to his comrades and advanced to meet him. He was flourishing a forked stick or staff which he had for propping up the stand when resting, and with this he caught a mighty cut Don Quixote made at him that severed it in two. But with the portion that remained in his hand he dealt such a whack on the shoulder of Don Quixote's sword arm (which the shield could not protect against the rustic assault) that poor Don Quixote came to the ground in a sad plight.

Sancho Panza, who was coming up close behind puffing and blowing, saw him fall and cried to his assailant not to strike him again, for he was a poor enchanted knight, who had never harmed anyone all the days of his life. But what checked the rustic was not Sancho's shouting but the fact that Don Quixote did not stir hand or foot. So, fancying he had killed him, he hastily hitched his tunic up to his waist and took to his heels across the country like a deer.

By this time all Don Quixote's companions had come up to where he lay. But the processionists seeing them running, and with them the officers of the Brotherhood with their crossbows, apprehended mischief. So clustering around the image, they raised their hoods and grasped their scourges, as the priests did their tapers, and awaited the attack. They were determined to defend themselves and even to take the offensive against their assailants if they could.

Fortune, however, arranged the matter better than they expected, for all Sancho did was to fling himself on his master's body, raising over him the most doleful and laughable lamentation that ever was heard, for he believed Don Quixote was dead. The priest was known to another priest who walked in the procession, and their recognizing one another set at rest the apprehensions of both parties. The first then told the other in two words who Don Quixote was, and he and the whole troop of penitents went to see if the poor gentleman was dead.

"Oh, flower of chivalry," Sancho Panza was saying, with tears in his eyes, "that one blow of a stick should have ended the course of your well-spent life! Oh pride of your race, honor and glory of all La Mancha, indeed, of all the world, that for lack of you will be full of evil-doers, no longer in fear of punishment for their misdeeds! Oh you, generous above all the Alexanders, since for only eight months of service you have given me the best island the sea girds or surrounds! Humble with the proud, haughty with the humble, encounterer of dangers, endurer of outrages, enamored without reason, imitator of the good, scourge of the wicked, enemy of the mean, in short, knight-errant, which is all that can be said!"

At the cries and moans of Sancho, Don Quixote came to. "He who lives separated from you, sweetest Dulcinea"—these were his first words—"has greater miseries to endure than these. Aid me, friend Sancho, to mount the enchanted cart, for I am not in a condition to press the saddle of Rocinante, as this shoulder is all knocked to pieces."

"That I will do with all my heart, señor," said Sancho. "Let us return to our village with these gentlemen, who seek your good. There we will prepare for another sally, which may turn out more profitable and creditable to us."

"You are right, Sancho," returned Don Quixote. "It will be wise to let the malign influence of the stars which now prevails pass off."

The canon, the priest, and the barber told him he would act very wisely in doing as he said. And so, highly amused at Sancho Panza's simplicities, they placed Don Quixote in the cart as before. The procession once more formed itself in order and proceeded on its road, the goathered took his leave of the party, the officers of the Brotherhood declined to go any farther, and the priest paid them their due. The canon begged the priest to let him know how Don Quixote did, whether he was cured of his madness or still suffered from it, and then begged leave to continue his journey. In short, they all separated and went their ways, leaving to themselves the priest and the barber, Don Quixote, Sancho Panza, and the good Rocinante, who regarded everything with as great resignation as his master.

The driver yoked his oxen and made Don Quixote comfortable on a bundle of hay and at his usual deliberate pace took the road the priest directed. At the end of six days they reached Don Quixote's village and entered it about the middle of the day, which it so happened was a Sunday, and the people were all in the square, through which Don Quixote's cart passed. They all flocked to see what was in the cart, and when they recognized their townsman they were filled with amazement, and a boy ran off to bring the news to his housekeeper and his niece that their master and uncle had come back all lean and yellow and stretched on a pile of hay on an oxcart. It was piteous to hear the cries the two good ladies raised, how they beat their breasts and poured out fresh maledictions on those accursed books of chivalry. All this was renewed when they saw Don Quixote coming in at the gate.

At the news of Don Quixote's arrival, Sancho Panza's wife came running, for she knew by this time that her husband had gone away with him as his squire. On seeing Sancho, the first thing she asked him was if the ass was well. Sancho replied that he was, better than his master was.

"Thanks be to God," said she, "for being so good to me. But now tell me, my friend, what have you made by your squirings? What gown have you brought me back? What shoes for your children?"

"I bring nothing of that sort, wife," said Sancho, "though I bring other things of more consequence and value."

"I am very glad of that," returned his wife. "Show me these things of more value and consequence, my friend, for I want to see them to cheer my heart that has been so sad and heavy all these ages that you have been away."

"I will show them to you at home, wife," said Sancho. "Be content for the present, for if it please God that we should again go on our travels in search of adventures, you will soon see me a count or governor of an island, and not one of those everyday ones, but the best that is to be had."

"Heaven grant it, husband," said she, "for indeed we have need of it. But tell me, what's this about islands, for I don't understand it?"

"Honey is not for the mouth of the ass," returned Sancho. "All in good time you shall see, wife. In fact, you will be surprised to hear yourself called 'your ladyship' by all your vassals."

"What are you talking about, Sancho, with your ladyships, islands, and vassals?" replied Teresa Panza—for so Sancho's wife was called, though they were not relations, for in La Mancha it is customary for wives to take their husbands' surnames.

"Don't be in such a hurry to know all this, Teresa," said Sancho. "It is enough that I am telling you the truth, so shut your mouth. But I may tell you this much by the way, that there is nothing in the world more delightful than to be a person of consideration, squire to a knight-errant, and a seeker of adventures. To be sure most of those one finds do not end as pleasantly as one could wish, for out of a hundred, ninety-nine will turn out cross and contrary. I know it by experience, for out of some I came blanketed and out of others beaten. Still, for all that, it is a fine thing to be on the look-out for what may happen, crossing mountains, searching woods, climbing rocks, visiting castles, putting up at inns, all free, and devil take the *maravedí* to pay."

While this conversation passed between Sancho Panza and his wife, Don Quixote's housekeeper and niece took him in and undressed him and laid him on his old bed. He eyed them askance, and could not make out where he was. The priest instructed the niece to be very careful to make her uncle comfortable and to keep a watch over him so that he wouldn't escape from them again, telling her what they had been obliged to do to bring him home. On this the pair once more lifted up their voices and renewed their maledictions upon the books of chivalry and implored heaven to plunge the authors of such lies and nonsense into the bottomless pit. They were, in short, kept in anxiety and dread lest their uncle and master should give them the slip the moment he found himself somewhat better, and as they feared, so it happened.

But the author of his history, though he has devoted research and industry to the discovery of the deeds achieved by Don Quixote on his third sally, has been unable to obtain any information respecting them, at any rate derived from authentic documents. Tradition has merely preserved in the memory of La Mancha the fact that Don Quixote, the third time he sallied forth from his home, betook himself to Zaragoza, where he was present at some famous jousts which took place in that city, and that he had adventures there worthy of his valor and high intelligence. Of his end and death he could learn no particulars, nor would he have ascertained it or known of it, if good fortune had not produced an old physician for him who had in his possession a leaden box, which, according to his account, had been discovered among the crumbling foundations of an ancient hermitage that was being rebuilt. In this box were found certain parchment manuscripts in Gothic character, but in Castilian verse, containing many of the knight's achievements and setting forth the beauty of Dulcinea, the form of Rocinante, the fidelity of Sancho Panza, and the burial of Don Quixote himself, together with sundry epitaphs and eulogies on his life and character. But all that could be read and deciphered were those which the trustworthy author of this new and unparalleled history here presents. And the said author asks of those that shall read it nothing in return for the vast toil which it has cost him in examining and searching the Manchegan archives in order to bring it to light, save that they give him the same credit that people of sense give to the books of chivalry that pervade the world and are so popular. For with this he will consider himself amply paid and fully satisfied and will be encouraged to seek out and produce other histories, if not as truthful, at least equal in invention and no less entertaining. The first words written on the parchment found in the leaden box were these.

The Academicians of Argamasilla, a Village of La Mancha, on the Life and Death of Don Quixote of La Mancha, *Hoc Scripserunt*[1]

Monicongo, Academician of Argamasilla, on the Tomb of Don Quixote

EPITAPH

The scatterbrain that gave La Mancha more
  Rich spoils than Jason's; who a point so keen
  Had to his wit, and happier far had been
If his wit's weathercock a blunter bore;
The arm renowned far as Gaeta's shore,
  Cathay, and all the lands that lie between;
  The muse discreet and terrible in mien
As ever wrote on brass in days of yore;
He who surpassed the Amadíses all,
  And who as naught the Galaors accounted,
    Supported by his love and gallantry:
Who made the Belianíses sing small,
  And sought renown on Rocinante mounted;
    Here, underneath this cold stone, doth he lie.

Paniaguado, Academician of Argamasilla,
in Laudem Dulcineæ Del Toboso[2]

SONNET

She, whose full features may be here descried,
  High-bosomed, with a bearing of disdain,
  Is Dulcinea, she for whom in vain
The great Quixote of La Mancha sighed.
For her, Toboso's queen, from side to side
  He traversed the grim sierra, the champaign
  Of Aranjuez, and Montiel's famous plain
On Rocinante, oft a weary ride.

1. "Wrote this." Literary academies, the members of which chose extravagant or allusive pen names, were common in Cervantes' day. There was of course no such "academy" in Argamasilla.
2. "In praise of Dulcinea."

Malignant planets, cruel destiny,
Pursued them both, the fair Manchegan dame
And the unconquered star of chivalry.
Nor youth nor beauty saved her from the claim
Of death; he paid love's bitter penalty,
And left the marble to preserve his name.

Caprichoso, a Most Witty Academician of Argamasilla, in Praise of Rocinante, Steed of Don Quixote of La Mancha

SONNET

On that proud throne of diamantine sheen,
Which the blood-reeking feet of Mars degrade,
The mad Manchegan's banner now hath been
By him in all its bravery displayed.
There hath he hung his arms and trenchant blade
Wherewith, achieving deeds till now unseen,
He slays, lays low, cleaves, hews; but art hath made
A novel style for our new paladin.
If Amadís be the proud boast of Gaul,
If by his progeny the fame of Greece
Through all the regions of the earth be spread,
Quixote crowned in grim Bellona's hall
Today exalts La Mancha over these,
And above Greece or Gaul she holds her head.
Nor ends his glory here, for his good steed
Doth Brigliador and Bayard far exceed;[3]
As mettled steeds compared with Rocinante,
The reputation they have won is scanty.

Burlador, Academician of Argamasilla, on Sancho Panza

SONNET

The worthy Sancho Panza here you see;
A great soul once was in that body small,
Nor was there squire upon this earthly ball
So plain and simple, or of guile so free.
Within an ace of being Count was he,
And would have been but for the spite and gall
Of this vile age, mean and illiberal,
That cannot even let a donkey be.
For mounted on an ass (excuse the word),
By Rocinante's side this gentle squire
Was wont his wandering master to attend.
Delusive hopes, that lure the common herd
With promises of ease, the heart's desire,
In shadows, dreams, and smoke ye always end.

3. The mounts of Orlando (Roland) and Rinaldo.

Cachidiablo, Academician of Argamasilla,
on the Tomb of Don Quixote

EPITAPH

The knight lies here below,
  Ill-errant and bruised sore,
  Whom Rocinante bore
In his wanderings to and fro.
By the side of the knight is laid
  Stolid man Sancho too,
  Than whom a squire more true
Was not in the esquire trade.

Tiquitoc, Academician of Argamasilla,
on the Tomb of Dulcinea Del Toboso

EPITAPH

Here Dulcinea lies.
  Plump was she and robust;
  Now she is ashes and dust:
The end of all flesh that dies.
A lady of high degree,
  With the port of a lofty dame,
  And the great Quixote's flame,
And the pride of her village was she.

These were all the verses that could be deciphered. The rest, the writing being worm-eaten, were handed over to one of the Academicians to make out their meaning conjecturally. We have been informed that at the cost of many sleepless nights and much toil he has succeeded and that he means to publish them, in expectation of seeing Don Quixote's third sally.

Forsi altro canterá con miglior plectro.[4]

THE END

4. Roughly, "Perhaps another more talented poet will recount [his deeds]." The Italian verse, slightly garbled, comes from *Orlando furioso,* xxx. 16.

Second Part of The Ingenious Gentleman Don Quixote of La Mancha

by

Miguel de Cervantes Saavedra,

Author of the First Part

Dedicated to Don Pedro Fernández de Castro,
Count of Lemos, of Andrade, and of Villalba,
Marquis of Sarria, Gentleman of His Majesty's Chamber,
Knight Commander of the Commandery of Peñafiel and of La Zarza of the Order of Alcántara
Viceroy, Governor, and Captain General of the Kingdom of Naples,
and President of the Supreme Court of Italy.

1615
With Copyright.

Printed in Madrid, by Juan de la Cuesta.
For sale at the shop of Francisco de Robles,
bookseller to the king our lord.

Price

I, Hernando de Vallejo, clerk of our lord the king's chamber and resident clerk in his majesty's Council, attest that, the members of the Council having examined a book entitled Don Quixote of La Mancha, Second Part, *by Miguel de Cervantes Saavedra, which was printed by permission of his majesty, they priced each sheet at four* maravedís, *the book having seventy-three sheets, at which rate it amounts and comes to two hundred and ninety-two* maravedís, *unbound. And they ordered this certificate of price to be placed at the beginning of each copy of the aforesaid book so that all may know and understand what price is to be asked and received for it, without exceeding it in any manner whatsoever, as is stated and appears in the original act and decree issued concerning it, which I have in my possession, to which I refer; and by order of the aforesaid members of the Council and by request of the aforesaid Miguel de Cervantes, I have issued this certificate at Madrid, on October 21, 1615.*

HERNANDO DE VALLEJO

Corrector's Statement

I have examined this book, entitled Second Part of Don Quixote of La Mancha, *written by Miguel de Cervantes Saavedra, and there is nothing in it worthy of note which does not correspond to its original.*

Issued at Madrid, on October 21, 1615.

THE LICENTIATE FRANCISCO MURCIA DE LA LLANA

Censor's Approval[1]

By commission and order of the members of the Council, I have had the book contained in this memorandum submitted to examination. It contains nothing against the faith or good morals; on the contrary, it is a work full of legitimate entertainment, mixed with sound moral philosophy. A license for printing it may be issued. At Madrid, November 5, 1616.

DOCTOR GUTIERRE DE CETINA

Censor's Approval

By commission and order of the members of the Council, I have examined the Second Part of Don Quixote of La Mancha, *by Miguel de Cervantes Saavedra. It contains nothing against our holy catholic faith or good morals; on the contrary, it contains decent recreation and harmless diversion which the ancients judged suitable for their states; for even in the austere republic of the Lacedemonians they put up a statue to laughter, and the Thessalians dedicated festivals to it, as Pausanias says (cited by Bosius[2] in Book II of* De Signis Ecclesiae, *ch. 10) thereby inspiring weary minds and melancholy spirits. Tully recalled this in book one of* De Legibus, *and so does the poet when he says,* Interpone tuis interdum gaudia curis.[3] *This is what the author does by mixing truth with jokes, the sweet with the useful, the moral with the facetious, by concealing the fish-hook of moral correction with the bait of humor, while pursuing his well-chosen subject, whereby he aspires to expel books of chivalry, for with his good diligence, he has cleverly*

1. Note that in the ten years between the publication of Parts I and II an ecclesiastical censor's approval had become necessary. The three censors are Gutierre de Cetina, who is not the celebrated poet; José de Valdivielso, a priest, poet, playwright, and friend of Lope de Vega, chaplain of various important personages; and Márquez Torres, otherwise unknown, whose approbation is one of the most interesting examples of such censor's opinions to be found in this period. The censor distinguishes between satire, which was considered generally to be harmful (for reasons Cervantes himself will state in the preface to the reader of Part II) and moral reproof, which was the main justification for fiction as a respectable art form. Cervantes' enemies had accused him of satirizing Lope de Vega in Part I, and Márquez Torres, without mentioning this directly, defends Cervantes' gentle humor, which he compares to mild medicines, while obliquely attacking the picaresque novel (*Guzmán de Alfarache* and *La pícara Justina*, probably), which is compared with traumatic cures and even accused of teaching rather than eradicating vice. The anecdote of the French courtiers who wanted to meet Cervantes is one of the earliest testimonies of the international fame which the author of *Don Quixote* enjoyed late in his life.

2. "Bosius" is a now-obscure Roman priest and author, Thomas Bozius (d. 1610), whose book *De signis Ecclesiae Dei libri XXIV* appeared in 1569. In spite of the references to Pausanias, the information on the Lacedemonian statue of Laughter comes from Apuleius's novel, *The Golden Ass.*

3. The "poet" mentioned is the author of a famous school text usually called "Cato's Couplets," *Disticha Catonis.* The quotation says, "Now and then mix pleasures with your business."

cleansed these realms of their contagious malady. This work is worthy of his great wit, which is the honor and light of our nation and the wonder and envy of foreign ones. This is my opinion, saving, etc. At Madrid, March 17, 1615.

MASTER JOSEF DE VALDIVIELSO

Approbation

By commission of Dr. Gutierre de Cetina, vicar-general of this city of Madrid, his majesty's capital, I have examined this book, the Second Part of the Ingenious Gentleman Don Quixote of La Mancha, *by Miguel de Cervantes Saavedra, and I do not find in it anything unworthy of Christian zeal or incompatible with the decency required of good example or moral virtues; on the contrary, it contains much erudition and edification, in the chastity of its well-developed theme (the eradication of worthless and mendacious books of chivalry, whose infection had spread more than was proper) as well as in the smoothness of its Castilian language, unadulterated by tedious and studied affectation, a vice rightly abhorrent to sensible men. And in the correction of vices, which he treats in a general way in the course of his witty discourses, the author so wisely respects the laws of Christian admonition that he who is touched by the infirmity which the author aspires to cure will have swallowed willingly, without the slightest hesitation or revulsion, before he realizes it, the beneficial cure of loathing for his particular vice with the sweetness and pleasant taste of its medicine; and he will discover that he is delighted* and *admonished —which is the most difficult thing to accomplish.*

There have been many who because they do not know how to temper or mix properly the useful with the pleasant have wasted all of their laborious efforts, since because they were unable to imitate Diogenes in philosophy and learning, they have foolhardily, not to say licentiously and ignorantly, attempted to imitate his cynicism, becoming maliciously critical, inventing examples which never occurred in order to give importance to the vice which they touch upon in their harsh reprehension; and perhaps they reveal ways, which were until then unknown, to follow such vices. And thus they come to be not admonishers but teachers of vice. They make themselves odious to the intelligent, they cause the common people to lose respect for their work—if indeed they ever had any—and the vices which they may have wished to correct in their irresponsible and imprudent way are more firmly established than ever. Not all abcesses are ready for prescriptions or cauterization at the same time; indeed some are much more receptive to gentle and mild medicines, by applying which the attentive, perceptive, and learned doctor achieves his object of curing them, a result which is often better than that achieved with the violent treatment of the cauterizing iron.

But our nation, as well as foreign nations, have had a very different opinion of the writings of Miguel de Cervantes; for everyone wants to see the author—as if he were something miraculous—of the books which Spain, France, Italy, Germany, and Flanders have received with universal applause, for their decorum and decency as well as for the gentleness and mildness of their discourses.

I can certify with truth that on the twenty-fifth of February of this year of 1615, when my master, his Eminence Don Bernardo de Sandoval y Rojas, the cardinal-archbishop of Toledo, went to call upon the ambassador of France, who had visited his Eminence, and who had come to discuss matters concerning the marriages of the French and Spanish princes, many French gentlemen who had come in the retinue of the ambassador, as courteous as they are intelligent and fond of literature, came up to me and to other chaplains of the cardinal interested to know what good books were most highly-regarded, and when by chance this one, which I was censoring, was mentioned, they had scarcely heard the name Miguel de Cervantes when they began to sing his praises, stressing the high regard in which his books are held in France as well as in the neighboring countries: the Galatea, *which one of them practically knew by heart, the first part of this work, and the* Novelas. *Their praises were such that I offered to take them to see the author, which they received with a great show of appreciation. They questioned me closely about his age, his profession, his rank, and condition. I was obliged to say that he was old, a soldier, a gentleman, and poor. To which one of them replied these exact words: "Do you mean that Spain does not support such a man generously from the public treasury?" Another of those gentlemen promptly replied with this thought and sharp observation, and he said, "If poverty has forced him to write, may God grant that he never have enough, so that he will make the whole world rich with his works, even though he is poor."*

I am aware that for a censor's statement, this one is rather long. Some will say that it verges on flattering eulogy. But the truth of what I briefly state relieves the critic of suspicion of my motives and me of concern. Besides, nowadays nobody praises a person who cannot grease the flatterer's palm, for although he says it in jest, affectedly and falsely, he expects to be paid in earnest.

Madrid, February 27, 1615.

THE LICENTIATE MÁRQUEZ TORRES.

Copyright

Whereas we were informed by you, Miguel de Cervantes Saavedra, that you had composed the Second Part of Don Quixote of La Mancha, *which you were submitting to us; and because it was a book of pleasant and decent fiction and cost you much effort and study, you begged us to issue a license to print it and a copyright for twenty years or whatever period might be our pleasure; and the members of our Council having examined it, seeing that the book fulfilled the requirements set forth in our regulations on the subject, it was agreed that we should issue this our permit for the above stated reason; and we have concurred.*

For which reason we grant license and permission to you that, for the time and space of ten full consecutive years, which shall begin and be counted from the date of this our permit, you or the person who acts as your agent, and no other, may print and sell the book which is mentioned above. And by means of this permit, we grant license and permission to any printer of our realms whom you may name, that during the aforesaid time he may print it according to the original copy examined by our Council, which is sealed and signed at the end by Hernando de Vallejo, the clerk of our Chamber and one of those resident in it; provided that first and before it is sold, you bring it before the members, together with the aforesaid original, so that it may be seen that the aforesaid printing is identical with it, or that you bring an affidavit in due form showing that it was examined and corrected by a corrector named by us.

And furthermore, the aforesaid printer who may print the aforesaid book shall not print the beginning and first sheet or release more than a single copy together with the original to the author and person at whose expense he is printing it, nor to any other person whomsoever, for effecting the aforesaid correction and pricing, until the aforesaid book has first and previously been corrected and priced by the members of our Council. This being done, and not otherwise, he may print the aforesaid beginning and first sheet, at the very beginning of which he shall put this our license and approbation, pricing, and errata; nor can you sell it, nor may you or any other person whosoever sell it until the aforesaid book is in the aforesaid form, on pain of falling under and incurring the penalties contained in the aforesaid regulations and laws of our realms which apply to this matter.

And furthermore, during the aforesaid period, no one without your permission may print or sell it; and he who prints or sells it shall lose whatever copies of it, types, and accessories that he may have, and in addition he shall incur a fine of 50,000 maravedís *for each infraction; of which fine one-third shall go to our Chamber, one-third to the judge who hears the case, and one-third to the person who denounces the crime.*

And furthermore, we command those of our Council, presiding judges, judges of our courts of appeals, magistrates, bailiffs of our household and court and chanceries, and all other justices whomsoever of all the cities, towns, and villages of our realms and seigniories, to each one in his jurisdiction, those who are so now as well as those who shall be henceforth, that you keep and comply with this our permit and favor which we grant, and not oppose or evade it in any way whatsoever, under pain of losing our favor and a fine of 10,000 maravedís *for our chamber. Issued at Madrid, March* 30, 1615.

I, THE KING.

By order of the king our lord: Pedro de Contreras.

Prologue to the Reader

God bless me, gentle or even plebeian reader, how eagerly must you be looking forward to this preface, expecting to find there retaliation, scolding, and abuse against the father of the second Don Quixote—I mean him who was, they say, begotten at Tordesillas and born at Tarragona![1] Well the truth is, I am not going to give you that satisfaction, for though injuries stir up anger in humbler breasts, in mine the rule must grant an exception. You would have me call him ass, fool, and insolent intruder, but I have no such intention. Let his offence be his punishment; 'with his bread let him eat it'; let him worry about it.

What I cannot help resenting is that he charges me with being old and one-handed, as if it had been in my power to hinder time's passage, or as if the loss of my hand had occurred in some tavern and not on the grandest occasion the past or present has seen or the future can hope to see.[2] If my wounds have no beauty to the beholder's eye, they are, at least, honorable in the estimation of those who know where they were received. The soldier shows to greater advantage dead in battle than alive in flight, and so strongly is this my feeling that, if now it were proposed to do the impossible for me, I would rather have taken part in that mighty action than be free from my wounds this minute and not have been there. The wounds the soldier shows on his face and breast are stars that direct others to the heaven of honor and the search for merited praise. It is to be observed, moreover, that one writes not with grey hairs but with the understanding, which commonly improves with years.

I resent, too, that he calls me envious and explains to me, as if I were ignorant, what envy is. For really and truly, of its two varieties, I only know that which is holy, noble, and high-minded. And if that be so, as indeed it is, I am not likely to attack a priest, above all if, in addition, he holds the rank of familiar of the Holy Office.[3] If he said what he did on account of the person on whose behalf it seems he spoke, he is entirely mistaken, for I worship the genius of that person and admire his works and his unceasing and strenuous industry. Yet all in all, I am grateful to this gentleman, the author,

1. In 1614, at Tarragona, there appeared a sequel to Cervantes' own *Part I* of *Don Quixote* written by a still unknown Alonso Fernández de Avellaneda, "a native of the town of Tordesillas." The preface of the work contains some coarse humor at Cervantes' expense, as he will explain in this "Prologue." (A portion of Avellaneda's sequel is reprinted in "Backgrounds and Sources," below.)

2. Cervantes lost the use of his left hand as a result of a wound received at the Battle of Lepanto, 1571, where a combined Christian fleet, under the command of Philip II's half-brother Don Juan of Austria, defeated the Turkish fleet near the modern Greek coastal town of Navpaktos.

3. Avellaneda charged Cervantes with attacking Lope de Vega, probably alluding to the passages on the drama in Part I, Ch. XLVIII, and attributed the attack to envy.

for saying that my stories are more satirical than exemplary, but that they are good. They could not be that unless there was a little of everything in them.

I suspect you will say that I am taking a very humble line and keeping myself too much within the bounds of my moderation from a feeling that additional suffering should not be inflicted upon a sufferer and that what this gentleman has to endure must doubtless be very great. He does not dare come out into the open field and broad daylight but hides his name and disguises his country as if he had been guilty of some sort of treason. If perchance you should come to know him, tell him from me that I do not consider myself insulted, I know well what the temptations of the devil are, and that one of the greatest is putting it into a man's head that he can write and print a book that will procure him as much fame as money and as much money as fame. To prove this I will beg you, in your own sprightly, pleasant way, to tell him this story.

There was a madman in Seville who hit on one of the funniest absurdities and manias that any madman in the world ever gave way to, and it was this. He made a tube of reed sharp at one end, and catching a dog in the street or wherever it might be, with his foot he held one of its legs and with his hand lifted up the other and as best he could inserted the tube where, by blowing, he made the dog as round as a ball. Then, holding it in this position, he gave it a couple of slaps on the belly and let it go.

"Do your worships think, now," he said to the bystanders, who were always there in abundance, "that it is an easy thing to blow up a dog?" Does your worship think now that it is an easy thing to write a book?

If that story does not suit him, you may, dear reader, tell him this one, which is likewise about a madman and a dog.

In Córdoba there was another madman, whose habit it was to carry on his head a piece of marble slab or a stone, and no light one at that. When he came upon any unwary dog, he used to approach it and let the weight fall right on top of it. The dog, in a rage, barking and howling, would run three streets without stopping. It so happened, however, that one of the dogs he dropped his load on was a cap-maker's dog, a great favorite with his master. The stone came down hitting it on the head, the dog raised a yell at the blow, the master saw the affair and was furious. Snatching up a measuring-yard he rushed out at the madman and did not leave a sound bone in his body.

"You dog, you thief! What have you done to my greyhound?" he exclaimed, as each blow fell. "Don't you see, you brute, that my dog is a greyhound?" And repeating the word "greyhound" again and again, he sent the madman away beaten to a powder.

The madman took the lesson to heart and vanished and for more than a month never once showed himself in public. But after that he came out again with his old trick and a heavier load than ever. He would come up to where there was a dog and examine it very carefully without venturing to let the stone fall.

"This is a greyhound, beware!" he would say.

In short, all the dogs he came across, whether mastiffs or terriers, he said were greyhounds, and he dropped no more stones. Maybe it will be the same with this historian, who will not venture again to drop the weight of his wit in books, which, being bad, are harder than stones.

Tell him too, that I do not care two cents for the threat of depriving me of my profit by means of his book. I say to him, quoting from the famous interlude, "The Trollop," "Long live my lord the alderman, and Christ be with us all." Long live the great Count of Lemos, whose Christian charity and well-known generosity support me against all the strokes of my parsimonious fortune, and long live the supreme benevolence of His Eminence of Toledo, Don Bernardo de Sandoval y Rojas.[4] What matter if there were no printing-presses in the world, or if they print more books against me than there are letters in the verses of Mingo Revulgo![5] These two princes, unsought by any adulation or flattery of mine, of their own goodness alone, have taken it upon themselves to show me kindness and protect me, and in this I consider myself happier and richer than if Fortune had raised me to her greatest height in the ordinary way. The poor man may retain honor, but not the vicious; poverty may cast a cloud over nobility but cannot hide it altogether. And as virtue of itself sheds a certain light, even though it be through the cracks and chinks of penury, it wins the esteem of lofty and noble spirits, and in consequence their protection.

You need say no more to him, nor will I say anything more to you except that you should bear in mind that this *Second Part of Don Quixote* which I offer you is cut by the same craftsman and from the same cloth as the *First*. In it I present Don Quixote continued and finally dead and buried, so that no one may dare bring forward any further evidence against him, for that already produced is sufficient. Suffice it, too, that some reputable person should have given an account of all these shrewd lunacies of his without going into the matter again. Abundance, even of good things, prevents them from being valued, and scarcity, even in the case of what is bad, confers a certain value.

I was forgetting to tell you that you may expect the *Persiles*, which I am now finishing, and also the Second Part of *Galatea*.[6]

4. Bernardo de Sandoval y Rojas was cardinal-archbishop of Toledo, primate of Spain and brother of the duke of Lerma, the prime minister.

5. *Las coplas de Mingo Revulgo* is the title given to a versified satire on the reign of Henry IV.

6. Cervantes published his *Galatea*, a pastoral romance, in 1585, but probably never finished the sequel. His Byzantine romance, called *Persiles* for short, appeared in 1617, posthumously.

Dedication
To the Count of Lemos

These days past, when sending Your Excellency my plays, that had appeared in print rather than on the stage, I said, if I remember well, that Don Quixote was putting on his spurs to go and render homage to Your Excellency. Now I say that he has put them on, and he is on his way. Should he arrive, I think I shall have rendered some service to Your Excellency, as from many parts I am urged to send him off, so as to dispel the loathing and disgust caused by another Don Quixote who, under the name of *The Second Part,* has run masquerading through the whole world. And he who has shown the greatest longing for him has been the great Emperor of China, who wrote me a letter in Chinese a month ago and sent it by a special courier. He asked me, or to be truthful, he begged me to send him Don Quixote, for he intended to found a college where the Spanish tongue would be taught, and it was his wish that the book to be read should be the story of Don Quixote. He also added that I should come and be the rector of this college.

I asked the bearer if His Majesty had provided a sum for my travel expenses. He answered that the thought had not even crossed his mind.

"Then, brother," I replied, "you can return to your China, post haste or at whatever haste you are bound to go, as I am not fit for so long a journey and, besides being ill, I am very much without money, while emperor for emperor and monarch for monarch, I have at Naples the great Count of Lemos, who, without so many petty titles of colleges and rectorships, supports me, protects me and does me more favor than I can wish for."

Thus, I gave him his leave, and I beg mine from you, offering Your Excellency the *Travails of Persiles and Sigismunda,* a book I shall finish within four months, God willing, and which will be either the worst or the best that has been composed in our language, I mean of those intended for entertainment. Yet I repent of having called it the worst for, in the opinion of friends, it is bound to attain the summit of possible excellence. May Your Excellency return in the health that I wish for you. Persiles will be ready to kiss your hand and I your feet, being as I am, Your Excellency's most humble servant.

From Madrid, this last day of October of the year one thousand six hundred and fifteen.

At the service of Your Excellency:

MIGUEL DE CERVANTES SAAVEDRA

Table of the Chapters in This Second Part of Don Quixote of La Mancha*

* In the first edition of *Don Quixote,* this Table of Contents was at the end of the book.

End of the Table

The Second Part of
The Ingenious Gentleman
Don Quixote of La Mancha

Chapter I

OF THE CONVERSATION WHICH THE PRIEST AND THE BARBER HAD WITH DON QUIXOTE ABOUT HIS MALADY

Cide Hamete Benengeli, in the Second Part of this history, and third sally of Don Quixote, says that the priest and the barber remained nearly a month without seeing him in order not to recall or bring back to his memory what had taken place. They did not, however, omit to visit his niece and housekeeper, urging them to be careful to treat him with attention and give him strengthening things to eat, and such as were good for the heart and the brain, from which it was plain to see all his misfortune proceeded. The niece and housekeeper replied that they did so and would do so with all possible care and assiduity, for they could perceive that their master was now and then beginning to show signs of being in his right mind. This gave great satisfaction to the priest and the barber, for they concluded they had taken the right course in bringing him home enchanted on the oxcart, as has been described in the First Part of his great as well as accurate history, in the last chapter. So they resolved to pay him a visit and test the improvement in his condition, though they thought it almost impossible that there could be any. And they agreed not to touch on any matter connected with knight-errantry, so as not to run the risk of reopening wounds which were still so tender.

They came to see him, consequently, and found him sitting up in bed in a green wool vest and a red Toledo cap, and so withered and dried up that he looked as if he had been turned into a mummy. They were very cordially received by him. They inquired about his health, and he talked to them about himself very naturally and in very well-chosen language. In the course of their conversation they fell to discussing what they call statecraft and systems of government, correcting this abuse and condemning that, reforming one practice and abolishing another, each of the three setting himself up as a new legislator, a modern Lycurgus or a brand-new Solon. So completely did they remodel the state that they seemed to have thrust it into a furnace and taken out something quite different from what they had put in. And on all the subjects they dealt with,

Don Quixote spoke with such good sense that the pair of examiners were fully convinced that he was quite recovered and in his full senses.

The niece and housekeeper were present at the conversation and could not find words enough to express their thanks to God at seeing their master so clear in his mind. The priest, however, changing his original plan, which was to avoid mentioning matters of chivalry, resolved to test Don Quixote's recovery thoroughly and see whether it was genuine or not. So, from one subject to another, he came at last to talk of the news that had reached them from the capital. Among other things, he said it was considered certain that the Turk was coming down with a powerful fleet and that no one knew what his purpose was or when the great storm would burst. All Christendom was apprehensive of this occurence, which almost every year calls us to arms, and his Majesty had made provision for the security of the coasts of Naples and Sicily and the island of Malta.

"His Majesty," Don Quixote replied, "has acted like a prudent warrior in providing for the safety of his realms in time, so that the enemy may not find him unprepared. But if my advice were taken I would recommend to him a measure which at present, no doubt, his Majesty is very far from thinking of."

"God keep you in his hand, poor Don Quixote," said the priest to himself, on hearing this, "for it seems to me you are plunging from the height of your madness into the profound abyss of your simplicity."

But the barber, who had the same suspicion as the priest, asked Don Quixote what ought, in his view, to be adopted. Perhaps it might prove to be one that should be added to the list of the many impertinent suggestions habit usually offered to princes.

"Mine, master shaver," said Don Quixote, "will not be impertinent but, on the contrary, pertinent."

"I don't mean that," said the barber, "but experience has shown that all or most of the expedients proposed to his Majesty are either impossible, or absurd, or harmful to the king and to the kingdom."

"Mine, however," replied Don Quixote, "is neither impossible nor absurd, but the easiest, the most reasonable, the readiest, and the most expeditious that anyone could imagine."

"You take a long time to tell it, Señor Don Quixote," said the priest.

"I don't choose to tell it here, now," said Don Quixote, "and have it reach the ears of the lords of the Council tomorrow morning, so that someone else will carry off the thanks and rewards of my trouble."

"For my part," said the barber, "I give my word here and before God that I will not repeat what your worship says 'to king or rook or earthly man.' That is the oath I learned from the ballad about the priest who, in the prelude, told the king about the thief who had robbed him of the hundred gold *doblas* and his pacing mule."

"I am no authority on stories," said Don Quixote, "but I know the oath is a good one, because I know the barber to be an honest fellow."

"Even if he were not," said the priest, "I will stand bail for him and guarantee that in this matter he will be as silent as a mute, under pain of paying any penalty that may be pronounced."

"And who will be security for you, señor priest?" said Don Quixote.

"My profession," replied the priest, "which is to keep secrets."

"By heaven!" said Don Quixote at this, "what more has his Majesty to do but to command, by public proclamation, the knights-errant scattered all over Spain to assemble on a fixed day in the capital. Even if no more than half a dozen come, there may be one among them who alone will suffice to destroy the entire might of the Turk. Give me your attention and follow what I have to say. Is it, I ask, any new thing for a single knight-errant to demolish an army of two hundred thousand men, as if they all had but one throat or were made of icing? Tell me, how many histories are there filled with these marvels? If only—in an evil hour for me, I don't speak for anyone else—the famous Don Belianís were alive now, or any one of the innumerable progeny of Amadís of Gaul! If any of these were alive today and were to come face to face with the Turk, by my faith, I would not give much for the Turk's chance. But God will have regard for his people and will provide some one who, if not so valiant as the knights-errant of yore, at least will not be inferior to them in spirit. But God knows what I mean, and I say no more."

"Alas!" exclaimed the niece at this, "may I die if my master does not want to turn knight-errant again."

"A knight-errant I shall die," Don Quixote rejoined, "and let the Turk come down or go up when he likes, and in as strong force as he can. Once more I say, God knows what I mean."

At this moment the barber spoke up. "I ask your worships' leave," he said, "to tell a short story of something that happened in Seville. It is so appropriate just now that I feel like telling it." Don Quixote gave him leave, the rest prepared to listen, and he began.

"In the madhouse at Seville was a man whose relations had placed him there as being out of his mind. He was a graduate of Osuna in canon law, but even if he had been a graduate of Salamanca, it was the opinion of most people that he would have been mad all the same. This graduate, after some years of confinement, took it into his head that he was sane and in his full senses, and under this impression wrote to the Archbishop, entreating him earnestly and in very correct language to have him released from the misery in which he was living. By God's mercy he had now recovered his lost reason, though his relations, in order to enjoy his property, kept him there and, in spite of the truth, would make him out to be mad until his dying day. The Archbishop, moved by repeated sensible, well-written letters, directed one of his chaplains to ask in the madhouse about the truth of the licenciate's statements and to have an interview with the madman himself. If it should appear that he was in his senses, then he should be taken out and set free. The chaplain did so, and the director assured him that the man was still mad and that, though he often spoke like a highly intelligent person, he would in the end break out into nonsense that in quantity and quality counterbalanced all the sensible things he had said before. This could easily be tested by talking to him.

"The chaplain resolved to try the experiment, and obtaining access to the madman conversed with him for an hour or more. During all this time no word was uttered that was either incoherent or absurd. On the contrary, the madman spoke so rationally that the chaplain was compelled to believe him to be sane. Among other things, he said the director was against him in order not to lose the presents his relations made him for reporting him still mad but with lucid intervals. The worst foe he had in his misfortune was his large property, for in order to enjoy it his enemies disparaged and threw doubts upon the mercy our Lord had shown him in turning him from a brute beast into a man. In short, he spoke in such a way that he cast suspicion on the director and made his relations appear covetous and heartless and himself so rational that the chaplain determined to take him away with him so that the Archbishop might see him and ascertain for himself the truth of the matter.

"Yielding to this conviction, the worthy chaplain begged the director to make available the clothes in which the licenciate had entered the house. The director again bade him beware of what he was doing, as the licenciate was beyond a doubt still mad. But all his cautions and warnings could not dissuade the chaplain from taking him away. The director seeing that it was on orders from the Archbishop, obeyed, and they dressed the licentiate in his own clothes, which were new and decent. He, as soon as he saw himself clothed like one in his senses and divested of the appearance of a madman, entreated the chaplain to permit him in charity to go and take leave of his comrades the madmen. The chaplain said he would go with him to see what madmen there were in the house, and so they went upstairs, with some of the others who were present. Approaching a cage in which there was a raving madman, though just at that moment calm and quiet, the licenciate spoke to him. 'Brother,' he said, 'think if you have any commands for me, for I am going home, as God has been pleased, in his infinite goodness and mercy, without any merit of mine, to restore me my reason. I am now cured and in my senses, for with God's power nothing is impossible. Have strong hope and trust in him, for as he has restored me to my original condition, so likewise he will restore you if you trust in him. I will take care to send you some good things to eat, and be sure you eat them. For I would have you know I am convinced, as one who has gone through it, that all this madness of ours comes of having the stomach empty and the brains full of wind. Take courage! take courage! for despondency in misfortune breaks down health and brings on death.'

"To all these words of the licenciate another madman in a cage opposite that of the raving one was listening. Raising himself up from an old mat on which he lay stark naked, he asked in a loud voice who it was that was going away cured and in his senses. 'It is I, brother,' the licenciate replied. 'I have now no need to remain here any longer, for which I return infinite thanks to Heaven that has had so great mercy upon me.'

" 'Mind what you are saying, graduate, and don't let the devil deceive you,' replied the madman. 'Keep quiet, stay where you are, and you will save yourself the trouble of coming back.'

" 'I know I am cured,' returned the graduate, 'and that I shall not have to do penance again.'

" 'You cured!' said the madman. 'Well, we shall see. God be with you, but I swear to you by Jupiter, whose majesty I represent on earth, that for this crime alone, which Seville is committing today in releasing you from this house and treating you as if you were in your senses, I shall have to inflict such a punishment on it as will be remembered for ages and ages, amen. Do you not know, you miserable little licenciate, that I can do it, being, as I say, Jupiter the Thunderer, who hold in my hands the fiery bolts with which I am able and accustomed to threaten and lay waste the world? But in one way only will I punish this ignorant town, and that is by not raining upon it, nor on any part of its district or territory, for three whole years, to be reckoned from the day and moment when this threat is pronounced. You free, you cured, you in your senses!—and I mad, I disordered, I bound! I will as soon think of sending rain as of hanging myself.'

"As those present stood listening to the words and exclamations of the madman, our licenciate turned to the chaplain and seized him by the hands. 'Do not be alarmed, señor,' he said to him. 'Pay no attention to what this madman has said, for if he is Jupiter and will not send rain, I who am Neptune, the father and god of the waters, will rain as often as it pleases me and may be needful.'

"The director and the bystanders laughed, and at their laughter the chaplain was half ashamed. 'For all that, Señor Neptune,' he replied, 'it will not do to vex Señor Jupiter. Remain where you are, and some other day, when there is a better opportunity and more time, we will come back for you.' So they stripped the licenciate, and he was left where he was. That's the end of the story."

"So that's the story, master barber," said Don Quixote, "which was so apropos that you could not help telling it? Master shaver, master shaver, how blind is he who cannot see through a sieve! Is it possible that you do not know that comparisons of wit with wit, valor with valor, beauty with beauty, birth with birth, are always odious and unwelcome? I, master barber, am not Neptune, the god of the waters, nor do I try to make anyone take me for an astute man, for I am not one. My only endeavor is to convince the world of the mistake it makes in not reviving in itself the happy time when the order of knight-errantry was in the field. But our depraved age does not deserve to enjoy such a blessing as those ages enjoyed when knights-errant took upon their shoulders the defense of kingdoms, the protection of damsels, the succor of orphans and minors, the chastisement of the proud, and the recompense of the humble.

"With the knights of these days, for the most part, it is the damask, brocade, and rich materials they wear that rustle as they go, not the chain mail of the armor. No knight nowadays sleeps in the open field exposed to the inclemency of heaven and in full panoply from head to foot. No one now takes a nap, as they call it, without drawing his feet out of the stirrups and leaning upon his lance, as the knights-errant used to do. No one now, issuing from the wood, penetrates yonder mountains, and then treads the barren, lonely shore of the sea—mostly a tempestuous and stormy one—and finding on the beach a little boat without oars, sail, mast, or tackling of any kind, in the intrepidity of his heart flings himself into it and commits himself to the wrathful billows of the deep sea, that one moment lift him up to heaven and the next plunge him into the depths; and opposing his breast to the irresistible gale, finds himself, when he least expects it, three thousand leagues and more away from the place where he embarked; and leaping ashore in a remote and unknown land has adventures that deserve to be written, not on parchment, but on brass. But now sloth triumphs over energy, indolence over exertion, vice over virtue, arrogance over courage, and theory over practice in arms, which flourished and shone only in the golden ages and in knights-errant.

"For tell me, who was more virtuous and more valiant than the famous Amadís of Gaul? Who more discreet than Palmerín of England? Who more gracious and easy-going than Tirante the White? Who more courtly than Lisuarte of Greece? Who more slashed or slashing than Don Belianís? Who more intrepid than Perión of Gaul? Who more ready to face danger than Felixmarte of Hircania? Who more sincere than Esplandián? Who more impetuous than

Don Cirongilio of Thrace? Who more bold than Rodamonte? Who more prudent than King Sobrino? Who more daring than Reinaldos? Who more invincible than Roland? And who more gallant and courteous than Ruggiero, from whom the dukes of Ferrara of the present day are descended, according to Turpin in his *Cosmography.*[1]

"All these knights, and many more that I could name, señor priest, were knights-errant, the light and glory of chivalry. These, or such as these, I would want to carry out my plan, and in that case his Majesty would find himself well served and would save great expense, and the Turk would be left tearing his beard. And so I will stay where I am, as the chaplain does not take me away. And if Jupiter, as the barber has told us, will not send rain, here am I, and I will rain when I please. I say this so that Master Basin may know that I understand him."

"Indeed, Señor Don Quixote," said the barber, "I did not mean it in that way and, so help me God, my intention was good, and your worship ought not to be annoyed."

"As to whether I ought to be annoyed or not," returned Don Quixote, "I myself am the best judge."

"I have hardly said a word as yet," remarked the priest at this, "and I would gladly be relieved of a doubt, arising from what Don Quixote has said, that worries and afflicts my conscience."

"The señor priest has leave for more than that," returned Don Quixote, "so he may declare his doubt, for it is not pleasant to have a doubt on one's conscience."

"Well then, with that permission," said the priest, "I say my doubt is that, do what I can, I cannot persuade myself that the whole pack of knights-errant you, Señor Don Quixote, have mentioned, were really and truly persons of flesh and blood that ever lived in the world. On the contrary, I suspect it to be all fiction, fable, and falsehood, and dreams told by men awakened from sleep, or rather still half asleep."

"That is another mistake," replied Don Quixote, "into which many have fallen who do not believe that there ever were such knights in the world, and I have often, with various people and on occasions, tried to expose this almost universal error to the light of truth. Sometimes I have not been successful in my purpose, sometimes I have, supporting it upon the shoulders of the truth. So clear is this truth that I can almost say I have with my own eyes seen Amadís of Gaul, who was a man of lofty stature, fair complexion, with a handsome though black beard, of a countenance between gentle and stern in expression, sparing of words, slow to anger, and

1. The first nine are heroes of Spanish romances, the others are from Boiardo and Ariosto. There never was any such book as Turpin's *Cosmography;* it was Ariosto himself who traced the descent of the dukes of Ferrara from Ruggiero.

quick to put it away from him. As I have depicted Amadís, so I could, I think, portray and describe all the knights-errant to be found in all the histories in the world, for by the perception I have that they were what their histories describe, and by the deeds they did and the dispositions they displayed, it is possible, with the aid of sound philosophy, to deduce their features, complexion, and stature."

"How big, in your worship's opinion, may the giant Morgante have been, Señor Don Quixote?" asked the barber.

"With regard to giants," replied Don Quixote, "opinions differ as to whether there ever were any or not in the world. But the Holy Scripture, which cannot err by a jot from the truth, shows us that there were, when it gives us the history of that big Philistine, Goliath, who was seven cubits and a half in height, which is a huge size. Likewise, in the island of Sicily, there have been found legbones and armbones so large that their size makes it plain that their owners were giants and as tall as great towers. Geometry puts this fact beyond a doubt. But, for all that, I cannot speak with certainty as to the size of Morgante, though I suspect he cannot be very tall. I am inclined to be of this opinion because I find in the history[2] in which his deeds are particularly mentioned, that he slept under a roof. Since he found houses to contain him, it is clear that his bulk could not have been anything excessive."

"That is true," said the priest, and yielding to the enjoyment of hearing such nonsense, he asked him what was his notion of the features of Reinaldos of Montalbán, and Don Roland and the rest of the Twelve Peers of France, for they were all knights-errant.

"As for Reinaldos," replied Don Quixote, "I venture to say that he was broad-faced, of ruddy complexion, with roguish and somewhat prominent eyes, excessively punctilious and touchy, and given to the society of thieves and riff-raff. With regard to Roland, or Rotolando, or Orlando (for the histories call him by all these names), I am of opinion, and hold, that he was of middle height, broad-shouldered, rather bow-legged, swarthy-complexioned, redbearded, with a hairy body and a severe expression of countenance, a man of few words, but very polite and well-bred."

"If Roland was not a more graceful person than your worship has described," said the priest, "it is no wonder that the fair Lady Angelica rejected him and left him for the gaiety, liveliness, and grace of that budding-bearded little Moor to whom she surrendered herself. She showed her sense in falling in love with the gentle softness of Medoro rather than the roughness of Roland."

"That Angelica, señor priest," returned Don Quixote, "was a giddy damsel, flighty and somewhat wanton, and she left the world

2. I.e., the *Morgante maggiore* of Pulci. The account of the bones found in Sicily is the *Jardín de flores curiosas* by Antonio de Torquemada.

as full of her vagaries as of the fame of her beauty. She treated with scorn a thousand gentlemen, men of valor and wisdom, and took up with a smooth-faced sprig of a page, without fortune or fame, except such reputation for gratitude as the affection he bore his friend got for him.[3] The great poet who sang her beauty, the famous Ariosto, not caring after her contemptible surrender to sing her adventures—they probably would have done her little credit—dropped her where he says

> How she received the sceptre of Cathay,
> Some bard of defter quill may sing some day.[4]

"This was no doubt a kind of prophecy, for poets are also called *vates*, that is to say diviners. Its truth has been made plain, for since then a famous Andalusian poet has lamented and sung her tears, and another famous and rare poet, a Castilian, has sung her beauty."[5]

"Tell me, Señor Don Quixote," said the barber here, "among all those who praised her, has there been no poet to write a satire on this Lady Angelica?"

"I can well believe," replied Don Quixote, "that if Sacripante or Roland had been poets they would have given the damsel a trimming. It is naturally the way with poets who have been scorned and rejected by their ladies, whether fictitious or not, in short by those whom they select as the ladies of their thoughts, to avenge themselves in satires and libels—a vengeance, to be sure, unworthy of generous hearts. But up to the present I have not heard of any defamatory verse against the Lady Angelica, who turned the world upside down."

"Strange," said the priest. But at this moment they heard the housekeeper and the niece, who had previously withdrawn from the conversation, exclaiming aloud in the courtyard, and at the noise they all ran out.

Chapter II

WHICH TREATS OF THE NOTABLE ARGUMENT WHICH SANCHO PANZA HAD WITH DON QUIXOTE'S NIECE AND HOUSEKEEPER, TOGETHER WITH OTHER DROLL MATTERS

The history relates that the outcry Don Quixote, the priest, and the barber heard came from the niece and the housekeeper as Sancho strove to force his way in to see Don Quixote while they held the door against him. "What does this vagabond want in this

3. The friend was his master, Dardinel, beside whose body he received the wound of which he was cured by Angelica, in the *Orlando furioso*.
4. *Orlando furioso*, xxx. 16.
5. The Andalusian was Barahona de Soto, *Primera parte de la Angélica*, Granada, 1586. The Castilian was Lope de Vega, *Hermosura de Angélica*, Madrid, 1602.

house?" they exclaimed. "Be off to your own, brother, for it is you, and no one else, that delude my master and lead him astray and take him tramping around the country."

"Devil's own housekeeper!" rejoined Sancho. "I am deluded and led astray and taken tramping around the country and not your master! He has taken me all over the world, and you are mightily mistaken. He lured *me* away from home by a trick, promising me an island, which I am still waiting for."

"May evil islands[1] choke you, Sancho, you wretch," said the niece. "What are islands? Is it something to eat, greedy glutton that you are?"

"It is not something to eat," replied Sancho, "but something to govern and rule, and better than four aldermanships or four judgeships."

"Nevertheless," said the housekeeper, "you don't enter here, you bag of dirty tricks and sack of mischief. Go govern your house and dig your garden and give up looking for islands or drylands."

The priest and the barber listened with great amusement to the words of the three. But Don Quixote, uneasy that Sancho might blab and blurt out a whole heap of mischievous stupidities and touch on points that might not be altogether to his credit, called to him and made the other two hold their tongues and let him come in. Sancho entered, and the priest and the barber took their leave of Don Quixote. They despaired of his recovery when they saw how convinced he was of his crazy ideas and how saturated with the nonsense of his accursed chivalry.

"You will see, my friend," the priest said to the barber, "that when we are least expecting it, our gentleman will be off once more for another flight."

"I have no doubt of it," returned the barber. "But I do not wonder so much at the madness of the knight as at the simple-mindedness of the squire, who has such a firm belief in all that about the island that I suppose no imaginable disillusionment could get it out of his head."

"God help them," said the priest. "Let us be on the lookout to see what comes of all these absurdities of knight and squire, for it seems as if they had both been cast in the same mold, and the madness of the master without the foolishness of the servant would not be worth a farthing."

"That is true," said the barber, "and I should like very much to know what the pair are talking about at this moment."

"I promise you," said the priest, "the niece or the housekeeper will tell us later, for they are not the ones to forget to listen."

1. The niece and housekeeper do not understand the word *ínsula*, the literary word for "island," and take it to be something edible. The word-play is lost in English.

Meanwhile Don Quixote shut himself up in his room with Sancho, and when they were alone he spoke his mind. "It grieves me greatly, Sancho, to hear you maintain that I took you away from your cottage," he said, "though you know I did not remain in my own house. We sallied forth together, we took the road together, we wandered abroad together, and have had the same fortune and the same luck. If they blanketed you once, they beat me a hundred times, and that is the only advantage I have over you."

"That was only reasonable," replied Sancho, "for, by what your worship says, misfortunes belong more properly to knights-errant than to their squires."

"You are mistaken, Sancho," said Don Quixote, "according to the maxim *quando caput dolet, &c.*"

"I don't understand any language but my own," said Sancho.

"I mean to say," said Don Quixote, "that when the head suffers all the members suffer and, being your lord and master, I am your head, and you a part of me since you are my servant. Thus any evil that affects or shall affect me should pain you, and what affects you give pain to me."

"Maybe so," said Sancho. "But when I was blanketed as a member, my head was on the other side of the wall looking on while I was flying through the air, and did not feel any pain whatever. If the members are obliged to feel the suffering of the head, it should be obliged to feel their sufferings."

"Do you mean to say now, Sancho," said Don Quixote, "that I felt nothing when they were blanketing you? If you do, you must not say so or think so, for I felt more pain then in spirit than you did in body. But let us put that aside for the present, for we shall have opportunities enough for considering and settling the point. Tell me, Sancho my friend, what are they saying about me in the village here? What do the common people think of me? What do the *hidalgos?* What do the *caballeros?*[1] What do they say of my valor, of my achievements, and of my courtesy? How do they regard the task I have undertaken to revive and restore to the world the now forgotten order of chivalry?

"In short, Sancho, I would have you tell me all you have heard on the topic. And you must tell me without adding to the good or taking away anything from the bad, for it is the duty of loyal vassals to tell the truth to their lords just as it is and in its proper shape, without letting flattery add to it or any idle deference lessen it. I assure you, Sancho, that if the naked truth, undisguised by flattery, reached the ears of princes, times would be different, and other ages would be reckoned iron ages rather than ours, which indeed I look on as the age of gold.[2] Profit by this advice, Sancho, and report to

1. The gentry and the nobility.
2. Don Quixote probably means an age in which money is more important than anything else.

me clearly and faithfully the truth of what you know concerning what I have asked."

"That I will do with all my heart, master," replied Sancho, "provided your worship will not get angry at what I say, since you want me to tell you the naked truth, without putting any more clothes on it than it had when I heard it."

"I will not be angry at all," returned Don Quixote. "You may speak freely, Sancho, and without any beating around the bush."

"Well then," said he, "first of all, I have to tell you that the common people consider your worship completely crazy and me no less a fool. The *hidalgos* say that, not content with being a gentleman, you have assumed the 'Don,' and made a knight of yourself when all you own is a few vines and a couple of acres of land and the shirt on your back.[3] The *caballeros* say they do not want to have *hidalgos* setting up in opposition to them, particularly poor *hidalgos* who polish their own shoes and darn their black stockings with green silk."

"That," said Don Quixote, "does not apply to me, for I am always well dressed and never patched. Ragged I may be, but ragged more from wear and tear of arms than of time."

"As to your worship's valor, courtesy, deeds, and goal, there is a variety of opinions. Some say, 'crazy but funny,' others, 'valiant but unfortunate,' others, 'courteous but out of place,' and they go into so many things that they don't leave a sound bone either in your worship or in myself."

"Remember, Sancho," said Don Quixote, "that wherever virtue exists in an eminent degree, it is persecuted. Few or none of the famous men that have lived escaped being calumniated by malice. Julius Cæsar, the boldest, wisest, and bravest of captains, was charged with being ambitious, and not particularly neat in his dress or pure in his morals. Of Alexander, whose deeds won him the name of Great, they say that he was something of a drunkard. Of Hercules, him of the many labors, it is said that he was lewd and effeminate. Of Don Galaor, the brother of Amadís of Gaul, it was whispered that he was too quarrelsome, and of his brother that he was a cry-baby. So, Sancho, among all these calumnies against good men, mine may pass, since they are no worse than you have said."

"That's just the trouble!"

"Is there more, then?" asked Don Quixote.

"There's the tail to be skinned yet," said Sancho. "So far you've heard only the good stuff. But if your worship wants to know all the lies they're saying about you, I'll bring you somebody this instant who can tell you all of them without missing an atom. Last night the son of Bartolomé Carrasco, who has been studying at Sala-

3. In the time of Cervantes, the title of *don* was restricted to titled nobles, their families, and high ecclesiastics.

manca, came home after having been made a bachelor, and when I went to welcome him, he told me that your worship's history is already in books, with the title of THE INGENIOUS GENTLEMAN DON QUIXOTE OF LA MANCHA. And he says they mention me in it by my own name, Sancho Panza, and the lady Dulcinea del Toboso too, and various things that happened to us when we were alone, so that I crossed myself in amazement at how the historian who wrote them down could have known them."

"I promise you Sancho," said Don Quixote, "the author of our history will be some sage enchanter, for to such as they nothing they choose to write about is hidden."

"A sage and an enchanter indeed!" said Sancho. "Why, the bachelor Sansón Carrasco (that is the name of the man I spoke of) says the author of the history is called Cide Hamete Berengena."

"That is a Moorish name," said Don Quixote.

"Maybe so," replied Sancho. "I have heard say that the Moors are mostly great lovers of eggplants."[4]

"You must have mistaken the surname of this 'Cide'—which means in Arabic 'Lord'—Sancho," observed Don Quixote.

"Very likely," replied Sancho, "but if your worship wants me to fetch the bachelor, I will go for him in a jiffy."

"You will give me great pleasure, my friend," said Don Quixote, "for what you have told me has amazed me, and I shall not eat a morsel that will agree with me until I have heard all about it."

"Then I'm off for him," said Sancho, and leaving his master he went in search of the bachelor. He returned with him in a short time, and all three together, they had a very amusing conversation.

Chapter III

OF THE LAUGHABLE CONVERSATION THAT TOOK PLACE BETWEEN DON QUIXOTE, SANCHO PANZA, AND THE BACHELOR SANSÓN CARRASCO

Don Quixote was extremely anxious while waiting for the bachelor Carrasco, from whom he would hear how he himself had been put into a book, as Sancho had said. He deemed it incredible that any such history could exist, for the blood of the enemies he had slain was not yet dry on his swordblade, and now they claimed that his mighty achievements were making the rounds in print. For all that, he fancied some sage, either a friend or an enemy, might by magic arts have given them to the press—if friendly in order to magnify and exalt them above the most famous ever achieved by any knight-errant, and if an enemy, to bring them to naught and degrade them below the meanest ever recorded of any low squire,

4. ***Berengena:*** "eggplant."

though, he reflected, the achievements of squires never were recorded. If, however, such a history did indeed exist, as the story of a knight-errant it was bound to be grandiloquent, lofty, imposing, splendid and true. With this he comforted himself somewhat, though he was uneasy at the thought that the author was a Moor, judging by the title of "Cide," and no truth was to be expected from Moors, as they are all impostors, cheats, and schemers. He was afraid the writer might have dealt with his love affairs in some indecorous fashion that might tend to the discredit and prejudice of the purity of his lady Dulcinea del Toboso. He would have had him set forth the fidelity and respect he had always observed towards her, spurning queens, empresses, and damsels of all sorts, and keeping in check the impetuosity of his natural impulses. Absorbed and wrapped up in these and various other cogitations, he was found by Sancho and Carrasco, whom Don Quixote received with great courtesy.

The bachelor, though he was named after Samson, was not very big, but he was a great joker. Of a sallow complexion, but very sharpwitted, he was about twenty-four years of age, with a round face, a flat nose, and a large mouth, all indications of a mischievous disposition and a love of fun and jokes. He gave a sample of this as soon as he saw Don Quixote, by falling on his knees before him. "Let me kiss your mightiness's hand, Señor Don Quixote of La Mancha," he said, "for by the habit of St. Peter that I wear, though I have no more than the first four orders,[1] your worship is one of the most famous knights-errant that have ever been, or will be, all the world over. A blessing on Cide Hamete Benengeli, who has written the history of your great deeds, and a double blessing on that connoisseur who took the trouble of having it translated out of Arabic into our Castilian tongue for the universal entertainment of the people!"

Don Quixote made him rise. "So, then," he said, "it is true that there is a book about me, and that it was a Moor and a sage who wrote it?"

"So true is it, señor," said Sansón, "that in my estimation there are more than twelve thousand volumes of this history in print this very day. Only ask Portugal, Barcelona, and Valencia, where they have been printed, and moreover there is a report that it is being printed at Antwerp, and I am persuaded there will not be a country or language in which there will not be a translation of it."[2]

"One of the things," here observed Don Quixote, "that ought to give most pleasure to a virtuous and eminent man is to find himself

1. Carrasco refers to his ecclesiastical dress (habit of St. Peter) and to the first stages of holy orders on the way to priesthood.

2. No editions had yet appeared at Barcelona or Antwerp. On the other hand, there were two editions at Brussels and one at Milan, of which Cervantes does not seem to have been aware when he wrote this.

in his lifetime in print and in type, familiar to the people and with a good name. I say with a good name, for if it is the opposite, then there is no death to be compared to it."

"If it is a question of good name and fame," said the bachelor, "your worship alone wins the palm from all the knights-errant. The Moor in his own language and the Christian in his have taken care to set before us your gallantry, your high courage in encountering dangers, your fortitude in adversity, your patience under misfortunes as well as wounds, the purity and continence of the platonic loves of your worship and my lady Doña Dulcinea del Toboso—"

"I never heard my lady Dulcinea called Doña," observed Sancho here, "only the lady Dulcinea del Toboso. So here already the history is wrong."

"That is not an objection of any importance," replied Carrasco.

"Certainly not," said Don Quixote. "But tell me, señor bachelor, what deeds of mine are made the most of in this history?"

"On that point," replied the bachelor, "opinions differ, as tastes do. Some swear by the adventure of the windmills that your worship took to be Briareuses and giants, and others by that of the fulling mills. One praises the description of the two armies that afterwards took the appearance of two herds of sheep, another that of the dead body on its way to be burried at Segovia, while a third says the liberation of the galley slaves is the best of all, and a fourth that nothing comes up to the affair with the Benedictine giants and the battle with the valient Biscayan."

"Tell me, señor bachelor," said Sancho at this point, "does the adventure with the Yangüesans come in, when our good Rocinante went hankering after tidbits where he shouldn't?"

"The sage has left nothing in the inkwell," replied Sansón. "He tells all and sets down everything, even to the capers that worthy Sancho cut in the blanket."

"I cut no capers in the blanket," returned Sancho. "In the air I did, and more of them than I liked."

"There is no human history in the world, I suppose," said Don Quixote, "that has not its ups and downs, especially such as deal with chivalry, for they can never be entirely made up of prosperous adventures."

"For all that," replied the bachelor, "some who have read the history say they would have been glad if the author had left out some of the countless beatings that were inflicted on Señor Don Quixote in various encounters."

"That's where the truth of the history comes in," said Sancho.

"At the same time they might fairly have kept silent about them," observed Don Quixote. "There is no need for record events which do not change or affect the truth of a history, if they tend to bring the hero of it into contempt. Aeneas was not in truth and earnest so pious as Virgil represents him, nor Ulysses so wise as Homer describes him."

"That is true," said Sansón, "but it is one thing to write as a poet, another to write as a historian. The poet may describe or sing things, not as they were, but as they ought to have been, while the historian has to write them down, not as they ought to have been, but as they were, without adding to or subtracting from the truth."

"Well then," said Sancho, "If this señor Moor has set out to tell the truth, no doubt among my master's drubbings mine are to be found, for they never took the measure of his worship's shoulders without doing the same for my whole body. But I have no right to wonder at that, for, as my master himself says, the members must share the pain of the head."

"You are a sly dog, Sancho," said Don Quixote. "Upon my word, you have an excellent memory when you choose to remember things."

"If I were to try to forget the whacks they gave me," said Sancho, "my welts would not let me, because they are still fresh on my ribs."

"Hush, Sancho," said Don Quixote, "and don't interrupt the bachelor, whom I entreat to go on and tell all that is said about me in this history."

"And about me," said Sancho, "for they say, too, that I am one of the principal presonages in it."

"*Personages*, not *presonages*, friend Sancho," said Sansón.

"What! Are you another of those people who criticize the way I talk?" said Sancho. "If that's to be the way, we won't finish in a lifetime."

"May God shorten my life, Sancho," returned the bachelor, "if you are not the second most important person in the history. There are even some who would rather hear you talk than the cleverest in the whole book—though there are some, too, who say you showed yourself over-credulous in believing you could possibly govern that island offered you by Señor Don Quixote."

"There is still sunshine on the wall," said Don Quixote. "When Sancho is somewhat more advanced in life, with the experience that years bring, he will be fitter and better qualified to be a governor than he is at present."

"By God, master," said Sancho, "the island that I can't govern with the age I have now, I won't be able to govern at the age of Methuselah. The difficulty is that this island keeps its distance somewhere, I don't know where, and not that I lack the wit to govern it."

"Leave it to God, Sancho," said Don Quixote, "all will come out right and perhaps better than you think. No leaf on the tree stirs but by God's will."

"That is true," said Sansón, "and if it is God's will, there will no lack of a thousand islands, much less one, for Sancho to govern."

"I have seen governors in these parts," said Sancho, "that are not fit to tie my shoe, but they're still called 'your lordship' and served on silver."

"Those are not governors of islands," observed Sansón, "and they have an easier task. Those that govern islands must at least know grammar."

"I could manage the *gram* well enough," said Sancho, "but for the *mar* I have neither leaning nor liking, for I don't know what it is. But leaving this matter of the government in God's hands, to send me wherever it may be most to his service, I may tell you, Señor Bachelor Sansón Carrasco, it has pleased me beyond measure that the author of this history should have spoken of me in such a way that what is said of me gives no offense. For, on the faith of a true squire, if he had said anything about me that was at all unbecoming an old Christian, as I am, the deaf would have heard of it."

"That would be working miracles," said Sansón.

"Miracles or no miracles," said Sancho, "let everyone watch how he speaks or writes about people and not set down at random the first thing that comes into his head."

"One of the faults they find with this history," said the bachelor, "is that its author inserted in it a story called 'Ill-advised Curiosity.' Not that it is bad or poorly told, but that it is out of place and has nothing to do with the history of his worship Señor Don Quixote."

"I will bet the son of a Moorish dog has mixed up the cabbages and the baskets," said Sancho.

"Then I say," said Don Quixote, "the author of my history was no sage but some ignorant chatterer who, in a haphazard and heedless way, set about writing it, let it turn out as it might. It was just what Orbaneja, the painter of Úbeda, used to do. When they asked him what he was painting, he answered, 'Whatever it turns out to be.' Sometimes he would paint a rooster in such a way, and so unrealistic, that he had to write alongside of it in capital letters, 'This is a rooster.' So it will be with my history, which will require a commentary to make it intelligible."

"No fear of that," returned Sansón, "for it is so plain that there is nothing in it to puzzle over; children turn its pages, young people read it, grown men understand it, old people praise it; in a word, it is so pored over and read and memorized by people of all sorts that the instant they see any skinny nag they say, 'There goes Rocinante.' And those that are most fond of reading it are pages, for there is not a lord's ante-chamber where there is not a *Don Quixote* to be found. One takes it up if another lays it down, this one pounces on it, and that one begs for it. In short, this history is the most delightful and least harmful entertainment that has been hitherto seen, for there is not to be found in the whole of it even the semblance of an immodest word or a thought that is other than Catholic."

"To write it any other way," said Don Quixote, "would be to write not truth, but falsehood, and historians who have recourse to falsehood ought to be burned, like those who coin false money. I do not know what could have led the author to make use of novelettes and irrelevant stories when he had so much to write about in mine. No doubt he must have followed the proverb 'with straw or with hay, etc.,'[3] for by merely setting forth my thoughts, my sighs, my tears, my lofty purposes, my enterprises, he might have made a volume as large or larger than all the works of El Tostado[4] would make up.

"In fact, my conclusion is, señor bachelor, that to write histories or books of any kind, there is need of great judgment and a ripe understanding. To give expression to humor and write in a strain of graceful pleasantry is the gift of great geniuses. The cleverest character in a comedy is the jester, for he who would make people take him for a fool must not be one. History is to some extent a sacred thing, for it should be true, and where the truth is, there God is. But notwithstanding this, there are some who write and toss out books as if they were fritters."

"There is no book so bad but it has something good in it," said the bachelor.

"No doubt of that," replied Don Quixote. "But it often happens that those who have acquired and attained a well-deserved reputation by their writings lose it entirely, or damage it in some degree, when they give them to the press."

"The reason for that," said Sansón, "is that as printed works are examined at leisure, their faults are easily seen, and the greater the fame of the writer, the more closely are they scrutinized. Men famous for their genius, great poets, illustrious historians, are always, or most commonly, envied by those who take a particular delight and pleasure in criticizing the writings of others, without having produced any of their own."

"That is no wonder," said Don Quixote, "for there are many clergymen who are no good for the pulpit but excellent in detecting the defects or excesses of those who preach."

"All that is true, Señor Don Quixote," said Carrasco, "but I wish such fault-finders were more lenient and less exacting, and did not pay so much attention to the spots on the bright sun of the work they are criticizing. For if *aliquando bonus dormitat Homerus*,[5] they should remember how long he remained awake to shed the light of his work with as little shade as possible. It may be that what they

3. ". . . fill my belly all the way."

4. A prolific author of devotional works.

5. "Worthy Homer sometimes dozes [forgets]" (Horace).

find fault with are moles, which sometimes heighten the beauty of the face that bears them. So I say that great is the risk to which he who prints a book exposes himself, for of all impossibilities the greatest is to write one that will satisfy and please all readers."

"A book about me must have pleased few," said Don Quixote.

"Quite the contrary," said the bachelor, "for, as *stultorum infinitus est numerus*,[6] innumerable are those who have enjoyed the book. But some have lodged a complaint against the author's memory, inasmuch as he forgot to say who the thief was who stole Sancho's Dapple. It is not stated there that he was stolen, but only to be inferred from what is set down, and a little farther on we see Sancho mounted on the same ass, without any reappearance of it. They say, too, that he forget to state what Sancho did with the hundred crowns he found in the valise in the Sierra Morena, as he never alludes to them again. There are many who would be glad to know what he did with them or what he spent them on, for it is one of the serious omissions of the work."

"Señor Sansón, I am not in a mood now for going into accounts or explanations," said Sancho. "I have a sinking feeling in my stomach, and unless I doctor it with a couple of swigs of old wine, I'll get St. Lucy's ailment.[7] I have it at home, and my old woman is waiting for me. After dinner I'll come back and answer you and all the world every question you may choose to ask, as well about the loss of the ass as about the spending of the hundred crowns." And without another word or waiting for a reply he made off home.

Don Quixote begged and entreated the bachelor to stay and take pot luck. The bachelor accepted the invitation and remained; a couple of young pigeons were added to the ordinary fare; at dinner they talked chivalry, Carrasco fell in with his host's humor, the banquet came to an end, they took their afternoon nap, Sancho returned, and their conversation was resumed.

Chapter IV

IN WHICH SANCHO PANZA GIVES A SATISFACTORY REPLY TO THE DOUBTS AND QUESTIONS OF THE BACHELOR SANSÓN CARRASCO, TOGETHER WITH OTHER MATTERS WORTH KNOWING AND TELLING

Sancho came back to Don Quixote's house and took up the conversation where he had left off.

"As to what Señor Sansón said," he declared, "that he would like to know by whom or how or when my ass was stolen, I say in reply that the same night we went into the Sierra Morena, running away from the Holy Brotherhood after that unlucky adventure with

6. "The number of fools is infinite."

7. An obscure expression which may mean "I'll waste away to skin and bones."

the galley slaves and the other one with the corpse that was going to Segovia, my master and I ensconced ourselves in a thicket. There, my master leaning on his lance and I seated on my Dapple, battered and weary with these recent encounters, we fell asleep as if it had been on four feather mattresses. I in particular slept so sound that, whoever he was, he was able to come and prop me up on four stakes, which he put under the four corners of the pack-saddle in such a way that he left me mounted on it, and took away Dapple from under me with out my feeling it."

"That is an easy matter," said Don Quixote, "and it is no new occurrence, for the same thing happened to Sacripante at the siege of Albracca. The famous thief, Brunello, by the same contrivance, took his horse from between his legs."[1]

"Day came," continued Sancho, "and the moment I stirred, the stakes gave way and I fell to the ground. I looked about for the ass but could not see him. The tears rushed to my eyes, and I raised such a lamentation that if the author of our history has not put it in, he may depend on it, he has left out a good thing. Some days after, I don't know how many, traveling with her ladyship the Princess Micomicona, I saw my ass, and mounted on him, in the dress of a gipsy, was that Ginés de Pasamonte, the great rogue and rascal that my master and I freed from the chain."

"That is not where the mistake lies," replied Sansón. "It is that, before the ass has turned up, the author speaks of Sancho as being mounted on it."

"I don't know what to say to that," said Sancho, "unless the historian made a mistake, or perhaps it might be a blunder of the printer's."

"No doubt that's it," said Sansón. "But what became of the hundred crowns? Did they vanish?"

"I spent them for my own good, and my wife's and my children's," Sancho replied to this, "and they're the reason that my wife bears so patiently all my wanderings on highways and byways in the service of my master, Don Quixote. If after all this time I had come back to the house without a cent and without the ass, it would have been a poor future for me. And if anyone wants to know anything more about me, here I am, ready to answer the king himself in person. It is no affair of anyone's whether I took or did not take, whether I spent or did not spend, for if the whacks that were given to me in these journeys were to be paid for in money, even if they were valued at no more than four *maravedís* apiece, another hundred crowns would not pay me for half of them. Let everybody take care of himself and not try to make white black, and black white. For each of us is as God made him, and often worse."

"I will take care," said Carrasco, "to impress upon the author of

1. *Orlando furioso,* xxvii. 84.

the history that, if he prints it again, he must not forget what worthy Sancho has said, for it will raise it a good six inches higher."

"Is there anything else to correct in the history, señor bachelor?" asked Don Quixote.

"No doubt there is," replied he, "but not anything of the same importance as those I have mentioned."

"Does the author promise a second part at all?" said Don Quixote.

"He does promise one," replied Sansón, "but he says he has not found it, nor does he know who has it, and we cannot say whether it will appear or not. So on that score, as some say that no second part has ever been good, and others that enough has been already written about Don Quixote, it is thought there will be no second part. Yet there are some who are jovial rather than saturnine. 'Let us have more Quixotic adventures, let Don Quixote charge and Sancho chatter,' they declare, 'and no matter how it may turn out, we shall be satisfied with that.' "

"And what does the author mean to do?" said Don Quixote.

"What?" replied Sansón. "Why, as soon as he has found the history which he is now searching for with extraordinary diligence, he will at once give it to the press, moved more by the profit that may accrue to him from doing so than by any thought of praise."

"The author looks for money and profit, does he?" observed Sancho, when he heard that. "It will be a wonder if he succeeds, because it will be only hurry, hurry, with him, like the tailor on Easter Eve, and works done in a hurry are never finished as perfectly as they ought to be. Let master Moor, or whatever he is, pay attention to what he is doing, and I and my master will give him enough material in the way of adventures and actions of all sorts that he can make up not only one second part, but a hundred. The good man fancies, no doubt, that we are fast asleep in the straw here, but let him hold up our feet to be shod and he will see which foot we're lame on. All I say is, that if my master would take my advice, we would be out there now, redressing outrages and righting wrongs, as is the use and custom of good knights-errant."

Sancho had hardly uttered these words when the neighing of Rocinante fell upon their ears. Don Quixote accepted this neighing as a happy omen and resolved to make another sally in three or four days from that time. Announcing his intention to the bachelor, he asked him in what region he ought to commence his expedition. The bachelor replied that in his opinion, Don Quixote ought to go to the kingdom of Aragon and the city of Zaragoza, where there were to be certain solemn joustings at the festival of St. George. There he might win renown above all the knights of Aragon, which would be winning it above all the knights of the world. The bachelor commended his very praiseworthy and gallant resolution but admonished him to proceed with greater caution in encountering dangers, because his life did not belong to him but to all those who had need of him to protect and aid them in their misfortunes.

"That's the part I hate, Señor Sansón," said Sancho here. "My master will attack a hundred armed men as a greedy boy would half a dozen melons. God help us, señor bachelor, there is a time to attack and a time to retreat, and it shouldn't be always 'Santiago, and close in, Spain!'[2] Besides, I have heard it said (and I think by my master himself, if I remember rightly) that the valor lies between the extremes of cowardice and rashness. If that is so, I don't want him to run away without having good reason or to attack when unfavorable odds make it better not to. But, above all things, I warn my master that if he is to take me with him, it must be on the condition that he is to do all the fighting and that I am not to be called to do anything except what concerns keeping him clean and comfortable. In that I will do my duty, but to expect me to draw sword, even against rascally peasants with hatchets, is useless. I don't set myself up to be a fighting man, Señor Sansón, but only the best and most loyal squire that ever served knight-errant. If my master Don Quixote, in consideration of my many faithful services, is pleased to give me some island of the many his worship says one may stumble on in these parts, I will take it as a great favor. If he does not give it to me, I was born like everyone else, and a man mustn't depend on anyone except God. What is more, my bread will taste as well, and perhaps even better, without a governorship than if I were a governor, and how do I know but that in these governments the devil may have prepared some trap for me, to make me lose my footing and fall and knock my teeth out? Sancho I was born and Sancho I expect to die. But still, if heaven were to make me a fair offer of an island or something else of the kind, without much trouble and without much risk, I am not such a fool as to refuse it. People say, 'when they offer you a heifer, run with a halter' and 'when good luck comes, take it home.' "

"Brother Sancho," said Carrasco, "you have spoken like a professor. But, for all that, put your trust in God and in Señor Don Quixote, for he will give you a kingdom, not to say an island."

"It is all the same, be it more or be it less," replied Sancho, "though I can tell Señor Carrasco that my master would not be throwing any kingdom he might give me into a torn sack. I have felt my own pulse and I find myself well enough to rule kingdoms and govern islands, and I have told my master as much before now."

"Take care, Sancho," said Sansón. "Honors change manners, and perhaps when you find yourself a governor you won't know the mother that bore you."

2. The old Spanish war cry.

"That may be true of those what are born in the ditches,"[3] said Sancho, "not of those who have the fat of an old Christian two inches deep on their souls, as I have. Only look at my disposition: is that likely to show ingratitude to anyone?"

"God grant it," said Don Quixote. "We shall see when the government comes. I seem to see it already."

He then begged the bachelor, if he were a poet, to do him the favor of composing some verses for him conveying the farewell he meant to take of his lady Dulcinea del Toboso, and to see that a letter of her name was placed at the beginning of each line, so that, at the end of the verses, "Dulcinea del Toboso" might be read by putting together the first letters. The bachelor replied that although he was not one of the famous poets of Spain, who numbered, they said, only three and a half, he would not fail to compose the required verses. Yet he saw a great difficulty in the task, as the letters which made up the name were seventeen. Thus, if he made four ballad stanzas of four lines each, there would be a letter over, and if he made them of five lines, what they called *décimas* or *redondillas*, there were three letters short. Nevertheless he would try to drop a letter as well as he could, so that the name "Dulcinea del Toboso" might be got into four ballad stanzas.

"It must be, by some means or other," said Don Quixote, "for unless the name stands there plain and manifest, no woman would believe the verses were made for her."

They agreed on this, and that the departure should take place in three days from that time. Don Quixote enjoined the bachelor to keep it a secret, especially from the priest and Master Nicolás and from his niece and the housekeeper, lest they should thwart him in his praiseworthy and valiant purpose. After promising all this, Carrasco took his leave and asked Don Quixote to inform him of his good or evil fortunes whenever he had an opportunity. Thus they bade each other farewell, and Sancho went away to make the necessary preparations for their expedition.

Chapter V

OF THE SHREWD AND DROLL CONVERSATION THAT TOOK PLACE BETWEEN SANCHO PANZA AND HIS WIFE TERESA PANZA, AND OTHER MATTERS WORTHY OF BEING DULY RECORDED

The translator of this history, when he comes to write this fifth chapter, says that he considers it apocryphal, because in it Sancho Panza speaks in a style unlike that which might have been expected from his limited intelligence and says things so subtle that he does not think it possible Sancho could have conceived them. However,

3. I.e., in disgraceful circumstances, those who don't know their fathers.

desirous of doing what the task called for, he was unwilling to leave it untranslated, and therefore he went on as follows.

Sancho came home in such glee and spirits that his wife noticed his happiness a bowshot off, so much so that it made her ask him about it.

"What do you have, Sancho my friend," she said, "that makes you so glad?"

"Wife," he rejoined, "if it were God's will, I would be very glad not to be so well pleased as I show myself."

"I don't understand you, husband," said she, "and I don't know what you mean by saying you would be glad, if it were God's will, not to be well pleased. Fool that I am, I don't know how one can find pleasure in not having it."

"Listen, Teresa," replied Sancho, "I am glad because I have made up my mind to go back to the service of my master Don Quixote, who plans to go out a third time to seek adventures. I am going with him again, because my poverty requires it and also because I am cheered by the thought that I may find another hundred crowns like those we have spent. Yet it makes me sad to have to leave you and the children, and if God would be pleased to let me have my daily bread, dry-shod and at home, without taking me out into the byways and crossroads—and he could do it at small cost by merely willing it—it is clear my happiness would be more solid and lasting, for the happiness I have is mingled with sorrow at leaving you, so that I was right in saying I would be glad, if it were God's will, not to be well pleased."

"Look here, Sancho," said Teresa, "ever since you joined up with a knight-errant you talk in such a roundabout way that there is no understanding you."

"It is enough that God understands me, wife," replied Sancho, "for he is the understander of all things, and that will do. But mind, sister, you must look after Dapple carefully for the next three days, so that he may be fit to take arms. Double his feed and see to the packsaddle and other harness, for it is not a wedding we are going to, but around the world, and to play at give and take with giants and dragons and monsters, and hear hissings and roarings and bellowings and howlings. And even all this would be nothing, if we didn't have to deal with Yangüesans and enchanted Moors."

"I know well enough, husband," said Teresa, "that squires-errant don't eat their bread for nothing. and so I will be always praying to our Lord to deliver you speedily from all that hard fortune."

"I can tell you, wife," said Sancho, "if I did not expect to see myself governor of an island before long, I would drop down dead on the spot."

"No, husband," said Teresa, " 'let the hen live, even if she has the pip." Live, and let the devil take all the governments in the world. You came out of your mother's womb without a government, you have lived until now without a government, and when it is God's will, you will go, or be carried, to your grave without a government. How many there are in the world who live without a government, and continue to live all the same, and are included in the number of the people. The best sauce in the world is hunger, and as the poor are never without that, they always eat with a will. But mind, Sancho, if by good luck you should find yourself with some government, don't forget me and your children. Remember that Sanchico is now full fifteen, and it is right he should go to school, if his uncle the abbot has a mind to have him trained for the Church. Consider, too, that your daughter Mari-Sancha will not die of grief if we marry her. For I have my suspicions that she is as eager to get a husband as you to get a government—and, after all, a daughter looks better ill married than as some rich man's mistress."

"By my faith," replied Sancho, "if God brings me to get any sort of a government, I intend, wife, to make such a high match for Mari-Sancha that there will be no approaching her without calling her 'my lady.' "

"No, Sancho," returned Teresa, "marry her to her equal; that is the safest plan. If you take her out of clogs and put her into high-heeled shoes, from her grey woolen skirt to hoopskirts and silk negligées, from plain 'Marica' and 'you,' to 'Doña So-and-so' and 'my lady,' the girl won't know where she is, and at every turn she will make a thousand blunders that will show the thread of her coarse homespun stuff."

"Hush, you silly woman," said Sancho. "She only needs to practice it for two or three years, and then dignity and decorum will fit her as easily as a glove. If not, what does it matter? Let her be 'my lady,' and never mind what happens."

"Keep to your own station, Sancho," replied Teresa, "and don't try to raise yourself higher. Remember the proverb that says, 'wipe the nose of your neighbor's son, and take him into your house.' A fine thing it would be, indeed, to marry our María to some fancy count or grand gentleman who, when the whim took him, would insult her and call her a peasant and the daughter of a sod-buster and a spinning wench. I have not been bringing up my daughter for that all this time, I can tell you, husband. You bring home money, Sancho, and leave marrying her to my care. There is Lope Tocho, Juan Tocho's son, a stout, sturdy young fellow that we know, and I can see he does not dislike the girl. With him, one of our own sort, she will be well married, and we will have her always under our eyes and be all one family, parents and children, grandchildren and sons-in-law, and the peace and blessing of God will dwell among us.

So don't you go marrying her in those courts and grand palaces where they won't know what to make of her, or she what to make of herself."

"Don't be stupid, Mrs. Barabbas," said Sancho. "What do you mean by trying, without why or wherefore, to keep me from marrying my daughter to one who will give me grandchildren that will be called 'your lordship'? Look, Teresa, I have always heard my elders say that he who does not know how to take advantage of luck when it comes to him has no right to complain if it passes him by. Now that it is knocking at our door, it will not do to shut it out. Let us go with the favoring breeze that blows upon us."

It is this sort of talk, and what Sancho says below, that made the translator of the history say he considered this chapter apocryphal.

"Don't you see, you animal," continued Sancho, "that it will be a good thing for me to find some profitable governorship that will lift us out of the mire, and then I'll marry Mari-Sancha to whom I please. And you will find yourself called 'Doña Teresa Panza,' and sitting in church on a fine carpet and cushions and draperies, in spite and in defiance of all the born ladies of the town. No, stay as you are, not getting any bigger or smaller, like a tapestry figure. Let us say no more about it, for Sanchica shall be a countess, say what you will."

"Do you realize what you're saying, husband?" replied Teresa. "Well, for all that, I am afraid this rank of countess for my daughter will be her ruin. You do as you like, make a duchess or a princess of her, but I can tell you it will not be with my will and consent. I was always a lover of equality, brother, and I can't bear to see people give themselves airs without any right. They called me Teresa at my baptism, a plain, simple name, without any additions or tags or fringes of Dons or Doñas. Cascajo was my father's name, and since I am your wife, I am called Teresa Panza, though by right I ought to be called Teresa Cascajo; but 'kings do what the law says.'[1] I am content with this name without having the 'Don' put on top of it to make it so heavy that I cannot carry it. I don't want to make people talk about me when they see me dressed like a countess or governor's wife. They will say at once, 'See what airs the swine-herding slut gives herself! Only yesterday she was always spinning flax and used to go to mass with the tail of her skirt over her head instead of a shawl, and there she goes today in a hoopskirt with her brooches and airs, as if we didn't know her!' If God keeps me in my seven senses, or five, or whatever number I have, I am not going to bring myself to such a pass. You go, brother, and be a government or an island man, and swagger as much as you like, for by the soul of my mother, neither my daughter nor I are going to stir a step from our village. 'A respectable woman should have a broken

1. Teresa inverts the proverb.

leg and keep at home,' and 'to be busy at something is a virtuous girl's holiday.' Be off to your adventures along with your Don Quixote, and leave us to our misadventures, for God will mend them for us according as we deserve it. I don't know, I'm sure, who fixed the 'Don' to him, that neither his father nor grandfather ever had."

"I declare you have a devil of some sort in your body!" said Sancho. "God help you, what a lot of things you have strung together, one after the other, without head or tail! What have Cascajo and the brooches and the proverbs and the airs to do with what I say? Look here, you crazy, ignorant thing—which I can call you, when you don't understand my words and run from good luck—if I had said that my daughter should throw herself out of a tower or go roaming the world like princess Doña Urraca,[2] you would be right in not giving in to my will. But if in an instant, in less than the twinkling of an eye, I put the 'Don' and 'my lady' on her, and take her out of the sticks and put her under a canopy, on a dais, and on a couch, with more velvet cushions than all the Almohadas of Morocco ever had in their family,[3] why won't you consent and agree to my wishes?"

"Do you know why, husband?" replied Teresa. "Because of the proverb that says 'a monkey in silk is a monkey still.' People only throw a hasty glance at a poor man; on the rich man they fix their eyes. And if this rich man was once poor, then there is sneering and gossip and spite of backbiters, and in the streets here they swarm as thick as bees."

"Look here, Teresa," said Sancho, "and listen to what I am now going to say to you. Maybe you never heard it in all your life, and I do not give my own notions; but what I am about to say are the opinions of his reverence the preacher who preached in this town last Lent and who said, if I remember rightly, that all things present that our eyes behold bring themselves before us and remain and fix themselves on our memory much better and more forcibly than things past."

These observations which Sancho makes here are the other ones on account of which the translator says he regards this chapter as apocryphal, inasmuch as they are beyond Sancho's capacity.

"Whence it arises," he continued, "that when we see any person well dressed and making a figure with rich garments and retinue of servants, it seems to lead and impel us perforce to respect him, though memory may at the same moment recall to us some lowly condition in which we have seen him, but which, whether it may have been poverty or low birth, being now a thing of the past, has

2. Doña Urraca was omitted in her father's will and threatened to disgrace him by taking to a disreputable life. He in consequence altered his will and left her the city of Zamora.

3. A confusion on Sancho's part of the word for cushion (*almohada*) and the Almohades, a North African sect of the twelfth and thirteenth centuries which invaded Spanish Islam.

no existence, while the only thing that has any existence is what we see before us. And if this person whom fortune has raised from his original lowly state (these were the very words the padre used) to his present height of prosperity, is well bred, generous, courteous to all, without seeking to vie with those whose nobility is of ancient date, depend upon it, Teresa, no one will remember what he was, and everyone will respect what he is, except the envious, from whom no good fortune is safe."

"I do not understand you, husband," replied Teresa. "Do as you like, and don't break my head with any more speechifying and rhetoric, and if you have revolved to do what you say—"

"*Resolved*, you should say, woman," said Sancho, "not *revolved*."

"Don't set yourself to argue with me, husband," said Teresa. "I speak as God pleases and don't use fancy language. And I say if you are determined to have a governorship, take your son Sancho with you and teach him from this time on how to hold a government, for sons ought to inherit and learn the trades of their fathers."

"As soon as I have the government," said Sancho, "I will send for him by post, and I will send you money, of which I'll have no lack, for there is never any want of people to lend it to governors when they haven't got it. And you dress him so as to hide what he is and make him look like what he is going to be."

"You send the money," said Teresa, "and I'll dress him up for you as fine as you please."

"Then we are agreed that our daughter is to be a countess," said Sancho.

"The day that I see her a countess," replied Teresa, "it will be the same to me as if I was burying her. But once more I say do as you please, for we women are born to this burden of being obedient to our husbands, even if they're blockheads," and with this she began to weep in earnest, as if she already saw Sanchica dead and buried.

Sancho consoled her by saying that though he must make her a countess, he would put it off as long as possible. Here their conversation came to an end, and Sancho went back to see Don Quixote, and make arrangements for their departure.

Chapter VI

OF WHAT TOOK PLACE BETWEEN DON QUIXOTE AND HIS NIECE AND HOUSEKEEPER; IT IS ONE OF THE MOST IMPORTANT CHAPTERS IN THE WHOLE HISTORY

While Sancho Panza and his wife, Teresa Cascajo, held the above irrelevant conversation, Don Quixote's niece and housekeeper were not idle, for by a thousand signs they began to perceive that their uncle and master meant to give them the slip the third time and once more betake himself to his, for them, ill conceived chivalry. They strove by all the means in their power to divert him from such an unlucky scheme, but it was all preaching in the wilderness and hammering cold iron. Nevertheless, among many other representations made to him, the housekeeper had this to say. "In truth, master, if you do not keep still and stay quietly at home and give up roaming mountains and valleys like a troubled spirit, looking for what they say are called adventures, but what I call misfortunes, I shall have to make complaint to God and the king with loud supplication to send some remedy."

To which Don Quixote replied, "What answer God will give to your complaints, housekeeper, I do not know, nor what his Majesty will answer either. I only know that if I were king I should decline to answer the numberless silly petitions they present every day, for one of the greatest among the many troubles kings have is being obliged to listen to all and answer all, and therefore I should be sorry that any affairs of mine should worry him."

"Tell us, señor," said the housekeeper at this point, "at his Majesty's court are there no knights?"

"There are," replied Don Quixote, "and plenty of them. It is right there should be, to enhance the dignity of the prince, and for the greater glory of the king's majesty."

"Then might not your worship," said she, "be one of those that, without stirring a step, serve their king and lord in his court?"

"Recollect, my friend," said Don Quixote, "that all knights cannot be courtiers, nor can all courtiers be knights-errant, nor need they be. There must be all sorts in the world, and though we may be all knights, there is a great difference between one and another. For the courtiers, without leaving their rooms, or the threshold of the court, range the world over by looking at a map, without its costing them a farthing and without suffering heat or cold, hunger or thirst. But we, the true knights-errant, measure the whole earth with our own feet, exposed to the sun, to the cold, to the air, to the inclemencies of heaven, by day and night, on foot and on horseback. Nor do we only know enemies in pictures, but in their own real shapes, and at all risks and on all occasions we attack them, without any regard to childish points or rules of single combat, whether one has or has not a shorter lance or sword, whether one carries relics or any secret contrivance about him, whether or not one of the combatants is facing the sun,[1] and other niceties of the sort that are observed in set combats of man to man, that you know nothing about, but I do.

"And you must know besides that the true knight-errant, though

1. One of the most important of the preliminaries in a formal combat was placing the men so that neither should be at a disadvantage by having the sun in his eyes.

he may see ten giants that not only touch the clouds with their heads but pierce them, and that walk, each of them, on legs like two tall towers, and whose arms are like the masts of mighty ships, and each eye like a great mill-wheel, and glowing brighter than a glass furnace, must not on any account be dismayed by them. On the contrary, he must attack and fall upon them with a gallant bearing and fearless heart, and, if possible, vanquish and destroy them, even though they have for armor the shells of a certain fish that they say are harder than diamonds, and in place of swords wield trenchant blades of Damascus steel or clubs studded with spikes also of steel, such as I have more than once seen. All this I say, housekeeper, that you may see the difference there is between the one sort of knight and the other. And it would be well if there were no prince who did not set a higher value on this second, or more properly speaking first, kind of knights-errant, for, as we read in their histories, there have been some among them who have been the salvation, not merely of one kingdom, but of many."

"Ah, señor," here exclaimed the niece, "remember that all this you are saying about knights-errant is fable and fiction. And their histories, if indeed they were not burned, would deserve, each of them, to have a *sambenito*[2] put on it, or some mark by which it might be known as infamous and a corrupter of morals."

"By the God that gives me life," said Don Quixote, "if you were not my full niece, daughter of my own sister, I would inflict a chastisement upon you for the blasphemy you have uttered that all the world should ring with. What? Can it be that a young hussy that hardly knows how to handle a dozen lace bobbins dares to wag her tongue and criticize the histories of knights-errant? What would Señor Amadís say if he heard of such a thing? He, however, no doubt would forgive you, for he was the most humble-minded and courteous knight of his time, and moreover a great protector of damsels.

"But some there are that might have heard you, and it would not have been well for you in that case, for they are not all courteous or mannerly. Some are ill-humored scoundrels, nor does everyone who calls himself a gentleman behave so in all respects.[3] Some are pure gold, others spurious, and all look like gentlemen, but not all can stand the touchstone of truth. There are men of low rank who strain themselves to bursting to pass for gentlemen, and exalted gentlemen who, one would think, were dying to pass for men of low rank. The former raise themselves by their ambition or by their virtues, the latter debase themselves by their lack of spirit or by

2. The garment worn by penitents who had been tried by the Inquisition and had confessed.

3. *Caballero* means both "knight" and "gentleman." It is in the latter sense that Don Quixote uses the word in the following passage, as the context will show.

their vices. One has need of experience and discernment to distinguish these two kinds of gentlemen, so much alike in name and so different in conduct."

"God bless me!" said the niece, "that you should know so much, uncle—enough, if need be, to get up into a pulpit and go preach in the streets—and yet that you should fall into a delusion so great and foolishness so manifest as to try to make yourself out to be vigorous when you are old, strong when you are sickly, able to put straight what is crooked when you yourself are bent by age, and, above all, a knight when you are not one. For though gentlemen[4] may become knights, it's impossible for poor ones!"

"There is a great deal of truth in what you say, niece," returned Don Quixote, "and I could tell you something about pedigrees that would astonish you. But I refrain, in order not to mix up things human and divine. Look, my dears, all the lineages in the world (attend to what I am saying) can be reduced to four sorts. There are those that had humble beginnings and went on spreading and extending themselves until they attained surpassing greatness, and those that had great beginnings and maintained them and still maintain and uphold the greatness of their origin. Again, there are those that from a great beginning have ended in a point like a pyramid, having reduced and lessened their original greatness till it has come to nought, like the point of a pyramid, which, relatively to its base or foundation, is nothing. And then there are those—and it is the kind that are the most numerous—that have had neither an illustrious beginning nor a remarkable mid-course, and will have an end without a famous name, like an ordinary plebeian line.

"Of the first, those that had an humble origin and rose to the greatness they still preserve, the Ottoman house may serve as an example, which from a humble and lowly shepherd, its founder, has reached the height at which we now see it. For examples of the second sort of lineage, that began with greatness and maintains it still without adding to it, there are the many princes who have inherited the dignity and maintain themselves in their inheritance, without increasing or diminishing it, keeping peacefully within the limits of their states. Of those that began great and ended in a point, there are thousands of examples, for all the Pharaohs and the Ptolemies of Egypt, the Cæsars of Rome, and the whole herd (if I may apply such a word to them) of countless princes, monarchs, lords, Medes, Assyrians, Persians, Greeks, and barbarians, all these lineages and lordships have ended in a point and come to nothing, they themselves as well as their founders. It would be impossible now to find one of their descendants, and, even should we find one, it would be in some lowly and humble condition. Of plebeian lineages I have

4. *Hidalgos,* i.e., like Alonso Quijano.

nothing to say, except that they merely serve to swell the number of those that live, without any eminence to entitle them to any fame or praise beyond this.

"From all I have said I would have you gather, my poor innocents, that great is the confusion among lineages, and that only those are seen to be great and illustrious that show themselves so by the virtue, wealth, and generosity of their possessors. I have said virtue, wealth, and generosity, because a great man who is vicious will be a great example of vice, and a rich man who is not generous will be merely a miserly beggar, for the possessor of wealth is made happy not by possessing it, but by spending it, and not by spending as he pleases, but by knowing how to spend it well. The poor gentleman has no way of showing that he is a gentleman but by virtue, by being affable, well-bred, courteous, gentle-mannered, and kindly, not haughty, arrogant, or censorious, but above all by being charitable. For by two *maravedís* given with a cheerful heart to the poor, he will show himself as generous as he who distributes alms with bellringing, and no one that perceives him to be endowed with the virtues I have named, even though he may not know him, will fail to recognize and set him down as one of good blood. It would be strange were it so, for praise has ever been the reward of virtue, and those who are virtuous cannot fail to receive commendation.

"There are two roads, my daughters, by which men may reach wealth and honors; one is that of letters, the other that of arms. I have more of arms than of letters in my composition, and, judging by my inclination to arms, was born under the influence of the planet Mars. I am, therefore, in a measure constrained to follow that road, and by it I must travel in spite of all the world, and it will be labor in vain for you to urge me to resist what heaven wills, fate ordains, reason requires, and, above all, my own inclination favors. Knowing as I do the countless toils that are the accompaniments of knight-errantry, I know, too, the infinite blessings that are attained by it. I know that the path of virtue is very narrow, and the road of vice broad and spacious. I know their ends and goals are different, for the broad and easy road of vice ends in death, and the narrow and toilsome one of virtue in life, and not transitory life, but in that which has no end. I know, as our great Castilian poet says, that—

> It is by rugged paths like these they go
> That scale the heights of immortality,
> Unreached by those that falter here below."[5]

"Woe is me!" exclaimed the niece, "my uncle is a poet, too! He knows everything, and he can do everything. I will bet, if he chose to become a mason, he could make a house as easily as a cage."

"I can tell you, niece," replied Don Quixote, "if these chivalrous

5. Garcilaso de la Vega's elegy on the death of Don Bernardino de Toledo.

thoughts did not engage all my faculties, there would be nothing that I could not do, nor any sort of knickknack that would not come from my hands, particularly cages, and toothpicks.

At this moment there came a knocking at the door, and when they asked who was there, Sancho Panza answered that it was he. The instant the housekeeper knew who it was, she ran to hide herself so as not to see him, in such abhorrence did she hold him. The niece let him in, and his master Don Quixote came forward to receive him with open arms, and the pair shut themselves up in his room, where they had another conversation not inferior to the previous one.

Chapter VII

OF WHAT PASSED BETWEEN DON QUIXOTE AND HIS SQUIRE, TOGETHER WITH OTHER VERY NOTABLE INCIDENTS

The instant the housekeeper saw Sancho Panza shut himself in with her master, she guessed what they were about and suspected that the consultation would have a third sally for its outcome. So she seized her shawl and, in deep anxiety and distress, ran to find the bachelor Sansón Carrasco. Since he was a well-spoken man and a new friend of her master's, she thought he might persuade him to give up any such crazy notion. She found him pacing the patio of his house, and, perspiring and flurried, she fell at his feet the moment she saw him.

"What is this, mistress housekeeper? What has happened to you?" said Carrasco, seeing how distressed and overcome she was. "One would think you were heartbroken."

"Nothing has happened, Señor Sansón," said she, "only that my master is breaking out, plainly breaking out."

"Whereabouts is he breaking out, señora?" asked Sansón. "On some part of his body?"

"He is only breaking out through the door of his madness," she replied. "I mean, dear señor bachelor, that he is going to break out again (and this will be the third time) to hunt all over the world for what he calls ventures, though I can't make out why he gives them that name.[1] The first time he was brought back to us slung across the back of an ass, and bruised all over. The second time he came in an oxcart, shut up in a cage, and convinced he was enchanted. The poor creature was in such a state the mother that bore him would not have known him, lean, yellow, with his eyes sunk deep into his skull. To bring him to his senses again, ever so little, cost me more than six hundred eggs, as God knows, and all the world and my hens too, that won't let me tell a lie."

1. *Venturas*, which the housekeeper mistakes for *aventuras*, would mean "strokes of good fortune."

"That I can well believe," replied the bachelor, "for they are so good and so fat and so well-bred that they would not say one thing for another, though they were to burst for it. So then, mistress housekeeper, that is all, and nothing is wrong, except what it is feared Don Quixote may do?"

"No, señor," said she.

"Well then," returned the bachelor, "don't be uneasy, but go home in peace. Get me ready something hot for breakfast, and while you are on the way say the prayer of Santa Apolonia, if you know it; for I will come presently, and you will see miracles."

"Woe is me," cried the housekeeper, "is it the prayer of Santa Apolonia you would have me say? That would do if it was the toothache my master had, but what he has got is in the brains."

"I know what I am saying, mistress housekeeper. Go, and don't set yourself to argue with me, for you know I am a graduate of Salamanca, and one can't be more of a bachelor than that," replied Carrasco, and with this the housekeeper retired, while the bachelor went to look for the priest, to arrange with him what will be told in its proper place.

While Don Quixote and Sancho were shut up together, they had a discussion which the history records with great precision and scrupulous exactness. "Señor," Sancho said to his master, "I have reduced my wife to let me go with your worship wherever you choose to take me."

"*Induced*, you should say, Sancho," said Don Quixote, "not *reduced*."

"Once or twice, as well as I remember," replied Sancho, "I have begged your worship not to correct my words as long as you understand what I mean by them. If you don't understand them say 'Sancho,' or 'devil, I don't understand you.' And if I don't make my meaning plain, then you may correct me, for I am so fossil—"

"I don't understand you, Sancho," said Don Quixote at once. "For I do not know what 'I am so fossil' means."

" 'So fossil' means I am so much that way," replied Sancho.

"I understand you still less now," said Don Quixote.

"Well, if you can't understand me," said Sancho, "I don't know how to put it. I don't know any more, God help me."

"Oh, now I have hit on it,' said Don Quixote. "You mean you are so *docile*, tractable, and gentle that you will accept whatever I tell you, and submit to what I teach you."

"I would bet," said Sancho, "that from the very first you understood me and knew what I meant, but you wanted to upset me so that you could hear me make another couple of dozen blunders."

"Maybe so," replied Don Quixote. "But to come to the point, what does Teresa say?"

"Teresa says," replied Sancho, "that I should be careful with your worship, and to 'let legal documents do all the talking,' because 'he who cuts the cards does not shuffle,'[2] and one 'take' is better than two 'I'll give you's.' I say a woman's advice is no great thing, but he who won't take it is a fool."

"And so say I," said Don Quixote. "Continue, Sancho my friend. Go on, for you are speaking pearls of wisdom today."

"The fact is," continued Sancho, "that, as your worship knows better than I do, we are all of us liable to death, and today we are, and tomorrow we are not, and the lamb goes to the slaughter as soon as the sheep, and nobody can promise himself more hours of life in this world than God may be pleased to give him. For death is deaf, and when it comes to knock at our life's door, it is always urgent, and neither prayers nor struggles nor scepters, nor miters, can keep it back, as common talk and report say, and as they tell us from the pulpits every day."

"All that is very true," said Don Quixote. "But I cannot make out what you are driving at."

"What I am driving at," said Sancho, "is that your worship decide on wages for me, to be paid monthly while I am in your service, to be paid to me out of your estate. I don't care to depend on rewards which either come late, or little, or never at all, God help me with my own. In short, I would like to know what I am earning, be it much or little. Because 'the hen will lay on one egg, and many littles make a much, and so long as one gains something, there is nothing lost.' To be sure, if it should happen—what I neither believe nor expect—that your worship were to give me that island you have promised me, I am not so ungrateful or so grasping but that I would be willing to have the revenue of such island appraised and my wages subtracted *pro cata*."

"Sancho, my friend," replied Don Quixote, "sometimes rat may be as good as cat."

"I see," said Sancho. "I bet I ought to have said *pro rata,* not *pro cata*. But it is no matter, as your worship has understood me."

"And so well understood," returned Don Quixote, "that I have seen into the depths of your thoughts and know the mark you are shooting at with the countless shafts of your proverbs. Look here, Sancho, I would gladly fix your wages if I had ever found any instance in the histories of the knights-errant to show or indicate, by the slightest hint, what their squires used to get monthly or yearly. But I have read all or the best part of their histories, and I cannot remember reading of any knight-errant having assigned fixed wages to his squire. I only know that they all served for reward, and that when they least expected it, if good luck attended their masters. they found themselves recompensed with an island or something

2. *Quien destaja no baraja.* This punning proverb means, "A man will not break a contract he himself has arranged."

equivalent to it, or at the least they were left with a title and lordship. If with these hopes and additional inducements you, Sancho, care to return to my service, well and good. But to suppose I am going to disturb or unhinge the ancient usage of knight-errantry is all nonsense. And so, my friend Sancho, go back to your house and explain my intentions to your Teresa, and if she likes and you wish to serve me for rewards, *bene quidem.*[3] If not, we remain friends, for 'if the pigeon-roost does not lack food, it will not lack pigeons.' And bear in mind, my son, that 'a good hope is better than a bad holding, and a good grievance better than a bad compensation.' I speak in this way, Sancho, to show you that I can rain proverbs just as well as yourself. In short, I mean to say, and do say, that if you don't want to come with me, trusting in my generosity, and run the same chance that I run, God be with you and make a saint of you. I shall find plenty of squires more obedient and painstaking, and not so thick-headed or talkative as you are."

When Sancho heard his master's firm, resolute language, a cloud came over the sky for him and the wings of his heart drooped, for he was sure that his master would not go without him for all the wealth of the world. As he stood there dumbfounded and depressed, Sansón Carrasco came in with the housekeeper and niece, who were anxious to hear by what arguments he was about to dissuade their master from going to seek adventures. Sansón, who was remarkably sly, came forward and embraced him as he had done before.

"O flower of knight-errantry! O shining light of arms! O honor and mirror of the Spanish nation!" he exclaimed loudly. "May God Almighty in his infinite power grant that any person or persons who would impede or hinder your third sally may find no way out of the labyrinth of their schemes or ever accomplish what they most desire!"

Then he turned to the housekeeper. "Mistress housekeeper may just as well give up saying the prayer of Santa Apolonia," he said, "for I know it is the positive determination of the spheres that Señor Don Quixote shall proceed to put into execution his new, lofty designs. I should lay a heavy burden on my conscience did I not urge and persuade this knight not to keep the might of his strong arm and the virtue of his valiant spirit any longer curbed and checked, for by his inactivity he is defrauding the world of the redress of wrongs, of the protection of orphans, of the honor of virgins, of the aid of widows, and of the support of wives, and other matters of this kind appertaining, belonging, proper, and peculiar to the order of knight-errantry.

"On, then, my lord Don Quixote, beautiful and brave, let your worship and highness set out today rather than tomorrow. If any-

3. "Well and good."

thing be needed for the execution of your purpose, here am I ready in person and purse to supply the want. Were it requisite to attend your magnificence as squire, I should esteem it the happiest good fortune."

At this, Don Quixote turned to Sancho.

"Did I not tell you, Sancho," he said, "that there would be squires enough and to spare for me? See now who offers to become one, none other than the illustrious bachelor Sansón Carrasco, the perpetual joy and delight of the courts of the Salamancan schools, sound in body, discreet, patient under heat or cold, hunger or thirst, with all the qualifications requisite to make a knight-errant's squire! But heaven forbid that, to gratify my own inclination, I should shake or shatter this pillar of letters and vessel of the sciences, and cut down this towering palm of the fair and liberal arts. Let this new Samson remain in his own country, and, bringing honor to it, bring honor at the same time on the grey heads of his venerable parents. I will be content with any squire that comes to hand, as Sancho does not deign to accompany me."

"I do deign," said Sancho, deeply moved and with tears in his eyes. "It shall not be said of me, master," he continued, "that I bit the hand that fed me. No, I don't come from ungrateful stock; all the world knows, but particularly my own town, who the Panzas that I am descended from were. What is more, I know and can see, from your many good words and deeds, your worship's desire to show me favor. If I have been bargaining more or less about my wages, it was only to please my wife who, when she sets herself to press a point, is like a hammer driving the hoops of a cask as she drives to do what she wants. But, after all, a man must be a man and a woman a woman. And as I am a real man, which I can't deny, I will be one in my own house too, whatever the consequences. So there's nothing more to be done but for your worship to make your will with its codicil in such a way that it can't be provoked, and let us set out at once, to save Señor Sansón's soul from suffering, as he says his conscience obliges him to persuade your worship to go out into the world a third time. So I again offer to serve your worship faithfully and loyally, as well and better than all the squires that served knights-errant in times past or present."

The bachelor was filled with amazement when he heard Sancho's phraseology and style of talk, for though he had read the first part of Don Quixote's history, he never thought that the squire could be so funny as he was there described. But now, hearing him talk of a "will and codicil that could not be provoked," instead of "will and codicil that could not be revoked," he believed all he had read about him, and set him down as one of the greatest simpletons of modern times. He said to himself that two such lunatics as master and servant the world had never seen.

In a word, Don Quixote and Sancho embraced one another and made up, and by the advice and with the approval of the great Carrasco, who was now their oracle, it was arranged that their departure should take place in three days' time. By then they would have made ready everything needed for the journey and procured a helmet, which Don Quixote said he must by all means take. Sansón offered him one, as he had a friend who would not refuse it to him, though it was more dingy with rust and mildew than bright and clean like burnished steel.

The curses which both housekeeper and niece poured out on the bachelor were past counting. They tore their hair, they clawed their faces, and, in the style of the hired mourners that were once in fashion, they raised a lamentation over the departure of their master and uncle as if it had been his death.

Sansón's intention in persuading the knight to sally forth once more was to do what the history relates farther on. All this was by the advice of the priest and barber, with whom he had previously discussed the subject. Finally, then, during those three days, Don Quixote and Sancho provided themselves with what they considered necessary, and Sancho pacified his wife and Don Quixote his niece and housekeeper. At night, unseen by anyone except the bachelor, who thought fit to accompany them half a league out of the village, they set out for El Toboso, Don Quixote on his good Rocinante and Sancho on his old Dapple, his saddlebags furnished with certain matters in the way of victuals, and his purse with the money Don Quixote had given him to meet emergencies. Sansón embraced the knight and entreated him to send word of his good or evil fortunes, so that he might rejoice over the former or bewail the latter, as the laws of friendship required. Don Quixote promised he would do so, and Sansón returned to the village, while the other two took the road for the great city of El Toboso.

Chapter VIII

WHEREIN IS RELATED WHAT BEFELL DON QUIXOTE ON HIS WAY TO HIS LADY DULCINEA DEL TOBOSO

"Blessed be Allah the all-powerful!" says Hamete Benengeli on beginning this eighth chapter. "Blessed be Allah!" he repeats three times, and he says he utters these thanksgivings at seeing that he has now got Don Quixote and Sancho afield, and that the readers of his delightful history may reckon that the achievements and witticisms of Don Quixote and his squire are now about to begin. He urges them to forget the ingenious gentleman's previous acts of chivalry and to fix their eyes on those still to come, which now begin on the road to El Toboso, as the others began on the plains of Montiel—a modest request, considering all he promises.

He goes on to relate that Don Quixote and Sancho were left alone, and the moment Sansón took his departure, Rocinante began to neigh and Dapple to sigh. Both knight and squire accepted this as a good sign and a very happy omen. However, if the truth be told, Dapple's sighs and brays were louder than the neighings of the hack. Sancho inferred that his good fortune was to exceed and surpass that of his master, building, perhaps, upon some judicial astrology that he may have known, though the history says nothing about it. All that can be said is that, when he stumbled or fell, he was heard to say he wished he had not left home, for nothing was gained by stumbling or falling but a damaged shoe or a broken rib. Fool though he was, he did not err in this.

"Sancho, my friend," said Don Quixote, "night is drawing in upon us as we go, and it will be too dark for us to reach El Toboso, where I am resolved to go before I engage in another adventure, in order to obtain the blessing and generous permission of the peerless Dulcinea. That being granted, I expect and feel assured that I shall conclude and bring to a happy termination every perilous adventure, for nothing in life makes knights-errant more valorous than to have gained their ladies' favor."

"That I believe," replied Sancho, "but I think it will be difficult for your worship to speak with her or see her, at any rate where you will be able to receive her blessing—unless she throws it over the wall of the yard where I saw her last time, when I took her the letter that told of the crazy acts and mad things your worship was doing in the heart of Sierra Morena."

"Did you take for a yard wall, Sancho," said Don Quixote, "the place where or at which you saw that never sufficiently extolled grace and beauty? It must have been the gallery, corridor, or portico of some rich and royal palace."

"It might have been all that," returned Sancho, "but to me it looked like a wall, unless I am short of memory."

"At all events, let us go there, Sancho," said Don Quixote. "Provided I see her, it is the same to me whether it be over a wall, or at a window, or through the clink of a door, or the railing of a garden. Any beam of the sun of her beauty that reaches my eyes will give light to my reason and strength to my heart, so that I shall be unmatched and unequaled in wisdom and valor."

"Well, to tell the truth, señor," said Sancho, "when I saw that sun of the lady Dulcinea del Toboso, it was not bright enough to throw out beams at all. It must have been because her grace was sifting the wheat I told you of, and the thick dust she raised came before her face like a cloud and dimmed it."

"What! do you still persist, Sancho," said Don Quixote, "in saying, thinking, believing, and maintaining that my lady Dulcinea was sifting wheat, that being an occupation and task entirely at variance with what is and should be the employment of persons of distinction, who are constituted and reserved for other avocations and pursuits that show their rank a bowshot off? You have forgotten, O Sancho, those lines of our poet wherein he paints for us how, in their crystal abodes, those four nymphs employed themselves who rose from their beloved Tagus? They seated themselves in a verdant meadow to embroider those tissues which the ingenious poet describes to us as being worked and woven with gold and silk and pearls.[1] Something of the kind must have been the employment of my lady when you saw her, except that the spite some wicked enchanter seems to have against everything concerning me changes all those things that give me pleasure and turns them into shapes unlike ther own. So I fear that in that history of my achievements which they say is now in print, if perchance its author was some sage who is an enemy of mine, he will have put one thing for another, mingling a thousand lies with one truth, and amusing himself by relating transactions which have nothing to do with a faithful relation of events. O envy, root of all countless evils, and cankerworm of the virtues! All the vices, Sancho, bring some kind of pleasure with them, but envy brings nothing but irritation, bitterness, and rage."

"I say so too," replied Sancho, "and I suspect in that legend or history of us that the bachelor Sansón Carrasco told us he saw, my honor is dragged in the dirt and knocked around sweeping the streets, as they say. And yet, on the faith of an honest man, I never spoke ill of any enchanter, and I am not so well off that I am to be envied. To be sure, I am rather sly, and I have a certain touch of the rogue in me, but all is covered by the great cloak of my simplicity, always natural and never acted. If I had no other merit except that I believe, as I always do, firmly and truly in God and all the holy Roman Catholic Church holds and believes, and that I am a mortal enemy of the Jews, the historians ought to have mercy on me and treat me well in their writings. But let them say what they like. 'Naked I came, naked I remain; I neither lose nor gain.' And even if I see myself in a book and passed around from hand to hand all over the world, I don't care what they say about me."

"That, Sancho," returned Don Quixote, "reminds me of what happened to a famous poet of our own day, who, having written a bitter satire against all the courtesan ladies,[2] did not insert or name in it a certain lady of whom it was questionable whether she was

1. Don Quixote is describing a famous passage from Garcilaso de la Vega's *Egloga III*.

2. Cervantes probably refers to Vicente Espinel, the author of "Satire against the ladies" or courtesans of Seville.

one or not. She, seeing she was not on the poet's list, asked him what he had seen in her that led him not to include her with the others, telling him he must add to his satire and put her in the new part, or else suffer the consequences. The poet did as she asked and left her without a shred of reputation, and she was satisfied by getting fame, though it was infamy.

"In keeping with this is what they relate of the shepherd who set fire to the famous temple of Diana, by repute one of the seven wonders of the world, and burned it with the sole object of making his name live in after ages. Though it was forbidden to name him or mention his name by word of mouth or in writing, lest the object of his ambition should be attained, nevertheless it became known that he was called Erostratus.

"Something of the same sort is what happened in the case of the great emperor Charles V and a gentleman in Rome. The emperor was anxious to see the famous temple of the Rotunda, called in ancient times the temple 'of all the gods,'[3] but nowadays, by a better nomenclature, 'of all the saints.' It is the best preserved building of all those of pagan construction in Rome, and best sustains the founders' reputation for mighty works and great magnificence. It is in the form of a half orange, of enormous dimensions, and well lighted, though no light penetrates it save that which is admitted by a window, or rather round skylight, at the top, and it was from there that the emperor examined the building. A Roman gentleman stood by his side and explained to him the skillful construction and ingenuity of the vast fabric and its wonderful architecture. When they had left the skylight he said to the emperor, 'A thousand times, your Sacred Majesty, the impulse came upon me to seize your Majesty in my arms and fling myself down from yonder skylight, so as to leave behind me in the world a name that would last for ever.' 'I am thankful to you for not carrying such an evil thought into effect,' said the emperor, 'and I shall give you no opportunity in future of again putting your loyalty to the test. I therefore forbid you ever to speak to me or to be where I am,' and he followed up these words by bestowing a liberal bounty upon him.

"My meaning is, Sancho, that the desire of acquiring fame is a very powerful motive. What, do you think, made Horatius in full armor jump from the bridge into the depths of the Tiber? What burned the hand and arm of Mucius? What impelled Curtius to plunge into the deep burning gulf that opened in the midst of Rome? What, in opposition to all the omens that declared against him, made Julius Caesar cross the Rubicon?[4] And to come to more

3. The Pantheon.
4. These classical examples of bravery are all self-explanatory except perhaps C. Mucius Scaevola, who burned off his right hand when he failed to kill King Porsena, who had besieged Rome.

modern examples, what scuttled the ships, and left stranded and cut off the gallant Spaniards under the command of the most courteous Cortés in the New World? All these and a variety of other great exploits are, were, and will be, the work of fame that mortals desire as a reward and a portion of the immortality their famous deeds deserve. Nevertheless we Catholic Christians and knights-errant look more to that future everlasting glory in the ethereal regions of heaven than to the vanity of the fame acquired in this present transitory life. However long that fame may last, it must after all end with the world itself, which has its own appointed end.

"Thus, O Sancho, in what we do we must not overstep the bounds assigned to us by the Christian religion we profess. In slaying giants we have to slay pride, just as we kill envy by generosity and nobleness of heart, anger by calmness of demeanor and equanimity, gluttony and sloth by the spareness of our diet and the length of our vigils, lust and lewdness by the loyalty we maintain toward those we have made the mistresses of our thoughts, indolence by traversing the world in all directions seeking opportunities of making ourselves, besides Christians, famous knights. Such, Sancho, are the means by which we reach those extremes of praise that fair fame carries with it."

"All that your worship has said so far," said Sancho, "I have understood quite well. Still I would be glad if your worship would dissolve a doubt which has just this minute come into my mind."

"Resolve, you mean, Sancho," said Don Quixote. "Say on, in God's name, and I will answer as well as I can."

"Tell me, señor," Sancho went on, "those courteouses and seizers[5] and all those venturous knights you say are now dead—where are they now?"

"The heathens," replied Don Quixote, "are, no doubt, in hell. The Christians, if they were good Christians, are either in purgatory or in heaven."

"All right," said Sancho, "but now I want to know—the tombs where the bodies of those great lords are, do they have silver lamps before them, or are the walls of their chapels ornamented with crutches, shrouds, locks of hair, legs, and eyes in wax?[6] Or what are they ornamented with?"

"The tombs of the heathens," said Don Quixote in reply, "were generally sumptuous temples. The ashes of Julius Cæsar's body were placed on the top of a stone obelisk of vast size, which they now call in Rome Saint Peter's needle. The emperor Hadrian had for a tomb a castle as large as a good-sized village, which they called the *Moles Adriani* and is now the castle of St. Angelo in Rome. Queen

5. I.e., Curtiuses and Caesars. An untranslatable pun. Sancho says, "all those Julios ["Juliuses" or "Julys"] and Agostos ["Augustuses or "Augusts"]."

6. Typical votive offerings to commemorate miraculous cures. Miniature wax or metal arms, legs, etc., are still commonly seen in churches in Mexico, for example.

Artemisia buried her husband Mausolus in a tomb which was considered one of the seven wonders of the world. But none of these tombs, or any of the many others of the heathens, were ornamented with shrouds or any of those other offerings and tokens that show that they who are buried there are saints."

"That's the point I'm coming to," said Sancho. "Now tell me, which is the greater work, to bring a dead man to life or to kill a giant?"

"The answer is easy," replied Don Quixote. "It is a greater work to bring to life a dead man."

"Now I have got you," said Sancho. "In that case, the fame of those who bring the dead to life, who give sight to the blind, cure cripples, restore health to the sick, and before whose tombs there are lamps burning, and whose chapels are filled with devout people on their knees adoring their relics will be a better fame in this life and in the next than that which all the heathen emperors and knights-errant that have ever been in the world have left or may leave behind them."

"That I grant, too," said Don Quixote.

"Then this fame, these favors, these privileges, or whatever you call it," said Sancho, "belong to the bodies and relics of the saints who with the approbation and permission of our holy mother Church, have lamps, tapers, shrouds, crutches, pictures, eyes, and legs, by means of which they increase devotion and add to their own Christian reputation. Kings carry the bodies or relics of saints on their shoulders, and kiss bits of their bones, and enrich and adorn their chapels and favorite altars with them."

"What would you have me infer from all you have said, Sancho?" asked Don Quixote.

"My meaning is," said Sancho, "let us set out to become saints, and we'll get the fame we are striving after more quickly. For you know, señor, yesterday or the day before yesterday (it is so recent you could say so) they canonized and beatified two little barefoot friars. It is now considered the greatest good luck to kiss or touch the iron chains with which they wrapped and tortured their bodies, and they are held in greater veneration, so it is said, than the sword of Roland in the armory of our lord the king—may God preserve him. So that, señor, it is better to be a humble little friar of no matter what order, than a valiant knight-errant. With God, two dozen lashings are worth more than two thousand lance-thrusts, be they given to giants, or monsters, or dragons."

"All that is true," returned Don Quixote, "but we cannot all be friars, and many are the ways by which God takes his own to heaven. Chivalry is a religion; there are sainted knights in glory."

"Yes," said Sancho, "but I have heard say that there are more friars in heaven than knights-errant."

"That," said Don Quixote, "is because those in religious orders are more numerous than knights."

"There are many errant ones," said Sancho.

"Many," replied Don Quixote, "but few are they who deserve the name of knights."

With these and similar discussions they passed that night and the following day, without anything worth mention happening to them. Don Quixote was not a little dejected at this, but at length the next day, at daybreak, they beheld the great city of El Toboso. At the sight of it Don Quixote's spirits rose and Sancho's fell, for he did not know Dulcinea's house, nor in all his life had he ever seen her, any more than his master. Thus they were both uneasy, the one in his desire to see her, the other at not having seen her, and Sancho could not imagine what he would do when his master sent him to El Toboso. In the end Don Quixote made up his mind to enter the city at nightfall, and they waited until the time came among some oak trees near El Toboso. When the moment they had agreed on arrived, they made their entrance into the city, where something happened to them that may fairly be called something.

Chapter IX

WHEREIN IS RELATED WHAT WILL BE SEEN THERE

'Twas at the very midnight hour'[1]—more or less—when Don Quixote and Sancho left the woods and entered El Toboso. The town was in deep silence for all the inhabitants were asleep and stretched out on their backs, as the saying is. The night was rather dark, though Sancho would have been glad had it been completely dark, so as to find in the darkness an excuse for his blundering. All over the place nothing was to be heard except the barking of dogs, which deafened the ears of Don Quixote and troubled the heart of Sancho. Now and then an ass brayed, pigs grunted, cats mewed, and the various noises they made seemed louder in the silence of the night. Though the enamored knight took all this to be of evil omen, he nevertheless turned to Sancho.

"Sancho, my son," he said, "lead on to the palace of Dulcinea; it may be that we shall find her awake."

"For God's sake! What palace am I to lead to?" said Sancho. "What I saw her highness in was only a very little house."

"Most likely she had then withdrawn into some small apartment of her palace," said Don Quixote, "to amuse herself with her maids, as great ladies and princesses are accustomed to do."

"Señor," said Sancho, "if your worship will have it in spite of me that the house of my lady Dulcinea is a palace, do you expect to

1. From the ballad of Conde Claros.

find the door open at this hour? And will it be right for us to go knocking till they hear us and open the door, making a disturbance and confusion all through the household? Do you think we are going to visit our mistresses, like lovers who come and knock and go in at any hour, however late it may be?"

"Let us first of all find the palace for certain," replied Don Quixote, "and then I will tell you, Sancho, what we had best do. But look, Sancho, for either I see badly, or that dark mass that can be seen ahead of us should be Dulcinea's palace."

"Then let your worship lead the way," said Sancho, "perhaps it may be so. Though I see it with my eyes and touch it with my hands, I'll believe it as much as I believe it is daylight now."

Don Quixote took the lead, and having gone a matter of two hundred paces, he came upon the mass silhouetted in the dark. He found it was a great tower, and then he perceived that the building in question was not a palace but the principal church of the town.

"It's the church we have come upon, Sancho," he said.

"So I see," said Sancho, "and God grant we may not come upon our graves. It's a bad omen to find oneself wandering in a graveyard at this time of night—especially when I told your worship, if I remember rightly, that the house of this lady will be in an alley without an outlet."

"The curse of God on you for a blockhead!" said Don Quixote. "Where have you ever heard of castles and royal palaces being built in alleys without an outlet?"

"Señor," replied Sancho, "every country has customs of its own. Perhaps here in El Toboso it is the custom to build palaces and important buildings in alleys, so I entreat your worship to let me search around these streets or alleys I see here and perhaps, in some corner or other, I may stumble on this palace—and I wish I saw the dogs eating it for leading us on such a wild goose chase."

"Speak respectfully of what belongs to my lady, Sancho," said Don Quixote. "Let us keep the feast in peace, and not throw the rope after the bucket."

"I'll hold my tongue," said Sancho, "but how am I to take it patiently when your worship wants me, after only once seeing our mistress's house, to be able to recognize it and find it in the middle of the night, when your worship can't find it, though you must have seen it thousands of times?"

"You will drive me to desperation, Sancho," said Don Quixote. "Look here, you heretic, have I not told you a thousand times that never once in my life have I seen the peerless Dulcinea or crossed the threshold of her palace, and that I am enamored solely by hearsay and by her great reputation for beauty and discretion?"

"I hear it now," returned Sancho, "and I may tell you that if you have not seen her, neither have I."

"That cannot be," said Don Quixote, "for you said, at any rate, when you brought back the answer to the letter I sent you with, that you saw her sifting wheat."

"Don't mind that, señor," said Sancho. "I must tell you that, as for my seeing her and bringing you back an answer, that was by hearsay too, for I can no more tell who the lady Dulcinea is than I can hit the sky."

"Sancho, Sancho," said Don Quixote, "there are times for jests and times when jests are out of place. If I tell you I have neither seen nor spoken to the lady of my heart, that is no reason why you should say you have not spoken to her or seen her when the contrary is the case, as you well know."

While the two were engaged in this conversation, they perceived someone with a pair of mules approaching the spot where they stood. From the noise the plow made, as it dragged along the ground, they guessed him to be some farm hand who had got up before daybreak to go to his work, and so it proved to be. He came along singing the ballad that says—

> Ill did ye fare, ye men of France,
> In Roncesvalles chase.[2]

"May I die, Sancho," said Don Quixote, when he heard him, "if any good will come to us tonight! Do you not hear what that rustic is singing?"

"I do," said Sancho, "but what has Roncesvalles chase to do with what we are doing? He might just as well be singing the ballad of Calaínos, for any good or ill it can bring us in our business."

By this time the farm hand had come up.

"Can you tell me, worthy friend, and God speed you," Don Quixote asked, "whereabouts here is the palace of the peerless princess Doña Dulcinea del Toboso?"

"Señor," replied the lad, "I am a stranger, and I have been only a few days in the town, doing farm work for a rich farmer. In that house opposite there live the priest of the village and the sacristan. Both or either of them will be able to give your worship some account of this princess, for they have a list of all the people of El Toboso. But it is my belief there is not a princess living here. Many ladies there are, of quality, and in her own house each of them may be a princess."

"Well, the lady I am inquiring for must be one of these, my friend," said Don Quixote.

"Maybe so," replied the lad. "God be with you, for here comes the daylight," and without waiting for more of questions, he whipped on his mules.

2. The beginning of one of the most popular of the ballads of the Carolingian cycle.

Sancho saw that his master was downcast and somewhat dissatisfied. "Señor," he said to him, "daylight will be here before long, and it will not do for us to let the sun find us in the street. It will be better for us to leave the city, and for your worship to hide in some forest in the neighborhood. I will come back in the daytime, and there won't be a nook or corner of the whole village I won't search for the house, castle, or palace, of my lady, and it will be hard luck for me if I don't find it. As soon as I have found it I will speak to her grace and tell her where and how your worship is waiting for her to arrange some plan for you to see her without any damage to her honor and reputation."

"Sancho," said Don Quixote, "you have delivered a thousand sentences condensed in the compass of a few words. I thank you for the advice you have given me and take it most gladly. Come, my son, let us go look for some place where I may hide, while you will return, as you say, to seek and speak with my lady, from whose discretion and courtesy I look for favors more than miraculous."

Sancho was in a fever to get his master out of the town, to prevent his discovering the falsehood of the reply Sancho had brought to him in the Sierra Morena on behalf of Dulcinea. So he hastened their departure, which was done at once. Two miles out of the village they found a forest or thicket where Don Quixote ensconced himself, while Sancho returned to the city to speak to Dulcinea. On this mission things happened to him which demand renewed attention and a new chapter.

Chapter X

WHEREIN IS RELATED THE DEVICE SANCHO ADOPTED TO ENCHANT THE LADY DULCINEA, AND OTHER INCIDENTS AS LUDICROUS AS THEY ARE TRUE

When the author of this great history comes to relate what is set down in this chapter he says he would have preferred to remain silent, fearing it would not be believed. For here Don Quixote's madness reaches the limits of everything imaginable, and even goes a couple of bowshots beyond. Yet in the end, though still under the same fear and apprehension, the author recorded it without adding to the truth of the story or leaving out a jot, and entirely disregarding the charges of falsehood he might have to face. He was right in this, for the truth may be spun fine but will not break and always rises above falsehood as oil above water.

So, going on with his story, he says that as soon as Don Quixote had ensconced himself in the forest, oak grove, or woods near El Toboso, he bade Sancho return to the city, nor should he present himself again without having first spoken on Don Quixote's behalf to his lady and begged that she might deign to let herself be seen by her enslaved knight, and bestow her blessing upon him, thus enabling him to anticipate a happy outcome in all his encounters and difficult enterprises. Sancho undertook to execute the task as he had been instructed and to bring back an answer as good as that he had brought back the first time.

"Go, my son," said Don Quixote, "and be not dazed when you confront the light of that sun of beauty you are about to seek. Happy are you above all the squires in the world! Note, and let it not escape your memory, how she receives you, if she changes color while you deliver my message, if she is agitated and disturbed at hearing my name, if she cannot rest upon her cushion, should you find her seated in the sumptuous state chamber proper to her rank. Should she be standing, observe if she rests now on one foot and now on the other, if she repeats her reply two or three times, if she passes from gentleness to austerity, from asperity to tenderness, or if she raises her hand to smooth her hair though it be not disarranged.

"In short, my son, observe all her actions and motions, for if you report them to me as they were, I will devine what she hides in the recesses of her heart as regards my love. For I would have you know, Sancho, if you do not already know, that with lovers the outward actions and motions they give way to when their loves are in question are the faithful messengers that proclaim what is going on in the depths of their hearts. Go, my friend, may better fortune than mine attend you, and bring you more success than I dare expect, torn between hope and dread in this harsh solitude."

"I will go and return quickly," said Sancho. "Cheer up that tiny heart of yours, master, for at this moment it seems no bigger than a hazel nut. Remember what they say, that a stout heart breaks bad luck, and that where nothing is ventured, nothing is gained. And they also say, the hare jumps up where it's least expected. I say this because if we could not find my lady's palaces or castles last night, now by daylight I count on finding them when I least expect it, and once found, leave it to me to manage her."

"Really, Sancho," said Don Quixote, "you always bring in your proverbs so appropriately, whatever we deal with! May God give me better luck in what I desire!"

With this, Sancho wheeled about and gave Dapple the stick. Don Quixote remained behind, seated on his horse, resting in his stirrups, and leaning on the end of his lance, filled with sad and troubled forebodings. There we will leave him and accompany Sancho, who went off no less serious and troubled than he left his master. Indeed, no sooner had he got out of the thicket and looked backward to make sure that Don Quixote was not within sight than he dismounted from his ass. Then, seating himself at the foot of a tree, he began to commune with himself.

"Now, brother Sancho," he said, "let us know where your worship is going. Are you going to look for some ass that has been lost? Not at all. Then what are you going to look for? I am going to look for a princess, that's all, and, in her, for the sun of beauty and the whole heaven in one. And where do you expect to find all this, Sancho? Where? Why, in the great city of El Toboso. Well, who sent you searching after her? The famous knight Don Quixote of La Mancha, who rights wrongs, gives food to those who thirst and drink to the hungry. That's all very well, but do you know her house, Sancho? My master says it will be some royal palace or grand castle. And have you ever seen her, by any chance? Neither I nor my master ever saw her. And does it strike you that it would be just and right if the people of El Toboso, finding out that you were here with the intention of tampering with their princesses and bothering their ladies, were to come and batter your ribs and not leave an unbroken bone in you? They would, indeed, have very good reason, if they did not see that I am under orders, and that 'you are a messenger, my friend, no blame belongs to you.'[1] Don't you depend on that, Sancho; Manchegan people are as hot-tempered as they are honest and won't put up with anything from anybody. By the Lord, if they get wind of you, it will be worse for you, I promise you: 'Get out of here, you son of a bitch!' 'Let lightning strike someone else's house!' Why should I go looking for three feet on a cat, to please another man—especially when looking for Dulcinea will be like looking for a girl named María in Ravenna or a bachelor in Salamanca? The devil, the devil and nobody else, has tangled me up in this!"

Such was the soliloquy Sancho held with himself. "Well," he repeated to himself, by way of conclusion, "there's a remedy for everything except death, under whose yoke we have all to pass, whether we like it or not, when life's finished. I have seen by a thousand signs that this master of mine is a madman fit to be tied, and I don't lag behind him in that respect. I'm a bigger fool than he is when I follow him and serve him, if there's any truth in the proverb that says, 'Tell me what company you keep, and I'll tell you what you are,' or in the other, 'Not with whom you are bred, but with whom you are fed.' Well then, if he is mad, as he is, and with a madness that mostly takes one thing for another, white for black and black for white, as when he said the windmills were giants and the monks' mules dromedaries, flocks of sheep armies of enemies, and much more to the same tune, it will not be very hard to make him believe that some country girl, the first I come across, is the lady Dulcinea. And if he does not believe it, I'll swear it, and if he should swear, I'll swear again, and if he insists I'll insist still more until I've out-argued him. Maybe, by holding out in this way, I may put a stop to his sending me on errands of this kind next time. Or

1. Two lines from one of the Bernardo del Carpio ballads.

maybe he will think, as I suspect he will, that one of those wicked enchanters, who he says have a spite against him, has changed her form in order to do him harm and injure him."

With this reflection Sancho made his mind easy, regarding the affair as good as settled, and stayed there till the afternoon so as to make Don Quixote think he had time enough to go to El Toboso and return. Things turned out so luckily for him that as he got up to mount Dapple he spied, coming from El Toboso toward the spot where he stood, three peasant girls on three colts or fillies; the author does not make the point clear. It is more likely they were she-asses, the usual mount with village girls, but as it is of no great consequence, we need not stop to prove it.

To be brief, the instant Sancho saw the peasant girls, he returned full speed to seek his master and found him sighing and uttering a thousand passionate lamentations.

"What news, Sancho, my friend," Don Quixote exclaimed when he saw him. "Am I to mark this day with a white stone or a black?"

"Your worship," replied Sancho, "had better mark it with red paint like the announcements on the walls of classrooms,[2] so that whoever sees it may see it plain."

"Then you bring good news," said Don Quixote.

"So good," replied Sancho, "that your worship has only to spur Rocinante and get out into the open field to see the lady Dulcinea del Toboso, who with two of her maids is coming to see your wor ship."

"Holy God! What are you saying, Sancho, my friend?" exclaimed Don Quixote. "Take care lest you deceive me or seek by false joy to cheer my real sadness."

"What could I get by deceiving your worship," returned Sancho, "especially when it will soon be obvious whether I am telling the truth or not? Come, señor, spur your horse, and you will see the princess our mistress coming, robed and adorned—in fact, like what she is. Her damsels and she are all one glow of gold, all bunches of pearls, all diamonds, all rubies, all cloth of brocade two inches thick with embroidery.[2] Their hair is loose on their shoulders like so many sunbeams playing with the wind. Moreover, they are mounted on three painted paltries, the finest sight ever you saw."

"*Palfreys*, you mean, Sancho," said Don Quixote.

"There is not much difference between paltries and palfreys," said Sancho. "But no matter what they're riding, there they are, the

1. Names of professors elected to university chairs were painted on the walls.

2. The importance of various types of cloth as an indication of wealth and status is obvious throughout this novel; but the shades of status revealed by buckram, baize, frieze, etc., are now lost on readers. In the original, Sancho exaggerates the quality of Dulcinea's imaginary dress by saying that she has on brocade which is re-embroidered or quilted ten layers deep, when three levels of embroidery or appliqué was the maximum.

finest ladies one could wish for, especially my lady the princess Dulcinea, who staggers one's senses."

"Let us go, Sancho, my son," said Don Quixote, "and in return for this news, as unexpected as it is good, I bestow upon you the best spoil I shall win in the first adventure I may have. Or if that does not satisfy you, I promise you the foals I shall have this year from my three mares that you know are in foal on our village common."

"I'll take the foals," said Sancho, "for it is not quite certain that the spoils of the first adventure will be good ones."

By this time they had left the wood and saw the three village lasses close at hand. Don Quixote looked all along the road to El Toboso, and as he could see nobody except the three peasant girls, he was completely puzzled. He asked Sancho if he had last seen them outside the city.

"What do you mean, outside the city?" returned Sancho. "Are your worship's eyes in the back of your head, that you can't see that they are coming our way, and shining like the sun itself at noonday?"

"I see nothing, Sancho," said Don Quixote, "but three country girls on three jackasses."

"Now, may God deliver me from the devil!" said Sancho. "Can it be that your worship takes three palfreys—or whatever they're called—as white as the driven snow, for jackasses? By the Lord, I could pull out my beard if that was the case!"

"Well, I can only say, Sancho, my friend," said Don Quixote, "that it is as plain they are jackasses—or jennies—as that I am Don Quixote and you Sancho Panza. At any rate, they seem to be so."

"Be quiet, señor," said Sancho, "don't talk that way, but open your eyes, and come and pay your respects to the lady of your thoughts, who is close to us now."

With these words he advanced to receive the three village lasses, and dismounting from Dapple, caught one of the mounts of the three country girls by the halter. "Queen and princess and duchess of beauty," he said, as he dropped on both knees to the ground, "may it please your haughtiness and greatness to receive into your favor and good will your captive knight who stands there turned into marble stone, and quite stupefied and benumbed at finding himself in your magnificent presence. I am Sancho Panza, his squire, and he the vagabond knight Don Quixote of La Mancha, otherwise called the Knight of the Mournful Countenance."

Don Quixote had by this time placed himself on his knees beside Sancho and, with eyes bulging out of his head and a troubled gaze, was staring at her whom Sancho called queen and lady. As he could see nothing in her except a village lass, and not a very good-looking one, for she was dish-faced and snub-nosed, he was perplexed and bewildered and did not venture to open his lips. The country girls, at the same time, were astonished to see these two men, so strange in appearance, on their knees, preventing their companion from going on. But the girl who had been stopped broke the silence.

"Get out of the way, bad luck to you," she said angrily and testily, "and let us pass. We are in a hurry."

"Oh, princess and universal lady of El Toboso," Sancho rejoined, "is not your magnanimous heart softened by seeing the pillar and prop of knight-errantry on his knees before your sublimated presence?"

"Try that line on somebody else!" one of the others exclaimed, when she heard this. "Watch those fancy gents try to make fun of us village girls, as if we couldn't tell 'em a thing or two. Go your own way, and let us go ours, and it will be healthier for you."

"Get up, Sancho," said Don Quixote at this. "I see that 'fortune, with evil done to me unsated still,'[3] has barricaded all the roads by which any comfort may reach this wretched soul I carry in my flesh.

"And thou O highest perfection of excellence that can be desired, utmost limit of grace in human shape, sole relief of this afflicted heart that adores thee, though the malign enchanter that persecutes me has brought clouds and cataracts on my eyes, and to them, and them only, transformed thy unparagoned beauty and changed thy features into those of a poor peasant girl, if so be he has not at the same time changed mine into those of some monster to render them loathsome in thy sight, refuse not to look upon me with tenderness and love. In this submission that I make on my knees to thy transformed beauty, discern the humility with which my soul adores thee."

"Tell that to my grandfather!" cried the girl. "I really like the way you flatter a girl! Now out of the way and let us pass, and we'll thank you."

Sancho stood aside and let her go, very pleased to have gotten out of the tangle he was in. The instant the village lass who had done duty for Dulcinea found herself free, she prodded her "paltry" with a sharp stick and set off at full speed across the field. The she-ass, however, feeling the point more acutely than usual, began cutting such capers that it flung the lady Dulcinea to the ground. Seeing this, Don Quixote ran to help her up, while Sancho fixed and adjusted the packsaddle, which had slipped under the ass's belly. The packsaddle being secured, Don Quixote was about to lift up his enchanted mistress in his arms and put her upon her mount. But the lady, getting up from the ground, saved him the trouble, for, going back a few paces, she took a short run, and putting both hands on the croup of the ass, she vaulted into the saddle more lightly than a falcon, and sat astride like a man.

3. A line from Garcilaso de la Vega's *Egloga III*.

"By St. Roque!" exclaimed Sancho at this. "Our lady is lighter than a hawk, and could teach the most experienced Cordoban or Mexican rider how to mount. She cleared the back of the saddle in one jump, and without spurs she is making the palfrey go like a zebra—and her damsels aren't far behind her, all flying like the wind."

It was true, indeed; for as soon as they saw Dulcinea mounted they pushed on after her and sped away without looking back for more than half a league. Don Quixote followed them with his eyes, and when they were no longer in sight he turned to Sancho.

"Now, Sancho," he said, "do you see how I am hated by enchanters! And see to what a length they go in their malice and spite against me, when they seek to deprive me of the happiness that would be mine in seeing my lady in her own proper form. The fact is I was born to be an example of misfortune, and the target and mark at which the arrows of adversity are aimed and directed. Observe too, Sancho, that these traitors were not content with changing and transforming my Dulcinea, but they transformed and changed her into a shape as vulgar and ugly as that of the village girl yonder, and at the same time they robbed her of that which is such a peculiar property of ladies of distinction, that is to say the sweet fragrance that comes of being always among perfumes and flowers. For I must tell you Sancho, when I approached to put Dulcinea upon her palfrey—as you say it was, though to me it appeared a she-ass—she gave me a whiff of raw garlic that made my head reel and poisoned my very heart."

"O scum of the earth!" cried Sancho at this, "O miserable, spiteful enchanters! O that I could see you all strung by the gills, like sardines on a twig! You know a great deal, you can do a great deal, and you do a great deal more. It ought to have been enough for you. you scoundrels, to have changed the pearls of my lady's eyes into oak galls, and her hair of purest gold into the bristles of a red ox's tail, and in short, all her features from beautiful to ugly, without meddling with her smell, for by that we might somehow have found out what was hidden underneath that ugly rind. Yet, to tell the truth, I never perceived her ugliness, but only her beauty, which was raised to the highest pitch of perfection by a mole she had on her right lip, like a moustache, with seven or eight red hairs like threads of gold, and more than nine inches long."

"From the correspondence which exists between those of the face and those of the body," said Don Quixote, "Dulcinea must have another mole resembling that on her thigh on the same side as the one on her face. But hairs of the length you mentioned are very long for moles."

"Well, all I can say is there they were as plain as could be," replied Sancho.

"I believe it, my friend," returned Don Quixote, "for nature bestowed nothing on Dulcinea that was not perfect and well-finished. Thus, had she a hundred moles like the one you have described, in her they would not be moles but moons and shining stars. But tell me, Sancho, what seemed to me to be a packsaddle while you were fixing it, was it a plain saddle or a sidesaddle?"

"It was neither," replied Sancho, "but a high-backed saddle, with a cover worth half a kingdom, so rich is it."

"And that I could not see all this, Sancho!" said Don Quixote. "Once more I say, and will say a thousand times, I am the most unfortunate of men."

Sancho, the rogue, had enough to do to hide his laughter at hearing the foolish talk of the master he had so skillfully deceived. At length, after a good deal more conversation had passed between them, they remounted their beasts and followed the road to Zaragoza, which they expected to reach in time to take part in a certain festival which is held every year in that illustrious city. But before they got there things happened to them, so many, so important, and so strange that they deserve to be recorded and read, as will be seen farther on.

Chapter XI

OF THE STRANGE ADVENTURE WHICH THE VALIANT DON QUIXOTE HAD WITH THE WAGON OR CART OF "THE PARLIAMENT OF DEATH"

Dejected beyond measure, Don Quixote pursued his journey. He turned over in his mind the cruel trick the enchanters had played on him by changing his lady Dulcinea into the vile shape of the village lass, nor could he think of any way of restoring her to her original form. These reflections so absorbed him that, without being aware of it he let go Rocinante's bridle. The hack, perceiving the liberty granted him, stopped at every step to crop the fresh grass with which the plain abounded. Sancho recalled his master from his reverie.

"Sadness, señor," said he, "was made not for beasts but for men, but if men give in to it they turn beasts. Control yourself, your worship, be yourself again, gather up Rocinante's reins. Cheer up, perk up, and show that gallant spirit that knights-errant ought to have. What the devil is this? What discouragement is this? Are we here or in France? The devil take all the Dulcineas in the world, for the well-being of a single knight-errant is of more consequence than all the enchantments and transformations on earth."

"Hush, Sancho," said Don Quixote in not too faint a voice, "hush and utter no blasphemies against that enchanted lady. I alone am to blame for her misfortune and hard fate; her calamity has come from the hatred the wicked bear me."

"That's what I say," returned Sancho. " 'His heart would weep, I vow, who saw her once, to see her now.' "

"You may well say that, Sancho," replied Don Quixote, "as you saw her in the full perfection of her beauty. The enchantment does not go so far as to pervert your vision or hide her loveliness from you; against me alone and against my eyes is the strength of its venom directed. Nevertheless, there is one thing which has occurred to me, and that is that you did not well describe her beauty to me, for, as I recollect, you said that her eyes were pearls. But eyes like pearls are rather the eyes of a sea bream than of a lady, and I am persuaded that Dulcinea's must be green emeralds, full and soft, with two rainbows for eyebrows. Take away those pearls from her eyes and transfer them to her teeth, for beyond a doubt, Sancho, you have taken the one for the other, the eyes for the teeth."

"Very likely," said Sancho, "for her beauty bewildered me as much as her ugliness did your worship. But let us leave it all to God, who alone knows what is to happen in this vale of tears, in this evil world of ours, where there is hardly a thing to be found without some mixture of wickedness, roguery, and rascality. But one thing, señor, troubles me more than all the rest, and that is thinking what is to be done when your worship conquers some giant or some other knight and orders him to go and present himself before the beauty of the lady Dulcinea. Where is this poor giant or this poor wretch of a vanquished knight to find her? I think I can see them wandering all over El Toboso looking stupid and asking for my lady Dulcinea. Even if they meet her in the middle of the street they won't know her any more than they would my father."

"Perhaps, Sancho," returned Don Quixote, "the enchantment does not go so far as to prevent conquered and presented giants and knights from recognizing Dulcinea. We will experiment with one or two of the first I vanquish and send to her, whether they see her or not, by commanding them to return and give me an account of what happened."

"I declare, I think what your worship has proposed is excellent," said Sancho, "and that by this plan we shall find out what we want to know. If it turns out that she is hidden only from your worship, the misfortune will be more yours than hers. But so long as the lady Dulcinea is well and happy, we for our part will make the best of it and get on as well as we can, seeking our adventures and leaving Time to take his own course. He is the best physician for these and greater ailments."

Don Quixote was about to reply to Sancho Panza when he noticed crossing the road a cart full of the strangest and most varied personages and figures that could be imagined. The creature who led the mules and acted as carter was a hideous demon; the cart was open to the sky, without any framework or covering. The first figure

Don Quixote's eyes lit upon was that of Death itself with a human face, next to it was an angel with large painted wings, and at one side an emperor with a crown, to all appearance of gold, on his head. At the feet of Death was the god called Cupid, not blindfolded, but with his bow, quiver, and arrows. There was also a knight in full armor, except that he had no morion or helmet, but only a hat decked with plumes of different colors, and along with these were others with a variety of costumes and faces.

All this, unexpectedly encountered, took Don Quixote somewhat aback and intimidated Sancho. But the next instant Don Quixote was glad of it, believing that some new perilous adventure was presenting itself to him. Under this impression, and with a spirit prepared to face any danger, he planted himself in front of the cart and spoke in a loud and menacing tone. "Carter, or coachman, or devil, or whatever thou art," he said, "tell me at once who thou art, whither thou art going, and who these folk are thou carriest in thy wagon, which looks more like Charon's boat than an ordinary cart."

At this the devil stopped the cart. "Señor," he answered quietly, "we are players of Angulo el Malo's[1] company. We have been acting the play of 'The Parliament of Death'[2] this morning, which is the octave of Corpus Christi, in a village behind that hill, and we have to act it this afternoon in that village which you can see from here. Because it is so near, and to save the trouble of undressing and dressing again we are in the costumes in which we perform. That lad there appears as Death, that other as an angel, that woman, the manager's wife, plays the queen, this one the soldier, that the emperor, and I am the devil. I am one of the principal characters of the play, for in this company I take the leading parts. If you want to know anything more about us, ask me and I will answer with the utmost exactitude, for as I am a devil I am up on everything!"

"By the faith of a knight-errant," replied Don Quixote, "when I saw this cart I fancied some great adventure was presenting itself to me, but I declare one must touch with the hand what appears to the eye, if illusions are to be avoided. God speed you, good people, keep your festival. And remember, if you ask of me any service I can render you, I will do it gladly, for as a child I was fond of plays and in my youth a keen lover of the actor's art."

While they were talking, fate so willed it that one of the company in a jester's costume, with a great number of bells and armed with three blown ox-bladders on the end of a stick, joined them. Approaching Don Quixote, this clown began flourishing his stick and banging the ground with the bladders and cutting capers with great jingling of the bells. The sinister apparition so startled Roci-

1. Andrés de Angulo, a real theatrical manager who flourished about 1580.

2. Perhaps the play of that name by Lope de Vega.

nante that, in spite of Don Quixote's efforts to hold him in, he took the bit between his teeth and set off across the plain with greater speed than the bones of his anatomy ever gave any promise of. Sancho, who thought his master was in danger of being thrown, jumped off Dapple, and ran in all haste to help him, but by the time he reached him Don Quixote was already on the ground. Beside him was Rocinante, who had come down with his master, the usual end and upshot of Rocinante's boldness and daring.

But the moment Sancho dismounted from his beast to go and help Don Quixote, the dancing devil with the bladders jumped up on Dapple. Beating him with them, and more by means of fright and the noise than by the pain of the blows, he made him fly across the fields toward the village where they were going to hold their festival. Sancho witnessed Dapple's race and his master's fall and did not know which of the two cases of need he should attend to first. In the end, like a good squire and good servant, he let his love for his master prevail over his affection for the ass, though every time he saw the bladders rise in the air and come down on the hind quarters of his Dapple he felt the pains and terrors of death, and would rather have had the blows fall on his own eyeballs than on the least hair of the ass's tail. In this trouble and perplexity he came to where Don Quixote lay in a far sorrier plight than he liked, and helped him to mount Rocinante.

"Señor," he said to him, "the devil has carried off my Dapple."

"What devil?" asked Don Quixote.

"The one with the bladders," said Sancho.

"Then I will recover him," said Don Quixote, "even if he be shut up with him in the deepest and darkest dungeons of hell. Follow me, Sancho, for the cart goes slowly, and with the mules of it I can make good the loss of Dapple."

"You need not take the trouble, señor," said Sancho. "Keep cool, for as I now see, the devil has let Dapple go, and he is coming back to his old quarters." So it turned out, for, having taken a fall with Dapple, in imitation of Don Quixote and Rocinante, the devil made off on foot to the town, and the ass came back to his master.

"For all that," said Don Quixote, "it will be well to avenge the discourtesy of that devil upon some of those in the cart, even if it were the emperor himself."

"Don't think of it, your worship," returned Sancho. "Take my advice and never meddle with actors, for they are a privileged class, and I myself have known an actor arrested for two murders, and let off scot-free. Remember that, as they are good-humored people who give pleasure, everyone favors and protects them, and helps and makes much of them, above all when they are those of royal companies and under patent, all or most of whom in dress and appearance look like princes."

"Still, for all that," said Don Quixote, "the player devil must not go off boasting, even if the whole human race favors him."

So saying, he headed for the cart, which was now very near the town, shouting out as he went. "Stay! halt! ye merry, jovial crew! I want to teach you how to treat asses and animals that serve as steeds to the squires of knights-errant."

So loud were the shouts of Don Quixote, that those in the cart heard and understood them. Guessing by the words what the speaker's intention was, Death in an instant jumped out of the cart. The emperor, the devil carter, and the angel followed after him, nor did the queen or the god Cupid stay behind. They all armed themselves with stones and formed a line, prepared to receive Don Quixote on the points of their pebbles. Don Quixote, when he saw them drawn up in such a gallant array with uplifted arms ready for a mighty discharge of stones, checked Rocinante and began to consider in what way he could attack them with the least danger to himself. As he halted Sancho came up and saw that he was about to attack this well-ordered squadron. "It would be the height of madness to attempt such an enterprise," Sancho declared. "Remember, señor, that against a shower of rocks there is no defensive armor in the world except to hide under a brass bell. Besides, one should remember that it is rashness, not valor, for a single man to attack an army that has Death in it, and where emperors fight in person with angels, good and bad, to help them. If this reflection will not make you keep quiet, perhaps the sure knowledge will suffice that among them all, though they look like kings, princes, and emperors, there is not a single knight-errant."

"Now indeed you have hit the point, Sancho," said Don Quixote, "which may and should turn me from the resolution I had already formed. I cannot and must not draw sword, as I have many a time before told you, against anyone who is not a dubbed knight. It is for you, Sancho, if you will, to avenge the wrong done your Dapple. I will help you from here by shouts and salutary counsels."

"There is no occasion to take vengeance on anyone, señor," replied Sancho. "It is not the part of good Christians to revenge wrongs, and besides, I will arrange it with my mount to leave his grievance to my good will and pleasure, which is to live in peace as long as heaven grants me life."

"Well," said Don Quixote, "if that is your resolve, good Sancho, sensible Sancho, Christian Sancho, honest Sancho, let us leave these phantoms alone and turn to the pursuit of better and worthier adventures. From what I see of this country, we cannot fail to find plenty of marvelous ones in it."

He at once wheeled about, Sancho ran to take possession of his Dapple, and Death and his flying squadron returned to their cart and pursued their journey. Thus the dread adventure of the cart of

Death ended happily, thanks to the advice Sancho gave his master, who had, the folowing day, a fresh adventure, of no less thrilling interest than the last, with an enamored knight-errant.

Chapter XII

OF THE STRANGE ADVENTURE WHICH BEFELL THE VALIANT DON QUIXOTE WITH THE BOLD KNIGHT OF THE MIRRORS

The night succeeding the day of the encounter with Death, Don Quixote and his squire spent under some tall shady trees. Don Quixote, at Sancho's persuasion, ate a little from the store carried by Dapple.

"Señor," Sancho said to his master as they were eating, "what a fool I would have been if I had chosen for my reward the spoils of the first adventure your worship achieved, instead of the foals of the three mares. After all, 'a bird in the hand is better than two in the bush.' "

"At the same time, Sancho," replied Don Quixote, "if you had let me attack them as I wanted, at the very least the emperor's gold crown and Cupid's painted wings would have fallen to you as spoils. I would have taken them by force and given them into your hands."

"The scepters and crowns of those play-actor emperors," said Sancho, "are never pure gold, but only brass foil or tin."

"That is true," said Don Quixote, "for it would not be right that the accessories of the drama should be real and not mere fictions and semblances like the drama itself. Toward that, Sancho—and, as a necessary consequence, toward those who represent and produce it—I would you were favorably disposed, for they are all instruments of great good to the State. At every step they set before us a mirror in which we may see vividly displayed what goes on in human life, nor is there any likeness that shows us more faithfully what we are and ought to be than play and players. Tell me, have you not seen a play acted in which kings, emperors, pontiffs, knights, ladies, and sundry other personages were introduced? One plays the villain, another the knave, this one the merchant, that the soldier, one the sharp-witted fool, another the foolish lover. And when the play is over, and they have put off the costumes they wore in it, all the actors become equal."

"Yes, I have seen that," said Sancho.

"Well then," said Don Quixote, "the same thing happens in the comedy and life of this world, where some play emperors, others popes and, in short, all the characters that can be brought into a play. But when it is over, that is to say when life ends, death strips them all of the garments that distinguish one from the other, and all are equal in the grave."

"A fine comparison!" said Sancho, "though not so new but that I have heard it quite a number of times, as well as the other from the game of chess. While the game lasts, each piece plays its own part, and when the game is finished they are all mixed, jumbled up, and shaken together, and stowed away in the bag, which is much like ending life in the grave."

"You are growing less stupid and more sensible every day, Sancho," said Don Quixote.

"Yes," said Sancho, "it must be that some of your worship's discretion sticks to me. Land that, of itself, is barren and dry, will yield good fruit if you fertilize it and till it. What I mean is that your worship's conversation is the fertilizer that has fallen on the barren soil of my dry wit, and the time I have spent in your service and company has been the tillage. With such help I hope to yield fruit in abundance that will not fall or slip away from those paths of good breeding your worship has made in my parched understanding."

Don Quixote laughed at Sancho's affected phraseology and realized that what he said about his improvement was true, for now and then he spoke in a way that surprised him. But always, or mostly, when Sancho tried to talk fine and attempted polite language, he wound up by toppling from the summit of his simplicity into the abyss of his ignorance. Where he showed his culture and his memory to the greatest advantage was in dragging in proverbs, whether or not they had any bearing on the subject in hand, as may have been seen already and will be noticed in the course of this history.

In conversation of this kind they passed a good part of the night, but Sancho felt a desire to let down the curtains of his eyes, as he used to say when he wanted to go to sleep. So he stripped Dapple and left him at liberty to graze his fill. He did not remove Rocinante's saddle, as his master's express orders were that so long as they were in the field or not sleeping under a roof, Rocinante was not to be stripped. It was the ancient usage established and observed by knights-errant to take off the bridle and hang it on the saddle-bow, but to remove the saddle from the horse—never! Sancho acted accordingly and gave him the same liberty he had given Dapple, between whom and Rocinante there was a friendship so unequaled and so strong that it is handed down by tradition from father to son.

The author of this true history devoted some special chapters to it which, in order to preserve the propriety and decorum due a history so heroic, he did not insert therein. Yet at times he forgets this resolution of his and describes how eagerly the two beasts would scratch one another when they were together and how, when they were tired or full, Rocinante would lay his neck across Dapple's, stretching half a yard or more on the other side. The pair would stand thus, gazing thoughtfully on the ground, for three days, or at least so long as they were left alone, or hunger did not drive them to go and look for food. I may add that they say the author left it on record that he likened their friendship to that of Nisus and Euryalus, and Pylades and Orestes.[1] If that is so it may be perceived, to the admiration of mankind, how firm the friendship must have been between these two peaceful animals, shaming men, who preserve friendships with one another so badly. This was why it was said—

> For friend no longer is there friend;
> The reeds turn lances now.[2]

And someone else has sung—

> Friend is wary of friend . . .[3]

Let no one fancy that the author was at all astray when he compared the friendship of these animals to that of men. Men have received many lessons from beasts and learned many important things, for example, the enema from the stork, vomit and gratitude from the dog, watchfulness from the crane, foresight from the ant, modesty from the elephant, and loyalty from the horse.[4]

Sancho at last fell asleep at the foot of a cork tree, while Don Quixote dozed beneath a sturdy oak. But only a short time had elapsed when a noise coming from the rear awoke him. He was startled and rose to his feet. Listening and looking in the direction of the noise, he perceived two men on horseback, one of whom let himself drop from the saddle.

"Dismount, my friend," he said to the other man, "and take the bridles off the horses. So far as I can see, this place will provide grass for them and the solitude and silence my lovesick thoughts have need of."

Saying this he stretched himself upon the ground. As he flung himself down, the armor he was wearing rattled, revealing to Don Quixote that he must be a knight-errant. Don Quixote went over to Sancho, who was asleep, shook him by the arm, and with no small difficulty brought him back to his senses. "Brother Sancho," he said to him in a low voice, "we have got an adventure."

"God send us a good one," said Sancho. "And where may her ladyship madam adventure be?"

1. Classical examples of friendship, the first made famous by the *Aeneid*, the second from various Greek writers.

2. Lines from a ballad on the civil wars among Moors of southern Spain. The "reeds" are untipped lances used in friendly war games.

3. The probable meaning of an obscure phrase.

4. These famous "bestiary" examples probably came from a popular miscellany called *Silva de varia lección*. The stork was supposed to use its beak as an enema, the dog to force itself to vomit, the crane to stand guard with a stone in one claw which it would drop if it dozed, the ant to store food, the elephant to mate in secret, etc.

"Where, Sancho?" replied Don Quixote. "Turn your eyes and look, and you will see a knight-errant stretched there. It strikes me that he is not overly happy. I saw him fling himself off his horse and throw himself on the ground with a certain air of dejection, and his armor rattled as he fell."

"Well," said Sancho, "how does your worship deduce that this is an adventure?"

"I do not mean to say," returned Don Quixote, "that it is a complete adventure, but that it is the beginning of one, for that is the way adventures begin. But listen, for it seems he is tuning a lute or guitar, and from the way he is spitting and clearing his throat he must be getting ready to sing something."

"Faith, you are right," said Sancho, "No doubt he is some enamored knight."

"Every knight-errant is enamored," said Don Quixote. "But let us listen to him for, if he sings, by that thread we shall be led to the spool of his thoughts. 'Out of the abundance of the heart the mouth speaketh.' "

Sancho was about to reply to his master, but he was stopped by the Knight of the Grove's voice, which was neither very bad nor very good. Listening attentively the pair heard him sing this

SONNET

Your pleasure, prithee, lady mine, unfold;
Declare the terms that I am to obey;
My will to yours submissively I mold,
And from your law my feet shall never stray.
Do you desire me dead, to grief a prey?
Then count me even now as dead and cold;
Would you I tell my woes in some new way?
Then shall my tale by Love itself be told.
The unison of opposites to prove,
Of softest wax and diamond hard am I;
But still, obedient to the laws of love,
Here, hard or soft, I offer you my breast,
Whate'er you grave or stamp thereon shall rest
Indelible for all eternity.

With an "Ah me!" that seemed to come from the inmost recesses of his heart, the Knight of the Grove brought his lay to an end. A little while later he spoke, in a melancholy and piteous voice. "O fairest and most ungrateful woman on earth!" he exclaimed. "Can it be, most serene Casildea de Vandalia, that you will suffer this your captive knight to waste away and perish in ceaseless wanderings and rude and arduous toils? It is not enough that I have compelled all the knights of Navarre, all the Leonese, all the Andalusians, all the

Castilians, and finally all the knights of La Mancha, to confess you the most beautiful in the world?"

"Not so," said Don Quixote at this, "for I am from La Mancha, and I have never confessed anything of the sort, nor could I nor should I confess a thing so much to the prejudice of my lady's beauty. You see how this knight is raving, Sancho. But let us listen, perhaps he will tell us more about himself."

"That he will," returned Sancho, "for he seems in a mood to bewail himself for a month at a stretch."

But this was not the case, for the Knight of the Grove, hearing voices near him, instead of continuing his lamentation, stood up and spoke in a distinct but courteous tone.

"Who goes there?" he asked, "And who are you? Do you belong to the number of the happy or of the miserable?"

"Of the miserable," answered Don Quixote.

"Then come to me," said he of the Grove, "and rest assured that you come to woe and to affliction itself."

Don Quixote, finding himself answered in such a soft and courteous manner, went over to him, as did Sancho, whereupon the doleful knight took Don Quixote by the arm.

"Sit down here, sir knight," he said. "For that you are such, and of those who profess knight-errantry, is sufficiently proved by my finding you in this place where solitude and night, the natural couch and proper retreat of knights-errant, keep you company."

"A knight I am," said Don Quixote in reply, "of the profession you mention, and though sorrows, misfortunes, and calamities have made my heart their abode, the compassion I feel for the misfortunes of others has not been thereby banished from it. From what you have just now sung I gather that yours spring from love, I mean from the love you bear that fair ingrate you named in your lament."

In the meantime they had seated themselves together on the hard ground peaceably and sociably, just as if, as soon as day broke, they were not going to break one another's heads.

"Are you, sir knight, in love perchance?" asked he of the Grove of Don Quixote.

"By mischance I am," replied Don Quixote, "though the ills arising from well-bestowed affections should be esteemed favors rather than misfortunes."

"That is true," returned the Knight of the Grove, "if rejection did not unsettle our reason and understanding, for if it is excessive it looks like revenge."

"I was never rejected by my lady," said Don Quixote.

"Certainly not," said Sancho, who stood close by, "for my lady is gentle as a lamb and softer than a roll of butter."

"Is this your squire?" asked the Knight of the Grove.

"He is," said Don Quixote.

"I never yet saw a squire," said the Knight, "who ventured to speak when his master was speaking. At least there is mine, who is as big as his father, and it cannot be proved that he has ever opened his lips when I am speaking."

"By my failth then," said Sancho, "I have spoken and am fit to speak in the presence of one as much, or even—but never mind—it only makes it worse to stir it."

At that, the Squire of the Grove took Sancho by the arm. "Let us two go where we can talk in squire style as much as we please," he said, "and leave these gentlemen our masters to fight it out over the story of their loves. Depend on it, daybreak will find them still at it without having made an end."

"By all means," said Sancho. "I will tell your worship who I am, and you will see whether I am to be reckoned among the number of the most talkative squires."

With this the two squires withdrew to one side, and between them there passed a conversation as funny as that between their masters was serious.

Chapter XIII

IN WHICH IS CONTINUED THE ADVENTURE OF THE KNIGHT OF THE GROVE, TOGETHER WITH THE CLEVER ORIGINAL, AND TRANQUIL COLLOQUY THAT PASSED BETWEEN THE TWO SQUIRES

The knights and the squires made up two groups, the latter telling the story of their lives and the former the story of their loves, but the history relates first of all the conversation of the servants and afterwards takes up that of the masters. It says that the Squire of the Grove withdrew a little from the others before speaking to Sancho.

"A hard life it is we lead and live, señor," he said, "we that are squires to knights-errant. Truly we eat our bread in the sweat of our faces, which is one of the curses God laid on our first parents."

"It may be said, too," added Sancho, "that we eat it in the chill of our bodies, for who gets more heat and cold than the miserable squires of knight-errantry? Even so it would not be so bad if we had something to eat, for troubles seem less serious if there's bread. But sometimes we go a day or two without breaking our fast, except with the wind that blows."

"All that," said the Squire of the Grove, "may be endured and put up with when we have hopes of reward. Unless the knight-errant he serves is excessively unlucky, after a few turns the squire will at least find himself rewarded with a fine government of some island or some fair county."

"I," said Sancho, "have already told my master that I shall be content with the government of some island, and he is so noble and generous that he has promised it to me many times."

"I," said he of the Grove, "will be satisfied with a canonry for my services, and my master has already assigned me one."

"Your master," said Sancho, "no doubt is a knight in the Church line, and can bestow rewards of that sort on his good squire. Mine is only a layman, though I remember some clever but, to my mind, designing people strove to persuade him to try and become an archbishop. He, however, desires only to be an emperor, but I was trembling all the time that he might take a fancy to go into the Church, not finding myself fit to hold office in it. For I may tell you, though I look like a man, I am no better than a beast for the Church."

"Well, you are wrong there," said the Squire of the Grove, "for those island governments are not all satisfactory. Some are misshapen, some are poor, some are gloomy, and, in short, the tallest and best looking brings with it a heavy burden of cares and troubles. The unhappy man to whose lot it has fallen bears all that upon his shoulders. It would be far better for us in this accursed service to return to our houses and there employ ourselves in pleasanter occupations—in hunting or fishing, for instance. What squire in the world is so poor as not to have a hack and a couple of greyhounds and a fishing pole to amuse himself with in his own village?"

"I don't lack any of those things," said Sancho. "It's true I don't have a horse, but I have an ass that is worth two of my master's. God send me a bad Easter, and the next one at that, if I would make the swap, even with four bushels of barley thrown in. You will laugh at the value I put on my Dapple—for dapple is the color of my beast. As for greyhounds, there's no lack of them, for there are enough and to spare in my town. Besides, it's more fun to hunt when it is at other people's expense."

"In truth and earnest, sir squire," said he of the Grove, "I am firmly resolved to have done with the drunken vagaries of these knights, to go back to my village and bring up my children. For I have three, like three Oriental pearls."

"I have two," said Sancho, "that might be presented before the Pope himself, especially a girl whom I am raising to be a countess, please God, though in spite of her mother."

"And how old is this lady that is being brought up to be a countess?" asked the Squire of the Grove.

"Fifteen, a couple of years more or less," answered Sancho. "But she is as tall as a lance, and as fresh as an April morning, and as strong as a porter."

"Such endowments fit her to be not only a countess but a nymph of the greenwood," said the Squire of the Grove. "By God, I'll bet the little bitch is as strong as an ox!"

"She's no bitch, nor was her mother, nor will either of them be, please God, while I live," replied Sancho, somewhat offended. "Speak more politely, for in a man raised among knights-errant, who are courtesy itself, your words don't seem to me to fit the occasion."

"How little you know about compliments, sir squire," rejoined the Squire of the Grove. "What, don't you know that when a horseman delivers a good lance thrust at the bull in the plaza, or when anyone does anything very well, people often say, 'Oh, the son of a bitch! How well he has done it!' and that what seems to be an insult in the expression is high praise? Disown sons and daughters, señor, who don't do what calls for compliments of this sort to be paid their parents."

"I do disown them," replied Sancho, "and in this way, and by the same reasoning, you could call me and my children and my wife bitches and sons of bitches, for all they do and say in the highest degree deserves such praise. To see them again I pray God deliver me from mortal sin or, what comes to the same thing, from this perilous calling of squire into which I have fallen a second time, lured and beguiled by a purse with a hundred ducats I found one day in the heart of the Sierra Morena. The devil is always putting a bag full of doubloons in front of my eyes, here, there, everywhere until I imagine at every step I am putting my hand on it and hugging it, and carrying it home with me, and making investments, and getting interest, and living like a prince. So long as I think of this I make light of all the hardships I endure with this crazy master of mine who, I well know, is more of a madman than a knight."

"That's why they say 'greed bursts the bag,' " said the Squire of the Grove. "But if we are to talk of them, there is not a bigger madman in the world than my master, for he is the kind that makes people say, 'other men's problems kill the ass.' The reason he is pretending to be crazy is to enable another knight to recover his lost senses. For all I can tell, when he finds what he's looking for, it may blow up in his face."

"And is he in love, by any chance?" asked Sancho.

"He is," said the Squire of the Grove, "with a certain Casildea de Vandalia, the cruelest and kindest lady the world could produce.[1] But the cruel mistress business is not the foot he limps on, for he has greater schemes rumbling in his innards, as will be seen before many hours are over."

"There's no road so smooth but it has some hole or rut in it," said Sancho. "We all have our troubles, even if I have them by the potful. Madness will have more followers and hangers-on than good sense. But if there is any truth in the common saying that to have

1. An untranslatable pun on *crudo,* "cruel" and "raw": "The rawest and most cooked lady in the world."

someone to share your troubles gives relief, I can take consolation from you, since you serve a master as crazy as my own."

"Crazy but valiant," replied the Squire of the Grove, "and more roguish than crazy or valiant."

"Mine is not that," said Sancho, "I mean he has nothing of the rogue in him. On the contrary, he is the soul of goodness, with no thought of doing harm to anyone, only good to all, nor has he any malice whatever in him. A child might persuade him it is night at noonday, and for this simplicity of mind I love him like my heart's core, and I can't bring myself to leave him, no matter what foolish things he may do."

"For all that, brother and señor," said the Squire of the Grove, "if the blind lead the blind, both are in danger of falling into the ditch. We had better beat a quiet retreat and get back to our own quarters, for those who seek adventures don't always find good ones."

Sancho kept spitting from time to time, and his spittle seemed somewhat thick and dry.

"It seems to me," said the compassionate Squire of the Grove, when he observed this, "that with all this talk of ours our tongues are sticking to the roofs of our mouths, but I have a pretty good loosener hanging from the saddle-bow of my horse."

He stood up and came back the next minute with a large flask of wine and a meat pie half a yard across. This is no exaggeration, for it was made of a white rabbit so big that Sancho, as he handled it, took it to be made of a goat, not to say a kid. "So this is what you carry with you, señor?" he asked, as he caught sight of it.

"Why, what are you thinking about?" said the other. "Do you take me for some paltry squire? I carry a better larder on my horse's croup than a general takes with him when he goes on a march."

Sancho ate without being urged, and in the dark bolted mouthfuls the size of knots on a tether.

"You are a trusty squire," he said, "one of the right sort, splendid and lavish, as this banquet shows. If it did not arrive by magic, at least it looks as if it had. Not like me, unlucky beggar, with no more in my saddlebags than a scrap of cheese, so hard one might brain a giant with it, and for company a few dozen carob beans and about as many filberts and walnuts. This I owe to my master's austerity, and to the idea he has and the rule he follows that knights-errant must not live or sustain themselves on anything except dried fruits and the herbs of the field."

"By my faith, brother," said the Squire of the Grove, "my stomach is not made for thistles or wild pears or roots of the woods. Let our masters do as they like, with their chivalrous notions and laws, and eat what is there ordained. I carry my food basket and this flask hanging from the saddle-bow, whatever they may say. It is such an object of worship with me, and I love it so, that there is hardly a moment but I am kissing and embracing it over and over again."

So saying he thrust it into Sancho's hands, who raised it, pointed it at his mouth, and gazed at the stars for a quarter of an hour. When he had done drinking, he let his head fall on one side and gave a deep sigh. "Oh, the son of a bitch, how good it is!" he exclaimed.

"There, you see," said he of the Grove, hearing Sancho's exclamation, "you called the wine a son of a bitch by way of praise."

"I admit that," said Sancho, "and grant it is no dishonor to call anyone a son of a bitch when it is to be understood as praise. But tell me, señor, by what you love best, is this Ciudad Real wine?"

"What a winetaster!" said the Squire of the Grove. "It's from there and nowhere else, and it has some years' age too."

"Trust me for that," said Sancho. "Never fear, I'll hit upon the place it came from somehow. What would you say, sir squire, to my having such a great natural instinct in judging wines that you need only let me smell one and I can tell positively its region, its kind, its flavor and age, the changes it will undergo, and everything that has to do with a wine? But it is no wonder, for I have had in my family, on my father's side, the two best winetasters seen in La Mancha for many a long year. To prove it, I'll tell you a thing that happened to them. They gave the two of them some wine out of a cask to taste, asking their opinion as to the condition, quality, goodness or badness of the wine. One of them tried it with the tip of his tongue, the other did no more than bring it to his nose. The first said the wine had a flavor of iron, the second said it had a stronger flavor of cordovan leather. The owner said the cask was clean, and that nothing had been added to the wine from which it could have got a flavor of either iron or leather. Nevertheless, these two great winetasters stuck by what they had said. Time went by, the wine was sold, and when they came to clean out the cask, they found in it a small key hanging to a thong of cordovan. Judge for yourself if one who comes of the same stock has not a right to give his opinion in such cases."

"That is why I say," said the Squire of the Grove, "we should give up seeking after adventures. Since we have loaves let us not go looking for cakes but return to our humble abodes, for God will find us there if it is his will."

"Until my master reaches Zaragoza," said Sancho, "I'll remain in his service. After that we'll see."

The end of it was that the two squires talked so much and drank so much that sleep had to tie their tongues and moderate their thirst, for to quench it was impossible. And so the pair of them fell asleep clinging to the now nearly empty flask and with half-chewed morsels in their mouths. There we will leave them for the present and relate what passed between the Knight of the Grove and the Knight of the Mournful Countenance.

Chapter XIV

WHEREIN IS CONTINUED THE ADVENTURE OF THE KNIGHT OF THE GROVE

Of the many things that were a matter for discussion between Don Quixote and the Knight of the Grove, the history relates that the latter addressed these words to Don Quixote.

"In a word, sir knight," he said, "I would have you know that my destiny or, more properly speaking, my choice led me to fall in love with the peerless Casildea de Vandalia. I call her peerless because she has no peer, whether it be in bodily stature or in the supremacy of rank and beauty. This same Casildea, then, that I speak of, requited my honorable passion and worthy aspirations by compelling me, as his stepmother did Hercules, to engage in many perils of various sorts. At the end of each she promised me that, with the end of the next, the object of my hopes should be attained, but my labors have increased link by link until they are past counting, nor do I know what will be the last that will signal the moment for the accomplishment of my chaste desires.

"On one occasion she bade me challenge the famous giantess of Seville, La Giralda by name, who is as mighty and strong as if made of brass, and though never stirring from one spot, is the most restless and changeable woman in the world.[1] I came, I saw, I conquered, and I made her stay quiet and behave herself, for nothing but north winds blew for more than a week. Another time I was ordered to lift those ancient stones, the mighty bulls of Guisando,[2] an enterprise that might more fitly be entrusted to porters than to knights. Again, she bade me fling myself into the cavern of Cabra[3] —an unparalleled and awful peril—and bring her a minute account of all that is concealed in those gloomy depths. I stopped the motion of the Giralda, I lifted the bulls of Guisando, I flung myself into the cavern and brought to light the secrets of its abyss, yet my hopes are as dead as dead can be, and her scorn and her commands as lively as ever.

"To be brief, last of all she has commanded me to go through all the provinces of Spain and compel all the knights-errant wandering therein to confess that she surpasses all women alive today in beauty, and that I am the most valiant and the most deeply enam-

1. The colossal brass statue standing on a globe that acts as a weathercock on the top of the belfry of the Cathedral of Seville.

2. Large pre-Roman statues of bulls, the most famous of a number of such Iberian sculptures, the purpose of which is unknown.

3. A chasm in the Sierra de Cabra, south of Córdoba, probably the shaft of an ancient mine.

ored knight on earth. In support of this claim I have already traveled over the greater part of Spain and have vanquished several knights who have dared to contradict me. But what I most plume and pride myself upon is having vanquished in single combat that famous knight Don Quixote of La Mancha, and made him confess that my Casildea is more beautiful than his Dulcinea. In this one victory I consider myself to have conquered all the knights in the world, for this Don Quixote that I speak of has vanquished them all, and now that I have vanquished him, his glory, his fame, and his honor have passed and are transferred to my person, for

> The more the vanquished hath of fair renown,
> The greater glory gilds the victor's crown.[4]

Thus the innumerable achievements of the said Don Quixote are now set down to my account and have become mine."

Don Quixote was amazed when he heard the Knight of the Grove and was a thousand times on the point of telling him he lied, and had the words already on the tip of his tongue. But he restrained himself as well as he could, in order to force him to confess the lie with his own lips.

"As to what you say, sir knight," he said to him quietly, "about having vanquished most of the knights of Spain, or even of the whole world, I say nothing, but that you have vanquished Don Quixote of La Mancha I consider doubtful. It may have been some other that resembled him, although there are few like him."

"What do you mean, not vanquished him?" said the Knight of the Grove. "By the heaven that is above us I fought Don Quixote and overcame him and made him yield. He is a man of tall stature, gaunt features, long, lank limbs, with hair turning grey, an aquiline nose rather hooked, and large black drooping mustache. He does battle under the name of 'The Knight of Mournful Countenance,' and has for squire a peasant called Sancho Panza. He presses the loins and rules the reins of a famous steed called Rocinante, and lastly he has for the mistress of his will a certain Dulcinea del Toboso, once upon a time called Aldonza Lorenzo, just as I call mine Casildea de Vandalia because her name is Casilda and she is from Andalusia. If all these tokens are not enough to vindicate the truth of what I say, here is my sword, that will compel incredulity itself to give credence to it."

"Calm yourself, sir knight," said Don Quixote, "and give ear to what I am about to say to you. I would have you know that this Don Quixote you speak of is the greatest friend I have in the world, so much so that I may say I regard him in the same light as my own person. From the precise and clear indications you have given, I cannot but think that he must be the very one you have van-

4. Lines from *La Araucana* of Ercilla.

quished. On the other hand, I see with my eyes and feel with my hands that it cannot possibly have been the same—unless indeed, since he has many enemies who are enchanters, and one in particular who is always persecuting him, one of them may have taken his shape in order to let himself be vanquished, so as to defraud him of the fame that his exalted achievements as a knight have earned and acquired for him throughout the known world. In confirmation of this, I must tell you, too, that it is but ten hours since these said enchanters his enemies transformed the shape and person of the fair Dulcinea del Toboso into a dirty and common village lass, and in the same way they must have transformed Don Quixote. If all this does not suffice to convince you of the truth of what I say, here is Don Quixote himself, who will maintain it by arms, on foot or on horseback or in any way you please."

So saying he stood up and laid his hand on his sword, waiting to see what the other would do.

"An honest man backs up his word," the Knight of the Grove replied in an equally calm voice. "He who has succeeded in vanquishing you once when transformed, Sir Don Quixote, may fairly hope to subdue you in your own proper shape. But as it is not becoming for knights to perform their feats of arms in the dark, like highwaymen and bullies, let us wait till daylight so that the sun may behold our deeds. The conditions of our combat shall be that the vanquished shall be at the victor's disposal, to do all that he may enjoin, provided the injunction be such as shall be becoming a knight."

"I am more than satisfied with these conditions and terms," replied Don Quixote. That having been said, they betook themselves to where their squires lay, and found them snoring and in the same posture as when sleep overcame them. They roused the squires up and told them to get the horses ready, as at sunrise they were to engage in a bloody and arduous single combat. At this piece of news Sancho was aghast and thunderstruck, trembling for his master's safety because of the mighty deeds he had heard the Squire of the Grove ascribe to his. But without a word the two squires went in quest of their beasts, for by this time the three horses and the ass had smelled one another out and were all together.

On the way, the Squire of the Grove spoke to Sancho. "You must know, brother," he said, "that it is the custom with the fighting men of Andalusia, when they are seconds in any duel, not to stand idle with folded arms while the principals fight. I say so to remind you that while our masters are fighting, we, too, have to fight and knock one another to pieces."

"That custom, sir squire," replied Sancho, "may hold good among those bullies and fighters you talk of, but certainly not among the squires of knights-errant. At least, I have never heard my master speak of such a custom, and he knows all the laws of knight-errantry by heart. But granting it true that there is an express law that squires are to fight while their masters are fighting, I don't intend to obey it but to pay any fine that may be laid on peacefully minded squires like myself. I am sure it cannot be more than two pounds of wax,[5] and I would rather pay that, for I know it will cost me less than the outlay for bandages to mend my head, which I consider as broken and split already. Another thing that makes it impossible for me to fight is the lack of a sword, for I never carried one in my life."

"I know a good solution for that," said the Squire of the Grove. "I have here two canvas bags of the same size. You take one, and I the other, and we will have a pillow fight with equal arms."

"If that's the way, so be it, with all my heart," said Sancho, "for that sort of battle will help to knock the dust out of us instead of hurting us."

"That will not do," said the other, "for we must put into the bags, to keep the wind from blowing them away, half a dozen nice smooth pebbles, all of the same weight. In this way we shall be able to baste one another without doing ourselves any harm or mischief."

"God in heaven!" said Sancho. "What soft fur and wads of carded cotton he is putting into the bags, so that our heads may not be broken and our bones beaten to a powder! But even if they are filled with cocoons, I can tell you, señor, I am not going to fight. Let our masters fight; that's their problem; and let us drink and live. Time will take care to relieve us of our lives, without our looking for excuses to end them before their proper time comes and they drop from ripeness."

"Still," returned he of the Grove, "we must fight, if only for half an hour."

"By no means," said Sancho. "I am not going to be so discourteous or so ungrateful as to have any quarrel, be it ever so small, with a man I have eaten and drunk with. Besides, who the devil could bring himself to fight in cold blood, without anger or provocation?"

"I can remedy that entirely," said he of the Grove, "and in this way. Before we begin the battle, I will come straight up to your worship and punch you three or four times, with which I will lay you at my feet and rouse your anger, even if it were sleeping sounder than a dormouse."

"To match that plan," said Sancho, "I have another that is not a bit worse. I will take a stick, and before your worship comes near enough to waken my anger, I will put yours so sound to sleep with

5. The fine imposed in some religious fraternities on absent members, to be used for candles.

whacks that it won't waken unless it is in the next world, where it is known that I am not a man to let my face be handled by anyone. Let every man look out for himself—though the best way would be to let everyone's anger sleep, for nobody knows another's heart, and a man may come looking for wool and go home shorn. God gave his blessing to peace and his curse to quarrels. If a hunted cat, surrounded and hard pressed, turns into a lion, God knows what I, who am a man, may turn into. So from now on, I warn you, sir squire, that all the harm and mischief that may come of our quarrel will be blamed on you."

"Very good," said the Squire of the Grove. "God will send the dawn's light, and we'll be all right."

And now gay-plumaged birds of all sorts began to warble in the trees and with their varied and gladsome notes seemed to welcome and salute the fresh morn that was beginning to show the beauty of her countenance at the doors and windows of the east, shaking from her locks a profusion of liquid pearls. Bathed in this dulcet moisture the plants, too, seemed to shed and shower down a pearly spray, the willows distilled sweet manna, the fountains laughed, the brooks babbled, the woods rejoiced, and the meadows arrayed themselves in all their glory at her coming.

But hardly had the light of day made it possible to see and distinguish things, when the first object that presented itself to the eyes of Sancho Panza was the Squire of the Grove's nose, which was so big that it almost overshadowed his whole body. It is, in fact, stated that it was of enormous size, hooked in the middle, covered with warts, and of a mulberry color like an egg-plant. It hung down an inch below his mouth, and the size, the color, the warts, and the bend of it made his face so hideous that Sancho, as he looked at him, began to tremble hand and foot like a child in convulsions. In his heart he vowed to let himself be given two hundred punches sooner than be provoked to fight that monster.

Don Quixote examined his adversary, and found that he already had his helmet on and the visor lowered, so that one could not see his face. He observed, however, that the Knight of the Grove was a sturdily built man, but not very tall in stature. Over his armor he wore a surcoat or tabard of what seemed to be the finest cloth of gold, all bespangled with glittering mirrors like little moons, which gave him an extremely gallant and splendid appearance. Above his helmet fluttered a great quantity of plumes, green, yellow, and white, and his lance, which was leaning against a tree, was very long and stout, and had a steel point more than four inches in length.

Don Quixote observed all and took note of all, and from what he saw and observed he concluded that this knight must be a man of great strength, but he did not for all that give way to fear, like Sancho Panza. On the contrary, with a composed and dauntless air he turned to the Knight of the Mirrors. "If, sir knight," he said, "your great eagerness to fight has not banished your courtesy, I would entreat you to raise your visor a little, in order that I may see if the comeliness of your countenance corresponds with that of your equipment."

"Whether you come victorious or vanquished out of this undertaking, sir knight," replied the Knight of the Mirrors, "you will have more than enough time and leisure to see me. If I do not comply with your request, it is because it seems to me a serious wrong would be done the fair Casildea de Vandalia, should I waste time by stopping to raise my visor before having compelled you to avow what you are already aware I maintain."

"Well then," said Don Quixote, "while we are mounting you can at least tell me if I am that Don Quixote whom you said you vanquished."

"To that we answer you," said the Knight of the Mirrors, "that you are as like the knight I vanquished as one egg is like another. However, since you say enchanters persecute you, I will not venture to say positively whether you are the said person or not."

"That," said Don Quixote, "is enough to convince me that you are mistaken. To relieve you of it altogether, let our horses be brought, and in less time than it would take you to raise your visor, if God, my lady, and my arm stand me in good stead, I shall see your face, and you shall see that I am not the vanquished Don Quixote you take me to be."

With this, they cut short the colloquy and mounted. Don Quixote wheeled Rocinante around to reach the proper distance before charging back upon his adversary, and the Knight of the Mirrors did the same. But Don Quixote had not moved away twenty paces when he heard himself called by the other. Each returned halfway, and the Knight of the Mirrors spoke to Don Quixote.

"Remember, sir knight," he said, "that in keeping with the terms of our combat, the vanquished, as I said before, shall be at the victor's disposal."

"I am aware of it already," said Don Quixote, "provided what is commanded and imposed upon the vanquished be things that do not transgress the limits of chivalry."

"That is understood," replied he of the Mirrors.

At this moment Don Quixote caught sight of the squire's extraordinary nose, and he was no less amazed than Sancho at the sight. Indeed, he set him down as a monster of some kind, or a human being of some new species or unearthly breed. Sancho, when he saw his master retiring to run his course, did not care to be left alone with the large-nosed man. With one flap of that nose against his own, the battle, he feared, would be all over for him, and he would be left stretched on the ground, either from the blow or with fright.

So he ran after his master, holding on to Rocinante's stirrup-leather.

"I implore your worship, señor," he said, when it seemed to him time for Don Quixote to turn his horse, "before you turn to charge, help me up into this cork tree, from which I will be able to witness the gallant encounter your worship is going to have with this knight. That is more to my taste and better than from the ground."

"It seems to me rather, Sancho," said Don Quixote, "that you prefer to mount a scaffold in order to see the bulls without danger."

"To tell the truth," returned Sancho, "the squire's monstrous nose has filled me with fear and terror, and I don't dare stay near him."

"It is such," said Don Quixote, "that were I not what I am it would terrify me too. Come, I will help you to climb up."

While Don Quixote waited for Sancho to ascend the cork tree, the Knight of the Mirrors measured off as much ground as he deemed necessary. Then, supposing Don Quixote to have done the same, and without waiting for any trumpet sound or other signal to direct them, he wheeled his horse, which was not more agile or better-looking than Rocinante, and at his top speed, which was an easy trot, he proceeded to charge his enemy. He drew rein, however, when he saw Don Quixote helping Sancho, and halted in mid career. His horse was very grateful for this, as he was already winded. Don Quixote, fancying that his foe was coming down upon him flying, drove his spurs vigorously into Rocinante's scrawny flanks and made him move out in such style that the history tells us that on this occasion only was he known to achieve something like running, for on all others it was a simple trot. With this unparalleled fury he bore down on the spot where the Knight of the Mirrors stood digging his spurs into his horse up to buttons,[6] without being able to make him stir an inch from the place where he had come to a standstill.

At this lucky moment and crisis Don Quixote came upon his adversary, in trouble with his horse and hindered by his lance, which he either could not manage or had no time to brace. Don Quixote, however, paid no attention to these difficulties, and in perfect safety to himself and without any risk hit the Knight of the Mirrors with such force that he brought him to the ground over the haunches of his horse, and with so heavy a fall that he lay to all appearance dead, not stirring hand or foot. The instant Sancho saw him fall he slid down from the cork tree and ran to where his master was. Don Quixote, dismounting from Rocinante, went and stood over the Knight of the Mirrors. Unlacing his helmet to see if he was dead, and to give him air if he should happen to be alive, he saw—who can say what he saw, without filling every hearer with

6. The old form of spur was a spike with a knob or button near the point to keep it from penetrating too far.

astonishment, wonder, and awe? He saw, the history says, the very countenance, the very face, the very look, the very physiognomy, the very effigy, the very image of the bachelor Sansón Carrasco!

"Make haste here, Sancho," he called out loudly, as soon as he saw this, "and behold what you may see but will not believe. Quick, my son, learn what magic can do, and what wizards and enchanters are capable of."

Sancho came up, and when he saw the countenance of the bachelor Carrasco, he started crossing himself a thousand times and blessing himself as many more. All this while the prostrate knight showed no signs of life.

"It is my opinion, señor," Sancho said to Don Quixote, "that in any case your worship should stick your sword into the mouth of this being here who looks like the bachelor Sansón Carrasco. Perhaps by doing so you will kill one of your enemies, the enchanters."

"Your advice is not bad," said Don Quixote, "for of enemies the fewer the better." He was drawing his sword to carry into effect Sancho's suggestion when the Squire of the Mirrors arrived. He was now without the nose which had made him so hideous. "Mind what you are about, Señor Don Quixote," he cried out in a loud voice, "your friend, the bachelor Sansón Carrasco, is at your feet, and I am his squire."

"And the nose?" said Sancho, seeing him without the hideous feature he had before. "I have it here in my pocket," the other replied.

Putting his hand into his right pocket, he pulled out a false nose of varnished pasteboard of the shape already described, while Sancho examined him ever more closely. "Holy Mary be good to me!" he shouted in amazement. "Aren't you Tomé Cecial, my neighbor and companion?"

"To be sure I am!" returned the now unnosed squire. "Tomé Cecial I am, companion and friend Sancho Panza. I'll tell you later about the means and tricks and falsehoods that have brought me here. But in the meantime, beg and entreat your master not to touch, mistreat, wound, or slay the Knight of the Mirrors there at his feet because, beyond all question, it is the rash and ill-advised bachelor Sansón Carrasco, our fellow townsman."

At this moment the Knight of the Mirrors came to. Don Quixote noticed it and held the naked point of his sword over his face. "You are a dead man, knight," he said to him, "unless you confess that the peerless Dulcinea del Toboso excels your Casildea de Vandalia in beauty. In addition to this you must promise, if you should survive this encounter and fall, to go to the city of El Toboso and present yourself before her on my behalf, that she may deal with you according to her good pleasure. If she leaves you free to do yours, you are in like manner to return and seek me out (for the trail of my mighty deeds will serve you as a guide to lead you to where I may be), and tell me what may have passed between you and her —conditions which, in accordance with what we stipulated before our combat, do not transgress the just limits of knight-errantry."

"I confess," said the fallen knight, "that the dirty tattered shoe of the lady Dulcinea del Toboso is better than the unkempt though clean beard of Casildea. I promise to go and to return from her presence to yours and to give you a full and particular account of whatever you ask."

"You must also confess and believe," added Don Quixote, "that the knight you vanquished was not and could not be Don Quixote of La Mancha, but some one else in his likeness, just as I confess and believe that you, though you seem to be the bachelor Sansón Carrasco, are not so, but some other resembling him, whom my enemies have here put before me in his shape, in order that I may restrain and moderate the vehemence of my wrath, and make a gentle use of the glory of my victory."

"I confess, hold, and think everything to be as you believe, hold, and think it," replied the battered knight. "Let me rise, I entreat you—if, indeed, the shock of my fall will allow me, for it has left me in a sorry plight."

Don Quixote helped him to rise, with the assistance of his squire Tomé Cecial. Sancho never took his eyes off the squire, and asked him questions the replies to which clearly established that this was really and truly the Tomé Cecial he had said he was. But the impression made on Sancho's mind by his master's declaration that the enchanters had changed the face of the Knight of the Mirrors into that of the bachelor Sansón Carrasco would not permit him to believe what he saw with his eyes. In a word, both master and servant remained beset by delusion, while down in the mouth and out of luck, the Knight of the Mirrors and his squire parted from Don Quixote and Sancho, the knight intending to seek some village where he could plaster and strap his ribs. Don Quixote and Sancho resumed their journey to Zaragoza, and here the history leaves them in order that it may relate who the Knight of the Mirrors and his long-nosed squire were.

Chapter XV

WHEREIN IT IS TOLD AND REVEALED WHO THE KNIGHT OF THE MIRRORS AND HIS SQUIRE WERE

Don Quixote went off satisfied, elated, and vainglorious in the highest degree at having won a victory over such a valiant knight as he imagined the Knight of the Mirrors to be. From his knightly word, moreover, he expected to learn whether the enchantment of his lady still continued, since the vanquished knight was bound, under the penalty of ceasing to be one, to return and relate what took place between them. But Don Quixote was of one mind and the Knight of the Mirrors of another, for just then his only concern was to find some village where he could treat himself with a plaster, as has been said already.

The history goes on to say, then, that when the bachelor Sansón Carrasco advised Don Quixote to resume his interrupted knight-errantry, this resulted from a conclave with the priest and the barber on what means to adopt that would induce Don Quixote to stay at home in peace and quiet and not agitate himself with his ill-fated adventures. On this occasion it was decided unanimously, in keeping with the view advanced by Carrasco, that Don Quixote should be allowed to go, as it seemed impossible to restrain him. Then Sansón should sally forth to meet him as a knight-errant and do battle with him, for a cause could readily be found, and vanquish him, that being looked upon as an easy matter. First it should be agreed and settled that the vanquished was to be at the victor's mercy and then, Don Quixote having been vanquished, the bachelor knight was to command him to return to his village and his house and not leave it for two years or until he received further orders. It was clear Don Quixote would unhesitatingly obey, rather than contravene or fail to observe the law of chivalry; and he might, perhaps, during the period of his seclusion, forget his folly, or there might be some hope of finding the right remedy to cure his madness.

Carrasco undertook the task, and Tomé Cecial, friend and neighbor of Sancho Panza's, a lively jolly fellow, offered himself as his squire. Carrasco armed himself in the fashion described, and Tomé Cecial, so as not to be recognized by his friend when they met, fitted on over his own natural nose the masquerade nose that has been mentioned. So they followed the same route Don Quixote took, almost arrived in time to be present at the adventure of the cart of Death, and finally encountered them in the grove, where all that the careful reader has been reading about took place. Had it not been for the extraordinary fancies of Don Quixote and his conviction that the bachelor was not the bachelor, señor bachelor would have been incapacitated forever from taking his degree of licentiate, through having exposed himself to the whims of fortune with his ill-considered scheme.

"Sure enough, Señor Sansón Carrasco, we are getting what we deserve," said Tomé Cecial, when he saw how their plans had been thwarted and how pitifully their expedition had petered out. "It is easy enough to plan and set out on an enterprise, but it is often difficult to come well out of it. Don Quixote a madman, and we sane; yet he goes off laughing, safe, and sound, and you are left sore and sorry! I'd like to know now which is the madder, the man who is mad because he cannot help it, or the man mad of his own free will?"

"The difference," Sansón replied, "between the two sorts of madmen is that he who is mad willy-nilly will always remain so, while he who is mad of his own accord can give it up whenever he likes."

"In that case," said Tomé Cecial, "I was a madman of my own accord when I volunteered to become your squire, and, of my own accord, I'll give it up and go home."

"That's your affair," returned Sansón, "but to suppose that I am going home until I have given Don Quixote a thrashing is absurd. What urges me on now is not any wish he may recover his senses but the desire for vengeance. With this terrible pain in my ribs, I can't think on more charitable lines."

Thus conversing, the pair proceeded until they reached a town where by good luck they found a bonesetter, with whose help the unfortunte Sansón was cured. Tomé Cecial went off home, while Sansón stayed behind meditating vengeance. The history will leave him until the proper time, so that it may not now fail to celebrate with Don Quixote.

Chapter XVI

OF WHAT BEFELL DON QUIXOTE WITH A DISCREET GENTLEMAN OF LA MANCHA

Don Quixote pursued his journey with the high spirits, satisfaction, and complacency already described, imagining himself the most valorous knight-errant of the age because of his recent victory. All the adventures that could befall him from that time forth he regarded as already done and brought to a happy conclusion. He sneered at enchantments and enchanters, and disregarded the countless beatings he had suffered in the course of his knight-errantry, and the volley of stones that had leveled half his teeth, and the ingratitude of the galley slaves, and the audacity of the Yangüesans, and the shower of stakes that fell upon him. In short, he said to himself that could he but discover some means, mode, or way of disenchanting his lady Dulcinea, he would not envy the highest fortune that the most fortunate knight-errant of yore ever reached or could reach.

He was going along entirely absorbed in these fancies, when Sancho spoke. "Isn't it odd, señor," he said, "that I have still before my eyes the monstrous enormous nose of my comrade, Tomé Cecial?"

"Do you then believe, Sancho," said Don Quixote, "that the

Knight of the Mirrors was the bachelor Carrasco and his squire Tomé Cecial your comrade?"

"I don't know what to say to that," replied Sancho. "All I know is that what he told me about my own house, wife, and children, nobody else but himself could have known. And the face, once the nose was off, was the very face of Tomé Cecial, as I have seen it many a time in my town and next door to my own house, and the sound of the voice was just the same."

"Let us reason this out, Sancho," said Don Quixote. "Come now, by what process of thinking can it be supposed that the bachelor Sansón Carrasco would come as a knight-errant, in arms offensive and defensive, to fight with me? Have I ever been by any chance his enemy? Have I ever given him any occasion to owe me a grudge? Am I his rival, or does he profess arms, that he should envy the fame I have acquired in them?"

"Well, but what are we to say, señor," returned Sancho, "about that knight, whoever he is, being so like the bachelor Carrasco, and his squire so like my comrade, Tomé Cecial? If that is enchantment, as your worship says, wasn't there some other pair in the world for them to take the the likeness of?"

"It is all," said Don Quixote, "a scheme and plot of the malignant magicians who persecute me. Foreseeing that I would be victorious in the conflict, they arranged that the vanquished knight should display the countenance of my friend the bachelor, so that my friendship for him should stay the edge of my sword and might of my arm, and temper the just wrath of my heart. In this way, the person who sought to take my life by fraud and falsehood would save his own. To prove this, you know already, Sancho, by experience which cannot lie or deceive, how easy it is for enchanters to change one countenance into another, turning fair into foul and foul into fair. It is not two days since you saw with your own eyes the beauty and elegance of the peerless Dulcinea in all its perfection and natural harmony, while I saw her in the repulsive and low form of a coarse country wench, with cataracts in her eyes and a foul smell in her mouth. When the perverse enchanter ventured to effect so wicked a transformation, it is no wonder he used the shapes of Sansón Carrasco and your neighbor to snatch the glory of victory out of my grasp. For all that, however, I console myself because, after all, in whatever shape he may have come, I have been victorious over my enemy."

"God knows what's the truth of it all," said Sancho.

Being fully aware that the transformation of Dulcinea had been a device and fraud of his own, his master's illusions gave him no satisfaction. But he hesitated to reply for fear he might say something that would reveal his trickery.

As they were talking thus, they were overtaken by a man who was following the same road. He was mounted on a very handsome gray mare and dressed in an overcoat and hood of fine green cloth, with tawny velvet trim and a cap with earflaps made of the same velvet. The trappings of the mare were for field use and the saddle had short stirrups, the whole being mulberry and green in color. He carried a Moorish cutlass hanging from a broad green and gold shoulder strap, with matching half-boots. The spurs were not gilt, but lacquered green and so brightly polished that, matching as they did the rest of his apparel, they looked better than if they had been of pure gold.

When the traveler caught up with them, he saluted them courteously and, spurring his mare, was about to pass without stopping. But Don Quixote called out to him. "Gallant sir," he said, "if your worship should be going our way and has no occasion for speed, it would please me greatly if we were to join company."

"In truth," replied he on the mare, "I would not pass you so hastily but for fear that your horse might get excited by the company of my mare."

"You may safely hold in your mare, señor," said Sancho in reply to this. "Our horse is the most virtuous and well-behaved horse in the world and never does anything wrong on such occasions. The only time he misbehaved, my master and I suffered for it sevenfold, so I say again your worship may pull up if you like. If she was offered to him on a platter, this horse would not show any interest in her."

The traveler drew rein, amazed at the appearance and features of Don Quixote, who rode without his helmet, which Sancho carried like a valise in front of Dapple's packsaddle. But if the man in green examined Don Quixote closely, still more closely did Don Quixote examine the man in green, who struck him as being a man of intelligence. In appearance he was about fifty years of age, with but few grey hairs, an aquiline cast of features, and an expression between grave and good-humored, while his dress and accouterments showed him to be a man of some importance. What the man in green thought of Don Quixote of La Mancha was that he had never yet seen anyone of that sort and shape. He marveled at the lankness of his horse, his lofty stature, the leanness and sallowness of his countenance, his armor, his bearing, and his gravity—a figure and apparition such as had not been seen in those regions for many a long day.

Don Quixote saw very plainly the attention with which the traveler was regarding him and read his curiosity in his astonishment. Since he was courteous and ready to please everybody, he spoke in anticipation of any question the other could ask.

"The appearance I present to your worship being so strange and so out of the common," he said, "I should not be surprised if it filled you with wonder. But you will cease to wonder when I tell you that I am one of those knights who, as people say, go seeking adventures. I have left my home, I have mortgaged my estate, I have given up my comforts and committed myself to the arms of Fortune, that she may bear me whithersoever she please. My desire was to restore to life knight-errantry that now is dead. For some time past, stumbling here, falling there, now coming down headlong, now raising myself up again, I have carried out a great portion of my design, aiding widows, protecting maidens, and offering help to wives, orphans, and minors, this being the proper and natural duty of knights-errant. Therefore, because of my many valiant and Christian achievements, I have been already found worthy to make my way in print to well-nigh all, or most, of the nations of the earth. Thirty thousand volumes of my history have been printed, and it is likely to be printed thirty thousand thousands of times, if heaven does not put a stop to it. In short, to sum up all in a few words, or in a single one, I may tell you I am Don Quixote of La Mancha, otherwise called 'The Knight of the Mournful Countenance.' Though self-praise is degrading, I must perforce sound my own sometimes, that is to say, when there is no one at hand to do it for me. So that, gentle sir, neither this horse, nor this lance, nor this shield, nor this squire, nor all these arms put together, nor the sallowness of my countenance, nor my gaunt leanness, will henceforth astonish you, now that you know who I am and what profession I follow."

With these words Don Quixote held his peace, and, from the time he took to answer, the man in green seemed to be at a loss for a reply. After a long pause, however, he spoke. "You were right when you saw curiosity in my amazement, sir knight," he said, "but you have not succeeded in removing the astonishment I feel at seeing you. Although you say, señor, that knowing who you are ought to remove it, it has not done so. On the contrary, now that I know, I am left more amazed and astonished than before. Is it possible that there are knights-errant in the world in these days, and histories of real chivalry printed? I cannot convince myself that anyone on earth nowadays aids widows, or protects maidens, or defends wives, or helps orphans, nor would I believe it had I not seen it in your worship with my own eyes. Blessed be heaven! By means of this history of your noble and genuine chivalrous deeds, which you say has been printed, the countless stories of fictitious knights-errant with which the world is filled, so much to the injury of morality and the prejudice and discredit of good histories,will have been driven into oblivion."

"There is a good deal to be said on that point," said Don Quixote, "as to whether the histories of the knights-errant are fiction or not."

"Why, is there anyone who doubts that those histories are false?" said the man in green.

"I doubt it" said Don Quixote. "But never mind that just now, for if our journey lasts long enough, I trust in God I shall show your worship that you do wrong in going along with those who regard it as a matter of certainty that they are not true."

From this last observation of Don Quixote's, the traveler began to have a suspicion that he was crazy and was waiting for him to confirm it by something further. But before they could turn to any new subject Don Quixote begged him to tell who he was, since he himself had avowed his condition and way of life.

"I, Sir Knight of the Mournful Countenance," replied the man in the green overcoat, "am a gentleman by birth and native of the village where, please God, we are going to today. I am more than fairly well off, and my name is Don Diego de Miranda. I spend my life with my wife, children, and friends, my pursuits are hunting and fishing, though I keep neither hawks nor greyhounds—nothing but a tame partridge[1] or a bold ferret or two. I have six dozen or so of books, some in our mother tongue, some Latin, some of them history, others devotional, while books of chivalry have not as yet crossed the threshold of my door. I am more given to leafing through the profane than the devotional, so long as they are books of honest entertainment that charm by their style and attract and interest by the invention they display, though of these there are very few in Spain. Sometimes I dine with my neighbors and friends, and often invite them, my entertainment being neat and well served without stint of anything. I have no taste for gossip nor do I allow gossiping in my presence. I do not pry into my neighbors' lives, nor do I guess at others' motives. I hear mass every day and share my substance with the poor, making no display of charitable works, lest I let hypocrisy and vainglory, those enemies that subtly take possession of the most watchful heart, find an entrance into mine. I strive to make peace between those whom I know to be at odds, I am the devoted servant of Our Lady, and my trust is ever in the infinite mercy of God our Lord."

Sancho listened with the greatest attention to the account of the gentleman's life and occupation. Thinking it a good and a holy life, and that he who led it ought to work miracles, he threw himself off Dapple, and running in haste seized his right stirrup and kissed his foot again and again with a devout heart and almost with tears.

"What are you about, brother? What are these kisses for?" the gentleman asked him, when he saw this.

1. Tame partridges are extensively used by Andalusian sportsmen as decoys.

"Let me kiss," said Sancho, "for I think your worship is the first saint with short stirrups I ever saw all the days of my life."

"I am no saint," replied the gentleman, "but a great sinner. You are the saint, brother, for you must indeed be good, as shown by your simplicity."

Sancho went back to his packsaddle, having extracted a laugh from his master's profound melancholy, arousing fresh amazement in Don Diego. Don Quixote then asked him how many children he had, and observed that one of the things wherein the ancient philosophers, who were without the true knowledge of God, placed the highest good was in the gifts of nature and of fortune, in having many friends and many good children.

"I, Señor Don Quixote," answered the gentleman, "have one son, without whom, perhaps, I should count myself happier than I am. Not that he is a bad son, but he is not so good as I could wish. He is eighteen years of age, and for six years he has been at Salamanca studying Latin and Greek. When I wished him to turn to the study of other subjects I found him so wrapped up in the science of poetry, if that can be called a science, that he will have nothing to do with law, which I wished him to study, or with theology, queen of them all. I would like him to be an honor to his family, as we live in days when our kings liberally reward learning that is virtuous and worthy; for otherwise learning is a pearl on a dunghill. He spends the whole day deciding whether Homer expresses himself correctly or not in such and such a line of the *Iliad*, whether Martial was indecent or not in such and such an epigram, whether such and such lines of Virgil are to be understood in this way or in that. In short, he talks of nothing but the works of these poets, and of those of Horace, Persius, Juvenal, and Tibullus. For the moderns in our own language he cares little, but with all his seeming indifference to Spanish poetry, just now his thoughts are absorbed in writing a gloss on four lines sent him from Salamanca, which I suspect are for some poetical tournament."[2]

"Children, señor," said Don Quixote in reply, "are portions of their parents' entrails and consequently, whether good or bad, should be loved as we love the souls that give us life. The parents must guide them from infancy in the ways of virtue, propriety, and worthy Christian conduct, so that when grown up they may be the staff of their parents' old age and the glory of their posterity. To force them to study this or that science I do not think wise, though

2. Literary competitions, in which the compositions of the competitors were recited in public and prizes awarded by appointed judges, were still frequent in the time of Cervantes. A "gloss" is a composition based on a short (in this case, four-line) poem, which attempts to develop the idea of the short poem in some novel fashion. In Ch. XVIII, below, Don Quixote discusses the rules for the gloss.

it may be no harm to persuade them. When there is no need to study for the sake of a livelihood, and the student is so fortunate that heaven has given him parents who can support him, I would advise them to let him pursue whatever science he appears to favor. Though that of poetry is less useful than pleasurable, it is not one of those that bring its possessor into disrepute.

"Poetry, gentle sir, is, as I take it, like a tender young maiden of supreme beauty, to array, bedeck, and adorn whom is the task of several other maidens, who are all other sciences. She must avail herself of the help of all, and all derive their luster from her. But this maiden will not bear to be handled, nor dragged through the streets, nor exposed either at the corners of the marketplace, or in the nooks of palaces. She is the product of an alchemy of such virtue that he who can effectuate it will turn her into pure gold of inestimable worth. He who possesses her must keep her within bounds, not permitting her to break out in ribald satires or soulless sonnets. She must on no account be offered for sale, unless, indeed, it be in heroic poems, moving tragedies, or sprightly and ingenious comedies. She must not be touched by the buffoons nor by the ignorant multitude, who are unable to comprehend or appreciate her hidden treasures. And do not suppose, señor, that I apply the term multitude here merely to plebeians and the lower orders, for everyone who is ignorant, be he lord or prince, may and should be included in the multitude. He, then, who embraces and cultivates poetry under the conditions I have named shall become famous and his name honored throughout all the civilized nations of the earth.

"And with regard to what you say, señor, of your son having no great opinion of Spanish poetry, I am inclined to think that he is not quite right there, and for this reason. The great poet Homer did not write in Latin, because he was a Greek, nor did Virgil write in Greek, because he was a Latin. In short, all the ancient poets wrote in the language they imbibed with their mother's milk and never went in quest of foreign ones to express their sublime conceptions. That being so, the usage should in justice extend to all nations, and the German poet should not be undervalued because he writes in his own language, nor the Castilian, nor even the Biscayan, for writing in his. But your son, señor, I suspect, is not prejudiced against Spanish poetry, but against those poets who are mere Spanish verse writers, without any knowledge of other languages or sciences to adorn and give life and vigor to their natural inspiration. Yet even in this he may be wrong for, according to a true belief, a poet is born one. That is to say, the poet by nature comes forth a poet from his mother's womb and, following the bent that heaven has bestowed upon him, without the aid of study or art, he produces things that show how truly he spoke who said, '*Est Deus in nobis*,' etc.[3] At the same time, I say that the poet by nature who calls in art to his aid will be a far better poet and will surpass him who tries to be a poet while relying upon his knowledge of art alone. The reason is that art does not surpass nature but only brings it to perfection. Thus nature combined with art, and art with nature, will produce a perfect poet.

"To bring my argument to a close, I would say then, gentle sir, let your son go on as his star leads him, for being so studious as he seems to be, and having already successfully surmounted the first step of the sciences, which is that of the languages, with their help he will by his own exertions reach the summit of polite literature. This well befits an independent gentleman, and adorns, honors, and distinguishes him, as much as the miter does the bishop, or the gown the learned counselor. If your son writes satires reflecting on the honor of others, chide and correct him, and tear them up. But if he composes discourses in which he rebukes vice in general, in the style of Horace, and with elegance like his, commend him. It is legitimate for a poet to write against envy and scourge the envious in his verse, and the other vices too, provided he does not single out individuals. There are, however, poets who, for the sake of saying something spiteful, would run the risk of being banished to the isles of Pontus.[4] If the poet be pure in his morals, he will be pure in his verses too, for the pen is the tongue of the mind, and like the thought engendered there, so will be the things that it writes down. And when kings and princes observe this marvelous science of poetry in wise, virtuous, and thoughtful subjects, they honor, value, exalt them, and even crown them with the leaves of that tree which the thunderbolt strikes not,[5] as if to show that they whose brows are honored and adorned with such a crown are not to be assailed by anyone."

The wearer of the green overcoat was filled with astonishment at Don Quixote's argument, so much so that he began to abandon his suspicion that the speaker was crazy. But in the middle of the discourse, Sancho, liking it little, had turned aside out of the road to beg a little milk from some shepherds who were milking their ewes close by. The gentleman, highly pleased, was about to renew the conversation when Don Quixote, raising his head, saw a cart covered with royal flags coming along the road. Convinced that this must be some new adventure, he called aloud to Sancho to come and bring him his helmet. Sancho, hearing himself called, left the shepherds and, prodding Dapple vigorously, rejoined his master, to whom there befell a terrific and desperate adventure.

3. "There is a god in us . . ." (Ovid).
4. Like Ovid, banished to Tomos in Pontus.
5. The laurel.

Chapter XVII

WHEREIN IS SHOWN THE FURTHEST AND HIGHEST POINT WHICH THE UNEXAMPLED COURAGE OF DON QUIXOTE REACHED OR COULD REACH—TOGETHER WITH THE HAPPILY ACHIEVED ADVENTURE OF THE LIONS

The history tells that when Don Quixote called out to Sancho to bring him his helmet, Sancho was buying some curds the shepherds agreed to sell him. Flurried by the great haste his master was in he did not know what to do with them or what to carry them in. In order not to lose them, for he had already paid for them, he thought it best to dump them into his master's helmet. Having acted on this bright idea, he went to see what his master wanted.

"Give me that helmet, my friend," Don Quixote called out, as Sancho came near, "for either I know little of adventures, or what I observe yonder is one that will and does require me to arm myself."

The gentleman in the green overcoat, on hearing this, looked in all directions but could see only a cart coming towards them with two or three small flags. This led him to conclude it must be carrying His Majesty's funds, and he said so to Don Quixote. The latter, however, would not believe it, his firm conviction being that whatever happened to him must be adventures and still more adventures.

"Forewarned is forearmed," he answered. "I lose nothing preparing myself, for I know by experience that I have enemies, visible and invisible, and never know when, or where, or what moment, or in what shapes they will attack me."

With that he turned to Sancho and called for his helmet. Sancho, having no time to take out the curds, had to hand it over just as it was. Don Quixote took it and, without noticing what was in it, clapped it on his head with all speed. As the curds were pressed and squeezed, the whey began to run all over his face and beard, which greatly startled him.

"Sancho, what's this?" he cried out. "I think my head is softening, or my brains are melting, or I am sweating from head to foot! If I am sweating it is certainly not from fear. I have no doubt that the adventure about to befall me is a terrible one. Give me something to wipe myself with, if you have it, for this profuse sweat is blinding me."

Sancho held his tongue and gave him a cloth, thanking God at the same time that his master had not hit upon the truth. Don Quixote wiped himself and took off his helmet to see why his head felt so cool. When he saw all that white mash inside his helmet, he put it to his nose.

"By the life of my lady Dulcinea del Toboso," he exclaimed, as soon as he had smelled it, "you have put curds in it, you treacherous, impudent, ill-mannered squire!"

Sancho replied to this with great composure and feigned innocence. "If they are curds," he said, "let me have them, your worship, and I'll eat them—or let the devil eat them, for he must have put them there. Would I dare to dirty your worship's helmet? You have found the daring culprit, you have! Faith, sir, by the light God gives me, I must have enchanters too. They persecute me as a servant and part of your worship. They must have put that mess there to provoke your patience to anger and make you beat my ribs as you so often do. Well, this time, they have missed their aim, for I trust to my master's good sense to see that I have no curds or milk or anything of the sort. If I had, I would put it in my stomach and not in the helmet."

"Maybe so," said Don Quixote.

All this the gentleman was observing, and with astonishment, more especially when, after having wiped clean his head, face, beard, and helmet, Don Quixote put on the helmet, settled himself firmly in his stirrups, checked his sword, and gasped his lance.

"Now, come who will," he cried, "here am I, ready to take on Satan himself in person!"

By this time the cart with the flags had come up, unattended except by the carter on a mule and a man sitting in front. Don Quixote planted himself in front of it.

"Where are you going, brothers?" he asked. "What cart is this? What have you got in it? What are those flags?"

"The cart is mine," replied the carter. "In it is a pair of wild caged lions, which the governor of Orán is sending to court as a present to His Majesty. And the flags are our lord the King's, to show that what is here is his property."

"Are the lions large?" asked Don Quixote.

"So large," replied the man who sat at the door of the cart, "that larger, or as large, have never crossed from Africa to Spain. I am the keeper, and I have brought over others, but never any like these. They are male and female, the male in that first cage and the female in the one behind, and they are hungry, for they have eaten nothing today. So let your worship stand aside, for we must hurry to the place where we will feed them."

"Lion whelps against me?" Don Quixote exclaimed, smiling slightly. "Lion whelps against me? And at such a time! Then, by God, the gentlemen who send them here shall see if I am a man to be frightened by lions. Get down, my good fellow, and as you are the keeper, open the cages and release those beasts for me. In the midst of this plain I will let them know who Don Quixote of La

Mancha is, despite and in the teeth of the enchanters who have sent them."

"So," said the gentleman to himself at this, "our worthy knight has shown of what sort he is. The curds, no doubt, have softened his skull and ripened his brains."

At this instant Sancho came up to the man in green. "Señor, for God's sake," he said, "do something to keep my master, Don Quixote, from tackling these lions. If he does, they'll tear us all to pieces here."

"Is your master so mad," asked the gentleman, "that you think and fear he will fight such fierce animals?"

"He is not mad," said Sancho, "but he is daring."

"I will prevent it," said the gentleman, and he went over to Don Quixote, who was insisting on the keeper's opening the cages.

"Sir knight," he said, "knights-errant should attempt adventures which offer some prospect of a successful outcome, not those which preclude it. Valor that borders on temerity savors of madness rather than of courage, and these lions, moreover, have not attacked you, nor do they dream of such a thing. They are presents for His Majesty, and it would not be right to stop them or delay their journey."

"Gentle sir," replied Don Quixote, "you go and mind your tame partridge and your bold ferret, and let each man look to his own affairs. This is my business, and I know whether these lions have been sent to attack me or not." With that he turned to the keeper.

"By all that's good, sir scoundrel," he exclaimed, "if you don't open the cages this very instant, I'll pin you to the cart with this lance."

"Please your worship," said the carter, when he saw the resolve of this fantasy in armor, "for charity's sake, señor, let me unyoke the mules and place myself in safety along with them before the lions are turned out. If they kill them I am ruined for life, for all I possess is this cart and mules."

"O man of little faith," replied Don Quixote, "get down and unyoke. You will soon see that you are exerting yourself for nothing and that you might have spared yourself the trouble."

The carter got down and with all speed unyoked the mules, and the keeper called out at the top of his voice. "I call all here," he shouted, "to witness that against my will and under compulsion I open the cages and let the lions loose. I warn this gentleman that he will be accountable for whatever mischief which these beasts may do, and for my salary and dues as well. You, gentlemen, place yourselves in safety before I open, for I know they will do me no harm."

Once more the gentleman strove to persuade Don Quixote not to do such a mad thing, as it was tempting God to engage in such a piece of folly. To this, Don Quixote replied that he knew what he was doing. The gentleman in return entreated him to reflect, for he knew he was under a delusion.

"Well, señor," answered Don Quixote, "if you do not care to be a spectator of this tragedy, as in your opinion it will be, spur your gray mare and place yourself in safety."

When he heard this, Sancho with tears in his eyes entreated Don Quixote to give up an enterprise which dwarfed the adventure with the windmills, the awful one with the fulling mills, and in fact, every feat he had attempted throughout his life, making trifles out of them by comparison.

"Look, señor," said Sancho, "there's no enchantment here, nor anything of that sort, because between the bars and chinks of the cage I have seen the paw of a real lion. Judging by that, I reckon the lion such a paw could belong to must be bigger than a mountain."

"Fear at any rate," replied Don Quixote, "will make him look bigger to you than half the world. Retire, Sancho, and leave me. If I should die here you know our old agreement. You will hasten to Dulcinea—I say no more." To this he added some further words that banished all hope of his giving up his insane project. The gentleman in the green overcoat would have offered resistance but found himself ill-matched as to arms, nor did he think it prudent to come to blows with a madman, for such Don Quixote now showed himself to be in every respect. The latter, renewing his commands to the keeper and repeating his threats, warned the gentleman to spur his mare, Sancho his Dapple, and the carter his mules.

All of them tried to get away from the cart as far as they could before the lions broke loose. Sancho was weeping over his master's death, for this time he firmly believed it was in store for him from the claws of the lions. He cursed his fate and called it an unlucky hour when he thought of taking service with him again, but for all his tears and lamentations he did not forget to thrash Dapple so as to put a good space between himself and the cart. The keeper, seeing that the fugitives were now some distance off, once more uttered his warnings and entreaties. The reply was that he had been heard and need not trouble himself with any further warnings or entreaties, as they would be fruitless. He was advised to make haste.

While the keeper was busy opening the first cage, Don Quixote was considering whether it would not be well to do battle on foot, instead of on horseback. Finally he resolved to fight on foot, fearing that Rocinante might take fright at the sight of the lions. So he sprang from his horse, flung his lance aside, slipped his shield on his arm, and drew his sword. Then, with marvelous intrepidity and resolute courage he advanced slowly to plant himself in front of the cart, commending himself with all his heart to God and to his lady Dulcinea.

It is to be observed that, on coming to this passage, the author of this true history breaks out into exclamations. "O brave Don Quixote, valiant past extolling! Mirror, wherein all the heroes of the world may see themselves! Second modern Don Manuel de León, once the glory and honor of Spanish knighthood![1] In what words shall I describe this dread exploit, by what language shall I make it credible for ages to come, of what eulogies would you not be worthy, though they be hyperboles piled on hyperboles! On foot, alone, undaunted, stout-hearted, with but a simple sword, and that no trenchant blade of the Perrillo brand,[2] a shield, but no bright polished steel one, there you stood, biding and awaiting the two fiercest lions that Africa's forests ever bred! May your own deeds be your praise, O valiant Manchegan! Here I leave them as they stand, for words fail me wherewith to glorify them!"

Here the author's outburst came to an end, and he proceeded to take up the thread of his story. He relates how the keeper, seeing that Don Quixote had taken up his position and that it was impossible for him to avoid letting out the male without incurring the enmity of the fiery and daring knight, flung open the doors of the first cage. It contained, as has been said, the lion, which was now seen to be of enormous size, and grim and hideous to look upon. The first thing it did was to turn round in the cage in which it lay and extend its claws and stretch itself thoroughly. It then opened its mouth and yawned very leisurely. With the nearly eighteen inches of tongue it had stuck out, it licked the dust out of its eyes and washed its face. This done, it put its head out of the cage and looked all around with eyes like glowing coals, offering a spectacle and demeanor that could strike terror into temerity itself. Don Quixote merely observed the lion steadily, longing for it to leap from the cart and come to close quarters with him, when he hoped to hew it in pieces.

So far did his unparalleled madness go. But the noble lion, more courteous than arrogant, not troubling himself about silly bravado, after having looked all round, as has been said, turned around and presented its hindquarters to Don Quixote, and very coolly and tranquilly lay down again in the cage. Seeing this, Don Quixote ordered the keeper to take a stick to it and provoke it to make it come out.

"That I won't," said the keeper, "for if I anger it, the first man it'll tear in pieces will be myself. Be satisfied, sir knight, with

1. A famous knight of the court of Ferdinand and Isabel who retrieved a lady's glove from a lion's cage.

2. The *perrillo*, i.e., the "little dog," was the trademark of a famous swordsmith.

what you have done, which leaves nothing more to be said on the score of courage, and do not seek to tempt fortune a second time. The lion has the door open and is free to come out or not to come out, but as it has not come out so far, it will not come out today. Your worship's great courage has been fully manifested already. No brave champion, so it strikes me, is bound to do more than challenge his enemy and wait for him on the field. The disgrace falls on the adversary who does not come, and the knight who has waited for him carries off the crown of victory."

"That is true," said Don Quixote. "Close the door, my friend, and by way of certificate let me have, in the best form you can, what you have seen me do. Namely, you opened the lion's cage, I waited for him, he did not come out, I still waited for him, he still did not come out, and lay down again. I am not bound to do more. Enchantments begone, and God uphold the right, the truth, and true chivalry! Close the door as I have said, while I make signals to the fugitives, so that they may learn this exploit from your lips."

The keeper obeyed, and Don Quixote, fixing on the point of his lance the cloth he had wiped his face with after the deluge of curds, proceeded to recall the others. They were still in full flight, all together, and looked back at every step, the gentleman bringing up the rear. It was Sancho, however, who happened to observe the signal of the white cloth. "May I die," he exclaimed, "if my master has not overcome the wild beasts, for he is calling to us."

They all stopped and saw that it was Don Quixote who was making signals. Shaking off their fears to some extent, they approached slowly until they were near enough to hear distinctly Don Quixote's voice as he called to them. At length they returned to the cart.

"Harness your mules once more, brother," Don Quixote was saying to the carter as they arrived, "and continue your journey. As for you, Sancho, give him two gold crowns for himself and the keeper, to compensate them for the delay for which I am responsible."

"I will give it with all my heart," said Sancho. "But what has become of the lions? Are they dead or alive?"

The keeper, in full detail and bit by bit described the end of the contest. To the best of his power and ability he extolled the valor of Don Quixote, at sight of whom the lion quailed and would not and dared not come out of the cage, though the door had been held open ever so long. He had pointed out to the knight that it was tempting God to provoke the lion in order to force him out, as the knight had wished. Don Quixote, in consequence, though only reluctantly and altogether against his will, had allowed the door to be closed.

"What do you think of this, Sancho?" said Don Quixote. "Are there any enchantments that can prevail against true valor? The enchanters may be able to rob me of good fortune, but not of fortitude and courage."

Sancho paid the crowns, the carter yoked the mules, the keeper kissed Don Quixote's hands for the bounty bestowed upon him and promised to give an account of the valiant exploit to the King himself, as soon as he saw him at court.

"Then," said Don Quixote, "if His Majesty should happen to ask who performed it, you must say the Knight of the Lions. It is my desire that the name which I have hitherto borne, Knight of the Mournful Countenance, be from this time forward changed, altered, transformed, and turned into Knight of the Lions. In this I follow the ancient usage of knights-errant, who changed their names when they pleased, or when it suited their purpose."

The cart went its way, and Don Quixote, Sancho, and the gentleman in the green overcoat went theirs. All this time Don Diego de Miranda had not spoken a word, being entirely taken up with observing and noting all that Don Quixote did and said. The opinion he formed was that he was a man of good sense who had gone mad, and a madman on the verge of rationality. The first part of his history had not yet reached him for, had he read it, the amazement with which Don Quixote's words and deeds filled him would have vanished, as he would then have understood the nature of this madness. Knowing nothing of it, he took him to be rational one moment and crazy the next, for what Don Quixote said was sensible, elegant, and well expressed, and what he did, absurd, rash, and foolish. "What could be madder," he said to himself, "than to put on a helmet full of curds and then persuade oneself that enchanters are softening one's skull. Or what could be greater rashness and folly than to strive to fight lions tooth and nail?"

Don Quixote roused him from these reflections and this soliloquy. "No doubt, Señor Don Diego de Miranda," he said, "you look on me as a fool and a madman. It would be no wonder if you did, for my deeds bear witness to nothing else. But for all that, I would have you note that I am neither so mad nor so foolish as you must have thought. A gallant knight shows to advantage when he adroitly turns his lance against a fierce bull under the eyes of his sovereign, in the midst of a spacious plaza. A knight shows to advantage arrayed in glittering armor, pacing the lists before the ladies in some joyous tournament, as do all those knights who entertain, divert, and, if we may say so, honor the courts of their rulers by warlike exercises or the semblance of them. But all these knights have a lesser luster when compared with the knight-errant who traverses deserts, solitudes, crossroads, forests, and mountains in quest of perilous adventures, bent on bringing them to a happy and successful issue, in order to win glorious and lasting renown. Greater, I maintain, is the renown of the knight-errant who aids a widow in some lonely waste than that of the court knight dallying with some city damsel.

"All knights have their special parts to play. Let the courtier devote himself to the ladies, let him add luster to his sovereign's court by his liveries, let him entertain poor gentlemen with the sumptuous fare of his table and arrange joustings, preside over tournaments, and prove himself noble, generous, and magnificent, and above all a good Christian. So doing, he will fulfil the duties that are especially his—but let the knight-errant explore the corners of the earth and penetrate the most intricate labyrinths. At each step let him attempt impossibilities, on desolate heaths let him endure the burning rays of the midsummer sun and the bitter inclemency of the winter winds and frosts. Let no lions daunt him, no monsters terrify him, no dragons make him quail, for to seek the latter, to attack the former, and to vanquish all, are in truth his main duties.

"I, then, since my lot has placed me among the knights-errant must needs undertake whatever seems to fall within the sphere of my duties. Thus it was my bounden duty to attack the lions I attacked just now, though I knew it to be the height of rashness. I know well the nature of valor, that it is a virtue situated between two vicious extremes, cowardice and temerity. But it will be a lesser evil for the valiant man to rise till he reaches the point of rashness, rather than sink to the point of cowardice. Just as it is easier for the prodigal than for the miser to become generous, so it is easier for a rash man to prove truly valiant than for a coward to rise to true valor. Believe me, Señor Don Diego, in attempting adventures it is better to lose by a card too many than by a card too few. It is better to hear it said, 'such a knight is rash and daring,' rather than 'such a knight is timid and cowardly.' "

"I avow, Señor Don Quixote," said Don Diego, "that all you have said and done is proved correct by the test of reason itself. And I believe that, if the laws and ordinances of knight-errantry should be lost, they might be found in your worship's breast as in their own proper depository and treasure house. But let us hasten on to my village, where you shall rest after your recent exertions. These, if not of the body, have been of the spirit, which may induce bodily fatigue."

"I take the invitation as a great favor and honor, Señor Don Diego," replied Don Quixote.

Moving onward at a better pace than before, at about two in the afternoon they reached the village and house of Don Diego or, as Don Quixote called him, "The Knight of the Green Overcoat."

Chapter XVIII

OF WHAT HAPPENED TO DON QUIXOTE IN THE CASTLE OR HOUSE OF THE KNIGHT OF THE GREEN OVERCOAT, TOGETHER WITH OTHER MATTERS OUT OF THE ORDINARY

Don Quixote found Don Diego de Miranda's house to be large, built in village style, with his coat-of-arms in rough stone over the street door. The patio served as a storeroom and the entry way as a cellar. Standing around were plenty of wine jars which, since they came from El Toboso, brought back to his memory his enchanted and transformed Dulcinea. With a sigh, and not thinking what he was saying, or in whose presence he was, he exclaimed,

> "O you sweet treasures to my sorrow found!
> Once sweet and welcome when 'twas heaven's will.[1]

O Tobosan jars, how you bring back to my memory the sweet object of my bitter regrets!"

The student poet, Don Diego's son, had come out with his mother to receive him. When they heard this exclamation, both mother and son were filled with amazement at the extraordinary figure of Don Quixote, who dismounted from Rocinante and advanced with great politeness to ask permission to kiss the lady's hand. "Señora," said Don Diego, "pray receive with your accustomed kindness Señor Don Quixote of La Mancha, whom you see before you. He is a knight-errant, and the bravest and wisest in the world."

The lady, whose name was Doña Cristina, received him with every sign of good will and great courtesy, while Don Quixote placed himself at her service with an abundance of well-chosen, polished phrases. Almost the same civilities were exchanged between him and the student who, listening to Don Quixote, took him to be a sensible, clear-headed person.

Here the author paints a detailed picture of Don Diego's mansion, displaying for us the whole contents of a rich gentleman farmer's house. But the translator of the history thought it best to pass over these and other details of the same sort in silence, as they were not in harmony with the main purpose of the story, the strong point of which is truth rather than dull digressions.

They led Don Quixote into a room, and Sancho removed his armor, leaving him in loose Walloon breeches and chamois-leather vest, all stained with rust from the armor. He wore a soft, schoolboy collar, without starch or lace, his half-boots were brown, and his

1. The beginning of Garcilaso's Sonnet X, the most famous in Spanish, which according to tradition was inspired by the poet's discovering a lock of his dead mistress's hair.

overshoes waxed.[2] He wore his good sword, which hung from a sealskin shoulder strap, for he had suffered for many years, they say, from an ailment of the kidneys.[3] Over all this he threw a long cloak of good grey cloth. But first of all, with five or six buckets of water (for as to the number of buckets there is some dispute), he washed his head and face. Yet the water remained whey-colored, because of Sancho's greediness and the buying of those accursed curds that had so whitened his master.

Thus arrayed, and with a sprightly, gallant air, Don Quixote passed into another room where the student was waiting to entertain him while the table was being laid. With the arrival of so distinguished a guest, Doña Cristina was anxious to show that she was well able to receive becomingly those who entered her house.

While Don Quixote was taking off his armor, Don Lorenzo (as Don Diego's son was called) used the occasion to question his father. "What are we to make of this gentleman you have brought home to us, sir?" he asked. "His name, his appearance, and the fact that you call him a knight-errant have completely puzzled my mother and me."

"I don't know what to say, my son," replied Don Diego. "All I can tell you is that I have seen him act like the greatest madman in the world, and heard him make observations so sensible that they efface and cancel everything he does. Talk to him yourself and take the pulse of his intelligence. You are discerning, so exercise your best judgment concerning his wisdom or folly—though, to tell the truth, I am more inclined to regard him as mad than sane."

With this Don Lorenzo went off to entertain Don Quixote, as has been said.

"Your father, Señor Don Diego de Miranda," Don Quixote said to Don Lorenzo, in the course of the conversation, "has told me of your rare abilities and subtle intellect and, above all, he assures me you are a great poet."

"A poet maybe," replied Don Lorenzo, "but by no means a great one. I am indeed somewhat given to poetry and to reading good poets, but in no way does this justify the title of 'great' used by my father."

"Your modesty is not displeasing," said Don Quixote, "for every poet is filled with conceit and thinks he is the best poet in the world."

"There is no rule without an exception," said Don Lorenzo. "Perhaps some are poets who do not think they are."

"Very few," said Don Quixote. "But tell me, what verses are you

2. It was customary to wear soft shoes indoors and overshoes or clogs out of doors.

3. Sufferers from ailments in the region of the loins found a strap passing over the shoulder easier than the ordinary sword belt.

working on at present? Your father tells me they leave you somewhat restless and absorbed. If it is a gloss, I know something about glosses and should like to hear them. If they are for a poetry competition, try to win the second prize, for favoritism or the author's standing determines the first, while justice alone accounts for the second award. Thus the third comes to be the second, and the first, reckoning in this way, will be third, just as licentiate degrees are confered at the universities. Nevertheless, the title of first is a great distinction."

"So far," said Don Lorenzo to himself, "I would not take you to be a madman; but let us go on." Addressing Don Quixote, he said, "Your worship has apparently attended the university. What sciences have you studied?"

"That of knight-errantry," said Don Quixote, "which is as good as that of poetry, and even an inch or two above it."

"I do not know what science that is," said Don Lorenzo, "and until now I have never heard of it."

"It is a science," said Don Quixote, "that comprehends in itself all or most of the sciences in the world. He who professes it must be a jurist and must know the rules of justice, distributive and equitable, so as to give to each one what belongs to him and is his due. He must be a theologian, so as to be able to give clear and distinctive reason for the Christian faith he professes, wherever it may be asked of him. He must be a physician, and above all an herbalist, so as in wilderness and solitudes to know the herbs that have the property of healing wounds, for a knight errant must not go looking for some one to cure him at every step. He must be an astronomer, so as to know by the stars how many hours of the night have passed, and what clime and quarter of the world he is in. He must know mathematics, for at every turn some need for it will present itself to him. Putting aside the fact that he must be adorned with all the virtues, cardinal and theological, to come down to minor particulars, he must, I say, be able to swim as well as Nicholas or Nicolao the Fish could, as the story goes.[4] He must know how to shoe a horse and repair his saddle and bridle. To return to higher matters, he must be faithful to God, and to his lady, he must be pure in thought, decorous in words, generous in works, valiant in deeds, patient in suffering, compassionate towards the needy, and, lastly, an upholder of the truth though its defense should cost him his life. Of all these qualities, great and small, is a true knight-errant made up. Judge then, Señor Don Lorenzo, whether it be a contemptible science which the knight who studies and professes it has to learn, and whether it may not compare with the very loftiest that are taught in the schools and universities."

4. A legendary "merman" sometimes identified with a famous Italian swimmer of the fifteenth century.

"If that is so," replied Don Lorenzo, "this science, I confess, surpasses all."

"What do you mean, if that is so?" said Don Quixote.

"What I mean to say is," said Don Lorenzo, "that I doubt whether there are now, or ever were, any knights-errant, and that they professed such virtues."

"Many a time,'" replied Don Quixote, "have I said what now I repeat, that most people in the world believe that there never were any knights-errant in it. As it is my opinion that, unless heaven by some miracle brings home to them the truth that there were and are, all the pains one takes will be in vain, as experience has often shown me. So I will not now stop to disabuse you of the error you share with the multitude. All I shall do is to pray to heaven to deliver you from it and show you how beneficial and necessary knights-errant were in days of yore and how useful they would be in these days were they but in vogue. But now, for the sins of the people, sloth and indolence, gluttony and soft living are triumphant."

"Our guest has broken away from us," said Don Lorenzo to himself at this point, "but for all that he is a glorious madman, and I would be a dull blockhead to doubt it."

Here, having been summoned to dinner, they brought their discussion to a close. Don Diego asked his son what insight he had gained into their guest's wits. "All the doctors and clever scribes in the world," Don Lorenzo answered, "will not make sense of his madness, for it is an illegible scrawl. His is a madness streaked with lucid intervals."

They went in to dinner, and the repast was neat, plentiful, and tasty, of the sort Don Diego had said on the road he was in the habit of giving to his guests. But what pleased Don Quixote most was the marvelous silence that reigned throughout the house, for it was like a Carthusian monastery.

When the cloth had been removed, grace said, and their hands washed, Don Quixote earnestly requested Don Lorenzo to repeat his verses for the poetry tournament.

"Not to be like those poets," the young man replied, "who refuse when they are asked to recite their verses and when they are not asked for them spew them out, I will repeat my gloss. I do not expect any prize for it and composed it merely as an exercise of ingenuity."

"A discerning friend of mine," said Don Quixote, "was of opinion that no one should waste his time glossing verses. His reasoning was that the gloss can never approach the text and that, more often than not, it departs from the meaning and purpose of the glossed lines. Besides, the laws of the gloss were too strict, allowing no interrogations, nor 'said he,' nor 'I say,' nor turning verbs into nouns, nor any change in construction, not to speak of other restrictions and limitations that hobble gloss-writers, as you no doubt know."

"I very much wish, Señor Don Quixote," said Don Lorenzo, "that I could catch your worship committing a blunder, but I cannot, for you slip through my fingers like an eel."

"I don't understand what you mean by this 'slipping,' " said Don Quixote.

"I will explain myself another time," said Don Lorenzo. "At present please listen to the glossed verses and the gloss, which run thus:

Could 'was' become an 'is' for me,
  Then would I ask no more than this;
  Oh could, for me, the time that is
Become the time that is to be!

GLOSS

Dame Fortune once upon a day
  To me was bountiful and kind;
  But all things change; she changed her mind,
And what she gave she took away.
O Fortune, long I've sued to thee;
  The gifts thou gavest me restore,
  For, trust me, I would ask no more,
Could 'was' become an 'is' for me.

No other prize I seek to gain,
  No triumph, glory, or success,
  Only the long-lost happiness,
The memory whereof is pain.
One taste, methinks, of bygone bliss
  The heart-consuming fire might stay;
  And, so it come without delay,
Then would I ask no more than this.

I ask what cannot be, alas!
  That time should ever be, and then
  Come back to us, and be again,
No power on earth can bring to pass;
For fleet of foot is he, I wis,[5]
  And idly, therefore, do we pray
  That what for age hath left us may
Become for us the time that is.

Perplexed, uncertain, to remain
  'Twixt hope and fear, is death, not life;
  'Twere better, sure, to end the strife,
And dying, seek release from pain.
And yet, thought were the best for me.
  Anon the thought aside I fling,
  And to the present fondly cling,
And dread the time that is to be."

5. I know.

When Don Lorenzo had finished reciting his gloss, Don Quixote stood up and, speaking in a loud voice, almost a shout, grasped Don Lorenzo's right hand. "By the highest heavens, O noble youth," he exclaimed, "you are the best poet on earth, and deserve to be crowned with laurel, not by Cyprus or by Gaeta—as a certain poet, God forgive him, said[6]—but by the Academies of Athens, if they still flourished, and by those that flourish now at Paris, Bologna, and Salamanca. Heaven grant that the judges who rob you of the first prize—that Phoebus may pierce them with his arrows, and the Muses never cross the thresholds of their doors. Repeat for me some of your long line verses, señor, if you will be so good, for I want thoroughly to feel the pulse of your rare genius."

Is there any need to say that Don Lorenzo enjoyed hearing himself praised by Don Quixote, though he looked upon him as a madman? O power of flattery, how far you reach, and how wide are the bounds of your pleasant jursidiction! Don Lorenzo gave a proof of it, for he complied with Don Quixote's request and entreaty, and repeated to him this sonnet on the fable or story of Pyramus and Thisbe.

SONNET

"The lovely maid, she pierces now the wall;
Heart-pierced by her young Pyramus doth lie;
And Love spreads wing from Cyprus isle to fly,
A chink to view so wondrous great and small.
There silence speaketh, for no voice at all
Can pass so strait a strait; but love will ply
Where to all other power 'twere vain to try;
For love will find a way whate'er befall.
Impatient of delay, with reckless pace
The rash maid wins the fatal spot where she
Sinks not in lover's arms but death's embrace.
So runs the strange tale, how the lovers twain
One sword, one sepulchre, one memory,
Slays, and entombs, and brings to life again."

"Blessed be God," said Don Quixote when he heard Don Lorenzo's sonnet, "that among the hosts of poets consumed by their own spleen I have found one consummate poet, señor, as the art of this sonnet proves you to be!"

For four days Don Quixote was most sumptuously entertained in Don Diego's house. He asked his permission to depart, expressing gratitude for the kindness and hospitality he received in his house, but saying that it did not become knights-errant to give themselves up for long to idleness and luxury. Thus he was anxious to fulfill

6. Juan Bautista de Bivar.

the duties of his calling by seeking adventures which, he was informed, the neighborhood could provide in abundance. There he hoped to employ his time until the day arrived for the jousts at Zaragoza, that being his proper destination. But first of all he meant to enter the cave of Montesinos, of which so many marvelous things were reported all through the country, and at the same time to investigate and explore the origin and true source of the seven lakes commonly called the lakes of Ruidera.

Don Diego and his son commended his laudable resolve and asked him to take whatever he wanted from their house and belongings, as they would most gladly be of service to him. Indeed, his personal worth and his honorable profession made this incumbent upon them.

The day of his departure came at length. It was as welcome to Don Quixote as it was sad and sorrowful for Sancho Panza, who was very well satisfied with the abundance of Don Diego's house and had no wish to return to the starvation of the woods and wilds and the short rations of his ill-stocked saddlebags. Yet he filled and packed them with what he considered needful.

"I do not know whether I have told you already," said Don Quixote, as he took leave of Don Lorenzo, "but if so I tell you again that, if you would spare yourself fatigue and toil in reaching the inaccessible summit of the temple of fame, all you need do is turn aside from the somewhat narrow path of poetry and take the still narrower one of knight-errantry. It is wide enough, however, to make you an emperor in the twinkling of an eye."

In this speech Don Quixote completed the evidence of his madness, but what he went on to say was even more conclusive. "God knows," he said, "how gladly I would take Don Lorenzo with me to teach him how to spare the humble and trample the proud under foot, virtues that are part and parcel of the profession I belong to. But since his tender age and praiseworthy pursuits do not permit it, I will content myself with impressing upon your worship that you will become famous as a poet if you are guided by the opinion of others rather than by your own. No fathers or mothers ever think their own children ill-favored, and this sort of deception prevails still more strongly in the case of the children of the brain."

Both father and son were amazed afresh at the strange medley Don Quixote talked, sense at one moment and nonsense the next, and at his pertinacity and persistence in going through thick and thin in quest of his unlucky adventures, the end and goal of his desires. There was a renewal of offers of service and civilities and then, with the gracious permission of the lady of the castle, they took their departure, Don Quixote on Rocinante and Sancho on Dapple.

Chapter XIX

IN WHICH IS RELATED THE ADVENTURE OF THE ENAMORED SHEPHERD, TOGETHER WITH OTHER TRULY AMUSING INCIDENTS

Don Quixote had gone but a short distance beyond Don Diego's village when he fell in with a couple of either priests or students, and a couple of peasants, mounted on four beasts of the asinine kind. One of the students carried, wrapped up in a piece of green material, by way of a suitcase, what seemed to be a little linen and a couple of pairs of ribbed stockings, the other carried nothing but a pair of new fencing-foils with buttons. The peasants carried various articles that showed they were on their way from some large town where they had bought them and were taking them home to their village.

Both students and peasants were struck with the same amazement that everybody felt who saw Don Quixote for the first time and were dying to know who this man, so different from ordinary men, could be. Don Quixote saluted them, and after ascertaining that their road was the same as his, offered them his company and asked them to slacken their pace, as their young asses traveled faster than his horse. Then, to gratify them, he related in a few words who he was and the calling and profession he followed, which was that of a knight-errant seeking adventures in all parts of the world. He informed them that his own name was Don Quixote of La Mancha and that he was called, by way of surname, the Knight of the Lions. All this was Greek or gibberish to the peasants, but not so to the students, who very soon perceived the crack in Don Quixote's brain. For all that, however, they regarded him with amazement and respect.

"If you, sir knight, have no fixed road," one student said to him, "as is the custom with those who seek adventures, your worship should come with us. You will see one of the finest and richest weddings that up to now have ever been celebrated in La Mancha or for many a league round."

Don Quixote asked him if the bridegroom was some prince, since he spoke of it in this way.

"Not at all," said the student. "It is the wedding of a farmer and a farmer's daughter. He is the richest in the whole region, and she is the most beautiful that ever mortal set eyes on. The accompanying festivities will be something rare and out of the common, for it will all take place in a meadow adjoining the town of the bride. She is always called Quiteria the beautiful and the bridegroom Camacho the rich. She is eighteen, he twenty-two, and they are fairly matched, though some busy-bodies, who have all the pedigrees in the world by heart, maintain that the family of the fair Quiteria is better than Camacho's. But no one minds that nowadays, for wealth can solder a great many flaws.

"At any rate, Camacho is open-handed, and it occurred to him to have the whole meadow screened with boughs and covered overhead, so that the sun will have hard work getting in to reach the grass that covers the soil. He has provided dancers too, not only sword but also bell-dancers, for in his own town there are people who ring and jingle the bells to perfection. No need to speak of shoe-dancers, for he had engaged a whole crowd of them.[1] But none of these things, nor the many others I have failed to mention, will do more to make this wedding memorable than the part I suspect the despairing Basilio will play in it.

"This Basilio is a young man from Quiteria's village, who lived next door to her parents' house. Love seized this opportunity to reproduce to the letter the long-forgotten loves of Pyramus and Thisbe. Basilio loved Quiteria from his earliest years, and she responded to his passion with countless modest proofs of affection, so that the loves of the two children, Basilio and Quiteria, were the talk and the amusement of the town. As they grew up, the father of Quiteria made up his mind to refuse Basilio his habitual freedom of access to the house; and, to put an end to his own unceasing doubts and suspicions, he arranged a match for his daughter with the rich Camacho. He did not approve of marrying her to Basilio, who had not so large a share of the gifts of fortune as of nature, for, if the truth be told ungrudgingly, he is the most agile youth we know, a mighty thrower of the bar, a first-rate wrestler, and a great ballplayer. He runs like a deer and leaps better than a goat, bowls over the ninepins as if by magic, sings like a lark, plays the guitar so as to make it speak, and, above all, handles a sword as well as the best."

"For that skill alone," said Don Quixote, "the youth deserves to marry, not merely the fair Quiteria, but Queen Guinevere herself, were she alive now, in spite of Launcelot and all who would try to prevent it."

"Say that to my wife," said Sancho, who had until now listened in silence. "She won't hear of anything but each one marrying his equal, holding with the proverb 'two by two, ram and ewe.' What I would like is that this good Basilio (for I am beginning to take a fancy to him already) should marry this lady Quiteria. A blessing and good luck—I meant to say the opposite—on people who would prevent those who love one another from marrying."

"If all those who love one another were to marry," said Don Quixote, "it would deprive parents of the right to choose and to

1. In the sword-dances the dancers made cuts and passes at each other, the art of the performance consisting in going as near as possible without doing any injury. The bell-dancers wore a costume hung with little bells. The peculiar agility of the shoe-dancers, *zapateadores,* was shown by striking the sole of the shoe with the palm of the hand.

marry off their children to the proper person at the proper time. If it was left to daughters to choose husbands as they pleased, one would be for choosing her father's servant, and another, some one she has seen passing in the street and thinks gallant and dashing, though he may be a drunken bully. Love and fancy easily blind the eyes of the judgment, so essential in choosing one's way of life, and the matrimonial choice is very liable to error, requiring great caution and the special favor of heaven to make it a good one. The man who sets out on a long journey will, if he is wise, seek some trusty and pleasant companion to accompany him before he departs. Why, then, should not a man do likewise for the whole journey of life down to the final halting place of death, more especially when the companion has to be his companion in bed, at board, and everywhere, as the wife is to her husband? The companionship of one's wife is no article of merchandise, that, after it has been bought, may be returned, or bartered, or changed. It is an inseparable quality that lasts as long as life lasts; it is a noose that, once you put it around your neck, turns into a Gordian knot. If it is not severed by the scythe of Death, there is no untying it. I could say a great deal more on this subject, were I not prevented by my eagerness to find out if the señor licentiate has anything more to tell about the story of Basilio."

The student, bachelor, or, as Don Quixote called him, licentiate, responded to this request. "I have nothing whatever to say further," he said, "except that the moment Basilio learned the beautiful Quiteria was to marry Camacho the rich, he has never been seen to smile or heard to utter a rational word. He always goes around moody and dejected, talking to himself in a way that shows plainly he is out of his senses. He eats little and sleeps little, and all he eats is fruit. When he sleeps, if he sleeps at all, it is in the field on the hard earth like a brute beast. Sometimes he gazes at the sky, at other times he fixes his eyes on the earth in such an abstracted way that he might be taken for a clothed statue with its drapery stirred by the wind. In short, he shows such signs of a heart crushed by suffering, that all of us who know him believe that when tomorrow the fair Quiteria says 'I do,' it will be his sentence of death."

"God will do better than that," said Sancho, "for God who gives the wound gives the salve, nobody knows what will happen, and there are a good many hours between today and tomorrow, and at any one of them or any moment, the house may fall, I have seen the rain coming down and the sun shining all at one time, and many a man goes to bed in good health who can't stir the next day. Tell me, is there anyone who can boast of having driven a nail into the wheel of fortune? No, faith, and between a woman's 'yes' and 'no' I wouldn't venture to put the point of a pin, because there would not be room for it. If you tell me Quiteria loves Basilio heart and soul, then I'll give him a bag of good luck. Love, I have heard say, looks through spectacles that make copper seem gold, poverty wealth, and bleary eyes pearls."

"What are you driving at, Sancho, curses on you?" said Don Quixote. "When you take to stringing proverbs and sayings together, no one can understand you but Judas himself, and I wish he had you. Tell me, you animal, what do you know about nails or wheels or anything else?"

"Oh, if you don't understand me," replied Sancho, "no wonder my words are taken for nonsense. No matter, I understand myself and know there is nothing very foolish in what I have said. Only your worship, señor, is always obstructing to everything I say, no, everything I do."

"*Objecting,* not *obstructing,*" said Don Quixote, "God confound you, you prevaricator of honest language!"

"Don't find fault with me, your worship," returned Sancho. "You know I was not brought up at court or trained at Salamanca, to know whether I am adding or dropping a letter or so in my words. Why, God bless me, it's not fair to force a Sayago peasant to speak like a Toledan.[2] Maybe there are Toledans who aren't too good when it comes to polished talk."

"That is true," said the licentiate, "for those who have been brought up in the Tanneries and the Zocodover[3] cannot talk like those who are almost all day pacing the cathedral cloisters, and yet they are all Toledans. Pure, correct, elegant, and lucid language will be met with in men of courtly breeding and discrimination, though they may have been born in Majalahonda. I say, men of discrimination, because there are many lacking in it, and discrimination is the grammar of good language, when practice goes alongside. I, sirs, for my sins have studied canon law at Salamanca, and I rather pride myself on expressing my meaning in clear, plain, and intelligible language."

"If you did not pride yourself more on your skill with those foils you carry than on the skill of your tongue," said the other student, "you would have been head of your class where you are now tail."

"Look here, bachelor Corchuelo," returned the licentiate, "you have the most mistaken idea in the world about skill with the sword, if you think it useless."

"It is not an idea as far as I'm concerned, but an established truth," replied Corchuelo, "and if you want me to prove it to you by experiment, you have swords there, and this is a good opportunity. I have a steady hand and a strong arm, and these, together with my resolution, which is not negligible, will make you confess

2. Sayago is a district between Zamora and the Portuguese frontier. Its speech was considered the essence of rusticity. The Castilian of Toledo was regarded as the standard.

3. The Zocodover is the main plaza of Toledo.

I am not mistaken. Dismount and put in practice your positions and circles and angles and science,[4] for I hope to make you see stars at noonday with my crude, uneducated swordmanship. In it, next to God, I place my trust that the man is yet to be born who will make me turn my back, and that there is no one in the world I will not compel to give ground."

"As to whether you turn your back or not, I do not concern myself," replied the swordsman, "though your grave might perhaps be dug on the spot where you planted your foot the first time. I mean that you would be stretched dead there for despising swordsmanship."

"We shall soon see," replied Corchuelo, and getting off his donkey briskly, he furiously drew out one of the swords the licentiate carred on his beast.

"It must not be that way," said Don Quixote at this point. "I will be the director of this fencing match and judge of this often disputed question."

Dismounting from Rocinante and grasping his lance, he planted himself in the middle of the road, just as the licentiate, with an easy, graceful bearing and step advanced towards Corchuelo, who came on against him, with blood in his eye, as the saying is. The other two in the group, the peasants, without dismounting from their asses, served as spectators of the mortal tragedy.

The cuts, thrusts, down strokes, back strokes, and doubles that Corchuelo delivered were past counting, and came thicker than hops or hail. He attacked like an angry lion, but he was met by a tap on the mouth from the button of the licentiate's sword that checked him in the midst of his furious onset and made him kiss it as if it were a relic, though not as devoutly as relics are and ought to be kissed. The end of it was that the licentiate counted with his sword every one of the buttons of the short cassock Corchuelo wore, tore the tail into strips like the tentacles of an octopus, and knocked off his hat twice. So completely did he tire him out that Corchuelo, in vexation, anger, and rage, took the sword by the hilt and flung it away with such force that one of the peasants, who was a notary, and who went for it, made an affidavit afterwards that it had been hurled nearly three-quarters of a league. This testimony will serve, and has already served, to show and establish with certainty that strength is overcome by skill.

"By my faith, señor bachelor," said Sancho, approaching the wearied Corchuelo where he sat, "if your worship takes my advice, you will never challenge anyone to fence again, only to wrestle and throw the bar, for you have the youth and strength for that. But as

4. Books on "scientific" fencing, with geometrical terminology, elaborate diagrams, etc., are satirized by other Golden Age writers, e.g., Quevedo; but Cervantes seems to favor the theoretical approach.

for these fencers as they call them, I have heard say they can put the point of a sword through the eye of a needle."

"I am satisfied with having tumbled off my high horse," said Corchuelo, "and with having had the truth I was so ignorant of proved to me by experience."

Getting up he embraced the licentiate, and they were better friends than ever. They did not care to wait for the notary who had gone for the sword, as they saw he would be a long time about it, and resolved to push on so as to reach in good time the village of Quiteria, to which they all belonged.

During the remainder of the journey the licentiate held forth to them on the excellences of the sword, with such conclusive arguments, and such figures and mathematical proofs, that all were convinced of the value of the science and Corchuelo cured of his stubborn doubt.

It grew dark, but before they reached the town it seemed to them all as if a heaven full of countless glittering stars were in front of it. They heard, too, the pleasant mingled notes of a variety of instruments, flutes, drums, psalteries, pipes, tabors, and rattles, and as they drew near, they perceived that the trees of a leafy arcade that had been constructed at the entrance of the town were filled with lights unaffected by the wind, for the breeze at the time was so gentle that it had not power to stir the leaves on the trees. The musicians were the life of the wedding, wandering through the pleasant grounds in separate bands, some dancing, others singing, others playing the various instruments already mentioned. In short, it seemed as through mirth and gaiety were frisking and gamboling all over the meadow. Several other persons were engaged in erecting a platform from which people might conveniently see the plays and dances that were to be performed the next day on the spot dedicated to the celebration of the marriage of Camacho the rich and the obsequies of Basilio. Don Quixote would not enter the village, for all the urgings of peasant and bachelor alike. He excused himself on the grounds, amply sufficient in his opinion, that knights-errant customarily slept in the fields and woods in preference to towns, even were it under gilded ceilings. So he turned aside a little from the road, very much against Sancho's will, as the good quarters he had enjoyed in the castle or house of Don Diego came back to his mind.

Chapter XX

WHERE AN ACCOUNT IS GIVEN OF THE WEDDING OF CAMACHO THE RICH, TOGETHER WITH THE INCIDENT OF BASILIO THE POOR

Scarce had the fair Aurora given bright Phœbus time to dry the liquid pearls upon her golden locks with the heat of his fervent rays, when Don Quixote, shaking off sloth from his limbs, sprang to his feet and called to his squire Sancho, who was still snoring. Seeing which, Don Quixote ere he roused him addressed him thus. "Happy are you, above all the dwellers on the face of the earth, who without envying or being envied sleep with tranquil mind, and whom neither enchanters persecute nor enchantments affright. Sleep, I say, and will say a hundred times, without any jealous thoughts of your mistress to make you keep ceaseless vigils, or any cares as to how you may repay your debts or find tomorrow's food for yourself and your needy little family, to interfere with your repose. Ambition does not break your rest, nor this world's empty pomp disturb you, for the utmost extent of your anxiety is to provide for your donkey, since upon my shoulders you have laid the support of yourself, the counterpoise and burden that nature and custom have imposed upon masters. The servant sleeps and the master lies awake thinking how he is to feed him, advance him, and reward him. The distress of seeing the sky turn brazen and withhold its needful moisture from the earth is not felt by the servant but by the master, who in time of scarcity and famine must support him who has served him in times of plenty and abundance."

To all this Sancho made no reply because he was asleep, nor would he have waked up so soon as he did had not Don Quixote brought him to his senses with the butt of his lance. He awoke at last, drowsy and lazy, and casting his eyes about in every direction. "Unless I am mistaken," he observed, "from the direction of that arcade there comes a steam and a smell a great deal more like broiled bacon than rushes or thyme. A wedding that begins with smells like that, by my faith, ought to be plentiful and generous."

"Have done, you glutton," said Don Quixote. "Come, let us go and witness this wedding and see what the rejected Basilio does."

"Let him do what he likes," returned Sancho. "If he were not poor, he would marry Quiteria. Does he expect to make a grand match for himself when he hasn't a cent to his name? Faith, señor, it's my opinion the poor man should be content with what he can get, and not go chasing rainbows. I will bet my arm that Camacho could bury Basilio in *reales*, and if that is so, as no doubt it is, what a fool Quiteria would be to refuse the fine dresses and jewels Camacho must have given her and will give her, and take Basilio's bar-throwing and swordplay. They won't give a pint of wine at the tavern for a good throw of the bar or a neat thrust of the sword. Talents and accomplishments that can't be turned into money, let Count Dirlos have them.[1] But when such gifts are bestowed on a man possessing hard cash, I wish my own life looked as good as they do. On a good foundation you can raise a good building, and the best foundation in the world is money."

1. I.e., they are useless. Count Dirlos was the hero of a popular ballad.

"For God's sake, Sancho," said Don Quixote here, "stop that harangue. If you were allowed to continue all you begin to say every instant, I believe you would have no time left for eating or sleeping, for you would spend it all talking."

"If your worship had a good memory," replied Sancho, "you would remember the articles of our agreement before we started from home this last time. One of them was that I was to be allowed to say all I liked, so long as it was not against my neighbor or your worship's authority. So far, it seems to me, I have not broken the said article."

"I remember no such article, Sancho," said Don Quixote. "And even if that were so, I desire you to hold your tongue and come along. The instruments we heard last night are already beginning to enliven the valleys again, and no doubt the marriage will take place in the cool of the morning, and not in the heat of the afternoon."

Sancho did as his master ordered, putting the saddle on Rocinante and the packsaddle on Dapple. Then they both mounted and entered the arcade at a leisurely pace. The first thing that Sancho's eyes lit upon was a whole ox spitted on a whole elm tree. In the fire on which it was to be roasted there was burning a middling-sized mountain of wood, and the six stewpots that stood around the blaze had not been made in the ordinary mold of common pots, because they were six half wine-vats, each fit to hold the contents of a slaughterhouse, and could swallow up whole sheep and hide them away in their insides with no more display than if they had been pigeons. Countless were the hares ready skinned and the plucked fowls that hung on the trees for burial in the pots, numberless the fowl and game of various sorts suspended from the branches that the air might keep them cool. Sancho counted more than sixty wineskins of over six gallons each, all filled, as it proved afterwards, with noble wines. There were, besides, piles of the whitest bread, like the heaps of wheat one sees on the threshing floors. There was a wall made of cheeses arranged like open brickwork, and two cauldrons full of oil, bigger than those in a dyer's shop, for cooking fritters which, when fried, were taken out with two mighty shovels and plunged into another cauldron of prepared honey that stood close by. Of cooks and cookmaids there were over fifty, all clean, brisk, and blithe. In the capacious belly of the ox were a dozen soft little sucking-pigs which, sewn up there, served to give it tenderness and flavor. The spices of different kinds did not seem to have been bought by the ounce but by the pound, and all lay open to view in a great chest. In short, all the preparations made for the wedding were in rustic style, but abundant enough to feed an army.

Sancho observed all, contemplated all, and everything won his heart. The first to captivate and take his fancy were the stewing pots, out of which he would have very gladly taken a moderate helping. Then the wineskins secured his affections and lastly, the produce of the frying pans, if, indeed, such imposing cauldrons may be called frying pans. Unable to control himself or bear it any longer, he approached one of the busy cooks and civilly but hungrily begged permission to soak a scrap of bread in one of the pots.

"Brother," the cook answered him, "this is not a day on which hunger is to rule, thanks to the rich Camacho. Get down and look about for a ladle and skim off a hen or two, and much good may they do you."

"I don't see one," asid Sancho.

"Wait a bit," said the cook. "Sinner that I am, how finicky and helpless you are!"

So saying, he seized a bucket and plunging it into one of the half vats took up three hens and a couple of geese. "Fall to, friend," he said to Sancho, "and take the edge off your appetite with these skimmings until dinner time comes."

"I have nothing to put them in," said Sancho.

"Well then," said the cook, "take spoon and all. Camacho's wealth and happiness furnish everything."

While Sancho fared thus, Don Quixote was watching some twelve peasants come in at one end of the arcade. They were all in holiday and gala dress and mounted on twelve beautiful mares with rich handsome field trappings and a number of little bells attached to their breastplates. Drawn up in regular order, they ran not one but several courses over the meadow, raising jubilant shouts. "Long live Camacho and Quiteria!" they cried. "He is as rich as she is fair, and she is the fairest on earth!"

"It is easy to see these people have never seen my Dulcinea del Toboso," Don Quixote said to himself, on hearing this. "If they had they would be more moderate in their praises of this Quiteria of theirs."

Shortly after this, several bands of dancers of various sorts began to enter the arcade at different points, among them a group of sword-dancers composed of some twenty-four lads of gallant and high-spirited mien, clad in the finest and whitest of linen, and with handkerchiefs embroidered in various colors with fine silk. One of the men on the mares asked an active youth who led them if any of the dancers had been wounded.

"As yet, thank God, no one has been wounded," was the reply. "We are all safe and sound."

He at once began to execute complicated figures with the rest of his comrades, with so many turns and such great dexterity that, though Don Quixote had often seen such dances, he thought he had never seen any so good as this. He also admired another group that came in. It was made up of fair young maidens, none of whom seemed to be under fourteen or over eighteen years of age, all dressed in green stuff, with their hair partly braided, partly flowing loose, but all of such bright gold as to vie with the sunbeams, and over it they wore garlands of jasmine, roses, amaranth, and honeysuckle. At their head were a venerable old man and an ancient dame, more brisk and active, however, than might have been expected from their years. The notes of a Zamora bagpipe accompanied them, and with modesty in their countenances and in their eyes, and lightness in their feet, they seemed the best dancers in the world.

Following these there came an artistic dance of the sort they call "speaking dances." It was composed of eight nymphs in two files, with the god Cupid leading one and Wealth the other, the former furnished with wings, bow, quiver, and arrows, the latter in a rich dress of gold and silk of various colors. The nymphs that followed Love bore their names written on white parchment in large letters on their backs. "Poetry" was the name of the first, "Wit" of the second, "Birth" of the third, and "Valor" of the fourth. Those that followed Wealth were distinguished in the same way, the badge of the first announcing "Liberality," that of the second "Largess," the third "Treasure," and the fourth "Peaceful Possession."

In front of them all came a wooden castle drawn by four wild men, all wearing ivy and burlap stained green, and looking so natural that they nearly terrified Sancho. On the front of the castle and on each of the four sides of its frame it bore the inscription "Castle of Caution." Four skillful drum and flute players accompanied them, and the dance having been opened, Cupid, after executing two figures, raised his eyes and aimed his bow at a damsel who stood between the turrets of the castle. Then he spoke to her:

"I am the mighty God whose sway
  Is potent over land and sea.
The heavens above us own me; nay,
  The shades below acknowledge me.
I know not fear, I have my will,
  Whate'er my whim or fancy be;
For me there's no impossible,
  I order, bind, forbid, set free."

Having concluded the stanza he discharged an arrow at the top of the castle and went back to his place. Wealth then came forward, went through two more figures, and spoke as soon as the drums ceased:

"But mightier than Love am I,
  Though Love it be that leads me on,
Than mine no lineage is more high,
  Or older, underneath the sun.
To use me rightly few know how,
  To act without me fewer still,

For I am worldly Wealth, and I vow
For evermore to do thy will."

Wealth retired, and Poetry came forward, and when she had gone through her figures like the others, she fixed her eyes on the damsel of the castle and addressed her:

"With many a fanciful conceit,
Fair Lady, winsome Poesy
Her soul, an offering at thy feet,
Presents in sonnets unto thee.
If thou my homage wilt not scorn,
Thy fortune, watched by envious eyes,
On wings of poesy upborne
Shall be exalted to the skies."

Poetry withdrew, and on the side of Wealth, Liberality advanced, went through her figures, and spoke:

"To give, while shunning each extreme,
The sparing hand, the over-free,
Therein consists, so wise men deem,
The virtue Liberality.
But thee, fair lady, to enrich,
Myself a prodigal I'll prove,
A vice not wholly shameful, which
May find its fair excuse in love."

In the same manner all the characters of the two bands advanced and retired, and each executed its figures and delivered its verses, some of them graceful, some burlesque, but Don Quixote's memory (though he had an excellent one) only carried away those that have been just quoted. All then mingled together, forming chains and breaking off again with graceful, unconstrained gaiety. Whenever Love passed in front of the castle he shot his arrows up at it, while Wealth broke gilded money boxes against it. At length, after they had danced a good while, Wealth drew out a great purse, made of the skin of a large brindled cat and to all appearance full of money, and flung it at the castle, and with the force of the blow, the boards fell asunder and tumbled down, leaving the damsel exposed and unprotected. Wealth and the characters of his band advanced, and throwing a great chain of gold over her neck pretended to take her and lead her away captive. Seeing this, Love and his supporters made as though they would release her, the whole action being accompanied by the drums and having the form of a regular dance. The wild men made peace between them, and with great dexterity readjusted and fixed the boards of the castle, and the damsel once more ensconced herself within. With this the dance wound up, to the great enjoyment of the beholders.

Don Quixote asked one of the nymphs who it was that had

composed and arranged it. She replied that it was a priest of the town who had a nice taste in devising things of the sort. "I will lay a wager," said Don Quixote, "that the same priest or bachelor is a greater friend of Camacho's than of Basilio's, and that he is better at satire than at vespers. He has introduced the accomplishments of Basilio and the riches of Camacho very neatly into the dance."

" 'My gamecock is the winner.' I stick to Camacho," exclaimed Sancho Panza, who had been listening to all this,

"It is easy to see you are a rustic, Sancho," said Don Quixote, "and of the sort that cry 'Long live the conqueror.' "

"I don't know what sort I am," returned Sancho, "but I know very well I'll never get such choice skimmings off Basilio's pots as these I have got off Camacho's"—and he showed him the bucketful of geese and hens, and seizing one began to eat with great gaiety and appetite.

"To hell with the accomplishments of Basilio!" he said. "As much as you have, so much are you worth, and as much as you are worth, so much do you have. As a grandmother of mine used to say, there are only two families in the world, the Haves and the Have Nots, and she stuck to the Haves. To this day, Señor Don Quixote, people would sooner feel the pulse of 'Have' than of 'Know,' for an ass covered with gold looks better than a horse with a packsaddle. So once more I say I stick to Camacho, the bountiful skimmings of whose pots are geese and hens, hares and rabbits. But the skimmings of Basilio's, if any ever come to hand, or even to foot, they'll be only watery wine."

"Have you finished your harangue, Sancho?" said Don Quixote.

"Of course I have finished it," replied Sancho, "because I see your worship takes offense at it. But if it was not for that, there was work enough cut out for three days."

"God grant I may see you dumb before I die, Sancho," said Don Quixote.

"At the rate we are going," said Sancho, "I'll be chewing clay before your worship dies. And then, maybe, I'll be so dumb that I'll not say a word until the end of the world or, at least, till the day of judgment."

"Even should that happen, Sancho," said Don Quixote, "your silence will never come up to all you have talked, are talking, and will talk all your life. Moreover, it naturally stands to reason that my death will come before yours. So I never expect to see you dumb, not even when you are drinking or sleeping, and that is the utmost I can say."

"In good faith, señor," replied Sancho, "there's no trusting the fleshless one, I mean Lady Death, who eats the lamb as soon as the sheep and, as I have heard our priest say, 'treads with equal foot upon the lofty towers of kings and the lowly huts of the poor.'

That lady is more mighty than dainty, she is no way squeamish, she devours all and is ready for all, and fills her saddlebags with people of all sorts, ages, and ranks. She is no reaper to sleep out the siesta; at all times she is reaping and cutting down, the dry grass as well the green. She never seems to chew, but bolts and swallows everything put before her, for she has a canine appetite that is never satisfied. And though she has no belly, she knows she has a dropsy and is thirsty to drink the lives of all that live, as one would drink a jug of cold water."

"Say no more, Sancho," said Don Quixote at this, "don't try to better it and risk a fall. For in truth what you have said about death in your rustic speech is what a good preacher might have said. I tell you Sancho, if you had discretion equal to your mother wit, you might take a pulpit in hand, and go about the world preaching fine sermons."

"He preaches well who lives well," said Sancho, "and I know no more theology than that."

"Nor need you," said Don Quixote, "but I cannot conceive or make out how it is that, since the fear of God is the beginning of wisdom, you who are more afraid of a lizard than of God, know so much."

"Pass judgment on your chivalries, señor," returned Sancho, "and don't set yourself up to judge of other men's fears or braveries, for I am as good a fearer of God as my neighbors are. But let me despatch these skimmings, for all the rest is only idle talk that will be called to account for in the other world."

So saying, he began a fresh attack on the bucket, with such a hearty appetite that he aroused Don Quixote's, who no doubt would have helped him had he not been prevented by what must be told farther on.

Chapter XXI

IN WHICH CAMACHO'S WEDDING IS CONTINUED, WITH OTHER DELIGHTFUL INCIDENTS

While Don Quixote and Sancho were engaged in the discussion set forth in the last chapter, they heard loud shouts and a great noise, which were uttered and made by the men on the mares as they went at full gallop. Their shouts welcomed the bride and bridegroom, who were approaching with musical instruments and pageantry of all sorts around them, and accompanied by the priest and the relatives of both, and all the most distinguished people of the surrounding villages.

"By God," Sancho exclaimed, when he saw the bride, "as well as I can make out she's wearing an expensive coral necklace instead of the usual medalions, and the material of her dress is velvet an inch deep instead of green Cuenca cloth. And the white linen trimming —my word, it's satin! Look at her hands! Are they set off with jet rings? May I never have any luck if they're not gold—solid gold—with pearls as white as curdled milk, and every one of them worth an eye of your head. Son of a bitch, what hair she has! If it's not a wig, I never saw longer or fairer in my life. Tell me she isn't elegant and doesn't have a good figure and that she doesn't remind you of a palm tree loaded with clusters of dates! The trinkets she has hanging from her hair and neck look just like them. I swear in my heart she is a fine looking lass fit to be bedded down."[1]

Don Quixote laughed at Sancho's rustic eulogies and thought that, saving his lady Dulcinea del Toboso, he had never seen a more beautiful woman. The fair Quiteria appeared somewhat pale, no doubt because of the bad night brides always have getting ready for the next day's wedding. The bridal party advanced towards a theater that stood on one side of the meadow decked with carpets and boughs. There they were to plight their troth, and from it they were to watch the dances and plays, but just as they arrived at that spot they heard a loud outcry behind them.

"Wait a little," a voice called out, "you, as inconsiderate as you are hasty!"

At these words everyone turned around and saw that the speaker was a man dressed in what seemed to be a loose black coat sprinkled with crimson patches like flames. He was crowned, as it soon appeared, with a crown of gloomy cypress, and in his hand he held a long staff. As he approached he was recognized by everyone as the gallant Basilio, and all waited anxiously to see what would come of his words, for they feared that his appearance at such a moment might lead to some catastrophe. He came up at last, weary and breathless. Planting himself in front of the bridal pair, he drove his staff, which had a steel spike at the end, into the ground. With pale face and eyes fixed on Quiteria, he addressed her in a hoarse, trembling voice.

"Well do you know, ungrateful Quiteria," he said, "that according to the holy law we acknowledge, so long as I live you can take no husband. Nor are you unaware that, since I hoped that time and my own exertions would improve my fortunes, I have never failed to observe the respect due to your honor. But you, casting behind you all you owe my true love, would surrender what is mine to another whose wealth serves to bring him not only good fortune but supreme happiness. To complete that happiness—not that I think he deserves it, but inasmuch as heaven is pleased to bestow it upon

1. An obscure expression which says literally, "who can pass the sand banks (or trestles) of Flanders." Trestles of "Flemish pine" were used to make beds, and Sancho appears to be making an oblique allusion to the wedding night.

him—I will, with my own hands, do away with the obstacle that may interfere with it and remove myself from between you. Long live the rich Camacho! Many a happy year may he live with the ungrateful Quiteria! And let poor Basilio die, die, Basilio whose poverty clipped the wings of his happiness and brought him to the grave!"

So saying, he seized the staff he had driven into the ground and, leaving one half of it fixed there, showed that it was a sheath concealing a fairly long rapier. With what may be called its hilt planted in the ground, he swiftly, coolly, and deliberately threw himself upon it. In an instant the bloody point and half the steel blade appeared at his back, the unhappy man falling to the earth bathed in his blood and transfixed by his own weapon.

His friends at once ran to his aid, filled with grief at his misery and sad fate.

Don Quixote, dismounting from Rocinante, hastened to help him and took him in his arms, discovering that he had not yet ceased to breathe. They were about to draw out the rapier, but the priest who was standing by objected to its being withdrawn before Basilio had confessed, as the instant of its withdrawal would be that of his death. Basilio, however, revived slightly and spoke in a weak voice, as though in pain.

"If you would consent, cruel Quiteria," he said, "to give me your hand as my bride in this last fatal moment, I might still hope that my rashness would find pardon, as by its means I attained the bliss of being yours."

Hearing this, the priest urged him to think of his soul's welfare rather than of the cravings of the body, and in all earnestness to implore God's pardon for his sins and for his rash deed. Basilio replied to this that he was determined not to confess unless Quiteria first gave him her hand in marriage, for that happiness would compose his mind and give him courage to make his confession.

Don Quixote, hearing the wounded man's entreaty, exclaimed aloud that what Basilio asked was just and reasonable, and moreover a request that might be easily complied with. It would be as much to Señor Camacho's honor to receive the lady Quiteria as widow of the brave Basilio as if he received her direct from her father.

"In this case," said he, "it will be only a matter of saying 'I do,' and no consequences can follow the utterance of the word, for the nuptial couch of this marriage must be the grave."

Camacho was listening to all this, perplexed and bewildered and not knowing what to say or do. But so urgent were the entreaties of Basilio's friends, imploring him to allow Quiteria to give him her hand, so that his soul, leaving this life in despair, should not be lost, that they moved and, indeed, forced him to say that if Quiteria should consent he would be satisfied, as it was only putting off the fulfillment of his wishes for a moment. At once all assailed Quiteria and besought her, some with prayers, others with tears, and others with persuasive arguments, to give her hand to poor Basilio. She, however, harder than marble and more unmoved than any statue, seemed unable or unwilling to utter a word, nor would she have given any reply had not the priest bade her decide quickly what she meant to do, as Basilio's soul was now at his teeth, and there was no time for hesitation.

At this the fair Quiteria, to all appearance distressed, grieved, and repentant, advanced without a word to where Basilio lay, his eyes already turned in his head, his breathing short and painful. He was murmuring the name of Quiteria between his teeth and apparently was about to die like a heathen and not like a Christian. Quiteria approached him, knelt down, and demanded his hand by signs without speaking. Basilio opened his eyes, gazing fixedly at her.

"O Quiteria," he said, "why have you turned compassionate at a moment when your compassion will serve as a dagger to rob me of life? I have not now the strength left either to bear the happiness you give me by accepting me as yours, or to suppress the pain that is rapidly drawing the dread shadow of death over my eyes. What I entreat of you, star so fatal to me, is that the hand you ask of me and would give me, be not given out of indulgence or to deceive me afresh. Confess, rather, and declare that without any constraint upon your will you give it to me as to your lawful husband. It is not fitting that you should trifle with me at such a moment, or resort to falsehoods with one who has dealt so truly with you."

While uttering these words he showed such weakness that the bystanders expected each return of faintness would take his life with it. Then Quiteria, overcome with modesty and shame, held in her right hand the hand of Basilio and spoke. "No force would bend my will," she said. "As freely, therefore, as it is possible for me to do so, I give you the hand of a lawful wife, and take yours if you give it to me of your own free will, untroubled and unaffected by the calamity your hasty act has brought upon you."

"Yes, I give it," said Basilio, "neither agitated nor distracted, but with the unclouded reason heaven is pleased to grant me, I give myself to be your husband."

"And I give myself to be your wife," said Quiteria, "whether you live many years, or they carry you from my arms to the grave."

"For one so badly wounded," observed Sancho at this point, "this young man has a great deal to say. They should make him leave off billing and cooing, and attend to his soul, for to my thinking he has it more on his tongue than at his teeth."

Basilio and Quiteria having thus joined hands, the priest, deeply moved and with tears in his eyes, pronounced the blessing upon them and implored heaven to grant an easy passage to the soul of the newly wedded man. He, however, the instant he received the blessing, jumped nimbly to his feet and with unparalleled effrontery pulled out the rapier that had been sheathed in his body. All the bystanders were astounded and some, more simple than inquiring, exclaimed aloud.

"A miracle, a miracle!" they shouted.

"No miracle, no miracle," Basilio replied, "only a trick, a trick!"

The priest, perplexed and amazed, hastened to examine the wound with both hands and found that the blade had passed, not through Basilio's flesh and ribs but through a hollow iron tube full of blood, which he had adroitly fixed at the place, the blood, as was afterwards ascertained, having been so prepared as not to congeal.

In short, the priest and Camacho and most of those present saw that they were tricked and made fools of. The bride showed no signs of displeasure at the deception. On the contrary, hearing them say that the marriage, being fraudulent, would not be valid, she said that she confirmed it afresh. This led everyone to conclude that the affair had been planned by agreement and understanding between the pair. Camacho and his supporters were so mortified that they proceeded to take a violent revenge. Drawing their swords, a great number of them attacked Basilio, in whose defense as many more swords were in an instant unsheathed while Don Quixote, assuming the lead on horseback, with his lance over his arm and well covered with his shield, made all give way before him. Sancho, who never found any pleasure or enjoyment in such doings, retreated to the wine vats from which he had taken his delectable skimmings, considering that, as a holy place, that spot would be respected.

"Hold, sirs, hold!" cried Don Quixote in a loud voice. "We have no right to take vengeance for wrongs that love may do to us. Remember that love and war are the same thing, and as in war it is allowable and common to make use of wiles and stratagems to overcome the enemy, so in the contests and rivalries of love the tricks and devices employed to attain the desired end are justifiable, provided they be not to the discredit or dishonor of the loved object. Quiteria belonged to Basilio and Basilio to Quiteria by the just and beneficent disposal of heaven. Camacho is rich and can purchase his pleasure when, where, and as it pleases him. Basilio has but this ewe-lamb, and no one, however powerful he may be, shall take her from him. These two whom God hath joined man cannot separate, and he who attempts it must first pass the point of this lance."

So saying, he brandished it so stoutly and dexterously that he overawed all who did not know him.

But so deep an impression had the rejection of Quiteria made on Camacho's mind that it banished her at once from his thoughts. Thus he let himself be swayed by the counsels of the priest, a wise and kindly disposed man, so that he and his partisans were pacified and calmed. To prove it they put up their swords and took to blaming Quiteria's inconstancy rather than Basilio's craftiness. Camacho asserted that if Quiteria, while still a maiden, loved Basilio so much, she would have loved him too as a married woman, and that he ought to thank heaven for having taken her from him rather than for having given her.

Camacho and his followers being thus consoled and pacified, those on Basilio's side also calmed down. The rich Camacho, to show that he felt no resentment for the trick and cared not a whit, ordered the festival to go on just as if he had actually married. Neither Basilio, however, nor his bride, nor their followers would take any part in it, and they withdrew to Basilio's village. The poor, too, if they are persons of virtue and good sense, have those who follow, honor, and uphold them, just as the rich have those who flatter and dance attendance on them.

With them they carried off Don Quixote, regarding him as a man of worth and a stout one. Sancho alone had a cloud on his soul, for he found himself debarred from waiting for Camacho's splendid feast and festival, which lasted until night. Thus dragged away, he moodily followed his master, who accompanied Basilio's party, and left behind him the fleshpots of Egypt. Yet in his heart he took them with him, and the now nearly finished skimmings he carried in the bucket conjured up visions before his eyes of the glory and abundance of the good cheer he was losing. And so, vexed and dejected though not hungry, without dismounting from Dapple he followed in the footsteps of Rocinante.

Chapter XXII

WHEREIN IS RELATED THE GREAT ADVENTURE OF THE CAVE OF MONTESINOS IN THE HEART OF LA MANCHA, WHICH THE VALIANT DON QUIXOTE BROUGHT TO A HAPPY TERMINATION

Many and great were the attentions shown to Don Quixote by the newly married couple, who felt themselves under an obligation to him for coming forward in defense of their cause. They deemed his wisdom the equal of his courage, rating him as a Cid in arms and a Cicero in eloquence. The worthy Sancho enjoyed himself for three days at the expense of the pair, who revealed that the sham wound had not been planned jointly with the fair Quiteria but was a scheme of Basilio's, who counted upon the very outcome they had witnessed. He confessed, it is true, that he had explained his plan to some of his friends, so that at the proper time they might aid him and see to it that the deceit would succeed.

"Deceit," said Don Quixote, "is not and ought not to be the term used when the end envisaged is a virtuous one." The marriage of lovers, he maintained, was a most excellent end.

He reminded them, however, that love has no greater enemy than hunger and constant want, for love is all gaiety, enjoyment, and happiness, especially when the lover possesses the object of his love, and of all this, poverty and want are the declared enemies.

He was saying this in order that Señor Basilio might abandon the accomplishments he was skilled in, for though they brought him fame, they brought him no money. He should apply himself to the acquisition of wealth by legitimate industry, which will never fail those who are prudent and persevering. The poor man who is a man of honor, if indeed a poor man can be a man of honor, has a jewel when he has a fair wife, and if she is taken from him, his honor is taken from him and slain. The fair woman who is a woman of honor, and whose husband is poor, deserves to be crowned with the laurels and crowns of victory and triumph. Beauty by itself attracts the desires of all who behold it, and the royal eagles and birds of towering flight swoop down on it as on a dainty lure. But if beauty is accompanied by want and penury, then the ravens and kites and other birds of prey assail it, and she who stands firm against such attacks well deserves to be called the crown of her husband.

"Remember, prudent Basilio," added Don Quixote, "it was the opinion of a certain sage, I know not whom, that there was only one good woman in the whole world. His advice was that each one should think and believe that this one good woman was his own wife, and in this way he would live happy. I myself am not married nor, so far, has it ever entered my thoughts to be so. Nevertheless I would venture to give advice to anyone who might ask it, as to the way he should seek a wife he would be satisfied to marry. The first thing I would recommend would be to pay attention to good name rather than to wealth, for a good woman does not win a good name merely by being good, but by letting it be seen that she is so, whereas open looseness and freedom do much more damage to a woman's honor than secret depravity. If you take a good woman into your house, it will be an easy matter to keep her good and even to make her still better. But if you take a bad one, you will find it hard work to mend her, for it is no very easy matter to pass from one extreme to another. I do not say it is impossible, but I look upon it as difficult."

"This master of mine," said Sancho to himself, as he listened to all this, "when I say anything that has weight and substance, says I could take a pulpit in hand, and go around preaching fine sermons. But I say of him that, when he begins stringing maxims together and giving advice, not only could he take a pulpit in hand, but two on each finger, and go into the marketplaces to his heart's content. Devil take you for a knight-errant, what a lot of things you know! I used to think in my heart that the only thing he knew was what belonged to his chivalry, but there is nothing he hasn't tasted or dipped his spoon in."

Sancho muttered this rather audibly, so that his master overheard him.

"What are you muttering there, Sancho?"

"I'm not saying anything or muttering anything," said Sancho. "I was only saying to myself that I wish I had heard what your worship has said just now before I married. Perhaps I'd say now, 'The unhitched ox licks himself well.' "

"Is your Teresa so bad then, Sancho?"

"She is not very bad," replied Sancho, "but she is not very good. At least, she is not as good as I could wish."

"It is wrong of you, Sancho," said Don Quixote, "to speak ill of your wife, for after all she is the mother of your children."

"We are even," returned Sancho, "because she speaks ill of me whenever she takes it into her head, especially when she is jealous. Satan himself could not put up with her then."

In short, they remained three days with the newly married couple, who entertained them and treated them like kings. Don Quixote begged the fencing licentiate to find him a guide to show the way to the cave of Montesinos, as he had a great desire to enter it and see with his own eyes if the wonderful tales told of it all over the country were true. The licentiate said he would get him a cousin of his own, a famous scholar very much given to reading books of chivalry, who would take great pleasure in conducting him to the mouth of the cave. He would show him, too, the lakes of Ruidera, which were famous all over La Mancha, and even all over Spain. He assured Don Quixote that he would find the cousin entertaining, for he was a youth who could write books good enough to be printed and dedicated to princes. The cousin arrived at last, leading an ass in foal, with a packsaddle covered with a gaily colored carpet or cloth. Sancho saddled Rocinante, got Dapple ready, and stocked his saddlebags, accompanied by those of the cousin, likewise well filled. So, commending themselves to God and bidding farewell to all, they set out, taking the road for the famous cave of Montesinos.

On the way Don Quixote asked the cousin about the nature of his pursuits, avocations, and studies, to which the cousin replied that he was by profession a humanist, and that his pursuits and studies were writing books for the press, all of great utility and no less entertainment to the nation. One was called *The Book of Liveries,* in which he described seven hundred and three liveries, with their colors, mottoes, and rebuses, from which gentlemen of the court might pick and choose any they fancied for festivals and revels, without having to beg them from anyone, or puzzle their brains, as the saying is, to have them match their objects and purposes.

"For," said he, "I give the jealous, the rejected, the forgotten, the absent, what will suit them and fit them without fail.[1] I have another book, too, which I shall call *Metamorphoses*, or *The Spanish Ovid*. It is of rare and original invention, for imitating Ovid in burlesque style, I show who the Giralda of Seville and the Angel of the Magdalena were, what the sewer of Vecinguerra at Córdoba was, and the bulls of Guisando, the Sierra Morena, the Leganitos and Lavapiés fountains at Madrid, not forgetting those of the Piojo, of the Caño Dorado, and of the Priora—all with their allegories, metaphors, and changes, so that they are amusing, interesting, and instructive all at once.[2]

Another book I have which I call *The Supplement to Polydore Vergil*. It deals with the invention of things, and is a work of great erudition and research, for I establish and elucidate elegantly some things of great importance which Polydore omitted to mention.[3] He forgot to tell us who was the first man in the world that had a cold in his head, and who was the first to use mercurial ointment for the French disease, but I give it accurately set forth, and quote more than twenty-five authors in proof of it, so you may perceive I have labored to good purpose and that the book will be of service to the whole world."

"Tell me, señor," said Sancho, who had been listening attentively to the cousin, "—and God give you luck in printing your books—can you tell me (for of course you know, as you know everything) who was the first man that scratched his head? To my thinking it must have been our father Adam."

"So it must," replied the cousin, "for there is no doubt but Adam had a head and hair, and being the first man in the world he would have scratched himself sometimes."

"So I think," said Sancho. "But now tell me, who was the first tumbler in the world?"

"Really, brother," answered the cousin, "I could not at this moment say positively without having investigated it. I will look it

1. Wealthy gentlemen (and ladies) appeared at tournaments and other festivities in costumes allusive of their love affairs, and a number of books appeared with suggestions for clever rebuses, mottoes, puns, designs for embroideries, for fancy helmet crests, etc., to help in designing these "liveries."

2. Ovid collected and versified in his Latin *Metamorphoses* ("transformations") Greco-Roman legends, many of which explain the origin of place-names, rivers, etc. Ovid was sometimes studied for its well-hidden allegorical or moral content. Thus the cousin explains who or what were transformed into various Spanish landmarks: the weathervanes of two famous churches, prehistoric stone animals, and five fountains, etc., and reveals their "allegories."

3. Polydore Vergil (1470–1550), an Italian historian, compiled a widely read book on the discovery of important arts, sciences, religious practices, laws, and so on, from classical sources. It includes some things that now seem frivolous, such as the inventors of games, the wearing of finger-rings, etc.—the sort of trivia which inspire the cousin's scholarly efforts.

up when I go back to where I have my books and will answer you the next time we meet, for this will not be the last time."

"Look here, señor," said Sancho, "don't give yourself any trouble about it, for I have just this minute hit upon what I asked you. The first tumbler in the world, you must know, was Lucifer, when they threw or pitched him out of heaven, for he came tumbling into the bottomless pit."

"You are right, friend," said the cousin.

"Sancho," Don Quixote interjected, "that question and answer are not your own. You heard them from someone else."

"Hold your peace, señor," said Sancho. "Faith, if I take to asking questions and answering, I'll go on from now until tomorrow morning. Why, to ask foolish things and answer nonsense I don't have to go looking for help from my neighbors."

"You have said more than you are aware of, Sancho," said Don Quixote. "There are some who wear themselves out learning and proving things that once known and proved, are not worth a penny to the understanding or memory."

In this and other pleasant conversation the day went by, and that night they put up at a small hamlet not more than two leagues distant from the cave of Montesinos, as the cousin told Don Quixote. He added that, if Don Quixote was bent upon entering it, ropes would be needed, so that he might be tied and lowered into its depths. Don Quixote said that even if it reached to the bottomless pit he meant to see where it went to. So they bought about six hundred feet of rope, and next day at two in the afternoon they arrived at the cave. Though the mouth is spacious and wide, it is full of thorn and wild fig bushes and brambles and briars, so thick and matted that they completely close it up and cover it.

On coming within sight of it all three dismounted, and the cousin and Sancho immediately tied Don Quixote very firmly with the ropes. "Mind what you are about, master," said Sancho, as they were girding and belting him. "Don't go burying yourself alive, or putting yourself where you'll be like a bottle put to cool in a well. It's no affair or business of your worship's to explore down there, where it must be worse than a dungeon."

"Tie me and hold your peace," said Don Quixote, "for an undertaking like this, friend Sancho, was reserved for me."

"I beg you, Señor Don Quixote," said the guide, "observe carefully and examine with a hundred eyes everything within. Perhaps there may be some things for me to put into my book of *Transformations.*"

" 'The tambourine is in good hands.' My master knows what he's doing," said Sancho Panza, who with this remark had finished the tying, which went not over the armor but only over the vest.

"It was careless of us," Don Quixote observed, "not to have provided ourselves with a small cowbell to be tied on the rope close to me. The sound would show that I was still descending and alive, but as that is out of the question now, in God's hand be it to guide me." Forthwith he fell on his knees and in a low voice offered up a prayer to heaven, imploring God to aid him and grant him success in this to all appearance perilous and untried adventure. "O mistress of my actions and movements, illustrious and peerless Dulcinea del Toboso," he then exclaimed aloud, "if so be the prayers and supplications of this fortunate lover can reach your ears, by your incomparable beauty I entreat you to hear them, for they but ask you not to withhold your favor and protection now that I stand in such need. I am about to precipitate, to sink, to plunge myself into the abyss here before me, only to let the world know that while you favor me there is no impossibility I will not attempt and accomplish."

With these words he approached the cavern and saw that it was impossible to let himself down or effect an entrance except by sheer force or by cleaving a passage. So, drawing his sword, he began to demolish the brambles at the mouth of the cave. At the noise, a vast multitude of crows and rooks flew out of it so thick and so fast that they knocked Don Quixote down. Indeed, if he had been as much of a believer in augury as he was a Catholic Christian he would have taken it as a bad omen and declined to bury himself in such a place. He got up, however, and as there rose up no more crows or nightbirds like the bats that flew out along with the crows, the cousin and Sancho gave him rope and he lowered himself into the depths of the dread cavern. As he entered it Sancho sent his blessing after him and made a thousand crosses over him.

"God," he said, "and the Virgin of La Peña de Francia, and the Trinity of Gaeta[4] guide you, O flower and cream of knights-errant. There you go, you daredevil of the earth, heart of steel, arm of brass. Once more, God guide you and send you back safe, sound, and unhurt to the light of this world you are leaving to bury yourself in the darkness you are seeking." And the cousin offered up almost the same prayers and supplications.

Don Quixote kept calling to them to give him rope and more rope, and they gave it out little by little. By the time the calls, which came out of the cave as out of a pipe, could no longer be heard, they had let down the six hundred feet of rope. They were inclined to pull Don Quixote up again, as they could give him no more rope. However, they waited about half an hour, and then began to gather in the rope with great ease and without feeling any weight, so that they fancied Don Quixote was remaining below.

4. La Peña de Francia is a mountain near Ciudad Rodrigo, and one of the holy places of Spain in consequence of the discovery of an image of the Virgin there in the fifteenth century. The Trinity of Gaeta is the chapel dedicated to the Trinity above the harbor of Gaeta.

Convinced that this was so, Sancho wept bitterly and hauled away in great haste, in order to settle the question. When, however, they had taken in, as it seemed, about five hundred feet, they felt a weight, at which they were greatly delighted. At last, at sixty feet more, they saw Don Quixote distinctly, and Sancho called out to him. "Welcome back, señor," he said, "for we had begun to think you were going to stay there to found a family."

But Don Quixote answered not a word. When they had drawn him out entirely they saw he had his eyes shut and gave every appearance of being fast asleep.

They stretched him on the ground and untied him, but still he did not awake. They rolled him back and forwards and shook and pulled him about, so that after some time he came to. Stretching himself just as if he were waking up from a deep and sound sleep, he looked about him. "God forgive you, friends," he said, "you have taken me away from the sweetest, most delightful existence and spectacle that ever human being enjoyed or beheld. Now indeed I know that all the pleasures of this life pass away like a shadow and a dream, or fade like the flower of the field. O ill-fated Montesinos! O sore-wounded Durandarte! O unhappy Belerma! O tearful Guadiana, and you O hapless daughters of Ruidera who show in your waves the tears that flowed from your beauteous eyes!"

The cousin and Sancho Panza listened to the words of Don Quixote, who uttered them as though with immense pain he drew them up from his very innards. They begged him to explain himself and tell them what he had seen in that hell down there.

"Hell do you call it?" said Don Quixote. "Call it by no such name, for it does not deserve it, as you shall soon see."

He then begged them to give him something to eat, as he was very hungry. They spread the cousin's saddle cover on the grass and delved into the stores contained in the saddlebags. Then all three sat down lovingly and sociably and made a luncheon and a supper of it all in one. After the cloth was removed, Don Quixote of La Mancha spoke.

"Let no one rise," he said, "and listen to me, my sons, both of you."

Chapter XXIII

OF THE WONDERFUL THINGS THE INCOMPARABLE DON QUIXOTE SAID HE SAW IN THE DEEP CAVE OF MONTESINOS, THE IMPOSSIBILITY AND MAGNITUDE OF WHICH CAUSE THIS ADVENTURE TO BE DEEMED APOCRYPHAL

It was about four in the afternoon when the sun, veiled in clouds, with subdued light and tempered beams, enabled Don Quixote to relate, without heat or inconvenience, what he had seen in the cave of Montesinos to his two illustrious hearers, and he began as follows:

"Some twelve or fourteen times a man's height down in this pit, and on the right-hand side, there is a recess or space, roomy enough to contain a large cart with its mules. A little light reaches it through some chinks or crevices, communicating with it and open to the surface of the earth. This recess or space I perceived when I was already growing weary and disgusted at finding myself hanging suspended by the rope, traveling downwards into that dark region without any certainty or knowledge of where I was going. I resolved to enter it and rest myself for a while. I called out, telling you not to let out more rope until I bade you, but you must not have heard me. I then gathered in the rope you were sending me, and making a coil or pile of it I seated myself upon it, ruminating and considering what I was to do to lower myself to the bottom, having no one to hold me up.

"As I was thus deep in thought and perplexity, suddenly and without provocation a profound sleep fell upon me, and when I least expected it, I do not know how, I awoke and found myself in the midst of the most beautiful, delightful meadow that nature could produce or the most lively human imagination conceive. I opened my eyes, I rubbed them, and found I was not asleep but thoroughly awake. Nevertheless, I felt my head and breast to satisfy myself whether I myself was there or some empty delusive phantom. But touch, feeling, and the collected thoughts that passed through my mind all convinced me that I was the same then and there as I am at this moment.

"I next caught sight of a stately royal palace or castle, with walls that seemed built of clear transparent crystal. Through two great doors that opened wide I saw coming toward me a venerable old man clad in a long gown of mulberry-colored serge that trailed upon the ground. On his shoulders and breast he had a green satin collegiate hood, and covering his head a black Milanese cap, and his snow-white beard fell below his belt. He carried no arms whatever, nothing but a rosary of beads bigger than good-sized filberts, each tenth bead being like a moderate ostrich egg. His bearing, his gait, his dignity, and imposing presence held me spellbound and wondering. He approached me, and the first thing he did was to embrace me closely.

" 'For a long time now, O valiant knight Don Quixote of La Mancha,' he said to me, 'we who are here enchanted in these solitudes have been hoping to see you, so that you may make known to the world what is shut up and concealed in this deep cave, called the cave of Montesinos, which you have entered. It was an achievement reserved for your invincible heart and stupendous courage alone to attempt. Come with me, illustrious sir, and I will show you the marvels hidden within this transparent castle, whereof I am the governor and perpetual warden. I am Montesinos himself, from whom the cave takes its name.'[1]

"The instant he told me he was Montesinos, I asked him if the story they told in the world above was true, that he had taken out the heart of his great friend Durandarte from his breast with a little dagger and carried it to the lady Belerma, as his friend when at the point of death had commanded him. He replied that they spoke the truth in every respect except as to the dagger, for it was not a dagger, nor little, but a burnished knife sharper than an awl."

"That knife must have been made by Ramón de Hoces the Sevillian," said Sancho.

"I do not know," said Don Quixote. "It could not have been by that knife-maker, however, because Ramón de Hoces was a man of yesterday, and the affair of Roncesvalles, where this mishap occurred, was long ago. But the question is of no great importance, nor does it affect or alter in any way the truth or substance of the story."

"That is true," said the cousin. "Continue, Señor Don Quixote, for I am listening to you with the greatest pleasure in the world."

"And with no less pleasure do I tell the tale," said Don Quixote. "And so, to proceed: the venerable Montesinos led me into the palace of crystal where, in a lower chamber, strangely cool and entirely of alabaster, was an elaborately wrought marble tomb. Upon it I beheld, stretched at full length, a knight, not of bronze, or marble, or jasper, as are seen on other tombs, but of actual flesh and bone. His right hand (which seemed to me somewhat hairy and sinewy, a sign of great strength in its owner) lay on the side of his heart. Before I could put any question to Montesinos, he saw how I gazed at the tomb in amazement.

" 'This,' he said to me, 'is my friend Durandarte, flower and mirror of the true lovers and valiant knights of his time. He is held enchanted here, as I myself and many others are, by that French enchanter Merlin, who, they say, was the devil's son. My belief is, not that he was the devil's son, but that he knew, as the saying is, a bit more than the devil. How or why he enchanted us, no one knows; but time will tell, and I suspect that time is not far off. What I marvel at is, for I know this as surely as that it is now day,

1. Montesinos is the hero of half a dozen ballads belonging to the Carolingian cycle but does not figure in any of the French romances. According to the ballads he was one of the Peers, and son of Count Grimaltos, or Grimaldos, by a daughter of Charlemagne. He owed his name to having been born in a forest (*monte*), where his father and mother were wandering, banished from court by the machinations of the traitor Tomillas. It appears to have been connected with this cave from a very early period.

that Durandarte ended his life in my arms and that, after his death, I took out his heart with my own hands. Indeed it must have weighed more than two pounds; for, according to naturalists, he who has a large heart is more largely endowed with valor than he who has a small one. Then, as this is the case, and as the knight did really die, how comes it that he now moans and sighs from time to time, as if he were still alive?'

"As he said this, the wretched Durandarte cried out in a loud voice:

> 'O cousin Montesinos!
> 'T was my last request of thee,
> When my soul hath left the body,
> And that lying dead I be,
> With thy knife or with thy dagger
> Cut the heart from out my breast,
> And bear it to Belerma.
> This was my last request.'

On hearing this, the venerabled Montesinos fell on his knees before the unhappy knight.

" 'O Señor Durandarte, my beloved cousin,' he exclaimed, 'long since have I done what you bade me on that sad day when I lost you. I took out your heart as well as I could, and left not an atom of it in your breast. I wiped it with a lace handkerchief, and I took the road to France with it, having first laid you in the bosom of the earth with tears enough to wash and cleanse my hands of the blood that covered them after they had plunged into your breast. Furthermore, O cousin of my soul, at the first village I came to after leaving Roncesvalles, I sprinkled a little salt on your heart so that it would not smell and I could bring it, if not fresh, at least pickled, into the presence of the lady Belerma.

" 'She, like you, myself, Guadiana your squire, the dueña Ruidera and her seven daughters and two nieces, and many more among your friends and acquaintances, have been kept here under enchantment by the sage Merlin these many years, and though more than five hundred have gone by, not one of us has died. Ruidera and her daughter and nieces alone are missing, and that is because of the tears they shed. Merlin, who seems to have felt for them, changed each one into a lake, and to this very day in the world of the living, and in the province of La Mancha, these are called the Lakes of Ruidera. The seven daughters belong to the kings of Spain and the two nieces to the knights of a very holy order called the Order of St. John.

" 'Guadiana your squire, who likewise bewailed your fate, was changed into a river bearing his own name, but when he came to the surface and beheld the sun of this other heaven, so great was his grief at the thought of leaving you that he plunged into the bowels of the earth. However, as he cannot help following his natural course, from time to time he comes out and shows himself where the sun and people can see him. The lakes I spoke of send him their waters, and with these, and others that flow to him, he makes a grand and imposing entrance into Portugal. Yet, wherever he goes, he shows his melancholy and sadness, and takes no pride in breeding dainty choice fish but only coarse and tasteless sorts, very different from those of the golden Tagus.

" 'Everything I tell you now, O cousin, I have told you many times before, and as you do not answer, I fear that either you refuse to believe me or do not hear me, and God knows how much this grieves me. But now I have news to give you. It may not greatly diminish your sufferings, but it will do nothing to worsen them. Be instructed that you have here before you (open your eyes and you will see) that great knight of whom the sage Merlin has prophesied such great things—I mean Don Quixote of La Mancha, who in these days has again, and to better purpose than in past times, revived the long-forgotten practice of knight-errantry. With his intervention and aid it may come about that we shall be disenchanted, for great deeds are reserved for great men.

" 'And if that may not be,' said the wretched Durandarte in a low and feeble voice, 'if that may not be, then, O cousin, I say "patience and shuffle the cards." ' Then, turning over on his side, he relapsed into his former silence without uttering another word.

"And now there was heard a great outcry and lamentation, accompanied by deep sighs and bitter sobs. I looked around, and through the crystal wall I saw passing through another chamber a procession of fair damsels in two rows. All of them were clad in mourning and had white turbans of Turkish fashion on their heads. Behind, in the rear of the procession, there came a lady, for so from her dignity she seemed to be. She too was clad in black, with a white veil so long and ample that it swept the ground, and her turban was twice as large as the largest of any of the others. Her eyebrows met, her nose was rather flat, her mouth was large but with ruddy lips, and her teeth, when she revealed them, appeared to be few and not well placed, though white as peeled almonds. In her hands she held a fine cloth, and in it, as well as I could make out, was a mummified heart, all dried up and shriveled.

"Montesinos told me that those in the procession were the attendants of Durandarte and Belerma, enchanted like their master and mistress, and that the last one, carrying the heart and cloth in her hands, was the lady Belerma. With her damsels she went four days in the week in procession singing, or rather weeping, dirges over his cousin's body and pitiable heart. If she appeared to me somewhat ill-favored or less beautiful than renown declared, it was because of the bad nights and worse days she passed in this enchantment, as was shown by the great dark circles around her eyes, and her sickly complexion.

" 'Her sallowness, and the rings round her eyes,' said Montesinos, 'are not due to the periodical ailment usual with women, for it is many months and even years since she has had any. It is the grief her own heart suffers for the heart she ceaselessly holds in her hand, and which freshens and brings back to her mind the sad fate of her lost lover. But for this, even the great Dulcinea del Toboso, so celebrated in all these parts, and indeed throughout the world, could hardly equal her for beauty, grace, and gaiety.'

" 'Hold hard!' said I at this, 'tell your story as you ought, Señor Don Montesinos, for you know very well that all comparisons are odious, and there is no occasion to compare one person with another. The peerless Dulcinea del Toboso is what she is, and the lady Doña Belerma is what *she* is and has been, and that's enough.'

" 'Forgive me, Señor Don Quixote,' he said in reply. 'I admit I was wrong and spoke unthinkingly in saying that the lady Dulcinea could scarcely match the lady Belerma. To have learned, by what means I do not know, that you are her knight would be enough to make me bite my tongue out rather than compare her to anything save heaven itself.'

"After this apology offered me by the great Montesinos, my heart recovered from the shock inflicted when I heard my lady compared with Belerma."

"I am amazed," said Sancho, "that your worship didn't jump on the old fellow and break every bone in his body with kicks, and pull out his beard until you didn't leave a hair in it."

"No, Sancho, my friend," said Don Quixote, "it would not have been right in me to do that, for we are all bound to respect the aged, even when they are not knights, but especially those who are both knights and enchanted. I only know that neither he nor I owed each other anything after the many other questions and answers we exchanged."

"I cannot understand, Señor Don Quixote," remarked the cousin at this point, "how your worship, in the short time you were below, could have seen so many things, and said and answered so much."

"How long is it since I went down?" asked Don Quixote.

"Little better than an hour," replied Sancho. "That cannot be," returned Don Quixote, "because night overtook me while I was there, and day came, and it was night again and day again three times. So, by my reckoning, I have been three days in those remote regions hidden from your sight."

"My master must be right," replied Sancho, "for since everything that has happened to him is by enchantment, maybe what seems to us an hour would seem three days and nights there."

"That's it," said Don Quixote.

"And did your worship eat anything all that time, señor?" asked the cousin.

"I never touched a morsel," answered Don Quixote, "nor did I feel hunger, or think of it."

"And do the enchanted eat?" said the cousin.

"They neither eat," said Don Quixote, "nor are they subject to the greater excretions, though it is thought that their nails, beards, and hair grow."

"And do the enchanted sleep, now, señor?" asked Sancho.

"Certainly not," replied Don Quixote. "At least, during the three days I was with them not one of them closed an eye, nor did I either."

"The proverb, 'Tell me what company you keep and I'll tell you who you are,' is to the point here," said Sancho. "Your worship keeps company with enchanted people who are always fasting and watching. What wonder, then, that you neither eat nor sleep while you are with them? But forgive me, señor, if I say, may God take me—I was just going to say the devil—if I believe a single word of what you have just told us."

"What!" said the cousin. "Do you think Señor Don Quixote has been lying? Why, even if he wanted to, he has not had the time to imagine and put together such a host of lies."

"I don't believe my master is lying," said Sancho.

"Then what do you believe?" asked Don Quixote.

"I believe," replied Sancho, "that this Merlin, or those enchanters who enchanted the whole crew your worship says you saw and talked with down there, stuffed your imagination or your mind with all this rigmarole you have been telling us, and whatever is still to come."

"All that might be so, Sancho," replied Don Quixote, "but it is not, for everything I have told you I saw with my own eyes and touched with my own hands. Among the countless other marvelous things Montesinos showed me—I will give you an account of them at leisure and at the proper time in the course of our journey, for they would not all be in place here—he showed me three country girls who went skipping and capering like goats over the pleasant fields. The instant I saw them I knew one of them was the peerless Dulcinea del Toboso and the others the two country girls who were with her and with whom we spoke on the road from El Toboso! I asked Montesinos if he knew them, and he told me he did not, but he thought they must be some enchanted ladies of distinction, for it was only a few days before that they had made their appearance in those meadows, and that I should not be surprised, because there were a great many other ladies there of times past and present, enchanted and in various strange shapes. Among them he had recognized Queen Guinevere and her dame Quintañona, who had poured out the wine for Lancelot when he came from Britain."

When Sancho Panza heard his master say this, he was ready to take leave of his senses or die with laughter, for he knew the real truth about the pretended enchantment of Dulcinea, in which he himself had been the enchanter and had concocted all the evidence. So he made up his mind at last that, beyond all doubt, his master was out of his wits and stark mad. "It was an evil hour, a worse season, and a sorrowful day," he said to him, "when your worship, my dear master, went down to the other world, and an unlucky moment when you met with Señor Montesinos, who has sent you back to us like this. You were all right here above, in your full senses, such as God had given you, quoting maxims and giving advice at every turn, but now you are talking the greatest nonsense that can be imagined."

"Since I know you, Sancho," said Don Quixote, "I pay no heed to your words."

"Nor I to your worship's," said Sancho, "whether you beat me or kill me for those I have spoken and will speak, if you don't correct and mend your own. But tell me, while we are still at peace, how or by what sign did you recognize this lady as our mistress. And if you spoke to her, what did you say, and what did she answer?"

"I recognized her," said Don Quixote, "because she was wearing the same garments as when you pointed her out to me. I spoke to her, but she did not utter a word in reply. On the contrary, she turned her back on me and took to flight, at such a pace that a crossbow bolt could not have overtaken her. I was about to follow her, and would have done so had not Montesinos advised me not to take the trouble as it would be useless, particularly as the time was drawing near when I would have to leave the cavern. He told me too, that in time he would let me know how he and Belerma and Durandarte and everyone there were to be disenchanted. But what pained me most of all I observed down there was this. While Montesinos was speaking to me, one of the two companions of the hapless Dulcinea came up to me on one side, without my having seen her coming. There were tears in her eyes, and she spoke to me, in a low agitated voice.

" 'My Lady Dulcinea del Toboso,' she said, 'kisses your worship's hands and entreats you to do her the favor of letting her know how you are. Since she is in great need, she also entreats your worship as earnestly as she can to be so good as to lend her half a dozen *reales*, of whatever you have about you, against this new cotton skirt I have here. She promises to repay them very promptly.' I was amazed and taken aback by such a message, so I turned to Señor Montesinos.

" 'Is it possible, Señor Montesinos,' I asked, 'that persons of distinction under enchantment can be in need?'

" 'Believe me, Señor Don Quixote,' he replied, 'that which we all need is to be met with everywhere. It penetrates all quarters and reaches everyone, and does not spare even the enchanted. As the lady Dulcinea del Toboso has sent her servant to beg those six *reales*, and the pledge is to all appearance a good one, there is nothing for it but to give them to her, for no doubt she must be in some difficulty.'

" 'I will take no pledge from her,' I replied, 'but I cannot give her the sum she asks for, for all I have is four *reales*.'

"These I gave her—they were the coins that you, Sancho, gave me the other day to bestow in alms upon the poor I met along the road.

" 'Tell your mistress, my dear,' I said, 'that I am grieved to the heart at her distress, and wish I was a Fugger[2] to remedy them. I would have her know that I cannot be, and ought not be, in health while deprived of the happiness of seeing her and enjoying her discreet conversation. I implore her, as earnestly as I can, to allow herself to be seen and addressed by her captive servant and forlorn knight. Tell her, too, that when she least expects it she will hear it proclaimed that I have made an oath and vow after the fashion of the Marquis of Mantua when he found his nephew Baldwin at the point of death in the heart of the mountains, and swore to avenge him. He refused to eat bread off a tablecloth, and other trifling matters which he added, until vengeance was done. Even so will I swear to take no rest, and to roam the seven regions of the earth more thoroughly than the Infante Don Pedro of Portugal ever roamed them, until I have disenchanted her.'

" 'All that and more, you owe my lady,' was the damsel's answer. She took the four *reales*, and instead of making me a curtsy she cut a caper, springing two full yards into the air."

"O blessed God!" exclaimed Sancho aloud at this, "is it possible that such things can be in the world, and that enchanters and enchantments can have such power as to change my master's right senses into such mad ravings! O señor, señor, for God's sake, consider yourself, look out for your reputation, and don't believe this silly stuff that has left you weak and short of wits."

"You talk in this way because you love me, Sancho," said Don Quixote. "Since you lack experience in worldly matters, everything that offers some difficulty seems impossible to you. But time will pass, as I said before, and I will relate some of the things I saw down there which will make you believe what I have just told you, and the truth of which allows neither reply nor question."

2. The Fuggers were a German banking family whose wealth reached its height during the sixteenth century.

Chapter XXIV

WHEREIN ARE RELATED A THOUSAND TRIFLING MATTERS, AS TRIVIAL AS THEY ARE NECESSARY TO THE RIGHT UNDERSTANDING OF THIS GREAT HISTORY

He who translated this great history from the original written by its first author, Cide Hamete Benengeli, says that on coming to the chapter that dealt with the adventures in the cave of Montesinos, he found written on the margin, in Hamete's own hand, these exact words:

"I cannot in any way persuade myself that everything related in the preceding chapter could have actually happened to the valiant Don Quixote. The reason is that all the adventures that have occurred up to this moment have been possible and plausible. But as for this story of the cave, I see no way of accepting it as true, as it so much exceeds all reasonable bounds. It is impossible for me to believe that Don Quixote could lie, since he is the most truthful gentleman and the noblest knight of his time. He would not tell a lie though he were shot to death with arrows. On the other hand, when I consider how he related the story in minute detail, he could not in so brief a time have put together such a vast network of absurdities."

"If, then, this adventure seems apocryphal, it is no fault of mine. So, without declaring it false or true, I write it down. Use your own wisdom, reader, to decide as you see fit, for I am not required, nor is it in my power, to do more. Some maintain, however, that at the time of his death he retracted and said he had invented it all, thinking it a perfect match for the adventures he had read in his histories." And then he goes on to say:

The cousin was amazed at Sancho's boldness as well as at the patience of his master, and concluded that the latter's good temper was due to the happiness he felt at having seen his lady Dulcinea, even when enchanted. Otherwise, Sancho's words and language would have deserved a thrashing, for indeed he thought Sancho had been rather impudent to his master.

"Señor Don Quixote of La Mancha," he said to him, "I look upon the time spent in traveling with your worship as very well employed, for it has made me the richer by four things. First, I have made your acquaintance, which I consider good fortune indeed. Second, I have learned what the cave of Montesinos contains, together with the transformations of Guadiana and of the lakes of Ruidera, and this will be of use to me for the *Spanish Ovid* I am working on. Third, I have discovered the antiquity of cards, which were in use at least in the time of Charlemagne, as may be inferred from the words you say Durandarte uttered at the end of that long spell while Montesinos was talking to him, when he woke up and said, 'Patience and shuffle the cards.' This phrase and expression he could not have learned while he was enchanted, but only previously in France, in the time of the emperor Charlemagne aforesaid.

"This demonstration is the very thing I need for the other book I am writing, the *Supplement to Polydore Vergil on the Invention of Antiquities.* I believe he never thought of inserting the invention of cards in his book, as I mean to do in mine. That will be a matter of great importance, particularly when I can cite so grave and trustworthy an authority as Señor Durandarte. And the fourth thing is that I have ascertained the source of the river Guadiana, heretofore unknown to mankind."

"You are right," said Don Quixote. "Yet I should like to know, if by God's favor they grant you a licence to print those books of yours—which I doubt—to whom you intend to dedicate them."

"There are lords and grandees in Spain to whom they can be dedicated," said the cousin.

"Not many," said Don Quixote. "Not that they are unworthy of it, but because they do not care to accept books and display the generosity that the author's labor and courtesy seem to require. One prince I know who makes up for all the rest, and so splendidly, that if I were to speak of him, envy might be aroused in many a noble breast.[1] But leave the matter for some more convenient time, and let us go and look for a place of shelter for the night."

"Not far from here," said the cousin, "is a hermitage. People say that the hermit who lives there was a soldier, and he is reputed to be a good Christian and a very intelligent and charitable man. Close to the hermitage he has a small house built at his own expense. Though small, it is large enough to receive guests."

"Has this hermit any hens, do you think?" asked Sancho.

"Few hermits are without them," said Don Quixote. "Those we see nowadays are not like the hermits in the Egyptian deserts who wore palm leaves and lived on the roots of the earth. But do not think that by praising them I am disparaging the others. What I mean is that the penances of present-day hermits do not equal the asceticism and austerity of former times. Yet it does not follow that they are not all worthy men, and such I believe them to be. At the worst, the hypocrite who pretends to be good does less harm than the shameless sinner."

At this point they saw approaching them at a brisk pace a man on foot, who kept on beating a mule loaded with lances and halberds. When he came up to them, he greeted them and was about to continue on his way.

1. A compliment to Cervantes' patron, the Count of Lemos.

"Stop, my good man," Don Quixote called to him. "You seem to be in more of a hurry than suits that mule."

"I cannot stop, señor," answered the man. "The arms you see me carrying are to be used tomorrow, so I must not delay. God be with you. But if you want to know why I am carrying them, I will be spending the night at the inn beyond the hermitage, and if that is your road you will find me there, and I will tell you some curious things. Once more, God be with you."

He urged on his mule at such a pace that Don Quixote had no time to ask about the curious things he had to relate. Being himself somewhat inquisitive and always anxious to learn something new, he decided to set out at once and spend the night at the inn instead of the hermitage, where the cousin wanted them to stay. Accordingly they mounted, and all three took the direct road for the inn, which they reached a little before nightfall. On the road, the cousin proposed going to the hermitage for a drink. The instant Sancho heard this, he steered his Dapple towards it, and Don Quixote and the cousin did the same. But Sancho's bad luck so ordered it, apparently, that the hermit was not at home, as a female sub-hermit they found in the hermitage told them.[2] They called for some wine. She replied that her master had none, but that if they liked water she would give it with great pleasure.

"If I found any pleasure in water," said Sancho, "there are wells along the road where I could have had enough. Ah, Camacho's wedding and plentiful house of Don Diego, how often do I miss you!"

Leaving the hermitage, they pushed on toward the inn, and a little farther on they came upon a youth who was pacing along in front of them at no great speed, so that they overtook him. He carried a sword over his shoulder, and slung on it was, probably, a bundle of his clothes, most likely his breeches or trousers, and his cloak and a shirt or two. He was wearing a short jacket of velvet with a gloss like satin, and had his shirt out. His stockings were of silk, and his shoes square-toed, as they wear them at court. He might have been eighteen or nineteen years old. His expression was merry, and he seemed to be agile. As he went along he sang *seguidillas*[3] to while away the tedium of the journey. As they came up with him he was just finishing one, which the cousin learned by heart. They say it went like this:

I'm off to the wars
  For the want of pence,
Oh, had I but money
  I'd show more sense.

2. The suggestion is that the absent hermit has a concubine.

3. Verses of shorter lines than the ballad and generally of a humorous or satirical cast.

"You travel very airily, sir gallant," said Don Quixote, who was the first to address him. "Where are you going, may we ask, if it is your pleasure to tell us?"

"The heat and my poverty are the reason I travel so airily," the youth replied, "and the wars are my destination."

"What has poverty to do with it?" asked Don Quixote. "The heat one can understand."

"Señor," replied the youth, "in this bundle I carry velvet breeches to match this jacket. If I wear them out on the road, I shall not be able to make a fine show with them in the city, and I have no money to buy others. That is the reason, as well as to keep cool, why I travel in this way to overtake some companies of infantry that are less than twelve leagues off. When I enlist, there will be no lack of baggage trains to travel with to the place of embarkation, which they say will be Cartagena. I would rather have the king for a master and serve him in the wars, than serve some pauper at court."

"And did you get any travel money, now?" asked the cousin.

"If I had been in the service of some grandee of Spain or personage of distinction," replied the youth, "I would surely have had some; that's the advantage of serving rich masters; and out of the servants' hall men come to be lieutenants or captains, or get a good pension. But it was my bad luck always to serve job hunters and adventurers, whose keep and wages were so scanty that half went to pay for the starching of one's collars. It would be a miracle indeed if a page leaving to seek his fortune ever got anything like a reasonable tip."

"And tell me, for heaven's sake," asked Don Quixote, "is it possible, my friend, that all the time you served you never got any uniforms?"

"They gave me two," replied the page, "but just as when a man quits a religious community before making profession, they strip him of the habit of the order and give him back his own clothes, so did my masters return me mine. As soon as the business that brought them to court was finished, they went home and took back the liveries, which were only for show."

"What *spilorceria!*[4]—as an Italian would say," said Don Quixote. "But for all that, consider yourself fortunate to have left the court with so worthy an aim, for there is nothing on earth more honorable or profitable than serving, first of all God, and then one's king and natural lord, particularly in the profession of arms, by which, if not more wealth, at least more honor is to be won than by letters, as I have said many a time. Though letters may have founded more great houses than arms, still those founded by arms

4. Stinginess.

have a certain superiority over those founded by letters, and a certain splendor that sets them above all others. And bear in mind what I am about to say to you, for it will be of great use and comfort to you in time of trouble. It is, not to let your mind dwell on the misfortunes that may befall you, for the worst of all is death, and if it be a good death, the best of all is to die.

"They asked Julius Cæsar, the valiant Roman emperor, what was the best death. He answered, the unexpected death, which comes suddenly and unforeseen. Though he answered like a pagan, without the knowledge of the true God, yet, as far as sparing our feelings is concerned, he was right. Suppose you are killed in the first engagement or skirmish, whether by a cannon ball or blown up by mine, what matter? It is only dying, and all is over, and according to Terence, a soldier dead in battle cuts a better figure than when alive and safe in flight. And the good soldier wins fame in proportion as he is obedient to his captains and those in command over him.

"Remember, my son, that it is better for the soldier to smell of gunpowder than of civet, and that if old age should come upon you in this honorable calling, though you may be covered with wounds and crippled and lame, it will not find you without honor, and of a kind that poverty cannot lessen, especially now that provisions are being made for supporting and relieving old and disabled soldiers. It is not right to treat them in the manner of those who set free and get rid of their black slaves when they are old and useless. Turning them out of the house under the pretense of making them free, they make them slaves to hunger, from which they can be released only by death. But for the present I won't say more than for you to get up behind me on my horse as far as the inn, and dine with me there. Tomorrow you can continue your journey, and God give you as good speed as your intentions deserve."

The page did not accept the invitation to mount, though he did agree to supper at the inn. And here they say Sancho said to himself, "God be with you for a master! Is it possible that a man who can say so many and such good things as he has said just now, can say that he saw the impossible absurdities he reports about the cave of Montesinos? Well, well, we shall see."

And now, just as night was falling, they reached the inn, and Sancho observed with great satisfaction that his master took it for a real inn, and not for a castle, as he usually did. The instant they entered Don Quixote asked the landlord about the man with the lances and halberds and was told that he was in the stable seeing to his mule. Sancho and the cousin proceeded to do the same for their beasts, giving the best manger and the best place in the stable to Rocinante.

Chapter XXV

WHEREIN IS SET DOWN THE BRAYING ADVENTURE, AND THE AMUSING ONE OF THE PUPPETEER, TOGETHER WITH THE MEMORABLE DIVINATIONS OF THE DIVINING APE

Don Quixote's bread would not bake, as the common saying is, until he had heard the curious things the man who carried the arms had promised to reveal. He went looking for him where the innkeeper said he was, and having found him, he asked him now by all means to give his answer to the question he had been asked on the road.

"The tale of my wonders must be heard at greater leisure and not standing," said the man. "Let me finish foddering my mount, good sir, and then I'll tell you things that will astonish you."

"Don't wait for that," said Don Quixote. "I'll help you with everything." And so he did, sifting the barley for him and cleaning out the feedbox. This degree of humility made the other feel bound to tell him with a good grace what he had asked. So he sat down on a bench, with Don Quixote beside him and the cousin, the page, Sancho Panza, and the landlord, for a senate and an audience.

"You must know," said the man, beginning his story, "that in a village four leagues and a half from this inn, it so happened that one of the aldermen, by the tricks and roguery of a servant girl of his (it's too long a tale to tell), lost a donkey. He did all he possibly could to find it, but it was no use. Two weeks might have gone by, so the story goes, since the ass had been missing, when, as the alderman who had lost it was standing in the plaza, another alderman of the same town said to him, 'Reward me for good news, friend; your donkey has turned up.'

" 'That I will, and willingly,' said the other. 'But tell me, where has it turned up?'

" 'In the forest,' said the finder. 'I saw it this morning without packsaddle or harness of any sort, and so lean that it went to one's heart to see it. I tried to drive it ahead of me and bring it to you, but it is already so wild and shy that when I went near, it made off into the thickest part of the forest. If you want the two of us to look for it, let me put up this she-ass at my house. I'll be back at once.'

" 'You will be doing me a great kindness,' said the owner of the ass, 'and I'll try to pay you back in the same coin.'

"It is with all these details, and just as I am telling it now, that those who know all about it tell the story. Well then, the two aldermen set off on foot, arm in arm, for the forest. When they came to the place where they hoped to find the ass they could not find it, nor was it to be seen anywhere, search as they might. Since there was no sign of it, the alderman who had seen it had another idea.

" 'Look here,' he said, 'a plan has occurred to me which beyond a doubt will enable us to locate the animal, even if it is hidden in the bowels of the earth, not to say the forest. This is it. I am wonderful at braying, and if you are any good at it, the thing's as good as done.'

" 'Any good, did you say?' said the other. 'By God, I won't be outdone by anybody, not even by the asses themselves.'

" 'We'll soon see,' said the second alderman, 'for my plan is for you to go to one side of the forest, and I the other, so as to go all around it. Every now and then you will bray and I will bray, and the ass cannot fail to hear us and will answer us if it is in the forest.'

" 'I declare, friend, that it's an excellent plan and worthy of your great genius.'

Thus they agreed to separate, and it so happened that they brayed almost at the same moment. Each of them was deceived by the other's braying and ran to look, believing the ass had turned up at last.

" 'Is it possible,' said the loser, after they caught sight of one another, 'that it was not my ass that brayed?'

" 'No, it was I,' said the other.

" 'Well then, I can tell you, friend,' said the ass's owner, 'that between you and an ass there's no difference as far as braying goes, for I never in all my life heard anything more natural.'

" 'Those praises and compliments belong to you more justly than to me, my friend,' said the inventor of the plan. 'By the God that made me, you could give a couple of brays by way of a handicap to the best and most accomplished brayer in the world. Your tone is deep, your voice is well sustained in both time and pitch, and your finishing notes come thick and fast. In fact, I consider myself beaten, and I yield the palm and banner to you in this rare accomplishment.'

" 'Well then,' said the owner, 'I'll set a higher value on myself for the future and consider that I know something, since I possess an excellence of some sort. Though I always thought I brayed well, I never supposed I reached the pitch of perfection you say I do.'

" 'And I say too,' said the other, 'that there are rare gifts going begging in the world, and that they are not properly used by those who don't know what to do with them.'

" 'Our gifts,' said the owner of the ass, 'except in cases like the one we have in hand, cannot be of any use to us, and even now God grant they may do some good.'

"With that they separated and took to their braying once more. But every instant they deceived one another and kept coming to meet one another. At last, by way of countersign, so as to know that it was they and not the ass, they agreed to give two brays, one after the other. So, with a double bray at every step, they made the complete circuit of the forest, but the lost ass never gave them an answer or even the sign of one. How could the poor unfortunate brute have answered, when they found it, devoured by wolves, in the thickest part of the forest?

" 'I was wondering,' said the owner, as soon as he saw it, 'why it did not answer. If it wasn't dead it would have brayed when it heard us, or it would have been no ass. But for the sake of having heard you bray to such perfection, my friend, I count the trouble I took to find it no loss, even though I have found it dead.'

" 'But you set the standard, my friend,' said the other. 'If the abbot sings well, the acolyte is not far behind him.'

"So they returned disconsolate and hoarse to their village, where they told their friends, neighbors, and acquaintances what had happened in their search for the ass, each vying to praise the other's skill in braying. The whole story came to be told and spread about through the neighboring villages. The devil, who never sleeps, with his love for sowing dissension and scattering discord everywhere, blowing mischief about and making quarrels out of nothing, ordained that the people of the other towns would start braying whenever they saw anyone from our village, as if to mock us for the braying of our aldermen. Then the boys took it up, which was the same as getting into the hands and mouths of all the devils of hell. The braying spread from one town to another in such a way that the men of the braying town can be distinguished as easily as blacks from whites. So far has it gone with this miserable joke that several times the scoffed have come out armed and arrayed to do battle with the scoffers. Neither king nor rook, nor fear nor shame, can improve matters.

"Tomorrow or the day after, I believe, the men of my town, that is, the braying town, will take the field against another village two leagues away, and one of our worst persecutors. I have bought these lances and halberds you have seen so that we may turn out well prepared. These are the strange things I told you I had to tell, and if you don't think they are, I have got no others."

With this the worthy fellow brought his story to a close, and at that very moment there came in at the gate of the inn a man entirely clad in chamois leather, hose, breeches, and jacket.

"Señor host, have you room?" he asked in a loud voice. "Here's the divining ape and the show of the *Freeing of Melisendra.*"

"God bless us!" said the landlord. "Why, it's Master Pedro! We're in for a great night!" (I forgot to mention that this Master Pedro had his left eye and nearly half his cheek covered with a patch of green taffeta, showing that something ailed all that side.)

"Your worship is welcome, Master Pedro," continued the landlord, "but where are the ape and the show? I don't see them."

"They are near," said the man in leather, "but I came on first to ask if there was any room."

"I'd make the Duke of Alba himself clear out to make room for Master Pedro," said the landlord. "Bring in the ape and the show; there's company in the inn tonight that will pay to see it and the cleverness of the ape."

"Good!" said the man with the patch. "I'll lower the price and be well pleased if I take in only what it costs me. Now I'll go back and see to it that the cart arrives with the ape and the show." With this, he went out of the inn.

Don Quixote at once asked the landlord who this Master Pedro was, and what the show and the ape he had with him were like.

"This is a famous puppeteer," the landlord answered, "who for some time past has been going about La Mancha de Aragón[1] with a show of the freeing of Melisendra by the famous Don Gaiferos. It is one of the best and best acted stories that have been seen in this part of the kingdom for many a year. And he has with him an ape with the most extraordinary ability ever seen in an ape or imagined in a human being. Ask him anything, and he listens attentively to the question, then jumps on his master's shoulder and whispers into his ear the answer which Master Pedro then speaks out aloud. He has much more to say about things from the past than about things to come, and though he doesn't always hit the target, most times he is right enough and gives us the notion that the devil is in him. He gets two *reales* for every question if the ape answers, I mean, if his master answers for him after he has whispered into his ear. So people believe that this Master Pedro is very rich. He is a 'gallant man' as they say in Italy, and good company, and leads the finest life in the world. He talks more than six and drinks more than a dozen, thanks to all his tongue, his ape, and his show."

At this moment Master Pedro returned, and in a cart followed the show and the ape—a big one, without a tail and with buttocks as bare as felt, but not vicious looking.

"Can you tell me, sir fortune-teller," said Don Quixote to the ape as he saw him, "what fish we will catch, and what is in store for us? See, here are my two *reales*"—and he told Sancho to give them to Master Pedro, who answered for the ape.

"Señor," he said, "this animal gives no answer or information about things that are to come. Of things past he knows something, and more or less of things present."

"I swear I would not give two cents," said Sancho, "to be told my own past. Who knows that better than I do? And to pay for being told what I know would be mighty foolish. But since he

1. The eastern part of La Mancha.

knows the present, here are my two *reales*. Tell me, señor ape, what my wife Teresa Panza is doing now, and what she does to amuse herself."

"I will not receive payment in advance or until the service has been rendered," said Master Pedro, refusing the money. Then with his right hand he twice slapped his left shoulder, and with one spring the ape perched himself upon it, put his mouth to his master's ear, and began chattering his teeth rapidly. Having kept this up for the length of a Creed, he sprang to the ground again. At the same instant Master Pedro in great haste ran and fell upon his knees before Don Quixote, and embraced his legs.

"I embrace these legs," he exclaimed, "as I would embrace the two pillars of Hercules, O illustrious reviver of knight-errantry, so long consigned to oblivion! O never yet duly extolled knight, Don Quixote of La Mancha, courage of the faint-hearted, prop of the tottering, arm of the fallen, staff and counsel of all who are unfortunate!"

Don Quixote was thunderstruck, Sancho astounded, the cousin staggered, the page astonished, the man from the braying town agape, the landlord in perplexity, and, in short, everyone amazed at the words of the puppeteer.

"And you, worthy Sancho Panza," he went on, "best squire and squire to the best knight in the world! Be of good cheer, for your good wife Teresa is well, and she is at this moment combing a pound of flax. By way of further proof, she has at her left hand a jug with a broken spout that holds a drop of wine, with which she refreshes herself at her work."

"That I can well believe," said Sancho. "She is a lucky one, and except for her jealousy, I would not change her for the giantess Andandona,[2] who by my master's account was a very clever and worthy woman. My Teresa is of the kind that won't let themselves go without anything, though their heirs may have to pay for it."

"Now I declare," said Don Quixote, "that the man who reads and travels much sees and knows a great deal. I say so because what amount of persuasion could have persuaded me that there are apes in the world able to divine things, as I have seen now with my own eyes? For I am that very Don Quixote of La Mancha this worthy animal refers to, though he has gone rather too far in my praise. But whatever I may be, I thank heaven that it has endowed me with a tender and compassionate heart, always disposed to do good to all and harm to none."

"If I had money," said the page, "I would ask señor ape what will happen to me on the journey I am making."

By this time Master Pedro had risen from Don Quixote's feet.

"I have already said," he replied, "that this little beast says noth-

2. A giantess in *Amadís of Gaul*.

ing about the future. If he did, your not having any money would not matter. To oblige Señor Don Quixote here present, I would give up all the profits in the world. And now, because I owe it to him, and in order to give him pleasure, I will set up my show and entertain everyone in the inn without any charge whatever."

As soon as he heard this, the delighted landlord pointed out a place where the show might be set up, and it was done at once.

Don Quixote was not too happy with the ape's abilities, for he did not think it proper that an ape should divine anything, either past or future. So while Master Pedro was arranging the show, he went off with Sancho to a corner of the stable where he could speak without being overheard.

"Look here, Sancho," he said, "I have been pondering this ape's extraordinary powers, and I have come to the conclusion that beyond any doubt his master, Master Pedro, has a pact, tacit or express, with the devil."

"If the packet is express from the devil," said Sancho, "it must be a very dirty packet no doubt; but what good can it do Master Pedro to have such packets?"

"You do not understand me, Sancho," said Don Quixote. "My meaning is that he must have made some compact with the devil to infuse this power into the ape, so that he may earn a living by it. After he has grown rich he will hand over his soul, which is what the enemy of mankind wants. I am led to believe this by observing that the ape only answers about things past or present, and the devil's knowledge extends no further. He knows the future only by guesswork, and that not always, for it is reserved for God alone to know the times and the seasons. For him there is neither past nor future, all is present.

"This being true, as it is, it is clear that this ape speaks in the devil's style. I am astonished that they have not denounced him to the Holy Office and put him to the question, and forced him to say from whom he has these powers. For it is certain that this ape is no astrologer. Neither his master nor he casts, or knows how to cast those figures they call horoscopes, which are now so common in Spain that there is not a servant girl or page boy or old cobbler that will not undertake to cast a horoscope as if it were the easiest thing in the world. In this way they reduce to nothing the marvelous truth of astrological science by their lies and ignorance. I know of a lady who asked one of these astrologers whether her little lapdog would become pregnant and would breed, and how many and what color the little pups would be. To which señor astrologer, after having made his calculations replied that the bitch would be pregnant, and would drop three pups, one green, another bright red, and the third speckled, provided she conceived between eleven and twelve either of the day or night, and on a Monday or Saturday. As things turned out, two days after this the bitch died of overeating, and señor horoscope caster won local renown as a most profound astrologer, as most of these persons do."

"Still," said Sancho, "I would be glad if your worship would make Master Pedro ask his ape whether what happened to your worship in the cave of Montesinos is true. For begging your worship's pardon, I, for my part, take it to have been all moonshine and lies, or at any rate something you dreamed."

"That may be," replied Don Quixote. "However, I will do what you suggest, though I have my own scruples on that score."

At this point Master Pedro came up in search of Don Quixote, to tell him the show was now ready and to come and see it, for it was worth seeing. Don Quixote explained his wish, and begged Master Pedro to ask his ape at once to say whether certain things which had happened to him in the cave of Montesinos were dreams or realities, for to him they appeared to partake of both. Upon this Master Pedro, without answering, fetched the ape and put it down in front of Don Quixote and Sancho.

"See here, señor ape," he said, "this gentleman wishes to know whether certain things which happened to him in the cave called the cave of Montesinos were false or true."

On his making the usual sign the ape mounted on his left shoulder and seemed to whisper in his ear. "The ape," Master Pedro declared at once, "says that the things you saw or that happened to you in the cave are false in part and true in part. He only knows this and no more about the matter. But if your worship wishes to know more, on Friday next he will answer whatever he is asked, for his power is at present exhausted and will not return to him till Friday, as he has said."

"Did I not say, señor," said Sancho, "that I could not convince myself that all your worship said about the adventures in the cave was true, or even the half of it?"

"The course of events will tell, Sancho," replied Don Quixote. "Time, that discloses all things, leaves nothing that it does not drag into the light of day, though it is buried in the bosom of the earth. But enough of that for the present. Let us go and see Master Pedro's show, for I am sure there must be something novel in it."

"Something!" said Master Pedro. "This show of mine has sixty thousand novel things in it. Let me tell you, Señor Don Quixote, it is one of the things most worth seeing in the world today. But *operibus credite et non verbis*,[3] so now let's get to work. It is growing late, and we have a great deal to do and to say and show."

Don Quixote and Sancho obeyed him and went to where the puppet theater was already set up and uncovered, surrounded with small candles which made it look bright and attractive. When they

3. "Though ye believe not me, believe the works." John 10:38.

had come, Master Pedro ensconced himself inside it, for it was he who had to work the puppets, and a boy, a servant of his, posted himself outside. He acted as commentator and explained the mysteries of the exhibition, having a wand in his hand to point to the figures as they came out.

And so, after everyone in the inn had taken his place in front of the theater, some of them standing, and Don Quixote, Sancho, the page, and cousin, occupying the best places, the interpreter began to say what he who reads or hears the next chapter will hear and see.

Chapter XXVI

WHEREIN IS CONTINUED THE DROLL ADVENTURE OF THE PUPPETEER, TOGETHER WITH OTHER THINGS THAT ARE TRULY QUITE GOOD

"All were silent, Tyrians and Trojans"[1]—I mean, all who were watching the puppet theater were hanging on the lips of the boy who was to explain its wonders, when drums and trumpets were heard inside it and cannon went off. The noise was soon over, and then the boy raised his voice. "This true story," he said, "which is acted here for your worships is taken word for word from the French chronicles and from the Spanish ballads that everybody knows and the boys in the streets sing. Its subject is the rescue by Señor Don Gaiferos of his betrothed, Melisendra, who was a captive in Spain at the hands of the Moors in the city of Sansueña, as they called what is now Zaragoza. Here you see Don Gaiferos playing *tablas*, just as they sing it:

> Playing at *tablas* Don Gaiferos sits,
> For Melisendra is forgotten now.[2]

And that personage who appears there with a crown on his head and a scepter in his hand is the Emperor Charlemagne, the supposed father of Melisenda, who, angered to see his future son-in-law's inaction and unconcern, comes in to chide him. Observe with what vehemence and energy he chides him, so that you would think he was going to give him half a dozen raps with his scepter. Indeed, there are authors who say he did so, and hard ones too. After having said a great deal to him about imperiling his honor by not setting his fiancée free, he said, so the tale runs,

> 'Enough I've said, see to it now.'

Note how the emperor turns away and leaves Don Gaiferos fuming.

1. A line from a translation of the *Aeneid*.
2. *Tablas* is an old game like backgammon. The commentator recites lines from popular ballads, here and below, as he narrates.

Now Gaiferos, in a burst of anger, flings the board and pieces down and calls in haste for his armor. He asks his cousin Don Roland for the loan of his sword, Durindana, but Don Roland refuses to lend it, offering instead to accompany him in the difficult enterprise he is undertaking. Gaiferos, in his valor and anger, will not accept it, and says that he alone will suffice to rescue his betrothed, even though she were imprisoned deep in the center of the earth. With this he retires to arm himself and set out on his journey at once.

"Now your worships, turn your eyes to that tower that appears there, which is supposed to be one of the towers of the fortress of Zaragoza, now called the Aljafería. That lady who appears on the balcony dressed in Moorish fashion is the peerless Melisendra, for many a time she used to gaze from there upon the road to France and seek consolation in her captivity by thinking of Paris and her husband. Observe, too, a new incident which now occurs, such as, perhaps, never was seen. Do you not see that Moor, who silently and stealthily, with his finger on his lip, approaches Melisendra from behind? Observe now how he plants a kiss upon her lips, and what a hurry she is in to spit and wipe them with the white sleeve of her blouse, and how she bewails herself and tears her fair hair as though it were to blame for the wrong.

"Observe, too, that the stately Moor who is in that gallery is King Marsilio of Sansueña. Having seen the Moor's insolence, he at once orders him (though his kinsman and a great favorite of his) to be seized and given two hundred lashes, while carried through the streets of the city according to custom:

> With criers going before him
> And justices behind.[3]

And here you see them come out to execute the sentence, although the offense has just been committed, for among the Moors there are no indictments nor appeals as with us."

"Boy, boy," Don Quixote called out at this point, "go on with your story, and don't go off on tangents, for to establish the truth clearly there is need of a great deal of proof and confirmation."

Master Pedro also spoke from within:

"Boy, stick to your text and do as the gentleman says; that's the best plan. Keep to your plainsong and don't attempt harmonies, which tend to break down when they are too elaborate."

"I will," said the boy. "This figure you see here on horseback," he went on, "wearing a Gascon cloak, is Don Gaiferos himself. His wife, avenged of the insult of the amorous Moor, and taking her stand on the balcony of the tower with a calmer and more tranquil countenance, has seen him but does not recognize him. She speaks

3. Verses from a ballad by Quevedo.

to her husband, supposing him to be some traveler, and has that long discussion with him as it runs in the ballad:

> 'If you, sir knight, to France are bound,
> Oh! for Gaiferos ask.'

I do not repeat it here because long-windedness begets disgust. Suffice it to observe how Don Gaiferos reveals himself, and that by her joyful gestures Melisendra shows us she has recognized him. What is more, we now see how she lowers herself from the balcony to place herself on the haunches of her good husband's horse. But ah, unhappy lady! The edge of her petticoat has caught on one of the bars of the balcony and she is left hanging in the air, unable to reach the ground.

"But you see how compassionate heaven sends aid in our sorest need. Don Gaiferos advances, and without minding whether the rich petticoat is torn or not, he seizes her and by force brings her to the ground. Then with one jerk he places her on the haunches of his horse, astraddle like a man, and bids her hold on tight and clasp her arms around his neck, crossing them on his breast so as not to fall, for the lady Melisendra was not used to that style of riding. You see, too, how by neighing the horse shows his satisfaction with the gallant and beautiful burden he bears in his lord and lady. You see how they wheel around and leave the city and in joy and gladness take the road to Paris. Go in peace, O peerless pair of true lovers! May you reach your longed-for fatherland in safety, and may fortune raise no hindrance to your properous journey. May the eyes of your friends and kinsmen behold you enjoying in peace and tranquillity the remaining days of your life—may they be as numerous as those of Nestor!"

"Simplicity, boy!" Master Pedro called out again, when he heard this. "None of your high flights. All affectation is bad."

The interpreter did not reply, but went on with what he had to say. "There is no shortage of idlers, who see everything, to see Melisendra come down and mount, and word was brought to King Marsilio. He at once gave orders to sound the alarm, and see what a stir there is, and how the city is drowned with the sound of the bells pealing in the towers of all the mosques."

"No, indeed!" said Don Quixote at this. "With regard to the bells Master Pedro is very inaccurate, for bells are not in use among the Moors, only kettledrums, and a kind of small horn somewhat like our oboe. To ring bells this way in Sansueña is unquestionably a great absurdity."

On hearing this, Master Pedro stopped ringing. "Don't pay attention to trifles, Señor Don Quixote," he said, "or expect to raise things to a pitch of perfection that is out of reach. Are there not almost every day a thousand comedies acted all around us full of thousands of inaccuracies and absurdities? Yet, for all that, they have a successful run and are listened to not only with applause but with admiration and all the rest of it. Go on, boy, and don't mind; as long as I fill my pocket, it's no matter if I show as many inaccuracies as there are motes in a sunbeam."

"True enough," said Don Quixote, and the boy went on. "See what a numerous and glittering crowd of horsemen issues from the city in pursuit of the two faithful lovers, what a blowing of trumpets there is, what sounding of horns, what beating of drums and tabors. I fear they will overtake them and bring them back tied to the tail of their own horse, which would be a dreadful sight."

Don Quixote, however, seeing such a swarm of Moors and hearing such a din, thought it was time to aid the fugitives, and up he stood.

"Never while I live," he exclaimed in a loud voice, "will I permit treachery to be practiced in my presence on such a famous knight and fearless lover as Don Gaiferos. Halt, ye ill-born rabble; follow him not nor pursue him, or ye will have to reckon with me in battle!"

Suiting the action to the word, he drew his sword and with one bound placed himself close to the puppet stage. With unexampled rapidity and fury he began to shower down blows on the puppet troop of Moors, knocking over some, decapitating others, maiming this one and demolishing that.[4] Among many more, he delivered one downstroke which, if Master Pedro had not ducked, made himself small, and got out of the way, would have sliced off his head as easily as if it had been made of almond paste.

"Stop! Señor Don Quixote!" Master Pedro kept shouting. "Can't you see they're not real Moors you're knocking down and killing and destroying, but only little pasteboard figures! Look—sinner that I am!—how you're wrecking and ruining all my property!"

In spite of this, Don Quixote did not stop raining cuts, slashes, downstrokes, and backstrokes, and at length, in less time than it takes to say two Creeds, he brought the whole show to the ground. All the fittings and figures were smashed and knocked to pieces, King Marsilio was badly wounded, and the Emperor Charlemagne had his crown and head split in two. The whole audience was thrown into confusion, the ape fled out the window to the roof of the inn, the cousin was frightened, and even Sancho Panza himself was in extreme fear; for, as he swore after the storm was over, he had never seen his master in such a furious passion.

The complete destruction of the show having been thus accomplished, Don Quixote became a little calmer. "I wish I had here

4. In Ch. 26 of Avellaneda's sequel, Don Quixote is present at the rehearsal of a play by Lope de Vega and draws his sword to challenge the actor who has slandered the innocent queen of Navarre. It would appear that Cervantes is outdoing his imitator and at the same time taking a crack at Lope de Vega by slyly comparing Lopa's play to a cheap puppet show. Not all scholars agree with this explanation, however.

before me now," he said, "all those who do not or will not believe how useful knights-errant are in the world. Just think, if I had not been here, what would have become of the brave Don Gaiferos and the fair Melisendra! Depend upon it, by this time those dogs would have overtaken them and inflicted some outrage upon them. So, then, long live knight-errantry beyond everything living on earth this day!"

"Let it live, and welcome," said Master Pedro in a feeble voice, "and let me die, for I am so unfortunate that I can say with King Don Rodrigo,

> 'Yesterday was I lord of Spain
> Today I've not a turret left
> That I may call mine own.'

Not half an hour, no, barely a minute ago, I saw myself lord of kings and emperors. My stables were filled with countless horses and my trunks and bags with showy costumes beyond reckoning. Now I find myself ruined and laid low, destitute and a beggar, and above all without my ape. By my faith, I'll have to sweat blood before I catch him—and all this through the reckless fury of sir knight here who, they say, protects the fatherless, and rights wrongs, and does other charitable deeds. In my case only have his generous intentions been found wanting, blessings and praise to the highest heavens! Oh well, he lives up to his name, Knight of the Mournful Countenance. He has made mine mournful, all right!"[5]

Sancho Panza was touched by Master Pedro's words. "Don't weep and lament, Master Pedro," he said to him. "You are breaking my heart. My master Don Quixote, let me tell you, is so catholic and scrupulous a Christian that, if he sees he has done you wrong, he will admit it. He will agree to pay for it and make it good, with something over and above."

"Only let Señor Don Quixote pay me for part of the damage he has done," said Master Pedro, "and I would be content, and his worship would ease his conscience. No man can be saved if he keeps what is another's against the owner's will and makes no restitution."

"That is true," said Don Quixote, "but at present I am not aware that I have got anything of yours, Master Pedro."

"How can that be?" rejoined Master Pedro. "What about these relics lying here on the bare hard ground? Were they not scattered and shattered by the invincible strength of that mighty arm? And whose were the bodies they belonged to but mine? And what did I get my living by but by them?"

"Now am I fully convinced," said Don Quixote, "of what I had many a time before believed. The enchanters who persecute me

5. Master Pedro's black humor depends on a pun: the knight of the mournful *figura* ("face") has disfigured my figures, i.e., puppets.

simply put figures like these before my eyes and then change them into whatever they please. In very truth I assure you gentlemen now listening to me that everything that has taken place here seemed to me to take place literally. Melisendra was Melisendra, Don Gaiferos Don Gaiferos, Marsilio Marsilio, and Charlemagne Charlemagne. That was why my anger was roused, and to be faithful to my calling as a knight-errant I tried to aid and protect those who fled. These good intentions of mine produced what you have seen. If the exact opposite has occurred, the fault is not mine, but that of the wicked beings who persecute me. Nevertheless, I am willing to shoulder the expenses of this error of mine, though no ill will lay behind it. Let Master Pedro see what he wants for the spoiled figures, for I agree to pay it at once in good Castilian currency."

Master Pedro bowed low. "I expected no less," he said, "of the rare Christianity of the valiant Don Quixote of La Mancha, true helper and protector of all destitute and needy vagabonds. The landlord here and the great Sancho Panza shall be the arbiters and appraisers between your worship and me, and decide what these dilapidated figures may be worth."

The landlord and Sancho having consented, Master Pedro picked up from the ground King Marsilio of Zaragoza with his head off.

"Here you see," he said, "how impossible it is to restore this king to his former state, so I think, saving your better judgments, that for his death, decease, and demise, four *reales* and a half may be given to me."

"Proceed," said Don Quixote.

"Well then, for this cleavage from top to bottom," continued Master Pedro, taking up the split Emperor Charlemagne, "it would not be much if I were to ask five *reales* and a quarter."

"It's not little," said Sancho.

"Nor is it much," said the landlord. "Make it even, and say five *reales*."

"Let him have the whole five and a quarter," said Don Quixote, "for the sum total of this notable disaster does not depend on a quarter more or less. Be quick about it, Master Pedro, for it's getting on to supper time, and my appetite is beginning to stir."

"For this figure," said Master Pedro, "which lacks a nose and an eye, and is the fair Melisendra, I ask the very reasonable sum of two *reales* and twelve *maravedís*."

"The devil must be in it," said Don Quixote, "if Melisendra and her husband are not by this time at least on the French border, for the horse they rode on seemed to me to fly rather than gallop. So don't try to sell me the cat for the hare by showing me a noseless Melisendra when she is now, no doubt, enjoying herself at her ease with her husband in France. God help every one to his own, Master Pedro, and let us all proceed fairly and honestly. Now go on."

Master Pedro realized that Don Quixote was beginning to

wander and was returning to his original fantasies. But he was not inclined to let him escape.

"This cannot be Melisendra," he said. "It must be one of the damsels that waited on her. If I'm given sixty *maravedís*, I'll be content and sufficiently paid."

And so he went on, putting values on many more smashed figures. After the two arbiters had adjusted them to the satisfaction of both parties, it all came to forty *reales* and three-quarters. And over and above this sum, which Sancho at once disbursed, Master Pedro asked for two *reales* for his trouble in catching the ape.

"Let him have them, Sancho," said Don Quixote, "not to catch the ape, but to get drunk. I would give two hundred this minute for the good news, to anyone who could tell me positively, that the lady Doña Melisendra and Señor Don Gaiferos were now in France and with their own people."

"No one could tell us that better than my ape," said Master Pedro, "but no devil could catch him now. Yet I suspect that affection and hunger will drive him to look for me tonight. Tomorrow will soon be here and we shall see."

In short, the puppet-show storm passed off, and all dined in peace and good fellowship at Don Quixote's expense, for he was the height of generosity. Before it was daylight, the man with the lances and halberds took his leave, and soon after daybreak the cousin and the page came to bid Don Quixote farewell. The former returned home, and the latter resumed his journey, Don Quixote giving him twelve *reales* by way of help. Master Pedro did not care to engage in any more palaver with Don Quixote, for he knew him very well. So he rose before the sun, and having gathered the remains of his show and caught his ape, he too went off to seek his adventures. The landlord, who did not know Don Quixote, was as much astonished at his mad actions as at his generosity.

To conclude, Sancho, by his master's orders, paid him very liberally, and taking leave of him they left the inn at about eight in the morning and took to the road. There we will leave them to pursue their journey, for this is necessary in order to take up certain other matters that have their place in this famous history.

Chapter XXVII

WHEREIN IT IS SHOWN WHO MASTER PEDRO AND HIS APE WERE, TOGETHER WITH THE MISHAP DON QUIXOTE HAD IN THE BRAYING ADVENTURE, WHICH HE DID NOT CONCLUDE AS HE WOULD HAVE LIKED OR AS HE HAD EXPECTED

Cide Hamete, the chronicler of this great history, begins this chapter with these words: "I swear as a Catholic Christian." With regard to this oath, his translator says that Cide Hamete's swearing as a Catholic Christian (he being—as no doubt he was—a Moor) only meant that just as a Catholic Christian taking an oath swears, or ought to swear, what is true and tell the truth in what he avers, so Cide Hamete was telling the truth, as much as if he swore as a Catholic Christian, in all he chose to write about Quixote, especially in declaring who Master Pedro was and the secret of the trained ape that astonished all the villages with his divinations.

Cide Hamete says, then, that he who has read the First Part of this history will remember well enough the Ginés de Pasamonte whom Don Quixote set free in the Sierra Morena along with the other galley slaves, and that for his good deed he afterwards got poor thanks and worse payment from the wicked, evil-living set. It was this very Ginés de Pasamonte—Don Ginesillo de Parapilla, Don Quixote called him—who stole Dapple from Sancho Panza. This robbery, of which (by the fault of the printers) neither the how nor the when was stated in the First Part, has been a puzzle to a good many people, who attribute to the bad memory of the author what was the error of the press. In fact, however, Ginés stole him while Sancho Panza was asleep on his back, adopting the plan and device that Brunello used when he stole Sacripante's horse from between his legs at the siege of Albracca. As has been told, Sancho afterwards recovered him.

This Ginés, then, afraid of being caught by the officers of justice, who were looking for him to punish him for his innumerable swindles and crimes (which were so many and so great that he himself wrote a big book giving an account of them), resolved to move to the kingdom of Aragón, cover up his left eye, and take up the trade of a puppetshowman. He knew how to do this, as well as sleight-of-hand tricks, extremely well.

From some released Christians returning from Barbary, it so happened, he bought the ape, which he taught to mount upon his shoulder when he made a certain sign, and to whisper, or seem to do so, in his ear. Thus prepared, before entering any town with his show and his ape, he used to inform himself at the nearest village, or from the most likely person he could find, as to what particular things had happened there, and to whom. Bearing them well in mind, the first thing he did was to exhibit his show, sometimes performing one story, sometimes another, but all lively, amusing, and familiar. As soon as the performance was over he would praise the talents of his ape, assuring the public that he could see all the past and the present, but as to the future he had no skill. For each question answered he asked two *reales*, and for some he made a reduction, just as he happened to feel the mood of the questioners. Now and then he came to houses where things that he knew of had happened to the people living there, and even if they did not ask him a question, not wanting to pay for it, he would make the sign to the ape and then declare that it had said so and so, which fitted the case exactly. In this way he acquired a prodigious reputation, and everybody sought him out.

On other occasions, being very crafty, he would answer in such a way that the answers suited the questions; and as no one cross-examined him or pressed him to tell how his ape knew such things, he made monkeys of them all and filled his pockets. The instant he entered the inn he knew Don Quixote and Sancho, and with that knowledge it was easy for him to astonish them and all who were there. But it would have cost him dear had Don Quixote brought down his hand a little lower when he cut off King Marsilio's head and destroyed all his horsemen, as related in the preceding chapter.

So much for Master Pedro and his ape. And now to return to Don Quixote of La Mancha. After he had left the inn he determined to visit, first of all, the banks of the Ebro and that neighborhood before entering the city of Zaragoza. For there was still time to spare before the jousts. With this object in view he followed the road and traveled along it for two days without meeting any adventure worth committing to writing.

On the third day, as he was ascending a hill, he heard a great noise of drums, trumpets, and musket shots. At first he imagined some regiment of soldiers was passing that way, and to see them he spurred Rocinante and mounted the hill. On reaching the top he saw at the foot of it over two hundred men, as it seemed to him, armed with weapons of various sorts: lances, crossbows, spears, pikes, and a few muskets and a great many shields. He descended the slope and approached the band near enough to see distinctly the flags, make out the colors, and distinguish the devices they carried, especially one on a standard or pennant of white satin, on which there was painted in a very lifelike style an ass like a little Sardinian pony with its head up, its mouth open, and its tongue out, as if it were in the act and attitude of braying; and around it were inscribed in large characters these two lines—

> They did not bray in vain,
> Our magistrates twain.

From this device Don Quixote concluded that these people must be from the braying town, and he said so to Sancho, explaining to him what was written on the standard. At the same time he observed that the man who had told them about the matter was wrong in saying that the two who brayed were aldermen, for according to the lines of the standard they were magistrates. To which Sancho replied, "Señor, there's nothing contradictory in that. Maybe the aldermen who brayed then got to be magistrates of their town afterwards, and so they can use both titles. Besides it has nothing to do with the truth of the story whether the brayers were magistrates or aldermen, provided at any rate they did bray; for a magistrate is just as likely to bray as an alderman." They perceived, in short, that the town which had been twitted had turned out to do battle with some other village that had jeered it more than was fair or neighborly.

Don Quixote proceeded to join them, not a little to Sancho's uneasiness, for he never relished mixing himself up in expeditions of that sort. The members of the troop made room for him, taking him to be some one who was on their side. Don Quixote, putting up his visor, advanced with an easy bearing and demeanor to the standard with the ass, and all the chief men of the army gathered around him to look at him, staring at him with the usual amazement that everybody felt on seeing him for the first time.

Don Quixote, seeing them examining him so attentively and that none of them spoke to him or put any question to him, determined to take advantage of their silence; so, breaking his own, he raised his voice and said, "Worthy sirs, I entreat you as earnestly as I can not to interrupt a speech which I wish to address to you, until you find it displeases or annoys you; and if that comes to pass, at the slightest hint you give me I will put a seal upon my lips and a gag in my mouth."

They all told him to say what he liked, for they would listen to him willingly.

With this permission, Don Quixote went on to say, "I, sirs, am a knight-errant whose calling is that of arms and whose profession is to protect those who require protection and give help to such as stand in need of it. Some days ago I became acquainted with your misfortune and the cause which impels you to take up arms again and again to revenge yourselves upon your enemies. Having many times thought over your business in my mind, I find that, according to the laws of combat, you are mistaken in holding yourselves insulted. A private individual cannot insult an entire community unless it be by challenging it collectively as a traitor, because he cannot tell who in particular is guilty of the treason for which he defies it.

"Of this we have an example in Don Diego Ordóñez de Lara, who challenged the whole town of Zamora, because he did not know that Vellido Dolfos alone had committed the treachery of slaying his king; and therefore he challenged them all, and the vengeance and the reply concerned all. Though, to be sure, Señor Don Diego went rather too far, indeed very much beyond the limits of a challenge; for he had no occasion to challenge the dead, or the waters, or the loaves, or those yet unborn, and all the rest of it as set forth. But let that pass, for when anger breaks out there's no father, governor, or bridle to check the tongue.

"The case being, then, that no one person can insult a kingdom, province, city, state, or entire community, it is clear there is no reason for going out to avenge the defiance of such an insult, inasmuch as it is *not* one. A fine thing it would be if the people of 'Clock Town' were to be at loggerheads every moment with everyone who called them by that name,—or the Casserolers, Eggplanters, Whalers, Soapers,[1] or the bearers of all the other names and titles that are always in the mouth of the boys and common people! It would be a nice business indeed if all these illustrious cities were to take offense and revenge themselves and go about perpetually drawing their swords in every petty quarrel! No, no; God forbid!

"There are four things for which sensible men and well-ordered States ought to take up arms, draw their swords, and risk their persons, lives, and properties. The first is to defend the Catholic faith; the second, to defend one's life, which is in accordance with natural and divine law; the third, in defense of one's honor, family, and property; the fourth, in the service of one's king in a just war; and if to these we choose to add a fifth (which may be included in the second), in defense of one's country. To these five capital causes, there may be added some others that may be just and reasonable, and make it a duty to take up arms. But to take them up for trifles and things to laugh at and be amused by rather than offended, suggests that he who does so is completely lacking in common sense.

"Moreover, to take an unjust revenge (and there cannot be any just one) is directly opposed to the sacred law that we acknowledge, wherein we are commanded to do good to our enemies and to love them that hate us; a command which, though it seems somewhat difficult to obey, is only so to those who have in them less of God than of the world and more of the flesh than of the spirit. For Jesus Christ, God and true man, who never lied, and could not and cannot lie, said, as our lawgiver, that his yoke was easy and his burden light. He would not, therefore, have laid any command upon us that it was impossible to obey. Thus, sirs, you are bound to keep quiet by human and divine law."

"The devil take me," said Sancho to himself at this, "but this master of mine is a tologian; or, if not, he's as like one as one egg is like another."

Don Quixote stopped to take breath, and, observing that silence was still preserved, had a mind to continue his speech, and would have done so if Sancho had not butted in. Seeing his master pause, he took the lead, saying, "My lord Don Quixote of La Mancha,

1. A number of towns were known for their clock towers. The other nicknames refer to Valladolid, Toledo, Madrid, and probably Seville.

who once was called the Knight of the Mournful Countenance, but now is called the Knight of the Lions, is a gentleman of great intelligence who knows Latin and his mother tongue like a bachelor of arts. In everything that he deals with or advises, he proceeds like a good soldier, and he has all the laws and ordinances of what they call combat at his fingertips. So you have nothing to do but to let yourselves be guided by what he says, and you can blame me if you go wrong. Besides, you have been told that it is foolishness to take offence at merely hearing a bray. I remember when I was a boy I brayed as often as I had the urge, without anyone's trying to stop me, and so beautifully and naturally that when I brayed all the asses in the town would bray. But I was none the less for that the son of my parents, who were greatly respected. And though I was envied because of my ability by several important people in the town, I didn't give a hoot. And so that you can see I am telling the truth, just listen, because this skill is like swimming: once you learn it, you never forget it."

And then, putting his hand over his nose, he began to bray so vigorously that all the valleys around rang again.

One of those, however, that stood near him, believing that Sancho was mocking them, lifted up a long staff he had in his hand and gave him such a blow with it that Sancho dropped to the ground unconscious.

Seeing him so roughly handled, Don Quixote, lance in hand, attacked the man who had struck him. But so many thrust themselves between them that he could not avenge Sancho. Far from it, finding a shower of stones rained upon him, and crossbows and muskets unnumbered leveled at him, he turned Rocinante around and, as fast as his best gallop could take him, he left them behind, commending himself to God with all his heart to deliver him out of this peril, in dread every step that some bullet would hit his back and come out through his breast. Every minute he took a deep breath to see whether he still could.

The members of the band, however, were satisfied with seeing him run away, and did not fire at him. They sat Sancho, barely restored to his senses, on his ass, and let him go after his master. Not that he was sufficiently recovered to guide the beast, but Dapple followed the footsteps of Rocinante, from whom he could not remain separated for a moment. Don Quixote having got some way off looked back, and seeing Sancho coming, waited for him, since he observed that no one was following him.

The men of the troop stood their ground till night, and as the enemy did not come out to battle, they returned to their town triumphant and happy. Had they been aware of the ancient custom of the Greeks, they would have erected a monument on the spot.

Chapter XXVIII

OF MATTERS THAT BENENGELI SAYS HE WHO READS THEM WILL KNOW, IF HE READS THEM WITH ATTENTION

The brave man flees when he discovers treachery, and wise men reserve themselves for better occasions. This proved to be the case with Don Quixote, who, giving way before the fury of the townsfolk and the hostile intentions of the angry troop, took to flight and, without a thought of Sancho or the danger in which he was leaving him, retreated to such a distance as he thought made him safe.

Sancho, lying across his donkey, followed him, as has been said, and finally caught up, having by this time recovered his senses. When he joined Don Quixote, he let himself drop off Dapple at Rocinante's feet, sore, bruised, and belabored. Don Quixote dismounted to examine his wounds, but finding him unharmed from head to foot, he said to him quite angrily, "In an evil hour you started to bray, Sancho! Where did you learn that it is good to mention rope in the house of a man who has been hanged? To the music of brays what harmonies could you expect to get but blows? Give thanks to God, Sancho, that they made the sign of the cross on you with a stick and did not mark you *per signum crucis* with a cutlass."

"I'm not up to answering," said Sancho. "I feel as if I was speaking through my shoulders. Let's mount and get away from here. I'll keep from braying, but not from saying that knights-errant run away and leave their good squires to be ground to a fine powder at the hands of their enemies."

"He who retreats does not run away," returned Don Quixote, "for I would have you know, Sancho, that the valor which is not based upon a foundation of prudence is called rashness, and the exploits of the rash man are to be attributed rather to good fortune than to courage. I admit that I retreated, but not that I fled. I have followed the example of many valiant men who have reserved themselves for better times; histories are full of instances of this, but as it would not be any good to you or pleasure to me, I will not recount them to you now."

Sancho was by this time mounted with the help of Don Quixote, who then himself mounted Rocinante, and at a leisurely pace they proceeded to take shelter in a grove which was in sight about a quarter of a league off. Every now and then Sancho uttered deep sighs and dismal groans. When Don Quixote asked him what caused such acute suffering, he replied that from the end of his backbone up to the nape of his neck he was so sore that it nearly drove him out of his senses.

"The cause of that soreness," said Don Quixote, "is, no doubt, that the pole with which they struck you being a very long one, it caught you all down the back, where all the parts that are sore are situated, and had it reached any further you would be sorer still."

"By God," said Sancho, "your worship has relieved me of a great doubt and explained it very clearly! Is the cause of my soreness such a mystery that there's any need to tell me I am sore everywhere the staff hit me? If it was my ankles that pained me, there might be something in trying to guess why they did, but it doesn't take brains to figure out that I'm sore where they thrashed me. By my faith, master, 'nobody cares about his neighbor's sad affairs.'

"Every day I am discovering more and more how little I have to hope for from keeping company with your worship. If you let them beat me up this time, the next time, or a hundred times more, we'll have more blanketings like the other day, and other pranks. Now it's my back; next time it'll be my face. I would do a great deal better (if I wasn't an ignorant brute that will never do any thing right in my life), I would do a great deal better, I say, to go home to my wife and children and support them and bring them up on what God may give me, instead of following your worship along roads and paths that lead nowhere, with little to drink and less to eat. And then when it comes to sleeping! Measure out seven feet on the earth, brother squire, and if that's not enough for you, take as many more, for you may have it all your own way and stretch yourself to your heart's content. Oh that I could see the first man that meddled with knight-errantry burned to ashes—or at any rate the first man who chose to be squire to such fools as all the knights-errant of past times must have been! Of those of the present day I say nothing, because, as your worship is one of them, I respect them, and because I know your worship knows a bit more than the devil in all you say and think."

"I would lay a good wager with you, Sancho," said Don Quixote, "that now that you are talking on without anyone to stop you, you don't feel a pain in your whole body. Talk away, my son, say whatever comes into your head or mouth, for so long as you feel no pain, the irritation your impertinences give me will be a pleasure to me. And if you are so anxious to go home to your wife and children, God forbid that I should prevent you. You have money of mine; see how long it is since we left our village this third time, and how much you should have been able to earn every month, and pay yourself."

"When I worked for Tomé Carrasco, the father of the bachelor Sansón Carrasco that your worship knows," replied Sancho, "I used to earn two ducats a month besides my food. I don't know what I should earn with your worship, though I know a knight-errant's squire has harder times of it than a man who works for a farmer; for after all, we who work for farmers, however much we slave all day, at the worst, at night, we have our stew for supper and sleep in a bed, which I have not slept in since I have been in your worship's service, if it wasn't the short time we were in Don Diego de Miranda's house, and the feast I had with the skimmings I took off Camacho's pots, and what I ate, drank, and slept in Basilio's house. All the rest of the time I have been sleeping on the hard ground under the open sky, exposed to what they call the inclemencies of heaven, keeping alive with scraps of cheese and crusts of bread and drinking water either from the brooks or from the springs we come to on these back roads we travel."

"I admit, Sancho," said Don Quixote, "that all you say is true; how much do you think I ought to give you over and above what Tomé Carrasco gave you?"

"I think," said Sancho, "that if your worship was to add on two *reales* a month I'd consider myself well paid; that is, as far as the wages of my labor go; but to make up to me for your worship's pledge and promise to make me governor of an island, it would be fair to add six *reales* more, making thirty in all."

"Very good," said Don Quixote. "It is twenty-five days since we left our village; so calculate, Sancho, and see how much I owe you, and pay yourself, as I said before, out of our treasury."

"My word!" said Sancho, "but your worship is very much off in his calculations. When it comes to the promise of the island, we must count from the day your worship promised it to me to this present hour we are at now."

"Well, how long is it, Sancho, since I promised it to you?" said Don Quixote.

"If I remember rightly," said Sancho, "it must be over twenty years, plus or minus three days."

Don Quixote gave himself a great slap on the forehead and began to laugh heartily, and said he, "Why, I have not been wandering, either in the Sierra Morena or in the whole course of our expedition but barely two months, and you say, Sancho, that it is twenty years since I promised you the island. I believe now you would have all that money you have of mine for your wages. If so, and if that is your pleasure, I give it to you now, once and for all, and much good may it do you, for so long as I see myself rid of such a good-for-nothing squire I'll be glad to be left a pauper without a cent.

"You perverter of the squirely rules of knight-errantry, where have you ever seen or read that any knight-errant's squire made terms with his lord: 'You must give me so much a month for serving you'? Plunge, O scoundrel, rogue, monster—for such I take you to be—plunge, I say, into their endless histories. If you find that any squire ever said or thought what you have said now, I will let you nail it to my forehead, and give me, over and above, four sound slaps in the face. Turn the rein or the halter of your Dapple and begone home; for one single step further you shall not take in my company.

"O bread thanklessly received! O promises ill-bestowed! O man more beast than human being! Now, when I was about to raise you to such a position, that, in spite of your wife, they would call you 'my lord,' you are leaving me? You are going now when I had a firm and fixed intention of making you lord of the best island in the world? Well, as you yourself have said before now, honey is not for the mouth of the ass. Ass you are, ass you will be, and ass you will end when the course of your life is run; for I know it will come to its close before you perceive or discern that you are a beast."

Sancho regarded Don Quixote earnestly while he was giving him this scolding and was so touched by remorse that the tears came to his eyes, and in a piteous and broken voice he said to him, "Master, I confess that, to be a complete ass, all I lack is a tail. If your worship will only fix one on to me, I'll consider it rightly placed and I'll serve you as an ass all the remaining days of my life. Forgive me and have pity on my foolishness, and remember I know little, and, if I talk much, it's more from a weak mind than meanness. But 'he who sins and mends, himself to God commends.' "

"I should have been surprised, Sancho," said Don Quixote, "if you had not introduced some proverb into your speech. Well, well, I forgive you, provided you mend and not show yourself in future so fond of your own interest, but try to be of good cheer and take heart, and encourage yourself to look forward to the fulfillment of my promises, which, by being delayed, does not become impossible."

Sancho said he would do so and keep up his spirits as best he could. They then entered the grove, and Don Quixote settled himself at the foot of an elm, and Sancho at that of a beech, for trees of this kind and others like them always have feet but no hands. Sancho passed the night in pain, for with the evening dews the blow from the pole made itself felt all the more. Don Quixote passed it in his never-failing meditations; but, for all that, they had some winks of sleep, and with the appearance of daylight they pursued their journey in quest of the banks of the famous Ebro, where the adventure which will be told in the following chapter befell them.

Chapter XXIX

OF THE FAMOUS ADVENTURE OF THE ENCHANTED BOAT

By easy stages, two days after leaving the grove Don Quixote and Sancho reached the river Ebro, and the sight of it was a great delight to Don Quixote as he contemplated and gazed upon the charms of its banks, the clearness of its stream, the gentleness of its current, and the abundance of its crystal waters; and the pleasant view revived a thousand tender thoughts in his mind. Above all, he dwelt upon what he had seen in the cave of Montesinos; for though Master Pedro's ape had told him that of those things part was true, part false, he clung more to their truth than to their falsehood, the very reverse of Sancho, who held them all to be downright lies.

As they were thus proceeding, then, they discovered a small boat, without oars or any other gear, that lay at the water's edge tied to the trunk of a tree growing on the bank. Don Quixote looked all around, and seeing nobody, at once, without more ado, dismounted from Rocinante and ordered Sancho to get down from Dapple and tie both beasts securely to the trunk of a poplar or willow that stood there. Sancho asked him the reason of this sudden dismounting and tying.

Don Quixote replied, "You must know, Sancho, that this boat is plainly, and without the possibility of any alternative, calling and inviting me to enter it, and in it go to give aid to some knight or other person of distinction in need of it, who is no doubt in some dire predicament; for this is the way of the books of chivalry and of the enchanters who appear and speak in them. When a knight is involved in some difficulty from which he cannot be delivered save by the hand of another knight, though they may be at a distance of two or three thousand leagues or more one from the other, they either take him up in a cloud, or they provide a boat for him to get into, and in less than the twinkling of a eye they carry him where they will and where his help is required; and so, Sancho, this boat is placed here for the same purpose. This is as true as that it is now day, and before this one passes, tie Dapple and Rocinante together, and then in God's hand be it to guide us; for I would not hold back from embarking, though barefoot friars were to beg me."

"As that's the case," said Sancho, "and your worship chooses to give in to these—I don't know if I may call them absurdities—at every turn, there's nothing for me to do but to obey and bow my head, bearing in mind the proverb, 'Do as thy master bids thee, and sit down to table with him.' But for all that, for the sake of easing my conscience, I warn your worship that in my opinion this boat is not enchanted but belongs to some of the fishermen of this river. They catch the best shad in the world here."

As Sancho said this, he tied the animals, leaving them to the care and protection of the enchanters, with sorrow in his heart. Don Quixote told him not to be uneasy about leaving the animals behind, for the enchanter who had led them "over such longinquous roads" and regions would take care to feed them.

"I don't understand *logiquous*," said Sancho, "nor have I ever heard the word all the days of my life."

"*Longinquous,*" replied Don Quixote, "means far off; but it is no wonder you do not understand it, for you are not expected to know Latin, like some who pretend to know it and don't."

"Now they are tied," said Sancho. "What are we to do next?"

"What?" said Don Quixote, "cross ourselves and weigh anchor; I mean, embark and cut the moorings by which the boat is held." And jumping into the boat, with Sancho behind him, he cut the rope, and the boat began to drift away slowly from the bank. When Sancho saw himself somewhere about two yards out in the river, he began to tremble and give himself up for lost. But nothing distressed him more than hearing Dapple bray and seeing Rocinante struggling to get loose, and he said to his master, "Dapple is braying in grief at our leaving him, and Rocinante is trying to escape and jump in after us. O dear friends, peace be with you, and may this madness that is taking us away from you be turned into sober sense and bring us back to you." And with this he began crying so bitterly, that Don Quixote said to him, sharply and angrily, "What are you afraid of, cowardly creature? What are you weeping at, chicken heart? Who pursues or molests you, you soul of a timid mouse? What do you want, unsatisfied in the very heart of abundance? Are you, perchance, tramping barefoot over the Riphæan mountains, instead of being seated on a bench like an archduke on the tranquil current of this pleasant river, from which in a short space we shall come out upon the broad sea? But we must have already emerged and gone seven hundred or eight hundred leagues; and if I had here an astrolabe to take the altitude of the polestar, I could tell you how many we have traveled, though either I know little, or we have already crossed or shall shortly cross the equinoctial line which parts the two opposite poles midway."

"And when we come to that line your worship speaks of," said Sancho, "how far will we have gone?"

"Very far," said Don Quixote, "for of the three hundred and sixty degrees that this terraqueous globe contains, as computed by Ptolemy, the greatest cosmographer known, we shall have traveled one-half when we come to the line I spoke of."

"By God," said Sancho, "your worship quotes a fine source for what you say: 'putrid by Tolly Me or Trollopy the great cousin-grabber' or whatever it is."

Don Quixote laughed at the interpretation Sancho put upon "computed," and the name of the cosmographer Ptolemy. "You must know, Sancho," he continued, "that with the Spaniards and those who embark at Cádiz for the East Indies, one of the signs they have to show them when they have passed the equinoctial line I told you of, is that the lice die upon everybody on board the ship, and not a single one is left, or to be found in the whole vessel if they gave its weight in gold for it. So, Sancho, pass your hand down your thigh, and if you come upon anything alive we shall be no longer in doubt; if not, then we have crossed."

"I don't believe it," said Sancho. "Still, I'll do as your worship says, though I don't know what need there is for trying these experiments, for I can see with my own eyes that we have not moved five yards away from the bank, or shifted two yards from where the animals stand. There are Rocinante and Dapple in the very same place where we left them. And when I look at some fixed object, as I am doing now, I swear by all that's good, we are not stirring or moving at the pace of an ant."

"Try the test I told you of, Sancho," said Don Quixote, "and don't mind any other, for you know nothing about colures, lines, parallels, zodiacs, ecliptics, poles, solstices, equinoxes, planets, signs, bearings, the measures of which the celestial and terrestrial spheres are composed. If you were acquainted with all these things, or any portion of them, you would see clearly how many parallels we have cut, what signs we have seen, and what constellations we have left behind and are now leaving behind. But again I tell you, feel and hunt, for I am certain you are cleaner than a sheet of smooth white paper."

Sancho felt, and passing his hand gently and carefully down to the hollow of his left knee, he looked up at his master and said, "Either the test is unreliable or we have not come to where your worship says, not by many leagues."

"Why, how so?" asked Don Quixote. "Have you found something?"

"Yes, several somethings," replied Sancho. And shaking his fingers he washed his whole hand in the river along which the boat was quietly gliding in midstream, not moved by any occult intelligence or invisible enchanter, but simply by the current, which was smooth and gentle at that point.

They now came in sight of some large water mills that stood in the middle of the river,[1] and the instant Don Quixote saw them he cried out, "See there, my friend? There stands the castle or fortress where there is, no doubt, some oppressed knight or ill-used queen or infanta or princess, in whose aid I am brought here."

"What city, fortress, or castle is your worship talking about, señor?" said Sancho. "Don't you see that those are mills moored in the river to grind wheat?"

"Hold your peace, Sancho," said Don Quixote. "Though they look like mills, they are not. I have already told you that enchantments transform things and change their proper shapes. I do not mean to say they really change them from one form into another, but that it seems as though they did, as experience proved in the transformation of Dulcinea, sole refuge of my hopes."

1. Floating mills, moored in midstream, were common on the Ebro.

By this time, the boat, having reached the middle of the stream, began to move less slowly than before. When the workers on the mill-barge saw the boat coming down the river and on the point of being sucked into the millrace, several of them ran out quickly with long poles to stop it, and being all powdery, with faces and garments covered with flour, they presented a sinister appearance. They raised loud shouts, crying, "You damned fools, where are you going? Are you mad? Do you want to drown yourselves or dash yourselves to pieces on these wheels?"

"Did I not tell you, Sancho," said Don Quixote at this, "that we had reached the place where I am to show what the might of my arm can do? See what ruffians and villains come out against me; see what monsters oppose me; see what hideous countenances come to frighten us? Ye shall soon see, scoundrels!"

And then standing up in the boat he began in a loud voice to hurl threats at the millers, exclaiming, "Wicked and misguided rabble, restore to liberty and freedom the person ye hold in durance in this your fortress or prison, high or low or of whatever rank or quality he be, for I am Don Quixote of La Mancha, otherwise called the Knight of the Lions, for whom, by decree of heaven above, it is reserved to give a successful conclusion to this adventure!" And so saying he drew his sword and began making passes in the air at the millers, who, hearing but not understanding all this nonsense, were trying, with their poles, to stop the boat, which was now getting into the rushing channel of the wheels.

Sancho fell upon his knees devoutly appealing to heaven to deliver him from such imminent peril; which it did by the activity and quickness of the millers, who, pushing against the boat with their poles, stopped it, not, however, without upsetting the boat and throwing Don Quixote and Sancho into the water. It was lucky for Don Quixote that he could swim like a fish, though the weight of his armor pulled him to the bottom twice; and had it not been for the millers, who plunged in and pulled them both out, it would have been disaster for the pair of them. As soon as they had been pulled out on the bank, more drenched than thirsty, Sancho went down on his knees and with clasped hands and eyes raised to heaven, prayed a long and fervent prayer to God to deliver him evermore from the rash projects and attempts of his master.

The fishermen who owned the boat, which the millwheels had knocked to pieces, now came up, and seeing it smashed, they proceeded to strip Sancho and to demand payment for it from Don Quixote. With great calmness, just as if nothing had happened him, he told the millers and fishermen that he would pay for the boat most cheerfully, on condition that they delivered up to him, free and unhurt, the person or persons that were imprisoned in that castle of theirs.

"What persons or what castle are you talking about, you lunatic! Do you want to carry off the people who come to grind wheat in these mills?"

"Enough," said Don Quixote to himself. "It would be preaching in the desert to attempt by entreaties to induce this rabble to do any virtuous action. In this adventure two mighty enchanters must have encountered one another, and one frustrates what the other attempts; one provided the boat for me, and the other overturned me. God help us; this world is all machinations and schemes at cross purposes one with the other. I can do no more." And then turning towards the mills he said aloud, "Friends, whoe'er ye be that are immured in that prison, forgive me that, to my misfortune and yours, I cannot deliver you from your misery; this adventure is doubtless reserved and destined for some other knight."

So saying he settled up with the fishermen and paid fifty *reales* for the boat, which Sancho handed to them very much against his will, saying, "With a couple more boat affairs like this, we'll sink our whole capital."

The fishermen and the millers stood staring in amazement at the two figures, so very different to all appearance from ordinary men, and were wholly unable to make out the drift of the observations and questions Don Quixote addressed to them. Concluding that they were madmen, they left them, the millers returning to their mills and the fishermen to their huts. Don Quixote and Sancho returned to their animals—and to their beastly life—and so ended the adventure of the enchanted boat.

Chapter XXX

OF DON QUIXOTE'S ADVENTURE WITH A FAIR HUNTRESS

Knight and squire reached their mounts in rather low spirits and bad humor, Sancho particularly, for with him what touched the money supply touched his heart, and when any was taken from him he felt as if he were robbed of the apples of his eyes. Finally, without exchanging a word, they mounted and turned away from the famous river, Don Quixote absorbed in thoughts of his love, Sancho in thinking of his advancement, which just then, it seemed to him, he was very far from securing. For, fool that he was, he saw clearly enough that his master's acts were all or most of them utterly senseless, and he began to cast about for an opportunity of retiring from his service and going home some day, without entering into any explanations or saying good-bye to his master. Fortune, however, ordered matters very much the opposite of what he contemplated.

It so happened that the next day towards sunset, on coming out of a wood, Don Quixote cast his eyes over a green meadow and at the far end of it observed some people, and as he drew nearer he saw that it was a hawking party. Coming closer, he distinguished among them an elegant lady on a pure white palfrey or hackney caparisoned with green trappings and a silver-mounted sidesaddle. The lady was also in green, and so richly and splendidly dressed that splendor itself seemed personified in her. On her left hand she bore a hawk, proof to Don Quixote's mind that she must be some great lady and the mistress of the whole hunting party, which was the fact.

So he said to Sancho, "Run Sancho, my son, and say to that lady on the palfrey with the hawk that I, the Knight of the Lions, kiss the hands of her exalted beauty, and if her excellency will grant me leave I will come and kiss them in person and place myself at her service for whatever lies within my power and her highness may command; and mind, Sancho, how you speak, and take care not to drag any of your proverbs into your message."

"Drag in any of my proverbs!" said Sancho. "How can you say that to me? Why, this is not the first time in my life I have carried messages to high and exalted ladies."

"Except for the one you carried to the lady Dulcinea," said Don Quixote, "I am not aware that you have carried any other, at least in my service."

"That is true," replied Sancho, "but 'a reliable payer doesn't mind leaving security,' and 'in a house where there's' plenty, supper is soon cooked.' I mean there's no need of telling or warning me about anything. I'm ready for everything and know a little of everything."

"That I believe, Sancho," said Don Quixote. "Go and good luck to you, and God speed you."

Sancho went off at top speed, forcing Dapple out of his regular pace, and came to where the beautiful huntress was standing, and dismounting knelt before her and said, "Fair lady, that knight that you see there, the Knight of the Lions by name, is my master, and I am his squire, and at home they call me Sancho Panza. This same Knight of the Lions, who was called not long since the Knight of the Mournful Countenance, sends me to say may it please your highness to give him leave that, with your permission, approbation, and consent, he may come and carry out his wishes, which are, as he says and I believe, to serve your exalted loftiness and beauty. And if you give it, your ladyship will do a thing which will redound to your honor, and he will receive a most distinguished favor and satisfaction."

"You have indeed, worthy squire," said the lady, "delivered your message with all the formalities such messages require. Rise up, for it is not right that the squire of a knight so great as he of the

Mournful Countenance, of whom we have heard a great deal here, should remain on his knees; rise, my friend, and bid your master welcome to the services of myself and the duke my husband, in a country house we have here."[1]

Sancho got up, charmed as much by the beauty of the good lady as by her well-bred air and her courtesy, but, above all, by what she had said about having heard of his master, the Knight of the Mournful Countenance; for if she did not call him Knight of the Lions it was no doubt because he had so recently taken the name. "Tell me, my dear squire," asked the duchess (whose title, however, is not known), "this master of yours, is he the one about whom there is a history in print, called *The Ingenious Gentleman, Don Quixote of La Mancha,* who has for the lady of his heart a certain Dulcinea del Toboso?"

"He's the one, señora," replied Sancho, "and that squire of his who appears, or ought to appear, in the said history under the name of Sancho Panza, is myself, unless they have changed me in the cradle, I mean in the press."

"I am delighted by all this," said the duchess. "Go, my dear Panza, and tell your master that he is welcome to my estate and that nothing could happen to me that could give me greater pleasure."

Sancho returned to his master mightily pleased with this gratifying answer, and told him all the great lady had said to him, lauding to the skies, in his rustic phrase, her rare beauty, her charm, and her courtesy. Don Quixote drew himself up briskly in his saddle, fixed himself in his stirrups, settled his visor, gave Rocinante the spur, and with an easy bearing advanced to kiss the hands of the duchess, who, having sent to summon the duke her husband, told him all about the message while Don Quixote was approaching. And as both of them had read the First Part of this history, and from it were aware of Don Quixote's strange ideas, they awaited him with the greatest delight and desire to make his acquaintance, meaning to humor him and agree with everything he said, and, so long as he stayed with them, to treat him as a knight-errant, with all the ceremonies usual in the books of chivalry they had read, for they themselves were very fond of such books.

Don Quixote now came up with his visor raised, and as he seemed about to dismount, Sancho made haste to go and hold his stirrup for him. But in getting down off Dapple, Sancho was so unlucky as to hitch his foot in one of the ropes of the packsaddle in such a way that he was unable to free it, and he was left hanging by it with his face and breast on the ground. Don Quixote, who was

1. Many scholars believe that Cervantes modeled his aristocrats on the Duke and Duchess of Luna and Villahermosa, who had a country house at Pedrola, near Zaragoza.

not used to dismounting without having the stirrup held, assuming that Sancho had by this time come to hold it for him, threw himself off with a lurch and brought Rocinante's saddle—which was no doubt badly girthed—after him, and saddle and he both came to the ground, not without embarrassment to himself and abundant curses muttered against the unlucky Sancho, who still had his foot in the shackles.

The duke ordered his huntsmen to go to the aid of knight and squire, and they raised Don Quixote, badly shaken by his fall. Limping, he advanced as best he could to kneel before the noble pair. This, however, the duke would by no means permit; on the contrary, dismounting from his horse, he went and embraced Don Quixote, saying, "I am grieved, Sir Knight of the Mournful Countenance, that your first experience on my property should have been such an unfortunate one as we have seen. But the carelessness of squires is often the cause of worse accidents."

"That which has happened me in meeting you, mighty prince," replied Don Quixote, "cannot be unfortunate, even if my fall had not stopped short of the depths of the bottomless pit, for the glory of having seen you would have lifted me up and delivered me from it. My squire, God's curse upon him, is better at unloosing his tongue in talking impertinence than in tightening the girth of a saddle to keep it steady; but however I may be, fallen or raised up, on foot or on horseback, I shall always be at your service and that of my lady the duchess, your worthy consort, worthy queen of beauty and paramount princess of courtesy."

"Careful, Señor Don Quixote of La Mancha," said the duke. "Where my lady Doña Dulcinea del Toboso is, it is not right that other beauties should be praised."

Sancho, by this time released from his entanglement, was standing near, and before his master could answer he said, "There is no denying, and it must be maintained, that my lady Dulcinea del Toboso is very beautiful. But 'the hare jumps up where one least expects it,' I have heard tell that what people call Mother Nature is like a potter that makes clay pots, and a person who makes one nice pot can as well make two, or three, or a hundred. I say so because, by my faith, my lady the duchess is in no way behind my mistress the lady Dulcinea del Toboso."

Don Quixote turned to the duchess and said, "Your highness may conceive that never had knight-errant in this world a more talkative or a more amusing squire than I have, and he will prove the truth of what I say, if your highness is pleased to accept my services for a few days."

To which the duchess replied, "That the worthy Sancho is amusing, I consider a very good thing, because it is a sign that he is shrewd; for drollery and humor, Señor Don Quixote, as you very well know, do not take up their abode with dull wits; and as the good Sancho is droll and witty, I thus conclude that he is shrewd."

"And talkative," added Don Quixote.

"So much the better," said the duke, "for so many clever things cannot be said in few words; but not to lose time in talking, come, great Knight of the Mournful Countenance—"

"Of the Lions, your highness must say," said Sancho, "for there is no Mournful Countenance nor any such character now."

"He of the Lions be it," continued the duke. "I say, let Sir Knight of the Lions come to a castle of mine close by, where he shall be given that reception which is due to so exalted a personage, and which the duchess and I are accustomed to give to all knights-errant who come there."

By this time Sancho had straightened and girthed Rocinante's saddle, and Don Quixote having gotten on his back and the duke mounted a fine horse, they placed the duchess in the middle and set out for the castle. The duchess desired Sancho to come to her side, for she found infinite enjoyment in listening to his shrewd remarks. Sancho required no urging but pushed himself in between them and the duke, who thought it rare good fortune to receive such a knight-errant and such an errant squire in their castle.

Chapter XXXI

WHICH TREATS OF MANY AND GREAT MATTERS

Supreme was the satisfaction that Sancho felt at seeing himself, as it seemed, an established favorite with the duchess, for he looked forward to finding in her castle what he had found in Don Diego's house and in Basilio's. He was always fond of good living and always seized by the forelock any opportunity of feasting whenever it presented itself.

The history informs us, then, that before they reached the country house or castle, the duke went on in advance and instructed all his servants how they were to treat Don Quixote. And so the instant he came up to the castle gates with the duchess, two lackeys or equerries, clad in what they call dressing gowns of fine crimson satin reaching to their feet, hastened out, and catching Don Quixote in their arms before he saw or heard them, said to him, "Your excellency should go and help my lady the duchess off her horse."

Don Quixote obeyed, and great bandying of compliments followed between the two over the matter. But in the end the duchess's determination carried the day, and she refused to get down or dismount from her palfrey except in the arms of the duke, saying she did not consider herself worthy to impose so unnecessary a burden on so great a knight.

At length the duke came out to help her down, and as they entered a spacious courtyard, two fair damsels came forward and threw over Don Quixote's shoulders a big cloak of the finest scarlet cloth, and at the same instant all the galleries overlooking the courtyard were lined with the men-servants and women-servants of the household, crying, "Wecome, flower and cream of knight-errantry!" while all (or most of them) sprinkled scented water on Don Quixote and the duke and duchess—at all which Don Quixote was greatly astonished. And this was the first time that he thoroughly felt and believed himself to be a real knight-errant and not an imaginary one, now that he saw himself treated in the same way as he had read of such knights being treated in days of yore.

Sancho, deserting Dapple, hung on to the duchess and entered the castle, but feeling some twinges of conscience at having left the ass alone, he approached a dignified dueña who had come out with the rest to receive the duchess, and in a low voice he said to her, "Señora González, or whatever your grace may be called—"

"I am called Doña Rodríguez de Grijalba," replied the dueña. "What is your will, my friend?" To which Sancho made answer, "I'd be grateful if your worship would do me the favor of going out to the castle gate, where you will find a grey ass of mine; make them, if you please, put him in the stable, or put him there yourself, for the poor little thing is a bit nervous and won't like being alone at all."

"If the master is as wise as the man," said the dueña, "we have a fine bargain. Be off with you, my friend, and bad luck to you and him who brought you here. Take care of your own donkey for we, the dueñas of this house, are not used to work of that sort."

"Well," replied Sancho, "I have heard my master, who knows all kinds of stories, telling the story of Lancelot when he came from Britain, say that 'ladies waited upon him and dueñas upon his hack'; and, if it comes to my donkey, I wouldn't change him for Señor Lancelot's hack."

"If you are a jester, brother," said the dueña, "keep your jokes for some place where they'll be appreciated and paid for; for you'll get nothing from me but a fig."[1]

"At any rate, it will be a very ripe one," said Sancho. "If years were points, you'd win your card games with no trouble."

"Son of a bitch," said the dueña, all aglow with anger, "whether I'm old or not, it's with God I have to reckon, not with you, you garlic-stuffed lout!" And she said it so loud that the duchess heard it, and turning round and seeing the dueña in such a state of excitement, and her eyes flaming so, asked whom she was arguing with.

1. The "fig" was a gesture of contempt made by sticking the thumb between the index and third finger of the fist.

"With this good fellow here," said the dueña, "who has earnestly requested me to go and put an ass of his that is at the castle gate into the stable, holding up to me as an example that they did it somewhere or other—that some ladies waited on Lancelot, and dueñas on his hack; and what is more, to wind up with, he called me old."

"That," said the duchess, "I should have considered the greatest affront that could be offered me." And addressing Sancho, she said to him, "You must know, friend Sancho, that Doña Rodríguez is very youthful and that she wears that hood more for dignity and custom than because of her years."

"May all the rest of mine be unlucky," said Sancho, "if I meant it that way. I only spoke because the affection I have for my donkey is so great, and I thought I could not commend him to a more kind-hearted person than the lady Doña Rodríguez."

Don Quixote, who was listening, said to him, "Is this proper conversation for the place, Sancho?"

"Señor," replied Sancho, "every one must mention what he wants wherever he may be. I thought of Dapple here, and I spoke of him here. If I had thought of him in the stable, I would have spoken there."

On which the duke observed, "Sancho is quite right, and there is no reason at all to find fault with him. Dapple shall be fed to his heart's content, and Sancho may rest easy, for he shall be treated like himself."

While this conversation, amusing to all except Don Quixote, was proceeding, they ascended the staircase and ushered Don Quixote into a chamber hung with rich cloth of gold and brocade. Six damsels relieved him of his armor and waited on him like pages, all of them prepared and instructed by the duke and duchess as to what they were to do, and how they were to treat Don Quixote, so that he might see and believe they were treating him like a knight-errant. When his armor was removed, there stood Don Quixote in his tight-fitting breeches and chamois doublet, lean, lanky, and long, with cheeks that seemed to be kissing each other inside; such a figure, that if the damsels waiting on him had not taken care to control their merriment (which was one of the particular directions their master and mistress had given them), they would have burst with laughter.

They asked him to let himself be stripped that they might put a shirt on him, but he would not on any account, saying that modesty became knights-errant just as much as valor. However, he said they might give the shirt to Sancho; and shutting himself in with him in a room where there was a sumptuous bed, he undressed and put on the shirt. Finding himself alone with Sancho, he said to him, "Tell me, you novice buffoon and veteran nitwit: do you think it right to offend and insult a dueña so deserving of reverence and respect as that one just now? Was that a time to remember your Dapple, or are these noble personages likely to let the beasts fare badly when they treat their owners in such elegant style?

"For God's sake, Sancho, restrain yourself, and don't show the thread so as to let them see what coarse, vulgar stuff you're made of. Remember, sinner that you are: the master is the more esteemed the more respectable and well-bred his servants are, and one of the greatest advantages that princes have over other men is that they have servants as good as themselves to wait on them. Do you not see—miserable wretch that you are, and unlucky mortal that I am!—that if they perceive you to be a coarse clown or an amusing simpleton, they will think I am some imposter or swindler? No, Sancho my friend, keep clear, oh, keep clear of these stumbling blocks; for he who falls into the way of being a chatterbox and clever, becomes a wretched buffoon the first time he trips. Bridle your tongue, consider and weigh your words before they escape your mouth, and bear in mind we are now in quarters whence, by God's help and the strength of my arm, we shall come forth mightily advanced in fame and fortune."

Sancho promised him with much earnestness to keep his mouth shut and to bite off his tongue before he uttered a word that was not altogether to the purpose and well considered, and told him he might make his mind easy on that point, for he would never do anything to embarrass them.

Don Quixote dressed himself, put on his sword belt and sword, threw the scarlet mantle over his shoulders, placed on his head a cap of green satin that the damsels had given him, and thus arrayed entered the large room, where he found the damsels drawn up in double file, the same number on each side, all with the vessels for washing the hands, which they presented to him with profuse curtsies and ceremonies. Then came twelve pages, together with the steward, to lead him to dinner, as his hosts were already waiting for him. They placed him in the middle, and with much pomp and stateliness they conducted him into another room, where there was a sumptuous table laid with only four places. The duchess and the duke came out to the door of the room to receive him, and with them a grave ecclesiastic, one of those who rule noblemen's houses; one of those who, not being born magnates themselves, never know how to teach those who are, how to behave as such; one of those who would have the greatness of the great measured by their own narrowness of mind; one of those who, when they try to introduce economy into the household they rule, lead it into stinginess. One of this sort, I say, must have been the grave churchman who came out with the duke and duchess to receive Don Quixote.

A vast number of polite speeches were exchanged, and at length, taking Don Quixote between them, they proceeded to sit down to table. The duke pressed Don Quixote to take the head of the table, and, though he refused, the entreaties of the duke were so urgent that he had to accept it.

The ecclesiastic took his seat opposite to him, and the duke and duchess those at the sides. All this time Sancho stood by, gaping with amazement at the honor he saw shown to his master by these illustrious persons. Observing all the ceremonious urging that had passed between the duke and Don Quixote to induce him to take his seat at the head of the table, he said, "If your worship will give me leave, I will tell you a story of what happened in my village about this matter of seats."

The moment Sancho said this, Don Quixote trembled, convinced that he was about to say something foolish. Sancho glanced at him, and guessing his thoughts, said, "Don't be afraid of my going astray, senōr, or saying anything inappropriate. I haven't forgotten the advice your worship gave me just now about talking much or little, well or ill."

"I have no recollection of anything of the sort, Sancho," said Don Quixote. "Say what you will, only say it quickly."

"Well then," said Sancho, "what I am going to say is so true that my master Don Quixote, who is here present, will keep me from lying."

"Lie as much as you want for all I care, Sancho," said Don Quixote, "for I am not going to stop you; but consider what you are going to say."

"I have considered and reconsidered it so much," said Sancho, "that I know I'm on safe ground (like the bellringer who's safe in his belfry), as will be seen by what follows."

"It would be well," said Don Quixote, "if your highnesses would order them to turn out this idiot, for he will talk a heap of nonsense."

"By the life of the duke, Sancho shall not be taken away from me for a moment," said the duchess. "I am very fond of him, for I know he is very clever."

"God bless your holiness," said Sancho, "for the good opinion you have of my wit, though there's none in me. But the story I want to tell is this. There was an invitation given by a gentleman from my town, a very rich one, and one of quality, for he was one of the Alamos of Medina del Campo, and married to Doña Mencía de Quiñones, the daughter of Don Alonso de Marañón, Knight of the Order of Santiago, that was drowned at the Herradura—the one there was that quarrel about years ago in our village, that my master Don Quixote was mixed up in, to the best of my belief, that Tomasillo the mischief-maker, the son of Balbastro the smith, was wounded in. Isn't all this true, master? For heaven's sake, say so, that these lords and ladies may not take me for some lying wind-bag."

"So far," said the ecclesiastic, "I take you to be more of a wind-bag than a liar; but I don't know what I shall take you for later."

"You cite so many witnesses and proofs, Sancho," said Don Quixote, "that I have no choice but to say you must be telling the truth. Go on, and cut the story short, for at this rate, you will not make an end for two days."

"He is not to cut it short," said the duchess. "On the contrary, for my gratification, he is to tell it as he knows it, even if he should not finish it in six days; and if he took that many, they would be the pleasantest I ever spent."

"Well then, sirs, I say," continued Sancho, "that this same gentleman, that I know as well as I do my own hands, for it's not a bowshot from my house to his, invited a poor but respectable farmer—"

"Get on, brother," said the churchman. "At the rate you are going you won't finish your story short of the next world."

"I'll stop less than halfway, please God," said Sancho. "And so I say this farmer, coming to the house of the gentleman I spoke of that invited him—rest his soul, he is dead now; and apparently he died like a saint, so they say; I was not there, because just at that time I had gone to reap at Tembleque—"

"As you live, my son," said the churchman, "hurry back from Tembleque, and finish your story without burying the gentleman, unless you want to have more funerals."

"Well then, it so happened," said Sancho, "that as the pair of them were going to sit down to table—and I think I can see them now plainer than ever—"

Great was the enjoyment the duke and duchess derived from the irritation the worthy churchman showed at the long-winded, halting way Sancho had of telling his story, while Don Quixote was chafing with rage and vexation.

"So, as I was saying," continued Sancho, "as the pair of them were going to sit down to table, as I said, the farmer insisted on the gentleman's taking the head of the table, and the gentleman insisted on the farmer's taking it, as his orders should be obeyed in his house; but the farmer, who prided himself on his politeness and good breeding, wouldn't on any account, until the gentleman, peeved, putting his hands on his shoulders, compelled him by force to sit down, saying 'Sit down, you stupid lout, for wherever I sit will be the head to you.' And that's the story, and, frankly, I think it hasn't been brought in amiss here."

Don Quixote turned all colors, which, on his sunburnt face, mottled it till it looked like marble. The duke and duchess suppressed their laughter so as not to mortify Don Quixote, for they saw through Sancho's impertinence; and to change the conversation, and keep Sancho from uttering more absurdities, the duchess asked Don Quixote what news he had of the lady Dulcinea, and if he had sent her any presents of giants or scoundrels lately, for he must certainly have vanquished a good many.

To which Don Quixote replied, "Señora, my misfortunes, though they had a beginning will never have an end. I have vanquished giants, and I have sent her caitiffs and miscreants; but where are they to find her if she is enchanted and turned into most ill-favored peasant wench that can be imagined?"

"I don't know," said Sancho Panza. "To me she seems the most beautiful creature in the world; at any rate, in agility and jumping she'd beat a tumbler. By my faith, señora duchess, she leaps from the ground on to the back of an ass like a cat."

"Have you seen her enchanted, Sancho?" asked the duke.[2]

"What, seen her!" said Sancho. "Why, who the devil was it but myself that first thought of the enchantment business? She is about as enchanted as my father."

The ecclesiastic, when he heard them talking of giants and caitiffs and enchantments, began to suspect that this must be Don Quixote of La Mancha, whose story the duke was always reading; and he had himself often reproved him for it, telling him it was foolish to read such fooleries; and becoming convinced that his suspicion was correct, addressing the duke, he said very angrily to him, "Señor, your excellency will have to give account to God for what this good man does. This Don Quixote, or Don Demented, or whatever his name is, cannot, I imagine, be so crazy as your excellency would have him, holding out encouragement to him to go on with his vagaries and follies."

Then turning to address Don Quixote he said, "And you, you poor fool, who put it into your head that you are a knight-errant, and vanquish giants and capture 'miscreants'? Goodbye and good riddance! Go home and bring up your children if you have any, and attend to your business, and stop wandering about the world, gaping and making a laughing-stock of yourself to all who know you and all who don't. Where, in heaven's name, have you discovered that there are or ever were knights-errant? Where are there giants in Spain or miscreants in La Mancha, or enchanted Dulcineas, or all the rest of the silly things they tell about you?"

Don Quixote listened attentively to the reverend gentleman's words, and as soon as he perceived he had finished speaking, in spite of the presence of the duke and duchess, he sprang to his feet with angry looks and an agitated expression and said—but the reply deserves a chapter to itself.

2. The duke's question and Sancho's answer are apparently delivered in an aside.

Chapter XXXII

OF THE REPLY DON QUIXOTE GAVE HIS CENSURER, WITH OTHER INCIDENTS, GRAVE AND DROLL

Don Quixote, then, having risen to his feet, trembling from head to foot like a man dosed with mercury, said in a hurried, agitated voice, "The place I am in, the presence in which I stand, and the respect I have and always have had for the profession to which your worship belongs, hold and bind the hands of my just indignation. And for these reasons as well as because I know, as everyone knows, that a cleric's weapon is the same as a woman's, the tongue, I will with mine engage in equal combat with your worship, from whom one might have expected good advice instead of foul abuse.

"Pious, well-meant reproof requires other circumstances and arguments of another sort. At any rate, to have reproved me in public, and so harshly, exceeds the bounds of proper reproof, for that comes better with gentleness than with rudeness; and it is not right to call the sinner roundly foolish and stupid without knowing anything of the sin that is reproved. Come, tell me, for which of the stupidities you have observed in me do you condemn and abuse me, and bid me go home and look after my house and wife and children, without knowing whether I have any? Is nothing more needed to fit one to lay down the law for chilvalry and pass judgment on knights-errant, than to get a foothold, by hook or by crook, in other people's houses to rule over the masters (and that, perhaps, after having been brought up in all the strictness of some seminary, and without having ever seen more of the world than may lie within twenty or thirty leagues round)?

"Is it, perhaps, an idle occupation, or is the time ill-spent that is spent in roaming the world in quest, not of its enjoyments, but of those arduous toils whereby the good mount upwards to the abodes of everlasting life? If gentlemen, great lords, nobles, men of high birth, were to consider me as a fool I should take it as an irreparable insult; but I care not a whit if clerics who have never entered upon or trod the paths of chivalry should think me foolish. Knight I am, and knight I will die, if such be the pleasure of the Most High. Some take the broad road of overweening ambition; others that of low and servile flattery; others that of deceitful hypocrisy, and some that of true religion; but I, led by my star, follow the narrow path of knight-errantry, and in pursuit of that calling I despise wealth, but not honor. I have redressed injuries, righted wrongs, punished insolences, vanquished giants, and crushed monsters. I am in love, for no other reason than that it is incumbent on knights-errant to be so; but though I am, I am no carnal-minded lover, but one of the chaste, platonic sort. My intentions are always directed to worthy ends, to do good to all and evil to none; and if he who intends this, does this, and makes this his business deserves to be called a fool, it is for your highnesses to say, O most excellent duke and duchess."

"Good, by God!" cried Sancho. "Say no more in your own defence, my lord and master, for there's nothing more in the world to be said, thought, or insisted on; and besides, when this gentleman denies, as he has, that there are or ever have been any knights-errant in the world, is it any wonder if he knows nothing of what he has been talking about?"

"Perhaps, brother," said the ecclesiastic, "you are that Sancho Panza that is mentioned, to whom your master has promised an island?"

"Yes, I am," said Sancho, "and what's more, I deserve it as much as anyone; I am one of those who say 'stick with the good and you'll become good' and who believe that 'what counts is your friends not your background' and that 'a man who sits by a good tree finds good shade.' I've 'sat by' a good master, and I have been going around with him for months, and God willing, I'll be just like him. Long life to him and long life to me, for he won't lack empires to rule, or I islands to govern."

"No, Sancho my friend, certainly not," said the duke, "for in the name of Señor Don Quixote I confer upon you the government of one of no small importance that I have at my disposal."

"Go down on your knees, Sancho," said Don Quixote, "and kiss the feet of his excellency for the favor he has bestowed upon you."

Sancho obeyed, and on seeing this, the ecclesiastic stood up from table completely out of temper, exclaiming, "By the habit I wear, I am almost inclined to say that your excellency is as great a fool as these sinners. No wonder they are mad, when people who are in their senses sanction their madness! I leave your excellency with them, for so long as they are in the house, I will remain in my own and spare myself the trouble of reproving what I cannot correct." And without uttering another word or eating another morsel, he went off, the entreaties of the duke and duchess being entirely unavailing to stop him—not that the duke said much to him, for he could not, because of the laughter his uncalled-for anger provoked.

When he had done laughing, he said to Don Quixote, "You have replied on your own behalf so stoutly, Sir Knight of the Lions, that there is no occasion to seek further satisfaction for this, which, though it may look like an offense, is not so at all, for, as women can give no offense, neither can ecclesiastics, as you very well know."

"That is true," said Don Quixote, "and the reason is, that he who cannot be offended cannot give offense to anyone. Women, children, and ecclesiastics, as they cannot defend themselves, though they may receive offense cannot be insulted, because between the offense and the insult there is, as your excellency very well knows, this difference: the insult comes from one who is capable of offering it, and does so, and maintains it; the offense may come from any quarter without carrying insult.

"To take an example: a man is standing unsuspectingly in the street and ten others come up armed and beat him; he draws his sword and defends himself as well as he can, but the number of his antagonists makes it impossible for him to effect his purpose, which is to avenge himself. This man suffers an offense but not an insult. Another example will make the same thing plain: a man is standing with his back turned, another comes up and strikes him, and after striking him runs off without waiting an instant, and the other pursues him but does not overtake him. He who received the blow received an offense, but not an insult, because an insult must be maintained. If he who struck him, though he did so treacherously, had drawn his sword and stood and faced him, then he who had been struck would have received offense and insult at the same time: offense because he was struck treacherously, insult because he who struck him maintained what he had done, standing his ground without taking to flight.

"And so, according to the laws of the accursed duel, I may have received offense, but not insult, for neither women nor children can maintain it, nor can they wound, nor have they any way of standing their ground, and it is just the same with those connected with religion; for these three sorts of persons are without arms offensive or defensive, and so, though naturally they are bound to defend themselves, they have no right to offend anybody. And though I said just now I might have received offense, I say now certainly not, for he who cannot receive an insult can still less give one; for which reasons I ought not to feel, nor do I feel, aggrieved at what that good man said to me. I only wish he had stayed a little longer, that I might have shown him the mistake he makes in supposing and maintaining that there are not and never have been any knights-errant in the world. Had Amadís or any of his countless descendants heard him say as much, I am sure it would not have gone well with his worship."

"I'll swear to that," said Sancho. "They would have given him a slash that would have slit him down from top to toe like a pomegranate or a ripe melon; they were too touchy to put up with jokes like that! By my faith, I'm sure if Reinaldos of Montalbán had heard the little man's words he would have punched him in the mouth so hard that he wouldn't have spoken for the next three years. Let him tackle them, and he'll see how he'll get out of their hands!"

The duchess, as she listened to Sancho, was dying laughing, and in her own mind she set him down as funnier and madder than his master; and there were a good many just then who were of the same opinion.

Don Quixote finally calmed down, and dinner came to an end, and as the cloth was removed four damsels came in, one of them with a silver basin, another with a jug also of silver, a third with two fine white towels on her shoulder, and the fourth with her arms bared to the elbows, and in her white hands (for white they certainly were) a round ball of Naples soap. The one with the basin approached and gracefully and confidently thrust it under Don Quixote's chin, who puzzled at such a ceremony, said never a word, supposing it to be the custom of that region to wash beards instead of hands. He therefore stuck his chin out as far as he could, and at the same instant the jug began to pour and the damsel with the soap rubbed his beard briskly, scattering snowflakes—for the soap lather was no less white—not only over the beard, but all over the face and over the eyes of the submissive knight, who was perforce obliged to keep them shut.

The duke and duchess, who had not known anything about this, waited to see what would come of this strange washing. The barber damsel, when she had him four inches deep in lather, pretended that there was no more water and ordered the one with the jug to go and fetch some, while Señor Don Quixote waited. She did so, and Don Quixote was left with the strangest and most ludicrous appearance that could be imagined. All those present, and there were a good many, were watching him, and as they saw him there with half a yard of neck, and that uncommonly brown, his eyes shut, and his beard full of soap, it was a great wonder, and only by great discretion, that they were able to restrain their laughter. The young ladies who had thought up the joke kept their eyes down, not daring to look at their master and mistress. And as for them, laughter and anger struggled within them, and they did not know what to do, whether to punish the audacity of the girls or to reward them for the amusement they had received from seeing Don Quixote in such a plight.

Finally, the damsel with the jug returned and they finished washing Don Quixote, and the one who carried the towels very sedately wiped him and dried him; and all four together making him a profound obeisance and curtsey, they were about to go, when the duke, lest Don Quixote should see through the joke, called out to the one with the basin saying, "Come and wash me, and see that you don't run out of water." The girl, sharp-witted and prompt, came and placed the basin for the duke as she had done for Don Quixote, and they soon had him well soaped and washed, and having wiped him dry they bowed and left. It appeared afterwards that the duke had sworn that if they had not washed him as they had Don Quixote he would have punished them for their impudence, which they adroitly atoned for by soaping him as well.

Sancho observed the ceremony of the washing very attentively and said to himself, "God bless me, I wonder if it's the custom in this region to wash squires' beards too as well as knights'? For by God and upon my soul I need it badly; and if they gave me a scrape of the razor besides I'd take it as a bigger favor."

"What are you saying to yourself, Sancho?" asked the duchess.

"I was saying, señora," he replied, "that in the courts of other princes, when the cloth is taken away, I have always heard say they give water for the hands, but not lye soap for the beard. That's why it's good to live long so that you can see a lot. Although they say also that he who lives a long life must undergo much evil, though to undergo a washing like this one is a pleasure rather than a hardship."

"Don't be uneasy, friend Sancho," said the duchess. "I will see that my ladies wash you, and even rinse and bleach you if necessary."

"I'll be content with the beard," said Sancho, "at least for now; and as for the future, God knows."

"Attend to worthy Sancho's request, steward," said the duchess, "and do exactly what he wishes."

The steward replied that Señor Sancho would be obeyed in everything; and with that he went off to dinner and took Sancho along with him, while the duke and duchess and Don Quixote remained at table discussing a great variety of things, but all bearing on the calling of arms and knight-errantry.

The duchess begged Don Quixote, as he seemed to have a retentive memory, to describe and portray to her the beauty and features of the lady Dulcinea del Toboso, for, judging by what fame trumpeted abroad of her beauty, she felt sure she must be the fairest creature in the world, nay, in all La Mancha.

Don Quixote sighed on hearing the duchess's request and said, "If I could pluck out my heart and lay it on a plate on this table here before your highness's eyes, it would spare my tongue the pain of telling what can hardly be thought of, for in it your excellency would see her portrayed in full. But why should I attempt to depict and describe in detail, and feature by feature, the beauty of the peerless Dulcinea, the burden being one worthy of other shoulders than mine, an enterprise wherein the brushes of Parrhasius, Timantes, and Apelles, and the graver of Lysippus[1] ought to be employed, to paint it in pictures and carve it in marble and bronze, and Ciceronian and Demosthenian eloquence to sound its praises?"

"What does Demosthenian mean, Señor Don Quixote?" said the duchess. "It is a word I never heard in all my life."

1. Ancient Greek artists.

"Desmothenian eloquence," said Don Quixote, "means the eloquence of Demosthenes, as Ciceronian means that of Cicero, who were the two most eloquent orators in the world."

"True," said the duke. "You show your ignorance with such a question. Nevertheless, Señor Don Quixote would greatly gratify us if he would depict her to us; for surely, even in an outline or sketch she will be something to make the most beautiful women envious."

"I would do so certainly," said Don Quixote, "had she not been erased from my mind by the misfortune that fell upon her a short time ago, one of such a nature that I am more ready to weep over it than to describe it. For your highnesses must know that, going a few days back to kiss her hands and receive her benediction, approbation, and permission for this third sally, I found her altogether a different being from the one I sought. I found her enchanted and changed from a princess into a peasant, from fair to foul, from an angel into a devil, from fragrant to pestiferous, from refined to common, from a dignified lady to a jumping tomboy, from light to darkness, and, in a word, from Dulcinea del Toboso into a coarse Sayago wench."

"God bless me!" said the duke aloud at this, "who can have done the world such an injury? Who can have robbed it of the beauty that gladdened it, of the grace and gaiety that charmed it, of the modesty that shed a luster upon it?"

"Who?" replied Don Quixote. "Who could it be but some malignant enchanter of the many that persecute me out of envy—that accursed race born into the world to obscure and bring to naught the achievements of the good and glorify and exalt the deeds of the wicked? Enchanters have persecuted me, enchanters persecute me still, and enchanters will continue to persecute me until they have sunk me and my lofty chivalry in the deep abyss of oblivion; and they injure and wound me where they know I feel it most. For to deprive a knight-errant of his lady is to deprive him of the eyes he sees with, of the sun that gives him light, of the food whereby he lives. Many a time before have I said it, and I say it now once more, a knight-errant without a lady is like a tree without leaves, a building without a foundation or a shadow without the body that causes it."

"There is no denying it," said the duchess. "But still, if we are to believe the history of Don Quixote that has recently appeared and has been generally well received, it is to be inferred from it (if I remember rightly) that you have never seen the lady Dulcinea and that the said lady is nothing in the world but an imaginary lady that you begot and gave birth to in your brain and adorned with whatever charms and perfections you chose."

"There is a good deal to be said on that point," said Don Quixote. "God knows whether there is any Dulcinea or not in the world, or whether she is imaginary or not imaginary. These are things the proof of which must not be pushed to extreme lengths. I have not begotten nor given birth to my lady, though I behold her as she must necessarily be, a lady who contains in herself all the qualities to make her famous throughout the world, beautiful without blemish, dignified without haughtiness, tender and yet modest, gracious out of courtesy and courteous out of good breeding, and lastly, of exalted lineage, because beauty shines forth and excels with a higher degree of perfection upon good blood than in the fair of lowly birth."

"That is true," said the duke. "But Señor Don Quixote will give me leave to say what I am constrained to say by the story of his exploits that I have read, from which it is to be inferred that, granting there is a Dulcinea in El Toboso, or out of it, and that she is in the highest degree beautiful as you have described her to us, as regards the loftiness of her lineage she is not on a par with the Orianas, Alastrajareas, Madásimas, or others of that sort, with whom, as you well know, the histories abound."

"To that I may reply," said Don Quixote, "that Dulcinea is the daughter of her own accomplishments, and that virtues rectify blood, and that lowly virtue is more to be regarded and esteemed than exalted vice. Dulcinea, besides, has that within her which may raise her to be a crowned and sceptered queen; for the merit of a fair and virtuous woman is capable of performing greater miracles; and virtually, though not formally, she has in herself higher fortunes."

"I protest, Señor Quixote," said the duchess, "that in all you say, you go most cautiously 'sounding the depths as you go,' as the saying is; henceforth I will believe, and I will see to it that everyone in my house believes, even my lord the duke, that there is a Dulcinea in El Toboso, and that she is living today, and that she is beautiful and nobly born and deserves to have such a knight as Señor Don Quixote in her service, and that is the highest praise that it is in my power to give her or that I can think of. But I cannot help entertaining a doubt and having a certain grudge against Sancho Panza. The doubt is this, that the history I have mentioned declares that Sancho Panza, when he carried a letter on your worship's behalf to the lady Dulcinea, found her sifting a sack of wheat; and it says it was in all probability red wheat, which makes me doubt the loftiness of her lineage."

To this Don Quixote replied, "Señora, your highness must know that everything or almost everything that happens to me transcends the ordinary limits of what happens to other knights-errant, whether it be that it is directed by the inscrutable will of destiny or by the malice of some jealous enchanter. Now it is an established fact that all or most famous knights-errant have some special gift: one has the gift of being safe from enchantment, another that of being made of such invulnerable flesh that he cannot be wounded, as was the famous Roland, one of the twelve peers of France (of whom it is related that he could not be wounded except in the sole of his left foot, and that it must be with the point of a stout pin and not with any other sort of weapon whatever; and so, when Bernardo del Carpio slew him at Roncesvalles, finding that he could not wound him with steel, he lifted him up from the ground in his arms and strangled him, calling to mind at that time the death which Hercules inflicted on Antæus, the fierce giant that they say was the son of Terra.

"I would infer from what I have mentioned that perhaps I may have some gift of this kind, not that of being invulnerable, because experience has many times proved to me that I am of tender flesh and not at all impenetrable; nor that of being safe from enchantment, for I have already seen myself thrust in a cage, in which all the world would not have been able to confine me except by force of enchantments. But as I delivered myself from that one, I am inclined to believe that there is no other that can hurt me. And so, these enchanters, seeing that they cannot exert their vile craft against my person, revenge themselves on what I love most and seek to rob me of life by mistreating that of Dulcinea in whom I live; and therefore I am convinced that when my squire carried my message to her, they changed her into a common peasant girl, engaged in such a low occupation as sifting wheat. I have already said, however, that that wheat was not red wheat, nor wheat at all, but grains of orient pearl. And as a proof of all this, I must tell your highnesses that, coming to El Toboso a short time back, I was altogether unable to discover the palace of Dulcinea, and that the next day, though Sancho, my squire, saw her in her own proper shape, which is the fairest in the world, to me she appeared to be a coarse, ill-favored farm wench, and by no means a well-spoken one, she who is propriety itself.

"And so, as I am not and, so far as one can judge, cannot be enchanted, she it is that is enchanted, that is smitten, that is altered, changed, and transformed; in her have my enemies revenged themselves upon me, and for her shall I live in ceaseless tears, until I see her in her pristine state. I have mentioned this lest anybody should question what Sancho said about Dulcinea's winnowing or sifting; for, as they changed her to me, it is no wonder if they changed her to him. Dulcinea is illustrious and well born and of one of the gentle families of El Toboso, which are many, ancient, and good. Therein, most assuredly, not small is the share of the peerless Dulcinea, through whom her town will be famous and celebrated in ages to come, as Troy was through Helen, and Spain through La Cava, though with a better title and tradition.[2]

"For another thing; I would have your graces understand that

2. La Cava is the name of the daughter of Count Julian, seduced by Rodrigo, the last Gothic ruler. Julian called in the North Africans, who defeated Rodrigo.

Sancho Panza is one of the most amusing squires that ever served knight-errant. Sometimes there is a simplicity about him so shrewd that it is an amusement to try and make out whether he is simple or sharp; he has mischievous tricks that show him to be a rogue, and blundering ways that prove him to be a fool. He doubts everything and believes everything; when I think he is about to fall headlong from sheer stupidity, he comes out with something shrewd that raises him up to the skies. Finally, I would not exchange him for another squire, though I were given a city to boot, and therefore I am in doubt whether it will be well to send him to the government your highness has bestowed upon him; though I perceive in him a certain aptitude for the work of governing, so that, with a little trimming of his understanding, he would manage any government as easily as the king does his taxes. And moreover, we know already by ample experience that it does not require much cleverness or much learning to be a governor, for there are a hundred around us that scarcely know how to read and yet govern like experts. The main point is that they should have good intentions and be desirous of doing right in all things, for they will never be at a loss for persons to advise and direct them in what they have to do, like those gentlemen-governors who, being no lawyers, pronounce sentences with the aid of an adviser. My advice to him will be to take no bribe and surrender no right, and some other little matters that I have in my craw which will be produced in due season for Sancho's benefit and the advantages of the island he is to govern."

The duke, duchess, and Don Quixote had reached this point in their conversation when they heard voices and a great hubbub in the palace, and Sancho burst abruptly into the room all in a fright, with a straining-cloth as a bib, followed by several servants, or, more properly speaking, kitchen-boys and other underlings, one of whom carried a small dishpan full of water, that from its color and impurity was plainly dishwater. The one with the dishpan pursued him and followed him everywhere he went, endeavoring with the utmost persistence to thrust it under his chin, while another kitchen-boy seemed anxious to wash his beard.

"What is all this, friends?" asked the duchess. "What is it? What do you want to do to this good man? Do you forget he is a governor-elect?"

To which the barber kitchen-boy replied, "The gentleman will not let himself be washed as is customary, and as my lord the duke and the señor his master have been."

"Yes, I will," said Sancho, in a great rage. "But I'd like it to be with cleaner towels, clearer lye-water, and not such dirty hands; for there's not so much difference between me and my master that he should be washed with perfumed water and I with devil's lye. The customs of regions and princes' palaces are only good so long as they give no annoyance; but the way of washing they have here is worse than doing penance. I have a clean beard, and I don't need such refreshments, and whoever comes to wash me or touch a hair of my head, I mean to say my beard, with all due respect be it said, I'll give him a punch that will leave my fist sunk in his skull; for *cirimonies* and soapings like this are more like jokes than entertainments for guests.

The duchess was ready to die with laughter when she saw Sancho's rage and heard his words. But it was no pleasure to Don Quixote to see him in such sorry shape, with the stained towel and surrounded by the hangers-on of the kitchen. So making a low bow to the duke and duchess, as if to ask their permission to speak, he addressed the rabble in a dignified tone: "Hail, gentlemen! You let that youth alone, and go back to where you came from, or anywhere else you like; my squire is as clean as any other person, and those troughs are too small for him. Take my advice and leave him alone, for neither he nor I appreciate joking."

Sancho took the word out of his mouth and went on, "No, let them come and play tricks on this country boy, for it's about as likely I'll stand them as that it's now midnight! Let them bring me a comb here, or whatever they please, and curry my beard, and if they get anything out of it that offends against cleanliness, let them shave an X on my head."

At this, the duchess, laughing all the while, said, "Sancho Panza is right, and always will be in all he says. He is clean, and, as he says himself, he does not require to be washed; and if our ways do not please him, he is free to choose. Besides, you promoters of cleanliness have been excessively careless and thoughtless, I don't know if I ought not to say audacious, to bring troughs and wooden utensils and kitchen dishcloths, instead of basins and jugs of pure gold and towels of holland, to such a person and such a beard. But, after all, you are wicked and ill-bred, and spiteful as you are, you cannot help showing the grudge you have against the squires of knights-errant."

The impudent servants, and even the steward who came with them, took the duchess to be speaking in earnest, so they removed the straining-cloth from Sancho's neck, and with something like shame and confusion went off all of them and left him. Seeing himself safe out of that extreme danger, as it seemed to him, he ran and fell on his knees before the duchess, saying, "From great ladies you can expect great favors. This one which your grace has done for me today can't be repaid with less than wishing I was dubbed a knight-errant, to devote myself all the days of my life to the service of so exalted a lady. I am a peasant, my name is Sancho Panza, I am married, I have children, and I am serving as a squire; if in any one of these ways I can serve your highness, I will not be longer in obeying than your grace in commanding."

"It is easy to see, Sancho," replied the duchess, "that you have learned to be polite in the school of politeness itself. I mean to say it is easy to see that you have been nursed in the bosom of Señor Don Quixote, who is, of course, the cream of good breeding and flower of ceremony—or cirimony, as you would say yourself. God bless such a master and such a servant, the one the model of knight-errantry, the other the star of squirely fidelity! Rise, Sancho, my friend. I will repay your courtesy by taking care that my lord the duke makes good to you the promised gift of the government as soon as possible."

With this, the conversation came to an end, and Don Quixote retired to take his midday nap; but the duchess begged Sancho, unless he had a very great desire to go to sleep, to come and spend the afternoon with her and her ladies in a very cool chamber. Sancho replied that, though he certainly had the habit of sleeping four or five hours in the heat of the day in summer, to serve her excellency he would try with all his might not to sleep even one that day, and that he would come in obedience to her command, and with that he went off. The duke gave fresh orders with respect to treating Don Quixote as a knight-errant, without departing in the smallest particular from the style in which, as the stories tell us, they used to treat the knights of old.

Chapter XXXIII

OF THE DELECTABLE DISCOURSE WHICH THE DUCHESS AND HER DAMSELS HELD WITH SANCHO PANZA, WELL WORTH READING AND NOTING

The history records that Sancho did not sleep that afternoon, but in order to keep his word came, when he had eaten, to visit the duchess, who, finding enjoyment in listening to him, made him sit down beside her on a low seat, though Sancho, out of pure good breeding, did not want to sit down. The duchess, however, told him he was to sit down as governor and talk as squire, as in both respects he was worthy of even the chair of the Cid Ruy Díaz the Champion. Sancho shrugged his shoulders, obeyed, and sat down, and all the duchess's damsels and dueñas gathered around him, waiting in profound silence to hear what he would say. It was the duchess, however, who spoke first, saying:

"Now that we are alone and that there is nobody to overhear us, I would like for the señor governor to resolve certain doubts I have, rising out of the history of the great Don Quixote that is now in print. One is that since the worthy Sancho never saw Dulcinea, I mean the lady Dulcinea del Toboso, or took Don Quixote's letter to her, for it was left in the memorandum book in the Sierra Morena, how did he dare to invent the answer and all that about finding her sifting wheat? The whole story was a joke and lies—and very harmful to the peerless Dulcinea's good name—which are not at all becoming the character and fidelity of a good squire."

At these words, Sancho, without uttering one in reply, got up from his chair, and with noiseless steps, with his body bent and his finger on his lips, went all round the room lifting up the hangings. Having done this, he came back to his seat and said, "Now, señora, that I have seen that there is no one (except present company) listening to us on the sly, I will answer what you have asked me, and all you may ask me, without fear or dread. And the first thing I have got to say is, that I consider my master Don Quixote to be completely crazy, though sometimes he says things that, to my mind, and indeed everybody's that listens to him, are so wise and run in such a straight furrow that the devil himself couldn't have said them better. But for all that, really, and beyond all question, it's my firm belief he is cracked. Well, then, as this is clear to my mind, I'm not afraid to make him believe things that have neither head nor tail, like that business about the answer to the letter, and the one that happened six or eight days ago, which is not yet in history, that is to say, the business about the enchantment of my lady Dulcinea. I made him believe she is enchanted, though there's no more truth in it than in a fairy tale."

The duchess begged him to tell her about the enchantment or joke, so Sancho told the whole story exactly as it had happened, and his hearers were not a little amused by it. And then resuming, the duchess said, "In consequence of what worthy Sancho has told me, a doubt starts up in my mind, and there comes a kind of whisper to my ear that says, 'If Don Quixote is mad, crazy, and cracked, and Sancho Panza his squire knows it, and notwithstanding, serves and follows him, and believes his empty promises, there can be no doubt he must be even madder and sillier than his master. And that being so, people will disapprove, señora duchess, if you give the said Sancho an island to govern; for how will he who does not know how to govern himself know how to govern others?' "

"By God, señora," said Sancho, "that doubt is timely; but your grace may tell it to speak plainly, or as it sees fit. I know what it says is true, and if I were wise I would have left my master long ago. But this was my fate, this was my bad luck. I can't help it; I must follow him. We're from the same village, I've eaten his bread, I'm fond of him, I'm grateful, he gave me his ass-colts, and above all I'm faithful. So it's quite impossible for anything to separate us, except the pick and shovel. And if your highness does not want to give me the government you promised, God made me without it, and maybe your not giving it to me will be all the better for my conscience. Fool that I am I know the proverb 'pride goeth before a fall,' and it may be that Sancho the squire will get to heaven sooner than Sancho the governor. 'They make as good bread here as in France,' and 'by night all cats are grey,' and 'he who must fast till afternoon will perish soon' and 'all stomachs are the same size' and can be filled 'with straw or hay,' as the saying is, and 'our heavenly Father feedeth the fowls of the air,' and 'four yards of coarse wool keeps you warmer than four of fine broadcloth' and 'when we quit this world and are put underground, the prince travels by as narrow a path as the journeyman,' and 'the Pope's body does not take up more feet of earth than the sacristan's,' though the one is higher than the other. When we go to our graves we all pack ourselves up and makes ourself small, or rather they pack us up and make us small in spite of ourselves, and then—good night to us. And I say once more, if your ladyship doesn't want to give me the island because I'm a fool, like a wise man I won't worry about it. I have heard say that 'behind the cross there's the devil,' and that 'all that glitters is not gold,' and that they took Wamba the farmer away from his oxen, ploughs, and yokes to be made King of Spain, and from among brocades, and pleasures, and riches, Rodrigo was taken to be eaten by snakes, if the verses of the old ballads don't lie."

"To be sure they don't lie!" exclaimed Doña Rodríguez, the dueña, who was one of the listeners. "Why, there's a ballad that says they put King Rodrigo alive into a tomb full of toads, and snakes, and lizards, and that two days later the king, in a plaintive, feeble voice, cried out from the tomb,

> 'They gnaw me now, they gnaw me now,
> There where I most did sin.'

And according to that, the gentleman has good reason to say he would rather be a farmer than a king, if vermin are to eat him."

The duchess could not help laughing at the simplicity of her dueña or wondering at the language and proverbs of Sancho, to whom she said, "Worthy Sancho knows very well that when once a knight has made a promise, he strives to keep it, though it may cost him his life. My lord and husband the duke, though not one of the errant sort, is nevertheless a knight, and for that reason will keep his word about the promised island, in spite of the envy and malice of the world. Let Sancho be of good cheer, for when he least expects it he will find himself seated on the throne of his island and seat of dignity and will take possession of his government which he won't ever want to give up even for a better one. The charge I give him is to be careful how he governs his vassals, bearing in mind that they are all loyal and well born."

"As to governing them well," said Sancho, "there's no need of telling me to do that, for I'm kind-hearted by nature, and I feel sorry for the poor: 'The loaf thou shalt not take from them who knead and bake.' By my faith they won't throw loaded dice with me. I'm an old dog, and you can't fool me easily. I can be wide-awake if need be, and I don't let spots come before my eyes, for I know where the shoe pinches.

"I say so, because with me the good will have support and protection and the bad neither footing nor access. And it seems to me that in governments, the hardest thing is to get started; and maybe, after having been a governor a couple of weeks, I'll take kindly to the work and know more about it than the field work I've grown up with."

"You are right, Sancho," said the duchess, "for no one is born educated, and bishops are made out of men and not out of stones. But to return to the subject we were discussing just now, the enchantment of the lady Dulcinea, I look upon it as certain and more than evident, that Sancho's idea of tricking his master, making him believe that the peasant girl was Dulcinea and that if he did not recognize her it must be because she was enchanted, was all a device of one of the enchanters that persecute Don Quixote. For really and truly, I know from good authority that the peasant girl who jumped on the ass was and is Dulcinea del Toboso, and that worthy Sancho, though he fancies himself the deceiver, is the one that is deceived and that there is no more reason to doubt the truth of this than of anything else we never saw. Señor Sancho Panza must know that we too have enchanters here that are well disposed to us and tell us what goes on in the world, plainly and distinctly, without subterfuge or deception; and believe me, Sancho, that agile country lass was and is Dulcinea del Toboso, who is as enchanted as possible; and when we least expect it, we shall see her in her own proper from, and then Sancho will be disabused of the error he is under at present."

"All that's very possible," said Sancho Panza. "Now I'm willing to believe what my master says about what he saw in the cave of Montesinos, where he says he saw the lady Dulcinea del Toboso in the very same dress and costume that I said I had seen her in when I enchanted her just to please myself.

"It must all have been the other way around as your ladyship says; because it is impossible to believe that out of my poor wit such a clever trick could be concocted in a moment, nor do I think my master is so mad that by my weak and feeble persuasion he could be made to believe anything so out of all reason. But, señora, your excellency must not think that I am wicked, because a numbskull like me is not bound to see into the thoughts and plots of those vile enchanters. I invented all that to escape my master's scolding, and not with any intention of hurting him; and if it has turned out differently, there is a God in heaven who judges our hearts."

"That is true," said the duchess. "But tell me, Sancho, what is this you say about the cave of Montesinos, for I should like to know."

Then Sancho related to her, word for word, what has been said already touching that adventure, and having heard it the duchess said, "From this occurrence it may be inferred that, as the great Don Quixote says he saw there the same farm girl Sancho saw on the way from El Toboso, it is, no doubt, Dulcinea, and that there are some very active and exceedingly busy enchanters about."

"That's what I say," said Sancho, "and if my lady Dulcinea is enchanted, too bad for her. I'm not going to pick a quarrel with my master's enemies, who seem to be numerous and spiteful. The truth is that the one I saw was a farm girl and I took her for a farm girl; and if that was Dulcinea, it's not my fault nor should I be called to answer for it or take the consequences. But they must go nagging at me at every step—'Sancho said it, Sancho did it, Sancho here, Sancho there'—as if Sancho was some nobody and not that same Sancho Panza that's now going all over the world in books (so Sansón Carrasco told me, and he's at any rate a bachelor of Salamanca; and people of that sort can't lie, except when they feel like it or they have some very good reason for it). So there's no reason for anybody to quarrel with me. And since I have a good reputation, and, as I have heard my master say, 'a good name is better than great riches,' let them hand over this government and they'll see miracles, for one who has been a good squire will be a good governor."

"All of worthy Sancho's observations," said the duchess, "are Catonian sentences, or at any rate out of the very heart of Michael Verini himself, who *florentibus occidit annis.*[1] In fact, to speak in Sancho's own style, 'under a ragged coat there's often a good drinker.'"

"Indeed, señora," said Sancho, "I never yet drank from vice; from thirst, I confess that I have, because I'm no hypocrite. I drink when I feel like it, or, if I don't feel like it, when they offer it to me, so as not to look either strait-laced or rude; for when a friend drinks one's health what heart can be so hard as not to return it? But if I put on boots, I don't dirty them;[2] besides, squires to knights-errant mostly drink water, for they are always wandering around in woods, forests and meadows, mountains and crags, without a drop of wine to be had if they gave their eyes for it."

"So I believe," said the duchess. "And now let Sancho go and rest, and we will talk later at greater length and settle how he may soon go and have the government 'handed over,' as he says."

1. "Died in the flower of youth." Michael Verini was the author of *De puerorum moribus disticha,* in the style of Cato's *Disticha,* and, like it, a well-known schoolbook at the time.

2. A proverbial way of describing drinking without getting drunk.

Sancho once more kissed the duchess's hand and begged her to take good care of his Dapple, for he was the light of his eyes.

"What Dapple are you talking about?" said the duchess.

"My ass," said Sancho. "So as not to mention him by that name, I'm accustomed to call him Dapple. I begged this lady dueña here to take care of him when I came into the castle, and she got as angry as if I had said she was ugly or old, though it ought to be more natural and proper for dueñas to feed asses than to sit around looking dignified. God bless me! what a grudge a gentleman of my village had against these ladies!"

"He must have been some peasant," said Doña Rodríguez the dueña, "for if he had been a gentleman and well born he would have exalted them higher than the horns of the moon."

"That will do," said the duchess. "No more of this. Hush, Doña Rodríguez, and let Señor Panza rest easy and leave the treatment of Dapple to me, for as he is a treasure of Sancho's, I'll care for him as if he were my own."

"It will be enough for him to be in the stable," said Sancho, "for neither he nor I are worth your grace's trouble, and I'd as soon stab myself as consent to it. For though my master says that in politeness it is better to lose by a card too many than a card too few, when it comes to politeness to asses, we must mind what we are about and keep within due bounds."

"Take him to your government, Sancho," said the duchess, "and there you will be able to make as much of him as you like, and even retire him from work."

"Don't think, señora duchess, that you have said anything absurd," said Sancho. "I have seen more than two asses go into government, and for me to take mine with me would be nothing new."

Sancho's words made the duchess laugh again and gave her fresh amusement, and dismissing him to sleep, she went away to tell the duke the conversation she had had with him, and between them they plotted and arranged to play a joke on Don Quixote that was to be a good one and entirely in knight-errantry style, and in that same style they played several upon him, so much in keeping and so clever that they form the best adventures this great history contains.

Chapter XXXIV

WHICH RELATES HOW THEY LEARNED THE WAY IN WHICH THEY WERE TO DISENCHANT THE PEERLESS DULCINEA DEL TOBOSO, WHICH IS ONE OF THE MOST FAMOUS ADVENTURES IN THIS BOOK

Great was the pleasure the duke and duchess took in the conversation of Don Quixote and Sancho Panza; and, more determined than ever to play some jokes on them that would have the look and appearance of adventures, they took as their basis of action what Don Quixote had already told them about the cave of Montesinos in order to play a really good one on him.[1]

But what the duchess marveled at above all was that Sancho's simplicity could be so great as to make him believe as absolute truth that Dulcinea had been enchanted, when it was he himself who had been the enchanter and trickster in the business.

Having, therefore, instructed their servants in everything they were to do, six days later they took Don Quixote out to hunt with as great a retinue of huntsmen and beaters as a crowned king.

They presented Don Quixote with a hunting suit and Sancho with another of the finest green cloth; but Don Quixote declined to put his on, saying that he must soon return to the hard pursuit of arms and could not carry a wardrobe or stores with him. Sancho, however, took what they gave him, meaning to sell it at the first opportunity.

The appointed day having arrived, Don Quixote armed himself, and Sancho arrayed himself, and mounted on his Dapple (for he would not give him up, though they offered him a horse), he placed himself in the middle of the troop of huntsmen. The duchess came out splendidly attired, and Don Quixote, in pure courtesy and politeness, held the rein of her palfrey, though the duke tried to prevent it.

At last they reached a wood that lay between two high mountains, where, after occupying posts, blinds, and paths, and distributing the party in different positions, the hunt began with great noise, shouting, and uproar, so that, between the barking of the hounds and the blowing of the horns, they could not hear one another. The duchess dismounted and with a sharp boar-spear in her hand posted herself where she knew the wild boars were in the habit of passing. The duke and Don Quixote likewise dismounted and placed themselves one at each side of her. Sancho took up a position behind everybody without dismounting from Dapple, whom he dared not leave for fear that some accident might happen to him. Scarcely had they taken their stand in a line with several of their servants, when they saw a huge boar, closely pursued by the hounds and followed by the huntsmen, coming towards them, gnashing his teeth and tusks, and scattering foam from his mouth. As soon as he saw it, Don Quixote, slipping his shield on his arm and drawing his sword, advanced to meet it. The duke with boar-spear did the same; but the duchess would have gone in front of them all had not the duke stopped her.

Sancho alone, deserting Dapple at the sight of the mighty beast,

1. Don Quixote had actually told them nothing about the cave of Montesinos; all they knew of it was through Sancho.

took to his heels as hard as he could and struggled in vain to climb a tall oak. Halfway up, as he was taking hold of a branch in his effort to reach the top, he was so unlucky and unfortunate that it gave way, and, caught in his fall by a broken limb of the oak, he hung suspended in the air unable to reach the ground. Finding himself in this position, and that the green coat was beginning to tear, and reflecting that if the fierce animal came that way it might be able to get at him, he began to utter such cries and call for help so urgently that all who heard him and did not see him felt sure he must be in the teeth of some wild beast.

Finally the tusked boar fell, pierced by the blades of the many spears that blocked his escape. Don Quixote, turning around at the cries of Sancho, for he knew by them that it was he, saw him dangling from the oak head downwards, with Dapple, who had not forsaken him in his distress, close behind him. (Cide Hamete observes that he seldom saw Sancho Panza without seeing Dapple, or Dapple without seeing Sancho Panza, such was their attachment and loyalty one to the other.) Don Quixote went over and unhooked Sancho, who, as soon as he found himself on the ground, looked at the tear in his hunting coat and was heartsick, for he believed that the garment was worth a fortune.

Meanwhile they had slung the mighty boar across the back of a mule, and having covered it with sprigs of rosemary and branches of myrtle, they carried it off as the spoils of victory to some large field-tents which had been pitched in the middle of the wood, where they found the tables set and dinner served in such grand and sumptuous style that it was easy to see the rank and magnificence of those who had provided it. Sancho, as he showed the holes in his torn suit to the duchess, observed, "If we had been hunting hares or small birds, my coat would never have been in danger. I don't know what pleasure you get from lying in wait for an animal that can kill you with his tusk if he gets at you. I remember hearing an old ballad that says,

> By bears may you be eaten
> Like Favila the renownèd."

"He was a Gothic king," said Don Quixote, "who was devoured by a bear while hunting."

"That's what I mean," said Sancho. "I don't like kings and princes exposing themselves to such dangers just for a pleasure which ought not to be one, to my mind, since it consists in killing an animal that has committed no crime whatever."

"Quite the contrary, Sancho; you are wrong there," said the duke. "For hunting is more suitable and necessary for kings and princes than for anybody else. The chase is the image of war; it has strategy, plans, ambushes for defeating the enemy in safety; you must endure extreme cold and intolerable heat; indolence and sleep are reduced, the bodily powers are invigorated, the limbs of him who engages in it become agile, and, in a word, it is a sport which may be followed without injury to anyone and with enjoyment to many. And most important, it is not for everybody, like other kinds of hunting—except hawking, which also is only for kings and great lords. Reconsider your opinion therefore, Sancho, and when you are governor take up hunting, and it will do you a world of good."

"Never," said Sancho. "A good governor should have a broken leg and stay at home. It would be a fine thing if, after people had gone to the trouble of coming to look for him on business, the governor were away in the forest enjoying himself. The government would go to pot that way. By my faith, señor, hunting and amusements are more fit for loafers than for governors; what I intend to amuse myself with is playing cards on holidays and bowling on Sundays and feast days. These 'chases' or whatever don't suit my rank or sit well with my conscience."

"God grant it may turn out so," said the duke, "because 'there's many a slip twixt the cup and the lip.' "

"Be that as it may," said Sancho, " 'a reliable payer doesn't mind leaving a security' and 'God's help is better than diligence' and 'it's the guts that support the feet and not the feet that support the guts.' I mean to say that if God gives me help and I do my duty honestly, no doubt I'll govern like an expert. Let them put a finger in my mouth, and they'll see whether I can bite or not."

"The curse of God and all his saints on you, Sancho!" exclaimed Don Quixote. "When will the day come—as I have often said to you—when I shall hear you make one single coherent, rational remark without proverbs? Pray, your highnesses, leave this fool alone, for he will grind your souls between, not to say two, but two thousand proverbs, dragged in at the wrong time and as much to the purpose as—may God grant as much health to him, or to me if I want to listen to them!"

"Sancho Panza's proverbs," said the duchess, "though more numerous than those in Professor Núñez's collection are not therefore less to be esteemed for the conciseness of the maxims. For my own part, I can say they give me more pleasure than others that may be more to the point and more timely."

In pleasant conversation of this sort they passed out of the tent into the wood, and the day was spent in visiting some of the posts and blinds, and then night closed in, not, however, as brilliantly or tranquilly as might have been expected at the season, for it was then midsummer, but bringing with it a kind of haze that greatly aided the project of the duke and duchess.

And thus, as night began to fall, and a little after twilight set in, suddenly the whole wood on all four sides seemed to be on fire, and shortly after, here, there, on all sides, a vast number of trumpets and other military instruments were heard, as if several troops of cavalry were passing through the wood. The blaze of the fire and the noise of the warlike instruments almost blinded the eyes and deafened the ears of those that stood by, and indeed of all who were in the wood. Then there were heard repeated cries like the Moors' when they rush to battle. Trumpets and clarions brayed, drums beat, fifes played, so unceasingly and so fast that the party almost lost their senses with the confused din of so many instruments.

The duke was astounded, the duchess amazed, Don Quixote wondering, Sancho Panza trembling, and indeed, even they who were aware of the cause were frightened. In their fear, they fell silent, and a postillion, in the guise of a demon, passed in front of them, blowing, in stead of a bugle, a huge hollow horn that gave out a horrible hoarse sound.

"Ho there! courier," cried the duke, "who are you? Where are you going? What troops are these that seem to be passing through the wood?"

To which the courier replied in a harsh, discordant voice, "I am the devil. I am in search of Don Quixote of La Mancha. Those who are coming this way are six troops of enchanters who are bringing on a triumphal car the peerless Dulcinea del Toboso. She comes under enchantment, together with the gallant Frenchman Montesinos, to give instructions to Don Quixote as to how the lady may be disenchanted."

"If you were the devil, as you say and as your appearance indicates," said the duke, "you would already have recognized the knight Don Quixote of La Mancha, for you have him here before you."

"By God and upon my conscience," said the devil, "I never noticed for my mind is occupied with so many different things that I was forgetting the main thing I came about."

"This demon must be an honest fellow and a good Christian," said Sancho. "If he wasn't he wouldn't swear by God and his conscience. I feel sure now there must be good souls even in hell itself."

Without dismounting, the demon then turned to Don Quixote and said, "The unfortunate but valiant knight Montesinos sends me to thee, the Knight of the Lions (would that I might see thee in their claws), bidding me to tell thee to wait for him wherever I may find thee, as he brings with him her whom they call Dulcinea del Toboso, that he may show thee what is needful in order to disenchant her. Since I came for no more, I need stay no longer; demons of my sort be with thee, and angels with these lords and ladies." And so saying he blew his huge horn, turned about, and went off without waiting for a reply from anyone.

They all felt fresh wonder, but particularly Sancho and Don Quixote; Sancho to see how, in defiance of the truth, they insisted that Dulcinea was enchanted; Don Quixote because he could not feel sure whether what had happened to him in the cave of Montesinos was true or not. As he was deep in these cogitations, the duke said to him, "Do you mean to wait, Señor Don Quixote?"

"Why not?" replied he. "Here will I wait, fearless and firm, though all hell should come to attack me."

"Well, if I see another devil or hear another horn like the last one, nothing will make me wait here," said Sancho.

Night now closed in more completely, and many lights began to flit through the wood, just as those fiery exhalations from the earth, that look like shooting stars to our eyes, flit through the heavens. A frightful noise, too, was heard, like that made by the solid wheels that oxcarts usually have, by the harsh, ceaseless creaking of which, they say, the bears and wolves are put to flight, if there happen to be any where they are passing. In addition to all this commotion, there came a further disturbance to increase the tumult, for now it seemed as if in truth, on all four sides of the wood, four skirmishes or battles were going on at the same time; in one quarter resounded the dull noise of a terrible cannonade, in another numberless muskets were being discharged, the shouts of the combatants sounded almost close at hand, and farther away the Moorish war cries were raised again and again.

In a word, the bugles, the horns, the clarions, the trumpets, the drums, the cannon, the musketry, and above all the tremendous noise of the carts, all made up together a din so confused and terrific that Don Quixote had need to summon up all his courage to brave it; but Sancho's gave way, and he fell fainting on the skirt of the duchess's dress, who let him lie there and promptly ordered them to throw water in his face. This was done, and Sancho came to by the time that one of the carts with the creaking wheels reached the spot. It was drawn by four plodding oxen all covered with black drapery. On each horn they had fixed a large lighted wax taper, and on the top of the cart was constructed a raised seat, on which sat a venerable old man with a beard whiter than the very snow, and so long that it fell below his waist. He was dressed in a long robe of black linen; for as the cart was thickly set with a multitude of candles it was easy to make out everything that was on it. Leading it were two hideous demons, also clad in linen with faces so ugly that Sancho, having once seen them, shut his eyes so as not to see them again. As soon as the cart had drawn up to the spot, the old man rose from his lofty seat, and standing up said in a loud voice, "I am the sage Lirgandeo," and without another word the cart then passed on. Behind it came another of the same form, with another aged man enthroned, who, stopping the cart, said in a voice no less solemn than that of the first, "I am the sage Alquife, the great friend of Urganda the Unknown," and passed on. Then another cart came by at the same pace, but the occupant of the throne was not old like the others, but a large, robust man of a forbidding countenance, who as he came up said in a voice hoarser and more devilish, "I am the enchanter Arcalaus, the mortal enemy of Armadís of Gaul and all his kindred," and then passed on.

Having gone a short distance the three carts halted, and the monotonous noise of their wheels ceased. Soon they heard another, not noise, but sound of sweet, harmonious music, of which Sancho was very glad, taking it to be a good sign; and he said to the duchess, from whom he did not stir a step, or for a single instant, "Señora, where there's music there can't be anything bad."

"Nor where there are lights and it is bright," said the duchess; to which Sancho replied, "Fire gives light, and it's bright where there are bonfires, as we see by those that are all around us and perhaps may burn us; but music is a sign of celebrations and merrymaking."

"That remains to be seen," said Don Quixote, who was listening to everything. And he was right, as is shown in the following chapter.

Chapter XXXV

WHEREIN IS CONTINUED THE INSTRUCTION GIVEN TO DON QUIXOTE TOUCHING THE DISENCHANTMENT OF DULCINEA, TOGETHER WITH OTHER MARVELOUS INCIDENTS

They saw advancing towards them, to the sound of this pleasing music, what they call a triumphal car, drawn by six grey mules with white linen trappings, on each of which was mounted a penitent, robed also in white, with a large lighted wax taper in his hand. The car was twice or perhaps three times as large as the former ones, and in front and on the sides stood twelve more penitents, all as white as snow and all with lighted tapers, a spectacle to excite fear as well as wonder; and on a raised throne was seated a nymph draped in a multitude of silver-tissue veils with an embroidery of countless gold sequins glittering all over them, that made her appear, if not richly, at least brilliantly appareled. She had her face covered with thin transparent veiling, the texture of which did not prevent the fair features of a maiden from being distinguished, while the numerous lights made it possible to judge of her beauty and of her years, which seemed to be not less than seventeen but not to have yet reached twenty.

Beside her was a figure in a robe—a flowing robe, as they say—reaching to the feet, while the head was covered with a black veil. But the instant the car drew up in front of the duke and duchess and Don Quixote, the music of the oboes ceased, and then that of the lutes and harps on the car, and the figure in the robe rose up, and flinging it apart and removing the veil from its face, disclosed to their eyes the shape of Death itself, fleshless and hideous, at which sight Don Quixote felt uneasy, Sancho frightened, and the duke and duchess displayed a certain trepidation. Having risen to its feet, this living death, in a trance-like voice and with a rather sluggish tongue began to speak as follows:

"I am that Merlin who the legends say
The devil had for father, and the lie
Hath gathered credence with the lapse of time.
Prince of magic, of Zoroastrian lore
Monarch and treasurer, I have outlived
The envious centuries which strive to hide
The gallant deeds of valiant errant knights,
Who are, and ever have been, dear to me.
  Enchanters and magicians and their kind
Are mostly hard of heart; not so am I;
For mine is tender, soft, compassionate,
And its delight is doing good to all.
In the dim caverns of the gloomy Dis,
Where, tracing mystic lines and characters,
My soul was concentrating, there came to me
The sorrow-laden plaint of her, the fair,
The peerless Dulcinea del Toboso.
I knew of her enchantment and her fate,
From high-born dame to peasant wench transformed;
And touched with pity, first I turned the leaves
Of countless volumes of my devilish craft,
And then, in this grim grisly skeleton
Myself encasing, hither have I come
To show where lies the fitting remedy
To give relief in such a piteous case.
  O thou, the pride and joy of all that wear
The adamantine steel! O shining light,
O beacon, polestar, path, and guide of all
Who, scorning slumber and the lazy down,
Adopt the toilsome life of bloodstained arms!
To thee, great hero who all praise transcends,
La Mancha's luster and Iberia's star,
Don Quixote, wise as brave, I say
For peerless Dulcinea del Toboso
Her pristine form and beauty to regain,
'T is needful that thy esquire Sancho shall,
On his own sturdy buttocks bared to heaven,
Three thousand and three hundred lashes lay,

> And that they smart and sting and hurt him well.
> Thus have the authors of her woe resolved.
> And this is, noble lords, wherefore I come."

"By all that's holy," exclaimed Sancho at this, "I'll just as soon give myself three stabs with a dagger as three, not to say three thousand, lashes. The devil take such a way of disenchanting! I don't see what my rump has got to do with enchantments. By God, if Señor Merlin hasn't found some other way of disenchanting the lady Dulcinea del Toboso, she can go to her grave enchanted."

"I'll take you, you garlic-stuffed peasant," said Don Quixote, "and tie you to a tree as naked as the day you were born, and give you, not to say three thousand three hundred, but six thousand six hundred lashes, and so well laid on that it will require three thousand three hundred tugs to pull the whip loose; don't answer me a word or I'll tear your heart out."

On hearing this, Merlin said, "That will not do, for the lashes, which worthy Sancho has to receive must be given of his own free will and not by force, and at whatever time he pleases, for there is no fixed limit assigned to him; but it is permitted, if he wishes to commute half the pain of this whipping, to let them be given by the hand of another, though it may be somewhat weighty."

"Not a hand, my own or anybody else's, weighty or weighable is going to touch me," said Sancho. "Did I dream up the lady Dulcinea del Toboso? Why should my rump have to pay for her mistakes? My master, that's a part of her—he's always calling her 'my life' and 'my soul,' and his 'stay and prop'—can and should whip himself for her and take all the trouble necessary for her disenchantment. But for me to whip myself! Never!"

As soon as Sancho had spoken, the nymph in silver that was at the side of Merlin's ghost stood up, and removing the thin veil from her face disclosed one that seemed to all a bit too pretty; and with a mannish freedom from embarrassment and in a not very lady-like voice, addressing Sancho directly, said, "O wretched squire, soulless and insensitive, stony, flinty-hearted! If, impudent thief, they had commanded you to jump from some lofty tower; if, enemy of the human race, they had asked you to swallow a dozen toads, two dozen lizards, and three dozen adders; if they wanted you to murder wife and children with a sharp cruel scimitar, it would be no wonder for you to act stubborn and squeamish. But to balk at a mere three thousand three hundred lashes, what every poor little orphan gets every month—it is enough to amaze, astonish, astound the compassionate hearts of all who hear it, nay, all who come to hear it in the course of time.

"Turn, O miserable, hard-hearted animal, turn, I say, those frightened calf's eyes upon these of mine that are compared to radiant stars, and you will see them weeping trickling streams and rills, and tracing furrows, tracks, and paths over the fair fields of my cheeks. Let it move you. O sneaky, foul-tempered monster, to see my blooming youth—still in its teens, for I am not yet twenty—wasting and withering away beneath the husk of a rustic peasant wench. And if I do not appear in that shape now, it is a special favor Señor Merlin here has granted me, to the sole end that my beauty may soften you. For the tears of beauty in distress turn rocks into cotton and tigers into ewes.

"Whip, O whip that hide of yours, you great untamed brute, rouse up the lusty vigor that only urges you to eat and eat, and set free the softness of my flesh, the gentleness of my nature, and the fairness of my face. And if you will not relent or come to reason for me, do so for the sake of that poor knight beside you—your master I mean, whose heart I can this moment see, how he has it stuck in his throat, not five inches from his lips, and only waiting for your inflexible or yielding reply to make its escape by his mouth or go back again into his breast."

Don Quixote, on hearing this, felt his throat, and turning to the duke he said, "By God, señor, what Dulcinea says is true; I have my heart stuck here in my throat like the nut of a crossbow."

"What do you say to this, Sancho?" said the duchess.

"I say, señora," returned Sancho, "what I said before: as for the lashes, never! *Abernuncio*!"

"*Abrenuncio*, you should say, Sancho, and not as you do," said the duke.

"Let me alone, your highness," said Sancho. "I'm not in the humor now to pay attention to grammar or to a letter more or less. These lashes that I'm to get or I'm to give myself have so upset me that I don't know what I'm saying or doing. But I'd like to know where my lady Dulcinea del Toboso learned this way she has of asking favors. She comes to ask me to cut my flesh with lashes, and she calls me soulless and great untamed brute and a string of foul names that the devil is welcome to. Does she think my skin doesn't feel pain? What do I care whether she is enchanted or not? Is she bringing a basket of linens, shirts, kerchiefs, socks—not that I wear any—to soften me up? No, nothing but one insult after another, when everybody knows the proverb that 'an ass loaded with gold goes lightly up a mountain,' and that 'gifts break rocks,' and 'praying to God and plying the hammer,' and that 'one *take* is better than two *I'll give thee*'s.'

"Then there's my master, who should be stroking me and petting me to soften me up like wool and carded cotton. He says if he gets hold of me he'll tie me naked to a tree and double the number of lashes on me. These tender-hearted gentlemen should consider that it's not merely a squire but a governor they are asking to whip himself, as if it were nothing at all. Let them learn, damn them, the right way to ask and beg and behave themselves. You have to wait for the proper time, and people are not always in good humor. I'm ready to burst with grief at seeing my green coat torn, and they come to ask me to whip myself of my own free will, when I have no more interest in whipping myself than in becoming an Indian chief."

"Well the fact is, friend Sancho," said the duke, "that unless you become softer than a ripe fig, you shall not get your hands on that government. It would be a fine thing for me to send my islanders a cruel governor with a heart of stone, who won't yield to the tears of afflicted damsels or to the prayers of wise, lordly, ancient enchanters and sages! In short, Sancho, either you must whip yourself, or they must whip you, or you won't be governor."

"Señor," said Sancho, "will you let me have two days' grace to consider what is best for me?"

"No, certainly not," said Merlin. "Here, this minute, and on the spot, the matter must be settled. Either Dulcinea will return to the cave of Montesinos and to her former condition of peasant wench, or else in her present form she shall be carried to the Elysian fields, where she will remain waiting until the number of lashes is completed."

"Now then, Sancho!" said the duchess, "show courage and proper gratitude for your master Don Quixote's bread that you have eaten. We are all bound to oblige and please him for his benevolent disposition and lofty chivalry. Consent to this whipping, my son; to hell with the devil and chicken-hearted fear, for 'a stout heart overcomes bad luck,' as you very well know."

To this Sancho replied with the following irrelevant remark, addressing Merlin: "Will your worship tell me, Señor Merlin—when that courier devil came up, he gave my master a message from Señor Montesinos, charging him to wait here, because Montesinos was coming to arrange how the lady Doña Dulcinea del Toboso was to be disenchanted. But up to now we have not seen Montesinos, nor anything like him."

To which Merlin made answer:"The devil, Sancho, is a blockhead and a great scoundrel. I sent him to look for your master, not with a message from Montesinos but from myself. Montesinos is in his cave expecting, or more properly speaking, waiting for his disenchantment. The hardest part is still to come. If he owes you anything or you have any business to transact with him, I'll bring him to you and put him down wherever you want. But for the present make up your mind to consent to this penance, and believe me it will be very good for you, for soul as well for body—for your soul because of the charity with which you perform it, for your body because I know that you are of a sanguine character and it will do you no harm to draw a little blood."

"There are too many doctors in the world; even the enchanters are doctors," said Sancho. "However, since everybody tells me the same thing—though I can't see it myself—I say I am willing to give myself the three thousand three hundred lashes, provided I can do it whenever I like, without a limit on days or times. I'll try to get out of debt as quickly as I can, so that the world can enjoy the beauty of the lady Dulcinea del Toboso. It seems, contrary to what I thought, that she is beautiful after all. On condition, too, that I don't have to draw blood with the whip and that if any of the lashes happen to be mere flicks, they are to count. Furthermore, in case I should make any mistake in counting, Señor Merlin, as he knows everything, is to keep count, and let me know how many are still lacking or over the number."

"There will be no need to let you know of any over," said Merlin, "because, when you reach the full number, the lady Dulcinea will at once, and that very instant, be disenchanted, and will come in her gratitude to seek out the worthy Sancho and thank him, and even reward him for the good work. So you have no cause to be uneasy about lashes too many or too few; heaven forbid I should cheat anyone by even the smallest number."

"Well God's will be done," said Sancho. "I give up! I accept the penance on the conditions laid down."

The instant Sancho uttered these last words the music of the oboes struck up once more, and again a host of muskets were discharged, and Don Quixote threw his arms around Sancho's neck, kissing him again and again on the forehead and cheeks. The duchess and the duke expressed the greatest satisfaction, the car began to move on, and as it passed, the fair Dulcinea bowed to the duke and duchess and made a low curtsy to Sancho.

And now bright smiling dawn came on apace; the flowers of the field, revived, raised their heads, and the crystal waters of the brooks, murmuring over the grey and white pebbles, hastened to pay their tribute to the awaiting rivers; the glad earth, the unclouded sky, the fresh breeze, the clear light, each and all showed that the day that came treading on the skirts of morning would be calm and bright. The duke and duchess, pleased with their hunt and at having carried out their plans so cleverly and successfully, returned to their castle resolved to follow up their joke; for to them there was no reality that could afford them more amusement.

Chapter XXXVI

WHEREIN IS RELATED THE STRANGE AND UNDREAMED ADVENTURE OF THE DISTRESSED DUEÑA, ALIAS THE COUNTESS TRIFALDI, TOGETHER WITH A LETTER WHICH SANCHO PANZA WROTE TO HIS WIFE, TERESA PANZA

The duke had a majordomo of a very facetious and easy-going disposition, and it was he that played the part of Merlin, made all the arrangements for the recent adventure, composed the verses, and got a page to act the part of Dulcinea. And now, with the assistance of his master and mistress, he got up another of the funniest and strangest plans that can be imagined.

The duchess asked Sancho the next day if he had begun the task which he had to perform for the disenchantment of Dulcinea. He said he had, and had given himself five lashes during the night.

The duchess asked him what he had whipped himself with.

He said with his hand.

"That," said the duchess, "is more like giving yourself slaps than lashes. I am sure the sage Merlin will not be satisfied with such gentleness. The worthy Sancho must make a scourge with thorns in it or a cat-o'-nine tails that will make itself felt. 'Don't spare the rod.' The release of so great a lady as Dulcinea will not be granted so cheaply or at such a paltry price; and remember, Sancho, that works of charity done in a lukewarm and half-hearted way are without merit and of no avail."

To which Sancho replied, "If your ladyship will give me a proper whip or cord, I'll beat myself with it, provided it doesn't hurt too much. For your information, I may be a peasant, but my flesh is more cotton than hemp, and it won't do for me to destroy myself for the good of anybody else."

"By all means," said the duchess. "Tomorrow I'll give you a scourge that will be just the thing for you and will adjust to the tenderness of your flesh as if it were made for it."

Then Sancho said, "Your highness must know, my dear lady, that I have written a letter to my wife, Teresa Panza, giving her an account of all that has happened me since I left her; I have it here inside my shirt, and all that's left is to put the address on it. I'd be glad if your grace would read it, for I think it's written in a governor-like style; I mean the way governors ought to write."

"And who dictated it?" asked the duchess.

"Who could have dictated but myself, sinner as I am?" said Sancho.

"And did you write it yourself?" said the duchess.

"That I didn't," said Sancho, "for I can neither read nor write, though I can sign my name."

"Let us see it," said the duchess. "You undoubtedly display in it the quality and quantity of your wit."

Sancho drew an unsealed letter from his shirt, and the duchess, taking it, found that it read in this fashion:

SANCHO PANZA'S LETTER TO HIS WIFE, TERESA PANZA

'I may have been flogged, but at least I rode in style.'[1] If I have got a good governorship, it is at the cost of a good whipping.

1. Criminals sentenced to flogging were led through the streets, mounted on a horse. Poor people had little opportunity to ride, hence the irony.

You won't understand this just now, my Teresa. Later, you'll know what it means. I want you to know, Teresa, that I intend for you to have a coach, for that is a matter of importance, because any other way of travel is like crawling. You're a governor's wife. Nobody is going to have a reason to criticize you! I'm sending you a green hunting suit that my lady the duchess gave me; alter it and make a skirt and bodice for our daughter.

Don Quixote, my master, if I am to believe what I hear in these parts, is a sane madman and a clever fool—and I am no better.

We have been in the cave of Montesinos, and the sage Merlin is using me for the disenchantment of Dulcinea del Toboso (who is called Aldonza Lorenzo back there). With three thousand three hundred lashes, minus five, that I'm to give myself, she will be left as disenchanted as the day she was born. Say nothing of this to anyone: 'put your business in the public light, and some will say it's black and others will say it's white.'

I'm leaving here in a few days for my governorship, to which I am going with a mighty great desire to make money, for they tell me all new governors set out with the same desire. I'll see how the land lies and will let you know if you're to come and live with me or not.

Dapple is well and sends his regards. I wouldn't leave him behind if they were taking me away to be Grand Turk.

My lady the duchess kisses your hands a thousand times; send back two thousand, for as my master says, nothing costs less or is cheaper than good manners. God has not been pleased to provide me with another valise with another hundred crowns, like the one the other day. But never mind, my Teresa, 'the one who sounds the alarm is safe from harm,' and 'everything will come out in the wash' of the government. What they tell me worries me—that once I have tasted it, I will 'eat my hands along with it.' If that is so, it'll not come cheap, though the maimed and crippled have a benefice of their own in the alms they beg for; so that one way or another you'll be rich and fortunate.

May God, who can do it, give you good fortune and keep me to serve you. From this castle, the 20th of July, 1614.

Your husband, the governor,

SANCHO PANZA

When she had read the letter, the duchess said to Sancho, "On two points the worthy governor goes rather astray: one is in saying or hinting that this governorship has been bestowed upon him for the lashes that he is to give himself, when he knows (and he cannot deny it) that when my lord the duke promised it to him nobody ever dreamed of such a thing as lashes; the other is that he shows himself here to be very greedy. I would not have him turn out to be a bad choice. 'Avarice bursts the bag,' and a greedy governor carries out ungoverned justice."

"I don't mean it that way, señora," said Sancho, "and if you think the letter doesn't say what it should, I'll tear it up and write another; and maybe it will be a worse one if it's left up to me."

"No, no," said the duchess, "this one will do, and I want the duke to see it."

With this, they went around to a garden where they were to dine, and the duchess showed Sancho's letter to the duke, who was extremely pleased with it. They dined, and after the table had been cleared and they had amused themselves for a while with Sancho's rich conversation, the melancholy sound of a fife and harsh discordant drum made itself heard. All seemed somewhat agitated by this confused, martial, and gloomy music, especially Don Quixote, who could not keep his seat from pure excitement. As for Sancho, it is needless to say that fear drove him to his usual refuge, the side or the skirts of the duchess. And really and truly, the sound they heard was a most doleful and melancholy one.

While they were still in uncertainty, they saw advancing towards them through the garden two men clad in mourning robes so long and flowing that they trailed along the ground. As they marched, they beat two great drums which were likewise draped in black, and beside them came the fife player, pitch-black like the others. Following these came a personage of gigantic stature enveloped rather than clad in a gown of the deepest black, the train of which was of prodigious dimensions. Over the gown, girdling and crossing his figure, he had a broad sword-belt which was also black, and from which hung a huge scimitar with a black scabbard and fittings. He had his face covered with a transparent black veil, through which might be glimpsed a very long beard as white as snow. He advanced, keeping step to the sound of the drums with great gravity and dignity; and, in short, his stature, his gait, his blackness, and his retinue might well have struck with astonishment, as they did, all who beheld him without knowing who he was.

With this measured pace and in this guise he approached to kneel before the duke, who, with the others, awaited him standing. The duke, however, would not on any account allow him to speak until he had risen. The prodigious apparition obeyed and, standing up, removed the veil from his face and disclosed the most enormous, the longest, the whitest, and the thickest beard that human eyes had ever beheld until this moment, and then, producing a grave, sonorous voice from the depths of his broad, bulging chest, and fixing his eyes on the duke, he said:

"Most high and mighty señor, my name is Trifaldín of the White Beard. I am squire to the Countess Trifaldi,[2] otherwise called the Distressed Dueña, on whose behalf I bear a message to your highness, which is that your magnificence kindly grant her leave and

2. "Trifaldin" and "Trifaldi" are based on the words for "three" and "skirt" or "train" (*falda*).

permission to come and tell you her trouble, which is one of the strangest and most remarkable that the world's most distressed mind could have imagined. But first she desires to know if the valiant and never vanquished knight, Don Quixote of La Mancha, is in this your castle, for she has come in quest of him on foot and without breaking her fast from the kingdom of Candaya to your realms here; a thing which may and ought to be regarded as a miracle or attributed to enchantment. She is even now at the gate of this fortress or country house and only waits for your permission to enter. I have spoken."

And with that he coughed and stroked his beard from top to bottom with both hands, and stood very tranquilly waiting for the response of the duke, which was to this effect: "Many days ago, worthy squire Trifaldín of the White Beard, we heard of the misfortune of my lady the Countess Trifaldi, whom the enchanters have caused to be called the Distressed Dueña. Bid her enter, O stupendous squire, and tell her that the valiant knight Don Quixote of La Mancha is here, and from his generous disposition she may safely promise herself every protection and assistance. And you may tell her, too, that if she needs my help, it will not be withheld, for I am bound to give it to her by my knighthood, which involves the protection of women of all sorts, especially widowed, wronged, and distressed dueñas, such as her ladyship seems to be."

On hearing this Trifaldín bent his knee to the ground, and making a sign to the fifer and drummers to strike up, he turned and marched out of the garden to the same notes and at the same pace as when he entered, leaving them all amazed at his bearing and solemnity. Turning to Don Quixote, the duke said, "After all, renowned knight, the mists of malice and ignorance are unable to hide or obscure the light of valor and virtue. I say so, because your excellency has been barely six days in this castle, and already the unhappy and the afflicted come in quest of you from lands far distant and remote, and not in coaches or on dromedaries, but on foot and fasting, confident that in that mighty arm they will find a cure for their sorrows and troubles, thanks to your great achievements, which fly and circle over all the known earth."

"I wish, señor duke," replied Don Quixote, "that the saintly ecclesiastic, who at table the other day showed such ill will and bitter spite against knights-errant, were here now to see with his own eyes whether such knights are needed in the world. He would at any rate learn by experience that those suffering any extraordinary affliction or sorrow, in extreme cases and unusual misfortunes, do not go to look for a remedy to the houses of jurists or village sacristans, or to the knight who has never attempted to pass the bounds of his own town, or to the indolent courtier who only seeks for news to repeat and talk of, instead of striving to do deeds and exploits for others to relate and record. Relief in distress, help in need, protection for damsels, consolation for widows, are to be found in no sort of persons better than in knights-errant. And I give unceasing thanks to heaven that I am one, and regard any misfortune or suffering that may befall me in the pursuit of so honorable a calling as endured for a good purpose. Let this dueña come and ask what she will, for I will effect her relief by the might of my arm and the dauntless resolution of my bold heart."

Chapter XXXVII

WHEREIN IS CONTINUED THE NOTABLE ADVENTURE OF THE DISTRESSED DUEÑA[1]

The duke and duchess were extremely glad to see how readily Don Quixote fell for their scheme, but at this moment Sancho observed, "I hope this señora dueña won't be putting any difficulties in the way of the promise of my government. I have heard a Toledo apothecary, who talked like an orator, say that where dueñas were mixed up nothing good could happen. God bless me, how that apothecary hated them! And so what I'm thinking is, if all dueñas, of whatever sort or condition they may be, are troublemakers and busybodies, what must the distressed ones, like this Countess Three-skirts or Three-tails be like?—for in my country skirts or tails, tails or skirts, it's all one."

"Hush, Sancho my friend," said Don Quixote. "Since this lady dueña comes in quest of me from such a distant land she cannot be one of those the apothecary meant; moreover this is a countess, and when countesses serve as dueñas, it is in the service of queens and empresses, for in their own houses they are mistress and have other dueñas to wait on them."

To this, Doña Rodríguez (who was present) made answer, "My lady the duchess has dueñas in her service that might be countesses if it was the will of fortune; 'but law decrees what kings please.' Let nobody speak ill of dueñas, above all of elderly maiden ladies; for though I am not one myself, I know and am aware of the advantage a maiden dueña has over one that is a widow; but 'he who clipped us has kept the scissors.' "

"For all that," said Sancho, "there's so much to be clipped about dueñas, so my barber said—but 'let sleeping dogs lie.' "

"These squires," returned Doña Rodríguez, "are always our enemies; and as they haunt the antechambers and watch us at every step, whenever they are not saying their prayers (and that's often

1. A *dueña,* which means "matron," roughly, was a respectable married woman or widow whose duty was to chaperon wealthy ladies, as squires served their male counterparts. The age, nunlike dress, evil temper, and ignorance of dueñas are satirized by many Spanish writers of this period.

enough), they spend their time gossiping about us, digging up our skeletons, and burying our good name. But I can tell these walking blocks that we will live in spite of them, and in great houses too, though we die of hunger and cover our flesh, be it delicate or not, with widow's weeds, as one covers or hides a garbage heap with a tapestry on a procession day. By my faith, if it were permitted me and time allowed, I could prove, not only to those here present, but to all the world, that there is no virtue that is not to be found in a dueña."

"I have no doubt," said the duchess, "that my good Doña Rodríguez is right, and very much so; but she had better wait for some appropriate time to defend herself and the rest of the dueñas, so as to crush the calumny of that wicked apothecary and root out the prejudice in the great Sancho Panza's mind."

To which Sancho replied, "Ever since I began to feel like a governor, I have lost my squirish humor, and I don't give a damn for all the dueñas in the world."

They would have carried this dueña-dispute further had they not heard the notes of the fife and drums once more, from which they concluded that the Distressed Dueña was making her entrance. The duchess asked the duke if it would be proper to go out to receive her, as she was a countess and a person of rank.

"In so far as she is a countess," said Sancho, before the duke could reply, "I am for your highnesses going out to receive her; but in so far as she is a dueña, it is my opinion you should not stir a step."

"Who asked you to meddle in this, Sancho?" said Don Quixote.

"Who, señor?" said Sancho. "I meddle, and I have a right to meddle, as a squire who has learned the rules of courtesy in the school of your worship, the most courteous and best-bred knight in the whole world of courtliness; and in these things, as I have heard your worship say, 'as much is lost by a card too many as by a card too few,' and 'a word to the wise is sufficient.' "

"Sancho is right," said the duke. "We'll see what the countess is like, and by that, measure the courtesy that is due to her."

And now the drums and fife made their entrance as before; and here the author brought this short chapter to an end and began the next, following up the same adventure, which is one of the most notable in the history.

Chapter XXXVIII

WHEREIN IS TOLD THE DISTRESSED DUEÑA'S ACCOUNT OF HER MISFORTUNES

Following the melancholy musicians, there filed into the garden as many as twelve dueñas, in two lines, all dressed in ample mourning robes apparently of serge, with white veils of thin gauze so long that they allowed only the border of the robe to be seen. Behind them came the Countess Trifaldi, the squire Trifaldín of the White Beard leading her by the hand, clad in the finest shaggy black baize, such that, had it been tufted, every tuft would have appeared to be as big as a Martos chickpea.

The countess's train, or skirt, or whatever it might be called, ended in three points which were held up by the hands of three pages, likewise dressed in mourning, forming an elegant geometrical figure with the three acute angles made by the three points, from which all who saw the peaked skirt concluded that it must be because of it the countess was called Trifaldi, as though it were Countess of the Three Skirts. And Benengeli says it was so, and that by her right name she was called the Countess Lobuna, because wolves bred in great numbers in her country; and if, instead of wolves, they had been foxes, she would have been called the Countess Zorruna,[1] as it was the custom in those parts for lords to take distinctive titles from the thing or things most abundant in their dominions; this countess, however, in honor of the new fashion of her skirt, dropped Lobuna and took up Trifaldi.

The twelve dueñas and the lady came on at processional pace, their faces being covered with black veils, not transparent ones like Trifaldín's, but so closely-woven that they allowed nothing to be seen through them. As soon as the band of dueñas was fully in sight, the duke, the duchess, and Don Quixote stood up, as well as all who were watching the slow-moving procession. The twelve dueñas halted and formed a lane, along which the Distressed One advanced, Trifaldín still holding her hand. On seeing this, the duke, the duchess, and Don Quixote went some twelve paces forward to meet her. She then, kneeling on the ground, said in a voice coarse and rough, rather than fine and delicate, "May it please your highnesses not to offer such courtesies to this your servant—I mean, this your handmaid—for I am in such distress that I shall never be able to make a proper reply, because my strange and unparalleled misfortune has carried off my wits, and I know not whither; but it must be a long way off, for the more I look for them the less I find them."

"He would lack wits, señora countess," said the duke, "who did not perceive your worth by your person, which obviously deserves all the cream of courtesy and flower of polite usage." And raising her up by the hand he led her to a seat beside the duchess, who likewise received her with great urbanity. Don Quixote remained silent, while Sancho was dying to see the features of Trifaldi and

1. The puns turn os *loba*: "she-wolf" and "cassock"; and *zorra*: "fox" and "whore." There may be a very sly reference to the analogy with the name of the ducal house of Osuna, *oso* meaning "bear."

one or two of her many dueñas. But there was no possibility of it until they themselves showed their faces of their own accord and free will.

All kept still, waiting to see who would break silence, which the Distressed Dueña did in these words: "I am confident, most mighty lord, most fair lady, and most discreet company, that my most miserable misery will be accorded a reception no less dispassionate than generous and condolent in your most valiant bosoms, for it is one that is enough to melt marble, soften diamonds, and mollify the steel of the most hardened hearts in the world. But before it is proclaimed to your hearing, not to say your ears, I would like to be enlightened whether there be present in this society, circle, or company, that knight immaculatissimus, Don Quixote of la Manchissima, and his squirissimus Panza."[2]

"The Panza is here," said Sancho, before anyone could reply, "and Don Quixotissimus too; and so, most distressed Dueñissima, you may say what you willissimus, for we are all readissimus to do you any servissimus."

On this Don Quixote rose, and addressing the Distressed Dueña, said, "If your sorrows, afflicted lady, can indulge in any hope of relief from the valor or might of any knight-errant, here are mine, which, feeble and limited though they be, shall be entirely devoted to your service. I am Don Quixote of La Mancha, whose calling it is to give aid to the needy of all sorts. And that being so, it is not necessary for you, señora, to make any appeal to benevolence or compose preambles, but only to tell your woes plainly and straightforwardly: for you have hearers that will know how, if not to remedy them, to sympathize with them."

On hearing this, the Distressed Dueña looked as though she wanted to throw herself at Don Quixote's feet, and actually did fall before them and said, as she struggled to embrace them, "Before these feet and legs I cast myself, O unconquered knight, as before the foundations and pillars of knight-errantry; these feet I desire to kiss, for upon their steps hangs and depends the sole remedy for my misfortune, O valorous errant, whose veritable achievements leave behind and eclipse the fabulous ones of the Amadíses, Esplandiáns, and Belianíses!"

Then turning from Don Quixote to Sancho Panza, and grasping his hands, she said, "O thou, most loyal squire that ever served knight-errant in this present age or ages past, whose goodness is more extensive than the beard of Trifaldín my companion here present, well mayest thou boast that, in serving the great Don Quixote, thou art serving, summed up in one, the whole host of knights that have ever borne arms in the world. I conjured thee, by

2. The humor of these lines in Spanish depends on the Dueña's pompous rhetoric, full of Latinate superlatives (*-ísimo*), incorrectly imitated by Sancho.

what thou owest to thy most loyal goodness, that thou wilt become my kind intercessor with thy master, that he speedily give aid to this most humble and most unfortunate countess."

To this Sancho made answer, "As to my goodness, señora, being as long and as great as your squire's beard, it matters very little to me. 'May my soul have hairy cheeks when heaven it seeks,'[3] that's the point; about beards here below I care little or nothing. But without all this wheedling and begging I will ask my master—for I know he loves me, and, besides, he has need of me just now for a certain business—to help and aid your worship as far as he can. Unpack your woes and lay them before us, and leave us to deal with them, for we'll be all of one mind."

The duke and duchess, as it was they who had contrived this adventure, were ready to burst with laughter at all these things and between themselves they commended the clever acting of Trifaldi, who, returning to her seat, said, "Queen Doña Maguncia reigned over the famous kingdom of Candaya, which lies between the great Trapobana and the Southern Sea, two leagues beyond Cape Comorin. She was the widow of King Archipiela, her lord and huband, and of their marriage they had issue the Princess Antonomasia,[4] heiress of the kingdom; which Princess Antonomasia was reared and brought up under my care and direction, I being the oldest and highest in rank of her mother's dueñas.

"Time passed, and the young Antonomasia reached the age of fourteen and such a perfection of beauty that nature could not raise it higher. And what can I say of her intelligence! She was as intelligent as she was fair, and she was fairer than all the world and is so still, unless the envious fates and hard-hearted Sisters Three have cut the thread of her life. But that they have not, for Heaven will not suffer so great a wrong to Earth as to pluck unripe the grapes of the fairest vineyard on its surface.

"Of this beauty, to which my poor feeble tongue has failed to do justice, countless princes, not only of that country, but of others, were enamored, and among them a private gentleman, who was at the court, dared to raise his thoughts to the heaven of so great beauty, trusting to his youth, his gallant bearing, his numerous accomplishments and graces, and his quickness and readiness of wit. For I may tell your highnesses, if I am not boring you, that when he played the guitar he could make it speak, and he was, in addi-

3. A proverbial expression; one explanation of it connects it with the story of a eunuch who replied to taunts with "May our souls have mustaches, for the other sort do not interest us."

4. A mixture of real and absurd names which parodies those in the romances of chivalry: "Maguncia" is the Latin name for Mainz, a city in Germany; "Candaya" is imaginary; "Trapobana" is an old name for Ceylon; the "Southern Sea" is the Indian Ocean; "Cape Comorin" is at the southern tip of India; "Archipiela" is based on "archipelago"; "Antonomasia" is a rhetorical term.

tion, a poet and an excellent dancer, and he could make birdcages so well, that he could have earned his living just by making them, if he had found himself reduced to utter poverty; and talents and charms of this kind are enough to bring down a mountain, not to say a tender young girl.

"But all his gallantry, wit, and gaiety, all his graces and accomplishments, would have been of little or no avail towards gaining the fortress of my protégée, had not the impudent thief taken the precaution of winning me over first. First, the villain and heartless vagabond sought to win my good will and purchase my compliance, so as to get me, like a treacherous warden, to hand over to him the keys of the fortress I had in charge. In a word, he gained an influence over my mind and overcame my resolutions with I know not what trinkets and jewels he gave me.

"But it was some verses I heard him singing one night from a grating that opened on the street where he lived, that, more than anything else, made me give way and led to my fall; and if I remember rightly they ran thus:

> 'From that sweet enemy of mine
> My bleeding heart has had its wound;
> And to increase the pain I'm bound
> To suffer and to make no sign.'

The lines seemed priceless to me and his voice sweet as syrup. And afterwards, I may say ever since then, looking at the misfortune into which I have fallen, I have thought that poets, as Plato advised, ought to be banished from all well-ordered States; at least the amatory ones, for they don't write verses like the ballad of 'The Marquis of Mantua,' that delight and draw tears from the women and children, but sharp-pointed conceits that pierce your heart like soft thorns and like the lightning, strike it, leaving the body untouched. Another time he sang:

> 'Come Death, so subtly veiled that I
> Your coming know not, how or when,
> Lest it should give me life again
> To find how sweet it is to die.'

—and other songs and refrains of the same sort, such as enchant when sung and fascinate when written.

"And then, when they condescend to compose a sort of verse that was at that time in vogue in Candaya, which they call *seguidillas!* Then hearts leap and laughter breaks forth and the body grows restless and all the senses turn to quicksilver.

"And so I say, sirs, that these troubadours richly deserve to be banished to desert isles. Though it is not they that are in fault, but the simpletons that praise them and the foolish girls that believe them; and had I been the faithful dueña I should have been, his stale conceits would have never moved me, nor should I have been taken in by such phrases as 'in death I live,' 'in ice I burn,' 'in flames I shiver,' 'hopeless I hope,' 'I go and stay,' and paradoxes of that sort which their writings are full of. And then when they promise the Phœnix of Arabia, the crown of Ariadne, the horses of the Sun, the pearls of the South, the gold of Tibar, and the balsam of Panchaia! Then it is they give free rein to their pens, for it costs them little to make promises they have no intention or power of fulfilling.

"But where am I wandering to? Woe is me, unfortunate being! What madness or folly leads me to speak of the faults of others when there is so much to be said about my own? Again, woe is me, hapless that I am! It was not verses that conquered me but my own stupidity; it was not music that made me yield but my own imprudence; my own great ignorance and little caution opened the way and cleared the path for Don Clavijo's advances, for that was the name of the gentleman I have referred to. And so, with my help as go-between, he found his way many a time into the chamber of the deceived Antonomasia (deceived not by him but by me) under the title of a lawful husband; for, sinner though I was, I would not have allowed him to approach the edge of her shoe sole without being her husband. No, no, not that; marriage must come first in any business of this sort that I take in hand. But there was one hitch in this case, which was that of inequality of rank, Don Clavijo being a private gentleman, and the Princess Antonomasia, as I said, heiress to the kingdom.

"The entanglement remained for some time a secret, kept hidden by my cunning precautions, until I perceived that a certain expansion of waist in Antonomasia must before long disclose it, the dread of which made us all three take counsel together, and it was agreed that before the mischief came to light, Don Clavijo should demand Antonomasia as his wife before the Vicar, in virtue of an agreement to marry him made by the princess and drafted by my wit in such binding terms that the might of Samson could not have broken it. The necessary steps were taken; the Vicar saw the agreement and took the lady's confession; she confessed everything in full, and he ordered her into the custody of a very respectable bailiff of the court."

"Are there bailiffs of the court in Candaya, too," said Sancho at this, "and poets, and *seguidillas*? I swear I think the world is the same all over! But hurry up, Señora Trifaldi; it's late, and I am dying to know the end of this long story."

"I will," replied the countess.

Chapter XXXIX

IN WHICH THE TRIFALDI CONTINUES HER MARVELLOUS AND MEMORABLE STORY

By every word that Sancho uttered, the duchess was as much delighted as Don Quixote was driven to desperation. He ordered him to hold his tongue, and the Distressed One went on to say: "Finally, after much questioning and answering, as the princess held to her story without changing or varying her previous declaration, the Vicar gave his decision in favor of Don Clavijo, and she was delivered over to him as his lawful wife; which so distressed the Queen Doña Maguncia, the Princess Antonomasia's mother, that within the space of three days we buried her."

"She died, no doubt," said Sancho.

"Of course," said Trifaldín. "They don't bury living people in Candaya, only the dead."

"Señor Squire," said Sancho, "a man in a faint has been known to be buried, in the belief that he was dead; and it struck me that Queen Maguncia ought to have fainted rather than died. Because if you keep on living, a great many things turn out all right, and the princess's mistake was not so great that she needed to get so upset.

"If the lady had married one of her pages or some other servant of the house, as many others have done (so I have heard say), then the mischief would have been past curing. But to marry such an elegant, accomplished gentleman as has been just now described to us—certainly, certainly even if it was a foolish mistake, it was not such a big one as you think; for according to the rules of my master here (and he won't allow me to lie) if scholars can become bishops, then gentlemen (especially if they are knights-errant) can become kings and emperors."

"You are right, Sancho," said Don Quixote, "for with a knight-errant, if he has but an ounce of good fortune, it is in the cards to become the mightiest lord on earth. But let the Distressed One proceed; for I suspect she has yet to tell us the bitter part of this so far sweet story."

"The bitter is indeed to come," said the countess, "and so bitter that castor oil is sweet and hemlock tasty in comparison. The queen, then, being dead, and not in a swoon, we buried her; and hardly had we covered her with earth, hardly had we said our last farewells, when (*Quis talia fando temperet a lachrymis?*)[1] over the queen's grave there appeared, mounted upon a wooden horse, the giant Malambruno, Maguncia's first cousin. Besides being cruel, he is an enchanter, and to revenge the death of his cousin, punish the

1. "Who speaking such things might restrain his tears" (Virgil, *Aeneid*, II).

audacity of Don Clavijo, and in wrath at the impudence of Antonomasia, he left them both enchanted by his art on the grave itself, she being changed into a brass monkey and he into a horrible crocodile of some unknown metal.

"Between the two there stands a pillar, also of metal, with certain characters in the Syriac language inscribed upon it, which, being translated into Candayan, and now into Castilian, contain the following sentence: 'These two rash lovers shall not recover their former shape until the valiant Manchegan comes to do battle with me in single combat; for the Fates reserve this unexampled adventure for his mighty valor alone.'

"This done, he drew from its sheath a huge, broad scimitar, and seizing me by the hair, he made as though he meant to cut my throat and shear my head clean off. I was terror-stricken, my voice stuck in my throat, and I was in the deepest distress; nevertheless I summoned up my strength as well as I could, and in a trembling and piteous voice I addressed such words to him as induced him to stay the infliction of a punishment so severe. He then caused all the dueñas of the palace, those that are here present, to be brought before him; and after having dwelt upon the enormity of our offense and denounced dueñas, their characters, their evil ways and worse intrigues, blaming all for what I alone was guilty of, he said that he did not wish to chastise us with capital punishment but with others of a slow nature which would be in effect civil death forever; and the very instant he ceased speaking we all felt the pores of our faces opening and pricking us, as if with the points of needles. We at once put our hands up to our faces and found ourselves in the state you now see."

Here the Distressed One and the other dueñas raised the veils with which they were covered and disclosed countenances all bristling with beards, some red, some black, some white, and some mixed, at which spectacle the duke and duchess made a show of being filled with wonder. Don Quixote and Sancho were overwhelmed with amazement, and the bystanders lost in astonishment, while Trifaldi went on to say: "Thus did that malevolent villain Malambruno punish us, covering the tenderness and softness of our faces with these rough bristles! Would to heaven that he had lopped off our heads with his enormous scimitar instead of obscuring the light of our countenances with this fuzz that covers us!

"For if we look into the matter, sirs (and what I am now going to say, I would say with eyes flowing like fountains, only that the thought of our misfortune and the oceans they have already wept keep them as dry as barley spears, and so I say it without tears), where, I ask, can a dueña with a beard go? What father or mother will feel pity for her? Who will help her? For, if even when she has a smooth skin, and a face tortured by a thousand kinds of lotions and cosmetics, she can hardly get anybody to love her, what will she do when she shows a countenance turned into a thicket? Oh dueñas, companions mine! It was an unlucky moment when we were born and an ill-starred hour when our fathers begot us!" And as she said this she showed signs of being about to faint.

Chapter XL

OF MATTERS RELATING AND BELONGING TO THIS ADVENTURE AND TO THIS MEMORABLE HISTORY

Really and truly all those who find pleasure in histories like this ought to show their gratitude to Cide Hamete, its original author, for the scrupulous care he has taken to set before us all its minute particulars, not leaving anything, however trifling it may be, that he does not make clear and plain. He portrays the thoughts, he reveals the fancies, he answers implied questions, clears up doubts, sets objections at rest, and, in a word, makes plain the smallest points the most inquisitive can desire to know. O renowned author! O happy Don Quixote! O famous Dulcinea! O witty Sancho Panza! All and each, may you live countless ages for the delight and amusement of the dwellers on earth!

The history goes on to say that when Sancho saw the Distressed One faint he exclaimed, "I swear by the faith of an honest man and the lives of all my ancestors the Panzas, that I never did see or hear of, nor has my master related or conceived in his mind, such an adventure as this. A thousand devils—not that I mean to curse you—take you, Malambruno, for an enchanter and a giant! Couldn't you find some other sort of punishment for these poor things but bearding them? Wouldn't it have been better—it would have been better for them—to have taken off half their noses from the middle upwards, even though they'd have snuffled when they spoke, than to have put beards on them? I'll bet they can't afford to pay anybody to shave them."

"That is the truth, señor," said one of the twelve. "We have no money to get ourselves shaved, and so some of us have taken to using adhesive or sticking-plasters by way of an economical remedy. By applying them to our faces and pulling them off with a jerk, we are left as bare and smooth as the bottom of a stone mortar. There are, to be sure, women in Canadaya that go from house to house to remove fuzz and pluck eyebrows and make cosmetics for the use of the women, but we, the dueñas of my lady, would never let them in, for most of them look suspiciously like procurers who have retired from prostitution. If we are not relieved by Señor Don Quixote, we shall be carried to our graves with beards."

"I will pluck out my own in the land of the Moors," said Don Quixote, "if I don't cure yours."

At this instant Trifaldi recovered her from swoon and said, "The echo of that promise, valiant knight, reached my ears in the midst of my swoon and has been the means of reviving me and bringing back my senses; and so once more I implore you, illustrious errant, indomitable sir, to let your gracious promises be turned into deeds."

"There shall be no delay on my part," said Don Quixote. "Tell me, señora, what I must do, for my heart is most eager to serve you."

"The fact is," replied the Distressed One, "it is five thousand leagues, a couple more or less, from here to the kingdom of Candaya, if you go by land. But if you go through the air and in a straight line, it is three thousand two hundred and twenty-seven. You must know, too, that Malambruno told me that, whenever fate provided the knight who would be our deliverer, he himself would send him a steed far better and with fewer tricks than a rented mule; for it will be that same wooden horse on which the valiant Pierres carried off the fair Magalona. The horse is guided by a peg it has in its forehead that serves for a bridle, and it flies through the air with such speed that you would think the very devils were carrying it. This horse, according to ancient tradition, was made by Merlin. He lent it to Pierres, who was a friend of his, and who made long journeys with it, and, as has been said, carried off the fair Magalona, bearing her through the air on its haunches and making all who beheld them from the earth gape with astonishment; and Merlin only lent it to those whom he loved or those who paid him well; and since the great Pierres, we know of no one having mounted it until now. From him, Malambruno stole it by his magic art, and he has it now in his possession and makes use of it in his journeys which he constantly makes through different parts of the world. He is here today, tomorrow in France, and the next day in Potosí. And the best of it is, the horse neither eats nor sleeps nor wears out shoes, and goes at an ambling pace through the air without wings, so that a man mounted on it can carry a cup full of water in his hand without spilling a drop, so smoothly and easily does it go, for which reason the fair Magalona enjoyed riding it greatly."

"For going smoothly and easily," said Sancho at this, "give me my Dapple, though he can't go through the air. But on the ground I'll back him against all the amblers in the world."

They all laughed, and the Distressed One continued: "And this same horse (if Malambruno is disposed to put an end to our sufferings) will appear here before night shall have advanced half an hour; for he announced to me that the sign he would give me, so that I might know that I had found the knight I was in quest of, would be to send me the horse, wherever it might be, speedily and promptly."

"And how many is there room for on this horse?" asked Sancho.

"Two," said the Distressed One, "one in the saddle and the other on the croup, and generally these two are knight and squire, when there is no damsel that's being carried off."

"I'd like to know, Señora Distressed One," said Sancho, "what is the name of this horse?"

"His name," said the Distressed One, "is not the same as Bellerophon's horse that was called Pegasus, or Alexander the Great's, called Bucephalus, or Orlando the Mad's, the name of which was Brigliador, nor Bayard, the horse of Reinaldos of Montalbán, nor Frontino like Ruggiero's, nor Bootes or Peritoa, as they say the horses of the sun were called, nor is he called Orelia, like the horse on which the unfortunate Rodrigo, the last king of the Goths, rode to the battle where he lost his life and his kingdom."

"I'll bet," said Sancho, "that since they haven't given him any of these famous names of well-known horses, they haven't given him the name of my master's Rocinante, which for being apt surpasses all that have been mentioned."

"That is true," said the bearded countess. "Still it fits very well, for he is called Clavileño the Swift, in accordance with his being made of wood, with the peg he has in his forehead,[1] and with the swift pace at which he travels; and so, as far as name goes, he may compare with the famous Rocinante."

"I have nothing to say against his name," said Sancho, "but what kind of bridle or halter is he managed with?"

"I have said already," said Trifaldi, "that it is with a peg. By turning it to one side or the other, the knight who rides him makes him go as he pleases, either through the upper air, or skimming and almost sweeping the earth, or else in the middle course that is sought and followed in all well-regulated proceedings."

"I'd like to see him," said Sancho. "But to expect one to mount him, either in the saddle or on the croup, is to ask the impossible. I can hardly keep my seat on Dapple and on a pack-saddle softer than silk and here they'd have me sit on wooden haunches without pad or cushion of any sort! By God, I have no intention of bruising myself to get rid of anyone's beard. Let each one shave himself as best he can. I'm not going to accompany my master on any such long journey. Besides, I can't be any help to the shaving of these beards as I can to the disenchantment of my lady Dulcinea."

"Yes, you can, my friend," replied Trifaldi, "and so much, that without you, so I understand, we shall be able to do nothing."

"In the king's name!" exclaimed Sancho, "what have squires got to do with the adventures of their masters! Are they to have the fame of the adventures they go through and we the hardships? Lord! If the historians would only say, 'Such and such a knight

1. *Clavo*: "a nail or spike"; *leño*: "wood."

finished such and such an adventure, but with the help of so and so, his squire, without which it would have been impossible for him to accomplish it.' But they write simply, 'Don Paralipomenón of the Three Stars accomplished the adventure of the six monsters,' without mentioning such a person as his squire, who was there all the time, just as if there was no such person in the world. Once more, sirs, I say my master may go alone, and much good may it do him; and I'll stay here in the company of my lady the duchess; and maybe when he comes back, he will find the lady Dulcinea's affairs much advanced; for I mean in free hours and at idle moments to give myself a spell of whipping that will leave me scarred for life."

"Nevertheless, you must go if it is necessary, my good Sancho," said the duchess, "for they are honorable people who ask you; and the faces of these ladies must not remain overgrown in this way because of your idle fears; that would be a terrible thing indeed."

"In the king's name, once more!" said Sancho. "If this charitable work were to be done for the sake of modest damsels or orphan girls, a man might expose himself to some hardships; but to bear it for the sake of stripping beards off dueñas! Devil take it! I'd sooner see them all bearded, from the highest to the lowest, and from the most prudish to the most affected."

"You are very hard on dueñas, Sancho my friend," said the duchess. "You incline very much to the opinion of the Toledo apothecary. But indeed you are wrong; there are dueñas in my house that may serve you as models for dueñas; and here is my Doña Rodríguez, who will not allow me to say otherwise."

"Your excellency may say it if you like," said Rodríguez, "for God knows the truth of everything; and whether we dueñas are good or bad, bearded or smooth, we are our mothers' daughters like other women. And as God sent us into the world, he knows why he did, and on his mercy I rely, and not on anybody's beard."

"Well, Señora Rodríguez, Señora Trifaldi, and present company," said Don Quixote, "I trust in Heaven that it will look with kindly eyes upon your troubles, for Sancho will do as I bid him. Only let Clavileño come and let me find myself face to face with Malambruno, and I am certain no razor will shave you more easily than my sword shall shave Malambruno's head off his shoulders; for God suffers the wicked, but not for ever."

"Ah!" exclaimed the Distressed One at this, "may all the stars of the celestial regions look down upon your greatness with benign eyes, valiant knight, and shed every prosperity and valor upon your heart, that it may be the shield and safeguard of the abused and downtrodden race of dueñas, detested by apothecaries, sneered at by squires, and tricked by pages. Ill betide the girl that in the flower of her youth would not sooner become a nun than a dueña! Unfortunate beings that we are, we dueñas! Though we may be descended in the direct male line from Hector of Troy himself, our mistresses never fail to address us as '*vos*' if they think it makes queens of them.[2] O giant Malambruno, though you are an enchanter, you are true to your promises. Send us now the peerless Clavileño, that our misfortune may be brought to an end; for if the hot weather sets in and these beards of ours are still there, alas for our lot!"

Trifaldi said this in such a pathetic way that she drew tears from the eyes of all, and even Sancho's filled up, and he resolved in his heart to accompany his master to the uttermost ends of the earth, if the removal of the wool from those venerable countenances depended upon it.

Chapter XLI

OF THE ARRIVAL OF CLAVILEÑO AND THE END OF THIS PROTRACTED ADVENTURE

And now night came, and with it the appointed time for the arrival of the famous horse Clavileño, the non-appearance of which was already beginning to make Don Quixote uneasy, for it struck him that, as Malambruno was so long about sending it, either he himself was not the knight for whom the adventure was reserved or else Malambruno did not dare to meet him in single combat. But lo! suddenly there came into the garden four wildmen all clad in green ivy bearing on their shoulders a great wooden horse. They placed it on its feet on the ground, and one of the wildmen said, "Let the knight who has the courage to do it mount this machine."

Here Sancho exclaimed, "I'm not mounting, for I don't have the courage, and I'm not a knight."

"And let the squire, if he has one," continued the wildman, "take his seat on the croup, and let him trust the valiant Malambruno; for by no sword except Malambruno's, nor by the malice of any other, shall he be assailed. They have only to turn this peg the horse has in his neck, and he will bear them through the air to where Malambruno awaits them. But so that the vast elevation of their course may not make them dizzy, their eyes must be covered until the horse neighs, which will be the sign of their having completed their journey."

With these words, leaving Clavileño behind them, they retired with graceful bearing the way they came. As soon as the Distressed One saw the horse, almost in tears she exclaimed to Don Quixote, "Valiant knight, the promise of Malambruno has proved trustworthy. The horse has come, our beards are growing, and by every

2. *Vos* was a form of address used with inferiors.

hair in them all of us implore you to shave and shear us, since all you have to do is mount him with your squire and begin your new journey."

"That I will, Señora Countess Trifaldi," said Don Quixote, "most gladly and with right good will, without stopping to take a cushion or put on my spurs, so as not to lose time, such is my desire to see you and all these dueñas shaved clean."

"That I won't," said Sancho, "with good will or bad will, or any way at all; and if this shaving can't be done without my mounting on the croup, my master had better look for another squire to go with him, and these ladies for some other way of making their faces smooth. I'm no witch to have a taste for traveling through the air. What will my islanders say when they find out that their governor walks around on the winds? And another thing: it is three thousand and odd leagues from here to Candaya. If the horse tires or the giant gets angry, we'll be half a dozen years getting back, and there won't be isle or island in the world that will know me. And so, as it is a common saying 'in delay there's danger,' and 'when they offer you a heifer, run with a halter,' these ladies' beards must excuse me. 'Saint Peter is at home in Rome.' I mean I am very comfortable in this house where so much is made of me and from whose owner I expect the great favor of seeing myself a governor."

"Friend Sancho," said the duke at this, "the island that I have promised you is not a moving one or one that will run away; it has roots so deeply buried in the bowels of the earth that it will be no easy matter to pluck it up or shift it from where it is. You know as well as I do that there is no sort of office of any importance that is not obtained by a bribe of some kind, great or small; well, what I want in return for this governorship is that you go with your master Don Quixote and bring this memorable adventure to a conclusion. And whether you return on Clavileño as quickly as his speed seems to promise, or adverse fortune brings you back on foot traveling as a pilgrim from hostel to hostel and from inn to inn, on your return you will always find your island where you left it and your islanders with the same eagerness they have always had to receive you as their governor, and my good will will remain the same. Doubt not the truth of this, Señor Sancho, for that would be grievously wronging my disposition to serve you."

"Say no more, señor," said Sancho. "I am a poor squire and not equal to carrying so much courtesy; let my master mount; blindfold my eyes and commit me to God's care and tell me if I can commend myself to our Lord or call on the angels to protect me when we go towering up there."

To this Trifaldi answered, "Sancho, you may freely commend yourself to God or whom you will; for Malambruno though an enchanter is a Christian and works his enchantments with great circumspection, taking care not to offend anyone."

"Well then," said Sancho, "God and the most holy Trinity of Gaeta give me help!"

"Since the memorable adventure of the fulling mills," said Don Quixote, "I have never seen Sancho in such a fright as now; were I as superstitious as others, his abject fear would cause me some little trepidation of spirit. But come here, Sancho, for with the leave of these lords and ladies I would say a word or two to you in private."

And drawing Sancho aside among the trees of the garden and seizing both his hands he said, "You see, brother Sancho, the long journey we have before us, and God knows when we shall return or what leisure or opportunities this business will allow us. I wish you therefore to retire now to your chamber, as though you were going to fetch something required for the road, and in a trice give yourself at least five hundred lashes toward the three thousand three hundred to which you are committed. It will be all to the good, and to begin a thing is to have it half finished."

"By God," said Sancho, "your worship must be out of your senses! This is like the saying, 'You see me with child, and you want me a virgin.' Just as I'm about to go sitting on a bare board, your worship would have me hurt my backside! Your worship is certainly not reasonable. Let's be off to shave these dueñas; and on our return I promise on my word to fulfil my obligation so quickly that it will satisfy your worship. I can't say more."

"Well, I will comfort myself with that promise, my good Sancho," replied Don Quixote, "and I believe you will keep it; for indeed though simple, you are a veracious man."

"I'm not voracious," said Sancho, "but even if I was a little, still I'd keep my word."

With this they went back to mount Clavileño, and as they were about to do so Don Quixote said, "Cover your eyes, Sancho, and mount; for one who sends for us from lands so far distant cannot mean to deceive us for the sake of the paltry glory to be derived from deceiving persons who trust in him; though all should turn out the contrary of what I hope, no malice will be able to dim the glory of having undertaken this exploit."

"Let's go, señor," said Sancho, "for I have taken the beards and tears of these ladies deeply to heart, and I won't enjoy a bite of food until I have seen them restored to their former smoothness. Mount, your worship, and blindfold yourself, for if I am to go on the croup, it is plain the rider in the saddle must mount first."

"That is true," said Don Quixote, and, taking a handkerchief out of his pocket, he begged the Distressed One to cover his eyes very carefully; but after having them covered he uncovered them again, saying, "If my memory does not deceive me, I have read in Virgil of the Palladium of Troy, a wooden horse the Greeks offered to the goddess Pallas, which was filled with armed knights, who were afterwards the destruction of Troy; so it would be as well to see, first of all, what Clavileño has in his stomach."

"There is no occasion," said the Distressed One. "I will vouch for him, and I know that Malambruno has nothing tricky or treacherous about him. You may mount without any fear, Señor Don Quixote; on my head be it if any harm befalls you."

Don Quixote thought that to say anything further with regard to his safety would be putting his courage in an unfavorable light; and so, without more words, he mounted Clavileño and tried the peg, which turned easily; and as he had no stirrups and his legs hung down, he looked like nothing so much as a figure in some Roman triumph painted or embroidered on a Flemish tapestry.

Much against his will and very slowly, Sancho proceeded to mount, and, after settling himself as well as he could on the croup, he found it rather hard, and not at all soft, and asked the duke if it would be possible to oblige him with a pad of some kind or a cushion, even if it were off the couch of his lady the duchess or the bed of one of the pages, as the haunches of that horse were more like marble than wood. On this Trifaldi observed that Clavileño would not bear any kind of harness or trappings and that his best plan would be to sit sideways like a woman, as in that way he would not feel the hardness so much.

Sancho did so, and, bidding them farewell, allowed his eyes to be covered, but immediately afterwards he uncovered them again, and looking tenderly and tearfully on those in the garden, asked them help him in his present strait with a Paternoster and an Ave Maria apiece, so that God might provide some one to say as many for them, if they should ever find themselves in a similar emergency.

At this Don Quixote exclaimed, "Are you on the gallows, thief, or at your last moment, to use pitiful entreaties of that sort? Cowardly, spiritless creature, are you not in the very place the fair Magalona occupied, and from which she descended, not into the grave, but to become Queen of France, unless the histories lie? And I who am here beside you, may I not put myself on a par with the valiant Pierres, who pressed this very spot that I now press? Cover your eyes, cover your eyes, abject animal, and let not your fear escape your lips, at least in my presence."

"Blindfold me," said Sancho. "Since you won't let me commend myself or be commended to God, is it any wonder if I am afraid that a region of devils may carry us off to Peralvillo?"[1]

They were then blindfolded, and Don Quixote, finding himself

1. Peralvillo was a town where the Holy Brotherhood executed their prisoners. Sancho, of course, means a *legion* of devils.

settled to his satisfaction, felt for the peg, and the instant he placed his fingers on it, all the dueñas and all who stood by lifted up their voices exclaiming, "God guide you, valiant knight! God be with you, intrepid squire! Now, now you are flying through the air more swiftly than an arrow! Now you begin to amaze and astonish all who are gazing at you from the earth! Sit still, brave Sancho; you are swaying! Look out: don't fall! Your fall will be worse than that rash youth's who tried to steer the chariot of his father the Sun!"

As Sancho heard the voices, clinging tightly to his master and winding his arms round him, he said, "Señor, why do they say we are going up so high, if their voices reach us here and they seem to be speaking here close to us?"

"Don't mind that, Sancho," said Don Quixote, "for as affairs of this sort and flights like this are out of the common course of things, you can see and hear as much as you like a thousand leagues offi; but don't squeeze me so tight or you will upset me; and really I know not what you have to be uneasy or frightened at, for I can safely swear I never mounted a smoother-going steed all the days of my life. One would think we are not moving from one place. Banish fear, my friend, for indeed everything is going as it ought, and we have the wind astern."

"That's true," said Sancho, "for such a strong wind is blowing against me on this side that it seems as if people were blowing on me with a thousand pairs of bellows"—which was the case. They were puffing at him with a great pair of bellows; for the whole adventure was so well planned by the duke, the duchess, and their majordomo that nothing was omitted to make it a perfect success.

Don Quixote now, feeling the blast, said, "Beyond a doubt, Sancho, we must have already reached the second region of the air, where the hail and snow are generated. The thunder, the lightning, and the thunderbolts are engendered in the third region, and if we go on ascending at this rate, we shall shortly come into the region of fire, and I know not how to regulate this peg, so as not to mount up where we shall be burned."

And now the duke's men began to warm their faces, from a distance, with tow that could be easily set on fire and extinguished again, fixed on the end of a cane. On feeling the heat Sancho said, "May I die if we are not already in that fire place, or very near it because a good part of my beard has been singed, and I have a mind, señor, to uncover and see where we are."

"Do nothing of the kind," said Don Quixote. "Remember the true story of the licentiate Torralba that the devils carried flying through the air riding on a stick with his eyes shut. In twelve hours he reached Rome and dismounted at Torre di Nona, which is a street of the city, and saw the whole sack and storming and the death of Bourbon, and was back in Madrid the next morning, where he gave an account of all he had seen.[2] And he said moreover that as he was going through the air, the devil told him to open his eyes, and he did so and saw himself so near the body of the moon, so it seemed to him, that he could have laid hold of it with his hand, and that he did not dare to look at the earth lest he should be seized with dizziness.

"So, Sancho, it will not do for us to uncover our eyes, for he who has us in charge will be responsible for us; and perhaps we are gaining altitude to enable us to descend at one swoop on the kingdom of Candaya, as the falcon does on the heron, so as to seize it however high it may soar; and though it seems to us not half an hour since we left the garden, believe me we must have traveled a great distance."

"I don't know about that," said Sancho. "All I know is that if the Señora Magellan or Magalona was satisfied with this croup, she could not have had very tender flesh."

The duke, the duchess, and all in the garden were listening to the conversation of the two heroes and were greatly amused by it; and now, desirous of putting a finishing touch to this rare and well-contrived adventure, they applied a light to Clavileño's tail with some tow, and the horse, being full of exploding rockets, immediately blew up with a prodigious noise and brought Don Quixote and Sancho Panza to the ground half singed.

By this time the bearded band of dueñas, Trifaldi and all, had vanished from the garden, and those that remained lay stretched on the ground as if in a swoon. Don Quixote and Sancho got up rather shaken, and looking about them, were filled with amazement at finding themselves in the same garden from which they had started and at seeing such a number of people stretched on the ground. Their astonishment was increased when at one side of the garden they perceived a tall lance planted in the ground and hanging from it by two cords of green silk a smooth white parchment on which there was the following inscription in large gold letters: "The illustrious knight Don Quixote of La Mancha has, by merely attempting it, finished and concluded the adventure of the Countess Trifaldi, otherwise called the Distressed Dueña. Malambruno is now satisfied on every point, the chins of the dueñas are now smooth and clean, and King Don Clavijo and Queen Antonomasia in their original form. And when the squirely whipping shall have been completed, the white dove shall find herself delivered from the pestiferous gerfalcons that persecute her and in the arms of her beloved mate; for such is the decree of the sage Merlin, arch-enchanter of enchanters."

As soon as Don Quixote had read the inscription on the parch-

2. Torralba was tried in 1528 on charges of dealing in magic. The Bourbon mentioned is the duke killed during the Sack of Rome in 1527.

ment he perceived clearly that it referred to the disenchantment of Dulcinea, and returning hearty thanks to heaven that he had with so little danger achieved so grand an exploit as to restore to their former complexion the countenances of those venerable dueñas, he advanced towards the duke and duchess, who had not yet come to, and taking the duke by the hand he said, "Be of good cheer, worthy sir, be of good cheer; it's nothing at all; the adventure is now over and without any harm done, as the inscription fixed on this post shows plainly."

The duke came to slowly and like one recovering consciousness after a heavy sleep, and the duchess and all who had fallen prostrate about the garden did the same, with such demonstrations of wonder and amazement that they would have also persuaded one that what they pretended so adroitly in jest had happened to them in reality. The duke read the placard with half-shut eyes, and then ran to embrace Don Quixote with open arms, declaring him to be the best knight that had ever been seen in any age. Sancho kept looking about for the Distressed One, to see what her face was like without the beard and if she was as fair as her elegant person promised. But they told him that the instant Clavileño descended flaming through the air and came to the ground, the whole band of dueñas with Trifaldi vanished, and that they were already shaved and without any stubble left.

The duchess asked Sancho how he had fared on that long journey, to which Sancho replied, "I felt, señora, that we were flying through the region of fire, as my master told me, and I wanted to uncover my eyes for a bit. But my master, when I asked permission to uncover them, would not let me; but as I have a little bit of curiosity and a desire to know what is forbidden and kept from me, quietly and without anyone seeing me I raised the handkerchief covering my eyes just a little, close to my nose, and from underneath looked towards the earth, and it seemed to me that it was no bigger than a mustard seed and that the men walking on it were little bigger than hazel nuts; so you can see how high we must have been going then."

To this the duchess said, "Sancho, my friend, watch what you are saying. It seems you could not have seen the earth, but only the men walking on it; for if the earth looked to you like a mustard seed and each man like a hazel nut, one man alone would have covered the whole earth."

"That is true," said Sancho, "but for all that I got a glimpse of a bit of one side of it, and saw it all."

"Look, Sancho," said the duchess, "with a 'bit of one side' one does not see the whole of what one looks at."

"I don't know about that way of looking at things," said Sancho. "I only know that your ladyship will do well to bear in mind that since we were flying by enchantment, I might have seen the whole earth and all the men by enchantment whatever way I looked.

"And if you won't believe this, you won't believe that, uncovering my eyes close to my eyebrows, I saw myself so near to the sky that there was not a foot between me and it; and by everything that I can swear by, señora, it is mighty big! And it so happened we came by where the Seven Goats are,[3] and by God and upon my soul, since I was a goatherd in my own country when I was a boy, as soon as I saw them I felt an urge to play with them for a little, and if I hadn't given in, I think I'd have burst. So I make up my mind, and what do I do? Without saying anything to anybody, not even to my master, softly and quietly I got down from Clavileño and amused myself with the goats—which are like gilly flowers and like blossoms—for almost three-quarters of an hour. And Clavileño never stirred or moved from one spot."

"And while the good Sancho was amusing himself with the goats," said the duke, "how was Señor Don Quixote occupied?"

To which Don Quixote replied, "As all these things and such like occurrences are out of the ordinary course of nature, it is no wonder that Sancho says what he does; for my own part I can only say that I did not uncover my eyes either above or below, nor did I see sky or earth or sea or shore. It is true I felt that I was passing through the region of the air, and even that I touched that of fire. But that we passed farther I cannot believe; for the region of fire being between the heaven of the moon and the last region of the air, we could not have reached that heaven where the Seven Goats Sancho speaks of are without being burned; and as we were not burned, either Sancho is lying or Sancho is dreaming."

"I am neither lying nor dreaming," said Sancho. "Only ask me to describe those same goats, and you'll see whether I'm telling the truth or not."

"Describe them then, Sancho," said the duchess.

"Two of them," said Sancho, "are green, two blood-red, two blue, and one a mixture of all colors."

"That's a strange kind of goat," said the duke. "In this earthly region of ours we have no such colors; I mean goats of such colors."

"That's very plain," said Sancho. "Of course there must be a difference between the goats of heaven and the goats of the earth."

"Tell me, Sancho," said the duke, "did you see any he-goat among those goats?"

"No, señor," said Sancho. "But I have heard say that none ever passed the horns of the moon."[4]

They did not care to ask him anything more about his journey,

3. The Pleiades.
4. The humor of this passage depends on the double meanings of *cabrón*, "he-goat" and "complacent husband," and *cuernos*, "horns" and "cuckold."

for they saw he was in the humor to go rambling all over the heavens giving an account of everything that went on there, without having ever stirred from the garden. Such, in short, was the end of the adventure of the Distressed Dueña, which gave the duke and duchess laughing matter not only for the time being but for all their lives, and Sancho something to talk about for ages, if he lived so long; but Don Quixote, coming close to his ear, said to him, "Sancho, as you would have us believe what you saw in heaven, I require you to believe me as to what I saw in the cave of Montesinos. I say no more."

Chapter XLII

OF THE COUNSELS WHICH DON QUIXOTE GAVE SANCHO PANZA BEFORE HE SET OUT TO GOVERN THE ISLAND, TOGETHER WITH OTHER WELL-CONSIDERED MATTERS

The duke and duchess were so well pleased with the successful and amusing result of the adventure of the Distressed One that they resolved to continue the joke, seeing what a fit subject they had for making it all pass for reality. So having laid their plans and given instructions to their servants and vassals how to behave to Sancho in his government of the promised island, the next day (that following Clavileño's flight), the duke told Sancho to prepare and get ready to go and be governor, for his islanders were already looking out for him as for the showers of May.

Sancho made him a bow and said, "Ever since I came down from heaven, and from the top of it looked at the earth and saw how little it is, the great desire I had to be a governor has been partly cooled in me. What is grand about being ruler on a grain of mustard seed, or what dignity or authority in governing half a dozen men about as big as hazel nuts; because so far as I could see, there were no more on the whole earth? If your lordship would be so good as to give me a small bit of heaven, even if it were no more than half a league, I'd rather have it than the best island in the world."

"Look, Sancho," said the duke, "I cannot give a bit of heaven, not so much as the breadth of my nail to anyone; rewards and favors of that sort are reserved for God alone. What I can give, I give you, and that is a real, genuine island, compact, well proportioned, and uncommonly fertile and fruitful, where, if you know how to use your opportunities, you may, with the help of the world's riches, gain those of heaven."

"Well then," said Sancho. "I'll take the island, and I'll try to be such a governor that in spite of scoundrels I'll go to heaven; and it's not from any craving to rise above my station or better myself, but from the desire I have to see what it tastes like to be a governor."

"Once you taste it, Sancho," said the duke, "you'll want to eat it all, it is so sweet to command and be obeyed. Depend upon it, when your master comes to be emperor (as he will beyond a doubt from the course his affairs are taking), it will be no easy matter to take it away from him, and he will be sore and sorry at heart to have been so long without becoming one."

"Señor," said Sancho, "I imagine it's a good thing to be in command, if it's only over a herd of cattle."

"May I be buried with you, Sancho," said the duke. "You know everything. I hope you will make as good a governor as your good sense promises; and that is all I have to say. Now remember, tomorrow is the day you must set out for the governorship of the island, and this evening they will provide you with the proper attire for you to wear, and all the things necessary for your departure."

"Let them dress me as they like," said Sancho. "However I'm dressed I'll be Sancho Panza."

"That's true," said the duke. "But one's dress must be suited to the office or rank one holds; for it would not do for a jurist to dress like a soldier, or a soldier like a priest. You, Sancho, shall go partly as a lawyer, partly as a captain, for, in the island I am giving you, arms are needed as much as letters, and letters as much as arms."

"I don't know much about letters," said Sancho, "for I don't even know the A B C; but it is enough for me to have the Christus[1] in my memory to be a good governor. As for arms, I'll handle those they give me till I drop, and then, God be my help!"

"With so good a memory," said the duke, "Sancho cannot go wrong in anything."

Here Don Quixote joined them; and learning what was happening and how soon Sancho was to go to his government, he with the duke's permission took Sancho by the hand and retired to his room with him for the purpose of giving him advice as to how he was to behave himself in office. As soon as they had entered the chamber, he closed the door and almost by force made Sancho sit down beside him, and in a quiet tone thus addressed him: "I give infinite thanks to heaven, friend Sancho, that, before I have met with any good luck, fortune has come forward to meet you. I, who counted upon my good fortune to repay you for your services, find myself still waiting for advancement, while you, before the time and contrary to all reasonable expectation, see yourself blessed in the fulfillment of your desires. Some will bribe, beg, solicit, rise early, entreat, persist, without attaining the object of their suit; while another comes, and without knowing why or wherefore, finds himself invested with the place or office so many have sued for; and here it

1. The cross prefixed to the alphabet in schoolbooks.

is that the common saying, 'There is good luck as well as bad when a job's to be had,' applies. You, who, to my thinking, are beyond all doubt a dullard, without early rising or losing sleep or taking any trouble, with the mere breath of knight-errantry that has breathed on you, see yourself without more ado governor of an island, as though it were a mere matter of course. This I say, Sancho, that you not attribute the favor you have received to your own merits, but give thanks to heaven that disposes matters beneficently, and secondly thanks to the great power the profession of knight-errantry contains in itself. With a heart, then, inclined to believe what I have said to you, attend, my son, to your Cato here who would counsel you and be your pole star and guide to direct and pilot you to a safe haven out of this stormy sea on which you are about to set sail; for offices and great trusts are nothing else but a deep sea of troubles.

"First of all, my son, you must fear God, for in the fear of him is wisdom, and being wise you cannot err in anything.

"Secondly, you must keep in view that you are striving to know yourself, the most difficult thing to know that the mind can imagine. If you know yourself, it will follow you will not puff yourself up like the frog that strove to make himself as large as the ox; if you do, the recollection of having kept pigs in your own country will serve as the ugly feet for the peacock's tail of your folly."[2]

"That's the truth," said Sancho. "But that was when I was a boy; later when I was bigger, it was geese I kept, not pigs. But to my thinking that has nothing to do with it. Not all governors come from royal stock."

"True," said Don Quixote, "and for that reason those who are not of noble origin should take care that the dignity of the office they hold be accompanied by a gentle manner, which wisely managed will save them from the sneers of malice that no station escapes.

"Glory in your humble birth, Sancho, and be not ashamed of saying you are peasant-born; for when it is seen you are not ashamed, no one will set himself to embarrass you; and pride yourself rather on being one of lowly virtue than a lofty sinner. Countless are they who, born of low parentage, have risen to the highest dignities, pontifical and imperial, and of the truth of this I could give you instances enough to weary you.

"Remember, Sancho, if you make virtue your aim and take pride in doing virtuous actions, you will have no cause to envy princes and lords, for blood is an inheritance but virtue an acquisition, and virtue has in itself alone a worth that blood does not possess.

"This being so, if perchance anyone of your kinsfolk should come

2. An allusion to the fable that the peacock's pride in his tail is tempered when he contemplates his ugly feet.

to see you when you are on your island, you are not to reject or slight him but on the contrary to welcome him, entertain him, and make much of him; for in so doing you will be approved of heaven (which is not pleased that any should despise what it has made) and will comply with the laws of well-ordered nature.

"If you take your wife with you (and it is not well for those that administer governments to be long without their wives), teach and instruct her, and strive to smooth her natural roughness; for all that may be gained by a wise governor may be lost and wasted by a boorish, stupid wife.

"If perchance you are left a widower—a thing which may happen —and in virtue of your office seek a consort of higher degree, choose not one to serve you for a hook and fishing rod or a receptacle for improper gifts. Verily, I tell you, for all the judge's wife receives, the judge will be held accountable at the general calling to account, where he will have to repay in death, fourfold, items that in life he regarded as naught.

"Never go by arbitrary law, which is so much favored by ignorant men who pride themselves on cleverness.

"Let the tears of the poor man find in you more compassion, but not more justice, than the pleadings of the rich.

"Strive to lay bare the truth, as well amid the promises and gifts of the rich man as amid the sobs and entreaties of the poor.

"When equity may and should be brought into play, press not the utmost rigor of the law against the guilty; for the reputation of the stern judge stands not higher than that of the compassionate.

"If perchance you permit the staff of justice to bend, let it be not by the weight of a gift, but by that of mercy.

"If it should happen to you to give judgment in the cause of one who is your enemy, turn your thoughts away from your injury and fix them on the justice of the case.

"Let not your own self-interest blind you in another man's case; for the errors you will thus commit will be most frequently irremediable, or if not, only to be remedied at the expense of your good name and even of your fortune.

"If any handsome woman comes to seek justice of you, turn away your eyes from her tears and your ears from her lamentations, and consider deliberately the merits of her demand, if you would not have your reason swept away by her weeping, and your rectitude by her sighs.

"Abuse not by word him whom you have to punish in deed, for the pain of punishment is enough for the unfortunate without the addition of your insults.

"Bear in mind that the culprit who comes under your jurisdiction is but a miserable man subject to all the propensities of our depraved nature, and so far as may be in your power, show yourself lenient and forbearing; for though the attributes of God are all equal, to our eyes that of mercy is brighter and loftier than that of justice.

"If you follow these precepts and rules, Sancho, your days will be long, your fame eternal, your reward abundant, your felicity unutterable; you will marry your children as you wish; they and your grandchildren will bear titles; you will live in peace and concord with all men; and, when life draws to a close, death will come to you in calm and ripe old age, and the gentle and loving hands of your great-grandchildren will close your eyes.

"What I have thus far addressed to you are instructions for the adornment of your mind; listen now to those which tend to that of the body."

Chapter XLIII

OF THE SECOND SET OF COUNSELS DON QUIXOTE GAVE SANCHO PANZA

Who, hearing the foregoing discourse of Don Quixote, would not have set him down for a person of great good sense and greater rectitude of purpose? But, as has been frequently observed in the course of this great history, he only talked nonsense when he touched on chivalry, and in discussing all other subjects he showed that he had a clear and unbiased understanding; so that at every turn his acts gave the lie to his intellect, and his intellect to his acts; but in the case of these second counsels that he gave Sancho, he showed himself to have a lively turn of humor and displayed conspicuously his wisdom and his folly.

Sancho listened to him with the deepest attention and tried to fix his counsels in his memory, like one who meant to follow them and by their means bring the full promise of his governorship to a happy issue. Don Quixote, then, went on to say:

"With regard to the mode in which you should govern your person and your house, Sancho, the first charge I have to give you is to be clean and to cut your nails, not letting them grow as some do, whose ignorance makes them fancy that long nails are an ornament to their hands, as if those excrescences they neglect to cut were nails and not the talons of some lizard-catching hawk—a filthy and unnatural abuse.

"Go not unbelted and loose, Sancho; for disordered attire is a sign of an unstable mind, unless indeed the slovenliness and slackness is to be set down to slyness, as was the opinion in the case of Julius Cæsar.

"Ascertain cautiously what your office may be worth; and if it will allow you to give liveries to your servants, give them respectable and serviceable, rather than showy and gaudy ones, and divide them between your servants and the poor; that is to say, if you can clothe six pages, clothe three and three poor men, and thus you will have pages for heaven and pages for earth; the vainglorious never think of this new mode of giving liveries.

"Eat not garlic nor onions, lest they find out your boorish origin by the smell; walk slowly and speak deliberately, but not in such a way as to make it seem you are listening to yourself, for all affectation is bad.

"Eat sparingly and dine more sparingly still; for the health of the whole body if forged in the workshop of the stomach.

"Be temperate in drinking, bearing in mind that wine in excess keeps neither secrets nor promises.

"Take care, Sancho, not to chew with both cheeks full, and not to eruct in anybody's presence."

"Eruct?" said Sancho. "I don't know what that means."

"*To eruct*, Sancho," said Don Quixote, "means *to belch*, and that is one of the vulgarest words in the Spanish language, though a very expressive one; and therefore polite persons have had recourse to the Latin, and instead of *belch* say *eruct*, and instead of *belches* say *eructations*. And if some do not understand these terms it matters little, for custom will bring them into use in the course of time, so that they will be readily understood. This is the way a language is enriched; custom and the public are all-powerful there."

"In truth, señor," said Sancho, "one of the counsels and cautions I intend to bear in mind will be not to belch, for I'm constantly doing it."

"*Eruct*, Sancho, not *belch*," said Don Quixote.

"Eruct. I'll say it from now on, and I swear not to forget it," said Sancho.

"Likewise, Sancho," said Don Quixote, "you must not mingle such a quantity of proverbs in your speech as you do; for though proverbs are short maxims, you drag them in so often by the head and shoulders that they savor more of nonsense than of maxims."

"God alone can cure that," said Sancho, "for I have more proverbs in me than a book, and when I speak they come so thick together into my mouth that they fall to fighting among themselves to get out; that's why my tongue lets fly the first that come, though they may not be very suitable. But I'll take care from now on to use such as befit the dignity of my office; for 'in a house where there's plenty, supper is soon cooked,' and 'he who cuts the cards doesn't shuffle,' and 'he who sounds the alarm is safe from harm,' and 'he who gives or retains needs brains.' "

"That's it, Sancho!" said Don Quixote. "Pack, tack, string proverbs together; nobody is hindering you! 'My mother beats me, and I go on with my deceits.' I am advising you to avoid proverbs, and here in a second you have shot out a whole litany of them, which have as much to do with what we are talking about as 'over the hills of Úbeda,' Mind, Sancho, I do not say that a proverb aptly brought in is objectionable; but to pile up and string together proverbs at random makes conversation dull and vulgar.

"When you ride on horseback, do not go lolling with your body on the back of the saddle, nor carry your legs stiff or sticking out from the horse's belly, nor yet sit so loosely that one would suppose you were on Dapple; for the seat on a horse makes gentlemen of some and grooms of others.

"Be moderate in your sleep; for he who does not rise early does not get the benefit of the day; and remember, Sancho, diligence is the mother of good fortune, and indolence, its opposite, never yet attained the object of an honest ambition.

"The last counsel which I will give you now, though it does not tend to bodily improvement, I would have you carry carefully in your memory, for I believe it will be no less useful to you than those I have given you already, and it is this—never engage in a dispute about families, at least in the way of comparing them one with another; for necessarily one of those compared will be better than the other, and you will be hated by the one you have disparaged and get nothing from the one you have exalted.

"Your dress should be hose of full length, a long jacket, and a cloak a trifle longer; loose breeches by no means, for they are becoming neither for gentlemen nor for governors.

"For the present, Sancho, this is all that has occurred to me to advise you; as time goes by and occasions arise my instructions shall follow, if you take care to let me know how you are getting on."

"Señor," said Sancho, "I see well enough that all these things your worship has said to me are good, holy, and profitable. But what use will they be to me if I don't remember any of them? Of course the business about not letting my nails grow and marrying again if I have the chance will not slip my mind. But all that other mess and muddle and jumble—I don't and can't recollect any more of it than of last year's clouds; so it must be given to me in writing. And though I can't read or write, I'll give it to my confessor, to drive it into me and remind me of it whenever it is necessary."

"Ah, sinner that I am!" said Don Quixote, "how bad it looks in governors not to know how to read or write; for let me tell you, Sancho, when a man knows not how to read, or is left-handed, it suggests one of two things; either that he was the son of exceedingly humble and lowly parents, or that he himself was so incorrigible and naughty that neither good company nor good teaching could make any impression on him. It is a great defect that you labor under, and therefore I would have you learn at any rate to sign your name."

"I can sign my name well enough," said Sancho, "because when I was steward of a brotherhood in my village, I learned to make some letters, like the marks on bales of goods, which they told me spelled my name. Besides I can pretend my right hand is crippled and make some one else sign for me, for 'there's a remedy for everything except death.' And since I'll be in command and hold the staff, I can do as I like. Besides, you know what they say about 'the magistrate's son. . . ,'[1] and since I'll be governor, and that's higher than a magistrate, 'gather round and see the show!' Let them insult me and abuse me: 'they'll come for wool and go back shorn'; 'God knows where to find those he loves'; 'the silly sayings of the rich pass for wisdom in the world'; and since I'll be rich, being a governor and at the same time generous, as I mean to be, no fault will be seen in me. 'Only make yourself honey and the flies will come to you;' 'you're only worth as much as you possess,' as my grandmother used to say; and 'you can have no revenge of a man of substance.' "

"Oh, God's curse upon you, Sancho!" exclaimed Don Quixote. "Sixty thousand devils fly away with you and your proverbs! For the last hour you have been stringing them together and inflicting the pangs of torture on me with every one of them. Those proberbs will bring you to the gallows one day, I promise you. Your subjects will take the government from you, or there will be revolts among them. Tell me, where do you pick them up, you ignoramus? How do you apply them, you idiot? For with me, to utter one and make it apply properly, I have to sweat and labor as if I were digging."

"By God, master," said Sancho, "your worship is making a fuss about very little. Why the devil should you get mad if I make use of what is my own? And I've got nothing else or any other capital except proverbs and more proverbs; and I have just thought of four perfect for this occasion and like pears in a basket; but I won't repeat them, for 'silence is saintly.' "[2]

"That, Sancho, you are not," said Don Quixote, "for not only are you not 'saintly silence,' but you are pestilent prattle and perversity. Still, I would like to know what four proverbs have just now come into your memory, for I have been going through my own—and it is a good one—and none occurs to me."

"What can be better," said Sancho, "than 'never put your thumbs between two back teeth'; and 'to "get out of my house" and "what do you want with my wife?" there is no answer'; and 'whether the pitcher hits the stone, or the stone the pitcher, it's a bad business for the pitcher'; all of which fit to perfection? For no one should quarrel with his governor or anyone in authority, because he will come off the worst, like the man who puts his finger between two back teeth, and if they are not back teeth it makes no

1. The full proverb is, "The magistrate's son goes into court with an easy mind."
2. Literally, "Good silence is called Sancho," perhaps from a variant form of *santo*, "holy." The following jokes depend on this pun on *Sancho*.

difference, so long as they are teeth; and to whatever the governor may say there's no answer, any more than to 'get out of my house' and 'what do you want with my wife?' And then, as for that about the stone and the pitcher, a blind man could see that. So that he 'who sees the mote in another's eye should see the beam in his own,' or it will be 'the pot calling the kettle black.' And your worship knows that 'the fool knows more in his own house than the wise man in another's.' "

"No, Sancho," said Don Quixote, "the fool knows nothing, either in his own house or in anybody else's, for no wise structure of any sort can stand on a foundation of folly; but let us say no more about it, Sancho, for if you govern badly, yours will be the fault and mine the shame. But I comfort myself with having done my duty in advising you as earnestly and as wisely as I could; and thus I am released from my obligations and my promise. God guide you, Sancho, and govern you in your government, and deliver me from the misgiving I have that you will turn the whole island upside down, a thing I might easily prevent by explaining to the duke what you are and telling him that all that fat little person of yours is nothing but a sack full of proverbs and impudence."

"Señor," said Sancho, "if your worship thinks I'm not fit for this government, I give it up on the spot; for one dirty nail of my soul is dearer to me than my whole body, and I can live just as well plain Sancho, on bread and onions, as governor, on partridges and capons. And what's more, while we're asleep we're all equal, great and small, rich and poor. But if your worship looks into it, you will see it was your worship alone that put me on to this business of governing, for I know no more about the government of islands than a buzzard. And if there's any reason to think that because of my being a governor the devil will get hold of me, I'd rather go to heaven as Sancho than to hell as a governor."

"By God, Sancho," said Don Quixote, "for those last words you uttered alone, I consider you deserve to be governor of a thousand islands. You have good natural instincts, without which no knowledge is worth anything; commend yourself to God, and try not to swerve in the pursuit of your main object; I mean, always make it your aim and fixed purpose to do right in all matters that come before you, for heaven always helps good intentions; and now let us go to dinner, for I think my lord and lady are waiting for us."

Chapter XLIV

HOW SANCHO PANZA WAS CONDUCTED TO HIS GOVERNMENT, AND OF THE STRANGE ADVENTURE THAT BEFELL DON QUIXOTE IN THE CASTLE

They say that in the true original of this history, as Cide Hamete wrote this chapter—which his interpreter did not translate as he wrote it—there was a kind of complaint the Moor made against himself for having taken in hand a story so dry and of so little variety as this one about Don Quixote, because he found himself forced to speak perpetually of him and Sancho, without venturing to indulge in digressions and episodes more serious and more interesting. He said, too, that to go on with his mind, hand, and pen always restricted to writing on one single subject and speaking through the mouths of a few characters was intolerable drudgery, the result of which was never equal to the author's labor, and that to avoid this he had in the First Part availed himself of the device of stories like "The Ill-advised Curiosity" and "The Captive Captain," which stand, as it were, apart from the story, the others that are given there being incidents which occurred to Don Quixote himself and could not be omitted.

He also thought, he says, that many, engrossed by the interest attaching to the exploits of Don Quixote, would take none in the stories and pass them over hastily or impatiently without noticing the elegance and art of their composition, which would be very manifest were they published by themselves and not as mere adjuncts to the antics of Don Quixote or the foolishness of Sancho. Therefore in this Second Part he thought it best not to insert stories, either separate or interwoven, but only episodes, something like them, arising out of the circumstances the facts present, and even these sparingly, and with no more words than suffice to make them plain; and as he confines and restricts himself to the narrow limits of the narrative, though he has ability, capacity, and brains enough to deal with the whole universe, he requests that his labors may not be despised, and that credit be given him, not for what he writes, but for what he has refrained from writing.

And so he goes on with his story, saying that the day Don Quixote gave the counsels to Sancho, the same afternoon after dinner he handed them to his squire in writing so that he might get some one to read them to him. They had scarcely, however, been given to Sancho when he let them drop, and they fell into the hands of the duke, who showed them to the duchess, and they were both amazed afresh at the madness and wit of Don Quixote.

To carry on the joke, then, the same evening they despatched Sancho with a large following to the village that was to serve him for an island. It happened that the person who had him in charge was a majordomo of the duke's, a man of great discretion and humor—and there can be no humor without discretion—and the same who played the part of the Countess Trifaldi in the comical way that has been already described; and thus qualified, and instructed by his master and mistress as to how to deal with Sancho, he carried out their scheme admirably. Now it came to pass that as soon as Sancho saw this majordomo, he seemed in his features to recognize those of Trifaldi, and turning to his master, he said to him, "Señor, either the devil will carry me off, here on this spot, righteous and believing, or your worship will admit to me that the face of this majordomo of the duke's here is the same as the Distressed One's."

Don Quixote regarded the majordomo attentively, and having done so, said to Sancho, "There is no reason why the devil should carry you off, Sancho, either righteous or believing—and what you mean, I know not. The face of the Distressed One is that of the majordomo, but for all that, the majordomo is not the Distressed One; for his being so would involve a great contradiction. But this is not the time for going into questions of the sort, which would take us into an inextricable labyrinth. Believe me, my friend, we must pray earnestly to our Lord that he deliver us both from wicked wizards and enchanters."

"It is no joke, señor," said Sancho, "because before this, I heard him speak, and it seemed as if the voice of Trifaldi was sounding in my ears. Well, I'll keep quiet. But I'll take care to be on the look-out from now on for any sign that may confirm or do away with my suspicion."

"You will do well, Sancho," said Don Quixote, "and you will let me know all you discover and all that befalls you in your governorship."

Sancho at last set out attended by a great number of people. He was dressed like a lawyer, with a very full, brown plush camel's hair overcoat and a cap of the same material, and mounted Moorish-style on a mule. Behind him, in accordance with the duke's orders, followed Dapple with brand new ass-trappings and ornaments of silk, and from time to time Sancho turned round to look at his donkey, so well pleased to have him with him that he would not have changed places with the emperor of Germany. On taking leave, he kissed the hands of the duke and duchess and got his master's blessing, which Don Quixote gave him with tears and he received blubbering.

Let worthy Sancho go in peace, and good luck to him, Gentle Reader; and look out for two bushels of laughter, which the account of how he behaved himself in office will give you. In the meantime turn your attention to what happened to his master the same night, and if you do not laugh at it, at any rate you will stretch your mouth with a grin; for Don Quixote's adventures must be honored either with wonder or with laughter.

It is recorded, then, that as soon as Sancho had gone, Don Quixote felt his loneliness; and had it been possible for him to revoke the mandate and take away the government from Sancho, he would have done so. The duchess observed his dejection and asked him why he was melancholy; because, she said, if it was for the loss of

Sancho, there were squires, dueñas, and damsels in her house who would wait on him to his full satisfaction.

"The truth is, señora," replied Don Quixote, "that I do feel the loss of Sancho. But that is not the main cause of my looking sad. And of all the offers your excellency makes me, I accept only the good will with which they are made, and as to the remainder, I entreat of your excellency to permit and allow me alone to wait on myself in my chamber."

"Indeed, Señor Don Quixote," said the duchess, "that must not be; four of my damsels, as beautiful as flowers, shall wait on you."

"To me," said Don Quixote, "they will not be flowers but thorns to pierce my heart. They, or anything like them, shall as soon enter my chamber as fly. If your highness wishes to gratify me still further, though I deserve it not, permit me to please myself and wait upon myself in my own room; for I place a barrier between my inclinations and my virtue, and I do not wish to break this rule through the generosity your highness is disposed to display towards me; and, in short, I will sleep in my clothes rather than allow anyone to undress me."

"Say no more, Señor Don Quixote, say no more," said the duchess. "I assure you I will give orders that not even a fly, much less a damsel, shall enter your room. I am not the one to undermine the propriety of Señor Don Quixote, for it strikes me that among his many virtues, the one that is preeminent is that of modesty. Your worship may undress and dress in private and in your own way, as you please and when you please, for there will be no one to hinder you; and in your chamber you will find the vessels necessary for the needs of one who sleeps with his door locked, to the end that no natural needs compel you to open it.

"May the great Dulcinea del Toboso live a thousand years, and may her fame extend all over the surface of the globe, for she deserves to be loved by a knight so valiant and so virtuous; and may kind heaven infuse zeal into the heart of our governor Sancho Panza to finish his whipping speedily, so that the world may once more enjoy the beauty of so grand a lady."

To which Don Quixote replied, "Your highness has spoken like what you are; from the mouth of a noble lady nothing bad can come; and Dulcinea will be more fortunate and better known to the world by the praise of your highness than by all the eulogies the greatest orators on earth could bestow upon her."

"Well, well, Señor Don Quixote," said the duchess, "it is nearly supper time, and the duke is probably waiting; come let us go to supper and retire to rest early, for the journey you made yesterday from Candaya was not such a short one but that it must have caused you some fatigue."

"I feel none, señora," said Don Quixote, "for I would go so far as to swear to your excellency that in all my life I never mounted a quieter beast or a pleasanter paced one than Clavileño; and I don't know what could have induced Malambruno to discard a steed so swift and so gentle and burn it so recklessly as he did."

"Probably," said the duchess, "repenting of the evil he had done to Trifaldi and company and others, and the crimes he must have committed as a wizard and enchanter, he resolved to make away with all the instruments of his craft; and so he burned Clavileño as the chief one and that which mainly kept him restless, wandering from land to land. And by its ashes and the trophy of the placard, the valor of the great Don Quixote of La Mancha is established for ever."

Don Quixote renewed his thanks to the duchess, and having supped, retired to his chamber alone, refusing to allow anyone to enter with him to wait on him, such was his fear of encountering temptations that might lead or drive him to forget his chaste fidelity to his lady Dulcinea. For he had always present to his mind the virtue of Amadís, that flower and mirror of knights-errant.

He locked the door behind him, and by the light of two wax candles undressed himself, but as he was taking off his stockings—O disaster unworthy of such a personage!—there came a burst, not of sighs or anything belying his delicacy or good breeding, but of some two dozen stitches in one of his stockings that made it look like a window lattice. The worthy gentleman was distressed beyond measure, and at that moment he would have given an ounce of silver to have had a bit of green silk thread there; I say green silk, because the stockings were green.

Here Cide Hamete exclaimed as he was writing, "O poverty, poverty! I know not what could have possessed the great Cordoban poet[1] to call you 'holy gift ungratefully received.' Although a Moor, I know well enough from the dealings I have had with Christians that holiness consists in charity, humility, faith, obedience, and poverty; but for all that, I say he must have a great deal of godliness who can find any satisfaction in being poor; unless, indeed, it be the kind of poverty one of their greatest saints refers to, saying, 'possess all things as though ye possessed them not;' which is what they call poverty in spirit.

"But that other poverty—for it is of you I am speaking now—why do you love to fall out with gentlemen and men of good birth more than with other people? Why do you compel them to smear the cracks in their shoes, and to have the buttons of their coats, one silk, another hair, and another glass? Why must their ruffs be always wrinkled like endive leaves, and not crimped with a crimping iron?" (From this we may perceive the antiquity of starch and crimped ruffs.) Then he goes on: "Poor gentleman of good family!

1. Juan de Mena.

always nourshing his honor, dining miserably and in secret, and making a hypocrite of the toothpick with which he sallies out into the street after eating nothing to oblige him to use it! Poor fellow, I say, with his nervous honor, fancying that people perceive a league off the patch on his shoe, the sweatstains on his hat, the shabbiness of his cloak, and the hunger of his stomach!"

All this was brought home to Don Quixote by the bursting of his stitches. However, he comforted himself on perceiving that Sancho had left behind a pair of traveling boots, which he resolved to wear the next day. At last he went to bed, out of spirits and heavy at heart, as much because he missed Sancho as because of the irreparable disaster to his stockings, the stitches of which he would have even taken up with silk of another color, which is one of the greatest signs of poverty a gentleman can show in the course of his never-failing embarrassments.

He put out the candles; but the night was warm and he could not sleep. He rose from his bed and opened slightly a grated window that looked out on a beautiful garden, and as he did so he perceived and heard people walking and talking in the garden. He set himself to listen attentively, and those below raised their voices so that he could hear these words:

"Urge me not to sing, Emerencia, for you know that ever since this stranger entered the castle and my eyes beheld him, I cannot sing but only weep. Besides my lady is a light rather than a heavy sleeper, and I would not for all the wealth of the world that she found us here. And even if she were asleep and did not waken, my singing would be in vain, if this strange Æneas, who has come into my country in order to humiliate me, sleeps on and wakens not to hear it."

"Heed not that, dear Altisidora," replied a voice. "The duchess is no doubt asleep, and everybody in the house save the lord of your heart and disturber of your soul. For just now I perceived him to open the grated window of his chamber, so he must be awake. Sing, my poor sufferer, in a low sweet tone to the accompaniment of your harp; and even if the duchess hears us, we can lay the blame on the heat of the night."

"That is not the point, Emerencia," replied Altisidora. "But I would not want my singing to lay bare my heart or to be thought a light and wanton maiden by those who know not the mighty power of love. But come what may; better a blush on the cheeks than a sore in the heart." And here a harp softly played made itself heard.

As he listened to all this, Don Quixote was in a state of breathless amazement, for immediately the countless adventures like this, with windows, gratings, gardens, serenades, lovemakings, and languishings that he had read of in his trashy books of chivalry, came to his mind. He at once concluded that some damsel of the duchess's was in love with him and that her modesty forced her to keep her passion secret. He feared that she might overcome his resistance, and made an inward resolution not to yield. And commending himself with all his might and soul to his lady Dulcinea, he made up his mind to listen to the music; and to let them know he was there, he gave a pretended sneeze, at which the damsels were not a little delighted, for all they wanted was that Don Quixote should hear them. So having tuned the harp, Altisidora, running her hand across the strings, began this ballad:

O thou that art above in bed,
  Between the holland sheets,
A-lying there from night till morn,
  With outstretched legs asleep;

O thou, most valiant knight of all
  The famed Manchegan breed,
Of purity and virtue more
  Than gold of Araby;

Give ear unto a suffering maid,
  Full-grown but evil-starr'd,
For those two suns of thine have lit
  A fire within her heart.

Adventures seeking thou dost rove,
  To others bringing woe;
Thou scatterest wounds, but, ah, the balm
  To heal them dost withhold!

Say, valiant youth, and so may God
  Thy enterprises speed,
Didst thou the light mid Libya's sands
  Or Jaca's rocks first see?

Did scaly serpents give thee suck?
  Who nursed thee when a babe?
Wert cradled in the forest rude,
  Or gloomy mountain cave?

O Dulcinea may be proud,
  That plump and lusty maid;
For she alone hath had the power
  A tiger fierce to tame.

And she for this shall famous be
  From Tagus to Jarama,
From Manzanares to Genil,
  From Duero to Arlanza.

Fain would I change with her, and give
  A petticoat all fringed
The best and bravest that I have,
  With golden braided trim.

O for to be the happy maid
Thy mighty arms enfold,
Or even sit beside thy bed
And scratch thy flaky poll!

I rave, to favors such as these
Unworthy to aspire;
Thy feet to tickle were enough
For one so low as I.

What caps, what slippers silver-laced,
Would I on thee bestow!
What damask breeches make for thee;
What fine long holland cloaks!

And I would give thee pearls that should
As big as oak-galls show;
So matchless big that each might well
Be called the great "Alone."[2]

Manchegan Nero, look not down
From thy Tarpeian Rock
Upon this burning heart, nor add
The fuel of thy wrath.

A virgin soft and young am I,
Not yet fifteen years old
(I'm only three months past fourteen,
I swear upon my soul).

I hobble not nor do I limp,
All blemish I'm without,
And as I walk my lily locks
Are trailing on the ground.

And though my nose be rather flat,
And though my mouth be wide,
My teeth like topazes exalt
My beauty to the sky.

Thou knowest that my voice is sweet,
That is if thou dost hear;
And I am molded in a form
Somewhat below the mean.

These charms, and many more, are thine,
Spoils won by thy sword, ah!
A damsel of this house am I,
By name Altisidora.

Here the song of the lovesick Altisidora came to an end, while the warmly wooed Don Quixote began to feel alarm; and with a

2. Apparently a reference to a pearl so large it was called *La Sola*, the "alone" or "unique."

deep sigh he said to himself, "O that I should be such an unlucky knight that no damsel can set eyes on me but falls in love with me! O that the peerless Dulcinea should be so unfortunate that they cannot let her enjoy my incomparable constancy in peace! What would ye with her, ye queens? Why do ye persecute her, ye empresses? Why do ye pursue her, ye virgins of from fourteen to fifteen? Leave the unhappy creature to triumph, rejoice, and glory in the lot love has been pleased to bestow upon her in surrendering my heart and yielding up my soul to her. Ye love-smitten throng, know that to Dulcinea only I am soft dough and sugar-paste, but flint to all others; for her I am honey, for you bitter aloes. For me Dulcinea alone is beautiful, wise, virtuous, graceful, and high-bred, and all others are ugly, foolish, frivolous, and low-born.

"Nature sent me into the world to be hers and no other's. Altisidora may weep or sing, the lady for whose sake they beat me in the castle of the enchanted Moor may give way to despair, but I must be Dulcinea's, boiled or roasted, pure, courteous, and chaste, in spite of all the magic-working powers on earth."

And with that he shut the window with a bang and, as much out of temper and out of sorts as if some great misfortune had befallen him, stretched himself on his bed, where we will leave him for the present, as the great Sancho Panza, who is about to set up his famous government, now demands our attention.

Chapter XLV

OF HOW THE GREAT SANCHO PANZA TOOK POSSESSION OF HIS ISLAND, AND OF HOW HE BEGAN TO GOVERN

O perpetual discoverer of the antipodes, torch of the world, eye of heaven, sweet agitator of wine-coolers! Thimbræus here, Phœbus there, now archer, now physician, father of poetry, inventor of music; thou that always risest and, notwithstanding appearances, never settest! To thee, O Sun, by whose aid man begetteth man, to thee I appeal to help me and lighten the darkness of my wit that I may be able to proceed with scrupulous exactitude in giving an account of the great Sancho Panza's government; for without thee I feel myself weak, feeble, and uncertain.

To come to the point, then—Sancho with all his attendants arrived at a village of some thousand inhabitants, and one of the largest the duke possessed. They informed him that it was called the island of Barataria, either because the name of the village was Baratario, or because of the way in which the government had been conferred upon him.[1]

When he reached the gates of the town, which was a walled one,

1. A *barato* (hence Barataria) was a tip which winning gamblers gave to the casino servants. *Barato* is also an adjective meaning "cheap."

the municipality came forth to meet him, the bells rang out a peal, and the inhabitants showed every sign of general satisfaction; and with great pomp they conducted him to the principal church to give thanks to God. Then with burlesque ceremonies they presented him with the keys of the town and acknowledged him as perpetual governor of the island of Barataria. The costume, the beard, and the fat, squat figure of the new governor astonished all those who were not in on the secret, and even all who were, and they were not a few.

Finally, leading him out of the church, they carried him to the judgment seat and seated him on it, and the duke's majordomo said to him, "It is an ancient custom in this island, señor governor, that he who comes to take possession of this famous island is bound to answer a question which shall be put to him, and which must be a somewhat knotty and difficult one; and by his answer the people take the measure of their new governor's wit, and hail with joy or deplore his arrival accordingly."

While the majordomo was making this speech Sancho was gazing at several large letters inscribed on the wall opposite his seat, and as he could not read, he asked what was painted on the wall. The answer was, "Señor, there is written and recorded the day on which your lordship took possession of this island, and the inscription says, 'This day, the so-and-so of such-and-such a month and year, Señor Don Sancho Panza took possession of this island; many years may he enjoy it.' "

"And whom do they call Don Sancho Panza?" asked Sancho.

"Your lordship," replied the majordomo. "For no other Panza but the one who is now seated in that chair has ever entered this island."

"Well then, let me tell you, brother," said Sancho, "I haven't got the 'Don,' nor has any one of my family ever had it. My name is plain Sancho Panza, and Sancho was my father's name, and Sancho was my grandfather's, and they were all Panzas, without any Dons or Doñas tacked on. I suppose that on this island there are more Dons than stones; but never mind; God knows what I mean, and maybe if my government lasts four days I'll weed out these Dons that probably are as big a nuisance as mosquitos, there are so many.[2] Let the majordomo go on with his question, and I'll give the best answer I can, whether the people deplore it or not."

At this instant there came into court two men, one dressed as a farmer, the other as a tailor, for he had a pair of scissors in his hand, and the tailor said, "Señor governor, this farmer and I come before your worship because this honest man came to my shop yes-

2. As has been said in connection with "Don" Quixote, the title was legally restricted to noblemen and prelates, but it was beginning to be assumed by persons who had no claim to it.

terday (for saving everybody's presence I'm a licensed tailor, God be thanked), and putting a piece of cloth into my hands asked me, 'Señor, will there be enough in this cloth to make me a cap?' Measuring the cloth, I said there would. He probably suspected—as I supposed, and I supposed right—that I wanted to steal some of the cloth, led to think so by his own dishonesty and the bad opinion people have of tailors; and he told me to see if there would be enough for two. I guessed what he was thinking, and I said 'yes.' He, still following up his original unworthy notion, went on adding cap after cap, and I 'yes' after 'yes,' until we got as far as five. He has just this moment come for them. I gave them to him, but he won't pay me for my labor; on the contrary, he calls upon me to pay *him* or else return his cloth."

"Is all this true, brother?" said Sancho.

"Yes," replied the man, "but will your worship make him show the five caps he has made me?"

"Willingly," said the tailor. And drawing his hand from under his cloak, he showed five caps stuck on the five fingers of it, and said, "There are the caps this good man asks for; and by God and upon my conscience I haven't a scrap of cloth left, and I'll let the work be examined by the inspectors of the trade."

All present laughed at the number of caps and the novelty of the lawsuit. Sancho set himself to think for a moment and then said, "It seems to me that in this case it is not necessary to deliver long-winded arguments but only to give the judgment of an honest man; and so my decision is that the tailor lose his labor and the farmer the cloth, and that the caps go to the prisoners in the jail; and let there be no more about it."

If the decision which he delivered later concerning the cattle dealer's purse[1] excited the admiration of the bystanders, this provoked their laughter; however, the governor's orders were carried out.

Two old men appeared before the governor, one carrying a cane by way of a walking-stick, and the one who had no stick said, "Señor, some time ago I lent this good man ten crowns in gold as a favor and to do him a service on the condition that he was to return them to me whenever I should ask for them. A long time passed before I asked for them, in order not to put him to any greater difficulties to return them than he was in when I lent them to him. But thinking he was growing careless about payment, I asked for them once and several times; and not only will he not give them back, but he denies that he owes them, and says I never lent him any such crowns, or if I did, that he repaid them. And I have no witnesses either of the loan or the payment, for he never paid me. I

1. See below. Cervantes apparently altered the order of Sancho's judgments, and the word "later" has been added to make sense of the passage.

want your worship to put him under oath, and if he swears he returned them to me, I forgive him the debt here and before God."

"What do you say to this, old man, you with the stick?" said Sancho.

To which the old man replied, "I admit, señor, that he lent them to me; but let your worship lower your staff, and as he leaves it to my oath, I'll swear on it that I gave them back and paid him really and truly."

The governor lowered the staff, and as he did so the old man who had the stick handed it to the other old man to hold for him while he swore, as if he found it in his way; and then laid his hand on the cross of the staff, saying that it was true the ten crowns that were demanded of him had been lent him but that he had with his own hand given them back into the hand of the lender, who, not recollecting it, was always asking for them.

Seeing this, the great governor asked the lender what answer he had to make to what his opponent said. He said that no doubt his debtor had told the truth, for he believed him to be an honest man and a good Christian, and he himself must have forgotten when and how he had given him back the crowns, and that from that time forth he would make no further demand on him.

The debtor took his stick again, and bowing his head left the court. Observing this, and how, without another word, he left, and observing too the resignation of the plaintiff, Sancho buried his head in his bosom and remained for a short space in deep thought, with the forefinger of his right hand on his brow and nose; then he raised his head and ordered them to call back the old man with the stick, for he had already taken his departure. They brought him back, and as soon as Sancho saw him he said. "My good man, give me that stick, for I want it."

"Willingly," said the old man. "Here it is, señor," and he put it into Sancho's hand.

Sancho took it and, handing it to the other old man, said to him, "Go, and God be with you; for now you are paid."

"I, señor!" returned the old man. "Why, is this cane worth ten gold crowns?"

"Yes," said the governor, "or if not I'm the biggest fool in the world. Now you'll see whether I have the brains to govern a whole kingdom." And he ordered the cane to be broken in two, there, in the presence of all. It was done, and in the middle of it they found ten gold crowns. All were filled with amazement and looked upon their governor as another Solomon. They asked him how he had come to the conclusion that the ten crowns were in the cane. He replied that observing how the old man who swore gave the stick to his opponent while he was taking the oath, and swore that he had really and truly given him the crowns, and how as soon as he had finished swearing he asked for the stick again, it came into his head that the sum demanded must be inside it. And from this, Sancho said it might be seen that God sometimes guides those who govern in their judgments, even though they may be fools; besides he had himself heard the curate of his village mention just such another case, and he had so good a memory, that if it were not that he forgot everything he wished to remember, there would not be such a memory on all the island.

To conclude, the old men went off, one crestfallen and the other pleased, all who were present were astonished, and he who was recording the words, deeds, and movements of Sancho could not make up his mind whether he was to look upon him and set him down as a fool or as a man of sense.

As soon as this case was disposed of, there came into court a woman holding on with a tight grip to a man dressed like a well-to-do cattle dealer, and she came forward making a great outcry and exclaiming "Justice, señor governor, justice! and if I don't get it on earth I'll go look for it in heaven. Señor governor, this wicked man caught me in the middle of the fields here and used my body as if it were a filthy rag and, woe is me! got from me what I had preserved for twenty-three years and more, defending it against Moors and Christians, natives and outsiders; and I always as hard as an oak and keeping myself as pure as a salamander in the fire or wool among the brambles, for this good fellow to come now with his clean hands to handle me!"

"It remains to be proved whether this gentleman has clean hands or not," said Sancho. And turning to the man he asked him what he had to say in answer to the woman's charge.

He, in embarrassment, answered "Sirs, I am a poor pig dealer, and this morning I left the village to sell (saving your presence) four pigs, which, between taxes and swindling, I sold for a little less than they were worth. As I was returning to my village I met this lady on the road, and the devil who makes a mess out of everything, made us lie together. I paid her fairly, but she was not satisfied and grabbed me and never let go until she brought me here. She says I raped her, but she lies by the oath I swear or am ready to swear; and this is the whole truth and every particle of it."

The governor then asked him if he had any money in silver; he said he had about twenty ducats in a leather purse inside his shirt. The governor ordered him to take it out and hand it to the plaintiff; he obeyed trembling; the woman took it, and making a thousand salaams to all and praying to God for the long life and health of the señor governor who had such regard for distressed orphans and virgins, she hurried out of court with the purse grasped in both her hands, first looking, however, to see if the money it contained was silver.

As soon as she was gone Sancho said to the cattle dealer, whose tears were already starting and whose eyes and heart were following his purse, "Good fellow, go after that woman and take the purse from her, by force if necessary, and come back with it here." And he did not say it to one who was a fool or deaf, for the man was off like a flash, and ran to do as he was told.

All the bystanders waited anxiously to see the end of the case, and presently both man and woman came back at even closer grips than before, she with her skirt up and the purse in the lap of it, and he struggling hard to take it from her, but all to no purpose, so stout was the woman's defense, she all the while crying out, "Justice from God and the world! See here, señor governor, the shamelessness and boldness of this villain, who in the middle of the town, in the middle of the street, wanted to take from me the purse your worship made him give me."

"And did he take it?" asked the governor.

"Take it!" said the woman, "I'd let my life be taken from me sooner than the purse. Does he think I'm just a little girl? It'll take more than this repulsive wretch to frighten me! Pincers and hammers, mallets and chisels would not get it out of my grip; no, nor lions' claws; the soul from out of my body first!"

"She is right," said the man. "I admit I'm beaten and powerless; I confess I haven't the strength to take it from her." And he let go of her.

Upon this the governor said to the woman, "Let me see that purse, my worthy and sturdy friend." She handed it to him at once, and the governor returned it to the man and said to the rough and unraped damsel, "Sister, if you had shown as much, or only half as much, spirit and vigor in defending your body as you have shown in defending that purse, the strength of Hercules could not have forced you. Be off; God speed and good riddance, and don't show your face on this island or within six leagues of it, under pain of two hundred lashes; be off at once, I say, you shameless, cheating slut."

The woman was cowed and went off disconsolately, hanging her head; and the governor said to the man, "My good man, go home with your money, and God speed you; and in the future, if you don't want to lose it, see that you don't take it into your head to lie with anybody." The man thanked him as clumsily as he could and went his way, and the bystanders were again filled with admiration at their new governor's judgments and sentences.

All this, having been taken down by his chronicler, was at once despatched to the duke, who was looking for it with great eagerness; and here let us leave the good Sancho; for his master, sorely troubled in mind by Altisidora's music, has pressing claims upon us now.

Chapter XLVI

OF THE TERRIBLE BELL-AND-CAT FRIGHT THAT DON QUIXOTE GOT IN THE COURSE OF THE ENAMORED ALTISIDORA'S WOOING

We left Don Quixote wrapped up in the reflections which the music of the enamored maid Altisidora had given rise to. He went to bed with them, and like fleas they would not let him sleep or get a moment's rest, and the runs of his stockings helped them. But as Time is fleet and no obstacle can stay his course, he came riding on the hours, and morning very soon arrived.

Seeing which, Don Quixote left the soft down, and, by no means slothful, dressed himself in his chamois suit and put on his traveling boots to hide the disaster to his stockings. He wrapped himself in his scarlet mantle, put on his head a green velvet cap trimmed with silver, flung across his shoulder the sword belt with his good trenchant sword, took up a large rosary that he always carried with him, and with great solemnity and swagger proceeded to the antechamber where the duke and duchess were already dressed and waiting for him.

But as he passed through a gallery, Altisidora and the other damsel, her friend, were lying in wait for him, and the instant Altisidora saw him she pretended to faint, while her friend caught her in her lap, and began hastily unlacing the bosom of her dress.

Don Quixote observed it, and approaching them said, "I know very well what this seizure arises from."

"I know not from what," replied the friend, "for Altisidora is the healthiest damsel in all this house, and I have never heard her complain all the time I have known her. A plague on all the knights-errant in the world, if they are all ungrateful! Go away, Señor Don Quixote, for this poor child will not come to herself again so long as you are here."

To which Don Quixote returned, "Do me the favor, señora, to let a lute be placed in my chamber tonight, and I will comfort this poor maiden to the best of my power. For in the early stages of love, a prompt disillusion is an approved remedy." And with this he retired, so as not to be recognized by any who might see him there.

He had scarcely withdrawn when Altisidora, recovering from her swoon, said to her companion, "The lute must be left, for no doubt Don Quixote intends to give us some music, and being his, it will not be bad."

They went at once to inform the duchess of what was going on and of the lute Don Quixote asked for, and she, delighted beyond measure, plotted with the duke and her two damsels to play a trick on him that should be amusing but harmless. In high glee they waited for night, which came quickly as the day had come; and as for the day, the duke and duchess spent it in delightful conversation with Don Quixote.

That day the duchess really and truly dispatched one of her pages (who had played the part of the enchanted Dulcinea in the forest) to Teresa Panza, with the letter from her husband Sancho Panza and with the bundle of clothes which he had left to be sent to her. And the duchess charged the page to bring back a good account of everything that happened with Teresa.

When this had been done, and when eleven o'clock came, Don Quixote found a guitar in his chamber. He tuned it, opened the window, and perceived that some persons were walking in the garden. Having passed his fingers over the frets of the guitar and adjusted it as well as he could, he spat and cleared his chest, and then with a voice a little hoarse but on pitch, he sang the following ballad, which he had himself that day composed:

Mighty Love the hearts of maidens
  Doth unsettle and perplex,
And the instrument he uses
  Most of all is idleness.

Sewing, stitching with the needle,
  Having always work to do,
To the poison Love instilleth
  Is the antidote most sure.

And to proper-minded maidens
  Who desire the matron's name
Modesty's a marriage portion,
  Modesty their highest praise.

Men of prudence and discretion,
  Courtiers gay and gallant knights,
With the wanton damsels dally,
  But the modest take to wife.

There are passions, transient, fleeting,
  Loves in hostelries declar'd,
Sunrise loves, with sunset ended,
  When the guest hath gone his way.

Love that springs up swift and sudden,
  Here today, tomorrow flown,
Passes, leaves no trace behind it,
  Leaves no image on the soul.

Painting that is laid on painting
  Maketh no display or show;
Where one beauty's in possession
  There no other can take hold.

Dulcinea del Toboso
  Painted on my heart I wear;

Never from its panel, never,
Can her image be erased.

The quality of all in lovers
Most esteemed is constancy;
'T is by this that love works wonders;
This exalts them to the skies.

Don Quixote had gotten to this point in his song, to which the duke, the duchess, Altisidora, and nearly the whole household of the castle were listening, when all of a sudden from a gallery above, that was exactly over his window, they let down a cord with more than a hundred bells attached to it and immediately after that dumped out a great sack full of cats, which also had bells of smaller size tied to their tails. Such was the din of the bells and the squalling of the cats, that though the duke and duchess were the contrivers of the joke, they were startled by it, while Don Quixote stood paralyzed with fear. And as luck would have it, two or three of the cats made their way in through the grating of his chamber, and flying from one side to the other, made it seem as if there was a legion of devils at large in it. They extinguished the candles that were burning in the room and rushed about seeking some way of escape. The cord with the large bells never ceased rising and falling; and most of the people of the castle, not knowing what was really the matter, were at their wits' end with astonishment.

Don Quixote sprang to his feet, and drawing his sword, began making passes at the grating, shouting out, "Avaunt, malignant enchanters! Avaunt, ye witchcraft-working rabble! I am Don Quixote of La Mancha, against whom your evil machinations avail not nor have any power." And turning upon the cats that were running about the room, he slashed away at them. They dashed at the grating and escaped by it, except one that, finding itself hard pressed by the thrusts of Don Quixote's sword, lept at his face and held on to his nose with tooth and nail, from the pain of which he began to shout his loudest.

The duke and duchess hearing this and guessing what it was ran with all haste to his room, and as the poor gentleman was striving with all his might to detach the cat from his face, they opened the door with a master-key, entered with lights, and witnessed the unequal combat. The duke ran forward to part the combatants, but Don Quixote cried out aloud, "Let no one take him from me; leave me hand to hand with this demon, this wizard, this enchanter; I will teach him, man to man, who Don Quixote of La Mancha is." The cat, however, ignoring these threats, growled and held on; but at last the duke pulled it off and flung it out of the window.

Don Quixote was left with a face as full of holes as a sieve and a nose not in very good condition, and greatly vexed that they did not let him finish the battle he had been so stoutly fighting with that villain of an enchanter. They sent for some medicated oil, and Altisidora herself with her own fair hands bandaged all the wounded parts. As she did so she said to him in a low voice, "All these mishaps have befallen you, stony-hearted knight, for the sin of your hardheartedness and obstinacy; and God grant your squire Sancho may forget to whip himself, so that your dearly beloved Dulcinea may never be released from her enchantment, that you may never come to her marriage bed at least while I who adore you am alive."

To all this Don Quixote made no answer, except heave deep sighs, and then stretched himself on his bed, thanking the duke and duchess for their kindness, not because he stood in any fear of that bell-ringing rabble of enchanters in feline shape, but because he recognized their good intentions in coming to his rescue. The duke and duchess left him to repose and withdrew greatly grieved at the unfortunate result of the joke. For they never thought the adventure would have fallen so heavy on Don Quixote or cost him so dear, because it cost him five days of confinement to his bed, during which he had another adventure, pleasanter than the previous one, which his chronicler will not relate just now in order that he may turn his attention to Sancho Panza, who was proceeding with great diligence and cleverness in his government.

Chapter XLVII

WHEREIN IS CONTINUED THE ACCOUNT OF HOW SANCHO PANZA CONDUCTED HIMSELF IN HIS GOVERNMENT

The history says that from the courtroom they carried Sancho to a sumptuous palace where in a spacious chamber there was a spotless table laid out with royal magnificence. Oboes sounded as Sancho entered the room, and four pages came forward to present him with water for his hands, which Sancho received with great dignity. The music ceased, and Sancho seated himself at the head of the table, for there was only one chair and no other place set on it. A personage, who it appeared afterwards was a physician, came and stood by his side with a whalebone wand in his hand. They then lifted up a fine white cloth covering fruit and a great variety of dishes of different sorts. A man who looked like a student said grace, and a page put a lace-trimmed bib on Sancho, while another who performed the duties of steward placed a dish of fruit before him.

But hardly had he tasted a morsel when the man with the wand touched the plate with it, and they took it away with the utmost speed. The steward, however, brought him another dish, and Sancho proceeded to try it. But before he could get at it, not to say taste it, already the wand had touched it, and a page had carried it off with the same promptitude as the fruit. Sancho seeing this was puzzled and looking from one to another asked if his dinner was to be a disappearing act.

To this the personage with the wand replied, "It is to be eaten, señor governor, as is usual and customary on other islands where there are governors. I, señor, am a physician, and I am paid a salary on this island to serve its governors as such, and I have a much greater regard for their health than for my own, studying day and night and making myself acquainted with the governor's constitution, in order to be able to cure him when he falls sick. The chief thing I have to do is to attend his dinners and suppers and allow him to eat what appears to me to be fit for him and keep from him what I think will do him harm and be injurious to his stomach. That is why I ordered the plate of fruit to be removed as being too moist, and that other dish I ordered to be removed as being too hot and containing many spices that stimulate thirst. For he who drinks much kills and consumes the radical moisture wherein life consists."

"Well then," said Sancho, "that dish of roast partridges there that seems properly seasoned will not do me any harm."

To this the physician replied, "Of those my lord the governor shall not eat so long as I live."

"Why so?" said Sancho.

"Because," replied the doctor, "our master Hippocrates, the pole star and beacon of medicine, says in one of his aphorisms *omnis saturatio mala, perdicis autem pessima,* which means 'all repletion is bad, but that of partridge is the worst of all.' "

"In that case, señor doctor," said Sancho, "please indicate among the dishes that are on the table what will do me most good and least harm, and let me eat it, without tapping it with your stick. For by the life of the governor, and so may God suffer me to enjoy it, I'm dying of hunger. And in spite of the doctor and all he may say, to deny me food is the way to take my life instead of prolonging it."

"Your worship is right, señor governor," said the physician. "And therefore your worship, in my opinion, should not eat those stewed rabbits there, because it is a furry kind of food. If that veal were not roasted and pickled, you might try it; but it is out of the question."

"That big steaming dish beyond it," said Sancho, "seems to me to be a stew, and out of the variety of things in such stews, I can't fail to find something tasty and good for me."

"*Absit,*" said the doctor. "Far from us be any such foolish idea! There is nothing in the world less nourishing than a stew. Let canons, or rectors of colleges, or peasants' weddings have stews, but let us have none of them on the tables of governors, where everything that is present should be delicate and refined. And the reason is that always, everywhere, and by everybody, simple medicines are more esteemed than compound ones, for we cannot go wrong in those that are simple, while in the compound we may, by merely altering the quantity of the things composing them.

"But what I am of opinion the governor should eat now in order to preserve and fortify his health is a hundred or so crisp wafers and a few thin slices of quince preserve, which will settle his stomach and help his digestion."

Sancho on hearing this leaned back in his chair and surveyed the doctor steadily, and in a solemn tone asked him what his name was and where he had studied.

He replied, "My name, señor governor, is Doctor Pedro Recio de Agüero, I am a native of a place called Tirteafuera which lies between Caracuel and Almodóvar del Campo, on the right-hand side, and I have the degree of doctor from the university of Osuna."

To which Sancho, glowing all over with rage, returned, "Then let Doctor Pedro Recio de Malagüero, native of Tirteafuera,[1] a place that's on the right-hand side as we go from Caracuel to Almodóvar del Campo, graduate of Osuna, get out of my sight at once; or I swear by the sun I'll take a stick, and beginning with him, I'll beat every doctor off the whole island; at least those I know to be ignorant. I respect learned, wise, sensible doctors and honor them as divine persons. I repeat: if Pedro Recio doesn't get out of here, I'll take this chair I am sitting on and break it over his head. And if they call me to account for it, I'll clear myself by saying I served God in killing a bad doctor—a public executioner. And now give me something to eat or else take your government; for a trade that does not feed its master is not worth two beans."

The doctor was dismayed when he saw the governor in such a rage, and he would have left the room but that the same instant a post-horn sounded in the street. The steward put his head out of the window and then turned around and said, "It's a courier from my lord the duke, no doubt with some despatch of importance."

The courier came in all sweating and flurried, and taking a paper from his bosom, placed it in the governor's hands. Sancho handed it to the majordomo and ordered him to read the address, which ran thus: *To Don Sancho Panza, Governor of the Island of Barataria, into his own hands or those of his secretary.* Sancho when he heard this said, "Which of you is my secretary?" "I am, señor," said one of those present, "for I can read and write, and am a Biscayan."[2] "With that addition," said Sancho, "you might be secretary to the emperor himself. Open this paper and see what it says." The new-born secretary obeyed, and having read the contents, said the matter was one to be discussed in private. Sancho ordered the chamber to be cleared, the majordomo and the steward only remaining; so the doctor and the others withdrew, and then the secretary read the letter, which was as follows:

It has come to my knowledge, Señor Don Sancho Panza, that certain enemies of mine and of the island are about to make a

1. *Recio* means "harsh," *Agüero* means "omen," and *mal agüero*, "evil omen." *Tirteafuera* means something like "Get out of the way!"

2. Biscayans were known for their loyalty.

furious attack upon it some night, I do not know when. It behooves you to be on the alert and keep watch, that they may not surprise you. I also know by trustworthy spies that four persons have entered the town in disguise in order to take your life, because they stand in dread of your great capacity; keep your eyes open and take heed who approaches you to address you, and eat nothing that is presented to you. I will take care to send you aid if you find yourself in difficulty, but in all things you will act as may be expected of your judgment. From this place, the sixteenth of August, at four in the morning.

Your friend,
THE DUKE

Sancho was astonished, and those present appeared to be so too. Turning to the majordomo, Sancho said to him, "What we have got to do first, and it must be done at once, is to put Doctor Recio in jail, because he'll be the one, if anybody is going to kill me, and by a slow death and the worst of all, which is hunger."

"Furthermore," said the steward, "it is my opinion your worship should not eat anything that is on this table, for it was a present from some nuns; and as they say, 'behind the cross there's the devil.' "

"I don't deny it," said Sancho. "So for the present give me a piece of bread and four pounds or so of grapes; no poison can come in them. The fact is I can't go on without eating, and if we are to be prepared for these battles that are threatening us, we must be well provisioned. 'A full belly makes a stout heart.'

"And you, Mr. Secretary, answer my lord the duke and tell him that all his commands will be obeyed to the letter, as he directs. And say from me to my lady the duchess that I kiss her hands, and that I beg her not to forget to send my letter and bundle to my wife Teresa Panza by a messenger. I will take it as a great favor and will make every effort to serve her in all that lies within my power. While you are about it you may enclose greetings to my master Don Quixote that he may see I am grateful. And as a good secretary and a good Biscayan you may add whatever you like and whatever will come in best. Now clear the table and give me something to eat, and I'll be ready to meet all the spies and assassins and enchanters that may come against me or my island."

At this instant a page entered saying, "Here is a farmer on business, who wants to speak to your lordship on a matter of great importance, he says."

"It's very odd," said Sancho, "the ways of these men of business. Is it possible they can be such fools as not to see that an hour like this is no hour for coming on business? We who govern and we who are judges—are we not men of flesh and blood, and are we not to be allowed the time required for taking rest, unless they'd have us made of marble? By God and on my conscience, if the government remains in my hands (which I have a notion it won't), I'll cut some of these businessmen down to size. However, tell this good man to come in; but make sure first of all that he is not some spy or one of my assassins."

"No, my lord," said the page. "He looks like a simple fellow, and either I know very little or he is as good as good bread."

"There is nothing to be afraid of," said the majordomo, "for we are all here."

"Would it be possible, Mr. Steward," said Sancho, "now that Doctor Pedro Recio is not here, to let me eat something solid and substantial, even if it were only a piece of bread and an onion?"

"Tonight at supper," said the steward, "the shortcomings of the dinner will be made good, and your lordship shall be fully contented."

"God grant it," said Sancho.

The farmer now came in, a nice-looking man that one could tell a mile off was an honest fellow and a good soul. The first thing he said was, "Which one is the lord governor here?"

"Who else could it be," said the secretary, "but the one who is seated in the chair?"

"Then I humble myself before him," said the farmer; and going down on his knees he asked for his hand to kiss. Sancho refused, and ordered him stand up and say what he wanted. The farmer obeyed and then said, "I am a farmer, señor, a native of Miguelturra, a village two leagues from Ciudad Real."

"Another Tirteafuera!" said Sancho. "Go on, brother; I know Miguelturra very well, I can tell you, for it's not very far from my own town."

"The case is this, señor," continued the farmer. "By God's mercy I am happily married with the blessing of the holy Roman Catholic Church. I have two sons, students, and the younger is studying to become bachelor, and the elder to be licentiate. I am a widower, for my wife died, or more properly speaking, an incompetent doctor killed her by giving her a purge when she was pregnant. And if it had been God's will for the child to be born, and it had been a boy, I would have put him to study to be a doctor, so that he might not envy his brothers the bachelor and the licentiate."

"So that if your wife had not died, or had not been killed, you would not now be a widower," said Sancho.

"No, señor, certainly not," said the farmer.

"We've got that much settled," said Sancho. "Get on with it, brother, because this is more like bed-time than business-time."

"Well then," said the farmer, "this son of mine who is going to be a bachelor fell in love with a local girl called Clara Palsy, daughter of Andrés Palsy, a very rich farmer. This name Palsy does not come to them by ancestry or descent, but because all the family are paralytics, and for a better name they call them Palsy. Though to tell the truth the girl is as fair as an oriental pearl and like a flower of the field, if you look at her on the right side; on the left not so much, because on that side she lacks an eye that she lost from small-pox; and though her face is thickly and deeply pitted, those who love her say they are not pits but the graves where the hearts of her lovers are buried. She is so neat that not to soil her face she carries her nose turned up, as they say, as if it was running away from her mouth. And with all this she looks extremely well, for she has a wide mouth; and except for ten or twelve missing teeth and molars, she might compare and compete with the most beautiful. Of her lips I say nothing, for they are so fine and thin that, if lips could be rolled like yarn, you could make a skein of them; but being of a different color from ordinary lips, they are wonderful, for they are mottled, blue, green, and purple.

"I hope my lord governor will pardon me for painting so minutely the charms of a girl who sooner or later will be my daughter; for I love her, and I don't find her unattractive."

"Paint what you will," said Sancho. "I enjoy your painting, and if I had eaten, there could be no dessert more to my taste than your portrait."

"The dessert is yet to come," said the farmer. "There will be time enough for it later. I can tell you, señor, if I could paint her gracefulness and her tall figure, it would astonish you; but that is impossible because she is bent double with her knees up to her mouth. Nevertheless it is easy to see that if she could stand up she'd knock her head against the ceiling. And she would have given her hand to my bachelor before now, only that she can't stretch it out, for it's shriveled; but still one can see its elegance and fine make by its long ridged fingernails."

"That will do, brother," said Sancho. "Consider her described from head to foot. What is it you want now? Come to the point without all this beating around the bush and all these scraps and additions."

"I want your worship, señor," said the farmer, "to do me the favor of giving me a letter of recommendation to the girl's father, begging him to be so good as to let this marriage take place, as we are not ill-matched either in the gifts of fortune or of nature; for to tell the truth, señor governor, my son is possessed, and there is not a day but the evil spirits torment him three or four times. And from having once fallen into the fire, he has his face puckered up like a piece of parchment and his eyes watery and always running. But he has the disposition of an angel, and if he were not always hitting and punching himself, he'd be a saint."

"Is there anything else you want, my good man?" said Sancho.

"There's another thing I'd like," said the farmer, "but I'm afraid to mention it; however, out with it! I've got to get it off my chest, come what may. I mean, señor, that I'd like your worship to give me three hundred or six hundred ducats as a help to my bachelor's dowry—I mean, to help him in setting up house. Because after all, they have to live by themselves, without being subject to the interference of their in-laws."

"Is there anything else you'd like?" said Sancho. "Don't hold back from mentioning it out of bashfulness or modesty."

"No, indeed there is not," said the farmer.

The moment he said this, the governor rose to his feet, and seizing the chair he had been sitting on exclaimed, "By all that's good, you ill-bred, boorish clod, if you don't get out of here at once and hide yourself from my sight, I'll lay your head open with this chair. You shifty son-of-a-bitch, you devil's own painter; you come to ask me for six hundred ducats at this hour? Where would I get them, you stinking lout? And why should I give them to you if I had them, you sly numbskull? What have I to do with Miguelturra or the whole Palsy family? Get out I say, or by the life of my lord the duke I'll do as I said. You're not from Miguelturra, but some crafty devil sent here from hell to tempt me. Why, you wretch, I have not yet had the governorship half a day, and you expect me to have six hundred ducats already!"

The steward made signs to the farmer to leave the room, which he did with his head down, and to all appearance in terror that the governor might carry his threats into effect, for the rogue knew very well how to play his part.

But let us leave Sancho in his wrath, and peace be with them all; and let us return to Don Quixote, whom we left with his face bandaged and doctored after the cat wounds, of which he was not cured for eight days; and on one of these there befell him what Cide Hamete promises to relate with that exactitude and truth with which he is accustomed to set forth everything connected with this great history, however minute it may be.

Chapter XLVIII

OF WHAT BEFELL DON QUIXOTE WITH DOÑA RODRÍGUEZ, THE DUCHESS'S DUEÑA, TOGETHER WITH OTHER OCCURRENCES WORTHY OF RECORD AND ETERNAL REMEMBRANCE

Exceedingly moody and dejected was the sorely wounded Don Quixote, with his face bandaged and marked, not by the hand of God, but by the claws of a cat, mishaps incidental to knight-errantry. Six days he remained without appearing in public, and one night as he lay awake thinking of his misfortunes and of Altisidora's pursuit of him, he perceived that some one was opening the door of his room with a key, and he at once assumed that the enamored damsel was coming to make an assault upon his chastity and put him in danger of being unfaithful to his lady Dulcinea del Toboso.

"No," said he, firmly persuaded of the truth of his idea (and he said it loud enough to be heard), "the greatest beauty upon earth shall not avail to make me renounce my adoration of her whom I bear stamped and graved in the core of my heart and the secret depths of my breast. Whether thou, oh lady mine, art transformed into an onion-eating country wench or into a nymph of golden Tagus weaving a web of silk and gold, whether Merlin or Montesinos holds thee captive where they will; where'er thou art, thou art mine, and where'er I have been or shall be, I am thine."

The very instant he had uttered these words, the door opened. He stood up on the bed wrapped from head to foot in a yellow satin coverlet, with a cap on his head, and his face and his mustache bandaged—his face because of the scratches, and his mustache to keep it from drooping and falling down—in which attire he looked like the most extraordinary phantom that could be conceived. He kept his eyes fixed on the door, and just as he was expecting to see the love-smitten and unhappy Altisidora make her appearance, he saw coming in a most venerable dueña, in a white hemmed veil, so long that it covered and enveloped her from head to foot. Between the fingers of her left hand she held a short lighted candle, while with her right she shaded it to keep the light from her eyes, which were covered by spectacles of great size. She advanced with noiseless steps, treading very softly.

Don Quixote kept an eye upon her from his watchtower, and observing her costume and noting her silence, he concluded that it must be some witch or sorceress that was coming in such a guise to work him some mischief, and he began crossing himself at a great rate. The specter gradually advanced, and on reaching the middle of the room, looked up and saw the energy with which Don Quixote was crossing himself. And if he was scared by seeing such a figure as hers, she was terrified at the sight of his. The moment she saw his tall yellow form with the coverlet and the bandages that disfigured him, she gave a loud scream, and exclaiming, "Jesus! what's this I see?" let the candle fall in her fright, and then finding herself in the dark, turned to leave, but stumbling on her skirts in her consternation, she fell flat.

Don Quixote in his trepidation began saying, "I conjure thee, phantom, or whatever thou art, tell me what thou art and what thou wouldst with me. If thou art a soul in torment, say so, and all that my powers can do I will do for thee; for I am a Catholic Christian and love to do good to all the world, and to this end I have embraced the order of knight-errantry to which I belong, the province of which extends to doing good even to souls in purgatory."

The unfortunate dueña hearing herself thus conjured, by her own fear guessed Don Quixote's, and in a low plaintive voice answered, "Señor Don Quixote—if you are indeed Don Quixote—I am no phantom or specter or soul in purgatory, as you seem to think, but Doña Rodríguez, dueña of honor to my lady the duchess, and I come to you with one of those grievances your worship is always redressing."

"Tell me, Señora Doña Rodríguez," said Don Quixote, "do you perchance come to transact any go-between business? Because I must tell you I am not available for anybody's purpose, thanks to the peerless beauty of my lady Dulcinea del Toboso. In short, Señora Doña Rodríguez, if you will leave out and put aside any love messages, you may go and light your candle and come back, and we will discuss all the commands you have for me and whatever you wish, except, as I say, any suggestive communications."

"I carry somebody's messages, señor?" said the dueña. You don't know me very well. No, I'm not far enough advanced in years to take to any such childish tricks. God be praised I have a soul in my body still, and all my teeth and molars in my mouth, except one or two that the colds, so common here in Aragón have robbed me of.

"But wait a little, while I go and light my candle, and I will return immediately and lay my sorrows before you as before one who relieves those of all the world." And without staying for an answer she left the room and left Don Quixote tranquilly meditating while he waited for her.

A thousand thoughts at once suggested themselves to him on the subject of this new adventure, and it struck him as being ill done and worse advised in him to expose himself to the danger of breaking his plighted faith to his lady; and said he to himself, "Who knows but that the devil, being wily and cunning, may be trying now to entrap me with a dueña, having failed with empresses, queens, duchesses, marchionesses, and countesses? Many a time have I heard it said by many a man of sense that he will sooner tempt you with some flat-nosed wench than a beautiful Roman-nosed one. Who knows but this privacy, this opportunity, this silence, may awaken my sleeping desires and lead me in these my latter years to fall where I have never stumbled? In cases of this sort it is better to flee than to await the battle. But I must be out of my senses to think and utter such nonsense; for it is impossible that a long, white-hooded, spectacled dueña could stir up or excite a wanton thought in the most immoral bosom in the world. Is there a dueña on earth that has fair flesh? Is there a dueña in the world who is not meddlesome, sour-faced, and prudish?

"Avaunt, then, ye dueña crew, useless when it comes to human pleasures! Oh, but that lady did well who, they say, had at the end of her sitting room a couple of statues of dueñas with spectacles and lace-maker's cushions, as if at their needlework, and those statues served quite as well to give an air of propriety to the room as if they had been real dueñas."

So saying he leaped off the bed, intending to close the door and not allow Señora Rodríguez to enter; but as he went to shut it Señora Rodríguez returned with a wax candle lighted, and having a closer view of Don Quixote, with the coverlet round him and his bandages and nightcap, she was alarmed afresh, and retreating a couple of paces, exclaimed, "Am I safe, sir knight? For I don't look upon it as a sign of very great chastity that your worship should have got up out of bed."

"I may well ask the same, señora," said Don Quixote. "And I do ask whether I shall be safe from being assaulted and ravished."

"Of whom and against whom do you demand that security, sir knight?" said the dueña.

"Of you and against you I ask it," said Don Quixote. "For I am not marble, nor are you brass, nor is it now ten o'clock in the morning, but midnight—or a trifle past it I fancy—and we are in a room more secluded and retired than the cave could have been where the treacherous and daring Æneas enjoyed the fair, soft-hearted Dido. But give me your hand, señora. I require no better protection than my own continence and my own sense of propriety, as well as that which is inspired by that venerable headdress." And so saying he kissed his own right hand and took Doña Rodríguez', she yielding it to him with similar ceremonies.[1] (And here Cide Hamete inserts a parenthesis in which he says that to have seen the pair marching from the door to the bed, linked hand in hand in this way, he would have given the better of the two cloaks he owned.)

Don Quixote finally got into bed, and Doña Rodriguez took her seat on a chair at some little distance from his couch, without taking off her spectacles or putting aside the candle. Don Quixote wrapped the bedclothes round him and covered himself up completely, leaving nothing but his face visible, and as soon as they had both regained their composure he broke silence, saying, "Now, Señora Doña Rodríguez, you may unbosom yourself and express everything you have in your sorrowful heart and afflicted breast, for I shall listen to you with chaste ears and aid you with sympathetic efforts."

"I believe it," replied the dueña. "From your worship's gentle and winning presence only such a Christian answer could be expected. The fact is, then, Señor Don Quixote, that though you see me seated in this chair, here in the middle of the kingdom of Aragón, and in the attire of a despised, outcast dueña, I am from the Asturias of Oviedo, and from a family with which many of the best of the province are connected by blood.

1. Apparently an oath, like "cross my heart."

"But my bad luck and the improvidence of my parents, who, without knowing how, were unexpectedly reduced to poverty, brought me to the court of Madrid, where as a provision and to avoid greater misfortunes, my parents placed me as seamstress in the service of a lady of quality, and I would have you know that for hemming and sewing I have never been surpassed by any all my life.

"My parents left me in service and returned to their own country, and a few years later went, no doubt, to heaven, for they were extremely good Catholic Christians. I was left an orphan with nothing but the miserable wages and trifling presents that are given to servants of my sort in palaces. But about this time, without any encouragement on my part, one of the squires of the household fell in love with me, a man somewhat advanced in years, full-bearded and respectable, and above all as blue-blooded as the king himself, for he came from an old family from La Montaña.

"We did not carry on our loves with such secrecy but that they came to the knowledge of my lady, and she, not to have any fuss about it, had us married with the full sanction of the holy mother Roman Catholic Church, of which marriage a daughter was born to put an end to my good fortune, if I had any; not that I died in childbirth, for I passed through it safely and in due time, but because shortly afterwards my husband died of a certain shock he received, and had I time to tell you of it I know your worship would be surprised." And here she began to weep bitterly and said, "Pardon me, Señor Don Quixote, if I am unable to control myself, for every time I think of my unfortunate husband my eyes fill up with tears.

"God bless me, with what an air of dignity he used to carry my lady behind him on a stout mule as black as jet! For in those days they did not use coaches or sedan-chairs, as they do now, and ladies rode behind their squires. This much at least I cannot help telling, so that you may observe the good breeding and punctiliousness of my worthy husband. As he was turning into Santiago Street in Madrid, which is rather narrow, one of the city magistrates with two bailiffs before him was coming out of it, and as soon as my good squire saw him he wheeled his mule around, as if he would turn and accompany him. My lady, who was riding behind him, said to him in a low voice, 'What are you doing, you wretch? Don't you see that I am here?' The magistrate like a polite man pulled up his horse and said to him, 'Proceed, señor, for it is I who ought to accompany my lady Doña Casilda'—for that was my mistress's name.

"Still my husband, cap in hand, persisted in trying to accompany the magistrate, and seeing this, my lady, filled with rage and vexation, pulled out a big pin, or, I rather think, an awl, out of her needle case and drove it into his back with such force that my husband gave a loud yell and twisted his body so that he knocked his mistress to the ground. Her two lackeys ran to help her up, and the magistrate and the bailiffs did the same; the Guadalajara Gate was all in commotion—I mean the idlers congregated there. My mistress came back on foot, and my husband hurried to a barber's shop protesting that he was run right through the guts. The courtesy of my husband was so talked of that the boys gave him no peace in the street; and on this account, and because he was somewhat shortsighted, my lady the duchess dismissed him. And it was his sorrow over this I am convinced beyond a doubt that brought on his death.

"I was left a helpless widow, with a daughter on my hands increasing in beauty like the foam on the sea. At length, however, as I had the reputation of being an excellent needlewoman, my lady the duchess, then newly married to my lord the duke, offered to take me with her to this kingdom of Aragón, and my daughter also. And here as time went by my daughter grew up and with her all the charm in the world: she sings like a lark, knows all the fast court dances and does all the popular steps like some street wench, reads and writes like a schoolmaster, and does sums like a miser. Of her neatness I say nothing, for the running water is not purer; and her age is now, if my memory serves me, sixteen years five months and three days, one more or less.

"To come to the point, the son of a very rich farmer, living in a village of my lord the duke's not very far from here, fell in love with this girl of mine; and in short, I do not know how they came together, and under the promise of marrying her he made a fool of my daughter, and will not keep his word. And though my lord the duke is aware of it (for I have complained to him, not once but many and many a time, and entreated him to order the farmer to marry my daughter), he turns a deaf ear and will scarcely listen to me; the reason being that as the deceiver's father is so rich, and lends him money, and is constantly going security for his debts, he does not like to offend or annoy him in any way.

"Now, señor, I want your worship to take it upon yourself to redress this wrong either by entreaty or by arms; for by what everybody says, you came into it to redress grievances and right wrongs and help the unfortunate. Let your worship consider the unprotected condition of my daughter, her beauty, her youth, and all the perfections I have said she possesses; and before God and on my conscience, out of all the damsels my lady has, there is not one that comes up to the sole of her shoe. And the one they call Altisidora and look upon as the boldest and gayest of them, in comparison with my daughter, does not come within two leagues of her. For I would have you know, señor, that all that glitters is not gold; because this little Altisidora has more forwardness than good looks and more impudence than modesty. Besides being not very healthy, for she has such a disagreeable breath that one cannot bear to be near her for a moment; and even my lady the duchess—but I'll hold my tongue, for they say that walls have ears."

"For heaven's sake, Doña Rodríguez, what ails my lady the duchess?" asked Don Quixote.

"Since you put it that way," replied the dueña, "I cannot help answering the question and telling the whole truth. Señor Don Quixote, have you observed the beauty of my lady the duchess, that complexion of hers like a smooth, polished sword, those two cheeks of milk and roses—for in the one she has the sun and in the other the moon—that liveliness with which she walks or rather seems to skim the earth, so that she seems to radiate health wherever she passes? Well, let me tell you she may first of all thank God for this, and next, two running sores that she has, one in each leg, by which all the evil humors, of which the doctors say she is full, are discharged."[2]

"Blessed Virgin!" exclaimed Don Quixote. "And is it possible that my lady the duchess has drains of that sort? I would not have believed it if barefoot friars had told me; but as the lady Doña Rodríguez says so, it must be so. But surely such sores, and in such places, do not discharge humors, but perfume. Verily, I do believe now that this practice of making sores is a very important matter for the health."

Don Quixote had hardly said this, when the chamber door flew open with a loud bang, and with the start the noise gave her, Doña Rodríguez dropped the candle from her hand, and the room was left as dark as a wolf's mouth, as the saying is. Suddenly the poor dueña felt two hands seize her by the throat, so tightly that she could not croak, while some one else, without uttering a word, very briskly lifted her petticoats, and with what seemed to be a slipper began to spank her so heartily that anyone would have felt pity for her. And although Don Quixote felt it, he never stirred from his bed. He did not know what it could be, and he lay quiet and silent, apprehensive that his turn for a drubbing might be coming.

Nor was the apprehension an idle one; for leaving the dueña (who did not dare to cry out) well paddled, the silent executioners fell upon Don Quixote, and stripping him of the sheet and the coverlet, they pinched him so fast and so hard that he was driven to defend himself with his fists, and all this in marvelous silence. The battle lasted nearly half an hour, and then the phantoms fled; Doña Rodríguez gathered up her skirts, and bemoaning her misfortune went out without saying a word to Don Quixote. He, sorely pinched, puzzled, and dejected, remained alone, and there we will

2. Doctors made these sores in the belief that the fluids which drained out were harmful humors.

leave him, wondering who could have been the perverse enchanter who had reduced him to such a state. But that shall be told in due time, for Sancho claims our attention, and the methodical arrangement of the story demands it.

Chapter XLIX

OF WHAT HAPPENED TO SANCHO IN MAKING THE ROUNDS OF HIS ISLAND

We left the great governor angered and irritated by that portrait-painting rogue of a farmer who, instructed by the majordomo, as the majordomo was by the duke, tried to play a joke on him. He however, stupid, rough, and stocky as he was, held his own against them all, saying to those around him and to Doctor Pedro Recio, who as soon as the private business of the duke's letter was disposed of had returned to the room, "Now I see plainly that judges and governors ought to be and must be made of brass to endure the demands of petitioners that at all hours and all times insist on being heard, and having their business despatched, and their own affairs and no others attended to, come what may. And if the poor judge does not hear them and settle the matter—either because he can't or because that is not the time set apart for hearing them—they immediately criticize him, and run him down, and ruin his reputation, and even pick holes in his pedigree.

"You silly, stupid petitioner, don't be in a hurry; wait for the proper time and opportunity for doing business. Don't come at dinner time or at bedtime. Judges are only flesh and blood and must give to Nature what she naturally demands of them; all except myself, for in my case I give her nothing to eat, thanks to Señor Doctor Pedro Recio Tirteafuera here, who wants me to die of hunger and declares that this form of death is life. And I hope God gives the same sort of life to him and all his kind—I mean the bad doctors; for the good ones deserve palms and laurels."

All who knew Sancho Panza were astonished to hear him speak so elegantly and did not know what to attribute it to unless perhaps duties and grave responsibility either sharpen or dull men's wits. At last Doctor Pedro Recio Agüero of Tirteafuera promised to let him have supper that night, though it might go against all the aphorisms of Hippocrates. With this the governor was satisfied and looked forward to the approach of night and supper time with great eagerness. And though time, to his mind, stood still and made no progress, nevertheless the hour he so longed for came, and they gave him a beef salad with onions and some rather stale boiled calves' feet. At this he fell to with more enthusiasm than if they have given him quails from Milan, pheasants from Rome, veal from Sorrento, partridges from Morón, or geese from Lavajos.

Turning to the doctor at supper he said to him, "Look here, señor doctor; in the future don't trouble yourself about giving me dainty things or fancy dishes to eat, for it will only upset my stomach. It is accustomed to goat, cow, bacon, dried beef, turnips, and onions; and if by any chance it is given this palace food, it gets queasy and sometimes nauseated. What the steward can do is to serve me what they call 'leftovers stew' (and the riper they are the better they smell); and he can cram whatever he likes into them, so long as it is good to eat, and I'll be obliged to him and will pay him back some day. But let nobody play any tricks on me. Live and let live. Let's eat together in peace, for when God sends the dawn, he sends it for all. I mean to govern this island without giving up a right or taking a bribe; let everyone keep his eyes open and look out for himself. I can tell you that I'm as mean as the devil when I'm riled,[1] and if you drive me to it you'll see something that will astonish you. No; play fair with me, and I'll play fair with you.

"Señor governor," said the carver, "your worship is certainly right in everything you have said; and I promise you in the name of all the inhabitants of this island that they will serve your worship with all zeal, affection, and goodwill, for the mild form of government you have begun with leaves them no reason for doing or thinking anything to your worship's disadvantage."

"That I believe," said Sancho, "and they would be fools if they did or thought anything else. Again I say, see to my feeding and my Dapple's, for that is the great point and what is most to the purpose; and when the time comes, let's make the rounds, for it is my intention to rid this island of any kind of immorality and of vagrants, loafers, and idlers. I would have you know, my friends, that lazy good-for-nothings are the same thing in a State as the drones in a hive, that eat up the honey the worker-bees make. I mean to protect the peasants, to preserve the gentleman's privileges, to reward the virtuous, and above all to respect religion and honor its ministers. What do you say to that, my friends? Is there anything in what I say, or am I talking through my hat?"

"There is so much in what your worship says, señor governor," said the majordomo, "that I am filled with wonder when I see a man like your worship, entirely without learning (for I believe you have none) say such things, and so full of maxims and sage remarks, very different from what was expected of your worship's intelligence by those who sent us or by us who came here. Every day we see something new in this world; jokes become realities, and the jokers find the tables turned on them."

Night came, and with the permission of Doctor Pedro Recio, the

1. A conjecture; Sancho says, "The devil is in Cantillana, and if you drive me to it, . . ." etc. Some interpret it to mean, roughly, "There's something wrong here."

governor had supper. They then got ready to make the rounds, and he started with the majordomo, the secretary, the steward, the chronicler charged with recording his deeds, and bailiffs and notaries enough to form a fair-sized squadron. In the middle marched Sancho with his staff, as fine a sight as one could wish to see. Only a few streets of the town had been traversed when they heard the noise of clashing swords. They hastened to the spot and found that the combatants were but two, who seeing the authorities approaching stood still, and one of them exclaimed, "Help in the name of God and the king! Are men to be allowed to rob in the middle of this town, and rush out and attack people in the very streets?"

"Be calm, my good man," said Sancho, "and tell me what the cause of this quarrel is; for I am the governor."

Said the other combatant, "Señor governor, I will tell you in a very few words. Your worship must know that this gentleman has just now won more than a thousand *reales* in that gambling house opposite, and God knows how. I was there and gave more than one doubtful point in his favor, very much against what my conscience told me. He made off with his winnings, and when I thought he was going to give me an *escudo* or so at least as a tip, as it is usual and customary to give men of quality like me, who stand by to see fair or foul play, and back up swindles, and prevent quarrels, he pocketed his money and left the house. Indignant at this, I followed him, and speaking fairly and courteously asked him to give me at least eight *reales*, for he knows I am a respected man and that I have neither profession nor property, for my parents never taught me one or left me any. But the rogue, who is a bigger thief than Cacus and a worse cheater than Andradilla, refused to give me more than four *reales*. Your worship can see how little shame and conscience he has. But by my faith if you had not come up I'd have made him disgorge his winnings, and he'd have learned how to balance the scales."[2]

"What do you say to this?" asked Sancho. The other replied that all his antagonist said was true, and that he did not choose to give him more than four *reales* because he very often gave him money; and that those who expected presents ought to be civil and take what is given them with a cheerful face, without haggling over tips with the winners unless they know them for certain to be cheaters and their winnings to be unfairly won; and that there could be no better proof that he himself was an honest man and not a thief, as his opponent said, than his having refused to give anything; for cheaters always pay hush money to the onlookers who know their tricks.

"That is true," said the majordomo. "Let your worship consider what is to be done with these men."

2. Putnam's rendering of an obscure saying.

"What is to be done," said Sancho, "is this: you, the winner, be you good, bad, or indifferent, give this assailant of yours a hundred *reales* at once, and you must hand out thirty more for the poor prisoners. And you who have neither profession nor property and hang around the island in idleness, take these hundred *reales* now, and some time tomorrow leave the island under sentence of banishment for ten years and under pain of completing it in another life if you violate the sentence, for I'll hang you on a gibbet, or at least the hangman will by my orders. Not a word from either of you, or I'll make you feel my hand."

The one paid the money; the other took it; the latter left the island; the former went home; and then the governor said, "Either I am not good for much, or I'll get rid of these gambling houses, for it strikes me they are very harmful."

"This one at least," said one of the notaries, "your worship will not be able to get rid of, for an influential person owns it, and what he loses every year is beyond all comparison more than what he makes by the cards. On the minor gambling houses your worship may exercise your power. It is they that do most harm and conceal the most abuses. In the houses of lords and gentlemen of quality the notorious swindlers do not dare play their tricks; and as the vice of gambling has become common, it is better that men should play in houses of repute than in some tradesman's, where they catch an unlucky fellow in the small hours of the morning and skin him alive."

"I know already, notary, that there is a good deal to be said on that point," said Sancho.

And now a constable came up with a young man in custody, and said, "Señor governor, this boy was coming towards us, and as soon as he saw the officers, he turned and ran like a deer, which shows that he must be a lawbreaker. I ran after him, and if he had not stumbled and fallen, I would never have caught him."

"What did you run for, fellow?" said Sancho.

To which the young man replied, "Señor, it was to avoid answering all the questions officers ask."

"What are you by trade?"

"A weaver."

"And what do you weave?"

"Lance heads, with your worship's good leave."

"You're being clever with me! You pride yourself on being a joker? Very good. And where were you going just now?"

"To take the air, señor."

"And where do you 'take the air' on this island?"

"Where it blows."

"Good! Your answers are very much to the point. You are a smart young man. But take notice that I am the air and that I am blowing on you astern and sending you straight to jail. Ho there! Take him and lead him off. I'll make him sleep there tonight without air."

"By God," said the young man, "your worship can't make me sleep in jail any more than you can make me king."

"Why can't I make you sleep in jail?" said Sancho. "Don't I have the power to arrest you and release you whenever I like?"

"All the power your worship has," said the young man, "won't be able to make me sleep in jail."

"Oh no?" said Sancho. "Take him away at once where he'll see his mistake with his own eyes, even if the jailer wants to go easy on him—for the usual price. I'll lay a penalty of two thousand ducats on him if he allows you to stir a step from the prison."

"That's ridiculous," said the young man. "The fact is, all the men on earth will not make me sleep in prison."

"Tell me, you devil," said Sancho. "Do you have some angel that will deliver you and take off the irons I am going to order them to put upon you?"

"Now, señor governor," said the young man in a sprightly manner, "let us be reasonable and come to the point. Granted your worship may order me to be taken to prison, and to have irons and chains put on me, and to be shut up in a dungeon, and may lay heavy penalties on the jailer if he lets me out, and granted that he obeys your orders; still, if I don't choose to sleep and choose to remain awake all night without closing an eye, will your worship with all your power be able to make me sleep if I don't want to?"

"Certainly not," said the secretary, "and the fellow has made his point."

"So then," said Sancho, "you will refuse to go to sleep entirely of your own free will, and not in opposition to mine?"

"No, señor," said the youth, "certainly not."

"Well then, go, and God be with you," said Sancho. "Go home to your own bed, and God give you sound sleep, for I don't want to rob you of it. But for the future, let me advise you not to joke with the authorities, because you may come across some one who will bring down the joke on your skull."

The young man went his way, and the governor continued his round, and shortly afterwards two constables came up with a man in custody, and said, "Señor governor, this person, who seems to be a man, is a woman, and not a bad-looking one, in men's clothes."

They raised two or three lanterns to her face, and by their light they distinguished the features of a woman of about sixteen or a little more, with her hair gathered into a gold and green silk net, and fair as a thousand pearls. They scanned her from head to foot and observed that she had on red silk stockings with garters of white taffeta bordered with gold and pearls; her breeches were of green and gold, and under a loose, sleeveless jacket or vest of the same she wore a blouse of the finest white and gold cloth; her shoes were white and such as men wear. She carried no sword at her belt, but only a richly ornamented dagger, and on her fingers she had several handsome rings. In short, the girl seemed fair to look at in the eyes of all, and none of those who saw her knew her. The people of the town said they could not imagine who she was, and those who were in on the secret of the jokes that were to be played on Sancho were the ones who were most surprised, for this incident and discovery had not been arranged by them, and they watched anxiously to see how the affair would end.

Sancho was fascinated by the girl's beauty, and he asked her who she was, where she was going, and what had induced her to dress herself in that garb. She with her eyes fixed on the ground answered in modest embarrassment, "I cannot tell you, señor, in front of so many people what must remain a private matter, for my own sake. One thing I wish to be known, that I am no thief or lawbreaker, but only an unhappy girl whom the power of jealousy has led to disregard the respect that is due to propriety."

Hearing this, the majordomo said to Sancho, "Make the people stand back, señor governor, so that the lady may say what she wishes with less embarrassment."

Sancho gave the order, and all except the majordomo, the steward, and the secretary fell back. Finding herself then in the presence of no more, the young lady went on to say, "I am the daughter, sirs, of Pedro Pérez Mazorca, the wool-tax collecter of this town, who is in the habit of coming very often to my father's house."

"That won't do, señora," said the majordomo, "for I know Pedro Pérez very well, and I know he has no child at all, either son or daughter; and besides, though you say he is your father, you add then that he comes very often to your father's house."

"I had already noticed that," said Sancho.

"I am confused just now, sirs," said the young woman, "and I don't know what I am saying; but the truth is that I am the daughter of Diego de la Llana, whom you must all know."

"Yes, that will do," said the majordomo, "for I know Diego de la Llana, and know that he is a gentleman of position and a rich man, and that he has a son and a daughter, and that since he was left a widower nobody in all this town can speak of having seen his daughter's face, for he keeps her locked up so tight that he does not give even the sun a chance of seeing her; and even so, the report says she is extremely beautiful."

"It is true," said the girl, "and I am that daughter. Whether the report lies or not as to my beauty, you, sirs, will have decided by this time, as you have seen me." And with this she began to weep bitterly.

On seeing this the secretary leaned over to the steward's ear and said to him in a low voice, "Something serious has no doubt happened to this poor girl, since she goes wandering from home in such dress and at such an hour, and one of her rank too." "There can be no doubt about it," returned the steward, "and moreover her tears confirm your suspicion."

Sancho gave her the best comfort he could and entreated her to tell them without any fear what had happened her, as they would all earnestly and by every means in their power try to solve her problem.

"The fact is, sirs," said she, "that my father has kept me shut up for ten years, the time since the earth received my mother. Mass is said at home in a sumptuous chapel, and all this time I have seen nothing but the sun in the heaven by day and the moon and the stars by night. Nor do I know what streets are like, or plazas, or churches, or even men, except my father and a brother I have, and Pedro Pérez the tax collector, whom, because he came frequently to our house, I took it into my head to call my father, to avoid naming my own.

"This confinement and the restrictions on my going out, even to church, have been making me unhappy for many months. I longed to see the world, or at least the town where I was born, and it did not seem to me that this wish was inconsistent with proper behavior for young ladies of quality. When I heard them talking of bullfights and mock battles on horseback and of acting plays, I asked my brother, who is a year younger than myself, to tell me what sort of things these were, and many more that I had never seen. He explained them to me as well as he could, but the only effect was to arouse in me a still stronger desire to see them. At last, to cut short the story of my disgrace, I begged and entreated my brother—I had never made such an entreaty—" And she began to weep again.

"Proceed, señora," said the majordomo, "and finish the story of what has happened to you, for your words and tears are keeping us all in suspense."

"I have only a little more to tell, though I have many tears to shed," said the girl. "For that is the consequence of indulging foolish wishes."

The maiden's beauty had made a deep impression on the steward's heart, and he again raised his lantern for another look at her and thought they were not tears she was shedding but tiny pearls or dew of the meadow; indeed, he exalted them still higher, and made Oriental pearls of them, and fervently hoped her misfortune might not be so great a one as her tears and sighs seemed to indicate.

The governor was losing patience at the length of time the girl was taking to tell her story and told her not to keep them waiting any longer; for it was late, and there still remained a good deal of the town to be gone over.

She, with broken sobs and half-suppressed sighs, went on to say,

"My misfortune, my misadventure, is simply this, that I begged my brother to dress me up as a man in a suit of his clothes and take me some night, when our father was asleep, to see the whole town. He, overcome by my entreaties, consented, and dressing me in this suit and himself in clothes of mine that fitted him as if made for him (he he doesn't have a hair on his face and might pass for a very beautiful young girl), tonight, about an hour ago, more or less, we left the house. Led by our youthful and foolish impulse, we have made the circuit of the whole town. And then, as we were about to return home, we saw a great troop of people coming, and my brother said to me, 'Sister, this must be the nightwatch. Use your feet and put wings on them, and follow me as fast as you can so they won't recognize us, for that would be bad business.' And with that, he turned and began, I cannot say to run but to fly. In less than six paces I fell down from fright, and then the officer came up and brought me before your worships, where I find myself humiliated in front of all these people because I am bad and frivolous."

"So then, señora," said Sancho, "you've had no other misfortune, and it wasn't jealousy that made you leave home, as you said at the beginning of your story?"

"Nothing has happened to me," said she, "and it was not jealousy that brought me out, but merely a longing to see the world, which did not go beyond seeing the streets of this town."

The appearance of the constables with her brother in custody, whom one of them had overtaken as he ran away from his sister, now fully confirmed the truth of what the girl said. He was wearing an elegant skirt and a short blue damask cloak with fine gold lace, and his head was bare and adorned only with its own hair, which looked like rings of gold, so blond and curly was it.

The governor, the majordomo, and the steward took him aside, and, unheard by his sister, asked him how he came to be in that dress, and he with no less shame and embarrassment told exactly the same story as his sister, to the great delight of the infatuated steward. The governor, however, said to them, "Young lady and gentleman, this has certainly been a very childish affair, and to explain this foolishness and rashness there was no need for all this delay and all these tears and sighs. If you had said, 'We are so-and-so, and we sneaked out of our parents' house in this way in order to amuse ourselves, out of mere curiosity and with no other object,' there would have been an end of the tale, and none of these little sobs and tears and all the rest of it."

"That is true," said the young lady, "but you see, I was so embarrassed that I couldn't help myself."

"No harm has been done," said Sancho. "Come on, we will leave you at your father's house; perhaps he will not have missed you. Next time don't be so childish or eager to see the world; for 'a respectable young lady should have a broken leg and stay at home'; hens and women are ruined by roaming'; and 'she who is eager to see is also eager to be seen.' I say no more."

The young man thanked the governor for his kind offer to take them home, and they directed their steps towards the house, which was not far off. On reaching it, the youth threw a pebble up at a grating, and immediately a woman-servant who was waiting for them came down and opened the door for them, and they went in, leaving the party marveling as much at their grace and beauty as at the fancy they had for 'seeing the world' by night and without leaving the village; which, however, they attributed to their youth.

The steward was left with a heart pierced through and through, and he made up his mind to ask the young lady's father for her hand the very next day, sure she would not be refused him as he was a servant of the duke's. And even Sancho had ideas and schemes of marrying the youth to his daughter Sanchica, and he resolved to open the negotiation at the proper time, persuading himself that no husband could be refused to a governor's daughter. And so the night's round came to an end, and a couple of days later the governorship, whereby all his plans were overthrown and swept away, as will be seen farther on.

Chapter L

WHEREIN IS SET FORTH WHO THE ENCHANTERS AND EXECUTIONERS WERE WHO SPANKED THE DUEÑA AND PINCHED AND SCRATCHED DON QUIXOTE, AND WHAT BEFELL THE PAGE WHO CARRIED THE LETTER TO TERESA SANCHA, SANCHO PANZA'S WIFE

Cide Hamete, the very painstaking investigator of the minute points of this true history, says that when Doña Rodríguez left her quarters to go to Don Quixote's, another dueña who roomed with her observed her, and as all dueñas are fond of prying, listening, and sniffing, she followed her so silently that the good Rodríguez never perceived it. And as soon as the dueña saw her enter Don Quixote's room, not to fail in a dueña's invariable practice of tattling, she hurried off that instant to report to the duchess how Doña Rodríguez was closeted with Don Quixote.

The duchess told the duke and asked him to let her and Altisidora go and see what the dueña wanted with Don Quixote. The duke gave them permission, and the pair cautiously and quietly crept to the door of the room and posted themselves so close to it that they could hear all that was said inside. But when the duchess heard how Rodríguez had made her sores public, she could not restrain herself, nor Altisidora either. And so, filled with rage and thirsting for vengeance, they burst into the room and tormented

Don Quixote and flogged the dueña in the manner already described. For insults directed at their beauty and self-esteem greatly provoke the anger of women and make them eager for revenge.

The duchess told the duke what had happened, and he was much amused by it. She, carrying out her plan for playing jokes on Don Quixote and amusing herself, dispatched the page who had played the part of Dulcinea in the negotiations for her disenchantment (which Sancho Panza in the cares of government had forgotten all about) to Teresa Panza, his wife, with her husband's letter and another from herself, and also a great string of fine coral beads as a present.

Now the history says this page was very sharp and quick-witted; and eager to serve his lord and lady he set off very willingly for Sancho's village. Before he entered it he observed a number of women washing in a brook and asked them if they could tell him whether a woman called Teresa Panza, wife of one Sancho Panza, squire to a knight called Don Quixote of La Mancha lived there. At the question, a young girl who was washing stood up and said, "Teresa Panza is my mother, and that Sancho is my father, and that knight is our master."

"Well then, young lady," said the page, "come and show me where your mother is, for I bring her a letter and a present from your father."

"I will be glad to, señor," said the girl, who seemed to be about fourteen, more or less. And leaving the clothes she was washing to one of her companions, and without putting anything on her head or feet, for she was bare-legged and wind-blown, away she skipped in front of the page's horse, saying, "Come, your worship, our house is at the entrance of the town, and my mother is there, very depressed at not having had any news of my father for a long time."

"Well," said the page, "I am bringing her such good news that she will have reason to thank God."

And then, skipping, running, and capering, the girl reached the town, but before going into the house she called out at the door, "Come out, mother Teresa, come out, come out; here's a gentleman with letters and other things from my dear father." At these words her mother Teresa Panza came out spinning a bundle of flax, in a grey skirt (so short that it looked as if "they'd cut it off to shame her"),[1] a grey bodice, and a blouse. She was not very old, though plainly past forty, strong, healthy, vigorous, and tanned; and seeing her daughter and the page on horseback, she exclaimed, "What's this, child? Who is this gentleman?"

1. Docking the skirts was a punishment for misconduct.

"A servant of my lady, Doña Teresa Panza," replied the page; and suiting the action to the word, he quickly dismounted from his horse, and with great humility advanced to kneel before the lady Teresa, saying, "Let me kiss your hand, Señora Doña Teresa, as the lawful and only wife of Señor Don Sancho Panza, rightful governor of the island of Barataria."

"Oh, sir, get up! Don't do that!" said Teresa. "I'm not a court lady, but only a poor country woman, the daughter of a clodbuster, and the wife of a squire-errant and not of any governor."

"You are," said the page, "the most worthy wife of a most arch-worthy governor; and as a proof of what I say, accept this letter and this present." And at the same time he took out of his pocket a string of coral beads with gold clasps, and placed it on her neck and said, "This letter is from his lordship the governor, and the other, as well as these coral beads, from my lady the duchess, who sends me to your worship."

Teresa stood lost in astonishment, and her daughter as well, and the girl said, "I'll bet our master Don Quixote's at the bottom of this; he must have given father the governorship or county he so often promised him."

"That is the truth," said the page. "For it is through Señor Don Quixote that Señor Sancho is now governor of the island of Barataria, as will be seen by this letter."

"Will your worship read it to me, noble sir?" said Teresa. "For though I can spin, I can't read a word."

"Nor I either," said Sanchica. "But wait a bit, and I'll go and fetch some one who can read it, either the curate himself or the bachelor Sansón Carrasco, and they'll come gladly to hear any news of my father."

"There is no need to fetch anybody," said the page. "For though I can't spin I can read, and I'll read it." And so he read it through. But as it has been already given it is not inserted here; and then he took out the other one from the duchess, which ran as follows:

> Friend Teresa: Your husband Sancho's good qualities, of heart as well as of head, induced and compelled me to request my husband the duke to give him the governorship of one of his many islands. I am told he governs exceptionally well, of which I am very glad, and my lord the duke, of course, also. And I am very thankful to heaven that I have not made a mistake in choosing him for that government; for I would have Señora Teresa know that a good governor is hard to find in this world, and may God make me as good as Sancho's way of governing.
>
> Enclosed I send you, my dear, a string of coral beads with gold clasps. I wish they were Oriental pearls; but "he who gives you a bone does not wish to see you dead and gone."
>
> A time will come when we shall become acquainted and meet

one another, but God knows the future. Remember me to your daughter Sanchica, and tell her from me to be prepared, for I mean to find a rich husband for her when she least expects it.

They tell me there are big acorns in your village; send me a couple of dozens or so, and I shall value them greatly as coming for your hand; and write to me at length to assure me of your health and well-being; and if there is anything you need, you have only to open your mouth, and yours needs will be met. And so God keep you.

From this place.

Your loving friend,
THE DUCHESS

"Ah, what a good, plain, humble lady!" said Teresa when she heard the letter. "May I may be buried with ladies of that sort, and not the gentlewomen we have in this town, who think that because they are gentlewomen the wind must not touch them, and they go to church with as many airs as if they were queens, no less, and seem to think they are disgraced if they look at a farmer's wife! And see here how this good lady, though she's a duchess, calls me 'friend,' and treats me as if I was her equal—and equal may I see her with the tallest church tower in La Mancha! And as for the acorns, señor, I'll send her ladyship a peck and such big ones that people can come to see them as a show and a wonder.

"And now, Sanchica, see that the gentleman is comfortable. Put up his horse, and get some eggs out of the stable, and cut plenty of bacon, and let's give him a dinner fit for a prince; for the good news he has brought us and his honest face deserve it all. And meanwhile I'll run out and give the neighbors the news of our good luck, and the priest, and Master Nicolás the barber, who are and always have been such friends of your father's."

"I will, mother," said Sanchica. "But you must give me half of that string; for I don't think my lady the duchess could have been so simple as to send it all to you."

"It is all for you, my child," said Teresa. "But let me wear it round my neck for a few days; for it really seems to make my heart glad."

"You will be glad, too," said the page, "when you see the bundle there is in this suitcase, for it is a suit of the finest cloth, that the governor only wore one day out hunting and now sends, all for Señora Sanchica."

"May he live a thousand years," said Sanchica, "and the man who brings it, just as many, or even two thousand, if need be."

With this Teresa hurried out of the house with the letters and with the string of beads round her neck, and went along drumming on the letters as if they were a tambourine, and meeting the priest and Sansón Carrasco by chance, she began dancing and saying,

"We're not poor relations now! We've got a little government! Yes, let the finest fine lady tackle me, and I'll make her over!"

"What's all this, Teresa Panza? What madness is this, and what papers are those?"

"The madness is this: these are the letters from duchesses and governors, and these I have around my neck are fine coral beads, with big beads of beaten gold, and I am a governor's wife."

"God help us," said the priest, "we don't understand you, Teresa, or know what you are talking about."

"There, you can see for yourselves," said Teresa, and she handed them the letters.

The priest read them out for Sansón Carrasco to hear, and Sansón and he regarded one another with looks of astonishment at what they had read, and the bachelor asked who had brought the letters. Teresa in reply told them to come with her to her house and they would see the messenger, a very elegant young man, who had brought another present which was worth as much more. The priest took the coral beads from her neck and examined them again and again, and having satisfied himself as to their fineness, he expressed his amazement again and said, "By the habit I wear, I don't know what to say or think of these letters and presents; on the one hand I can see and feel the fineness of these coral beads, and on the other I read how a duchess sends for a couple of dozens of acorns."

"Make sense out of *those* facts!" said Carrasco. "Well, let's go and see the bearer of this letter, and from him we'll learn something about the contradictions that we see."

They did so, and Teresa returned with them. They found the page sifting a little barley for his horse, and Sanchica cutting bacon to be embedded in eggs for his dinner. His looks and his handsome apparel pleased them both greatly; and after they had greeted him courteously, and he them, Sansón begged him to give them his news, as well of Don Quixote as of Sancho Panza. For, he said, though they had read the letters from Sancho and her ladyship the duchess, they were still puzzled and could not make out what was meant by Sancho's governorship, particularly of an island, when all or most of those in the Mediterranean belonged to his Majesty.

To this the page replied, "As to Señor Sancho Panza's being a governor, there is no doubt whatever. But whether it is an island or not that he governs, with that I have nothing to do; suffice it to say that it is a town of more than a thousand inhabitants. With regard to the acorns, I may tell you my lady the duchess is so unpretentious and unassuming that, not to speak of asking for acorns from a country woman, she has been known to send to ask for the loan of a comb from one of her neighbors; for I would have your worships know that the ladies of Aragón, though they are just as aristocratic, are not so punctilious and haughty as the Castilian ladies; they treat people with greater familiarity."

In the middle of this conversation, Sanchica appeared with her skirt full of eggs, and said she to the page, "Tell me, señor, does my father wear hose since he has become a governor?"

"I have not noticed," said the page, "but no doubt he wears them."

"Ah! my God!" said Sanchica, "what a sight it must be to see my father in tights! Isn't it odd that ever since I was born I have wanted to see my father in hose?"

"Your worship will see him with just such things, if you live long enough," said the page. "By God, it won't be long before he's going around in a scholar's cap, if the governorship only lasts him two more months."[2]

The priest and the bachelor could see plainly enough that the page spoke in irony; but the fineness of the coral beads and the hunting suit that Sancho sent (for Teresa had already shown it to them) put them in doubt, and they could not help laughing at Sanchica's wish, and still more when Teresa said, "Señor priest, see if there's anybody here going to Madrid or Toledo, to buy me a real hoopskirt, a fashionable one of the best quality. Because I really and truly intend to be a credit to my husband's government as well as I can; and if I take a notion, I'll go to Madrid and show off in a coach like everybody else. A woman who has a governor for her husband may very well have one and keep one."

"And why not, mother!" said Sanchica. "I wish to God it was today instead of tomorrow, even if people said when they saw me seated in the coach with my mother, 'Look at so-and-so, the garlic-eater's daughter, stretched out in a coach as if she was a she-pope!' Let them tramp through the mud, and me go in my coach with my feet off the ground. Bad luck to all the vicious gossips in the world; 'as long as I get my way, I don't care what people say.' Am I right, mother?"

"You certainly are, my child," said Teresa. "And all this good luck, and even more, my dear Sancho foretold me; and you'll see, my daughter, he won't stop till he has made me a countess; for getting started is everything in luck; and as I have heard your dear father say many a time (for besides being your father he's the father of proverbs too), 'When they offer you a heifer, come running with a halter; when they offer you a government, take it; when they offer you a county, seize it; when they say, "Here, here!" to you with something good, swallow it.' It would be stupid to go to

2. "Scholar's cap" is a rough equivalent for *papahigo*, a cap affected by older men of status with a flap which could be turned down to protect the ears and the nape of the neck. (Sir Thomas More, in the portrait by Holbein, and Erasmus, in the Dürer portrait, wear caps of this type.)

sleep and not to answer the good fortune and the lucky chances that are knocking at the door of your house!"

"And what do I care," added Sanchica, "if anybody says when he sees me holding my head up, 'You can't make a silk purse,' and the rest of it?"

Hearing this the priest said, "I do believe that all the members of the Panza clan are born with a sackful of proverbs in their insides. I never saw one of them that does not pour them out at all times and on all occasions."

"That is true," said the page, "for Señor Governor Sancho utters them at every step; and though a great many of them are not appropriate, still they amuse one, and my lady the duchess and the duke praise them highly."

"Then you still maintain that all this about Sancho's government is true, señor," said the bachelor, "and that there actually is a duchess who sends her presents and writes to her? Because we, although we have handled the presents and read the letters, don't believe it and suspect it to be the doings of our fellow townsman Don Quixote, who thinks that everything is done by enchantment. And for this reason I am almost ready to say that I'd like to touch and feel your worship to see whether you are an ambassador of the imagination or a man of flesh and blood."

"All I know, sirs," replied the page, "is that I am a real ambassador, and that Señor Sancho Panza is really a governor, and that my lord and lady the duke and duchess can give, and have given him, this government, and that I have heard that Sancho Panza is getting along extremely well. Whether there is any enchantment in all this or not, it is for your worships to settle between you. And that's all I know, by the oath I swear, which is by the life of my parents, who are still alive, and whom I love dearly."

"It may be so," said the bachelor, "but *dubitat Augustinus*."[3]

"Let him doubt who will," said the page. "What I have told you is the truth, and that will always rise above falsehood, as oil above water; *operibus credite, et non verbis*.[4] Let one of you come with me, and he will see with his eyes what he does not believe with his ears."

"It's for me to make that trip," said Sanchica. "Take me with you, señor, behind you on your horse; for I'll very willingly go to see my father."

"Governors' daughters," said the page, "must not travel along the roads alone, but accompanied by coaches and litters and a great number of attendants."

"By God," said Sanchica, "I can go just as well mounted on a

3. "Augustine doubts it." Carrasco uses a cliché of theological debate to mean, "I am unconvinced."

4. "Believe in my actions, not my words," an allusion to John 10:38.

she-ass as in a coach; what a delicate thing you must take me for!"

"Hush, girl," said Teresa. "You don't know what you're talking about; the gentleman is right: 'when in Rome, do as the Romans do.' When it was 'Sancho' it was 'Sancha'; when it is 'Señor Governor' it's 'señora'; I don't know if I make my point."

"Señora Teresa says more than she realizes," said the page. "And now give me something to eat and let me go at once, for I intend to return this evening."

"Come and have a bite with me," said the priest at this. "Señora Teresa has more will than means to serve so worthy a guest."

The page refused, but had to consent at last for his own convenience; and the priest took him home with him very gladly, in order to have an opportunity of questioning him at leisure about Don Quixote and his doings.

The bachelor offered to write the letters in reply for Teresa; but she did not care to let him mix himself up in her affairs, for she thought him somewhat given to joking; and so she gave a roll and a couple of eggs to a young acolyte who knew how to write, and he wrote for her two letters, one for her husband and the other for the duchess, dictated out of her own head, which are not the worst inserted in this great history, as will be seen farther on.

Chapter LI

OF THE PROGRESS OF SANCHO'S GOVERNMENT, AND OTHER SUCH ENTERTAINING MATTERS

Day came after the night of the governor's round, a night which the steward passed without sleeping, so full were his thoughts of the face and spirit and beauty of the disguised maiden, while the majordomo spent what was left of it in writing an account to his lord and lady of all Sancho said and did, being as much amazed at his sayings as at his doings, for there was a mixture of shrewdness and simplicity in all his words and deeds.

The señor governor finally got up, and by Doctor Pedro Recio's directions, they made him break his fast with a bite of preserves and four sips of cold water, which Sancho would have readily exchanged for a piece of bread and a bunch of grapes. But seeing there was no help for it, he submitted with no little sorrow of heart and discomfort of stomach, Pedro Recio having persuaded him that light and delicate food stimulated the brain, which was most essential for persons placed in command and in responsible situations, where they have to employ not only the bodily powers but those of the mind also.

By means of this sophistry Sancho was made to endure hunger, and hunger so keen that in his heart he cursed the governorship and even him who had given it to him. However, with his hunger and his preserves he undertook to deliver judgments that day, and the first thing that came before him was a question that was submitted to him by an outsider, in the presence of the majordomo and the other attendants, and it was in these words:

"Señor, a large river separated two districts of one domain. (Will your worship please to pay attention, for the case is an important and a rather knotty one?) Well then, over this river there was a bridge, and at one end of it a gallows, and a sort of tribunal, where four judges commonly sat to administer the law which the lord of river, bridge, and the domain had enacted, and which was to this effect: 'If anyone crosses by this bridge from one side to the other, he shall declare on oath where he is going and with what object; and if he swears truly, he shall be allowed to pass, but if falsely, he shall be put to death for it by hanging on the gallows erected there, without reprieve.' Though the law and its severe penalty were known, many persons crossed, but in their declarations it was easy to see at once they were telling the truth, and the judges let them pass free. It happened, however, that one man, when they came to take his declaration, swore and said that by the oath he took he was going to die on the gallows that stood there, and nothing else. The judges held a consultation over the oath, and they said, 'If we let this man pass free, he has sworn falsely, and by the law he ought to die; but if we hang him, as he swore he was going to die on that gallows, and therefore swore the truth, by the same law he ought to go free.' I ask your worship, señor governor, what are the judges to do with this man? For they are still in doubt and perplexity; and having heard of your worship's keen and exalted intellect, they have sent me to entreat your worship on their behalf to give your opinion on this very intricate and puzzling case."

To this Sancho answered, "Certainly those judges that have sent you to me might have saved themselves the trouble, for I have more of the dull than the keen in me; but repeat the case over again in a way that I can understand it, and then perhaps I might be able to find a solution."

The questioner repeated again and again what he had said before, and then Sancho said, "I believe that I can state the business clearly and quickly like this: the man swears that he is going to die upon the gallows, and if he dies on it, he has sworn the truth, and by the law enacted deserves to go free and pass over the bridge. But if they don't hang him, then he has sworn falsely, and by the same law deserves to be hanged."

"It is as the señor governor says," said the messenger, "and as regards a complete comprehension of the case, there is nothing left to desire or hesitate about."

"Well then I say," said Sancho, "that of this man they should let the part that has sworn truly pass, and hang the part that has lied; and in this way the conditions of the passage will be fully complied with."

"But then, señor governor," replied the questioner, "the man will have to be divided into two parts, a lying part and a truthful one. And if he is divided of course he will die; and so none of the requirements of the law will be carried out, and it is absolutely necessary to comply with it."

"Look here, my good sir," said Sancho. "Either I'm a numbskull or else there is the same reason for this traveler's dying as for his living and crossing the bridge; because if the truth saves him the lie equally condemns him. And that being the case, I think you should tell the gentlemen who sent you to me that as the arguments for condemning him and for absolving him are exactly balanced, they should let him pass freely, since it is always more praiseworthy to do good than to do evil. I would issue this opinion signed with my name, if I knew how to sign. And what I have said in this case is not out of my own head, but one of the many precepts my master Don Quixote gave me the night before I left to become governor of this island, that came into my mind, and it was this, that when there was any doubt about the justice of a case, I should lean to mercy; and it is God's will that I should recollect it now, for it fits this case as if it was made for it."

"That is true," said the majordomo. "And I maintain that Lycurgus himself, who gave laws to the Lacedemonians, could not have pronounced a better decision than the great Panza has given. Let the morning's audience close with this, and I will see that the señor governor has dinner entirely to his liking."

"That's all I ask for—fair play," said Sancho. "Give me my dinner, and then let it rain cases and questions on me, and I'll dispatch them in a jiffy."

The majordomo kept his word, for he felt it against his conscience to kill so wise a governor by hunger; particularly as he intended to put an end to Sancho's governorship that very night with the last joke he was commissioned to play on him.

It came to pass, then, that after he had dined that day, in opposition to the rules and aphorisms of Doctor Tirteafuera, as they were clearing the table there came a courier with a letter from Don Quixote for the governor. Sancho ordered the secretary to read it to himself, and if there was nothing in it that demanded secrecy to read it aloud. The secretary did so, and after he had skimmed the contents he said, "It may well be read aloud, for what Señor Don Quixote writes to your worship deserves to be printed or written in letters of gold, and it is as follows."

DON QUIXOTE OF LA MANCHA'S LETTER TO SANCHO PANZA, GOVERNOR OF THE ISLAND OF BARATARIA

Whereas I expected to hear of your stupidities and blunders, friend Sancho, I have received intelligence of your displays of good sense, for which I give special thanks to heaven, that can raise the poor from the dunghill and make wise men of fools. They tell me you govern like a man but are as humble as if you were a beast. But I would have you bear in mind, Sancho, that very often it is fitting and necessary, for the dignity of office, to resist the humility of the heart; for the appearance of one who is invested with grave duties should be in keeping with such duties and not measured by what his own humble tastes may lead him to prefer. Dress well; a stick dressed up does not look like a stick. I do not say you should wear trinklets or flashy clothes, or that being a judge you should dress like a soldier, but that you should dress yourself in the apparel your office requires, and that at the same time it be neat and handsome.

To win the good will of the people you govern there are two things, among others, that you must do; one is to be civil to all (this, however, I told you before), and the other to take care that food be abundant, for there is nothing that troubles the heart of the poor more than hunger and high prices.

Do not make many laws; but see to it that those which you make are good ones and, above all, that they are observed and carried out; for laws that are not observed are the same as if they did not exist. Indeed, they encourage the idea that the prince who had the wisdom and authority to make them had not the power to enforce them. Laws that threaten and are not enforced come to be like the log, the king of the frogs, that frightened them at first, but that in time they despised and mounted upon.

Be a father to virtue and a stepfather to vice. Be not always strict, nor yet always lenient, but observe a mean between these two extremes, for in that is the aim of wisdom. Visit the jails, the slaughterhouses, and the marketplaces; for the presence of the governor is of great importance in such places. It comforts the prisoners who are in hopes of a speedy release; it is a warning to the butchers, who balance their scales for the moment; and it is the terror of the female vendors, for the same reason.

Do not show yourself (even if perchance you are, which I do not believe) covetous, a follower of women, or a glutton; for when the people and those that have dealings with you become aware of your special weakness, they will attack you in that quarter till they have brought you down to the depths of perdition.

Consider and reconsider, study and restudy over again the advice and the instructions I gave you before your departure to your government, and you will see that in them, if you follow them, you have a help at hand that will lighten for you the troubles and difficulties that beset governors at every step. Write to your lord and lady and show yourself grateful to them, for ingratitude is the offspring of pride, and one of the greatest sins we know of; and he who is grateful to those who have been good to him shows that he will be so to God also, who has bestowed and still bestows so many blessings upon him.

My lady the duchess sent off a messenger with your suit and another present to your wife Teresa Panza; we expect the answer every moment.

I have been a little indisposed from a certain scratching I received, not very much to the benefit of my nose; but it was nothing. If there are enchanters who try to harm me, there are also some who defend me.

Let me know if the majordomo who is with you had any share in the Trifaldi performance, as you suspected; and keep me informed of everything that happens to you, as the distance is so short; all the more as I am thinking of giving up, very soon, this idle life I am now leading, for I was not born for it. A thing has occurred to me which I am inclined to think will put me out of favor with the duke and duchess; but though I am sorry for it, I do not care; after all I must obey my calling rather than their pleasure, in accordance with the saying, *amicus Plato, sed magis amica veritas.*[1] I quote this Latin to you because I assume that since you became a governor you no doubt have learned it.

God be with you, and may He keep you from being an object of pity to anyone.

Your friend,
DON QUIXOTE OF LA MANCHA

Sancho listened to the letter with great attention, and it was praised and considered wise by all who heard it. He then rose up from table, and calling his secretary shut himself in with him in his own room, and without putting it off any longer set about answering his master Don Quixote at once; and he ordered the secretary to write down what he told him without adding or suppressing anything, which he did, and the answer was to the following effect.

SANCHO PANZA'S LETTER TO DON QUIXOTE OF LA MANCHA

The pressure of business is so great that I have no time to scratch my head or even to cut my nails; and I have them so long God send a remedy for it. I say this, my dear master, so that you will not be surprised if I have not until now sent you word of how I am doing—well or badly—in this governorship, in which I am suffering more hunger than when we two were wandering through the woods and wilderness.

My lord the duke wrote to me the other day to warn me that certain spies had entered this island to kill me; but up to the present I have not discovered any except a certain doctor who receives a salary in this town for killing all the governors that

1. "Plato is a friend, but Truth is a better friend."

come here. He is called Doctor Pedro Recio and is from Tirteafuera; so you see what a name he has to make me dread dying under his hands. This doctor says of himself that he does not cure diseases when there are any, but prevents their coming, and the medicines he uses are diet and more diet until he reduces you to bare bones; as if leanness were not worse than fever.

In short he is killing me with hunger, and I am dying of discouragement, because when I thought I was coming to this government to get hot food and cold drinks, and take my ease between holland sheets on feather beds, I find I have come to do penance as if I was a hermit; and as I don't do it willingly, I suspect that in the end the devil will carry me off.

So far I have not touched a fee or received any bribes, and I don't know what to think of it. Here they tell me that the governors that come to this island, before entering it have plenty of money either given to them or lent to them by the people of the town, and that this is the usual custom not only here but with all who receive governorships.

Last night going the rounds I caught a beautiful young lady in men's clothes, and a brother of hers dressed as a woman. My steward has fallen in love with the girl and has in his own mind chosen her for a wife, so he says, and I have chosen the young man for a son-in-law. Today we are going to explain our intentions to the father of the pair, who is one Diego de la Llana, a gentleman and as pure-blooded a Christian as you please.

I visit the marketplace, as your worship advises me, and yesterday I found a vendor selling new hazel nuts and discovered that she had mixed a bushel of old rotten nuts with a bushel of new. I confiscated the whole batch for the children of the charity school, who will know how to separate them well enough, and I sentenced her not to come into the marketplace for two weeks. They told me I did right. I can tell your worship it is commonly said in this town that there are no people worse than female vendors, for they are all shameless, ruthless, and impudent, and I can well believe it from what I have seen of them in other towns.

I am very glad my lady the duchess has written to my wife Teresa Panza and sent her the present your worship speaks of; and I will try to show myself grateful when the time comes. Kiss her hands for me, and tell her I say she has not cast her bread upon the waters in vain, as she will see.

I would not like your worship to have any quarrel with my lord and lady; for if you fall out with them it is plain it will do me harm. And as you give me advice to be grateful, it will not do for your worship not to be grateful yourself to those who have shown you such kindness, and by whom you have been treated so hospitably in their castle.

I don't understand about the scratching but I suppose it must be one of the evil deeds the wicked enchanters are always doing to your worship. When we meet I will learn all about it.

I wish I could send your worship something; but I don't know what to send except some very well-made enema nozzles, to be used with a bag, that they make on this island; but if I stay on in this job, I'll find something to send, one way or another.

If my wife Teresa Panza writes to me, pay the postage and send me the letter, for I have a very great desire to hear how my house and wife and children are getting on. And so, may God deliver your worship from evil-minded enchanters, and bring me well and peacefully out of this government, which I doubt, for I expect to take leave of it and my life together, from the way Doctor Pedro Recio treats me.

Your worship's servant,
SANCHO PANZA THE GOVERNOR

The secretary sealed the letter and immediately dispatched the courier; and those who were carrying out the joke on Sancho, putting their heads together, arranged how he was to be dispatched from the government.

Sancho spent the afternoon in drawing up certain ordinances relating to the good government of what he thought was an island; and he ordained that there were to be no food retailers in the State, and that men might import wine into it from any place they pleased, provided they declared where it came from, so that a price might be put on it according to its quality, reputation, and the estimation it was held in; and he that watered his wine or changed the name was to forfeit his life for it. He reduced the prices of all footwear, but of shoes in particular, as they seemed to him to run extravagantly high. He established a ceiling on servants' wages, which were becoming recklessly exorbitant. He laid extremely heavy penalties upon those who sang lewd or satirical songs either by day or night. He decreed that no blind man should sing about any miracle in verse, unless he could produce authentic evidence that it was true, for it was his opinion that most of those the blind men sing about are imaginary, to the detriment of the true ones. He established and created a bailiff of the poor, not to harass them, but to examine them and see whether they really were poor; for many a sturdy thief or drunkard goes about under cover of a make-believe crippled limb or a sham sore. In a word, he made so many good rules that to this day they are preserved there, and are called *The ordinances of the great governor Sancho Panza.*

Chapter LII

WHEREIN IS RELATED THE ADVENTURE OF THE SECOND DISTRESSED OR AFFLICTED DUEÑA, OTHERWISE CALLED DOÑA RODRÍGUEZ

Cide Hamete relates that Don Quixote, being now cured of his scratches, felt that the life he was leading in the castle was entirely inconsistent with the order of chivalry he professed, so he determined to ask the duke and duchess to permit him to leave for Zaragoza, as the time of the festival was now drawing near, and he hoped to win there the suit of armor which is the prize at festivals of the sort.

But one day at table with the duke and duchess, just as he was about to carry his resolution into effect and ask for their permission, lo and behold suddenly there came in through the door of the great hall two women, as they afterwards proved to be, draped in mourning from head to foot, one of whom approaching Don Quixote threw herself at full length at his feet, pressing her lips to them and uttering moans so sad, so deep, and so doleful that she put all who heard and saw her into a state of perplexity. And though the duke and duchess supposed it must be some joke their servants were playing on Don Quixote, still the earnest way the woman sighed and moaned and wept puzzled them and made them feel uncertain, until Don Quixote, touched with compassion, raised her up and made her unveil herself and remove the mantle from her tearful face.

She complied and disclosed what no one could have ever anticipated, for she revealed the face of Doña Rodríguez, the dueña of the house, and the other female in mourning was her daughter, who had been made a fool of by the rich farmer's son. All who knew her were filled with astonishment, and the duke and duchess more than any; for though they thought her a simpleton and naïve, they did not think her capable of crazy pranks. Doña Rodríguez, at length, turning to her master and mistress said to them, "Will your excellencies allow me to speak to this gentleman for a moment, for it is necessary I should do so in order to conclude successfully an affair in which the boldness of a peasant with dishonorable intentions has involved me?"

The duke said that he gave her leave and that she might speak with Señor Don Quixote as much as she liked.

She then, turning to Don Quixote and addressing herself to him said, "Some days since, valiant knight, I gave thee an account of the injustice and treachery of a wicked peasant to my dearly beloved daughter, the unhappy damsel here before thee, and thou promised me to take her part and right the wrong that has been done her. But now it has come to my attention that thou art about to depart from this castle in quest of such fair adventures as God may provide thee. Therefore, before thou takest the road, I would that thou shouldst challenge this unruly rustic and compel him to marry my daughter in fulfillment of the promise he gave her to become her husband before he seduced her. For to expect that my lord the duke will do me justice is to ask pears from the elm tree, for the reason I stated privately to thee. And so may our Lord grant thee good health and forsake us not."[1]

To these words Don Quixote replied very gravely and solemnly, "Worthy dueña, hold back your tears, or rather dry them, and save your sighs; for I take it upon myself to obtain redress for your daughter, for whom it would have been better not to have been so ready to believe lovers' promises, which are for the most part quickly made and very slowly performed. And so, with my lord the duke's leave, I will at once go in quest of this heartless youth and will find him out and challenge him and slay him, if he refuses to keep his promised word; for the chief object of my profession is to spare the humble and chastise the proud; I mean, to help the distressed and destroy the oppressors."

"There is no necessity," said the duke, "for your worship to take the trouble of seeking out the rustic of whom this worthy dueña complains, nor is there any necessity, either, for asking my leave to challenge him; for I consider him duly challenged and will see that he is informed of the challenge and accepts it and comes to answer it in person to this castle of mine. I shall provide both of you with a safe field, observing all the conditions which are usually and properly observed in such trials, and observing too justice to both sides, as all princes who offer a free field to combatants within the limits of their domains are bound to do."

"Then with that assurance and your highness's leave," said Don Quixote, "I hereby for this once waive the privilege of nobility and put myself on a level with the lowly birth of the wrongdoer, making myself equal with him and enabling him to enter into combat with me. And so, I challenge and defy him, though absent, because he did wrong in breaking faith with this poor damsel, who was a maiden and now by his fault is no longer. And I say that he shall fulfill the promise he gave her to become her lawful husband, or else die in combat."

And then plucking off a glove, he threw it down in the middle of the hall, and the duke picked it up, saying, as he had said before, that he accepted the challenge in the name of his vassal, and fixed six days later as the time, the courtyard of the castle as the place, and for arms the customary ones of knights, lance and shield and dueling armor, with all the other accessories, without deception, trickery, or charms of any sort, and examined and passed by the judges of the field.

"But first of all," he said, "it is necessary that this worthy dueña and naughty damsel should place their claim for justice in the hands of Don Quixote; for otherwise nothing can be done,

1. Doña Rodríguez addresses Don Quixote in the high-flown speech of romances of chivalry, but note that he replies in normal Spanish.

nor can the said challenge be brought to a proper conclusion."

"I do so place it," replied the dueña.

"And I too," added her daughter, all in tears and covered with shame and confusion.

This declaration having been made, and the duke having settled in his own mind what he would do in the matter, the ladies in black withdrew, and the duchess gave orders that for the future they were not to be treated as servants of hers but as lady adventurers who came to her house to demand justice; so they gave them a room to themselves and waited on them as they would on strangers, to the consternation of the other women-servants, who did not know where the folly and imprudence of Doña Rodríguez and her unfortunate daughter would stop.

And now, to complete the enjoyment of the feast and bring the dinner to a satisfactory end, lo and behold the page who had carried the letters and presents to Teresa Panza, the wife of the governor Sancho, entered the hall. The duke and duchess were very well pleased to see him, being anxious to know the result of his journey; but when they asked him, the page said in reply that he could not give it before so many people or in a few words and begged their excellencies to let it wait for a private opportunity, and in the meantime amuse themselves with these letters; and taking out the letters, he placed them in the duchess's hand. One had by way of address, *Letter for my lady the Duchess So-and-so, of Such-and-Such*; and the other *To my husband Sancho Panza, governor of the island of Barataria; God prosper him longer than me.* The duchess's bread would not bake, as the saying is, until she had read her letter; and having looked over it herself and seen that it might be read aloud for the duke and all present to hear, she read out as follows.

TERESA PANZA'S LETTER TO THE DUCHESS

The letter your highness wrote me, my lady, gave me great pleasure, for indeed I found it very welcome. The string of coral beads is very fine, and my husband's hunting suit does not fall short of it. All this village is very much pleased that your ladyship has made a governor of my husband Sancho; though nobody will believe it, particularly the priest, and Master Nicolás the barber, and the bachelor Sansón Carrasco. But I don't care. As long as it is true, as it is, they may all say what they like. Though, to tell the truth, if the coral beads and the suit had not come, I would not have believed it either; because in this village everybody thinks my husband is stupid, and except for governing a flock of goats, they can't imagine what sort of governorship he can be fit for. God grant it, and direct him, as He sees that his children stand in need of it.

I have decided with your worship's permission, dear lady, to make the most of this opportunity and go to Court[2] to stretch out in a coach and make all those who envy me already pop their eyes out. So I beg your excellency to order my husband to send me a small sum of money, but not too small, because one's expenses are heavy at Court. A loaf costs a *real,* and meat thirty *maravedís* a pound, which is outrageous. If he doesn't want me to go let him tell me in time, for my feet are itching to take to the road; and my friends and neighbors tell me that if my daughter and I are fancy and dignified at Court, my husband will come to be known far more on account of me than I on account of him. Of course plenty of people will ask, "Who are those ladies in that coach?" and some servant of mine will answer, "The wife and daughter of Sancho Panza, governor of the island of Barataria." And in this way Sancho will become known, and I'll be well thought of, and everything will be perfect. I am as sorry as can be that they have gathered no acorns this year in our village. Nevertheless, I am sending your highness about half a peck that I went to the wood to gather and pick out one by one myself, and I could find no bigger ones. I wish they were as big as ostrich eggs.

Don't forget to write to me, your high and mightiness, and I will take care to answer, and let you know how I am, and whatever news there may be in this place, where I remain, praying our Lord to keep your highness and not to forget me.

Sancha, my daughter, and my son kiss your worship's hands.

She who would rather see your ladyship than write to you,

Your servant,
TERESA PANZA

All were greatly amused by Teresa Panza's letter, but particularly the duke and duchess; and the duchess asked Don Quixote's opinion whether they might open the letter that had come for the governor, which she suspected must be very good. Don Quixote said that to gratify them he would open it, and did so, and found that it ran as follows.

TERESA PANZA'S LETTER TO HER HUSBAND SANCHO PANZA

I got your letter, my dearest Sancho, and I promise you and swear as a Catholic Christian that I almost went crazy I was so happy. I can tell you, brother, when I heard that you were a governor I thought I would drop dead with pure joy; and you know they say sudden joy kills as well as great sorrow. As for Sanchica your daughter, she leaked from sheer happiness.

I had the suit you sent me right in front of me, and the coral beads my lady the duchess sent me around my neck, and the letters in my hands, and there was the bearer of them, and in spite of all this I really believed and thought that what I saw and han-

2. Teresa says, "go to court." The Spanish word *corte* means court, capital, big city, or *the* Court, i.e., Madrid. Teresa seems to have no desire to go to Barataria; perhaps she believes that Barataria and Madrid are close together.

dled was all a dream. Who could have thought that a goatherd would come to be a governor of islands? You know, my love, what my mother used to say, that one must live long to see much. I say it because I expect to see more if I live longer; for I don't expect to stop until I see you a collector of taxes or revenues. Those are jobs where, though the devil carries off those who make a bad use of them, still they make and handle money.

My lady the duchess will tell you how I want to go to Court; think about it and let me know your pleasure; I will try to be a credit to you by riding in a coach.

Neither the priest, nor the barber, nor the bachelor, nor even the sacristan, can believe that you are a governor, and they say the whole thing is an illusion or some sort of enchantment, like everything that has to do with your master Don Quixote. And Sansón says he will come in search of you and drive the governorship out of your head and the madness out of Don Quixote's skull. I only laugh and look at my string of beads and plan the dress I am going to make for our daughter out of your suit.

I sent some acorns to my lady the duchess; I wish they had been made of gold. Send me some strings of pearls if they are in fashion on that island.

Here is the news of the village: La Berrueca has married her daughter to a good-for-nothing painter who came here to paint anything that might turn up. The council gave him an order to paint his Majesty's arms over the door of the town hall. He asked two ducats, which they paid him in advance; he worked for eight days, and at the end of them had nothing painted, and then said he simply couldn't paint such trifling things. He returned the money, and, in spite of everything, has married on the pretence of being a good worker. It is true that he has now laid aside his paint brush and taken up a spade and goes to the field like a gentleman.

Pedro Lobo's son has received the first orders and tonsure, with the intention of becoming a priest. Minguilla, Mingo Silvato's granddaughter, found it out and has gone to court with him on the score of having given her promise of marriage. Gossip has it that she is pregnant by him, but he denies it flatly.

There are no olives this year, and there is not a drop of vinegar to be had in the whole village. A company of soldiers passed through here; when they left they took away with them three of the girls of the village; I won't tell you who they are; perhaps they will come back, and they'll find someone who'll marry them with all their blemishes, good or bad.

Sanchica is making lace; she earns eight *maravedís* a day clear, which she puts into a bank toward her trousseau; but now that she is a governor's daughter you'll give her a dowry without her working for it.

The fountain in the plaza has run dry. A bolt of lightning struck the pillory, and I wish they all lit there.

I look for an answer to this letter and your decision about my going to Court; and so, God keep you longer than me, or as long, for I would not want to leave you in this world without me.

Your wife,
TERESA PANZA

The letters were applauded, laughed over, relished, and admired; and then, as if to put the seal to the business, the courier arrived, bringing the one Sancho sent to Don Quixote, and this, too, was read out, and it raised some doubts as to the governor's simplicity. The duchess retired to hear from the page about his adventures in Sancho's village, which he narrated at full length without leaving a single circumstance unmentioned. He gave her the acorns and also a cheese which Teresa had given him as being particularly good and superior to those of Tronchón. The duchess received it with greatest delight, in which we will leave her, to describe the end of the government of the great Sancho Panza, flower and mirror of all governors of islands.

Chapter LIII

OF THE TROUBLOUS END AND TERMINATION OF SANCHO PANZA'S GOVERNMENT

To believe that in this life anything will remain for ever in the same state is an idle fancy; on the contrary, everything seems to go in a circle, I mean around and around. The spring goes looking for summer, the summer the fall, the fall the autumn, the autumn the winter, and the winter the spring, and so time rolls on without stopping. Human life alone, swifter than time, speeds onward to its end without any hope of renewal, unless it be in that other life which is boundless. So says Cide Hamete the Mohammedan philosopher; for there are many that by the light of nature alone, without the light of faith, have a comprehension of the fleeting nature and instability of this present life and the duration of that eternal life we hope for. But our author is here speaking of the rapidity with which Sancho's government came to an end, melted away, disappeared, vanished as it were in smoke and shadow.

For as he lay in bed on the night of the seventh day of his governorship, sated, not with bread and wine, but with delivering judgments and giving opinions and making laws and proclamations, just as sleep, in spite of hunger, was beginning to close his eyelids, he heard such a noise of bell-ringing and shouting that one would have thought the whole island was sinking. He sat up in bed listening intently, trying to make out what could be the cause of so great an uproar. Not only, however, was he unable to discover what it was, but as countless drums and trumpets now helped to swell the din of the bells and shouts, he was more puzzled than ever and filled with fear and terror; and getting up, he put on a pair of slippers because of the dampness of the floor, and without putting on a dressing gown or anything of the kind, he rushed to the door of his room just in time to see aproaching along a corridor a band of more than twenty persons with lighted torches and naked swords in their hands, all shouting out, "To arms, to arms, señor governor, to arms! The enemy is on the island in countless numbers, and we are lost unless your skill and valor come to our support."

Keeping up this noise, tumult, and uproar, they came to where Sancho stood dazed and bewildered by what he saw and heard, and as they approached one of them called out to him, "Arm at once, your lordship, if you would not have yourself destroyed and the whole island lost."

"What have I to do with arming?" said Sancho. "What do I know about arms or reinforcements? Better leave all that to my master Don Quixote, who will settle it and make all safe in two shakes; for I, sinner that I am, God help me, don't understand these fights."

"Ah, señor governor," said another, "what timidity this is! Arm yourself; here are arms for you, offensive and defensive; come out to the plaza and be our leader and captain; it is your prerogative by right, for you are our governor."

"Arm me then, in God's name," said Sancho, and they at once produced two long shields they had come provided with, and fitted them on him over his nightshirt, without letting him put on anything else, one shield in front and the other behind, and passing his arms through openings they had made, they bound him tight with ropes, so that there he was walled and boarded up as straight as a spindle and unable to bend his knees or stir a single step. In his hand they placed a lance, on which he leaned to keep himself from falling, and as soon as they had him ready, they told him to march forward and lead them on and give them all courage; for with him for their north pole and beacon and morning star, they were sure to bring their business to a successful conclusion.

"How am I to march, unlucky that I am?" said Sancho, "when I can't move my kneecaps, for these boards I have bound so tight to my body won't let me. What you must do is carry me in your arms and lay me across or set me upright at some entry, and I'll hold it either with this lance or with my body."

"Oh, señor governor!" cried another, "it is fear more than the boards that keeps you from walking; hurry up! Move! There is no time to lose; the enemy is increasing in numbers, the shouts grow louder, and the danger is pressing."

Urged by these exhortations and reproaches, the poor governor tried to move but fell to the ground with such a crash that he thought he had broken himself all to pieces. There he lay like a tortoise enclosed in its shell, or a side of bacon between two kneading-troughs, or a boat bottom up on the beach; nor did the gang of jokers feel any compassion for him when they saw him down. On the contrary, extinguishing their torches, they began to shout again and to repeat the calls to arms with such energy, trampling on poor Sancho, and slashing at his shields with their swords in such a way that, if he had not pulled himself in and made himself small and drawn in his head between the shields, it would have gone badly with the poor governor. Squeezed into that cramped space, he lay sweating and sweating again, and commending himself with all his heart to God to deliver him from his present peril.

Some stumbled over him, others fell upon him, and there was one who stood on top of him for some time, and from there as if from a watchtower issued orders to the troops, shouting out, "Over here, men! The enemy is concentrating in this direction! Guard the door there! Shut that gate! Push back those ladders! Bring pots of pitch and resin, and kettles of boiling oil! Block the streets with mattresses!" In short, in his ardor he mentioned every piece of equipment and every implement and engine of war by means of which an attack on a city is warded off, while the bruised and battered Sancho, who heard and suffered all, was saying to himself, "O if it would only please the Lord to let the island be conquered soon and me see myself either dead or out of this torture!" Heaven heard his prayer, and when he least expected it, he heard voices exclaiming. "Victory, victory! The enemy is beaten! Come, señor governor, get up, and come and enjoy the victory, and divide the spoils that have been won from the foe by the might of that invincible arm."

"Lift me up," said the wretched Sancho in a woebegone voice. They helped him to rise, and as soon as he was on his feet he said, "I'll be damned if I have beaten any enemies. I don't want to divide the spoils of the foe. I beg and entreat some friends, if I have one, to give me a sip of wine, for I'm drying up, and dry my sweat, because I'm dripping wet."

They rubbed him down, fetched him wine, and untied the shields. He seated himself on his bed, and with fear, agitation, and fatigue he fainted away. Those who had taken part in the joke were now sorry they had pushed it so far. However, the anxiety which his fainting had caused them was relieved by his coming to. He asked what time it was; they told him it was just daybreak. He said no more, and in total silence began to dress himself, while all watched him, waiting to see why he was putting on his clothes in such haste.

He got himself dressed at last, and then, slowly, for he was bruised and could not go fast, he proceeded to the stable, followed by all who were present, and going up to Dapple embraced him and gave him a kiss on the forehead and said to him, not without tears in his eyes, "Come here, comrade and friend and partner of my hardships and sorrow! When I was with you and had no cares to trouble me except mending your harness and feeding your little carcass, my hours, my days, and my years were happy. But since I left you and climbed the towers of ambition and pride, a thousand troubles, a thousand hardships, and four thousand worries have entered into my soul." While he was speaking in this strain, he was fixing the packsaddle on the ass, without a word from anyone. Then having Dapple saddled, he, with great pain and difficulty, got up on him, and addressing himself to the majordomo, the secretary, the steward, and Pedro Recio the doctor and several others who stood by, he said, "Make way, gentlemen, and let me go back to my old freedom; let me go look for my past life, and resurrect from this present death. I was not born to be a governor or protect islands or cities from the enemies that want to attack them. Ploughing and digging, dressing and pruning grapevines are more in my line than defending provinces or kingdoms. 'Saint Peter is at home in Rome.' I mean each of us is best following the trade he was born to. A sickle fits my hand better than a governor's scepter; I'd rather have my fill of gazpacho than be dependent on the stinginess of a meddling doctor who kills me with hunger, and I'd rather lie in summer under the shade of an oak, and in winter wrap myself in a double sheepskin jacket in freedom, than go to bed between holland sheets and dress in sables under the burden of a governorship. God be with your worships, and tell my lord the duke that 'naked I came, naked I remain, I neither lose nor gain.' I mean that without a cent I came into this government, and without a cent I go out of it, very different from the way governors usually leave other islands. Stand aside and let me go; I have to poultice myself, for I believe every one of my ribs is crushed, thanks to the enemies that have been trampling on me tonight."

"That is unnecessary, señor governor," said Doctor Recio, "for I will give your worship a potion for falls and bruises that will soon make you as sound and strong as ever; and as for your diet, I promise your worship to behave better and let you eat plentifully of whatever you like."

"You spoke too late," said Sancho. "I'd as soon turn Turk as stay any longer. Those jokes are not funny the second time. By God I'd as soon stay on in this governorship, or take on another, even if it was offered me on a platter, as fly to heaven without wings. I am a Panza, and they are all obstinate, and if they once say 'odds,' odds it must be, no matter if it is evens, in spite of everybody. Here in this stable I leave the ant's wings that lifted me up into the air for the swifts and other birds to eat, and let's get our feet back on the ground; and if they're not in perforated cordovan shoes, they won't lack rough hemp-soled sandals. 'Stick to your own kind' and 'Don't go in over your head.' And now let me pass; it's getting late."

To this the majordomo said, "Señor governor, we would glady let your worship go, though it grieves us very much to lose you, for your wit and Christian conduct naturally make us want to keep you; but it is well known that every governor, before he leaves the place where he has been governing, is bound first of all to render an account. Let your worship do so for the ten days you have held the governorship, and then you may go and the peace of God go with you."

"No one can demand it of me," said Sancho, "but the person my lord the duke appoints; I am going to meet him, and to him I'll give an exact one; besides, when I leave naked as I do, there is no other proof needed to show that I have governed like an angel."

"By God, the great Sancho is right," said Doctor Recio, "and we should let him go, for the duke will be delighted to see him."

They all agreed to this and allowed him to go, first offering to keep him company and furnish him with all he wanted for his own comfort or for the journey. Sancho said he did not want anything more than a little barley for Dapple and half a cheese and half a loaf for himself; for the distance being so short there was no reason for any better or bigger provisions. They all embraced him, and he with tears embraced all of them and left them filled with admiration not only at his remarks but at his firm and sensible resolution.

Chapter LIV

WHICH DEALS WITH MATTERS RELATING TO THIS HISTORY AND NO OTHER

The duke and duchess resolved that the challenge Don Quixote had given their vassal, for the reason already mentioned, should proceed. And as the young man was in Flanders, to which he had fled to escape having Doña Rodríguez for a mother-in-law, they arranged to substitute for him a Gascon lackey named Tosilos, first of all carefully instructing him in all he had to do.

Two days later the duke told Don Quixote that in four days from that time his opponent would present himself on the field of battle armed as a knight and would maintain that the damsel lied through her teeth if she affirmed that he had given her a promise of marriage. Don Quixote was greatly pleased at the news and promised himself to do wonders in this affair, and he considered it fortunate that an opportunity should have arisen for letting his noble hosts see what the might of his strong arm was capable of. And so in high spirits and satisfaction he awaited the expiration of the four days, which, measured by his impatience seemed four hundred ages.

Let us leave them to pass, as we do other things, and go and keep Sancho company, as mounted on Dapple, half glad, half sad, he paced along on his road to join his master, in whose society he was happier than in being governor of all the islands in the world.

Well then, it so happened that before he had gone a great way from the island of his government (and whether it was island, city, town, or village that he governed, he never troubled himself to inquire) he saw coming along the road he was traveling six pilgrims with staffs, foreigners of the sort that beg for alms singing. As they drew near they arranged themselves in a line and lifting up their voices all together began to sing in their own language something that Sancho could not understand, with the exception of one word which was plainly "alms." From which he gathered that it was alms they asked for in their song; and being, as Cide Hamete says, excessively charitable, he took out of his saddlebags the half loaf and half cheese he had been provided with and gave it to them, explaining to them by signs that he had nothing else to give. They received it very gladly, but exclaimed, "Geld! Geld!"

"I don't understand what you want of me, good people," said Sancho.

Then one of them took a purse out of his bosom and showed it to Sancho, by which he comprehended they were asking for money, and putting his thumb to his throat and spreading his hand upwards[1] he gave them to understand that he had not the sign of a coin about him, and urging Dapple forward he broke through them. But as he was passing, one of them who had been examining him very closely rushed towards him, and flinging his arms around his waist exclaimed in a loud voice and good Spanish, "God bless me! What's this I see? Is it possible that I hold in my arms my dear friend, my good neighbor Sancho Panza? But there's no doubt about it, for I'm not asleep, nor am I drunk just now."

Sancho was surprised to hear himself called by his name and find himself embraced by a foreign pilgrim, and after examining him steadily without speaking, he was still unable to recognize him; but the pilgrim seeing his perplexity cried, "What? Is it possible, Sancho Panza, that you do not know your neighbor Ricote, the Morisco shopkeeper of your village?"

Sancho, looking at him more carefully, began to recall his features, and at last recognized him perfectly, and without getting off the donkey threw his arms round his neck saying, "Who the devil could have recognized you, Ricote, in the disguise you're wearing? Tell me, who turned you into a Frenchy? How do you dare to return to Spain? If they catch you and identify you, you'll be in bad trouble."

"If you don't betray me, Sancho," said the pilgrim, "I am sure that in this dress no one will recognize me. Let's get off the road into that grove there where my comrades are going to eat and rest,

1. Apparently a universal gesture, as our own shrug is now.

and you can eat with them there, for they are very good fellows. I'll have time to tell you then all that has happened to me since I left our village in obedience to his Majesty's edict that threatened such severities against the unfortunate people of my nation, as you have heard."

Sancho complied, and Ricote having spoken to the other pilgrims, they withdrew to the grove they saw, a considerable distance from the road. They threw down their staffs, took off their pilgrim's cloaks, and remained in their shirtsleeves. They were all good-looking young fellows, except Ricote, who was a man somewhat advanced in years. They carried knapsacks, all of them, and all apparently well filled, at least with things provocative of thirst, such as would summon it from two leagues off. They stretched themselves on the ground, and making a tablecloth of the grass, they spread on it bread, salt, knives, walnuts, scraps of cheese, and well-picked ham-bones which if they were past gnawing were not past sucking. They also set out a black edible called, they say, caviar, and made of the eggs of fish, a great thirst-wakener. Nor was there any lack of olives, dry, it is true, and without any seasoning, but for all that tasty and pleasant.

But what made the best show on the field of the banquet was half a dozen leather bottles of wine, for each of them produced his own from his knapsack. Even the good Ricote, who from a Morisco had transformed himself into a German or Dutchman, took out his, which in size might have vied with the five others. They then began to eat with great enjoyment and very leisurely, making the most of each morsel—very small ones of everything—that they took up on the point of the knife. And then all at the same moment, they raised their arms and *botas* aloft, the mouths of the leather bottles placed in their mouths and all eyes fixed on heaven just as if they were taking aim at it. And in this position they remained ever so long, wagging their heads from side to side as if in acknowledgment of the pleasure they were enjoying while they decanted what was inside the bottles into their own stomachs.

Sancho beheld all, "and nothing gave him pain."[2] On the contrary, acting on the proverb he knew so well, "when in Rome do as the Romans do," he asked Ricote for his *bota* and took aim like the rest of them, and with no less enjoyment. Four times were the *botas* raised, but the fifth it was all in vain, for they were drier and more sapless than a rush by that time, which made the jollity that had been kept up so far begin to flag.

Every now and then one of them would grasp Sancho's right hand in his own saying, "Spanish people, German people all same;

2. A line from a ballad, *Mira Nero de Tarpeya*.

good friend." And Sancho would answer, "Good friend, by Gott!"[3] and then go off into a fit of laughter that lasted an hour, without a moment's thought of anything that had happened to him in his governorship; for cares have very little sway over us while we are eating and drinking. At length, the wine having been exhausted, drowsiness began to come over them, and they fell asleep on their very table and tablecloth. Ricote and Sancho alone remained awake, for they had eaten more and drunk less, and Ricote drawing Sancho aside, they seated themselves at the foot of a beech, leaving the pilgrims buried in sweet sleep; and without once falling into his own Morisco tongue, Ricote spoke as follows in pure Castilian:

"You know, neighbor and friend Sancho Panza, how the proclamation or edict his Majesty commanded to be issued against those of my nation filled us all with terror and dismay;[4] me at least it did, to such a degree that I think before the time granted us for leaving Spain was up, the full force of the penalty had already fallen on me and on my children. I decided, then, and I think wisely (just like one who knows that at a certain date the house he lives in will be taken from him, and looks out beforehand for another to change into), I decided, I say, to leave the town, alone and without my family, and to go seek out some place to move them to comfortably and not in the hurried way in which the others took their departure. For I saw very plainly, and so did all the older men among us, that the proclamations were not mere threats, as some said, but laws which would be enforced at the appointed time. And what made me believe this was what I knew of the treacherous ill-considered schemes which our people harbored, schemes of such a nature that I think it was a divine inspiration that moved his Majesty to carry out so bold a resolution. Not that we were all guilty, for some were true and steadfast Christians; but they were so few that they could not hold out against those who were not; and it was not prudent to cherish a viper in the bosom by allowing enemies to remain in the house. In short it was with just cause that we were punished with banishment, a mild and lenient penalty in the eyes of some, but to us the most terrible that could be inflicted upon us.

"Wherever we are, we weep for Spain; for after all we were born there, and it is our native land. Nowhere do we find the reception our unhappy condition needs; and in Barbary and all the parts of Africa where we counted upon being received, assisted, and welcomed, it is there they insult and ill-treat us most. We did not

3. The pilgrim speaks broken Italian. His remark probably alludes to the political connections between Hapsburg Spain and the German Holy Roman Empire, a reference appropriate to a German Catholic traveler in the anti-Protestant Spain of this period.

4. The edict Ricote refers to was that published on September 22, 1609, commanding the Moriscos under pain of death to hold themselves in readiness to embark for Africa at three days' notice.

know our good fortune until we lost it; and such is the longing we almost all of us have to return to Spain, that most of those who like myself know the language, and there are many who do, come back to it and leave their wives and children behind, unprovided for, so great is their love for it; and now I know by experience the meaning of the saying, 'sweet is the love of one's country.'

"I left our village, as I said, and went to France, but though they gave us a kind reception there I was anxious to see all I could. I crossed into Italy and reached Germany, and there it seemed to me we might live with more freedom, as the inhabitants are not very particular; everyone lives as he likes, for in most parts they enjoy freedom of religion. I took a house in a town near Augsburg and then joined these pilgrims, who are in the habit of coming to Spain in great numbers every year to visit the shrines here, which they look upon as their Indies and a sure and certain source of profit. They travel nearly all over it, and there is no town out of which they do not go well fed and well drunk, as the saying is, and with a *real*, at least in money, and they come out at the end of their travels with more than a hundred crowns saved, which, changed into gold, they smuggle out of the kingdom either in the hollow of their staffs or in the patches of their pilgrim's cloaks or by some device of their own, and carry to their own country in spite of the guards at the posts and passes where they are searched.

"Now my purpose is, Sancho, to carry away the treasure that I left buried, which, as it is outside the town, I'll be able to do without risk, and to write, or cross over from Valencia, to my daughter and wife, who I know are at Algiers, and find some means of bringing them to some French port and from there to take them to Germany. There we will await what it may be God's will to do with us; for, after all, Sancho, I know well that Ricota my daughter and Francisca Ricota my wife are Catholic Christians, and though I am not such a good one, still I am more of a Christian than a Moor, and it is always my prayer to God that he will open the eyes of my understanding and show me how I am to serve Him. But what amazes me and I cannot understand is why my wife and daughter should have gone to Barbary rather than to France, where they could live as Christians."

To this Sancho replied, "Remember, Ricote, that may not have been possible for them, because Juan Tiopieyo your wife's brother took them, and being a true Moor he went where he could go most easily. And I can tell you something else: it is my belief you are going in vain to look for what you left buried, for we heard they took from your brother-in-law and your wife a great quantity of pearls and money in gold which they were carrying out of the country, undeclared."

"That may be," said Ricote, "but I know they didn't touch my hoard, because I didn't tell them where it was, for fear of what might happen. So, if you'll come with me, Sancho, and help me to take it away and conceal it, I will give you two hundred crowns. With such a sum you can take care of your needs, because you know that I know they are many."

"I would do it," said Sancho, "but I am not at all greedy, because I gave up a job this morning in which I could have made the walls of my house out of gold and eaten off silver plates before six months were over. And so for this reason, and because I feel I would be guilty of treason to my king if I helped his enemies, I wouldn't go with you if, instead of promising me two hundred crowns, you gave me four hundred here in cash."

"And what job is this you have given up, Sancho?" asked Ricote.

"I have given up being governor of an island," said Sancho, "and such a one, faith, as you won't find the like of easily."

"And where is this island?" said Ricote.

"Where?" said Sancho. "Two leagues from here, and it is called the island of Barataria."

"Nonsense! Sancho," said Ricote. "Islands are way out in the sea; there are no islands on the mainland."

"What? No islands!" said Sancho. "I tell you, Ricote my friend, I left it this morning, and yesterday I was governing there as I pleased like a hanging judge,[5] but for all that I gave it up, for a governor's job seemed to me a dangerous office."

"And what have you gained by the government?" asked Ricote.

"I have gained," said Sancho, "the knowledge that I am no good for governing, unless it is a herd of cattle, and that the riches that come from these governments are obtained at the cost of one's rest and sleep, and even one's food; for on islands the governors must eat little, especially if they have doctors to look after their health."

"I don't understand you, Sancho," said Ricote, "but it seems to me that you are talking nonsense. Who would give you islands to govern? Is there any scarcity in the world of smarter men than you for governors? Hold your tongue, Sancho, and come back to your senses, and consider whether you'll come with me as I said to help me to take away the treasure I left buried (for in fact it may be called a treasure, it is so large), and I will give you something to live on, as I told you."

"And I have told you already, Ricote, that I will not," said Sancho. "Be satisfied that I won't betray you, and be on your way in God's name and let me go mine; for I know that well-gotten gain may be lost, but ill-gotten gain is lost, itself and its owner likewise."

"I won't argue, Sancho," said Ricote. "But tell me, were you in our village when my wife and daughter and brother-in-law left it?"

"I was," said Sancho, "and I can tell you your daughter left it

5. Literally, "like a Sagittarius." The meaning is not clear.

looking so lovely that all the village turned out to see her, and everybody said she was the prettiest creature in the world. She cried as she went, and embraced all her friends and acquaintances and those who came out to see her, and she begged them all to commend her to God and Our Lady his mother, in such a touching way that it made me cry myself, though I'm not much given to tears. And, faith, some would have liked to hide her, or follow her along the road and take her away from the officials; but the fear of going against the king's command kept them back. The one who showed himself most upset was Don Pedro Gregorio, the rich young heir you're acquainted with, and they say he was deeply in love with her. Since she left he has not been seen in our village again, and we all suspect he has gone after her to kidnap her, but so far nothing has been heard of it."

"I always had a suspicion that gentleman had a passion for my daughter," said Ricote, "but as I felt sure of my Ricota's virtue it gave me no uneasiness to know that he loved her; for you must have heard it said, Sancho, that Morisco women seldom or never have affairs with Old Christians; and my daughter, who I believe thought more of being a Christian than of being in love, would not trouble herself about the attentions of this heir."

"God grant it," said Sancho, "for it would be a bad business for both of them; but now let me leave, friend Ricote, for I want to reach where my master Don Quixote is tonight."

"God be with you, brother Sancho," said Ricote. "My comrades are beginning to stir, and it is time, too, for us to continue our journey."

Then they both embraced, and Sancho mounted Dapple, and Ricote leaned on his staff, and so they parted.

Chapter LV

OF WHAT HAPPENED TO SANCHO ON THE ROAD, AND OTHER THINGS THAT CANNOT BE SURPASSED

The length of time he delayed with Ricote prevented Sancho from reaching the duke's castle that day, though he was within half a league of it when night, somewhat dark and cloudy, overtook him. This, however, as it was summer time, did not give him much uneasiness, and he turned off the road intending to wait for morning. But his ill luck and hard fate decreed that as he was searching about for a place to make himself as comfortable as possible, he and Dapple fell into a deep, dark hole among some very old buildings. As he fell he commended himself with all his heart to God, believing he was not going to stop until he reached the depths of the bottomless pit. But it did not turn out so, for a little more than three times a man's height Dapple touched bottom, and Sancho found himself sitting on him without having received any hurt or damage whatever.

He felt himself all over and held his breath to see whether he was quite sound or had a hole made in him anywhere, and finding himself all right and whole and in perfect health, he was profuse in his thanks to God our Lord for the mercy that had been shown him, for he was sure he had been broken into a thousand pieces. He also felt along the sides of the pit with his hands to see if it were possible to get out of it without help, but he found they were quite smooth and afforded no hold anywhere, at which he was greatly distressed, especially when he heard how pathetically and dolefully Dapple was groaning, and no wonder he complained, nor was it from ill temper, for in truth he was not in very good shape. "Oh," said Sancho, "what unexpected accidents happen at every step to those who live in this miserable world! Who would have said that a man who was sitting on a throne yesterday, governor of an island, giving orders to his servants and his vassals, would find himself today buried in a pit without a soul to help him or servant or vassal to come to his aid? My donkey and I will die of hunger here, if he doesn't die of his bruises and injuries, and I of grief and sorrow. At any rate I won't be as lucky as my master Don Quixote of La Mancha, when he went down into the cave of that enchanted Montesinos, where he found people to make more of him than if he had been in his own house; for it seems as if they had a table laid out and a bed ready made for him. He saw pretty and pleasant visions there, but here I imagine I'll see toads and adders. Unlucky wretch that I am, what an end my foolishness and fancies have come to! They'll take my bones out of here, when it is heaven's will that I'm found, picked clean, white, and polished, and poor Dapple's with them. That way perhaps they'll discover who we are, at least those who have heard that Sancho Panza is never separated from his donkey, nor his donkey from Sancho Panza. Unlucky wretches, I say again, that our cruel fate should not let us die in our own country and among our own people, where if there was no help for our misfortune, at any rate there would be some one to grieve for it and to close our eyes as we passed away!

"O comrade and friend, how badly have I repaid your faithful services! Forgive me, and ask Fortune, as well as you can, to deliver us out of this miserable plight we are both in; and I promise to put a crown of laurel on your head, and make you look like a poet laureate, and give you double rations."

In this way did Sancho lament, and his ass listened to him without answering him a word, such was the distress and anguish the poor beast found himself in. At length, after a night spent in bitter moanings and lamentations, day came, and by its light Sancho perceived that it was wholly impossible to escape from that pit without help, and he began to complain and utter loud shouts to find out if there was anyone within hearing. But all his shouting was only crying in the wilderness, for there was not a soul anywhere in the neighborhood to hear him, and he gave himself up for dead.

Dapple was lying on his back, and Sancho helped him to his feet, though he was scarcely able to stand. Then taking a piece of bread out of his saddlebags, which had shared their fortunes in the fall, he gave it to the ass, to whom it was not unwelcome, saying to him as if he understood, "As long as you have food, even troubles seem good."

And now he observed on one side of the pit an opening large enough to admit a person if he stooped and held himself in. Sancho rushed to it and crawled through. He saw that it was wide and spacious inside, which he was able to see because a ray of sunlight that penetrated what might be called the roof showed it all plainly. He observed too that it opened and widened out into another spacious cavity; seeing which he made his way back to where the ass was, and with a stone began to pick away the dirt from the opening until in a short time he had made room for the beast to pass easily, and this accomplished, taking him by the halter, he began to follow the cavern to see if there was any outlet at the other end. He advanced in the gloom, sometimes without any light, but never without fear. "God Almighty help me!" said he to himself. "This misfortune would make a good adventure for my master Don Quixote. He would certainly have taken these depths and dungeons for flowery gardens or the palace of Galiana,[1] and would expect to come out of this darkness and narrow passage into some blooming meadow. But poor unlucky me, with no one to guide me, discouraged, I expect at every step another pit deeper than the first to open under my feet and swallow me up for good. 'Welcome, evil, if you come alone.' "

In this way and with these reflections, he seemed to himself to have traveled rather more than half a league when at last he perceived a dim light—it was apparently morning already—that was entering somewhere showing that this road, which appeared to him the road to the other world, led to some opening.

Here Cide Hamete leaves him, and returns to Don Quixote, who in high spirits and satisfaction was looking forward to the day fixed for the battle he was to fight with the man who had robbed Doña Rodríguez's daughter of her honor, for whom he hoped to obtain satisfaction for the wrong and injury shamefully done to her.

It came to pass, then, that having sallied forth one morning to practice and exercise himself in what he would have to do in the

1. A legendary Moorish princess, the remains of whose palace are still pointed out near the bridge of Alcántara in the city of Toledo.

encounter he expected the next day, as he was putting Rocinante through a short run or charge, he brought his horse's feet so close to a pit that but for reining in tightly it would have been impossible for him to avoid falling into it. He pulled him up, however, without a fall, and coming a little closer examined the hole without dismounting. But as he was looking at it he heard loud cries proceeding from it, and by listening attentively was able to make out that he who uttered them was saying, "Ho, above there! Is there any Christian that hears me, or any charitable gentleman that will take pity on a sinner buried alive, on an unfortunate disgoverned governor?"

It struck Don Quixote that it was the voice of Sancho Panza he heard, at which he was astounded and amazed, and shouting as loudly as he could, he cried out, "Who is down there? Who is that crying?"

"Who else would be here or would be crying," was the answer, "but poor Sancho Panza, for his sins and for his bad luck, governor of the island of Barataria, formerly squire to the famous knight Don Quixote of La Mancha?"

When Don Quixote heard this his amazement was redoubled and his astonishment grew greater than ever, for it came to his mind that Sancho must be dead and that his soul was in torment down there; and carried away by this idea he exclaimed, "I conjure thee by everything that as a Catholic Christian I can conjure thee by, tell me who thou art; and if thou art a soul in torment, tell me what thou wouldst have me do for thee; for as my profession is to give aid and succor to those that need it in this world, I shall as a Catholic aid and succor the distressed of the other, who cannot help themselves."

"In that case," answered the voice, "your worship who speaks to me must be my master Don Quixote of La Mancha. From the tone of the voice it can undoubtedly be nobody else."

"I am Don Quixote," replied Don Quixote, "he whose profession it is to aid and succor the living and the dead in their necessities; wherefore tell me who thou art, for thou art keeping me in suspense; because, if thou art my squire Sancho Panza, and art dead, since the devils have not carried thee off, and thou art by God's mercy in purgatory, our holy mother the Roman Catholic Church has intercessory means sufficient to release thee from the pains thou art in; and I for my part will plead with her to that end, so far as my means will go; without further delay, therefore, declare thyself, and tell me who thou art."

"By all that's good," was the answer, "and by the birth of anyone your worship chooses, I swear, Señor Don Quixote of La Mancha, that I am your squire Sancho Panza, and that I have never died in all my life. But I have given up my governorship, for reasons that would take too long to explain, and last night Dapple and I fell into this pit where I am now, and Dapple won't let me lie, for as more proof he is here with me."

Nor was this all; one would have thought the ass understood what Sancho said, because that moment he began to bray so loudly that the whole cave echoed.

"A splendid witness!" exclaimed Don Quixote. "I know that bray as well as if I were its mother, and your voice too, my Sancho. Wait while I go to the duke's castle, which is nearby, and I will bring some one to take you out of this pit into which your sins no doubt have brought you."

"Go, your worship," said Sancho, "and come back quick for God's sake; I can't stand being buried alive any longer, and I'm dying of fear."

Don Quixote left him and hastened to the castle to tell the duke and duchess what had happened to Sancho, and they were not a little astonished at it. They could easily understand his having fallen, because the cave had been in existence there from time immemorial; but they could not imagine how he had given up the government without their receiving any warning of his coming.

To be brief, they brought 'some cords and ropes,' as the ballad says, and by dint of many hands and much labor they pulled Dapple and Sancho Panza out of the darkness into the light of day. A student who saw him remarked, "That's the way all bad governors should come out of their governments, as this sinner comes out of the depths of the abyss, dead with hunger, pale, and I suppose without a cent."

Sancho overheard him and said, "It is eight or ten days, brother critic, since I began to govern the island they gave me, and all that time I was never full, not even for an hour; doctors persecuted me, and enemies crushed my bones; I had no opportunity of taking bribes or collecting my fees; and if that is the case, as it is, I don't deserve, I think, to come out in this fashion. But 'man proposes and God disposes,' and God knows what is best, and what suits each one best. 'When in Rome . . .' and don't ever say 'That'll never happen to me,' and 'When she got there, the cupboard was bare.' God knows my meaning and that's enough; I say no more, though I could."

"Don't be angry or annoyed at what you hear Sancho," said Don Quixote, "or this will never end. As long as your conscience is clear, let them say what they like; for trying to stop slanderers' tongues is like trying to put a fence around the countryside. If a governor comes out of his government rich, they say he has been a thief; and if he comes out poor, that he has been shiftless and stupid."

"They'll be pretty sure this time," said Sancho, "to consider me a fool rather than a thief."

Thus talking, and surrounded by boys and a crowd of people, they reached the castle, where on one of the galleries the duke and duchess stood waiting for them. But Sancho would not go up to see the duke until he had first put up Dapple in the stable, for he said the donkey had spent a very bad night in its last quarters. Then he went upstairs to see his lord and lady, and kneeling before them he said, "Because it was your highnesses' pleasure, not because of any merits of my own, I went to govern your island of Barataria, to which 'naked I came and naked I remain; I neither lose nor gain.' Whether I have governed well or badly, I have had witnesses who will say what they think fit. I have answered questions, I have decided cases, and always dying of hunger, for Doctor Pedro Recio of Tirteafuera, the island- and governor-doctor, would have it so. Enemies attacked us by night and pressed us hard, but the people of the island say they came out safe and victorious by the might of my arm; and may God give them as much health as there's truth in what they say.

"In short, during that time I have weighed the cares and responsibilities governing brings with it, and I find my shoulders can't bear them, nor are they a load for my back or arrows for my quiver; and so, before the government threw me out, I preferred to throw the government out; and yesterday morning I left the island as I found it, with the same streets, houses, and roofs it had when I entered it. I asked nobody for a loan, nor did I try to fill my pocket; and though I meant to pass some useful laws, I made hardly any, as I was afraid they would not be obeyed; for in that case it comes to the same thing to pass them or not to pass them. I left the island, as I said, without any escort except my donkey. I fell into a cavern; I followed it until this morning by the light of the sun I saw a way out. But it was not so easy. If heaven had not sent me my master Don Quixote, I'd have stayed there till the end of the world.

"So now my lord and lady duke and duchess, here is your governor Sancho Panza, who in the ten days he has held the governorship has come to the knowledge that he would not give anything to be governor, not only of an island, but of the whole world. And now that that's settled, I kiss your worships' feet. And like a boy in a game of leapfrog, I'm jumping out of government and into the service of my master Don Quixote. After all, though in it I eat my bread in fear and trembling, at any rate I eat my fill; and for my part, so long as I'm full, it's all alike to me whether it's with carrots or with partridges."

Here Sancho brought his long speech to an end, Don Quixote having been the whole time in dread that he would utter thousands of absurdities; and when he saw him conclude with so few, he thanked heaven in his heart. The duke embraced Sancho and told him he was heartily sorry he had given up the government so soon, but that he would see that he was provided with some other post on his estate less onerous and more profitable. The duchess also embraced him, and gave orders that he should be taken good care of, as it was plain to see he had been badly bruised and was in bad shape.

Chapter LVI

OF THE PRODIGIOUS AND UNPARALLELED BATTLE THAT TOOK PLACE BETWEEN DON QUIXOTE OF LA MANCHA AND THE LACKEY TOSILOS IN DEFENCE OF THE DAUGHTER OF DOÑA RODRÍGUEZ

The duke and duchess had no reason to regret the joke that had been played upon Sancho Panza in giving him the government, especially as their majordomo returned the same day and gave them a minute account of almost every word and deed that Sancho uttered or did during the time. And to wind up with, he eloquently described to them the attack on the island and Sancho's fright and departure, with which they were not a little amused.

After this, the history goes on to say that the day fixed for the battle arrived and that the duke, after having repeatedly instructed his lackey Tosilos how to deal with Don Quixote so as to vanquish him without killing or wounding him, gave orders to have the iron points removed from the lances, telling Don Quixote that Christian charity, on which he prided himself, could not suffer the battle to be fought with so much risk and danger to life; and that he must be content with the offer of a battlefield on his territory (though that was against the decree of the holy Council,[1] which prohibits all challenges of the sort) and not push such an arduous venture to its extreme limits.

Don Quixote told his excellency to arrange all matters connected with the affair as he pleased and that he would obey him in everything. The dread day, then, having arrived and the duke having ordered a spacious stand to be erected facing the court of the castle for the judges of the field and the appellant dueñas, mother and daughter, vast crowds flocked from all the villages and hamlets of the neighborhood to see the novel spectacle of the battle, nobody, dead or alive, in those parts having ever seen or heard of such a one.

The first person to enter the field and the lists was the master of ceremonies, who surveyed and paced the whole ground to see that there was nothing unfair and nothing concealed to make the combatants stumble or fall. Then the dueñas entered and seated themselves, enveloped in shawls down to their eyes and even their bosoms, and displaying no slight emotion. Don Quixote appeared in

1. The Council of Trent (Canon xix, session xxv).

the lists; shortly afterwards, accompanied by several trumpets and mounted on a powerful steed that shook the whole place, the great lackey Tosilos made his appearance on one side of the courtyard with his visor down and stiffly cased in a suit of stout shining armor. The horse turned out to be a Frisian, broad-backed and gray, and with twenty-five pounds of wool hanging from each of his fetlocks.

The gallant combatant came well primed by his master the duke as to how he was to bear himself against the valiant Don Quixote of La Mancha. He had been warned that he must on no account kill him, but try to avoid the first encounter so as to run no risk of killing him, as he was sure to do if he met him head on. He crossed the courtyard at a walk, and coming to where the dueñas were, he stopped for a moment to look at her who demanded him for a husband. The marshal of the field summoned Don Quixote, who had already presented himself in the courtyard, and joining Tosilos he addressed the dueñas and asked them if they consented that Don Quixote of La Mancha should do battle for their right. They said they did and whatever he should do in their behalf they declared rightly done, final, and valid.

By this time the duke and duchess had taken their places in a gallery commanding the enclosure, which was ringed by a multitude of people eager to see this perilous and unparalleled encounter. The conditions of the combat were that if Don Quixote proved the victor, his antagonist was to marry the daughter of Doña Rodríguez; but if he should be vanquished, his opponent was released from the promise that was claimed against him and from all obligations to give satisfaction.

The master of ceremonies stationed them so that neither would face the sun and led each to the spot where he was to stand. The drums beat, the sound of the trumpets filled the air, the earth trembled under foot, the hearts of the gazing crowd were full of anxiety, some hoping for a happy outcome, some apprehensive of an unfortunate ending to the affair. And lastly, Don Quixote, commending himself with all his heart to God our Lord and to the lady Dulcinea del Toboso, stood waiting for them to give the necessary signal for the charge. Our lackey, however, was thinking of something very different; he only thought of what I am now going to mention.

It seems that as he stood contemplating his enemy, she struck him as the most beautiful woman he had ever seen all his life; and the little blind boy whom in our streets they commonly call Love had no mind to let slip the chance of triumphing over a lackey heart and adding it to the list of his trophies. And so, stealing gently upon him unseen, he drove an arrow two yards long into the poor lackey's left side and pierced his heart through and through;

which he was able to do quite at his ease, for Love is invisible and comes and goes as he likes, without anyone calling him to account for what he does.

Well then, when they gave the signal for the charge, our lackey was in a daze, thinking about the beauty of her whom he had already made mistress of his liberty, and so he paid no attention to the sound of the trumpet, unlike Don Quixote, who took off the instant he heard it, and, at the highest speed Rocinante was capable of, headed for his enemy, his good squire Sancho shouting lustily as he saw him start, "May God guide you, cream and flower of knights-errant! May God give you the victory, for you have justice on your side!"

But though Tosilos saw Don Quixote coming at him, he never stirred a step from the spot where he was posted, and instead of doing so, called loudly to the marshal of the field. When the latter came up to see what Tosilos wanted, he said, "Señor, is not this battle to decide whether I marry or do not marry that lady?" "Just so," was the answer. "Well then," said the lackey, "I feel qualms of conscience, and I would lay a heavy burden upon it if I were to proceed any further with the combat; I therefore declare that I yield myself vanquished and that I am willing to marry the lady at once."

The marshal of the field was lost in astonishment at the words of Tosilos; and as he was one of those who knew the plot behind the affair, he did not know what to say in reply. Don Quixote pulled up in mid career when he saw that his enemy was not attacking. The duke could not make out the reason why the battle did not go on. But the marshal of the field hastened to let him know what Tosilos said, and he was amazed and extremely angry at it.

In the meantime Tosilos advanced to where Doña Rodríguez sat and said in a loud voice, "Señora, I am willing to marry your daughter, and I have no wish to obtain by litigations and fighting what I can obtain in peace and without any risk to my life."

The valiant Don Quixote heard him, and said, "As that is the case, I am released and absolved from my promise. Let them marry by all means, and as 'God our Lord has given her to him, may Saint Peter add his blessing.' "

The duke had now descended to the courtyard of the castle, and going up to Tosilos he said to him, "Is it true, sir knight, that you yield yourself vanquished, and that moved by scruples of conscience you wish to marry this damsel?"

"It is, señor," replied Tosilos.

"And he does well," said Sancho. " 'Give to the cat what the mouse would steal, and he will rid you of the problem.' "

Tosilos meanwhile was trying to unlace his helmet, and he begged them to help him at once, as he was having trouble breathing and he could not tolerate being shut up for such a long time in that confined space. They removed it quickly, and his lackey features were revealed to the public gaze. At this sight Doña Rodríguez and her daughter raised a mighty outcry, exclaiming, "This is a trick! This is a trick! They have put Tosilos, my lord the duke's lackey, in place of the real husband. The justice of God and the king against such trickery, not to say roguery!"

"Do not distress yourselves, ladies," said Don Quixote. "For this is no trickery or roguery; or if it is, it is not the duke who is at the bottom of it, but those wicked enchanters who persecute me, and who, jealous of my reaping the glory of this victory, have turned your husband's features into those of this person, who you say is a lackey of the duke's. Take my advice, and notwithstanding the malice of my enemies, marry him, for beyond a doubt he is the one you wish for a husband."

When the duke heard this, all his anger was on the point of vanishing in a fit of laughter, and he said, "The things that happen to Señor Don Quixote are so extraordinary that I am ready to believe this lackey is not mine. But let us adopt this plan and scheme: let us put off the marriage for, say, two weeks, and let us keep this person about whom we are uncertain under lock, and perhaps in the course of that time he may return to his original shape. For the spite which the enchanters entertain against Señor Don Quixote cannot last so long, especially as it is of so little advantage to them to practice these deceptions and transformations."

"Oh, señor," said Sancho, "those scoundrels are well used to changing whatever concerns my master from one thing into another. A knight that he overcame some time back, called the Knight of the Mirrors, they turned into the shape of the bachelor Sansón Carrasco of our town and a great friend of ours; and my lady Dulcinea del Toboso they have turned into a farm girl. So I suspect this lackey will have to live and die a lackey all the days of his life."

Here the Rodríguez's daughter exclaimed, "Whoever this man who asks me to be his wife may be, I am grateful to him for it. I had rather be the lawful wife of a lackey than the jilted lover of a gentleman; though he who seduced me is nothing of the kind."

To be brief, all the talk and all that had happened ended in Tosilos' being shut up until it was seen how his transformation turned out. All hailed Don Quixote as victor, but most of the spectators were glum and disappointed at finding that the combatants they had been so anxiously waiting for had not torn one another to pieces, just as the boys are disappointed when the man they are waiting to see hanged does not come out because the prosecution or the court has pardoned him. The people dispersed; the duke and Don Quixote returned to the castle; they locked up Tosilos; Doña Rodríguez and her daughter remained perfectly contented when they saw that one way or another the affair must end in marriage; and Tosilos wanted nothing else.

Chapter LVII

WHICH TREATS OF HOW DON QUIXOTE TOOK LEAVE OF THE DUKE, AND OF WHAT FOLLOWED WITH THE WITTY AND IMPUDENT ALTISIDORA, ONE OF THE DUCHESS'S DAMSELS

Don Quixote now felt it was time to abandon a life of such idleness as he was leading in the castle; for he fancied that he was making himself sorely missed by remaining shut up and inactive amid the countless luxuries and enjoyments his hosts lavished upon him as a knight-errant; and he felt too that he would have to render a strict account to heaven of that indolence and seclusion. And so one day he asked the duke and duchess to grant him permission to take his departure. They gave it, showing at the same time that they were very sorry he was leaving them.

The duchess gave his wife's letters to Sancho Panza, who shed tears over them, saying, "Who would have thought that the great hopes which the news of my governorship raised in my wife Teresa Panza's breast would end like this, with my returning to the endless adventures of my master Don Quixote of La Mancha? Still I'm glad to see my Teresa behaved as she ought in sending the acorns, for if she had not sent them, I'd have been sorry and she'd have shown herself ungrateful. It is a comfort to me that they can't call that present a bribe because I already had the governorship when she sent them, and it's reasonable that those who have received a favor should show their gratitude, if it's only with a trifle. After all, I went into the government naked, and I come out of it naked; so I can say with an easy conscience— and that's no small matter— 'naked I came, naked I remain; I neither lose nor gain.' "

Thus did Sancho soliloquize on the day of their departure, as Don Quixote, who had the night before taken leave of the duke and duchess, made his appearance at an early hour in full armor in the courtyard of the castle. The whole household of the castle was watching him from the galleries, and the duke and duchess, too, came out to see him. Sancho was mounted on his Dapple, with his saddlebags, valise, and provisions, supremely happy because the duke's majordomo, the same that had acted the part of Trifaldi, had given him a little purse with two hundred gold crowns to meet the necessary expenses of the road, but of this Don Quixote knew nothing as yet. While all were, as has been said, observing him, suddenly from among the dueñas and handmaidens the impudent and witty Altisidora lifted up her voice and said in pathetic tones:

Give ear, cruel knight;
Draw rein; where's the need
Of spurring the flanks
Of that ill-broken steed?
From what art thou flying?
No dragon I am,
Not even a ewe,
But a tender young lamb.
Thou hast jilted a maiden
As fair to behold
As nymph of Diana
Or Venus of old.
Bireno,[1] Aeneas, what worse shall I call thee?
Barabbas go with thee! All evil befall thee!

In thy claws, ruthless robber,
Thou bearest away
The heart of a meek
Loving maid for thy prey;
Three kerchiefs thou stealest,
And garters a pair,
From legs than the whitest
Of marble more fair;
And the sighs that pursue thee
Would burn to the ground
Two thousand Troys
If so many were found.
Bireno, Aeneas, what worse shall I call thee?
Barabbas go with thee! All evil befall thee!

May no feelings of mercy
To Sancho be granted,
And thy Dulcinea
Be left still enchanted,
May thy falsehood to me
Find its punishment in her,
For in my land the just
Often pays for the sinner.
May thy grandest adventures
Disasterous prove,
May thy joys be all dreams,
And forgotten thy love.
Bireno, Aeneas, what worse shall I call thee?
Barabbas go with thee! All evil befall thee!

May thy name be abhorred
For thy conduct to ladies,

1. Bireno, Duke of Zealand, who deserted Olimpia, daughter of the Count of Holland, very much as Theseus deserted Ariadne. (*Orlando furioso*, Cantos IX and X.)

From London to England,
From Seville to Cádiz;
May thy cards be unlucky,
Thy hands contain ne'er a
King, seven, or ace
When thou playest *primera*;
When thy corns are pared down
May it be to the quick;
When thy molars are pulled
May the roots of them stick.
Bireno, Aeneas, what worse shall I call thee?
Barabbas go with thee! All evil befall thee!

All the while the unhappy Altisidora was lamenting in the above strain, Don Quixote stood staring at her; and without replying a word to her, he turned to Sancho and said. "Sancho my friend, I conjure you by the life of your forefathers tell me the truth: do you by any chance have the three kerchiefs and the garters this love-sick maid is talking about?"

To this Sancho answered, "The three kerchiefs I have; but the garters—she's out of her mind."

The duchess was amazed at Altisidora's brazenness; she knew that she was bold, lively, and impudent, but not so much so as to venture to such extremes of impudence; and not being prepared for the joke, her astonishment was all the greater. The duke had a mind to keep the joke going, so he said, "It does not seem to me proper, sir knight, that after receiving the hospitality that has been offered you in this castle, you should have cared to carry off even three kerchiefs, not to say my handmaid's garters. It is a sign of ingratitude and does not tally with your reputation. Return her garters, or else I defy you to mortal combat, for I am not afraid of wicked enchanters changing or altering my features as they changed those of my lackey Tosilos, who did battle with you."

"God forbid," said Don Quxiote, "that I should draw my sword against your illustrious person, from which I have received such great favors. The kerchiefs I will restore, as Sancho says he has them. As to the garters that is impossible, for I have not got them; neither has he. And if your handmaiden here will look in her hiding places, depend upon it, she will find them. I have never been a thief, my lord duke, nor do I mean to be so long as I live, if God cease not to have me in his keeping. This damsel by her own confession speaks as one in love, for which I am not to blame, and therefore need not ask pardon, either of her or of your excellency, whom I entreat to have a better opinion of me, and once more to give me leave to pursue my journey."

"And may God so prosper it, Señor Don Quixote," said the duchess, "that we may always hear good news of your exploits. God speed you; for the longer you stay, the more you inflame the hearts of the damsels who behold you. And as for this one of mine, I will so chastise her that she will not transgress again, either with her eyes or with her words."

"One word and no more, O valiant Don Quixote, I ask you to hear," said Altisidora, "and that is that I beg your pardon about the theft of the garters. For by God and upon my soul I have got them on, and I have fallen into the same blunder as he did who went looking for his donkey being all the while mounted on it."

"Didn't I say so?" said Sancho. "I'm a likely one to hide stolen goods! Why if I had wanted to deal in them, I would have had plenty of opportunities in my government."

Don Quixote bowed his head and saluted the duke and duchess and all the bystanders, and wheeling Rocinante around, Sancho following him on Dapple, he rode out of the castle, heading for Zaragoza.

Chapter LVIII

WHICH TELLS HOW ADVENTURES CAME CROWDING ON DON QUIXOTE IN SUCH NUMBERS THAT THEY GAVE ONE ANOTHER NO REST

When Don Quixote saw himself in the open country, free, and relieved of the attentions of Altisidora, he felt at his ease and ready to take up the pursuit of chivalry once more with renewed vigor.

Turning to Sancho he said, "Freedom, Sancho, is one of the most precious gifts that heaven has bestowed upon men; no treasures that the earth holds buried or the sea conceals can compare with it. For freedom, as for honor, life may and should be risked. And on the other hand, captivity is the greatest evil that can fall to the lot of man. I say this, Sancho, because you have seen the luxury, the abundance we have enjoyed in this castle we are leaving. Yet amid those delicious banquets and snow-cooled beverages I felt as though I were surrounded by deprivation and hunger, because I did not enjoy them with the same freedom as if they had been my own; because the sense of being under an obligation to return benefits and favors received is a restraint that checks the independence of the spirit. Happy is he, to whom heaven has given a piece of bread for which he is not bound to give thanks to any but heaven itself!"

"For all your worship says," said Sancho, "it is not becoming that there should be no thanks on our part for two hundred gold crowns that the duke's majordomo has given me in a little purse which I wear over my heart, like a warming poultice or strengthening medication, to meet any emergencies. For we won't always find castles where they'll entertain us; now and then we may come across roadside inns where they'll beat us."

In conversation of this sort the knight- and squire-errant were pursuing their journey, when, after they had gone a little more than half a league, they saw some dozen men dressed like farmers stretched out on their cloaks on the grass of a green meadow eating their dinner. They had beside them what seemed to be white sheets concealing some objects under them, standing upright or lying flat, and arranged at intervals. Don Quixote approached the diners, and, greeting them courteously first, he asked them what it was those cloths covered. "Señor," answered one of the party, "under these cloths are some images carved in relief and some wooden supports intended for an altarpiece we are putting up in our village. We carry them covered so that they won't get soiled, and on our shoulders so that they won't get broken."

"With your leave," said Don Quixote, "I should like to see them; for images that are carried so carefully no doubt must be fine ones."

"I should say they are!" said the other. "Let the money they cost speak for that; for as a matter of fact there is not one of them worth less than fifty ducats. And so that your worship may judge, wait a moment, and you shall see with your own eyes." And getting up from his dinner he went and uncovered the first image, which proved to be one of Saint George on horseback with a serpent writhing at his feet and the lance thrust down its throat with all that fierceness that is usually depicted. The whole group was one blaze of gold, as the saying is. On seeing it Don Quixote said, "That knight was one of the best knights-errant the army of heaven ever had; he was called Don Saint George, and he was moreover a defender of maidens. Let us see this next one."

The man uncovered it, and it was seen to be that of Saint Martin on his horse, dividing his cloak with the beggar. The instant Don Quixote saw it he said, "This knight too was one of the Christian adventurers, and I believe he was even more generous than valiant, as you may observe, Sancho, by his dividing his cloak with the beggar and giving him half of it. No doubt it was winter at the time, for otherwise he would have given him the whole of it, so charitable was he."

"It was not that, most likely," said Sancho, "but that he was heeding the proverb that says, 'You need good sense to know when to give and when to withhold.' "

Don Quixote laughed and asked them to take off the next cloth, underneath which was seen the image of the patron saint of the Spanish kingdoms seated on horseback, his sword stained with blood, trampling on Moors and treading heads underfoot; when he saw it Don Quixote exclaimed, "Ah, this is a knight, and of the squadrons of Christ! This one is called Don Saint James the Moorslayer, one of the bravest saints and knights the world ever had or heaven has now."

They then raised another cloth which it appeared covered Saint Paul falling from his horse, with all the details that are usually given in representations of his conversion, rendered in such lifelike style that one would have said Christ was speaking and Paul answering. "This," said Don Quixote, "was in his time the greatest enemy that the Church of God our Lord had, and the greatest champion it will ever have; a knight-errant in life, a steadfast saint in death, an untiring laborer in the Lord's vineyard, a teacher of the Gentiles, whose school was heaven, and whose instructor and master was Jesus Christ himself."

There were no more images, so Don Quixote told them to cover them up again, and said to those who had brought them, "I take it as a happy omen, brothers, to have seen what I have; for these saints and knights were of the same profession as myself, which is the calling of arms. Only there is this difference between them and me, that they were saints, and fought with divine weapons, and I am a sinner and fight with human ones. They won heaven by force of arms, for heaven suffereth violence; and I, so far, know not what I have won by dint of my sufferings; but if my Dulcinea del Toboso were released from hers, perhaps with improved luck and a sounder mind I might direct my steps in a better path than I am following at present."

"May God hear and the devil be deaf," said Sancho to this.

The men were filled with wonder, as well at the appearance as at the words of Don Quixote, though they did not understand one half of what he meant by them. They finished their dinner, took their images on their backs, and bidding farewell to Don Quixote resumed their journey.

Sancho was amazed afresh at the extent of his master's knowledge, as much as if he had never known him, for it seemed to him that there was no story or event in the world that he did not have at his fingertips and fixed in his memory, and he said to him, "Really, master, if what has happened to us today is to be called an adventure, it has been one of the sweetest and pleasantest that have happened to us in the whole course of our travels; we have come out of it without a beating or fright, and we haven't drawn sword or hit the earth with our bodies, nor have we been left hungry. Blessed be God that he has let me see such a thing with my own eyes!"

"What you say is true, Sancho," said Don Quixote, "but remember all times are not alike nor do they always run the same way; and these things the vulgar commonly call omens, which are not based upon any natural reason, will by him who is wise be esteemed and reckoned fortunate accidents. One of these believers in omens will get up in the morning, leave his house, and meet a friar of the order of the blessed Saint Francis, and, as if he had met a griffin, he will turn around and go home. If a member of the Mendoza clan spills salt on his table, gloom is spilled on his heart, as if nature were obliged to give warning of coming misfortunes by means of such trivial things as these. The wise man and the Christian should not trifle with what it may please heaven to do. Scipio on coming to Africa stumbled as he leaped on shore. His soldiers took it as a bad omen; but he, clasping the soil with his arms, exclaimed, 'You cannot escape me, Africa, for I hold you tight between my arms.' Thus, Sancho, meeting those images has been to me a most happy occurrence."

"I can well believe it," said Sancho. "But I wish your worship would tell me why Spaniards, when they are about to do battle, call on that Saint James the Moorslayer, saying 'Santiago and close in, Spain!' Is Spain open, so that it is necessary to close it? What is the meaning of this custom?"

"You are very simple, Sancho," said Don Quixote. "Look, God gave that great knight of the Red Cross to Spain as her patron saint and protector, especially in those hard struggles the Spaniards had with the Moors; and therefore they invoke and call upon him as their defender in all their battles; and in these he has been seen many times beating down, trampling under foot, destroying and slaughtering the Hagarene[1] squadrons in the sight of all; of which fact I could give you many examples recorded in truthful Spanish histories."

Sancho changed the subject, and said to his master, "I am amazed, señor, at the boldness of Altisidora, the duchess's maid. The one they call Love must have cruelly pierced and wounded her. They say he is a little blind urchin who, though blear-eyed, or more properly speaking sightless, if he aims at a heart, be it ever so small, hits it and pierces it through and through with his arrows. I have heard it said too that the arrows of Love are blunted and dulled by maidenly modesty and reserve; but with this Altisidora it seems they are sharpened rather than blunted."

"Bear in mind, Sancho," said Don Quixote, "that love is influenced by no consideration, recognizes no restraints of reason, and is of the same nature as death, that assails alike the lofty palaces of kings and the humble cabins of shepherds; and when it takes entire possession of a heart, the first thing it does is to banish timidity and modesty from it; and so without shame Altisidora declared her passion, which caused me to feel embarrassment rather than pity."

"What cruelty!" exclaimed Sancho. "Unheard-of ingratitude! I can only say for myself that the very smallest loving word of hers would have subdued me and made a slave of me. Son of a bitch! What a heart of marble, what a breast of bronze, what a soul of

1. Moors, the descendants of Hagar.

mortar! But I can't imagine what this damsel saw in your worship that could have conquered and captivated her so. What charm, what elegance, what grace, what handsome face, which of these things by itself, or what all together, could have made her fall in love with you? For indeed and in truth often I stop to look at your worship from the sole of your foot to the topmost hair of your head, and I see more to frighten a person than to make one fall in love. And I have heard people say that beauty is the first and main thing that excites love, and as your worship has none at all, I don't know what the poor creature fell in love with."

"Recollect, Sancho," replied Don Quixote, "there are two sorts of beauty, one of the soul, the other of the body; that of the soul displays and exhibits itself in intelligence, in chastity, in honorable conduct, in generosity, in good breeding; and all these qualities are possible and may exist in an ugly man. And when it is this sort of beauty and not that of the body that is the attraction, love is apt to spring up suddenly and violently. I, Sancho, realize that I am not handsome, but at the same time I know I am not hideous; and it is enough for an honorable man not to be a monster to be an object of love, if only he possesses the endowments of soul I have mentioned."

While engaged in this discourse they were making their way through a wood that lay beyond the road, when suddenly, without expecting anything of the kind, Don Quixote found himself caught in some nets of green cord stretched from one tree to another; and unable to conceive what it could be, he said to Sancho, "Sancho, it strikes me this business of the nets will prove one of the strangest adventures imaginable. May I die if the enchanters that persecute me are not trying to entangle me in them and delay my journey, by way of revenge for my harsh behavior towards Altisidora. Well then let me tell them that if these nets, instead of being green cord, were made of the hardest diamonds, or stronger than that with which the jealous god of blacksmiths enmeshed Venus and Mars, I would break them as easily as if they were made of rushes or cotton threads."

But just as he was about to press forward and break through all, suddenly from among some trees two shepherdesses of surpassing beauty presented themselves to his sight—or at least damsels dressed like shepherdesses, except that their jackets and skirts were of fine brocade; that is to say, the skirts were rich hoopskirts of gold-embroidered silk. Their hair, that in its golden brightness vied with the beams of the sun itself, fell loose on their shoulders and was crowned with garlands twined with green laurel and red amaranth; and their years to all appearance were not under fifteen nor above eighteen.

Such was the spectacle that filled Sancho with amazement, fascinated Don Quixote, made the sun halt in his course to behold them, and held all four in a strange silence. One of the shepherdesses, at length, was the first to speak and said to Don Quixote, "Stop, sir knight, and do not break these nets; for they are not spread here to do you any harm, but only for our amusement; and as I know you will ask why they have been put up, and who we are, I will tell you in a few words.

"In a village some two leagues from this, where there are many people of quality and rich gentlefolk, it was agreed upon by a number of our friends and relations to come with their wives, sons and daughters, neighbors, friends, and kinsmen, and take a holiday in this spot, which is one of the pleasantest in the whole neighborhood, setting up a new pastoral Arcadia among ourselves, we girls dressing ourselves as shepherdesses and the boys as shepherds. We have been practicing two eclogues, one by the famous poet Garcilasso, the other by the most excellent Camoens, in his own Portuguese tongue, but we have not as yet acted them. Yesterday was our first day here; we have a few of what they say are called field-tents pitched among the trees on the bank of an ample brook that fertilizes all these meadows; last night we spread these nets in the trees here to snare the silly little birds that startled by the noise we make may fly into them. If you would like to be our guest, señor, you will be welcomed hospitably and courteously, for here just now neither care nor melancholy shall enter."

She held her peace and said no more, and Don Quixote answered, "Truly, fairest lady, Actæon when he unexpectedly saw Diana bathing in the stream could not have been more fascinated and amazed than I at the sight of your beauty. I commend your mode of entertainment, and thank you for the kindness of your invitation; and if I can serve you, you may command me with full confidence of being obeyed, for my profession is none other than to show myself grateful and ready to serve persons of all conditions, but especially persons of quality such as your appearance indicates. And if, instead of taking up, as they probably do, but a small space, these nets took up the whole surface of the globe, I would seek out new worlds through which to pass, so as not to break them. And that you may give some degree of credence to this exaggerated language of mine, know that it is no less than Don Quixote of La Mancha that makes this declaration to you, if such a name has reached your ears."

"Oh, my dearest friend," instantly exclaimed the other shepherdess, "what great good fortune has befallen us! Do you see this gentleman we have before us? Well then let me tell you he is the most valiant and the most lovesick and the most courteous gentleman in all the world, unless a history of his achievements that has been printed and I have read is telling lies and deceiving us. I will bet that this man who is with him is Sancho Panza his squire, whose witty sayings none can equal."

"That's true," said Sancho. "I am the witty person and squire you speak of, and this gentleman is my master Don Quixote of La Mancha, the same one that's in the history and that they talk about."

"Oh, my friend," said the other, "let's beg him to say; for it will give our fathers and brothers infinite pleasure. I too have heard of the bravery of the one and the wit of the other, as you have said. And what is more, they say that he is the most constant and loyal lover that was ever heard of, and that his lady is a certain Dulcinea del Toboso, to whom all over Spain the prize for beauty is awarded."

"And justly awarded," said Don Quixote, "unless, indeed, your unequalled beauty makes it a matter of doubt. But spare yourselves the trouble, ladies, of pressing me to stay, for the urgent calls of my profession do not allow me to take rest under any circumstances."

At this moment there came up to the spot where the four stood a brother of one of the two shepherdesses, like them in shepherd costume, and as richly and showily dressed as they were. They told him that their companion was the valiant Don Quixote of La Mancha and the other, Sancho his squire, about whom he knew already from having read their history. The elegant shepherd offered his services and begged the knight to accompany him to their tents, and Don Quixote had to give in and comply.

And now the beaters arrived and the nets were filled with a variety of birds which, fooled by the color, fell into the danger they were fleeing from. More than thirty persons, all gaily attired as shepherds and shepherdesses, assembled on the spot and were at once informed who Don Quixote and his squire were, at which they were not a little delighted, since they knew about him already through his history. They returned to the tents, where they found tables set richly, plentifully, and neatly. They treated Don Quixote as a person of distinction, giving him the place of honor. All observed him and were full of astonishment at the spectacle. At last, when the table had been cleared, Don Quixote with great composure lifted up his voice and said:

"One of the greatest sins that men are guilty of is—some will say pride—but I say ingratitude, in accord with the common saying that hell is full of ingrates. This sin, so far as it has lain in my power, I have endeavored to avoid ever since I have had the faculty of reason. And if I am unable to repay good deeds that have been done to me with other deeds, I substitute the desire to do so. And if that is not enough, I make them known publicly; for he who declares and makes known the good deeds done to him would repay them with others if it were in his power, because for the most part those who receive are the inferiors of those who give. Thus, God is superior to all because He is the supreme giver, and the offerings of man fall short by an infinite distance of being a full return for the gifts of God. But gratitude in some degree makes up for this deficiency and shortcoming.

"I therefore, grateful for the favor that has been extended to me here, and unable to make a return in the same measure, restricted as I am by the narrow limits of my power, offer what I can and what I have to offer in my own way; and thus I declare that for two full days I will maintain, in the middle of this highway leading to Zaragoza, that these ladies disguised as shepherdesses, who are here present, are the fairest and most courteous maidens in the world, excepting only the peerless Dulcinea del Toboso, sole mistress of my thoughts, be it said without offence to those who hear me, ladies and gentlemen."

On hearing this Sancho, who had been listening with great attention, cried out in a loud voice, "Is it possible that there is anyone in the world who will dare to say and swear that my master is crazy? Tell me, you gentlemen shepherds, is there a village priest, however wise or learned, who could say what my master has said; or is there knight-errant, whatever renown he may have as a man of valor, that could offer what my master has offered now?"

Don Quixote turned on Sancho, and with a face glowing with anger said to him, "Is it possible, Sancho, that there is anyone in the whole world who will say you are not a fool, with a lining to match, and who knows what trimmings of malice and cunning? Who asked you to meddle in my affairs or to inquire whether I am a wise man or a blockhead? Silence. Do not answer me a word. Saddle Rocinante if he is unsaddled; and let us go to put my offer into execution; for with the justice that I have on my side, you may consider as vanquished all who shall venture to question it."

And in a great rage, and showing his anger plainly, he rose from his seat, leaving the company lost in wonder, and making them feel doubtful whether they ought to regard him as crazy or sane. In the end, though they tried to dissuade him from involving himself in such a challenge, assuring him they admitted his gratitude as fully established and needed no fresh proofs to be convinced of his valiant spirit, as those related in the history of his exploits were sufficient, still Don Quixote persisted in his resolve; and mounted on Rocinante, slipping his shield on his arm and grasping his lance, he posted himself in the middle of a highway that was not far from the green meadow. Sancho followed on Dapple, together with all the members of the pastoral gathering, eager to see what would be the upshot of this vainglorious and extraordinary proposal.

Don Quixote, then, having, as has been said, planted himself in the middle of the road, made the air ring with words to this effect:

"Ho ye travellers and wayfarers, knights, squires, folk on foot or on horseback, who pass this way or shall pass in the course of the next two days! Know that Don Quixote of La Mancha, knight-errant, is posted here to maintain by arms that the beauty and courtesy enshrined in the nymphs that dwell in these meadows and groves surpass all upon earth, putting aside the lady of my heart, Dulcinea del Toboso. Wherefore, let him who is of the opposite opinion come on, for here I await him."

Twice he repeated the same words, and twice were they unheard by any adventurer. But fate, that was guiding affairs for him better and better, so ordered it that shortly afterwards there appeared on the road a crowd of men on horseback, many of them with lances in their hands, all riding in a compact body and in great haste. No sooner had those who were with Don Quixote seen them than they turned about and withdrew to some distance from the road, for they knew that if they stayed some harm might come to them. But Don Quixote with intrepid heart stood his ground, and Sancho Panza shielded himself with Rocinante's hindquarters. The troop of lancers came up, and one of them who was in advance began shouting to Don Quixote, "Get out of the way, you son of the devil, or these bulls will tear you to pieces!"

"Rabble!" returned Don Quixote, "I care nothing for bulls, be they the fiercest that Jarama breeds on its banks. Confess at once, scoundrels, that what I have declared is true; else ye have to deal with me in combat."

The herdsman had no time to reply nor Don Quixote to get out of the way even if he wished; and so the drove of fierce bulls and tame steers, together with the crowd of herdsmen and others who were taking them to be penned up in a village where there was to be a bullfight the next day, passed over Don Quixote and over Sancho, Rocinante, and Dapple, hurling them all to the earth and rolling them over on the ground. Sancho was left crushed, Don Quixote scared, Dapple battered, and Rocinante in no very sound condition. They all got up, however, at length, and Don Quixote in great haste, stumbling and falling, started off running after the drove, shouting out, "Stop! Wait! Ye wicked rabble, a single knight awaits you, and he is not of the temper or opinion of those who say, 'For a fleeing enemy, make a bridge of silver.' "

The retreating party in their haste, however, did not stop or pay any more attention to his threats than to last year's clouds. Weariness brought Don Quixote to a halt, and more enraged than avenged he sat down on the road to wait until Sancho, Rocinante, and Dapple came up. When they reached him, master and servant mounted once more, and without going back to bid farewell to the mock or imitation Arcadia, and more in humiliation than contentment, they continued their journey.

Chapter LIX

WHEREIN IS RELATED THE STRANGE THING, WHICH MAY BE REGARDED AS AN ADVENTURE, THAT HAPPENED TO DON QUIXOTE

A clear limpid spring which they discovered in a cool grove relieved Don Quixote and Sancho of the dust and fatigue due to the impolite behavior of the bulls, and by the side of this, having turned Dapple and Rocinante loose without halter or bridle, the forlorn pair, master and servant, seated themselves. Sancho had recourse to the larder of his saddlebags and took out of them what he called the grub.[1] Don Quixote rinsed his mouth and bathed his face, by which cooling process his flagging spirits were revived.

Out of pure vexation Don Quixote did not eat, and out of pure politeness Sancho did not venture to touch the food in front of him but waited for his master to begin. Seeing, however, that, absorbed in thought, he was forgetting to raise bread to his mouth, Sancho said nothing, but completely ignoring good manners, he began to stow away in his paunch the bread and cheese at hand.

"Eat, Sancho my friend," said Don Quixote. "Sustain your life, which is of more consequence to you than to me, and leave me to die from my worries and the pressure of my misfortunes. I was born, Sancho, to live dying, and you to die eating. And to prove the truth of what I say, look at me, printed in histories, famed in arms, courteous in behavior, honored by princes, courted by maidens; and after all, when I looked forward to palms, triumphs, and crowns, won and earned by my valiant deeds, I have this morning seen myself trampled, kicked, and crushed by the feet of unclean and filthy animals. This thought blunts my teeth, paralyzes my jaws, numbs my hands, and robs me of all appetite for food; so much so that I have a mind to let myself die of hunger, the cruelest death of all deaths."

"So then," said Sancho, munching hard all the time, "your worship does not agree with the proverb that says, 'Let Martha's life be snuffed, but let her die stuffed.' I, at any rate, don't plan to kill myself; instead, I intend to do as the cobbler does, who stretches the leather with his teeth until he makes it reach as far as he wants. I'll stretch out my life by eating until it reaches the end heaven has fixed for it. And let me tell you, señor, there's no greater madness than to think of dying of despair as your worship does; take my advice, and after eating, lie down and sleep a while on this green grass-mattress, and you will see that when you awake you'll feel somewhat better."

Don Quixote did as he recommended, for it struck him that Sancho's reasoning was more like a philosopher's than a fool's, and he

1. Putnam's translation for an old peasant term meaning, roughly, "cold cuts."

said, "Sancho, if you will do for me what I am going to ask of you, my mind would be more eased and my heaviness of heart not so great; and it is this: you go a short distance away from here, while I am sleeping as you advise, and exposing your flesh to the air, give yourself three or four hundred lashes with Rocinante's reins, towards the three thousand and odd you are to give yourself for the disenchantment of Dulcinea; for it is a great pity that the poor lady should be left enchanted through your carelessness and negligence."

"There is a good deal to be said on that point," said Sancho. "Let's both go to sleep now, and after that, God has decreed what will happen. Let me tell your worship that for a man to whip himself in cold blood is a hard thing, especially if the lashes fall on an undernourished and worse-fed body. Let my lady Dulcinea have patience, and when she is least expecting it, she will see me whipped to shreds, and 'until death it's all life.' I mean that I have life in me still, and the desire to make good what I have promised."

Don Quixote thanked him and ate a little, and Sancho a good deal, and then they both lay down to sleep, leaving those two inseparable friends and comrades, Rocinante and Dapple, to their own devices and to feed unrestrained on the abundant grass with which the meadow was furnished. They woke up rather late, mounted once more and resumed their journey, pushing on to reach an inn which was in sight, apparently a league off. I say an inn, because Don Quixote called it so, contrary to his usual practice of calling all inns castles.

They reached it and asked the innkeeper if there was room. He said yes, with as much comfort and as good fare as they could find in Zaragoza. They dismounted, and Sancho stowed away his larder in a room to which the innkeeper gave him the key. He took the beasts to the stable, fed them, and came back to see what orders Don Quixote, who was seated on a bench at the door, had for him, giving special thanks to heaven that this inn had not been taken for a castle by his master.

Supper time came, and they went up to their room, and Sancho asked the innkeeper what he had to give them for supper. To this the innkeeper replied that 'his mouth would be the measure'; he had only to ask for what he wanted, for that inn was provided with the birds of the air and the fowls of the earth and the fish of the sea.

"There's no need of all that," said Sancho. "If they'll roast us a couple of chickens we'll be satisfied, for my master has a delicate stomach and eats little, and I'm not overly gluttonous."

The landlord replied he had no chickens, because hawks had stolen them.

"Well then," said Sancho, "let señor landlord tell them to roast a pullet, so that it is a tender one."

"Pullet! My father!" said the innkeeper. "Indeed and in truth, only yesterday I sent over fifty to the city to sell. Aside from pullets, ask what you will."

"In that case," said Sancho, "you must have veal or kid."

"Just now," said the landlord, "there's none in the house, because it's all gone; but next week there will be more than enough."

"Much good that does us," said Sancho. "I'll bet that all these shortcomings are going to wind up in plenty of bacon and eggs."

"By God," said the landlord, "my guest must be joking! I tell him I have neither pullets nor hens, and he expects me to have eggs! Think of some other fancy dish, if you please, and don't ask for hens again."

"Damnation!" said Sancho. "Let's settle the matter; say at once what you have, and let's have no more discussion."

"Really and truly, señor guest," said the landlord, "all I have is a couple of cow's feet that look like calves' feet, or a couple of calves' feet like cow's feet. They are boiled with chickpeas, onions, and bacon, and at this moment they are saying, 'Eat me, eat me.' "

"I'll brand them as mine right now," said Sancho. "Don't let anybody touch them; I'll pay better for them than anyone else, because I couldn't wish for anything more to my taste; and I don't care whether they are calves' feet or cow's feet."

"Nobody shall touch them," said the landlord, "for the other guests I have, being persons of high quality, bring their own cook and butler and provisions with them."

"When it comes to people of quality," said Sancho, "there's nobody more so than my master. But the calling he follows does not allow for provisions or supplies. We lay ourselves down in the middle of a meadow and fill ourselves with acorns or medlars."

Here ended Sancho's conversation with the landlord, Sancho not caring to carry it any farther by answering him; for he had already asked him what calling or what profession it was his master followed.

Supper time having come, then, Don Quixote betook himself to his room, the landlord brought in the stew-pot just as it was, and the knight sat himself down to dine very resolutely. It seems that from another room, which was next to Don Quixote's, with nothing but a thin partition to separate it, he overheard these words, "As you live, Señor Don Jerónimo, while they are bringing supper, let us read another chapter of the *Second Part of Don Quixote of La Mancha.*

The instant Don Quixote heard his own name, he started to his feet and listened intently to what they said about him, and he heard the Don Jerónimo who had been addressed say in reply, "Why would you have us read that absurd stuff, Don Juan, when it is impossible for anyone who has read the first part of the history of Don Quixote of La Mancha to take any pleasure in reading this *Second Part?*"

"Nevertheless," said he who was addressed as Don Juan, "we may as well read it, for there is no book so bad that there is not something good in it. What displeases me most in it is that it represents Don Quixote as now cured of his love for Dulcinea del Toboso."[2]

On hearing this Don Quixote, full of wrath and indignation, raised his voice and said, "Whoever he may be who says that Don Quixote of La Mancha has forgotten or can forget Dulcinea del Toboso, I will teach him with equal arms that what he says is very far from the truth; for neither can the peerless Dulcinea del Toboso be forgotten, nor can forgetfulness have a place in Don Quixote; his motto is constancy, and his profession to maintain the same with gentleness and without violence."

"Who answers us?" they asked from the next room.

"Who else," said Sancho, "but Don Quixote of La Mancha himself, who will make good all he has said and all he will say; for 'a reliable payer doesn't mind leaving a security.' "

Sancho had hardly uttered these words when two gentlemen, for such they seemed to be, entered the room, and one of them, throwing his arms round Don Quixote's neck, said to him, "Your appearance cannot leave any question as to your name, nor can your name fail to identify your appearance; unquestionably, señor, you are the real Don Quixote of La Mancha, north pole and morning star of knight-errantry, despite and in defiance of him who has sought to usurp your name and annihilate your achievements, as the author of this book which I here present to you has done." And with this he put a book which his companion carried into the hands of Don Quixote, who took it and without replying began to leaf through it; but he presently returned it saying, "In the little I have seen I have discovered three things in this author that deserve to be censured. The first is some words that I have read in the preface; the next that the language is Aragonese, for sometimes he writes without articles; and the third, which above all stamps him as ignorant, is that he goes wrong and departs from the truth in the most important part of the history, for here he says that my squire Sancho Panza's wife is called Mari Gutiérrez, when she is called nothing of the sort, but Teresa Panza; and when a man errs on such an important point as this, there is good reason to fear that he is in error on every other point in the history."

"A fine sort of historian!" exclaimed Sancho at this. "He must know a lot about our affairs when he calls my wife Teresa Panza,

2. Avellaneda in Chapter II of his continuation has Aldonza Lorenzo write Don Quixote threatening him with a beating for calling her "Princess" and "Dulcinea." Don Quixote, stung by her ingratitude, resolves to look for another mistress.

Mari Gutiérrez. Take the book again, señor, and see if I am in it and if he has changed my name."

"From your talk, friend," said Don Jerónimo, "no doubt you are Sancho Panza, Señor Don Quixote's squire."

"Yes, I am," said Sancho, "and I'm proud of it."

"Faith, then," said the gentleman, "this new author does not handle you with the decency that your person displays; he makes you a glutton and a fool, and not in the least witty, and very different from the Sancho described in the First Part of your master's history."

"God forgive him," said Sancho. "He should have left me in my corner without troubling his head about me: 'let him who knows how, ring the bells'; 'Saint Peter is at home in Rome.' "

The two gentlemen asked Don Quixote to come into their room and have supper with them, as they knew very well there was nothing in that inn fit for one of his sort. Don Quixote, who was always polite, yielded to their request and dined with them. Sancho stayed behind with the stewpot and, invested with absolute authority, seated himself at the head of the table, and the landlord sat down with him, for he was no less fond of cows' and calves' feet than Sancho was.

While at supper Don Juan asked Don Quixote what news he had of the lady Dulcinea del Toboso, was she married, had she given birth or was she with child, or if she was still a virgin, preserving her modesty and delicacy, did she cherish the remembrance of the tender passion of Señor Don Quixote?

To this he replied, "Dulcinea is a virgin still, and my passion more firm than ever, our relationship as unsatisfactory as before, and her beauty transformed into that of a foul country wench."

And then he proceeded to give them a full and particular account of the enchantment of Dulcinea, and of what had happened to him in the cave of Montesinos, together with what the sage Merlin had prescribed for her disenchantment, namely the scourging of Sancho.

The amusement the two gentlemen derived from hearing Don Quixote recount the strange incidents of his history was exceedingly great; and if they were amazed by his absurdities, they were equally amazed by the elegant style in which he delivered them. On the one hand they regarded him as a sensible man, and on the other he seemed to them a madman, and they could not make up their minds where between wisdom and folly they ought to place him.

Sancho, having finished his supper and left the landlord tipsy, entered the room where his master was and as he came in said, "May I die, sirs, if the author of this book your worships have wants us to enjoy ourselves. Since he already calls me a glutton (according to what your worships say) I wouldn't want him to call me drunkard too."

"But he does," said Don Jerónimo. "I can't remember, however, in what way, though I know his words are offensive, and what is more, untrue, as I can see plainly by the physiognomy of the worthy Sancho before me."

"Believe me," said Sancho, "the Sancho and the Don Quixote of this history must be different from the ones who appear in the one Cide Hamete Benengeli wrote, namely my master, valiant, wise, and true in love, and myself, simple, witty, and neither glutton nor drunkard."

"I believe it," said Don Juan. "And if it were possible, an order should be issued that no one should have the presumption to deal with anything relating to Don Quixote except his original author Cide Hamete, just as Alexander commanded that no one should presume to paint his portrait except Apelles."

"Let him who will, paint me," said Don Quixote, "but let him not abuse me; for patience often collapses when they heap insults upon it."

"No one can insult Señor Don Quixote," said Don Juan, "from whom he himself will not be able to demand satisfaction, unless he prefers to ward it off with the shield of his patience, which, I take it, is great and strong."

A considerable portion of the night passed in conversation of this sort, and though Don Juan wanted Don Quixote to read more of the book to see what he would say, he was not to be prevailed upon, saying that he considered it as read and pronounced it utterly stupid; and, if by any chance its author should learn that he had had it in his hand, he did not want him to flatter himself with the idea that he had read it; for we should keep our thoughts, and still more our eyes, away from what is obscene and filthy.

They asked him where he intended to go. He replied, to Zaragoza, to take part in the jousts which were held in that city every year. Don Juan told him that the new history described how Don Quixote, whoever he might be, had been there also, tilting at the ring, but that the description was utterly devoid of originality, had few clever mottoes, very few liveries, but many idiocies.

"For that very reason," said Don Quixote, "I will not set foot in Zaragoza; and by that means I shall expose to the world the lie of this new history writer, and people will see that I am not the Don Quixote he speaks of."

"You will do quite right," said Don Jerónimo. "There are other jousts at Barcelona in which Señor Don Quixote may display his valor."

"That is what I mean to do," said Don Quixote. "I pray your worships to excuse me, since it is time for me to go to bed. And please consider and number me among your greatest friends and servants."

"And me too," said Sancho. "Maybe I'll be good for something."

With this they said farewell, and Don Quixote and Sancho retired to their room, leaving Don Juan and Don Jerónimo amazed to see the medley he made of his good sense and his craziness; and they felt thoroughly convinced that these, and not the ones their Aragonese author described, were the genuine Don Quixote and Sancho.

Don Quixote rose early and said good-bye to his hosts by knocking on the wall of the other room. Sancho paid the landlord magnificently and recommended that either he say less about the accommodations of his inn or keep it better supplied.

Chapter LX

OF WHAT HAPPENED TO DON QUIXOTE ON HIS WAY TO BARCELONA

It was a fresh morning giving promise of a cool day as Don Quixote left the inn, first of all ascertaining the most direct road to Barcelona without passing through Zaragoza, so anxious was he to show that this new historian, who they said abused him so, was a liar. Well, as it turned out, nothing worthy of being recorded happened to him for six days, at the end of which, having left the highway, he was overtaken by night in a thicket of oak or cork trees; for on this point Cide Hamete is not as precise as he usually is on other matters.

Master and servant dismounted from their beasts, and as soon as they had settled themselves at the foot of the trees, Sancho, who had had a good noon meal that day, let himself, without more ado, enter the gates of sleep. But Don Quixote, whom his thoughts, far more than hunger, kept awake, could not close his eyes and roamed in his imagination to and fro through all sorts of places. At one moment it seemed to him that he was in the cave of Montesinos; then he saw Dulcinea, transformed into a country wench, skipping and mounting her she-ass. Again it seemed that the words of the sage Merlin were sounding in his ears, setting forth the conditions to be observed and the exertions to be made for the disenchantment of Dulcinea.

He lost all patience when he considered the laziness and uncharitableness of his squire; for to the best of his knowledge, Sancho had only given himself five lashes, a number paltry and out of proportion to the vast number required. At this thought he felt such vexation and anger that he reasoned the matter thus: "If Alexander the Great cut the Gordian knot, saying, 'To cut comes to the same thing as to untie,' and thereby managed to become lord of all Asia, something similar could happen now in Dulcinea's disenchantment if I whip Sancho against his will. For if it is the condition of the remedy that Sancho receive three thousand and some-odd lashes, what does it matter to me whether he inflicts them himself or some one else inflicts them, when the essential point is that he receive them, wherever they come from?"

With this idea he went over to Sancho, having first taken Rocinante's reins and arranged them so as to be able to flog with them, and began to untie the string (the common belief is he had but one in front) by which his squire's breeches were held up. But the instant he approached him, Sancho woke up in his full senses and cried out, "What is this? Who is touching me and untying me?"

"It is I," said Don Quixote, "and I come to make up for your shortcomings and relieve my own distress. I have come to whip you, Sancho, and wipe out some portion of the debt you owe. Dulcinea is perishing; you are living free of cares; I am dying of hope deferred; therefore unlace yourself willingly, for it is my intention, here in this retired spot, to give you at least two thousand lashes."

"Oh, no, you won't," said Sancho. "Your worship had better not move, or else by the living God the deaf will hear us; the lashes I agreed to must be voluntary and not forced, and right now I have no urge to whip myself; it is enough if I give you my word to flog and whip myself when I have a mind."

"It will not do to leave it to your courtesy, Sancho," said Don Quixote, "for you are hard of heart and, even though a peasant, tender of flesh." And at the time time he was struggling and fighting to untie the squire's pants.

Seeing this Sancho got to his feet, and lunging at his master, he gripped him with all his might. Hooking one leg behind him, he threw him to the ground on his back. Sancho then put his right knee on Don Quixote's chest and held down his hands so that he could neither move nor breathe.

"So, traitor!" exclaimed Don Quixote. "You revolt against your master and natural lord? You dare attack him who gives you his bread?"

" 'I neither overthrow a king, nor make a king,' "[1] said Sancho. "I am only standing up for myself; I am my own lord. If your worship promises me to be quiet and not to try to whip me now, I'll let you go free and unhindered; if not—

Traitor and Doña Sancha's foe,
Thou diest on the spot."

Don Quixote gave his promise, and swore by the life of the lady of his thoughts not to touch so much as a hair of his garments, and to leave him entirely free and to his own discretion to whip himself whenever he pleased.

Sancho got up and went some distance from the spot, but as he was about to lean against another tree, he felt something touch his

1. A faithful page helped Henry of Trastamara kill his brother the king by tripping the latter. An old ballad has the page say this line quoted by Sancho.

head, and raising his hands, he encountered somebody's two feet with shoes and stockings on them. He trembled with fear; he moved to another tree; and the same thing happened to him. He began to shout, calling Don Quixote to come and protect him. Don Quixote did so and asked him what had happened to him and what he was afraid of. Sancho replied that all the trees were full of human feet and legs. Don Quixote felt them and guessed at once what it was; and he said to Sancho, "You have nothing to be afraid of, for these feet and legs that you feel but cannot see belong no doubt to some outlaws and bandits that have been hanged on these trees; for the authorities in these parts hang them up by twenties and thirties when they catch them; whereby I conjecture that I must be near Barcelona." And it was, in fact, as he supposed; with the first light they looked up and saw that the fruit hanging on those trees were the bodies of bandits.

And now day dawned; and if the dead bandits had scared them, they were no less troubled by more than forty living ones, who all of a sudden surrounded them and ordered them, in the Catalan tongue, to stand still and wait until their captain came up. Don Quixote was on foot, his horse was unbridled, and his lance leaning against a tree, and in short he was completely defenseless. He thought it best therefore to fold his arms and bow his head and reserve himself for a more favorable occasion and opportunity.

The robbers hurried to search Dapple and did not leave him a single thing of all he carried in the saddlebags and in the valise. And it was lucky for Sancho that the duke's crowns and those he brought from home were in a belt that he wore. Even so, these good people would have frisked him and would even have looked to see what he had hidden between the hide and flesh but for the arrival at that moment of their captain. He was about thirty-four years of age, apparently, strongly built, above average height, of stern aspect and swarthy complexion. He was mounted on a powerful horse, and had on a coat of mail, with four of the pistols they call *pedreñales* in that country at his waist. He saw that his squires (for so they call those who follow that trade) were about to strip Sancho Panza, but he ordered them to desist and was at once obeyed, so the belt escaped. He was amazed to see a lance leaning against the tree, a shield on the ground, and Don Quixote in armor and dejected, with the saddest and most melancholy face that sadness itself could produce; and going up to him he said, "Don't be so sad, my good man, for you have not fallen into the hands of some inhuman Busiris,[2] but into Roque Guinart's, which are more merciful than cruel."[3]

2. Legendary king of Egypt who sacrificed foreigners to his gods.

3. This character is modeled on a famous Catalan bandit, Perot Roca Guinarda (1582–?), who after a dashing career as an outlaw, won a pardon and a captaincy in the Spanish army in Naples. Roca Guinarda took part in the violent political struggles of early seventeenth century Catalonia, and Cervantes also alludes to these factions later in this chapter.

"The cause of my sadness," replied Don Quixote, "is not that I have fallen into your hands, O valiant Roque, whose fame is bounded by no limits on earth, but that my carelessness should have been so great that your soldiers should have caught me unbridled, when it is my duty, according to the rule of knight-errantry which I profess, to be always on the alert and at all times my own sentinel; for let me tell you, great Roque, had they found me on my horse, with my lance and shield, it would not have been very easy for them to subdue me, for I am Don Quixote of La Mancha, he who has filled the whole world with his achievements."

Roque Guinart at once perceived that Don Quixote's weakness was more akin to madness than to boastfulness; and though he had several times heard him spoken of, he never regarded his deeds as true, nor could he persuade himself that such a humor could become dominant in the heart of man. He was extremely glad, therefore, to meet Don Quixote and test at close quarters what he had heard of him at a distance; so he said to him, "Do not despair, valiant knight, nor regard as misfortune the position in which you find yourself. It may be that by these slips your crooked fortune will make itself straight; for heaven by strange circuitous ways, mysterious and incomprehensible to man, raises up the fallen and makes the poor rich."

Don Quixote was about to thank him, when they heard behind them a noise as of a troop of horses. There was, however, but one, and riding it at a furious pace was a youth, apparently about twenty years of age, clad in sleeveless jacket of gold-trimmed green damask and breeches and a cocked hat, with plumes, tight-fitting polished boots, gilt spurs, dagger, and sword, and in his hand a small gun, and a pair of pistols at his waist.

Roque turned his head at the noise and perceived this handsome figure, which drawing near thus addressed him, "I came in search of you, valiant Roque, to find if not a remedy at least relief in my misfortune. And not to keep you in suspense, for I see you do not recognize me, I will tell you who I am: I am Claudia Jerónima, the daughter of Simón Forte, your good friend and special enemy of Clauquel Torrellas, who is your enemy, since he belongs to the faction opposed to you.

"You know that this Torrellas has a son who is called, or at least was not two hours ago, Don Vicente Torrellas. Well, to cut short the tale of my misfortune, I will tell you in a few words what this young man has done to me. He saw me, he courted me, I listened to him, and, unknown to my father, I fell in love with him; for there is no woman, however secluded she may live or shy she may be, who will not have more than enough opportunities to carry out her rash impulses. In a word, he promised to be my husband, and I promised to be his wife, without carrying matters any further. Yesterday, I learned that, ignoring his pledge to me, he was about to marry another and that this morning he was going to be betrothed. The news stunned me and made me desperate. My father not being at home, I was able to dress as you see. Riding as fast as my horse would go, I overtook Don Vicente about a league from here, and without waiting to accuse him or hear excuses, I fired this musket at him, and these two pistols besides, and I believe that I must have lodged more than two bullets in his body, opening doors to release my honor, drenched in his blood.

"I left him there in the hands of his servants, who did not dare and were not able to defend him. I have come looking for you so that you may help me get to France, where I have relatives with whom I can live, and also to implore you to protect my father, so that Don Vicente's numerous kinsmen may not try to wreak their lawless vengeance on him."

Roque, filled with admiration at the gallant bearing, high spirit, handsome figure, and plight of the fair Claudia, said to her, "Come, señora, let's see whether your enemy is dead; and then we will consider what will be best for you."

Don Quixote, who had been listening to what Claudia said and Roque Guinart said in reply, exclaimed, "Nobody need trouble himself with the defense of this lady, for I take it upon myself. Give me my horse and arms, and wait for me here; I will go in quest of this knight, and dead or alive, I will make him keep the promise made to so great a beauty."

"Nobody need have any doubt about that," said Sancho, "for my master is very good at matchmaking; not many days ago he forced another man to marry, who in the same way backed out of his promise to another young lady; and if the enchanters who persecute him hadn't changed the man's proper shape into a lackey's, that maiden would not be one this minute."

Roque, who was paying more attention to the fair Claudia's situation than to the words of master or servant, did not hear them; and ordering his squires to restore to Sancho everything they had taken from Dapple, he directed them to return to the place where they had been quartered during the night, and then set off with Claudia at full speed in search of the wounded or slain Don Vicente. They reached the spot where Claudia met him but found nothing there except freshly spilled blood; looking all around, however, they spotted some people moving up the slope of a hill and concluded, as indeed it proved to be, that it was Don Vicente, whom either dead or alive his servants were removing to attend to his wounds or to bury him. They made haste to overtake them, which, as the party moved slowly, they were able to do with ease. They found Don Vicente being carried by his servants, whom he was entreating in a broken, feeble voice to leave him there to die, as the pain of his wounds would not suffer him to go any farther.

Claudia and Roque leaped off their horses and approached him. The servants were overawed by the appearance of Roque, and Claudia was moved by the sight of Don Vicente, and going up to him half tenderly, half sternly, she took his hand and said to him, "If you had given me this, according to our agreement, you would never have come to this pass."

The wounded gentleman opened his half-closed eyes, and recognizing Claudia said, "I see clearly, fair and mistaken lady, that it is you who have slain me, a punishment not merited or deserved by my feelings towards you, for never did I mean to, nor could I, wrong you in thought or deed."

"It is not true, then," said Claudia, "that you were going this morning to betroth yourself to Leonora, the daughter of the rich Balvastro?"

"Certainly not," replied Don Vicente. "My cruel fortune must have carried those tidings to you to drive you in your jealousy to take my life. But since I leave my life in your hands and in your arms, I consider my fate a happy one. And to assure yourself of this, press my hand and take me for your husband if you will; I have no better satisfaction to offer you for the wrong you think you have received from me."

Claudia pressed his hand, and her own heart was so oppressed that she fainted on the bleeding breast of Don Vicente, whom a death spasm seized the same instant.

Roque was in perplexity about what to do. The servants ran to fetch water to sprinkle their faces, and brought some and bathed them with it. Claudia recovered from her fainting fit, but not so Don Vicente from the paroxysm, for his life had come to an end. On perceiving this, Claudia, when she had convinced herself that her beloved husband was no more, rent the air with her sobs and made the heavens ring with her laments; she tore her hair and scattered it to the winds, she beat her face with her hands and showed all the signs of grief and sorrow that could be conceived to come from an afflicted heart. "Cruel, rash woman!" she cried, "how easily were you moved to carry out so wicked a thought! O raging force of jealousy, to what desperate lengths do you lead those that give you lodging in their bosoms! O husband, whose unhappy fate in being mine has taken you from the marriage bed to the grave!"

So vehement and so piteous were the lamentations of Claudia that they drew tears from Roque's eyes, unused as they were to shed them on any occasion. The servants wept, Claudia swooned away again and again, and the whole place seemed a field of sorrow and an abode of misfortune. In the end Roque Guinart directed Don Vicente's servants to carry his body to his father's village, which was close by, for burial. Claudia told him she wanted to go to a convent of which an aunt of hers was abbess, where she intended to pass her life with a better and everlasting spouse. He applauded her pious resolution and offered to accompany her wherever she wished and to protect her father against the kinsmen of Don Vicente and all the world, should they seek to injure him. Claudia would not on any account allow him to accompany her; and thanking him for his offers as well as she could, she took leave of him in tears. The servants of Don Vicente carried away his body, and Roque returned to his comrades, and so ended the love affair of Claudia Jerónima. But what wonder, when it was the invincible and cruel might of jealousy that wove the web of her sad story?

Roque Guinart found his squires at the place to which he had ordered them, and Don Quixote on Rocinante in their midst, making a speech to them in which he urged them to give up a mode of life so full of peril, as well to the soul as to the body. But as most of them were Gascons, rough lawless fellows, his speech did not make much impression on them. Roque on coming up asked Sancho if his men had returned and restored to him the treasures and jewels they had stripped off Dapple. Sancho said they had, but that three kerchiefs which were worth three cities were missing.

"What are you talking about, man?" said one of the bystanders. "I've got them, and they're not worth three *reales*."

"That is true," said Don Quixote. "But my squire values them as he says because of the person who gave them to me."

Roque Guinart ordered them to be restored at once; and making his men fall in in line, he directed all the clothing, jewelry, and money that they had taken since the last distribution to be produced; and making a hasty valuation, and exchanging what could not be divided for money, he distributed it among all his companions so equitably and carefully that in no case did he exceed or fall short of strict distributive justice.

When this had been done and all left content, satisfied, and pleased, Roque observed to Don Quixote, "If this scrupulous exactness were not observed with these fellows, there would be no living with them."

Upon this Sancho remarked, "From what I have seen here, justice is such a good thing that there is no doing without it, even among thieves themselves."

One of the squires heard this, and raising the butt-end of his gun would no doubt have broken Sancho's head with it had not Roque Guinart called out to him to hold his hand. Sancho was frightened out of his wits and vowed not to open his lips so long as he was in the company of these people.

At this instant one or two of those squires who were posted as sentinels on the roads, to watch who came along them and report what passed to their chief, came up and said, "Señor, there is a great troop of people not far off coming along the road to Barcelona."

To which Roque replied, "Have you made out whether they are the kind that are looking for us, or are they the kind of people we are looking for?"

"The kind we are after," said the squire.

"Well then, away with you all," said Roque, "and bring them here to me at once without letting one of them escape."

They obeyed, and Don Quixote, Sancho, and Roque, left by themselves, waited to see what the squires brought, and while they were waiting Roque said to Don Quixote, "Ours must seem a strange sort of life to Señor Don Quixote: strange adventures, strange incidents, and all full of danger. And I don't wonder that it should seem so, for in truth I must confess there is no way of life more restless or anxious than ours.

"What led me into it was a certain thirst for vengeance, which is strong enough to disturb the quietest hearts. I am by nature kind-hearted and benevolent, but, as I said, the desire to revenge myself for a wrong that was done me so overcomes all my better impulses that I keep on in this way of life in spite of what my conscience tells me; and as 'one depth calls to another,' and one sin to another sin, revenges have linked themselves together, and I have taken upon myself not only my own but those of others: it pleases God, however, that, though I see myself in this maze of entanglements, I do not lose all hope of escaping from it and reaching a safe port."

Don Quixote was amazed to hear Roque utter such excellent and just sentiments, for he did not think that among those who followed such trades as robbing, murdering, and waylaying there could be anyone capable of a virtuous thought, and he said in reply, "Señor Roque, the beginning of health lies in recognizing the disease and in the patient's willingness to take the medicines which the physician prescribes. You are sick, you know what ails you, and heaven, or more properly speaking God, who is our physician, will administer medicines that will cure you, and cure gradually and not all of a sudden or by a miracle. Besides, intelligent sinners are nearer repentance than those who are simple-minded; and as your worship has shown good sense in your remarks, all you have to do is keep up your spirits and trust that the sickness of your conscience will improve. And if you have any desire to shorten the journey and put yourself easily on the road to salvation, come with me, and I will show you how to become a knight-errant, a calling where so many hardships and mishaps are encountered that if they are taken as penance, they will have you in heaven in a jiffy."

Roque laughed at Don Quixote's advice, and changing the subject, he related the tragic affair of Claudia Jerónima, at which

Sancho was extremely grieved; for he had been favorably impressed by the young woman's beauty, boldness, and spirit.

And now the squires dispatched to make the capture came up, bringing with them two gentlemen on horseback, two pilgrims on foot, and a coach full of women with some six servants on foot and on horseback in attendance, and a couple of muleteers whom the gentlemen had with them. The squires made a ring round them, both victors and vanquished maintaining profound silence, waiting for the great Roque Guinart to speak. He asked the gentlemen who they were, where they were going, and what money they carried with them. "Señor," replied one of them, "we are two captains of Spanish infantry; our companies are at Naples, and we are on our way to embark in four galleys which they say are at Barcelona under orders for Sicily. We have about two or three hundred crowns, with which we are, by our standards, rich and contented, for a soldier's poverty does not allow a bigger fortune."

Roque asked the pilgrims the same questions he had put to the captains and was answered that they were going to take ship for Rome and that between them they might have about sixty *reales*. He asked also who was in the coach, where they were going, and what money they had, and one of the men on horseback replied, "The persons in the coach are my lady Doña Guiomar de Quiñones, wife of the chief justice of the ecclesiastical court at Naples, her little daughter, a maid, a dueña; we six servants are in attendance upon her, and the money amounts to six hundred crowns."

"So then," said Roque Guinart, "we have here nine hundred crowns and sixty *reales*; my soldiers must number about sixty; see how much goes to each, for I am a poor accountant." As soon as the robbers heard this they raised a shout of "Long life to Roque Guinart, in spite of the crooks that seek his ruin!"

The captains showed plainly the concern they felt, the judge's wife was downcast, and the pilgrims did not at all enjoy seeing their property confiscated. Roque kept them in suspense in this way for a while; but he had no desire to prolong their misery, which was obvious a bowshot off, and turning to the captains he said, "Sirs, will your worships be courteous enough to lend me sixty crowns, and her ladyship the judge's wife eighty, to satisfy this band that follows me, for 'it is by his singing the abbot gets his dinner'; and then you may at once proceed on your journey, free and unhindered, with a safe-conduct which I will give you, so that if you come across any other bands of mine that I have scattered in these parts, they will do you no harm; for I have no intention of doing injury to soldiers, or to any woman, especially ladies of quality."

Profuse and eloquent were the expressions of gratitude with

which the captains thanked Roque for his courtesy and generosity; for such they regarded his leaving them their own money. Señora Doña Guiomar de Quiñones wanted to leap out of the coach to kiss the feet and hands of the great Roque, but he would not allow it on any account; on the contrary, he begged her pardon for the wrong he had done her under pressure of the inexorable necessities of his unfortunate calling. The judge's lady ordered one of her servants to give the eighty crowns that had been assessed as her share at once, for the captains had already paid down their sixty. The pilgrims were about to hand over their pittance, but Roque told them to stop, and turning to his men he said, "Of these crowns two go to each man and twenty remain over; let ten be given to these pilgrims, and the other ten to this worthy squire that he may be able to speak favorably of this adventure." And then having writing materials, with which he always went provided, brought to him, he gave them in writing a safe-conduct to the leaders of his bands; and bidding them farewell, he let them go free, filled with admiration at his magnanimity, his generous disposition, and his unusual conduct, and inclined to regard him as an Alexander the Great rather than a notorious robber.

One of the squires observed in his mixture of Gascon and Catalan, "This captain of ours would make a better friar than highwayman; if he wants to be so generous in the future, let it be with his own property and not ours."

The unlucky fellow did not speak so low but that Roque overheard him, and drawing his sword he split his head almost in two, saying, "That is the way I punish those who are impudent and disrespectful." They were all taken aback, and not one of them dared to utter a word, such deference did they pay him.

Roque then withdrew to one side and wrote a letter to a friend of his at Barcelona, telling him that the famous Don Quixote of La Mancha, the knight-errant of whom there was so much talk, was with him, and was, he assured him, the funniest and wisest man in the world; and that in four days from that date, that is to say, on Saint John the Baptist's Day, he was going to deposit him in full armor mounted on his horse Rocinante, together with his squire Sancho on an ass, in the middle of the beach of the city. Roque also asked him to notify his partisans, the Niarros, so that they might amuse themselves with him. He hoped, he said, that his enemies the Cadells[4] could be deprived of this pleasure; but that was impossible, because the crazy behavior and shrewd sayings of Don Quixote and the humors of his squire Sancho Panza could not help giving general pleasure to all the world. He dispatched the letter by

4. The Niarros and Cadells were the two factions in the internecine wars mentioned in the previous note. The real Roca Guinarda was also a *nyerro*.

one of his squires, who, exchanging the costume of a highwayman for that of a peasant, made his way into Barcelona and gave it to the person to whom it was addressed.

Chapter LXI

OF WHAT HAPPENED TO DON QUIXOTE ON ENTERING BARCELONA, TOGETHER WITH OTHER MATTERS THAT PARTAKE OF THE TRUE RATHER THAN OF THE INGENIOUS

Don Quixote spent three days and three nights with Roque, and had he passed three hundred years he would have found enough to observe and wonder at in his mode of life. At daybreak they were in one spot, at dinner time in another; sometimes they fled without knowing from whom, at other times they lay in wait, not knowing for what. They slept standing, breaking their slumbers to shift from place to place. They were constantly sending out spies, posting sentinels, and blowing on the fuses of matchlock guns, though they carried but few, for all of them used flintlocks.

Roque passed his nights in some place or other apart from his men so that they might not know where he was, for the many proclamations the viceroy of Barcelona had issued against his life kept him uneasy and fearful, and he did not dare to trust anyone, afraid that even his own men would kill him or hand him over to the authorities: truly a miserable, uncomfortable life!

At length, by unfrequented roads, short cuts, and secret paths, Roque, Don Quixote, and Sancho, together with six squires, set out for Barcelona. They arrived at the beach on Saint John's Eve during the night; and Roque, after embracing Don Quixote and Sancho (to whom he presented the ten crowns he had promised but had not until then given), left them with many expressions of goodwill on both sides.

Roque went back, while Don Quixote remained on horseback, just as he was, waiting for day, and it was not long before the countenance of the fair Aurora began to appear at the windows of the east, gladdening the grass and flowers, if not the ear, though to gladden that too there came at the same moment a sound of oboes and drums, a din of bells, and cries of "Clear the way there!" of some runners, that seemed to issue from the city. The dawn made way for the sun that with a face broader than a shield began to rise slowly above the low line of the horizon.

Don Quixote and Sancho gazed all around them; they beheld the sea, a sight until then unseen by them; it struck them as exceedingly spacious and broad, much more so than the lakes of Ruidera which they had seen in La Mancha. They saw the galleys along the beach, which, lowering their awnings, displayed themselves decked with streamers and pennants that fluttered in the breeze and kissed and swept the water, while on board sounded bugles, trumpets, and oboes which far and near played a tune with melodious, warlike notes. Then they began to move and execute a kind of skirmish on the calm water, while a vast number of horsemen on fine horses and in showy liveries, issuing from the city, matched it with a somewhat similar movement. The soldiers on board the galleys kept up a ceaseless fire, which those on the walls and in the forts of the city returned, and the heavy artillery rent the air with the tremendous noise they made, to which the gangway cannon of the galleys replied. The bright sea, the smiling earth, the clear air—though at times darkened by the smoke of the guns—all seemed to fill the whole multitude with unexpected delight. Sancho could not make out how it was that those great hulks that moved over the sea should have so many feet.

And now the horsemen in livery came galloping up with shouts and Moorish war cries and cheers to where Don Quixote stood amazed and wondering; and one of them, the person to whom Roque had sent word, addressing him exclaimed, "Welcome to our city, mirror, beacon, star, and north pole of all knight-errantry in its widest extent! Welcome, I say, valiant Don Quixote of La Mancha; not the false, the fictitious, the apocryphal, that recent days have offered us in lying histories, but the true, the legitimate, the real one that Cide Hamete Benengeli, flower of historians, has described to us!"

Don Quixote made no answer, nor did the horsemen wait for one, but wheeling about and rejoining their followers, they began spiraling around Don Quixote, who, turning to Sancho, said, "These gentlemen have plainly recognized us. I will wager they have read our history, and even the newly printed one by the Aragonese."

The cavalier who had addressed Don Quixote again approached him and said, "Come with us, Señor Don Quixote, for we are all at your service and great friends of Roque Guinart's." To which Don Quixote replied, "If courtesy breeds courtesy, yours, sir knight, is an offspring or a very near relative of the great Roque's. Take me where you please; I shall have no will but yours, especially if you wish to employ it in your service."

The cavalier replied with words no less polite, and then, all closing in around him, they set out with him for the city, to the music of the oboes and the drums. As they were entering it, the Evil One, who is the author of all mischief, and young boys, who are worse than the devil, appeared on the scene. A couple of audacious, mischievous urchins forced their way through the crowd, and one of them lifting up Dapple's tail and the other Rocinante's, inserted a bunch of furze under each. The poor beasts felt the strange spurs and added to their discomfort by pressing their tails tight and bucking, as a result of which they flung their masters to the ground. Don Quixote, embarrassed and humiliated, hurried to remove the plume from his poor nag's tail, while Sancho did the same for Dapple. His conductors tried to punish the audacity of the boys, but there was no possibility of doing so, for they hid themselves among the hundreds of others that were following them. Don Quixote and Sancho mounted once more, and with the same acclamations and music reached their guide's house, which was large and stately, that of a rich gentleman, in short; and there for the present we will leave them, for such is Cide Hamete's pleasure.

Chapter LXII

WHICH DEALS WITH THE ADVENTURE OF THE ENCHANTED HEAD, TOGETHER WITH OTHER TRIVIAL MATTERS WHICH CANNOT BE LEFT UNTOLD

Don Quixote's host was one Don Antonio Moreno by name, a gentleman of wealth and intelligence, and very fond of diverting himself in any fair and good-natured way; and having Don Quixote in his house, he set about devising modes of making him exhibit his mad traits in some harmless fashion; for jests that give pain are not jests, and no amusement is worth anything if it hurts another. The first thing he did was to make Don Quixote take off his armor, and lead him, in that tight chamois suit we have already described and depicted more than once, out on a balcony overhanging one of the principal streets of the city, in full view of the crowd and of the boys, who gazed at him as they would at a monkey. The cavaliers raced their horses before him again as though it were for him alone and not to enliven the festival of the day that they wore their uniforms, and Sancho was extremely contented, for it seemed to him that, without knowing how, he had discovered another Camacho's wedding, another house like Don Diego de Miranda's, another castle like the duke's. Some of Don Antonio's friends dined with him that day, and all showed honor to Don Quixote and treated him as a knight-errant, and he, becoming puffed up and conceited as a result, could not contain himself for satisfaction. So numerous were Sancho's clever remarks that all the servants of the house and all who heard him were hanging on his every word. While at the table, Don Antonio said to him, "We hear, Sancho, that you are so fond of chicken-breast pudding and meat balls that if you have any left, you keep them inside your shirt for the next day."

"No, señor, that's not true," said Sancho, "for I am more neat then greedy, and my master Don Quixote here knows well that we often live for a week on a handful of acorns or walnuts. Of course, if it happens that they offer me a heifer, I come running with a halter. I mean, I eat what they give me and take advantage of opportunities as I find them. But whoever says that I'm a greedy eater or not neat, let me tell him that he is wrong; and I'd put it in a different way if I did not respect the honorable beards that are at the table."

"Indeed," said Don Quixote, "Sancho's moderation and cleanliness in eating might be inscribed and engraved on plates of brass, to be kept in eternal remembrance in ages to come. It is true that when he is hungry there is a certain appearance of voracity about him, for he eats fast and chews with both cheeks full. But cleanliness he is always mindful of; and when he was governor he learned how to eat with such refinement that he ate grapes, and even pomegranate seeds, with a fork."

"What!" said Don Antonio, "has Sancho been a governor?"

"Yes," said Sancho, "and of an island called Barataria. I governed it to perfection for ten days; and lost my peace of mind and learned to detest all the governorships in the world. I ran away from it and fell into a pit, where I gave myself up for dead, and out of which I escaped alive by a miracle."

Don Quixote then gave them a minute account of the whole affair of Sancho's government, with which he greatly amused his hearers.

When the cloth had been removed, Don Antonio, taking Don Quixote by the hand, led him into a distant room in which there was nothing in the way of furniture except a table, apparently of marble, resting on a pedestal of the same, upon which was set up, after the fashion of the busts of the Roman emperors, a head which seemed to be of bronze. Don Antonio walked around the whole apartment with Don Quixote and circled the table several times, and then said, "Now, Señor Don Quixote, that I am satisfied that no one is listening to us and that the door is shut, I will tell you about one of the rarest adventures, or more properly speaking, remarkable objects, that can be imagined, on condition that you will keep what I say to you in the remotest recesses of secrecy."

"I swear it," said Don Quixote, "and for greater security I will bury it; for I would have you know, Señor Don Antonio" (he had by this time learned his name), "that you are addressing one who, though he has ears to hear, has no tongue to speak; so that you may safely transfer whatever you have in your bosom into mine, in confidence that you have consigned it to the depths of silence."

"In reliance upon that promise," said Don Antonio, "I will astonish you with what you shall see and hear, and relieve myself of some of the vexation it gives me to have no one to whom I can confide my secrets, for they are not of a sort to be entrusted to everybody."

Don Quixote was puzzled, wondering what could be the object of such precautions. Then taking his hand Don Antonio passed it over the bronze head and the whole table and the pedestal of marble on which it stood, and then said, "This head, Señor Don Quixote, has been made and fabricated by one of the greatest enchanters and sorcerers the world ever saw, a Pole, I believe, by birth, and a pupil of the famous Escotillo of whom such marvellous stories are told.[1] He was here in my house, and for a consideration of a thousand crowns that I gave him, he constructed this head, which has the property and virtue of answering whatever questions are put to its ear. He observed the angles of the planets, he traced figures, he studied the stars, he watched favorable moments, and at length brought it to the perfection we shall see tomorrow, for on Fridays it is mute, and this being Friday we must wait till the next day. In the meanwhile, your worship may consider what you would like to ask it; for I know by experience that in all its answers it tells the truth."

Don Quixote was amazed at the powers and qualities of the head, and was inclined to disbelieve Don Antonio; but seeing what a short time he had to wait to test the matter, he did not choose to say anything except to thank Don Antonio for having revealed so important a secret. They then left the room, Don Antonio locked the door, and they returned to the chamber where the rest of the gentlemen were assembled. In the meantime Sancho had recounted to them several of the adventures and accidents that had happened to his master.

That afternoon they took Don Quixote out for a ride, not in his armor but in street clothes and wearing a tan overcoat that at that season would have made ice itself sweat. Orders were left with the servants to entertain Sancho so as not to let him leave the house. Don Quixote was mounted, not on Rocinante, but on a large, smooth-gaited mule, handsomely caparisoned. They put the overcoat on him, and on the back, without his perceiving it, they stitched a parchment on which they wrote in large letters, "This is Don Quixote of La Mancha." When they set out on their excursion, the placard attracted the eyes of all who chanced to see him, and as they read out, "This is Don Quixote of La Mancha," Don Quixote was amazed to see that everybody who saw him called him by his name and knew him, and turning to Don Antonio, who rode at his side, he observed to him, "Great are the privileges of knight-errantry, for it makes him who professes it known and famous in every region of the earth. See, Don Antonio, even the boys of this city know me without ever having seen me."

"True, Señor Don Quixote," returned Don Antonio. "For as fire

1. Probably Michael Scotus, called Escotillo in some Spanish authors, a sixteenth-century magician, whose tricks are confused with those of his thirteenth-century namesake.

cannot be hidden or kept secret, virtue cannot escape being recognized; and that which is attained by the profession of arms shines and is distinguished above all others."

It came to pass, however, that as Don Quixote was proceeding amid the acclamations that have been described, a Castilian, reading the inscription on his back, cried out in a loud voice, "The devil take you, Don Quixote of La Mancha! How have you lasted this long, without being killed by all the beatings you've taken! You're crazy, and if you were crazy by yourself and kept your craziness to yourself, it wouldn't be so bad. But you have the gift of making fools and madmen of all who have anything to do with you or to say to you. Why, look at these gentlemen who are keeping you company! Go home, you fool, and look after your affairs and your wife and children, and give up this foolishness that is sapping your brains and skimming off your wits."

"Go your own way, brother," said Don Antonio, "and don't offer advice to those who don't ask you for it. Señor Don Quixote is perfectly sane, and we who keep him company are not fools; virtue is to be honored wherever it may be found; go, and bad luck to you, and don't meddle where you are not wanted."

"By God, your worship is right," replied the Castilian. "For to advise this poor man is to kick against the pricks. Nevertheless, it fills me with pity that the good sense they say this blockhead has in everything should go down the drain of his knight-errantry. But may the bad luck your worship talks of follow me and all my descendants, if, from this day on, though I should live longer than Methuselah, I ever give advice to anybody even if he asks me for it."

The advice-giver went off, and they continued their ride; but so great was the press of the boys and people to read the placard, that Don Antonio was forced to remove it as if he were taking off something else.

Night came, and they went home, and there was a ladies' dancing party, for Don Antonio's wife, a woman of rank, gay, beautiful, and witty, had invited some friends of hers to come and do honor to her guest and amuse themselves with his strange delusions. Several of them came, they dined sumptuously, and the dance began at about ten o'clock. Among the ladies were two of a mischievous and joke-loving turn, and, though perfectly proper, somewhat free in playing tricks for harmless diversion. These two were so indefatigable in getting Don Quixote to dance that they tired him out, not only in body but in spirit. It was a sight to see the figure Don Quixote made, long, lank, lean, and sallow in his tight-fitting clothes, ungainly, and above all anything but agile. The ladies flirted with him on the sly, and he discouraged them, also very discreetly, but finding himself hard pressed by their attentions raised his voice and exclaimed, "*Fugite, partes adversae*![2] Leave me in peace, unwelcome thoughts! Keep your passion to yourselves, ladies, for she who is queen of mine, the peerless Dulcinea del Toboso, suffers none but hers to lead me captive and subdue me." And so saying he sat down on the floor in the middle of the room, tired out and broken down by all this exertion in the dance.

Don Antonio directed him to be taken up bodily and carried to bed, and the first that laid hold of him was Sancho, saying as he did so, "It serves you right for dancing so much! Do you think that just because men are valiant or knights-errant they make good dancers? If you do, I can tell you you are mistaken; there's many a man would rather kill a giant than attempt a fancy dance step. If it had been country dancing you were doing, I could take your place, for I can dance those like an expert; but I'm no good at these fancy courtier's steps."

With these and other observations Sancho set the whole ballroom laughing and then put his master to bed, covering him up well so that he might sweat out any chill caught dancing.

The next day Don Antonio thought he might as well test the enchanted head, and with Don Quixote, Sancho, and two others, friends of his, besides the two ladies that had tired out Don Quixote at the ball, who had remained for the night with Don Antonio's wife, he locked himself up in the chamber where the head was. He explained to them the quality it possessed and swore them to secrecy, telling them that now for the first time he was going to try the power of the enchanted head. No one except Don Antonio's two friends knew about the trick of the enchantment, and if Don Antonio had not first revealed it to them, they would have been inevitably reduced to the same state of amazement as the rest, so artfully and skilfully was it contrived.

The first to approach the ear of the head was Don Antonio himself, and in a low voice but not so low as not to be audible to all, he said to it, "Head, tell me by the power that lies in you what am I thinking of at this moment?"

The head, without any movement of the lips, answered in a clear and distinct voice, so as to be heard by all, "I cannot judge thoughts."

All were thunderstruck at this, and all the more so as they saw that there was nobody anywhere near the table or in the whole room that could have answered. "How many of us are here?" asked Don Antonio once more; and it was answered in the same way, softly, "You and your wife, with two friends of yours and two of hers, and a famous knight called Don Quixote of La Mancha, and a squire of his, Sancho Panza by name."

Now there was fresh astonishment; now everyone's hair was

2. An exorcism: "Begone, adversaries!"

standing on end with fright. Don Antonio, moving away from the head, exclaimed, "This suffices to show me that I have not been deceived by him who sold you to me, O wise head, talking head, answering head, wonderful head! Let some one else ask it whatever he wants."

And as women are usually impulsive and inquisitive, the first to come forward was one of the two friends of Don Antonio's wife, and her question was, "Tell me, head, what should I do to be very beautiful?" and the answer she got was, "Be very modest."

"I will not ask you anything else," said the questioner.

Her companion then came up and said, "I would like to know, head, whether my husband loves me or not." The answer given to her was, "Consider how he treats you, and you will discover the answer." And the married lady went off saying, "That answer did not need a question; for of course the treatment one receives shows the feelings of him from whom it is received."

Then one of Don Antonio's two friends advanced and asked it, "Who am I?" "You know," was the answer. "That is not what I ask," said the gentleman, "but I want you to tell me if you know me." "Yes, I know you; you are Don Pedro Noriz," was the reply.

"I do not seek to know more," said the gentleman, "for this is enough to convince me, O head, that you know everything." And as he retired the other friend came forward and asked it, "Tell me, head, what are the wishes of my eldest son?"

"I have said already," was the answer, "that I cannot judge wishes; however, I can tell you the wish of your son is to bury you."

"How true," said the gentleman. "It's so obvious one can point to it with his finger!" And he asked no more.

Don Antonio's wife came up and said, "I don't know what to ask you, head; I would only like to know if I shall have many years of enjoyment of my good husband." And the answer she received was, "You shall, for his vigor and his temperate habits promise many years of life, which by their intemperance others so often cut short."

Then Don Quixote came forward and said, "Tell me, you who answer, was that which I describe as having happened to me in the cave of Montesinos the truth or a dream? Will Sancho's whipping be accomplished without fail? Will the disenchantment of Dulcinea be brought about?"

"As to the question of the cave," was the reply, "there is much to be said; there is something of both in it. Sancho's whipping will proceed slowly. The disenchantment of Dulcinea will attain its due consummation."

"I seek to know no more," said Don Quixote. "Let me but see Dulcinea disenchanted and I will consider that all the good fortune I could wish for has come upon me all at once."

The last questioner was Sancho, and his questions were, "Head, shall I by any chance have another government? Shall I ever escape from the hard life of a squire? Shall I get back to see my wife and children?" To which the answer came, "You will govern in your house; and if you return to it you will see your wife and children; and on ceasing to serve you will cease to be a squire."

"That's good, by God!" said Sancho Panza. "I could have told myself that; the prophet Perogrullo couldn't have said it better!"[3]

"What did you expect it to answer, oaf?" said Don Quixote. "Is it not enough that the replies this head has given suit the questions put to it?"

"Yes, it is enough," said Sancho. "But I would have liked it to have spoken plainer and told me more."

The questions and answers came to an end here, but not the wonder with which all were filled, except Don Antonio's two friends who were in on the secret. This, Cide Hamete Benengeli thought fit to reveal at once, not to keep the world in suspense, believing that the head had some strange, magical mystery in it. He says, therefore, that in imitation of another head, the work of a printer, which he had seen at Madrid, Don Antonio made this one at home for his own amusement and to astonish ignorant people; and its mechanism was as follows. The tabletop was of wood painted and varnished to imitate marble, and the pedestal on which it stood was of the same material, with four eagles' claws projecting from it to support the weight more steadily. The head, which resembled a bust or figure of a Roman emperor, and was colored like bronze, was hollow throughout, as was the table, into which it was fitted so exactly that no trace of the joining was visible. The pedestal of the table was also hollow and connected with the throat and chest of the head, and the whole apparatus was connected with another room underneath the chamber in which the head stood. Through the entire cavity in the pedestal, table, throat and chest of the bust or figure, there passed a tube of tin carefully adjusted and concealed from sight. In the room below corresponding to the one above was placed the person who was to answer, with his mouth to the tube; and the voice, as in an ear-trumpet, passed up and down, the words coming clearly and distinctly. It was impossible, thus, to detect the trick.

A nephew of Don Antonio's, a smart sharp-witted student, was the answerer, and as he had been told beforehand by his uncle who the persons were that would come with him that day into the chamber where the head was, it was an easy matter for him to answer the first question at once and correctly; the others he answered by guesswork, and, being clever, cleverly.

3. Perogrullo was a legendary personage who dealt in prophecies that were truisms.

Cide Hamete adds that this marvelous contrivance stood for some ten or twelve days; but that, as it became known through the city that he had in his house an enchanted head that answered all who asked questions of it, Don Antonio, fearing it might come to the ears of the watchful sentinels of our faith, explained the matter to the inquisitors, who commanded him to dismantle it and have done with it, lest the ignorant should be misled. By Don Quixote, however, and by Sancho the head was still held to be an enchanted one and capable of answering questions, though more to Don Quixote's satisfaction than Sancho's.

The gentlemen of the city, to gratify Don Antonio and also to entertain Don Quixote and give him an opportunity for displaying his silly behavior, made arrangements for a tilting at the ring in six days from that time, which, however, for a reason that will be mentioned hereafter, did not take place.

Don Quixote took a fancy to stroll about the city quietly and on foot, for he feared that if he went on horseback the boys would pester him; so he and Sancho and two servants that Don Antonio gave him went out for a walk. Thus it came to pass that going along one of the streets Don Quixote lifted up his eyes and saw written in very large letters over a door, "Books printed here," at which he was very pleased, for until then he had never seen a print shop and he was curious to know what it was like. He entered with all his following and saw them printing pages in one place, correcting in another, setting up type here, revising there; in short all the work that is to be seen in great printing firms. He went up to one case and asked what they were doing there; the workmen told him, he watched them with wonder, and passed on. He approached a man at another set of cases and asked him what he was doing. The workman replied, "Señor, this gentleman here" (pointing to a man of impressive appearance and a certain gravity of look) "has translated an Italian book into our Spanish tongue, and I am setting it up in type for the press."

"What is the title of the book?" asked Don Quixote. To which the author replied, "Señor, in Italian the book is called *Le Bagatelle.*"

"And what does *Le Bagatelle* mean in Spanish?" asked Don Quixote.

"*Le Bagatelle,*" said the author, "means in Spanish *Trifles*; but though the book is humble in name it has good solid matter in it."

"I," said Don Quixote, "have some little smattering of Italian, and I pride myself on singing some of Ariosto's stanzas. But tell me, señor—I do not say this to test your ability, but merely out of curiosity—have you ever met with the word *pignatta* in your book?"

"Yes, often," said the author.

"And how do you render that in Spanish?"

"How would I render it," replied the author, "but by *pot*?"

"My word," exclaimed Don Quixote, "how proficient you are in the Italian language! I would lay a good wager that where they say in Italian *piace* you say in Spanish *pleases*, and where they say *più* you say *more*, and you translate *sù* by *above* and *giù* by *below*."

"I translate them that way of course," said the author, "for those are their proper equivalents."

"I would venture to swear," said Don Quixote, "that your worship is not known in the world, which always begrudges rewarding brilliant minds and praiseworthy labors. What talents lie wasted there! What minds shoved into corners! What real virtues rejected! Still it seems to me that translation from one language into another, except from the queens of languages, Greek and Latin, is like looking at Flemish tapestries on the wrong side; for though the figures are visible, they are full of threads that make them indistinct, and they do not show with the smoothness and texture of the right side; and translation from easy languages demonstrates neither ingenuity nor command of words, any more than transcribing or copying one document from another. But I do not mean by this to imply that no credit is to be allowed for the work of translating, for a man may employ himself in ways worse and less profitable to himself. This estimate does not include two famous translators, Doctor Cristóbal de Figueroa, in his *Pastor Fido*, and Don Juan de Jáuregui, in his *Aminta*, where their skill leaves in doubt which is the translation and which the original. But tell me, are you printing this book at your own expense or have you sold the copyright to some bookseller?"

"I print at my own expense," said the author, "and I expect to make a thousand ducats at least by this first edition, which is to be of two thousand copies that will go in no time for six *reales* apiece."

"Your worship is mistaken!" said Don Quixote. "It is plain you don't know the ins and outs of the printers and the collusion among them. I promise you when you find yourself saddled with two thousand copies you will feel so sore that it will astonish you, particularly if the book is a little out of the common and not in any way spicy."

"Then what?" said the author. "Would your worship have me give it to a bookseller who will give three *maravedís* for the copyright and think he is doing me a favor? I do not print my books to win fame in the world, for I am known already through my works; I want to make money, without which reputation is not worth a cent."

"God send your worship good luck," said Don Quixote, and he moved on to another case, where he saw them correcting a sheet of a book with the title *Light of the Soul*. Noticing it he observed, "Books like this, though there are many of the kind, are the ones that deserve to be printed, for there are many sinners in these days, and innumerable lights are needed for all that are in darkness."

He passed on and saw they were also correcting another book, and when he asked its title they told him it was called, *The Second Part of the Ingenious Gentleman Don Quixote of La Mancha,* by a citizen of Tordesillas.

"I have heard of this book already," said Don Quixote, "and verily and on my conscience I thought it had been by this time burned to ashes as useless; but its Martinmas will come to it as it does to every pig;[4] for fictions are better and more entertaining the more nearly they approach the truth or what looks like it; and true stories, the truer they are the better they are." And so saying, he walked out of the print shop with a certain amount of displeasure in his looks. That same day Don Antonio arranged to take him to see the galleys that lay at the beach, at which Sancho was delighted as he had never seen any in his life. Don Antonio sent word to the commandant of the galleys that he intended to bring his guest, the famous Don Quixote of La Mancha, of whom the commandant and all the citizens had already heard, that afternoon to see them; and what happened to him on board will be told in the next chapter.

Chapter LXIII

OF THE MISHAP THAT BEFELL SANCHO PANZA ON THE VISIT TO THE GALLEYS, AND THE STRANGE ADVENTURE OF THE BEAUTIFUL MORISCO GIRL

Profound were Don Quixote's reflections on the reply of the enchanted head, though none of them deduced that it was a trick, and all concentrated on the promise, which he regarded as a certainty, of Dulcinea's disenchantment. This he turned over in his mind again and again with great satisfaction, fully persuaded that he would shortly see its fulfillment. And as for Sancho, though, as has been said, he hated being a governor, still he had a longing to be giving orders and finding himself obeyed once more; this is the misfortune that being in authority, even in jest, brings with it.

To resume: that afternoon their host Don Antonio Moreno and his two friends, with Don Quixote and Sancho, went to the galleys. The commandant had been already made aware of his good fortune in seeing two such famous persons as Don Quixote and Sancho, and the instant they came to the shore, all the galleys struck their awnings and the oboes rang out. A skiff covered with rich carpets and

4. I.e., doom, St. Martin's Day being the traditional day for pig-slaughtering in Spain.

cushions of crimson velvet was immediately lowered into the water, and as Don Quixote stepped on board, the leading galley fired her gangway gun, and the other galleys did the same; and as he mounted the starboard ladder the whole crew saluted him (as is the custom when a personage of distinction comes on board a galley) by exclaiming, "Hu, hu, hu," three times. The admiral, for so we shall call him, a Valencian gentleman of rank, gave him his hand and embraced him, saying, "I shall mark this day with a white stone as one of the happiest I can expect to enjoy in my lifetime, since I have seen Señor Don Quixote of La Mancha. It will recall the occasion that reveals to us that in him we see contained and condensed all that is worthy in knight-errantry."

Don Quixote, delighted beyond measure with such a lordly reception, replied to him in words no less courteous. All then proceeded to the stern, which was very handsomely decorated, and seated themselves on the bulwark benches. The boatswain passed along the gangway and piped all hands to strip to the waist, which they did in an instant. Sancho, seeing such a number of men stripped to the skin, was taken aback, and still more when he saw them spread the awning so briskly that it seemed to him as if all the devils were at work on it; but all this was nothing to what I am going to tell now. Sancho was seated on the captain's stage, close to the last rower on the right-hand side. This rower, previously instructed in what he was to do, laid hold of Sancho, hoisting him up in his arms, and the whole crew, who were standing ready, beginning on the right, proceeded to pass him on, tumbling him along from hand to hand and from bench to bench with such rapidity that it took the sight out of poor Sancho's eyes, and he no doubt thought that the devils themselves were flying away with him; nor did they stop with him until they had sent him back along the left side and deposited him on the stern. The poor fellow was left bruised and panting and all in a sweat, and unable to comprehend what it was that had happened to him.

Don Quixote when he saw Sancho's flight without wings asked the admiral if this was a usual ceremony with those who came on board the galleys for the first time; for, if so, as he had no intention of adopting them as a profession, he had no desire to perform such exercises, and if anyone tried to lay hold of him to tumble him about, he vowed to God he would kick his soul out; and as he said this he stood up and clapped his hand on his sword. At this instant they struck the awning and lowered the yard with a prodigious noise. Sancho thought heaven was coming off its hinges and going to fall on his head, and full of terror he ducked and put it between his knees. Nor was Don Quixote altogether under control, for he too shook a little, hunched his shoulders and paled. The crew then hoisted the yard with the same rapidity and clatter as when they lowered it, all the while keeping silence as though they had neither voice nor breath. The boatswain gave the signal to weigh anchor, and leaping into the middle of the gangway began to flick the shoulders of the crew with his lash or whip, and to put gradually to sea.

When Sancho saw so many red feet (for such he took the oars to be) moving all together, he said to himself, "It's these that are the real enchanted things, and not the ones my master talks about. What can these wretches have done to be whipped like that? And how does that one man who goes along there whistling dare to whip so many? I say this is hell, or at least purgatory!"

Don Quixote, observing how attentively Sancho regarded what was going on, said to him, "Ah, Sancho my friend, how quickly and cheaply might you finish up the disenchantment of Dulcinea if you would strip to the waist and take your place among those gentlemen! Amid the pain and sufferings of so many you would not feel your own much; and moreover perhaps the sage Merlin would allow each of these lashes, because they are being laid on vigorously, to count for ten of those which you must give yourself eventually."

The admiral was about to ask what these lashes were and what was Dulcinea's disenchantment when a sailor exclaimed, "The fort on Montjuich is signaling that there is an oared vessel off the coast to the west."

On hearing this the admiral sprang up on the gangway crying, "Now then, boys, don't let her give us the slip! It must be some Algerian corsair brigantine that the watchtower signals to us." The three others immediately came alongside the flagship to receive their orders. The admiral ordered two to put out to sea while he with the other kept to the shore, so that in this way the vessel could not escape them. The crews plied the oars driving the galleys so furiously that they seemed to fly.

The two that had put out to sea, after a couple of miles, sighted a vessel which, so far as they could make out, they judged to be one of fourteen or fifteen banks of rowers, and so she proved. As soon as the vessel discovered the galleys, she took to flight with the object and in the hope of making her escape by her speed. But the attempt failed, for the flagship was one of the fastest vessels afloat and overtook her so rapidly that those on board the brigantine saw clearly there was no possibility of escaping, and the Moorish captain therefore wanted them to drop their oars and give themselves up so as not to provoke the captain in command of our galleys to anger.

But chance, directing things otherwise, so ordered it that just as the flagship came close enough for those on board the enemy vessel to hear the shouts from her calling on them to surrender, two *Toraquis*, that is to say two Turks, both drunk, that with a dozen more were on board the brigantine, discharged their muskets, killing two of the soldiers that lined the sides of our vessel. Seeing this the admiral swore he would not leave one of those he found on board the vessel alive, but as he bore down furiously upon her, she slipped away from him underneath the oars. The galley shot a good way ahead; those on board the brigantine saw their situation was desperate; and while the galley was coming about, they made sail, and by sailing and rowing once more tried to flee. But their activity did not do them as much good as their rashness did them harm, for the galley catching up with them in a little more than half a mile threw her oars over them and took the whole of them alive. The other two galleys now joined them, and all four returned with the prize to the beach, where a vast multitude stood waiting for them, eager to see what they brought back.

The admiral anchored close in and perceived that the viceroy of the city was on the shore. He ordered the skiff to push off to fetch him and the yard to be lowered for the purpose of hanging immediately the Moorish captain and the rest of the men taken on board the vessel—about thirty-six in number, all good-looking fellows and most of them Turkish musketeers. He asked which was the captain of the brigantine and was answered in Spanish by one of the prisoners (who afterwards proved to be a Spanish renegade), "This young man, señor, that you see here is our captain," and he pointed to one of the handsomest and most gallant-looking youths that could be imagined. He did not seem to be twenty years of age.

"Tell me, foolhardy infidel," said the admiral, "what led you to kill my soldiers, when you saw it was impossible for you to escape? Is that the way to respect flagships? Don't you know that rashness is not valor? Faint prospects of success should make men bold, but not rash."

The captain was about to reply, but the admiral could not at that moment listen to him as he had to hasten to receive the viceroy, who was now coming on board the galley, and with him certain of his attendants and some of the people.

"You have had good hunting, señor admiral," said the viceroy.

"Your excellency shall soon see how good, by the game strung up to this yard," replied the admiral.

"How so?" returned the viceroy.

"Because," said the admiral, "against all law, reason, and usages of war they have killed two of my best soldiers on board these galleys, and I have sworn to hang every man that I have taken, but above all this young man, who is the captain of the brigantine," and he pointed to him as he stood with his hands already bound and the rope round his neck, ready for death.

The viceroy looked at him, and seeing him so handsome, so graceful, and so submissive, he felt a desire to spare his life, the good looks of the youth furnishing him at once with a letter of recommendation. He therefore questioned him, saying, "Tell me, captain, are you a Turk, Moor, or renegade?"

To which the youth replied, also in Spanish, "I am neither a Turk, nor Moor, nor renegade."

"What are you, then?" said the viceroy.

"A Christian woman," replied the youth.

"A woman and a Christian, in such a dress and in such circumstances! It is more marvelous than credible," said the viceroy.

"Suspend the execution of the sentence," said the youth. "Your vengeance will not lose much by waiting while I tell you the story of my life."

What heart could be so hard as not to be softened by these words, at any rate so far as to listen to what the unhappy youth had to say? The general told him to say what he pleased, but not to expect pardon for his flagrant offence. With this permission the youth began in these words.

"Born of Morisco parents, I am of that nation, more unhappy than wise, upon which recently a sea of woes has poured down. In the course of its misfortune I was carried to Barbary by an uncle and aunt, for it was in vain that I declared I was a Christian, as in fact I am, and not a mere pretended one, or outwardly, but a true Catholic Christian. It availed me nothing with those charged with our sad exile to protest this, nor would my uncle and aunt believe it; on the contrary, they treated it as a lie and a scheme to enable me to remain behind in the land of my birth; and so, more by force than of my own will, they took me with them. I had a Christian mother, and a father who was a man of sound sense and a Christian too. I imbibed the Catholic faith with my mother's milk. I was well brought up, and neither in word nor in deed did I, I think, show any sign of being a Morisco.

"To accompany these virtues, for such I hold them, my beauty, if I possess any, increased with my years; and great as were the modesty and seclusion in which I lived, they were not so great but that a young gentleman, Don Gaspar Gregorio by name, eldest son of a gentleman who is lord of a village near ours, found opportunities of seeing me. How he saw me, how we met, how his heart was lost to me and mine not kept from him, would take too long to tell, especially at a moment when I am afraid that the cruel rope that threatens me will cut off my breath between tongue and throat. I will only say, therefore, that Don Gregorio chose to accompany me in our banishment. He joined the Moriscos who were leaving from other villages, for he knew their language very well, and on the voyage he struck up a friendship with my uncle and aunt who were taking me with them; for my father, like a wise and far-sighted man, as soon as he heard the first edict for our expulsion, left the village and went in search of some refuge for us abroad.

"He left hidden and buried, at a spot of which I alone have knowledge, a large quantity of pearls and precious stones of great value, together with a sum of money in gold *cruzados* and doubloons. He ordered me on no account to touch the treasure, if by any chance they expelled us before his return. I obeyed him, and with my uncle and aunt, as I have said, and relatives and neighbors, crossed over to Barbary, and the place where we settled was Algiers, much the same as if we had settled in hell itself.

"The king heard of my beauty, and rumor told him of my wealth, which was in some degree fortunate for me. He summoned me before him and asked me what part of Spain I came from and what money and jewels I had. I mentioned the place and told him the jewels and money were buried there but that they might easily be recovered if I myself went back for them. All this I told him, in dread that my beauty and not his own covetousness might blind him.

"While he was engaged in conversation with me, they brought him word that with me was one of the handsomest and most graceful youths that could be imagined. I knew at once that they were speaking of Don Gaspar Gregorio, whose manly beauty can hardly be exaggerated. I was troubled when I thought of the danger he was in, for among those barbarous Turks a handsome boy or young man is more esteemed than a woman, however beautiful she may be. The king immediately ordered him to be brought before him that he might see him and asked me if what they said about the youth was true. I then, almost as if inspired by heaven, told him it was, but that I would have him to know 'he' was not a man, but a woman like myself, and I begged him to allow me to go and dress her in appropriate clothing, so that her beauty might be seen to perfection and that she might present herself before him with less embarrassment. He told me go by all means and said that the next day we would discuss the plan to be adopted for my return to Spain to bring out the hidden treasure.

"I spoke to Don Gaspar, I told him the danger he was in if he let it be seen he was a man, I dressed him as a Moorish woman, and that same afternoon I brought him before the king, who was charmed when he saw 'her' and resolved to keep the damsel and make a present of her to the Sultan. To avoid the risk she might run among the women of his seraglio, and distrustful of himself, he commanded her to be placed in the house of some Moorish ladies of rank who would protect and attend to her; and there she was taken at once. What we both suffered (for I can't deny that I love him) may be left to the imagination of those who are separated if they love one another dearly. The king then arranged for me to return to Spain in this brigantine and for two Turks, those who killed your soldiers, to accompany me. This Spanish renegade also came with me"—and here she pointed to the man who had first spoken—"who I know is secretly a Christian and more anxious to be left in Spain then to return to Barbary. The rest of the crew of the brigantine are Moors and Turks, who merely serve as rowers. The two Turks, greedy and insolent, instead of obeying the orders we had to land me and this renegade in Christian dress (with which we came provided) on the first Spanish ground we came to, chose to sweep the coast and capture some prize if they could, fearing that if they put us ashore first, we might, in case of some accident befalling us, make it known that the brigantine was at sea, and thus, if there happened to be any galleys on the coast, they might be taken. We sighted this beach last night, and knowing nothing of these galleys, we were discovered, and the result was what you have seen.

"To sum up, there is Don Gregorio in woman's dress, among women, in imminent danger of his life; and here am I, with hands bound, in expectation, or rather in dread, of losing my life, of which I am already weary. Here, sirs, ends my sad story, as true as it is unhappy; all I ask of you is to allow me to die like a Christian, for, as I have already said, I am not guilty of the offense with which those of my nation are charged." And she stood silent, her eyes filled with tears, accompanied by plenty of tears from the bystanders. The viceroy, touched with compassion, went up to her without speaking and untied the cord that bound the hands of the Moorish girl.

But all the while the Moorish Christian girl was telling her strange story, an elderly pilgrim, who had come on board the galley at the same time as the viceroy, kept his eyes fixed upon her; and the instant she ceased speaking, he threw himself at her feet and embracing them said in a voice broken by sobs and sighs, "O Ana Félix, my unhappy daughter, I am your father Ricote, come back to look for you, unable to live without you who are dearer than my soul!"

At these words of his, Sancho opened his eyes and raised his head, which was drooping, as he thought over his unlucky excursion; and looking at the pilgrim, he recognized in him that same Ricote he met the day he gave up his government, and he was convinced that this was his daughter. She being now unbound embraced her father, mingling her tears with his, while he addressing the admiral and the viceroy said, "This, sirs, is my daughter, more unhappy in her adventures than in her name. She is Ana Félix, surnamed Ricote, celebrated as much for her own beauty as for my wealth. I left my native land in search of some shelter or refuge for us abroad, and having found one in Germany, I returned in this pilgrim's dress, in the company of some other German pilgrims, to seek my daughter and dig up a large quantity of treasure I had left buried. My daughter I did not find, the treasure I found and have with me; and now, in this strange roundabout way you have seen, I find the treasure that more than all makes me rich, my beloved daughter. If our innocence and her tears and mine can with strict justice open the door to clemency, extend it to us, for we never had any intention of injuring you, nor do we sympathize with the aims of our people, who have been justly banished."

"I know Ricote well," said Sancho at this, "and I know too that what he says about Ana Félix being his daughter is true; but as to those other particulars about going and coming, and having good or bad intentions, I say nothing."

While all present stood amazed at this strange occurrence, the admiral said, "At any rate your tears will not allow me to keep my oath; live, fair Ana Félix, all the years that heaven has allotted you; but these rash and insolent fellows must pay the penalty of the crime they have committed." And with that he gave orders to have the two Turks who had killed his two soldiers hanged at once from the yardarm. The viceroy, however, begged him earnestly not to hang them, as their behavior had more of madness than of defiance. The admiral yielded to the viceroy's request, for revenge is not easily taken in cold blood.

They then tried to devise some scheme for rescuing Don Gaspar Gregorio from the danger in which he had been left. Ricote offered for that object more than two thousand ducats that he had in pearls and gems. They proposed several plans, but none so good as that suggested by the renegade already mentioned, who offered to return to Algiers in a small vessel of about six banks, manned by Christian rowers, as he knew where, how, and when he could and should land, nor was he unfamiliar with the house in which Don Gaspar was staying. The admiral and the viceroy had some hesitation about placing confidence in the renegade and entrusting him with the Christians who were to row, but Ana Félix said she could answer for him, and her father offered to pay the ransom of the Christians if by any chance they should be captured. This, then, being agreed upon, the viceroy landed, and Don Antonio Moreno took the Morisco girl and her father home with him, the viceroy charging him to give them the best reception and welcome in his power, while on his own part he offered all that his house contained for their entertainment, so great was the good will and kindliness the beauty of Ana Félix had inspired in his heart.

Chapter LXIV

TREATING OF THE ADVENTURE WHICH GAVE DON QUIXOTE MORE UNHAPPINESS THAN ALL THAT HAD HITHERTO BEFALLEN HIM

The wife of Don Antonio Moreno, so the history says, was extremely happy to see Ana Félix in her house. She welcomed her with great kindness, charmed as well by her beauty as by her intelligence; for in both respects the Morisco girl was richly endowed, and all the people of the city flocked to see her as though they had been summoned by the ringing of the bells.

Don Quixote told Don Antonio that the plan adopted for releasing Don Gregorio was not a good one, for its risks were greater than its advantages, and that it would be better to land him with his arms and horse in Barbary; for he would rescue the young man in spite of the whole Moorish host, as Don Gaiferos carried off his wife Melisendra.

"Remember, your worship," observed Sancho on hearing him say so, "Señor Don Gaiferos carried off his wife from the mainland and took her to France by land; but in this case, if by chance we free Don Gregorio, we have no way of bringing him to Spain, because the sea is in between."

"There's a remedy for everything except death," said Don Quixote. "If they bring the vessel close to the shore we shall be able to get on board though all the world strive to prevent us."

"Your worship makes it sound very easy," said Sancho. "But 'there's many a slip 'twixt the cup and the lip,' and I am relying on the renegade, who seems to me to be an honest good-hearted fellow."

Don Antonio then said that if the renegade did not prove successful, they would adopt the expedient of sending the great Don Quixote to Barbary.

Two days afterwards the renegade put to sea in a light vessel of six oars to a side manned by a stout crew, and two days later the galleys made sail eastward, the admiral having begged the viceroy to let him know all about the freeing of Don Gregorio and about Ana Félix, and the viceroy promised to do as he requested.

One morning as Don Quixote went out for a ride along the beach, arrayed in full armor (for, as he often said, that was "his only dress, his only rest the fray," and he never was without it for a moment), he saw coming towards him a knight, also in full armor, with a shining moon painted on his shield, who, on approaching sufficiently near to be heard, said in a loud voice, addressing himself to Don Quixote, "Illustrious knight and never sufficiently extolled Don Quixote of La Mancha, I am the Knight of the White Moon, whose unheard-of achievements will perhaps have brought me to thy notice. I come to do battle with thee and prove the might of thy arm, to the end that I make thee acknowledge and confess that my lady, let her be who she may, is incomparably fairer than thy Dulcinea del Toboso. If thou dost acknowledge this fairly and openly, thou shalt escape death and save me the trouble of inflicting it upon thee. If thou fightest and I vanquish thee, I demand no other satisfaction than that, laying aside arms and abstaining from going in quest of adventures, thou shouldst withdraw and betake thyself to thine own village for the space of a year and live there without putting hand to sword, in peace and quiet and beneficial repose, the same being needful for the increase of thy substance and the salvation of thy soul. And if thou dost vanquish me, my head shall be at thy disposal, my arms and horse thy spoils, and the renown of my deeds transferred to thine. Consider which will be thy best course, and give me thy answer speedily, for this day is all the time I have for the dispatch of this business."

Don Quixote was amazed and astonished, as well at the Knight of the White Moon's arrogance, as at his reason for delivering the defiance, and with calm dignity he answered him, "Knight of the White Moon, of whose achievements I have never heard until now, I will venture to swear thou hast never seen the illustrious Dulcinea; for hadst thou seen her, I know thou wouldst have taken care not to venture thyself upon this issue, because the sight would have removed all doubt from thy mind that there ever has been or can be a beauty to be compared with hers; and so, not saying thou liest, but merely that thou art not correct in what thou sayest, I accept thy challenge, with the conditions thou hast proposed, and at once, that the day thou hast fixed may not expire; and from thy conditions I except only that of the renown of thy achievements being transferred to me, for I know not of what sort they are nor what they may amount to; I am satisfied with my own, such as they be. Take, therefore, the side of the field thou choosest, and I will do the same; and to whom God shall give the victory may Saint Peter add his blessing."

The Knight of the White Moon had been seen from the city, and it was told to the viceroy how he was in conversation with Don Quixote. The viceroy, fancying it must be some fresh adventure thought up by Don Antonio Moreno or some other gentleman of the city, hurried out at once to the beach accompanied by Don Antonio and several other gentlemen, just as Don Quixote was wheeling Rocinante around in order to take up the necessary distance. The viceroy upon this, seeing that the pair of them were evidently preparing to charge, put himself between them, asking them what it was that led them to engage in combat all of a sudden in this way. The Knight of the White Moon replied that it was a question of precedence of beauty; and briefly told him what he had said to Don Quixote and how the conditions of the defiance agreed upon by both sides had been accepted. The viceroy went over to Don Antonio and asked in a low voice whether he knew who the Knight of the White Moon was, or was it some joke they were playing on Don Quixote. Don Antonio replied that he neither knew who he was nor whether the challenge was a joke or in earnest. This answer left the viceroy in a state of perplexity, not knowing whether he ought to let the combat go on or not; but unable to persuade himself that it was anything but a joke, he fell back, saying, "If there is no other way out of it, gallant knights, except to confess or die, and Don Quixote is inflexible, and your worship of the White Moon still more so, in God's hand be it, and you may give battle."

He of the White Moon thanked the viceroy in courteous and well-chosen words for the permission he gave them, and so did Don Quixote, who then, commending himself with all his heart to heaven and to his Dulcinea, as was his custom on beginning any combat that awaited him, proceeded to take a little more distance, as he saw his antagonist was doing the same. Then, without blast of trumpet or other warlike instrument to give them the signal to charge, both at the same instant wheeled their horses; and he of the White Moon, being the swifter, met Don Quixote after having traversed two-thirds of the course and there encountered him with such violence that, without touching him with his lance (for he held it high, to all appearance purposely), he hurled Don Quixote and Rocinante to the earth in a perilous fall. He sprang upon him at once, and placing the lance over his visor said to him, "Thou art vanquished, sir knight, nay dead unless thou admitest the conditions of our challenge."

Don Quixote, bruised and dazed, without raising his visor said in a weak, feeble voice as if he were speaking out of a tomb, "Dulcinea del Toboso is the fairest woman in the world, and I the most unfortunate knight on earth. It is not fitting that this truth should suffer by my feebleness; drive thy lance home, sir knight, and take my life, since thou hast taken away my honor."

"That will I certainly not do," said he of the White Moon. "Long live the fame of the lady Dulcinea's beauty; all I require is that the great Don Quixote retire to his own home for a year, or for so long a time as shall by me be enjoined upon him, as we agreed before engaging in this combat."

The viceroy, Don Antonio, and several others who were present heard all this, and heard too how Don Quixote replied that so long as nothing in prejudice of Dulcinea was demanded of him, he would observe all the rest like a true and loyal knight. The promise given, he of the White Moon wheeled about, and making obeisance to the viceroy with a movement of the head, rode away into the city at a slow gallop. The viceroy ordered Don Antonio to hasten after him and by some means or other find out who he was. They lifted Don Quixote up and uncovered his face and found him pale and bathed with sweat. Rocinante from the jolt he had received lay unable to stir for the present. Sancho, wholly dejected and woebegone, knew not what to say or do. He thought it was all a dream, that the whole business was a piece of enchantment. Here was his master defeated and bound not to take up arms for a year. He saw the light of the glory of his achievements dimmed; the hopes of the promises lately made swept away like smoke before the wind. Rocinante, he feared, was crippled for life, and his master's bones out of joint; for if he were only shaken out of his madness it would be no small luck. In the end they carried Don Quixote into the city in a sedan-chair which the viceroy sent for, and there the viceroy himself returned, eager to know who this Knight of the White Moon was who had left Don Quixote in such a sad plight.

Chapter LXV

WHEREIN IS MADE KNOWN WHO THE KNIGHT OF THE WHITE MOON WAS; LIKEWISE DON GREGORIO'S RELEASE, AND OTHER EVENTS

Don Antonio Moreno followed the Knight of the White Moon, and a number of boys followed him too, or rather pursued him, until they had him cornered in an inn in the heart of the city. Don Antonio, eager to make his acquaintance, entered also. A squire came out to meet the knight and remove his armor, and he shut himself into a lower room, still attended by Don Antonio, whose bread would not bake until he had found out who he was. He of the White Moon, seeing then that the gentleman would not leave him, said, "I know very well, señor, what you have come for. It is to find out who I am; and as there is no reason why I should conceal it from you, while my servant here is taking off my armor, I will tell you the true state of the case, without leaving out anything. You must know, señor, that I am called the bachelor Sansón Carrasco. I am from the same village as Don Quixote of La Mancha, whose madness and folly make all of us who know him feel pity for him, and I am one of those who have felt it most. And persuaded that his chance of recovery lay in rest and staying at home and in his own house, I hit upon a scheme for keeping him there. Three months ago, therefore, I went out to meet him as a knight-errant, under the assumed name of the Knight of the Mirrors, intending to engage him in combat and overcome him without hurting him, making it the condition of our combat that the vanquished should be at the disposal of the victor. What I meant to demand of him (for I regarded him as vanquished already) was that he should return to his own village and not leave it for a whole year, by which time he might be cured. But fate ordered it otherwise, for he vanquished me and unhorsed me, and so my plan failed. He went his way, and I came back conquered, covered with shame, and badly bruised from my fall, which was a particularly dangerous one. But this did not take away my desire to meet him again and overcome him, as you have seen today. And as he is so scrupulous in his observance of the laws of knight-errantry, he will, no doubt, in order to keep his word, obey the command that I have given him. This, señor, is how the matter stands, and I have nothing more to tell you. I implore of you not to betray me or tell Don Quixote who I am, so that my well-meaning plans may be successful and that a man of excellent wits—were he only rid of the nonsense of chivalry —may get them back again."

"O señor," said Don Antonio, "may God forgive you the wrong you have done the whole world in trying to bring the most amusing madman in it back to his senses. Do you not see, señor, that what is gained by restoring Don Quixote's sanity can never equal the enjoyment his delusions give? But my belief is that all your efforts, sir, will be of no avail to bring a man so hopelessly crazy to his senses again. And if it were not uncharitable, I would say may Don Quixote never be cured, for by his recovery we lose not only his amusing remarks but his squire Sancho Panza's too, any one of which is enough to turn melancholy itself into merriment. However, I'll keep silent and say nothing to him, and we'll see whether I am right in my suspicion that Señor Carrasco's efforts will be fruitless."

The bachelor replied that at all events the affair was going well, and he hoped for good results from it. Don Antonio then offered to do whatever else he might request, and he said good-bye. The bachelor had his armor packed at once on a mule. He rode away from the city the same day on the horse he rode to battle and returned to his own country without meeting any adventure calling for record in this veracious history.

Don Antonio reported to the viceroy what Carrasco told him, and the viceroy was not very well pleased to hear it, for with Don Quixote's retirement there was an end to the amusement of all who knew anything of his mad doings.

Six days did Don Quixote keep to his bed, sick, melancholy, moody, and out of sorts, brooding over the unhappy event of his defeat. Sancho tried to comfort him, and among other things he said to him, "Hold up your head, señor, and cheer up, if you can, and thank heaven that if you have had a tumble you haven't come out with a broken rib. Since you know that 'if you get in a fight, you may get hit' and 'you can't make an omelet without breaking eggs,' to hell with the doctor; you don't need him to cure this ailment. Let us go home and give up going around in search of adventures in strange lands and places. If you think about it, I'm the great loser, though your worship is in worse shape. With the governorship I gave up all wish to be a governor again, but I did not give up wanting to be a count; and that will never happen if your worship gives up becoming a king by renouncing the calling of chivalry; and so my hopes are going up in smoke."

"Be quiet, Sancho," said Don Quixote. "You see my suspension and retirement is not to exceed a year; I shall soon return to my honored calling, and I shall not be at a loss for a kingdom to win and a county to bestow on you."

"May God hear it and the devil be deaf," said Sancho. "I have always heard say that 'a good prospect is better than a bad possession.' "

As they were talking, Don Antonio came in looking extremely pleased and exclaiming, "Good news, Señor Don Quixote! Don Gregorio and the renegade who went for him have come ashore—ashore do I say? They are by this time in the viceroy's house and will be here immediately."

Don Quixote cheered up a little and said, "To tell the truth I am almost ready to say I should have been glad that it turned out the other way, for it would have obliged me to cross over to Barbary, where by the might of my arm I would have restored to liberty, not only Don Gregorio, but all the Christian captives there are in Barbary. But what am I saying, miserable thing that I am? Am I not the one who has been conquered? Am I not the one who has been overthrown? Am I not the one who must not take up arms for a year? Then what am I making promises for; what am I bragging about, when it is fitter for me to handle the distaff than the sword?"

"No more of that, señor," said Sancho. "We all have crosses to bear. 'Today for thee and tomorrow for me.' You shouldn't pay any attention to this business of collisions and blows; he that falls today may get up tomorrow, unless he chooses to lie in bed, I mean gives way to weakness and doesn't pluck up fresh spirit for fresh battles; let your worship get up now to receive Don Gregorio; for the household seems to be in an uproar, and no doubt he has come by this time."

And so it proved, for as soon as Don Gregorio and the renegade had given the viceroy an account of the voyage there and back, Don Gregorio, eager to see Ana Félix, came with the renegade to Don Antonio's house. When they carried him away from Algiers, he was in woman's dress; on board the vessel, however, he exchanged it for that of a captive who escaped with him; but in whatever dress he might be he looked like a person to be sought after and served and esteemed, for he was exceptionally handsome, and to judge by appearances some seventeen or eighteen years of age. Ricote and his daughter came out to welcome him, the father with tears, the daughter with bashfulness. They did not embrace each other, for where there is deep love there is usually restraint. Seen side by side, the comeliness of Don Gregorio and the beauty of Ana Félix were the admiration of all who were present. It was silence that spoke for the lovers at that moment, and their eyes were the tongues that declared their pure and happy feelings.

The renegade explained the plan and means he had adopted to

rescue Don Gregorio, and Don Gregorio at no great length, but in a few words, in which he showed that his intelligence was in advance of his years, described the peril and embarrassment he found himself in among the women with whom he had stayed. To conclude, Ricote liberally payed and rewarded the renegade as well as the men who had rowed; and the renegade was once again received into the Church and was reconciled with it, and from a corrupt limb became by penance and repentance a clean and sound one.

Two days later the viceroy discussed with Don Antonio the steps they should take to enable Ana Félix and her father to stay in Spain, for it seemed to them there could be no objection to a daughter who was so good a Christian and a father to all appearance so well-intentioned remaining there. Don Antonio offered to arrange the matter at the capital, where he was compelled to go on some other business, hinting that many a difficult affair is settled there with the help of favor and presents.

"No," said Ricote, who was present during the conversation, "it will not do to rely upon favor or presents, because with the great Don Bernardino de Velasco, Count of Salazar, to whom his Majesty has entrusted our explusion, neither entreaties nor promises, bribes nor appeals to compassion, are of any use. For though it is true he mingles mercy with justice, still, seeing that the whole body of our nation is tainted and corrupt, he applies to it the cautery that burns rather than the salve that soothes. And thus, by prudence, sagacity, care, and the fear he inspires, he has borne on his mighty shoulders the weight of this great policy and carried it into effect, all our schemes and plots, importunities and wiles, being ineffectual to blind his Argus eyes, ever on the watch lest one of us should remain behind in concealment, and like a hidden root eventually come to sprout and bear poisonous fruit in Spain, now cleansed and relieved of the fear in which our vast numbers kept it. Heroic resolve of the great Philip the Third, and unparalleled wisdom to have entrusted it to Don Bernardino de Velasco!"

"At any rate," said Don Antonio, "when I am there I will make all possible efforts, and let heaven do as pleases it best. Don Gregorio will come with me to relieve the anxiety which his parents must be suffering on account of his absence. Ana Félix will remain in my house with my wife, or in a nunnery; and I know the viceroy will be glad that the worthy Ricote should stay with him until we see what terms I can make."

The viceroy agreed to all that was proposed; but Don Gregorio on learning what had occurred declared he could not and would not on any account leave Ana Félix. However, as it was his purpose to go and see his parents and devise some way of returning for her, he went along with the proposed arrangement. Ana Félix remained with Don Antonio's wife, and Ricote in the viceroy's house.

The day for Don Antonio's departure came, and two days later that for Don Quixote's and Sancho's; for Don Quixote's fall did not allow him to take the road sooner. There were tears and sighs, swoonings and sobs, at the parting between Don Gregorio and Ana Félix. Ricote offered Don Gregorio a thousand crowns if he would have them, but he would not take any but five which Don Antonio lent him and he promised to repay at the capital. So the two of them left, and Don Quixote and Sancho afterwards, as has been already said, Don Quixote without his armor and in traveling gear, and Sancho on foot, Dapple being loaded with the armor.

Chapter LXVI

WHICH TREATS OF WHAT HE WHO READS WILL SEE, OR WHAT HE WHO HAS IT READ TO HIM WILL HEAR

As he left Barcelona, Don Quixote turned to gaze at the spot where he had fallen. "Here was Troy," he said. "Here my ill luck, not my cowardice, robbed me of all the glory I had won; here Fortune made me the victim of her caprices; here the luster of my achievements was dimmed; here, in a word, fell my happiness never to rise again."

"Señor," said Sancho on hearing this, "brave hearts are as patient in adversity as they are glad in prosperity. I judge by myself, because, if when I was a governor I was glad, now that I'm a squire and on foot I'm not sad. And I have heard tell that what people commonly call Fortune is a drunken, fickle woman and, what is more, blind, and so she neither sees what she does nor knows what person she knocks down or sets up."

"You are very philosophical, Sancho," said Don Quixote. "You are talking very sensibly; I don't know who teaches you such things. But I can tell you there is no such thing as Fortune in the world, nor does anything which takes place, be it good or bad, come about by chance, but by the special preordination of heaven; and hence the common saying that 'each of us is the maker of his own Fortune.' I have made mine, but not with the proper amount of prudence, and my presumption has therefore made me pay dearly; for I ought to have realized that Rocinante's feeble strength could not resist the power and size of the Knight of the White Moon's horse. In a word, I took a chance, I did my best, I was knocked off, but though I lost my honor, I did not lose nor can I lose the virtue of keeping my word. When I was a knight-errant, daring and valiant, I backed up my achievements by hand and deed, and now that I am a humble squire I will back up my words by keeping the promise I have given. Forward then, Sancho my friend, let us go to keep the year of the noviciate in our own country, and in that seclusion we shall acquire new strength to return to the by me never-forgotten calling of arms."

"Señor," returned Sancho, "traveling on foot is not such a pleasant thing that it makes me feel disposed or tempted to make long marches. Let's leave this armor strung up on some tree, like someone that has been hanged; and then with me on Dapple's back and my feet off the ground we can make the journey in stages however your worship pleases to measure them out. But if you think I'm going to travel on foot in long days' marches, you're wrong."

"A good idea, Sancho," said Don Quixote. "Let my armor be hung up for a trophy, and under it or around it we will carve on the trees what was inscribed on the trophy of Roland's armor:

These let none move
Who dareth not his might with Roland prove."

"That's the very thing," said Sancho. "And if we didn't need Rocinante on the road, it would be as well to leave him hung up too."

"No, I'd rather not have either him or the armor hung up," said Don Quixote, "that it may not be said, 'for good service a bad reward.' "

"Your worship is right," said Sancho, "for, as wise people say, 'Don't punish the packsaddle for the ass's mistake.' And, as in this affair the fault is your worship's, punish yourself and don't vent your anger on the already battered and bloody armor, or the meekness of Rocinante, or the tenderness of my feet, trying to make them travel more than is reasonable."

In conversation of this sort the whole of that day went by, as did the four succeeding ones, without anything occurring to interrupt their journey, but on the fifth as they entered a village they found a great number of people at the door of an inn enjoying themselves, as it was a holiday. Upon Don Quixote's approach a peasant called out, "One of these two gentlemen approaching, who don't know the parties, will tell us what we ought to do about our wager."

"That I will, certainly," said Don Quixote, "with all fairness, if I can manage to understand what it's about."

"Well, here it is, worthy sir," said the peasant. "A man of this village who is so fat that he weighs two hundred seventy-five pounds challenged another, a neighbor of his, who does not weigh more than a hundred twenty-five to run a race. The agreement was that they were to run a distance of a hundred paces with equal weights; and when the challenger was asked how the weights were to be equalized, he said that the other, as he weighed one hundred twenty-five pounds, should put one hundred fifty in iron on his back, and that in this way the weight of the thin man would equal that of the fat one."

"Hold it!" exclaimed Sancho at once, before Don Quixote could answer. "It's for me, who only a few days ago gave up being a governor and a judge, as all the world knows, to settle these doubtful questions and give an opinion in disputes of all sorts."

"Answer in God's name, Sancho my friend," said Don Quixote, "for I'm in no condition to give crumbs to a cat, my judgment is so confused and upset."

With this permission Sancho said to the peasants who stood clustered round him, waiting with open mouths for the decision to come from his, "Brothers, what the fat man asks is not reasonable nor is it the least bit fair, because if it is true, as they say, that the challenged may choose the weapons, then it is not fair for the fat man to choose—and such as will prevent and keep the thin man from winning. My decision, therefore, is that the fat challenger lighten, peel, thin, trim, and correct himself, and take one hundred fifty pounds of his flesh off his body, here or there as he pleases and as suits him best; and being in this way reduced to one hundred twenty-five pounds, he will be equal and even with his opponent, and they will be able to run on equal terms."

"By golly," said one of the peasants as he heard Sancho's decision, "the gentleman has spoken like a saint and given judgment like a canon! But the fat man certainly won't part with an ounce of his flesh, not to say one hundred fifty pounds."

"The best plan will be for them not to race," said another, "so that the thin man doesn't break down under the weight or the fat one strip himself of his flesh. Let half the wager be spent on wine, and let's take these gentlemen to the tavern where there's the best, and 'devil take the hindmost.' "

"I thank you, sirs," said Don Quixote, "but I cannot stop for an instant. Sorrows and unhappy circumstances force me to seem discourteous and to travel as speedily as possible." And spurring Rocinante he pushed on, leaving them wondering at what they had seen and heard, at his own strange appearance as well as at the shrewdness of his servant, for such they took Sancho to be. And another of them observed, "If the servant is so clever, what must the master be? I'll bet, if they go to Salamanca to study, they'll get to be magistrates at Court in no time. Everything else is a waste of time except studying and more studying—and knowing someone influential and having a little luck! And before a man knows where he is, he finds himself with a magistrate's staff in his hand or a miter on his head."

That night master and servant spent out in the fields in the open air, and the next day as they were pursuing their journey, they saw coming towards them a man on foot with a mail pouch over his shoulder and a javelin or pike in his hand, the very picture of a foot-courier, who, as soon as he came close to Don Quixote, increased his pace and half running came up to him, and embracing his right thigh, for he could reach no higher, exclaimed with evident pleasure, "O Señor Don Quixote of La Mancha, what happiness it will bring to the heart of my lord the duke when he knows your worship is coming back to his castle, for he is still there with my lady the duchess!"

"I do not recognize you, friend," said Don Quixote, "nor do I know who you are, unless you tell me."

"I am Tosilos, my lord the duke's lackey, Señor Don Quixote," replied the courier, "the one who refused to fight your worship about marrying the daughter of Doña Rodríguez."

"God bless me!" exclaimed Don Quixote. "Is it possible that you are the one whom my enemies the enchanters changed into the lackey you speak of in order to rob me of the honor of that battle?"

"Nonsense, sir!" said the messenger. "There was no enchantment or transformation at all; I entered the lists just as much Tosilos the lackey as I came out of them Tosilos the lackey. I hoped to marry without fighting, for the girl had attracted me. But my scheme had a very different result, for as soon as your worship had left the castle, my lord the duke had me given a hundred strokes for having acted contrary to the orders he gave me before engaging in the combat. And the end of the whole affair is that the girl has become a nun, and Doña Rodríguez has gone back to Castile, and I am now on my way to Barcelona with a packet of letters for the viceroy which my master is sending him. If your worship would like a drop of pure wine, though warm, I have a gourd here full of the best, and some scraps of Tronchón cheese that will serve as a stimulator and wakener of your thirst if by chance it is asleep."

"I accept the offer," said Sancho. "Forget the compliments. Fill the cups, good Tosilos, in spite of all the enchanters in the Indies."

"You are unquestionably the biggest glutton in the world, Sancho," said Don Quixote, "and the biggest fool on earth, not to be able to see that this courier is enchanted and this Tosilos a fake. Stay with him and drink your fill; I will go on ahead slowly and wait for you to catch up with me."

The lackey laughed, unsheathed his gourd, unpouched his scraps of cheese, and taking out a small loaf of bread, he and Sancho seated themselves on the green grass, and in peace and good fellowship finished off the contents of the mail pouch down to the bottom, so resolutely that they licked the wrapper of the letters, merely because it smelled of cheese.

Said Tosilos to Sancho, "Beyond a doubt, Sancho my friend, this master of yours must be a complete madman."

" 'Must be,' indeed!" said Sancho. He owes no man anything;[1]

1. There is a pun on the Spanish *debe,* which means both "must be" and "owes."

he pays for everything, particularly when the coin is madness. I see it clearly enough, and I tell him so plain enough; but what's the use? Especially now that it is all over with him, for he has been beaten by the Knight of the White Moon."

Tosilos begged him to explain what had happened to him, but Sancho replied that it was impolite to leave his master waiting for him and that some other day if they met there would be time enough for that. And then getting up, after shaking out his jacket and brushing the crumbs out of his beard, he led Dapple away and saying good-bye to Tosilos left him and rejoined his master, who was waiting for him under the shade of a tree.

Chapter LXVII

OF THE RESOLUTION DON QUIXOTE FORMED TO TURN SHEPHERD AND TAKE UP LIFE IN THE FIELDS WHILE THE YEAR FOR WHICH HE HAD GIVEN HIS WORD WAS RUNNING ITS COURSE; WITH OTHER EVENTS TRULY DELECTABLE AND HAPPY

If a multitude of reflections troubled Don Quixote before he was knocked off his horse, a great many more harassed him after his fall. He was under the shade of a tree, as has been said, and there, like flies to honey, thoughts came crowding upon him and stinging him. Some of them had to do with the disenchantment of Dulcinea, others with the life he was about to lead in his enforced retirement. Sancho came up and spoke in high praise of the generous disposition of the lackey Tosilos.

"Is it possible, Sancho," said Don Quixote, "that you still think that he is a real lackey? Apparently it has escaped your memory that you have seen Dulcinea turned and transformed into a peasant wench, and the Knight of the Mirrors into the bachelor Carrasco, all the work of the enchanters that persecute me. But tell me now, did you ask this Tosilos, as you call him, what has become of Altisidora, did she weep over my absence, or has she already consigned to oblivion the love thoughts that used to afflict her when I was present?"

"The thoughts that I had," said Sancho, "were not such as to leave time for asking foolish questions. Good Lord, señor! Is this the time to be inquiring into other people's thoughts, especially love thoughts?"

"Look, Sancho," said Don Quixote, "there is a great difference between what is done out of love and what is done out of gratitude. A knight may very possibly be proof against love; but it is impossible, strictly speaking, for him to be ungrateful. Altisidora, to all appearance, loved me truly; she gave me the three kerchiefs you know about; she wept at my departure; she cursed me; she abused me; casting shame to the winds she bewailed in public—all signs that she adored me; for the wrath of lovers always ends in curses. I had no hopes to give her nor treasures to offer her, for mine are given to Dulcinea, and the treasures of knights-errant are like those of the fairies, illusory and deceptive. All I can give her is the place in my memory I keep for her, without prejudice, however, to that which I keep for Dulcinea, whom you are wronging by your neglect in whipping yourself and scourging that flesh—oh that I might see it eaten by wolves—which would rather save itself for the worms than relieve that poor lady."

"Señor," replied Sancho, "if the truth is to be told, I can't persuade myself that the whipping of my backside has anything to do with the disenchantment of the enchanted. It's like saying, 'If your head aches rub ointment on your knees.' At any rate I'll bet that in all the histories dealing with knight-errantry that your worship has read, you have never come across anybody disenchanted by whipping. However that may be, I'll whip myself when I feel like it and there is time for scourging myself comfortably."

"God grant it," said Don Quixote. "And heaven give you grace to see and realize the obligation you have to help my lady, who is yours also, inasmuch as you are mine."

As they pursued their journey talking in this way they came to the very same spot where they had been trampled by the bulls. Don Quixote recognized it and said to Sancho, "This is the meadow where we came upon those gay shepherdesses and gallant shepherds who were trying to revive and imitate rustic Arcadia, an original and clever idea. Let us imitate their plan, and if you approve of it, Sancho, I would like for us to become shepherds, at any rate for the time I must live in retirement. I will buy some ewes and everything else requisite for the pastoral calling; and I under the name of the shepherd Quixotiz and you as the shepherd Pancino, we will roam the woods and groves and meadows singing songs here, lamenting in elegies there, drinking the crystal waters of the springs or limpid brooks or flowing rivers. The oaks will yield us their sweet fruit with bountiful hand, the trunks of the hard cork trees a seat, the willows shade, the roses perfume, the broad meadows carpets tinted with a thousand dyes; the clear pure air will give us breath, the moon and stars lighten the darkness of the night for us, song shall be our delight, lamenting our joy, Apollo will supply us with verses, and love with conceits whereby we shall make ourselves eternally famous, not only in this but in ages to come."

"By golly," said Sancho, "but that sort of life suits me to a tee. And what is more, as soon as the bachelor Sansón Carrasco and Master Nicolás the barber have seen what we're doing, they'll want to live that way and turn shepherds along with us. I hope to God it doesn't enter the curate's head to join the sheepfold too, he's so jolly and fond of enjoying himself."

"Well said, Sancho," said Don Quixote. "And the bachelor Sansón Carrasco, if he enters the pastoral fraternity, as no doubt he will, can call himself the shepherd Sansonino, or perhaps the shepherd Carrascón; Nicolás the barber may call himself Miculoso, as Boscán formerly was called Nemoroso.[1] As for the priest, I don't know what name we can give him unless it is something derived from his title as curate and we call him the shepherd Curiambro.

"For the shepherdesses whose lovers we shall be, we can pick names as we would pears; and as my lady's name does just as well for a shepherdess's as for a princess's, I need not trouble myself to look for one that will suit her better. You can give whatever name you want to your beloved."

"I don't think I'll give her any but Teresona," said Sancho, "which will go well with her stoutness and with her real name, as she is called Teresa;[2] that way, when I sing her praises in my verses, I'll show how chaste my passion is, for I'm not 'looking for fancy bread in other men's houses.' It won't do for the curate to have a shepherdess, for the sake of good example; and if the bachelor wants one, he can do as he pleases."

"God bless me, Sancho my friend!" said Don Quixote, "what a life we shall lead! What oboes and Zamora bagpipes we shall hear, what drums, rattles, and fiddles! And then if among all these different sorts of music that of the *albogues* is heard, almost all the pastoral instruments will be there."

"What are *albogues*?" asked Sancho, "for I never in my life heard tell of them or saw them."

"*Albogues*," said Don Quixote, "are tin plates like candlesticks that struck against one another on the hollow side make a noise which, if not very pleasing or harmonious, is not disagreeable and goes very well with the rude notes of the bagpipe and drum.

"The word *albogue* is Morisco, as are all those in Spanish that begin with *al*; for example, *almohaza, almorzar, alhombra, alguacil, alhucema, almacén, alcancía,* and others of the same sort, of which there are not many more; our language has only three that are Morisco and end in *í*, which are *borceguí, zaquizamí,* and *maravedí. Alhelí* and *alfaquí* are seen to be Arabic, as well by the *al* at the beginning as by the *í* they end with. I mention this incidentally, the chance allusion to *albogues* having reminded me of it.

1. Garcilaso de la Vega, the most famous and admired pastoral poet of the Spanish Renaissance, wrote an eclogue in which there is a character, Nemoroso, formerly thought to represent his friend Boscán. (Both names, Nemoroso and Boscán, suggest the words for "grove" in Latin and Spanish.) Modern scholars believe Nemoroso represents Garcilaso himself.

2. Teresona means "Big Teresa."

"It will be of great assistance to us in the perfect practice of this calling that I am something of a poet, as you know, and that besides the bachelor Sansón Carrasco is an accomplished one. Of the priest I say nothing; but I will wager he has a bit of the poet in him, and no doubt Master Nicolás too, for all barbers, or most of them, are guitar players and writers of verses. I will bewail my separation; you will sing your praises as a constant lover; the shepherd Carrascón will figure as a rejected one, and the curate Curiambro as whatever may please him best; and so all will go as well as one could wish."

To this Sancho made answer, "I am so unlucky, señor, that I'm afraid the day will never come when I'll see myself at such a calling. O what polished spoons I'll make when I'm a shepherd! What pastoral food, rich cream, garlands, and such things! And if these things don't make me famous for wisdom, at least they'll make me famous for ingenuity.

"My daughter Sanchica will bring our dinner to the sheepfold. But wait—she's good-looking, and some shepherds are more evil-minded than innocent. I wouldn't want her to 'come for wool and go back shorn'; lovemaking and immoral desires are just as common in the fields as in the cities, and in shepherds' huts as in royal palaces: 'do away with the cause, you do away with the sin'; 'if eyes don't see, hearts don't break.' It's best to avoid the problem: 'staying out of jail is the best kind of bail.' "

"No more proverbs, Sancho," exclaimed Don Quixote. "Any one of those you have uttered would suffice to explain your meaning. I have often recommended to you not to be so lavish with proverbs and to exercise some moderation in quoting them; but it seems to me it is only 'preaching in the desert'; 'my mother gives me good advice, but I do as I please on the sly.' "

"It seems to me," said Sancho, "that your worship is like the pot that calls the kettle black in the common saying. You criticize me for quoting proverbs, and you string them by twos yourself."

"Observe, Sancho," replied Don Quixote, "that I bring in proverbs to the purpose, and when I quote them they fit like a ring on the finger. You drag them in by the hair, rather than introduce them. If I am not mistaken, I have told you already that proverbs are short maxims drawn from the experience and observation of our wise men of old; but the proverb that is not to the purpose is nonsense and not a maxim. But enough of this; as nightfall is drawing on let us retire some little distance from the royal highway to pass the night. What is in store for us tomorrow God knows."

They left the road and ate supper late and poorly, very much against Sancho's will, who turned over in his mind the hardships attendant upon knight-errantry in woods and forests, even though at times abundance presented itself in castles and houses, as at Don

Diego de Miranda's, at the wedding of Camacho the Rich, and at Don Antonio Moreno's. He reflected, however, that it could not be always day or always night; and so that night he passed in sleeping, and his master in waking.

Chapter LXVIII

OF THE BRISTLY ADVENTURE THAT BEFELL DON QUIXOTE

The night was somewhat dark, for though there was a moon in the sky, she was not in a place where she could be seen; for sometimes the lady Diana goes on a stroll to the antipodes and leaves the mountains all black and the valleys in darkness. Don Quixote obeyed nature so far as to sleep his first sleep, but did not give way to the second, very different from Sancho, who never had any second, because with him sleep lasted from night till morning, showing what a sound constitution and few cares he had. Don Quixote's cares kept him restless, so much so that he awoke Sancho and said to him, "I am amazed, Sancho, at the unconcern of your temperament. I believe you are made of marble or hard brass, incapable of any emotion or feeling whatever. I lie awake while you sleep, I weep while you sing, I am faint with fasting while you are sluggish and torpid from overeating. It is the duty of good servants to share the sufferings and feel the sorrows of their masters, if only for the sake of appearances. See the calmness of the night, the solitude of the spot, inviting us to break our slumbers by a vigil of some sort. Get up, for heaven's sake, and retire a little distance, and with boldness and cheerful courage give yourself three or four hundred lashes toward Dulcinea's disenchantment. I beg you to do this, making it a request, for I have no desire to come to grips with you a second time, as I know you have a heavy hand. As soon as you have laid them on, we will spend the rest of the night, I singing about my separation, you about your constancy, thus beginning at once with the pastoral life we are to follow at our village."

"Señor," replied Sancho, "I'm no monk to get up in the middle of my sleep and scourge myself, and it doesn't seem to me that one can pass from one extreme of the pain of whipping to the other of music. Will your worship let me sleep and not worry me about whipping myself? You'll make me swear never to touch a hair of my jacket, much less my flesh."

"O hard heart!" said Don Quixote, "O pitiless squire! O bread ill-bestowed and favors ill-considered, both those I have done for you and those I mean to do for you! On account of me, you have seen yourself a governor, and through me you see yourself in immediate expectation of being a count, or obtaining some other equivalent title, and the fulfillment of these expectations will be delayed no longer than this year, for I *post tenebras spero lucem.*"[1]

"I don't know what that means," said Sancho. "All I know is that so long as I am asleep, I have neither fear nor hope, trouble nor joy. God bless the man that invented sleep, the cloak that covers all human worries, the food that removes hunger, the drink that drives away thirst, the fire that warms the cold, the cold that tempers the heat, and, to wind up, the universal coin with which everything is bought, the weight and balance that makes the shepherd equal with the king and the fool with the wise man. Sleep, I have heard say, has only one fault, that it is like death; for between a sleeping man and a dead man there is very little difference."

"Never have I heard you speak so elegantly as now, Sancho," said Don Quixote. "And here I begin to see the truth of the proverb you sometimes quote: 'Not with whom you are bred, but with whom you are fed.' "

"Damn it, master," said Sancho, "I'm not the one that's stringing proverbs now, for they drop from your worship's mouth in pairs faster than from mine; only there is this difference between mine and yours, probably, that yours are well-timed and mine are untimely; but anyhow, they are all proverbs."

At this point they became aware of an indistinct rumble and a harsh noise that seemed to spread through all the valleys around. Don Quixote stood up and laid his hand upon his sword, and Sancho crouched under Dapple and put the bundle of armor on one side of him and the ass's packsaddle on the other, in fear and trembling as great as Don Quixote's excitement. Each instant the noise increased and came nearer to the two terrified men, or at least to one, for as to the other, his courage is known to all.

The fact of the matter was that some men were taking over six hundred pigs to sell at a fair and were on their way with them at that hour, and so great was the noise they made and so loud their grunting and snorting that they deafened the ears of Don Quixote and Sancho, who could not make out what it was. The scattered, grunting herd approached in a surging mass, and without showing any respect for Don Quixote's dignity or Sancho's, passed right over the pair of them, demolishing Sancho's defenses and not only knocking Don Quixote down but sweeping Rocinante off his feet into the bargain. And what with the trampling and the grunting and the pace with which the unclean beasts had arrived, packsaddle, armor, Dapple, Rocinante, Sancho, and Don Quixote were left in a confused jumble on the ground.

Sancho got up as well as he could and begged his master to give

1. "I look for light after darkness" (Job 17:12, Vulgate). This was also the motto of the first printer of *Don Quixote.*

him his sword, saying he wanted to kill half a dozen of those unmannerly pigs, for he had by this time realized that that was what they were.

"Let them be, my friend," said Don Quixote. "This insult is the penalty of my sin; and it is the righteous chastisement of heaven that jackals should devour a vanquished knight and wasps sting him and pigs trample him under foot."

"I suppose it is the chastisement of heaven, too," said Sancho, "that flies should prick the squires of vanquished knights, and lice eat them, and hunger attack them. If we squires were the sons of the knights we serve, or their very near relations, it would be no wonder if the penalty of their misdeeds extended to us, even to the fourth generation. But what have the Panzas to do with the Quixotes? Oh, well, let's lie down again and sleep out what little of the night is left, and God will send us dawn, and things will be better tomorrow."

"Sleep, Sancho," returned Don Quixote, "for you were born to sleep as I was born to watch; and from now until dawn, I will give free rein to my troubled thoughts and seek a release for them in a little madrigal which, unknown to you, I composed in my head last night."

"It seems to me," said Sancho, "that thoughts that allow you to write verses can't be too troubled. Your worship can write verses as much as you like, and I'll sleep as much as I can." And taking the space of ground he required, he muffled himself up and fell into a sound sleep, undisturbed by bond, debt, or sorrows of any sort. Don Quixote, propped up against the trunk of a beech or a cork tree—for Cide Hamete does not specify what kind of tree it was—sang in this strain to the sound of his own sighs:

> When in my mind
> I muse, O Love, upon thy cruelty,
> To death I flee,
> In hope therein the end of all to find.
>
> But drawing near
> That welcome haven in my sea of woe,
> Such joy I know,
> That life revives, and still I linger here.
>
> Thus life doth slay,
> And death again to life restoreth me;
> Strange destiny,
> That deals with life and death as with a play!

He accompanied each verse with many sighs and not a few tears, as one whose heart was pierced with grief at his defeat and his separation from Dulcinea.

And now daylight came, and the sun shone in Sancho's eyes with his beams. He awoke, roused himself, shook himself, and stretched his sluggish limbs, and seeing the havoc the pigs had made with his supplies cursed the herd and then some. Finally the pair resumed their journey, and as evening closed in they saw coming towards them some ten men on horseback and four or five on foot. Don Quixote's heart beat faster and Sancho's quailed with fear, for the persons approaching them carried lances and shields and were in very warlike guise. Don Quixote turned to Sancho and said, "If I could make use of my weapons and my promise had not tied my hands, I would consider this host that comes against us child's play; but perhaps it may turn out to be something different from what we assume."

The men on horseback now came up, and raising their lances, surrounded Don Quixote in silence and pointed them at his back and breast, menacing him with death. One of those on foot, putting his finger to his lips as a sign to be silent, seized Rocinante's bridle and led him off the road, and the others leading Sancho and Dapple, and all maintaining a strange silence, followed in the steps of the one who led Don Quixote. The latter two or three times attempted to ask where they were taking him and what they wanted, but the instant he began to open his lips they threatened to close them with the points of their lances; and Sancho fared the same way, for the moment he seemed about to speak one of those on foot punched him with a goad, and Dapple likewise, as if he too wanted to talk.

Night set in, they quickened their pace, and the fears of the two prisoners grew greater, especially as they heard themselves addressed from time to time with "Get on, Troglodytes"; "Silence, barbarians"; "You'll pay, cannibals"; "No murmuring, Scythians"; "Don't open your eyes, murderous Polyphemuses, bloodthirsty lions," and suchlike names, with which their captors harassed the ears of the wretched master and servant. Sancho went along saying to himself, "Trolley-dites, barbers, carnivals, sithiuns? I don't like those names at all: 'It's a bad wind our wheat is being winnowed in'; 'misfortune comes all at once like blows on a dog's back,' and God grant that this unlucky adventure has nothing worse in store for us."

Don Quixote rode along completely perplexed, unable with the aid of all his wits to make out what could be the meaning of these abusive names, and the only conclusion he could arrive at was that there was no good to be hoped for and much evil to be feared. And now, about an hour after midnight, they reached a castle which Don Quixote saw at once was the duke's, where they had been but a short time before. "God bless me!" said he, as he recognized the mansion, "what does this mean? It is all courtesy and politeness in this house; but with the vanquished good turns into bad and bad into worse."

They entered the principal courtyard of the castle and found it prepared and decorated in a way that added to their amazement and doubled their fears, as will be seen in the following chapter.

Chapter LXIX

OF THE STRANGEST AND MOST EXTRAORDINARY ADVENTURE THAT BEFELL DON QUIXOTE IN THE WHOLE COURSE OF THIS GREAT HISTORY

The horsemen dismounted, and, together with the men on foot, without a moment's delay picking up Sancho and Don Quixote, they carried them into the courtyard, around which nearly a hundred torches fixed in their sockets were burning, besides above five hundred lamps along the galleries, so that in spite of the night, which was somewhat dark, the absence of daylight could not be perceived. In the middle of the courtyard was a bier, raised about two yards above the ground and covered completely by an immense canopy of black velvet, and on the steps all around it white wax tapers burned in more than a hundred silver candlesticks. On the bier was the dead body of a young woman so beautiful that by her beauty she made death itself look beautiful. She lay with her head resting upon a cushion of brocade and crowned with a garland of sweet-smelling flowers of various kinds, her hands crossed over her bosom, and between them a yellowed, triumphant palm branch.[1] On one side of the courtyard was a stage, where on two chairs were seated two persons who from the crowns on their heads and scepters in their hands appeared to be kings of some sort, whether real or mock ones. By the side of this stage, which was reached by steps, were two other chairs on which the men carrying the prisoners seated Don Quixote and Sancho, all in silence, and by signs giving them to understand that they too were to be silent; which, however, they would have been without any signs, for their amazement at all they saw held them tongue-tied.

And now two persons of distinction, who were at once recognized by Don Quixote as his hosts the duke and duchess, ascended the stage attended by a numerous suite, and seated themselves on two ornate chairs close to the two kings, as they seemed to be. Who would not have been amazed at this? Nor was this all, for Don Quixote had perceived that the dead body on the bier was that of the fair Altisidora. As the duke and duchess mounted the stage Don Quixote and Sancho rose and made them a deep bow, which they returned by nodding their heads slightly. At this moment an official crossed over and approaching Sancho threw over him a robe of black material painted all over with flames of fire, and taking off

1. A symbol of virginity.

his cap put upon his head a pointed hat such as those being punished by the Holy Inquisition wear. And he whispered in Sancho's ear that he must not open his mouth or they would put a gag upon him or take his life. Sancho surveyed himself from head to foot and saw himself all ablaze with flames, but as they did not burn him, he did not give a hang for them. He took off the pointed hat and seeing it painted with devils he put it on again, saying to himself, "Well, so far those don't burn me and these haven't carried me off." Don Quixote surveyed him too, and though fear had dulled his faculties, he could not help laughing at Sancho's appearance.

And now from underneath the bier, so it seemed, there rose a low, sweet sound of flutes, which, not being overshadowed by human voice (for there, silence itself kept silence), had a soft and amorous effect. Then, beside the pillow of the apparently dead body, suddenly there appeared a fine-looking young man wearing a toga, who, to the sound of a harp which he himself played, sang in a sweet and clear voice these two stanzas:

> While fair Altisidora, who the sport
> Of Don Quixote's cruelty has been,
> Returns to life, and in this magic court
> The dames in mourning come to grace the scene;
> While of her matrons all, in seemly sort,
> My lady robes in black the somber mien,
> Her beauty and her sorrows will I sing
> With defter quill than touched the Thracian string.[2]
>
> But not in life alone, I feel, to me
> Belongs the office; Lady, when my tongue
> Is cold in death, believe me, unto thee
> My voice shall raise its tributary song.
> My soul, from this strait prison-house set free,
> As o'er the Stygian lake it floats along,
> Thy praises singing still shall hold its way,
> And make the waters of oblivion stay.

At this point one of the two that looked like kings exclaimed, "Enough, enough, divine singer! It would be an endless task to put before us now the death and the charms of the peerless Altisidora, not dead as the ignorant world imagines, but living in the voice of fame and in the penance which Sancho Panza, here present, has to undergo to restore her to the long-lost light. Do thou, therefore, O Rhadamanthus, who sittest in judgment with me in the murky caverns of Dis, as thou knowest all that the inscrutable fates have decreed regarding the resuscitation of this damsel, announce and declare it at once, that the happiness we look forward to from her restoration be no longer deferred."

2. I.e., that of Orpheus.

No sooner had Minos, the fellow judge of Rhadamanthus, said this, than Rhadamanthus rising up said:

"Ho, servants of this house, high and low, great and small, come here one and all, and print on Sancho's face twenty-four smacks, and give him twelve pinches and six pin-pricks in the back and arms; for on this ceremony depends the salvation of Altisidora."

On hearing this Sancho broke silence and cried out, "I swear to God I'd as soon let my face be smacked or handled as turn Moor. In heaven's name! What was handling my face got to do with the resurrection of this girl? 'When it rains, it pours.' They enchant Dulcinea and whip me to disenchant her; Altisidora dies of ailments God was pleased to send her, and to bring her to life again they must give me twenty-four smacks and punch holes in my body with pins and raise welts on my arms with pinches! Try those jokes on somebody's brother-in-law. 'I'm an old dog, and you can't catch me with kind words.' "

"Thou shalt die," said Rhadamanthus in a loud voice. "Relent, thou tiger; humble thyself, proud Nimrod; suffer and be silent, for nothing impossible is asked of thee; it is not for thee to inquire into the difficulties in this matter; smacked thou must be, pricked thou shalt see thyself, and with pinches thou must be made to howl. Ho, I say, servants, obey my orders; or by the word of an honest man, ye shall see what ye were born for."

At this some six dueñas, advancing across the court, made their appearance in procession, one after the other, four of them with spectacles, and all with their right hands uplifted, showing two inches of wrist to make their hands look longer, as is the fashion nowadays. No sooner had Sancho caught sight of them than, bellowing like a bull, he exclaimed, "I might let myself be handled by all the world; but allow dueñas to touch me—never! Scratch my face, as they did my master's in this very castle; run me through the body with sharp-pointed daggers; pinch my arms with red-hot pincers; I'll bear all in patience to please these gentlemen. But I won't let dueñas touch me, even if the devil would carry me off!"

Here Don Quixote, too, broke silence, saying to Sancho, "Have patience, my son, and gratify these noble persons, and give all thanks to heaven that it has granted you such powers that by the torment of your person you can disenchant the enchanted and restore to life the dead."

The dueñas were now close to Sancho, and he, having become more tractable and reasonable, settling himself well in his chair, presented his face and beard to the first, who delivered a very well-placed smack and then made him a low curtsy.

"Less politeness and less cosmetics, señora dueñas," said Sancho. "By God your hands smell of vinegar lotion."

Finally, all the dueñas smacked him, and several others of the household pinched him; but what he could not stand was being pricked by the pins. So, apparently annoyed, he got up out of his chair and seizing a lighted torch that stood near him took after the dueñas and the whole set of his tormentors, exclaiming, "Get away from me, you ministers of hell. I'm not made of brass, so that I don't feel such extreme tortures."

At this instant Altisidora, who probably was tired of having lain so long on her back, turned on her side; seeing which the bystanders cried out almost with one voice, "Altisidora is alive! Altisidora lives!"

Rhadamanthus commanded Sancho to temper his wrath, as the object they had sought was now attained. When Don Quixote saw Altisidora move, he went on his knees to Sancho saying to him, "Now is the time, son of my loins and not my squire, for you to give yourself some of those lashes required for the disenchantment of Dulcinea. Now, I say, is the time when the power that is in you is ripe and strong enough to accomplish the good that is expected from you."

To which Sancho made answer, "That's trick on trick, it seems to me, and not syrup on pancakes. It would be a fine thing for a whipping to come now, on the top of pinches, smacks, and pin-pricks! You might as well take a big stone and tie it around my neck and pitch me into a well. I wouldn't mind it much, if I'm always going to be the scapegoat in order to cure other people's ailments. Leave me alone; or by God I'll upset the whole applecart, come what may."

Altisidora had by this time sat up on the bier, and as she did so the oboes sounded, accompanied by the flutes and the voices of all present exclaiming, "Long live Altisidora! long live Altisidora!" The duke and duchess and the kings Minos and Rhadamanthus stood up, and all, together with Don Quixote and Sancho, advanced to receive her and take her down from the bier. And she, as though recovering from a swoon, bowed her head to the duke and duchess and to the kings, and looking sideways at Don Quixote, said to him, "God forgive you, heartless knight, for through your cruelty I have been, to me it seems, more than a thousand years in the other world; and to you the most compassionate squire on earth, I give thanks for the life I now possess. From this day on, friend Sancho, consider as yours six chemises of mine which I bestow on you, to make as many shirts for yourself, and if they are not all in perfect condition, at any rate they are all clean."

Sancho kissed her hands in gratitude, kneeling, and with his pointed hat in his hand. The duke ordered them take it from him and give him back his cap and jacket and remove the flaming robe. Sancho begged the duke to let them leave him the robe and miter, as he wanted to take them home for a souvenir and memento of that unexampled adventure. The duchess said he could certainly keep them, for he knew already what a great friend of his she was. The duke then gave orders that the courtyard should be cleared and that all should retire to their chambers, and that Don Quixote and Sancho should be conducted to their old quarters.

Chapter LXX

WHICH FOLLOWS SIXTY-NINE AND DEALS WITH MATTERS INDISPENSABLE FOR THE CLEAR COMPREHENSION OF THIS HISTORY

Sancho slept that night on a trundle bed in the same room with Don Quixote, a thing he would have gladly avoided if he could, for he knew very well that with questions and answers his master would not let him sleep, and he was in no humor for talking much, as he still felt the pain of his recent martyrdom, which interfered with his speech; and it would have been more to his taste to sleep in a hovel alone than in that luxurious chamber in company. And so well founded did his apprehension prove, and so correct was his anticipation, that scarcely had his master gotten into bed when he said, "What do you think of tonight's adventure, Sancho? Great and mighty is the power of cold-hearted scorn, for you with your own eyes have seen Altisidora killed not by arrows or the sword or any warlike weapon or deadly poisons, but by the thought of the sternness and disdain with which I have always treated her."

"She was welcome to die," said Sancho, "when she pleased and how she pleased; but she might have left me alone, because I never made her fall in love or scorned her. I don't know, and I can't imagine, how the recovery of Altisidora, a young lady more capricious than sensible, can have, as I have said before, anything to do with the torture of Sancho Panza. Now I begin to see plainly and clearly that there are enchanters and enchantments in the world; and may God deliver me from them, since I can't deliver myself. But I beg your worship to let me sleep and not ask me any more questions, unless you want me to throw myself out of the window."

"Sleep, Sancho my friend," said Don Quixote, "if the pin-pricks and pinches you have received and the smacks administered to you will let you."

"No pain equaled the insult of the smacks," said Sancho, "for the simple reason that it was dueñas, confound them, that gave them to me. But once more I beg your worship to let me sleep, for sleep is relief from miseries for those who have them when they are awake."

"So be it, and God be with you," said Don Quixote.

They fell asleep, both of them, and Cide Hamete, the author of this great history, took this opportunity to record and relate what it was that induced the duke and duchess to set up the elaborate plot that has been described. The bachelor Sansón Carrasco, he says, not forgetting how he as the Knight of the Mirrors had been vanquished and overthrown by Don Quixote, which defeat and overthrow upset all his plans, resolved to try his hand again, hoping for better luck than he had before. And so, having learned where Don Quixote was from the page who brought the letter and present to Sancho's wife, Teresa Panza, he got himself new armor and another horse, and put a white moon upon his shield, and to carry his arms he had a mule led by a peasant, not by Tomé Cecial his former squire, for fear he should be recognized by Sancho or Don Quixote. He came to the duke's castle, and the duke informed him of the road and route Don Quixote had taken with the intention of being present at the jousts at Zaragoza. He told him, too, of the jokes he had played on him, and of the scheme for the disenchantment of Dulcinea at the expense of Sancho's backside. Finally he gave him an account of the trick Sancho had played on his master, making him believe that Dulcinea was enchanted and turned into a country wench, and of how the duchess, his wife, had persuaded Sancho that it was he himself who was deceived, because Dulcinea really was enchanted. The bachelor laughed not a little and marveled at the shrewdness and simple-mindedness of Sancho as well as at the length to which Don Quixote's madness went. The duke begged the bachelor if he found Don Quixote (whether he overcame him or not) to return that way and let him know the result. This the bachelor did. He set out in search of Don Quixote, and not finding him at Zaragoza, he went on; and how he fared has been already told. He returned to the duke's castle and told him all, what the conditions of the combat were, and how Don Quixote was now, like a loyal knight-errant, returning to keep his promise of retiring to his village for a year, by which time, said the bachelor, he might perhaps be cured of his madness. For that was the object that had led him to adopt these disguises, as it was a sad thing for so well-informed a gentleman as Don Quixote to be crazy. And so he took his leave of the duke and went home to his village to wait there for Don Quixote, who was following him.

Hence the duke seized the opportunity of playing this joke on him, so much did he enjoy everything connected with Sancho and Don Quixote. He had the roads about the castle, far and near, everywhere he thought Don Quixote was likely to pass on his return, watched by large numbers of his servants on foot and on horseback. These were to bring him to the castle, by fair means or foul, if they met him. They did meet him, and sent word to the duke, who, having already arranged what was to be done, as soon as he heard of his arrival, ordered the torches and lamps in the court to be lit and Altisidora to be placed on the bier with all the pomp and ceremony that has been described, the whole affair being so well arranged and acted that it differed little from reality.

And Cide Hamete says, moreover, that personally he considers the concocters of the joke as crazy as the victims of it, and that the duke and duchess came very close to looking like fools themselves when they took such pains to make fun of a pair of fools.

As for the latter, one was sleeping soundly and the other lying awake occupied with his untrammeled thoughts when daylight came, bringing with it the desire to rise; for lying in bed was never a delight to Don Quixote, victor or vanquished. Altisidora—returned from death to life, or so Don Quixote fancied—humoring her lord and lady, entered the chamber, crowned with the garland she had worn on the bier and wearing a robe of white taffeta embroidered with gold flowers, her hair flowing loose over her shoulders, and leaning upon a staff of fine black ebony. Don Quixote, disconcerted and in confusion at her appearance, huddled himself up and well-nigh covered himself entirely with the sheets and quilts of the bed, tongue-tied, and unable to show her any courtesy. Altisidora seated herself on a chair at the head of the bed, and, after a deep sigh, said to him in an amorous, feeble voice, "When women of rank and modest maidens trample their honor and permit themselves to speak in spite of every impediment, revealing the inmost secrets of their hearts, they are in a desperate situation. Such a one am I, Señor Don Quixote of La Mancha, desperate, conquered, lovesick, but yet patient under suffering and virtuous, so much so that my heart broke because of my silence, and I lost my life. For the last two days I have been dead, killed by the thought of the cruelty with which you have treated me, stony-hearted knight, 'O harder thou than marble to my plaint,' or at least believed to be dead by all who saw me. And had it not been that Love, taking pity on me, let my recovery depend on the sufferings of this good squire, there I should have remained in the other world."

"Love might very well have let it depend on the sufferings of my jackass, and I would have been obliged to him," said Sancho. "But tell me, señora—and may heaven send you a more soft-hearted lover than my master—what did you see in the other world? What goes on in hell? For of course that's where one who dies in despair is bound for."

"To tell you the truth," said Altisidora, "I must not have died completely, for I did not go into hell; had I gone in, it is very certain I would never have come out again, do what I might. The truth is, I came to the gate, where about a dozen devils were playing tennis, all in breeches and jackets, with Walloon collars trimmed with Flemish lace, and ruffles of the same that served them for cuffs, with two inches of arm exposed to make their hands look longer. In their hands they held rackets of fire. But what amazed me still more was that books, apparently full of hot air and padding, served them for tennis balls, a strange and marvelous thing. This, however, did not astonish me so much as to observe that, although with players it is usual for the winners to be glad and the losers sorry, in that game all were growling, all were snarling, and all were cursing one another."

"That's no wonder," said Sancho, "for devils, whether playing or not, can never be content, win or lose."

"Very likely," said Altisidora. "But there is another thing that surprises me too, I mean surprised me then, and that was that no ball outlasted the first serve or was of any use a second time; and it was wonderful to see the constant succession of books, new and old. To one of them, a brand-new, well-bound one, they gave such a stroke that they knocked the guts out of it and scattered the leaves about. 'Tell me what book that is,' said one devil to another, and the other replied, 'It is the *Second Part of the History of Don Quixote of La Mancha,* not by Cide Hamete, the original author, but by an Aragonese who by his own account is from Tordesillas.' 'Take it away,' said the first, 'and send it to the depths of hell out of my sight.' 'Is it that bad?' said the other. 'It is so bad,' said the first, 'that if I had set myself deliberately to make a worse one, I could not have done it.' They then went on with their game, knocking other books back and forth; and I, having heard them mention the name of Don Quixote whom I love and adore so, took care to retain this vision in my memory."

"A vision it must have been, no doubt," said Don Quixote, "for I am the only Don Quixote in the world. This history has for some time been passed around from hand to hand, but it does not stay long in any, for everybody gives it the boot. I am not disturbed to hear that I am wandering like a ghost in the darkness of the abyss or in the daylight above, for I am not the one that history is about. If it is good, faithful, and true, it will have ages of life; but if it is bad, from its birth to its burial will not be a very long journey."

Altisidora was about to proceed with her complaint against Don Quixote, when he said to her, "I have several times told you, señora, that it grieves me you should have set your affections upon me, as from mine they can only receive gratitude, but no return. I was born to belong to Dulcinea del Toboso, and the fates, if there are any, dedicated me to her; and to suppose that any other beauty can take the place she occupies in my heart is to suppose an impossibility. This frank declaration should suffice to make you retire within the bounds of your modesty, for no one can oblige himself to do impossibilities."

Hearing this, Altisidora, becoming angry and upset, exclaimed, "God's life! You dried up, insensitive nobody! You are more obstinate and hard-headed than some peasant who's been asked a favor when he has his mind made up. If I get my hands on you I'll tear your eyes out! Do you really believe, you loser, you beat-up wretch, that I died for your sake? Everything you saw last night was make-believe. I'm not the woman to let the end of my fingernail suffer for such a camel, much less die!"

"I can well believe that," said Sancho. "All that about lovers pining to death is absurd; they may talk about it, but as for doing it —let Judas believe that!"

While they were talking, the musician, singer, and poet, who had sung the two stanzas quoted above came in and making a deep bow to Don Quixote said, "Will your worship, sir knight, consider me and count me among your most faithful servants? For I have long been a great admirer of yours, because of your fame as well as because of your achievements."

"Will your worship tell me who you are," replied Don Quixote, "so that my courtesy may correspond to your merits?"

The young man replied that he was the musician and singer of the night before.

"Of a truth," said Don Quixote, "your worship has a most excellent voice; but what you sang did not seem to me very appropriate. What have Garcilaso's stanzas to do with the death of this lady?"

"Don't be surprised at that," returned the musician. "For with the novice poets of our day, the practice is for every one to write as he pleases and pilfer where he chooses, whether it applies to the subject or not, and nowadays there is no piece of silliness they can sing or write that is not excused as poetic licence."

Don Quixote was about to reply but was prevented by the duke and duchess, who came in to see him, and with them there followed a long and delightful conversation, in the course of which Sancho said so many clever and mischievous things that he left the duke and duchess amazed not only at his simple-mindedness but at his shrewdness. Don Quixote begged their permission to leave that same day, since for a vanquished knight like himself it was fitter he should live in a pig-sty than in a royal palace. They gave it very readily, and the duchess asked him if Altisidora was in his good graces.

He replied, "Señora, let me tell your ladyship that this damsel's ailment comes entirely from idleness, and the cure for it is proper and constant employment. She herself has told me that they wear lace in hell; and since she must certainly know how to make it, let it never be out of her hands. When she is occupied manipulating the bobbins, the image or images of what she loves will not occupy her thoughts. This is the truth, this is my opinion, and this is my advice."

"And mine," added Sancho. "I have never in all my life seen a lacemaker that died for love; when young women are at work their minds are more set on finishing their tasks than on thinking about their love affairs. I speak from my own experience; when I'm digging I never think if my old woman; I mean my Teresa Panza, that I love better than my own eye lashes."

"You are right, Sancho," said the duchess, "and I will take care that my Altisidora employs herself henceforward in needlework of some sort; for she is extremely good at it."

"There is no need to use that remedy, señora," said Altisidora. "The mere thought of the cruelty with which this wandering good-for-nothing has treated me will suffice to blot him out of my memory without any other device. With your highness's leave I will retire, not to have before my eyes, I won't say his 'rueful countenance,' but his abominable, ugly looks."

"That reminds me of the common saying, that 'the lover who says hurtful things is ready to forgive,' " said the duke.

Altisidora then, pretending to wipe away her tears with a handkerchief, made a curtsy to her master and mistress and left the room.

"Hard luck, you poor girl," said Sancho, "hard luck! You've been up against a soul as dry as a rush and a heart as hard as oak. If you had tried me, by golly, 'another cock would have crowed for you.' "

So the conversation came to an end, and Don Quixote dressed himself and dined with the duke and duchess and set out the same evening.

Chapter LXXI

OF WHAT HAPPENED TO DON QUIXOTE AND HIS SQUIRE SANCHO ON THE WAY TO THEIR VILLAGE

The vanquished and afflicted Don Quixote went along very downcast in one respect and very happy in another. His sadness arose from his defeat and his satisfaction from the thought of the powers possessed by Sancho, as had been proved by the resurrection of Altisidora, though it was with difficulty he could persuade himself that the love-smitten damsel had really been dead.

Sancho went along anything but cheerful, for it grieved him that Altisidora had not kept her promise by giving him the chemises; and turning this over in his mind, he said to his master, "Surely, señor, I'm the most unlucky doctor in the world, where there are many physicians who, though they are killing the sick man they are treating, want to be paid for their work, which is only signing a silly prescription for some medicines that the apothecary and not he makes up, and there's the poor patient, fleeced. But with me, though to cure somebody else costs me drops of blood, smacks, pinches, pin-pricks, and whippings, nobody gives me a cent. Well, I swear by all that's good if they put another patient into my hands, they'll have to grease them before I cure him. As they say, 'it's by his singing the abbot gets his dinner,' and I refuse to believe that heaven has bestowed on me the powers I have for me to hand them out to others for nothing."

"You are right, Sancho my friend," said Don Quixote, "and Altisidora has behaved very badly in not giving you the chemises she promised. And although your power is *gratis data*—as it has cost you no effort whatever—it is more than an effort to have to endure bodily torture. I can say for myself that if you want payment for the lashes toward the disenchantment of Dulcinea, I would have given it to you liberally before this. I am not sure, however, whether payment will interfere with the treatment, and I would not have the reward counteract the medicine. Still, I think there will be nothing lost by trying it; decide what you want, Sancho, and whip yourself at once; then pay yourself with your own hand, since you have some of my money."

At this proposal Sancho opened his eyes wide and pricked up his ears and in his heart agreed to whip himself willingly, and said he to his master, "Very well then, señor, I am prepared to gratify your worship's wishes, if I profit by it; the love of my wife and children forces me to seem mercenary. Tell me, your worship: how much you will pay me for each lash I give myself?"

"If, Sancho," replied Don Quixote, "I were to pay you according to the importance and nature of the cure, the treasures of Venice and the mines of Potosí would be insufficient to pay you. See what you have of mine, and put a price on each stroke."

Sancho said, "There are three thousand, three hundred and some odd lashes, of which I have given myself five; the rest remain. Forget about the five, and let's take the three thousand, three hundred, which at a quarter *real* apiece (for I won't take less if the whole world asked me) make three thousand, three hundred quarter *reales*; the three thousand are one thousand, five hundred half *reales*, which make seven hundred and fifty *reales*; and the three hundred make a hundred and fifty half *reales*, which come to seventy-five *reales*, which added to the seven hundred and fifty make eight hundred and twenty-five *reales* in all. These I will subtract from what I have belonging to your worship, and I'll return home rich and content, though well whipped, because 'you can't make an omelet . . .'—you get my meaning."

"O blessed Sancho! O dear Sancho!" said Don Quixote. "How we shall be obliged to you, Dulcinea and I, all the days of our lives that heaven may grant us! If she returns to her lost shape (and she certainly will), her misfortune will have been good fortune and my defeat a most happy triumph. Decide, Sancho, when you are going to begin the whipping, because I will throw in another hundred *reales* if you'll do it quickly."

"When?" said Sancho. "Tonight, without fail. Let your worship arrange for us to spend it out of doors and in the open air, and I'll flay myself."

Night, longed for by Don Quixote with the greatest anxiety in the world, came at last, though it seemed to him that the wheels of Apollo's car had broken down and that the day was drawing itself out longer than usual, just as is the case with lovers, who never make the reckoning of their desires agree with time. They finally made their way in among some pleasant trees that stood a little distance from the road, and there vacating Rocinante's saddle and Dapple's packsaddle, they stretched themselves on the green grass and ate their supper from Sancho's provisions. The latter, after making a powerful and flexible whip out of Dapple's rope halter, retreated about twenty paces from his master among some beech trees. Don Quixote seeing him march off with such resolution and spirit, said to him, "Take care, my friend, not to cut yourself to pieces; allow the strokes to wait for one another, and do not be in so great a hurry that you run out of breath midway; I mean, do not lash yourself so strenuously that your life fails before you have reached the desired number. And so that you may not lose by a card too much or too little, I will station myself apart and count on my rosary here the lashes you give yourself. May heaven help you as your good intention deserves."

"'A reliable payer doesn't mind leaving a security,'" said Sancho. "I mean to thrash myself in such a way as to hurt myself without killing myself, for that, no doubt, is the essence of this miracle."

He then stripped himself from the waist up, and snatching up the rope he began to lay on and Don Quixote to count the lashes. He might have given himself six or eight when he began to think the joke was not funny and the price very low; and stopping for a moment, he told his master that he had made a bad bargain, for each stroke ought to be paid for at the rate of half a *real* instead of a quarter.

"Go on, Sancho my friend, and don't weaken," said Don Quixote, "for I double the stake."

"In that case," said Sancho, "it's in God's hand, and let it rain lashes." But the crafty peasant no longer laid them on his shoulders but on to the trees, with such groans every now and then that one would have thought at each of them his soul was being pulled up by the roots. Don Quixote, touched to the heart and fearing Sancho might kill himself, and that through Sancho's imprudence he might miss his own object, said to him, "On your life, my friend, let the matter rest where it is, for the remedy seems to me a very rough one, and it will be well to have patience. 'Zamora was not won in an hour.' If I have not counted wrong, you have given yourself over a thousand lashes; that is enough for the present; 'the ass,' to put it in homely phrase, 'can carry the load, but not the overload.' "

"No, no, señor," replied Sancho. "Let it never be said of me, 'Advance money to a worker and you get a shirker.' Move back a little further, your worship, and let me give myself at least a thousand lashes more. With a few more strokes like these we'll have finished this fencing match, and there will even be cloth to spare."

"Since you are in such a willing mood," said Don Quixote, "may heaven help you; lay on and I'll retire."

Sancho returned to his task with so much resolution that he soon had the bark stripped off several trees, such was the severity with which he whipped himself; and one time, raising his voice, and giving a beech a tremendous lash, he cried out, "Here let mighty Samson fall and those who throng this pagan hall!"

At the sound of his tormented voice and of the stroke of the cruel lash, Don Quixote ran to him at once, and seizing the twisted halter that served him for a scourge, said to him, "Heaven forbid, Sancho my friend, that to please me you should lose your life, which is needed for the support of your wife and children; let Dulcinea wait for a better opportunity, and I will content myself with a hope soon to be realized and have patience until you have gained fresh strength so as to finish this business to the satisfaction of everybody."

"Since your worship wants it that way, señor," said Sancho, "so be it. Throw your cloak over my shoulders, for I'm sweating, and I don't want to take cold; it's a risk that beginners run in this kind of discipline."

Don Quixote complied and, taking off his cloak, covered Sancho, who slept until the sun woke him. They then resumed their journey, which they terminated—for the time being—at a village that lay three leagues farther on. They dismounted at an inn which Don Quixote recognized as such and did not take to be a castle with moat, turrets, portcullis, and drawbridge; for ever since he had been vanquished, he talked more rationally about everything, as will be shown presently. They lodged him in a room on the ground floor, where in place of the usual decorations there were some old painted hangings such as they commonly use in villages. On one of them was painted by some very poor hand the Rape of Helen, when the bold guest carried her off from Menelaus, and on the other was the story of Dido and Aeneas, she on a high tower, waving with half a sheet to her fugitive guest who was out at sea fleeing in a frigate or brigantine. He noticed in the two pictures that Helen did not go very reluctantly, for she was laughing slyly to herself; but the fair Dido was shown shedding tears the size of walnuts from her eyes. Don Quixote as he looked at them observed, "Those two ladies were very unfortunate not to have been born in this age, and I unfortunate above all men not to have been born in theirs. Had I encountered those gentlemen, Troy would not have been burned or Carthage destroyed, for I had only to slay Paris, and all these misfortunes would have been avoided."

"I'll bet," said Sancho, "that before long there won't be a tavern, roadside inn, hostelry, or barbershop where there isn't a picture of our deeds. But I'd like it painted by the hand of a better painter than painted these."

"You are right, Sancho," said Don Quixote, "for this painter is like Orbaneja, a painter who was at Úbeda, who when they asked him what he was painting, used to say, 'Whatever turns out.' And if he happened to be painting a rooster, he would write under it, 'This is a rooster,' for fear they might think it was a fox. The painter or writer, for it's all the same, who published the history of this new Don Quixote that has appeared must have been one of this sort I think, Sancho, for he painted or wrote 'whatever turns out.' Or perhaps he is like a poet called Mauleón that was at Court some years ago, who used to answer off the top of his head whatever he was asked, and when someone asked him what *Deum de Deo* meant, he replied *Dé donde diere.*[1] But, leaving this aside, tell me, Sancho, do you intend to have another turn at whipping yourself tonight, and would you rather have it indoors or in the open air?"

"By God, señor," said Sancho, "for what I'm going to give myself, it's all the same to me whether it's in a house or in the fields; still I'd like it to be among trees; for they seem to be keeping me company, and they help me to bear my pain wonderfully."

"Well, I won't allow it, Sancho my friend," said Don Quixote. "We'll save it until we get to our village, so that you can recover your strength. At the latest we shall get there the day after tomorrow."

Sancho said that Don Quixote might do as he pleased but that he would like to finish the business quickly before his blood cooled and while he had an appetite, because one should "never put off till tomorrow," and "pray to God and ply the hammer," "one *take* is better than two *I'll give you*'s," and "a bird in the hand is worth two in the bush."

"For God's sake, Sancho, no more proverbs!" exclaimed Don Quixote. "It seems that you are going back to your old ways. Speak in a plain, simple, straightforward way, as I have often told you, and you will see that 'one plain loaf is worth a hundred fancy tidbits.' "

1. *Deum de Deo*: "God from God," a phrase from the Creed. *Dé donde diere*: "Let me (or him) strike wherever I (or he) can," which is roughly equivalent to "whatever turns out." There is an aural similarity between the Latin and Spanish phrases that is not apparent in print.

"I don't know what bad luck it is of mine," said Sancho, "but I can't utter a word without a proverb, for a proverb seems as good as an argument to me. However, I'll do better, if I can." And so for the present the conversation ended.

Chapter LXXII

OF HOW DON QUIXOTE AND SANCHO REACHED THEIR VILLAGE

All that day Don Quixote and Sancho remained in the village and inn waiting for night, the one in order to finish up his task of scourging in the open country, the other in order to see it accomplished, for therein lay the fulfillment of his desires. Meanwhile there arrived at the inn a traveler on horseback with three or four servants, one of whom said to the person who appeared to be the master, "Señor Don Álvaro Tarfe, your worship can take your siesta here today; the quarters seem clean and cool."

When he heard this, Don Quixote said to Sancho, "Look here, Sancho; when I leafed through that book of the Second Part of my history, I think I came across this name of Don Álvaro Tarfe."

"That's possible," said Sancho. "We had better let him dismount, and then we can ask about it."

The gentleman dismounted, and the landlady gave him a room on the ground floor opposite Don Quixote's and adorned with painted hangings of the same sort. The newly arrived gentleman, dressed for summer weather, came out to the gateway of the inn, which was wide and cool, and addressing Don Quixote, who was pacing up and down there, he asked, "In what direction is your worship headed, sir?"

"To a nearby village which is my home," replied Don Quixote. "And your worship, where are you bound for?"

"I am going to Granada, señor," said the gentleman, "to my own country."

"And good country it is," said Don Quixote. "But will your worship do me the favor of telling me your name, for it strikes me it is of more importance to me to know it than I can tell you."

"My name is Don Álvaro Tarfe," replied the traveler.

To which Don Quixote returned, "I have no doubt whatever that your worship is that Don Álvaro Tarfe who appears in print in the Second Part of the history of Don Quixote of La Mancha, lately printed and published by a new author."

"I am the same," replied the gentleman, "and that same Don Quixote, the principal personage in the history, was a very great friend of mine, and it was I who took him away from home, or at least induced him to come to some jousts that were to be held at Zaragoza, where I was going myself. Indeed, I showed him many kindnesses and saved him from a beating by the executioner because of his extreme rashness."

"Tell me, Señor Don Álvaro," said Don Quixote, "am I at all like that Don Quixote you talk of?"

"No indeed," replied the traveler, "not a bit."

"And that Don Quixote," said ours, "had he with him a squire called Sancho Panza?"

"He had," said Don Álvaro, "and though he had the reputation of being very funny, I never heard him say anything that had anything amusing in it."

"That I can well believe," said Sancho at this, "because being funny is not in everybody's line. That Sancho your worship speaks of, gentle sir, must be some great scoundrel, bore, and thief, all in one; for I am the real Sancho Panza, and I have tons of clever remarks. If you don't believe me, your worship can test me. Follow me around for a year or so, and you will find they fall from me at every step, and so rich and so plentiful that though mostly I don't know what I am saying, I make everybody that hears me laugh. And the real Don Quixote of La Mancha, the famous, the valiant, the wise, the lover, the righter of wrongs, the guardian of minors and orphans, the protector of widows, the disdainer of damsels, he who has for his sole mistress the peerless Dulcinea del Toboso, is this gentleman before you, my master; all other Don Quixotes and all other Sancho Panzas are deceptions and illusions."

"By God I believe it," said Don Álvaro, "for you have uttered more witticisms, my friend, in the few words you have spoken than the other Sancho Panza in all I ever heard from him, and they were not a few. He was more of a glutton than a wit, and more dull than funny. I am convinced that the enchanters who persecute Don Quixote the Good have been trying to persecute me with Don Quixote the Bad. But I don't know what to say, for I am ready to swear I left him shut up in the Nuncio's Asylum at Toledo, to be treated, and here another Don Quixote turns up, though a very different one from mine."

"I don't know whether I am good or not," said Quixote, "but I can safely say I am not the bad one. And to prove it, let me tell you, Señor Don Álvaro Tarfe, I have never in my life been in Zaragoza. In fact, when I was told that this imaginary Don Quixote had been present at the jousts in that city, I declined to enter it, in order to reveal his imposture before the face of the world; and so I went on straight to Barcelona, the storehouse of courtesy, haven of strangers, asylum of the poor, fatherland of the valiant, champion of the wronged, pleasant home of true friendships, and city unrivaled in site and beauty. And though the adventures that befell me there are not by any means matters of enjoyment, but rather of regret, I do not regret them, simply because I have seen it."

"In a word, Señor Don Álvaro Tarfe, I am Don Quixote of La Mancha, the one that fame speaks of, and not that unfortunate person who has attempted to usurp my name and take credit for my ideas. I entreat your worship on your honor as a gentleman to be so good as to make a statement before the magistrate of this village that you never in all your life saw me until now, and that neither am I the Don Quixote in print in the Second Part, nor is this Sancho Panza, my squire, the one your worship knew."

"That I will do most willingly," replied Don Álvaro, "though it amazes me to find two Don Quixotes and two Sancho Panzas at once, as much alike in name as different in action; and again I say and declare that what I saw I cannot have seen, and that what happened me cannot have happened."

"No doubt your worship is enchanted, like my lady Dulcinea del Toboso," said Sancho, "and I wish to heaven your disenchantment depended on my giving myself another three thousand and some odd lashes like what I'm giving myself for her, because I'd lay them on without expecting any payment."

"I don't understand the business about lashes," said Don Álvaro. Sancho replied that it was a long story, but that he would tell him if they happened to be going the same way.

By now dinner time had arrived, and Don Quixote and Don Álvaro dined together. The village magistrate came by chance into the inn together with a notary, and Don Quixote laid a petition before him, requesting that to protect his rights, Don Álvaro Tarfe, the gentleman there present, should make a statement before the magistrate that he did not know Don Quixote of La Mancha, also there present, and that he aforesaid Don Quixote was not the one that was in print in a history entitled *Second Part of Don Quixote of La Mancha*, by one Avellaneda of Tordesillas. The magistrate finally put it in legal form, and the statement was made with all the formalities required in such cases, at which Don Quixote and Sancho were highly pleased, as if such a document were of great importance to them, and as if their words and deeds did not plainly show the difference between the two Don Quixotes and the two Sanchos. Many civilities and offers of service were exchanged by Don Álvaro and Don Quixote, in the course of which the great Manchegan displayed such good sense that he disabused Don Álvaro of his error. The latter was convinced he must have been enchanted, since he had actually touched two such opposite Don Quixotes.

Evening came, they set out from the village, and after about half a league two roads branched off, one leading to Don Quixote's village, the other the road Don Álvaro was to follow. In this short interval Don Quixote told him of his unfortunate defeat and of Dulcinea's enchantment and the remedy, all which caused Don

Álvaro fresh amazement, and embracing Don Quixote and Sancho he went his way, and Don Quixote went his. That night he spent among trees again in order to give Sancho an opportunity of working out his penance. This he did in the same fashion as the night before, at the expense of the bark of the beech trees much more than of his back, of which he took such good care that the lashes would not have knocked off a fly had there been one there.

The gullible Don Quixote did not miss a single stroke of the count, and he found that together with those of the night before they made up three thousand and twenty-nine. The sun apparently rose early to witness the sacrifice, and with his light they resumed their journey, discussing Don Álvaro's mistake and saying how clever it was to have taken his statement before a magistrate in such an unimpeachable form. That day and night they traveled on, nor did anything worth mentioning happen to them, unless it was that in the course of the night Sancho finished up his task, which delighted Don Quixote beyond measure. He looked forward to daylight, to see if along the road he should meet his already disenchanted lady Dulcinea; and as he pursued his journey there was no woman he met that he did not approach to see if she was Dulcinea del Toboso, as he held it absolutely certain that Merlin's promises could not lie.

Full of these thoughts and anxieties, they ascended a hill from which they could see their own village, at the sight of which Sancho fell on his knees exclaiming, "Open your eyes, beloved home, and see your son Sancho Panza returning to you, if not very rich, very well whipped! Open your arms and receive also your son Don Quixote, who, if he comes vanquished by the arm of another, comes victorious over himself, which, as he himself has told me, is the greatest victory anyone can desire. I'm bringing back money: 'I may have been flogged, but at least I rode in style.' "[1]

"Leave off this foolishness," said Don Quixote. "Let us enter our village with our right foot forward. There we will give free range to our fancies and settle our plans for our future pastoral life."

With this they descended the slope and went straight to their village.

Chapter LXXIII

OF THE OMENS DON QUIXOTE HAD AS HE ENTERED HIS VILLAGE, AND OTHER INCIDENTS THAT EMBELLISH AND AUTHENTICATE THIS GREAT HISTORY

At the entrance of the village, so says Cide Hamete, Don Quixote saw two boys quarreling on the village threshing floor, one of

1. See Ch. XXXVI, note 1.

whom said to the other, "Give up, Periquillo; you'll never see it again as long as you live."

Don Quixote heard this, and said he to Sancho, "Did you hear, my friend, what that boy said, 'You'll never see it again as long as you live'?"

"Well," said Sancho, "what does it matter if the boy said so?"

"What!" said Don Quixote. "Don't you see that, applied to the object of my desires, the words mean that I am never to see Dulcinea again?"

Sancho was about to answer, when his attention was diverted by seeing a hare come flying across the fields pursued by several greyhounds and hunters. In its terror it ran to take shelter and huddle under Dapple. Sancho picked it up easily and presented it to Don Quixote, who was saying, "*Malum signum, malum signum!*[1] A hare flies, greyhounds chase it, Dulcinea appears not."

"Your worship's a strange man," said Sancho. "Let's suppose that this hare is Dulcinea and these greyhounds chasing it the wicked enchanters who turned her into a country wench. She flees, and I catch her and put her into your worship's hands, and you hold her in your arms and pet her. What bad sign is that, or what ill omen is to be found here?"

The two boys who had been quarreling came over to look at the hare, and Sancho asked one of them what their quarrel was about. He was answered by the one who had said, "You'll never see it again as long as you live," that he had taken a cage full of crickets from the other boy and did not intend to give it back to him as long as he lived. Sancho took out four *cuartos* from his pocket and gave them to the boy for the cage, which he placed in Don Quixote's hands, saying, "There, señor! There are the omens broken and destroyed, and they have no more to do with our affairs, to my thinking, fool that I am, than with last year's clouds. And if I remember rightly, I have heard the priest of our village say that it does not become Christians or sensible people to pay attention to these silly things. Even you yourself said the same to me some time ago, telling me that all Christians who heeded omens were fools. But there's no need to make an issue of it; let us push on and go into our village."

The hunters came up and asked for their hare, which Don Quixote gave them. They then went on, and in the small meadow at the entrance of the town they came upon the priest and the bachelor Sansón Carrasco busy with their breviaries. It should be mentioned that in place of a packsaddle cover, Sancho had thrown over Dapple and over the bundle of armor, the robe painted with flames which they had put on him at the duke's castle the night Altisidora came back to life. He had also fixed the pointed hat on Dapple's head,

1. "A bad omen, a bad omen."

the most novel decoration—and metamorphosis—of any ass in the world. They were at once recognized by both the priest and the bachelor, who came toward them with open arms. Don Quixote dismounted and gave them a friendly embrace; and the sharp-sighted boys, whom nothing escapes, spied the ass's miter and came running to see it, calling out to one another, "Come here, boys, and see Sancho Panza's jackass dressed up fit to kill, and Don Quixote's beast skinnier than ever."

So at length, with the boys capering around them and accompanied by the priest and the bachelor, they made their entrance into the town and proceeded to Don Quixote's house, at the door of which they found his housekeeper and niece, whom the news of his arrival had already reached. It had been brought to Teresa Panza, Sancho's wife, as well, and she with her hair all loose and half naked, dragging Sanchica her daughter by the hand, ran out to meet her husband. But seeing him not quite so well dressed as she thought a governor ought to be, she said to him, "Why have you arrived like this, husband? You look as if you've walked until you're worn out, and you resemble a vagabond rather than a governor."

"Hold your tongue, Teresa," said Sancho. "There's more than meets the eye. Let's go into the house, and there you'll hear strange things. I bring money, which is the main thing, earned by my own industry without harming anybody."

"You bring the money, my good husband," said Teresa, "and I don't care how it was earned. However you came by it, you won't have done anything new in the world."

Sanchica embraced her father and asked him if he brought her anything, for she had been waiting for him as for the showers of May; and she taking hold of him by the belt on one side, and his wife by the hand, while the daughter led Dapple, they headed for their house, leaving Don Quixote in his, in the hands of his niece and housekeeper and in the company of the priest and the bachelor.

Don Quixote at once, without any regard to time or season, drew the bachelor and the pirest aside and in a few words told them of his defeat and of the obligation he was under not to leave his village for a year, which he meant to keep to the letter without departing a hair's breadth from it, as became a knight-errant bound by scrupulous good faith and the laws of knight-errantry. He also told them of how he planned to become a shepherd for that year and spend his time in the solitude of the fields, where he could with perfect freedom give range to his thoughts of love while he followed the virtuous pastoral calling; and he begged them, if they had not a great deal to do and were not prevented by more important business, to consent to be his companions, for he would buy sheep and cattle enough to qualify them for shepherds. And the most important point of the whole affair, he could tell them, was settled, for he had given them names that would fit them to a tee. The priest asked what they were. Don Quixote replied that he himself was to be called the shepherd Quixotiz, and the bachelor the shepherd Carrascón, and the priest the shepherd Culiambro, and Sancho Panza the shepherd Pancino.

Both were astounded at Don Quixote's new madness; however, in order to prevent his running away from the village again in pursuit of his chivalry, trusting that in the course of the year he might be cured, they went along with his new project, applauded his crazy idea as a bright one, and offered to share the life with him.

"And what's more," said Sansón Carrasco, "I am, as all the world knows, a very famous poet, and I'll be always making verses, pastoral or courtly or whatever may come into my head, to pass the time in those secluded regions where we shall be roaming. But what is most necessary, sirs, is that each of us should choose the name of the shepherdess he plans to glorify in his verses, and that we should not leave a tree, be it ever so hard, without inscribing and carving her name on it, as is the habit and custom of love-sick shepherds."

"That's the very thing," said Don Quixote, "though I have no need of looking for the name of an imaginary shepherdess, for there's the peerless Dulcinea del Toboso, the glory of these riverbanks, the ornament of these meadows, the mainstay of beauty, the cream of all the graces, and, in a word, the being to whom all praise is appropriate, be it ever so hyperbolical."

"Very true," said the priest "but we the others must look about for willing shepherdesses that will answer our purpose one way or another."

"And," added Sansón Carrasco, "if we can't find appropriate names, we'll give them the names of the ones in print who are so well known: Fílidas, Amarilises, Dianas, Fléridas, Galateas, Belisardas. Since they sell these ladies in the marketplaces, we may certainly buy them and make them our own. If my lady, or I should say my shepherdess, happens to be called Ana, I'll sing her praises under the name of Anarda, and if Francisca, I'll call her Francenia, and if Lucia, Lucinda, for it all comes to the same thing; and Sancho Panza, if he joins this fraternity, may glorify his wife Teresa Panza as Teresaina."

Don Quixote laughed at the adaptation of the name, and the priest bestowed vast praise on the worthy and honorable resolution he had made and again offered to keep him company all the time that he could spare from his pressing duties. And so they took their leave of him, recommending and beseeching him to take care of his health and treat himself to a suitable diet.

It so happened that his niece and the housekeeper overheard what the three of them said, and as soon as they were gone, the two women came in to Don Quixote, and the niece said, "What's this, uncle? Now that we were thinking you had come back to stay at home and lead a quiet respectable life here, are you going to get into fresh entanglements by becoming a 'young shepherd, thou that comest here, young shepherd going there?' No! Indeed 'the barley stalk is too hard now to be turned into shepherd's pipes.' "

"And," added the housekeeper, "will your worship be able to stand the hot afternoons of summer and the night air of winter and the howling of the wolves out in the fields? Certainly not. That's a life and a business for hardy men, bred and seasoned to such work almost from the time they were in diapers. Why, considering the disadvantages, it's better to be a knight-errant than a shepherd! Look here, señor; take my advice—and I'm not giving it to you full of bread and wine, but fasting, and with fifty years behind me—stay at home, look after your affairs, go often to confession, be good to the poor, and upon my soul be it if any evil comes to you."

"Hold your peace, my daughters," said Don Quixote. "I know very well what my duty is; help me to bed, for I don't feel very well; and rest assured that, knight-errant now or wandering shepherd to be, I shall never fail to care for your needs, as you will see by my actions." And the good daughters (for that they undoubtedly were), the housekeeper and niece, helped him to bed, where they gave him something to eat and made him as comfortable as possible.

Chapter LXXIV

OF HOW DON QUIXOTE FELL SICK, AND OF THE WILL HE MADE, AND HOW HE DIED

Since human affairs are not eternal but all tend ever downwards from their beginning to end, and above all man's life, and as Don Quixote's enjoyed no special dispensation from heaven to slow its course, its end and close came when he least expected it. For—whether from the melancholy his defeat produced, or by heaven's will that so ordered it—a fever settled upon him and kept him in his bed for six days, during which he was often visited by his friends the priest, the bachelor, and the barber, while his good squire Sancho Panza never left his bedside. They, believing that it was grief at finding himself vanquished and the object of his heart, the liberation and disenchantment of Dulcinea, unattained, that kept him in this state, tried by all the means in their power to cheer him up; the bachelor telling him take heart and get up to begin his pastoral life, for which he himself, he said, had already composed an eclogue that would outshine all Sannazaro had ever written, and had bought with his own money two splendid dogs to guard the flock, one called Barcino and the other Butrón, which a herdsman of Quintanar had sold him.

But for all this Don Quixote could not shake off his sadness. His friends called in the doctor, who felt his pulse and was not very pleased with it, and said that in any case it would be well for him to attend to the health of his soul, as that of his body was in a bad way. Don Quixote heard this calmly; but not so his housekeeper, his niece, and his squire, who began weeping bitterly, as if they had him lying dead before them. The doctor's opinion was that melancholy and depression were bringing him to his end. Don Quixote begged them to leave him by himself, as he had a wish to sleep a little. They obeyed, and he slept at one stretch, as the saying is, more than six hours, so that the housekeeper and niece thought he was going to sleep forever. But at the end of that time he woke up and in a loud voice exclaimed, "Blessed be Almighty God, who has shown me such goodness. In truth his mercies are boundless, and the sins of men can neither limit them nor keep them back!"

The niece listened with attention to her uncle's words, and they struck her as more coherent than usual, at least during his illness, so she asked, "What are you saying, señor? Has anything happened? What mercies or what sins of men are you talking about?"

"The mercies, niece," said Don Quixote, "are those that God has this moment shown me, and with him, as I said, my sins are no impediment. My reason is now free and clear, rid of the dark shadows of ignorance that my deplorable constant study of those detestable books of chivalry cast over it. Now I see through their absurdities and deceptions, and it only grieves me that this revelation has come so late that it leaves me no time to make some amends by reading other books that might be a light to my soul.

"Niece, I feel myself at the point of death, and I would like to die in such a way as to show that my life has not been so bad that I should be remembered as a madman; for though I have been one, I would not like to perpetuate that fact with my death. Call, dear niece, my good friends the priest, the bachelor Sansón Carrasco, and Master Nicolás the barber, for I wish to confess and make my will."

But his niece was saved the trouble by the entrance of the three. The instant Don Quixote saw them he exclaimed, "Good news for you, good sirs: I am no longer Don Quixote of La Mancha, but Alonso Quixano, whose way of life won for him the name of Good. Now am I the enemy of Amadís of Gaul and of the whole countless troop of his descendants; odious to me now are all the profane stories of knight-errantry; now I perceive my folly, and the peril into which reading them brought me; now, by God's mercy, in my right senses, I loathe them."

When the three heard him speak in this way, they had no doubt whatever that some new madness had taken possession of him; and Sansón said, "What? Señor Don Quixote! Now that we have news of the lady Dulcinea's being disenchanted, how can you say such a thing? Now, just as we are on the point of becoming shepherds, to spend our lives singing, like princes, are you thinking of becoming a hermit? Hush, for heaven's sake, be rational, and let's have no more tales."

"The tales," said Don Quixote, "that until now have been real, and have done me such harm, I hope now that I am dying, with heaven's help, to turn to my good. I feel, sirs, that I am rapidly drawing near death. Stop joking, and bring me a confessor to confess me, and a notary to make my will; for in extremities like this, man must not trifle with his soul; and while the priest is confessing me, let some one, I beg, go for the notary."

They looked at one another, amazed at Don Quixote's words; but, though uncertain, they were inclined to believe him, and one of the signs by which they concluded that he was dying was this sudden and complete return to his senses after having been mad; for to the words already quoted he added much more, so well expressed, so devout, and so rational, as to banish all doubt and convince them that he was sound of mind.

The priest asked them all to go, and left alone with him confessed him. The bachelor went for the notary and returned shortly afterwards with him and with Sancho, who, having already learned from the bachelor the condition his master was in, and finding the housekeeper and niece weeping, began to blubber and shed tears.

The confession over, the priest came out saying, "Alonso Quixano the Good is indeed dying and is indeed in his right mind; we may now go in to him while he makes his will."

This news gave a tremendous impulse to the brimming eyes of the housekeeper, niece, and Sancho Panza his good squire, making the tears burst from their eyes and a host of sobs from their breasts, for in truth, as has been said more than once, whether as plain Alonso Quixano the Good or as Don Quixote of La Mancha, Don Quixote was always of a gentle disposition and kindly in all his ways, and hence he was beloved, not only by those of his own house, but by all who knew him.

The notary came in with the rest, and as soon as the preamble of the will had been set out and Don Quixote had commended his soul to God with all the devout formalities that are usual, coming to the bequests, he said, "Item, it is my will that, regarding certain moneys in the hands of Sancho Panza (whom in my madness I made my squire), inasmuch as between him and me there have been certain accounts and debits and credits, no claim be made against him, nor any account demanded of him; but that if anything remains over and above after he has paid himself what I owe him, the balance, which will be small, shall be his, and much good may it do him; and if, as when I was mad I had a share in giving him the government of an island, now that I am in my senses, I could give him that of a kingdom, it should be his, for the simplicity of his character and the fidelity of his conduct deserve it."

And then, turning to Sancho, he said, "Forgive me, my friend, that I led you to seem as mad as myself, making you fall into the same error I myself fell into, that there were and still are knights-errant in the world."

"Ah!" said Sancho weeping, "don't die, master, but take my advice and live many years; for the most foolish thing a man can do in this life is to let himself die without rhyme or reason, without anybody killing him or any hands but melancholy's doing him in. Come on, don't be lazy; get up from that bed and let's take to the fields in shepherd's clothes as we agreed. Perhaps behind some bush we'll find the lady Dulcinea disenchanted, as fine as fine can be. If you are dying of grief at having been defeated, blame me and say you were unseated because I had tightened Rocinante's girth badly. Besides, you must have seen in your books of chivalry that it is a common thing for knights to upset one another and for him who is conquered to be conqueror tomorrow."

"Very true," said Sansón, "and good Sancho Panza's view of these cases is quite right."

"Sirs, not so fast," said Don Quixote. "'In last year's nests there are no birds this year.' I was mad, now I am in my senses; I was Don Quixote of La Mancha, I am now, as I said, Alonso Quixano the Good. And may my repentance and sincerity restore me to the esteem you used to have for me; and now let Master Notary proceed.

"Item, I leave all my property absolutely to Antonia Quixana my niece, here present, after all has been deducted from the most available portion of it that may be required to satisfy the bequests I have made. And the first disbursement I desire to be made is the payment of the wages I owe for the time my housekeeper has served me, plus twenty ducats for a dress.

"The priest and the bachelor Sansón Carrasco, now present, I appoint my executors.

"Item, it is my wish that if Antonia Quixana, my niece, desires to marry, she shall marry a man of whom it shall be first of all ascertained that he does not know what books of chivalry are; and if it should be proved that he does, and if, in spite of this, my niece insists upon marrying him, and does marry him, then she shall forfeit the whole of what I have left her, which my executors shall devote to works of charity as they please.

"Item, I entreat the aforesaid gentlemen my executors, that, if good fortune should lead them to discover the author who is said to have written a history now going about under the title of *Second Part of the Deeds of Don Quixote of La Mancha,* they beg of him on my behalf as earnestly as they can to forgive me for having been, without intending it, the cause of his writing so many and such monstrous absurdities as he has written in it; for I am leaving the world with a feeling of remorse at having provoked him to write them."

With this he closed his will, and a faintness coming over him he stretched himself out at full length on the bed. All were in consternation and made haste to relieve him, and during the three days he lived after that on which he made his will, he fainted very often. The house was all in confusion; but still the niece ate, and the housekeeper drank, and Sancho Panza enjoyed himself; for inheriting property wipes out or softens in the heir the feeling of grief the dead man might be expected to leave behind him.

At last Don Quixote's end came, after he had received all the sacraments and had in full and forcible terms expressed his detestation of books of chivalry. The notary was there at the time, and he said that in no book of chivalry had he ever read of any knight-errant dying in his bed so calmly and so like a Christian as Don Quixote, who amid the tears and lamentations of all present yielded up his spirit, that is to say, died. On perceiving it the priest begged the notary to bear witness that Alonso Quixano the Good, commonly called Don Quixote of La Mancha, had passed away from this present life and died; and he said he desired this testimony in order to remove the possibility that any other author but Cide Hamete Benengeli should bring him to life again falsely and making interminable stories out of his achievements.

Such was the end of the Ingenious Gentleman of La Mancha, whose village Cide Hamete would not indicate precisely, in order to leave all the towns and villages of La Mancha to contend among themselves for the right to adopt him and claim him as a son, as the seven cities of Greece contended for Homer. The lamentations of Sancho and the niece and housekeeper are omitted here, as well as the new epitaphs on his tomb. Sansón Carrasco, however, put the following lines there:

A valiant gentleman lies here,
A stranger all his life to fear,
Nor in his death could Death prevail,
In that last hour, to make him quail.
He for the world but little cared,
And at his feats the world was scared.
A crazy man his life he passed,
But in his senses died at last.

And the most sage Cide Hamete said to his pen, "Rest here,

hung up by this brass wire upon this rack, O my pen, whether of skilful make or clumsy cut I know not; here shalt thou remain long ages, unless presumptuous or malignant historians take thee down to profane thee. But ere they touch thee, warn them and, as best thou canst, say to them:

> Beware, ye cowards; stay your hands!
> Let it be touched by none.
> For this adventure, O good king,
> Was meant for me alone.

"For me alone was Don Quixote born, and I for him; it was his to act, mine to write; we two together make but one, notwithstanding and in spite of that pretended Tordesillesque writer who has ventured or would venture with his great, coarse, ill-trimmed ostrich quill to write the achievements of my valiant knight. For it is no burden for his shoulders nor subject for his sluggish wit. If perchance thou shouldst come to know him, thou shalt warn him to leave at rest where they lie the weary moldering bones of Don Quixote and not to attempt to carry him off, in opposition to all the laws of death, to Old Castile, making him rise from the grave where in reality and truth he lies stretched at full length, powerless to make any third expedition or new sally; for the two that he has already made, so much to the enjoyment and approval of everybody to whom they have become known, in this as well as in foreign countries, are quite sufficient for the purpose of ridiculing all those made by the whole set of the knights-errant. And so doing, shalt thou comply with thy Christian calling, giving good counsel to one that bears thee ill will.

"And I shall remain satisfied and proud to have been the first who has ever enjoyed the fruit of his writings as fully as he could desire; for my desire has been no other than to cause mankind to abhor the false and foolish tales of the books of chivalry, which, thanks to that of my true Don Quixote, are even now tottering and doubtless doomed to fall for ever. Farewell."

THE END

Backgrounds and Sources

MANUEL DURÁN

Cervantes' Harassed and Vagabond Life†

We can think of many great writers whose lives have left only a few traces upon their work. This is not so with Cervantes: his biography sheds light upon his masterpieces. He was seldom a cold and distant observer of his world. His presence as a witness and occasionally as a judge of what he saw is discreet yet undeniable. He made good use of his experience: he went so far as to include himself, as a minor character, in several of his works—much in the same way as one of our contemporary film directors, Alfred Hitchcock, appears fleetingly in his own movies. His presence is discreet yet insistent: he will not deny or betray his own personality; he begs us to take it into account when reading his texts. Pride and humility go hand in hand in him, helping him to become a good witness of his time—and of the human condition of all time.

Cervantes was born in Alcalá de Henares, a small university city not far from Madrid, in 1547, probably on September 29, St. Michael's day, since it was often the custom to bestow the name of the saint in the calendar upon a child born on that day. He was baptized in the church of Santa María la Mayor on Sunday, October 9.

His father, Rodrigo de Cervantes, was an impecunious hidalgo. He had become a practical surgeon after a few months of hurried studies at the University of Alcalá, where he had excellent friends among the medical faculty; not too long after acquiring his degree, Rodrigo married (in 1543) Leonor de Cortinas, a young girl born in Barajas, near Madrid, also a member of the gentry, also impecunious. They had seven children, all but the last two born in Alcalá de Henares.

Nothing is known about the first years of Miguel de Cervantes' life except that his family moved often. Miguel was only three and a half years old when his family moved away from Alcalá de Henares. The family was going through a period of hardship. Rodrigo's income was meager. With nine mouths to feed and little or no income, the family moved to Valladolid. Debts accumulated: Mi-

† From Manuel Durán, *Cervantes* (Boston: Twayne Publishers, 1974), pp. 21–30. Cervantes' life has been the object of intense study since the early eighteenth century, when Spaniards began generally to acknowledge him as the greatest of their "classical" prose-writers. In his own day, however, Cervantes was not an important person, even in literary circles, and his biography is full of gaps that especially tormented nineteenth-century historians, who made virtually every likely source of information yield its bit of fact. There is, of necessity, a great deal of imaginative reconstruction of Cervantes' life, of interpretation of his financial and legal difficulties, his unstable family life, his shadowy ancestry, etc. The reader should note how often Professor Durán must deduce the facts of Cervantes' life from meager evidence. [*Editor.*]

guel's father went to jail for a few months. We find the family in Córdoba (where they settled in 1553); Córdoba was but a shadow of its former size and opulent past under the Moors, but it must still have been a fascinating city. It is in Córdoba that Miguel de Cervantes went to an elementary school (he was seven years old when his family settled there) and acquired the rudiments of learning, perhaps at the school conducted by Father Alonso de Vieras. Later on, in 1555, he probably began the study of Latin at the Jesuit College of Santa Catalina. But 1557 was a bad year: the family was pressed by debts. There is no trace of Rodrigo and his family from that date until they reappear in Seville in 1564. Miguel was by then a handsome youth of seventeen. He must have enjoyed life in Seville, then on the verge of becoming a "boom town." He probably continued his studies at the Jesuit College. Much later, one of his characters, the wise dog Cipión, would state: "I have heard it said [he describes the Jesuit teachers at Seville] of those saintly ones that in the matter of prudence there is not their like in the world, while as guides and leaders along the heavenly path few can come up to them. They are mirrors in which are to be viewed human decency, Catholic doctrine, and extraordinary wisdom, and, lastly, a profound humility that is the basis upon which the entire edifice of a holy life is reared."[1] Later, Cervantes would describe the agreeable character of student life: "In short, I led the life of a student, without hunger and without the itch—and I can give it no higher praise than that. For if it were not that the itch and hunger are the student's constant companions, there would be no life that is pleasanter or more enjoyable, since virtue and pleasure here go hand in hand, and the young find diversion even as they learn."[2] Miguel loved to read: he was a voracious reader, and we may assume that his long lasting love affair with literature had already begun. The theatre fascinated him: it must have been a glorious day for him when Lope de Rueda, a famous actor who also wrote plays (among them his famous *pasos*, one-act plays or curtain raisers, that the modern reader finds still fresh and amusing) came to Seville and gave several performances there. This took place probably in 1564. In a prologue he later wrote to a collection of his own plays, he reminisces about that happy day. He is discussing the theatre in general, and his own childhood memories, with some of his friends: "I, as the oldest one there, said that I remembered having seen on the stage the great Lope de Rueda, a man distinguished in both acting and understanding. He was a native of Seville, and a goldsmith by trade, which means he was one of those that make gold leaf. He was admirable in pastoral poetry; and in this genre neither then nor since has anybody surpassed him."[3]

1. *Three Exemplary Novels,* tr. Samuel Putnam (New York, 1950), p. 151.
2. *Ibid.,* p. 152.
3. In *Obras completas* (Madrid, 1949), p. 179.

Bad luck once more besieged Cervantes' family. A certain Rodrigo de Chaves instituted a suit against Rodrigo, his father, and attached his goods. The family moved to Madrid in 1566. Miguel was now twenty. He probably continued his education there with private tutors and at the City School of Madrid under the learned López de Hoyos, who, as a follower of Erasmus, may have inculcated in his young pupil some of Erasmus' progressive and liberal ideas. Cervantes' culture was becoming broader and more solid. Nevertheless, as Richard L. Predmore states in his biography, "by the most generous estimate that the available facts will allow, young Cervantes cannot have enjoyed much more than six years of formal schooling. In most men this amount of study could not have created a sufficient base for the very considerable literary culture visible in Miguel's later writings, which reveal a good knowledge of the outstanding Latin authors, a smattering of Greek literature, a close familiarity with some of the great writers of the Italian Renaissance and the kind of acquaintance with his own literature that one might expect a boy with strong literary inclinations to possess. What he knew of the Latin language and literature was certainly grounded in his schooling; the rest must have been the product of his own reading. The five years he was soon to spend in Italy contributed decisively to his continued education and account for his extensive reading in Italian literature."[4]

At twenty Cervantes had a wandering spirit which had been formed in his adolescence perhaps by his frequent travels through Spain. He also felt an intense yearning for both knowledge and freedom. All of this undoubtedly influenced his decision to go to Italy, which was then the mecca of all lovers of culture and of a free life. Nevertheless his trip to Italy may well have been the result of less lofty goals: it has been suggested that at this time Miguel first ran afoul of the law—since there exists in the General Record Office in Simancas a document dated September, 1569, which begins thus: "An Order to Arrest against Miguel de Cervantes. Without Right to Appeal. [signed by] Secretary Padreda. [Motive] A Crime." According to the document, he had stabbed a certain Antonio de Segura in Madrid during a challenge to a duel. No one knows for sure whether the Miguel de Cervantes alluded to in this document is *our* Miguel de Cervantes. The biographer Luis Astrana Marín, in his six learned volumes on the life of Cervantes, thinks this to be the case. In support of his charge, he cites in particular a verse of the *Voyage to Parnassus* in which the author confesses to a "youthful imprudence," from which many of his later misfortunes ensued. It is not wholly clear that we should pay much attention to this accusation, whether truly directed against our writer or not. If true, even if we conclude that Cervantes was guilty,

4. *Cervantes*, by Richard L. Predmore (New York, 1973), p. 49.

it would only be a question of confirming one more trial, or rather one more accusation, of the many that the writer endured throughout his life. Finally, "it would not be defaming the author to admit that on occasion he was quick to reach for his sword. A gentleman at that time never went forth without strapping on his sword, and its purpose was not simply for display alone."[5]

Towards 1569 we find Cervantes in Italy, where he had travelled as a member of the retinue of Cardinal Acquaviva. Shortly afterwards he enlisted in the Spanish army and was sent to sea. He fought heroically under the command of Don John of Austria in the sea battle of Lepanto in 1571 and was twice wounded: one wound paralyzed his left hand. He later took part in other campaigns, especially the raids against Tunis and the nearby fortress of La Goleta. In 1575 he embarked for Spain with his brother Rodrigo.[6] He carried with him warm letters of recommendation from his superiors. The galley in which he travelled was seized by Turkish pirates. Thus began five years of captivity, as a slave to his captor, the Greek renegade Dali Mamí. At the end of this period, and after several frustrated attempts to escape, he was ransomed by some Trinitarian monks and was able to return to Spain. Thus Cervantes had passed some twelve years outside Spain—and these were the decisive years in the life of any man, the years between twenty and thirty-three. He returned enriched by his experience; his thirst for adventure had been partially quenched; he longed for stability, a career, some kind of stable success. Success, however, was to prove out of reach.

When he returned to Spain in 1580, several unpleasant experiences still awaited him. He soon realized there was no hope of obtaining any reward for his services. A military career seemed hopeless since one of his arms was no longer useful. Thus began a ceaseless struggle against poverty and neglect. First he lived in Madrid, then he moved to Portugal for a short time. He found no place to root himself. He became a writer almost out of desperation: what else could he do? How could he earn a living? He began to write out of love for literature but also, probably, out of desperation, hoping to find in his literary career a source of income. He was thus from the very beginning a professional writer, although an unsuccessful one at first. The most popular genres were then the pastoral novel and the theater: he tried them both to little avail. A brief love affair made him a father: an illegitimate daughter, Isabel de Saavedra, was the consequence of his affair. In 1584 he married

5. *Cervantes: His Life, his Times, his Works. Created by the Editors of Arnoldo Mondadori* (New York, 1970), p. 25.

6. The date traditionally given for Cervantes' departure from Naples is 20 September 1575. Professor Juan Bautista Avalle-Arce, however, has corrected this date and proved that Cervantes must have departed early in September. See "La Captura de Cervantes," *Boletín de la Real Academia Española*, 1968, p. 237–80.

Catalina de Salazar, a woman somewhat younger than himself, and it seems that he found no happiness in his marriage. He lived for a time in Esquivias, a village of La Mancha where his wife had a farm. It was the heart of arid Spain, a poor land almost impossible to idealize: its inhabitants were ignorant and backward. From his memories of life in La Mancha, he would later create Don Quixote and his environment. Cervantes then turned to humble jobs, since literature had proved incapable of providing him with a living. He became quartermaster for the Invincible Armada: for ten years he was an itinerant buyer, living in Seville and other towns in Andalusia. He had separated from his wife, whom he never mentioned in his works. In 1597, because of the bankruptcy of a financier with whom he had deposited some state funds, he was jailed in Seville. In these years he became acquainted with people of the lower class: it seems obvious that he found them more outgoing and decent than the people of the middle and upper classes with whom he had dealings. He did not lack for occasion to study at first hand the myriad forms of picaresque life, since Seville was the capital of the picaroons. The city was growing fast, having become the economic center of Spain and the main port of the overseas fleets. Gold and silver poured into Spain from Seville. Industry flourished. Rapid growth and change—plus a transient population—made for a minimum of social constraints. It is in Seville that Cervantes must have known the real-life counterpart of Monipodio, the good-tempered, humane Al Capone of the Golden Age.

There was another Spain, much less glamorous than the pageant of Seville, that also attracted his attention: life in the villages of Andalusia and along the winding, sun-drenched roads leading to these villages. Cervantes came to know it well: the poor inns, the wandering artisans and shepherds, the long convoys of mule trains, the humble yet proud peasants. It was another strand in the huge tapestry that unfolded before him. Cervantes was the perfect witness, observing every detail, noticing the delicate balance and the constant interaction between human beings, taking mental notes about their foibles and their moments of happiness.

Life was never boring. Yet Cervantes was always on the verge of bankruptcy: he was not a businessman, his records were not accurate, the financial rewards of his jobs were meager. It is not surprising, therefore, that in 1590 he petitioned to find a position in the Spanish colonies overseas. His hopes were dashed: an ungrateful administration rejected his petition. Perhaps his troubles with the law had convinced the bureaucrats that he was basically unreliable. Cervantes had pleaded: "Sire: Miguel de Cervantes Saavedra says that he has served Your Majesty for many years in the sea and land campaigns that have occurred over the last 22 years, particularly in the Naval Battle [Lepanto], where he received many wounds, among which was the loss of a hand from gunfire . . . and he has since continued to serve in Seville on business of the Armada, under the orders of Antonio de Guevara, as is on record in the testimonials in his possession. In all this time he has received no favors at all. He asks and begs as humbly as he can that Your Majesty be pleased to grant him the favor of a position in America, of the three or four currently vacant, namely, the accountant's office in the new Kingdom of Granada, or the governorship of the province of Soconusco in Guatemala, or the office of ship's accountant in Cartagena, or that of corregidor in the city of La Paz . . ."[7] As Richard Predmore observes, "influence and money won more jobs than merit, it seems. On 6 June 1590, an official of the Council of the Indies scribbled on the back of Cervantes' memorial: 'Let him look on this side of the water for some favor that may be granted him.' Perhaps the sympathetic reader will console himself with the proverb about the ill wind that blows no good. The action of the Council of the Indies unwittingly favored the birth of Don Quixote."[8]

There can be no doubt about Cervantes' honesty. Each new supervisor confirmed him in his job. There can be no doubt either about his bad luck. In 1602 he was again, for a short time, in jail at Seville. In 1604 he decided to move to Valladolid. The decisive moment was at hand: early in 1605 the first part of *Don Quixote* appeared. Yet Cervantes' joy at the instantaneous success of his novel was short-lived. Again he became involved with the police: a gentleman, Gaspar de Ezpeleta, was fatally wounded in a duel at the entrance of Cervantes' house. The investigation proved Cervantes and his family had nothing to do with this incident—yet it also revealed that Cervantes' sister and daughter led somewhat irregular lives, were frequently visited by male friends and received gifts from them.

Cervantes' huge literary success did not bring him riches: his publisher and several pirate publishers kept most of the profits. But it did motivate him to go on writing.

In 1606 the Court settled again in Madrid: Cervantes and his family moved with it. Cervantes wanted to be in touch with other writers and was looking for new publishers; the women in his household, busy with fashion designing and sewing, were looking for customers. Miguel's last years in Madrid were relatively serene. He overcame through patience and wisdom all his adversities, the neglect of famous writers such as Lope de Vega—who seldom had a good word for his works—and the sadness of family crises: his daughter married but soon became the mistress of a wealthy middle-aged businessman; when Cervantes intervened in the interest of preventing scandal, she became estranged and never again visited

7. Quoted by Predmore, *op. cit.*, p. 138. 8. *Ibid.*

him. Cervantes immersed himself in his work. It was harvest season for him: late in life, yet in full command of his talent, he produced in quick succession his *Exemplary Novels* (1613), the second part of *Don Quixote* (1615), and finally *Persiles and Sigismunda*, a novel in which his imagination and his love for adventure found almost limitless scope. Cervantes knew his days were numbered. He suffered from a disease which was diagnosed as dropsy—some modern biographers think it was diabetes—and had to stay in bed for long periods. He could not stop writing until the very end. Early in April, 1616, his doctor recommended a trip to Esquivias, in the hope that country air would reinvigorate him. On April 19 he was back in Madrid he busied himself with the final pages of his *Persiles* and the Prologue to the novel. In the Prologue he describes an encounter with a student on his way back from his recent visit to Esquivias. The student is very pleased to meet, as he says, "the famous one, the merry author, the jubilation of the Muses." They ride along for a while and the conversation turns to Cervantes' health. The student diagnoses Cervantes' disease as "dropsy" and advises him to curb his drinking. He replies, "Many have told me . . . but I find it as difficult not to drink my fill as though I had been born for that purpose alone. My life is coming to an end, and by the tempo of my pulse beats, I judge that their career and mine will be over on Sunday at the latest." He goes on to describe the parting of the new friends and closes with a general farewell: "Farewell to the Graces, farewell to wit, farewell to cheerful friends, for I am dying in the desire to see you soon contented in the other life."[9] He died in Madrid on April 23, 1616, at peace with himself and with the world, having received the last sacraments, and was buried in the convent of the Trinitarian nuns. He died without bitterness or regrets since he had been fully conscious of his merit, indeed of his genius, and was aware that his literary creations would endure: a writer cannot hope for a greater source of consolation.

Objectively, Cervantes' life was not a success story. He was seldom in full control: he was too poor; for many years he lacked public recognition. Yet, as Angel del Río points out, "there is no reason to lament Cervantes' misfortunes nor the mediocrity of his daily life. He could thus, through an experience which is seldom obtained when the writer is successful and wealthy, know, observe and feel the beat of Spanish life in its greatness and its poverty, in its heroic fantasy and in the sad reality of an imminent decadence. He was to leave in his books the most faithful image of this life, reflected in multiple perspectives with bittersweet irony and penetrating humor."[1]

9. *Obras completas, ed. cit.*, p. 1529.

1. *Historia de la literatura española. Edición revisada* (New York, 1963), I. 288.

If Cervantes' biography teaches us anything, it is that he was at the same time *inside* and *outside* the mainstream of Spanish life. As an insider, he took part in the battle of Lepanto and wrote at least two successful books, *Don Quixote* and the *Exemplary Novels*. This is certainly much more than the level of achievement of most middle-class hidalgos of his time. As an outsider, he was always poor —almost to the point of being destitute—and not infrequently in jail; he lacked influential friends in a society where nothing could be done without them and without money; he was often unable to protect adequately the female members of his family; the influential critics and writers of his time did not recognize the quality of his work; his accomplishments as a soldier and as a loyal member of the Administration were ignored—while his every minor transgression was punished harshly. A complete outsider would have rebelled or subsided into depression and silence. A complete insider would have seen only the rosiest aspects of Spanish life. It was his fate, and our gain, that he saw both sides. Out of his twofold experience a complex picture of Spanish society was born. It was a picture that included irony and parody, idealism and criticism, realism and fantasy: it was so rich and complex that we can still see ourselves mirrored in it. This is what makes him a classic. He knew that criticism without love created a distorted image, love without criticism a bland, fuzzy image. Luckily for him—and for us—he was plentifully endowed with a critical eye and a compassionate heart.

A last footnote to his biography seems necessary, so much the more as most of his biographers (and this is the case even with his most recent ones, such as Richard Predmore) have chosen to ignore or neglect this point. It is a mere detail, almost meaningless to the modern reader, yet all-important to the inhabitant of Golden Age Spain: was Cervantes an "Old Christian"? In other words, are we sure (and was he sure) that he did not belong to a "New Christian" family, a *converso* family, in other words, a family in which some ancestors were converted Jews? A critical, ironic bent, plus an affinity for the ideas of Erasmus seem to point in the direction of a *converso* ancestry. The documentary proofs are lacking. Yet some of the best modern Hispanists, Américo Castro and Stephen Gilman among them, lean towards the idea that Cervantes came from a *converso* family. As Gilman states, "Salvador de Madariaga was first to give printed expression to a suspicion that those readers who had perceived Cervantes' constant mockery of pretensions to lineage (not only in the *Retablo de las maravillas* [*The Marvelous Pageant*], but also in the *Persiles* and the *Quixote*) had fleetingly entertained. . . . Since then Castro in his *Cervantes y los casticismos* (*Cervantes and the Caste System*), Madrid, 1966, has brought additional information to the fore. . . . The presence of no less than five physicians in Cervantes' immediate family will seem highly significant to those familiar with the social history of the time."[2] We may never know for certain. If these suspicions were to be confirmed, they would help to explain Cervantes' official neglect, his failure to achieve social status, his ironic vision. Be it as it may, he was a "marginal man," according to the sociologists' cliché, and his work bears witness to this fact. Of course, a "marginal man" usually becomes a humorist—when at all possible, if bitterness or depression do not interfere. This was his case. His merry vision transcended each personal crisis, each disappointment. His robust laughter and his ironic smile can still help us to achieve the same goals.

ANONYMOUS

The Ballad Farce

This anonymous playlet must have been written in the last years of the sixteenth century. It first appeared in a collection of Lope de Vega's works, *Tercera parte de las comedias de Lope de Vega* (Madrid, 1613), on which the free translation (by Joseph R. Jones) is given below.

The plot is similar to that of *Don Quixote*: a man goes mad from reading too many ballads, most of which deal with the exploits of Christian and Saracen knights, and he leaves home to become a knight-errant in imitation of his heroes, only to be brought back after an inglorious defeat at the hands of an irate shepherd. The author of the farce has very cleverly strung together pieces of, parodies of, or allusions to, thirty-one ballads. Since modern readers of the translation lose the humor that depends on a knowledge of the poems satirized, they can only appreciate the amusing situation. The playlet is important, however, in the study of Cervantes, because it shows that the theme of insanity induced by literature was not unique in *Don Quixote*; and many scholars believe that the farce provided Cervantes with the nuclear idea for his own book, which began as a short novel satirizing the romances of chivalry but which developed far beyond such a simple plan, once Cervantes became aware of possibilities only hinted at in the *entremés*.

In the seventeenth century, farces such as this were regularly presented between the acts of longer *comedias*.

In order to suggest the rhythm and antiquated language of the ballads, the translator has put Bartolo's speeches into pseudo-Tudor blank verse, indicating the divisions with a slash (/).

LIST OF CHARACTERS

PERO TANTO, *an old peasant, father of Teresa and Perico, husband of Mari Crespa*

MARI CRESPA, *wife of Pero Tanto*

TERESA, *a young peasant woman, wife of Bartolo*

PERICO, *younger brother of Teresa*

2. *The Spain of Fernando de Rojas. The Intellectual and Social Landscape of La Celestina* (Princeton, 1972) p. 20.

ANTÓN, *an old peasant, Bartolo's father*
BARTOLO, *a young peasant, husband of Teresa*
BANDURRIO, *Bartolo's stupid servant*
DOROTEA, *Bartolo's younger sister*
SIMOCHO, *a shepherd*
MARICA, *a shepherdess*

Enter MARI CRESPA, TERESA, PERICO, *and* PERO TANTO, *an old man, dressed as peasants.*

MARI CRESPA. Is it really true, Señor Pero Tanto?

PERO TANTO. I'm amazed that you should doubt my word.

MARI CRESPA. Don't be angry. I don't doubt you.

PERO TANTO. Nevertheless, I'm telling you that your son-in-law and friend wants to go off to the war and leave his wife and farm; he discussed it with me. He has started *pretending* to be a knight-errant from reading too many ballads, but I believe that before long he'll be a *real* madman. And even though I tried to persuade him to stay, he is so out of his senses that he is leaving Teresa.

PERICO. I'm sorry for my sister!

TERESA. Alas! Wretched wife that I am! Bartolo my husband wants to become a soldier. Mother, what kind of a man did you marry me to?

MARI CRESPA. Is it my fault?

PERICO. Alas! My brother-in-law is going away!

TERESA. Oh, my darling Bartolo! What will I do alone?

PERICO. And I, what will I do alone, without you?

MARI CRESPA. Oh, Bartolo!

PERICO. Here he comes, to say good-bye.

ALL. Alas!

Enter BARTOLO, *dressed as a peasant, and* BANDURRIO.

BARTOLO. Saddle me the gray pony—the one that belongs to my father Antón Llorente—and bring me the big cork pot-cover, the green overcoat, and the rusty cattle-prod, the helmet made from a gourd shell, and my Basque machete. Get me some thrush's feathers for my crest; they'll do for heron's plumes. And put on it the blue braid that my wife Teresa del Villar, who is here, gave me to wear. Now go, Bandurrio, and see that everything is ready.

BANDURRIO. I'm ready to go, because we soldiers have got to be diligent.

Exit BANDURRIO.

MARI CRESPA. What's this, Bartolo, my son? What's this you're doing to us? Married for four days, and you want to leave my daughter?

PERICO. My dear brother-in-law, don't go off to fight the English. My sister will be afraid to go to bed at night.

PERO TANTO. What do you say, Bartolo? Don't go! See how unhappy Teresa is, because you're leaving her when she is so young and all alone!

TERESA. He's got to stay here, now more than ever!

BARTOLO. My dearest Teresa, stop complaining and nagging! There are ways to stop barking dogs! Though my business may take long, my stay will be short: next St. Ciruelo's Day or the thirty-first of February. Remember the look in my eyes, which, when I am away from you, are on either side of my nose and below my eyebrows.

Enter BANDURRIO.

BANDURRIO. Let's go, sir.

BARTOLO. What did you say, Bandurrio?

BANDURRIO. I said, get ready. We still have three times twenty leagues to go if we're going to make sixty.

BARTOLO. Goodby, Teresa. Adieu, gentlemen. Goodby, Brother Perico; good-bye, Pero Tanto.

Exit BANDURRIO *and* BARTOLO.

TERESA. I wish I could die, so that I wouldn't have to suffer such humiliations!

PERO TANTO. Everybody knows that beauty is unlucky, as the proverb says.

PERICO. If that's true, my sister must be the prettiest girl in our village.

MARI CRESPA. The poor little thing! What bad luck! She barely got married yesterday and today she's a widow and all alone.

TERESA. I don't know why I don't drop dead, mother, when I see my sweetheart going off to war.

PERO TANTO. [*aside*] Poor Teresa, all she does is cry; she's asking her mother to listen to her troubles.

TERESA. Dear mother, who wouldn't cry, even if she had a heart of stone?

MARI CRESPA. For heaven's sake hush! We'll find a solution.

PERO TANTO. What solution?

MARI CRESPA. We'll go see Bartolo's father. When we tell him, he'll bring Bartolo back to the village tied up, if he doesn't come quietly.

TERESA. Mother has a very good idea. Let's go find him. You can stay at home, Perico.

PERICO. All right.

PERO TANTO. Let's go quickly. I'm sure he'll do it.

TERESA. If we don't find him, let me sit by the seashore and weep.

Exeunt omnes except PERICO.

PERICO. Who would believe that Bartolo is so crazy from reading ballads that he is going to become a soldier and ship out! [*Enter* DOROTEA.]

DOROTEA. Perico, my friend, sitting here by the door with your clean shirt and new cap! My brother Bartolo is going to England to kill Drake and capture the queen. He's going to bring me a little Protestant boy on a chain, and a Protestant girl for grandmother.

PERICO. Let's go up on the roof terrace. From there, we can see the scenery. If you come with me, I'll tell you a story about a Greek woman who kidnapped a blond girl.[1]

DOROTEA. I have some honey and lard.

1. The next few lines of dialogue are puzzling and probably full of double meanings which are no longer apparent.

PERICO. I have some nougat candy and some pine-nuts.

DOROTEA. We'll make something delicious out of all that!

PERICO. Let's go, Dorotea, and spend our siesta time there. We can play where nobody will see us. You can be the little girl and I'll be your teacher. I'll inspect your sampler and your needlework, and I'll do what teachers do to bad little girls who make mistakes in their needlework!

DOROTEA. I have a toy coach with four wheels for our dolls to ride in.

PERICO. I have a bag of limes and a mechanical toy that I bought at the fair. When I grow up, Miss Dorotea, I'm going to have a pony. I'll race it up and down the street, and you'll come to your window to look at me from behind the grille.

DOROTEA. You'll marry me, and there will be a wedding and a party. We'll sleep together in a silk bed.

PERICO. And we'll make a baby that will go to school.

Exeunt TERESA *and* PERICO.

Enter BANDURRIO [*who has lost his way*].

BANDURRIO. Bartolo and I were in such a hurry to get out of the village and get to the seaport that we got lost in this forest. He is following me. I can't find a path or a track or even a shepherd who can tell me where to find the road. I see a shepherd, who seems to be sad and depressed, resting his elbow on a boulder.

Exit BANDURRIO.

Enter MARICA *and* SIMOCHO.

SIMOCHO. Oh faithless shepherdess! Crueler than wolf traps, harder than tortoises—the shell, not the insides. You believe that people still think of you as some kind of Penelope, but everybody knows you don't love me. You took off your fancy blouse and the necklace I gave you and put on your apron—the one you wear when you're washing tripe. If you thought you could hide it, you were wrong! It's as plain as the nose on your face.

MARICA. Simocho, it's your fault. The other day when we were all together, you stepped on Menga's foot.

SIMOCHO. Stupid jealousy!

MARICA. Yes, jealousy!

SIMOCHO. Marica, if I offended you, I hope to God that all my mares die and that they never have another foal.

MARCIA. I hope your curses—and a lot worse—fall on you, Simocho. I hope crows peck out your eyes, like some dead jackass's—which is what you are. Let me go!

SIMOCHO. Wait, Marica!

MARICA. Let me go!

SIMOCHO. Don't be angry.

MARICA. I'll scream.

SIMOCHO. You can scream until the deaf hear you!

Enter BARTOLO, *dressed in ridiculous paper armor, riding a stick horse.*

BARTOLO. Now hear me, Tarfe: seek not/ nor address the beauteous Daraja!/ She is the soul of my senses;/ she liveth in my blood./ The best boon my sorrow can give/—if this my love be sorrow—/ is that I live in sorrow/ for her who is my joy./ To whom better can she surrender/ herself, this Moorish damsel?/ For six years have I served her ?/ (This said Almoradí,/ and Tarfe heeded him.)

SIMOCHO. My friend, if you're drunk, go sleep it off somewhere else. There are no Moors around here. We're a couple of county people who want to get married.

MARCIA. Don't count on that!

BARTOLO. Retract, Almoradí, /—for it is only right—/ your coward's words and deeds./ Leave deeds to men of courage!/Sayest thou that she is thine?/ Release her, craven Moor!

SIMOCHO. Make me!

BARTOLO. By heav'n above, this lance/ shall pierce thee through and through!

SIMOCHO. Ow! He got me in the buttocks!

MARICA. I hope the devil gets 'em.

Exit MARICA.

SIMOCHO. Why am I not getting even, with the same lance?

BARTOLO. Avaunt brave steed!

SIMOCHO. [*mimicking* BARTOLO] Dismount from off thy horse/ and pay for what thou'st done!

SIMOCHO *seizes the lance, beats* BARTOLO, *knocks him to the ground, and runs off.* [BARTOLO *is face down.*]

BARTOLO. Ah, wicked, cruel fortune/ Now scarcely can I move./ Thou wilt be glad to see me/ thus prostrate on the grass./ But mine is not the fault/ for such a great mishap./ It is my ass's fault,/ who would not charge when urged./ Oh Holy Mary, help me./ I cannot even rise./ Bad luck to any knight/ that rides without his spurs!/ Still, am I not Baldovinos?/ And is that not Carloto/ who like a traitor left me/ here among these thorns?

ANTÓN. [*offstage*] They went this way, as the footprints show.

PERO TANTO. [*offstage*] We'll find them, like good hunting dogs.

BARTOLO. Where are you, my beloved?/ Have pity on my ills./ You used to feel compassion/ for all my trifling wounds,/ and now, when they are mortal/ you show no care at all./ I do not blame you, madam,/ and I must cease to speak;/ my suffering is such/ that now I rave and wander.

TERESA. [*offstage*] Keep going, mother. I heard a voice.

ANTÓN. [*offstage*] Head for where you heard the voice.

BARTOLO. Oh my cousin, Montesinos,/ Oh Don Merián, the prince,/ Oh good Count Oliveros/ Oh Durandarte brave!/ Poor mother, woe to thee!/ May God console thee now,/ for broken is the mirror/ whereon thou once didst look.

Enter PERO TANTO, ANTÓN, MARI CRESPA, *and* TERESA.

PERO TANTO. I'm cutting the branches in order to find the way.

ANTÓN. Look in every direction to see what it can be.

MARI CRESPA. I see a knight at the foot of a tall grove.

TERESA. With some armor on, but without a sword or dagger.

ANTÓN. Let's go see who it is.

TANTO. By St. John, it's your son!

BARTOLO. Oh, noble Count of Mantua,/ my uncle and blood-relation!

ANTÓN. What's wrong with you, son? Do you want to tell me?

BARTOLO. (This man must be my squire.)

TERESA. He tried to raise his head up.

BARTOLO. What are you saying, my friend?/ Have you brought me a clerk to shrive me?/ For my soul is now departing,/ and I would leave this life./ My body grieves me ought;/ my soul's my only care.

PERO TANTO. [*to* TERESA] Did his father understand him?

ANTÓN. He took me for somebody else. [*to* BARTOLO] I'm not your servant; I never worked for you. I'm your father, Bartolo. I've come to get you.

TERESA. Are you hurt?

MARI CRESPA. Tell the truth, my son.

BARTOLO. With two and twenty blows,/ the least of which was mortal,/ the villains left me here.

ANTÓN. Let's pick him up and take him to the village.

PERO TANTO. Good idea.

BARTOLO. Sir knight, in troth I tell thee,/ I am the fleshly son/ of the noble king of Lacia./ Queen Armelina is my dam./ And the beauteous Sevilla/ is my betrothèd spouse.

TERESA. What does he mean, "spouse" and "Armelina"?

PERO TANTO. He's reciting the ballad about the Count of Mantua.

BARTOLO. He was my blood relation,/ the brother of my sire,/ in very truth.

Enter BANDURRIO.

BANDURRIO. Where can Bartolo be?

ANTÓN. Over here, Bandurrio! Come here!

BARTOLO. And while they thus debated,/ his faithful squire appeared./ Hail, good Bandurrio!

PERO TANTO. Let's get this over with.

ANTÓN. Catch hold there, Bandurrio, and start walking.

MARI CRESPA. You go on ahead, daughter.

TERESA. I'll fly back to the village. [*Exit.*]

ANTÓN. What is all this, my son? Stop this crazy talk.

PERO TANTO. Damn those ballads! They're what made you this way. Bartolo, aren't you ashamed to pretend that you're Baldovinos.

BARTOLO. Me? Baldovinos? Nay!/For thou art Bencerraje,/ and I am Baza's warden.

PERO TANTO. A new mania!

ANTÓN. The poor boy, in such a state!

BARTOLO. Tell me, Bencerraje,/ what dost thou think of Zaida?/ She is an easy wench,/ and faithless, to my sorrow./ I've writ to her this missive./ Keep still and hear its words:/ "If you wore manly armor/ instead of silk and satin,/ and if you fought in battles/ instead of making lace . . ."

ANTÓN. He's stark raving mad.

PERO TANTO. That's clear from the way he talks.

BARTOLO. "If thou art tender-hearted,/ Zaide, as well as proud/and haughty . . ."

PERO TANTO. Another crazy notion! A different tune!

BARTOLO. [*delirious*] Upon another occasion,/ Tarfe sees that Reduán/ is enamored of Daraja . . ./ And from the hills of Jaca,/ Elicio, a simple shepherd,/ inside his wretched hut,/ with countenance most scornful,/ while leaning on his crook . . ./ Brabonel of Zaragoza,/ charging into the battle,/ wounded in many places,/ his bloody armor torn . . ./ Venus, evening star,/ rising from the Spanish sea, . . ./ And then the unhappy woman,/ in great dismay appeared,/ mounted on a roan . . ./ Begone, begone! Away, away!

ANTÓN. Hold him tight, Bandurrio.

PERO TANTO. Hold him so he won't get away. That's it; slowly; we're almost home.

MARI CRESPA. The poor thing. I'm already weeping for him as if he were dead.

BANDURRIO. What a shame!

BARTOLO. They all think I am dead;/ but tell me, mountain maid,/ does Azarque, fierce and furious,/ bare his strong right arm?

MARI CRESPA. Who is Azarque, my boy?

BARTOLO. Azarque lives in Ocaña.

Enter TERESA.

TERESA. Welcome everybody. The bed is ready for him.

BANDURRIO. Then let's put him to bed. Madmen calm down when they've had some sleep.

PERO TANTO *and* BANDURRIO *carry him off.*

TERESA. Mother! Guess what! Periquillo and that girl are up on the roof terrace making . . .

MARI CRESPA. What's going on?

TERESA. Dorotea and Periquillo! He's undressed and she's in her petticoat.

ANTÓN. My daughter?

TERESA. Yes, father-in-law. [*Exit.*]

Enter PERO TANTO *with* PERICO *and* DOROTEA.

TANTO. What a family! [*to* ANTÓN] My friend, this young man and this fine young lady are going to disgrace us all if we don't marry them as soon as possible.

ANTÓN. It would be better to whip them!

PERO TANTO. It would be better to have a wedding, if they love each other like Abindarráez and Fátima.

MARI CRESPA. Let them get engaged!

PERO TANTO. And let the fathers shake hands on it. Bandurrio, find some musicians to enliven the wedding festivities.

ANTÓN. Let's do it your way!

PERICO. Will you marry me?

DOROTEA. Yes!

ANTÓN. I pledge my word that they may get married.

MARI CRESPA. And I accept your word with pleasure. How's the patient?

Enter TERESA.

TERESA. Snoring like a pig.

ANTÓN. If he sleeps, he will undoubtedly recover his senses.

Enter BANDURRIO *and the musicians.*

BANDURRIO. The musicians have arrived. God keep you, honest people! Sing something. And you, little Teresa, dance!

The musicians sing the following verses, and TERESA *dances.*

MUSICIANS. Gentle breeze, I need your help; I am becalmed on the sea of forgotten love.

As they finish singing, BARTOLO *appears at a window, in his nightshirt.*

BARTOLO. Troy's engulfed in flames,/ her towers and her merlons;/ for the fires of love at times/ can burn the very stones.

ALL. Fire, fire, fire, fire!

Exeunt omnes.

BARTOLO. 'Fire,' they cry; 'Troy's burning!'/ And Paris says, 'May Helen/ burn with the fire of love.'

THE END.

GARCI RODRÍGUEZ DE MONTALVO

From Amadis of Gaul

Two important Iberian romances of chivalry appeared in English in the early nineteenth century through the efforts of Robert Southey (1774–1843), who translated *Amadís* and revised a sixteenth-century version of *Palmerin of England* (see below). Southey, who was Coleridge's brother-in-law and a close friend of Walter Scott, became poet laureate in 1813. He deserves to be remembered also as an early Hispanist and historian of Portugal.

There is an excellent new translation of *Amadís* by E. B. Place (Lexington: University of Kentucky Press, 1974). But the antiquated language, spelling, and punctuation of these older translations is analogous to the quaint Spanish of the romances which Don Quixote read and tried to imitate. The selection reprinted here is from the 1872 edition (London: John Russell Smith) of Southey's version. It chronicles the meeting of Amadis's royal parents, his ill-starred birth, exposure, adoption, precocious childhood and knighting, love for Oriana, early achievements, and penance on Peña Pobre ("Wretched Rock"). It is useful to re-read the Canon of Toledo's remarks, Part I, Ch. XLVII, in connection with these pages from *Amadís*, and to recall Don Quixote's experience with Maritornes in Part I, Ch. XVI, his penance beginning in Part I, Ch. XXV, and his adventure with the lion in Part II, Ch. XVII.

Not many years after the passion of our Redeemer, there was a Christian king in the lesser Britain, by name Garinter, who, being in the law of truth, was of much devotion and good ways. This king had two daughters by a noble lady his wife. The eldest was married to Languines King of Scotland; she was called the Lady of the Garland, because her husband taking great pleasure to behold her beautiful tresses, would have them covered only with a chaplet of flowers. Agrayes and Mabilia were their children, a knight and damsel of whom in this history much mention is made. Elisena the other daughter was far more beautiful, and although she had been demanded in marriage by many great princes, yet she would wed with none, but for her solitary and holy life was commonly called the Lost Devotee, because it was considered that for one of such rank, gifted with such beauty and sought in marriage by so many chiefs, this way of life was not fitting.

King Garinter, who was somewhat stricken in years, took delight in hunting. It happened one day, that having gone from his town of Alima to the chace, and being separated from his people, as he went along the forest saying his prayers, he saw to the left a brave battle of one knight against two. Soon had he knowledge of the twain, in that they were his own vassals, who being proud men and of powerful lineage had often by their evil customs offended him. Who the third was he knew not, but not relying so much in the worth of the one, as he feared the two, he drew aside and waited the event, which sorted to such effect, as by the hand of that one the others were both slain. This done the stranger came towards the king, and seeing him alone, said, Gentle sir, what country is this wherein knights errant are thus assailed? The king replied, Marvel not at this, knight, for our country yields as others do, both good and bad: as for these men, they have often offended, even against their lord and king, who could do no justice upon them, because of their kindred, and also because they harboured in this covered mountain. This king you speak of, replied the stranger, I come to seek him from a far land, and bring him tidings from a dear friend. If you know where he may be found, I pray you tell me. The king answered, Befal what may, I shall not fail to speak what is true. I am the king. The knight then loosing his shield and helmet gave them to his squire, and went to embrace Garinter, saying that he was King Perion of Gaul who had long desired to know him. Greatly were these kings contented that their meeting was in such a manner, and conferring together they took their way through the wood towards the city, when suddenly a hart ran before them which had escaped the toils. They followed at full speed, thinking to kill it, but a lion springing from a thicket before them, seized the hart, and having torn it open with his mighty claws, stood fiercely looking at the kings. Fierce as you are, said King Perion, you shall leave us part of the game! and he took his arms and alighted from his horse, who being affrighted at the wild beast would not go near him, and placing his shield before him went towards the lion sword in hand. The lion left his prey and came against him, they closed, and Perion at the moment when he was under the beast and in most danger, thrust his sword into his belly. When Garinter saw him fall, he said within himself, Not without cause is that knight famed to be the best in the world. Meanwhile their train came up, and then was their prey and venison laid on two horses and carried to the city.

The queen being advised of her guest, they found the palace richly adorned, and the tables covered. At the highest the kings seated themselves: at the other sate the queen with Elisena her daughter, and there were they served, as in the house of such a man beseemed. Then being in that solace, as that princess was so beautiful and King Perion on his part equal, in that hour and point they so regarded each other, that her great modesty and holy life could not now avail, but that she was taken with great and incurable love; and the king in like manner, though till then his heart had been free, so that during the meal both the one and the other appeared absent in thought. When the tables were removed, the queen would depart to her chamber; Elisena rising dropt a ring from her lap, which she had taken off when she washed her hands, and in her confusion of mind forgotten. She stooped for it and Perion who was near her stooped down also, so that their hands met, and he taking her hand prest it. She coloured deeply and thanked the king for his service. Ah, lady, said he, it shall not be the last, for all my life shall be spent in your service.

She followed her mother, but so disturbed that her sight was dizzy, and now not able to endure her feelings, she went and disovered them to the damsel Darioleta in whom she confided, and with tears from her eyes and from her heart, besought her to find out if King Perion loved any other woman. Darioleta surprized at this alteration, pitied and comforted her mistress, and went to King Perion's chamber. She found his squire at the door with the King's garments, which he was about to give him. Friend, said she, go you about your other affairs, for I must wait upon your master. The squire, thinking it was the custom of the country, gave her the garments and went away. She then entered the chamber where the king was in bed. He, who had seen her converse with Elisena confidently, now hoped that she might bring some remedy to his passion, and said to her all in trembling, Fair friend, what demand ye? I bring you wherewith to cloathe yourself, she replied. That should be for my heart, said Perion, which is now stript and naked of all my joy. As how? said the damsel. Thus, quoth he, coming into this land with entire liberty, and apprehending nothing but the chance of arms, here in this house I have been wounded by a mortal wound, for which if you, fair damsel, can procure me remedy, you shall be well recompensed. He then charged her not to discover him but where it was requisite, and told her his love for Elisena. Then said Darioleta, My lord, promise me on the faith of a king and a knight, that you will take to wife my Lady Elisena, when time shall serve, and right soon will I bring ye, where not only your heart shall be satisfied, but hers also, who, it may be, is in as much or more thought and dolour than you, with the same wound. But without this promise you shall never win her. The king whose will was already disposed by God that that which ensued might come to pass, took his sword which was by him, and laying his right hand upon the cross of its hilt, pronounced these words: I swear by this cross, and this sword wherewith I received the order of knighthood, to perform whatever you shall require for the Lady Elisena. Be you then of good cheer, said she, for I also will effect my promise.

Darioleta returned to the Princess and told her how she had sped. You know, said she, that in the chamber where King Perion lodgeth there is a door opening to the garden, whence your father used to go out, and which at this present is covered with the hangings; but I have the key thereof, and we can go in at night, when all in the palace are at rest. When Elisena heard this she was highly contented, but recollecting herself, she replied, How shall this be brought to pass, seeing that my father will lodge in the chamber with King Perion? Leave that to me said the damsel, and with that they parted.

When it was night Darioleta drew aside the squire of Perion, and asked him if he was of gentle birth. Aye, said he, the son of a knight! but why ask ye? For the desire I have, quoth she, to know one thing, which I beseech you by the faith you owe to God and to the king your master, not to hide from me. Who is the lady whom your master loveth best? My master, replied the squire, loves all in general, and none as you mean. While they thus talked Garinter came nigh, who seeing Darioleta in conference with Perion's squire, called her and asked what he had to say to her. In sooth my lord, quoth she, he tells me that his master is wont to be alone, and certainly I think he will feel himself embarrassed by your company. Garinter hearing that went to King Perion and said, My lord, I have many affairs to settle, and must rise at the hour of matins, and that you may not be disturbed, you had better be alone in your chamber. King Perion replied, Do as shall seem best to your liking. Then Garinter understood that Darioleta had told him rightly of his guest's inclination, and ordered his bed to be removed from Perion's apartment. These tidings Darioleta carried to her mistress, and they waited the hour when all should retire to sleep.

At night when all was husht, Darioleta rose, and threw a mantle over her mistress, and they went into the garden. When Elisena came to the chamber door her whole body trembled, and her voice that she could not speak. King Perion had fallen asleep; he dreamt that some one, he knew not who, entered his chamber by a secret door, who thrusting a hand between his ribs, took out his heart and threw it into the river. He asked why that cruelty was committed, and was answered, It is nothing! There is another heart left there which I must take from you, though against my will. Then the king suddenly awoke in great fear, and blessed himself. At this moment the two damsels had opened the door, and were entering; he heard them, and being full of his dream suspected treason, when he saw a door open behind the hangings, of which he had not known, and leaping from the bed he caught up his sword and shield. What is this? cried Darioleta. The king then knew her, and saw Elisena his beloved; he dropt his shield and sword, and throwing a mantle about him which was ready by the bed, he went and embraced her whom he loved. Darioleta then took up the sword in token of his promise and oath, and went into the garden, and Perion remained alone with Elisena in whom as he beheld her by the light of the three torches, he thought all the beauty of the world was centered.

When it was time that they should part, Darioleta returned to the chamber. I know, lady, said she, that heretofore you have been better pleased with me than you are now; but we must go, for time calleth us. Elisena rose. I beseech you, said Perion, do not forget the place! And she departed with the damsel. He remained in his room, and recollecting his dream, which still affrighted him, a wish to know its signification made him desirous to return to his own country, where were many wise men skilful in the solution of such things.

Ten days King Perion sojourned at Alima, and every night his beloved mistress visited him. Then it was necessary that he should depart, despite of his own inclination, and the tears of Elisena. He took leave of Garinter and the queen, and having armed himself, when he looked for his sword to gird it on, he missed it; though the loss grieved him, for it was a tried and goodly weapon, he durst not enquire for it, but, making his squire procure him another, he departed straight for his own kingdom. Albeit, before his departure, Darioleta came and told him of the great affliction and loneliness in which his lady was left. I commend her to you my friend, said he, as mine own proper heart. Then taking from his finger a ring of two which he wore, each resembling the other, he bade her carry it to his love.

So Elisena remained, leading a solitary life, and in great grief. Darioleta comforted her the best she could, and the time past on, till she felt herself great with child, and lost the appetite for food and the pleasure of sleep, and the fresh colour of her countenance. Then was her sorrow and carefulness greater, and not without cause, for in that time was there a law, that any woman, of what quality or estate soever, offending in such sort, could not excuse herself from death. This so cruel and abominable a custom endured, till the coming of the good King Arthur, who was the best king that ever there reigned, and he revoked it at the time when he slew Floyon in battle, before the gates of Paris. And albeit because of the words which Perion swore upon his sword, she was without fault before God, yet was she not before the world, for they had been so secret. To let him know her condition, was what she could not think, for he was young and proud of heart, and took no delight elsewhere than where renown was to be gained, and so was for ever going an errant knight from one place to another. So she found no remedy for her life; yet did not the loss of life afflict her so much as that of her dear and beloved lord. But God, by whose permission all this had come to pass for his holy service, gave such discretion to Darioleta, that she remedied all.

In the palace of King Garinter there was an arched chamber separated from the rest, which overlooked the river; it had a little iron door through which the damsels sometime were wont to go out by the water side, but now none inhabited the apartment. This chamber by Darioleta's advice, did Elisena request of her father, as suiting her disposition and solitary life, where she might perform her prayers undisturbed, with no companion but Darioleta, who had always served and accompanied her. This request she lightly obtained, and hereupon was the key of the iron door given to Darioleta, to open when it pleased the princess to recreate herself by the river. Here was Elisena somewhat comforted, to find herself in a place so convenient for her purpose, and she required council of her damsel what should be done with the fruit that she travailed withal? What? replied Darioleta, it must suffer to save you. Holy Mary, then said Elisena, shall I consent to destroy the child of him whom I love best in the world? Leave alone those thoughts, the damsel answered, if they kill you they will not spare the infant: it were great folly to destroy yourself and your lover, who could not live after you, for the sake of saving the child, who, if you die, must die also.

As this damsel was of quick mind herself, and now guided by the grace of God, she determined to have the remedy ready before the need; and it was in this guise: she took four boards and with them made an ark large enough to contain a new born child and its garments, and long enough for the sword; she fastened them together with bitumen, in such sort as the water should have no place to enter. She hid all this under her bed till she had compleated it; and it was even and close as if a master had made it. Then she showed it to Elisena and asked for what she thought it was designed? She answered, I know not. You shall know, said the damsel, when need is. Elisena replied, But little do I care to know what is done or what is said, for I am near to lose all my joy and comfort. Then had Darioleta great grief, and she went apart, not bearing to see her mistress weep.

It was not long before her travail came, and in those new and strange pains, in bitterness of heart, and not daring to cry out or groan, it pleased the Lord that she was safely delivered of a son. The damsel took him in her arms, and saw that the boy was a fair boy had he not been borne to hard fortune, but she delayed not to execute what of necessity had been resolved. She wrapt him in rich garments, and laying him by his mother, brought the ark. Elisena cried, What will you do? Place him here, she answered, and launch him down the stream, and belike he may escape. Then the mother took him in her arms, and wept bitterly over him. But Darioleta took ink and parchment, and wrote upon it, This is Amadis, son of a king. It was the name of her saint, and of great reverence in that country. She covered the parchment with wax, and hung it by a string round the neck of the babe, and Elisena fastened upon the string the ring which King Perion had given her at his departure. Darioleta then placed the infant in the ark and laid his father's sword beside him; this done, she covered the ark, which was securely joined and calked, and, opening the iron door, took it in her arms, and placed it in the river, commending it to God.

The tide ran strong, and soon carried the ark into the sea, which was not more than a half-league distant. Now the dawn appeared, and it pleased God that there was a knight of Scotland sailing on that sea, returning from the lesser Britain to his country, with his wife, who had newly been delivered of a son called Gandalin. The morning was both calm and clear, whereby the knight Gandales saw the ark floating among the waves, and he ordered the mariners to put out a boat and take it up. They speedily overtook it, and Gandales opened the cover, and beholding the babe within, he cried, This is from no mean place! And this he said because of the rich garments, and the ring and the good sword, and he cursed the mother who had for fear abandoned so fair a child. He carefully laid aside all the things that were contained in the ark, and desired his wife to breed up the infant, and she ordered the nurse of her own child Gandalin to suckle him. So they went their way through the sea with a favourable time, and took port in a town in Scotland called Antalia, and from thence departing they came to his castle, which was one of the good ones of the land; there he had the child brought up like his own son, and such he was believed to be, because the mariners who took up the ark, had sailed away to other parts.

* * *

He was called the Child of the Sea, for so they had named him, and with much care was he brought up by that good knight and his wife, and he grew and became so fair, that all who saw him marvailed. One day Gandales rode forth, for he was a right good knight and strong, and always accompanied King Languines at such time as they followed arms, and though the king had ceased to follow them, yet Gandales ceased not. He, as he rode along, met a damsel, that thus spake to him: Ah, Gandales if many great personages knew what I know, they would cut off thy head! Wherefore? quoth he. She replied, because thou nourishest their death.

* * *

Then tell me, said he, the meaning of what you said, that I nourished the death of many great personages. She made him swear that none should know it from him till she permitted, and then said, I tell thee, he whom thou foundest in the sea shall be the flower of knighthood in his time; he shall cause the strongest to stoop, he shall enterprize and finish with honour that wherein others have failed, and such deeds shall he do as none would think could be begun nor ended by body of man. He shall humble the proud, and cruel of heart shall he be against those who deserve it, and he shall be the knight in the world who most loyally maintains his love, and he shall love one answerable to his high prowess. And I tell you that on both sides he is of kingly parentage. Now go thy way, and believe that all this shall come to pass, and if thou discoverest it, there shall happen to thee therefore more evil than good. Ah, lady! said Gandales, tell me for God's sake where I can find you to talk with you upon this child's affairs! She answered, That shalt thou never know. Tell me then your name I beseech you by the faith you owe to the thing in the world that you love best. Thou conjurest me so that I will tell. My name is Urganda the Unknown; mark me well, and know me again if you can! And he who first saw her a damsel in her spring time, as one of eighteen years, now beheld her so old and overspent, that he marvailed how she could sit upon her horse, and he crost himself. She took a perfume box from her bosom and touching it became as she was before. Now, said she, think you to find me hereafter though you should seek me? Weary not yourself for that, for though all living creatures go about it, if I list, they should lose their labour. As God shall save me, I believe it, lady! but I pray you remember the child who is forsaken of all but myself. Doubt not that, said Urganda, I love him more than thou canst think, for I shall soon receive aid from him twice, which none else could give me, and he shall receive two guerdons to his joy. Now God be with thee! Thou shalt see me sooner than thou expectest.

* * *

When he[1] was seven years old, King Languines and his queen and household, passing through his kingdom from one town to

1. **Amadis.**

another, came to the castle of Gandales, where they were well feasted; but the Child of the Sea, and Gandalin and the other children were removed to the back court that they might not be seen. It fortuned that the queen was lodged in one of the highest apartments of the castle, and looking from her window she saw the children at play with their bows, and among them remarked the Child of the Sea for his shapeliness and beauty, and he was better clad than his companions, of whom he looked like the lord. The queen called to her ladies and damsels, Come and see the fairest creature that ever was seen! While they were looking at him, the child, who was thirsty, laid down his bow and arrows, and went to a water-pipe to drink. A boy bigger than the rest took up his bow to shoot with it; this Gandalin would not suffer; the other struck him angrily, and Gandalin cried out, Help me, Child of the Sea! He hearing this ran to him, and snatched the bow and crying, In an ill minute did you strike my brother, struck him on the head with all his force. They fought awhile till the other was fain to run away, and meeting their tutor, who asked what was the matter, replied, that the Child of the Sea had beat him. The tutor went towards him with the strap in his hand. How is this, Child of the Sea, said he, that you dare beat the boys? I shall punish you! But the child fell upon his knees. I had rather you would strike me, said he, than that any one before me should dare to beat my brother; and the tears came in his eyes. The tutor was moved, and told him to do so no more. All this the queen saw and she wondered why they called him the Child of the Sea.

At this time the king and Gandales entered, and the queen asked their host if that fair child was his? He answered, Yes. Why, then, said she, is he called the Child of the Sea?—Because he was born on the sea, when I returned from Brittany. Truly he is but little like you, said the queen; and this she said because the child was beautiful to a wonder, and Gandales was more good than handsome. The king, who was looking at him likewise, bade Gandales call him, For I will take him with me, said he, and have him brought up. So let it be, said Gandales, but he is not yet of an age that he should leave his mother. Then he went and brought him, and said, Child of the Sea, will you go with the king my master? Wherever you bid me, he replied, and my brother shall go with me. And I, quoth Gandalin, will not stay without him. Gandales then looked at the king. I believe, sire, you must take them both. I am the better pleased, answered the king, and calling Agrayes, he said, My son I would have you love these boys as well as I love their father.

When Gandales saw that the Child of the Sea was placed in the hands of another, the tears came into his eyes, and he said within himself, Fair son, thou art a little one to begin to go into adventure and danger! and now I see thee in the service of those who may one day serve thee. God guard thee, and fulfil what the wise Urganda foretold, and let me live to see the great wonders which in arms are promised thee. When the king saw that his eyes were full, he said, I did not think thou hadst been so foolish. Nor am I, answered Gandales, but if it please you, do you and the queen hear me. The rest then withdrew, and he told them how he had found the child; and he would have told what he knew from Urganda, but for his promise. And now, said he, deal ye with the child as ye ought, for as God shall save me by the way in which he came to me, I believe he is of great lineage. Then the queen said, he should be her's so long as he was of an age to obey women; and the next morning they departed, taking the children with them. Now I tell you that the queen brought up the Child of the Sea as carefully as if he had been her own son; and the trouble she took with him was not in vain, for such was his talent and so noble his nature, that better and more quickly than any besides he learnt every thing. And he was so fond of the chace, that if they would have let him, he would have been always shooting with the bow, or training the dogs. And the queen loved him so that she would scarce suffer him to be out of her sight.

Now King Perion abode in his kingdom. After some time, he being in his palace, there came a damsel and gave him a letter from Elisena his love, whereby she gave him to know that her father was dead, and she was unprotected, and for this cause he should pity her, for the queen of Scotland her sister was coming with her husband to take possession of the land. King Perion though he was sorrowful for Garinter's death, yet rejoiced to think that he should go for his mistress whom he never ceased to love; and he said to the damsel, Return and tell your lady that without delaying a single day, I shall speedily be with her. And the damsel returned joyfully. The king then collecting a suitable retinue, set forth, and journied till he came to the lesser Britain, where he found news that Languines was in mastery of all the land, except those towns which her father had left to Elisena. So hearing that she was at a town called Arcarte he went there, and if he was well received need not be said, and she also by him who so dearly loved her. The king told her to call together all her friends and kindred, for he would take her to wife, the which Elisena did with great joy, for in that consisted the end of all her wishes. Now when King Languines knew the coming of King Perion, and how he would marry Elisena, he summoned all the noblemen of the land, and went with them to meet him, and when the marriage and the feasts were concluded, the kings agreed to return into their own dominions.

Perion returning with Elisena his wife, came to a river side where he would rest that night, and while the tents were erecting, he rode alone along the banks, thinking how he might learn something from Elisena about the child of whom Ungan the Picard[2] had told

2. A wise "clerk" who had interpreted the king's dream.

him. So long went he on in his mood till he came to a hermitage, and fastening his horse to a tree, he went in to say his prayers. There was an old man within in the habit of his order, who asked him, Knight is it true that King Perion has married the daughter of our king? Yea verily, answered the king. Praised be God! said the good hermit, for I know certainly that she loved him with all her heart.—How know you that? By her own mouth, said he. The king then thinking to hear of him the thing he most desired to know, made himself known, and besought the hermit to tell him all he had heard from her. Truly, sir, answered the good man, therein should I greatly fault, and you would hold me for a heretic if I should divulge what was said in confession: suffice what I tell you, that she loves you with true and loyal love. But I would have you know what a damsel, who seemed very wise, said to me at the time when you came first into this country, and I could not understand her: that from the Lesser Britain should come two dragons, who should hold their sway in Gaul, and their hearts in Great Britain; and from hence they should go to devour the beasts of other countries, and against some they should be so fierce and furious, and against others so gracious and mild, as if they had neither talons nor hearts. The king wondered at this, which he could not understand, but there came a time when he knew the prophecy was true. So he returned to his tents.

When they were in bed together, he told the queen what had been interpreted of his dream, and asked her if she had brought forth a son. The queen hearing him, had so great shame that she wished herself dead, and she altogether denied it, so that at this time the king could not learn what he desired. They continued their journey till they arrived in Gaul, and those of the land were well pleased with their queen, who was a most noble lady, and the king had by her a son and a daughter, whom he called Galaor and Melicia.

* * *

King Lisuarte set sail with a great fleet, and on their way they put into Scotland, where he was honourably received by King Languines. Brisena his wife was with him, and their daughter Oriana, born in Denmark, and then about ten years old, the fairest creature that ever was seen, wherefore she was called the one without a peer. And because she suffered much at sea it was determined to leave her there. Right gladly did King Languines accept this charge, and his queen said, Believe me, I will take care of her like her own mother. So Lisuarte proceeded; and, when he arrived at Great Britain, he found those who disturbed him,[3] as is common in such cases, and for this cause he did not send for his daughter. And

3. I.e., rebels.

with great trouble that he took he was king at last, and he was the best king that had yet been, nor was there ever one who better maintained chivalry till King Arthur reigned, who passed in goodness all kings that were before him.

The Child of the Sea was now twelve years old, but in stature and size he seemed fifteen, and he served the queen; but now that Oriana was there, the queen gave her the Child of the Sea that he should serve her, and Oriana said that *it pleased her*, and that word which she said the child kept in his heart, so that he never lost it from his memory, and in all his life he was never weary of serving her, and his heart was surrendered to her, and this love lasted as long as they lasted, for as well as he loved her did she also love him. But the Child of the Sea, who knew nothing of her love, thought himself presumptuous to have placed his thoughts on her, and dared not to speak to her; and she who loved him in her heart was careful not to speak more with him than with another; but their eyes delighted to reveal to the heart what was the thing on earth that they loved best. And now the time came that he thought he could take arms if he were knighted, and this he greatly desired, thinking that he would do such things, that, if he lived, his mistress should esteem him. With this desire he went to the king, who was at that time in the garden, and fell upon his knees before him, and said, Sire, if it please you, it is time for me to receive knighthood. How, Child of the Sea! said Languines, are you strong enough to maintain knighthood? It is easy to receive, but difficult to maintain; and he who would keep it well, so many and so difficult are the things he must achieve, that his heart will often be troubled; and if, through fear, he forsakes what he ought to do, better is death to him than life with shame. Not for this, replied he, will I fail to be a knight: my heart would not require it, if it were not in my will to accomplish what you say. And since you have bred me up, compleat what you ought to do in this; if not, I will seek some other who will do it. The king, who feared lest he should do this, replied, Child of the Sea, I know when this is fitting better than you can know, and I promise you to do it, and your arms shall be got ready; but, to whom did you think to go?—To King Perion, who they say is a good knight, and has married the sister of your queen. I would tell him how I was brought up by her, and then he would willingly fulfil my desire. Now, said the king, be satisfied, it shall be honourably done.

* * *

When the Child of the Sea heard this, he called Gandalin, and said to him, My brother, take all my arms secretly to the queen's chapel, for this night I think to be knighted, and, because it behoves me to depart right soon, I would know if you wish to bear me company? Believe me, quoth Gandalin, never with my will shall I depart from ye. The tears came in the eyes of the Child at this, and he kissed him in the face, and said, Do now what I told you. Gandalin laid the arms in the chapel, while the queen was at supper; and, when the cloths were removed, the Child of the Sea went there, and armed himself all, save his head and his hands, and made his prayer the altar, beseeching God to grant him success in arms, and in the love which he bore his lady.

When the queen had retired, Oriana and Mabilia went with the other damsels to accompany him, and Mabilia sent for Perion as he was departing; and, when he came, she besought him to do what Oriana the daughter of King Lisuarte should request. Willingly, said King Perion, for her father's sake. Then Oriana came before him; and when he saw her, how fair she was, he thought there could not be found her equal in the world. She begged a boon, and it was granted. Then, said she, make this my Gentleman knight; and she showed him to Perion, kneeling before the altar. The king saw him how fair he was, and approaching him, said, Would you receive the order of knighthood?—I would.—In the name of God. then! and may He order it that it be well bestowed on you, and that you may grow in honour as you have in person. Then, putting on the right spur, he said, Now are you a knight, and may receive the sword. The king took the sword, and gave it to him, and the child girded it on. Then said Perion, According to your manner and appearance, I would have performed this ceremony with more honours, and I trust in God that your fame will prove that so it ought to have been done. Mabilia and Oriana then joyfully kissed the king's hands, and he, commending the Child of the Sea to God, went his way.

But he who was now a knight, took leave of the damsels who had watched with him, and Oriana, whose heart was bursting though she dissembled. He found Gandalin at the palace-door holding his lance and his shield, and his horse; and he mounted and went his way, unseen of any, for it was yet night.

* * *

They had not ridden far when they saw a damsel coming on her palfrey, and she had in hand a lance with its belt, and presently another damsel, who came by a different path, joined her, and they both came on communing together. When they reached him, she with the weapon said, Take this lance sir, and I tell you that within three days it will stand ye in good stead, as therewith ye shall deliver from death the house whence ye are descended. He, wondering at her words, replied, How damsel, can a house live or die? She answered, So it will be; and this lance I give you for some services which from you I expect; the first whereof shall be when you shall do an honour to one of your friends, whereby he shall be put into the worst danger that any knight hath been these ten years space. Damsel, said he, such honour, if God please, I will not do any friend. She answered, So it will be,—and spurred her palfrey, and departed. Now this was Urganda the Unknown.

* * *

When it was day, a knight looked from a window and asked Amadis, Art thou he who hast slain my jaylor and my servants?[4] Art thou he, answered Amadis, who so treacherously murderest knights and imprisonest dames and damsels? Thou art the most disloyal and cruellest knight in the world! As yet you know not all my cruelty, Arcalaus replied, and left the window; and soon they saw him enter the court well armed, upon a lusty courser. Now this was one of the largest knights in the world who were not giants, and Amadis looked at him with admiration, thinking that he must needs be of great strength. Why lookest thou at me so earnestly? quoth the Castellan.—Because thou wouldst be so good a knight were it not for thy foul disloyalty. I come in good time, quoth Arcalaus, to be preached at by one like thee! And with that he laid lance in rest, and ran the charge. The spears brake; horses and bodies met, and both horses were driven to the ground. Quickly the knights arose, and began a fierce combat which lasted long; at length the Castellan drew back, Knight, said he, thou art in the chance of death, and I know not who thou art: tell me that I may know, for I think rather to slay than take thee. My death, Amadis replied, is in the will of God, whom I fear; and thine is in the will of the devil, who is weary of helping thee, and will now let thy soul and body perish together. You ask my name: I am Amadis of Gaul, the knight of Queen Brisena. Then renewed they their combat with fresh fury till about the hour of tierce;[5] then Arcalaus waxed faint, and Amadis smote him down; and, as he rose, staggered him with another blow on the helmet, so that seeing himself near to die, he fled into the palace, and Amadis followed. But he running into a little chamber, at the door whereof stood a lady beholding the battle, took up a sword, for he had dropt his own in the court, and called to Amadis, Come in and finish the fight! This hall is larger, answered Amadis: let it be here. I will not come out, quoth the Castellan. What! quoth he of Gaul, thinkest thou so to save thyself? and placing his shield before him he entered the chamber, his sword being raised to strike; immediately the strength of all his limbs was gone, and he lost his senses, and fell to the ground like a dead man. Thou shalt die by no other death than this, said Arcalaus: What say you, my lady, have I well avenged myself? And with that he disarmed Amadis, who knew nothing of what was doing, and put on the

4. In one of his first adventures, Amadis grants a boon to a dwarf, who leads him to a castle owned by Amadis' future arch-enemy, the wicked sorcerer Arcalaus.

5. Nine in the morning.

armour himself, and said to his lady, As you regard yourself, let none remove this knight till his soul shall have forsaken his body. Then he descended into the court, and said to her whom Amadis had delivered, Seek for some other to release you, for this champion is dispatched. And when Gandalin heard these words, he fell down senseless. Arcalaus took the lady, and led her where Amadis lay in that deadly trance; and she seeing him in such plight, wanted no tears to express the abundance of her grief. As soon as he is dead, said Arcalaus to that other lady who was his wife, place this woman again in her prison. I will go to the court of King Lisuarte, and there relate how I performed this battle, upon condition that he who conquered should cut off his enemy's head, and within fifteen days publish his victory at that court. By these means none shall challenge me about his death, and I shall obtain the greatest glory in the world, having overcome him who conquered every one.

Then he went into the court, and ordered Gandalin and the dwarf to prison; but Gandalin reviled him with the names of traitor and villain, and provoked him to kill him, desiring death. Arcalaus made his men drag him by the leg to a dungeon. If I killed thee, said he, thou wouldst endure no farther pain, and there thou shalt have worse than death. He then mounted upon the horse of Amadis, and accompanied by three squires set forth for the court.

Grindalaya, the lady whom Amadis had delivered, made such dole over him as was pitiful to hear. The wife of Arcalaus comforted her so well as she could, for she was of disposition clean contrary to her husband, and always besought God in her prayers to turn his heart. As they were thus together, they saw two damsels enter the hall, each bearing in her hands many lighted candles, which they placed along the sides of the chamber wherein Amadis lay; the ladies beheld this while being neither able to speak nor move. One of the damsels took a book from a casket which she brought under her arm, and read from it aloud, and at times a voice answered her, and presently the answers were made by many voices together, as tho' an hundred, and all in the chamber. Then there came another book through the floor of the chamber, whirling as if driven by the wind, and it stopt at the feet of her who read, and she took and broke it into four parts, and burnt them at the sides of the chamber where the candles stood. Then she went to Amadis, and took him by the hand—Arise, Sir, for you lie uneasily! and Amadis arose and cried, Holy Mary! what is this? I was well nigh dead. Certes, sir knight, replied the damsel, such a man as you should not perish in this sort, for by your hand must others die who better deserve it! And with that, without more words, both damsels returned thither from whence they came.

Then Amadis asked what had past, and Grindalaya told him all. I felt him disarm me, said he, but all seemed as in a dream. Then arming himself in the harness of Arcalaus, he said to his wife, look to this lady well till I return; and he went to deliver Gandalin. The men of Arcalaus seeing him thus armed, ran all ways; but he descended the steps, and through the hall where he had slain the jaylor, and so to the dungeon: a dreadful place it was for the captives: in length, an hundred times as far as a man's spread arms can reach; one only and a half of that span wide; dark, for neither light nor air could enter, and so full that it was crowded. Amadis came to the door and called, Gandalin! But he, who was like one dead, hearing the voice was greatly terrified, and made no answer, for he believed that his master was slain, and he himself enchanted. Gandalin? where art thou? again cried Amadis. O God! will he not answer? And he said to the prisoners, Tell me for God's sake is the squire living whom they have just now cast here? But then the dwarf knew his voice, and answered, Here we are! Thereat greatly rejoicing, Amadis went to the lamp in the hall, and kindled torches and took them to the dungeon, and loosed Gandalin's chain, for he lay nearest the door, and bade him deliver his comrades.

They came from the dungeon, an hundred and fifteen men in all, of whom thirty were knights, and they followed Amadis, exclaiming, O fortunate knight! even so did our Saviour go out from hell, leading away his servants whom he had delivered. Christ give thee thy reward! And, when they came to the sun-light and open sky, they fell upon their knees, and with lifted hands blest God who had given that knight strength to their deliverance.

* * *

Amadis and Galaor[6] were within two leagues of London when they saw Ardian the dwarf coming towards them as fast as horse could gallop. Never trust me, quoth Amadis, if he comes not with the news of some great mishap to seek us. Presently the dwarf came up and related all his tidings, and how Oriana was carried away. Holy Mary, help me! cried Amadis: Which way did they take her? —By the city is the nearest road. Amadis immediately spurred his horse, and galloped amain towards London, so confounded with the terror of this news that he never spoke a word to Galaor, who followed him full speed. They passed close by the town without stopping a minute, only Amadis enquired of all he saw which way the Princess had been taken; but as Gandalin passed under the windows where the queen and her ladies were, the queen called him, and threw the king's sword to him, which was the best sword that ever knight girded on: Take it to your master, quoth she, and God speed him with it! and tell Galaor that the king went from hence with a damsel this morning, and is not yet returned, and we know not where she has led him. Gandalin took the sword and rode

6. The brother of Amadis. Arcalaus has by trickery forced King Lisuarte to hand over Oriana while Amadis is absent from London.

as fast as he could after Amadis, who coming to a brook missed the bridge in his hurry, and forcing the horse to leap, the tired animal fell short into the mud; then Gandalin came up to him and gave him the sword, and the horse which he himself rode. Presently they turned aside from the road to follow the track of horsemen, and there they saw some woodmen, who asked them if they came from London. For if a knight and a damsel be missing there, said they, we have seen an adventure; and then they told them what they had beheld. Who is it that has taken them? quoth Amadis; for he knew it was Lisuarte by the description. They answered, The damsel who led the knight here called loudly for Arcalaus. Lord God! quoth Amadis, let me but find that traitor!—The woodmen then told them how the party had separated, and said that one of the five knights who went with the damsel was the biggest knight they had ever seen. Amadis knew that that was Arcalaus; and bidding Galaor follow where the king went, he spurred on after Oriana. By sunset the horse could carry him no farther, and he being greatly distressed, saw a little to the right of the road a knight lying dead, and a squire by him holding his horse. Who slew that knight? cried Amadis. A traitor that passed by, carrying the fairest damsel in the world by force, and he slew my master only for asking who they were, and here is no one to help me to remove the body.—My squire shall help you: give me, your master's horse: I promise to give you two better in return. He told Gandalin to follow him after the body was disposed of, and gallopped on. Towards day-break he came to a hermitage in a valley, and asked the hermit if he had seen five knights pass carrying with them two damsels? Do you see yonder castle? he replied. My nephew tells me that Arcalaus the enchanter is lodged there, and with him two fair damsels whom he hath taken by violence. By God the very villain whom I seek!—He hath done much evil in this land, replied the hermit. God remove him or mend him!—Then Amadis asked him if he had any barley for his horse; and while the horse was feeding, enquired who was the lord of the castle. Grumen, said the good man, cousin to Dardan who was slain in Lisuarte's court, and therefore the king's enemies put up there. Now God be with you, father! quoth Amadis, I beseech you remember me in your prayers! Which way to the castle? Amadis followed the path which the good man had pointed out, and came up to it, and saw that the wall was high and the towers strong. He listened and could hear no sound within, and that pleased him, for he knew that Arcalaus was not going forth; and he rode round, and saw that it had only one issue. Then he retired among some crags, and dismounting stood holding the bridle, and with his eyes fixed upon the gate, like one who had no will to sleep. By this the morning broke, and he removed farther across a valley to a hill that was well wooded, for he feared that if those of the castle saw him they would suspect there were others at hand, and therefore not come out. Presently the gate opened, and a knight came out, and went to a high eminence and looked all round; then returned into the castle. It was not long before he saw Arcalaus and his four companions come out, all well armed, and among them Oriana. Ah, God! quoth he, now and for ever help me in her defense! They drew near him, and he heard Oriana say, Dear friend, I shall never see thee more, for I go to my death. The tears came into his eyes; he descended the hill as fast as he could, and came after them into a great plain, and then cried, Arcalaus! traitor! it becomes not one like thee to carry away so excellent a lady! Oriana knew the voice, and shook all over; but Arcalaus and the other ran at him. He took his aim at Arcalaus, and bore him right over the crupper; then turned his horse and smote at Grumen, so that the point and part of the stave of the spear came out at his back, and he fell down dead, and the spear broke in him. Then he drew the king's sword, and laid about with such rage and violence, and felt such strength in himself, that he thought if the whole plain were full of knights they could not stand before him. We are succoured! quoth the damsel of Denmark: it is the fortunate knight! look at the wonders he performeth! Ah, God protect thee, dear friend! cried Oriana: none other in the world can save us. The squire who had her in his keeping seeing what had passed, cried out, Certes I shall not wait till those blows come upon my head which shields and helmets cannot resist! And he put the princess down, and rode off full speed. By this Amadis had cut thro' the arm of another, and sent him away howling with the agony of death; and he cleft a third down to the neck. The fourth began to fly, and Amadis was after him, when he heard his lady cry: and looking round, saw that Arcalaus had mounted again, and was dragging her up by the arm. Amadis soon came up to them, and lifting up his sword dared not put forth his strength lest he should slay both, but with a half-blow he smote him on the shoulder, and cut away part of the cuirass and the skin; then Arcalaus let Oriana fall, that he might escape the better. Turn, Arcalaus, cried Amadis, and see if I be dead as thou hast reported! But he in fear of death spurred on, and threw his shield from off his neck for speed. The blow made at him just reached his loins with the sword-end, and fell upon the horse's flank and wounded it, so that the beast rode away more furiously. Amadis, albeit he so hated the enchanter, did not pursue him further, lest he should lose his mistress; he turned towards her, and alighted and knelt before her, and kissed her hand, saying, Now let God do with me what he will! I never thought to see you again. She being among the dead was in great terror, and could not speak, but she embraced him. The damsel of Denmark going to hold his horse saw the sword of Arcalaus on the ground, and admiring its beauty gave it to Amadis; but he seeing it was right glad thereof, for it was King Perion's sword which had been placed in his cradle, and which Arcalaus had taken when he enchanted him. Presently Gandalin came up, who had travelled all night long: a joyful man was he seeing how the quest had ended.

Amadis then placed Oriana upon the damsel's palfrey, while Gandalin caught one of the loose horses for the damsel, and taking her bridle they left the place of battle. But Amadis as they went along reminded Oriana how she had promised to be his. Hitherto, said he, I have known that it was not in your power to show me more favour than you did; but now that you are at full liberty, how should I support disappointments without the worst despair that ever destroyed man! Dear friend, quoth she, never for my sake shall you suffer, for I am at your will: though it be an error and a sin now, let it not be so before God. When they had proceeded about three leagues they entered a thick wood, and about a league farther there was a town. Oriana, who had not slept a wink since she left her father's house, complained of fatigue: Let us rest in that valley, said Amadis. There was a brook there and soft herbage; there Amadis took her from her palfrey. The noon, said he, is coming on very hot; let us sleep here till it be cooler, and meantime Gandalin shall go bring us food from the town. He may go, replied Oriana, but who will give him food?—They will give it him for his horse, which he may leave in pledge, and return on foot. No, said Oriana, let him take my ring, which was never before so useful; and she gave it to Gandalin, who, as he went by Amadis, said to him, He who loses a good opportunity, sir, must wait long before he find another. Oriana laid herself down upon the damsel's cloak, while Amadis disarmed, of which he had great need, and the damsel retired farther among the trees to sleep. Then was his lady in his power, nothing loth; and the fairest damsel in the world became a woman. Yet was their love encreased thereby, as pure and true love always is.

When Gandalin returned, the damsel prepared the food; and, though they had neither many serving-men, nor vessels of gold and silver, yet was that a sweet meal upon the green grass in the forest.

* * *

This history has related to you how Amadis promised Briolania to revenge her father's death, and how she gave him a sword, and that when in his combat with Gasinan he broke the sword, he gave the pieces to Gandalin's care: you shall now hear how the battle was performed, and what great danger he underwent because of that broken sword, not from any fault of his own, but for the ignorance of his dwarf Ardian.

Amadis now recollecting that the time was come to perform his promise, acquainted Oriana, and requested her leave, though to him it was like dividing his heart from his bosom to leave her; and she granted it, albeit with many tears, and a sorrow that seemed to presage what evil was about to happen. Amadis took the queen's leave for form's sake, and departed with Galaor and Agrayes. They had gone about half a league, when he asked Gandalin if he had brought the three pieces of the sword which Briolania had given him, and finding he had not, bade him return and fetch them. The dwarf said he would go, for he had nothing to delay him; and this was the means whereby Amadis and Oriana were both brought into extreme misery, neither they nor the dwarf himself being culpable.

The dwarf rode back to his master's lodging, found the pieces of the sword, put them in his skirt, and was retiring, when, as he passed the palace, he heard himself called. Looking up, he saw Oriana and Mabilia, who asked him why he had not gone with his master. I set out with him, said he, but returned for this; and he showed her the broken sword. What can your master want a broken sword for? quoth Oriana. Because, said the dwarf, he values it more than the two best whole ones, for her sake, who gave it him.—And who is she?—The lady for whom he undertakes this combat, and though you are daughter to the best king in the world, yet, fair as you are, you would rather win what she has won, than possess all your father's lands.—What gain so precious hath she made? Perchance she hath gained your master?—Yes, she has, his whole heart! and he remains her knight to serve her! Then, giving his horse the lash, he galloped away, little thinking the wrong he had done. Oriana remained pale as death; she burst into bitter reproaches against the falsehood of Amadis, and wrung her hands, and her heart was so agitated that not a tear did she shed. It was in vain that Mabilia and the damsel of Denmark strove to allay her rage with reasonable words: as passionate women will do, she followed her own will, which led her to commit so great an error, that God's mercy was necessary to repair it.

* * *

You have heard in the first part of this great history, how Oriana was moved to great anger and rage by what the Dwarf had said to her concerning the broken sword, so that neither the wise counsels of Mabilia nor of the Damsel of Denmark aught availed her. From that time she gave way to her wrath, so that wholly changing her accustomed manner of life, which was to be altogether in their company, she now forsook them, and for the most part chose to be alone, devising how she might revenge herself for what she suffered, upon him who had caused her sufferings. So recollecting that she could by writing make him sensible in her displeasure, even at a distance, being alone in her chamber, she took ink and parchment from her coffer, and wrote thus:

My frantic grief, accompanied by so great a reason, causes my weak hand to declare what my sad heart cannot conceal against you, the false and disloyal knight, Amadis of Gaul; for the disloyalty and faithlessness are known which you have committed against me, the most ill-fortuned and unhappy of all in the world, since you have changed your affection for me, who loved you above all things, and have placed your love upon one who by her years cannot have discretion to know and love you. Since then I have no other vengeance in my power, I withdraw all that exceeding and misplaced love which I bore towards you; for great error would it be to love him who has forsaken me, when in requital for my sighs and passion I am deceived and deserted. Therefore, as the wrong is manifest, never appear before me! for be sure the great love I felt is turned into raging anger. Go, and deceive some other poor woman as you deceived me with your treacherous words, for which no excuse will be received, while I lament with tears my own wretchedness, and so put an end to my life and unhappiness.

Having thus written, she sealed the letter with the seal of Amadis, and wrote on the superscription, I am the damsel wounded through the heart with a sword, and you are he who wounded me. She then secretly called a squire, who was named Durin, and was brother to the Damsel of Denmark, and bade him not rest till he had reached the kingdom of Sobradisa, where he would find Amadis; and she bade him mark the countenance of Amadis while he was reading the letter, and stay with him that day, but receive no answer from him, if he wished to give one.

Durin, in obedience to the command of Oriana, presently departed, and hasted so well that on the tenth day he arrived at Sobradisa, where he found the new Queen Briolania, whom he thought the fairest woman, except Oriana, that ever he had seen; and learning from her that Amadis had departed two days before, he followed him. Amadis took him apart from his brethren and from all others into a garden, and asked him if he came from the court of King Lisuarte, and what tidings. Sir, said he, the court is as when you left it: I come from thence by the command of my Lady Oriana; by this letter you will know the cause of my coming. Amadis took the letter, and he concealed the joy that was in his heart, that Durin might know nothing of his secret; but his grief he could not conceal when he had read those strong and bitter words, for neither his courage nor reason could support him then, for he seemed struck with death. When Durin saw him so disordered, he cursed himself and his ill fortune, and death, that had not overtaken him on the way. Amadis, for he could not stand, sate down upon the grass, and took the letter which had fallen from his hands, and, when he saw the superscription, again his grief became so violent that Durin would have called his brethren, but feared to do so, observing what secresy Amadis had chosen. Presently Amadis exclaimed, O Lord, wherefore does it please thee that I should perish, not having deserved it! And then again, Ah, truth, an ill guerdon dost thou give him who never failed thee! Then he took the letter again, saying, You are the cause of my unhappy end; come here that it may be sooner! And he placed it in his bosom. He asked Durin if he had aught else to say; and hearing that he had not, replied, Well then, thou shalt take my answer. Sir, quoth he, I am forbidden to receive any.—Did neither Mabilia nor thy sister bid thee say anything?—They knew not my coming: my lady commanded me to conceal it from them. Holy Mary help me! I see now my wretchedness is without remedy. He then went to a stream that proceeded from a fountain, and washed his face and eyes, and bade Durin call Gandalin, and bid him bring Ysanjo, the governor; and he said to the governor, Promise me, as you are a loyal knight, to keep secret all that you shall see till after my brothers have heard mass tomorrow. And the same promise he exacted from the two squires. Then he commanded Ysanjo to open privately the gate of the castle, and Gandalin to take his horse and arms out, privately also. Then he said to Ysanjo, It grieves me, my friend Ysanjo, to leave you before I could honour you according to your deserts; but I leave you with those who will do it. Ysanjo answered, Let me go with you, sir, and suffer what you suffer. Friend, answered Amadis, it must be as I say; God only can comfort me! I will be guided by his mercy, and have no other company. He then said to Gandalin, If thou desirest knighthood, take my arms; for, since thou hast kept them so well, it is right they should be thine. I shall little need them: if not, my brother Galaor shall knight thee. Tell him this, Ysanjo, and serve and love him as thou hast me, for I love him above all my lineage, because he is the best, and hath ever been humble towards me. Tell him, too, that I commit Ardian the dwarf to his care. They for great sorrow could make him no answer. Then Amadis embraced them, and commended them to God, saying that he never thought to see them more, and he forbade them to follow him; and with that spurred his horse and rode away, forgetting to take either shield, or helmet, or spear. He struck into the mountain, going whither his horse would. Thus he kept till midnight, being utterly lost in thought; his horse came then to a little stream of water, and proceeded upward to find a place so deep that he could drink thereat. The branches struck Amadis in the face, and so recalled him to himself, and he looked round, and seeing nothing but thickets, rejoiced, thinking that he was hidden in that solitude. So he alighted, and fastened his horse to a tree, and sate upon the green herb by, and wept till his head became giddy, and he fell asleep.

* * *

Good sir,[7] replied Amadis, I am now in such extremity that I cannot live any long time: I beseech you, by that God whose faith you hold, take me with you for the little while I have to live, that

7. Amadis, still grieving, meets an old priest who is returning to his hermitage and who agrees to take Amadis with him.

I may have comfort for my soul. My horse and arms I need no longer: I will leave them here, and go with you on foot, and perform whatever penitence you enjoin. If you refuse, you will sin before God, for else I shall wander and perish in this mountain. When the good man saw him thus resolute, he said to him, with a heart wholly bent to his good, Certes, sir, it becomes not a knight like you to abandon himself as if he had lost the whole world, by reason of a woman: their love is no longer than while they see you with their eyes, and hear such words as you say to them, and that past, presently they forget you; especially in those false loves that are begun against the Lord; the same sin which makes them sweet at first, gives them a bitterness in the end, as you experience. But you, who are of such prowess, and have such power, you who are the true and loyal protector of such as are oppressed, great wrong would it be to the world if you thus forsake it. I know not what she is who hath brought you to this extremity, but if all the worth and beauty of the sex were brought together in one, I know that such a man as you ought not to be lost for her. Good sir, quoth Amadis, I ask not your counsel upon this, where it is not wanted; but, for my soul's sake, I pray you take me in your company, for else I shall have no remedy, but to die in this mountain. The old man hearing this, had such compassion on him that the tears fell down his long white beard. Sir, my son, said he, I live in a dreary place, and a hard life; my hermitage is full seven leagues out at sea, upon a high rock, to which no ship can come except in summer time. I have lived there these thirty years, and he who lives there must renounce all the pleasures and delights of the world, and all my support is the alms which the people of the land bestow upon me. I promise you, said Amadis, this is the life I desire for the little while I shall live, and I beseech you, for the love of God, let me go with you. The good man, albeit against his will, consented; and Amadis said, Now, father, command me what to do, and I will be obedient. The good man gave him his blessing, and said vespers, and then taking bread and fish from his wallet, he bade Amadis eat; but Amadis refused, though he had been three days without tasting food. You are to obey me, said the good man, and I command you to eat, else your soul will be in great danger if you die. Then he took a little food; and when it was time to sleep, the old man spread his cloak and laid him down thereon, and Amadis laid himself down at his feet.

* * *

I pray you then, said Amadis, that so long as we are together you will not tell any man who I am, nor anything concerning me, and that you will call me by some other name, not my own; and when I am dead you tell my brethren of me, that they may take my body into their country. Your life and death, said the good man, are in the hands of God, so talk no more of this; he will help you if you know and love and serve him as you ought; but tell me, by what name will you be called?—Even by whatever it shall please you.—So the old man, seeing how fair he was, and in how forlorn a condition, replied, I will give you a name conformable to your appearance and distress, Beltenebros. Now Beltenebros being intrepreted, signifyeth, the fair forlorn. The name pleased Amadis, and he admired the good sense of the old man in chusing it; so by this name he was long known till it became as renowned as that of Amadis. Thus communing they reached the seaside just as the night closed in; there they found a bark, wherein the good man might cross to his hermitage. Beltenebros gave his horse to the mariners, and they gave him in exchange a cloak of goat skin, and a garment of coarse grey woollen. They embarked, and Beltenebros asked the good man what was the name of his abode. They call my dwelling place, said he, the Poor Rock, because none can live there without enduring great poverty; for thirty years I have never left it, till now that I went to the burial of my sister. At length they reached the rock and landed, and the mariners returned to the mainland.

* * *

Here Beltenebros dwelt in penitence and great grief, and he past the night most frequently under some large trees in the garden near the chapel, that he might there lament, without the knowledge of the hermit or the boys;[8] and calling to mind the great wrong he endured, he made this song in his passion:

Sith that the victory of right deserved
By wrong they do withhold for which I served;
Now sith my glory thus hath had a fall,
Glorious it is to end my life withall.
By this my death, likewise my woes' release,
My hope, my joy, my inflamed love doth cease.
But ever will I mind my during pain,
For they, to end my glory and my gain,
Myself have murdered, and my glory slain.

* * *

FRANCISCO DE MORAES CABRAL

From Palmerin of England

The selections from *Palmerin* illustrate the sort of "doubtful" adventures Don Quixote hopes to have when he and Sancho get into the boat in Part II, Ch. XXIX, and when he confronts the lion in Part II, Ch. XVII. The mysterious island ("Perilous Isle") is one of the *ínsulas* which Don Qui-

8. Nephews of the hermit.

xote has in mind when he promises Sancho an island. The adventure of the funeral procession was probably Cervantes' inspiration for the beginning of Part I, Ch. XIX. The selection is reprinted from the four-volume 1817 edition (London: Longman, Hurst, Reese, and Orme).

The Adventure of the Perilous Isle

When Palmerin was departed from the castle of Darmaco, he rode without any adventure for the space of three days together. On the fourth, when it was nigh sun-set, he heard upon the right the sound of waters, and turning that way came to the sea side, which by reason of distemperature made a great raging; the wind lifted and lashed its waves against the rocks, and drove them into the caverns which they had hollowed out in length of time, with a roaring which was heard far off; but within the caverns was such that it seemed to shake them like an earthquake. He went along the shore watching these works of Nature, and turning his eyes on all sides, that their occupation might drive other pensive matters forth of his mind, espied presently between two rocks, which made a quiet little bay, a large boat fastened by a rope on shore, and in it two oars laid in their places without any person to ply them, whereat he marvelled greatly: then bidding Selviam take his horse, for he would get into the boat, not being able to conceive why it should be there without hands. Selviam besought him to change his mind from so fond an enterprize, urging, that in an adventure of no better countenance, it was but mere folly to hazard his person; but when he saw his words might attain no persuasion from his attempt, he suffered him to use his will; for where will is mistress reason is set at little: and taking his horse, Palmerin entered the boat. He was scarcely in before Selviam called to him to come out again because he was unarmed; but turning his eyes toward the shore he perceived that he was already a stone's throw off, and laying hands on the oars to row back, all his strength was not so great but that the spell was stronger which bore him away; the wind was off shore, and it freshened, and soon carried the boat to a distance. Palmerin left the oars, thinking that all this was not without some cause; and it was not long before he lost sight of land.

* * *

Palmerin, travelling over that sea as ye have heard, went on all day and night, and on the following morning at daybreak found himself at the foot of a high and ragged rock, which in process of time the sea had wrought into an island. It was to appearance uninhabited, for he could see nothing but high trees. There landing from the boat in a port between two hills, he began to ascend by a narrow path in the rock, so steep that he who might slip would have far to fall. This was so painful a path, that before he had reached the half way up, he was fain to rest three or four times. At last he found himself in a fair green meadow, in the midst whereof was placed a marble stone of the height of a man, with an inscription upon it; Go NO FURTHER. When he had read this, the stone being placed there, as he supposed, to cause all passengers to be afraid they knew not of what. So thinking there was nothing here to fear, and that the words upon the marble were but vanity, he went on till at last he was benighted; for the time which it had taken him to climb the rock was so great that it had fairly finished the day, and now it became so dark that he could see nothing. Then laying him down on the grass to take his rest, he made his helmet his pillow, and so determined to sleep there for the night. But such were the motions in his mind, that the more he thought to take quiet rest, the farther off he was from his intent. For the remembrance of his lady Polinarda presented itself as best worthy his memory, because he had been so long absent from her, yet durst not enterprize to come into her presence, and the loss of Selviam, whose counsel always served as an especial remedy to these thoughts, left love at liberty to bring to mind a thousand recollections.

Thus spent he all that night in restless fancies, and seeing the day break at last, laced on his helmet, that if any danger should occur he might be better prepared for it. The farther he advanced into the isle, the fairer it seemed; and it grieved him to see it uninhabited: for as for the words he had read upon the marble, he now esteemed them to be flat mockage, because he could perceive nothing that deserved such a sore warning. But at length, among the thickest of those trees he found himself in a great field, open like the great square of some city, encompassed on all sides by the forest, and in no part, disproportioned. In the middle of this plain was a fountain raised upon a font of stone upon a marble basement; the water issued from the mouths of certain animals which were placed on the font, and it was in such quantity, that that which ran over into the field formed a little river. What most amazed him was, that this place was on the summit of the mountain, and yet the water rose there; a thing which seemed to him against all reason and rule of nature. At the foot of the marble basement two lions and two tygers were fastened, fearful to behold, and in truth of fierceness which might well be feared. Their chains were long enough to let them go three fathom length from the fountain, made of metal links of such thickness as was needed for their strength, fastened at one end unto large rings, which were rivetted into the marble, and at the other round the neck of the beasts. Palmerin well knew, that whoever would drink at that fountain must needs ask leave of these keepers, who would give it to none; and thinking it folly to make the attempt and provoke the hazard, would have passed on. But some red letters upon the stone of the font stopt him: it was written, THIS IS THE FOUNTAIN OF THE WISHED WATER. And going a little farther, he espied another inscription, which was thus: HE THAT DRINKETH OF THIS FOUNTAIN SHALL BRING TO END ANY ENTERPRISES OF STRENGTH. But farther on was a third writing which said, PASS, AND DRINK NOT. This made him not a little astonished, in that as the one gave him encouragement to approach the fountain, so the other stood in the way to hinder his determination. This last advice however he resolved to follow, remembering and holding it certain, that needless rashness is not accounted courage.

Palmerin had determined to depart from thence, and not approach the fountain, because the boon which the one inscription promised he held as nothing, and to attack those animals was rather folly than valour. So passing on into a path among the trees, he felt such shame of himself as compelled him to return: And covering himself with his shield and taking sword in hand, he advanced towards one of the tygers at the fountain, who received him with terrible fierceness, and sprung upon him; and though the activity and readiness of the knight were great, yet could he not prevent the tyger from tearing away the shield with his claws, breaking off all the straps short: howbeit this was not done so cheaply but that the beast took one of his legs with him with a cut in it well nigh through flesh and bone, so that he could no longer move at will.

Presently up came the other three beasts, all at once; and because Palmerin was without a shield, this was the greatest fear and the most doubtful adventure in which he had ever seen himself in all his life. Nevertheless, as in brave men such fear doubles their resolution, that which he felt was such, that, nothing remembering the greatness of the danger, he waited for the lion who was nearest him, the others not coming up so soon by reason of their chains, and gave him such a cut over the paws which he had lifted up to seize him with, that he cut them both clean off, and the lion fell to the ground, being unable to rise again. Then stooping down to recover his shield which the tyger had abandoned, the other lion approached so near unto him, that catching hold upon the strings of his helmet, he tore it from his head, and drew him after it so violently that he was enforced to fall upon his knees; when the other tyger catching him as he fell, crushed him with his paws so cruelly, that had not his armour been strong, he had torn him in pieces. Not only however did the goodness of his armour stand Palmerin in good stead, but he availed himself also of his sword, wherewith he made a thrust in such point of time and place, that it ran the tyger through the heart, and he fell to the earth clean bereft of life. By this time the lion who had been busied with the helmet, came at him again. Palmerin, now aware of him, held out the shield that he might seize it, and the moment he had fixed his claws in it. delivered him a stroke under it which brought his bowels out, and he fell dead. Still the access to the fountain was not secure, for the first tyger with the wounded leg was close to it, raging with such fury, that while he was there is was not possible to reach it. Palmerin seeing this, and how much of his work was done, went towards him covered with his shield; and though the tyger could but ill stand, he rose to seize him, laying one claw upon the shield and the other upon the sword, perceiving that it was from that his hurt came. The shield he plucked away, but with the edge of the sword he cut himself so sore that he could do no further hurt with that claw; and Palmerin then with another blow lopping the leg off, he stretched himself in the pains of death, howling with so loud a cry that it sounded over the whole island. The knight remained in such plight that he was fain to sit himself down and rest, thinking that verily all his bones had been broken by that first tyger. After he had rested him a while, he went to the fountain to quench his thirst, and he read the letters again and could not gather the meaning of the first inscription, but thought the advice which the last gave was the safest for those who chose to follow it. So having read them again he drank, and the water seemed no better than that of other fountains; he thought the whole was the work of some enchanter desirous of novelties; and seeing nothing more to be done, went on in the path which he had before taken.

Presently he came before a goodly and well fortified castle, than which he had never seen fairer or stronger, well edified, with goodly towers, and pleasantly seated, and moated round about, with a draw-bridge at the entrance. Round about it stood four jasper pillars, and upon each was hanged a shield; Palmerin went up to the first to see its colours, no longer holding the things of this island to be illusions, and he saw upon it certain letters in a field sable, saying, LET NO ONE TAKE ME DOWN. Certes, quoth Palmerin, I will try the end of these threats; and taking the shield from the pillar placed it upon his shoulders, for his own was lying quite demolished at the foot of the fountain. While he fastened it to his arm he heard a voice say, Don Cavalier, see that this boldness do not cost you dear! And looking that way he espied a knight coming from the castle over the draw-bridge, armed at all points, and so large and strong limbed, that he was much to be feared. He drawing nigh, and seeing Palmerin without a helmet, for the lion had bruised it in such sort that he could not use it, cried out with a voice of more threatening than courtesy, He that will bear this shield ought to have more arms than ordinary to defend him, and not come without that piece of which he has most need.

With these words, not staying to hear an answer, he delivered him such a stroke as brought a quarter of the shield on which it was received to the ground. Palmerin being in such danger, and seeing him so near, grappled with him, and because his heart was great, and from thence oftentimes strength comes to the limbs, he, besides that he was strong by nature, found himself at that hour so much so, that he overthrew him, and taking his sword from him, the knight yielded to his mercy. Palmerin demanded of him if he had any more to deal withal, to which he answered, that the chiefest danger was behind. Whereupon arming his head with the helmet of the vanquished knight, he went to the second pillar, being now resolved to go on and try whatever adventure might befal him. Here upon the shield in a field azure, he read as thus: I AM, MORE PERILOUS. Be as perilous as thou wilt, cried he, I shall not leave thee for that! So leaving the fragment of the first shield, he took down the second, when presently came forth another knight, in vermilion arms, over the same bridge, saying, Ill counsel have you taken in meddling with that shield. Ill or good, replied Palmerin, here am I, on whom you may take vengeance for the displeasure done you in so doing. Both at this met together with up-lifted swords, and a battle began between them of such hard strife and well-delivered strokes, that it had been in any part a thing to have been looked at. It did not last long, for he of the Castle not being able to endure the heavy blows of Palmerin, began to wax weak, so that his own strokes were now of little effect, and all his care was to defend himself. Palmerin perceiving this, and taking his sword in both hands, reached him such a sure warrant on the crest, that the sword pierced into his head, and he fell to the earth discharged of his life.

Then Palmerin, seeing that this combat was achieved also, went on to the third pillar, where, in the midst of the shield upon a field vert in azure letters was written these words: BY ME IS HONOUR GAINED. This also he took as he had done the others, and forthwith another knight sallied out, in arms of the same colour as the shield, as furious and melancholick as one who had great confidence in himself; and without using any words, entered a more dangerous combat than the other two passed, so that the difference between him and the former knights of the castle was manifest. Palmerin seeing that each new enemy was mightier than the last, did his utmost to bring this battle to an end, fearing the other which was yet to be achieved, according to the order of the shields; but this knight was of such signal prowess, that the proof of it made Palmerin more alert than he had yet been, enforcing him to make use of all his strength and activity. So not to delay myself in enumerating blows, the battle continued some time, but the victory remained with him who was alway wont to carry it, and the knight fell at his feet with an arm the less, of which wound he presently died; the conqueror being so sound, because he knew well how to defend himself, that of all these combats he felt nothing except the labour.

Anon he went to the last shield, where in a field argent were these letters of gold: IN ME IS THE VICTORY. He took it from the pillar, designing to use it, for his other was now of no defence. The fourth knight tarried not, but issued out of the castle in great haste, in arms of grey and white bordered with gold, saying, I did not think your folly would have gone so far, but since you are not contented with the past, wait and see what you have gained by it. Palmerin, not accustomed to make answer in place where knightly strength ought to shew itself, delivered him his mind in a blow upon the helmet, so well laid on, that he made him vaile his head upon his breast; but the knight of the castle requited him with another, which taking his shield in the middle, cut it clean through to the handles; so they began to smite each other with mortal strokes, without pity, as men who had none for themselves; each one putting forth all his strength and skill, seeing that both were needed. Their blows were so fearful and so well laid on, that for the most part they made way through the arms; their shields were of little avail, little indeed being left to shield them. He of the Castle was of such worth in arms, that no weakness was seen in him, nor any vantage in Palmerin, though that day was one of those in which he proved his person to the utmost. Long time this lasted, till the knight, not able to bear up against the blows of Palmerin, which seemed to fall thicker and faster, foredone with heat and toil and wounds, fell down as dead as one whom life had utterly deserted. Palmerin seeing this, kneeled down, and hearily gave thanks to God for this great victory. Then demanded he of the knight whom he had first conquered, if that there were any thing more to be done in the castle: to which he answered, Yes; but that nothing could be much for him to achieve.

These battles being ended, Palmerin went to the castle, and entering without let or hindrance into the court below, beheld the manner thereof, which was as marvellous as the perils which he had past through were fearful. All about the court were pillars of jasper stone, ten cubits in height, whereon all the chambers and towers were built, the court paved with precious stones of green and white, in chequers equally laid, like a chess board. In the middle were spouts of water playing up with such force that they ascended as high as the top of the buildings; the whole of the wood-work was of so new and subtle an invention, that the art of no man could comprehend either the beginning or end thereof. After Palmerin had surveyed these edifices from below, he ascended by a great staircase into a hall of such singular workmanship, that all which he had yet seen appeared little in comparison of it. At the entrance was a giant, so great and terrible that he had never yet seen other like him, holding in his hand a heavy iron mace, which, when Palmerin advanced to enter, he whirled about with a countenance which would have stricken fear into any other knight. But he, in which they of this quality caused little fear, remembering how fortunately he had begun without, determined to end as valiantly within. And so settling him to the giant, and giving him one stroke with the sword, he found him to be a thing artificial and fantastic, which fell at once to the ground without life. Then he entered the hall, and having admired the work thereof, he found a little door which opened into a varanda, from whence there was no passage to any part, except to another edifice opposite; but between them was a chasm of such depth that it was a fearful thing to behold. At the bottom thereof ran a river of black water, so dark and dolorous, that it seemed to be the very same which is called from Charon the boatman of hell. From this varanda to the one opposite there was no other passage than by a beam not broader than the hand; which was not only passing thin, but appeared so worn by time and so rotten, that it could not sustain the slightest weight. Fain he would have been on the further side, to see what farther was to be found in these edifices; but seeing no other way, and that this bridge was so perilous, he was thrown into the greatest confusion in the world. Nevertheless, remembering that the emperor Palmerin, his grandfather, had achieved a like adventure, he determined to try the passage; wherefore disarming himself lest the heaviness of his armour might break the plank, with a good courage he began to venture upon it, having nothing to defend him withal but his sword, whatever might happen. When he had attained the midst, the plank began to bend and crack, so that Palmerin verily supposed he must fall, and held himself for lost. So pausing a moment, he said within himself, Lady, if in great dangers I look for your succour, in what greater than this can Fortune ever place me? If I did not desire life for the sake of serving you therewith, little should I care for losing it here; deliver it now from this peril, and afterwards ordain any thing in which I may lose it for your service, and then shall you be served and I contented.

Then proceeding along the plank, he cared as little for its motion as if he had been walking along a firm and broad bridge; but before he had quite gained the opposite side, out from those buildings came a woman, to appearance of great age, her hair loose and her face torn, exclaiming, What avails my art if it is so often to be baffled by one man? and laying hold on Palmerin to drag him after her, she threw herself headlong into that deep river, there meeting the end which her deeds deserved. But he kept his footing so well that he stood, remaining astonished at what he had seen.

Then entering those buildings, he found none but women and serving men, of whom he asked the way down; they showed it him, and then he sent for the knight with whom he had fought the first battle, who came to him by another way, and Palmerin desired him to shew the name of this castle, as also what she was that had so desperately drowned herself. Sir, answered the knight, I cannot conceal any thing from you. This is called the Perilous Isle, whereof some hold opinion, that the sage Urganda was the first founder and lady, and that in this place she hid herself, and that after her death this castle remained enchanted, so that no person could attain to inhabit here. In this order she left this fair palace, and the fountain which you saw. And this we may the easier believe, seeing that no person, neither in our time nor before us, ever knew tidings of this isle, being a thing so worthy to be spoken of.

* * *

[*The Adventure of the Dead Body*]

They[1] went on throughout that kingdom, achieving feats which extended their renown; and going towards a city which was a sea port, where they might embark for Greece, they came upon a great and wide field, and looking about them, regaling their eyes with their fair flowers wherewith it was covered, they saw coming towards them a litter covered with a black pall, and accompanied by three esquires, who were making very doleful and grievous lamentations over a dead body which was upon the bier.

Drawing near, Florian, who was always desirous of novelties, wished to know the reason of this sorrow; and lifting up the cloth he beheld a knight lying in green armour, so embrued with blood, that one could hardly judge of what colour it was, and bearing the marks of so many blows, that it was plain he had received them in some great battle. This moved him to great compassion; and being desirous to know the cause of this he staid one of the esquires, willing him to report by what mischance the knight was slain, while the litter went on. The esquire having small leisure to stay, made him a short answer in this sort: If you wish to know, follow me, and I will tell you along the road; and if you have courage you may adventure your arms and person, where great honour may be gained with great peril. Certes, quoth Florian, hap what may I shall see the end of this. So taking leave of his brethren, who would fain have gone with him, he followed the litter, desirous to see the end of that the esquire had told him. Palmerin and Pompides seeing him gone, went their way along the field, talking of what had chanced. . . .

Florian of the Desert following the bier after he had parted from his brethren, the squire who was with him began thus: Sir, seeing you desire so much to know the knight who is slain, and thinking that you will not refuse to revenge his wrong if need should be, give ear, and I will discourse thereof to you at large. For as arms are

1. Palmerin and his brothers.

borne for the sake of redressing wrongs, assure yourself that in this adventure better than in any other you may employ them. You shall understand that this knight was named Sortibran the Strong, first cousin of king Frisol, whose worthiness hath been such, that he ever bare the name of the most redoubted knight in all his kingdom. So it was, that yesterday a squire came to his castle, who with tears desired him to assist him in a doubtful cause; whereto he courteously gave his consent, never having denied succour when it was asked at his hand, and went with him, not suspecting the treacherous intent of the squire, who brought him into a place where four of his enemies awaited his coming; and though Sortibran, my lord, did in battle against them all, all that a brave knight should do, nevertheless, as odds of number oftentimes overcometh valour, by dint of many wounds, in the end he was there cruelly slain. We being advertised of this great mishap, came with this bier to fetch him to his castle, where we might see his body honourably interred. In the mean while one of his young sons is gone to the court, to seek some knight that will revenge his father's death. Therefore, if you dare undertake this you shall not only enlarge your renown, but also shall work such occasion, that none may presume hereafter to commit any such treason. Florian, who desired nothing more, offered his person for this service, being grieved at the death of Sortibran, whom he had beforetime heard named as a right good knight. So riding on with them they came to the sea coast, where they entered a boat, that attended their coming, and having there shipped the body of Sortibran, they took the horses by land, and rowed along shore.

There they went on till night, when as they were crossing a bay which the sea made in those parts, they fell in with four Turkish galleys, which were lying there at anchor; and as there was no time to turn back, and none but Florian to fight, the boat was entered without resistance by Auderramete, a chief captain among the Moors, who beholding the rich armour of Florian, and judging him to be a noble knight, entertained him courteously, commanding the esquires to cast the dead body of their lord into the sea; and the next morning they hoisted sails to go on their voyage.

* * *

LUDOVICO ARIOSTO

From Orlando Furioso

The Italian verse romances of chivalry were perhaps the most admired and widely read examples of early sixteenth-century European literature, and among them, Ariosto's *Orlando furioso* (*Roland's Madness*) was the best, by general acclaim. Cervantes knew these romances at first hand in some cases and apparently by hearsay in others. Many of the elements of *Don Quixote* are analogous to those of such romances as the *Orlando furioso*: Ariosto's refined irony, his asides to the audience, the parodic elements (e.g., Archbishop Turpin, the chronicler of the deeds of Orlando and his peers, an obvious ancestor of Cide Hamete), and the strong personality of the author have led many readers to conclude that Cervantes was influenced by the Italian romances and their imitations. There are two episodes in *Don Quixote* which depend for their humor on a knowledge of these romances. There are others which gain dimensions when the reader can perceive amusing parallels if not outright parody. The two famous examples are Don Quixote's seizure of "Mambrino's helmet" and the subsequent controversy over the barber's basin and saddlebags, and Don Quixote's antics in the Sierra Morena, partly in imitation of the berserk Orlando's feats. The following selections illustrate the object of the parody and, in the case of Astolpho's aerial ride, a possible antecedent of the Clavileño episode, though there are numerous other sources of the idea, some much closer in detail than the passage from Ariosto.

The aristocratic Ludovico Ariosto (1474–1533) was a retainer of the Este family of Ferrara, in whose service he associated with some of the most famous, influential, and talented persons of his day: popes, the emperor, rulers, generals, painters, scholars. He was admired as a poet of Italian and Latin verse, a playwright, a satirist. Ariosto chose as the subject of his "epic" the *matière de France*, the deeds of Charlemagne's Twelve Peers, their friends and enemies, Christian and Saracen, which had already provided material for two earlier Italian poets, Pulci and Boiardo. Ariosto worked on his poem from about 1506 to 1532, the year in which he published the definitive edition.

Reprinted here are excerpts from William Stuart Rose's two-volume translation (London: H. G. Bohn, 1858). It is remarkably literal and even imitates the Italian stanza. (An excellent prose translation by Guido Waldman was published by Oxford University Press in 1974.)

Roland's Madness

Charlemagne's nephew Roland (or in Italian, Orlando), the invulnerable Christian champion, searching for his beloved Angelica, discovers a carved inscription which reveals that she has given herself to a rival, the handsome blond Saracen Medoro, whom she had encountered in the forest recovering from wounds.

Canto 23

CXI

Three times, and four, and six, the lines imprest
Upon the stone that wretch perused, in vain
Seeking another sense than was exprest,
And ever saw the thing more clear and plain;
And all the while, within his troubled breast,
He felt an icy hand his heart-core strain.
With mind and eyes close fastened on the block,
At length he stood, not differing from the rock.

CXII

Then well-nigh lost all feeling; so a prey
Wholly was he to that o'ermastering woe.
This is a pang; believe the experienced say[1]
Of him who speaks, which does all griefs outgo.[2]
His pride had from his forehead passed away,
His chin had fallen upon his breast below;
Nor found he, so grief barred each natural vent,
Moisture for tears, or utterance for lament.

CXVI

Languid, he lit, and left his Brigliador
To a discreet attendant: one undrest
His limbs, one doffed the golden spurs he wore,
And one bore off, to clean, his iron vest.
This was the homestead where the young Medore
Lay wounded, and was here supremely blest.
Orlando here, with other food unfed,
Having supt full of sorrow, sought his bed.

CXXIV

In him, forthwith, such deadly hatred breed
That bed, that house, that swain,[3] he will not stay
Till the morn break, or till the dawn succeed,
Whose twilight goes before approaching day.
In haste, Orlando takes his arms and steed,
And to the deepest greenwood wends his way.
And, when assured that he is there alone,
Gives utterance to his grief in shriek and groan.

CXXIX

All night about the forest roved the count,
And, at the break of daily light, was brought
By his unhappy fortune to the fount,
Where his inscription young Medoro wrought.
To see his wrongs inscribed upon that mount,
Inflamed his fury so, in him was nought
But turned to hatred, frenzy, rage, and spite;
Nor paused he more, but bared his faulchion[4] bright;

CXXX

Cleft through the writing; and the solid block,
Into the sky, in tiny fragments sped.

1. Statement.
2. Surpass.
3. The shepherd at whose house Orlando has stopped.
4. Sword.

Wo worth[5] each sapling and that caverned rock,
Where Medore and Angelica were read!

* * *

CXXXII

Wearied and woe-begone, he fell to ground,
And turned his eyes toward heaven; nor spake he aught,
Nor ate, nor slept, till in his daily round
The golden sun had broken thrice, and sought
His rest anew; nor ever ceased his wound
To rankle, till it marred his sober thought.
At length, impelled by frenzy, the fourth day,
He from his limbs tore plate and mail away.

CXXXIII

Here was his helmet, there his shield bestowed;
His arms far off, and, farther than the rest,
His cuirass; through the greenwood wide was strowed
All his good gear, in fine; and next his vest
He rent; and, in his fury, naked showed
His shaggy paunch,[6] and all his back and breast.
And 'gan that frenzy act, so passing dread,
Of stranger folly never shall be said.

CXXXIV

So fierce his rage, so fierce his fury grew,
That all obscured remained the warrior's sprite;[7]
Nor, for forgetfulness, his sword he drew,
Or wonderous deeds, I trow,[8] had wrought the knight:
But neither this, nor bill,[9] nor axe to hew,
Was needed by Orlando's peerless might.
He of his prowess gave high proofs and full,
Who a tall pine uprooted at a pull.

CXXVI

The shepherd swains, who hear the tumult nigh,
Leaving their flocks beneath the greenwood tree,
Some here, some there, across the forest hie,
And hurry thither, all, the cause to see.

* * *

5. Woe betide.
6. Hairy stomach.
7. Spirit.
8. Believe.
9. A weapon like a pole-axe.

Canto 24

V

Viewing the madman's wonderous feats more near,
The frightened band of rustics turned and fled;
But they, in their disorder, knew not where,
As happens oftentimes in sudden dread.
The madman in a thought is in their rear,
Seizes a shepherd, and plucks off his head!
And this as easily as one might take
Apple from tree, or blossom from the brake.

VI

He by one leg the heavy trunk in air
Upheaved, and made a mace the rest to bray.[1]
Astounded, upon earth he stretched one pair,
Who haply may awake at the last day.
The rest, who well advised and nimble are,
At once desert the field and scour[2] away:
Nor had the madman their pursuit deferred,
Had he not turned already on their herd.

X

Twice he ten peasants slaughtered in his mood,
Who, charging him in disarray, were slain;
And this experiment right clearly showed
To stand aloof was safest for the train.
Was none who from his body could draw blood;
For iron smote the impassive skin in vain.
So had heaven's King preserved the count from scathe,
To make him guardian of his holy faith.

Astolfo's Aerial Journey

Orlando's cousin, the English prince Astolfo, after a series of marvelous adventures, takes the hippogryph, a winged creature part griffon, part horse, from the magician Atlas and flies to Ethiopia, where he rids the kingdom of destructive harpies. He then goes to the highest point on earth, to the Terrestrial Paradise, whence he flies to the moon in Elijah's chariot with St. John the Evangelist, in order to recover Orlando's lost wits. One recalls Don Quixote's observation that he has never read of a knight's being transported in an ox-cart, as he is; they are usually sped through the air in a fiery chariot or on some hippogryph or similar beast (Part I, Ch. XLVII).

1. Break. 2. Run.

Canto 33

XCVI

Astolpho in his flight will I pursue,
That made his hippogryph like palfrey flee,
With reins and sell,[3] so quick the welkin[4] through
That hawk and eagle soar a course less free.
O'er the wide land of Gaul the warrior flew
From Pyrenees to Rhine, from sea to sea.
He westward to the mountains turned aside,
Which France's fertile land from Spain divide.

XCVII

To Arragon he past out of Navarre,
—They who beheld, sore[5] wondering at the sight—
Then leaves he Tarragon behind him far
Upon his left, Biscay upon his right:
Traversed Castile, Gallicia, Lisbon, are
Seville and Cordova, with rapid flight;
Nor city on sea-shore, nor inland plain,
Is unexplored throughout the realm of Spain.

XCVIII

Beneath him Cadiz and the strait he spied,
Where whilom[6] good Alcides[7] closed the way;
From the Atlantic to the further side
Of Egypt, bent o'er Africa, to stray;
The famous Balearic isles descried,
And Ivica,[8] that in his passage lay;
Toward Arzilla then he turned the rein,
Above the sea that severs it from Spain.

ALONSO FERNÁNDEZ DE AVELLANEDA

From Don Quixote

An unknown author wrote a sequel to Cervantes' own Part I, entitled *The Second Volume of the Ingenious Gentleman Don Quixote of La Mancha,* which appeared in Tarragona in 1614. An interesting work in its own right, it enjoyed little popularity in the seventeenth century; but in the eighteenth, it attained a modest success in French and English translations and was eventually reprinted in Spanish. Cervantes makes use of it in Part II.

3. Saddle.
4. Sky.
5. Greatly.
6. Once.
7. Hercules.
8. Ibiza.

In the opening chapters of this continuation, four noble gentlemen pass through Argamasilla on their way to Zaragoza, and one of them, Don Álvaro Tarfe, leaves a suit of parade armor in the care of Don Quixote, who has been his host for the night. Don Quixote is immediately inspired to follow the gentlemen and take part in the tournament, but he arrives too late. Don Álvaro and the other gentlemen, however, arrange a display of skill called Running at the Ring, in which a rider charges with his lance at a small metal circle suspended from a gallows-like support, as a test of accuracy and control useful in battle.

In Cervantes' own Part II, Don Quixote refuses to set foot in Zaragoza in order to discredit the "false" Quixote whose adventures are also circulating in print.

Cervantes takes a number of episodes from Avellaneda, skillfully improving their comic effect as a sort of challenge to his pseudonymous continuer. One of the most celebrated is the puppet show in Part II, Chs. XXV–XXVII, which outdoes Avellaneda's clever idea in Ch. XII below: Don Quixote interrupts a play by Lope de Vega in order to defend the unjustly accused heroine.

With these selections from Avellaneda in mind, one should reread Part II, Ch. LXXII and following, in which Don Álvaro Tarfe admits that the Don Quixote he met in Argamasilla was not the real one but a "bad" Quixote. The authentic knight asks Don Álvaro to give him a sworn statement that he and Sancho are not the same as the persons in the sequel.

The selections come from the 1784 version of William Augustus Yardley (London: Harrison & Company), which was based not on the Spanish of Avellaneda but on a widely-read French revision of the novel made by A. R. Lesage in 1704. The spelling, vocabulary, and punctuation of Yardley's translation have been slightly modernized.

Chapter IV. Which Shows How Don Quixote Won the Prize at the Course of the Ring.

The day for running at the ring being now arrived, the gentlemen who were to exhibit made themselves ready and gave all necessary orders for rendering the sport pleasant and magnificent. On the two sides of the square, two triumphal arches were erected, through which they were to pass to the lists; and on the triumphal arches were engraved several inscriptions in the praise of love. The windows and balconies were adorned with the most beautiful ladies of Saragossa and the neighbouring country, whose native charms were heightened by every embellishment of art and whose sparkling eyes discovered their hopes of receiving the prize at the hands of their lovers. The most distinguished place was appropriated for the reception of the viceroy and his family; after whom the prime nobility of the kingdom were seated, according to their rank and employments. The procession commenced by the judges of the field, who, after having paraded round the place three times, richly clad and followed by a numerous retinue, took their stations at the end of the course, amidst the sound of trumpets, in a magnificent theatre. Immediately as they were seated, there entered the place twenty cavaliers of graceful demeanor; they were divided into two troops and marched by pairs, arrayed in sumptuous liveries, with all the brilliant equipage of a superb and gallant solemnity. By the side of Don Alvaro, as his brother in arms, appeared the invincible Don Quixote, who entered the lists with a resolved and martial countenance. He wore his helmet on his head and was armed at all points, ready to fight all the giants in the world. The multitude, who do not always interpret things in the most favourable manner, set up a loud hooting at the curious appearance of Don Quixote and his peaceable courser. The two troops, passing before the ladies, performed the usual salute of gallantry by showing off the curvettings and prancing of their horses; in which particular, Rocinante, though untaught, played his part to admiration. When Don Quixote and Don Alvaro arrived before the judges and had saluted them, the chief of the judges, directing his discourse to the knight, said, with much gravity, "Most famous prince of La Mancha, flower and mirror of knight-erranty! We look upon it as a great favour of fortune that you have vouchsafed to honour with your presence the diversion we have prepared for the ladies on this day." The knight, with no less gravity, replied, "Great judge of martial exercises, though this be but mere sport, in comparison of the mighty enterprises I daily attempt, yet I will not deny you the satisfaction of seeing my dexterity." Having so said, he went on with Don Alvaro, who, when he came up to his troop, gave Don Quixote to understand that he must not run till the last, lest he should deprive the other knights of the hopes of winning any of the prizes; and, since his course must needs be the finest and most pleasing of all, it was fit to reserve it for the last, that the sport might conclude with something extraordinary. Don Quixote could not offer anything against such plausible reasons, but, drawing off to one side, became a spectator of the diversion.

The trumpets and kettle-drums now struck up amain, and the cavaliers ran their courses, every one in his turn, as had been appointed by lot, showing admirable skill and dexterity. Don Alvaro was admired above all the rest; he bore away the first prize and gave good proof that he was descended from the ancient Abencerrajes (a noble race of Moors), who first brought into Spain the custom of tilting and running at the ring, with other noble sports intended for the diversion of the ladies. When they had all run, Don Alvaro went up to Don Quixote, who began to be out of patience, and, leading him to the starting-place, the trumpets gave the signal. Don Quixote clapped his heels to the meagre sides of Rocinante, who, being ready to contribute as much as in him lay to his master's honour, appeared on this occasion uncommonly mettlesome and, after he had received about twenty memorandums from the spur, set out with more than ordinary swiftness. But here, alas, let us bewail the mutability of fortune, who delights in destroying, in a moment, the best-grounded hopes. Rocinante had now traversed half the course; he was now near the place where the ring was suspended on high, when his mighty mettle failing, he made a false step and fell down under his master. This accident set all the spectators a-laughing; and Don Quixote having helped up his horse, returned foaming with anger to the place from whence he set out. Don Alvaro, who was there ready to receive him, said to him, "Be not cast down, Sir Knight, since it was your horse's fault alone that you did not bear away the ring; your career was beautiful to admiration; and, if you take my advice, you must begin it again before Rocinante cools." Don Quixote, without answering one word, set forward the second time, and, being beside himself with passion and concern, missed the ring; but the Granadine,[1] who had expected this mishap, rectified it in an instant; for, having followed upon a hand-gallop, he raised himself on his stirrups, and taking off the ring with his hand, clapt it so adroitly upon the point of Don Quixote's lance that our knight did not perceive the deception. At the same time he cried out, with a loud voice, "Victory! victory! The illustrious Don Quixote, the ornament of knight-errantry, has borne away the ring!" The knight cast his eyes upon his lance, and seeing the ring there, concluded that he had finished his course with honour; then, turning to Don Alvaro, he said, "You see how dangerous it is to be idle. Rocinante, for want of being kept in his wind, has notoriously scandalized me." "It is true," said Don Alvaro, smiling, "but you have made good amends for it, and you must now go up to the judges to demand the prize." Don Quixote followed his advice, and advancing before the judges, held out his lance to them, saying, "Your lordships may be pleased to look upon this lance; methinks it says enough in my behalf." The same judge who had spoken to him before now undertook for his brethen, and having made fast to the end of his lance two dozen leather thongs which he had caused to be brought for the purpose and which were worth about a groat or threepence, he said to him, "Invincible knight-errant, as a prize for the skill and dexterity you have shown in your incomparable career, I present you with that precious jewel! The wise Lirgandus, your friend, brought it from the Indies for you. In short, these wonderful garters are made of the real skin of the Phoenix, that celebrated bird, the only one of his species. And, since you style yourself the Loveless Knight, I would advise you to

1. I.e., Don Álvaro.

present them to the lady in this assembly whom you shall judge the most insensible of that passion. But I do order you, upon pain of my displeasure, to come and sup with me tonight with Don Alvaro and to bring your faithful squire, who alone deserves to be servant to a knight of your worth." "I return you most humble thanks," answered Don Quixote, "for the noble present the wise Lirgandus sends me by your equitable hands; and you shall soon perceive how much I value your counsel." This said, he turned off to take an exact view of all the windows and balconies about the square. At last he halted at a low window where he saw an old woman between two courtesans, scurvily painted. This was the honourable lady he pitched upon. He drew near, and, resting the end of his lance, with the thongs hanging at it, on the edge of the window, said to her, in a grave and audible voice, "Most wise Urganda the Unknown, you see here before you the knight, so entirely yours, whom you have so often defended against the wiles of your malignant brother enchanters! In return for these favours, I beseech you to accept, at my hands, these precious garters, which I have gained with your favourable assistance and which are made of the very skin of that self-begotten bird, so much celebrated by our poets." The wise Urganda and her virtuous companions, wondering at this discourse, and at the present of the leather thongs, hearing also the rabble shout continually, discharged a volley of abusive language against the knight and instantly shut the window. Don Quixote, surprised at this incivility, knew not what to think and stood silent, as doubting how he should behave himself. Sancho, who had come up to his master in the Square after the course was over, seeing what small account the old woman made of the thongs, raised his voice and cried out, "O the old branded, excommunicated witch! What can she mean by refusing such curious delicate thongs? Poor jade! What a fool she is! By my father's soul, if I catch up a stone, I will soon make her open the window. But pray, Sir, let us leave the old hen and her chickens. Give me those laces; for these I have in my breeches are almost worn out, and the rest of them will serve in our errantry to mend Dapple's saddle-cloth and Rocinante's saddle." "Take, my son," replied Don Quixote in a melancholy mood (holding down the point of his lance), "take those rare garters, and lay them up carefully. I plainly perceive the wise Urganda is more friendly to my enemies than to me. She has sufficiently convinced me by the ill language I have just heard." "Od's my life, Sir!" quoth Sancho, "as for the ill language, never mind that; for it is all but words, and the wind carries them away. The crow cannot be blacker than his wings, and an old whore's curses are as good as prayers."

* * *

Chapter XII. [Which continues Don Quixote's Adventure with the Players]

The players, both men and women, made ready to rehearse the play in the hall, which they were to act the next day at Alcala. They lighted some candles that were stuck in little wooden candlesticks and drew a line on the floor to divide the stage from the audience. Don Quixote, Barbara, Sancho, and the scholars, and some others that were in the inn, took their places to hear the rehearsal, which soon began. A prince of Cordova appeared first, accompanied by his confidante, to whom he said, "Yes, my dear Henriquez! It is resolved: a disdained lover becomes an implacable enemy. I will be revenged of the Queen of Leon! The king her husband, whom you know I govern, is already prepossessed against her and contrives her death!" The Prince of Cordova would have proceeded, but seeing the queen appear, he withdrew. That princess stepped forward alone, with a handkerchief in her hand and, after wiping her eyes, which seemed bathed in tears, and stepping a few paces forward in silence, she said, "Perfidious Prince of Cordova, who, not able to corrupt my virtue with your love, dost contrive to blacken it by your artifices! Can you, without remorse, accuse my innocence? Alas, it is not death I fear! It is the dread of dying dishonoured! Great God, who seest the secrets of my soul, compassionate my sorrows! And will you, then, permit falsehood to triumph over virtue?" The actress, entering into her part with great energy, touched to the quick the susceptible Knight of La Mancha. He started up abruptly from his seat, drew his sword, and foaming with fury, cried out, "The Prince of Cordova is a traitor, a villain, and a slanderer! And as such I here challenge him to single combat; and I will soon, with the sole edge of my keen sword, cause him to confess that the Queen of Leon is not less chaste than the Princess Zenobia[1] herself!" The players, who were not prepared for this adventure, burst out laughing; but the knight going on with his challenge to the Prince of Cordova, the player who represented him drew his sword and, stepping up to Don Quixote, said, "There is no need, Sir Knight, of so much noise for so small a matter; and since you will espouse the queen's quarrel, whose chastity you are not so well acquainted with as I am, I consent to fight you, not here, but in the Great Square of Madrid, before the king and all the court!" As he was thus speaking, he espied a mule's crupper, which hung to the ceiling of the room; this he took down, and, tendering it to Don Quixote, went on, saying, "There, Sir Knight, since I have neither glove nor gauntlet to give you as a gage, take one of my garters, which may serve in the stead; and remember the combat shall be twenty days hence." All the company fell a-laughing at the player's

1. An old whore whom Don Quixote has taken under his wing.

contrivance, which so highly offended Don Quixote, that he said, "Really, gentlemen, I wonder that such wise and courageous princes should laugh to see a traitor accept my challenge; you ought rather to weep with the queen, who has so much cause to be troubled, but who ought now to take comfort, since she has had the good fortune to meet with me." Then turning to his squire and giving him the crupper, he said, "Here, Sancho, keep this gage safe." "By my faith!" cried Sancho, "the crupper is none of the worst! I'll e'en make it fast to my ass's saddle-cloth, where it shall stay till we can find out the owner." "Fool!" quoth Don Quixote, "to call that a crupper!" "What the devil is it, then," replied Sancho, "if it is not a mule's crupper?" "It is the Prince of Cordova's garter," answered the knight. "Why, sure, you will make me renounce Antichrist!" said the squire. "One would think I had never seen a crupper. Look ye, Sir, I have handled more cruppers than there are stars in Limbo!" "Here, blockhead!" quoth Don Quixote, "see whether ever there was a richer garter! Observe those golden fringes; and mark how a diamond, or a ruby, or an emerald of inestimable value, terminatres every thread." "Then I am certainly drunk," said Sancho, "for let me be hanged, if I see any of the gold fringes you talk of, but only little packthreads knotted at the ends! In short, it is possible this may be a garter in the other world, for the devil is a sad rogue; but in this, I do affirm it is a crupper." "Friend Sancho," quoth the director," do you banter us in calling this a crupper? I can assure you it is a garter of great value." "Nay, if you have any hand in it, Mr. Skiff," cried Sancho, "I say no more to it; for you gentlemen enchanters will turn white black, and, if you have it in your head, this must needs be a garter, though it smells so strong of a crupper."

Whilst they were in this pleasant contest, not unlike that about the helmet of Mambrino, a mule-driver coming into the room and seeing the crupper in Sancho's hand, said, "Cousin, pr'ythee leave the crupper where you found it; I did not buy it for your diversion." "Gentlemen," cried Sancho, "do not you hear what this honest man says? I am sure I did not bid him say so. Then it is a crupper, by Jove! I am glad of it. You may see by this, that enchanters and knights-errant are no such conjurors as they take themselves to be." Thus saying, he gave the crupper to the mule-driver; but Don Quixote, having no mind to part with it, went up to him, and snatching it away rudely, said, "Is it likely, clown, such a rich garter was made for you, then?" The mule-driver, who did not understand jesting and was much stronger than Don Quixote, laid hold of his arm, and giving him a thrust in the stomach, threw him over; then jumping upon him, he soon forced the crupper out of his hands. The squire, seeing his master fall, ran to his assistance and greeted the mule-driver with two furious cuffs, one of which took him in the nape of the neck and the other on the right ear. The mule-driver was stunned for a while, but soon revenged himself; for he laid on three or four smart strokes with the crupper across the chaps of the squire, after which he went out of the room, because the players and the scholars threatened to second Sancho if he did not give over. Sancho feigned great eagerness to follow him, crying aloud to the scholars, who held his hands, "Ay, ay! that's right! Pray hold me, gentlemen. I beseech you, for if I go after that discourteous mule-driver, I shall kill him and all his race, to the twentieth generation!" "No, Sancho," answered Don Quixote, "let the wretch go, since he flies before us; he is not worth our anger. Knights are not to make ill use of their valour and ought rather to make slight of, than to revenge a wrong when it comes from a man of no note, one of the meanest of the rabble." "You are in the right, Don Quixote," said the director, "you take just measures in this affair: great men must show moderation and calmness, that they may not do all the harm that is in their power to the little ones." "Well, then," said Sancho, "God speed the mule-driver with the two raps I laid him on about the ears!" Night being now far advanced, the director led Don Quixote into a room where he double-locked him in, after which he returned to the actors, who performed their rehearsal, and then went to bed.

Criticism

MARTÍN DE RIQUER

Cervantes and the Romances of Chivalry†

It is perfectly possible that Cervantes had ulterior motives which led him to conceive and write *Don Quixote*. One may question the writer's object and propose yet another interpretation among the many which the great novel has suggested; and one may accept or deny that the novel should be classified as esoteric literature. It is all possible and perhaps necessary; but even the most elementary critical approach demands, above all, that we heed, examine, and explain the stated purpose which guided the writer, particularly since he repeats with tedious insistence, in a clear, straightforward way, the reasons which led him to write *Don Quixote*. And though some readers might interpret this reiterated profession as a hypocritical excuse or a screen with which the author tries to conceal other objectives; and even though it were possible to prove or reveal in a totally convincing way Cervantes' hidden intentions; even so, as earnest critics we are bound to take into consideration what the writer declares so clearly, throughout the two parts of the novel, and to make what to many may seem a useless effort (or proof that we have fallen into the trap): to read *Don Quixote* ingenuously, to believe what Cervantes says, and to see whether the stated purpose is justifiable and is a response to some circumstance of its milieu.

In the prologue of the first part of the novel, the imaginary friend says to Cervantes: "[Your book] is from beginning to end an attack upon the books of chivalry, of which Aristotle never dreamed or St. Basil said a word or Cicero had any knowledge. . . . keep your aim fixed on the destruction of that ill-founded edifice of the books of chivalry, hated by so many yet praised by many more; for if you succeed in this you will have achieved no small success" (Part I, Prol.). *Don Quixote* ends, in the last lines of Part II, with the following words: "My desire has been no other than to cause mankind to abhor the false and foolish tales of the books of chivalry, which, thanks to that of my true Don Quixote, are even now tottering and doubtless doomed to fall for ever. Farewell." (Part II, Ch. LXXIV). Such clear, decisive statements, repeated often in the course of the novel, were understood perfectly by contemporary readers, as is logical. Avellaneda, in the prologue of his own *Quixote* writes, "But let Cervantes complain about my work because of the earnings I will take away from his second part; because he will have to admit at least that we both have the same

† Translated by Joseph R. Jones from "Cervantes y la caballeresca," in *Suma cervantina*, ed. J. B. Avalle-Arce and E. C. Riley (London: Tamesis Books, 1973), pp. 273–292. (All footnotes are Riquer's, unless otherwise noted.)

object, which is to banish the pernicious reading of worthless books of chivalry, so common in ignorant and idle people . . ." (Tarragona, 1614 ed., folio c *recto*). A year after the printing of these words, the second part of the authentic *Don Quixote* appears prefaced (among other official documents) by Master José de Valdivielso's *aprobación* (censor's approval) and by a second, longer *aprobación* by the Licentiate Márquez Torres. Valdivielso writes, "The author . . . pursuing his well-chosen subject, whereby he aspires to expel books of chivalry, for with his good diligence, he has cleverly cleansed these realms of their contagious malady." Márquez Torres tells us that in Don Quixote there is nothing undesirable from the Christian, moral point of view, "but on the contrary, it contains much erudition and edification, in the chastity of its well-developed theme (the eradication of worthless and mendacious books of chivalry, whose infection had spread more than was proper). . . ."

Three centuries later, Ortega says, "Cervantes claims that he is writing to attack books of chivalry. In recent times, critics have paid little attention to this purpose. Perhaps they believe it was a manner of speaking, a conventional presentation of the work, like the *soupçon* of exemplarity with which he shields his novellas. Nevertheless, we must return to this point of view. For esthetic reasons it is necessary to see the work of Cervantes as a polemic against books of chivalry."[1]

Chivalry in Real Life and in Literature

Sebastián de Covarrubias, in his *Treasury of the Castilian or Spanish Language*, published in 1611 (i.e., between the first and second parts of *Don Quixote*), defines books of chivalry as works "which deal with the deeds of knights-errant; pleasant and skillful fiction which provides much entertainment and little profit, such as the books about Amadís, Don Galaor, the Knight of Phoebus, etc."[2] These brief lines indicate that the books of chivalry are narratives which have a knight-errant as protagonist, that the action or plot is basically a series of "deeds," and that they are fictitious. The last qualification seems essential: if the elements are not fictitious, that is, if the protagonist has existed or the deeds have taken place, the narrative is no longer a "book of chivalry" but of history and deserves the weighty name of chronicle. As is well known, Castilian has not, until very recent times, made use of the term *novel* to designate a long fictional narrative. It could not adopt the cognate terms *roman* from French or *romanzo* from Italian because the

1. J. Ortega y Gasset, *Meditaciones del Quijote* (Madrid, 1914), 170.
2. S. de Covarrubias, *Tesoro de la lengua castellana o española*, ed. M. de Riquer (Barcelona, 1943), 324a.

Spanish word *romance* meant something quite different: a poem of eight-syllable verses, etc.[3] I suspect (in matters of this sort it is foolhardy and pedantic to affirm) that this centuries-old absence of a Castilian word for novel may have contributed to the confusion obvious in the mind of Don Quixote and of certain flesh-and-blood Quixotes about which we have information. A French writer makes it plain that he is going to narrate a fictional action when he entitles his work *Roman de Tristan, Roman dou Graal, Roman de Balain, Roman de Jean de Paris,* etc. He can of course disguise his fiction as reality and call his novel an *estoire,* or leave the question undecided with a vague *livre;* but the Castilian writer of the Middle Ages and the sixteenth and seventeenth centuries (the age which concerns us here) did not have such options and was forced to use, imprecisely, the names *historia* and *crónica* for works as "fantastic and preposterous" as the *History of the Invincible Knight Don Olivante de Laura, Part One of the Great History of the Very Brave and Courageous Prince Felixmarte of Hircania,* or the *Chronicle of the Very Valiant and Courageous Knight Platir, The Chronicle of Lepolemo,* etc. (The title *Las sergas de Esplandián* [*Deeds of Esplandián*] is admittedly a stroke of genius.) Simultaneous with the publication of books like these is the publication of others which were strictly true, with the titles *History of the Emperor Charles* V, or the *Chronicle of the Great Captain Gonzalo Hernández de Córdoba.* No doubt all this helped increase the confusion between accounts of imaginary matters and accounts of real events. It is a central question in the discussion between the priest and the innkeeper Palomeque (Part I, Ch. XLIX), to mention only two of the many passages in Cervantes' novel where this equivocation is debated.

In spite of its obviousness, this problem, which is inextricably linked with the invention of *Don Quixote,* can help us identify concepts and points of view which clarify Cervantes' attitude toward the literature of chivalry. In the chat between Don Quixote and the canon, we observe that the latter, a cultivated, sensible person, has a clear, unshakable idea of which books are historical and which are fiction. Don Quixote, a cultivated but unbalanced person who has gone mad precisely as a result of reading books, labors in his mind under the same delusion as the illiterate innkeeper Palomeque: all books which have a knight as the hero are true. Don Quixote tries to demonstrate, with arguments which the reader knows perfectly well are false (and in which Cervantes' refined irony always surfaces), that Amadís de Gaula existed, that the affair of Fierabrás at the bridge of Mantible was true, that King Arthur still lives in the shape of a raven, and that the love of Tristan and Iseult and Guin-

3. On the matter of terminology, see E. C. Riley, "Teoría literaria," *Suma cervantina* (London, 1973), 310–311.

evere and Lancelot were real. (He goes so far as to claim that his grandmother knew the lady Quintañona, the go-between in Lancelot's affair.) But Don Quixote, who has his sane moments, leaves the priest gaping with amazement when he concludes his case with this phrase: "Or perhaps I shall be told, too, that there was no such knight-errant as the valiant Lusitanian Juan de Merlo, who went to Burgundy and in the city of Arras fought with the famous lord of Charney, Monsieur Pierres by name, and afterwards in the city of Basle with Monsieur Enrique de Remestán, coming out of both encounters covered with fame and honor, or adventures and challenges achieved and delivered, also in Burgundy, by the valiant Spaniards Pedro Barba and Gutierre Quixada (of whose family I come in the direct male line), when they vanquished the sons of the Count of San Polo. I shall be told, too, that Don Fernando de Guevara did not go in quest of adventures to Germany, where he engaged in combat with Messire George, a knight of the house of the Duke of Austria. I shall be told that the jousts of Suero de Quiñones, of the *Paso*, and the adventures of Mosén Luis de Falces against the Castilian knight, Don Gonzalo de Guzmán, were mere mockeries, as well as many other achievements of Christian knights of these and foreign realms, which are so authentic and true that, I repeat, he who denies them must be totally wanting in reason and good sense." (Part I, Ch. XLIX). All of this is strictly true, and all these names and brief references come from the *Chronicle of John II*, which is apparently Cervantes' only source for these real Spanish knights-errant of the fifteenth century.[4]

One can compare Don Quixote's words quoted above with those of Fernando del Pulgar, in the biography of Rodrigo de Narváez included in Pulgar's *Illustrious Men of Castile* in a passage which, because it was composed at the end of the fifteenth century, sounds perfectly normal; it would occur to no one to attribute it to a madman: "I certainly never saw in my day or read that in the past there came so many knights from other realms and lands to these, your majesty's realms of Castile and León to do mortal combat, as I saw knights from Castile go seek adventures in other parts of Christendom. I knew Count Gonzalo de Guzmán and Juan de Merlo; I knew Juan de Torres and Juan de Polance, Alfarán de Vivero, Mosén Pero Vázquez de Sayavedra, Gutierre Quijada, and Mosén Diego de Valera; and I heard tell of other Castilians who with the bravery of true knights went through foreign kingdoms to do battle with any knight who wanted to fight and who thereby won honor for themselves and a reputation for the gentlemen of Castile as valiant and brave knights."[5]

It is appropriate to note that Fernando del Pulgar errs on the

4. See M. de Riquer, *Vida caballeresca en la España del siglo XV* (Madrid, 1965); inaugural speech before the Royal Spanish Academy.

5. Fernando del Pulgar, *Claros varones de Castilla*, ed. J. Domínguez Bordona (Clásicos castellanos, Madrid, 1923), 115.

side of brievity and modesty, because throughout the fifteenth century not only are numerous foreign knights-errant well documented in Spain, taking parts in jousts and passages of arms, but there are many Spanish knights-errant (Castilians, Galicians, Catalans, Valencians, Aragonese) who wandered over a great part of Europe (France, Burgundy, Flanders, England, Germany, Italy, Huugary, the Byzantine Empire, the Kingdom of Granada, etc.), all of them attested in trustworthy archival documents and chronicles.

The knight-errant existed and still wandered the roads of Europe, from court to court, in search of adventures (jousts, passages of arms, tournaments, mortal combat) only a century before Cervantes set himself to writing *Don Quixote*. And there existed a literature about these knights which can be divided into two categories: the biography of the knight, and the novel of chivalry. As examples of the first category we have the *Livre des faits du bon messire Jean le Maingre, dit Bouciquaut*, the *Livre des faits de Jacques de Lalaing*, and the *Victorial*, the biography of Don Pero Niño; and we could add the *Book of the Honorable Passage of Arms*, which, though it is simply a very extensive notarial account of a passage of arms, is perfectly representative of Spanish knight-errantry in 1434. To the second category belong certain novels—I cannot recall one in Castilian—in which the protagonist is imaginary and the plot is the author's invention, but which because of the description of the hero as well as because of the characteristics of the work, are realistic accounts of fifteenth-century knight-errantry and its enterprises. The Catalan novels *Curial e Güelfa* and *Tirant lo Blanch* and the French *Jean de Saintré* and the *Roman de Jean de Paris* conform to this type of narrative. Take for example the biography of a perfectly historical knight like Jacques de Lalaing, who accomplished his first knightly feats at Valladolid, which shows a great similarity with the novel that has as protagonist the fictitious Jean de Saintré, who accomplishes his first feats of arms at Barcelona. This type of novel, which is appropriately called the novel of chivalry, in contradistinction to the "books of chivalry," was understood by Cervantes, as his praise of *Tirant lo Blanch* demonstrates. The great writer was aware that this novel is different from the romances of chivalry and that it is characterized by naturalness, verisimilitude, and humor; and thus he writes, "[One of the books fell at the feet] of the barber. Curious to know whose it was, he picked it up and found it to read, *History of the Famous Knight, Tirante the White*. 'God bless me!' said the priest with a shout, 'Tirante the White here! Hand it over, friend, for in it I have found a treasury of enjoyment and a mine of recreation. Here is Don Quirieleison of Montalbán, a valiant knight, and his brother Tomás of Montalbán, and the knight Fonseca, with the battle the bold Tirante fought with the mastiff, and the witticisms of the damsel Placerdemivida, and the loves and wiles of the widow Reposada, and the empress in love with the squire Hipólito. In truth, my friend, by right of its style it is the best book in the world. Here knights eat and sleep and die in their beds, and make their wills before dying, and a great deal more of which there is nothing in all the other books' " (Part I, Ch. VI).[6]

Tirant lo Blanch—the living models for the protagonist of which may be Roger de Flor, John Hunyadi, voivode of Hungary and father of Matthias Corvinus, the Burgundian Geoffrey de Thoisy, Pedro Vázquez de Saavedra, etc.—is a novel which resembles the *Victorial* much more than it does *Amadís de Gaula.* The reason is that *Tirant* is a novel of chivalry and *Amadís* is a "book of chivalry."

The term "books of chivalry" for reasons of methodology and because the difference is evident, must be reserved for works of imagination that descend in a clear artistic line which we can trace from the verse narrative of Chrétien de Troyes and that found its most resounding success in the lengthy French prose romance *Lancelot,* the so-called "Vulgate," and in the likewise extensive prose *Tristan.* This line—as opposed to the family of works which make up what we call the novel of chivalry—is characterized essentially by the presence of marvelous elements (dragons, monsters, serpents, dwarfs, edifices built by magic, bottomless inhabited lakes, greatly exaggerated strength of the knights, mysterious atmosphere, etc.) and by location in exotic or distant lands and in a very remote past. There is not the least doubt that when Cervantes enunciates his intention to banish the reading of "books of chivalry," he is referring to this class of literary work, which begins around the mid-twelfth century and continues to his own day, with the natural variations of a four-centuries-old genre.

The element of chivalry in *Don Quixote* has many different nuances. The authentic historical knight is respected, from the figure of the warrior Cid to the real knights-errant of the fifteenth century, the Great Captain, García de Paredes, and—why not?—the generation of Lepanto, symbolized by the figure of the Captive, whose story (one should remember) comes right after the discourse on arms and letters. Cervantes praises the novel of chivalry, as the eulogy of Tirant reveals, and does not adopt a negative attitude toward the Renaissance epic of the sort made famous by Ariosto. On the other hand, he attacks and parodies the romances of chivalry, though he has no recourse but to set aside *Amadís de Gaula* and *Palmerín de Ingalaterra,* saved from the fire in the famous examination of Don Quixote's library. But his negative attitude

6. I omit the much-discussed final portion of this eulogy of *Tirant.* See G. E. Sansone, "Ancora del giudizio di Cervantes sul *Tirant lo Blanch,*" *Studi Mediolatini e Volgari,* VIII (1960). I still maintain the interpretation which I published in *RFE,* XXVII (1943). See also G. B. Palacín, "El pasaje más oscuro del *Quijote,*" *Duquesne Hispanic Review,* III (1964), and M. Bates, "Cervantes and Martorell," *HR,* XXXV (1967).

toward the romances of chivalry is not something new; on the contrary, it corresponds to the clearly stated position of serious Spanish writers, which had already emerged at the end of the fourteenth century and which was most persistent and systematic throughout the sixteenth.

Serious Authors against the Romances of Chivalry

There is a famous strophe in the *Rimado del palacio* [*Poem About Court*] in which the Chancellor Don Pero López de Ayala laments the time he wasted reading "books of fantasies and proven lies" like *Amadís* and *Lancelot.* Also at the end of the fourteenth century, the Dominican friar Antoni Canals, in the prologue of his Catalan version of the epistle *De Bene Vivendi,* thought to be by St. Bernard, states that one should not read frivolous books, and he uses as an example of such "the tales of *Lancelot* and *Tristan,*" the *Roman de Renart* (which he calls the *Romanc de la guineu*), Ovid's *Ars Amandi,* and the Pseudo-Ovidian *De Vetula.*[7] These early forerunners of what we are going to examine below are no less curious for the different origins of the authors, contemporaries of one another, who made such judgments: Chancellor Ayala, who was a knight (one should recall his participation in the principal battles of his day) and the Senecan writer Antoni Canals, who apparently speaks to an audience of courtiers capable of enthusiasm for Ovid and of reading and appreciating the *Roman de Renart* in French, since there is no evidence of a Catalan translation of this work, which would in any case be unlikely. For our purposes, what is really interesting is the attacks on the romances of chivalry throughout the sixteenth century by what we shall call "serious" authors, under which title I include philosophers, moralists, historians, and monastic writers from various orders. Let us first examine, in chronological order of composition or publication, a list of such attacks. indicating the work in which the romances of chivalry are censured:[8]

7. *Colección de documentos inéditos del Archivo de la Corona de Aragón,* XIII (Barcelona, 1857), 420.

8. I include data collected by Menéndez y Pelayo, *Orígnes de la novela,* I (Madrid, 1943), 440–447; Américo Castro, *El pensamiento de Cervantes* (Madrid, 1925), 26, n. 2; Werner Krauss, "Die Kritik des Siglo de Oro am Ritter- und Schaeferroman," *Homenage a Antoni Rubió i Lluch* (Barcelona, 1936), I, 225–246; Marcel Bataillon, *Erasmo y España* (México, 1966), 622–623, n. 1; M. de Riquer, prologue to the edition of *Tirante el Blanco* (Barcelona, 1947), I, XXXII–XLI; E. Glaser, "Nuevos datos sobre la crítica de los libros de caballerías en los siglos XVI y XVII," *Anuario de Estudios Medievales,* III (Barcelona, 1966). See also E. Asensio, "El erasmismo y las corrientes espirituales afines (conversos, franciscanos, italianizantes)," *RFE,* XXXVI (1952), 94. This list could no doubt be extended, but it is already very eloquent as it is, on the basis of these studies. Pedro Sainz Rodríguez, "Una fuente posible de *El Criticón* de Gracián," *Archivo Teológico Granadino,* XXV (1952), 13, n. 12, gives a "nomenclator" of authors who wrote against the romances of chivalry, some not represented on the list which I present her, but he does not indicate in what works the censures appear.

1524: Juan Luis Vives, *De institutione christianae feminae* (and 1528 trans. Jerónimo Justiniano, *Instrucción de la mujer cristiana*).
1529: Fray Antonio de Guevara, *Libro del emperador Marco Aurelio*.
1531: Juan Luis Vives, *De causis corruptarum artium*.
1533-1535: Juan de Valdés, *Diálogo de la lengua*.
1539: Fray Antonio de Guevara, *Aviso de privados y doctrina de cortesanos*.
1544: Francisco de Monzón, *Espejo del príncipe cristiano*.
1544: Francisco Cervantes de Salazar, in additions to his version of *Instrucción y camino para la sabiduría* by Juan Luis Vives.
1544: Pedro Mexía, *Historia imperial y cesárea*.
1545: Francisco Díaz Romano in the prologue to *Hábito y armadura espiritual* by Diego de Cabranes.
1546: Alejo de Venegas in the prologue to *Apólogo de la Ociosisidad y del Trabajo* by Luis Mexía.
1547: Luis de Alarcón, *Camino del Cielo*.
1547: Alonso de Fuentes, *Summa de philosophía natural*.
1548: Diego Gracián, *Morales de Plutarco*.
1552: Diego Gracián, *Historia de la entrada de Ciro Menor en Asia*.
1553: Alejo de Venegas in the preface to Agustín de Almazán's translation of *La moral y muy graciosa historia del Momo* by L. B. Alberti.
1553: Alfonso García Matamoros, *Pro adserenda Hispanorum eruditione*.
1553: Francisco de Barcelos, *Salutiferae crucis triumphus in Christi Dei gloriam*.
1555: Gonzalo Fernández de Oviedo, *Las quinquagenas de la nobleza de España*.
¿1556?: João de Barros, *Espelho de casados*.
1557: Andrés Laguna, *Cuatro elegantísimas y gravísimas oraciones de M. T. Cicerón, contra Catilina*.
1563: Melchor Cano, *De locis theologicis*.
1569: Arias Montano, *Rhetoricorum libri IV*.
¿1573?: Fray Agustín Salucio, *Aviso para los predicadores del santo Evangelio*.
1574: Gonzalo de Illescas, *Historia pontifical y católica*.
1580: Miguel Sánchez de Lima, *El arte poética en romance castellano*.
1582: Fray Luis de Grandada, *Introducción al Símbolo de la Fe*.
1588: Malón de Chaide, *La conversión de la Magdalena*.
1589: Fray Juan de Tolosa, *Aranjuez del alma*.

1589: Fray Francisco Ortiz Lucio, *Jardín de amores santos.*
1593: Fray Francisco de Ribera, *In XII prophetarum commentarii.*
1595: Fray Marco Antonio de Camós, *Microcosmia y gobierno universal del hombre cristiano.*
1597: Gaspar de Astete, *Tratado del gobierno de la familia y estado de las viudas y doncellas.*
1599: Fray Luis de Granada, *Compendio de doctrina cristiana.*
1599: Fray Pedro de la Vega, *Declaración de los siete psalmos penitenciales.*
1599: Fray Juan de la Cerda, *Vida política de todos los estados de mujeres.*

One must observe in the first place that the censures are not limited to books of chivalry. The majority of these authors include in their attacks the pastoral novel, the poetry of Boscán and even of Garcilaso, the *Celestina,* and at times the sentimental novel, such as the *Cárcel de amor* [*Prison of Love*]. In spite of this, the books of chivalry are usually the most abused, and the one which is most often the object of censure is *Amadís de Gaula* (although not all authors name it, and Juan de Valdés praises it), followed by *Las sergas de Esplandián* [*The Deeds of Esplandián*] and *Palmerín de Inglaterra,* and in a smaller proportion of attacks, *Primaleón, Florisando, Lisuarte de Grecia, Clarín de Landanís,* and *Reinaldos de Montalván* (a work different from the others.) Note also that in spite of passages which might appear to the moralists of the sixteenth century to be scabrous and lascivious, *Tirant lo Blanc* only appears in a long list of books made by Juan Luis Vives in *De Institutione Christianae Feminae,* when *Tirant* had already been published in two Catalan editions (1490 and 1497), in Italian (1501), and Castilian (1511), and would be reprinted three more times in Italian (1538, 1566, and 1611).

The above-mentioned list of serious authors who censured books of chivalry could be extended, let us not forget. And such a list of attacks is not a unique phenomenon. Suffice it to mention the attacks of the Church Fathers on pagan authors; and a roster of detractors of the cinema in the twentieth century would be interminable. But the list permits us to gather together the principal arguments brandished by the enemies of that literary genre. And since Miguel de Cervantes professes so many times that he is writing *Don Quixote* in order to make people forget books of chivalry, it is necessary to point out on what questions or judgments the views of the great novelist are in accord with those of the serious authors.

Sometimes the censures are aimed at the authors of the books of chivalry, sometimes at their readers. With regard to the authors, it is said that they are ignorant and write poorly. Fray Agustín Salucio (1573?), lumping together authors of romances and of "farces," is emphatic: "no Spaniard of talent has held it so cheap that he would waste it upon such trifles; and so those who have applied themselves to these accounts of imaginary subjects in prose or verse are garrulous, silly ignoramuses, with no education or acquaintance with good authors or *belles lettres*; their works are nothing but lies, without rhyme or reason, without polished language and without style, without the skill to maintain decorum or even to develop their wretched subject . . ."[9] Cervantes, who coincides in this opinion several times, makes the Toledan canon say that the books of chivalry "are harsh in their style, . . . long-winded in battle-descriptions, silly in speeches, preposterous in describing journeys, and finally, devoid of any intelligent artistry" (Part I, Ch. XLVII).[1]

Serious authors, with great frequency, accuse the authors of romances of chivalry of being enemies of truth, since they recount untrue and impossible events, which ignorant people may accept as true, to the detriment of authentic history. As an example of this widely-held opinion, observe what Diego Gracián writes (1552): ". . . at least with the reading of this work [Xenophon's *Anabasis*] I shall dull Spanish readers' taste for reading books of chivalry, of which there is greater abundance in our Spain than in other countries, when there should be fewer; for they serve no other purpose than to waste time and detract from other, truthful works, full of sound doctrine and profit, because the shapeless, disjointed yarns which one reads in these books of lies weaken belief in the true deeds which one reads about in authentic history." This criticism is constant, in both an explicit and implicit fashion, in *Don Quixote*, the madness of its protagonist being in great part the result of this error, that is, of believing, as we have already seen, that Lancelot, Tristan, and Amadís are as historical as Juan de Merlo, Suero de Quiñones, and the Great Captain.

That the books of chivalry incite readers to sensuality is, without doubt, the criticism that appears most frequently in serious authors, many of whom are moralists and clerics, and without doubt one of the accusations which have been most persistently leveled at every type of literature of chivalry, from Dante, who made Paolo Malatesta and Francesca de Rimini sin because of reading *Lancelot*, to the not very fastidious Brantôme, who declares in the *Les Dames galantes*, that he would like to have as many hundreds of *écus* in his pocket as there are women, secular and religious, perverted by the reading of *Amadís*. Cervantes at times points out the immorality of

9. Cited by E. Glaser, "Nuevos datos,"
1. See E. C. Riley, "Teoría literaria," *Suma*, 311 ff.

the romances of chivalry with ironical observations typical of his humor; and the words from the mouth of the writer himself say more than moralist's reflections: " . . . our famous Spaniard, Don Quixote de la Mancha, light and mirror of Manchegan knighthood and the first who in our age and in these calamitous times undertook the travail and exercise of arms-errant, and of undoing grievances, succoring widows, and protecting damsels, like those who with their whips and palfreys and with all their virginity about them, wandered from hill to hill and valley to valley; and unless some miscreant or some boor, with hood and hatchet, or some monstrous giant ravished them, there were damsels in past ages who after eighty years, during which they never slept under a roof a single day, went to their graves as untouched as the mothers who bore them" (Part I, Ch. IX). Obviously, making fun of immorality is much more effective than censure. In his serious moments, Cervantes agrees with the attitude of the moralists when he says of books of chivalry that "this genre of writing and composition comes under the heading of Milesian fable" (Part I, Ch. XLVII), since the so-called fables of Miletus were considered lewd in the extreme.[2]

There existed official prohibitions and efforts at prohibition of romances of chivalry in Spain as well as in the Indies,[3] an important aspect but one which interests us less than the parallels between the critical attitude of Cervantes and that of the serious authors of the sixteenth century previously enumerated. Beyond the anecdotal and circumstantial similarities, a great number of these writers and the author of *Don Quixote* share certain tendencies typical of Spanish Erasmism,[4] concerning which—and doubtless oversimplifying—one could point out facts of considerable importance. If we accept the theory that the favorite novel of the Erasmists was *Theagenes and Charicleia* by Heliodorus,[5] the end of Cervantes' literary career seems to have a very clear meaning: with *Don Quixote*, he parodies, satirizes, and ridicules the "old-fashioned" novel, the romance of chivalry born in the French twelfth century; with the *Persiles*, "a book which dares to compete with Heliodorus" (prologue to the novellas), he sets out in the direction which he doubtless thought most appropriate for the contemporary novel.

Books of Chivalry and the Public

The list of serious authors who attacked the books of chivalry presupposes an obvious conclusion: the books were very widely read.

2. On this question, see Schevill's note in his edition of *Don Quixote*, II, 457; and Bataillon, *Erasmo*, 616 and note.
3. See A. E. Serrano Redonnet, "Prohibición de libros en el primer sínodo santiagueño," *RFE*, V (1943), 162–166; I. A. Leonard, *Los libros del Conquistador* (Mexico, 1953), 76–88.
4. Cf. Bataillon, *Erasmo*, 614–615.
5. *Ibid.*, 620.

And even though the list increases each time some critic takes up the subject again, analyzing what we have may enlighten us on certain aspects of the problem. I believe that it is illogical to say that such attacks continued to be made out of habit after the vogue of the books of chivalry had greatly diminished (it would be hard for us to find a moralist nowadays who would warn us against reading Pedro Mata [an immensly popular novelist of the twenties and thirties] or a preacher who would speak of the immorality of the waltz). The list includes thirty-five attacks in seventy-five years (from 1524 to 1599). Taking into account the arbitrary and provisional nature of such estimates, one should note that the ten-year period in which the condemnations are most numerous is 1540–49 (eight censures), followed by 1550–59 (seven), the decade of Cervantes' childhood. In this spread of seventy-five years, the decades richest in the number of critical statments are 1580–89 (five censures) and 1590–99 (six); and we might point out that the latter coincides with the conception and beginning of *Don Quixote*. When Cervantes conceives and begins to write Part I of his great novel, serious works are still being published which contain attacks against the books of chivalry.

A delicate, provisional point also is estimating the number of editions of books of chivalry which Spanish booksellers issued. According to recent statistics.[6] and concentrating on the period which we have taken into account for the condemnation by serious authors, the data are as follows: 1530–39, thirty-five editions; 1540–49, forty-nine editions; 1550–59, twenty editions; 1560–69, twenty-nine editions; 1570–79, seven editions; 1580–89, thirty-one editions; 1590–99, four editions. We observe that as in the case of the attacks, the decade with most editions is 1540–49, and that in third place is the decade 1580–89. In censures as well as in editions, it appears that one can detect a decline in the decade 1570–79 (two censures and seven editions), but in the ten years which follow, the curve rises once more.

The most important datum, and unquestionably the hardest to establish, is the number of readers of books of chivalry. We have documentary evidence of a few noblemen and gentlemen who were fans of this type of literature, either because inventories of their libraries exist or because someone tells an anecdote which illustrates

6. See the useful charts, pp. 2–4, in the work of Maxime Chevalier, *Sur le public du roman de chevalerie* (Bordeaux, 1968). The author states that he has compiled them using Simón Díaz's *Bibliografía* and, for *Amadís de Gaula*, Place's bibliography in his edition. Chevalier states that between 1508 and 1630, eighteen eds. of *Amadís* appeared. But in papers left by Diego Clemencín, dated 1805, and the notes with which Juan Givanel published them, one deduces that between 1508 and 1589 at least twenty-eight eds. of this romance were published. Cf. Clemencín, "Biblioteca de libros de caballerías (año 1805)," *Publicaciones cervantinas* (Barcelona, 1942), 2–5. Doubtless both numbers are exaggerated (Place-Chevalier's too low, Clemencín-Givanel's too high), which makes the statistics very approximate. It is important to consider, in this sort of statistics, that for a considerable number of editions there is no known copy.

the social importance of such books. We have no information regarding lower-class readers because they have not left a trace of documentary evidence. It is of course self-evident that a book is reprinted because it is sold out. Various data lead one to believe that an edition of a book of chivalry was usually around a thousand copies:[7] a conservative, probably low, estimate of the number. And if conservative calculations permit eighty-six editions between 1551 and 1600,[8] this gives us eighty-six thousand copies, at a time when the population of the Spanish realms, including Portugal but not the Indies, was around nine and half million. This suggests that it was not only the upper classes that read the books of chivalry, but also the middle and lower. I do not believe that we should minimize the datum which Cervantes himself gives us when he makes Palomeque the innkeeper say the following words: "Because during the harvest, a lot of reapers gather here on holidays, and there are always some who know how to read; and one of them picks up one of these books, and more than thirty of us gather around him; and we listen to him with such pleasure that it makes us feel young again; at least I can say for myself that when I hear about those furious and terrible blows that the knights give each other, I have an urge to do it myself; and I would like to listen to these stories all day and all night" (Part I, Ch. XXXII). And a few lines later we learn that even Maritornes herself becomes sentimental when she listens to passages from the books of chivalry. This is not Cervantes' imagination, because we have already cited, above, Avellaneda's intention "to banish the pernicious reading of vain books of chivalry which is so common in ignorant, idle people [*gente rústica y ociosa*]."

One must bear in mind, furthermore, that a good number of books of chivalry, especially the short ones like *Tablante de Ricamonte, Pierres de Provenza, Clamades*, etc., enjoyed exceptionally wide circulation in broadsides and chap books printed on cheap paper, intended for an uncultivated public, and that most of them have disappeared without trace, though we have proof of their existence thanks to the catalogues of book collectors (beginning with Ferdinand Columbus) and to the advertisements of booksellers. This shows us also that reading books of chivalry did not disappear after the publication of *Don Quixote*; for a great number of these works continued to be published in this modest way until the beginning of the twentieth century.[9] Let us not forget, besides, that

7. See L. Pfandl, *Cultura y costumbres del pueblo español de los siglos XVI y XVII: Introducción al estudio del Siglo de Oro* (Barcelona, 1942), 1881-91; and the data and bibliography on this matter by J. Rubió in J. M. Madurell Marimón and J. Rubió Balaguer, *Documentos para la historia de la imprenta y librería en Barcelona* (1474–1553) (Barcelona, 1955), 88-89.

8. Chevalier, *op. cit.*, 5.

9. See A. Rodríguez-Moñino, *Construcción critica y realidad histórica en la poesía española de los siglos XVI y XVII* (Madrid, 1965), 45–49, and his *Diccionario de pliegos sueltos poéticos* (siglo XVI) (Madrid, 1970), 85–126; E. M. Wilson, *Some Aspects of Spanish Literary History* (Oxford, 1967), 23; and J. Caro Baroja, *Ensayo sobre la literatura de cordel* (Madrid, 1969), 317–331.

what interests us is the audience of the books of chivalry, part of which was the reader and part the listener, like the illiterate reapers of whom Palomeque the innkeeper speaks.

Everything leads us to conclude that when Cervantes conceived and began to write *Don Quixote*, the books of chivalry still enjoyed great prestige and had a considerable number of readers of all social classes. Otherwise, the stated purpose of the great novel, so often emphasized by Cervantes, would be pointless and outdated, even if we should admit that it is a screen to conceal loftier aspirations.

Parody of Books of Chivalry in Don Quixote

Cervantes's imaginary friend, in the prologue of Part I of *Don Quixote*, gives him the following advice: "Since your writing aims only at destroying the authority and acceptance which books of chivalry have in the world and among the common people, all you have to do . . . is try to make your sentences and periods harmonious and amusing, with meaningful, modest, and well-placed words. Try, also, to make the melancholy man laugh when he reads your story and the laughing man increase his merriment . . ." (Part I, Prologue). It is thus a matter of putting an end to the books of chivalry; but not with severe diatribes or moral discourses, as serious authors had been doing during the whole century, but with the more effective weapon of irony. Master José de Valdivielso had already noted it when in the *aprobación* of Part II of *Don Quixote*, recalling that the Lacedemonians had reared a statue to Laughter, he says that Cervantes, "by mixing the truth with jokes, the sweet with the useful, the moral with the facetious; by concealing the fishhook of moral correction with the bait of humor and by pursuing his well-chosen subject, whereby he aspires to expel books of chivalry . . . with his good diligence, has skilfully cleansed these realms of their contagious malady. . . ." A series of reliable testimonies shows that the reaction which *Don Quixote* produced among its contemporaries was, invariably, laughter.[1] Spaniards of 1605 roared with delight when they read the adventures of the Ingenious Gentleman, and they acclaimed Cervantes as a witty, amusing author. Fortunately, the reader of our own day who is not overwhelmed by life's problems—or by literary preoccupations—still laughs when he reads *Don Quixote*. But it is obvious that in numerous episodes and passages he is not aware of Cervantine irony, as were readers at the beginning of the seventeenth century.[2] The fact is that *Don Quixote* is, among

1. Cf. A. Bonilla, "¿Qué pensaron de Cervantes sus contemporáneos?" *Cervantes y su obra* (Madrid, 1916), and P. E. Russell, "*Don Quixote* as a Funny Book," *MLR*, LXIV (1969).

2. Each generation recognizes fewer and fewer of the comic elements of *Don Quixote*. For some years, I have had to explain in class what a barber's basin is, because there are students who believe that it was actually some sort of helmet used in Cervantes' day. Thus the episode of Mambrino's helmet and above all the extremely funny controversy over the

many other things—some doubtless of greater importance—a parody of the books of chivalry; and this special nuance can only be detected by someone familiar with the literary genre in question. Cervantes wrote for readers of books of chivalry; hence, in *Don Quixote* there are innumerable details which are explainable if one bears this in mind.

In the history of world literature, there are other cases of parody of heroic and chivalresque literature. Without going back to the *Batrachomyomachia* one might recall in passing the French *Audigier*, from the end of the twelfth century, a grotesque, scatological poem which clearly parodies the *chansons de geste*, especially *Girart de Rousillon;* and there is also a short Gallacio-Portuguese *gesta* by Alfonso López de Bayán which parodies the French epics so closely that each of its strophes ends with the letters EOI, like the mysterious AOI of the *Chanson de Roland.*[3] Needless to say, Cervantes knew none of these works.

The great ambiguity of *Don Quixote*, cleverly thought out by Cervantes, and one of the fundamental bases of the novel's parodic technique, appears in Chapter III of Part I, "where is told the amusing manner in which Don Quixote was armed a knight." Here there is something more than parody or grotesque distortion of passages from books of chivalry in which the youthful heroes receive knighthood. In Cervantes' day everyone accepted the idea that some men were simple gentlemen (*hidalgos*) and others knights (*caballeros*); that confusing one group with the other was unthinkable; and that simple gentlemen who wanted to pass themselves off as knights were as ludicrous as those who added "don" to their names without the right to do so (like Alonso Quijano, who made people call him "Don" Quixote). The Manchegan gentleman, when he sets out on his adventures, realizes that he has not been knighted; and as everyone knows, he persuades a wily innkeeper to act out the farce of giving him the accolade while pretending to pray certain prayers, in the presence of La Tolosa, who girds on his sword, and La Molinera, who puts on his spur. It is obvious that Don Quixote was never a knight, since the ceremonies in the hostelry are nothing but a joke and a farce. Spaniards of 1605 knew perfectly well that King Alphonse the Learned had decreed in his *Segunda Partida* (Second Division of the Code of Law) the following: "A person who has once received knighthood as a joke may not become a knight. This occurs [for example] . . . when he who gives

"helmet" and the saddlebags lose all their humor. In Spanish cities forty years ago, the basin was still familiar because it was used as a sign for barbershops.

3. See O. Jodogne, "Audigier et la chanson de geste, avec une édition nouvelle du poème." *Le Moyen Âgé*, XLVI (1960); and J. Horrent, "Un écho de la *Chanson de Roland* au Portugal: la geste de médisance de D. Alfonso Lopes de Baiam, "*Revue des Langues Vivantes*, XIV (1948), 133–141; and M. Rodrigues Lapa, *Cantigas d'escarnho e de mal dizer* (Coimbra, 1965), 96–99.

the accolade has no authority to do so . . . Hence it was established by law in former times that anyone who tried to dishonor the noble institution of knighthood should be dishonored by it; thus he could never receive knighthood" (II part., tit. xxi, law 12). Alonso Quijano, even though he might have recovered his senses, would never have been able to become a knight because he had once received knighthood "as a joke."

Don Quixote's bookish madness manifests itself, among other ways, in his nostalgia for a former time in which knight-errantry existed in what may appear a novelesque fashion. But, as we have seen, only a century earlier, Spain was the home of numerous genuine knights-errant. The Manchegan knight is actually a living relic, wandering the highways of Spain at the beginning of the seventeenth century. And one of the many aspects which the modern reader most easily overlooks is Don Quixote's old-fashioned costume. He wore "some armor that had belonged to his great-grandfathers, which, covered with rust and full of mold had been put away in a corner, and forgotten for long centuries" (Part I, Ch. I). The great-grandfather of a person who, in 1605, "bordered on fifty," would have worn a suit of armor from the period of the Wars of Granada. If we compare Ferdinand the Catholic's suit of war-armor, made between 1480 and 1500, which is on display in the arms collection of the Vienna Museum of Art History, with the Milenese armor of Philip III kept in the Royal Armory in Madrid, we can see the enormous difference between the defensive armor of the end of the fifteenth and that from the beginning of the seventeenth.[4] The outward appearance of Don Quixote produces either laughter or astonishment in everyone he meets on the road—as a battalion of parachusists led by a commander dressed like General Prim in the Moroccan Wars [1859–60] might produce in us. The quaintness of Don Quixote's outfit (the absurdity of which is later increased by the barber's basin) is complemented by the antiquated language which the Manchegan knight frequently uses, especially in Part I; it is a Castilian with a medieval tinge, typical of the books of chivalry. The unsuspecting modern reader unprepared by philological studies does not perceive Cervantes' irony when he makes Don Quixote say *non fuyades, fecho, la vuestra fermosura* ["flee ye not," "deed," "thy beauty," i.e., obsolete verb forms, the retention of etymological *f* where it had disappeared in speech, the use of the article with a possessive adjective, etc.], since the writer himself pronounced them exactly as today: *no huyáis, hecho, vuestra hermosura,* etc. This sort of pseudo-medieval Castilian is one more aspect of the parody of the

4. For photos of Ferdinand's armor, see M. de Riquer, *L'arnès del Cavaller* (Barcelona-Esplugues de Llobregat, 1968), plate 219; for Philip III's, see Valencia de Don Juan, *Catálogo de la Real Armería de Madrid* (Madrid, 1898), plate XVI.

style of books of chivalry, some of which were really ancient and others pretentiously "antique." Miguel Sánchez de Lima, in one of the censures (1580) enumerated above, says that "in most of [the romances] one does not find good speech, since it is all antiquated." Don Quixote, for example, constantly promises his servant the governorship of an island, always using the obsolete form *ínsula*, in the style of Ínsula Triste, Ínsula Fuerte, or Ínsula Sagitaria in the romances; and since Sancho does not understand the word, when in Part II the duke and duchess make him governor of a town far from the coast, in the very heart of Aragón, he is convinced that he is ruling an *ínsula* because he does not know that the term is a synonym for *island*.

In spite of the fact that in Don Quixote's library there were more than three hundred books, only a few books of chivalry are cited in the novel; these are *Amadís de Gaula, Las sergas de Esplandián, Amadís de Grecia, El caballero Platir, Palmerín de Oliva, Palmerín de Ingalaterra, Olivante de Laura, Felixmarte de Hircania, Lepolemo, Belianís de Grecia, Cirongilio de Tracia, Pierres de Provenza, Enrique fi de Oliva, Guarino Mezquino*, and *Tablante de Ricamonte*, in addition to the chivalresque novel *Tirant lo Blanch*. But Cervantes was familiar with many more: *Primaleón y Polendos* (in which the *hidalgo* Camilote appears), *Clamades y Claramonda* (the probable source of Clavileño), and *Clarián de Landanís* (where the deeds of Prince Diocleciano, called "the Knight of the Mournful Countenance" are told), etc.

The reader of the early seventeenth century, thoroughly imbued with the themes, style, and tone of books of chivalry, met humorous allusions to such books at every step in *Don Quixote*. The romances were usually set in exotic distant kingdoms, remote in time, such as Persia or the empire of Trapisonda; and just as *Amadís de Gaula* begins, "Not many years after the passion of our Lord and Savior, Jesus Christ, there was a Christian king in Brittany . . ." so *Don Quixote* begins, "In a village in La Mancha . . . not long ago, there lived a gentleman . . ." Everything becomes modern, normal, and commonplace, in a contrast intended to ridicule the exotic, antique, and extraordinary elements of the romances. The fiction that *Don Quixote* is a translation made by Cervantes from Cide Hamete Benegeli's Arabic original—which offers the novelist the two magnificent narrative levels—is likewise a satire of an old custom in books of chivalry with which their authors tried to give their fantasies respectability.[5]

5. For these points of contact between the books of chivalry and *Don Quixote*, see Clemencín's splendid comments and the short notes in my edition of Cervantes' work (Clásicos Planeta, Barcelona 1962, 1967, 1968). With regard to the custom of offering books of chivalry as translations, one might note that *Tirant lo Blanch*, in the dedication, is said to be a translation from English to Por-

The most common themes of the books of chivalry reappear in *Don Quixote* distorted by parody and irony. The oft-repeated episodes where the knight triumphs over monstrous giants, vast armies, or ferocious animals become ridiculous as Don Quixote prepares to fight windmills, flocks, and sleepy lions on their way to the royal zoo. The knight-errant's mission was to defend the helpless, free captives, and protect widows and maidens. Don Quixote knows this better than anyone; but he fails miserably when he saves Andrés from the wrath of Juan Haldudo, when the prisoners he frees are callous galley-slaves who show their thanks with a shower of stones, and when he plays the fool by becoming the champion of Doña Rodríguez's daughter. The encounter, dialogue, and combat between Don Quixote and the Knight of the Woods ridicules one of the most commonplace events of the books of chivalry.

Some episodes of *Don Quixote* are ironical imitations or parodies of passages in identifiable books of chivalry. The adventure of the dead body (Part I, Ch. XIX) is a conscious, intentional replica of the knight Floriano's adventure in *Palmerín de Ingalaterra* (Part I, Ch. LXXVI). The general outline of the adventure in Montesinos's cave (Part II, Ch. XXIII) was inspired by an episode in the *Sergas de Esplandián*,[6] as the Clavileño episode was inspired by the most noteworthy element in *Clamades y Clarmonda*.[7] Don Quixote's penance in the Sierra Morena (Part I, Ch. XXV), besides being an explicit imitation of Amadís, who had taken the name Beltenebrós (Beltenebros in Cervantes), is a recollection of an ancient theme seen, e.g., in Ivain's half-wild state in the *Li chevaliers au lion* of Chrétien de Troyes and in the lengthy accounts of the penitential retirement of Lancelot and of Tristan.[8] In Fierabrás's balm, Cervantes burlesques the wonder-working relic in the twelfth-century French *chanson de geste* which, revised and recast, became the *Historia del emperador Carolomagno . . . e de la cruda batalla que hubo Oliveros con Fierabrás* [*The history of the Emperor Charlemagne . . . and the fierce battle between Oliveros and Fierabrás*]. When Don Quixote is put on the ox-cart, at the end of Part I, he says, "I have read many reputable histories of knights-errant, but I have never read or seen or heard of enchanted knights being carried in this fashion or as slowly as these lazy, sluggish animals are

---

tuguese to Valencian. In this case, however, there may be some truth to the claim, since the author, Joanot Martorell, lived in London and dedicated the work to Prince Fernando of Portugal.

6. See M. R. Lida de Malkiel, "Dos huellas del *Esplandián* en el *Quijote* y el *Persiles*," *RPh*, IX (1955), 156–162.

7. See P. Aebischer, "Paleozoologie de *l'Equus clavileñus Cervant.*," *Etudes et Lettres*, II (Lausanne, 1962).

8. See also W. Pabst, "Die Selbstbestrafung auf dem Stein. Verwandtschaft von Amadis, Gregorius und Oedipus," *Der Vergleich . . . Festgabe für Hellmuth Petriconi* (Hamburg, 1955), 33–49.

likely to do, because they are always carried through the air, with remarkable speed, enclosed in some dark, black cloud, or in some fiery chariot or on some hippogryph or other similar beast. But to be transported in an ox-cart, as I am! God help me, I am confounded! But perhaps chivalry and the enchantments of our day follow another path than that the ancients followed" (Part I, Ch. XLVII). Though knights are generally transported in swift and marvelous vehicles, Don Quixote is wrong in supposing that it is an unheard-of-novelty to ride in a cart under humiliating circumstances. The first surviving novel of the deeds of Lancelot is Chrétien de Troyes's work entitled *Li chevaliers de la charrette*, in which the protagonist undergoes the humiliating trial of being carried in a cart driven by a loathsome dwarf; the knight considers it dishonorable; for as Chrétien says, malefactors were exhibited to the public in similar carts.

The episodes which occur in the palace of the duke and duchess (including the Clavileño episode) have a special slant, since in Part II of *Don Quixote* Cervantes feels obliged to focus the parody of the books of chivalry in a different way. In the first part, the technique was very clear: Don Quixote distorted reality in his mind; it was sufficient to convert a windmill into a giant, an inn into a castle, a flock into an army. But in the second part of the novel, Don Quixote always sees reality just as it is; he no longer takes any inn for a castle, and it is those who surround him who create chivalresque fiction for him: Sancho insisting that the coarse farm girl in the princess Dulcinea, Sansón disguising himself as the Knight of the White Moon, etc. The ducal pair organize the monumental and well-planned farces of Merlin's procession, the quest of the Distressed Dueña, Clavileño, Altisidora's lovesickness, the singular combat with Tosilos, etc., because they have read Part I of *Don Quixote* and know perfectly well what the Manchegan gentleman's weakness is. It is no longer Cervantes who parodies the books of chivalry but the persons of his novel. Doubtless it is for this reason that the archaisms in Don Quixote's Castilian decrease considerably and Cervantes no longer notes parodies of the style of the books of chivalry in passages like "Scarcely had rosy Apollo . . ." (Part I, Ch. II), so similar to a passage in *Belianís de Grecia*, or in the letter from Don Quixote to Dulcinea (Part I, Ch. XXV), so similar to the love letters in *Florisel de Niquea* or *Olivante de Laura*.

When Don Quixote recovers his wits, parody ceases altogether, since it is no longer necessary and has accomplished its mission. Alonso Quijano makes his confession, dictates his will, and dies. Cervantes had praised *Tirant lo Blanch*—the novel, not book of chivalry—"because among other things, in this book knights eat, and die in their beds, and make wills before they die."

E. C. RILEY

Novel and Romance in *Don Quixote*†

No attentive reader of Cervantes nowadays would maintain, as Fitzmaurice-Kelly did in his day, that Cervantes was "the least critical of men."[1] There can be no doubt of his knowledge of the literary theory of his time and of his concern with poetry, drama, and prose fiction. His interest in the last of these is even of historical importance. No earlier theorist that we know of had given it closer attention. Moreover, in *Don Quixote* literary theory itself is a fundamental theme, inseparable from the imaginative creation, because it is rooted in the protagonist's madness. The genesis of Cervantes' *Persiles* likewise owes not a little to theoretical speculations.

The observations of Cervantes on literature are expressed through the body of his work, either *in propria persona* or through his narrators and literary characters. His propensity for seeing both sides of the question, which finds expression in his equivocal irony and his preference for critical dialogue over direct statement, can make it a delicate task to determine his personal opinions with any precision. But behind the murmur of partial and possible answers given by his interlocutors we can hear the voice of Cervantes asking the right questions.

An important recent study has underlined the difference between Cervantes' "classical" and "normative" voice and its opposite, a subtle innuendo which shows up the limitations and undermines the norms of contemporary classical criticism.[2] The effect, it seems to me, is a double one. Cervantes appears to us as a more acute and original critic, and also as a more ambivalent one, than we had imagined. His irony turns and turns again, even on itself. By a typical paradox he shows his critical subtlety in the most striking fashion, bouncing the ball back to literary criticism by using artistic procedures which are normally the object of criticism. In the same way as Don Quixote subjects chivalric theory to the test of experience, the novel *Don Quixote* puts literary theory to the test of art. In the

† From *Suma Cervantina*, ed. J. B. Avalle-Arce and E. C. Riley (London: Tamesis Books, 1973), pp. 310–322. Professor Riley attempts to systematize Cervantes' opinions about literature by analyzing his observations and his practices as an author. Of particular interest are Riley's conclusions regarding the two modes of fiction used by Cervantes to produce the unique counterpoint of fantasy and "reality" in Don Quixote's world. (The editor gratefully acknowledges Professor Riley's translation of the selection; all notes are by Professor Riley.)

1. Quoted by George Saintsbury, *A History of Criticism and Literary Taste in Europe* (Edinburgh, 1900–1904), II, 348 n. This opinion was more or less typical of the nineteenth century. A notable exception was J. M. Guardia, in his introduction to the French translation of Cervantes's *Journey to Parnassus* (*Le Voyage au Parnasse* (Paris, 1864). Later, Menéndez y Pelayo, R. Schevill, and A. Bonilla paid some attention to Cervantes's literary theory; but it was Toffanin, De Lollis, and Américo Castro—the latter in particular—who established its importance.

2. Alban K. Forcione, *Cervantes, Aristotle and the "Persiles"* (Princeton, 1970).

last resort criticism is absorbed by artistic creation, but the work would not be what it is if its critical side did not exist.

Despite the unusual form and ambivalence of Cervantes' literary theory, it would be quite wrong to conclude that he had no firm convictions. The reiteration of certain principles, the persistence of certain points of view, affirmations with enough signs to show that they are to be taken seriously (Cervantes is not always joking): all these things together make it possible to reach a substantial body of conclusions.

* * *

Cervantes greatest originality as a theorist lies in his development of a theory of prose fiction which, though it was firmly rooted in contemporary poetics, went far beyond them. By conscious thought, intuition, and the example of *Don Quixote*, he laid the foundation of a valid theory of the modern novel. He could not have done this had he not perceived a difference between two types of prose fiction which critics did not begin to recognize until a century later, one of which is more freely imaginative, while the other is more closely bound to historical probability and actuality. English critical terminology makes an adequate distinction between the two: the first is *prose romance*, the second, *novel.*

* * *

There is probably no such thing as a chemically pure novel or romance. Nevertheless, we can very summarily distinguish the Medieval and Renaissance romance from the novel in the following important respects. The romance subordinates character to action. Its protagonists are heroic or exceptional, rather than average human beings. Action is subject to coincidence and to poetic justice, which, ultimately stand for the will of Providence, rather than to a causality that has its origin in human character in its relations with society. Romance thus presents an idealized world rather than the world of historical reality. As such, it reflects the image of the Ancient and Medieval world, not the modern empirically oriented view of the world. (This does not mean that romance has disappeared from modern literature. Its relative proximity to myth, the perennial attraction of fantasy and the supernatural, its element of wish-fulfilment, have assured its survival in renewed forms.)[3] It helps to understand Cervantes' theory if one bears in mind this dif-

3. The difference between novel and romance is noted, in general terms, in René Wellek and Austin Warren, *Theory of Literature*, 2nd ed. (New York, 1956), pp. 205–6. The English and American bibliography on the subject is enormous. A good introduction is Maurice Z. Shroder, "The Novel as Genre," *Massachusetts Review* (1963), reprinted in *The Theory of the Novel*, ed. Philip Stevick (New York, 1967), of special interest because of the attention devoted to *Don Quixote*. Also pp. 303–314 of Northrup Frye, *Anatomy of Criticism* (Princeton, 1957), likewise published in Stevicks' anthology. See also Frye's ambitious study of romance, *The Secular Scripture* (Cambridge, Mass. 1976).

I should observe that I did not make the due distinction between romance and novel in my *Cervantes' Theory of the Novel.* I now consider it fundamental.

ference, toward which he groped in his theoretical speculations, and which he gave form to, marvelously, with the creation of his great novel. In general, one can say that as a novelist and theorist, he criticizes romances; that as a lover of, and writer of romances, he defends them; and that he uses his theoretical knowledge and literary experience to find ways and devices for making them acceptable to the discerning reader.

The theoretical discussion of prose fiction in Cervantes is centered in the discussion of the Canon of Toledo, first with the Priest and then with Don Quixote, in Part I, Chs. XLVII–L. It is a dialogue on the romances of chivalry which contains a formula for the ideal romance which is too similar to Cervantes' *Persiles* to be pure coincidence. It is, of course, far from being a summary of Cervantes' opinions on prose fiction; in order to reach conclusions about his theories, one must also consult his other works. His discovery of a theoretical basis for the novel, as has happened in so many scientific discoveries, sprang from his speculations on related but different problems.

* * *

Only in *Don Quixote* does Cervantes find a completely satisfactory solution to the problem of the relationship between poetic ideal and historical reality. He puts the ideal in the only place where it is really to be found in an imperfect world: in the human mind. In a philosophical and psychological sense, *Don Quixote* deals with the complex relations between the interior world of the mind and the exterior, physical world. In a literary sense, it contrasts idealized poetic fiction, providentially ordered, with novelistic fiction, historically and empirically oriented. Expressed in critical terms, the book reveals the difference between the two aspects of verisimilitude: what "should be" and what "could be," the ideal and the possible—a difference to which critics had hitherto paid little attention. From the beginning of the seventeenth century, what "should be," the purely ideal, was destined to become essentially the province of poetry, and what "could be," that of the modern realistic novel. But Cervantes did more than merely separate them; other authors had often done that. His achievement in *Don Quixote* was to illuminate the mysterious interdependence of the two. He showed, with a depth unprecedented in prose fiction, human actions motivated by ideals, beliefs, aspirations, and illusions—man's inner life.

* * *

The essence of Don Quixote's madness is his inability to distinguish chivalresque fiction from real life. Hence his aspirations to become the hero of a poetic romance. Cervantes thus puts one form of prose fiction to the test by contrasting it with real life. But this "real life" is, of course, only another kind of fiction: novelistic fiction, which is closer to history than to the romances which fill Don Quixote's head.

The distinction made by modern criticism between romance and the novel, however difficult to define, was intuitively sensed by Cervantes. The first, a fantastic or idealized literary world, the second a historico-empirical literary world; dream of life, and life as it is lived: both of them literary fiction. The distinction of species within a single genre is fundamental, I think. Using quite a common comparison, Cervantes associates romance and literary fantasy with dream.[4] The Priest calls the books of chivalry "dreams told by men awakened from sleep, or rather still half asleep" (Part II, Ch. I); and the narrator in the first chapter of *Don Quixote* speaks of "the fabric of those celebrated, dreamed up inventions" (Part I, Ch. I); Berganza calls the pastoral romances "things that have been dreamed up" (*Coloquio*, p. 166[5]); and referring to the *Colloquy of the Dogs* itself, the Subaltern speaks of "those dreams or bits of nonsense" (p. 152). Don Quixote sleeps while the scrutiny of his library takes place, and again in the inn while the chivalric romances are being discussed. There is a clear association of dream with the Cave of Montesinos, with the marvelous island in Periandro's tale in *Persiles*, and with the play *The House of Jealousy*, all of them loaded with reminiscences of romance.

Where Cervantes expatiates most on fantasy is at the start of Chapter VI of the *Journey to Parnassus* (pp. 83–85). Here the author falls asleep, has a dream—note that it is a dream within the overall dream of the poem—and ponders on dreams. His own is of the third type mentioned "touching on revelations." He gives himself over to sleep and, he says, "I threw wide open the gates of my soul and let dream come in through my eyes with glory and pleasure assured." He enjoys "the spoils of four thousand pleasures," and then "Unleashed fantasy set me down in a flower-filled meadow that breathed the scents of Panchaia and Saba. This pleasant place captivated the eye, whose vision was much keener asleep than awake, as far as it could see." There is no doubt that for Cervantes literary fantasy can be art, and of the most delectable kind. Like a well-trained writer he does not forget "common decorum" even in dreams, and he dreams "discreetly." So it is not surprising that his scruples over lack of verisimilitude should now surface again. He goes on: "Palpably I saw . . . But I do not know whether to write it down, for my pen has always shied away from things that smack of the impossible; those with a glimmering of possibility, which are

4. As Forcione, op. cit., 14, observes, this goes back to Petrarch at least and perhaps to Horace.

5. Page-numbers in parentheses refer to the standard edition of the complete works of Cervantes, edited by Rodolfo Schevill and Adolfo Bonilla y San Martín (Madrid: Gráficas Reunidas, 1914–1941). [*Editor.*]

sweet and mild and sure, explain my pleasant scribbling." His wit never opens its doors "indiscriminately" but only to what is "concordant," because only an absurdity which is "deliberate" and guided by "humour" is pleasing. "For that is when falsehood satisfies: when it looks like truth and is written in a delightful way that will please both the simple and the discreet." The "possible" undoubtedly had a powerful attraction for Cervantes, and so did his taste for the fantastic. The writer may write impossible things, so long as he represents them as such, accommodating his manifest intention to the reader's intelligence. With the above words from Cervantes himself in the *Journey to Parnassus* we are very close to those of the Canon of Toledo on the need for fabulous plots to be wedded to the intelligence of the reader. To the awakened mind, unbridled literary fantasy corresponds to dream.

Romance and novel are two species of fiction, but since novelistic representation is likewise illusion, Cervantes wants the reader to be aware of the fact. So the story of Don Quixote's life is presented as a historical document attributed, in the main, to the totally incredible figure of Cide Hamete Benengeli. The aim and effect of this artifice—and of some other lesser devices—is to leave no room for the smallest doubt in the reader's mind that this "history" is invention. Cervantes underlines his intention at the beginning of Part I, contrasting its "fabulous nonsense" with the truth of mathematics, science, and logic (Prologue), and again at the end when he asks that his book be given just the same credence as discerning readers (*los discretos*) give to the books of chivalry (Part I, Ch. LII). His lively deception was so contrived as not to deceive the simple reader while making the discerning willingly suspend disbelief. He must have wished us to be, like himself, both involved in his work and detached from it. His own sense of involvement and detachment are expressed in those remarkable words, attributed to Benengeli's pen—words whose implications go so far beyond the immediate context that they may be included among the more notable statements made by novelists about their creations: "For me alone Don Quixote was born and I for him; he knew how to act, and I knew how to write; we two are as one" (Part II, Ch. LXXIV).

Cervantes discovered through prose fiction that art is a kind of illusion in which the reader joins, as in a game, with complete consciousness of its unreality, and that the more powerful the appearance of reality is, the greater the illusion. Romances are contained in *Don Quixote* as dreams are contained in real life, which for its part is a greater dream, just as the novel is an illusory fiction. By dint of recognizing the difference between them Cervantes came to know their mysterious, inextricable interaction. The equivocation of *Don Quixote* goes farther than Angel del Río thought when he said: "The equivocation is not in the novel, but in life, which the novel with complete fidelity reflects."[6] Inside the illusion of art there is a lasting reality which helps us to correct our own perspectives as we confront the shifting illusions of life.

JOHN J. ALLEN

Levels of Fiction in *Don Quixote*†

> This is a false awakening, being merely the next layer of your dream, as if you were rising up from stratum to stratum but never reaching the surface, never emerging into reality. . . . Yet who knows? Is this reality, *the* final reality or just a new deceptive dream?
>
> —Vladimir Nabokov, *King, Queen, Knave*; trans. Dmitri Nabokov (New York, 1968), pp. 20–21

There is a vast amount of "acting" in Don Quixote, quite apart from the possibility suggested by Mark Van Doren that this is in fact Don Quixote's real profession—actor, and not knight-errant.[1] From the very first episodes of Part I, the characters often accept the roles assigned them by Don Quixote, beginning with the innkeeper who knighted him, and the second part abounds with elaborately staged productions designed to deceive and mock both Don Quixote and Sancho. The appearance of Merlin and his entourage with instructions for the disenchantment of Dulcinea, the governorship of Sancho, the puppet show of Maese Pedro, and the reception given to Don Quixote in Barcelona are a few examples. The roles assumed by the characters are at times given an ironic twist, as in the encounter in the Sierra Morena between Don Quixote and Dorotea, when the mad knight acts the part of a crazed lover in imitation of Amadís and Roland. Dorotea has taken the role of the Princess Micomicona in an effort to lure Don Quixote back home, and the result is a confrontation between a mad knight playing the

6. A. del Río, "El equívoco del Quijote," HR, XXVII (1959), 215.

† From *Don Quixote: Hero or Fool?*, Part I, University of Florida Monographs: Humanities No. 29 (Gainesville: University of Florida Press, 1971), pp. 67–79. Contemporary critics have become increasingly interested in Cervantes' handling of fiction-within-fiction. In this essay, Professor Allen analyzes the "profusion of layers which separates us from our starting point in the fictional depths of the novel," a profusion of which every reader is aware, if only dimly, and which has always produced a curiously unsettling effect in admirers of the novel. Many critics have pointed out how a reader begins to feel the "reality" of the fictional characters at the point in Part I where they listen to the priest read them a story at Palomeque's inn. This sense of their actual existence grows when Part I of the novel—a book which does in fact exist in print, in twelve thousand copies—stimulates action in Part II. Professor Allen leads us beyond these observations to appreciate the unsuspectedly profound and refined effects achieved by Cervantes' juggling of his "sources" (an untrustworthy Moorish historian—or an enchanter, after all?—and a skeptical translator), of literature (such as the short story of Part I or the apocryphal sequel examined in Part II), and so on. The result of this brilliant manipulation is "an unprecedented illusion of autonomy" of the characters that has yet to be surpassed in world literature. (Quotations from *Don Quixote* are from the translation by Samuel Putnam [New York: Viking Press, 1949].)

1. *Don Quixote's Profession* (New York, 1958).

part of a mad knight, and a damsel in distress playing a damsel in distress. These brief indications will suffice to recall the abundance of acting in the novel. It is necessary here to penetrate the book at the deepest level of fiction-within-fiction, and reconstruct the various layers from that point to the surface, as preparation for an examination of the peculiar interpenetration which develops between two of the levels.

The last and smallest in this series of Chinese boxes is to be found in the "Story of the One Who Was Too Curious for His Own Good," from Part I of the novel. The story, apparently drawn in part from Ariosto's *Orlando Furioso*, Canto 43, has been left behind by a guest at the inn of Juan Palomeque, and is read by the curate to the assembled travelers. This "exemplary novel" is the story of Lotario and Anselmo, "the two friends," as they were known in Florence, where the action takes place, and of Anselmo's bride Camila. Anselmo begs Lotario to attempt to seduce Camila, as a test of her fidelity. Lotario reluctantly accepts, and the story runs its logical course to the tragedy which follows Anselmo's discovery that his friend and his bride are lovers.

The moment of interest here occurs when Anselmo, having pretended to leave his house, conceals himself to await the arrival of Lotario, who has told him in a fit of jealousy that Camila has indeed fallen. By the time of the meeting, Lotario has repented of the disclosure, and he and Camila, aware that Anselmo is watching, are prepared to offer him a convincing display of Camila's conjugal fidelity.

The principal actors in this little play, then, are Lotario and Camila, with Lotario acting the part of Camila's lover. At the next level, however—that of Anselmo, the spectator—Lotario is Anselmo's friend. Anselmo, and indeed the whole town, consider this to be the level of reality. The third level is that of the "real" Lotario, Camila's lover. Just as the mad Don Quixote decided to assume the role of mad knight in the Sierra Morena, so Lotario the lover has seen fit to superimpose the *role* of lover on his basic pose as Anselmo's friend. Of course, all of this is fiction for the characters at the fourth level, that of Don Quixote and the others at the inn. It is a short story, criticized by the curate for its lack of plausibility and praised for its style.

Perhaps the relationship among the various levels thus far will be clearer if it is put in terms of a more familiar use of the play within a play. In *Hamlet*, had Claudius himself played the part of the murderous king in the traveling players' production, the levels would correspond, and the reader of Shakespeare's play would stand at the same remove from the play within as Don Quixote and the others at the inn stand from the scene with which we began. This is the level of *Don Quixote*, Part I, which must be seen in the light of the next level as Don Quixote's life story, for Part I and Part II are *different* levels of fiction.

The relationship between Part I and Part II is analogous to that between the interpolated story with which we began and Part I. In chapters III and IV of Part II, Part I is commented on and criticized, and in much greater detail than was the "Story of the One Who Was Too Curious for His Own Good" in Part I. It is even corrected, modified, and amplified by Don Quixote and Sancho. Part II is the level of the "real" Don Quixote. Of course, this, too, is fiction, and its immediate casing is the manuscript of Cid Hamete. Between Cervantes and Cid Hamete stands the Moor who translated the manuscript into Spanish, and finally the reader's source is, of course, Cervantes' version. We have now arrived at our level of reality, or fiction, as the case may be, and are in a position to see the profusion of layers which separates us from our starting point in the fictional depths of the novel.

It is obvious that the components of the outer shell which includes the versions of Cid Hamete, the translator, and Cervantes, are not levels in the same sense as the others. But they are more than the superficial layers of the novels of chivalry which they parody. The thirteenth-century *Caballero Cifar*, for example, is presented by its author as a Spanish version of a Latin translation of a Chaldean original, but none of these has any real existence within the work. Cid Hamete is a *character* in *Don Quixote*, who, as he says, would have given his best coat to witness the encounter between Don Quixote and Doña Rodríguez in the duke's palace. His account is repeatedly placed under suspicion because he is Moorish. The translator, too, as was indicated in Chapter 1, edits and enters the text to make comments, as in this excerpt from Part II: "As he comes to set down this fifth chapter of our history, the translator desires to make it plain that he looks upon it as apocryphal, since in it Sancho Panza speaks in a manner that does not appear to go with his limited intelligence and indulges in such subtle observations that it is quite impossible to conceive of his saying the things attributed to him. However, the translator in question did not wish to leave his task unfinished. . . ."

It should be pointed out also that the juxtaposition of levels is not necessarily consistent throughout. The level of Cid Hamete is, in a fundamental sense, equidistant from Part I and Part II, although *within Part II* the illusion of one further remove is created.

The primary effect of these devices is the enhancement of the illusion of reality, as has been pointed out by more than one critic in discussing isolated relationships within the series here presented. Predmore, for example, on the effect of the "Story of the One Who Was Too Curious for His Own Good": "Since everything in *Don*

Quixote is really literature, this relationship [between literature and life] is an artistic illusion achieved by establishing two fictional levels so separated that the difference which separates them seems to the reader to be the difference between literature and life."[2] And further: "The story of the *Man Too Curious for His Own Good* contributes to the same illusion. . . . It establishes another fictional level, which we regard from the same point of view as the Priest and his listeners. One might say that for a time we sit down beside them and lend them some of our reality."[3] The principle is valid, although, as we have seen, not one but several other levels of fiction have been established.

Aubrey Bell, in his book on Cervantes, felt the same effect at another point in the series, the existence of Part I within Part II: "In the Second Part of *Don Quixote*, the Knight of the Lions is accompanied by his shadow, the Knight of the Sorrowful Countenance, now crystallized in the printed page of Part I, so that any doubts we may entertain concerning the reality of the shadow only make the living Don Quixote more real."[4]

As several critics have observed, it is *here*, in the relationship between the fifth and sixth levels, as they have just been presented, between Part I and Part II, that the most fertile interpenetration of levels lies. Luis Rosales dedicates more than sixty pages of his monumental *Cervantes y la libertad* to the investigation of the extremely complex implications of this relationship, and Américo Castro has considered his 1924 article on the subject, "Cervantes y Pirandello," important enough to re-edit for inclusion in a 1960 volume. The contribution of Castro, and of Rosales along lines suggested by Castro's original article, lies in the detailed analysis of the new dimension given to Don Quixote and Sancho in Part II, through the introduction of the historical account of their previous activities which Part I represents. The new situation begins to develop at the close of Chapter II of the second part, with Sancho's report to Don Quixote:

> "Bartolomé Carrasco's son came home last night. He has been studying at Salamanca and has just been made a bachelor. When I went to welcome him, he told me that the story of your Grace has already been put into a book called *The Ingenious Gentleman, Don Quixote de la Mancha*. And he says they mention me in it, under my own name, Sancho Panza, and the lady Dulcinea del Toboso as well, along with things that happened to us when we were alone together. I had to cross myself, for I could not help wondering how the one who wrote all those things down could have come to know about them."

2. Richard L. Predmore, *The World of "Don Quixote"* (Cambridge, Mass., 1967), pp. 2–3.
3. *Ibid.*, p. 10.
4. Aubrey F. G. Bell, *Cervantes* (Norman, Okla., 1947), p. 97.

"I can assure you, Sancho," said Don Quixote, "that the author of our history must be some wise enchanter."

At this point, as Castro points out, "the main characters of *Don Quixote* begin to show us the double personalities of real beings who live and move to and fro, and of literary characters, at the mercy of the 'second' existence which a writer was pleased to concede to them."[5]

But the relationship between the "story" of Don Quixote and his "real" existence does not remain one of simple juxtaposition:

> Don Quixote remained in a thoughtful mood as he waited for the bachelor Carrasco, from whom he hoped to hear the news as to how he had been put into a book, as Sancho had said. . . . If it was true that such a history existed, being about a knight-errant, then it must be eloquent and lofty in tone, a splendid and distinguished piece of work and veracious in its details.
>
> This consoled him somewhat, although he was a bit put out at the thought that the author was a Moor, if the appellation "Cid" was to be taken as an indication, and from the Moors you could never hope for any word of truth, seeing that they are all of them cheats, forgers, and schemers. He feared lest his love should not have been treated with becoming modesty but rather in a way that would reflect upon the virtue of his lady Dulcinea del Toboso.

We are presented here, as Castro says, with "the character's fear of not being understood by the author."[6] The final step in this illusion of the emancipation of the character from the author's control is taken in Chapter LIX, when someone comments that the spurious Part II contains an account of Don Quixote's participation in the jousts of Saragossa, and the knight's reply is as follows: "I will not set foot in Saragossa but will let the world see how this new historian lies, by showing people that I am not the Don Quixote of whom he is speaking." Thus the character, in Castro's words, "has rebelled against the author, and aspires to live his own life as he sees fit."[7]

Luis Rosales clarifies the significance of Cervantes' achievement by a comparison of the similar devices employed by Pirandello in *Six Characters in Search of an Author* and by Miguel de Unamuno in his novel *Niebla.* On Pirandello, he concludes: "One could say —and it is true—that they are not the ones who originate their own drama; rather, on the contrary, they originate in it. They are not

5. "Cervantes y Pirandello," in Américo Castro, *Hacia Cervantes,* 3rd ed. (Madrid, 1967), p. 480. This point is also taken up from another perspective by Casalduero: "We are [involved] in the theme of the play within a play . . . the union of the real figure and the artistic figure through humor" (*Sentido y forma del "Quijote,"* pp. 219–24).

6. P. 481.

7. P. 485.

defined by their character; they are defined by the life situation in which they are dramatized. . . . What matters to Pirandello is the consciousness of the character *as character*."[8]

Unamuno, deeply influenced by Cervantes, as his *Life of Don Quixote and Sancho* reveals, succeeds in *Niebla* in advancing still further along the same lines,. as Rosales convincingly demonstrates. Augusto Pérez, the principal character in the novel, decides to commit suicide, and consults with the author, who informs him that this would be impossible, since Pérez does not exist. Augusto Pérez, as Rosales says, "does not feel *fixed* to certain acts [as do the characters of Pirandello]. He thinks he can change them, although he may not do so. . . . Without ceasing to consider himself a fictional character, he does not identify his personality with his 'role.' "[9]

Don Quixote breaks through all of these restrictions and affirms his freedom over against the fixed, possibly inaccurate, representation of him in Part I.

We have seen, then, that the novel presents a complex series of different levels of fiction, and that the relationship between two of these levels (Part I and Part II) provides the vehicle for an unprecedented illusion of autonomy for Don Quixote, unequaled even by those who have employed similar devices in our own times.

But something else is happening with the appearance of Part I within Part II which bears directly upon the problem of the nature of reality in the world of *Don Quixote*. As we saw above in Chapter 1, Don Quixote coexists in the same world with Madame Bovary, Raskolnikov, and the rest of us. It is *our* world, however distinctively Don Quixote may interpret it. If there are enchanters at work in Don Quixote's world, surely their reality and *modus operandi* are those of Santa Claus in ours.

This is true right up to the point in Part II that we have been discussing. Cervantes, or Cid Hamete, tells us that Don Quixote fought windmills, stole a barber's basin, and engaged in a number of other rather unconventional activities, all of them undertaken in *our* world, and governed by the same physical and psychological principles which define our activity. The enchanters work only through the mind of the knight, as they do in our world. For those who would take issue with this basic fact about the book, one can only recommend Predmore's book, which clearly separates the firm ground of reality in the novel from its very considerable liability to misinterpretation by the characters.

What Predmore, and, for that matter, Castro and Rosales, neglect to discuss is the conclusive manner in which that reality, the phenomenal world of *Don Quixote*, is totally unhinged precisely at

8. *Cervantes y la libertad. La libertad soñada* (Madrid, 1960), II, 205.

9. Pp. 214–15.

the point which we have been examining, and that this results not from the creative activity of Don Quixote, but from a trick played by Cervantes on the reader. As we have seen above in Chapter 1, Cervantes is obviously a master at deliberate confusion. Who wrote Part I? Who wrote this partial biography of Don Quixote and Sancho, of which there are 12,000 copies in print already, according to Sansón Carrasco, who has just finished reading it? We may cite Don Quixote's answer to that question: "I can assure you, Sancho, that the author of our history must be some wise enchanter." It is all very well for Don Quixote to say this. The idea that an omniscient Moor has written an account of his activities and private thoughts of not thirty days before, and that the account is already translated into Spanish and published all across western Europe is no strain on his credulity. It is consistent with his view of the nature of reality. The trouble is, of course, that this time he is right. There is no explanation for this state of affairs but enchantment. Enrique Moreno Báez has noticed this anomaly, "wholly fictitious, and so artfully interwoven with the rest of the narration that only when we analyze it do we realize its complete inverisimilitude," but he seems to see only the inverisimilitude of the rapid appearance in print and the fact that it was known, for example, to Roque Guinart, "who, because of the hazards of his profession, could not be up on the latest literary novelties."[1] Edward Riley seems to see most clearly the significance of what has happened: "The Knight invents an enchanter-chronicler and proceeds to believe in him. . . . He is miraculously realized in fact and presents proof of his existence through the publication of Part I. The implications of this are formidable. It is a vindication of all his beliefs, for it means that chivalresque enchanters do exist outside the Knight's fancy—a point which Cervantes wisely refrains from pursuing, however. . . . The existence of Cide Hamete is a joke—and such a successful one that the significance of his absurdity is almost invariably passed over. He offers the one instance of total inverisimilitude in the book, with the exception of Don Alvaro Tarfe, who is a comparably peculiar case."[2]

But Riley, having grasped the "formidable implications" of this situation, notes only that "by making a patently unbelievable character supposedly responsible for the story, Cervantes wraps his vivid simulacrum of historical reality safely in an envelope of fiction." The implications are more formidable yet, because more is at stake than the immediate reader-author relationship affected by the point to which Riley refers. For even if the reader is able to suspend not only his disbelief, but any consistent and rational understanding of

1. "Arquitectura del *Quijote*," *Revista de Filología Española,* XXXII (1948), 283.

2. Edward C. Riley, *Cervantes's Theory of the Novel* (Oxford, 1962), p. 209.

the world in which the characters live, what can be the attitude of Sansón Carrasco, of the duke and duchess, of Antonio Moreno in Barcelona, of all the characters in the second part who have read the book and now meet the knight in his travels? The attitudes and activities of all of these characters in Part II are based upon a disbelief in enchanters, yet all accept the Don Quixote they meet as the same knight faithfully presented in the account of the Moorish enchanter.

If Don Quixote were to appear now at the door, could one accept him, and the novel as well? We are not dealing here with Hickock and Smith, in Capote's *In Cold Blood*, or Mailer's *Armies of the Night*. *Don Quixote* is a novel by an omniscient author, and is accepted *as such* by the characters in the second part. Surely we have passed through the looking glass into an impossible world. Américo Castro said in the article to which reference has already been made that Cervantes has presented us with "a play within a play, in such a subtle manner that it leaves in the reader the disturbing uncertainty of not knowing where one plane ends and the other begins."[3] We are in a position now to explain that "disturbing uncertainty." It arises from the unobtrusive, but nonetheless total, violation of the hitherto realistic world of the novel, through the intervention of an enchanter.

A poor writer might *tell* the reader that one's perspective conditions and distorts the perception of reality. A good writer could make the proposition *implicitly* evident in the relationships between the characters and their world. Cervantes seduces the reader into *acquiescing* in a wholly untenable perspective. Is not what Cervantes has accomplished here a sounder basis for the much discussed "perspectivism" in *Don Quixote* than the "basin-helmet" episode? Is it not much easier to identify with Don Quixote if one has, however superficially, shared his delusions? It may be objected that for Cervantes to make his point, the reader must become aware at some point that he has been fooled, and we have seen that the inverisimilitude is not usually perceived, but one has only to reread the quotation from Castro above to see that the "disturbing uncertainty" to which he refers arises precisely because the reader does not know just what has happened. Nor is Castro alone in this reaction to the novel. Others have noted that "one would not always need to have his head full of chivalric chimeras to wander off the road of reason,"[4] and decided that "the more one reads *Don Quixote* the more one is driven to the conclusion that this mystification [about the nature of *Don Quixote*] is of Cervantes' own making. The author seems . . . to delight in pulling the wool over his readers' eyes."[5] In Chapter 1 we have seen how Cervantes' mys-

3. "Cervantes y Pirandello," p. 480.

4. Predmore, *The World of "Don Quixote,"* p. 31.

5. Bruce Wardropper, "The Pertinence of *El curioso impertinente*," *PMLA*, LXXII (1957), 588.

tification about Don Quixote's real name and about the truth of the Cave of Montesinos episode produced a similar disorientation of the reader. Exposition of a proposition is outside, if not beneath, the art of the novel. Demonstration through action is the usual province of fiction. But *participation* on the reader's part is surely the highest aim of fiction, and this is clearly the effect of the situation we have been discussing.

Why does this total violation of the world of *Don Quixote* so often pass unnoticed by reader and critic alike? One can only conjecture. For one thing, the very profusion of levels discussed above probably lulls the reader into accepting yet another play within a play, without realizing that this case is radically different. For another, and this is the ultimate irony, *Don Quixote*, Part I, is the only specific object in the phenomenal world of Part II which exists literally, and lies ready at hand for our confirmation of its objective reality, yet it is precisely the presence of this book, *Don Quixote*, Part I, which violates the realistic terms of that world.

HERMAN MEYER

[The Poetics of Quotation in *Don Quixote*]†

* * *

It is clear that the device of pedantic quoting, which in countless works of Renaissance and Baroque poetry belongs to the reverently venerated set of decorative literary forms, has become meaningless for the author of *Don Quixote*. It has been debased to the function of a piece in a puzzle of literary fictions, along with—their range can only be briefly indicated here—the panegyric dedicatory poems at the conclusion of the prologue which are attributed to famous figures from the *Amadis* cycle and even to Rosinante; the frequent references to the ostensible Arabic "source" *Cid Hamet Benengeli*; and, most delightful of all, the use of two existing books (namely, the first part of *Don Quixote*, which appeared in 1605, and the

† From "Miguel de Cervantes' *Don Quixote*," in Herman Meyer, *The Poetics of Quotation in the European Novel*, trans. Theodore and Yetta Ziolkowski (Princeton University Press, 1968), pp. 59–71. An aspect of *Don Quixote* which many critics have studied is Cervantes' use of existing literary genres and practices as material for his novel. Herman Meyer believes that these older literary forms become "subject matter" and "dramatis personae" of the novel in a way that is even more important than the plot and characters, or the ideology (e.g., the criticism of the romances of chivalry), which is now antiquated. What makes Cervantes' system of quotation so effective is that it follows logically from Don Quixote's malady. As Meyer says, "The whole existence of our hero is to a certain extent a quotation, a quoting *imitatio* of the form of existence 'realized' . . . in courtly romances. . . ." Thus constant references to literature are a "natural emanation of his nature." Cervantes also parodies such traditional elements as the formal prologue, or stylistic traits such as the language of the romances or their fictional sources. Quotations from *Don Quixote* are from Ozell's revision of the translation by Peter Motteux (Modern Library edition).

"false" continuation, in 1614, by Avellaneda of Tordesillas) as pragmatic elements of motivation in the second part of the novel that appeared in 1615. Several adventures in the second part grow out of the literary fame enjoyed by Don Quixote and Sancho Panza thanks to "their" romance, that is to say the published first part. Through this collision of the empirical book and the imaginative world within the book, the fictive quality of the literary imagination is not lessened, but on the contrary vigorously underscored.

It is demonstrated once and for all, that the literary quotation is for the author of *Don Quixote* far more than a mere ornament attached to or imposed upon his novel with no organic connection. We shall see that he finds, rather, a much more artful possibility of exploiting the quotation, one which adapts itself organically to the overall style of the novel and contributes essentially to its structure. To make this evident, let us begin with the fundamental stylistic fact of this novel: the tension between two levels of style, the "lofty" and the "lowly," and the constant antithetical play among the various stylistic elements proper to these levels. From a genetic point of view, of course, this contrast consists by no means only of a simple opposition. It embraces the most varied shadings of influence from the entire Spanish literature of the day—from the realism of the picaresque novel to the idealistic sublimity of the Arcadian novel and the strident bombast of the courtly romances. To these are joined no less disparate elements from classical literature and Italian Renaissance poetry. But from a structural point of view this whole variety can be reduced to the simple contrast of high and low or, in other words, of pompous and simple. Yet these two styles are not equal partners. In the prologue the simple style is clearly represented, through the mouth of that "friend," as the true one that best serves the purpose of narrative:

> And since this writing of your's aims at no more than to destroy the Authority and Acceptance the Books of Chivalry have had in the World and among the Vulgar, you have no need to go begging Sentences of Philosophers, Passages out of Holy Writ, Poetical Fables, Rhetorical Orations, or Miracles of Saints. Do but take care to express yourself in a plain, easy Manner, in well-chosen, significant, and decent Terms, and to give an harmonious and pleasing Turn to your Periods: Study to explain your Thoughts, and set them in the truest Light, labouring, as much as possible, not to leave 'em dark nor intricate, but clear and intelligible. (Part I, Prol.)

The simple style is the one with which the poet feels at home; in the high style he generally speaks, as it were, with a borrowed voice. Naturally one should not oversimplify to the point of implying that Cervantes was a genuine "opponent" of the high style. This would not agree with the obvious pleasure with which he composes such rhetorical models as Don Quixote's speeches on the Golden Age (Part I, Ch. XI), and on weapons and the sciences (Part I, Chs. XXXVII–XXXVIII). It must be stressed, however, that in the contextual and formal texture of this novel the statements in high style represent a world devoid of meaning in which one no longer believes. This explains the paradox that the same author who works out the speech to the Golden Age as a proud sample of his rhetorical ability immediately thereafter characterizes it as "a speech which might very well have been omitted" and as "pointless words." Furthermore, in the high style it is not difficult to distinguish between a relatively straightforward and a bombastic type; the writer regards the latter in a completely negative light. Early in the exposition of the novel it is said:

> But among them all, none pleas'd him like the Works of the famous Feliciano de Sylva; for the clearness of his Prose, and those intricate Expressions in which 'tis interlac'd, seem'd to him so many Pearls of Eloquence, especially when he came to read the Challenges, and the amorous Addresses, many of them in this extraordinary Stile. "The Reason of your unreasonable Usage of my Reason, does so enfeeble my Reason, that I have Reason to expostulate with your Beauty": And this, "The sublime Heavens, which with your Divinity divinely fortify you with the Stars, and fix you the Deserver of the Desert that is deserv'd by your Grandeur." These and such like Expressions, strangely puzzled the poor Gentleman's Understanding, while he was breaking his Brain to unravel their Meaning, which Aristotle himself could never have found, though he should have been rais'd from the Dead for that very Purpose. (Part I, Ch. I)

The stylistic parody with its empty display of rhetorical splendors —hyperbole, polyptoton, *annominatio*, and so forth—lets the reader conclude by the principle of contraries what is meant in the prologue by "significant" and "decent" words.

The use of borrowed language, expressly satirical and with index finger raised in admonition, is at this point not yet very artful. It is adapted much more skillfully to the epic movement in the second chapter. During his departure, Don Quixote describes his setting out as he imagines that his future biographer will describe it:

> "Scarce had the ruddy-colour'd Phoebus begun to spread the golden Tresses of his lovely Hair over the vast Surface of the earthly Globe, and scarce had those feather'd Poets of the Grove, the pretty painted Birds, tun'd their little Pipes, to sing their early Welcomes in soft melodious Strains to the beautiful Aurora, who having left her jealous Husband's Bed . . ." (Part I, Ch. II)

and so forth. The fictitious description which activates the whole cosmic apparatus of classical mythology contrasts quite effectively with the realistic description of the actual departure. We see here

—and in general this holds true with very few exceptions—that the narrator does not move on his own into the lofty tone, but bestows it upon his figures in the reproduction of their speech or thoughts, thereby giving a pragmatic justification for the change in style. This motivation of stylistic shifts is not a restricting fetter. On the contrary, it enables this stylistic device to be spread out in inexhaustible epic variety. In order to bring about an interplay of two levels of style, Cervantes invents delightful interlacing or reflecting figures. In one instance Sancho must recapitulate from memory his master's letter to Dulcinea, composed in the sublimely lofty epistolary style of the time, and in doing so he distorts it grotesquely (Part I, Ch. XXV). On other occasions the author hands over his role of narrator for a moment to the fictive narrator of the "source," permitting the latter to speak in a superlative bombastic style that contrasts with the plaintiveness of the actual situation. A perfect example of this can be found in the adventure with the African lion, with its glaring mixture of genuine heroism and burlesque pitifulness. Still dripping with the curds that ooze down from his helmet, Don Quixote has taken a stand before the dangerous animal. At the moment of greatest tension the narrator interrupts himself:

> Here the Author of this faithful History could not forbear breaking the Thread of his Narration, and, rais'd by Wonder to Rapture and Enthusiasm, makes the following Exclamation. O thou most magnanimous Hero! Brave and unutterably Bold Don Quixote de la Mancha! Thou Mirror and grand Exemplar of Valour! Thou Second, and New Don Emanuel de Leon, the late Glory and Honour of all Spanish Cavaliers; What Words, what Colours shall I use to express, to paint in equal Lines, this astonishing Deed of thine! What Language shall I employ to convince Posterity of the Truth of this thy more than human Enterprise! (Part II, Ch. XVII)

The laudatory speech flows along at this stylistic level until the "real" narrator again takes over and reality sets in again with stark words. The king of the desert yawns, sticks out his tongue, and turns his rear to the challenger.

In this alternation between simple realism and ironically employed "high" speech, the literary quotation—and this means primarily the quotation in Don Quixote's own speeches—plays a key role. It is not dragged in but existentially determined as a natural emanation of his nature. For we should keep in mind that the whole existence of our hero is to a certain extent a quotation, a quoting *imitatio* of the form of existence "realized" (that is to say: imagined) in the courtly romances, and hence prescriptive for him. With reference to psychoanalysis Thomas Mann once brilliantly demonstrated to what a great extent "character" is only apparently a spontaneous uniqueness, since in reality it is determined by the *imitatio* of a prefigured model:

> His character is a mythical role which the actor just emerged from the depths to the light plays in the illusion that it is his own and unique; that he, as it were, has invented it all himself, with a dignity and security of which his supposed unique individuality in time and space is not the course, but rather which he creates out of his deeper consciousness in order that something which was once founded and legitimized shall again be represented and once more for good or ill, whether nobly or basely, in any case after its own kind conduct itself according to pattern.[1]

Men "quote" this given form, so to speak, in their lives and through their lives, thereby celebrating a mythic role. Thomas Mann does not mention *Don Quixote* in this connection, although the Hidalgo might have been his prize witness. For in the "character" of Don Quixote the "quotative life"—as a form of life and, by analogy, as a form of the novel—has come more completely into its own than almost anywhere else.

The fifth chapter provides a good example. Badly beaten by a mule-driver, Don Quixote lies in misery on the edge of the road. "Don Quixote perceiving that he was not able to stir, resolv'd to have recourse to his usual Remedy, which was to bethink himself what Passage in his Books might afford him some Comfort" (p. 26). Because of the similarity of the situation, he identifies himself with the wounded Baldwin from the popular *romance*[2] of the Marquess de Mantua, and in a weak voice quotes the latter's lament of love:

> "Alas, where are you, Lady dear,
> That for my Woe you do not moan?
> You little know what ails me here,
> Or are to me disloyal grown!" (Part I, Ch. V)

The stages of identification with the model can be clearly distinguished here. At first it is said only that Don Quixote finds the *romance* "as if made on purpose" for his circumstances: the relationship is still only analogical. But immediately afterwards he reaches a complete identification with the pattern, for when a sympathetic peasant wants to help him he mistakes him for "his" uncle from Mantua.[3] Nevertheless, this celebration of the mythic role contains an element of conscious choice. When the perplexed peasant raises a protest, Don Quixote answers:

1. Thomas Mann, "Freud und die Zukunft," *Adel des Geistes,* pp. 592f. Translated by H. T. Lowe-Porter: "Freud and the Future," *Freud, Goethe, Wagner* (New York: Alfred A. Knopf, 1937).

2. Ballad. [*Editor.*]

3. The entire episode goes back to the parodistic work *L'Entremés de los Romances* (1597); cf. Paul Hazard, *Don Quichotte de Cervantes* (Paris, n.d. [*ca.* 1938]), pp. 119ff.

> "I know very well who I am; and what's more, I know that I may not only be the Persons I have named, but also the Twelve Peers of France, nay, and the Nine Worthies all in One; since my Achievements will outrival not only the famous Exploits which made any of 'em singly illustrious, but all their mighty Deeds accumulated together." (Part I, Ch. V)

Since the awareness of "as though" does not disappear entirely, the identification is ruptured and the *imitatio* takes on an artistic quality. When Don Quixote decides to imitate the penance of Amadis in the desert and play the role of the desperate madman, Sancho asks him what his reason is, for his model certainly also had a reason. But Don Quixote gives him to understand that the *imitatio* is pure art for art's sake:

> "For, mark me, Sancho, for a Knight-Errant to run mad upon any just occasion, is neither strange nor meritorious; no, the Rarity is to run mad without a Cause, without the least Constraint or Necessity: There's a refin'd and exquisite Passion for you, Sancho! for thus my Mistress must needs have a vast Idea of my Love, since she may guess what I should perform in the Wet, if I do so much in the Dry." (Part I, Ch. XXV)

Now whether Don Quixote draws his quotations from the courtly books or—what is much more frequently the case—from the national store of *romances*, they all embody the world of chivalric illusion with which plain reality collides head-on. Thus they contribute to form that stylistic high level which, as we indicated above, sets itself in contrast to the low level of the realistic style of speech. One might ask whether this simple and direct contrast of reality and illusion and of high and low speech is not all too self-evident to be put through its paces for well-nigh a thousand pages. But the fluctuation between the two never becomes monotonous, thanks to the epic variety with which it is transformed. This is achieved especially by the sophisticated adaptation and assimilation of quotations in their new context. The second chapter offers a splendid example. Don Quixote comes into a miserable inn, which he takes to be an elegant castle. The innkeeper cannot even supply him with a bed. But that does not matter. Don Quixote answers magnanimously with the beginning lines of the well-known *romance*, "La Constancia":

> "For Arms are the only Things I value,
> And Combat is my Bed of Repose." (Part I, Ch. II)

The inn keeper obviously knows the *romance* also, for he is able to weave the next lines skillfully into his own answer:

> "At this rate, Sir Knight,
>
> Your Bed might be a Pavement
> And your Rest a constant Waking;

> you may then safely alight, and I dare assure you, you can hardly miss being kept awake all the year long in this house, much less one single Night." (Part I, Ch. II)

It is obvious that the primordial antithesis between the heroic world of fantasy and miserable reality has here been reduced to the specific contrast between idealistic asceticism and hardship from indigence, with the humoristic twist that the sly innkeeper goes so far as to capitalize on the opportunity he can offer for not sleeping! In the same hostel Don Quixote is disarmed by two slovenly but good-natured whores. He mistakes them for ladies of nobility and, while he is being disarmed, recites the *romance* of Lancelot, adapting it slightly to the situation at hand:

> "There never was on Earth a Knight
> So waited on by Ladies fair,
> As once was he, Don Quixote hight,
> When first he left his Village dear:
> Damsels t'undress him ran with Speed,
> And Princesses to dress his Steed." (Part I, Ch. II)

The antithetical device of high and low is rather simple here—poor camp followers instead of the illusory noble ladies—but it is enriched by an almost mirror-like correspondence in the thirty-first chapter of the second part, where knight and knave enter the ducal palace. In all innocence Sancho exhorts an aristocratic old duenna to go out before the gate and lead his dear ass Dapple into the stables. When she becomes highly indignant at his imputation, he quotes the same *romance*: "Damsels look'd after him, and Waiting-women after his Horse" (Part II, Ch. XXXI). The only result is that she berates him as the rascally son of a whore and garlic-eating stinkard. Again we find the antithesis of high and low, but the components have been turned about: the one who is addressed is now really a noble lady, but the peasant and his donkey have taken the place of the knight and his stallion. Figure and counterfigure, like a musical theme and its inversion, are related to one another by remote control over the space of a thousand pages.

Such thematic long-distance responses, which overarch the entire work with invisible bridges, are not at all rare. In the first part, as a confirmation and corroboration of his challenge to any man who might cast a dishonorable aspersion on his high mistress, Don Quixote cites the inscription on Roland's escutcheon (*Orlando furioso*, Canto XXIV):

> "Let none but he these Arms displace,
> Who dares *Orlando's* Fury face." (Part I, Ch. XIII)

When, having been defeated in a duel at the end of the second part, he has had to vow that he will refrain from further adventures and return to his village, he decides that now *his* weapons should be hung up on a tree and that the motto from Roland's escutcheon will stand beneath them (Part II, Ch. LXVI). Here the contrast between quotation and reality has been intensified. The first time, Don Quixote still had the right to speak in this manner. Now the challenging expression is highly out of keeping, because he has just lost the right to take any combat upon himself. This destroys the basic impulse of his life, and the whole bitter melancholy of the end of his life is concentrated in the inappropriately haughty quotation.

But even when a quotation is used only once, a rich elaboration of the basic antithesis is possible by means of parallel and contrary references. In the courtyard of an aristocratic house Don Quixote glimpses a row of earthen wine jugs which, because they come from Toboso, summon up in his mind the memory of his "enchanted" Dulcinea. In an ecstatic frame of mind he recites the introductory lines of a sonnet by Garcilaso de la Vega:

> "O! Pledges, once my Comfort and Relief,
> Though pleasing still, discover'd now with Grief!"
> (Part II, Ch. XVIII)

To the association based on the place of origin, Toboso, is added the aural association "*dulces prendas*"—"Dulcinea"; further, the comic parallel between the squat wine jug and the robust peasant maid ("Dulcinea" in the state of enchantment); and finally, the contrast of these two with the ethereal image of the beloved in his imagination.[4]

The use of quotations has shown us that the constant joining of elements related to one another by parallel and antithesis produces a finely balanced harmony of contrasts, by means of which the crass basic antithesis of delusion and reality is toned down. It is also part of this harmony of contrasts that Don Quixote's quotations find their antithetical correspondence in Sancho's brilliant use of popular expressions and proverbs. Quotation and proverb have as a common denominator the fact that both are preformed linguistic material. Proverbs in their totality constitute an unwritten literature, as it were, and represent a popular analogue to the quotations from written literature. Now, whereas Don Quixote's quotations are in general eminently inappropriate, Sancho's proverbs—despite their variegated disparity and apparent foolishness—are actually

4. This is not the only time that Garcilaso de la Vega, who was after all Cervantes' "pronounced and venerated favorite among the poets of Spain" (Hatzfeld, *Don Quijote als Wortkunstwerk*, p. 144), is treated parodistically. Here again is an indication that parody by no means requires a "hostile" attitude toward the object of parody and that it is misleading to conclude automatically that such an attitude exists.

with few exceptions quite relevant to the matter at issue. In Sancho's conversation with the duchess regarding the promised governorship, the whole pages-long potpourri of folksy sayings constitutes in essence nothing but an elaboration of his one main thought: that the distinction between poor and rich, lowly and aristocratic, is only vain appearance, for which reason he is gladly willing to renounce the governorship (Part II, Ch. XXXIII).

But even the contrast between literary quotation and proverb does not remain wholly at odds. Cross-connections emerge which are associated with the interlacing figures treated above. On the one hand Don Quixote condescends to express himself idiomatically in Sancho's fashion, although he does so only with a borrowed voice in order to make himself more comprehensible to his squire. When the latter wants to leave his master because he has not been paid, Don Quixote answers: " . . . and remember this, that if there be Vetches in my Dove-House, it will want no Pigeons. Good Arrears are better than ill Pay; and a Fee in Reversion is better than a Farm in Possession. Take notice too, there's Proverb for Proverb, to let you know that I can pour out a Volley of 'em as well as you" (Part II, Ch. VII). Conversely, Sancho, at the peak of his emotion in his lament after the supposed death of his master, imitates the latter's lofty manner of speech, only to slide back into his everyday language (Part I, Ch. LII). Likewise, he also makes occasional use of literary quotations, to which especially the popular literature of *romances* is suited. In these cases there is no lack of bowdlerization, but it affects only the outer form. Even when he mutilates the Latin text of the Mass, the contextual reference is astonishingly appropriate. Sancho's most brilliant achievement comes toward the end of the novel. Don Quixote tries to take off his trousers while his squire sleeps so that he can undertake the scourging which is supposed to release Dulcinea from the enchantment. But Sancho, overpowering him, kneels on his master and makes him promise to desist from his attempt. Otherwise:

> "Here thou diest,
> Traitor to Donna Sancha" (Part II, Ch. LX)

The eminently adapted and even more precisely literal quotation from the *romance* is disconcertingly appropriate, and the only impropriety lies in the contrast of its heroic atmosphere to the slapstick comedy of the situation.

We must forego any attempt to treat Don Quixote's "quoting" in a broader sense. There are many cases in which he ornaments his language with classical *topoi* or commonplaces or, in free form, summarizes large chunks of his courtly romances. It would turn out that the principle underlying these ornamental forms is the same as that in the literal quotation. They, too, are fitted consistently into the balanced harmony of contrasts that emerges from the interplay of antithetical elements. It suffices if we have succeeded in showing that the quotation in Cervantes' novel is a direct and pure expression of meaning, and that it succeeds in contributing to the establishment of that harmony of contrasts dominating the whole, in which the intended meaning finds its appropriate total epic form.

HARRY LEVIN

The Quixotic Principle: Cervantes and Other Novelists†

Our paradox is that a book about literary influence, and indeed against it, should have enjoyed so wide and decisive a literary influence. However, no one writes a book without hoping to influence his readers, even if his hope is to dissuade them from reading certain other books. Cervantes is by no means as obsessive as his monomaniacal protagonist, yet the writer returns to his proclaimed crusade in his final sentence: "I never desired any other thing, then that men would utterly abhor the fabulous impertinent and extravagant bookes of Chivalries: And to say truth, they begin already to stagger; for, undoubtedly, such fables and flam-flam tales will shortly faile, and I hope never rise again."[1] They were failing already, to be sure; there had been actual legislation to curb them; and he must have realized, with advancing commitment to his task, that he was not just dismissing an obsolescent genre; he was inventing a new one. Like any great invention, it had its forerunners and its congeners. Something like it had come out of the train of epic degeneration that produced the earlier Italian poems about the paladins of Charlemagne, notably that of Pulci. Rabelais had taken off from a folk tale to satirize not only the pedantries of scholasticism but the Arthurian quest for the Holy Grail. Classical mythology, reconsidered in sophisticated retrospect, had been fair game for the mocking commentary of Lucian and many others.

† From *The Interpretation of Narrative*, ed. M. W. Bloomfield (Cambridge: Harvard University Press, 1970), pp. 45–46, 50–52, 57–66.

In this abridged essay, Professor Levin sees a "Quixotic principle" in the "rivalry" between the actual world and our "novel-inspired" (*romanesque*) tendency to distort it. We require love, for example, to follow the patterns of romantic adventure repeated incessantly in books and, these days, television scripts. "Self-deception incited by literature"—the "principle" first used by Cervantes—is the subject of many of our greatest novels, and Levin demonstrates how the idea, in the hands of a great writer, can produce "a vehicle for testing hypotheses and breaking down preconceptions" which eventually leads the hero—and, one hopefully expects, the reader—to self-awareness.

1. *The History of Don Quixote*, trans. Thomas Shelton (London, 1896), IV, 278.

More specifically, the Cervantistas have pointed to a dramatic skit, which seems to have adumbrated *Don Quixote* a few years before: *El Entremés de los Romances*, the interlude of the ballads. Here the prototype is merely a dim-witted peasant whose head has been turned by the lore of the *Romancero* so that he identifies himself with some of its heroes. Could he have caught this disease as readily by listening as by reading? A number of the lines he quotes will be echoed by Don Quixote, who—like his predecessor Bartolo—will blame his horse for one of his discomfitures.

* * *

The *donnèe*[2] is not much more complex than the primitive farce about the blockhead whose daily round has been bemused with snatches of balladry. Cervantes made his vital innovation when he elevated this mock-hero to a sphere of excessive literacy. * * *

In the Knight of the Rueful Countenance we behold a full-length portrait of a single-minded reader for whom reading is believing, and whose consequent distortions of reality help to sharpen our apprehension of it. His malady, from which many have suffered during the five hundred years between Gutenberg and McLuhan, has been diagnosed by Ernest Renan as *morbus litterarius*.[3] Professor McLuhan seems to think that he has discovered a cure for it. Don Quixote's biography is the classic case of what Herman Meyer has named *das zitathafte Leben*, the quotation-oriented life.[4] All of our lives are more or less oriented to precepts and allusions. Sancho Panza relies on folk wisdom and pungent proverbs, in contradistinction to the book-learning and rhetorical speeches of his master. The contrasting textures of the language contributed to that intermixture of high and low styles which, as Erich Auerbach has shown, provides the textual basis for realism. It was a brilliant stroke for Cervantes to have settled upon his subject, to have tried it out in his first six chapters, to have launched his knight and brought him back in battered pride to his endangered library. But Cervantes manifested even greater brilliance by sustaining his theme through the second sally that takes up the rest of Part One, and thereafter through the third expedition which constitutes Part Two, without unduly repeating himself and with so resourceful a sequence of variations.

* * *

Cervantes, like all great writers, has acquired an extra dimension within his native culture, since he has done so much to delineate its patterns. But if he loses that quality when his work is exported,

2. The "basic idea" of *Don Quixote*. [*Editor.*]
3. "Literary disease." [*Editor.*]
4. Herman Meyer, *Das Zitat in der Erzählkunst: Zur Geschichte und Poetik des Europäischen Romans* (Stuttgart, 1967), p. 62.

something else may have been gained by its adaptation into another milieu and by the emulation it has stimulated.

* * *

No book has had a more spectacular fortune than the one whose relations with others I am considering. Since it assumed so prominent a place in the canon of European classics, and stood so near the beginnings of the novel, it was destined to figure in the formation of nearly all the other novelists. It was almost certain to be a milestone in their development; Stendhal testifies that his first encounter with it was "perhaps the greatest epoch of my life."[5] The all but countless imitations that it invited and sanctioned, the quasi-Quixotes adapted by other writers to other contexts, some of which we have been glancing at, have been systematically catalogued and amply documented in a number of studies.[6] What should concern us rather more centrally is not so much the direct line of Cervantes' impact as the basic process he discovered and its wider employment, which I shall venture to call the quixotic principle. Bernard Shaw, in one of his prefaces, berates the critics as usual—this time for attributing his technique of disillusionment to the influence of Ibsen or Nietzsche. Actually, he tell us, it was from a forgotten novel, *A Day's Ride, a Life's Romance,* by a minor novelist, Charles Lever, that Shaw learned "the tragicomic irony of the conflict between real life and the romantic imagination."[7] What he diagnoses as "Pott's" disease (for Lever's hero boasts that unromantic name) is the very malaise that had affected Don Quixote and Mr. Pickwick.

But Shaw did not gain his awareness of it from Cervantes, though he suggests that Lever might have got something through Stendhal; and we know well enough where Stendhal got it. In *The Counterfeiters* of André Gide, the novelist Edouard is writing a novel which will be entitled *The Counterfeiters.* What could be more appropriate, since fiction by definition is no more than a fabricated semblance of the truth it sets out to convey? The subject of this book-within-the-book is formulated in terms which come so close to Shaw's as to imply that each writer had independently come across the quixotic principle: "the rivalry between the real world and the representation that we make of it for ourselves."[8] That representation tends to be inherently romantic in the bookish sense of the word: *romanesque.* It has been argued—not to say overargued—by Denis de Rougemont that romance in the amatory

5. Stendhal, *Vie de Henry Brulard,* ed. Henri Martineau (Paris, 1927), I, 152.
6. Readers who are interested in translations, imitations, and other examples of Cervantes' influence on European literature might consult *Cervantes Across the Centuries,* ed. Angel Flores and M. J. Bernardete (New York: Dryden Press, 1947), Part Four. [*Editor.*]
7. G. B. Shaw, *John Bull's Other Island and Major Barbara* (New York, 1908), p. 158 (preface to *Major Barbara*).
8. André Gide, *Les Faux-monnayeurs* (Paris, 1925), p. 261.

sense, the cult of love between the sexes as we conceive and practice it, was superimposed upon the modern world by courtly troubadours and medieval romancers and sonneteering Christian Platonists.[9] Rougemont's thesis could be epitomized by La Rochefoucauld's maxim that some people would never fall in love if they had not heard about it. The passion of Paolo and Francesca was set aflame by a book they were reading together, the romance of Lancelot and Guinevere, which Dante curses as a go-between. Dante meanwhile has narrated the romance of Paolo with Francesca, and has revivified it by placing it in the contrasting context of a book-within-a-book.

Romances did not cease to exist when *Amadís* was put down, or when the Curate and the Barber burned Don Quixote's books. The Romantic Revival could be said to have suffused this spirit into all phases of human behavior. We should remember that the novel of its leading exponent, Rousseau, evokes another medieval love story; and if his Julie stands in the shadow of Héloïse, then her Abelard, Saint-Preux, might have been christened after some chivalric predecessor. The starting point for Scott—which means the starting point for Manzoni, Cooper, Balzac, and the nineteenth-century novel—was the library at Waverley Honour, where the quixotic young Edward indulged in "Castle-Building."[1] Scott has his realistic side, his lowlands as well as his highlands, his Hanoverian allegiance along with his Jacobite nostalgia. Yet he remains at heart a romanticist because, quite unlike Cervantes, he was less interested in exposing reality than in embellishing it. As daily life became more drably urbanized and uneventually uniform, much of fiction came to serve the desire to escape through fantasy into distant regions where the scenery was more picturesque and the prospect of adventure could still be held out. Many Anglo-American novelists, such as Hawthorne and the Brontës, expressly looked upon their works as romances, in order to claim more imaginative latitude. This Quixotism on the part of the author has its *preux chevalier* in the whimsical person of Lewis Carroll's White Knight.

It was the professed intent of Dickens to romanticize familiar things, but increasingly he comes out among the realists. The *donnée* of his first novel, *Pickwick Papers*, with its paunchy middle-class knight and its boot-shining cockney squire, is decidedly Cervantine. Don Quixote himself was not more chaste in resisting Maritornes during the bedroom farce at the inn than is Samuel Pickwick, Esq., when he blushes at being seen in his nightcap by the lady with the curling-papers at the Great White Horse in Ipswich. If he beams and bumbles his way toward an escape to the countryside and to the sentimentalities of Christmas, he comes back to

9. Denis de Rougemont, *L'Amour et l'occident* (Paris, 1939).

1. Walter Scott, *Waverley*, ch. iv.

London with a vengeance and to the terrain of future Dickensian satire, the lawcourt and the prison. Remote as Cervantes stands from the ground of Dickens' later writings, the two great caricaturists are linked by their common gifts of mimicry and powers of invention. I trust that the categories I have been using, for the sake of convenience, are understood to be relative rather than absolute. All narration involves some degree of interaction between realistic and romantic elements. Realism presupposes romanticism, and makes its sharpest points in juxtaposition with it, as I have been trying to demonstrate here and elsewhere. The novelist as we have known him, from Cervantes to—but not through—Joyce, and as contrasted with other storytellers working within the other narrative modes, has been primarily a realist.

This has not been the rule with the classic American tradition. One exception, H. H. Brackenridge in *Modern Chivalry*, made an amusing local extension of Cervantes' formula. But the primary emphasis has fallen upon the Gothic, upon the search for a past, or upon the exploitation of regional color. Melville hailed Cervantes as one of his personal demigods, associating him with John Bunyan and Andrew Jackson in a moving apostrophe. Yet the elaborate procedures of *Moby-Dick* are aimed at dignifying and amplifying a humble set of conditions, at conferring the honors of knighthood upon a crew of fishermen. A humorist must by nature be more of a realist, since his business is the perception of incongruities; and Mark Twain not infrequently seems to pursue the course of Cervantes, most straightforwardly with his *Connecticut Yankee in King Arthur's Court*. As an innocent abroad he played Sancho Panza, refusing to recognize the Old World's marvels and equating America with a modernity before which storied castles could do nothing but crumble. Whereas at home the romance-ridden South, spuriously gothicized by too long an immersion in the Waverley novels, was one of his principal targets. Its faded glories and its declining legends are intermingled with brute force and earthy cunning in Faulkner's darkly variegated chronicle of the Compsons and the Snopeses. It is not surprising to learn that he reread *Don Quixote* every year, as if it were the writer's Bible.[2]

With Hemingway, the revolt against literariness became a major stylistic premise. Its manifesto is his famous description of the retreat at Caporetto in *A Farewell to Arms*, where all the rhetoric of abstraction has been exploded on the battlefield. The experience of war has always tended to sharpen the edges of realism, as it must have done for Cervantes at Lepanto. It was crucial for Tolstoy at

2. William Faulkner, in *Writers at Work*, ed. Malcolm Cowley (New York, 1958), p. 136.

Sebastopol, and the quixotic principle can be seen at work throughout *War and Peace.* Consider the sturdy general Kutuzov, shrugging aside the complicated strategies of the military theorists and biding his time for the Battle of Borodino by dozing over a pallid historical novel of Madame de Genlis. The running contrast with Napoleon is highlighted by histrionic gestures and grandiose announcements. Even the frequent use of French in the novel, which underscores the artificiality of court circles, focuses attention on the immediacies of the Russian homeland, just as Pierre's dabblings in free-masonry pale before his initiation into the comradeship of battle. As for Napoleon himself, having realized his mad wishdreams and entrammeled Europe in misadventure, he was in no position to appreciate the irony of Cervantes. Afterward at Saint Helena, after dinner with his small entourage, we are told by his chronicler Las Cases: "He finished by reading to us from Don Quixote, stopped at several jests, and, putting down the book, remarked that it surely took courage to laugh in that moment at such trivialities."[3]

But, even as his youthful dreams of grandeur had been nourished by literature, so his private legend—as set down by Las Cases in the *Memorial of Saint Helena*—would stir the ambitions of the next generation. What *Amadís of Gaul* was to Don Quixote the *Mémorial* would be to Julien Sorel. When we first encounter Julien he is poring over it, astride a beam in his father's sawmill whence it is roughly knocked into the mill-race. No matter, for he has virtually memorized it; and, as he ascends the social scale in *The Red and the Black,* he patterns himself on two additional and somewhat contradictory models: Rousseau's *Confessions* and Moliere's *Tartuffe.* In *The Charterhouse of Parma* Fabrice de Dongo has a more urbane upbringing, yet it begins in the bedazzlement of the Napoleonic image and the baptism of fire at Waterloo—the pioneering treatment of war in modern fiction—which teaches him that being in the army is not like being a hero of Ariosto. The official biographer of the Napoleonides, those little would-be Napoleons whose quixotic aspirations so often culminated in mercenary defection and political compromise, was naturally Balzac. His catchphrase, Lost Illusions, might aptly stand as a generalization to cover all the instances that I have been reviewing, beginning with Don Quixote on his deathbed and extending far beyond the sentimental education of Frédéric Moreau. The case history that Balzac so designates, that of Lucien de Rubempré, is the object lesson of literary talent selling out.

The undergrowth of chastened romanticism, out of which such realism develops, is still fairly obtrusive in Balzac. It is more dis-

3. Comte Emmanuel de Las Cases, *Le Mémorial de Sainte-Hélène,* ed. Jean Prévost (Paris, 1935), p. 369.

ciplined, though by no means absent, in Flaubert. When Kierkegaard in 1843 called for a feminine version of *Don Quixote*,[4] he was unaware that this hiatus had been filled at least twice: in the mid-eighteenth century with *The Female Quixote* by the American-born Englishwoman Charlotte Lennox, and in 1800 with *Female Quixotism* by an American who sounds like an old-fashioned schoolmarm, Tabitha Tenney. Kierkegaard's suggestion was, at any rate, well taken; for the typical gentle reader, to be addressed and served and swayed by the novelist, would be a woman. The fictional heroines—Clarissas, Corinnes, and Consuelos—had all exhibited quixotic symptoms. The girlish reveries of Tatiana, in *Evgeni Onegin*, had been bibliographically footnoted. Through the interplay of sense and sensibility, Jane Austen had criticized Mrs. Radcliffe and Fanny Burney. E. S. Barrett, whose early pseudonym was Cervantes Hogg, had presented a paradigm in *The Heroine*, where a farmer's daughter sallies forth into a picaresque world, armed with no more than misleading assumptions about it, nurtured by the circulating libraries. "I sat down and read Ossian, to store my mind with ideas for conversation," she confides to us on one occasion, and on another: "Being in such distress, I though it incumbent on me to compose a sonnet."[5] Ultimately, but not before she has impulsively and repeatedly placed her virtue in danger, she is cured by reading *Don Quixote*.

The usual habits of novel-reading, of course, tended to spread such infections rather than cure them. Homeopathy could be efficacious only if the restorative book was molded in the Cervantine tradition. This particular delusion of grandeur, the self-portrait of the housewife as a heroine, was given the definitive stamp of Flaubert in *Madame Bovary*. * * * The female counterpart of Quixotism, or self-deception incited by literature, is known as *Bovarysme*; its ending can be tragic when not bathetic; but Flaubert, while modernizing the initial concept of Cervantes, vastly broadened it. * * *

Cervantes and Flaubert, then, rank together as the alpha and omega of the quixotic principle. In view of the span between them, perhaps we could generalize further by adapting an aphorism from Pascal. He was speaking of eloquence, which faces a similar problem: whenever words are used, they are abused, so that, if one genuinely seeks to carry conviction, one must begin by discrediting the verbal medium. Accordingly we could say: "Le vrai roman se moque du roman."[6] The true novel flouts the novel—or, to catch another nuance, the *romanesque*. Such mockery, focusing as it does on liter-

4. Søren Kierkegaard, *Either/Or*, trans. D. F. and M. L. Swenson (Princeton, 1944), I, 210.
5. E. S. Barrett, *The Heroine*, ed. Walter Raleigh (London, 1909), pp. 170, 21.
6. Blaise Pascal, *Pensées*, pref., 24. The original formulation is: "La vraie éloquence se moque de l'éloquence."

ary material, tends to take the form of parody. Fielding thus began by parodying Richardson, in "the Manner of Cervantes"; Jane Austen with divers parodies, memorably that of the Gothic novel in *Northanger Abbey*; Thackeray with his burlesques in *Punch* of Bulwer, Lever, Cooper, Disraeli—not to mention *Rebecca and Rowena*, subtitled A *Romance upon Romance*. It is not for nothing that we speak in this connection of a "take-off," or that so many novelists have started as parodists and played, in Stevenson's phrase, "the sedulous ape" to their forerunners.[7] Proust took off with a series of pastiches in *Le Figaro*, recounting a topical scandal *a la manière de* Balzac, Flaubert, Sainte-Beuve, Goncourt, and others. Through the posthumous fragment *Against Sainte-Beuve*, we now know that the *Remembrance of Things Past* (which contains purported excerpts from the Goncourt *Journal*) was helped into life by the midwifery of *The Human Comedy*.

Joyce's *Ulysses* constitutes a parody of parodies, both in its reductive relation to Homer's *Odyssey* and in such excursions as Gerty MacDowell's into the mawkish sphere of schoolgirl magazines, let alone the episode that stylistically recapitulates the evolution of English literature. But Joyce goes deeper, since he enters the minds of his leading characters so completely; he shows how consciousness is pieced together by reminiscence and how thought is patterned by echoes, whether these be Molly's songs or Bloom's advertisements or Stephen's scholastic formulations. By this stage, and in the mature fiction of the writers I have been citing, the novelist has taken us far beyond mere parody. But he had to make his breakthrough at the level of stylistic precedent. Through the parodic he moved on to the satiric, starting from a critique of literature and ending with a criticism of life. Hence Cervantes' explicit attack on books of chivalry can be read as an implicit renunciation of feudal institutions—or, better still, a salutation to the Renaissance. As historical circumstances changed, the central mechanism could be continually enlarged and rendered more flexible in meeting those changes. It was after all no more than some *idée fixe* which needed to become unfixed again and sharply detached in the light of fuller experience. It was, indeed, like falling out of love; and the infatuation that had preceded it could be likened, in Stendhal's terms, to the crystallization that dazzles the lover.

The overriding idea might assume the guise of an ideology to be challenged, of a doctrine which turned its believers into doctrinaires, or a frame of reference which proves inadequate for the phenomena it was intended to cover. The quest may take its hero to different regions in search of dissimilar objects, and yet still serve as a vehicle for testing hypotheses and breaking down preconceptions.

7. R. L. Stevenson, "A College Magazine," in *Memories and Portraits*.

Systems like that of Tristram Shandy's father or—more tragically—that of Richard Feverel's father, -isms and -ologies, hobby-horses and mental constructs of all sorts, must be verified and rectified by facts. And, since facts are not the same as words, our best means of gaining contact with actuality through them is to dramatize the processes of verification and rectification. The record is always having to be corrected in some particular. "Systems of metaphysics are to philosophers," wrote Voltaire, "what novels are to women . . . I have ventured to let the air out of some of those metaphysical balloons."[8] We watch this habit of deflation as it works through chapter after chapter with Candide, who is so naive that it takes a war, an inquisition, an earthquake, a tidal wave, and a disastrous tour of the world to disabuse him of his faith in the Leibnitzian optimism of Dr. Pangloss. Yet it would be a mistake to believe that the quixotic principle is a negative one simply because it operates through disillusionment. Rather, it is a register of development, an index of maturation. Its incidental mishaps can be looked back upon as milestones on the way to self-awareness.

Georg Lukács was therefore well warranted, fifty years ago in his *Theorie des Romans* when he made *Don Quixote* the crucial link in the chain of narrative extending from the ancient epic to the modern *Bildungsroman*, wherein the subjectivity of the individual develops into an ironic overview of life.[9] The path is clear, then, from Cervantes to Proust. Marcel is a young Quixote when he goes questing *à la recherche du temps perdu*. His *Amadis de Gaula* is the *Almanach de Gotha;* and that nostalgic magic-lantern vista of the baronial past, colored with all the heraldry, the genealogy, and the poetry of latter-day snobbism, is dispelled shortly after his duchess puts on the wrong shoes. His dubieties over his elusive Albertine bear a surprising likeness to the jealousies of Cervantes' Curious Impertinent. But, where Cervantes' book-within-the-book is a thoroughly outmoded document which somehow has the effect of launching Don Quixote into the world, Proust's ultimate book is the one that he will write upon his retirement from the world, the very work that is being created before our eyes. His last appeal is not from art to life but from life to art, an art which justifies life by rounding it out. It seems fitting that Proust should recall Cervantes, along with Dostoevsky and Tolstoy, and likewise Shakespeare and Sophocles, in his poignant memoir "Filial Sentiments of a Parricide." For the recognition-scene and the resolution of a novel must finally be what they were to Alonso Quixano the Good upon his deathbed: as Proust has summed it up, "a belated moment of lucidity."[1]

8. Voltaire, *Courte Réponse aux longs discours d'un docteur allemand.*
9. Georg Lukács, *Die Theorie des Romans* (Berlin, 1920), *passim.*
1. Marcel Proust, *Pastiches et mélanges* (Paris, 1919), p. 224.

RENE GIRARD

["Triangular" Desire in *Don Quixote*]†

"I want you to know, Sancho, that the famous Amadis of Gaul was one of the most perfect knights errant. But what I am saying, one of the most perfect? I should say the only, the first, the unique, the master and lord of all those who existed in the world. . . . I think . . . that, when a painter wants to become famous for his art he tries to imitate the originals of the best masters he knows; the same rule applies to most important jobs or exercises which contribute to the embellishment of republics; thus the man who wishes to be known as careful and patient should and does imitate Ulysses, in whose person and works Homer paints for us a vivid portrait of carefulness and patience, just as Virgil shows us in the person of Aeneas the valor of a pious son and the wisdom of a valiant captain; and it is understood that they depict them not as they are but as they should be, to provide an example of virtue for centuries to come. In the same way Amadis was the pole, the star, the sun for brave and amorous knights, and we others who fight under the banner of love and chivalry should imitate him. Thus, my friend Sancho, I reckon that whoever imitates him best will come closest to perfect chivalry."

Don Quixote has surrendered to Amadis the individual's fundamental prerogative: he no longer chooses the objects of his own desire—Amadis must choose for him. The disciple pursues objects which are determined for him, or at least seem to be determined for him, by the model of all chivalry. We shall call this model the *mediator* of desire. Chivalric existence is the *imitation* of Amadis in the same sense that the Christian's existence is the imitation of Christ.

In most works of fiction, the characters have desires which are simpler than Don Quixote's. There is no mediator, there is only the subject and the object. When the "nature" of the object inspiring the passion is not sufficient to account for the desire, one must turn to the impassioned subject. Either his "psychology" is examined or his "liberty" invoked. But desire is always spontaneous. It can

† From René Girard, *Deceit, Desire and the Novel* (Baltimore: Johns Hopkins University Press, 1965), pp. 1–18, 44–52. Girard offers rich insights into the psychology of Don Quixote and the relationship between Cervantes' masterpiece and other great novels often compared with it, such as *Madame Bovary*. The author believes that "all of the ideas of the Western novel are present in germ in *Don Quixote*," but that the absolutely fundamental idea is what he calls "triangular desire," desire inspired in the hero by his admiration for some ideal person, whose desires the hero also imitates. In Cervantes, Don Quixote imitates Amadís, principally, and adopts his goals. Other novelists have explored this "triangle" of subject, model, and jointly desired object, though none has ever gone beyond the "extreme forms of imitated desire" contained in *Don Quixote*: one pole being the mad knight's imitation of Amadís, the other, that of Lothario, in the tale of "Ill-advised Curiosity."

always be portrayed by a simple straight line which joins subject and object.

The straight line is present in the desire of Don Quixote, but it is not essential. The mediator is there, above that line, radiating toward both the subject and the object. The spatial metaphor which expresses this triple relationship is obviously the triangle. The object changes with each adventure but the triangle remains. The barber's basin or Master Peter's puppets replace the windmills; but Amadis is always present.

Don Quixote, in Cervantes' novel, is a typical example of the victim of triangular desire, but he is far from being the only one. Next to him the most affected is his squire, Sancho Panza. Some of Sancho's desires are not imitated, for example, those aroused by the sight of a piece of cheese or a goatskin of wine. But Sancho has other ambitions besides filling his stomach. Ever since he has been with Don Quixote he has been dreaming of an "island" of which he would be governor, and he wants the title of duchess for his daughter. These desires do not come spontaneously to a simple man like Sancho. It is Don Quixote who has put them into his head.

This time the suggestion is not literary, but oral. But the difference has little importance. These new desires form a new triangle of which the imaginary island, Don Quixote, and Sancho occupy the angles. Don Quixote is Sancho's mediator. The effects of triangular desire are the same in the two characters. From the moment the mediator's influence is felt, the sense of reality is lost and judgment paralyzed.

Since the mediator's influence is more profound and constant in the case of Don Quixote than in that of Sancho, romantic readers have seen in the novel little more than the contrast between Don Quixote the *idealist* and the *realist* Sancho. This contrast is real but secondary; it should not make us overlook the analogies between the two characters. Chivalric passion defines a desire *according to Another*, opposed to this desire *according to Oneself* that most of us pride ourselves on enjoying. Don Quixote and Sancho borrow their desires from the Other in a movement which is so fundamental and primitive that they completely confuse it with the will to be Oneself.

One might object that Amadis is a fictitious person—and this we must admit, but Don Quixote is not the author of this fiction. The mediator is imaginary but not the mediation. Behind the hero's desires there is indeed the suggestion of a third person, the inventor of Amadis, the author of the chivalric romances. Cervantes' work is a long meditation on the baleful influence that the most lucid minds can exercise upon one another. Except in the realm of chivalry, Don Quixote reasons with a great deal of common sense. Nor are his favorite writers mad: perhaps they do not even take their fiction seriously. The illusion is the fruit of a bizarre marriage of two lucid consciousnesses. Chivalric literature, ever more widespread since the invention of the printing press, multiplies stupendously the chances of similar unions.

Desire according to the Other and the "seminal" function of literature are also found in the novels of Flaubert. Emma Bovary desires through the romantic heroines who fill her imagination. The second-rate books which she devoured in her youth have destroyed all her spontaneity. We must turn to Jules de Gaultier for the definition of this "bovarysm" which he reveals in almost every one of Flaubert's characters: "The same ignorance, the same inconsistency, the same absence of individual reaction seem to make them fated to obey the suggestion of an external milieu, for lack of an autosuggestion from within." In his famous essay, entitled *Bovarysm*, Gaultier goes on to observe that in order to reach their goal, which is to "see themselves as they are not," Flaubert's heroes find a "model" for themselves and "imitate from the person they have decided to be, all that can be imitated, everything exterior, appearance, gesture, intonation, and dress."

The external aspects of imitation are the most striking; but we must above all remember that the characters of Cervantes and Flaubert are imitating, or believe they are imitating, the *desires* of models they have freely chosen. A third novelist, Stendhal, also underscores the role of suggestion and imitation in the personality of his heroes. Mathilde de la Mole finds her models in the history of her family; Julien Sorel imitates Napoleon. *The Memoirs of Saint-Helena* and the *Bulletins* of the Grand Army replace the tales of chivalry and the romantic extravagances. The Prince of Parma imitates Louis XIV. The young Bishop of Agde practices the benediction in front of a mirror; he mimics the old and venerable prelates whom he fears he does not sufficiently resemble.

Here history is nothing but a kind of literature; it suggests to all Stendhal's characters feelings and, especially, desires that they do not experience spontaneously. * * * Stendhal uses the word "vanity" (*vanité*) to indicate all these forms of "copying" and "imitating." The *vaniteux*—vain person—cannot draw his desires from his own resources; he must borrow them from others. Thus the *vaniteux* is brother to Don Quixote and Emma Bovary. And so in Stendhal we again find triangular desire.

* * *

A *vaniteux* will desire any object so long as he is convinced that it is already desired by another person whom he admires. The mediator here is a *rival*, brought into existence as a rival by vanity, and that same vanity demands his defeat. The rivalry between mediator and the person who desires constitutes an essential difference between this desire and that of Don Quixote, or of Emma Bovary. Amadis cannot vie with Don Quixote in the protection of orphans in distress, he cannot slaughter giants in his place. * * * In most of Stendhal's desires, the mediator himself desires the object, or could desire it: it is even this very desire, real or presumed, which makes this object infinitely desirable in the eyes of the subject. The mediation begets a second desire exactly the same as the mediator's. This means that one is always confronted with two *competing* desires. The mediator can no longer act his role of model without also acting or appearing to act the role of obstacle. Like the relentless sentry of the Kafka fable, the model shows his disciple the gate of paradise and forbids him to enter with one and the same gesture. * * *

In Cervantes the mediator is enthroned in an inaccessible heaven and transmits to his faithful follower a little of his serenity. In Stendhal, this same mediator has come down to earth. The clear distinction between these two types of relationship between mediator and subject indicates the enormous spiritual gap which separates Don Quixote from the most despicably vain of Stendhal's characters. The image of the triangle cannot remain valid for us unless it at once allows this distinction and measures this gap for us. To achieve this double objective, we have only to vary the *distance*, in the triangle, separating the mediator from the desiring subject.

Obviously this distance is greatest in Cervantes. There can be no contact whatsoever between Don Quixote and his legendary Amadis. Emma Bovary is already closer to her Parisian mediator. Travelers' tales, books, and the press bring the latest fashions of the capital even to Yonville. Emma comes still closer to her mediator when she goes to the ball at the Vaubyessards'; she penetrates the holy of holies and gazes at the idol face to face. But this proximity is fleeting. Emma will never be able to desire that which the incarnations of her "ideal" desire; she will never be able to be their rival; she will never leave for Paris.

Julien Sorel does all that Emma cannot do. At the beginning of *The Red and the Black* the distance between the hero and his mediator is as great as in *Madame Bovary*. But Julien spans this distance; he leaves his province and becomes the lover of the proud Mathilde; he rises rapidly to a brilliant position. Stendhal's other heroes are also close to their mediators. It is this which distinguishes Stendhal's universe from those we have already considered. * * * In the novels of Cervantes and Flaubert, the mediator remained beyond the universe of the hero; he is now within the same universe.

Romantic works are, therefore, grouped into two fundamental categories—but within these categories there can be an infinite number of secondary distinctions. We shall speak of *external media-*

tion when the distance is sufficient to eliminate any contact between the two spheres of *possibilities* of which the mediator and the subject occupy the respective centers. We shall speak of *internal mediation* when this same distance is sufficiently reduced to allow these two spheres to penetrate each other more or less profoundly.

Obviously it is not physical space that measures the gap between mediator and the desiring subject. Although geographical separation might be one factor, the *distance* between mediator and subject is primarily spiritual. Don Quixote and Sancho are always close to each other physically but the social and intellectual distance which separates them remains insuperable. The valet[1] never desires what his master desires. Sancho covets the food left by the monks, the purse of gold found on the road, and other objects which Don Quixote willingly lets him have. As for the imaginary island, it is from Don Quixote himself that Sancho is counting on receiving it, as the faithful vassal holds everything in the name of his lord. The mediation of Sancho is therefore an external mediation. No rivalry with the mediator is possible. The harmony between the two companions is never seriously troubled.

The hero of external mediation proclaims aloud the true nature of his desire. He worships his model openly and declares himself his disciple. We have seen Don Quixote himself explain to Sancho the privileged part Amadis plays in his life. Mme Bovary and Léon also admit the truth about their desires in their lyric confessions. The parallel between *Don Quixote* and *Madame Bovary* has become classic. It is always easy to recognize analogies between two novels of external mediation.

Imitation in Stendhal's work at first seems less absurd since there is less of that divergence between the worlds of disciple and model which makes a Don Quixote or an Emma Bovary so grotesque. And yet the imitation is no less strict and literal in internal mediation than in external mediation. If this seems surprising it is not only because the imitation refers to a model who is "close," but also because the hero of internal mediation, far from boasting of his efforts to imitate, carefully hides them.

The impulse toward the object is ultimately an impulse toward the mediator; in internal mediation this impulse is checked by the mediator himself since he desires, or perhaps possesses, the object. Fascinated by his model, the disciple inevitably sees, in the mechanical obstacle which he puts in his way, proof of the ill will borne him. Far from declaring himself a faithful vassal, he thinks only of repudiating the bonds of mediation. But these bonds are stronger than ever, for the mediator's apparent hostility does not diminish his prestige but instead augments it. The subject is convinced that the model considers himself too superior to accept him as a disciple.

1. Squire. [*Editor.*]

The subject is torn between two opposite feelings toward his model —the most submissive reverence and the most intense malice. This is the passion we call *hatred.*

Only someone who prevents us from satisfying a desire which he himself has inspired in us is truly an object of hatred. The person who hates first hates himself for the secret admiration concealed by his hatred. In an effort to hide this desperate admiration from others, and from himself, he no longer wants to see in his mediator anything but an obstacle. The secondary role of the mediator thus becomes primary, concealing his original function of a model scrupulously imitated.

* * *

As we have seen, the approach of the mediator tends to bring together the two spheres of *possibilities,* of which the rivals occupy the respective centers. The resentment they feel for each other is therefore always increasing. In Proust the birth of passion coincides with the birth of hate. As early as *Jean Santeuil* he gives an excellent triangular definition of hate, which is also a definition of desire:

> Of such a nature is hatred which compounds from the lives of our enemies a fiction which is wholly false. Instead of thinking of them as ordinary human beings knowing ordinary human happiness and occasionally exposed to the sorrows which afflict all mankind and ought to arouse in us a feeling of kindly sympathy, we attribute to them an attitude of arrogant self-satisfaction which pours oil upon the flames of our anger. For hatred transfigures individuals no less than does desire and like desire sets us thirsting for human blood. On the other hand since it can find satisfaction only in the destruction of the supposed self-satisfaction which so irritates us, we imagine that self-satisfaction, see it, believe it to be in a perpetual process of disintegration. No more than love does hatred follow the dictates of reason, but goes through life with eyes fixed on an unconquerable hope.

Proust constantly reveals hatred in desire, desire in hatred. But he remains faithful to the traditional language; he never eliminates the "like" and the "as much as's" which are strewn through the preceding quotation. He will never reach the highest level of internal mediation. This last stage was reserved for another novelist, the Russian, Dostoyevsky, who preceded Proust chronologically but succeeds him in the story of triangular desire.

Except for a few characters who entirely escape imitated desire, in Dostoyevsky there is no longer any love without jealousy, any friendship without envy, any attraction with repulsion. The characters insult each other, spit in each other's faces, and minutes later they fall at the enemy's feet, they abjectly beg mercy. This fascination coupled with hatred is not different in principle from Proustian snobbism and Stendhalian vanity. The inevitable consequences of desire copied from another desire are "envy, jealousy, and impotent hatred." As one moves from Stendhal to Proust and from Proust to Dostoyevsky, and the closer the mediator comes, the more bitter are the fruits of triangular desire.

* * *

The closer the mediator comes, the greater his role becomes and the smaller that of the object. Dostoyevsky by a stroke of genius places the mediator in the foregound and relegates the object to the background. At last novelistic composition reflects the real hierarchy of desire. * * * The transfer of the novelistic center of gravity is best and most spectacularly illustrated by *The Eternal Husband.* Veltchaninov, a rich bachelor, is a middle-aged Don Juan who is beginning to give in to weariness and boredom. For several days he has been obsessed by the fleeting apparitions of a man, at once mysterious and familiar, disturbing and odd. The character's identity is soon revealed. It seems he is a certain Pavel Pavlovitch Troussotzki, whose wife, a former mistress of Veltchaninov's, has just died. Pavel Pavlovitch has left his province in order to find in St. Petersburg the lovers of his dead wife. One of the lovers also dies, and Pavel Pavlovitch, in deep mourning, follows the funeral procession. There remains Veltchaninov on whom he heaps the most grotesque attentions and whom he wears out by his constant presence. The deceived husband makes very strange statements concerning the past. He pays his rival a visit in the middle of the night, drinks to his health, kisses him on the lips, and very cleverly tortures him, using an unfortunate little girl whose father remains unknown.

The woman is dead and the lover remains. There is no longer an object but the mediator, Veltchaninov, still exerts an irresistible attraction. This mediator makes an ideal narrator since he is the center of the action and yet scarcely participates in it. He describes events all the more carefully since he does not always succeed in interpreting them and is afraid of neglecting some important detail.

Pavel Pavlovitch considers a second marriage. Fascinated, he goes again to his first wife's lover; he asks him to help him choose a present for his latest choice; he begs him to go with him to her house. Veltchaninov demurs but Pavel Pavlovitch insists, begs, and ends by getting his way.

The two "friends" are given a warm reception at the young lady's house. Veltechaninov's conversation is entertaining and he plays the piano. His social ability arouses admiration: the whole family crowds around him, including the young lady whom Pavel Pavlovitch already looks on as his fiancée. The scorned suitor tries to be seductive without success. No one takes him seriously. He reflects on this new disaster, trembling with anguish and desire. Some years later Veltchaninov meets Pavel Pavlovitch again in a railroad station. The eternal husband is not alone; a charming lady, his wife, accompanies him, along with a dashing young soldier . . .

The Eternal Husband reveals the essence of internal mediation in the simplest and purest form possible. No digression distracts or misleads the reader. The text seems enigmatic only because it is too clear. It throws on the novelistic triangle a light so brilliant it dazzles us.

Confronted with Pavel Pavlovitch we can have no more doubts about the priority of the Other in desire, a principle first laid down by Stendhal. The hero is always trying to convince us that his relationship to the object of desire is independent of the rival. Here we clearly see that the hero is deceiving us. The mediator is immobile and the hero turns around him like a planet around the sun. The behavior of Pavel Pavlovitch seems strange to us but it is completely consistent with the logic of triangular desire. Pavel Pavlovitch can desire only through the mediation of Veltchaninov, *in* Veltchaninov as the mystics would say. He drags Veltchaninov along to the house of the lady he has chosen, so that he might desire her and thus guarantee her erotic value.

* * *

Triangular desire is *one*. We can start with Don Quixote and end with Pavel Pavlovitch, or we can begin with *Tristan and Isolde* as Denis de Rougemont does in *Love in the Western World* and quickly reach that "psychology of jealousy" which pervades our analyses. When he defines this psychology as a "profanation of the myth" embodied in the poem of Tristan, De Rougemont explicitly acknowledges the bond uniting the most "noble" forms of passion with morbid jealously, such as Proust or Dostoyevsky describe for us: "Jealousy, desired, provoked, and cunningly encouraged." De Rougemont correctly observes: "One reaches the point of wanting the beloved to be unfaithful so that one can court her again."

Such is—or very close to it—the desire of Pavel Pavlovitch. The eternal husband cannot do without jealousy. Trusting our analyses and the testimony of De Rougemont, we shall now see behind all forms of triangular desire the same diabolic trap into which the hero slowly sinks. Triangular desire is *one* and we think we are able to furnish a striking proof of its unity precisely where skepticism seems most jutified. The two "extremes" of desire, one illustrated by Cervantes, the other by Dostoyevsky, seem the hardest to incorporate in the same structure. We can accept that Pavel Pavlovitch is a brother to Proust's snob and even to Stendhal's *vaniteux*, but who would recognize in him a distant cousin of the famous Don Quixote? The impassioned eulogists of that hero cannot help but consider our comparison sacrilegious. For them Don Quixote lives only on the summits. How could the creator of this sublime being have an inkling of the swamps in which the eternal husband wallows?

The answer is to be found in one of the short stories with which Cervantes padded *Don Quixote*. Although they were all cast in a pastoral or chivalric mold these texts do not all fall back into the "romantic," nonnovelistic pattern. One of them, "The Curious Impertinent,"[2] portrays a triangular desire exactly like that of Pavel Pavlovitch.

Anselmo has just married the pretty young Camilla. The marriage was arranged with the help of Lothario, a very dear friend of the happy husband. Some time after the wedding Anselmo makes a curious request to Lothario. He begs him to pay court to Camilla, claiming that he wishes "to test" her faithfulness. Lothario refuses indignantly but Anselmo does not give up. He entreats his friend in a thousand different ways and in all his suggestions reveals the obsessive nature of his request. For a long time Lothario manages to put him off and finally pretends to accept in order to put him at ease. Anselmo arranges for the two young people to be alone together. He leaves on a journey, returns without warning, bitterly reproaches Lothario for not taking his role seriously. In short his behavior is so mad that he finally drives Lothario and Camilla into each other's arms. Learning that he has been betrayed, Anselmo kills himself in despair.

When one rereads the story in the light of *The Eternal Husband* and *The Captive*[3] it is no longer possible to consider it artificial and lacking in interest. Dostoyevsky and Proust enable us to dig down to its true meaning. "The Curious Impertinent" is Cervantes' *Eternal Husband;* the only difference between the two stories is in technique and the details of the intrigue.

Pavel Pavlovitch entices Veltchaninov to his fiancée's house; Anselmo asks Lothario to pay court to his wife. In both cases only the prestige of the mediator can certify the excellence of a sexual choice. Cervantes, at the beginning of his story, describes at length the friendship between the two protagonists, Anselmo's high opinion of Lothario, and the role of go-between which Lothario played with the two families on the occasion of the marriage.

It is clear that their ardent friendship is accompanied by a sharp feeling of rivalry. But this rivalry remains in the shadows. In *The Eternal Husband* the other side of the "triangular" feeling remains hidden. The hatred of the betrayed husband is obvious; we gradually guess at the admiration which this hatred hides. Pavel Pavlo-

2. The story of "Ill-Advised Curiosity." [*Editor.*]

3. By Marcel Proust. [*Editor.*]

vich asks Veltchaninov to choose the jewel he will give to his fiancée because to him Veltchaninov enjoys immense sexual prestige.

In both stories the hero seems to offer the beloved wife freely to the mediator, as a believer would offer a sacrifice to his god. But the believer offers the object in order that the god might enjoy it, whereas the hero of internal mediation offers his sacrifices to the god in order that he might not enjoy it. He pushes the loved woman into the mediator's arms in order to arouse his desire and then triumph over the rival desire. He does not desire *in* his mediator but rather *against* him. The hero only desires the object which will frustrate his mediator. Ultimately all that interests him is a decisive victory over his insolent mediator. Anselmo and Pavel Pavlovitch are driven by sexual pride, and it is this pride which plunges them into the most humiliating defeats.

* * *

No literary influence can explain the points of contact between "The Curious Impertinent" and *The Eternal Husband.* The differences are all differences of form, while the resemblances are resemblances of essence. No doubt Dostoyevsky never realized these similarities. Like so many nineteenth-century readers he saw the Spanish masterpiece only through romantic exegeses and probably had a most inaccurate picture of Cervantes. All his remarks on *Don Quixote* betray a romantic influence.

The existence of "The Curious Impertinent" next to *Don Quixote* has always intrigued critics. The question arises of whether the short story is compatible with the novel; the unity of the masterpiece seems somewhat compromised. It is this unity which is revealed by our journey through novelistic literature. Having begun with Cervantes, we return to Cervantes and ascertain that this novelist's genius has grasped the extreme forms of imitated desire. No small distance separates the Cervantes of Don Quixote and the Cervantes of Anselmo since it encompasses all the novels we have considered in this chapter. Yet the distance is not insuperable since all the novelists are linked to each other; Flaubert, Stendhal, Proust, and Dostoyevsky form an unbroken chain from one Cervantes to the other.

The simultaneous presence of external and internal mediation in the same work seems to us to confirm the unity of novelistic literature. And in turn, the unity of this literature confirms that of *Don Quixote.* One is proved by the other, just as one proves that the earth is round by going around it. The creative force of Cervantes is so great that it is exerted effortlessly throughout the whole novelistic "space." All the ideas of the Western novel are present in germ in *Don Quixote.* And the idea of these ideas, the idea whose central role is constantly being confirmed, the basic idea from which one can rediscover everything is triangular desire. And triangular desire is the basis of the theory of the *novelistic* novel for which this first chapter serves as an introduction.

ROBERT B. ALTER

The Mirror of Knighthood and the World of Mirrors†

> Why does it disturb us that Don Quixote be a reader of the *Quixote* and Hamlet a spectator of *Hamlet?* These inversions suggest that if the characters of a fictional work can be readers or spectators, we, its readers or spectators, can be fictitious.
>
> —J. L. Borges, "Partial Magic in the *Quixote*"

One of the most essential and unsettling qualities of modern culture is the geometric rate of increase in its dissemination. Ever since Gutenberg, when technology first intervened decisively in the reproduction of artifacts, the rapid expansion and development of Western culture have progressively sharpened a basic ambiguity. The artist, with new means of dissemination and new media of implementation at his disposal, could imagine enormous new possibilities of power in the exercise of his art. At the same time, the conditions of mechanical reproduction made it necessary for the individual artist to swim against a vast floodtide of trash out of all proportion to anything that had existed before in cultural history; and the reproduced art object itself, in its universal accessibility, could be cheapened, trivialized, deprived of its uniqueness, stripped of any claims it might have to be a model of value or a source of truth.[1] The transmission of artfully ordered words moves chronologically down a pyramid toward a broad numerical base, from the oral recitation of the traditional bard, who imparted an immemorial, or inspired, wisdom to a small circle of listeners actually gathered around him; to the handwritten word inscribed on scroll or tablet, still often thought of as magical or sacred, promulgated among a literate elite; to the printed text, made easily available in thousands

† Chapter 1 of Robert B. Alter, *Partial Magic: The Novel as a Self-Conscious Genre* (Berkeley: University of California Press, 1975), pp. 1–29. All quotations from *Don Quixote* are from the Samuel Putnam translation (New York: Viking Press, 1949). The numbers in parentheses refer to part and chapter. Alter's essay investigates "the nature of representation" in *Don Quixote* and the questions about art and existence raised by fiction. Cervantes constantly calls the reader's attention to the fictional status of his characters by having them discuss the authenticity of "facts" or the literary artistry of the numerous authors and reciters of stories who appear in the text, e.g., the Moorish translator's doubts about remarks attributed by one of the authors to Sancho, or Don Quixote's criticism of the puppet-show's verisimilitude—which overwhelms the knight's critical objectivity seconds later. By this device, Cervantes highlights the arbitrary nature of fiction, however "lifelike" it may appear at moments, and the obstacles which art puts in the way of a true understanding of nature.

1. For a brilliant discussion of this process, see Walter Benjamin, "The Work of Art in the Age of Its Mechanical Reproduction," *Illuminations* (New York: Harcourt, Brace and World, 1968).

upon thousands of copies, which at best preserves from its literary antecedents a flickering, intermittent aftersense that what it says *ought* to be true because it is written down in a book. The development, moreover, of still easier means of proliferation further dissipates even that vestigial sense of the authority of the written word: anyone now, with a walk to the nearest photocopy service and an investment often far smaller than the publisher's price, can "make" his own book from a borrowed copy, and with this convenience the qualitative distance in many people's minds between book and typescript or mimeographed text dwindles to a matter of clearer print and justified margins.

The novel as a genre provides a specially instructive measure of a culture caught up in the dynamics of its own technological instruments because it is the only major genre that comes into being after the invention of printing, and its own development—structural or thematic as well as economic—is intimately tied up with printing. I do not mean to fall into the error of certain voguish theorizers who assume that *all* important cultural changes are the result of modifications in the media of communication. On the contrary, I would take it as self-evident that the enormous social, political, and economic upheavals from the turn of the seventeenth century to the present, with the concomitant transformations in belief and world view, are not only reflected in the novel but also have very significantly determined the nature of the novel. All the good criticism, Marxist and non-Marxist, that connects the rise of the novel with the growth of the bourgeoisie, is surely not beside the point—it is only that it approaches the point from a bias, insisting that "realism" is the inherent goal of the novel and thus passing by much that deserves careful consideration.

The novel begins out of an erosion of belief in the authority of the written word and it begins with Cervantes. It fittingly takes as the initial target of its literary critique the first genre to have enjoyed popular success because of the printing press—the Renaissance chivalric romance. Although novelists were by no means the first writers to recognize clearly the fictional status of fictions, I think they were the first—and Cervantes of course the first among them—to see in the mere fictionality of fictions the key to the predicament of a whole culture, and to use this awareness centrally in creating new fictions of their own. For many novelists, to be sure, the crisis of belief in the written word of which I speak has been no more than an unregarded common cultural substratum for their work, while nowhere do they consciously exploit it in the solid-seeming fictional realities they create. Numerically, the novelists who write deliberately out of an undisguised skepticism about the status of fictions undoubtedly constitute a lesser tradition than that of the realists, but it is a brilliant tradition nevertheless, and one that throws a good deal of light on the nature of the novel as a genre. One measure of Cervantes' genius is the fact that he is the initiator of both traditions of the novel, his juxtaposition of high-flown literary fantasies with grubby actuality pointing the way to the realists, his zestfully ostentatious manipulation of the artifice he constructs setting a precedent for all the self-conscious novelists to come.[2]

Especially because so many generations of readers have rhapsodized over Don Quixote as a timeless image of humanity, it may be worth stressing that he exists simultaneously on two very different planes of being. On the one hand, the gaunt knight on his emaciated hack rides in the mind's eye across the plains of a very real La Mancha, appearing as a possible if bizarre figure of his time and place who in fact succeeds in becoming a general image of mankind in all the stubbornness of its idealism and the hopeless futility of its blind misdirections. Cervantes takes pains, on the other hand, to make us aware also that the knight is merely a lifelike model of papier-maché, a design in words, images, invented gestures and actions, which exists between the covers of a book by Miguel de Cervantes.[3] There is a perfect appropriateness in the fact that, toward the end of Don Quixote's adventures, when he comes to Barcelona, he should stumble into a printing shop where he witnesses the processes of proof-drawing, type-setting, revision, and is treated to a disquisition on the economics of publishing and bookselling (2:62). The effect is not very different from the cinematic device that has recently been put to such abundant and various use in which cameras, klieg lights, costumes, and props obtrude into the filmed scene. At such a moment we can hardly forget that Don Quixote himself is no more than the product of the very processes he observes, a congeries of words set up in type, run off as proof, corrected and rerun, bound in pages, and sold at so many reales a copy. Cervantes, moreover, repeatedly reminds us that without the rapid activity of presses like these churning out the first part of his hero's adventures, most of the adventures of the second part could never have taken place.

It is not only in the mind of the unhinged hidalgo that the reality of books and the reality of daily experience are hopelessly scrambled. Don Quixote's adventures, of course, begin in a library and frequently circle back to the contents of that library in thought or in speech, and more than once in action; but it is equally remarka-

2. The seminal essay on Cervantes as the paradigmatic novelist is Harry Levin's "The Example of Cervantes" in his *Contexts of Criticism* (Cambridge: Harvard University Press, 1957).

3. Shortly after writing this, I discovered the same point, though made from a different orientation and elaborated in Freudian terms, in Marthe Robert's "Toujours Don Quichotte" in her *Sur le papier* (Paris: Grasset, 1967). Mme Robert interestingly sees the tension between manifest fictionality and apparent reality as a generic dilemma of the novel on into the nineteenth and twentieth centuries.

ble that the world into which he sallies is flooded with manuscripts and printed matter. Sancho's ever-engaging presence reminds us that there is still a solid class of illiterates whose verbal culture is entirely—and pungently—oral; nevertheless, at times it begins to look as though all mankind were composed of two overlapping classes: readers and writers. It seems as if from behind every roadside bush and every wooded hill another author is waiting to spring out, clutching a sheaf of verses; even a dangerous convict is busy planning the second part of his autobiography as he marches off to the galleys; and the unlooked-for pleasures a traveler may find in the attic of his inn are as likely to be a trunk full of books as the embraces of a hospitable serving girl.

This novel, like so many others after it, presents us a world of role-playing, where the dividing lines between role and identity are often blurred, and almost everyone picks up the cues for his role from the literature he has read. Don Quixote could not be so successful in infecting the human world around him with quixotism if the chivalric romances did not enjoy such a large readership (again, the printing press would seem a precondition for his adventures): he repeatedly falls in with people who can play answering roles to his because they are almost as adept as he in the language, conventions, and actions of chivalric literature. Even so unlikely a person as the blanket-tossing innkeeper turns out to be such an enthusiastic reader of the chivalric romances that the shrewd Dorothea is moved to remark, "Our host could almost play a second to Don Quixote" (1:32). If we begin to wonder where literature stops and "reality" starts in a world so profuse in its mimickry of the printed page, Cervantes himself makes a point of compounding our confusion. Don Quixote at the printing shop may give us pause, but, still later in the novel, Don Quixote conversing with Don Alvaro Tarfe, a character from the spurious continuation of *Don Quixote* by Alonso de Avellaneda, is almost enough to induce ontological vertigo—a fictional character from a "true" fictional chronicle confronting a fictional character from a false one in order to establish beyond doubt his own exclusive authenticity.

Fictional characters, properly speaking, have no dimensions, since dimensions pertain to spatial existence and fiction exists in thought, not in the world of extension, but we are in the habit of applying the term "three-dimensional" metaphorically to characters that seem convincingly lifelike, a usage that may reflect something of the ambiguity with which we usually think about fictional characters. Cervantes, even before the currency of the metaphor, was finely aware of the ambiguity, and he illuminates it quite early in his novel when he pointedly reduces—or perhaps one should say raises—his protagonists to a two-dimensional plane. At the end of the eighth chapter, at the peak of a climactic adventure, when Don

Quixote is encountering his first armed adversary hand-to-hand—the formidable Biscayan astride his she-mule, sword aloft, cushion extended as shield—Cervantes suddenly freezes the action, leaving the bloody-minded antagonists with their swords hanging in mid-air, while he explains that the "author of this history" was unable to find any further documents pertaining to the exploits of Don Quixote. The chapter ends in this state of suspension, and a new one begins with the narrator ("the second author of this work") suddenly switching to the first-person singular to report in a relaxed anecdotal manner how one day in the marketplace of Toledo he ran across a series of notebooks written in Arabic characters which turned out to be none other than the *History of Don Quixote de la Mancha, Written by Cid Hamete Benengeli, Arabic Historian.* (The mediation of Cid Hamete is itself a complicated and intriguing matter to which we shall return later.) The first notebook, conveniently enough, contains a carefully drawn illustration of the very moment when the preceding narrative broke off. The coincidence is clearly to be marveled at; only the artificer who conceived both the first and the second authors of this history as well as the industrious Arabic historian could be responsible for such perfect synchronization of two discrete narratives and two different media. This is the way the illustration is described:

> There was a very lifelike picture of the battle between Don Quixote and the Biscayan, the two being in precisely the same posture as described in the history, their swords upraised, the one covered by his buckler, the other with his cushion. As for the Biscayan's mule, you could see at the distance of a crossbow shot that it was one for hire. Beneath the Biscayan there was a rubric which read: "Don Sancho de Azpeitia," which must undoubtedly have been his name; while beneath the feet of Rocinante was another inscription: "Don Quixote." Rocinante was marvelously portrayed: so long and lank, so lean and flabby, so extremely consumptive-looking that one could well understand the justness and propriety with which the name of "hack" had been bestowed upon him.
>
> Alongside Rocinante stood Sancho Panza, holding the halter of his ass, and below was the legend: "Sancho Zancas." The picture showed him with a big belly, a short body, and long shanks, and that must have been where he got the names of Panza y Zancas by which he is a number of times called in the course of the history. There are other small details that might be mentioned, but they are of little importance and have nothing to do with the truth of the story—and no story is bad so long as it is true.

The poised ambiguity with which Cervantes conceives the representation of reality here suggests why he stands at the beginning of a Copernican revolution in the practice and theory of mimesis. The whole passage, of course, is a representation within a representation within a representation of what one finally hesitates to call reality —a picture within a book within a narration by "the second author of this work." Its effect is like that of a mirror within a painting reflecting the subject of the painting, or the deployment of still photographs within a film: through a sudden glimpse of multiple possibilities of representation we are brought up short and thus moved to ponder the nature of representation and the presence of the artful representer.

Don Quixote, I would suggest, is impelled to his adventures by a nagging sense of the irreality of his own dull existence in the Iron Age. At any rate, he clearly draws an equation between being real and being recorded in literature. In the first part of the novel, he prepares for every action with an acute consciousness of "the sage who is to write the history" of his exploits, for it is only through the writing down that he can be sure he has become as real as Amadís, Don Belianís, Felixmarte, and all the rest. The traditional epic hero, of course, also desires his glory to be sung after him by the sons of men, but Don Quixote, a bookish man, actually wants to become a book. Instructively, in Part Two, when Don Quixote's ambition has precipitously caught up with him and he is pursued everywhere by the knowledge that he is already in a book, he begins to suspect that his chronicler may not be a sage after all but rather one of those willful sorcerers who are persecuting him. At this early point in the novel, however, we are offered a literally graphic image of the knight with his ambition already achieved, but the reality he has attained is a wavering fabric of contradictions.

The details of the illustration are brought forward to confirm the authenticity of the preceding narrative: if two independent sources, the unnamed first "author of this history" and Cid Hamete Benengeli, give us identical portraits, then this must be the "true" Don Quixote. Yet the authentication is really a transparent sleight-of-hand trick, for when the picture is described as "very lifelike," what this means in effect is that it is very like the picture at the end of the narrative that concluded with the previous chapter: internal consistency is quietly substituted for verisimilitude, though not so quietly that we do not reflect for a moment on the substitution. (Peculiarly, there is one small detail here that fails to jibe with the subsequent narrative. Sancho is not called "Panza y Zancas," or "paunch and shanks," a number of times in Cid Hamete's chronicle. Is this one of Cervantes' careless strokes, or a strategem for casting a faint shadow of doubt on the reliability of the Arabic notebooks, or of their translator?) In any case, by the time we are told at the end of the passage that only those details bearing on the truth of the story have been reported, we are likely to suspect that we no longer know what the truth of the story means, and the raising of such doubt may well be one purpose of the passage.

As for Don Quixote, with his aspirations to be translated into the sphere of literary reality, where does this whole graphic representation leave him? Fixed forever in a text, made the subject of a new iconography, he has achieved everything and almost nothing. He and Sancho have scarcely set out; all the "exploits" we are as yet aware of as readers are a handful of hilarious misconceptions of the knight's, and so the content of his immortality would seem to be the mere fact of being recorded on a printed page. Indeed, at this particular juncture, the page is not yet a printed one, since Cid Hamete's chronicle is set down in notebooks. The accompanying illustration, then, which seems so much like an engraving, would have to be a pen-and-ink drawing. Thus a notebook with sketches is imperceptibly metamorphosed into an illuminated volume, and we become aware of how tentative an affair the knight's immortality is, how much all reality in the novel is the product of the artist's *trompe l'oeil.*

The new novelistic reality that Cervantes created is real-seeming in many important respects yet avowedly arbitrary, and a central device for communicating an awareness of that double nature here and throughout the novel is the game played with the naming of names. Inventing and assigning names is the ruling passion of Don Quixote. As a corollary to the belief that to be real means to be recorded in literature, he is convinced that no identity can have reality until it is assigned an appropriate name. Yet, as several critics have observed, he knowingly chooses names that while euphonically appropriate to the new Golden-Age roles, are transparent revelations of Iron-Age identities, like Rocinante, who was a hack (*rocín*) before (*ante*), and is now supposed the first of all hacks.[4] A related doubleness of perspective is suggested in a different way here in the illustration, where each of the three human figures in the picture is carefully labeled with a rubric beneath it, and comment is devoted to the graphically demonstrated aptness of the name coinages "Rocinante" and "Panza y Zancas." Such rubrics, of course, were often used in Renaissance illustrations, and they serve here, at least ostensibly, as evidence of the narrative's veracity, each character scrupulously assigned his proper name. (Cid Hamete evidently has more documentary material at his disposal than the First Author, since he is able to give us the full name of the hitherto anonymous Biscayan.) At the same time, nothing could be more clearly a formal artifice, a contrivance of convention, than to represent personages with their identities neatly labeled below their feet, and this in turn may lead us to reflect on the sheer arbitrariness of the literary naming of names, on the purely verbal processes of authorial fiat through which characters come into being. In primitive culture, the

4. See Leo Spitzer, "Perspectivism in the *Quijote*," in *Linguistics and Literary History* (Princeton: Princeton University Press, 1948).

word is magical, exerting power over the physical world; in the biblical tradition it is sacred, instinct with unfathomable divine meaning. For Cervantes, the word simultaneously resonates with its old magical quality and turns back on itself, exposing its own emptiness as an arbitrary or conventional construct. The French critic, Marthe Robert, in her brilliant essay on *Don Quixote*, offers an elegant and precise formulation: "The quixotic Word [*la verbe donquichottesque*] . . . is invocation and critique, conjuration and radical probing, both the one and the other with their risks and perils.[5]

This ontological doubleness of language in Cervantes is mirrored in the new kind of narrative structure he devised: the fictional world is repeatedly converted into a multiple regress of imitations that call attention in various ways to their own status as imitations. The paradigm for this structure is clearest in the episode of Master Pedro and his puppets (2:26). Master Pedro's assistant stands out in front of the stage, narrating the action while his employer manipulates the puppets from behind. Imbedded in the boy's manifestly fictional narrative—which is, of course, enclosed in turn within the Second Author's version of a narrative by Cid Hamete Benengeli—are lines of old ballads, that is, fragments of another, preexistent body of literature. Don Quixote is the first to point out inadequacies in the management of its artifice, and in each case Master Pedro responds from behind the stage, either to confirm the judgment pronounced or to disagree with it. Thus, when the boy explains the arrest and punishment of one of the characters by a reference to Moorish legal practice, Don Quixote chides him, "Child, child, keep to the straight line of your story and do not go off on curves and tangents," and Master Pedro chimes in, shifting the metaphor, "Boy . . . do as this gentleman says . . . stick to your plain song and don't try any counterpoint melodies, for they are likely to break down from being overfine." The transparently fictional illusion, in other words, of the puppet-show narration, is again and again broken into by literary criticism from the "real" world. The critics, moreover, are themselves both masqueraders, though for very different reasons—Alonso Quijano the Good tricked out in armor as a medieval knight; the escaped convict of literary bent, Ginés de Pasamonte, disguised as an itinerant puppeteer.

Literary criticism, it should be noted, is intrinsic to the fictional world of the *Quixote* and of all the self-conscious novels that follow it. Such criticism is present not only in the parodistic exposure of the absurdities of chivalric romances and in the lengthy discussions of literary matters that take place among the protagonists several times in the novel, but it is also, to borrow Master Pedro's figure, a repeated counterpoint to the narrative plain song throughout the

5. *L'Ancien et le nouveau: de Don Quichotte à Kafka* (Paris: Petite Bibliothèque Payot, 1963), p. 25, note.

book, as the interruption of the puppet show illustrates with schematic clarity. In this self-conscious mode of fiction, literary criticism is not, as it may sometimes seem, interpolated, but is an essential moment in the act of imagination, an act that is at once "conjuration and radical probing."

Thus, Cid Hamete's chronicle is accompanied by the judgments of three commentators. The most prominent of these is of course the unnamed Second Author, who has much to say about the veracity of Cid Hamete, his dedication as a historian, the "hackled, twisting, winding thread of Benengeli's plot" (1:28), and so forth. Then the Arabic historian himself intervenes, either directly or through the report of the Spanish author, to marvel over the events he chronicles, to question the authenticity of Don Quixote's experience in the Cave of Montesinos, to complain of the monotony of Don Quixote's adventures with Sancho, and thus defend the practice of interpolated tales against the criticis of Part One. Even the distinctly subordinate Moorish translator gets into the act, making occasional comments about Cid Hamete and pronouncing one chapter to be apocryphal because Sancho's speech in it seems to him inconsistent with what we know of Sancho. Finally, various characters criticize tales told within the main narrative, questioning their probability, the motivation of their characters, the appropriateness of the language used in them. One of the most striking instances of this sort, again one in which role-playing and literary criticism are intertwined, is the romance within a play within the novel as told and commented on by the duke's major-domo masquerading as the Countess Trifaldi (2:38). In the course of the romance which she invents about herself, the countess quotes some verses sung by a lover, and then sharply observes on their style: "I should not have allowed myself to be moved by such labored conceits, nor should I have beleived that the poet was speaking the truth when he declared, 'I live dying, burn in ice, tremble in the fire, hope without hope, go and stay,' along with other contradictory conceptions of this sort with which their writing is filled."

But let us return briefly to Master Pedro's puppet show, for we have not yet considered what is surely the most remarkable thing about that episode—the way Don Quixote brings it to an abrupt end by suddenly leaping up to the stage and hacking the puppets to pieces with his sword while the puppet master cries in dismay, "Those are not real Moors that your Grace is knocking over, maiming, and killing, but pasteboard figures." On the level of farcical satire, the point of this dénouement is obvious enough: the infallible button connecting directly to the mad gentleman's *idée fixe* has again been pressed, and he responds like a comic doll, once again raising his valorous right arm to succor the distressed of an imaginary world of adventures. It is noteworthy, however, that this outburst of chivalric madness is immediately preceded by one of his most lucid moments in the critical discussion of mimesis. When bells ring from the towers of the mosques in the play, Don Quixote interrupts to object that this is utter nonsense because the Moors do not use bells. Master Pedro retorts that it is a picayune objection, since countless plays—such as Lope's, one gathers—are filled with much more glaring inaccuracies, and Don Quixote concedes the point, apparently willing to allow that in some sorts of imitations of reality, strictly consistent verisimilitude is not necessary. In the next moment, then, the knight leaps sword in hand from the clearest recognition of the puppet show as an artifice to a total acceptance of it as reality. Perhaps the best way to define the "lucid madness" attributed to him several times by the narrator is to say that he repeatedly polarizes within himself opposing attitudes toward fictions which most of us hold together in some sort of suspension. The moment when the impulse of consciousness darts from pole to pole is an illuminating one, for Cervantes understands that there is an ultimately serious tension between the recognition of fictions as fictions and the acceptance of them as reality, however easy it may seem to maintain these two awarenesses simultaneously. Knowing that a fiction is, after all, only a fiction, is potentially subversive of any meaningful reality that might be attributed to the fiction, while assenting imaginatively to the reality of a represented action is a step in a process that could undermine or bewilder what one ordinarily thinks of as his sense of reality. Cervantes' novel could be described as a comic acting-out of the ultimate implications, both moral and ontological, of this tension of attitudes.

If the *Quixote* calls into question the status of fictions and of itself as a fiction, it also affirms a new sense of the autonomy of the artist who has conceived it. I proposed the term *trompe l'oeil* in connection with the picture of Don Quixote and the Biscayan, and it may be helpful to imagine the whole novel for a moment as a series of *trompe l'oeil* panels that slide open consecutively to reveal the author peeping out at the end of the series. The Tale of the Captive, which occupies so many pages in Part One, provides a clear example of how this tricky structuring works. The Captive introduces his story, at the very end of Chapter 38, by announcing to his listeners that they will "hear a true tale which possibly cannot be matched by those fictitious ones that are composed with such cunning craftsmanship." He immediately proceeds, however, to begin his narrative with the most patently conventional of folktale beginnings—the father who divides his estate in three among his three sons, sending one to the Church, one to the sea, and one to a career of arms. By the end of the story (1:42), Cervantes is prepared to point out this conventionality to the reader. Thus, the curate remarks, "He told me a story about his father and his brothers which, if I had not known him to be so truthful a man, I should have taken to be one of those tales that old women tell by the fireside in wintertime," and the captive's brother, himself one of the protagonists of the beginning of the story, admits that it must seem "to be a fairy tale."

It is in the midst of this story, purportedly real in content, recalling a fairy tale in its form, that the narrator mentions another Spanish soldier who was imprisoned with him in North Africa, a certain Saavedra (1:40). Saavedra is, of course, Miguel de Cervantes Saavedra, the inventor of the captive and his story and of all the other obvious and devious narrators of this novel. The captive makes a few brief statements about the actual captivity of Cervantes, and then, with pointed coyness, Cervantes has him conclude, "If time permitted, which unfortunately it does not, I could tell you here and now something of that soldier's exploits which would interest and amaze you much more than my own story."

Many influential theories of fiction, like that of Ortega y Gasset in his *Notes on the Novel*, have contended that the "world" of a novel has to be hermetically sealed, for any penetration of untransformed materials from the world outside it would only shatter its compelling but fragile illusion of reality. The theory, I think, does not give the novel enough credit for its ability to confront *formally* the radical skepticism of the troubled historical period in which the genre has developed. It is, indeed, ironic that Ortega should have become one of the promulgators of such a theory; for a decade earlier, in his *Meditations on Quixote*, he shows a fine sense of the ontological duality of the genre, and in particular his comments on Master Pedro's puppet show in the Ninth and Tenth Meditation remain enormously suggestive.

Cervantes himself, as we see in this instance, did not hesitate to open up a loophole in the fictional reality looking out to the frankly autobiographical reality of the writer. (Elsewhere, of course, he introduces himself through references to his other works, and at one point, 1:47, the curate conjectures that the anonymous *Story of the One Who Was Too Curious for His Own Good*—a "fictitious" story because it is discovered within the narrative frame of the novel—might be by the same hand as *Riconete and Cortadillo*, one of Cervantes' *Exemplary Novels*, not yet published when Part One of the *Quixote* appeared.) That Saavedra should appear in the narrative of a fictional character invented by Saavedra is the author's way of affirming his absolute proprietorship over the fictional world he has created. If he chose, he could relate his own adventures as a soldier and prisoner instead of the captive's, for the act of fiction is purely a matter of the choice of the artist; it may resemble actual experience in a variety of ways, but it is not compelled in an Aristotelian sense to imitate, is not the slave of what common sense rather confusedly calls "reality."

It is perfectly appropriate, then, that the relationship of the writer to the reader at many junctures should be a teasing one. Cervantes' walk-on appearance as captive soldier anticipates the strategem of that archest of novelists, Vladimir Nabokov, who at the end of *Pale Fire* has his deranged homosexual hero affirm that he will continue to exist in some other form: "I may turn up yet, on another campus, as an old, happy, healthy, heterosexual Russian, a writer in exile, sans fame, sans future, sans audience, sans anything but his art." This is, of course, a portrait of Nabokov, though self-ironic in its echo of the Ages of Man speech from *As You Like It.* In any case, the momentary appearance of the author in his own work has the same basic implication as in Cervantes: these fictional materials, we are told in effect, however lifelike, however absorbing, have been assembled in the imagination of the writer, who is free to reassemble them in any number of ways, or to put them aside and tell his own story directly, and the fictional materials have no existence without the writer.

The intuition of life that, beginning with Cervantes, crystallized in the novel is profoundly paradoxical: the novelist lucidly recognizes the ways man may be painfully frustrated and victimized in a world with no fixed values or ideas, without even a secure sense of what is real and what is not, yet through the exercise of an autonomous art the writer boldly asserts the freedom of consciousness itself. The imagination, then, is alternately, or even simultaneously, the supreme instrument of human realization and the eternal snare of delusion of a creature doomed to futility.

The extraordinary complexity with which Cervantes sustains a full awareness of both sides of the paradox is worth considering further. It is most easily perceptible in the way he relates as the artist responsible for the novel to his protagonist, Don Quixote, and to his surrogate author, Cid Hamete. Many readers have regarded the device of the Arabic historian as gratuitous, and perhaps something of a nuisance, though I suspect that the perfect rightness of Cid Hamete as intermediary has recently come to be better understood. Benengeli is the demiurge of the world Cervantes has created, and, like the demiurge of gnostic theology, he is a somewhat ambiguous intermediary. The Second Author repeatedly extols his virtues as a faithful historian and at one point (2:40) addresses a rhapsodic tribute to him in a formal apostrophe. Yet Cid Hamete is first identified for us as the member of a nation of liars; he himself admits to having introduced the interpolated tales of Part One out of boredom with his main subject and in order to give his pen full scope to write what it chooses, and he occasionally expresses contradictory judgments or makes rather puzzling observations. If he begins one chapter (2:8) in proper Moorish fashion by exclaiming "Blessed be the mighty Allah!" three times, he is not averse from starting another chapter (2:27) with "I swear as a Catholic Christian." The Second Author makes no comment on this anomaly, but the translator offers a bizarre explanation which is, in its peculiar way, instructive: "the author merely meant that, just as a Catholic Christian when he takes an oath swears, or is supposed to swear, to tell the truth in all that he says, so in what he himself has to set down about Don Quixote he will adhere to the truth as if he were taking such a Christian oath." Whether all this actually confirms Cid Hamete's truthfulness or throws it into question is a matter over which the reader may puzzle. In any case, the translator's explanation illustrates a tendency shared with the protagonist of the novel by several of its narrators, which is to take metaphorical comparisons as literal equations. This odd practice is merely the reduction to the microscopic level—individual words and objects instead of actions and ideas—of the quixotic confusion between fiction and fact. In the same fashion, Don Quixote can transmute a meager codfish into veal and kid by juggling a series of similes (1:2), and the First Author can casually substitute dromedaries for she-mules by giving a comparison free reign (1:8). Who, one begins to wonder, is a reliable narrator here, or is language itself, with its constant need to extend its expressive scope through metaphor, intrinsically unreliable?

If figurative comparisons assume their own independent life, so, of course, do fictions, again for the dedicated historian as well as for the mad protagonist. When the mock-countess Trifaldi is first introduced (2:38), two observations are made on her name: "She was known as the Countess Trifaldi, as one might say, the Countess of the Three Skirts, an opinion that is supported by Benengeli, who asserts that the lady's right name was the Countess Lobuna and that she was so called on account of the many wolves in her country." This obviously parodies the devotion to precise nomenclature of a true epic chronicler, but it is nevertheless peculiar. By this point in the narrative, almost any reader would see, even here at the beginning of the episode, that the countess and her bizarrely costumed entourage are bogus, merely staging another in the series of elaborate practical jokes conceived by the duke and duchess. Cid Hamete inevitably knows this, in fact knows the countess's part is being played by a man, for he is the chronicler of the rest of the chapter, yet here he is reported gravely ascertaining her "right" name through his familiarity with the fauna of her non-existent country! Cid Hamete, the historian who both follows and controls his material, can also become its captive, slipping inside the frame of the world of masks and deceptions that he describes. The effect when the fiction begins thus to assume autonomy is the complementary opposite of *trompe l'oeil*, resembling the kind of transition between planes of reality recorded in the Chinese tale where the imperial architect, turning from the wrath of his emperor, opens the door in the drawing of the palace he has made and disappears inside.

It has recently been suggested by the Hispanist Ruth El Saffar that Cid Hamete is the artful means through which Cervantes interposes a necessary distance between himself and his work. This seems to me just, though one might add that Cid Hamete at the same time serves as a parodistic reflection of Cervantes' ambiguous relationship to his work. In any case, Mrs. El Saffar is apt in observing the effect on us of the paradoxical presence of the Arabic historian: as Benengeli's narrative point of view vacillates between following the protagonists and pulling back to an overview of retrospective omniscience, "the reader is successively drawn into the suspense and interest that the characters themselves provide and is wrenched away from them to an awareness of the pen which controls them."[6] This contradictory effect is precisely the one produced by virtually all self-conscious novels, from Cervantes onward. It is worth noting that Cervantes' principal means for achieving the effect is to split himself off into a fictional alter ego, the Moorish chronicler who is supposedly the true author of the history; Don Quixote himself is another kind of surrogate for the novelist, being prominent among the characters of the novel as an author manqué, who is impelled to act out the literary impulse in the world of deeds, to be at once the creator and protagonist of his own fictions.

Doubles, as we shall see, recur again in later developments of novelistic self-consciousness. This is hardly surprising in a kind of fiction repeatedly concerned with both the instructiveness and the deceptiveness of similitudes, with the ambiguity of identity and fictional character, and, above all, with the relation of the author to his work. A propos of the last of these concerns, Marthe Robert makes a shrewd observation about the *Quixote*: "Since the multiple oppositions embodied in the pair hero-author are far from being always superimposable, the play of antitheses is repeated through all the personages of the narrative, which, on the same account, is literally peopled with doubles."[7] This is immensely suggestive, though a little cryptic. What it means, I think, is that the novel is, both structurally and thematically, an unstable dialectic, working with a

6. "The Function of the Fictional Narrator in *Don Quijote*." *Modern Language Notes*, March 1968, p. 167. A more fully persuasive account of the various uses of Cid Hamete is offered by Mia I. Gerhardt in her finely intelligent *Don Quijote: La vie et les livres* (Amsterdam: Hollandsche Uitg. Mij., 1953). She sees the Moorish historian as Cervantes' principal means for making it clear that the author "is not the dupe of his own fiction" and for creating between the writer and the perceptive reader "a delectable complicity over this subtle fraud which is the novel" (p. 16).

7. *L'Ancien et le nouveau*, p. 22.

series of partly overlapping oppositions that might be conceptualized through such terms as art and nature, fiction and reality, ideal and actuality, role and identity, past and present, timelessness and temporality, belief and skepticism. Because the dialectic is inherently unstable, no opposition can produce the resolution of a synthesis, and so each set of antitheses, whether embodied in the characters of the novel or in its narrative structure, tends toward the invention of further antitheses. In the course of time, this dialectic within the novel-form produces in experimental modern writers like Alain Robbe-Grillet and Raymond Queneau fictional worlds where every event is represented as sheer hypothesis, to be dismantled and reassembled in new ways, the element of instability dominating all.

We have already noted how Cervantes projects segments of himself as a writer into two very different doubles, Cid Hamete and Don Quixote, the former acting as an intermediary between himself and the latter. Don Quixote, of course, proceeds to pair up with his opposite, Sancho, and the two enter into the most famous dialectic of the novel, in which the knight quixotizes the squire as the squire sanchifies the knight. At the same time, Don Quixote tends to convert those he encounters into amusingly distorted and opposing doubles of himself, beginning, in an external way, with the gallant Biscayan, culminating in the bachelor Sansón Carrasco, who as a reflection of Don Quixote appropriately assumes the sobriquet, Knight of the Mirrors. The interpolated stories, moreover, exhibit a fondness for antithetical pairings of characters—friends, rivals, lovers—many of whom stand in interesting relations of opposition and parallel to figures in the main narrative. As always, Cervantes has a sure instinct for parodying his own procedures, and at one point (2:12) he goes out of his way to remind us that he has even continued the principle of *dédoublement* from mankind to the animal kingdom. Rocinante and the gray ass are, of course, a doubling of the Quixote-Sancho pair, and Cervantes calls our attention to the fact here by devoting a page to the lofty friendship of the two beasts, comparing them to Nisus and Euryalus, Orestes and Pylades.

The proliferation of doubles in his first model of the novel as self-conscious genre can also be explained in another way. A double, of course, is a reflection or imitation, and often a covertly parodistic imitation that exposes hidden aspects of the original. (Thus, in the most familiar folkloristic use of the double motif, an ostensibly respectable person is confronted with the image of his demonic other self.) A mode of fiction, therefore, focused on the nature of imitation and its aesthetic or ontological implications may well find doubles to be of great utility. It should be emphasized, moreover, that the self-conscious novelist utilizes the double with a conscious quality of intellectual playfulness, in sharp contrast to writers like Poe, Dostoevski, and Conrad, who try to give the double its full mythic resonance as an embodiment of the dark Other Side of the self.

In *Don Quixote*, this utility of doubles as an experiment in imitation and a critique of fictions may be easier to see in doublings of plot than in those of character. Thus, Don Quixote's descent into the Cave of Montesinos is, to begin with, a parody of the portentous descent into the underworld of the traditional epic hero at a crucial midpoint of his journey, and both Sancho and Cid Hamete express considerable skepticism about the whole experience, while even the knight is led to wonder whether it may all have been a dream. This questionable adventure is in turn parodistically doubled in Sancho's fantastic aerial visions astride the wooden horse, Clavileño, an imaginary ascent matching the earlier imaginary descent, as Don Quixote himself makes clear in his final words to Sancho on the subject: "Sancho, if you want us to believe what you saw in Heaven, then you must believe me when I tell you what I saw in the Cave of Montesinos. I need say no more" (2:41). Not content with this parody of a parody of a descent into the underworld, Cervantes later makes Sancho go through another, more realistic, doubling of the same experience, when the squire stumbles into a pit and finds himself trapped in an underground cavern (2:55). Again, the writer draws our attention to the parallel between the episodes by causing Sancho, who can imagine nothing but treacherous holes in this underworld, to cry out: "This may be hard luck for me, but it would make a good adventure for my master Don Quixote. He would take these depths and dungeons for flowery gardens and Galiana's palace." (In the Spanish here there is a pointed pun: *Esta que para mí es desventura, mejor fuera para aventura de mi amo don Quijote*. That is, it needs only a turn of the screw of imagination, as small but crucial as the change of a prefix, to convert *desventura* to *aventura*, to transform the whole nature of what seems to impinge on one as reality. Yet, bumping against the hard rocks of a very palpable underground prison, Sancho must also suspect that such transformations are mere fictions, as arbitrary and inefficacious as the changing of a word to its opposite in the abstract realm of language through the shift of a letter or two.) Finally, close to the end of the novel, we are given a *third* parodistic repetition of the initial dubious descent into the underworld, when the maid Altisidora, who has been play-acting at being dead, manufactures a report of her experience in hell that is in effect a flamboyant spoof of both Sancho's concocted vision of his voyage on Clavileño and the knight's synthetic romance in the Cave of Montesinos (2:70). Altisidora's hell, in which planes of literary reality intersect, is a literary underworld in a different sense from Don Quixote's: in it, demons in fashionable dress play tennis using books "filled with wind and rubbish," among which the most swollen and empty turns out to be the spurious continuation of *Don Quixote.*

The world, in this multiplication of internal parodies, becomes an assemblage of mirrors—the armor of Sansón Carrasco, covered with small mirrors, could serve as its emblem—but since parody is precisely the literary mode that fuses creation with critique, the mirrors are in varying degrees distortive, so that the characters parade through a vast fun-house hall where even the most arresting figures can suddenly swell into monstrosities or shrink to absurdities. (The juncture of sharply etched verisimilitude and fantasy is one that will be characteristic of the whole self-conscious tradition of the novel.) Virtually everything, then, is composite, made up of fragmented images, refractions, and reflections of other things, which is to say that virtually everything is mediated by literature, whether the body of literary words and conventions outside this novel or the various literary inventions generated within the book itself. The novel creates a world at once marvelous and credible, but the most splendid evocations of character or action bear within them the visible explosive freight of their own parodistic negation.

This instability of fictional realities is most evident in Don Quixote's supreme fiction, Dulcinea. As many commentators have observed, Don Quixote is utterly clear about the fact that Dulcinea is his own invention yet deadly serious about his unswerving devotion to the ideal fiction he has made for himself. One of his early evocations of her aptly illustrates the new kind of relationship between literature and reality at work in this novel:

> Her name is Dulcinea, her place of residence El Toboso, a village of La Mancha. As to her rank, she should be at the very least a princess, seeing that she is my lady and my queen. Her beauty is superhuman, for in it are realized all the impossible and chimerical attributes that poets are accustomed to give their fair ones. Her locks are golden, her brow the Elysian Fields, her eyebrows rainbows, her eyes suns, her cheeks roses, her lips coral, her teeth pearls, her neck alabaster, her bosom marble, her hands ivory, her complexion snow-white. As for those parts which modesty keeps covered from the human sight, it is my opinion that, discreetly considered, they are only to be extolled and not compared to any other. [1:13]

Don Quixote begins from a town in La Mancha where of course, there are no princesses, but he immediately proceeds to affirm Dulcinea's royal rank, for the necessities of the literary convention from which she is drawn dictate absolutely what he understands to be the facts about her. What follows is essentially a catalogue of poetic clichés, virtually announced as such, which makes clear that Dulcinea is entirely a composite creature, assembled from the much-used materials of timeworn literary traditions. The effect of the passage, however, is strangely not that of a tired rehearsal of exhausted conventions. On the contrary, one senses that Don Quixote is making a fervent poem, however synthetic the poetry, out of Dulcinea, and the fact that she is composed of purely literary materials is precisely what endows her with prestige for him. (In the Spanish the passage has greater lyrical *élan,* reads a little less like a catalogue, because of the controlled rhythmic emphases and the variation of the long series with elegant poetic inversions.) If Dulcinea is too much a composite to be immediately present for us, the aura of her presence in the knight's imagination shines through the passage, and so we see how a manifest fiction can become a reality in the imagination of its beholder, even as he recognizes the materials from which the fiction has been composed.

The amusing pratfall of the final sentence—in the original, the final clause of a single long sentence and thus syntactically continuous with the string of poetic clichés—is instructive in another way. This most chaste of lovers slips, though decorously, from rosy cheeks and coral lips to incomparable genitalia, objects of amorous adulation that are decidedly outside the courtly literary conventions he has adopted. His violation of his own conventional framework in order to depict the "whole" Dulcinea suggests contradictory implications that push against one another in a precarious opposition. On the one hand, Dulcinea is so real for Don Quixote that she extends beyond the frame of literary convention in which he has created her. This incongruous physiological completeness, on the other hand, of his portrait of her hints that he himself exists in a flesh-and-blood world against which the divine Dulcinea, distilled as she is from familiar poetic hyperboles, must begin to seem purely a verbal concoction.

Perhaps it may help us see in perspective Cervantes' bold innovation in the management of fictions if we set this passage alongside another seventeenth-century composite of literary images of the ideal, Milton's evocation of Eden in *Paradise Lost* (4:235–287). Like so many Renaissance writers, Milton is also conscious of a tension between art and nature. The first paradise is the ultimate natural state, where "not nice Art . . . but Nature boon" pours forth a profusion of beauties. The poet, then, must struggle with the paradox of representing in art what transcends the merely human scope of art—he aspires to "tell how, if Art could tell," implying that it really cannot. Milton's solution to this difficulty is to flaunt the paradox, emphasizing the means of art he employs as he transforms prelapsarian nature into a brilliant artifact with sapphire fountains, golden sands and burnished fruit with golden rind, pebbles of orient pearl, crystal-mirror streams. Then he invokes a whole series of wondrous pleasure-gardens from the literature of antiquity only to suggest that all of them are no more than wavering, imperfect shadow images of the true Garden. Like Don Quixote, he represents the ideal by a grand synthesis of the imagery of a literary tradition—in this case, the pastoral tradition—though of course he brilliantly orchestrates the expressive possibilities of the tradition instead of simply stringing together traditional formulas. When Don Quixote, praising Dulcinea's beauty, says that "in it are realized all the impossible and chimerical attributes that poets are accustomed to give their fair ones," his words call our attention to her status as a fiction, to the fact that she is woven out of those impossible and chimerical attributes by a bookish mind that has come to believe in the possibility of their literal existence. When Milton writes, "*Hesperian* Fables true,/ If true, here only," the effect is quite the opposite. The truth of art may be doubted not because art is mere invention, but because art (or the human imagination) by its inherent limitations can offer only an intimation of the resplendent truth of divinely created nature.

Milton is perhaps the last great moment in a tradition of mimesis that begins for Western literature with Homer and the Bible. His poem memorably represents that aspect of the Renaissance which is the conscious culmination of a continuous cultural development through two and a half millennia. Cervantes' novel, on the other hand, is one of the supreme achievements of that impulse in the Renaissance which was already moving toward the troubled horizon of modernity. Cervantes cannot share Milton's Christian-humanist confidence in the power of language and the literary tradition to adumbrate the glory of God's nature. Revelation, after all, remains the bedrock of Milton's vision; and because revelation takes place through language—precisely in Scripture, by shadowy types in classical literature—it guarantees the possibility of some real correspondence between literary art and divinely wrought nature. For Cervantes, on the other hand, as a fundamentally secular skeptic (his hero's deathbed conversion notwithstanding), art is obviously questionable because it is understood to be ultimately arbitrary, while nature is still more problematic because it is so entrammeled with art, so universally mediated by art, shaped by art's peculiar habits of vision, that it becomes difficult to know what, if anything, nature in and of itself may be. From this point on, cultural creativity would proceed more and more through a recapitulative critique of its own past, and a major line of fiction would be avowedly duplicitous, making the paradox of its magically real duplicity one of its principal subjects. In these respects, Cervantes does not merely anticipate a later mode of imagination but fully realizes its possibilities; subsequent writers would only explore from different angles the imaginative potentialities of a kind of fiction that he authoritatively conceived. In this, as in other ways, *Don Quixote* is the archetypal novel that seems to encompass the range of what would be written afterward. Ironically reaching for the dream of a medieval world through Renaissance literary productions, it remains one of the most profoundly modern of all novels.

MIGUEL DE UNAMUNO

On the Reading and Interpretation of *Don Quixote*†

* * *

From time to time, some holy man from the camp of the wise and short-sighted pedants comes along and informs us that Cervantes neither could nor would mean to say what this or that symbolist[1] attributed to him, inasmuch as his sole object was to put an end to the reading of books of chivalry.

Assuming that such was his intent, what does Cervantes' intention in *Don Quixote*, if he had any intention, have to do with what the rest of us see in the book? Since when is the author of a book the person to understand it best?

Ever since *Don Quixote* appeared in print and was placed at the disposition of anyone who would take it in hand and read it, the book has no longer belonged to Cervantes, but to all who read it and feel it. Cervantes extracted Don Quixote from the soul of his people and from the soul of all humanity, and in his immortal book he returned him to his people and all humanity. Since then, Don Quixote and Sancho have continued to live in the souls of the readers of Cervantes' book and even in the souls of those who have never read it. There scarcely exists a person of even average education who does not have some idea of Don Quixote and Sancho.

Not long ago, a learned German, A. Kalthoff, in an interesting book, *Das Christusproblem*, returned once again to the ancient

† From *Selected Works of Miguel de Unamuno*, trans. Anthony Kerrigan, Bollingen Series, LXXXV (Princeton: Princeton University Press, 1967), vol. 3, *Our Lord Don Quixote*, pp. 445–462. Miguel de Unamuno (1864–1936) was a classical scholar, university professor and administrator, poet, essayist, novelist, a philosopher of sorts, and a gadfly of the Spanish conscience. He delighted in paradoxes and mildly shocking notions, of which this excerpt is a typical example. Unamuno believes that the value of *Don Quixote*, or any great piece of literature, depends on what may be read into it; the more its readers invest, the better the work, the greater its power to inspire and console. Efforts to limit the meaning of such a work are, in Unamuno's eyes, signs of what he calls "spiritual sloth," philosophical incapacity, and sterility—all of which he believes to be the particular vices of Spain. He reserves his worst criticism for literary scholars, whom he compares with the Masoretes, a medieval rabbinical school which compiled trivial and useless statistics about the Hebrew Bible. He dismisses Cervantes (who like Shakespeare, is something of a national saint) as unaware of the value of his own masterpiece, a mediocre stylist, coarse, insensitive, etc., etc. Yet Unamuno plainly loves Cervantes' work, to which he devotes so much of his thought and writing. Unamuno is always stimulating, whatever the position he happens to be defending.

1. Someone who has "attempted to plumb the depths and give our book a symbolic . . . sense . . ." [*Editor.*]

thesis, never altogether abandoned by all scholars, of the historical nonexistence of Jesus of Nazareth; Kalthoff maintains, with more or less well-founded arguments, that the Gospels are apocalyptic novels composed in Rome by Jewish Christians, that Christ is no more than a symbol of the Christian Church, itself born of the Jewish communities as the result of a socio-economic movement. And Kalthoff adds that this fact should matter little to Christians, for Christ is not the historical Jesus whom historians of the liberal Protestant school have attempted to re-establish with all historical exactitude through what the author calls a theology of the life of Jesus (*Leben-Jesu-Theologie*), but rather, Christ is the ethical and religious entity who has come down to us, living, growing, and adapting himself to the diverse needs of the times within the collective consciousness of Christendom.

I do not introduce this argument here because I agree with Kalthoff's doctrine, nor because I wish to refute it—I abhor refutations, which tend to be models of bad literature and worse philosophy—but only to clarify what I think of *Don Quixote*. Certainly it will occur to no one, unless it be to me, seriously to maintain that Don Quixote really and truly existed and did all the things that Cervantes tells us about, in the way that almost all Christians maintain and believe that Christ existed and did all the things the Gospels tell us about. Nevertheless, it can and should be maintained that Don Quixote existed and still exists with a life and existence perhaps more intense and effective than if he had lived and existed in the ordinary manner.

Each generation has added something to this Don Quixote, and he has been transformed and has grown greater all the time. Much more interesting than to sift all the minutiae that the Cervantist Masoretes have gone on collecting would be to gather together the diverse interpretations made of the figure of the Manchegan hidalgo by writers who have written about him. Don Quixote has been introduced into hundreds of works, and he has been made to say and do things he never said or did in the Cervantine text; all these writings could furnish us with the physiognomy of Don Quixote outside and apart from the pages of *Don Quixote*.

If Cervantes were to be resurrected and returned to the world, he would have no right whatsoever to complain of this Quixote, of which his own is no more than a hypostasis and point of departure. It would be just as legitimate for a mother who saw her child reach heights of which she did not even dream, or which were not to her liking, to attempt to make an infant of him once again and put him to her breast to suckle, if not return him to the womb. Cervantes brought Don Quixote into the world, and that same Don Quixote took it upon himself to live in it; though the good Don Miguel thought to kill him off and bury him, and though he had a notarized statement of his death drawn up so that no one should dare resurrect him and make him sally forth once more, Don Quixote has nevertheless resurrected himself, through his own devices, and he rides through the world doing as he did before.

Cervantes wrote his book in the Spain of the beginning of the seventeenth century and for the Spain of that time; but Don Quixote has traveled through all the countries of the world in the course of the three centuries that have passed since then. Inasmuch as Don Quixote could not be the same man, for example, in nineteenth-century England as in seventeenth-century Spain, he has been transformed and modified in England, giving proof thereby of his powerful vitality and of the intense realism of his ideal reality.

It is nothing more than pettiness of spirit (to avoid saying something worse) that moves certain Spanish critics to insist on reducing *Don Quixote* to a mere work of literature, great though its value may be, and to attempt to drown in disdain, mockery, or invective all who seek in the book for meanings more intimate than the merely literal.

If the Bible came to have an inestimable value it is because of what generations of men put into it by their reading, as their spirits fed there; and it is well known that there is hardly a passage in it that has not been interpreted in hundreds of ways, depending on the interpreter. And this is all very much to the good. Of less importance is whether the authors of the different books of the Bible meant to say what the theologians, mystics, and commentators see there; the important fact is that, thanks to this immense labor of generations through the centuries, the Bible is a perennial fountain of consolation, hope, and heartfelt inspiration. Why should not the same process undergone by Holy Scripture take place with *Don Quixote*? * * *

* * *

I have observed that whenever *Don Quixote* is cited with enthusiasm in Spain, it is most often the least intense and least profound passages that are quoted, the most literary and least poetic, those that least lend themselves to philosophic flights or exaltations of the heart. * * *

* * *

Instead of getting to the poetry in *Don Quixote*, the truly eternal and universal element in it, we tend to become enmeshed in its literature, in its temporal and particular elements. In this regard, nothing is more wretched than to consider *Don Quixote* a language text for Spanish. * * *

* * *

The story is told of a seventeenth-century English king who asked one of his courtiers if he knew Spanish; when the courtier told him he did not, the king exclaimed: "What a pity!" The courtier, thinking the king must have been considering appointing him to some embassy or mission to Spain, set about studying Spanish; once he had learned it, he went to see the king, to tell him he knew it; and the king answered: "I am happy to hear it, for now you can read *Don Quixote* in the original." Wherein the king demonstrated very little understanding of the value of *Don Quixote,* a book whose worth is clearly shown by the fact that it lends itself to successful translation. Eminently fit for translation, it loses nothing of its force and poetry when put into any other language whatever.

I have never been able to countenance the theory that *Don Quixote* will not yield to translation. Even more, I go so far as to believe that it gains in translation, and that if it has been understood better outside of Spain, it is in good part because a preoccupation with the language has not veiled its beauty in foreign lands. * * *

* * *

It sometimes occurs in literary history that the man is superior to the author; thus it is that we often cannot judge a writer who produced an enormous sensation among his contemporaries: we can only be surprised at the prestige he enjoyed and the influence he exerted. At other times, the author is superior to the man, and the works are more than the man who wrote them. There are men very much superior to their works, and there are works vastly superior to the men who carried them out. There are men who die without having used up all their spirit in their writings, but who lavished it in conversation, in spoken words and in deeds. It is surprising to find in the works of the ancients high-flown praise of some contemporary whose works leave us cold today; in such instances we must assume that the man was much superior to his works. In other cases, the contrary must be true.

I have no doubt in my mind but that Cervantes is a typical example of a writer enormously inferior to his work, to his *Don Quixote.* * * *

I suspect, in fact, that Cervantes died without having sounded the profundity of his *Don Quixote* and perhaps without even having rightly understood it. It seems to me that if Cervantes came back to life and read his *Don Quixote* once again, he would understand it as little as do the Cervantist Masoretes, and that he would side with them. Let there be no doubt that if Cervantes returned to the world he would be a Cervantist and not a Quixotist. It is enough to read our book with some attention to observe that whenever the good Cervantes introduces himself into the narrative and sets about making observations on his own, it is merely to give vent to some impertinence or to pass malevolent and malicious judgments on his hero. Thus, for example, when he recounts the beautiful exploit wherein Don Quixote addresses a discourse on the Golden Age to some goatherds who could not possibly understand it in the literal sense—and the harangue is of a heroic order precisely because of this incapacity—Cervantes labels it a "purposeless discourse." Immediately afterwards he shows us that it was not purposeless, for the goatherds heard him out with "open-mouthed fascination," and by way of gratitude they repaid Don Quixote with pastoral songs. Poor Cervantes did not attain to the robust faith of the hidalgo from La Mancha, a faith which led him to address himself to the goatherds in elevated language, convinced that if they did not understand the words they were edified by the music. And this passage is one of many in which Cervantes shows his hand.

None of this should surprise us, for as I have pointed out, if Cervantes was Don Quixote's father, his mother was the country and people of which Cervantes was part. Cervantes was merely the instrument by which sixteenth-century Spain gave birth to Don Quixote. In this work Cervantes carried out the most impersonal task that can be imagined and, consequently, the most profoundly personal in another sense. As author of *Don Quixote,* Cervantes is no more than the minister and representative of humanity; that is why his work was great.

* * *

In the season in which Cervantes was under the spiritual wing of his country, being incubated there, Don Quixote was born in his soul; that is to say, his country engendered Don Quixote in his soul; and thus, as soon as the hidalgo sallied forth into the world, his country abandoned Cervantes, and the author became once again the poor wandering writer, prey to all the literary preoccupations of his time. And thus are many things explained, among others the feebleness of Cervantes' critical sense and the poverty of his literary judgments, as Macaulay has already noted. Everything that is literary criticism in *Don Quixote* is of the most vulgar and poorest cast imaginable and reveals a vertiable stopping up of common sense.

And notice how a man so sane and so thoroughly compounded of common sense—and as coarse as they come, was our Cervantes—was able to beget a knight so mad and so rich in inner sense. Cervantes had no choice but to give us a madman so that in him he might personify the great and eternal soul of his people. The truth is that oftentimes, when the eternal humanity which sleeps in the depths of our spiritual being starts up in our souls to shout out its longings, we either appear mad or pretend to be mad so that we may be pardoned our heroism. Thousands of times will a writer resort to the artifice of pretending that he is saying in jest what he very seriously believes, or he will bring a madman on stage and make him say and do things he himself would very much like to do and say, and do and say with a will, if the miserable herd instinct of men did not drive them to throttle anyone who leaves the sheepfold they all want to escape—but which all lack the courage to do for fear of dying of hunger, thirst, and cold in the open country, without shepherd or sheep dog.

Consider what there is of genius in Cervantes, and consider what his inward relation is to his Don Quixote. Such considerations should indeed move us to leave Cervantism for Quixotism, and to pay more attention to Don Quixote than to Cervantes. God did not send Cervantes into the world for any other purpose than to write *Don Quixote*; and it seems to me that it would have been an advantage for us if we had never known the name of the author, and our book had been an anonymous work, like the old ballads of Spain and, as many of us believe, the *Iliad*.

I may indeed write an essay whose thesis will be that Cervantes never existed but Don Quixote did. In any case, inasmuch as Cervantes exists no longer, while Don Quixote continues alive, we should all abandon the dead and go off with the living, abandon Cervantes and follow Don Quixote.

* * *

And if some reader of this essay should say that it is made up of contrivances and paradoxes, I shall reply that he does not know one iota about matters of Quixotism, and repeat to him what Don Quixote said on a certain occasion to his squire: "Because I know you, Sancho, I pay no attention to what you say."

HELENA PERCAS DE PONSETI

The Cave of Montesinos: Cervantes' Art of Fiction†

The present essay is intended to show Cervantes' art of fiction as reflected in his stylistic techniques in one of the most suggestive and elusive episodes from *Don Quixote*:[1] the protagonist's descent

† Dr. Ponseti wrote the following study expressly for this edition. She has subsequently incorporated it into her book *Cervantes y su concepto del arte*. Dr. Ponseti believes that Cervantes carefully balances concrete descriptions with statements in ambivalent language and with partial or inconsistent explanations of events—a principle of organization which she terms "ambiguity"—in order to force the reader to consider more than one cause or motive for any given episode. She believes that this calculated avoidance of clarity is Cervantes' most original trait: he induces his readers to look for "the truth" of the narrative while he systematically frustrates their efforts to reach conclusions. This essay illustrates how many ways a sensitive reader may understand the intriguing episode of Montesinos' cave.

1. For a more detailed study of Cervantes' literary and autobiographical sources, see Helena Percas de Ponseti, *Cervantes y su concepto del arte* (Madrid: Gredos, 1974), pp. 448–583. Some recent investigations focusing on diverse aspects of the cave episode are those of Robert Hollander, "The Cave of Montesinos and the Key of Dreams," *The Southern Review*, IV (1968), 756–767; Alban K. Forcione, "The Cave of Montesinos," *Cervantes, Aristotle, and the "Persiles,"* Princeton: Princeton University Press, 1970, pp. 137–146; Juan Bautista Avalle-Arce, "Don Quijote, o la vida como obra de arte," *Cuadernos Hispano Americanos*, no. 242 (Feb., 1970), 247–280; Harry Sieber, "Literary Time in the 'Cueva de Montesinos,'" *Modern Language Notes*, LXXXVI (1971), 268–273; Peter N. Dunn, "La cueva de Montesinos por fuera y por dentro: estructura épica, fisonomía," *Modern Language Notes*, LXXXVIII (1973), 190–202; and André Labertit, "Estilística del testimonio apócrifo en el *Quijote* (Estudio del cap. XXIII de la 2a Parte)," in *Venezia nella Letteratura Spagnola e altri studi barocchi* (Pisa: Università degli Studi di Pisa, Facoltà di Lettere e Filosofia, 1973), pp. 139–161.

into Montesinos' cave, Part II, Chapter XXIII.[2] Cervantes' primary intent is to reflect and reveal life rather than describe or comment upon it. To achieve his objective he confronts the reader with Don Quixote's account of what he saw in the cave in such a way as to induce him to evaluate the veracity of the knight's tale.

Readers of *Don Quixote* may recall the events so vividly related by the knight after he emerges from the enchanted cave of Montesinos. He tells his squire and a scholar accompanying them that he fell asleep inside the cave and that when he awoke he saw "a crystal palace or castle." Montesinos himself, the warden of the castle, came out to greet him. In a lower-level chamber of the palace, the famous knight Durandarte was lying on his tomb, dead but moving and speaking. His lady, Belerma, was wailing over Durandarte's heart while parading it about in her hands. Other knights, squires, and ladies from Nordic epics and from the Breton and Carolingian cycles of medieval ballads were also there. Unexpectedly, Don Quixote's own lady, Dulcinea, appeared, still dressed in the peasant clothes she wore when Sancho 'enchanted' her. Don Quixote relates how Dulcinea fled from him, then sent him a message informing him that she was in great need, and requested a small loan against the security of a petticoat. He has also learned from Montesinos that Merlin, the magician, transformed Guadiana, Durandarte's squire, into the namesake river which runs through Castile and the Ruidera ladies into the lagoons by the river.

The story is so bizarre that the character-author of Don Quixote's biography (a Moor called Cide Hamete Benengeli) cannot ascertain whether Don Quixote has fabricated it or whether he relates things actually seen. He will limit himself to writing it down in full detail.

The invention of a character-author is an old rhetorical device, but Cervantes uses it in a unique way.[3] Cide Hamete Benengeli is a dispassionate historian—the narrator tells us—but we find him offering opinions on many subjects, including his suspicion that the cave episode he himself is writing is apocryphal. He even gives credit to hearsay about Don Quixote's supposed admission, at the

2. Miguel de Cervantes Saavedra, *El ingenioso hidalgo Don Quijote de la Mancha.* Nueva ed. crit. de Francisco Rodríguez Marín, 10 vols. (Madrid: Patronato del IV centenario de Cervantes, 1947–49), V, 163–189. Translations in the text and in the notes are mine. Other references to this text will be made by part and by chapter.

3. See Joseph E. Gillet, "The Autonomous Character in Spanish and European Literature," *Hispanic Review,* XXIV (1956), 179–190; also, Edward C. Riley, "The Fictitious-Authorship Device," in *Cervantes's Theory of the Novel* (Oxford: The Clarendon Press, 1964), pp. 205–212. For a more detailed treatment of Cervantes' independence from the prevalent seventeenth-century neo-Aristotelian theory of fiction writing, and of his use of the pseudo-author in the cave episode, see Alban K. Forcione, "The cave of Montesinos," in *Cervantes, Aristotle, and the "Persiles"* (Princeton: Princeton University Press, 1970), pp. 137–146. Wayne C. Booth considers *Don Quixote* as "really the first important novel using the self-conscious narrator" ("The Self-Conscious Narrator in Comic Fiction before *Tristram Shandy,*" *PMLA,* LXVII [1952], 1965).

time of his death, that he invented the tale. The translator of Cide Hamete's Arabic manuscript, a bilingual Moor who sometimes edits as he translates, reports finding on the margin of the historian's manuscript a handwritten notation casting doubts on the veracity of the knight's account.

As a matter of fact, Don Quixote's credibility can be questioned. At first, he firmly states he is telling the truth about what he saw in the cave. Sancho, Cide Hamete, and the reader know that the knight does not lie. As time goes on, however, Don Quixote appears to be less convinced. This is reflected by the way he puts the question of the veracity of his own story to a divining monkey and, later on, to a magic head. The monkey's reply ("parts of the tale are credible and parts are false") as well as the magic head's verdict ("there is much to be said on that score") fail to clarify the matter.

Finally, if there is anything unlikely or impossible in this true story (*"verdadera historia,"* Cervantes insists), it is the fault, we are told, of the author—Cide Hamete?, the translator?, the editor?—not the subject, Don Quixote.

In this manner Cervantes poses the problem of objectivity in fiction. He places entirely upon Don Quixote the responsibility of being consistent with himself and believable as a fictional character, and he explicitly appeals to the wisdom of the reader for judgment: "You the reader, who are so wise, judge for yourself" (Part II, Ch. XXIV). Thus, the reader is invited to become an active partner in the writing of the novel, a co-author. But, by that very fact, we can sense an implied substitution of terms in Cervantes' criticism of the "author," as if he were saying: "If there is anything unlikely or impossible in this true story, it's the reader's fault."

The Reader's First Considerations

Montesinos' cave is a real cave in la Mancha, and according to several critics[4] who have traced Don Quixote's footsteps to the very spot, Cervantes' description of its entrance is made with topographical accuracy and great realism down to the underbrush, brambles, crows, and bats. Don Quixote tells us that, as he was lowered into the darkness and silence, he found himself dangling, perplexed and confused. He describes how he reached a spot jutting from the side of the cave wall, sat down on the coiled rope, wondering how he

4. Mostly Spaniards, such as Fermín Caballero, *Pericia geográfica de Miguel de Cervantes demonstrada con la historia de Don Quijote de la Mancha* (Madrid: Yenes, 1840), pp. 96–100; and Azorín [José Martínez Ruiz], *La ruta de Don Quijote*, 3a ed. ilustrada (Madrid and Buenos Aires: Renacimiento, 1919), p. 139. Luis Astrana Marín informs us that today, as a result of landslides, there are no brambles or undergrowth but limestone rocks (*Vida ejemplar y heroica de Miguel de Cervantes Saavedra, con mil documentos hasta ahora inéditos y numerosas ilustraciones de la época*, 7 vols. [Madrid: Reus, 1948–1958], VII [1958], 360–364, more specifically, 363).

would manage to reach bottom (*calar al fondo*), and falls fast asleep.

All this description is precise on a literal level but suggests different possible interpretations on a figurative level. The words, together with the rope, a tie which may also be read figuratively, place Don Quixote in the realm of man's metaphysical solitude: the lack of communication directly or indirectly with others forces self-confrontation. In the Golden Age, one meaning of the word to "reach down," *calar*, was to penetrate a problem, to uncover something concealed. Don Quixote falls literally or figuratively asleep but remains inwardly awake. From the very beginning, therefore, there are two levels of reality: an external, literal level; and an internal, metaphorical level.

The beginning of Don Quixote's vision goes as follows:

> . . . unexpectedly and without knowing how it happened, I awoke and found myself in the midst of the most beautiful, pleasant, and delightful meadow that nature could create or the most fertile imagination could conceive. Opening my eyes, I rubbed them and discovered that I was not sleeping but really awake. Nevertheless, I felt my head and chest to make sure it was I who was there and not some empty and deceptive phantom. But my sense of touch, my feelings, and the coherence of my thoughts reassured me that I was the same then and there that I am here and now.

This passage seems to question man's existence and the meaning of reality much in the way Calderón did in *Life is a Dream*. However, the evolution of Don Quixote's beliefs from the first impact of his experience in the cave to the moment he dies suggests another dimension to the concept of life as a dream. Man's identity changes as his experiences force him to reappraise his visions of reality.

In the paragraph just quoted Cervantes accomplishes at least three aims. First, he stresses Don Quixote's concern with his own identity[5] which he attempts to establish pragmatically and inferentially (touch, feelings, coherence of thoughts): he is the same man awake and asleep (outside and inside the cave). Cervantes then confronts the reader with Don Quixote's experience directly, without the interference of the author, and forces the reader to identify himself with the character in order to understand him. Such identification takes place by analogy, through a spontaneous substitution of the symbols in Don Quixote's story with symbols from the

5. I agree with Américo Castro that Don Quixote feels his body to confirm his identity and not his existence to himself. Cervantes does not prefigure Descartes' "I think, therefore I am," as has been suggested (*El pensamiento de Cervantes* [Madrid: Impr. de la librería y casa ed. Hernando, 1925], p. 89).

reader's own life. Thus, along with the knight, the reader may experience the half-oppressive, half-comical progression from the spell-binding vision of the meadow and the crystal palace to the grotesque vision of the ideal, Dulcinea, making a material request for money. Finally, Cervantes makes the reader enter the world of literary creation by compelling him to reconstruct Don Quixote's reality, both analytically and intuitively. Now the reader is brought to disagree with the author Cide Hamete Benengeli: not only does Don Quixote's adventure seem possible but it rings true, for it betrays the knight's most intimate, unavowed apprehensions: Dulcinea may not exist.

After these considerations, the experience in Montesinos' cave may be read on three planes: literal, mythic-allegorical, and psychological, all of which are supported by symbolic detail.

The Literal Plane

On a predominantly literal plane, the episode may be read as a dream, a nightmare, or an hallucination, reflecting Don Quixote's obsession with his ideal world. Several descriptive details, possible but extraordinary or grotesque in nature, prompt this interpretation. For instance: Montesinos keeps passing between his fingers an enormous rosary with beads "larger than medium sized nuts," each tenth bead being the size of "an ostrich egg." His attire, a strange assortment of pieces of clothing, is inappropriate for the warden of a castle. Belerma, Durandarte's lady, wears an equally inappropriate Turkish turban on her Christian head. She is called beautiful, but she is quite ugly, with uneven teeth, circles under her eyes, and a sallow complexion, a result—Montesinos explains—of her bad nights and worse days in the enchanted cave. On Durandarte's tomb, in place of his effigy lies the knight himself. Dulcinea's messenger leaps two yards into the air instead of making a curtsy as she departs. The mummified heart that Belerma carries about is preserved with salt, so that it will not stink.

A number of external details also contribute to the possibility of reading the episode as a dream, a nightmare, or an hallucination. There are time discrepancies in the accounts of the length of Don Quixote's stay in the cave: one hour according to Sancho, half an hour according to the Scholar, and three days and nights according to Don Quixote. Furthermore, the knight believes that he awoke from a profound sleep inside the dark cave to find himself in broad daylight. The detachment with which he observes the events about him make him seem to be more a casual observer than an interested party. Such is the case when Dulcinea asks him for a few pennies. He replies flippantly that he is no banker. Then, as time goes on, the increasing vagueness of the vision—even to the extent that he appears to be less sure that the experience in the cave took place at all—is itself a characteristic of the oneiric.

In a literal reading of the cave episode the comically distorted dream symbols, together with factual discrepancies and unprecedented reactions, reveal the knight's emotional disturbance.

The Mythic-Allegorical Plane

The cave episode may be read on a mythic-allegorical plane which is not opposed to the literal plane but rather superimposed on it. Cervantes' contemporaries, better acquainted than ourselves with mysticism and its concepts, might have read the episode in this light.

Throughout his wanderings Don Quixote reveres Dulcinea and conceives of her as a spiritual force sustaining him in his lofty pursuits of knight-errantry—a religion to him. Prior to his descent into the cave, he invokes her favor and protection in a mystic language similar to that of the Soul's appeal to the Beloved for the concession of grace and courage. The analogy with the world of mysticism is further brought out by the choice of setting and imagery. The descent into a cave reminds us of Saint John's, Saint Theresa's, or Saint Ignatius of Loyola's descent into a cave for the purpose of shutting out the world and confronting the self. Many mystic visions were experienced in caves by sixteenth-century illuminists. In literary works, such as the *Song of Songs* and Saint John's *Living Flame of Love*, the cave is the image chosen to convey depth of concentration.

Analogies do not end here. We are reminded of the mystic imagery by the darkness and silence in Montesinos' cave, Don Quixote's tenacious will to explore it, his state of perplexity, his suspension by a rope and his subsequent disengagement from it, thereby severing all ties with the outer world. Before union with the Beloved, the soul of the mystic is enveloped in total darkness and silence, and is in a state of confusion, imprisoned in the body, in bondage to the world. A symbol found in mystic writings to convey the idea of bondage is a rope which binds arms and legs or holds the Soul suspended in the void, striving for freedom from the body through concentration and will power.

Don Quixote awakens in a setting of beauty and light in sight of a "sumptuous palace or castle . . . built of clear, transparent crystal." Saint Francis of Osuna, Saint Bernardino of Laredo, Saint Theresa, and other mystics conceive of union with the Beloved as taking place within a fortress, castle, palace, or walled city, built of "pure crystal" or "clear diamond." Recurrent words among mystics to refer to the Soul's illuminative way are: "crystal," "glass," "mirror," "clarity," "transparency."[6]

For the mystic, the road which the soul must travel presents great obstacles. In a work significantly entitled *The Inner Castle* (1587), Saint Theresa compares the Soul's struggle to the conquest of a fortified castle defended by all sorts of repugnant vermin and awesome creatures.[7] Saint Theresa's animal imagery and the mystics' accounts of tribulations and obstacles on the upward path to illumination and union are ironically brought to mind in Don Quixote's determination to brave the crows, jackdaws, and bats at the entrance of the cave, and in his efforts to cut a path through dense brambles and underbrush, leading downward (inverted image) to Montesinos' underground crystal castle.

The beginning of Don Quixote's experience suggests the first stage of a mystic vision. But just as he is about to behold the marvels announced by Montesinos, the vision transforms itself into a nightmare before his very eyes. The ideal knights and ladies in the enchanted cave have been transfigured beyond recognition. Dulcinea is not the beautiful lady of his dreams. She is recognizable to her knight by externals only, by her peasant clothes, which suggest her death as an ideal and as a spiritual source of strength. Montesinos compares Dulcinea to Durandarte's lady Belerma. While Don Quixote resents the comparison and refuses to accept it, he sounds unaccountably resigned as he retorts: "comparisons are odious. . . . The peerless Dulcinea is who she is, and lady Belerma is who she is and has been, and let the matter rest there." Nevertheless, Montesinos' parallel persists, reinforced by Don Quixote's denial of identity between both ladies.

There is also an intimation of identity between the dead Duran-

6. In their studies on mystic writings several critics explain the meaning of these mystic sumbols and imagery. Some other mystic symbols in Don Quixote's account are *castle warden, guard, heart, ray of light, closed eyes, hunger, thirst, changed identity, facelessness.* The interested reader may consult Helmut Hatzfeld, *Estudios literarios sobre la mística española* (Madrid: Gredos, 1955), pp. 172, 352–356; Jean Baruzi, *Saint Jean de la Croix et le problème de l'expérience mystique,* 2nd éd. rev. et augm. d'une préface nouvelle (Paris: F. Alcan, 1931), pp. 689–690; Robert Ricard, "Le symbolisme du *Château intérieur* chez Sainte Thérèse," *Bulletin Hispanique,* LXVII (1965), 29; *Medieval Mystical Tradition and Saint John of the Cross,* by a Benedictine monk of Stanbrook Abbey (London: Burns, Oates, & Washbourne, 1954), p. 123. As for the change of identity, Catherine of Siena clearly states: "I am no longer the same person I was yesterday . . . I have been changed into someone else" (Joseph M. Perrin, *Catherine of Siena,* trans. Paul Barrett [Westminster, Md.: Newman Press, 1965], p. 67). A good direct source for the interpretation of mystic symbols is the *Spiritual Canticle* by Saint John of the Cross, because the Saint was prevailed upon to attach to this work a formal commentary explaining the meaning of symbols. It can be read in *The Complete Works of Saint John of the Cross, Doctor of the Church,* II, trans. and ed. E. Allison Peers from crit. ed. P. Silverio de Santa Teresa (London: Burns, Oates, & Washbourne, 1953).

7. See *The Complete Works of Saint Teresa of Jesus,* II: *Way of Perfection. Interior Castle,* trans. and ed. E. Allison Peers, from crit. ed. P. Silverio de Santa Teresa (London: Sheed & Ward, 1946), p. 203.

darte and Don Quixote. It is suggested in several ways. Durandarte is "the flower and mirror" of knights-errant, as Montesinos refers to him. So, too, is Don Quixote "the flower and cream of knights-errant," as his squire calls him (Part II, Ch. XXII). The identity extends to Amadis, often proclaimed to be "the cream and flower of knights-errant," and to all brave knights. Don Quixote once asserted the identity of all men through character when he said that he could be any knight he wanted to be, and even all knights put together, by being as great as they, "for man is his works" (Part I, Ch. V).

But here in the cave, the enchanted Durandarte is no longer the gallant and spirited knight he was in the legend. When told by Montesinos that thanks to Don Quixote's favor and mediation they may all be disenchanted, he replies in a faint voice: "And even if it be not so . . . let's have patience and shuffle the cards." Through its humor, his unknightly remark sounds just as resigned and disenchanted as Don Quixote's protest at the comparison of "peerless" Dulcinea to lady Belerma.

Durandarte, of "actual flesh and bones" on his tomb, has a "hairy and sinewy" hand, "a sign of the strength of the owner." It resembles Don Quixote's hand, described by himself thus: "the structure of the sinews, the network of the muscles, the breadth and spaciousness of the veins" point to "the might of the arm that supports such a hand" (Part I, Ch. XLIII). Behind the linguistic variation the same idea prevails. What Don Quixote is witnessing is his own spiritual death, not the literal death of flesh and bones. The symbol is the graphic image of Durandarte's "mummified heart, all dried out and withered," like a shell or a flower without the juice of life.[8]

The reverent manner in which Belerma carries about her knight's heart brings to mind the Holy Grail, and, by association of ideas, projects the image of Don Quixote (identified with Durandarte) as Christ-figure. The Turkish turban worn by a Christian Belerma (identified with Dulcinea) evinces, by extension, Don Quixote's delusion concerning his ideal lady, symbol of his religion of knight-erranty. The three days and nights (an hour, or half-hour, in reality) that Don Quixote spends in the cave, like Christ in the realm of the dead, further strengthens the religious-mystic analogy but as a symbolic reversal: Don Quixote is powerless to restore the enchanted to their original shapes and forms, to rescue his ideals from

8. Compare Part II, Ch. XXXII, where Don Quixote speaks of his lady's beauty, erased from his memory, if not from his heart, in the following terms: "if only I could take my heart out and lay it before . . . your eyes . . . I should relieve my tongue of the trouble [of describing Dulcinea's beauty, for] in my heart your Excellency would see her fully portrayed."

perishing. What Don Quixote sees before him is a shattered world of chivalry of which he is a part. Sancho's teasing identification of his master with the enchanted, "tell me what company you keep, and I'll tell you what you are," confirms it.

The mythical and legendary knights and ladies have lost their attributes of immortality by being imprisoned in a world of sorcery which, for the reader, bears an uncomfortable resemblance to life. Ironically enough, their existence in the cave is identical to their mythical life in ballads. In these, however, their frustrations are unrecognizable as such, for they are concealed under the cloak of literary imagery and the embellishing linguistic conventions of the Middle Ages. Stripped of this cloak of language, the personages in the cave evoke scenes of hopelessness and living death. Montesinos' enormous rosary suggests the magnitude of its inefficacy.

The anticipated paradise has turned into a hell. Such is the name intuitively given by Sancho to the cave. Is this a Christian hell or even a pagan or a heathen hell? Or is it an intellectual hell, the search for truth with the eyes of the mind rather than those of the body? As Don Quixote is brought out of the cave his eyes are shut tight, a conceptual image exploited by the Renaissance, by the mystics in Spain, by Shakespeare in *King Lear.* Rather than a purgatory leading to a paradise, enchantment is a timeless hell without exit similar, for a present-day reader, to that of the existentialists.[9] The distortion of mystic symbols reveals a crumbling world of vanishing gods.

The Psychological Reading

Don Quixote's experience could be viewed as the result of a profound psychological shock.[1] The exact nature of this shock, however, lends itself to more than one interpretation. One view of its nature is that the disillusioned Don Quixote invents the vision in the cave for Sancho's benefit, with a didactic or vindictive intent motivated by Sancho's deception a few days earlier, when the squire

9. Two opposite readings of the episode suggesting hidden meanings of a theological nature are those of Denys Armand Gonthier and of Louis-Philippe May. The first proves Cervantes' orthodoxy (*El drama psicológico del Quijote* [Madrid: Ed. Studium, 1962], p. 43); the second proves Cervantes' precursory free-thinking tendencies (*Un Fondateur de la Libre-Pensée: Cervantès. Essai de déchiffrement de Don Quichotte* [Paris, 1947], p. 37).

1. Angel del Río stresses modern man's anguish over his existence ("El equívoco del *Quijote*," *Hispanic Review,* XXVII [1959], 211–216). Gloria Fry applies Kenneth Burke's theory of symbolic action to Don Quixote's descent into the cave to explain psychoanalytically the revelatory qualities of the vision ("Symbolic Action in the Episode of the Cave of Montesinos from *Don Quijote,*" *Hispania,* XLVIII [1965], 468–474. In "What Happened in the Cave of Montesinos?" (*Comparative Literature Symposium,* Lubbock, Texas, I [1968], 3–17), T. Earle Hamilton explains Don Quixote's experience on the basis of the psychoanalytical observations concerning the dream process made by Freud, Radestock, Strümpel, Jessen, and others.

had enchanted Dulcinea and her damsels and produced them in the form of three peasant girls.[2]

A number of details could sustain this interpretation. Don Quixote's eyes are exaggeratedly shut as he is pulled out of the cave. He emphatically protests that he has indeed seen what he describes. He delays relating his experience, asking for lunch first. He waits until the end of his story to bring up the sudden appearance of Dulcinea in peasant clothes to convince unbelieving Sancho that the events described were true and real. The Dulcinea in the cave imitates, in her flight, the Dulcinea enchanted by Sancho. The final clue to such a view would be Don Quixote's compromise with Sancho about the truth a few days later when he proposes to him that he will believe his squire's fantastic tale of what he saw in heaven if the squire, in turn, will believe Don Quixote's vision in the cave (Part II, Ch. XLI).

Such an interpretation, however plausible, is not entirely convincing, for it implies a premeditation quite out of character for Don Quixote. While premeditation might be consistent with the knight's growing suspiciousness, it is inconsistent with the integrity of his nature. Another factor discrediting this view is that even the considerable imaginative powers of Don Quixote would have required more time than one hour to construct a tale as elaborate and involved as this one, an opinion held by Sancho, the Scholar, and the author Cide Hamete Benengeli. I fully agree with them.

There is yet another possible interpretation of the nature of the shock suffered by Don Quixote, one in which the knight's motives are not in question at all. It is not a matter of deceit but of attaching more value to words and their conventional connotations than to the underlying realities which prompt them. With this in mind, the experience in the cave could be read more ingenuously, and also more ambiguously, adding a new dimension to our literal and mythic-allegorical readings. As Don Quixote relates his vision, his words cut out well-defined images (meadow, palace, dagger, tomb, money) from the complex background of his psychology. These words bring out precise meanings while the background from which they emerged recedes and fades away. As intuitions and feelings are translated into words, they are inevitably recreated as an interpretation. Don Quixote is giving us, therefore, an intuitive interpretation of his own vision which becomes meaningful to him as he recalls it through language. Some details in his story could have been recalled, or suggested by every interruption of Sancho and the

2. Salvador de Madariaga, "The Cave of Montesinos," *Don Quixote. An Introductory Essay in Psychology* (Newton, Wales: The Gregynog Press, 1934), pp. 157–165. Marc Van Doren does not hesitate to call the tale a "hoax." He says that Don Quixote invents Dulcinea's appearance in peasant clothes "to pull Sancho's leg." There is no other "plausible explanation of what happens in the cave" (*Don Quixote's Profession* [New York: Columbia Univ. Press, 1958], pp. 18, 56–57).

Scholar[3] requesting specific verification. The animation with which Don Quixote offers concrete information, especially Dulcinea's arrival and flight, could be explained as gratification for finding convincing evidence for his listeners as well as himself. The use of Dulcinea's peasant clothing as a proof of her identity is Cervantes' subtle way of catching Sancho in his own ruse regardless of whether Don Quixote has fabricated this detail, really dreamed it, or imagined it under his recent shock of seeing his lady under a spell. In any event, for a knight to conceive of his lady as a hapless peasant is an ideological distortion betraying mental anguish or, in Madariaga's view, cynicism.[4]

Don Quixote's mental anguish is further reflected in the fact that he draws conclusions within the framework of his own world of knighthood that are not supported by the facts. As he comes out of the cave his tone switches without transition from the ecstatic to the grieved. "You have robbed me of the most delightful existence mortal ever enjoyed and the sweetest vision human eyes ever rested upon," he exclaims (Part II, Ch. XXII). From this rapture he launches immediately into a lament for the enchanted personages in the cave and for their bitter fate.

The enchantment of knights and ladies and Dulcinea's metamorphosis from a beautiful lady into a grotesque peasant girl betray a sharpening awareness in Don Quixote's mind of the hollowness of his knight-errant world, although he would be unwilling to admit it openly. To do so would be to destroy the last stronghold of illusion. In retrospect, he may well have become aware of Sancho's deception. This would explain his change of attitude as he later talks with his squire about the cave, his compromise with him on the truth (i.e., "I'll believe you if you believe me," II, 41) and his subsequent disheartened silence about the whole matter.

Even if Don Quixote is semiconsciously playing a role, still he is revealing his state of mind. Alteration of detail, even complete invention, would be nothing other than a visual representation of the clash between his convictions and his doubts, between the idealist Don Quixote—his chosen name, his willed identity—and the realist Alonso Quijano—his conventional name, his social identity

3. Cervantes pokes fun at the Scholar, referred to in Spanish as *el Primo*, "the cousin" (of another scholar, that is), playing on this word which colloquially means "fool" and "dupe." Cervantes humorously calls him a humanist for believing that truth can be established by concensus of opinion.

4. This critic explains what he conceives to be Don Quixote's sudden cynical view of chivalry, as a momentary identification between a disillusioned Cervantes and a disillusioned Don Quixote (*op. cit.*, p. 161). Gerald Brenan points out that if it were a question of mere "intrusions of the author's wit" in Don Quixotes' dream they would "surely strike a false note." These intrusions are legitimate because they "throw some new light on Don Quixote's character" ("Novelist-Philosophers, XIII: Cervantes," *Horizon*, XVIII [1948], pp. 25–46, and particularly 38). Edward Sarmiento notes "the tenderness of the cave vision" as well as a sense of confrontation "with the truth" ("On the Interpretation of *Don Quixote*," *Bulletin of Hispanic Studies*, XXXVII [1960], 146–153, specifically, 152–153).

—which is beginning to emerge from within the committed man. The rise of Alonso Quijano within Don Quixote stresses the gradual transformation of the knight back into the country gentleman he was before. As Alonso Quijano looks back on Don Quixote's life, the substance of past thoughts, emotions, and convictions is appraised in the light of his changing beliefs. What might have been true yesterday is half true today and may be false in retrospect. Doubt is the evil magician destroying Don Quixote's inner world.

Cervantes' Approach to Facts

We may call the tale, wholly or partly, an invention, but never a lie! When Cervantes introduces contradictory data leading us on a quest for truth or falsehood which are impossible to establish with certainty, he is really insisting on the idleness of such a quest. Data, we are forced to conclude, are nothing but fiction, for, however precise or concrete, their interpretation differs with each individual's perspective and set of values.

Reality is, for Cervantes, whatever is consistent with human nature. On this basis, whatever Don Quixote senses, dreams, feels, or expresses—regardless of the words or images to which he resorts for communication—reveals his truth with all the ambiguity of emotions and thoughts inherent in humans. Even through fantasies and inventions man speaks the truth about himself. The moral, ethical, or factual clarity that is achieved by resorting to blacks and whites may be necessary for social communication. It is, nonetheless, a distortion of personal truth. When language symbols are stripped away, there appears a naked, shapeless, meaningless reality. By just telling what a man says or does, not what his words and actions mean, a glimpse of his truth may be captured. An interpretation, even the author's, is but one more deception.

Cervantes' Artistic Solution

The attainment of total objectivity is an almost unsurmountable difficulty for any author, irrespective of his method of approach. The very choice of materials constitutes a subjective focus. Cervantes' solution is to construct an image of life in which the relationship between art and nature is so balanced that it projects a semblance of reality.

Cervantes achieves this balance through ambiguity and restraint. Ambiguity is created by choosing words or images prompting multiple associations. Restraint is exercised through a careful screening out of details that might limit the possibilities for interpretation. The choice of setting and atmosphere (a cave, silence, solitude) and the workings of the subconscious (a dream, an obsession, mental turmoil) lend themselves to ambiguity and restraint since a logical sequence of events is no longer mandatory. Only those incidents and circumstances strictly relevant to meaningful thought associations appear. Incongruities and breaks in the flow of events then seem not only possible, but natural. The illusion of clarity is created by the visual, sculptured symbols: the crystal palace, the ornamented tomb, the mummified heart, the Turkish turban, the peasant clothing, etc.

The most original of Cervantes' techniques is, I believe, to choose materials prompting multiple associations. An example is the material relating to the suspension of bodily needs and of the passage of time in the enchanted cave. This could be Cervantes' reminiscence of Wolfram von Eschenbach's *Parzival* and of the Arthurian Grail legend (some of whose characters wander about in Montesinos' cave). In *Parzival,* the whole court in the subterranean castle is fed by the Grail's miraculous power and exists in a never-ending present without the usual human needs, as Philip Stephan Barto reminds us in his article, "Cervantes' Subterranean Grail Paradise."[5] Similar conditions exist in the epic tradition of classical descents into the underworld, as established by L. G. Salingar in "*Don Quijote* as a Prose Epic."[6] References to such descents are made several times in Cervantes' text. Miguel Cortacero y Velasco is reminded of Christ's ascent to Abraham's bosom.[7] Others might recall His descent into the realm of the dead, where there is no time, hunger, or thirst. Cervantes' descriptive choice may have no pagan, epic, or Christian allegorical meaning, but may be an embodiment of proverbial thought in Don Quixote's feverish and restless mind, a recollection of a folk saying, quoted by Sancho, to the effect that those in love are "exchanted and neither eat, drink, nor sleep" (Part I, Ch. XLIX). The reader readily connects the two descriptions in Cervantes' text and requires no other frame of reference to derive meaning.

Montesinos' palace or castle is another excellent example of an image prompting multiple associations—in this case with the mystic, the chivalrous, and the classical past. A palace, castle, or fortress is the divine abode of the mystic. It is sometimes made of crystal, like Montesinos' palace, other times of gems. The soul must brave the vermin, reptiles, and beasts to gain access to the abode, just as Don Quixtoe must fight the brambles, crows, and bats to gain entrance to the cave.

A parallel to these images is offered in the story Don Quixote made up (Part I, Ch. L) from his readings of chivalrous literature. A knight braves all sorts of beasts swimming in a lake before he can

5. *PMLA,* XXXVII (1923), 407.

6. *Forum for Modern Language Studies,* II (1966), 63–68.

7. *Cervantes y el Evangelio. Simbolismo del Quijote* (Madrid: Impr. Hijos de G. Fuentenebro, 1915), p. 212.

reach below its surface and come to a palace made of gold, diamonds, and other gems.

Classical literature has its counterparts. In the *Aeneid,* for instance, the classical lake, the Avernus, contains a cave defended by reptiles and other beasts that Aeneas must fight before he can gain access to the underworld.

In all three bodies of literature—the mystic, the chivalric, and the classic—the metaphysical world is represented by similar graphic images: inner, underground, and/or underwater realms containing palaces, castles, or fortresses.

Don Quixote's experience takes place in a hell-like paradise. The inner castle (palace or fortress) is the mystic's earthly paradise. Aeneas' underworld contains a sort of pagan hell, purgatory, and paradise. Don Quixote's invented story describes a knightly underwater paradise. This last reference suffices to justify and explain the palace or castle in Montesinos' cave in the context of Don Quixote's favorite readings. If, in addition, we have in mind a recollection of mystical, epic, or classical literature, the literal meaning of a dream experience becomes enriched with a diversity of philosophical overtones.

A third example is Durandarte's heart. In a ballad from the Carolingian cycle, known to Don Quixote as well as to seventeenth-century readers, Durandarte begged Montesinos to cut out his heart after he died and take it to his lady Belerma. In the process of so doing, Montesinos discovered—as he tells Don Quixote—that Durandarte's heart was very large, bearing out the truth of the folk belief that the braver the knight the bigger his heart. The salting of the heart grotesquely recalls practices for meat and fish preservation. It introduces a note of irony, overshadowing the pathos. The description of Durandarte's heart as "mummified . . . dried out and withered," recalls, perhaps only coincidentally, but certainly amusingly, Don Quixote's own appearance after his illness "looking withered and dried up like a mummy" (Part II, Ch. I). The suggested identity between Durandarte and Don Quixote, as pointed out in our second reading of the cave episode, is brought out further by this delightful touch of expressionistic technique. Symbol, literature, and life are deftly and naturally blended.

A fourth example is Durandarte's squire Guadiana. Guadiana is the name of a river in the vicinity of the cave of Montesinos which disappears into the ground for no apparent reason, according to the inhabitants of that region. In Don Quixote's cave-vision, the river disappears because Guadiana's grief for his dead master, Durandarte, is such that whenever the squire (metamorphosed into a river) comes to the surface of the earth he plunges under it again so as not to see the light of day. This transmutation has been granted to Guadiana by Merlin, the magician responsible for so many transformations in the Breton cycle of ballads or in Renaissance epics such as *Orlando furioso*, in which there is a cave[8] bearing the same characteristics as Montesinos' cave. On the other hand, Guadiana's transformation could be a reminiscence in Cervantes' mind of popular Spanish traditions or of earlier myths concerning the rivers, Darro and Genil, invented by the Spaniards Luis Barahona de Soto and Pedro Espinosa. It could be, equally as well, Cervantes' own imaginative myth, patterned after Ovid's *Metamorphoses*,[9] in which he combines a Carolingian ballad theme and a Renaissance epic theme with Castilian topography. Similarities between Cervantes' myth and other myths and the quest for the possible sources such as Ovid's *Metamorphoses*, suggested by the author himself, may delight scholars; the average reader requires none of this knowledge to enjoy the Guadiana myth, for it is delightful in itself.

A fifth example is that of Montesinos' attire, partly collegiate (the green satin sash around his shoulders); partly seminaristic (the hooded mulberry-colored cloak), and partly official (the black Milanese cap). Montesinos' clothing will impress readers in different ways. For some, there is irony tinged with religious overtones, heightened by Montesinos' almost superstitiously gigantic rosary. For others, the overtones are social or political. Readers with an orthodox theological background may view the purple of the enchanted castle-warden's cloak symbolically, in the context of man's insignificance and hopelessness when forsaken by divine grace. The ambiguity making such vastly diverging readings possible is derived from the fact that malice plays no role in incongruities that appear in dreams, and irony may or may not be present depending on the reader's mental make-up.

A final example of materials suggesting multiple associations is Dulcinea's money needs, a literalization of the allegory of Necessity.[1] Necessity and need are, in Spanish, the same word, *necesidad*. Necessity is, in Greek mythology, a throned deity presiding over human destinies. Necessity appears in the allegorical Vision of Er, in Book X of Plato's *Republic*. It appears also in Timarcus' vision, in Book VII of Plutarch's *Opera moralia*. Don Quixote is amazed that the enchanted should be subject to human needs—Necessity by philosophical extension. A reader associating Dulcinea's needs with the Necessity of the Greek myth would ponder over

8. Joseph G. Fucilla points out analogies of detail as well as verbal similarities between Sincero's descent into a crystal grotto (Prose XII of Sannazaro's *Arcadia*) and Don Quixote's descent into Montesinos' cave with its crystal palace. In the Sannazaro episode there are gods and nymphs transformed into rivers in analogous manner to Guadiana's transformation into a river ("The Cave of Montesinos," *Italica*, XXIX [1952], 171, 173).

9. The Scholar intends to use the information furnished by Don Quixote about the mutations of Guadiana and of the Ruidera Lagoons in his book entitled *Metamorphoses, or the Spanish Ovid*, an imitation 'in burlesque style' of Ovid's myths (Part II, Ch. XXII).

1. Arturo Marasso pointed out the existence of this allegory in his book: *Cervantes, la invención del Quijote* (Buenos Aires: Libr. Hachette, 1954), pp. 143–145.

man's inescapable subjection to his destiny and over the degree of free will or predestination playing a role in his life choices. A reader unaware of Plato's or Plutarch's allegories may simply be amused and moved by the plight and miseries of the enchanted, so similar to his own.

All these examples show that the reader may follow whichever lead is more to his taste, and reflect the episode in the mirror of his own beliefs, prejudices, aspirations, or spiritual tendencies. This is possible because Cervantes has created an episode deceivingly clear but, in fact, as ambiguous as life itself.

Cervantes artistic purpose is to present an authentic image of life by revelation rather than by description. He is far less concerned with establishing truth than with showing man's fruitless search for it.[2] His ultimate goal is to present the reader with the puzzle of human nature and the elusiveness of reality due to the vagaries of language, the deceptiveness of the senses, and the complex subtleties of the mind. The moment the critic commits himself to a clear-cut, single explanation of what happened in the cave of Montesinos he becomes, for future readers, one more character in the book.

STEPHEN GILMAN

The *Apocryphal Quixote*†

As any reader of Cervantes knows, in the fifty-ninth chapter of the second part of their adventures, Don Quixote and Sancho make a frightening discovery. They learn that they have been imitated, that caricatures of themselves have been unloosed upon the hapless towns of Spain, and that that part of their beings which exists in the minds of others, that very essential part which is known as fame, stands in immediate danger of destruction. For Don Quixote

2. Truth as a theme in Cervantes fiction has been a constant subject of debate among critics. Two conflicting views have been held to the present day: (1) For Cervantes truth is relative and a matter of ethical perspective. (2) For Cervantes truth is not relative nor a matter of perspective. It is simply difficult to discern on the moral plane owing to man's ethical limitations. Is there any essential contradiction between both views? I don't believe there is. The first view considers man's truth; the second absolute Truth. Both are accurate if we consider *Don Quixote* to be a moral but not a moralistic book about life, and if we don't identify human truth with divine truth.

† From *Cervantes Across the Centuries,* ed. Angel Flores and J. J. Bernardete (New York: Dryden Press, 1947), pp. 247–253. In some ways, the most brilliant passages in all of *Don Quixote* are those in Part II in which the author confronts his two characters with the astounding news that the history of a "false" Quixote and Sancho has appeared. With unequalled subtlety, Cervantes lets his "real" knight and squire refute the unauthorized account themselves. Stephen Gilman has used his familiarity with Fernández de Avellaneda's sequel to show that an examination of what this imitator rejects or alters in his model can help us to understand Cervantes' special appeal.

and Sancho Panza, living men within a literary environment, the appearance of the *Apocryphal Quixote* is clearly a case of calumny. Their reaction is natural: in order to distinguish themselves from their infamous imitators, they decide to change their plans, to alter their futures—to go to Barcelona, instead of to the jousts of Zaragoza, as they previously had intended. Later, when Don Quixote meets Don Alvaro Tarfe, a person from the rival history who had known his counterpart, he has him take a written oath affirming their lack of identity. It is a problem, like many of the other problems of Cervantes' second part, of being and will.

For Cervantes, the appearance of the *Apocryphal Quixote* had even more personal implications. Apparently without any forewarning, in the midst of the creation of the second part, he was confronted with a rival author who not only copied the first part of his book, but who also seemed to have a strange prescience as to the manuscript then in his hands, who in some way had managed to imitate and corrupt the adventures not yet published.[1] Furthermore, this unknown Alonso Fernández de Avellaneda, whoever he might be, had had the effrontery to preface his work with a series of insults to him. Cervantes was called "complaining, gossipy, impatient, and choleric as are all prisoners," and was taunted for his age, and even for his maimed hand, that glorious proof of his participation in the battle of Lepanto. Avellaneda even went so far as to gloat over the thought that his book might ruin the sale of the real second part and so cheat Cervantes of some much needed income. In addition to the spiritual trespass and the insults, there was the admitted intention of physical robbery.

Cervantes' reaction was not natural as had been that of Don Quixote and Sancho; it was typically Cervantine. After pointing out, in his own prologue, the injustice of some of his rival's remarks, he makes it clear that he disdains the polemic which was expected of him. He prefers to encompass Avellaneda in a web of irony. Hence, the anecdote of the madman and the dogs in the same prologue; the introduction and annihilation of Avellaneda's story within his own; and the finality of Don Quixote's death at the end of the book. Perhaps the darkest stain upon Avellaneda's soul is not the writing of his own version nor even his attacks upon Cervantes, but his share in the death of Don Quixote, his share in the death of meaning for man. In any case, it was not Cervantes but Cid Hamete Benengeli who permitted himself the luxury of polemic

1. The general scheme of the stay in the Duke's palace is present in Avellaneda's work, as well as that of such minor adventures as the puppet show of Ginés de Pasamonte. Rather than admit the unlikely and unsatisfactory explanation advanced by Menéndez Pidal to the effect that Cervantes imitated Avellaneda in parts, I prefer to accept the supposition of Fitzmaurice Kelly that Cervantes read chapters of his work in progress to his friends and that Avellaneda learned of his rival's plans through the consequent, and perhaps nationwide, gossip about what was going on.

reply, and called his fellow "historian," "presumptuous," and "perverse."

If Don Quixote and Sancho and if Cervantes had their own reactions to the *Apocryphal Quixote*, what has been and what should be the reaction of Cervantes' readers? In the first place, in 1614, when the false version appeared they were better equipped to judge its counterfeit nature than either Don Quixote or Sancho had dared to hope. Only one edition was printed before the appearance of the genuine second part in 1615, and none was printed afterwards. In the eighteenth century certain neo-classic critics, both in Spain and France, inspired by Lesage's translations, were not so sure. They seemed to feel that Avellaneda's caricatures, in that they did not develop and change novelistically with their circumstances, in that they were dead rather than living, were more "true to the truth" than the originals. The counter-quality of decorum must certainly have been rather difficult for them to find amid the extravagance and obscenity of the Avellanedan world.

The reaction of the nineteenth century was again typical; it represented an exaggeration not of doctrinaire but of positivistic criticism. Alonso Fernández de Avellaneda was not seen as a man with a pen in his hand who might imitate, who might criticize, or who, in doing both, might recreate. He became above all a problem, a mystery, a playground for erudites. Well over a hundred articles and books were published, naming this or that seventeenth-century figure as the unknown author, and almost every known personage of the time from Lope de Vega to Cervantes himself was accorded the dubious honor. It was a subject about which "cervantistas" could become passionate, and many long and bitter arguments were waged. Although from time to time, disparaging remarks were directed against the *Apocryphal Quixote*, very few critics took the trouble to judge the work on its own terms. If they had done so, they might have been surprised to find abundant support for the oldest theory of them all, that Avellaneda was a Dominican from Aragon.

Judging from the excesses of past criticism of Avellaneda's extraordinary book, it is perhaps now time to outline a fresh approach. The possibility that the imitation may surpass the imitated has long been discarded, and, on the basis of available evidence, the hazardous identifications of the artist have come to no conclusion. A major problem remains, however, among others. What is the imitative technique of Avellaneda? What does he discard and what does he keep and why? Or to state the problem differently, how can Avellaneda's changes be made to throw new light upon the way of Cervantes' creativity? When Menéndez y Pelayo called the *Apocryphal Quixote* a point of comparison which might serve for the "estimation" of the genius of Cervantes, he foresaw this problem, but unfortunately he did not investigate it. He returned instead to his generation's ceaseless quest for the name of Avellaneda.

If the problem of the *Apocryphal Quixote* is so to be redefined by the contemporary reader of Cervantes, he must first become aware of the centuries-old imitative tradition in Castilian literature that preceded Avellaneda. From the time of the medieval "juglar," like Juan Ruiz, who could dedicate his *Book of Good Love* to all and to anyone "who may add or change as he pleases," until that of the "comedia," with its numerous revisions and borrowings, imitation had become an accepted practice in the peninsula. As Avellaneda himself says:

> Let nobody be surprised that this second part should come from a different author, for it is not a new thing for different persons to pursue a single history. How many have spoken of Angelica's loves and of her fortunes? Arcadias have been written by many, and the *Diana* is not all from a single pen.[2]

It is a tradition which, according to Menéndez Pidal, corresponds integrally to the "popular" essence of Spanish culture. The reader is more important than the writer. The artist, as Avellaneda defines him above, becomes an historian and a servile one at that.

But Avellaneda has other things to say in his vicious prologue. In the first place, he modifies his self-justification, as the heir of a long tradition of imitation, by his attacks on Cervantes. Why insult the original author and at the same time admit his merit by the very fact of continuing his narrative? It is a delicate problem; Juan Ruiz certainly did not expect such treatment at the hands of the "juglares" who, he hoped, would carry on his inspiration. A further modification is the surprising statement by Avellaneda: "This part is somewhat different from his first, because I am of opposite humor to his . . ." He admits an antipathy here of such depth that it affects the creative process itself. He has gone beyond mere imitation, he says; he has recreated according to his own "humor," a humor profoundly hostile to that of Cervantes. The changes, then, that the reader will find in the apocryphal version correspond to something more than the incompetency of an imitator lacking Cervantes' genius; they represent a distinct artistic intent. It would be idle to deny that Avellaneda imitates and that, when he does so, he yields to the inevitable tendency of all those who copy, which is to caricature. Yet, if these were the only changes, consideration of the *Apocryphal Quixote* would merely emphasize Cervantes' poetic skill. It is when Avellaneda recreates that he throws light upon his rival's full poetic genius. It is possible to make a vital as well as a mechanical comparison.

2. Available translations of the *Apocryphal Quixote* in English are taken from Lesage's French version. The passages quoted here represent my own translation from the original.

The scope of this essay[3] does not allow for anything approaching a complete exploration of the Avellanedan world; it will be possible only to survey a few of its isolated landscapes, to sense the texture of its scenery, and to suggest routes for its future travelers. Although later the divergence of the two creative intents will be examined as they bring into relief different values from Don Quixote's familiar delusion that inns are castles, it would perhaps first be better to examine the initial escapade of the spurious knight. It holds a key to his future conduct. Don Quixote has buckled on a suit of new armor left in his care by Don Alvaro Tarfe, a gentleman who has recently passed through Argamasilla, and he stands before the mirror admiring himself for Sancho's benefit:

> "What do you think, Sancho? Does it look well on me? Do you not admire my gallantry and my warlike aspect?" This he said while walking up and down the room making faces and striking poses. . . . after which such an accident suddenly occurred within his fancy, that, putting his hand to sword with all speed, he drew near to Sancho with visible anger, saying: "Wait, cursed dragon, serpent of Libya, infernal basilisk; you shall know by experience the valor of Don Quixote, a second Saint George in strength . . ." Sancho, who saw him coming so ruthlessly, began to run around the room . . . fleeing from the fury of his master . . . Don Quixote meanwhile followed poor Sancho around the bed launching a thousand insults at him and with each one taking a long swing at him with his sword; and if the bed had not been as wide as it was, poor Sancho would have have had a bad time of it.

Sancho then pleads for mercy, which is granted him only after he has promised to relinquish all his enchanted damsels and hidden treasures. When Don Quixote ultimately reverts to his senses, his explanation for the outburst is curious:

> "Can you not see, Sancho, that it was feigned, in order that you might witness my great strength in combat, my skill in laying low my enemies, my craftiness in the charge?"

Here is a Don Quixote who, unlike the Knight of the Rueful Countenance, could feign his vocation, could play-act. He needs no inward belief, no comforting stimulus from aspectual reality; he could compose variations on the theme of knighthood with apt talent and dismiss the resulting tense situation a moment later as mere pretending. Here is to be the basic rhythm of the *Apocryphal Quixote*; a sudden aberration, an intensity of conflict, and an artificial dismissal of the whole matter. As soon as this scene has been played out, both Don Quixote and Sancho seem to have forgotten

3. From this point forward the material presented is a condensation and general revision of an article of mine published in Spanish in the *Revista de filología hispánica*, Buenos Aires, 1943.

it and converse awkwardly about going home to eat. But, as Avellaneda is careful to point out, the exaggeration of Don Quixote's madness corresponds to basic psychological change. The knight is now possessed of a crippled mind. As a literary character, he is not only imitated badly; he is conceived differently, and his madness now results from accidents "within the fancy." These are accidents which are to modify the very foundation of the novel.

The original Don Quixote's frequent delusion that inns were castles, when imitated by Avellaneda, will further illustrate the artistic metamorphosis. In the fourth chapter of the apocryphal version, the knight and the squire perceive an inn in the distance, where the inhabitants and their adventures are reminiscent of the inn of Juan Palomeque "the left-handed," and of Maritornes. In both cases the two disagree as to the identity of the building before them, but Avellaneda's hero is not interested, as is Cervantes', in defending the exactness of his perception. He sees, instead, an opportunity to fabricate, to take an imaginary inventory of insane details. He says to Sancho:

> "Stupid fool, can you not see from here the high turrets, the famous drawbridge, and the two very fierce griffins who forbid entrance to those who wish to enter against the will of the seneschal? . . . It would be well, Sancho, if you went up to that castle as if you were a real spy and if you noted with great care the width, height, and depth of the moat, the disposition of the gates and drawbridges, the towers, the platforms, the covered causeways, the dikes, the counter-dikes, the trenches, the portcullises, the sentry boxes, the parade grounds and guard posts that are there and the artillery possessed by the defenders . . ."

Just as in the attack on Sancho, the reaction overwhelms the slight original stimulus. Each incident and each encounter provokes an outpouring of absurd monologue in such proportions that Don Quixote's illusion that he is a knight, and the restricted set of chivalresque patterns that this belief can encompass, are lost from sight. The need for variation of entertainment that is the inherent problem of both *Quixotes* is solved in this way, by Avellaneda, in terms of quantity. (Cervantes, on the other hand, found a qualitative solution by interpolating other generic patterns, pastoral, picaresque, etc., and by allowing Don Quixote, still faithful to his vocation, to live in and react against them.) Thus the apocryphal Don Quixote is more comic madman than knight-errant.

Sancho Panza, too, is conceived of as an entertainer and has his own form of comic monologue. His speech is a blend of witticisms, puns, and simplicities which permit of no more interruption than the follies of his master, and consequently there can be no dialogue between them. Lacking the human understanding, the perspectivism, implied by Cervantes' dialogue technique, Avellaneda's protagonists can only exchange their interminable monologues. The fool fails to understand and the madman fails to heed. Don Quixote, for example, when flatly told by Sancho that his castle is only an inn, is unperturbed: "To the devil with you, then, for it is what I say, in spite of the whole world." He is neither saddened nor angered but stubborn; he does not argue, but holds his ground, even in the face of such an absolute contradiction. Later, after Don Quixote has entered the inn, he refuses to take off his helmet, stubbornly insisting the while that his hosts are "untrustworthy pagans." It is one of those innumerable minor crises that threaten to halt the forward movement of the narrative, and it has a typical solution. Sancho breaks down his master's perverse immovability by "repeated demanding." Don Quixote and Sancho may demand but they cannot argue; they may talk for the amusement of the reader, but cannot converse the one with the other. Their adoption by Avellaneda has affected the depths of their beings.

The inn itself, as Avellaneda portrays it, has very different contours from its Cervantean counterpart. Cervantes' frightful picaresque makeshift of a couch becomes a "reasonable bed"; Maritornes, with her almost sprightly ugliness, becomes a colorless Galician prostitute; Juan Palomeque "the left-handed," with all his jesting rascality, becomes an innkeeper whose only living reaction to Don Quixote is anger at his failure to pay for his lodging. Although the Galician girl solicits both Don Quixote and Sancho during the night, it is only a faint reverberation of the alarms and excursions of the Cervantean episode. Thus the counterpoint of picaresque versus chivalresque patterns, the ironic artistry of "being" as opposed to "seeming," that constituted the texture of the original incident, is lost. Don Quixote's make-believe is not inserted into a circumstance created for him, a circumstance of literature, but into a world having no relationship whatsoever with himself. Although Menéndez y Pelayo has compared the *Apocryphal Quixote* to the novels of Zola, such terms as "realism" or "naturalism" are not adequate for the world here presented. It is rather a world which is unevaluated, uncreated, in a sense unloved, the world of an historian but not of an artist. Of neither Zola nor Balzac can this be said. The frequent obscenity and filth of Don Quixote's surroundings is then, like the Galician prostitute, merely coincident with their meaninglessness. The "reasonableness" of the bed is a purely casual phenomenon; it could have as easily been, as it was so often to be, unspeakable. It is a world alien to Don Quixote in that it appears completely out of his, and his author's, artistic control.

So it seems that the spurious knight is ideally suited to the place of his existence. His stubborn insanity needs no carefully prepared excuses, no artificial configurations of circumstance for its delusions; and none are there. He needs no reference to enchanters to explain his failures, as in the first part, for he never admits them. He can desert Cervantes' pastoral countryside and travel through cities without risking the growing disillusion of the second part, because there is no continuity to his experience. His damaged "fancy" overrides his senses, and any too evident contradiction from the outside world can be dismissed merely by changing the subject. Without some dominant motivation which can give a functional value to his memory, it becomes unstrung, a kaleidoscope of past impressions and information. There can be no accumulation of disillusion, no experience in the novelistic sense. It is not that the false Don Quixote is clinically insane, as might first have been supposed, but that some stabilizer, some internal gyroscope of constant faith has been removed from his spiritual mechanism. But what is the name of the motivation, the stabilizer, the faith, that Avellaneda seems to have cut from the soul of Don Quixote? The name is Dulcinea. Avellaneda's knight no longer loves Dulcinea, and he changes his name to symbolize this new basis of his existence. He is not now the Knight of the Rueful Countenance but the Knight-without-Love (el Caballero Desamorado). When the real Don Quixote hears of this, his reaction demonstrates the immediacy of the coupling of his love and his memory: "Neither can the peerless Dulcinea del Toboso be forgotten, nor can forgetfulness exist in Don Quixote," he cries out. The Knight-without-Love, in contrast, must necessarily forget. He has nothing with which to evaluate the contents of his memory.

The deep purposefulness of Avellaneda's creative intent is made evident by this new title for Don Quixote. Avellaneda has not only imitated the *Quixote,* he has remade it by removing the basis of its transcendence. He has situated a loveless hero within a loveless world, a negative creation which helps to explain so much of the human consolation of Cervantes. Avellaneda's work can thus be considered as the other side of the Cervantean tapestry, and a comparison of the two reveals not the inspiration of the weaver but the excellence of what was woven.[4]

4. The reason why Avellaneda built a Don Quixote without a heart, why he despised the man he imitated, why he created a world without value, and perhaps these are all parts of the same question, cannot be answered here. I hope, however, to be able to answer it in the future.

Selected Bibliography

The following list presents for readers of English a brief selection of works on Cervantes, his writings, and his influence. It does not include books of which portions appear in this edition, or works summarized in Drake's recent bibliography on *Don Quixote* (also found below), though the editor particularly recommends Aubrey Bell's *Cervantes,* Salvador de Madariaga's *Don Quixote: An Introductory Essay in Psychology,* R. L. Predmore's *The World of Don Quixote,* A. Serrano-Plaja's *"Magic" Realism in Cervantes,* Mark Van Doren's *Don Quixote's Profession,* and the collections of essays compiled by Angel Flores and M. J. Bernardete, and by Lowry Nelson—all reviewed by Drake. (Readers of Spanish will find additional bibliography in all of the books listed.)

Allen, John J. *Don Quixote: Hero or Fool?* Part II. Gainesville: University of Florida Press, 1979.

Castro, Américo. *An Idea of History.* Columbus: Ohio State University Press, 1976. (Includes three essays on Cervantes and *Don Quixote.*)

Close, Anthony. *The Romantic Approach to Don Quixote.* Cambridge: Cambridge University Press, 1977.

Drake, Dana. *Don Quixote (1894–1970): A Selective Annotated Bibliography.* Vol. I. North Carolina Studies in Romance Languages and Literatures, No. 138. Valencia: Artes Gráficas Soler, 1974. (Detailed summaries of significant critical works.)

Effron, Arthur. *Don Quixote and the Dulcineated World.* Austin: University of Texas Press, 1971.

El Saffar, Ruth. *Distance and Control in Don Quixote: A Study in Narrative Technique.* North Carolina Studies in Romance Languages and Literatures, No. 147. Valencia: Artes Gráficas Soler, 1974.

Predmore, Richard L. *Cervantes.* New York: Dodd, Mead, 1973. (Beautifully illustrated.)

Robert, Marthe. *The Old and the New: From "Don Quixote" to Kafka.* Berkeley: University of California Press, 1977. ("Demonstrates how the model of Cervantes can illuminate the nature of the novel.")

NORTON CRITICAL EDITIONS

AUSTEN *Emma* edited by Stephen M. Parrish
AUSTEN *Pride and Prejudice* edited by Donald J. Gray
Beowulf (the Donaldson translation) edited by Joseph F. Tuso
Blake's Poetry and Designs selected and edited by Mary Lynn Johnson and John E. Grant
BOCCACCIO *The Decameron* selected, translated, and edited by Mark Musa and Peter E. Bondanella
BRONTË, CHARLOTTE *Jane Eyre* edited by Richard J. Dunn
BRONTË, EMILY *Wuthering Heights* edited by William M. Sale, Jr. *2nd Ed.*
Robert Browning's Poetry selected and edited by James F. Loucks
Byron's Poetry selected and edited by Frank D. McConnell
CARROLL *Alice in Wonderland* selected and edited by Donald J. Gray
CERVANTES *Don Quixote* (the Ormsby translation, substantially revised) edited by Joseph R. Jones and Kenneth Douglas
Anton Chekhov's Plays translated and edited by Eugene K. Bristow
Anton Chekhov's Short Stories selected and edited by Ralph E. Matlaw
CHOPIN *The Awakening* edited by Margaret Culley
CLEMENS *Adventures of Huckleberry Finn* edited by Sculley Bradley, Richmond Croom Beatty, E. Hudson Long, and Thomas Cooley *2nd Ed.*
CLEMENS *A Connecticut Yankee in King Arthur's Court* edited by Allison R. Ensor
CLEMENS *Pudd'nhead Wilson* and *Those Extraordinary Twins* edited by Sidney E. Berger
CONRAD *Heart of Darkness* edited by Robert Kimbrough *2nd Ed.*
CONRAD *Lord Jim* edited by Thomas C. Moser
CONRAD *The Nigger of the "Narcissus"* edited by Robert Kimbrough
CRANE *Maggie: A Girl of the Streets* edited by Thomas A. Gullason
CRANE *The Red Badge of Courage* edited by Sculley Bradley, Richmond Croom Beatty, E. Hudson Long, and Donald Pizer *2nd Ed.*
Darwin selected and edited by Philip Appleman *2nd Ed.*
DEFOE *Moll Flanders* edited by Edward Kelly
DEFOE *Robinson Crusoe* edited by Michael Shinagel
DICKENS *Bleak House* edited by George Ford and Sylvère Monod
DICKENS *Hard Times* edited by George Ford and Sylvère Monod
John Donne's Poetry selected and edited by A. L. Clements
DOSTOEVSKY *The Brothers Karamazov* (the Garnett translation revised by Ralph E. Matlaw) edited by Ralph E. Matlaw
DOSTOEVSKY *Crime and Punishment* (the Coulson translation) edited by George Gibian *2nd Ed.*
DREISER *Sister Carrie* edited by Donald Pizer
ELIOT *Middlemarch* edited by Bert G. Hornback
FIELDING *Tom Jones* edited by Sheridan Baker
FLAUBERT *Madame Bovary* edited with a substantially new translation by Paul de Man
BENJAMIN FRANKLIN'S AUTOBIOGRAPHY edited by J. A. Leo Lemay and P. M. Zall
GOETHE *Faust* translated by Walter Arndt and edited by Cyrus Hamlin
GOGOL *Dead Souls* edited by George Gibian
HARDY *Far from the Madding Crowd* edited by Robert C. Schweik
HARDY *Jude the Obscure* edited by Norman Page
HARDY *The Mayor of Casterbridge* edited by James K. Robinson
HARDY *The Return of the Native* edited by James Gindin
HARDY *Tess of the d'Urbervilles* edited by Scott Elledge *2nd Ed.*
HAWTHORNE *The Blithedale Romance* edited by Seymour Gross and Rosalie Murphy
HAWTHORNE *The House of the Seven Gables* edited by Seymour Gross

HAWTHORNE *The Scarlet Letter* edited by Sculley Bradley, Richmond Croom Beatty, E. Hudson Long, and Seymour Gross *2nd Ed.*
George Herbert and the Seventeenth-Century Religious Poets selected and edited by Mario A. Di Cesare
HOMER *The Odyssey* translated and edited by Albert Cook
HOWELLS *The Rise of Silas Lapham* edited by Don L. Cook
IBSEN *The Wild Duck* translated and edited by Dounia B. Christiani
JAMES *The Ambassadors* edited by S. P. Rosenbaum
JAMES *The American* edited by James W. Tuttleton
JAMES *The Portrait of a Lady* edited by Robert D. Bamberg
JAMES *The Turn of the Screw* edited by Robert Kimbrough
JAMES *The Wings of the Dove* edited by J. Donald Crowley and Richard A. Hocks
Tales of Henry James edited by Christof Wegelin
Ben Jonson and the Cavalier Poets selected and edited by Hugh Maclean
Ben Jonson's Plays and Masques selected and edited by Robert M. Adams
MACHIAVELLI *The Prince* translated and edited by Robert M. Adams
MALTHUS *An Essay on the Principle of Population* edited by Philip Appleman
MELVILLE *The Confidence-Man* edited by Hershel Parker
MELVILLE *Moby-Dick* edited by Harrison Hayford and Hershel Parker
MEREDITH *The Egoist* edited by Robert M. Adams
MILL *On Liberty* edited by David Spitz
MILTON *Paradise Lost* edited by Scott Elledge
MORE *Utopia* translated and edited by Robert M. Adams
NEWMAN *Apologia Pro Vita Sua* edited by David J. DeLaura
NORRIS *McTeague* edited by Donald Pizer
Adrienne Rich's Poetry selected and edited by Barbara Charlesworth Gelpi and Albert Gelpi
The Writings of St. Paul edited by Wayne A. Meeks
SHAKESPEARE *Hamlet* edited by Cyrus Hoy
SHAKESPEARE *Henry IV, Part I* edited by James L. Sanderson *2nd Ed.*
Bernard Shaw's Plays selected and edited by Warren Sylvester Smith
Shelley's Poetry and Prose edited by Donald H. Reiman and Sharon B. Powers
SOPHOCLES *Oedipus Tyrannus* translated and edited by Luci Berkowitz and Theodore F. Brunner
SMOLLET *Humphry Clinker* edited by James L. Thorson
SPENSER *Edmund Spenser's Poetry* selected and edited by Hugh Maclean *2nd Ed.*
STENDHAL *Red and Black* translated and edited by Robert M. Adams
STERNE *Tristram Shandy* edited by Howard Anderson
SWIFT *Gulliver's Travels* edited by Robert A. Greenberg *2nd Ed.*
The Writings of Jonathan Swift edited by Robert A. Greenberg and William B. Piper
TENNYSON *In Memoriam* edited by Robert H. Ross
Tennyson's Poetry selected and edited by Robert W. Hill, Jr.
THOREAU *Walden* and *Civil Disobedience* edited by Owen Thomas
TOLSTOY *Anna Karenina* (the Maude translation) edited by George Gibian
TOLSTOY *War and Peace* (the Maude translation) edited by George Gibian
TURGENEV *Fathers and Sons* edited with a substantially new translation by Ralph E. Matlaw
VOLTAIRE *Candide* translated and edited by Robert M. Adams
WATSON *The Double Helix* edited by Gunther S. Stent
WHITMAN *Leaves of Grass* edited by Sculley Bradley and Harold W. Blodgett
WOLLSTONECRAFT *A Vindication of the Rights of Woman* edited by Carol H. Poston
WORDSWORTH *The Prelude: 1799, 1805, 1850* edited by Jonathan Wordsworth, M. H. Abrams, and Stephen Gill
Middle English Lyrics selected and edited by Maxwell S. Luria and Richard L. Hoffman
Modern Drama edited by Anthony Caputi
Restoration and Eighteenth-Century Comedy edited by Scott McMillin